THE
TOWER OF RAVENS

BOOK ONE OF RHIANNON'S RIDE

KATE FORSYTH

RANDOM HOUSE AUSTRALIA

Random House Australia Pty Ltd
20 Alfred Street, Milsons Point, NSW 2061
http://www.randomhouse.com.au

Sydney   New York   Toronto
London   Auckland   Johannesburg

First published by Random House Australia 2004

National Library of Australia
Cataloguing-in-Publication Entry

Forsyth, Kate, 1966– .
The tower of ravens.

ISBN 1 74051 171 9.

1. Magic – Fiction. 2. Witches – Fiction.
3. Horses – Fiction. I. Title.
(Series: Forsyth, Kate, 1966–
Rhiannon's ride; bk. 1).

A823.3

Cover illustration by Neal Armstrong
Cover and internal design by Darian Causby/Highway 51
Typeset by Midland Typesetters, Maryborough, Victoria
Printed and bound by Griffin Press, Netley, South Australia

10 9 8 7 6 5 4 3 2 1

Kate Forsyth lives in Sydney with her husband Greg, their three children Benjamin, Timothy and Eleanor, a little black cat called Shadow and thousands of books. She has wanted to be a writer for as long as she can remember and has certainly been writing stories from the time she learnt to hold a pen. Being allowed to read, write and daydream as much as she likes and call it working is the most wonderful life imaginable and so she thanks you all for making it possible.

You can read more about Kate on her website at http://www.ozemail.com.au/~kforsyth or send a message to her at kforsyth@ozemail.com.au

ALSO BY KATE FORSYTH

THE WITCHES OF EILEANAN SERIES

Dragonclaw

The Pool of Two Moons

The Cursed Towers

The Forbidden Land

The Skull of the World

The Fathomless Caves

Full Fathom Five (writing as Kate Humphrey)

The Starthorn Tree

To my three beautiful children,
Benjamin, Timothy and Eleanor

CONTENTS

A PALE HORSE

TO THROW A PRINCE

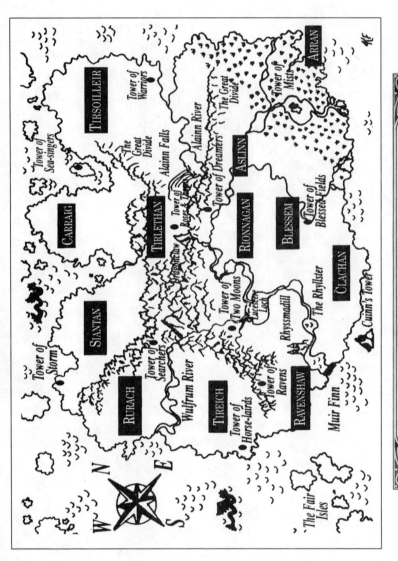

EILEANAN & THE FAR ISLANDS

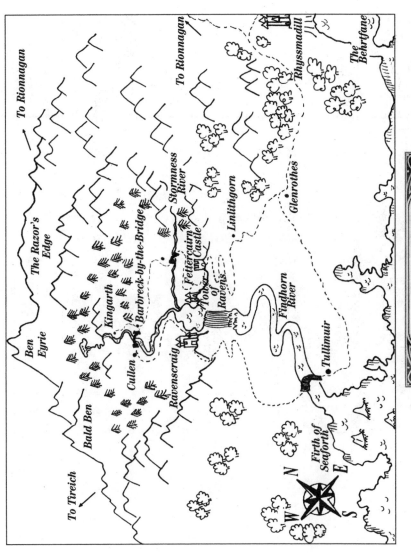

RAVENSHAW

'[Necromancy] has its name because it works
on the bodies of the dead, and gives answers
by the ghosts and apparitions of the dead, and
subterraneous spirits, alluring them into the
carcasses of the dead by certain hellish charms,
and infernal invocations, and by deadly
sacrifices and wicked oblations.'

Francis Barrett,
The Magus, 1801

'Through the Necromancer's magic words,
the dust in the decayed coffin takes shape
again and rises from a long forgotten past.'

Emile Grillot de Givry,
Witchcraft, Magic and Alchemy, 1931

A HORSE OF AIR

'With a heart of furious fancies
whereof I am commander
With a burning spear
And a horse of air
To the wilderness I wander.'

Tom o' Bedlam,
traditional folksong

ONE-HORN'S DAUGHTER

The girl crouched on the stone ledge, hugging her cloak of furs and skins close against the bite of the night. Far to the east, where the towering peaks of the mountains broke and fell away, the moons were rising. First the little moon, blue as a bruise, then the big blood-moon, glowing as orange as the leaping flames on the far side of the lake behind her.

She could hear the distant sound of voices and laughter across the ice as the wind shifted, carrying with it a shower of bright sparks. The pale circle of her face sank a little deeper into the dark huddle of her skins. She set her gaze resolutely to the east, where the snow-swollen river ran headlong towards the unknown future, towards freedom and the sea.

Tonight the inexpressible yearning was fierce in her. She could smell the bitter green coming of spring in the air, hear it in the clink of ice upon stone as the lake began to flex and test itself against the chains of winter, feel it all around her in the surge of sap and blood. These first few weeks of the green months were the cruellest of all, for they sang of joy to someone who had no understanding of the word. She could only sense it, like a deaf child hearing bells ringing all around her as a thrum of air against her skin. She did not know what she yearned for. She did not know why she sat here in the dark loneliness with a hot ache in her throat. She only knew that she could not bear to be with the herd tonight as they gloated over the spoils of their latest hunt, swaggering and boasting and wrestling about the fire while their new captive sat bound and bloodied, trying not to show his fear.

The girl was not driven away from her herd's carousing by any sense of compassion for the prisoner. She had no time to feel or wonder for anyone else. All her pity and terror were saved for herself. She sat on the ledge of stone and set her face to the east, wondering only if she should take the chance to creep away tonight, while the herd was busy carousing. If she ran all night, hiding her scent in the tumult of white water, running on stones so she would leave no footprints, if she ran till her heart was bursting, could she win her way free? The desire to escape was so fierce in her that she could only keep herself still by clenching her fingers so hard she cut purple crescents into her tough, calloused palms. For no matter how fast she ran, no matter how well she hid her tracks, the herd would find her in the end, and they would kill her for wanting to be free.

Below her, something moved. She tensed and looked down at once, for there were many wild and dangerous creatures in these mountains. At first she saw only darkness, but as her eyes adjusted from the brightness of the luminous moons, she began to see a dark shape emerging from the shadows. There was a round rump, the deep curve of a back, the long line of a graceful neck lowered

4

to drink from the river. Beyond she saw the vague shape of more horses, a whole herd of them, moving slowly along the stony bank of the river.

Behind her there was a burst of raucous laughter. The horses flung up their heads. One whickered. Moonlight glinted on the two long, scrolled horns that sprang from each forehead. She caught her breath in surprise. These were no wild ponies, but creatures out of myth and folklore. Whether it was the sound of her gasp, or a sudden shift in the wind that took her scent to the horses' quivering nostrils, she could not know, but suddenly the herd all flung out great shadowy wings and, with a rattle of hooves and a soft defiant whinny, took flight. For a moment she saw their soaring shapes outlined sharply against the red moon, the sound of their wings filling her ears. Then the herd of winged horses was gone, lost in the darkness.

The girl was on her feet, filled with exultation as sharp as thorns. *If I could only catch one*, she thought. *If I could only tame one. Then I could escape. They would never be able to stop me if I flew away on the back of a creature like that.*

She would not even admit the impossibility of such a plan. That she should see the fabled black winged horses on the very night that her need to escape had grown so urgent could hardly be coincidence. Those of her kind were ruled by superstition and omen. They did not believe in coincidences. The girl's brain boiled with ideas. Maybe if she tracked the winged horses to their lair, tried to tame one, make friends with it. She had tamed many a mountain pony that way.

Winged horses were notoriously wild, however, and she knew she did not have much time. The herd was growing tired of waiting for her horns to bud. Many younger girls had the buds of their horns swelling strongly, and had been bleeding at the rise of the full moons for months. Her first blood had come only that day, filling her with sick fear. She had scrubbed away the stain on her clothes with stones and icy water, and stuffed herself with a wad of crushed pine needles and sap so they could not smell her womb-blood and guess her secret.

She did not know how long she could hide the coming of her womanhood. Certainly no longer than a month. Today they had all been distracted by the man who had ridden into their territory and given them such a splendid chase. Next month she may not be so lucky. The herd had always viewed her with suspicion and disdain, for she had feet instead of hooves, and only two breasts instead of six. If she had grown a proud, strong horn like her mother, or even ten short, stubby ones like her cousin, the other deformities could have been ignored. A satyricorn without a horn was a freak, though, an embarrassment to the entire herd. They would scorn her and challenge her and, in the end, kill her for her lack. Four times already she had seen a hornless one hunted to their death. She knew there would be no mercy.

The girl put her hands up to her head and felt her smooth forehead, running her fingertips back into her hair. Not even the faintest suggestion of a horn. She gave an involuntary sigh, and turned reluctantly to head back to the camp. She had been away too long already. Soon someone would notice she was gone, and snuff the air for her scent. She wanted no-one to notice her tonight, with her skirts still damp from their scrubbing and the womb-blood seeping its way past the plug of pine needles.

She made her way silently round the lake, taking care to leap from stone to stone so as to leave no print in the mud, and then emerged casually from the bushes as if she had just visited the latrine and was now seeking her bed again.

The herd's camp was set in a wide clearing on the shore of the lake, sheltered to the west by a tall bluff. In the centre of the clearing the bonfire gnawed sullenly at the great log cast down across its ashes. A charred carcass was impaled upon a spit above it, its equine shape still recognisable despite the havoc the herd's knives had made upon its flesh. The sight grieved her. She had always loved horses and often used to leap onto the back of one of the wild mountain ponies, galloping it over the high meadows until at last it stopped trying to throw her off and submitted to her will. When she was twelve she had taught one of the shaggy little ponies to come to her whistle. On its broad back, she had explored all the hills around. It had been her one great pleasure, galloping along the sweeping green meadows, as swift as the wind, leaping over fallen logs and brooks, swimming with it in the lake. In those days she had not yet dreamt of escape. She had ridden the horse only for pleasure and for the satisfaction of at last being faster than the other girls in the herd. One-Horn had not approved, however. The herd had hunted down her friendly, shaggy pony, killed it and eaten it. She had never forgiven them.

Now, most of the herd was sleeping, worn out from the chase and too much *tia-tio*, the dark pungent ale they brewed from pine cones and honey. They lay where they had fallen, some still clutching their curved cups of bone.

Lying close to the fire, snoring loudly, were four horned men. Their hairy paunches were huge, and they had a sleek, well-fed air about them that the lean, muscular women did not share. Their brows were blunt and heavy, their noses flat and wide with flaring nostrils. Most had only two small curved horns, just peeking through their matted curls. One, though, had two much longer horns that curved up and out of his head in a perfect crescent. He was also the largest, with burly shoulders, a thick neck and heavy features. As First-Male, he was richly dressed, wearing a brown woollen kilt, a filthy jerkin, and many necklaces of bone and semi-precious stones. A golden brooch in the shape of a running horse was pinned to the jerkin. The girl knew the clothes and brooch had once belonged to her father, a human who had been captured by the herd many years ago. He had died in captivity when she had been only five.

In a stony corner, surrounded on two sides by the high walls of the bluff, lay two men without horns. One was dressed in a rough loincloth and cloak of hide, with very long, grey, matted hair and a straggly beard. He was so thin his ribs stood out against his wrinkled brown skin. He was tied to a stake with a long leash, his ankles hobbled for the night.

The other prisoner was young and fair, with thick curly hair the colour of summer grass. He was dressed in a dishevelled blue jacket over a white shirt and breeches, all much stained with mud and blood. His head slumped forward onto his chest, and congealing blood obscured most of one side of his face. His hands were tied tightly behind his back, and leather straps wrapped his arms and body from shoulder to waist.

Stepping quietly through the sleeping bodies, the girl saw his belongings scattered across the ground. There were the long, black boots, thrown away in disgust when no-one was able to make them fit over their hooves. The pretty painted box that magically played music when opened lay in the ashes, still tinkling away, while the silver goblet with the crystal set in its stem had fallen from One-Horn's hand as she snored by the fire. The blue cockaded hat was still on the head of Seven-Horns, though she slept with her face pressed into the dirt.

Hanging around the neck of First-Male was the little golden medal with its intriguing design of a hand radiating rays of light like the sun, while pinned to the fur cloak of Three-Horns was the silver badge cunningly forged in the shape of a charging stag.

The girl noticed all this with perturbation, for it showed who had won the squabbles. It was not a good sign that One-Horn had lost the hat and the brooch, for such spoils of war were marks of power and prestige. Since One-Horn was her mother and had offered her some protection from the scorn of the other women, it was just one more sign to the girl that she must make her escape quickly if she was to survive. Battles for supremacy were to the death, and One-Horn was beginning to lose her speed and aggression. There were many other women eager to take her place as leader of the herd.

The girl's sleeping furs were close to the prisoners, for she was nearly as low in prestige as they were, and not permitted to sleep near the fire. As she stepped past them to reach her bed, she was dismayed when a thin hand suddenly reached out and seized her ankle. She did not make any sound, but she paused and bent as if to pull a thorn from her foot.

'Lassie, this man they've caught, he's a Yeoman o' the Guard,' a reedy voice said urgently. 'It's treason to waylay him so. Any that lays a hand on the Rìgh's own body-guard will feel the tug o' the hangman's noose. Ye must let him go!'

'Me no fool,' the girl said softly and pulled her ankle out of his grasp, beginning to straighten up. She met the other prisoner's eyes. He had lifted his head and was staring at her pleadingly. His eyes were the colour of the lake in summer. He opened his swollen, blood-caked lips and managed to croak, 'Please!'

9

She looked away, shaking her head infinitesimally.

'But he's the Rìgh's own guard! He says he has news he must take to the court – the Rìgh is in dreadful danger.'

'So? What that to me?'

'Please!'

She shrugged a shoulder as if shaking away a mosquito and moved on to her bed, curling up with her back to the prisoners, pretending an indifference she did not feel. She could only hope no-one had heard Reamon speaking to her. Few of the herd had ever bothered to learn to speak his strange, lilting language, but One-Horn's daughter had always been an oddity with her soft feet and mobile toes, and her smooth torso. Because she looked so much like a human child, Reamon had looked to her first and sought to make her understand him. It was he who had taught her about the world outside and, once she began to dream of escape, she had learnt hungrily.

'Lassie!'

One-Horn's daughter heard his anguished whisper but drew her smelly furs closer about her, curling up like some small animal, instinctively trying to protect the deep, hidden parts of her body that had betrayed her so bitterly.

She slept badly. Her dreams were stained with blood and shadowed with dark wings. Her mind kept trying to come up with ways to capture a winged horse even while her exhausted body craved unconsciousness. *Nets*, she kept thinking. *Ropes. Though I must not injure it . . . they were so beautiful, so free . . .*

She came awake at some point in the hours before dawn, suddenly thinking of the saddle and bridle the herd had torn off the horse before cutting its throat. Surely if the prisoner had used such devices to ride his steed, they would help in retaining control of a winged horse? If she could just hide them before anyone woke, the herd might never realise they were gone. The satyricorn were in general rather self-absorbed, and paid little attention to anything outside their immediate concerns of hunting, eating, sleeping and fighting.

At once the girl rolled out of her skins and looked about her. All was quiet and dark. Mist hung across the steep, green hills. It was light enough for her to see the shape of her hands but dark enough that none were stirring. Cautiously she stood up. She saw the saddle lying in the dust to one side of the clearing, near the limp, discarded boots, but there was no sign of the bridle.

Swiftly she bent and picked the saddle up, settling it on her arm. It had a long, dangling girth and two small saddlebags hanging on either side. Many of the prisoner's belongings lay spilled out from the bags, as the herd had only taken those things they perceived to be of value. She stuffed everything back into the saddlebags, managing to work out how to fasten the buckles so they would not spill out again. There was a blue saddlecloth nearby, embroidered with gold. She picked that up as well, and then seized the boots on impulse. She knew well how much harder it was for her to run with her soft-fleshed feet. The boots could be of use.

As she hurried into the shelter of the forest, she cast a quick glance behind to make sure no-one was watching. The sight of the prisoner's intent blue gaze was like a lash across her nerves. It drove her forward, stumbling, hoping she was not betraying herself to danger.

She hid the saddle and boots in a fallen log she knew, and hurried back to the clearing, her pulse hammering with fear. Still no-one stirred, all satiated by the feast of horse meat and pine-cone ale the night before. Only the prisoner was awake, and he was busy sawing the leather that bound his hands against a sharp-edged rock he had somehow managed to prop upright behind him. She watched him for a while from the shelter of the trees. There was quiet desperation in every move he made. She wondered how he thought he could possibly escape, with his horse rounding the bellies of the herd, and blood still leaking from the wound on his temple. He would be better, she knew, to accept his fate and make the best of it, as Reamon had done ten years earlier. Yet she could not help a stirring of empathy. She too was desperate to escape.

Slowly the mist melted away and the sky grew lighter, while she stood there and hesitated, wondering if she should call the alarm. Then she realised the leather straps wrapping his arms were the reins of his bridle. He could never cut himself free in time, yet he could damage the reins given long enough and she did not want that to happen. The bridle could be of use to her.

Quickly she came up behind him. He heard her step and went quiet, every muscle tense. She bent over him, quickly unknotting the leather and unwinding his arms, whispering fiercely, 'Quiet, else me cut your throat.'

Once he understood that she was freeing him, he said hoarsely, 'The Rìgh will be grateful, he'll reward ye . . .'

'What use he to me?' she asked.

'I'll tell him what ye did . . .'

'If ye no' get catched again.'

'They will no' catch me!'

'They better no',' she said and stood back from him, holding the metal bits of the bridle so they would not betray her by jangling. She did not dare take the time to hide the bridle in the hollow log, thrusting it instead in the bushes and covering it with old leaves. Then she returned hurriedly to her skins, covering her head and trying to control the pounding of her heart. If anyone had seen, or if they guessed! She knew the prisoner had run stumbling towards the lake and had begun to make his faltering way across the thin, uneven ice. She was disappointed in him, if relieved. A drowned man could tell no tales. She heard the crack of ice and a splash a few minutes later and was surprised at how sorry she was.

The sound must have penetrated the drunken mists of some of those who slumbered nearby, for she heard a slow stirring and groaning, and a bad-tempered grumble as someone rolled over and tried to get comfortable again. Under the shelter of her skins the girl held her breath and waited for the sounds to die away. Instead, she heard someone get up and begin to lurch towards the latrine. For a minute or two there was silence and then came the inevitable cry of alarm.

Immediately the camp was in uproar. No matter how bad the hangover, a satyricorn would never allow a handsome young man to escape. Boys were rarely born to satyricorns and so were very highly prized. Once their horns grew, showing they were old enough to mate, their favours had to be shared among the many women of the herd, which led to many quarrels. It also, in time, led to the birth of weak and deformed babies. The satyricorns were therefore always eager to mate with males not of blood-kin.

Once, when there had been many herds of satyricorns in the mountains and forests, boy children had been exchanged between the herds. With few satyricorns left now, the males of the species were more respected and esteemed than ever. There were only a few of them, though, and the herd needed to raise children that were not too closely related to each other if they were to survive. Consequently, the women were always looking for men of other races with which to mate. There were few contenders for this honour. Ogres sufficed at times, though they were so ugly there was no pleasure to be had in the act, and the birthing of a half-ogre child was always painful and difficult due to their enormous size. Occasionally a seelie or Celestine was seized in a raid into the forest, but they never thrived in captivity. The herd would be lucky if they sired a child or two before they wasted away.

Most sought after of all were the horned men of the snowy heights, for they were lusty and strong and their children rarely failed to grow horns as they reached maturity. But the Children of the White Gods were fierce warriors, and it was very difficult to capture them or to keep them once they were caught, and so the satyricorn women would only seek to seize one in desperate circumstances.

A human male, however, was considered a fine prize. They often lived in captivity for many years and fathered many children, and usually they brought forged metal weapons and tools with them which the herd found very useful. Once it had been easy to catch a human male, but now they rarely rode alone into satyricorn territory. To have a young, strong, comely man come galloping through their valley had been the best thing that had happened to the herd in many years and no-one would allow him to escape easily.

One-Horn's daughter was dragged out of her skins by the hair, her mother screaming, 'Why you not hear? Where he gone?'

'Me sleep,' she responded, in the harsh, guttural language of the satyricorns. 'Me hear nothing. No-one hear nothing.'

Her mother dropped her and ran down the beach, her nostrils flaring wide as she snuffed the air, her eyes darting over the ground. 'Here! And here! He run here! In water.'

Everyone howled in dismay. Satyricorns hated water. It confused their senses and none of the herd could swim.

Beyond the lake, the river ran fast over sharp rocks. A shout went up as the man's head broke through the foam. He had flung one arm over a branch and was being swept along at breakneck speed.

One-Horn shrieked: 'Hunt!'

Quickly the women of the herd seized their weapons and began to run, circling round either side of the lake. Most had rough clubs of stone lashed to wood; one or two had metal-forged daggers which had once belonged to Reamon or other past prisoners. One-Horn's daughter hesitated for only a moment. She bent and picked up the curved bow that was her only legacy of her unknown father. He had not lived long enough to teach his daughter how to use the bow, but Reamon had had some knowledge of the weapon, enough to teach her the rudimentary skills. The rest she had taught herself, in the lonely meadows and forests around the lake, hewing herself arrows with the steel blade she had won gambling. Most of the girl's few possessions had been won gambling, for in feats of strength and speed she would always be the loser.

Fast as deer, the satyricorns leapt through the trees, howling and shouting with excitement. There were fourteen of them, led by the woman with the rapier horn, and they all carried crude weapons – clubs and stone axes and slingshots. Not one of the satyricorns was the same. Some had antlers like a stag, others thin twisting horns. One had ten stumpy horns like a goat's all over her head; another had two long, outward-curving horns above her ears and two small, curving horns above her eyebrows; yet another had three sets of down-curving tusks framing her face.

They had all discarded their long hide cloaks, some running naked, some wearing short skirts of animal skins. All of them were tall and muscular, with a ridge of coarse, wiry hair running down their backs and ending in a long, tufted tail. Necklaces of bones and teeth bounced on their six bare breasts. Their hooves rattled on the rocks and their bloodcurdling shrieks echoed round the valley. The girl ran after them, though the sharp stones cut her bare feet. She dared not fall too far behind, for that would draw attention to her, and might make them suspect she felt sympathy for the escaped prisoner. It was hard to keep up, though, for the satyricorn women were long-legged and swift.

The river began to force its way down the hill in a series of gushing rapids. They saw the man's head go under again and again, but he clung valiantly to his branch, fending himself off the rocks with his free arm. The branch spun round and round and at times was completely submerged. The river was swollen with melting snow, and flowing so fast the satyricorn were unable to keep up. They howled with rage and frustration, some coming to a halt on the ridge so they could shake their weapons. The girl came up behind them, panting, holding her side, her feet bruised and cut. For a moment she thought the prisoner was actually going to make it.

Then One-Horn took a dramatic flying leap down the ridge, landing on all fours on the pebbly shore below. With that one leap, she had cut across the curve of the river and got ahead of the man. She seized the end of a fallen log and heaved it into the water with one of the spectacular feats of strength that had won her the leadership of the herd. The effort obviously cost her. She rested her arms on her knees, her head hanging.

The man in the water tried desperately to swim round the obstacle, but the momentum of the river was too

16

strong. It swept him up hard against the fallen log and pinned him there. One-Horn drew her dagger and walked out along the log, bending down to seize the man's hair and twist his face up towards her. One-Horn's daughter could only watch, struggling to catch her breath. She felt an odd mixture of regret and relief. At least the knowledge of her treachery would die with him.

But One-Horn only menaced the escaped prisoner with her knife, before dragging the sodden, exhausted man out of the water. He was too valuable to kill. The girl's heart sank. Her mother would find out how he had escaped. The prisoner may not mean to betray her, but in the end, he would. Even a guilty glance at her would fire her mother's suspicions. She gripped her bow with shaking fingers and wondered if she dared kill him, to keep her secret safe. She dared not. One-Horn would kill her for snatching away her prey. They would suspect . . .

One-Horn was hauling the man along the log to the beach. Suddenly he spun and kicked out with one foot, sending her dagger flying out of her hand and into the river. Then he slammed his foot into the back of her knee, knocking One-Horn to the ground. Before anyone had time to react, he was kneeling on her back, his arm about her throat, bending her spine to breaking point.

Time seemed to slow. The satyricorn were leaping up and down on the ridge, howling and throwing rocks and spears, all of which clattered harmlessly on the stones below. One-Horn was fighting for breath, trying desperately to wrench the man's arm away from her throat. He was too strong. Any moment now he would snap her spine and she would be dead.

The girl fitted an arrow to her bow and lifted it. It seemed she gazed along the line of her arrow forever, its point aimed directly at the prisoner's straining back. For a moment she teetered on that moment of decision, seeing with a strange anguish all the possible ramifications of letting the arrow fly. The prisoner would be dead but her mother would be alive and perhaps even grateful. Her own prestige among the herd would be immeasurably enhanced. She would be able to add the prisoner's teeth and finger-bone to the necklace that hung down between her breasts, and she could claim with impunity whatever of his belongings she cared for. Secretly she would be sorry, though. He was young and fair and he had fought well for his freedom.

She let the string go. With a twang that caused her nerves to jolt, the arrow leapt free. She watched its pure and perfect arc, flying out from her taut bowstring, down, down, down through the clear morning air and deep into the back of the prisoner. He jerked upright, crying aloud, and then he fell. The girl stepped back, feeling sudden inexplicable nausea rising in her throat. Beside her, the satyricorns howled with blood-lust and the pleasure of the kill. On the beach below, One-Horn thrust the man's dead body away from her and leapt to her feet, her face twisted in a snarl of fury. She kicked the fallen body and then turned and looked up at her daughter. Begrudgingly she lifted one fist in acknowledgement.

One-Horn's daughter had to clench her hands together to hide their shaking. The herd was slapping her on the back, congratulating her for a fine shot, teasing her for stealing such a fine prize from her mother. They all bounded down along the curve of the ridge and onto the beach, where they hailed One-Horn with malicious glee.

'Why kill him?' One-Horn demanded furiously. 'No use dead. Can't mate a dead man. I would have thrown him off.'

'He too strong, he got you good,' Five-Horns chortled. 'You dead but for daughter. You owe daughter blood-debt. Kiss her feet.'

'No kiss anyone's feet,' One-Horn snarled. She cast her daughter a look of seething dislike and kicked the young man over so he lay on his back with his arms askew, staring blankly at the sky. The arrow protruded through his breast, clotted with blood. One-Horn's daughter averted her gaze.

But then Five-Horns began to rip off the man's clothes, and One-Horn angrily seized his other arm, shouting, 'Get off, he's mine!' The girl saw that she would lose everything if she was not careful. She wanted his clothes. They were beautiful, blue as the sky and white and soft as clouds. They would be warmer than her rough uncured skins, and would not smell so bad. Besides, if she followed the river east as she planned she would no doubt come in contact with other men and it would be best if she did not draw too much attention to herself. The man's clothes would be camouflage. So she lifted her dagger and leapt between One-Horn and Five-Horns, saying angrily, 'Get off! Me kill him, he mine.'

The two horned women looked at her in rage and surprise. One-Horn made a move as if to strike her daughter but the girl thrust her away, staring up into her mother's yellow eyes.

'Blood-right,' Seven-Horns said. 'She kill him, he hers.'

Five-Horns began to laugh. She stepped back mockingly. 'All yours, No-Horn.'

The name was an insult, but One-Horn's daughter could do nothing about it. Like a child, she had no horns and so the name was warranted. Besides, she had no desire to challenge Five-Horns to a duel, for the other woman was almost a foot taller and very strong. She swallowed the insult and bent to strip the man, trying not to let her fingers touch his clammy skin. She could not understand her revulsion and hoped no-one else would notice it. She had killed before, but never a creature that walked on two legs as she did, and spoke to her in a language she could understand. It seemed to make a difference.

It took a while to strip him naked, for he was heavy and his clothes were drenched. Then she had to cut off his finger and hack out his teeth, a task which made her feel utterly sick and wretched. By the time she had finished, the rest of the herd had lost interest and headed back to the camp. She did not know what to do with the body. It seemed wrong to leave him lying on the stones for the wolves and eagles to feast upon, so after a moment of indecision and anxiety she heaved him up and slid his body into the river. Then she toiled back up the hillside to the camp.

There One-Horn's daughter arrogantly demanded the return of all the dead man's belongings: the blue hat, the stag brooch and silver goblet, the golden medal, the music-box, the silver dagger he wore at his belt and the little black dagger he had worn inside his boot, and the warm hooded cloak, blue on one side, grey on the other. Angrily they were relinquished to her, for she had the blood-right and this was one law sacred to the satyricorn. She washed the white shirt and did her clumsy best to sew up the jagged rent, front and back, where her arrow had torn through the material. She sponged the blood and mud from the coat and breeches, then discarded her own smelly hides to dress herself in the dead man's clothes. Everything fitted her well, for she was as tall as the prisoner had been. She enjoyed the feel of the soft clothes against her skin.

She dusted off the soles of her filthy feet and pulled on the stockings and boots, slipped the double-edged black knife into its sheath inside the left boot, and twisted the tangled mass of her hair into a knot at the base of her neck. Then she pulled the cockaded blue hat onto her head, and strapped the silver dagger to her belt, feeling stronger and prouder than she had ever felt before. She wished she could look at herself. Was she as handsome as he had been, the young man whose clothes she wore with such satisfaction?

The rest of the day was spent carefully filing holes in his teeth so she could hang them on the thin leather thong around her neck. She already had a fair collection of teeth and bones – mainly those of birds and small mammals, but a few sharp yellow goblin fangs as well. She stripped his finger-bone of skin and flesh and scrubbed it well, then hung it in the centre with the goblin teeth on either side, then the other bones and teeth from the largest to the smallest, finishing with the dead man's small, white teeth. All the while she worked she was aware of Reamon's distress and revulsion but would not let it bother her.

The necklace looked good when she had finished, very full and heavy. She hung it around her neck, conscious of its weight against her skin. It rattled when she moved. She tried to keep her movements smooth, knowing she had aroused a lot of jealousy with her newfound glory. She told herself she would have aroused contempt and scorn instead of jealousy if she had not claimed the clothes and teeth, but the truth was she was enjoying the new respect in the eyes of the other satyricorns. Soon she would be gone. She did not need to fear their envy.

THE BLACK MARE

Many stories of the fabled flying horses were told around the campfire. It was said they could not be tamed, and that any who dared try would be thrown from a great height and killed.

Yet Reamon had once told her that some men of his race had succeeded in taming the golden winged horses of the west, and these men became great princes and warriors. The only way to tame a flying horse, he said, was to stay on its back for a year and a day, without dismounting once. If a rider managed this feat of skill and determination, then the respect of the flying horse was won and it would submit to its rider's will. Few ever succeeded, however, and many died trying.

One-Horn's daughter thought to herself that if a man like Reamon could stay on a winged horse's back for a year and a day, surely she could do it for a mere day or two. Just long enough to escape.

It was her plan to tie herself so firmly to the flying horse that it could not throw her off. She thought the horse's response would be to soar as high into the sky as it could. Eventually it must tire and come down to earth, and then she would cut herself free, letting the horse go. She did not care where she found herself, as long as it was many miles away from the herd.

Her big problem was how to capture the winged horse and keep it still and quiet long enough to saddle and bridle it, and to tie herself to the saddle. She had thought of rigging up a trap with a net but was afraid she might break the horse's leg or wings. She knew it was no use leaping from a tree trunk onto its back, because satyricorns had tried that in the past and had only been thrown off.

From the moment she had seen the horse, an idea had been brewing in her brain, but while the herd was still looking at her sideways and keeping track of her movements, she dared not see if the idea might bear fruit. She waited two full weeks, long enough for the herd to begin to forget. During that time she kept up her usual solitary habits, practising her archery in the high meadows, bringing in the occasional fish or bird, sleeping well away from the fire. Eventually the other women stopped spying on her, being too busy with the normal squabbles over the men and the food.

At last One-Horn's daughter felt free to return to her cache in the forest. She chose a chilly, misty evening when the herd was tired after a long day spent hunting, and filled with roast bear and *tia-tio*. Busy with their wrestling and boasting and gambling, they would not notice she had gone. Or so she hoped.

Going by a tortuous, labyrinthine route, and taking care to leave no trail, One-Horn's daughter came at last to the hollow log where she had hidden the saddle and saddle-bags. She paused there for a long moment, listening, before daring to drag out her prizes. She had brought with her a hot coal wrapped in a pouch of fur. She used it to kindle a fat-dipped reed which she stuck in a knothole, and then she quickly rummaged through the saddlebags.

On the day the herd had hunted down the rider and his horse, he had somehow managed to knock out three of his pursuers before the herd had dragged him down. He had done so from horseback, at a full gallop, and without apparently drawing a weapon. None of the herd had thought to wonder how he had done it, except for One-Horn's daughter. As usual she had been lagging behind the rest of the herd, not having their speed or stamina, and so she had seen the three women fall. While the others had raced on after the horse and rider, One-Horn's daughter had stopped and examined the fallen women. All three had had a sharp-pronged black thorn sticking out of their skin. She had pulled the thorns out and thrown them away, and all three women had woken some time later, red-eyed and grumpy and complaining of headaches. One-Horn's daughter thought the rider must have had some way of throwing or spitting out the thorn, since he had hit the women from quite a long distance and with amazing accuracy.

With satisfaction, she found a pouch of black barbs tucked in the front flap of one of the saddlebags. With them were two small bottles, one red and one green, and a long blowpipe. Over the next few days, she was able to establish that barbs anointed with liquid from the green bottle only knocked their target unconscious, while those doused in the liquid from the red bottle killed. The girl's plans crystallised.

She began to spend as much time as she dared searching for the herd of flying horses. Whenever she had a chance, she interrogated Reamon for all he knew about horses in general and winged horses in particular, although she feared him guessing her plans. She practised buckling and unbuckling the saddle and bridle, and whittled herself a quiver full of new arrows. She kept the blowpipe and pouch of barbs in her pocket, dousing the tips with the soporific liquid first. Whenever she could, she practised using the blowpipe, until she began to have a fair measure of accuracy.

Having a plan to work towards steadied her and made it easier to deal with the petty unkindness of the other women, though at times she found it hard to hide her excitement, which thrilled her blood like pine-cone ale.

One clear fine evening, she was hunting high in the alpine meadows when she heard the distant neigh of a horse. Her heart leapt so sharply in her breast that it pained her. She looked about quickly and saw the herd of black horses galloping along a far ridge. There were more than a dozen of them, led by a tall, deep-chested stallion with horns as long as swords springing from his brow. The mares that followed him were smaller and daintier, and their horns were not so long, but they were still far bigger than the wild ponies she was used to.

The girl gazed up at the herd for a long moment, enthralled by their beauty, but then, as they cantered out of sight behind the ridge, she dropped the brace of coneys she held and began to run after them.

She ran till her breath tore in her chest, clutching at the stitch in her side, bounding over boulders and between trees, tearing her flesh on brambles and bruising her feet. Her anxiety was acute. Two and a half weeks had passed since the last time she saw the winged horses, and she dared not lose her chance. As she came leaping and stumbling over the stony edge of the ridge, tears were beginning to blur her vision. She did not think she would be able to bear it if the horses had flown out of sight. She would just keep running, she swore to herself, and take her chances.

The horses were standing together in the meadow, heads bent to graze the sweet new grass. The stallion flung up his head and stared at her, his ears laid flat against his skull, his eyes ringed with white. Then he trumpeted a warning, rearing up on his hind legs before galloping about the herd, biting one mare on the flank when she was too slow to react. Black wings snapped open and the herd leapt up into the air, neighing in alarm. The stallion leapt with them, his wings so vast they blotted out the sun.

The girl flung up one pleading hand, calling silently, No, wait . . .

One of the mares turned to look at her, even as it launched itself into the air, tucking its legs up under its chest and belly. The stallion had soared over the ridge and the sky was again full of light, so the girl could see the mare clearly. She was very tall but delicately made, with slender limbs and a small, proud head. Her long, scrolled horns were opalescent blue, and more blue flashed at the tip of her sable wings.

The girl dragged out the blowpipe and the pouch of barbs, her fingers shaking so much she sent a spray of thorns cascading out as she fumbled to fit one into the pipe. She lifted the blowpipe to her mouth, struggling to drag oxygen into her lungs. The mare rose into the golden air, black and uncanny as a raven, and the girl expelled the barb with a great rush of air. It sang out into the sunset wind. Then there was no sound but the strong beat of wings. She let her hand drop. Tears rushed down her face. Her chest heaved in a great sob.

Then the surging movement of wing faltered. The mare dropped back down to the ground, her wings furling again along her side, her legs folding beneath her. She turned and collapsed to one side, her finely sculpted head drooping down to the ground. One-Horn's daughter stood there for a moment, frozen between triumphant joy and dread, then ran over and flung herself down beside the mare. She ran her hands along the drooping neck, down the long slender legs with their feathery fetlocks, back to the mare's soft velvety nose. The black skin was warm and silky; breath gusted out of the mare's large, sensitive nostrils and her eye quivered behind the closed lid. Relief weakened the girl's limbs so she could not move. She bent over the mare and laid her cheek against its soft skin. The horse's breath was warm and smelt of grass.

The girl did not linger long. Excitement filled her with new energy. She did not know how long the soporific would work. She covered the sleeping horse with her cloak, left her bow and quiver of arrows on the ground, and began to run back towards the valley. She did not need to go back to the camp. It was the saddlebags in the hollow log she wanted, packed with everything she thought she might need. Over the past two weeks she had prepared carefully, winning a new water-pouch, a whetting-stone and some tinder and flint in a gambling game. She had even challenged First-Male to a game of chance and for once had not allowed him to win, so that she could claim the brooch of the running horse that had belonged to her father. First-Male had been very affronted, for no-one ever let him lose, but One-Horn's daughter had not cared.

It did not take long to retrieve the saddle, bridle and bulging saddlebags but carrying them back through the forest, up the steep hills and over the ridge was an exhausting struggle. The boots were chafing her heels unbearably and her arms began to ache.

Much to her relief, the winged mare still slept. It was fully dark now, and the arch of night sky was freshly dusted with stars. A new anxiety constricted her breathing. Soon the herd would notice she was gone. Would they wait till morning before they began to hunt, or would they start looking for her straightaway? Surely she had a few more hours before they began to track her? Would the horse wake before then, or would she sleep on till dawn?

One-Horn's daughter began to make ready. It was incredibly difficult to strap on the saddle in the dark, with the mare lying down, but at last she managed to push the girth under the mare's belly with a stick, dragging it through and buckling it with stiff and unsure fingers. The bridle was no easier. It seemed to have far more straps than necessary, and she could not work out how to make the horse open its mouth for the bit. At last she wrenched the mare's jaw open, and the horse stirred and hurrumphed in its sleep, startling the girl so much she had to bite back a shriek. She rolled up the cloak and tied it to the pommel, then slung her bow and quiver of arrows on her back and clambered up into the saddle, gripping the pommel, afraid the horse would wake before she had time to tie herself on properly. The mare slept on, however, and so she was able to lash herself on tightly, using the reins to secure her arms to the horse's neck, and a coil of rope to tie her legs and body to the saddle and stirrups. It was not a comfortable position, but the girl knew her greatest danger was being flung to the ground from high in the air. She would rather endure an aching back and arms, and the cutting off of circulation in her hands and feet, than risk such a fall.

She was tired after her exertions and rested her head on the dark flowing mane, wondering how long she had before the horse woke up or the herd found her. She even

28

drifted off into an uneasy doze for a while, though the throbbing of her shoulder sockets and her wrists kept her from a deeper repose. At times she felt she was falling and would jerk awake, the leather biting into her flesh, only to drift asleep again. Then she heard a sound that brought her wide awake at once. It was the hullabaloo of the hunt. Although the sound was still faint, the girl knew how swift were the satyricorn. She had only a few minutes.

Frantically she began to kick the mare with her heels, and lash her neck with the end of the reins, rocking her body back and forth, urging the horse to wake, to flee. The shouts came closer. She lashed the mare harder. A convulsive shudder ran through the horse's body. She felt the satin-smooth skin ripple and twitch. Then the horse hurrumphed and suddenly jerked up onto its knees. The girl was rocked wildly, banging her chin on the pommel of the saddle and inadvertently biting her tongue as the mare bounded to her feet. She only had time to gasp and blink back tears, before the horse began to buck and rear wildly all round the clearing. One-Horn's daughter was jerked back and forth, up and down, bashing her face on its neck and withers, all the breath knocked out of her. The ropes cut her flesh cruelly. The horse galloped through the trees, trying to knock her off against a branch. She clung on grimly, trying to control her nausea and dizziness, feeling as battered and bruised as if she was being beaten with a club. One of her knees whammed so hard into a tree trunk that she thought it had been dislocated. Her skin was scraped and torn.

Fly, she silently urged the mare. *Fly away from here else they catch us . . .*

The mare spread her great feathery wings and leapt up into the air. The girl's stomach flip-flopped and she could not prevent a high-pitched scream from bursting out of her throat. Although it was still night-time, the moons had risen while she had dozed and the sky was bright with stars. She could see the dark shapelessness of the forest dropping away below her, incredibly fast, and feel the cold bite of the wind on her face. She shut her eyes and gripped tight every muscle in her aching arms and legs, determined not to fall.

As soon as the mare was in the air, the dreadful jolting and jarring was over. The mare flew smoothly and steadily, higher and higher. She could feel the smooth working of its muscles beneath her legs, and hear the rhythmic beat of its long wings. The sound was somehow soothing and after a while she dared to open her eyes. They seemed suspended in black fathomless space, stars all around and nothing below them. She shut her eyes again with a gasp, and rested her cheek against the horse's withers. *Don't let me fall*, she thought.

The mare's wings straightened and held steady. They hung there in the starry sky for an inestimably long moment, hovering. The girl took a deep painful breath and tightened her grip. Without warning the mare folded back her wings. They began to fall, hurtling towards the ground. Suddenly her wings snapped open again and the girl was flung backwards, crying aloud as the bonds jerked at her wrists and ankles. The mare neighed in distress as the jerk on the reins bruised her tender mouth. The girl fell back into the saddle with a painful thump, catching her breath with tears, and the mare neighed again and tried to buck. Again and again the mare sought to dislodge her, but the girl's knots held and she did not fall. So the mare flew on again, shaking her mane and neighing in distress, occasionally trying to buck off the heavy weight or shake away the hard, foul-tasting metal bit in her mouth.

30

They flew for an eternity. Then the sun was rising ahead of them, striking the girl's tired eyes like a silver-tipped whip. She shrank back, hiding her face in the flowing black mane. There was no sound but the steady beat of wings and the whistling of the wind. She guessed they were too high to hear birdsong. Without lifting her head she opened her eyes again and looked down past the sleek black shoulder. Below were wisps of rose-tinted clouds. They drifted apart and she could see a thin, shining curve of water winding through green forest. She could not believe how high they were. It hurt her lungs to breathe.

As the day wore on, the black mare grew weary and her attempts to throw the girl off grew feebler. The girl herself was near-fainting with exhaustion and pain. When at last the horse flew down to drink at the river and rest a while, she found she could not free herself. Her skin was so chafed and swollen that the leather reins had sunk deep into her flesh and she could not reach the knife strapped inside her boot, or unbuckle the dagger at her waist. They rested together, the mare lipping at the water, occasionally shuddering as she tried to shake the weight off, and the girl lying with her head resting on her bound arms, her arms and shoulders and knees and ankles throbbing unbearably. The sight of the water tortured her, for she was very thirsty. She tried again to reach the little black knife, but her movement spooked the horse and it shied and bucked. Helplessly she jerked and flopped around, and the horse neighed in terror and took off again, galloping through the forest, using its wings to leap through the underbrush or turn a sharp corner, bashing the girl against trees and rock-faces. One-Horn's daughter cracked her head hard against a stone cliff and felt pain lance down her neck and spine, then away she spun into a deep red, roaring unconsciousness. Time unravelled.

31

A THING OF BEAUTY

'Such are the horses on which gods and heroes ride, as represented by the artist. The majesty of men themselves is best discovered in the graceful handling of such animals. A horse so prancing is indeed a thing of beauty, a wonder and a marvel; riveting the gaze of all who see him.'

XENOPHON
On Horsemanship, 431–354 B.C.

KINGARTH

Lewen straightened his aching back, pushing the hair out of his eyes with a filthy, sweaty hand, and looked with some satisfaction on the large plot of rich dark earth before him. Although digging over the vegetable patch in preparation for the spring sowing was always hard work, he enjoyed working muscles stiff after the enforced inactivity of the winter, and he loved the smell of the sun-warmed earth.

He looked with keen pleasure across the lawns, through the grey filigree of branches just beginning to swell with flower buds, past pale stars of narcissus to the glimmering water of the loch. The forest lay beyond, green and deep and secret, with the grey, cloud-capped mountains brooding darkly beyond.

The knowledge that he would soon be leaving his parents' farm to travel back to the city only sharpened his acute sense of kinship with the wild, lovely landscape around him. Although he was looking forward to returning to his studies at the Tower of Two Moons, he knew he would miss his family and his home, this little glade of serenity surrounded on all sides by a dark snarl of wilderness.

I'll go out tramping this afternoon, he thought. *Take my dinner and walk up to the waterfall. Mam will understand.*

His mother looked up and smiled. She was a slender woman with eyes as green as the new leaves unfurling on the beech tree and a great mass of twiggy brown hair that was also just beginning to bud with leaves. Her bare feet were broad, brown and gnarled like tree roots.

'Sure, o' course ye can,' Lilanthe said. 'I'll keep Merry from following ye and teasing ye. I ken it's some peace ye be wanting.' She took a deep breath. 'Soil smells good.' Gracefully she lifted her brown homespun skirt and stepped into the dirt, her toes spreading and digging in. 'Mmm, tastes good too.'

Lewen grinned. 'Merry can sow her seeds now, if she wants.'

'Meriel!' Lilanthe called. 'Merry! Where are you?'

The branches of an apple tree at the far end of the garden shook violently and a girl dropped down, landing on hands and knees. She was only eleven years old, nine years younger than Lewen, for their mother had trouble carrying children to term. Three had died in her womb between Lewen and Meriel, and one had lived only a scant few hours before failing to take another breath. Their deaths had grieved Lilanthe deeply, and so she treasured this last child of hers all the more, keeping her close to home and teaching Meriel's lessons herself. The little girl was a bright, winsome child, as much at home in the forest as a squirrel, and with a deep connection to all growing things. Like her mother, she was small and slight, with long, twiggy brown hair and green eyes. Around her

36

head darted a tiny nisse, her iridescent wings whirring so fast they were merely a blur of light.

'Here I am, Mam,' Meriel sang out.

'Lewen has finished digging over the vegetable patch if you want to start planting,' Lilanthe said. 'Come and taste the soil, it's delicious!'

Meriel came bounding across the lawn, the nisse swooping ahead of her. When she came to the edge of the dug-over garden bed, she leapt in joyfully, squelching the damp earth between her bare toes. 'Yum, it is good,' she said. 'I'll go get my bags of seeds. Will ye help me, Lewen?'

'No' a chance,' he said. 'I've done my work for the day. I'm going to have a swim to get all this muck off me, then I'm going up the waterfall one last time.'

'I want to go too!' Meriel cried.

'Nay, it'll be late afore ye finish planting out those seeds, Merry,' Lilanthe said firmly. 'Ye can go into the forest anytime, but ye ken Nina will be here tomorrow and so this may be Lewen's last chance to go wandering in the forest afore he leaves for Lucescere.'

'No, I want to go,' Meriel wheedled. 'Oh, Lewen, must ye be going without me? Canna ye wait for me? I won't be long, I promise.'

'Aye, ye will, young lady. That's our vegetables for the summer ye've got rattling in that box o' yours, and I willna have ye spoil our harvest by being hasty in the planting. Leave Lewen be. He's worked hard this morning while ye were playing about and climbing trees and he deserves a few hours off.'

'Oh but Mam . . .'

'No buts about it, missy. Remember, I'm trusting ye to sow the seeds by yourself. Plant too deep or too shallow or too close together, and ye've lost your seed.'

'Aye, I ken that, Mam. It's just that it's our last afternoon alone with Lewen. Nina will have a whole caravan o' people with her and then he'll be going away with them and we willna see him again for ages . . .'

'No need to be reminding me, dear heart, I ken.' Lilanthe smiled at her and ruffled her wild brown locks. 'He'll be home for supper, though, and when ye've finished planting out the seeds ye can come and help me bake something special for him, if ye like.'

Meriel agreed begrudgingly. Lewen smiled at her, feeling rather guilty. It was not that he did not enjoy his little sister's company, it was just that she was so full of vitality. He felt a strong desire for quietness and reflection on his last afternoon in the forest.

After he had cleaned his tools and put them away in the barn, he went back through the garden towards the house. It was a very pretty little house, with rose briars climbing over the back porch and a stone shield over the arched front door with a design of a weeping greenberry tree carved upon it. It had been built of the local rough grey stone, but so carefully that all the stones fitted together harmoniously, making sure no draughts could sneak in through gaps and cracks. Its lichen-green roof was very steep, so that the heavy snows of winter would slide off easily, and the windows were all large and paned with glass, so that the rooms were filled with sunshine in the warm growing months. Long shutters with little heart shapes cut out in rows were now fastened securely back against the walls, but in winter they would be drawn across the windows, protecting the precious glass from hail and sleet, and keeping the warmth of the fire within. The doors and shutters and gables were all painted a soft green and the house was surrounded on all sides by a lovingly tended garden so it looked as if it had grown up from the earth rather than being assembled upon it.

Lewen came through the kitchen garden with its hedges of evergreen rosemary, grinning at Meriel as she knelt in the freshly dug garden beds, carefully planting out her seeds. His mother came out onto the porch, with a satchel of food in her hands and a bundle of clean clothes.

'Here ye are then, laddie. Do no' be late home now, do ye hear? Merry and I will be making ye a special supper for your last night at home. Will ye be home afore dark?'

'I'm just going up to the waterfall, Mam. I'm no' intending to climb auld Hoarfrost.'

'Aye, I ken. And I do no' fear ye doing something foolish. It's just . . . och, it's probably naught. Happen it's because I ken ye are leaving soon and I wish to keep ye close. I'm sorry. Ye enjoy your tramp and I'll see ye at supper.'

'Aye, sure, Mam. I'll be good, I promise.' He smiled at her cheekily, waved a quick goodbye and set off through the garden, rummaging in the satchel to see what she had packed for him. There was fresh baked bread and hard cheese and pickles, a fat wedge of fruitcake and, much to his satisfaction, a corked jar of cold ale.

On the grassy slope by the lake, he stripped off his damp, grimy clothes and plunged into the water, which was icy cold but invigorating. He swam vigorously across the lake to the island, parting the willow fronds to slide into the cool green cavern beneath, as he had done since he was just a boy. He floated there for a moment, but it was far too cold out of the sunshine and so he swam back towards the shore. Greatly refreshed, he towelled himself dry and dressed again, buckling his witch's dagger in its accustomed place at his belt and polishing his moonstone ring till it shone. He then followed a narrow green path into the woods, the nisse Kalea soaring swiftly ahead of him, her wings flashing.

It was an ancient forest, and very dark and tangled. Many of the trees had been growing since long before humans came to Eileanan. They ascended into the sky like massive columns, their trunks green and velvety with moss, their branches trailing shawls of fine grey lace. The path climbed past one old giant whose girth was so vast that a dozen men standing on its roots would not have been able to touch fingers, no matter how outstretched their arms.

It was quiet in the cool gloom, the only sound the occasional call of a bird or the subtle rustle of some creature in the undergrowth. Lewen walked swiftly, for the sun was already beginning to slant sideways through the tree trunks and it was a hike of an hour or more to the waterfall.

Kalea came down to perch on his shoulder, taking hold of his ear and raising herself on tiptoe so she could speak into it. 'Lewen tramp-stamp the green way, the forest way, Lewen sad-sorrowful?'

Lewen smiled ruefully. The nisse knew him well. He put up his hand and lifted her off his shoulder, holding her before his face so he could speak directly to her. Her eyes were the colour of the green heart of a flame, shining in the gloom like a cat's, and her face was triangular, with sharp-pointed ears poking through a mass of wild dark hair.

'I do feel rather sad,' he admitted. 'I'm going back to school, ye ken, and although I love the Theurgia and love being the Rìgh's squire, I still miss ye, and my kin, and the forest.'

'Why go? Stay-stop.'

'I canna,' he answered.

Her eyes blazed with fury. 'Canna? Why canna? Canna-willna.'

40

'I suppose that's true,' he said. 'I could stay, o' course. But I want to go to school, and learn; and I'm proud to serve my Rìgh and hope I'll be knighted after I graduate and happen even be appointed a Blue Guard like my da was, if I do well enough . . .'

Kalea reached out her tiny hand and seized his nose, tweaking it so hard tears sprang to his eyes. 'Fool-school,' she said scornfully. 'More learning-lore here, tree-wise, sky-wise, stone-wise, water-wise. No learning-lore at fool-school.'

Lewen had dropped her the moment she tweaked his nose, crying out in surprise. Now, as he rubbed it furiously, she hovered before him, her diamond-bright wings whirring.

'That hurt!' he said crossly.

She trilled derisively, showing her fangs, and darted away as he tried to catch her again.

'Canna catch me!' she called and buzzed about his head as exasperatingly as any mosquito. Every now and again she ducked closer to slap or pinch him. 'Canna catch me!'

'Stop it, Kalea!' Lewen cried. 'What's the matter with ye?'

'No go,' she suddenly cried, swooping down to clasp his finger with both arms. 'Lewen no go?'

He cupped her gently. 'I'll miss ye too, Kalea, indeed I will. But I truly do have to go. I've missed enough school these last few months, and I do no' want to fall behind. I'll come back when I can, though . . .'

Without warning she sank her sharp fangs into his hand. He yelped and shook her off, lifting his hand to suck at the blood leaking from the little puncture wounds.

'Kalea weep-wail, Kalea sob-snivel,' she cried, scrubbing at her eyes with tiny fists. 'Lewen go!' And she turned and flew away into the forest, swift and noisy as a hornet. Lewen stared after her, feeling angry and exasperated and a little bit guilty all at the same time. Kalea was the great-great-granddaughter of the nisse Elala whom Lilanthe had once rescued from children in a village square. Lewen's father Niall said that was when he first began to love Lilanthe, seeing her standing alone against a gang of bullies with the poor battered nisse cradled in her hands. Although the garden and forest around the house were infested with the great-great-grandchildren of Elala, Kalea was the youngest and the boldest. She was rarely far from Lewen, having developed an abiding affection for him ever since the time he had scooped her out of a particularly deep puddle one stormy day when she had been little more than a baby. Although nisses were by nature impish and quarrelsome, delighting in spiteful tricks and teasing games, Kalea had never tweaked his nose before, let alone bitten him. It upset him that she had done so now.

As he clambered over great, writhing roots, ducked under tangled vines, and slid down a slippery slope with the satchel bouncing on his back, Lewen's thoughts returned to the journey ahead of him. He had spent the last four years studying at the Theurgia and he loved it, but he did find the noise and crowds burdensome, and his duties as one of the Rìgh's squires took up a great deal of his spare time. He was so eager to be chosen as one of the Rìgh's personal bodyguards that he took his court duties very seriously, and by the end of the last term he had been exhausted in both body and mind. The Keybearer of the Coven had noticed, even if the Rìgh had not. So she had sent him home for the winter holidays. He had not been home to Kingarth since his sixteenth birthday, when he had sat the Second Test of Powers and had been accepted into the Theurgia as an apprentice-witch. Four long years spent in the midst of two hundred other apprentices, all jostling for attention, all noisy and opinionated, all hungry to prove their powers. No wonder he had been exhausted.

In the morning, the journeywitch Nina the Nightingale would be coming by the farm, so that Lewen could join her caravan of new apprentices on its way to the Theurgia. Journeywitches were a specially chosen band of witches who spent their days travelling around Eileanan looking for children with magical powers, and persuading their parents to send them to the Theurgia to be properly trained. They also performed rites for any village they passed that did not have a witch of its own.

Lewen could have easily ridden down to Ravenscraig, the castle of the ruling MacBrann clan, to meet Nina and her cavalcade, but the journeywitch was an old and dear friend of Lilanthe's and did not want to miss the chance to see her and Niall. So she and her band of apprentice-witches were all riding from Ravenscraig to Kingarth, even though the round trip would add a week to their journey.

Kingarth was the last croft before the wild mountains known as the Broken Ring of Dubhslain, which curved in a perfect crescent around the highlands of Ravenshaw. There were only two known paths through the great grim peaks. One path led west, over the exposed, wind-scoured flank of Bald Ben, to the rolling plains of Tìreich where the horse-lairds lived. The other climbed high past Dubhglais, 'the black lake', and up the steep, bare ridge of Ben Eyrie, the third highest mountain in Eileanan. Dragons were said to fly over Ben Eyrie, and ogres dwelled in the caves hidden within its cliffs. Although this road was by far the swiftest route to the north, it was considered so perilous that it was only used in times of great danger and need. It was called the Razor's Edge.

Under the shadow of Ben Eyrie was the loch known as Dubhglais, where the Findhorn River had its source. The river wound its way down to a tall waterfall called Hoarfrost's Beard that fell into the valley where Kingarth was nestled. It then tumbled and fell in swift rapids down the length of the highlands till it came to another steep cliff where it once again fell in a roaring mass of white water called the Findhorn Falls. Ravenscraig was built above these falls, and so for centuries it had been the stronghold of the MacBrann clan, secure against attack. Originally it had been the prionnsa's winter castle, but the family had taken up permanent residence there when their summer castle Rhyssmadill had proven too close to the dangerous and unpredictable sea.

Lewen had been to Ravenscraig many times, and in fact had only recently returned from a trip there with his family. The only thing it had in common with the great city of Lucescere in Rionnagan was that it was built above a waterfall too high for the Fairgean to leap. It was rather a small castle, damp and draughty and filled with dogs. Lucescere, on the other hand, was a vast warren of a place, filled with sorcerers, nobles, merchants, thieves and faeries. The Rìgh had his palace there, protected on either side by two deep, fast rivers. In the grounds of the palace was the Tower of Two Moons, where the Keybearer of the Coven of Witches had her headquarters, and where the Theurgia, the most famous school in the land, was based.

Although Lewen wanted desperately to be a Yeoman of the Guard, like his father had been, he had ambivalent feelings about Lucescere. He knew his mother had been unhappy there, shunned and mocked because of her faery blood. It was in the gardens of Lucescere that she had been attacked with an axe while sleeping in her tree-shape. Twenty years later she still walked with a limp, and the deep ugly scar still marred her smooth bark.

Although Lewen had not inherited the ability to shapechange into a tree, as his sister had done, he was certainly unhappy if he spent too much time away from the forest. If it had not been for the palace's famous gardens, Lewen would have left the Theurgia as soon as he got there. Although the gardens were very old and very beautiful, they were tamed and controlled, quite unlike the wild woods of northern Ravenshaw.

When Lewen had first gone to the Theurgia, at the age of sixteen, he had braced himself for the same sort of mockery and disdain his mother had faced, but to his relief his tree-changer ancestry had never been a problem. Either things had changed since Lachlan the Winged had won the throne, or else, as his father had laughingly said, he was simply too big for any of the other students to dare challenge him. Certainly Lewen had inherited his father's build, being a head above six foot tall, and broad across the shoulders. He had been taught to fight too, with fists and feet, dagger and claymore, and to shoot the longbow with uncanny accuracy. The longbowmen of Ravenshaw were famous, and Niall the Bear the most famous of them all. It was said only the Rìgh could bend a longer bow, or shoot as far or as truly, and Lachlan the Winged carried Owein's Bow, an ancient and magical weapon.

The cool, delicate touch of spray across his face roused him from his abstraction. Lewen glanced up, surprised, to see a wide curtain of white water tumbling down a high cliff. It fell sheer and foaming as a curtain of white muslin, the stone behind it dark and glistening. Here and there sunlight struck through the encircling trees and lit the spray as bright as diamonds, but most of the cliff-face and the pool below were in shadow and so the effect was curiously smooth and silent.

Lewen grinned and stretched and swung his satchel off his back. He felt a pleasant euphoric tiredness after his long walk, his exasperation at Kalea's antics having faded away. He pulled out the jar of ale first, uncorked it with his teeth, and took a long swig. After an hour in his rucksack it was not as cool as he would have liked and so he went down to the pool to set it in the icy water while he ate his bread and cheese. He knelt on the damp mossy stones and was just setting the jar securely between two rocks when he heard something that brought him swiftly to his feet.

In the dark underhang of rock by the cliff a horse was lying, its head drooping. Its breath was harsh and laboured, rasping in its throat. Its coat was so black it was hard to make out its shape in the gloom of the deep little dell, but Lewen was able to see at once that someone was draped over its withers. He scrambled over the rocks, his concern growing as he noticed the yellowish scum that streaked the horse's damp hide, the trembling of its limbs and the twitching of its hide, signs that it had been driven to exhaustion. Then Lewen was close enough to see and recognise the blue jacket and cockaded hat of a Yeoman of the Guard, and he broke into a run. The movement spooked the horse. It shook its head, eyes rolling white in terror, and tried to rise but was too weary, collapsing back to the ground. The attempt to rise had shown Lewen two more, very strange things. The horse had wings, magnificent black feathered wings, each as long as he himself was tall. And the body slumped heavily over the horse's back had been tied on with rope.

Lewen went forward slowly, holding out one hand, whickering softly under his breath. The horse's ears twitched and it rolled an eye towards him.

'Gently now,' he said. 'Gently.'

Slowly, step by step, Lewen came closer. Again the horse tried to rise and shy away but Lewen reached forward and caught it by the bridle, steadying it. He smoothed one hot, damp shoulder, distressed to see the slobber round the horse's mouth was stained with blood. Gently he eased the bit out of the horse's torn mouth, keeping a firm hand on the bridle as the horse tried to drag its head away, whinnying in distress.

Once he had calmed the horse again, Lewen turned his attention to the unconscious soldier. There was a nasty gash on one temple, with blood drying thick on one pale cheek, and the leather reins had cut deeply into the flesh at the wrists. Although Lewen had his witch's knife sheathed at his belt, he was reluctant to cut the bonds here in the gloom of the spray-misted basin, so far from home. He did not think he could carry the wounded soldier all the way home as well as lead the weary horse, and he knew his parents were the best people to tend both man and horse.

Gently Lewen urged the black mare to rise. He knew it was dangerous to let the horse lie still after such exertion, so he dragged on the cheek-band and pushed at the horse's flank until at last she summoned the energy to stand. He encouraged her to walk the few steps down the slope to the pool then, without letting go of the bridle, he reached down to the pool and cupped water in his hand, letting the horse drink from his palm. The poor beast drank thirstily, and would have drunk more if Lewen had not restrained her, knowing too much water could be danger-ous in her overheated and weakened state.

Keeping all his movements slow and steady, he rubbed the mare down with a handful of grass, then covered the horse and its unconscious rider as well as he could with

47

the warm woollen cloak tied before the pommel. Then, regretting his jar of ale growing nicely cold in the pool, he began the long, wearisome walk home.

It was fully dark by the time he and the exhausted horse plodded out of the forest and into the orchard by the lake. Both the moons were half-full, and their mingled radiance cast a cool, colourless light across the garden. The trees were all very black, the loch was a strange glimmery silver, and warm orange light streamed from Kingarth across the dark lawn. Lewen lifted his gaze to the light, finding new energy in the closeness of home. He was bone-weary himself. Many times it had only been the strength of his hand on the bridle and his shoulder against the horse's flank that had prevented the mare from foundering. The forest at night was a frightening place, besides, for it rustled and whimpered with mysterious sounds, and occasionally was rent by the howl of the hunter and the death-wail of the hunted. He was glad to have left the nerve-racking darkness of the forest behind.

Suddenly a huge shape loomed up out of the darkness beside him and he smelt the strong stench of bear. The horse did too, and reared and whinnied in terror, almost wrenching his arm out of its socket.

'Ursa! Back!' he cried.

'Ursa, down,' his father said gently. 'Go back.'

The bear gave a sad-sounding snuffle and lumbered away towards the house.

'What is it, laddie?' Niall said in his deep, calm voice. 'Ye're home so late, your mam was worried.' He came up out of the shadows, moving quietly for so tall a man. He saw at once the stumbling horse with its heavy burden and his son, trudging wearily at its bridle. 'What is this ye've found? A horse?'

'A winged horse,' Lewen said.

'Winged? With a thigearn astride?'

'He wears the coat o' a Yeoman.'

'Indeed?' Niall's voice rose in interest.

'He's been tied on cruelly tight. I dared not cut him loose; the bonds were too tight and the light too bad. I am afraid though . . .'

'Ye did well, my lad. Bring them to the stables. I'll call Lilanthe. She'll ken what to do.'

Lewen knew his mother had learnt her healing arts from Isabeau the Red, who was now Keybearer of the Coven. Lilanthe's knowledge was so deep, she was often called away to help at a difficult birthing, or to splint a shattered bone. His family's trip to Ravenscraig a few weeks earlier had been to help ease the last painful days of the old MacBrann, who had died slowly and with ever-increasing madness.

The final few yards to the stables seemed to take forever, with the horse barely able to put one hoof after another, and Lewen's boots seeming very hot and heavy. At last they were within the dim, hay-smelling vastness, and Niall was kindling lanterns and exclaiming aloud at the sight of the winged mare in the golden fullness of their light.

She was a magnificent beast, even as worn and tired as she was, with great black wings shading through blue to violet at the tips, and long scrolled horns with the irides-cence of dark mother-of-pearl. Every curve was beautiful and proud. She was delicately made for such a long-limbed animal, with a luxuriant mane and tail, and feathered hocks. She was so weary she hardly flinched as Niall drew his dagger and carefully sawed away at the ropes that bound the rider to the beast. At last the ropes frayed and fell away, and they were able to lift the rider down and lay him in the straw and lift the lantern to examine him.

There was a long silence.

'She's a girl,' Lewen breathed at last.

'And no' so very auld,' Niall said. 'What is she doing in the uniform o' a Yeoman?'

'And tied on to the back o' a winged horse?'

'Eà kens! Come, let us leave her for your mam and look to the horse. She's a noble beast and cruelly used. Look at her bleeding mouth.'

Niall had been a cavalier for many years and knew just what to do for the exhausted beast. He kept Lewen busy mixing warm mash, applying poultices and anointing the horse's many cuts and abrasions but, despite his fascination with the winged horse, Lewen could not help casting many a glance at the girl lying in the straw. She was so dirty and bloody it was hard to see much of her face, especially with all that black, matted hair straggling all over it, but her figure was tall and lithe with a deep curve from breast to hip, and her mouth had as sweet a shape as any he had seen on a girl. She was beginning to stir as Lilanthe gently bathed her swollen, lacerated wrists, and Lewen stopped to look again as her eyes slowly opened.

They were not black, as he might have expected with all that raven hair, but a clear blue-grey colour, and fringed with very long, dark lashes. For a moment she stared up at Lilanthe blankly, and then she glanced round the dimly lit stable, seeing the winged horse tethered in its stall, and the man and boy cleaning the tack nearby.

With a vicious snarl, the girl was on her feet, knocking Lilanthe over with the violence of her movement. The girl looked about desperately, seized a pitchfork from its place on the wall and raced at Niall, her lips drawn back from her teeth.

Niall dropped the saddle, holding up both his hands in a pacifying gesture, but the girl only growled and drove the pitchfork towards his heart. Niall lunged forward, caught the handle just below the tines, and wrested it from her. As he flung it away into the straw, she leapt at him with her nails raking at his eyes. He managed to block her with one arm, but he was knocked off balance by the speed of her attack and fell back onto the straw-scattered cobbles, the girl on top of him.

Lewen dropped his polishing rag and leapt to his father's aid.

THE WILD GIRL

Though he was able to drag the girl off his father, she turned on him, biting the tender skin where his neck met his shoulder. Lewen yelped and shoved her away. She kicked him hard behind the knee and he almost went over. Niall had scrambled to his feet again and caught her from behind but she kicked back with her heel, catching him smartly in the groin. He reeled back for a moment, as much shocked as pained, and the girl then turned on Lewen, grasping a lock of his curly brown hair and pulling so hard she almost ripped it out by the roots. Lewen had to wrap his arm about her throat, trapping one arm to her side, while he held her still against him with the other. She squirmed and wriggled like an eel, and he almost had to throttle her to keep her still.

Niall rubbed his abused private parts ruefully then took the pitchfork and threw it out the stable door. Lilanthe was trembling and he put one arm around her shoulders to comfort her. 'What a wildcat!' he said. 'I never thought

I'd be tempted to hit a woman before, let alone a wee slip o' a girl.'

'She's no' so wee,' Lewen panted, having to tighten his hold on the girl as she struggled again to break free. Indeed, she was near as tall as he was, though slim and softly curved. She kicked back savagely with one booted heel and he leapt back, inadvertently loosening his hold. She spun and tried to escape, but Lewen caught her again, holding both her hands in one hand and seizing her waist with the other. 'There's no need to fight and squirm so,' he said gently. 'We mean ye no harm. We're trying to help.'

She made a disbelieving noise but, when he tightened his grasp, stopped her desperate struggling, straining away from him, panting and trying to hold back tears. He loosened his bruising grip a little, moving away so she was not held so tightly against him. 'There's no need to fear,' he said in the same deep, gentle voice he had used to soothe the horse. 'Come, ye're sorely hurt. We do no' wish to harm ye any more than ye've already been harmed. Will ye no' sit and rest and let my mother tend ye?'

She looked up at him suspiciously, and he eased his grip and gestured to her to sit back down in the straw. 'Your wrists must be sore indeed,' he said kindly, 'and happen ye're thirsty? Can I get ye some water?'

She moistened her parched lips with the tip of her tongue but did not answer. Carefully he let her go and moved across to the barrel of water, scooping out a cup of water for her. She snatched it from him and scrambled away, then drank thirstily, staring at him through the tangle of filthy black hair.

Lilanthe regarded her with troubled eyes. 'She's like a snow-lion cub, all teeth and claws. I wonder where she came from.'

'What is your name, lassie?' Niall asked. 'And why do ye fight so? What do ye fear?'

She cast him a sideways look, wary and distrustful, then returned her gaze to Lewen's face.

'What is your name?' Lewen said very gently.

She licked her lips again, her eyes darting from one face to another, then said haltingly, 'Lassie.'

'Aye, we ken you're a lass, we've eyes in our head,' Niall said. 'But what is your name? What are ye called?'

'Lassie?' she said again.

Niall, Lewen and Lilanthe exchanged rueful glances.

'Happen she's a wee touched in the head,' Niall said.

The girl frowned and, with a puzzled air, lifted a hand to touch her head.

'Nay,' Lilanthe said. 'I dinna think so. There's intelligence in those fierce blue eyes. I wonder ... there's something strange about her. I'd say she's a faery child. Or at least, she has faery blood in her. And we are far from anywhere here. She must have come down out o' the mountains.'

'Then what is she doing wearing the uniform o' a Yeoman?' Niall said gruffly.

The girl stared at him uncomprehendingly. He bent and took a fold of her jacket between his fingers, saying, 'Where did ye get it? Who does it belong to?'

Immediately she flinched away, scrambling out of reach.

'Nay! Mine!' she cried.

'Yours?' Niall asked, his eyes on the silver stag badge of the Yeomen. 'Ye say the clothes are yours?'

She crossed her arms about her protectively. 'Mine! No touch.'

'Well, she seems to understand what we say well enough,' Niall said. He bent towards her. 'Lassie? Are ye hungry?'

She nodded her head voraciously, though she sidled back nervously, keeping a fair distance between them.

'Lewen, lad, why do ye no' go and find our guest something to eat? And happen make up a bed for her? She must be sick and weary. We can question her again in the morning. For now let her sleep and recover.'

'I'll fill up the bath too,' Lilanthe said with a quick smile. 'She's filthy.'

'Nay!' the girl said emphatically.

'Ye need a bath, my lass. Ye're no' sleeping in my good sheets until I have all that blood and muck off ye.'

'Nay!' the girl said again, gripping her hands into fists. She pointed one finger at the winged horse, now drowsily lipping at the bucket of warm mush with a blanket over its back. 'Me stay. She mine. Mine!'

'Ye want to stay here with the horse?' Lewen asked.

She glanced at him and nodded, her expression clearing for a moment. 'Mine.'

'We do no' seek to take your horse away from ye,' Niall said sternly. 'Though they say one canna own a winged horse. They canna be tamed with spur and whip, or broken to bridle and saddle, like ye have tried to do.' He gestured with one hand to the bridle in the straw where Lewen had dropped it, its bit befouled with blood and foam. 'A thigearn wins the trust and respect of his horse, he does no' bloody its mouth and whip it till it founders.'

It was clear she understood his meaning, for a crimson blush swept up her throat and face, and she dropped those disconcertingly luminous eyes. 'Dinna mean to hurt,' she said haltingly, searching for the right words. 'No . . . no other way.'

'No other way for what?' Lewen asked. 'Ye have ridden a long way. Where have ye come from? Are ye fleeing from someone?'

She shook her head, not looking at him, and made another emphatic gesture. 'Go away,' she said. 'Leave me. Me go. Soon me go.'

'But ye are hurt still,' Lewen said. 'Will ye no' let us tend ye, and give ye some food? And your mare? Ye canna mean to ride her anytime soon. She is sick and exhausted, and sorely hurt too.'

She looked at him in alarm. 'Hurt?'

'She's exhausted,' Niall said in cool tones of condemnation. 'And her flanks have been flayed cruelly.'

The girl flashed him an angry look. 'No' me. Thorns.'

Niall grinned, his teeth flashing white in his dark bushy beard. 'Ye're rather thorny yourself, my prickly lass. Nay, do no' look daggers at me. Ye may stay here in the stable if ye'd prefer. Indeed, somehow I think I'd sleep sounder tonight if ye did. It'd be like trying to cage a snow-lion cub to bring ye into the house. Lewen, lad, will ye go and get her some blankets and something to eat?'

Lewen nodded and tried to smother a yawn. He had to admit he was tired and hungry after the long walk through the forest.

As he turned to go, Lilanthe knelt down in the straw beside the girl, reaching for one lacerated wrist. At once the girl snarled at her, baring her teeth like a wolf. Lilanthe started back in alarm. Lewen turned back in sudden concern for his mother.

'Do no' be afraid,' Niall said, surprised. 'My wife is a healer. She shall no' hurt ye.'

The girl glared at them through the matted knots of her hair, her whole body tensed and ready to spring. Lilanthe made a tentative move towards her and the girl lashed out, raking Lilanthe's cheek with her filthy nails. Lilanthe gasped and shrank back, blood beading on her cheek. With a roar of outrage Niall strode forward, drawing his wife into the shelter of his arm with one hand and menacing the wild girl with his other fist. 'How dare ye?' he cried. 'Leave her be! She was only trying to help.'

The girl pressed herself back into the wall, her eyes blackly dilated, her hands held up before her face as if seeking to protect herself from a blow.

'Do no' fear,' Lewen said softly, stepping between his furious father and the wild-eyed girl. 'No-one here will hurt ye. Ye are safe, I promise ye. Will ye no' let us help ye? We mean ye no harm, there is no need to be afraid.'

She lifted her eyes to his face, her hands dropping. He took a few slow steps towards her, repeating his words in a low, gentle voice, and although she leant away from him she did not strike as he dropped to one knee before her. 'There, there, ye see? I mean ye no harm. We only want to help. Your poor wrists look so sore. See, the cool water feels good, doesn't it? It'll wash away the dirt and make sure your wounds heal cleanly.'

As he spoke, Lewen very gently took one hand and trickled the water over her abused wrist. She crouched very still, not taking her eyes off him. He turned her wrist in his big hand, and blotted it dry with the soft cloth, staining it with streaks of mud and blood. 'See, is that no' better? Let me wash the other one too. It must be so sore. Look how much it is swollen. Now let me put some lotion on it. Does that no' feel better?'

She breathed out in a long sigh, and nodded her head.

Then Niall moved, easing Lilanthe away from him so he could examine her scratched cheek. At once the girl shrank back, hands flying up in a protective gesture again.

'Sssh, sssh,' Lewen said. 'No need to fear. All is well.'

Niall sighed in exasperation. 'It's your mam who needs the lotion now,' he said. 'Do ye see how filthy that wildcat's claws are? It's your mam's cheek that'll fester, for sure.'

Lilanthe pressed her hand against her cheek. 'Nay, I'll be fine,' she said faintly. 'Lewen, let me do that. Ye're worn out.'

'Nay, no' ye,' the girl said. 'Me no like ye. Ye go away.'

Lilanthe was taken aback, and Niall was furious. 'Ungrateful brat,' he said. 'Fine, we'll go away. I hope ye're cold and hungry and your cuts and bruises throb all night.'

'Niall, no!' Lilanthe cried.

Lewen protested at the same time. '*Dai-dein*! She's sore hurt and she's afraid. Do no' be angry with her.'

Niall sighed. 'Fine. Ye stay and tend to her then. She seems to like ye, at least. I'll take your mother back to the house and tend to her. I'll send Merry out with some food for her –'

'Nay, no' Merry,' Lilanthe protested at once, looking askance at the filthy, wild-eyed, wild-haired creature crouched in the straw.

'Very well, no' Merry, me,' Niall agreed in a long-suffering tone. 'I willna be long, lad. Try to keep out o' reach o' those claws. I do no' want anyone else injured tonight.'

'All right, Da,' Lewen said.

'Make sure ye make up her bed well away from the winged horse,' Niall warned. 'That mare is as wild as the lass, remember, and though she is quiet enough now, she may no' be so docile once she recovers some o' her energy. A great beast like that can recuperate surprisingly quickly.'

'Aye, that I ken,' Lewen said, smiling.

'I'll be back in just a wee,' his father said. Still cradling the pale and shaken Lilanthe in one arm, he rather reluctantly went out into the darkness.

Lewen turned and looked at the wild-haired girl.

'Come, sit down,' he said gently. 'I shallna hurt ye,

I promise. Ye must be sick and dizzy with that head wound, and aching all over after the ride ye've had. Will ye no' trust me?'

She hesitated then very gingerly lowered herself back to the floor. 'Me do hurt. All over.'

'Ye must indeed. Here, let me finish salving your wrists. They're raw and bloody. Those ropes must've been tied very tight.'

'Had to be tight. Fall off if no' tight.'

'So ye tied them yourself? Ye tied yourself on the horse?'

After a long frowning moment, she nodded.

He said no more, kneeling in the straw before her and lifting up first one hand, then the other, turning them to examine the lacerated flesh. Her fingernails were torn and jagged and black with dirt, but the hands themselves were slender and long-fingered, with callouses he recognised as being caused by drawing back the string of a bow. He remembered the bow and quiver of roughly hewn arrows that had been tied onto her back, and felt his curiosity grow.

Very gently he applied the soothing cream and bandaged her wrists. Then he gathered up all her hair and swept it over her shoulder, smoothing it away from her brow so he could look at the wound on her temple. She sat quietly, almost as if spellbound, as he washed away the encrusted blood, and anointed the wound with his mother's salve.

'It is no' too bad,' he said softly. 'Head wounds often bleed a lot. Ye may have a headache for a day or two, but naught more serious. I'll no' bandage it, it's only a scrape and the air will do it good.'

She said nothing, just gazed at him with her dark brows drawn together over her eyes, though more in puzzlement than anger. With the mud and blood washed from her face, he was able to see her clearly for the first time. She had a long, thin face with bony temples and a patrician nose. Her cheekbones were so high there were little hollows beneath. Her mouth was soft and full-lipped with a deep indentation in the upper lip. It gave her a vulnerable air, at odds with the strength of the rest of her features. As he stared at her, her mouth quirked and set itself firmly. Lewen looked away quickly.

He moved back a little, taking up one of her feet and lifting an eyebrow in query. She tilted her head, then gave a little shrug and nodded. Gently he drew off the long, leather boots, and took her bare ankle in one hand, examining the bruised and swollen flesh carefully. 'The boots were some protection, at least,' he said. 'Let me wash your feet clean and put some arnica cream on, and then ye'll be more comfortable.'

She acquiesced silently. He washed her feet carefully, noting the hard soles and splayed toes of someone who customarily went barefoot, and the new red patches where the boots had rubbed skin not used to confinement. He had just finished massaging in the cream when he sensed someone watching and looked up. His mother stood just beyond the stable door, a pile of blankets in one arm, a basket in the other hand. She was watching them with a grave expression on her face. Lewen flushed but Lilanthe made no comment, limping in and putting her burdens down near her son, who lifted the girl's feet off his lap so that he could turn and reach to pick them up.

'I brought her a nightgown and some blankets,' Lilanthe said with the faintest trace of coolness in her voice. 'And there's some vegetable broth, and some new bread, and a slice of the whortleberry pie that Merry and I made this afternoon.'

Lewen was hot and uncomfortable in his skin. He found it hard to meet his mother's clear gaze. He busied himself winding up the unused bandages and tidying up the salves while the girl fell upon the soup and bread like a wild animal.

'Your supper is waiting for ye, when ye're ready,' Lilanthe said. 'Do no' be long, laddie. It's almost time for Merry to go to bed and she's eager to see ye, on your last night home with just us.'

Lewen bit his lip in chagrin. 'I'll no' be long, Mam. I'll just see her settled.'

Lilanthe nodded and shook out some warm blankets, then piled her basket high with her healing salves and bandages. 'Sleep well, lassie,' she said gently to the girl, who looked up briefly from her soup before lowering her face to the bowl again. 'Do no' fear. Ye are safe here. This house and garden are well protected. None will harm ye here.'

The girl looked up again, considering Lilanthe for a long moment, then she nodded in acknowledgement and went back to her meal.

'Ye're welcome,' Lilanthe said with gentle irony and went back into the darkness.

'It's usual to say "thanks" when someone does something for ye,' Lewen chided gently.

'Why?' she asked.

He was nonplussed. 'It just is. It's good manners. People get upset if ye do no' say thanks.'

'Why?'

'They just do. It's rude.'

'What rude?'

'Rude is . . . being rude is having bad manners.' Lewen was conscious of talking in circles. He made a big effort. 'Good manners are like the oil in the clogs of a clock, they keep things running smoothly,' he said.

The girl stared at him blankly. Lewen realised she would never have seen a clock before and cast around for some other way to explain.

'Being rude makes ye seem . . . ungrateful. No-one will like doing things for ye. If ye say things like "please" and "thank ye" and "bless ye" and "may I", then people will like ye more and like doing things for ye.'

'If me say . . . this thing, "thanks", then people like me?' she asked incredulously.

'Aye.'

'Ye too? Ye like me if me say "thanks"?'

'Aye, o' course. I mean . . .' Fearing his tongue getting into a tangle again, Lewen came to a halt.

'Then me say thanks,' she said.

'Ye're welcome,' he said. 'That's what you say when people have said thanks.'

'Why?' she asked.

'Ye just do,' he answered.

The girl absorbed this in silence.

Rather shyly Lewen directed the girl towards the clean clothes. 'Would you like to change? And there's a comb for your hair.' She stared at it in puzzlement as he held it up for her. He mimed combing his hair, then said, 'Though happen your hair is too knotted to comb by yourself. And it needs to be washed.'

He imagined himself washing it for her, and colour surged in his cheeks. He went on doggedly, 'Tomorrow, happen my mam will help you wash and comb it. Now ye should sleep. Ye are tired.'

She had put one hand up to her hair self-consciously. Now she dropped it, nodding and saying, 'Aye, me tired. No sleep last night.' She shook her head wonderingly and crammed another piece of whortleberry pie into her mouth.

62

'Why no'? Were ye riding the mare all night?'

She jerked her head in affirmation.

'How long? How long were ye on her back?'

She shrugged, then held up two fingers.

'Two days?'

'One day, one night,' she answered. 'Long time.'

'Aye, indeed. I'll leave ye to sleep then, for ye must be tired,' Lewen said, handing her the pile of soft blankets. 'I hope ye will be warm enough.'

She had been fingering the blankets rather dazedly. At his words she looked up at him, wiping her mouth with the back of her hand. Dimples suddenly flashed in her cheeks. She made a gesture that went from the blankets round the shadowy, lantern-lit stable with its straw-filled byres and sleepy, contented animals. 'Me never so warm,' she answered.

Lewen went back through the cool, moonlit garden to the house, feeling that hot, happy daze one gets from drinking too much ale at Hogmanay. His mind was so full of the girl that he had to stand outside the door in the darkness for a while to clear his head.

When he came into the kitchen, his parents and his sister were already seated at the table, eating their meal. Fires burnt at either end of the room, and candles were lit on the table and mantelpiece, filling the room with a golden glow. Ursa lay on her rug before one of the fires, her enormous bulk blocking most of its heat. She lifted her grey snout and looked at him with worried eyes, moaning a question. Both his parents scrutinised him closely too but he managed not to flush, pulling up his chair to the table and saying in his usual practical way, 'She's no' badly hurt, just tired and rather bruised,

I think. She'll be grand in the morning. What about the mare, though, *Dai-dein*?'

''Twas lucky ye found them when ye did,' Niall said gravely. 'The mare has been ridden hard, and then allowed to founder. She'll be lucky if she does no' take a chill.'

'I do no' think she meant to harm the mare in any way,' Lewen said eagerly. 'Ye ken the stories about winged horses, how difficult they are to tame. The mare would have fought the bit and saddle, and flown high to try to throw her off. She was bruised all over. I'd say the mare tried to knock her off against tree trunks and branches, ye ken the way they do.'

'How do ye ken she's bruised all over?' Lilanthe said sharply.

Lewen went red. 'I . . . she told me . . .'

'Here, lad, have some soup,' Niall said calmly. 'Dearling, will ye cut him some bread? He must be starving.'

'Aye, that I am,' Lewen responded, glad of the diversion. 'I managed to eat some of my cheese and bread on the way home, but it dinna even begin to fill the hole.'

He began to eat his soup hungrily, and when Lilanthe had cut him some bread he slathered it with butter.

Meriel bounced up and down in her chair with excitement. 'But who is she, this girl? Where did she come from? Did she catch the winged horse?'

'I dinna ken,' Lilanthe answered, taking her seat again and looking across at her son, raising her eyebrows. 'Lewen? Did she tell ye anything while ye were tending her?'

Lewen shrugged. 'She said she'd tied herself onto the horse, so I guess that means she caught it. She said she had to tie herself on tight so she would no' fall while the mare was in the air.'

Merry gave a sigh of happiness. 'Oh, I wish it had been me! Imagine, your own flying horse.'

'Thigearns do no' say they *own* their winged horses,' Niall said repressively. 'It is a friendship, a partnership. They say to win the respect o' a winged horse, a thigearn must ride it for a year and a day without once putting foot to ground. This girl is no thigearn.'

'She managed to stay on its back for a night and a day,' Lewen said. 'That's pretty amazing.'

His father regarded him for a moment, then nodded and smiled ruefully. 'I've done it myself on occasion, and I must admit I thought well o' myself afterwards, and I was no' riding a horse that can fly. She'll be stiff and sore for a day or two, particularly if she's no' used to riding astride.'

'I wonder where she came from,' Merry said, holding out her bowl for another serve of soup. 'I dinna see a winged horse flying over and I was out in the garden all day. Ye'd think I would've seen it.'

'Unless it came down out o' the mountains,' Lilanthe said.

'But there's naught in the mountains but goblins and ogres,' Merry said, wide-eyed. 'Did the lass look like a goblin?'

Lewen shut his mouth on his indignation and said nothing.

'Nay, o' course no',' his father said for him. 'She was a bonny lass, if rather wild.'

'There are other faeries in the mountains,' Lilanthe said quietly. 'Corrigans, satyricorns, nixies, cluricauns, even seelies. She is certainly wild enough and bonny enough to have seelie blood in her.' Lewen looked up and inadvertently met his mother's eyes. Her face was solemn, and he clamped his jaws together and looked away. 'I do no' think that is it, though.'

'But ye are sure she's o' faery blood?' Niall said. 'She looked human enough.'

Lilanthe nodded her brown twiggy head and got up, stacking the empty bowls and taking them away from the table. 'Aye, she's a half-breed, that I ken. Happen ye need to be one to ken one.' There was a faint shade of bitterness in her voice. 'She is hard to read, though. I canna hear her thoughts. I would say she has been harshly treated in the past, for her mind and heart are locked up tight indeed. She is well used to shielding her thoughts.'

She brought the next course to the table, an egg and onion tart served with steamed green leaves and roasted roots. Lewen and Merry passed up their plates to her and she served deftly, then sat down again with a sigh. Niall looked at her closely.

'Are ye troubled, *leannan*?'

She straightened her back and smiled at him rather wearily. 'Nay, nay, o' course no'.'

'I am,' Niall said. 'What is a strange, wild lass from the blue yonder doing wearing the coat and plaid o' a Yeoman?'

Lewen thought of his father's shabby old coat and stained white buckskin breeches, stored carefully in a large chest in the attic with the rest of his uniform, muslin bags of dried lavender and lemon verbena tucked between their folds. His father was proud indeed of his past standing as one of the Rìgh's personal guards. One of the few times Lewen had ever seen his father angry was when he and Merry had opened the chest and played dress-ups with their father's uniform to amuse themselves one snowy winter's day. Lewen had worn the silver mail shirt, cunningly made of metal links closely woven together, and the thick blue cloak and battered helmet, while Merry had dressed up in his court regalia, the blue tartan kilt and sporran, the cockaded blue tam-o'-shanter, the long-tailed blue coat. Finding them playing at soldiers, pretending to fight with old curtain rods and dragging the hems of his clothes through the dust, Niall had roared at them as angrily as any woolly bear. Merry had been so frightened she had begun to cry, but Niall was too angry to care. He had stripped the children of their costumes with hard and hasty hands, given them both resounding spanks on their bottoms and sent them sobbing down the stairs.

Later, with Lilanthe behind them to give them moral support, they had gone with some trepidation to apologise. The heat of Niall's anger had cooled but he was still displeased, and had told them, very sternly, that they must never touch his uniform again.

'To be chosen as a Yeoman o' the Guard is the greatest honour a soldier can be given,' he had said. 'I fought many a weary, bloody battle in those clothes, and watched many a comrade slain. I have slept in them many a time when we dared not remove even our boots in case the alarm was called, and I wore them as I stood behind my Rìgh with my eyes hot with tears o' pride as he was finally crowned. It took a very long time for us to bring peace to Eileanan and during all that time, those clothes were my second skin. Those stains on them are stains o' blood and mud and tears and sweat, and they are marks o' honour and courage. Do you understand me, bairns? For if I ever find ye playing with them again, I swear I'll give ye a whipping ye shall never forget.'

Lewen and Meriel had been contrite and overawed. Their father rarely spoke much about the long campaign to win the crown for Lachlan the Winged, and then to unite Eileanan under his banner. It was Lilanthe who had taught them their lessons, and she talked about it as if it had all happened long ago, in another lifetime. Niall's words made the Bright Wars seem vivid and immediate. Ever since then, Lewen had harboured a not-so-secret dream of becoming a Blue Guard himself.

'No Blue Guard would ever willingly relinquish his coat and cap,' Niall continued. 'I fear one o' my laird's men must have come to harm somewhere in the mountains, for this lass to have his gear. I must question her closely in the morning and find out how she came to be dressed so. His Highness will wish to ken if he has lost one o' his men. I wonder who it could be? I do no' ken all the Blue Guards like I used to. It has been some time since I was last in Lucescere.'

'So ye think he has fallen victim to foul play, whoever the Yeoman was?' Lilanthe asked.

Niall shrugged, frowning. 'I do no' ken. Happen there was an accident o' some kind. How can I tell? This lass, though, whoever she is, she has all his gear, his saddlebags and everything. Even the official saddlecloth, with the ensign o' the charging stag upon it. And she was wearing the badge o' the Yeomen.' His voice was thick with outrage.

Lilanthe chose her words with care. 'Do ye fear this lass may have killed the Yeoman?'

Niall's frown deepened. 'Did ye notice the coat has been torn at the breast and back, as if by an arrow? And the tear cobbled together again? And she carried bow and arrows.'

'They may no' be hers,' Lilanthe said.

Lewen remembered the callouses on her right palm but said nothing, staring at his plate in dumb misery.

'No, they may no'. And she is only a lass.' Niall sighed heavily.

'No' really,' Lilanthe said. 'She must be seventeen or eighteen. And certainly she kens how to fight.'

'No' to mention fight dirty,' Niall said.

'Aye. I'll never forget the look on her face as she went for ye with that pitchfork. I almost fainted!'

'Ye almost fainted! Think how I felt when she kicked me. I thought I was going to pass out. I'm afraid I willna be much use to ye for a day or two, *leannan*, I'm swollen up like a pair o' pumpkins.'

'Why? Where did she kick ye?' Meriel asked, wide-eyed.

Lilanthe gave her husband a reproving glance and got up to clear the plates.

'She bit me on the shoulder,' Lewen said, as much as to distract his little sister as because the wound was throbbing nastily.

Lilanthe put the plates down and hurried over to look. She pulled back the collar of his shirt and exclaimed at the round, purple-red bruise.

'What a wildcat,' Niall said admiringly.

'I'll put some arnica cream on it,' Lilanthe said. 'It's a nasty bite. What could make her behave so? It was no' as if we were threatening her or trying to hurt her. We were trying to help! She just went mad like a rabid dog.'

'Happen she was frightened,' Niall said.

'Or angry because ye held her saddlebags. Happen she thought ye were trying to steal her things. "Mine" seems to be her favourite word.'

'She had only just woken up,' Lewen said defensively. 'She dinna ken where she was or who we were.'

'Aye, that's true enough,' Niall said placatingly. 'Well, we'll question her in the morning. Let's leave the conjectures till then, shall we? Let's no' forget this is our last night together as a family for what may be a very long time. Merry, sweetling, why do ye no' serve us some of that special pie ye made for Lewen? And I'll get down

69

some goldensloe wine, to toast our lad on his last night at home.'

She'll probably be gone in the morning anyway, Lewen said to himself. The thought was cold and heavy as a stone, but he squared his shoulders and took the glass his father gave him with a grin of thanks. *No sense dreaming o' a lass I'll never see again.*

HER NAMING

Lewen woke early the next morning, and was at once sitting up and reaching for his clothes. The house was quiet and dim. He went down the stairs in his stockings, carrying his boots. His feet were numb by the time he reached the kitchen, for the stone floors were cold, and so he built a fire on the grey ashes in the hearth and willed it into life with a snap of his fingers. Flames roared up, and Lewen warmed the soles of his feet before pulling on his boots.

Ursa yawned and stretched, and raised her enormous head, gazing at him with questioning eyes. He reached up to rub her greying snout. 'Go back to sleep,' he said affectionately. 'All is well. I'm just going out to the stables.'

She moaned softly but put her head back down on her heavy paws, for she was a very old bear now and content to sleep before the fire and amble after Niall as he went about his chores. Lewen swung the kettle over the fire then, pulling on his coat and gloves, went quietly out into the early morning mist. The whole garden was wrapped in cloud. The silence was uncanny. Lewen moved with great gentleness, afraid to disturb the stillness. He eased open the door of the stable and stepped quietly inside.

The stall door had been smashed to pieces, and a length of frayed rope dangled from the ring where the mare's halter had been secured. The bucket of water had been kicked over, and the dirt floor was a churned mass of hoof prints. The stall was empty.

Yet in the mound of straw where he had made up a bed for the girl, she slept, curled within the curve of the winged horse's body, the blanket slipping from one shoulder, her hand tucked under her cheek. The horse slept too, its head resting on its forelegs. One wing sheltered the girl, like a black feathered quilt. In the other stalls, the horses all stood drowsily, Lewen's stallion Argent raising his head to look at him, the others sleeping on.

Lewen stood very still. Surely it was not safe for her to sleep there, so close to those sharp hooves? The mare was wild. Everyone knew it was near impossible to tame a winged horse, and this one must surely hate the rider that had ridden it so hard and so far. Yet there she slept, tucked up against the mare's side like a foal.

As if sensing his regard, the girl stirred and sighed and opened her eyes, lifting her hand to rub away the grit of sleep. Her movement roused the horse and it moved its head, blowing gustily through its nostrils. The girl looked up and saw Lewen standing there, gazing at her. Immediately she tensed, pushing herself away from him, pressing deeper into the horse's side. Lewen put up a warning hand, but it was too late. The mare at once scrambled to her feet, rearing back on her hind hooves. She trumpeted a defiant neigh, came down, and kicked out behind.

The girl had rolled herself nimbly away, and now stood

and stepped forward, her hand held out flat. 'Hush,' she said. 'No need to fear. Me here.'

The horse rolled a white-rimmed eye towards her and shied away, but the girl stepped closer still, one hand going to cup its velvet nose, the other moving up to seize the mare's ear. 'Ssssshhhh,' she crooned. 'Ssssshhhh. No need to fear.'

Amazingly, the winged horse quietened at once. It breathed in the girl's scent with flared nostrils, shivered a little and danced uneasily, but did not rear again or neigh. The girl moved closer still, smoothing the mare's satiny neck with her hand, whispering to her. The mare flicked her luxurious long tail and dropped her nose into the girl's hand, and the girl laid her cheek against the mare's neck, caressing one of the long scrolled horns, as blue as a dusk sky. 'Aye, ye're bonny, aye, ye are,' she whispered.

Lewen could only stand and stare. He had never seen anyone calm a horse so easily. Lewen was a horse-whisperer himself, and had tamed his own bad-tempered stallion in record time, but even that had taken him days, not hours. As he wondered and marvelled, she turned towards him and said coldly, 'Ye be more careful. She kick hard, she would. She afeared here.'

'It was ye I was worried about,' Lewen said defensively. 'What were ye thinking, sleeping up against her like that? She could've killed ye.'

'She mine,' she said flatly. 'I guard.'

'Guard? Guard her against what? There's naught to fear here.'

She gave him a contemptuous stare and turned back to the mare, stroking her nose and neck. At some point during the night she had removed the halter and blanket, for the mare was unfettered now. Lewen came forward a few small steps, fascinated by the mare's exotic beauty. The mare shook her mane and pranced a little. The girl laid her hand over the mare's nose again and she quietened so the girl could run her hands gently down her slender legs to check for hotness or swelling.

'Ye ken horses,' Lewen said. 'Ye've ridden them afore.'

'Sometimes,' she said. 'I call them, they come to me.'

'They just come? Any horse?'

She shrugged. 'All I've called.'

'The mare too? Then why . . .?'

She shook her head. 'Me no' ken if she carry me like the wild ponies do. And if she let me, me no' ken if me stay on long enough. Me fallen off afore. Me no' want to fall off while she flying.' She made a high, flowing gesture with her hand.

'Nay, o' course no',' Lewen said with a grin. He came forward another few steps and at once the girl backed away, fists clenching, baring her teeth at him warningly. The horse whinnied and sidestepped uneasily. Lewen put up both hands placatingly, stepping back. 'I mean ye no harm. I just wanted to check . . . I was worried. Are ye hungry? Would ye like some porridge?'

She was suspicious. 'What . . . porridge?' The word stumbled on her tongue.

'Ye do no' ken porridge?' Lewen said unbelievingly. 'It's oats . . . hot, and with milk and honey. It's good. If ye'll come . . .' He gestured out into the brightening morning. 'I can make ye some, and happen some griddle-cakes too, and tea.'

She narrowed her eyes. 'Why? What ye want?'

Lewen was distressed. 'Naught! I mean, I just . . . I thought ye might be hungry.'

'Me hungry, sure enough, but what ye care?'

'Ye're our guest here . . . ye're sore hurt . . . I wanted . . .'

'What?'

'Naught! Just to be kind.'

To his surprise and secret hurt, he saw contempt in her eyes. 'True me hungry. Bring food here,' she commanded.

He drew back, his eyes hardening. 'I am no' your servant,' he said. 'I thought ye might be hungry so I offered ye some breakfast, but if ye want it, ye can come and get it yourself.' He turned on his heel and began to walk out, his back very straight. She said nothing, but he could feel her gaze burning into his back.

He was out of the stable and halfway through the barnyard when he heard her say imperiously, 'Stop!'

He turned, still smouldering with anger. She stood in the doorway of the stable, dressed only in a long white nightgown and bare feet, her black hair a matted rat's nest. She looked so young and vulnerable his anger melted away, but he held himself stiffly still, meeting her gaze. 'Me very hungry,' she said forlornly, 'but canna leave what mine.' She gestured behind her.

'Ye mean, the horse?'

'All what mine.'

'Ye're afraid someone will steal your things?' Lewen did not know whether to feel anger or pity that she should be so filled with suspicion and distrust. He said more gently, 'No-one will steal your things, or even touch them, I promise. Ye and your things are safe here. Ye must learn to trust us if we are to help ye.'

'Why?'

'Why what?'

'Why ye want help me?'

Again Lewen could not find the words to explain. He said stiffly, 'Ye are our guest. Ye've broken our bread and tasted our salt. We may no' harm one who has partaken o' our hospitality.'

She seemed to accept this, for she nodded, turned back into the stable and said, with one imperiously pointed finger, 'Horse, stay. Me come back.'

Then she came out onto the dew-frosted grass, her bare feet leaving dark streaks.

'Wait! Ye must be cold. Where are your clothes, your shoes? Happen ye'd best get dressed first.' He tugged at his own clothes and indicated his own stout boots.

She looked surprised, but shrugged and went back inside, coming back a few minutes later with the long black boots pulled on under her nightgown and the plaid wrapped negligently about her shoulders. Lewen felt a now familiar bemusement. No other girl of his acquaintance would be so nonchalant about being seen in her nightgown, or so careless of her appearance. His curiosity about her continued to grow.

'So why did ye tie yourself to the mare? Did ye just wish to ride her, to tame her? Or are ye fleeing from someone?'

The girl's lips pressed together firmly and she did not answer.

'Did ye come down out o' the mountains? Where is your family?'

Still she would not answer. Lewen looked at her sideways, marvelling at the stubbornness of her patrician profile, the line of brow and nose so straight, the mouth below so softly and deeply curved. It was a face of contradictions, and he did not know which part to believe, the cold severity of the upper, or the warm sensuality of the lower.

They came into the warmth of the kitchen and at once Ursa lifted her snout and moaned a greeting, lumbering to her feet. The girl froze. Suddenly a sharp silver dagger was in her hand and she had dropped into a killer's crouch, her teeth bared. Ursa hardly noticed, so accustomed was she to gentleness and affection. She padded forward, lowering her head for a scratch behind the ears. Quick as a snake, the girl struck. Lewen was so taken aback his brain refused to respond. His muscles were well trained, however, and he lunged forward and caught her wrist, the sharp point of the dagger a scant inch away from Ursa's shaggy breast. For a moment they struggled silently, barely moving, but exerting their strength against each other. Then she submitted, allowing him to draw her away from the puzzled old bear, surrendering the knife into his hand as she rubbed at her bruised wrist.

'Ye strong,' she said with approval. 'Ye hurt me.'

Lewen swallowed his instinctive apology. 'Why did ye stab at poor auld Ursa like that?' he said.

She was regarding the enormous woolly bear with narrowed eyes. 'Bear,' she said, gesturing with one hand.

'Aye, o' course she's a bear, anyone can see that!'

He took a breath to berate her further, but the look on her face made him pause and reflect. 'Did ye think her a wild bear, strayed into our kitchen searching for food? I suppose she could have been, but . . . canna ye see how tame she is, how gentle?' He gave a low growl of frustration, unable to express how troubled he was by her fierceness, yet knowing he was being unfair. Anyone raised in the mountains knew to fear woolly bears, known as much for their savagery as their stupidity.

If he had not been raised by his parents, if he was someone else, someone normal, and he had walked into a strange house and seen such an immense, long-toothed, sharp-clawed, strong-shouldered creature in the kitchen, would he not have reacted instinctively to defend himself? And this strange feral girl from the mountains had clearly not been raised with gentleness as he had been. She flinched instinctively when anyone came too near, she carried a knife under her nightgown, she was the nastiest fighter he had ever seen, more unprincipled than even the beggar-boys down near the ports. It was wrong of him to wish her something different, it was wrong to long for her to have the gentleness of his father, the sensitivity of his mother, the merry heart and sweet trustfulness of his sister. She was what she was, and he should not want her to be different just because she had a mouth that fascinated him.

She was watching him now with a calculating expression, as if reading and interpreting the play of expressions on his face, and he took a deep breath and brought his thoughts back under control.

'Ursa is my father's familiar,' he said. When she clearly did not understand what he meant, he said rather vaguely, 'His friend, his helpmate, his . . .' He did not want to say 'pet', but could not think how to explain. 'Like your horse,' he said at last.

She moved her clear, intent gaze from his face to the bear's. Ursa was patiently waiting to be petted and Lewen choked back a laugh and put his hand up to scratch behind her ears. She slitted her eyes and growled deeply in her throat with pleasure. He stroked her snout and she ambled back to her place by the fire. 'She's very auld now,' he said, almost as if wanting to excuse her docility.

After that he did not know what to say to her. His hands suddenly felt large and clumsy, his face hot, and his tongue thick. He busied himself making breakfast, but even that felt wrong and difficult. He dropped the porridge pot, and slurped in too much milk and had to add more oats, which turned to glue, and then he forgot to add the salt and, when he hurried to remedy the omission, fumbled the opening of the canister and spilt in too much, and all the while his ears got hotter and hotter. She sat at the table in silence, watching him with interest, her arms wrapped round her knees, the nightgown slipping off one bare white shoulder as she did not know how to tie up the laces properly. By the time Lilanthe came in, the buds of her twiggy hair bursting into green overnight as if to signal the surge of spring that Lewen was feeling in his blood, her son was as red-cheeked and miserable as she had ever seen him. She tasted the porridge, cast him one whiplash glance but said nothing, swinging the pot off the fire and beginning to swiftly mix up some batter for griddle-cakes, all the while asking the girl gently how she had slept, and was she not cold in her nightgown still, and did she prefer honey or greengage jam? Lewen could only retire in grateful confusion.

Hand-in-hand with her father, Meriel came scampering in, bright-eyed with curiosity. Her chatter filled the silence so that Lewen was able to retreat to the table and busy himself eating and drinking. Meriel peppered the blue-eyed stranger with questions, not at all disconcerted by her reluctance to answer.

'Did ye sleep well? Were ye warm enough?'

'Aye.' The girl crammed a whole griddle-cake into her mouth.

'And ye really have a winged horse all o' your own? How did ye catch her?'

No answer.

'Can I have a ride o' her?'

'Nay,' she mumbled through her mouthful of crumbs.

'Oh, please? I've always wanted to have a winged horse o' my own. Please?'

'Nay.'

'Will she only let ye ride her? Are ye from Tìreich? How did ye get here? Did ye fly over the mountains?'

No answer. Another two griddle-cakes disappeared.

'Mam says ye were sore hurt by tying yourself on so tight. Do your wrists still hurt?'

'Aye.'

'Why did ye do it?'

'So no' fall off.' Her voice expressed weary contempt. She wiped jam away from her mouth and reached for another griddle-cake.

Meriel was not abashed. 'But if she's your horse, surely she wouldna let ye fall? Thigearns do no' tie themselves on.'

'She no' my horse *then*. Is now.' She flashed the little girl a sharp warning glance.

'So have ye only just caught her? She's no' really your horse then, is she?'

'Mine.'

'But, I mean, flying horses canna be tamed so easily. Thigearns must ride their flying horses for a year and a day. Ye only stayed on one day and one night. That canna count.'

'She mine!'

'How come ye talk so funny?'

The stranger gritted her jaw and stared at the little girl furiously.

'Meriel,' Lilanthe said warningly.

'But she does talk funny.'

'No' everyone grows up learning to speak our language,' Lilanthe said quietly. She served another platter of hot griddle-cakes, then turned to the girl. 'I must admit to curiosity also. We do no' even ken your name. What may we call ye?'

The girl shrugged, frowning. 'Lassie?' she said hesitatingly.

'But lassie is no' a name, it's . . . it's what ye are, like Lewen here is a lad. Or was, I should say,' Lilanthe said,

80

amending her sentence at a furious glance from her son. 'We canna just call ye "lassie". Do ye no' have a name? What did your family call ye?'

The girl's face closed up and she looked away, saying nothing.

'Ye have no family?'

She shrugged. 'Family like this?' An expansive gesture took in the warmly lit room, with its bright copper pans, bunches of dried herbs hanging from a rack, its collection of childish drawings tacked to the mantelpiece, the immense woolly bear snoozing by the fire. She uttered a bitter laugh. 'Nay, no family like this.'

'But your parents? Your mother? Your father?'

'Father dead.'

'Your mother?'

The girl laughed harshly again. 'Mother no' want me. No good.' She paused for a moment and then said, in a rush, as if she could no longer dam up the words. 'They kill me if me go back.'

They were all appalled.

'Kill ye?' Lewen cried. 'Why?'

'But, my lass, surely no'?' Niall said. 'A bonny lass like ye?'

'Me no good. No' strong enough, no' fast enough. Have no horns.'

'No horns?' Niall and Lilanthe exchanged swift glances.

The girl closed her mouth firmly and would not speak.

'A satyricorn?' Niall said. 'But . . .'

'It would explain the dirty fighting,' Lilanthe said dryly.

Lewen felt his heart sinking. The satyricorns were wild and fierce faeries indeed. Although the First-Horn of the largest known herd had signed the Pact of Peace, so that the satyricorns were theoretically vassals and allies of

Lachlan MacCuinn, many of the smaller, more remote herds continued to raid farms and villages just as they always had, killing indiscriminately and stealing food, weapons and young men.

'But I have seen satyricorns,' Niall said. 'The Rìgh has an infantry troop o' Horned Ones that serve him. They have hooves and a tail as well as horns, and yellow eyes. She is naught like them at all.'

'No horns, no hooves, and only one set o' dugs,' she said sadly.

There was a shocked silence. Despite himself, Lewen's eyes were drawn to the womanly swell of her thin cotton nightgown. He forced himself to look away. His father was regarding his plate, trying hard not to smile, Meriel's mouth was hanging open in amazement, and Lilanthe looked disconcerted, embarrassed and amused all at the same time.

'Happen she was a foundling child,' Lewen stumbled to fill the silence. 'Lost on the mountain or something.'

She gave a satiric snort. 'Horned Ones no' save lost lassie. Eat it if hungry enough. A lost laddie, they'd save. Some use for a lost laddie, at least when grown.' And she looked him up and down with such a knowing expression in her eyes that Lewen felt the blood surge up his body and into his face. He did not know where to look or what to say. Neither did his parents.

Luckily Meriel took the comment at face value, crying out, 'They'd *eat* a lost bairn? Do ye mean, they'd actually *eat* it?'

'If hungry enough,' she said indifferently.

'Urrgghh!'

The girl looked at her speculatively. 'Me ate goblin once. Rather eat nice, plump babe than foul, stinking goblin, wouldna ye?'

'Urrgghh, no! I wouldna want to eat either.'

'Ye would if hungry enough.'

'Nay, I would no'!'

'Bet ye would. If it meant ye'd get to live another day. Anyone would.'

'I'd rather die!'

'Proof ye've never really been hungry,' the girl said, and helped herself to another griddle-cake. They all hurried to pass her more butter and jam, and Lilanthe poured her another cup of fresh goat's milk, so full it almost brimmed over. The girl ate and drank greedily, wiping her mouth on her sleeve.

There was a long silence as they watched her eat, each busy with their own thoughts.

Then Niall leant forward, frowning, one hand scratching his bushy brown beard. 'So ye have run away from your family ... your herd. That is why ye caught the winged horse. To help ye escape.'

'Herd run fast, hunt good,' she said indistinctly, through a mouthful of food. 'Me slow. They catch me, they kill me.'

'So what about the saddle, the bridle? The clothes? Where did ye get them?'

She frowned, glaring at him suspiciously.

'Ye canna tell me they are what ye wore with a herd o' satyricorns,' Niall said. 'They are the uniform o' a Yeoman o' the Guard, the Rìgh's own regiment. Where did ye get them?'

Her frown deepened and for a moment it looked as if she would say nothing. Then she said reluctantly, 'Herd hunted down man, close on a moon ago. He dead. Me took his clothes. Liked better. Soft.'

Niall was watching her closely. 'Who was he? Do ye ken his name? How did he die?'

She did not answer.

'I thought satyricorns usually keep male prisoners alive,' he said slowly. 'Having a use for them, as ye said yourself.'

She did not drop her eyes, or blush, or fiddle with her knife, keeping her eyes steadily on his. 'Aye, true,' she answered.

'So how did the Yeoman die?'

'Try escape,' she said after a moment. 'Herd hunt him down.'

Niall nodded. 'I see.' He glanced at Lilanthe. 'I wonder who it could be? There'll be identification o' some kind in the saddlebags, I imagine, a family seal or signed reports. I'll look and see. We must send notice to His Highness . . .'

'Nay!'

They looked at the girl in surprise. She had leapt to her feet, sending the cup of milk cascading over the table. One fist was thrust under Niall's bearded chin. 'Mine! Ye no look, ye no touch. Mine now. No' yours.'

'But, lassie . . .'

'No touch.'

'But they are no' your things, lassie. They belong to that poor dead soldier. His family will be wanting to have his uniform and badge back, they are marks o' honour. They'll be wanting to ken how he died. We have plenty of clothes here that ye can have, ye do no' need his things anymore. I must see what news he was carrying, and send it on to my Rìgh. That Yeoman must have had dreadful need to reach the capital quickly, to ride through Dubhslain, canna ye see that? I must make sure the Rìgh kens what has happened.'

All the while Niall spoke, she was negating every sentence abruptly and forcefully. As he continued to argue with her, she reached down and drew the knife she wore hidden under her nightgown. She would have stabbed him if he had not had such quick reflexes, catching her wrist in both hands, leaning far back in his chair to avoid the snake-swift thrust. They wrestled silently for a few moments, her lips drawn back into a feral snarl, then at last Niall managed to knock the knife out of her hand, dragging her down to her knees.

He breathed heavily, trying to regain his temper as much as his breath. Lewen was frozen in shock and dismay, unable to believe he had forgotten her knife, realising how close his father had come to death because of his absent-mindedness. Lilanthe and Meriel were frozen likewise. Violence had erupted so quickly.

The girl took a deep shuddering breath perilously close to a sob. Niall released her wrists and she cradled them to her chest, her head bent. Still no-one spoke, not even Meriel, whose face had turned the colour of unbaked dough. Then Lilanthe gave a great sigh and went swiftly to her husband, bending over him, pressing his head to her breast. She said softly, brokenly, 'I canna believe . . . och, *leannan* . . . if she had killed ye . . .'

'I'm a hard man to kill,' Niall said with an attempt at a smile.

The girl raised her head. Though her face was smeared with tears and the bandages about her wrists were seeping with fresh blood, her expression was set hard with anger and determination.

'If ye touch me or mine again, me kill ye,' she said softly.

Niall sighed and put his arm about his wife's waist. After a moment he said, very sternly, 'Then let this be understood between us. If ye try to harm me or mine again while ye are here, I will have ye taken to the reeve and tried and punished. Ye do no' attack a man at his

85

own table, after ye have broken bread and tasted salt with him. Ye do no' seek to settle a disagreement by drawing your blade. This is dishonourable and unlawful. Ye may have been raised as a satyricorn, but ye are among men now, and ye must and will learn our ways.'

'How?' Lilanthe asked. 'What are we to do with her? We have no' had time to think what is best to do.'

The girl stood up, her blue-grey eyes blazing. 'Ye do naught with me! Me go. Me take horse and me go.'

'Where?' Lilanthe said gently. 'Where shall ye go? Back into the mountains? They are no' called Dubhslain for naught. Apart from the satyricorns, who ye say shall kill ye if they find ye, there are ogres and cursehags and dragons too. It is no place for anyone to live alone, no matter how doughty. And believe me, lassie, I ken. I ran away from my home too, when I was just a lass myself, and I lived in the wild mountains as best I could for quite a few years. Being able to change shape into a tree helped, o' course, but it was a cruel hard life, ye must understand that. And lonely. Bitterly lonely. It was that which drove me out o' the mountains in the end, a longing for those o' my own kind, for love and friendship.' She bent and pressed her cheek against Niall's beard and he put up one hand and caressed her leafy hair.

The girl was silent, though her chin was still raised defiantly and her hands clenched.

'Happen she should come to the Tower o' Two Moons with me?' Lewen said diffidently. His parents looked at him in surprise.

'It'll take us some time to travel to Lucescere,' he went on. 'Nina and Iven and I can try to teach her what we can on the way, and there'll be other apprentices too, for sure, and they'll help too. And then she can tell the Righ what she kens herself, I'm sure he'll have questions he'd want to ask her. And Aunty Beau will want to talk to her too, I ken.'

'Why, though, laddie?' Lilanthe sounded a little puzzled. 'Ye think the lassie has Talent?'

'She's tamed the winged horse,' Lewen said. When his father went to say something he held up his hand in entreaty. 'Nay, I mean, *really* tamed her, Dada. When I went in this morning, well, the mare had kicked out the door o' her stall and broken her headstall and torn up the whole place, but . . . well, they were sleeping together, like mare and foal, as sweetly as ye could imagine. And she talks to her. Tells the mare to stay and she does.'

Niall's brown eyes and Lilanthe's slanted green ones both swivelled to the girl's face. She stared back at them haughtily. 'She mine,' she said.

'She says she's tamed horses afore, in the mountains. She calls to them and they come.'

'Happen it's the Tower o' Horse-lairds we should be sending her to,' Niall said softly.

'Happen so,' Lewen agreed. 'But there's plenty o' time for that, if that's the right place for her to go, isn't there? There's no-one to take her there now, and she would ken no-one there nor how to go on. And the Rìgh would want to see her first, dinna ye think so?'

'Aye, he would.' Niall stroked his beard thoughtfully. 'I can see some merit in this plan o' yours, my lad. Though we must make sure news o' the Yeoman's death travels faster than ye will. It'll take ye a month or so to reach the palace, and my laird will be anxious for news o' his Yeoman. I wish we could scry to him, but the mountains stand in the way. What a shame the Tower o' Ravens is so infested with ghosts and we canna use the Scrying Pool there. It would be so much easier to keep in touch with the court and Coven.' Niall sighed and dug his fingers into his beard more vigorously.

'Come, we can work out the finer details later,' Lilanthe said. 'For now, I think it is a good plan. I would no' like to just send the lassie off somewhere all by herself, for all that she is so fierce and strong. The Tower o' Two Moons is interested in all Skills and Talents, and there are satyricorns at the royal court that may be able to help her find a place for herself.'

'Lewen's right, the Rìgh will want to question her about the Yeoman's death himself,' Niall said, almost as if he had not been listening to his wife. 'And happen on the way Lewen can make her realise that wearing the clothes o' a Blue Guard is treason!'

The girl had been listening to all this with narrow, suspicious eyes. At this last comment she flashed Niall a quick glance, but still said nothing, her jaw thrust out stubbornly.

Lilanthe turned to her and smiled, saying in her gentle voice, 'It is for ye to decide, o' course. We have no' rights over ye. I do no' ken if ye will like Lucescere, it is one o' the great cities o' Eileanan and very busy and noisy. They call it the Shining City because it is so beautiful. It is built on an island at the top o' the highest waterfall in Eileanan, a place where two great rivers meet. On sunny days the whole city is strung with rainbows from the spray. Ye would like to see it, I am sure. And the Tower o' Two Moons is very quiet and peaceful, for it is built away from the city, set in the heart o' acres o' the bonniest gardens. It too is one o' the grand sights o' this world. Ye will meet people o' all kinds there, both human and faery, and if ye wish, ye can try for a scholarship to study there and learn many new things, as Lewen does. Or ye can get back on to your winged horse and fly away from here, we shallna try and stop ye. It's up to ye, lassie.'

It was the right approach to take. The girl's face and stance relaxed as Lilanthe spoke, and a look of interest came into her eyes. She glanced once at Lewen and then back at Lilanthe, catching her lip between her teeth as she considered. Then she raised her head proudly.

'Me like to see this city,' she said. 'Me go.' As everyone sighed and relaxed a little, relieved to have a plan to work towards, she looked sternly at Niall. 'Ye, though – ye shallna touch what mine.'

'But . . .' Niall began.

'No touch! Else me kill ye.'

'Very well, then, lassie,' Lilanthe said quickly. 'We shall touch naught o' yours if ye do no' wish it. But can I give ye some other clothes to be wearing on your journey? For indeed, ye canna wear the uniform o' a Yeoman if ye have no' been chosen to serve the Rìgh. It is no' right and indeed, it is treasonable, as Niall said. If ye give me the clothes I will wash them for ye and pack them up, and ye can take them with ye.'

The girl nodded begrudgingly.

'Very well then. Now, we do no' have long. Nina and Iven will be here soon, if they left Barbreck-by-the-Bridge at daybreak like they said they would. How about a bath, lassie? Believe me, ye will feel much better when ye are clean. I'll wash your hair for ye and salve your wrists again and find ye some clothes, and then we can pack a bag for ye to take with ye. Lewen, dearling, I do no' ken how long they'll be able to stay so ye had best make ready.'

'He's already packed and repacked his bags about a hundred times,' Meriel teased.

'Well, I wanted to be ready,' Lewen said.

'Come on, my lad, let's go and get our chores done while the lassie has her bath,' Niall said. 'The poor auld horses must be wondering where their mash is, and I'm surprised we canna hear the pigs squealing from here.'

'I feed my horse, no' ye,' the satyricorn girl said, tensing up at once. 'I come now. Ye touch naught!'

Niall raised both his hands. 'I shallna touch a thing, lassie, I promise ye. Which reminds me. We canna keep on just calling ye "lassie". Ye sure ye do no' have a name? What did your mother call ye, and the other satyricorns?'

She flushed hotly. 'No-Horn,' she answered shortly. 'No' a nice name.' She struggled for words. 'Mean name.'

'We canna call ye that then,' he said, taken aback.

'Then we must give her one,' Lilanthe said. 'She needs a name.'

They all eyed her speculatively and she glared back at them, her jaw set firmly.

'Aye, but to choose a name that suits her, that's the trick,' Niall said, scratching his beard, a humorous glint in his eyes. 'Prickles? Bramble? Blackthorn?'

She tilted her chin even higher.

'Rosaleen? That means little dark rose,' Lilanthe said hastily.

'She's no' so little,' Niall said, grinning. 'What's a name that means enormous dark rose? No' that I think a rose is the right sort o' plant, thorny as it is. How about thistle?'

'Do no' even joke about that,' Lilanthe said with a little shudder. 'No' even Iain of Arran calls himself the Thistle, it brings back such dreadful memories. That's a name Margrit o' Arran took to the grave with her, thank Eà.'

'True enough,' Niall said soberly. 'I'd forgotten Margrit NicFóghnan was called the Thistle. Indeed, that would be a sorry name to give such a bonny lass. I suppose we should be serious about this. A name is a serious thing, one carries it all one's life. Are there no names ye like, lass?'

'Ken no names,' she answered.

'That makes things harder,' Niall said. 'Do ye ken any names to do with horses, *leannan*? A woman that rides a winged horse should have a name that suits. Is there a girlie form o' Ahearn? That means laird o' the horses and was a true naming indeed.'

'I do no' think so,' Lilanthe said, frowning. 'And we canna call her Ahearn, or any derivative, for it is a name that belongs to the MacAhern clan.'

'How about Rhiannon?' Lewen said quietly. They turned to him, surprised, having almost forgotten he was there, he had been so silent. 'From the auld story, ye ken the one,' he said. 'She rides past the king and he is so smitten with her beauty that he sends his cavaliers galloping after her, to bring her back to him. But she rides so swiftly none can catch her. The king canna forget her, and so day after day he returns to the same place in the forest, hoping to see her again. At last she gallops past and he pursues her. But not even his great war-charger can catch up with her, and so he calls out to her, telling her he has fallen in love with her. So she turns and reins in her horse, and lets him come near, and he makes her his wife.'

'Aye,' Niall said slowly. 'I remember that tale. Rhiannon.' He turned to the girl. She was gazing now at Lewen. Her face had softened, her mouth curving just enough for the elusive dimple to crease her cheek. 'Do ye like that name, lassie?' Niall asked gruffly.

'Rhee-ann-an.' She spoke the name slowly, haltingly, tasting the syllables on her tongue. 'She rides so swiftly none can catch her. Aye, I like. Rhee-ann-an.'

'Rhiannon it is, then,' Lilanthe said. Lewen caught the slight restraint in her voice and looked up at her. She smiled at him ruefully and tousled his curly brown hair, then stroked it back away from his brow. 'It's a lovely name, my lad, and well thought of. Why do ye no' all go and tend the horses now so Rhiannon can get her clothes for me to wash? Then ye can go round the farm with your father one more time and be saying your farewells.'

Lewen nodded, overcome by an unexpected wave of homesickness. Eà alone knew when he would be able to come back to Kingarth again. His eyes were suddenly hot and he had to swallow a lump in his throat.

'Go on, laddie,' Lilanthe said lovingly. 'Take your time. It's going to take a while to get Rhiannon clean, that's for sure!'

THE JONGLEURS

It was early afternoon when Meriel came skipping out to find her brother and father, who were busy grooming Lewen's big grey, Argent. The stallion was standing with one leg relaxed, his eyes half-closed in bliss, but as soon as he heard Meriel's quick footsteps, his ears went back and he lifted his top lip to smell the air suspiciously.

'Give over!' Lewen said affectionately, pushing the stallion with his shoulder. 'Ye should ken Merry's step by now.'

'We're ready!' Meriel cried. 'Gracious me, what a job! It was like trying to wash a litter o' piglets, the squealing and squirming we've had. My arms ache from hauling so much water, and then I had to mop up the floor, which looked like the floor o' the byre, it was so wet and muddy. And it took a whole bottle o' Mam's liquid soapwort to wash her hair, and then it was so matted Mam had to use up all the rosemary herb oil to get the knots out. It took forever.'

'Well, ye seem to have survived the experience,' Niall said, looking her over in mock concern. 'No black eyes, no bleeding nose, no bite marks that I can see. Is your mother all in one piece too?'

'Aye.' Laughing, Meriel snuggled up against her father's side. 'She fought a bit to begin with but Mam told her if she dared try again, Mam'd turn her into a tree and then she'd never be able to ride her winged horse again. Rhiannon dinna believe her, so Mam pretended to turn me into a tree just to show her.'

Lewen grinned. His mother could no more turn Rhiannon into a tree than he could, but Meriel had inherited her mother's tree-shifter abilities and needed only to dig her bare feet into the ground to change her shape. It was very disconcerting to watch if you were not used to it, though, and he could imagine Rhiannon's alarm.

'Well, thank Eà your mother couldna carry out her threat,' Niall said. 'Can ye imagine what kind o' tree our sweet Rhiannon would make? A very prickly goldengorse bush, perhaps. Or a blackthorn.'

'Ye are silly,' Meriel said. 'Anyway, she's very fidgety about her horse but Mam wouldna let her come out to check it 'cause she's all clean and dressed now, so I promised I'd make sure the mare's still all right.'

'She's grand,' Lewen said. 'I left her some warm mash and a bucket o' fresh water, and her ears pricked forwards with great interest, which is always a good sign. I think she'll be fine to set out tomorrow as long as Rhiannon does no' ride her too hard.'

'That's good. Mam said to tell ye that Nina and the caravans will be here soon – her little sunbird just flew in the window and trilled us such a bonny tune.'

'Almost here?' Lewen said in dismay.

'Aye, so ye'd better get hopping! Mam wants us all bonny and bright, she says. I'm to wear my new red dress and she wants ye to put on your good coat.'

'But I've packed it already! And right down the bottom o' my bag 'cause I dinna think I'd be needing it till we got to Lucescere.'

'Better go and unpack it, my lad,' Niall said. 'Your mam wants to show ye off to Nina, to be sure.'

'And there's so much o' him to show,' Meriel said cheekily. Lewen pretended to lunge for her and she danced away, laughing. 'And dinna think I'm hauling any water for your bath, laddie-boy. I never want to see that well-bucket again.'

Niall tousled his son's head affectionately. 'Go on, lad, go and get cleaned up. Tell your mam I'll be there in just a moment.'

Lewen nodded and gave Argent one more loving polish before putting away his curry-brush. With Meriel skipping beside him, chattering all the way, he went back through the gardens to the house, trying to imprint every aspect of the landscape upon his memory – the apple tree his mother had planted for him the day of his birth, the row of beehives under the cherry trees, the loch gleaming between the willow trees. It had seemed such a luxury, having three whole months of holiday, but it had rushed past him like a runaway horse and carriage.

Meriel left him in the kitchen garden, going to hang over the vegetable patch and make sure no bird had ravished her seeds away. Lewen had to clamber over Ursa, who was sleeping on the step in the sun, snoring loudly. He came into the kitchen, stopping abruptly inside the door. Rhiannon was sitting demurely by the fire, dressed in a leaf-green dress laced down the bodice with white satin ribbons. A frill of white embroidered cotton softened the square-cut neckline and the edge of the sleeves, which were folded back just below the elbow. Her hair was combed back from her face and tied in a simple knot at the back of her head, allowing the remainder to fall free in a shining black curtain that reached past the seat of her chair.

Lewen had seen the dress many times before, since it was a favourite of his mother's, but it was a very different dress on Rhiannon. Lilanthe was a slender woman, slight as a young willow tree. Rhiannon was far taller, and her waist was as deeply curved as a double bass. The silk clung closely to every curve, so that Lewen could see clearly the exact shape and dimension of her figure. The sight of her made the bones of Lewen's chest constrict so he had trouble taking a breath, and he was all too aware of a hot rush of blood to his groin.

She was frowning down at her bare feet, set neatly side by side, below the deep white frill edging her skirt. She looked up at Lewen, her eyes reflecting the green of the silk so that they looked the colour of water over pale sand. She scowled more deeply, saying abruptly, 'Me dare no' move in case it busts.'

He could find no words to answer her.

Lilanthe was busy laying the table but turned then to smile at her son. She was dressed in her best gown, a forest-green silk with gold embroidery and an underskirt of cream and gold brocade.

'Rhiannon is far too tall for my clothes! I did my best but we shall have to get her some other clothes. She certainly canna be wearing my auld green silk on the road.'

Lewen still could find nothing to say. He tried hard not to stare at Rhiannon but it was impossible to look anywhere else. His heart was swelling painfully in his chest, and his hands felt hot and heavy. He shoved them into his pockets.

Lilanthe regarded him shrewdly. 'Go on, laddie, ye havena time to waste. Nina will be here any moment and

96

she has a full caravan, she says. Go and get cleaned up, and then come and help me. It's been a long while since I've had a dozen guests for lunch.'

He nodded brusquely, trying hard not to show how powerfully the sight of a clean and silk-clad Rhiannon had affected him.

'And can ye dig out some o' your auld clothes for Rhiannon? She's near as tall as ye. She'll need some shirts and a jerkin, and some breeches to wear on the journey, for she'll be riding that winged horse o' hers, no doubt. Do ye ken what ye did with your auld riding cloak? For it'll rain, as sure as apples, and she'll need one.'

'Ye gave it away to the village jumble sale,' Lewen managed. His voice rasped in his throat.

'Och, aye, that I did. What a shame. I wonder if I can cut down one o' Niall's? But we've so little time . . .'

'Me have one,' the girl said sullenly, twisting her hands together in her lap. She looked angry and miserable.

'Aye, but . . . och, well, I suppose as long as ye do no' wear the plaid or the brooch, it canna matter. A cloak is a cloak, whether it be blue or no'. Ye can wear the tam-o'-shanter too, I suppose, as long as we take off the cockade. Och, so much to think o' and so little time! Go on, Lewen, my love, please! I want ye looking all bonny for Nina when she comes, for she hasna seen ye since she delivered ye to the Theurgia four years ago. She'll be so surprised to find ye so tall and doughty now. I ken I was.' Lilanthe sighed and smiled mistily at her son.

Lewen put his arms about his mother's slim waist and gave her a hearty squeeze, grateful that she had managed to cover his awkward silence and wondering if she under-stood all the things he found so hard to say. Then he made his escape, not meeting Rhiannon's sullen and ques-tioning gaze.

He was clean and dressed and engaged in rummaging through his wardrobe for old clothes when he heard a commotion outside, and went eagerly to his bedroom window to look out.

Two caravans were rolling up the elm-lined avenue towards the house. One was red and green, and the other was blue and yellow, the contrasting colour painted on decorative scrollwork around the windows and doors and roof. A big brown mare pulled the red caravan and a big grey gelding pulled the blue. A flaxen-haired man with a long, forked beard was lounging on the driver's seat of the blue caravan, playing a guitar, the reins knotted loosely over the dashboard. A little boy with curly chestnut hair was sitting up next to him, enthusiastically banging on a drum, with a small hairy creature sitting beside him, dressed in a short red dress and bonnet. The gelding plodded on placidly, occasionally twitching his ears back at the din. A woman drove the second caravan, dressed in green and vivid orange. As the caravans pulled up under Lewen's window, he saw a small iridescent green bird perched on her shoulder. Following the caravans were half a dozen horses and riders.

Lewen bundled together the clothes he had found on his bed then went leaping down the stairs, all his incipient homesickness drowned beneath a wave of excitement. It had been four years since he had last seen his mother's jongleur friends, but he remembered them clearly. They had come to give Lewen his Second Test of Powers and to accept him into the Coven as an apprentice-witch. At first all had been solemn and rather scary, but once Lewen had proven himself, the house had been full of music and laughter and dancing. Nina was nicknamed the nightingale for her gorgeous voice, and she had sung them many songs, merry, plaintive and droll in turn. Her husband

Iven was an acrobat and trickster, and knew more jokes and witty stories than anyone Lewen had ever met. Their son Roden had only been a toddler then and the arak Lulu no more than a round-eyed, wrinkle-faced baby. Nina had found her fallen out of a tree, and had nursed her back to health, saying she would teach her tricks when she was old enough. Although Nina now worked for the Coven, she had been a jongleur all her life and made no attempt to leave her past behind her.

As Lewen came out the front door, he saw Nina leap lightly down from the driving seat and seize Lilanthe in her arms, hugging her enthusiastically. Nina was a tall, slim woman with a mass of unruly chestnut hair and dark eyes. On her left hand she wore a vivid green emerald ring, the sign of a sorceress in the element of earth. Three other rings – green, white, and blue – decorated her right hand.

'Och, Nina, it's so lovely to see ye!' Lilanthe cried. 'Heavens, is that Roden? Look how big he's grown!'

'I could say the same about your laddie,' Nina said, smiling at Lewen. 'He's a man now! Is he a longbowman like Niall? He has the shoulders for it. Heavens, it makes me feel auld, to find Lewen so tall and doughty.'

Lewen grinned at his mother. 'That's exactly what Mam said ye'd say.'

Niall greeted Nina and Iven warmly then turned to the riders behind, saying with ritual ceremony, 'Welcome! Will ye no' stand down?'

The riders inclined their heads in acknowledgement, the three boys touching their caps. Two of the boys were tall and sturdy and brown-faced, and dismounted with customary ease. The other was pale and wan. He dismounted with difficulty, and winced as he moved.

The other three riders were girls. One was richly and fashionably dressed in a mud-spattered crimson velvet riding habit, brown leather boots and gloves, and a wide-brimmed brown velvet hat with a curled red feather. Long dark curls in wind-ruffled ringlets hung down her back and she had a mischievous smile.

Riding close beside her was a haughty-faced blonde girl dressed in dark brown the exact colour of her high-stepping nervous mare. Like her companion, she rode side-saddle and so carried a long whip in her left hand, but unlike her companion, her right boot was spurred. Lewen could tell at a glance that she rode her horse hard. The reins were held too tightly, so the mare fought the bit, dancing and sidestepping, her ears laid back flat. She was damp under her saddlecloth and Lewen could see the marks of whip and spur against her sweat-streaked hide.

The third girl was different again. She was plump and rosy-cheeked, with mousy hair tied in two wispy plaits. Wearing the plain homespun dress and wooden clogs of a country girl, she sat in the saddle like a sack of potatoes, and her short-legged, fat pony was on a leading-rein to the tallest of the boys. He paid her no attention, however, dropping the rein as he dismounted so he could rush forward to help down the girl in crimson. She had made no move to dismount herself but waited with absolute assurance that help would be forthcoming. The other brown-faced boy had also hurried forward, how-ever, and they collided at her stirrup. Lewen saw the girl's mouth curve in a little smile as they apologised to each other, both stiff and angry and very much on their dignity.

'Cameron helped me dismount yesterday so happen ye can hand me down today, Rafferty,' the girl said, holding out one small, gloved hand. The younger of the two boys took it proudly and assisted her down to the ground.

The sweat-lathered mare of the fair-haired girl shied and

bucked as if the hand clamped on the rein had tightened even further. Lewen moved quickly to take the rein and help the other girl down, before the horse kicked out at one of the others, or backed into the fat pony waiting so placidly behind.

'I thank ye,' she said coldly, shaking out her brown velvet skirts and casting a resentful look at the other boys. They did not notice.

Lewen nodded, smoothing the neck of her mare and murmuring in his deep, low voice until she had calmed. Then he went to help down the dumpy girl in clogs, who everyone seemed to have forgotten.

'Come on in, all o' ye, and welcome,' Lilanthe said. 'It's glad I am to see ye all.'

She led the group up the stairs and into the house, Meriel stricken into silence for a change and clinging close to her mother's side. The little boy, Roden, scampered happily beside Nina, holding the arak's hairy hand. She was an odd little creature, as small as a baby but with the sad, wizened face of a very old woman, and an extremely long, mobile tail. Soft grey-brown hair covered every part of her except her face, her hands and feet and the very tip of her tail.

Nina stopped halfway up the stairs to exclaim at the beautifully carved wooden doors. 'These are new since I was last here!' she cried. 'Oh, Lilanthe, they're exquisite. Dinna tell me Lewen made them? I had no idea he was so talented.'

Lilanthe smiled. 'He worked on them all winter. We're snowbound here, ye ken, and it was a bad winter, very cold and snowy. There's naught much else to do here. They're lovely, aren't they?'

'Indeed they are,' Nina replied, stopping to examine them closely before passing through into the house.

The door was split into two panels. A tree-changer had been carved on either side, their faces looking out from the leafy fronds of their hair. Birds and animals sheltered in their branches or looked out from behind their trunks – an owl, a lark, a squirrel, a donbeag, a wolf, an elven cat, a hare, the snout and sad eyes of a huge woolly bear. Flowers clustered around the tree-changers' roots, and when the doors were shut the fingers of the two forest faeries, man and woman, were entwined.

Lewen felt a warm glow of pleasure at Nina's words. He had worked on the doors for many days as a Hogmanay gift for his parents, and Nina was the first person outside his family to have seen them.

The apprentice-witches had all followed Nina up the steps.

Lewen noticed how the fair-haired girl's lip lifted in a condescending sneer as she glanced about, how the plump girl with plaits looked at the carved doors with wide-eyed admiration, and how the dark girl in crimson laughed and chatted with the two boys, who flanked her like a guard of honour. The other boy followed with a dreamy look of contentment as he gazed on the fresh green lawns, the narcissus and snowbells dancing under the bare branches of the trees, and the encircling ring of cloud-capped mountains.

'O mountains wild and high, where the eagle flies . . .' he murmured. 'No, no, that willna do. O mountains wild and high, where the eagles fly, frowning down upon us here, sear, dear, mere, yes, mere . . . frowning down upon us here, the garden green, the shining mere . . .'

Lewen led the nervous brown mare and the pony along the driveway towards the stables, wondering if the boy was mad.

Iven grinned at him.

102

'Young Landon fancies himself a poet,' he said. 'He's quite harmless and Nina thinks him very Talented. Och, no' at writing poetry. He stinks at that! But he is clear-seeing and clear-hearing, and very sensitive to atmosphere. Nina thinks he'll make a grand witch in time. Come, Sure, come, Steady.' He clicked his tongue and the carthorses followed him placidly like two big dogs, the caravans trundling along behind them.

'What about the others? Are they all apprentices too?' Niall asked, leading the other horses.

'Aye. Cameron is one o' the MacHamish clan and wants to be a Yeoman. He kens ye need to do your witch's training first, so he's submitting rather gracelessly to having to go to school for a few years. He's auld for it, being nineteen already, but he's been squire at Ravens-craig for four years or so, and trained as a soldier, and he has his heart set on serving the Rìgh, so the MacBrann is sponsoring him for the next few years to give him a chance.

'Rafferty is the son o' a clock-maker who shows some witch-talent, much to his family's surprise, nothing like that ever cropping up in their family afore. His father is hoping a few years at the Theurgia will help him climb a few rungs o' the social ladder. He's a good lad, though rather quick to throw a punch. They were rubbing along grandly till we picked up Lady Fèlice, but since then we've had a few punch-ups.'

'Is that the lass in the crimson?' Niall asked.

'Aye. She's the daughter o' the Earl o' Stratheden, one o' the MacBrann's courtiers, and has apparently caused some havoc with the hearts o' the young men in Ravenscraig. We picked her up there, and it's put the cat among the pigeons, I can tell ye. Until Lady Fèlice came, Lady Edithe o' Avebury queened over all o' us, but now her nose is quite out o' joint. She comes from the MacAven family, one o' the first families in Ravenscraig and famous for their witches. Edithe thinks herself quite the sorceress and far too good for us mere jongleurs.'

'Does she no' ken who Nina is?' Niall asked in surprise.

Iven shook his head, quirking his lip. 'She doesna think to look beyond the surface o' things, that one, and ye ken Nina would never tell her. I think Nina's taken a dislike to her ladyship and quite enjoys watching her make a fool o' herself. I must admit I find it rather amusing too. One minute, Lady Edithe's trying to ingratiate herself with Lady Fèlice because o' all her contacts at court, the next minute she's furious at all the attention she gets.'

'What about the lassie in the clogs?' Lewen asked.

'Och, aye,' Iven said, as if in sudden remembrance. 'Maisie. She's the granddaughter o' a village cunning man and a sweet wee thing. She's never been away from home afore and is quite overwhelmed. Nina says her Talent is quite strong, though.'

Iven's easy flow of conversation suddenly dried up, as he came to an abrupt halt just inside the stable door. The sturdy brown mare nudged his back with her nose. He did not seem to notice. He was staring at the winged mare, standing untethered in the wreck of her stall, contentedly lipping at a bucket of warm mash. At the sound and smell of the strange man, she flung up her horned head and shied away, showing the yellowish rim of her eye in sudden alarm.

'Easy, lassie,' Niall said in his low, warm voice. 'No need to fear. Easy now.'

The horse shook her head, hurrumphing, ears twitching back and forth. The black wings lifted and unfurled with a flash of iridescent blue at the tips.

'Eà's green blood!' Iven whispered.

'Aye, she's a bonny one, isn't she?' Niall said. 'Nervy, though. As ye can see, she's already kicked out the walls o' her stall. Happen we'd best untether the horses in the yard. They can graze in the garden and ye can leave the caravans there under the tree. It'll be cold tonight but they'll be fine once we blanket them.'

'What are ye doing with a winged horse?' the jongleur exclaimed. 'Ye canna be trying to tame it, surely?'

'Och, no' us,' Niall said. 'I do no' think I'd dare. Nay, we have a guest staying with us, a lassie named Rhiannon. She's the one that has dared cross her leg over the mare's back.'

'I do no' think I've ever heard o' a woman thigearn afore,' Iven said in interest. 'Is she one o' the MacAhern clan?'

'She's no' a NicAhern, nor a thigearn, nor even a woman,' Niall said. 'I said a lass and I meant it. She canna be much more than seventeen or eighteen.'

'Eà's green blood!' Iven said again. He shook his head in wonderment, unable to take his eyes off the mare, who was still dancing about on dark feathered hooves, ears laid back. 'We sing songs o' the black winged horses o' Ravenshaw. I thought it was only a story. I never thought I'd ever actually see one. Ye say this lassie has tamed it?'

'So it seems,' Niall said.

'Och, there's a tale in that, to be sure. Where is this lass?'

'Putting Lady Edithe and Lady Fèlice's noses out o' joint in the sitting room would be my bet,' Niall said rather dryly.

Iven raised an eyebrow. 'Bonny, is she then?'

'Aye, though no' in the manner o' your fine misses. She's bonny like a falcon is, or even yon winged horse.

Wild and fierce and dangerous to cross. Ye'll see what I mean when ye meet her.'

'I can hardly wait,' Iven replied.

Lewen thought of Rhiannon, sitting stiff and uncomfortable in her too-tight dress with her hands clenched in her lap and her bare feet set exactly side by side. His throat was suddenly dry. He wondered if he had done the right thing suggesting she come to the Tower of Two Moons with him. What would they make of her, those pretty fashionable girls, those rough and ready young men? He could not imagine any of them being as kind or accepting as his parents.

'Happen we'd best get the horses settled and then we can take Iven back to meet her?' he suggested.

'Aye, good idea, laddie. I'm sure Iven would care for a nice mug o' foaming ale.'

'To be sure,' Iven grinned.

They worked swiftly and competently to unharness the horses. The two sturdy carthorses were left free to graze where they willed, but the six other hacks were put into halters with a long rein that fastened to a spike in the ground. Although Lewen was eager to get back to the house, he gave them all a good currying, especially the tired brown mare with the painful welts on her side. As he brushed away the sweat and mud, he thought he too had conceived a strong dislike of the fair-haired girl with her whip and spurs. He wished he did not have to travel with her.

At last the horses were settled and the men walked back through the gardens towards the house, Iven bringing them up to date with news of the country. The biggest tidbit of gossip he had was that a date had been set for the wedding of the young heir to the throne, Donncan, to his cousin Bronwen, daughter of Maya the Ensorcellor.

The cousins had been betrothed as young children as a condition of the peace treaty between the Rìgh, Lachlan MacCuinn, and King Nila of the Fairgean, which ended decades of bloodshed. King Nila was Maya the Ensorcellor's half-brother, and had maintained a close interest in his niece, who had inherited the Fairgean ability to shapeshift in water, along with the smooth scaly skin, silvery eyes and finned limbs of the sea-dwelling faeries.

'They've set the wedding date for Midsummer's Eve, a most proper date,' Iven said. 'O' course His Highness wants Nina to sing at the wedding, so we have to make sure we're back in time.'

'Aye, I suppose it is time. Prionnsa Donncan would have turned twenty-four at Hogmanay, wouldn't he?' Niall looked at Lewen.

Lewen nodded. 'Aye. He would've sat his Third Test then. He canna join the Coven, o' course, being heir to the throne, but they will have wanted him to finish his studies afore he and Bronwen were married.'

Iven shrugged. 'The Banprionnsa Bronwen finished at the Theurgia last autumn, and by all accounts has been turning the court upside down with her tricks. Did ye ken it is all the fashion now for the young ladies to smear their skin with some kind o' silvery shimmering gel, to mimic the look o' Bronwen's scales? And they cut their dresses very low now, like Bronwen does, even though they have no gills to flaunt like she does. Some even go so far as to make false fins from muslin that they attach with ribbons to wrist and elbow. She has quite a clique o' her own now, that do naught but play and sing and dance, and stir up trouble. I heard one tale that she and her ladies have parties where they all swim naked in her pool, and do tricks like performing seals for the crowd.'

'Surely no'!' Niall was shocked.

Iven shrugged. 'Ye ken those ladies o' the court, all they do is clishmaclaver. Some say she's already with babe and she and Donncan need to be married afore the babe is born, which could be true. Others say the young prionnsa is hot for her, but she turns a cold shoulder on him, and His Highness wants to tie the knot afore she unravels all his treaties by running off with someone else. Who kens?'

Lewen listened with great interest. He knew the young heir to the throne very well, being only four years younger and seeing a great deal of him in the course of his duties as one of the Rìgh's squires. He knew Bronwen NicCuinn too, as well as anyone could know that cool, haughty young beauty.

'It's all the talk o' the countryside, though, which must relieve the pressure on the MacBrann,' Iven continued. 'Now he's inherited the crown o' Ravenshaw there's a good deal o' pressure on him to be marrying too and producing an heir. Ravenscraig was awash with eligible young ladies when we left. I fancy that is why Lady Fèlice is with us. I hear she tried her feminine wiles on him and was mortified when the MacBrann paid her no mind. Which is no' surprising, all things considered.'

At this last comment Lewen frowned and looked to his father, not liking to hear gossip about the MacBrann being repeated. Although Dughall MacBrann's lack of interest in women had been sniggered about for years, it was disconcerting hearing a friend of his father's discuss it so openly.

Niall smiled at him. 'Och, my lad, I ken ye think Iven as full o' clishmaclaver as the court ladies but indeed, his tongue does no' always run on wheels. It is his job to gather information for the Rìgh and he kens I'm still interested in court doings, although I live so far away. He can be the very soul o' discretion if needs be.'

'Indeed I can,' Iven said solemnly. 'All I'm telling ye is what ye could hear in any village inn. I ken far more than I've said, I promise ye.'

Lewen smiled but thought he would be sure never to confide any secrets to the fair-haired jongleur. His father must have read his expression for he put his hand on Lewen's shoulder and said quite seriously, 'Och, I mean it, laddie. Iven has worked in secret for the Rìgh since long afore Lachlan won back his throne. He was one o' Dide's men, and faced much danger in the days o' the Ensorcellor, when rebels and witches faced death by fire if they were caught. A single careless word would've been enough to condemn them all.'

Iven's face had darkened. 'Och, they were bad days. Let us hope we never see days like them again.'

'Eà turn her bright face upon us,' Niall said, just as sombrely.

They came silently through the kitchen garden, all busy with their own thoughts. Wood-smoke scented the cool, fresh air. The clouds on the mountains were slowly blowing down over the valley. Ursa ambled along behind Niall, raising her snout to sniff the air. Niall could hear voices from the sitting room, and then the sound of laughter.

Suddenly the nisse Kalea shot out of the sky like a maddened hornet. She tweaked one of Ursa's soft ears, so the old bear moaned in distress, tugged Niall's hair, and then grabbed hold of the two ends of Iven's long, plaited beard. She spun so fast in the air she was nothing but a blur of light. Iven cried out in pain and put up his hand to try to catch her. As suddenly as she had come, she was gone again. Iven's forked beard was now twisted into a spiral. He picked it up in his hand and looked at it ruefully. 'That hurt,' he said.

'That's nisses for ye,' Niall said. 'We get plagued by them a lot. They think o' the bairns as some kind o' pet, especially Lewen. Notice she did no' pull his hair?'

'Aye, so she dinna,' Iven said in mock resentment. 'That hardly seems fair. Doesna she ken I'm a guest and to be treated with deference?'

'What about me? I'm the master o' this wee domain and she pulls my hair and tugs on my nose all day long.'

'Aye, but she almost pulled my beard out by the roots. A man's beard should be sacred!'

'Would a nice cool ale make it feel better?' Niall asked, opening the door into the kitchen. 'Or happen a wee dram?'

'The sun is over the midline, make it a dram,' Iven said. 'Then take me to see this bonny lass that dares ride a winged horse. What a shame we canna bide a wee so I could have a chance to put her story into song. It's been a long while since we've had a new tale to tell.'

'We plan to send her with ye to Lucescere,' Niall said with a grin. 'Ye'll have plenty o' time for song-writing.'

'Will she be bringing her horse?'

'Just try to stop her.'

Iven tossed back his dram of whisky with a deep sigh of satisfaction. 'My beard and the Centaur's, I can hardly wait,' he said contentedly. 'I can tell it's going to be an interesting journey!'

THE APPRENTICE-WITCHES

Kingarth was only a small house and the sitting room was already uncomfortably crowded when the three men joined the others. Usually this room was reserved for Lilanthe, who did her sewing and the household accounts there, and wrote her letters. Beautifully worked tapestries of forests and gardens hung over the stone walls, and soft padded chairs covered in green velvet were drawn close about a low table. A sofa made comfortable with soft cushions and rugs was pushed against one wall, while a tall bookcase was crowded with books, a rare luxury so far from the city. On the mantelpiece was a collection of wooden animals Lewen had carved for his mother over the years. In moments of idleness he liked to sit and whittle, watching the shape that emerged from the wood as if it had been imprisoned inside.

The sofa and chairs were all occupied by the females, so Iven, Niall and Lewen went to crowd by the fire with the other males. As soon as Cameron and Rafferty saw Niall, they eagerly asked him if it was true he had once been one of Lachlan the Winged's own guard in the years before he had won the throne. Niall was happy to oblige them with tales of some of the Blue Guards' more romantic escapades from the days when the Ensorcellor ruled the land and Lachlan had been a young rebel, his wings concealed beneath a cloak of illusions so that all had thought him a poor hunchbacked cripple.

Lewen leant his shoulder against the wall and observed the members of the group with great interest. The young ladies were all drinking tea and listening politely to Nina as she brought Lilanthe up to date with the happenings of the royal court. Maisie was drinking in every word with rapt eyes, while Edithe was quick to express her opinion on everything from accounts of witch-taunting in Tîrsoilleir to the new tax on glass.

Meanwhile, the young poet Landon was absorbed in watching Rhiannon as she fiddled with a wooden box on the side table. Lewen grinned to himself. He had made the box at school and brought it home as a gift to his mother that Hogmanay. It was a cunningly designed puzzle box which looked as if it was merely a prettily carved cube of wood with no lid or hinge or clasp or lock that could be opened. However, it rattled when shaken, revealing something was hidden inside. Most people gave up in frustration after only a few moments, but it was possible to solve the puzzle if one looked long and hard enough. He wondered if Rhiannon would be one of the few to work it out, and by the determined expression on her face, he wagered that she would.

Meriel, Roden and Lulu the arak were busy playing spillikins on the floor, the little hairy creature showing amazing dexterity with fingers and toes and tail. Eventually she did knock over one of the sticks, however, and then the arak shrieked with rage and bounded all round the room, upsetting cups of tea and sending a plate of cakes flying. Hurriedly the children tidied up after her, apologising and trying to contain their giggles. When Edithe said haughtily that she would have thought the stable was the place for such a wild beast, and Lulu tipped her head upside down and made a rude face at her from between her hairy legs, Meriel and Roden lost control and fled the room, bubbling over with laughter. Lulu bounded after them, her long tail seizing one of the broken cakes and tossing it deftly into her mouth.

Edithe rolled her eyes and lifted her cup to her mouth, sipping delicately. 'Really, that animal! As if we were all no' in enough discomfort already. I must say, I do no' understand why we all must travel in this way. My father would have preferred me to travel in my own carriage, with outriders and my maid to attend me.'

'Students are no' permitted servants at the Theurgia,' Nina said in a tone of long suffering. 'Apprentices must learn to manage for themselves. Ye ken the rules, Edithe.'

Edithe sniffed and turned her gaze to Rhiannon, who had lifted the puzzle box to her ear and was shaking it vigorously. Something rattled inside, and she turned it in her hands, searching for a way to open it.

'So ye are to ride to the Tower o' Two Moons with us, Rhiannon? What is your Talent?'

Rhiannon shrugged, not looking up from the box in her hands.

'Ye have no Talent as yet? But ye are quite auld. Ye must have sat your first two Tests o' Powers. What element were ye strongest in?'

'Dinna ken.'

'Ye do no' ken? Ye mean ye have no' sat your Tests?'

'Nay.'

'But then, surely . . . what makes ye think ye can attend

the Theurgia if ye have no' even undertaken the First Test o' Powers? I ken, o' course, that the Coven are no' as strict as they once were about whom they allow to attend the Theurgia.' Edithe flicked a contemptuous glance towards Maisie, who coloured unhappily, and Landon, who did not notice. 'However, applicants must still have some form o' cunning, at the very least. I, o' course, was demonstrating unusually strong powers at a very young age and passed my First Test o' Powers with flying colours.'

She said this with a confidential smile to Fèlice, who smiled and murmured, 'O' course', with a laughing glance aside to Maisie.

Rhiannon was not listening. Her nimble fingers had found a loose edging of wood along the bottom of the box which, when pulled out, revealed a secret compartment. Hidden within was a tiny key. Rhiannon emptied it into her hand with a gleeful smile and at once began to look for a keyhole. She found it only a few moments later by swinging aside a carved scroll which had been made mobile by the removal of the piece of edging. She glanced up at Lewen in triumph and inserted the key into the lock. Once it was turned, the lid of the box swung open to reveal another, smaller, puzzle box inside. Lewen had to bite back a grin as her face changed from triumph to chagrin. At once she began to turn the smaller box in her hands, looking for the secret to opening it, but this box had been made differently to the first, and so presented a whole new conundrum.

Edithe did not like being ignored. She pressed her lips together, then said sharply, 'But ye? Ye have no' even sat your First Test o' Powers, that most sit at the age o' eight. How auld are ye now? What makes ye think ye can just turn up at the Theurgia and have them welcome ye with open arms? Have ye any Skills at all?'

Rhiannon did not answer, being still absorbed in the box.

Edithe leant forward and tapped her sharply on the knee. Rhiannon jumped violently and almost dropped the box.

'I said, do ye have any Skills at all?'

Every muscle in Rhiannon's body stiffened. She stared at Edithe warily, then slowly shook her head.

'Ye do no' go for training in witchcraft and witch-cunning then? Ye are naught but a common student? Are ye no' far too auld?'

'Dinna ken,' Rhiannon said, through clenched teeth.

'I see,' Edithe said. 'No Skills at all, and no learning either that I can see.'

'Edithe,' Nina said warningly.

Edithe smiled sweetly at her. 'I'm sorry. I'm just curious. Is the Theurgia really so desperate for students that they will accept just anyone?' She turned back to Rhiannon, running her gaze up and down the dress which had so obviously been made over to fit her. 'Your family must be eager indeed for ye to learn what ye can, and make many new friends and associates, if they are prepared to carry the costs of sending ye all the way to Lucescere to go to school.'

Lilanthe drew her brows together.

'Have no family,' Rhiannon said tersely.

'No family? But then who . . .?' Edithe glanced round at the small, simply furnished room, clearly wondering how Niall and Lilanthe could hope to pay for both their son and their strange guest to attend the Theurgia. 'Have ye a private independence?'

'Uh?'

'A private independence? Money o' your own? How do ye expect to pay for your board and tuition at the Tower?'

'Dinna ken.'

Edithe glanced at Fèlice, who shrugged, looking uncomfortable. 'I see,' Edithe said again with such a nasty innuendo in her voice that Lewen took a quick step forward, though he had no idea what he could say in Rhiannon's defence.

Before he could speak, his mother said in a chilly voice, 'Rhiannon shall be sitting for a scholarship. She shows unusual potential that we are certain shall flower into a true Talent. I have already written to the Keybearer about her and I am sure she shall be most pleased to welcome Rhiannon to the Theurgia. Isabeau is always excited at the discovery o' a possible new Talent.'

Edithe stared at her, both brows raised. 'Indeed?' she asked coolly. 'Ye ken the Keybearer well, do ye?'

'Ye must realise that Lilanthe is the Keybearer's dearest friend, Edithe,' Nina said. 'They have kent each other since they were lassies. Lilanthe once taught at the Theurgia. The Keybearer would love her to return and teach again but Lilanthe does no' care for cities.'

'Oh, I see,' Edithe cooed, pulling her chair a little closer to Lilanthe. 'I dinna realise. Och, please tell us more, madam. I would love to hear tales o' the Keybearer as a lass. I believe her powers were extraordinary even then?'

'Indeed they were,' Lilanthe said, 'but more extraordinary still were her kindness and compassion. Even today, when we are at peace with all, such consideration for the feelings o' others is rare.'

It was so clearly a snub that colour flamed into Edithe's cheeks and she sat back, at a loss for words. Lilanthe turned back to Nina, saying eagerly, 'Tell me, how is Dide? Is it true he has finally given up the travelling life?'

As Nina answered her with a laugh, Edithe excused herself stiffly and came over to the fire. To Lewen's surprise, Edithe did not join the laughing group round his father but came straight up to him, smiling sweetly. Up until this moment she had paid him no attention at all, but he soon realised that she had revised her earlier opinion of him as an unimportant country clodpole.

'I had no' realised your parents were so well acquainted with the court at Lucescere. Tell me, have ye visited there often?' she asked.

'Aye,' Lewen answered curtly, not wanting to tell her he waited on the Rìgh at table every night, and ran his messages, and carried his cloak and hat.

'Indeed? Tell me more,' she purred. 'Have ye met the Rìgh?'

'Aye,' he answered again, feeling torn between amusement and embarrassment. After a moment, realising she would find out in the end, he said reluctantly, 'I am one o' the Rìgh's squires, when time permits. I attend court every evening, after I have finished my studies, and I often ride out with him.'

Edithe leant closer. 'Ye must ken the young prionnsachan, then? Donncan and his brother Owein?'

'Aye, and the Banprionnsa Olwynne too,' Lewen said, irritated by the way she mentioned only the two sons of the family. Lewen was very close friends with the royal twins, being less than a year older than them, and in the same class at the Theurgia.

'Och, o' course,' she said now, smiling. 'I imagine we shall see a lot o' them once we are at the Theurgia.'

'I doubt it,' he answered. 'They are very busy with their own concerns. And the Theurgia is very large.'

She tried another tack. 'And the Keybearer, do ye see her often too?'

'No, no' very often,' he answered, looking for some way to escape.

117

'Oh? I had thought your mother was good friends with the Keybearer Isabeau NicFaghan? Did I misunderstand? Or perhaps their friendship was no' kept up?'

'Aunty Beau comes here often,' Lewen said unwillingly. 'She travels about a lot, ye ken. She'll always come by if she's in Ravenshaw.'

Edithe looked sceptical. 'But ye live so far away from anywhere here! It took us three days' hard riding to get here from Ravenscraig and the MacBrann told us there is nothing beyond your farm but the wild mountains.'

'Aye, that is true,' Lewen said. 'But Aunty Beau can take any shape she chooses, remember. It is no' far to come if ye are flying in the shape o' a golden eagle.'

Edithe was impressed despite herself. She leant even closer, laying one white hand on Lewen's sleeve. 'I am so glad to ken someone who will be able to teach me how to go on at the Theurgia.' She glanced down coyly, twisting the small moonstone ring on the middle finger of her right hand, symbol of her acceptance into the Coven as an apprentice. Lewen wore a ring very like it, as did all of the young apprentices. 'It will be so very large and overwhelming at first. It will be nice to have a friend, to help ease my first days there.'

Lewen was aware of Rhiannon's gaze fixed upon them, and blushed. He was saved from answering by Lilanthe, who stood up and said, 'Shall we go and eat? I can smell all is ready. Ye must be hungry.'

At once everyone stirred and looked up, beginning to make appreciative noises, for indeed the smell coming from the kitchen was delicious. They all followed Lilanthe eagerly, though Lewen noticed both Fèlice and Edithe looked rather affronted at having to eat in the kitchen.

Their look of outrage deepened as all three of the young men showed a marked inclination to sit next to Rhiannon

118

at the dinner table. Openly eyeing the voluptuous curves threatening to split the seams of her dress, Cameron scrambled to pull out a chair for her and then, when she sat, took the opportunity to gaze over her shoulder and down her cleavage. While he feasted his eyes, Rafferty slid deftly into the chair beside her, and tried to engage her in conversation, much to Cameron's chagrin. Cameron hurriedly took the seat on her other side, pushing the young poet Landon out of the way. Dejectedly Landon made his way round the other side of the table to sit next to Maisie, who smiled at him shyly in commiseration.

Edithe slipped her hand inside Lewen's arm and smiled at him, saying sweetly, 'Do ye always eat in the kitchen? How very quaint. Please, tell me where I should sit. I can see ye have no order o' precedence here.'

He pulled out a chair for her and then tried to make his escape but she was ruthless, pulling him down to sit next to her. Fèlice at once took the seat on his other side and both young ladies spent the whole meal laughing at every remark he made, leaning close to him so he could smell their perfumed hair, and generally making him very uncomfortable.

His only hope was that their attentions would make Rhiannon jealous, but she did not seem to notice, focusing all her attention on her food as if she had not eaten twenty-three griddle-cakes earlier in the day. Edithe and Fèlice exchanged a horrified roll of the eye when they saw her cramming her food into her mouth with both hands. Lewen managed to catch Rhiannon's eye and gently shook his head, showing her as unobtrusively as he could how to wield a knife and spoon. She scowled at him but tried to copy his actions, her elbows stuck out so far sideways the two boys had to lean the other way to avoid being poked in the face.

They were not put off, however, continuing to be assiduous in offering her more bread or another serve of pie. She did not soften with all their attention, answering only curtly, and often staring at them with scorn as if she thought their questions or comments more than usually stupid. The older boy, Cameron, was particularly attentive, leaning so close to her at times that Lewen had to grind his teeth together to stop himself from leaping up and protesting.

'I have no' seen ye at court afore. I ken I would remember ye if I had,' Cameron said with a winning smile.

She flashed him a glance but made no reply, being too busy eating.

'Am I right?' he said, leaning closer. 'If ye had been to the court at Ravenscraig, I am sure I must have noticed ye.'

She cast him a quizzical look, gave a perfunctory shake of her head, and reached for another bread roll.

'Never? Are ye a country lass then? Did ye grow up round here too?'

'Near enough,' she answered after a moment, cramming another wedge of cheese and leek pie into her mouth.

'So is this your first journey away from home?'

She nodded and elbowed him away so she could reach the jug of iced bellfruit juice. He sat back for a moment, disconcerted, then fortified himself with several large gulps of the juice and tried again. 'Ye must be rather daunted at the idea o' travelling all the way to the royal court at Lucescere then.'

'I think that's the understatement o' the day,' Edithe said to Fèlice, who giggled, then looked a little shamefaced.

'Ye must no' be nervous. I'll be happy to show ye round and tell ye how to get on,' Cameron continued.

'Like ye'd ken,' Edithe said with a snort of contempt.

Cameron glared at her. 'I may no' have been to the royal court afore but I've been a squire at Ravenscraig for years now.'

Edithe looked down her nose. 'Ye think anyone at Lucescere will care?'

Cameron turned his shoulder against her. 'Do no' listen to her,' he said warmly to Rhiannon. 'She hasna been to Lucescere either, she just likes to put on airs.'

Rhiannon stared at him blankly, shrugged and kept on eating. Cameron edged his chair closer to hers. 'So ye must no' be afraid,' he said in a low, confidential voice that Lewen had to strain to hear. 'I promise I'll keep an eye on ye. Ye shallna be lonely while I'm there to watch out for ye.'

Rhiannon laid down her knife and spoon. 'Me no afeared,' she said angrily, 'and me no lonely. Me have my horse.'

Cameron laughed, startled, then leant even closer, speaking in such a low voice that Lewen could not hear a word, despite all his efforts.

Rhiannon curled her lip. 'Rather have my horse,' she said.

Cameron sat back, colour rising in his cheeks. He looked dumbfounded.

Rhiannon grabbed another handful of roast potatoes, ate them hungrily, then wiped her greasy hands clean on her bodice. As she gulped down the rest of her juice, Rafferty took advantage of Cameron's sudden silence to try his hand at engaging her in conversation.

'I havena travelled much afore either,' he said. 'I'm so looking forward to it. I've always wanted to travel the world. What are ye looking forward to seeing the most?'

Rhiannon shrugged. 'Dinna ken.'

'I canna wait to see an ogre,' Rafferty said confidingly.

Her lip curled. 'Why? Ogres ugly, mean and stupid.'

'Ye've seen one afore?'

'Aye, o' course.' She spoke as if ogres were as common as dandelions.

'Well, I've never seen one. I come from down by the sea, though. I've seen the Fairgean come into harbour, riding on the back o' their sea-serpents.' He spoke rather defensively.

'Really?' Maisie squeaked.

'Aye, really.' Rafferty looked across the table at her.

'I'd love to see the Fairgean.' Maisie clasped her hands together. 'They're said to be bonny indeed.'

'If ye like that sort o' thing,' Edithe said cuttingly. 'Personally I find the idea o' scales and gills quite loathsome.'

'The Banprionnsa Bronwen is said to have scales and gills and they say she is the most beautiful girl at court,' Fèlice said. 'I canna wait to see her! I've heard her clothes are just divine.'

Cameron snorted in derision. 'Is that no' just like a lass? Who wants to look at clothes? It's the changing o' the guard that I'm dying to see. I hope the Rìgh's captain is there and no' off fighting somewhere. I've heard so many stories about him and his cursed sword.'

'Och, me too,' Rafferty said excitedly. He turned to Rhiannon. 'Have ye heard the tales? They say once he has drawn his sword, he canna sheathe it till all the enemy are dead. It doesna matter how many o' them there are, he'll just keep on fighting till nary a one is left.'

This sparked her interest and, encouraged, he went on. 'They call him Dillon o' the Joyous Sword, for the sword takes such joy in battle. He was one o' the League o' the Healing Hand, ye ken.' At Rhiannon's blank look, he said, 'Ye must've heard o' the League? There are so many stories about them. Ye ken, the band o' beggar children that helped the Rìgh win his throne?'

'Do ye think Jay the Fiddler will be at court?' Fèlice said with a sigh. 'I'd love to hear him play his *viola d'amore*. They say no-one can play the songs o' love like he can.'

'Very true,' Nina said with a mischievous smile. 'But I doubt whether Jay will be at court. He and Finn the Cat will be off somewhere on the Rìgh's business. Ye would think they had jongleurs' blood in them, those two, the way they travel around.'

'What about ye, Landon?' Lilanthe asked then in her soft, gentle voice, for the young poet had not said a word all meal. Indeed, he had hardly eaten a mouthful either, sitting with his chin resting in his hand and his eyes fixed on Rhiannon's face. Once or twice the wild girl had cast him an irritated glance, but he did not seem to care. He seemed to find her endlessly fascinating.

Landon did not respond, until Maisie tugged his darned and grubby shirt-sleeve. Then he looked round with an abstracted air, saying, 'I'm sorry?'

'What are ye most looking forward to seeing on your journey to Lucescere?' Lilanthe repeated.

He looked back at Rhiannon and smiled wistfully. 'My eyes have feasted upon the utmost pinnacle o' beauty, I have no desire to see aught else,' he answered without a trace of embarrassment.

Fèlice giggled, Maisie blushed, Edithe frowned and snorted, and the other boys looked down, discomfited and embarrassed on his behalf. Rhiannon herself stared across the table at her admirer in obvious puzzlement, then set about picking her teeth with a ragged but thankfully clean fingernail. The adults exchanged wry looks.

'What about ye, Maisie? Is there anything ye particularly want to see at court?' Lilanthe asked.

The country girl blushed and fiddled with her moonstone ring.

'I just want to see the Keybearer,' she whispered. 'And all the healers at work.'

'Ye are interested in herb-lore and the healing arts?' Lilanthe said. 'I must show ye my simple room afore ye go. I canna claim to be a healer like Isabeau or Johanna, her head healer, but I did learn what I ken from them and I do my best for the people o' the valley.'

'Och, I'd like that,' Maisie whispered, her face glowing.

'I guess ye're used to that sort o' thing,' Cameron said to Rhiannon, with a glowering look at Landon, who was once again regarding her with intense fascination.

'Uh?' Rhiannon said.

'All that flim-flammery and flattery,' he said. 'I bet all the lads ye ken follow ye round all the time, begging ye for a smile or a kiss.'

Rhiannon was surprised into laughter. 'Who, me? Nay!' she cried, shaking her head so her glossy hair swung.

If she was striking when sullen-faced and cross, she was quite breathtaking when smiling. Lewen could not take his eyes off her, even though he was aware of how cross this made both Edithe and Fèlice. He was not at all surprised when Cameron hitched his chair closer, sliding one arm around Rhiannon's waist as he whispered something in her ear. If Lewen had not been constrained by the rules of hospitality he would have leapt up and punched the good-looking boy right in his smiling mouth. As it was, his hands clenched into fists and he had to swallow the sour taste of rage.

All the warmth and spontaneity died out of Rhiannon's face. Sitting straight-backed and stiff as a poker, she hissed, 'Get your hand off me else me cut it off for ye!'

Her words rang out in one of those little lulls that sometimes come in a noisy room, and everyone turned and stared down the table. Cameron went scarlet and hurriedly moved his chair away. Rhiannon stared at him for a moment longer then went on eating as if nothing had happened, but Fèlice and Edithe gave little embarrassed titters and Lilanthe drew her brows together in a look of trouble.

After the meal had been cleared away, the group broke up. Lewen and his father showed the other men around the farm while Lilanthe took the girls out to her herb garden and then to her simple room, lined with bottles of home-made medicines and potions.

They met again for high tea in the kitchen, then all crammed together in the sitting room as dusk rolled over the garden.

Nina sang for them, her long-billed sunbird amusing everyone by accompanying her with melodious little trills and call notes. There was much animated talking and laughing, with Iven easily dominating the conversation, telling tales and teasing the others good-naturedly. He tried to draw Rhiannon out but she stared at him suspiciously and answered only in monosyllables, so at last he gave up and concentrated on entertaining his crowd. Rhiannon sat as still and wary as a bird hiding in bracken, frowning, her mouth set firmly, her luminous blue-grey eyes moving from face to face. It was clear to Lewen that she could understand little of what was said. They were all speaking too quickly, and at cross-currents, drowning out each other's voices as they insisted on having their say. The conversation was mostly concerned with politics and court gossip, none of which meant a thing to the wild girl from the mountains.

As the night wore on Edithe and Cameron, who had both obviously taken a strong dislike to Rhiannon, began to mock her more openly, asking her opinion on the appointment of the new Fealde in Tìrsoilleir or rumours that the treaty with the Fairgean was under strain. To each question Rhiannon said only, 'Dinna ken', which they seemed to find exquisitely funny. Edithe appeared most concerned about Rhiannon's lack of a private independence, and asked her a great many questions about how she hoped to manage in Lucescere without an allowance.

'But, my dear, ye simply must have some income,' she said. 'Although we all have to wear an apprentice robe while at school, there will be lots o' parties and balls and picnics and one must have clothes. It is the royal court, after all.' She looked Rhiannon up and down, and then said delicately, 'But happen ye do no' care for clothes?'

Cameron laughed.

Rhiannon said nothing.

Fèlice and Edithe then fell into an animated discussion about the latest fashions at court.

'I heard the Rìgh's niece wears her bodice cut very low, with barely a sleeve at all, to show off her fins and gills,' Edithe said. 'Who would have imagined fins and gills would become fashionable! And it is most unfair, for she does no' feel the cold, ye ken, so that she wears her dresses so even in the very midst o' winter.'

Rhiannon sat silently, listening, ignoring the fixed unfriendly gaze of Cameron and the fixed longing gaze of Landon as best she could. It was clear she was going to have to get used to Landon's eyes upon her face. He had spent all afternoon staring at her. Occasionally he dug out a scruffy little notebook from his pocket where he would scribble a few words, before staring in agony at the ceiling as he mouthed half-rhymes and mangled phrases. At one point Lewen heard him muttering, 'Breast, west, best, nest?' and he blushed for both Landon and himself.

126

He heard a burst of mocking laughter a little later, and looked across the room to find Fèlice and Edithe hiding their smiling mouths behind their hands, while Cameron grinned, looking very pleased with himself.

'What, naught to say?' Cameron was saying. 'What's the matter? Cat got your tongue?'

Rhiannon stared at him in obvious bewilderment. 'Uh? Cat? What cat? There no cat. And me have my tongue. See?' She poked it out at him.

They all broke into peals of laughter, even shy, sweet Maisie. Only Landon did not laugh, looking at Rhiannon in obvious pity and sympathy.

Glancing at Rhiannon, Lewen was surprised to see her eyes were swimming with tears. He got up at once and said gently, 'Rhiannon, ye must be weary still, would ye like to go to bed?'

She nodded at once and got up, so tall and awkward in her too-tight green dress that Edithe twisted her lip in scorn, hardening Lewen's dislike of her into something hotter and fiercer. He showed Rhiannon out of the room as quietly and unobtrusively as he could. Her fists were clenched and her cheeks were flushed, and she did not look at Lewen but caught up her mass of entangling skirts so she could stride out with ease. Lewen did not speak at all as he gathered up the clean nightgown Lilanthe had laid out for her, and the pile of warm blankets, and carried them all out to the stable. She went straight to the black mare, which turned its head and whinnied eagerly at the sight of her. Rhiannon flung her arm about its neck and buried her face in its silky flowing mane. The mare nudged her with its nose and blew gustily through its nostrils but she did not look up.

By the time Lewen had made up her bed for her, she was calm again, though her eyelashes were spiky with tears. She wiped her nose on her green silk sleeve.

'Thank ye,' she said with some difficulty.

'My pleasure. Sleep well,' Lewen answered. He hesitated, then said in a rush, 'And do no' fear. None o' those louts shall trouble ye tonight, for I'll set Ursa herself to guard your door.'

She laughed. 'That bear? Ye want horses mad with fear all night?'

Lewen said valiantly, 'Then I'll guard your door myself.'

'Me no afeared,' she said derisively. 'Those boys ken no more about mating than a babe.'

Lewen's blood surged. He had to turn away, pretending to busy himself checking the food and water of the other horses, until the heat in his face and his groin had subsided enough that he should not betray himself. In the meantime he could hear Rhiannon ripping off the despised green dress and splashing about in the water. He dared not turn round until all was quiet again. When at last he faced her she was sitting cross-legged in the straw, eyeing him speculatively, dressed only in the thin white nightgown, the laces at the bodice undone.

'I'd best get back.' He could not meet her eyes. 'Are ye sure ye're grand?'

She dragged up her nightgown to show her knife strapped to one long, pale thigh. 'Sure,' she said. 'What about ye? Need me to guard ye from those cursehags?'

Lewen grinned despite himself. 'I hope no',' he said.

'Call me if ye need me and me come,' she said.

'Ye too. Call me, I mean. If ye need me.'

'Me no need ye,' she said.

'I guess no',' he said, feeling miserable. 'Good night then.'

She wrinkled her brow. 'What this "good night"?'

'It's what ye say last thing at night, afore ye sleep,' Lewen said. 'It means have a good sleep, keep safe, have sweet dreams.'

She smiled, radiantly and unexpectedly. 'Me see. Good night to ye then.'

He nodded and went out into the darkness. He did not go back to the house at once, though, finding a tree to lean against in the chilly darkness of the garden, pressing his forehead against its smooth bark, crushing its new fresh leaves in his hands so he could smell their sharp smell. His body ached, his skin was hot, his mind was all confusion. He had heard of men addicted to moonbane, who kept on tasting it for its sweet, giddy delirium when all the time they knew it was poisoning their blood and destroying their reason. Rhiannon was like moonbane, he thought, and already it was too late for him. He was addicted.

BLACKTHORN

Rhiannon woke slowly, feeling deliciously warm and comfortable. She cuddled her cheek against the soft black feathers that lay over her like a counterpane, aware of a strange new feeling inside her. She did not know how to name this feeling, but when she thought of her horse it warmed and deepened within her, and when she thought of the boy, with his quiet, deep voice and steady, watching brown eyes, it caused her to curl her toes, her mouth lifting at the corners.

She stretched and reluctantly slipped out from underneath the sheltering wing. The mare lifted her head and regarded her with a great, black velvety eye. When Rhiannon stared into that eye, she saw within a greater blackness, a slit, an abyss without an end. It fascinated her, this black slit that did not reflect the light like the rest of the eye, but seemed to suck it inside. Everything about her mare fascinated and allured her. Every line and curve of her body, every movement she made, every twitch of ear or flare of nostril was filled with grace and strength and power, and it was hers, all hers. She did not care what the big bearded man said, the winged mare was hers.

The mare gave a soft whinny of agreement and nudged her with her nose.

Rhiannon had not had much time alone since arriving at Kingarth. When she was not sleeping, there was always someone watching her, talking at her, demanding her attention.

Even though Rhiannon was accustomed to having no personal privacy, having grown up in the midst of a large herd, nonetheless she was used to long periods of quiet and solitude. Satyricorns did not talk much. Their language was simple and used only when a grunt or gesture would not suffice. Rhiannon had always been isolated within the herd because she looked so different from the other satyricorn children. Their eyes were yellow with an oblong iris, not a soft grey-blue like the dawn sky. They had hard cloven hooves and a ridge of hair that ran down their spine, ending in a tufted tail. Her torso had been smooth and hairless, and her feet were soft and flexible. She had never been able to run as fast, or leap as far, or fight as roughly as any of the other satyricorn children, and so she had learnt to keep herself apart, spending her days roaming the high meadows alone.

Here there was no quiet and no solitude. Rhiannon had been spinning in a whirlwind of words from the moment she arrived, grabbing here and there at sounds she thought she understood, only to find they had many more meanings than she could ever have imagined. Eyes could be daggers, cats stole tongues, air could be put on like a garment. The only clue she had to meaning was the voice with which the words were uttered, and even that was deceitful. Many of these humans said one thing with their words, and quite another with their faces and bodies and voices. It was exhausting and bewildering trying to decipher it all, and to make it worse, Rhiannon did not believe them when they kept telling her she had nothing to fear. There were so many threatening undercurrents to the things that they said, so many traps in their words.

Lewen was the only one that she did not fear. His voice was deep and slow and thoughtful, and he never made any sudden jerky move to startle or frighten her. He smiled at her, and was kind, and he never said one thing with his words and another with his eyes. When Rhiannon was alone with him, she found herself relaxing the tension of her muscles and the fierceness of her concentration.

But for now she had only the drowsy horses for company. She could think over the happenings of the last few days and begin to prepare herself for the journey ahead. Rhiannon was conscious of trepidation, for she did not know what lay ahead of her, and she was suspicious of these shrill, noisy humans with their complicated ways. She meant to keep her dagger close to hand, and her wits about her, for she could see there were many pitfalls ahead if she was unwary. At least she could always escape any trouble on the back of her beautiful winged horse. As long as the flying horse was with her, Rhiannon would be safe.

She stroked the black velvety nose, then got down her saddlebags from their hooks. She had not had a chance to go through her things and make sure they had not been interfered with. She did not believe these humans when they said they would not touch her treasures. It did not matter that they had many strange and beautiful and useful things of their own. In Rhiannon's experience, the more you had, the more you wanted.

She spent a happy half-hour turning over her treasures and arranging them to her liking in the saddlebags. She caressed the gleaming brooch of the running horse, and hid it right down the bottom of the bag along with the music-box, the silver goblet, the medal with its device of a hand haloed in light and her other treasures. If anyone saw those they would take them, she knew. Anyone would.

Then she sharpened her two beautiful daggers and put them ready with her bow and quiver of arrows. She wanted them close to hand at all times. The blowpipe and pouches of poisoned barbs she tucked just inside the pocket of the saddlebag that hung on the right, so she could reach them easily. Everything else she stowed away neatly, all except her clothes and the grooming kit in its leather wallet. She was turning over the currying combs and brushes and sponges in puzzlement when she heard a noise and looked up, muscles tensing instinctively.

Lilanthe was in the doorway, carrying a basin and jug of warm water, a big portmanteau dangling awkwardly from the crook of her elbow. Outside, birds were beginning to test their voices for their coming hosanna to the sun, and mist was eddying in a rising breeze.

Rhiannon frowned and closed the flap of the saddlebag, thrusting it behind her.

Lilanthe came in and laid down her burdens. 'What is it ye wish to hide, lassie?'

Rhiannon did not answer.

Lilanthe sat next to her and wrapped her arms around her knees. 'I am troubled about ye, Rhiannon,' she said. 'I canna read your mind. Are ye so secretive and suspicious because ye have reason to fear honesty? Or is it just your nature? I wish I kent what it is ye are frightened o'.'

Her voice was so gentle and her eyes so filled with compassion, Rhiannon felt an urge to make her understand somehow.

'In herd, must fight for what yours,' she said.

'Aye, I understand that. But we are no' o' the herd, we have no desire to take what's yours away from ye.'

'Aye, ye do,' Rhiannon said fiercely. 'Ye say clothes no' mine, ye say horse no' mine.'

Lilanthe was quiet for a moment. 'I think ye can say the horse is yours,' she said at last. 'Certainly Lewen calls Argent "his" horse, and I call the garden "mine", and Niall calls Ursa "his" bear. I think it is natural in us to want to own things, to forge strong bonds with them. Niall's problem with ye calling the mare yours is a philosophical one, because a winged horse is no' like other horses. But he is no' acknowledging the fact that ye and the horse have clearly forged some kind o' bond, happen even the bond that is felt between thigearn and flying horse. Certainly none o' us would dream o' trying to separate ye.'

Rhiannon grasped at the words she understood. 'Ye say horse mine?'

'Aye, lassie. That is, if ye think ye belong to her as much as she belongs to ye.'

Rhiannon shrugged. 'O' course. She mine, me hers.'

Lilanthe smoothed her rough brown gown down over her knees. 'The clothes are a different matter, though, Rhiannon.' As the girl immediately stiffened, Lilanthe glanced up, smiling a little ruefully. 'Nay, hear me out, lassie. I understand that the clothes are important to ye, but ye canna keep them. They are no' yours, they belonged to the Yeoman, and after his death they belong to his family.'

'Me won them,' Rhiannon said, scarlet with suppressed fury. 'Blood-right!'

Lilanthe leant forward. 'What was that? Blood-right? What does that mean?'

'They mine,' she said flatly.

'Nay, Rhiannon, tell me, what does that mean? Did ye kill the soldier? Is that why ye claim the clothes as yours? Ye must tell me. Canna ye see how important it is that we ken? We saw the hole the arrow made in the cloth. He was shot through the back. Did ye shoot him? For that's a hanging offence, Rhiannon. That would be treason. Ye must tell me, ye must explain to me how it happened. For I do no' want . . . I would no' like to send ye to Lucescere without at least . . . canna ye tell me how it happened, Rhiannon?'

'Clothes mine,' she said sullenly.

Lilanthe sat back, her face setting hard. 'Nay, they are no', Rhiannon. Now, I have a compromise to offer ye, for I do no' wish to be taking anything away from ye against your will. Look what I have here.' She turned and opened the portmanteau she had brought from the house. 'See, these are auld clothes o' Lewen's. There are breeches and shirts, and quite a good coat, and an auld shawl o' mine, and some underclothes, and a few other things I think ye'll find useful.'

Lilanthe then turned and, before Rhiannon could stop her, picked up the blue cloak from where Rhiannon had laid it ready in the straw. She turned it in her hands. 'Now, look. Here is the cloak o' the Yeoman. It is no ordinary cloak. See how it is grey on one side and blue on the other? The cloaks o' the Blue Guards are woven with spells o' concealment and camouflage by the witches. In need, ye can turn it inside out and it will help ye blend into mist and darkness, or against grey stone and bracken.'

With an inarticulate growl, Rhiannon snatched back the cloak and huddled it against her. 'Mine!'

'No need to fret,' Lilanthe said with a smile. 'I have no other cloak for ye to wear and so my idea is ye should wear it till ye reach Lucescere and then give it to the Yeoman's family with everything else.'

Rhiannon looked stubborn, and Lilanthe went on quickly, persuasively, 'And the tam-o'-shanter too. If ye will give it to me for just a wee while, I'll unpick the cockade from it, and so then it will be a cap just like anybody else's. When ye get to Lucescere ye shall no' need them, for if ye are admitted to the Theurgia to study along with Lewen and the other apprentices, ye shall wear an apprentice's gown like everyone else. And if ye are no' . . . well, I have asked my friend Isabeau to give ye all ye will need. I will no' insist ye give these things up to me, Rhiannon, if ye will promise to submit them to Dillon, the captain o' the Yeomen, when ye arrive in Lucescere. Believe me, it is the best thing to do.'

The set look on Rhiannon's face did not relax.

'Please? Ye do no' need the soldier's uniform. I've given ye everything ye might need.'

'Very well then,' Rhiannon said ungraciously. 'Me no' wear them then, though no' fair, they mine . . .'

Lilanthe sighed. 'Happen ye will come to understand in time, lassie. It would be wise o' ye to try to understand our customs, if ye are to live among us. I ken what we do and what we believe must seem as strange to ye as ye seem to us. Ye have a long journey ahead o' ye, I would use it to learn what ye can if I were ye. Nina will teach ye, and Lewen too. He'll have a care for ye, no need to fear.'

'Me no' afeared,' Rhiannon said haughtily.

'Nay, I see ye are no',' Lilanthe said slowly. She paused, looking down at her hands, biting her lip. After a long moment she looked up at Rhiannon, saying hesitantly, 'I said that ye need no' fear, that Lewen will look out for ye and care for ye. I want ye to promise me, Rhiannon, that ye will have a care for him too.'

Rhiannon tilted an eyebrow in surprise. 'Lewen quick and strong,' she said approvingly. 'Stronger than me. He stop me killing bear.'

'I think ye understand me, Rhiannon.' Lilanthe's voice was a little uneven. 'Just promise me ye will no' hurt him . . .'

'He big and strong,' Rhiannon said dismissively. 'He no' let me hurt him.'

'I hope no',' Lilanthe said under her breath. 'But there are more ways than one to hurt a man.'

Rhiannon eyed her speculatively then nodded slowly in agreement.

After Lilanthe left, Rhiannon dragged the voluminous nightgown over her head and gave herself a cursory wash with the warm soapy water Lilanthe had poured into the basin for her. She had to admit it left her feeling refreshed, though she did find the older woman's insistence on constantly washing herself rather peculiar. Lilanthe had left her a comb as well, and Rhiannon made some attempt to drag it through her hair. It hurt, though, and so she gave up after only a moment, tossing the comb onto the floor.

This left Rhiannon with the puzzle of the clothes. She had never seen underclothes before and, after a long struggle trying to figure out which limb went through which hole, she managed to drag on the drawers. The chemise completely baffled her, however, and so she threw that at one of the horses who was laughing at her, and laughed herself when it landed over the horse's head, caught on one of its ears. The horse snorted and tossed its head, then rubbed its cheek against its leg, trying to dislodge the fragile scrap of cotton, without success.

Rhiannon managed to draw the breeches over her legs, having done that before, but found that these ones fastened with three small buttons, unlike the metal clasp of the dead soldier's pair. She had never seen buttons before and had no idea how to do them up. She stared at them and fiddled with them for quite a while, but then gave up, leaving the flap unfastened. The shirt she pulled over her head without too much trouble, managing to work out front from back eventually, but she could not tie the laces at the front and so left them loose, untroubled by the way the neckline hung loose, exposing the curve of her breasts.

All in all, Rhiannon was pleased with her new clothes. The white shirt was soft and warm against her skin, and the loose woollen breeches were more comfortable than the white leather pants the soldier had worn. The brown coat was a little too large, but had all sorts of useful pockets in which to store things, and she could move easily in it, unlike the tight green dress she had been forced to wear the day before. Most of all, she liked the cream-coloured shawl Lilanthe had given her, which was embroidered with a beautiful tracery of green tendrils and pink and red roses, now rather faded. She was so pleased with the shawl that she felt little regret over the loss of the dead soldier's clothes.

Lilanthe had left her the soldier's long black boots, not having any other shoes that would fit Rhiannon better, and so Rhiannon drew them on with pleasure, tucking the little black knife into its hidden sheath, and strapping the long silver dagger to her belt as before. She felt strong and brave again with her knives in place, and ready to face the mocking looks of those other boys and girls.

Now it was the mare's turn. Rhiannon had observed Niall and Lewen grooming the horses the previous day, and had seen how much the beasts had enjoyed the attention and how their coats had gleamed afterwards.

Rhiannon wanted her mare to look her very best before she showed her to the others. She picked up the grooming kit again, took out a brush and began to beat the dust out of the mare's coat.

She was engaged in trying to tug all the knots out of the luxuriant black mane when a sudden restiveness in the mare made her aware Lewen was leaning on the gate, watching her.

'Do ye and your mam always sneak around, spying on people?' she said without rancour.

'I'm sorry,' he said. 'Dinna mean to scare ye.'

'Och, me no afeared,' she said severely. 'Me just wonder how ye walk so quiet, being so big and all.'

He coloured.

She smiled. She liked making him blush.

'Being around animals so much, I suppose,' he said. 'They do no' like sudden noise or movement.'

'Nay,' she agreed, casting him a look from under her lashes. She had noticed that this sideways look often made him blush and stammer.

Lewen's colour was high and she saw his eyes were on the front of her shirt.

'Ye should tie up your shirt,' he said in a constricted voice. 'Ye do no' want to go out and about like that.'

'Like what?' she asked, looking down.

'Showing yourself like that. I ken ye mean naught by it, but . . . human lassies hide their . . . hide their . . .'

'My dugs, ye mean?'

'Their bosom,' Lewen said, blushing as hotly as anyone with such tanned skin could.

'Bosom,' she said, trying out the word.

'No-one will understand if ye do no' cover yourself up. Men will think ye are offering yourself to them . . .' He stumbled to a halt.

'To mate?'

'Aye, to mate.'

'And that bad?'

He nodded. 'Only whores do that. Ye do no' want them to think that o' ye, Rhiannon.'

'What whore?'

He searched for words. 'Whores are women . . . and men, too, o' course, who will . . . mate . . . with anyone, if they are paid enough for it. We . . . us humans . . . we do no' mate with just anyone . . . only with those we love . . . most o' us anyway. Usually, when we find someone we love enough, we promise to lie only with them, no' with anyone else, forever.'

Rhiannon was nonplussed. The satyricorn women always shared the men between them, and the idea of exclusivity was entirely foreign. Rhiannon had seen many ugly fights over the men, however, and thought she could see some sense in what Lewen said, as long as there were men enough for all the women. Certainly there seemed to be. The ratio of males and females among those staying at Kingarth was startlingly exact.

'So ye must try to remember to keep your laces tied, and no' show too much o' your body,' Lewen went on, keeping his gaze averted.

'No' ken how,' Rhiannon said flatly.

'Och, o' course. I should've thought. I'll have to teach ye.'

'Aye,' she said. 'What me do?'

He looked back at her, and swallowed. 'I'll show ye,' he said. Gently he reached out and took the laces in his hands, drawing her closer to him. She went obediently. She felt his fingers on her skin as he fumbled with the laces, and took a step closer to him. He smelt very clean and fresh, and she could see the pulse in his throat beating swiftly, and the burn of his blood under his skin. Slowly he knotted the laces together, explaining what he was doing while he did it. As she ducked her head to watch, her hair swung forward and brushed his hand, and she heard the sudden intake of his breath. For some reason her own blood heated, and she kept her gaze lowered, feeling shy with him for the first time.

He untied the laces then, and tried to make her do it herself, but her fingers were clumsy and she could not manage it. He smiled and said, with a warm huskiness to his voice that she had never heard before, 'Never mind. I'll tie it for ye now, and get some string for ye to practise on later. It's no' hard once ye get the hang o' it.'

'Hang o' it?' she repeated, puzzled.

'Once ye ken how.'

'Hang o' it,' she repeated again. 'Once ye get the hang o' it.'

'Aye. It must be hard for ye, all the bits o' slang we use. I'd never noticed it afore, but we do seem to use a lot.'

'Slang,' she repeated.

'Aye. Slang. Figures o' speech.'

She laughed. 'How speech have figure? This figure.' She gestured down her body with one hand.

'It is indeed,' he murmured. He took a deep breath and stepped away. His foot crunched on the comb she had tossed away and he bent and picked it up.

'I suppose ye canna manage combing your own hair either?' he said, glancing back at her with a rueful grin.

She shook her head.

'Would ye like me to do it for ye?'

She nodded.

His mouth quirked. He drew her to sit down on an upturned barrel and stood behind her, drawing the comb through the waterfall of silky black hair. For a while he worked in silence, gently unsnarling the tangles, and she sat still, enjoying the feel of his fingers in her hair and lingering on the nape of her neck.

'Tomorrow ye'll have to ask one o' the other girls to help ye with all this stuff,' he said after a long while.

'Why?'

'It'd be better.'

'Why? Me rather have ye.'

'Aye, I'm sure ye would, but it's no' seemly, Rhiannon, and besides, I do no' ken how long I could stand it. I'm only made o' flesh, ye ken.'

She twisted round to look up at him. 'Uh? O' course ye made o' flesh. We all made o' flesh.'

He nodded. 'Aye, I ken. I just mean . . . Never mind. Just ask one o' the lassies to help ye tomorrow, all right?'

Rhiannon sniffed. 'Me no like those lassies. Me like ye.'

Lewen took a deep breath, his hand twisting in her hair. For a moment he stood very still, holding her captive against him. She tensed all over and drew herself away, looking up at him warily. Her hair drew cruelly tight, like a rope between them. After a long moment that must have hurt her, he released his breath and his hand, stepping away. He stood with his back to her, his shoulders held stiffly, breathing with difficulty.

'I'm sorry,' he said at last. With great care, he laid the comb down on her saddlebags. 'I dinna mean to hurt ye.'

She shrugged. 'Ye no hurt me.'

'That's good. I'd better go.'

'Why?' she asked. 'Where go?'

'Anywhere,' he said with an unsteady laugh. 'The lake might be a good place.'

'Why?'

'Nice cold water,' he said with the same odd laugh.

She shrugged. 'Why ye all want wash so much? Ye smell clean enough.'

'Thank ye,' he said and began to move towards the door.

She remembered the buttons of her breeches and lifted her shirt. 'Afore ye go, ye help? Me no' ken how.'

He looked back at her and his breath caught. When he spoke his voice was unsteady. 'Rhiannon, do ye ken what ye do to me?'

'No, what me do?'

'Ye'd be a test to any man's resolve, do ye ken that?'

She did not understand. 'Too hard? Ye canna do?'

Lewen laughed a little. 'Och, I can do your buttons up all right, no problem there. Though I'd rather be undoing.'

'What ye mean?'

'Naught. Here, I'll show ye how to do it. Ye'd better learn to do it yourself, though, Rhiannon, for it's too much to ask me to be doing up your breeches for ye every day.'

He took a deep breath, grinned ruefully, and slipped his fingers inside the waistband of her breeches to button them up for her, slowly and with intense concentration. When he was finished he stood still for a while, his fingers hooked through her waistband, holding her against him. Then reluctantly he slipped his fingers free and stepped away, turning his back on her. 'Eà's green blood,' he said.

'Too hard?' she asked again.

He laughed unsteadily. 'Much too hard,' he agreed. 'Painfully so.'

She was puzzled, but shrugged. 'Me want clean horse,' she said, waving one hand at the winged mare. 'Me no ken how. Ye show?'

Lewen nodded, rubbing the back of his neck with one hand. 'Aye, that at least will be no hardship,' he answered. He went first to the water-trough and splashed his face and neck thoroughly with water, then took the dipper and poured more water over his head, gulping big mouthfuls of the icy cold fluid. She watched him in bemusement and he grinned at her.

'Ye're naught but trouble, Rhiannon, do ye ken that?'

She was indignant. 'Me no trouble!'

'Trouble through and through. Come on, where's that kit o' yours? It'll do me some good to burn some o' this excess energy away.'

He explained to her what each comb and brush was for, and demonstrated how to use the hoof pick on Argent, who picked up his huge hoof willingly enough.

Rhiannon then tried to do the same with the winged mare, who whinnied unhappily and danced away. Rhiannon tried again, then threw down the hoof pick in disgust. 'Me no good!'

'Do ye think she will let me help?' Lewen asked. 'For indeed ye are making a bad job o' it!'

'Thanks.'

Lewen's eyes gleamed appreciatively. Not only was Rhiannon learning human idioms fast, but also how a change in intonation could change a whole word's meaning. 'My pleasure,' he said just as ironically.

'Well, show me how then,' she said irritably. 'Me no' want to show her to those goblin-eyes till she looks bonny as can be. Then their eyes'll really stick out!'

'Will she let me come near? For she wouldna let me near her yesterday and I dinna want her to kick down any more walls.'

'Be nice, horse,' she said to the mare, which neighed and put back its ears, but allowed Lewen to come closer.

'Ye need to think o' a name for her,' Lewen said, gingerly laying one hand on the mare's shoulder. The skin

144

shivered under his touch but the horse did not shy away. 'Ye canna keep on calling her "horse".'

'Dinna ken any names,' Rhiannon said. 'In the herd, named for your . . . Me no ken how to say. Bigness.'

'Bigness? You mean height?'

Rhiannon shook her head impatiently. 'Nay, nay. Though, bigness o' body helps. Like, who gets first cut o' meat, that's First-Male, then other males, then my mother, One-Horn, she One-Horn and also First-Horn, for she kills best. Five-Horns is Second-Horn, but she has to fight hard against Three-Horns, who wants to kill her and my mother. Ye see?'

Lewen had taken up the curry-brush and was very gently brushing down the curve of the mare's back. 'Aye, I think so,' he said quietly. After a moment, he said, 'Do no' think o' the herd anymore. Ye have escaped them. Ye are free now. Think only o' what lies ahead. Ye have a lot to learn and no' only how to groom your own horse, but how to manage in society, and all sorts o' things about Eileanan.'

Rhiannon nodded and relaxed her grip on the comb, surprised to find it had pressed white ridges into her flesh.

'Your horse is the place to start, I think, since ye'll be riding her every day and so ye'll need to ken how to look after her. Come, I'll show ye her feet and how to clean them and stop her from bruising them. I wonder if she should be shod?' He slid his hand down the mare's leg and she at once lifted her hoof.

For the next half-hour they groomed the black mare until her coat gleamed like silk and she was relaxed and happy. As they brushed and combed her, and polished her hooves and horns, and worked the knots out of her mane and tail, they talked companionably. Lewen told Rhiannon about his first horse, a fat pony called Star for the white patch on its nose. He had soon outgrown Star and for many years rode a sweet-tempered strawberry roan called Aurora. Although he had loved it dearly, by his thirteenth birthday he was far too heavy for it, and so his father had given him Argent, who had been a large-boned, restive colt and now stood close on eighteen hands high, with powerful shoulders and rump. For three years Lewen had hand-fed and trained the young colt, and had begun to lunge him every day, so by the time he began to break the horse in to the saddle, they were well acquainted. Argent was bred from one of his father's own destriers, a warhorse taught to fight on the battlefield with his master. The line was famous, descended from Vervain, one of Cuinn Lionheart's six great stallions. With a pale, silvery-grey coat and tail, Argent was swift and strong with a savage temper, and he allowed no-one but Lewen to ride him.

'So ye named all your horses for . . . colour?' Rhiannon said, struggling to find the words for what she wanted to say.

'Aye, I suppose so, but ye do no' have to do that if ye do no' want.'

'Me want,' she said. 'Horse is black. What is good name for black horse?'

Lewen shrugged. 'I dinna ken. Sable, perhaps, or Jet.'

She screwed up her nose and shook her head emphatically. 'What did your father call me? Something sharp and cruel, he meant.'

'I do no' think he meant –'

'Aye, aye, he did, ye think me no understand? What was that?'

'Thistle?' Lewen replied tentatively.

'Nay, ye fool. Black something.'

'Och, aye. Blackthorn, another name for sloe. It grows wild round here. It has black thorny branches and pretty white flowers this time of year, that turn into a purply-blue fruit later. The villagers make sloe-gin out of it. Just now, this cold weather we've been having, they would call that a blackthorn winter, meaning winter in springtime.'

'Perfect,' Rhiannon said. 'That her name then. Blackthorn.'

Lewen looked at the tall, delicately built mare with her two long scrolled horns that were just the colour of the sloe, and nodded, pleased.

'Two good namings then.' Rhiannon smiled at him so that he blushed red and dropped his gaze, scuffing his boot against the straw-scattered floor. When he glanced up she was smiling radiantly still, but at her horse, which had tossed its head and was prancing, as if glad to be named.

The kitchen was bright and busy with activity, though outside it was all grey and hushed still. Rhiannon ate as greedily as ever, cramming in two bowlfuls of hot porridge with honey and goat's milk, and sixteen griddle-cakes with melted butter and cherry jam. After a life of lean provisions, she could not help herself. Although these last few days had been so very different from what she had known before, she could not believe she would not know hunger again. You ate when you could, even if you felt rather sick afterwards.

She was aware of scornful glances cast at her by the two other girls, who were dressed again in their ridiculous tight dresses with their hair in unnaturally perfect ringlets, like nothing she had seen before; and the yearning dreamy gaze of the youngest of the boys, who seemed to her quite mad; and the resentful, lustful glance of the oldest of the boys, which perturbed her as none of the others did. There was something very like hatred in his glance. She had seen it before and she knew it meant harm to come. All she could do was disdain his hot glance with coldness, and hope to keep away from him.

The third girl was eager to be kind, which Rhiannon was prepared to accept, though she thought the worse of her for offering it, and the second eldest of the boys was torn between his natural good nature and his desire to emulate the older, tougher boy. Rhiannon was used to reading intent in the body language of the herd. It had kept her safe and relatively unscathed for sixteen years. There was a fine balance to be kept between appearing too weak, so that you were scorned and bullied, and too strong, so that First-Horn thought it was time to take you down.

Lilanthe was hovering over her son, caressing his rough brown hair with one hand as she poured him more tea, or straightening his collar as she passed with a plate of fresh griddle-cakes. He smiled at her and did not shrug her hand away, knowing how hard this latest parting would be for her. At last she came and sat down and ate a little herself, gazing at her boy as if he had grown so tall and broad-shouldered overnight.

'Och, I wish ye did no' have to go so far away,' she said. 'I've missed ye these last four years! Lucescere is such a long way, all the way round the mountains and up into the highlands o' Rionnagan! I wish the Tower o' Ravens was no' such a ruin and ye could go there to study. It's only a few days from here and then I could be seeing ye often . . .'

Nina gave a little expressive shrug. 'Happen one day it will be restored. The Keybearer says she hopes the time will come when all thirteen towers o' learning are rebuilt again. Already there are seven, and a small enclave o' witches are camping in the ruins o' the Tower o' Dreamers and seeking to raise it high again, so soon there may be eight. No-one dares go near the Tower o' Ravens, though, ye ken. It is weird with ghosts and banshees and all sorts o' cruel and unhappy spirits, and they say it is only growing worse with time. The auld MacBrann sent some witches there a few months afore he died to see if it could be exorcised, saying he couldna sleep with all the ghosts flocking about his bed, but they came back in despair, saying the place reeked o' blood and death, and it was beyond their strength to cleanse it.'

'They dinna call him Malcolm the Mad for naught,' Iven said. 'Apparently he kept the whole castle in an uproar with his shrieks and curses and night terrors, and they got worse in the last few months afore he died.'

Lilanthe drew her brows together. 'Aye, he was troubled indeed, the poor auld man. We rode down to Ravenscraig to see if there was aught we could do to ease his last days, but he was rambling indeed by then and did no' ken us, or even his poor son. What o' Dughall? Does he no' plan to rebuild the tower? I ken Isabeau would come herself if he called, and bring a circle o' sorcerers to aid him.'

'Dughall says the best thing to do is pull the whole place down and cleanse it with fire. He says he had to spend a night there once during the Bright Wars and it was enough to turn his hair as white as his father's. It was always a dark place, ye ken, right from the time o' Brann the Raven himself. The MacBranns have always been a strange lot, with their experiments and machines . . .'

Niall leapt at once to the defence of his ruling clan. 'What about the auld MacBrann's seafire, then? That was one experiment the Rìgh found useful in the war against the Fairgean. And it was a MacBrann that built the locks at the mouth o' the Rhyssmadill, remember.'

Iven laughed, holding up both hands. 'Och, I ken. Ye must admit the MacBranns have always dabbled in the arcane, though. They have always loved the darker mysteries and that is why the Ensorcellor had so many followers here in Ravenshaw and why the attack on the Tower o' Ravens on the Day o' Betrayal was so very brutal.'

'Aye,' Niall agreed, sighing. 'That was a black day. Forty years or more ago it was, and I was naught but a bairn, but I remember it clearly. We could see the smoke from my parents' farm. It billowed up like a great dark pillar, higher than the mountains, and then hung over us all for days, choking us with ashes. No' one single witch escaped the massacre, they say, no' even the MacBrann's own wife, Dughall's mother. And she was a NicCuinn herself and aunt to the Rìgh. A Day o' Betrayal indeed.'

'Still, it was a long time ago and twenty-five years since the Ensorcellor was overthrown,' Nina said. She turned to the apprentices and said, 'Ye will see Maya the Mute at the Tower o' Two Moons, ye ken. She labours in the libraries there, helping to restore the knowledge that was lost when she ordered the great towers o' learning to be burnt. Ye must treat her with respect, for though she may be bound to silence and servitude, she is still the mother o' Bronwen NicCuinn, who will one day share the throne with Donncan the Winged.'

Not understanding a word that was said, Rhiannon had been growing impatient. Lilanthe must have noticed her restlessness for she turned to her and said, 'Ye must ask Nina and Iven to tell ye all the auld tales as ye travel, and sing ye some o' the songs, for ye have a lifetime o' learning to make up in just a short while.'

'Where does this lass come from, that she does no' ken the story o' Maya the Ensorcellor?' Edithe said scornfully.

'Does she no' have a mother, or an auld granny, to tell her bedtime stories? And even the meanest village sees a jongleur every once in a while, to tell the auld tales and sing the song cycles.'

'No' all,' Lilanthe said briefly.

'It must have been a hovel indeed,' Edithe said under her breath to Fèlice, who looked uncomfortable.

'Me learnt other things from my mother,' Rhiannon said clearly, glancing at the blonde girl with contempt. 'Like how to gut a goblin with a single slash o' my knife. Ye want me show you how?' And with a flick of her wrist her dagger was in her hand, its point hovering negligently near the pulse at the base of Edithe's throat. Edithe shrieked and shrank back. Rhiannon tossed the knife in her hand. 'I guess no',' she said and put the dagger away.

There was a shocked silence. Everyone stared at Rhiannon.

'Did ye see what she just did?' Edithe said in a squeaky voice. 'She threatened me!'

Nina put down her fork. 'I'm no' sure any o' us blame her,' she said testily. 'Ye have been unpardonably rude, Edithe. I would have thought better o' a NicAven o' Avebury.'

Edithe went crimson, and opened and shut her mouth a few times as she tried to think of a retort.

'Though Rhiannon does ken better than to draw her dagger at the dinner table,' Lilanthe said with a meaningful glance at her.

Rhiannon was unrepentant. 'Me no like that girl,' she said. 'She mean.'

'Well, I hope ye will learn to get on with one another,' Nina said impatiently. 'We have a long journey together ahead o' us, and it'll be unbearable if ye're at each other's throats. Can ye all no' try and be civil?'

'O' course,' Edithe said grandly. 'I am sorry if anything I have said was misunderstood.'

Lilanthe looked at the satyricorn girl. After a while she prompted her, saying, 'Rhiannon?'

'What?' she said.

'Edithe has just apologised. Should ye no' say sorry too?'

'Why? Me no' sorry.'

Edithe looked shocked.

'Rhiannon,' Lilanthe said wearily. 'Please.'

'It's considered good manners, lassie, to return the apology, even if ye do no' do so with sincerity,' Niall said with his usual humorous inflection.

'Me hate good manners,' Rhiannon said sullenly.

'We've noticed,' Niall responded and she flashed him an angry glance and then, surprisingly, laughed.

'Tell that girl to no' be so mean and me no kill her,' she said.

'I think that's Rhiannon's idea o' an apology,' Niall said to Edithe.

She looked down her nose, saying in an icy voice, 'I am sure my father would be horrified if he kent the sort o' company I was being forced to travel with. I shall write to him at the very first opportunity.'

'Ye do that,' Nina said. 'But just remember that this journey we are all about to embark upon is considered the first stage o' your learning as an apprentice-witch. The Coven believes humility, compassion and self-control are necessary attributes o' any witch. Ye may have all the craft and all the cunning in the world, but ye will never be allowed to join the Coven without showing forbearance and understanding towards others. Have I made myself clear, Edithe?'

'Aye, ma'am,' she said, looking crushed.

'And as for ye, Rhiannon, if ye wish to travel in my

care ye shall no' threaten any o' my students with harm again. Do ye understand me?'

'Aye, ma'am,' Rhiannon responded, not looking crushed at all.

'Good,' Nina said.

'Happen we'd best be on our way,' Iven said. 'It is light enough now to see the road. Is everyone packed up and ready?'

There was a chorus of answers, and everyone got up and started wrapping themselves in their riding cloaks and saying their farewells. Lilanthe was unable to hide her tears but she did not cling to Lewen, giving him a brief, hard hug before stepping back and saying huskily, 'Make sure ye send news o' yourself, ye hear, my lad?'

Niall embraced him too and then surprised Rhiannon by kissing her on the cheek and saying, 'Have a care for yourself, lassie, and keep that knife in your boot!'

'Unless I need it, o' course,' she replied cheekily, surprising him into laughter.

Lilanthe did not kiss Rhiannon goodbye, but detained her with a hand on her arm. 'I have written a letter o' introduction to my friend Isabeau, who is Keybearer o' the Coven,' she said gravely, giving Rhiannon a thick white envelope sealed with red wax. 'I have written her a full account o' ye, and I hope she will have a care for ye in Lucescere.'

'Thank ye,' Rhiannon said, taking the letter and stowing it away in one of the many pockets of her coat.

Lilanthe's expression softened. 'I hope all will be well with ye, Rhiannon. I am sorry I could no' help ye more.' She was silent for a moment, then said in a tumble, as Rhiannon turned to go, 'If ye have done no wrong, then no harm shall come to ye, that I am sure o'. Isabeau will find the truth o' it.'

Rhiannon's brows drew together, and she stared at Lilanthe, who looked white and tired. Then she said, very gruffly, 'Me done naught wrong!'

Lilanthe's gaze fell and colour rose in her cheeks. 'That's good, I'm glad. All will be well then.'

Rhiannon stared at her suspiciously, but Lilanthe just put her arm about her and gave her a brief hug, before turning to say her farewells to Nina and Iven.

Rhiannon followed the others out into the frosty morning, everyone shivering and complaining as they stowed their bags in the caravan and got out their tack to saddle up the horses. Meriel clung to her brother's hand, her cheeks wet with tears, and he looked down at her kindly and spoke quietly to her. After a while she nodded and let go of his hand, going to stand with her parents.

Only Lewen and Rhiannon had to go into the stable, since all the other horses had been pastured out for the night. He saddled up Argent quickly and then turned to help Rhiannon, who seemed to be having some trouble.

He found Rhiannon sitting on her backside in the straw, the saddle clutched to her chest, her face red. Blackthorn sidled about skittishly, her ears laid flat against her skull and an evil look in her dark eye.

'She doesna want to wear it,' Rhiannon said rather blankly. It was clear she had not expected the winged horse to resist her will.

'She's no' really been broken to the saddle and bridle yet, though, has she?' Lewen said. 'It took me a week to get Argent to accept the weight o' the saddle on his back.'

Rhiannon scowled. She got up and dusted off her bottom.

'Blackthorn, ye are my horse now, remember,' she said. 'Ye do what me say.'

The winged mare reared and neighed, shaking her

mane defiantly. Her magnificent wings unfurled, the muscles in her shoulders bunching.

'Ye do no' want to be mine anymore?' Rhiannon said miserably. 'But me thought . . .'

The mare stepped forwards delicately, pushing her black velvet nose into Rhiannon's shoulder and blowing slobber all over her. Then she turned her head and tried to bite the saddle.

'Ye do no' want saddle? But . . .'

'Well, they say a thigearn rides with neither saddle nor bridle. Happen ye're meant to be a true thigearn, after all,' Lewen said.

Rhiannon smiled.

'Me never rode with such things afore,' she said. 'Me no' now.'

'Ye'll have less control,' Lewen warned. 'And ye're bound to get rather bruised.'

She dismissed this with a gesture.

'The saddle and bridle belonged to the Yeoman, anyway,' he said. 'Ye can stow them in the caravan with the rest of his things.' He picked up the saddle and bridle, then slung the saddlebags over the top.

Immediately Rhiannon frowned. 'Nay! Mine . . . my things in there.' She turned back to the mare. 'Blackthorn? Just the bags? Me and my bags.'

Blackthorn hurrumphed and put her ears back.

'Happen ye should say "please",' Lewen murmured, trying not to laugh.

'Please? Why?'

'It's considered polite.'

'Hmmph. Very well. Please, Blackthorn?'

The mare inclined her head graciously.

'Ye will have to figure out some way to tie the saddlebags on if she willna wear the saddle. I wonder if she would accept wearing a pad? We use them for breaking in young horses. It's a soft saddle without a saddletree or stirrups. It has a girth and some hooks we could strap the saddlebags to. Let's see if she'll accept it.'

A short while later Lewen rode round the side of the house on the back of his tall, silver-dappled stallion. Argent was fighting the bit, eager for a gallop.

'What took ye so long, lad?' Iven called from the driving seat of his caravan, drawn up before the front steps. 'I thought the young ladies were slow!'

The laughter died out of his face as he saw the winged mare come stepping delicately through the mist-wreathed trees. The two long, scrolled horns springing from the mare's brow shone an unearthly blue, like the sky at dusk, and her wings were slightly unfurled, showing the subtle gradation of colour from black to iridescent blue. Rhiannon sat straight-backed and grave-faced on her back, wrapped in her long blue cloak, her black hair falling down her back, her quiver of arrows slung over one shoulder. Her longbow was strapped to the crown-embroidered saddlebags that hung over the mare's withers, while she wore her dagger strapped to her belt. She looked like the queen she had been named for.

There was a long astonished silence.

'O my heart moves in my breast, forever after I am denied all rest,' Landon whispered.

Rhiannon scowled.

A little mutter ran round the apprentices and their horses stirred restively beneath them.

'A thigearn,' Fèlice whispered. 'Och, I've always wanted –'

'A thigearn!' Edithe cried. 'But –'

'Och, she's so bonny,' Maisie said. 'I've never seen a

winged horse afore. Oh, I wish she'd fly. I'd love to see her fly!'

It was the longest speech any of them had heard the shy village girl say.

The boys were filled with exclamations of surprise too. 'How did she catch it?' Rafferty wanted to know. 'How does she control it without even a bridle, let alone whip or spurs?' He glanced sideways at Edithe, who as always had her long whip in her hand, and a sharp silver spur on her boot. Edithe looked displeased and tightened her rein, causing her mare to sidle sideways.

'I never heard o' a girl being a thigearn afore,' Cameron said gruffly. 'Are they allowed?'

'Why no', if she can ride it?' Nina said pleasantly. 'What a bonny creature, Rhiannon! I've heard o' the black winged horses o' Ravenshaw afore, o' course, but never thought to see one. Ye look like ye've ridden out of an auld tale, the two o' ye. Have ye ridden her long?'

'No' long,' Rhiannon answered, her face glowing.

'I thought ye had to ride for a year and a day without putting foot to ground afore ye could call yourself a thigearn,' Cameron said, his tone very near a jeer.

'Nay, all ye need do is tame a flying horse,' Niall said. 'It's just that it takes most men that long to break its will. Rhiannon did no' need to.' He smiled up at her. She smiled back.

'Well, we'll surely make a sensation in every village we ride through,' Edithe said in a voice of long suffering. 'We really are like a travelling circus now.'

'Aye, and isn't it a shame that all ken we ride on the Coven's business? Think o' the money we could make!' Iven said shamelessly, and winked at Nina. 'Come on, let's get this circus rolling!'

Barbreck-by-the-Bridge

A s they rode down the long elm-lined avenue, the sun struck down through the pale green blossoms flowering profusely on every bare twig and branch. The mist was drawn up like smoke, revealing lush lawns and copses of silver-barked birches. Away to the left were the orchards with their clouds of sweet-smelling blossoms in white and pink, while to the right lay the lake, lined with willow trees and flowering rushes.

Lewen was filled with a bittersweet sadness as he gazed about him, knowing it may be a year or more before he returned to Kingarth again. He turned to have one last look at the little stone house with its steep roof and gables, and saw his parents and sister waving madly. He waved back, then resolutely turned his face away, looking to the road ahead.

Suddenly a tiny shape came hurtling down out of the sky like a maddened hornet. Kalea caught Rhiannon's blue tam-o'-shanter and hurled it away, then seized hold of Rhiannon's hair in two tiny, determined hands and yanked with all her strength. Rhiannon yelped in pain and swatted at the little faery, sending her head over heels. Kalea crashed into an elm branch and hung there, whimpering. Rhiannon lifted both hands to her hair, her face white with fury. Blackthorn danced uneasily.

A babble of surprised voices rose.

'What is it?' Rafferty demanded. 'Did ye see how fast it came?'

'I thought we were being shot at,' Cameron exclaimed, dropping his hand from his sword.

'What on earth!' Iven cried, pulling up his grey carthorse. 'Och, it's the wee nisse!'

'Kalea!' Lewen said reprovingly. 'What in Eà's name do ye think ye are doing?'

'Look at the wee thing, is she no' adorable?' Fèlice cried.

Kalea showed her fangs.

'Ooh, how horrid!' Edithe cried and dragged her horse's head around so the brown mare wheeled sideways, almost trampling Maisie's fat pony.

Nina laughed and brought the blue tam-o'-shanter floating up from where it lay on the grass. 'Happen she's jealous,' she said, letting the tam-o'-shanter drop into Rhiannon's lap. Rhiannon seized it and put it on again, scowling ferociously.

'Kalea, ye must no' do things like that,' Lewen said helplessly. He held out his hand and the bright-winged faery came zooming down to cling to his finger, gibbering in distress. 'I'm sorry, did I no' say farewell to ye? Do no' cry. I'll be back soon enough.'

High-pitched screeches shrilled from the tiny throat. Lewen winced, but stroked the nisse's tangled mane of hair and smoothed down her indignant wings. 'I ken, I ken. Never mind. Ye kent I had to go.'

More screeches, and the nisse turned and shook a minuscule fist at Rhiannon. Lewen looked a little embarrassed, but did his best to soothe the enraged faery, while Rhiannon merely stared at her coldly, her mouth set hard.

Suddenly the faery swung away from Lewen's finger and hurtled towards Rhiannon again. As quickly as a striking snake, Rhiannon reached out and snatched her from the air. The speed and precision of her reflexes was extraordinary, making them all gasp. Imprisoned in Rhiannon's fist, Kalea shrieked in terror. No matter how she squirmed or wriggled, or how ferociously she sank her fangs into Rhiannon's hand, the satyricorn girl did not let go. Slowly, deliberately, holding Kalea close before her face, she began to squeeze her fingers closed. Kalea whimpered in pain.

'Rhiannon, let her go!' Lewen shouted.

She ignored him.

'Rhiannon, I mean it!' He kicked Argent forward and the stallion wheeled in close beside the nervous winged mare so Lewen could reach out and grasp Rhiannon's wrist. Holding her immobile, he used his other hand to prise open her fingers.

For a moment their strength and wills battled, then Rhiannon gasped and relaxed her hold. Kalea shot out of her hand and went flying to Lewen, nestling behind his ear, peering out to gibber at Rhiannon mockingly.

Lewen let go of her wrist.

Rhiannon looked down at the angry red marks on her still-bruised wrist. 'Ye strong,' she said in approval. 'Ye near broke my hand.'

'Ye should no' have hurt Kalea,' Lewen said, still furious.

'She hurt me.'

'She should no' have done that either.'

Rhiannon shrugged, cradling her abused wrist in her other hand. 'No' my fault.'

'No, happen so,' Lewen said, his anger cooling. 'But she's only a wee nisse, ye should no' have sought to kill her.'

'Tell her no' to hurt me again or me hurt her,' Rhiannon said indifferently and bent to stroke Blackthorn's damp neck, soothing the unsettled mare.

'Very well,' Lewen said coolly, and plucked the nisse from behind his ear. 'Go home, Kalea,' he said sternly. 'And let this be a lesson to ye!'

She made a derisive gibbering sound, then leant forward and kissed his nose. While Lewen was still recovering from his surprise and embarrassment, Kalea flew up into the air, made an extremely rude gesture towards Rhiannon, then shot off at high speed, her dragonfly wings whirring.

For a moment Rhiannon and Lewen were frozen in mutual surprise and consternation, then both broke into laughter.

'Nisses!' Lewen said, then said awkwardly, 'I'm sorry. She has absolutely no manners.'

'Me no manners either,' Rhiannon said cheerfully.

She looked round at the circle of faces. Edithe and Maisie both looked shocked, Fèlice, Iven and Nina were struggling to suppress amusement, and Roden and Rafferty were both laughing out loud. Landon had pulled out a grubby little notebook and was scribbling notes with a distastefully chewed quill, his ink bottle balanced most precariously on his saddle pommel, and Cameron was regarding Rhiannon with something very nearly approaching respect.

'What we wait for?' Rhiannon demanded. 'Ride on!'

Fèlice laughed. 'This journey is going to be fun,' she cried exuberantly. 'What will ye do next, Rhiannon?'

161

Without waiting for an answer, she dug her heel into her mare's side and moved off again down the road, Rafferty breaking into a trot to follow her.

'I can hardly wait to find out,' Iven said dryly and flicked his reins at the gelding's broad back. The caravans both moved off again, the apprentice-witches falling into formation behind them.

Lewen and Rhiannon followed suit, riding side by side at the very end of the cavalcade.

'I'm sorry if I hurt ye,' Lewen said remorsefully. 'I forgot how sore your wrists still are.'

Rhiannon gave her usual shrug, glancing at him under her lashes. 'Hurt worse afore,' she said dismissively and smiled at him, knowing full well she had just made him feel a whole lot worse.

The long avenue ended at a pair of massive iron gates, bounded on each side by tall thick hedges bristling with thorns. Beyond Kingarth was nothing but forest and mountains, filled with wild creatures and faeries of all kinds, many of them dangerous. The brambly hedge ran the whole perimeter of the farm, and was patrolled regularly by Ursa the Bear to make sure there were no gaps or holes through which even a polecat or hoar-weasel could squeeze its lithe shape. The gates themselves were guarded by the son of Niall's old gillie, who lived in a cottage just inside the gates with his wife and two young children.

Jock MacGhillie came out to unlock the gates for the cavalcade, saluting Iven smartly and wishing them good speed. They rode out smartly, so Jock could make sure all was secure behind them, and found themselves on a narrow dirt road that wound down through dense forest along the eastern bank of the Findhorn River. The river ran fast and white along its rocky course, tumbling down in foaming cataracts wherever the hill dropped away.

Looking back up the river, Rhiannon remembered how she used to sit on the ridge by the black lake, wondering where the river went and wishing she could follow it. The thought pleased her. She smiled and pressed her heels into Blackthorn's side so the mare lengthened her stride, cantering ahead of the others. Lewen's big grey stallion followed her at once, his heavy hooves sending up plumes of dust.

Rhiannon looked back over her shoulder at Lewen. 'Ye want race?'

'No flying allowed,' Lewen warned.

'What ye bet?'

His dark brown eyes sparkled. 'Ye're confident!'

'Me am.'

'Ye think your dainty wee mare can outrun Argent?' he scoffed.

'Try us.'

'All right then.'

'So what ye give me when me win?'

'I'll clean your tack for ye tonight,' he offered.

'Me clean own tack.'

'What then?'

'Me want money.'

Lewen raised his eyebrow. 'A gambling lass? What if ye lose? Ye havena any money to give me.'

'Me no lose.'

'Oh-ho, we are confident. All right, ye can owe me.'

'Me no need to.'

'Deal or no deal?'

'What ye mean?'

'That's what ye say when ye make a bet. Ye should say "deal", and then we each spit on our hands and shake on it.'

'Shake on it?' Rhiannon frowned in puzzlement. 'Shake? Like this?' And she began to shake all over, as if she was quivering with cold. Blackthorn put her ears back and sidestepped.

Lewen could not help himself. He burst out laughing. After a moment Rhiannon laughed too.

'Nay! No' like that! We shake hands. Like this.' He drew Argent close by Blackthorn's side and put out his hand to Rhiannon. After a moment's hesitation Rhiannon put her hand in his, and he pumped it up and down vigorously. 'That's shaking on it.'

'Me shake on it,' she said, and pretended to shake all over again.

He laughed out loud.

'All right, first to the big oak down there . . .' His voice died away as Blackthorn broke into a gallop. Startled, Lewen laughed and swore, and leant forward, slapping Argent's neck with his reins. The big stallion surged forward.

Shoulder to shoulder, the two horses galloped down the road, sending pebbles flying.

'Ye cheated!' Lewen panted. 'Ye're meant to start together.'

'Ye just slow,' Rhiannon teased. She crouched lower on Blackthorn's neck and the winged horse leapt forward, passing the big oak scant seconds before Argent.

'Me win, me win!' Rhiannon chanted.

'All right, all right,' he said, fumbling in his pocket for a coin, which he flipped to her. 'Though next time I'll make ye call the start.'

'Me still win,' Rhiannon crowed, cheeks pink, eyes bright with excitement. She rubbed the coin with her thumb, and then very carefully stowed it away inside her coat.

'No' a chance,' Lewen said. 'Ye only won because I'm too much o' a gentleman to call ye a cheat.'

'Och, sure,' she mocked.

They dismounted and rested in the shade, letting the horses graze at will, for neither wore a bit. In a few minutes, the big grey carthorse came shambling along, pulling the blue caravan. Iven lounged on the driving seat, his feet up, the reins looped and knotted over the rail. He was playing cards with Roden and Lulu. The arak was jumping up and down, gibbering with distress at her poor hand of cards, while Roden was looking smug, a heap of pebbles before him.

'I wouldna race too much if I were ye,' Iven said to Lewen and Rhiannon with a smile. 'We have a long way to ride and ye do no' want to be tiring out your horses.'

'Ye just jealous,' Rhiannon said. 'Ye wish ye racing too. That horse very slow.' She gestured towards the enormous carthorse with his patient dark eyes and shaggy hooves the size of dinner plates.

'Happen that's true,' Iven said with a sigh. 'Still, dinna ye look down upon auld Steady here. He may be slow, but he gets there. Anyway, no more racing, bairns. We really do have a long way to go today. Nina is keen to leave the Broken Ring o' Dubhslain behind us.'

'All right, Iven,' Lewen said readily. 'For today anyway. I have to have a chance to win back my honour tomorrow. We have a bet riding on it.'

'Och, well, in that case!' Iven laughed. 'I tell ye what, I'll make ye a bet o' my own. One week on the road and I bet neither o' ye will have the heart for racing!'

'What ye bet me?' Rhiannon said at once.

'A gambler in our midst. Well, Roden and I bet for pebbles, but that's only because I couldna afford to play with him otherwise, he's just too good.'

Roden grinned.

'Me no play for pebbles,' Rhiannon said.

'Ye are a gambling girl! All right then. If I win, ye have to cook dinner every night for a week. If I lose, I'll . . . hmmm . . . I'll . . .'

'Me want money,' Rhiannon said.

'Ye want hard coin? But I'm naught but a poor jongleur! All right then. A half-crown, if ye and Lewen are still racing every day after seven days on the road.'

'Deal,' Rhiannon said. She spat on her hand and held it out. Solemnly Iven spat on his hand and then shook hers. The caravans trundled on, and they mounted their horses again and fell into place behind the others. Lewen raised a quizzical eyebrow at her.

'Me need money,' Rhiannon explained. 'Me have none.'

Lewen smiled and shrugged. 'I guess ye could do with some money. We are going to Lucescere, the most expensive city in the world, after all.'

Rhiannon nodded. 'So me told.'

Lewen hesitated. 'Ye need no' worry about money,' he said. 'Isabeau, the Keybearer, will make sure ye have everything ye need. My mother has written to her, as ye ken. As a scholarship student, the Coven pays for all your day-to-day needs, your robes and books and food and lodging.'

'That girl say me need money. For balls . . . What ball?'

'A ball is a place where people go to dance and talk. It's also a round leather toy that bairns kick around. Lady Edithe would've meant the first, though.'

Rhiannon screwed up her face. 'Too many words. How ye ken them all?'

'I've had plenty o' time to learn,' Lewen answered. 'Do no' worry, ye'll pick them up soon enough.'

'Pick words up?' Rhiannon was more puzzled than ever.

Lewen sighed. 'Learn them, I mean.'

'So why me need money for balls?'

'Everyone gets dressed up in fancy clothes and jewels which cost a lot to buy.'

'Why?'

'I've often wondered. I wouldna worry too much, Rhiannon. I doubt whether ye'll go to many. Most students do no' have much to do with the court.'

Rhiannon frowned. 'Happen so,' she said. 'Still, if those cursehags are no' to laugh at me, me need money.'

'The Coven doesna like its students gambling,' Lewen warned.

'How will they ken?' Rhiannon lifted one expressive eyebrow. 'Unless ye mean to tell them?'

'I willna tell,' Lewen said uncomfortably. 'No-one likes a tittle-tattle.'

'Well then.' She flashed a smile at him.

'Witches are hard to trick,' Lewen warned. 'I'd be careful.'

'How else me get money?' Rhiannon asked. 'How ye get?'

'We royal squires are paid handsomely,' Lewen said, with a mock attempt to emulate Edithe's high-bred tone.

'Then me be squire too.'

Lewen shifted uncomfortably in his saddle. 'Lassies canna be squires.'

'Why no'?'

'They just canna.'

Rhiannon scowled.

'I make things too,' Lewen said hurriedly, eager to change the subject. 'We spend an awful lot o' time sitting around and waiting for His Highness. I hate to sit idle, so I got in the habit o' whittling to help pass the time. I've always liked to make my own arrows, they seem to fly more true than those made for me by others. The other squires used to want to buy them from me, and then the palace guards did too, and now I can sell as many as I make. Even the Rìgh likes my arrows best.' He spoke with quiet pride.

Rhiannon eyed the quiver bristling with arrows that hung from Argent's saddle. They did indeed seem beautifully made, being unusually long and formed from some white wood, fletched with green. They made hers seem clumsy and badly made.

'I make other things too. Chess sets, sometimes, or toys for the palace bairns. Boxes, or little figurines o' animals. I like making those.'

'Ye made the boxes back there? The tricky one?'

Lewen grinned. 'Aye, I made those. They were fun.'

'Very tricky.'

'There are lots o' things students can do to help support themselves while at the Theurgia. If ye show a Skill at something, like growing things or animals, ye can get a job working in the garden or in the stables or kennels. Ye're good with horses. When we get to Lucescere, I'll introduce ye to the stable-master. I'm sure he'd be happy to give ye some work. Horse-whisperers are always welcome there.'

Rhiannon smiled. 'Me like horses, me like that.'

'Ye should no' say "me like", ye should say "I". "I would like that" is the proper way to say it.'

'I would like that,' she repeated after a moment, even though it was clear she did not like being corrected.

He smiled at her. 'Very good. Ye learn fast.'

She nodded. 'Me try.'

'Ye mean, I try,' Lewen corrected her again.

She compressed her lips together, then said obediently, 'I mean, I try.'

Until now, the road had just been wide enough for two horses to ride comfortably side by side, but as they came down out of the forest the road widened and an eager Rafferty was able to ride up beside them and engage them in conversation. Lewen quite liked the young apprentice-witch but nonetheless he had to suppress a flash of irritation when he saw the glow of admiration in the boy's eyes when he gazed at Rhiannon.

'I say, ye can ride!' Rafferty cried. 'And that mare o' yours can really go! Will ye race with me?'

'What ye bet?' Rhiannon said at once.

Rafferty's eyes sparkled. 'Half a copper?'

'Ye promised Iven ye would no' race again today,' Lewen reminded Rhiannon, feeling like a stern big brother.

She hunched a shoulder at him and said to Rafferty, 'Me race . . . I race ye tomorrow then.'

'Grand,' he said. 'Ye ken, none o' the lasses I ken would ever ride like that. They'd be too afraid o' falling off.'

'I no' afraid o' aught,' Rhiannon boasted.

'More fool ye,' Lewen said, and leant forward a little in his saddle so Argent's stride lengthened, bringing him up beside Iven's caravan. He felt he had had enough of Rafferty's company.

The road wound down into softly rolling hills and pastures. Men and women were working together in every field, ploughing the rich dark earth, sowing seeds, cutting back the hedgerows and tending herds of goats and pigs. In nearly every dell was a small croft with its orchard just beginning to bud with spring flowers, and smoke wisping up from its chimney. The crofters waved at the caravans as they passed by, and the apprentices waved back, enjoying the fresh spring weather.

They reached the little village of Barbreck-by-the-Bridge late that afternoon. It was no more than a single street with an inn at one end and a mill with a water-wheel at the other, and two rows of small, grey houses with high-pitched roofs along either side, facing onto a village green where chickens wandered and children played. The Findhorn River came foaming down the hill to boil about the stone ramparts of a great bridge composed of six arches, with crenellated gatehouses at either end.

A crowd of grim-faced people milled about at one end of the bridge, all looking down at something that lay on the ground in their midst. A man wearing an enormous sword strapped to his back was ordering them about, his black eyebrows drawn close over his eagle nose.

'That's the reeve,' Lewen said in alarm. 'I wonder what the matter is?'

'Barbreck-by-the-Bridge has a reeve?' Iven asked in surprise.

'Och, nay, it's far too wee. Odran the reeve will have come over from Cullen, the town on the far side o' the bridge. I wonder what can have happened?'

'I guess we'll soon find out,' Iven answered, slapping the reins on Steady's back. The carthorse quickened his pace.

It was only a day since the caravans had driven through Barbreck-by-the-Bridge on their way to Kingarth, but still the sight of the gaudily painted vans was enough to draw the eye of everyone in the village. As they turned to stare, Rhiannon was able to see the naked body of a man lying on the ground, water spreading a dark stain across the pavement. Her heart jerked. She averted her eyes, trying to control the sudden rapid beating of her pulse, her ragged breathing. Around her were cries of alarm and horror.

Nina drew Roden against her, hiding his face in her skirt, though the little boy strained away, saying, 'But Mam, I wanna see! What happened to him? Is he dead?'

'Aye, honey,' she answered. 'Do no' look!'

Iven jumped down from the driver's seat and went to greet the reeve.

'Trouble?' he asked. 'What's the problem?'

'Murder,' the reeve said tersely. 'Man shot in the back, and thrown in the river. We havena had a murder in these parts for nigh on ten years, and this one looks a right nasty one.'

'I am Iven Yellowbeard, a courier in the Rìgh's service and a former Blue Guard,' Iven said. 'Can I be o' any assistance?'

The reeve cast a suspicious eye at the jongleur, noting his frivolous beard and brightly coloured clothes. Iven bowed ironically. 'No' all Blue Guards become farmers when they retire,' he said. 'I was born a jongleur and a jongleur I shall die, and all the life betwixt spent in service to Lachlan the Winged.'

Still the reeve looked unconvinced.

Lewen dismounted and went to join Iven, leaving Argent untethered. 'How are ye yourself, Odran?'

The reeve straightened his back, saluting smartly. 'Sore troubled, sir, and ye?'

'Well enough, until I saw what ye have here. May we take a look? Iven was once a Blue Guard, and he kens more than any man should ken about violent death. Also, I fear ... I suspect Iven may ken who it is. For we've had intimations o' a Blue Guard gone missing, shot through the back, we suspect. We would like to ken if this is he.'

'Indeed?' Odran raised one thick, black eyebrow. 'In that case, please, be my guest.'

Iven went down on one knee beside the naked corpse, and examined him carefully. There was evidently a strong stench for his nose wrinkled involuntarily, and he tried not to lean too close. 'Arrow wound here through the back,' he said in a voice stiff with distaste. 'And look, chafing here at wrists and ankles. He was bound up tightly. He's been badly beaten too. Looks like he may have a broken rib or two. I'd say the injuries occurred afore death. It's hard to tell, though, for he's been in the water a while. By the degree o' putrefaction, I'd say it's been a few weeks, happen even a month.'

There was an unhappy murmur from the crowd. A plump woman hid her face against a man's broad shoulder.

'Look at his hand,' Odran said gruffly. 'He looks like he's been tortured.'

Iven very gently picked up the dead man's right hand, which was missing its smallest finger. He frowned. 'I think the finger might have been cut off after death. I canna be sure though.' He laid the hand down again, and wiped his fingers on his handkerchief, looking very pale.

'But why?' Odran asked.

Iven shrugged. 'A souvenir?'

He carefully turned the dead man over, to examine the ragged exit wound in the chest. The corpse had once had corn-yellow curls, though now they were dark with water and bedraggled with water-weed. His face was a sickly grey and grossly swollen, and his glazed eyes were wide open and stared out from their sockets. His skin was marked with putrefaction like mould-flowers on canvas. His mouth hung open and they could see the blackened ruin of his toothless gums.

'Eà's green blood!' Lewen cried, and gagged.

'Nay! Och, nay!' Nina cried from the caravan. 'Nay, it canna be!'

'Do ye ken who it is?' Odran the reeve asked.

Iven and Lewen both nodded. Lewen was sallow with shock. 'It is Connor the Just, one o' the Rìgh's general staff,' he answered. 'He was once squire to the Rìgh, as I am now. He is brother to Johanna the Healer.'

'Och, it will break her heart to lose him,' Nina cried. 'He is all she had.' Tears streamed down her face. She wiped them away and got down slowly from the caravan, making her way through the crowd, which drew back respectfully. She knelt beside the dead body, taking the slack hand in hers.

'His teeth have all been drawn,' she said in a constricted voice. 'Why? Why?'

'Torture?' Odran asked. 'Or souvenirs, taken after death? I dinna ken. I've never seen aught like it.'

Nina sobbed and Iven put his arm about her, drawing her head down onto his shoulder. Fèlice and Edithe both looked sick and upset, and Maisie had her hand pressed against her mouth. Landon had climbed down from his horse and hidden his face against its hot hide. Even Cameron and Rafferty, normally so cocky, were white under their tans.

Rhiannon, meanwhile, sat very still, wanting to look away, but so fascinated by the sight of the limp, grey body that she could not force her eyes to move. Her stomach felt like it had been turned upside down. Lewen had turned to stare at her in miserable doubt and suspicion, and hot tears stung her eyes. She had never expected to be faced with the corpse of what she had done, or for it to affect her so powerfully. She thought of the necklace of teeth and bones coiled at the bottom of her bag, and suddenly her stomach heaved. She bent over, trying to control her revulsion, but it won out and she vomited her breakfast in a vile splatter on the road.

'Yurk!' Edithe cried and spurred her horse away.

'Nina, the girls should no' be seeing this, or Roden either. Will ye take them away? Lewen and I will come and join ye when we can.'

Nina nodded and got up, wiping her eyes. 'Poor, poor Johanna,' she said. 'I remember what she was like after Tòmas died, and he was no' even her true brother. To lose Connor too, and in such a horrible way. Och, it's just too awful.'

She came up to the caravans, looking white and woeful, and lifted Roden down, saying, 'Come, my wee dearling, let's get ye away from here. Ye're too young to see yet the evil men can do to other men. Let us go to the inn and warm ourselves by the fire, and have a hot toddy.'

Roden nodded soberly, staring back at the dead man with huge dark eyes, and Lulu slipped her paw into his hand, making little whimpering sounds. With Sure and Steady following along behind, Nina walked slowly towards the little grey inn with its steep roof and bright red shutters. She looked as bowed and spiritless as an old woman. Rhiannon followed close behind, her hand on Blackthorn's warm silky hide. She had never seen sorrow before, and it gave her a strange feeling inside, as if she had been punched in the stomach and was now all sore and tender.

They tethered the horses outside the inn, loosening their girths and pumping the trough with water, then traipsed inside. Rhiannon took her saddlebags with her, feeling as if the dead man's plundered bones glowed with guilty heat, threatening to accuse her. When she sat with the other apprentices at the table, she shoved the bags underneath and put her feet on them.

'A murdered Yeoman!' Edithe murmured. 'Who would do such a thing?'

'They'll hang the murderer if they catch him,' Cameron said grimly. 'It's treason to even waylay a Yeoman, let alone kill one.'

Rhiannon did not know what it meant to be hanged, but to drive his point home, Cameron mimed it for her. He hung an imaginary rope around his neck, then demonstrated the sudden jerk, the choking and gargling, and then the cruel death, eyes bulging, tongue protruding, head awry on the limp neck. Feeling faint and nauseous, Rhiannon looked away.

'Why would they kill him? And beat and torture him?' Maisie said pitifully. Her face was blotched white and red, and her eyes swam with tears. 'He was only young too, did ye see? He canna have been more than thirty.'

'I kent him when he was just a lad, no' much more than Roden here,' Nina said, sitting down beside them and resting her head in her hands. 'He was a bonny, bright lad, and so brave. He was one o' the very first pupils o' the new Theurgia. Och, His Highness will be furious! Heads will roll, I guarantee it. Connor was his page and then his squire, and then one o' his bodyguards, and now one o' his most trusted lieutenants. They called him the Just because he had such a way o' enforcing law and order wherever he went. Everyone liked him and trusted him. Who can have killed him, and why?'

'He was at Ravenscraig a month or so ago,' Fèlice said in a tear-choked voice. 'I danced with him. He was such a bonny dancer.'

'Happen he discovered a plot against the Rìgh,' Edithe said. 'So the plotters killed him.'

'But why torture him?' Nina cried. She looked ravaged with grief. 'Why!'

'Happen to discover how much he knew,' Rafferty said. He was quickly recovering his spirits, and was beginning to look rather excited. 'Will the Rìgh send soldiers, do ye think? To discover who the murderer is?'

Nina nodded. 'I would say so. Or perhaps he will ask the MacBrann to look into it, since it happened here in Ravenshaw. It will take a long time to get news o' Connor's death to the Rìgh. Witches canna scry over high mountains, ye ken, no' without a Scrying Pool o' great power. The MacBrann will have to send messengers, and that could take weeks. Even carrier-pigeons have trouble getting over the mountains here, they are so high and wild. Och, they will all be distraught when they hear the news. Connor was well loved.' She wiped her eyes and blew her nose, and smiled wanly at the innkeeper as he brought a tray of steaming mugs. 'Drink up, bairns, it'll do ye good. We've all had a nasty shock.'

Cameron reached for his mug eagerly. 'That hit the spot,' he said with a sigh after taking a long draught. 'Naught like a wee dram to calm the nerves, or settle the stomach.' He cast Rhiannon a mocking glance.

'I'm not much o' a whisky drinker,' Nina said, 'but ye're right, Cameron, hot like this, with honey and spices in it, it's the best thing for us all now.' She passed a mug to Rhiannon, saying gently, 'Here ye are, this'll help. Never mind, Rhiannon, a sight like that is enough to give anyone the shivers.'

Rhiannon nodded and tried to smile, taking the cup in her trembling hands. She wondered if Nina would be so kind if she knew it was terror that caused her hands to shake. All their talk of treason and hanging frightened her terribly. She resolved to get rid of the damning necklace at the very first opportunity. No-one must guess that she was the one who had shot the Yeoman dead.

She lifted the cup and tasted the hot whisky toddy cautiously. It was like drinking liquid fire. At first she coughed and choked, but by the third sip, it went down her throat easily enough and warmed her body all through.

'Connor the Just was with the auld MacBrann when he died,' Fèlice said. 'He rode out that very night, he did no' even stop to say goodbye. We were all rather chagrined, all us lassies o' the court, when we heard, for he was rather a favourite among us. I canna believe he is dead.'

'What was he doing up here, in the highlands?' Edithe asked. 'There's naught up here but goats and peasants.'

Nina sighed. 'Happen he was trying to cross the Razor's Edge.'

'The what?'

'It's a pass through the mountains to Rionnagan,' she answered. 'Though pass is no' quite the right word. It's more like a high bridge o' stone, very dangerous to cross. It is by far the quickest way to Rionnagan. Few go that way, however, unless their need is desperate. A dragon roosts at Ben Eyrie, ye ken, and the mountains are filled with ogres and goblins and wild satyricorn.'

Rhiannon thought Nina's eyes turned towards her as she spoke, and hurriedly she lifted the cup to her mouth and drank again, afraid her face would give her away.

Fèlice shuddered. 'How horrid! Surely he wouldna have gone that way!'

'If his need was great enough, he might have,' Nina said. She gave a little shiver. 'I must say, the ripping out o' his teeth could be the work o' satyricorns. I do no' ken much about them, but I'm sure I've seen them wear necklaces made o' teeth and bones. I wish Lilanthe were here, she would ken.'

'Surely Lewen's mother is no' a satyricorn?' Edithe asked, scandalised. 'I mean, I ken she's some kind o' faery, ye only have to look at her to ken that, but surely no' one o' those dreadful wild horned women?'

Nina was exasperated. 'Lilanthe is a tree-shifter, do ye ken naught?' she snapped. 'Eà's green blood! Nay, I say Lilanthe would ken because she's an expert in the faeries o' the forest. She raised them to fight for Lachlan in the Bright Wars, did ye no' ken? Then, after peace was won, she lectured in their ways at the Theurgia. She was the one who persuaded them all to sign the Pact o' Peace, tree-changers, seelies, satyricorns too. She kens their customs better than anyone.' Again she glanced at Rhiannon, with frowning black eyes.

'How strange,' Edithe murmured. 'Though, o' course, she is a faery too.'

Rhiannon gritted her teeth and looked down into her cup. She was torn between a hysterical need to laugh, and a desire to grind Edithe's face into the table. She wondered what the fair-haired girl would say if she realised she was sitting at the same table as one of those dreadful wild horned women. She could just imagine how Edithe's nostrils would flare and her lip would curl with distaste.

Iven and Lewen came slowly into the inn. Roden ran to his father and Iven lifted him up to his shoulder, hugging him closely.

'Well, what a dark end to our day,' he said, coming to sit near his wife. 'Nina, my love, how are ye yourself?'

'Terrible,' she answered. 'I canna believe it is true. Was that really Connor lying there all battered and bruised, or was it all just a bad dream?'

'No dream,' he answered shortly, signalling to the innkeeper to bring them more mulled whisky.

'To think we have lost one more o' the gallant League o' the Healing Hand!' Nina said. 'There is only Finn and Jay left, and Johanna, and Dillon.' Tears welled up in her eyes and she pressed the heels of her hands to her face.

'Come, it is getting late,' Iven said. 'I do no' think we should ride any further today. Have they enough room here at the inn for the girls at least to sleep in comfort? I see they have a field where we can let the horses graze, and where we can make camp.'

'What have they done with Connor?' Nina asked. Her voice was so piteous Lulu stopped spinning the apple she had been given, and came to her side anxiously, looking up into her face and making little whining noises. Nina petted her absent-mindedly, her eyes fixed pleadingly on Iven's face.

'One o' the boatmen has taken him to Ravenscraig, to show the MacBrann,' Iven said unwillingly. 'He needs to be buried fast, he's in bad shape after all that time in the water, but we thought the prionnsa should see him first.'

'I've had a thought,' Nina said. 'Iven, could Connor have been trying to cross the Razor's Edge? And if so, what news drove him to take such a risk? Do ye ken if there were any papers among his things?'

Iven glanced at Rhiannon, and shook his head.

Rhiannon pressed her feet into the bags under the table, feeling a slow burn creep up her face. Nina and Iven both knew, then, how she had come riding down out of the mountains, dressed in the stolen clothes of a dead soldier. She should have guessed they would be told. She wondered if they knew she was the daughter of a satyricorn too. Unable to help herself, she gazed at Lewen pleadingly, and he refused to meet her gaze. Apprehension slithered through the pit of her stomach. Was she to stand accused of murder? Would they hang her? She slid her hand down to the knife she wore strapped to her belt.

Nina sighed. 'I guess it was too much to hope for. We're lucky any o' his things were found at all.' Once again her eyes returned to Rhiannon's face, filled with questions. Rhiannon looked back warily, her jaw thrust forward. 'Och, well, it is almost dusk already and I feel weary unto my very soul. Let us have an early night, and we'll ride out with the dawn.'

'My love, I've been thinking. Happen we should ride down the eastern side o' the Findhorn River. I ken the roads are said to be bad that way, but we need to get back to Lucescere just as soon as we can. The Rìgh will want to hear all we ken about Connor's death.'

'But, Iven, should we no' go back past Ravenscraig, as we planned? The MacBrann may wish to question us.'

Iven shrugged. 'This is a matter for the Rìgh, Nina, no' for the MacBrann, even though it happened here in his land. Even if we go to Ravenscraig we will need to hurry on to Lucescere just as fast as we can. The murder o' a Yeoman is a matter for the royal courts.'

Rhiannon gripped her knife hilt. She was amazed how Iven and Nina were able to speak of one thing and seem to speak of another. To her, and to Lewen, she imagined, it was clear they were debating whether it was best to take her, Rhiannon, to Ravenscraig to face the reckoning, or head straight to the capital, for her to explain herself to the mysterious and powerful Rìgh they all seemed to admire so much. To the other apprentices, though, there can have been no trace of the dark undercurrent of suspicion that Rhiannon heard so clearly.

'We will head down the eastern bank then,' Nina said tiredly. 'We'll save a week or more if we do no' have to cross the Findhorn.'

Iven nodded. 'More, probably, for once we get to Ravenscraig we'd have to stay for days, no doubt. Ye ken how slowly things move there, with all the confusion after Malcolm's death. The Rìgh will want the news as fast as possible. Which reminds me, my love, do ye think ye can send a bird across the mountains with a message?'

Nina sighed. 'I do no' want to be the one to tell the news. It'll break Johanna's heart.'

'They must be anxious about Connor already. Surely it's kinder to let them ken than keep Johanna in a fret o' worry for the weeks it'll take any message to get there from Ravenscraig.'

'I suppose so,' Nina said unhappily.

She got up and shook out her skirts. 'I'll need a hawk at the very least. I had better go and start calling.'

Fascinated, the apprentices all followed her outside. As Rhiannon went past Lewen, she cast him a look from under her lashes. His set expression suddenly broke. His hand shot out and caught her arm, in the crook of her elbow, and he pulled her aside, letting the others pass by.

'Rhiannon,' he whispered, his voice breaking. 'Ye had naught to do with Connor's death, did ye? Did ye?'

She dropped her eyes, saying, 'Nay, it was no' me.'

He lifted her hand in both of his, smoothing his thumb over the callouses on her palm. 'Ye have the hands o' an archer.'

Her colour deepened. 'I can shoot a bow and arrow, aye. I bet I can outshoot ye! That does no' mean I killed him.'

He dropped her hand, and very gently touched the saddlebags she had clasped under her arm. 'Are there papers in there?'

She shook her head. 'Nay.' A memory returned to her. 'He had papers. They used them to feed the fire.'

He sighed and dropped his hand. 'Rhiannon?'

'Aye?'

He shook his head. 'Naught. I'm just glad it was no' ye who killed him. I kent him well, ye see. When ye spoke o'

181

a Blue Guard that the herd took prisoner, I never imagined it would be Connor. I saw him only a month or so ago, at Ravenscraig. I canna believe he rode right past Kingarth and did no' stop to see us. He must've had urgent news indeed!'

Rhiannon said nothing. She remembered how Reamon had begged her to help the captured soldier. 'He has news he must take to the court – the Rìgh is in dreadful danger,' he had said. But the soldier was dead and his news lost. There was nothing she could do about it now.

'Rhiannon, the Rìgh will want to ken all ye can tell him about Connor's death,' Lewen said. 'He will be angry and upset, he loved Connor well. Ye . . . ye will tell all ye can, won't ye? And be polite and respectful? I would no' wish . . .' His voice trailed off, and he sighed. 'Happen we had best try to teach ye some court manners afore we arrive in Lucescere.'

Rhiannon nodded her head. 'Aye, happen so,' she answered, surprising him. His head came up and he scrutinised her face closely.

'I no' want offend him,' Rhiannon explained.

'Nay,' Lewen said and laughed. 'Very wise, wild girl.'

Together they went out of the warm inn and into the chilly afternoon. The sun was setting behind the mountains and long blue shadows were cast by every tree and hill. Nina was standing out in the centre of the field behind the inn, her eyes closed, her hands loose by her side. Her long chestnut curls were blown about wildly by the wind. The others all sat on the fence, a respectful distance away, watching in silence. The sunbird perched beside them, occasionally giving a little questioning trill. Whenever it did so, Iven tapped its beak with his finger and it would quieten, though it never took its bright eyes off Nina.

'What she doing?' Rhiannon whispered after a while.

'Calling a bird,' Edithe answered curtly.

'But she's no' making any sound.'

'She's calling it with her mind,' Fèlice explained with a quick smile.

A few minutes later, Rhiannon heard a high, yelping call. She looked up into the sky but could see nothing. The sun was balanced in a cleft in the mountains, sending wide golden rays high up into the colourless sky. The yelping cry came again, and then Rhiannon saw, far up above, the shape of an eagle. It swung in the air as if suspended from a string. Without opening her eyes, Nina suddenly raised one hand. The eagle folded its wings and came plummeting down. Involuntarily everyone flinched back as it landed heavily on Nina's hand. It was enormous, with strong talons, a cruel beak and golden-bronze feathers. Only Nina did not recoil. She opened her eyes and stared into the fierce golden eye so close to hers. For a long moment they communed in silence, then Nina brought it to stand on the fence so she could attach a message-tube to its great clenched claws. Then it spread its beautiful, barred wings and launched itself into the air, climbing swiftly up into the grey vault of the evening sky.

'If anyone can cross the mountains and come safely to Lucescere, it will be her,' Nina said, sounding tired. 'I wish she carried happier news.'

Iven nodded and put his arm about her waist, and slowly they made their way back to the inn.

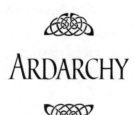

ARDARCHY

They were up and away early the next morning, leaving the river behind them as the road swung east through the hills. Occasionally they saw a small huddle of houses round a village green, or a solitary croft set among old plum trees, and midmorning they saw a goose-girl driving a flock of great white indignant birds along the road, hissing and honking, and terrifying the horses with their aggressively held heads on long, snaky necks.

Blackthorn was startled into the air, the first time she had flown since Rhiannon had captured her. Rhiannon was almost jerked off her saddle-pad, clinging to the mare's mane so desperately the coarse hair cut her flesh. She had refused to admit she was frightened of flying on the mare's back again, and so she hoped no-one noticed how pale and cold her skin was when at last Blackthorn dropped down to the ground again. To her relief, no-one seemed to have noticed, being too full of the mare's beauty and grace to pay her rider any heed at all.

The sun had slipped behind the mountains by the time Iven finally called the halt, drawing up his gaudy caravan in the shelter of a copse of trees by the road. The riders were all stiff and tired and cold, but the horses had to be attended to and firewood gathered before they could at last sit down and rest. Iven and Nina made camp with swift efficiency, and so it was not long before the campfire was burning merrily and the enticing smell of hot stew was filling the air.

While Nina stirred the big iron cooking pot, Fèlice showed Rhiannon where she was to sleep. The blue caravan which Iven drove was the one set aside for the journey-apprentices. Inside were four hard, narrow bunks, one set above the other on either side. Fèlice had lit a lantern hanging by the door. By its smoky, uneven light, Rhiannon peered into the dimness, noting the girls' clothes hanging from the rails, the shoes and bags shoved under the bunks, the piles of securely bound trunks and barrels and sacks of supplies. It was all very cramped and dark and smelly, and Rhiannon did not like it at all.

'Where others sleep?' she demanded.

'Nina and Iven and Roden sleep in the red caravan,' Fèlice said, 'and the boys sleep round the fire generally. I dinna ken what they'll do if it rains. Sleep under the caravan, I guess. It's no' very salubrious, is it?'

Rhiannon did not know what salubrious meant, but she agreed with Fèlice's tone.

'Me no sleep here,' she said flatly.

'But where else would ye sleep?' Fèlice asked in surprise.

'Me sleep outside.'

'With the boys? Surely no'? It wouldna be seemly, Rhiannon.'

'What this seemly?'

Fèlice was lost for words. 'No' . . . no' proper. No' appropriate. Boys and girls do no' sleep together. I mean, no' unless they . . . no' unless they're married.' She blushed rosily.

'Why?'

'It's just no' appropriate.'

'Me no care . . .'

'Ye should say "I do no' care",' Fèlice said.

Rhiannon cast her a look of irritation. 'I dinna care! I no' sleeping here.'

'But why no'? I mean, I ken it's small and rather crowded with all our luggage . . . and I must admit I'm used to having a room to myself and found it hard to grow accustomed to sharing.' She giggled. 'I hardly slept a wink the first few nights for Maisie's snoring. And Edithe kept banging on the bottom o' her bed to try to make her stop. But I've got used to it now, I hardly notice it anymore. Or maybe I'm just so tired from riding so far. And it's only for sleeping in. We spend all our time till we go to bed sitting round the campfire, talking and listening to Iven's stories and songs. It's rather fun, actually.'

'I canna sleep in here,' Rhiannon said. 'It's too small, too close.' She gave a little shiver and backed out of the caravan, into the fresh air. Above her was a vast arch of starry sky, and a sharp cold wind blew through the leaves, making the flames dance. Rhiannon took a deep breath and a tension she had not known was there seeped away.

'Nina, Rhiannon says she canna sleep in the caravan,' Fèlice said, sounding troubled. 'She wants to sleep out here with the boys.'

'I always sleep out here,' Rhiannon said, indicating the wind and the stars and the trees with a sweeping gesture of her arm. 'I do no' like being all . . .'

'Cooped up?' Nina said, when Rhiannon's vocabulary failed her.

'Makes I feel . . . trapped,' Rhiannon said.

'Makes *me* feel trapped,' Fèlice corrected automatically.

'Makes *me* feel trapped? Why me? And no' I? I all other times.'

Nina smiled. 'Do ye ken, Rhiannon, I have no idea why. But Fèlice is right. Happen I should set her to teaching ye the rules o' grammar, for to tell ye the truth I've never really understood them. I grew up naught but a jongleur lass, ye ken. I probably make Fèlice and Edithe shudder with the way I speak too.'

'Oh, no,' Fèlice said, horrified. 'I mean, I would no' presume . . .'

'Och, no need to blush. I'm no lady, no' me. Or should that be "no' I"?'

'No' I,' Fèlice said apologetically.

'There ye go. Ye're hereby appointed as Rhiannon's language teacher.'

Fèlice looked at Rhiannon a little dubiously but could not help laughing at Rhiannon's scowling expression. 'I'll be gentle, I promise,' she said.

'And about sleeping outside, I see no reason why Rhiannon canna sleep under the stars if she so wishes. I often do in summer, I must admit. The ground's a little too cold for me at this time o' year but if Rhiannon does no' mind, I do no' see why we should.'

'But . . .' Fèlice said doubtfully.

'Are ye worried about the proprieties? I wouldna be concerned, Fèlice. Witches rarely worry about such things. I for one ken Rhiannon can look after herself.'

Rhiannon smiled at her radiantly. 'So I can,' she asserted. 'Or should that be "So me can"?'

Fèlice sighed.

The other apprentice-witches were all huddled by the fire in their cloaks, surreptitiously rubbing at their bruises and complaining about their aches and pains. Nina passed around a jar of salve and promised to warm up bags of dried herbs for the girls to take to bed with them, apologising for the hard pace they were being set.

'Weather's chancy in the highlands,' she said, 'and we want to make good time while we can. Last time Iven and I were in the Broken Ring o' Dubhslain, we ended up being stuck in a goatherd's cottage for two weeks while a snowstorm raged.'

'But it's springtime,' Fèlice cried. 'Surely we shallna get snowed in now?'

Nina shrugged. 'Like I said, the weather's unpredictable here. It's something to do with being circled by mountains on all sides.'

'Cold the wind blows and bleak the raven cries, down the stony glens o' black Dubhslain,' Landon murmured. 'What rhymes with "slain"? Wane? Fain? Pain?'

'I think ye could do something with "pain",' Fèlice murmured, rubbing her backside ruefully. Everyone laughed.

'Do ye ken why it's called the Broken Ring o' Dubhslain?' Iven asked. 'I dinna ken if it be true, but they say there was a great act o' sorcery in these hills, many years ago, in the time o' Brann the Raven himself.'

He paused for effect, taking a sip of ale. 'Now Brann was one o' the First Coven, as ye ken. But many o' his people hated and feared him, for he was a cold-hearted ruthless man and much given to dabbling in mysteries that would have best been left undisturbed. One summer, it was said, Brann and his retinue were here in the highlands for he had decided to hunt down and capture the fabled black winged stallion for himself.'

He nodded and smiled at Rhiannon, who was listening, rapt. 'Some o' his men decided to lay a trap for him and murder him, making it seem like an accident. Brann's son Dugald was only thirteen then and they thought they could rule through him. Brann saw into their hearts, though, and laid a trap of his own. In those days this valley was surrounded on all sides by mountains in a perfect ring. They had a hard journey climbing up here, but Brann urged them on, taunting them with their cowardice and weakness until at last they climbed the last cliff and came inside the ring. On they travelled, towards the high peak o' Ben Eyrie where it was said the black winged horses flew. Three days they travelled, and always the rebels waited for their chance to slay the Raven. He never seemed to sleep, however, and they dared not face him awake.

'On the third night, Brann at last seemed to rest and they drew their knives and crept upon him. Just as the ringleader raised his blade, Brann leapt up and sent him flying back with the force o' his magic. The rebels turned to flee but Brann struck the ground with his staff, enacting a great spell o' incredible strength by using the perfect ring o' mountains as his circle o' power. The earth itself groaned and shook, and a great crack opened up in its flank.

'A fountain o' water burst up from the deepest depths o' the earth and swept away all that lay afore it, including all o' Brann's men, traitorous or no'. And the ring o' mountains was broken and the land cleared all the way to the sea, farms and villages and towns all drowned in the flood. And where Brann's staff had struck was a great black fathomless lake, which he called Dubhglais.

'Then Brann came down alone from the mountains, following the new river, which he named the Findhorn. And where the river fell through the broken ring in a great roaring waterfall he built a castle and named it

Ravenscraig. And on the far shore, in the shadow o' the broken mountain, he built his witches' tower. And no-one ever dared rebel against him again.'

'I'm no' surprised,' Landon said, looking up from the fire with dreamy eyes. 'He was a cold, strange man, by all accounts. Did ye ken he swore he would outwit Gearradh in the end, and live again?'

Everyone sighed and shivered and looked up at the tall icy peaks surrounding them on all sides but one, and hunched closer to the fire.

'Who that?' Rhiannon whispered to Lewen.

'Brann? He was one o' the sorcerers from the Other World, who brought humankind here to Eileanan. We call them the First Coven. Ravenshaw – this country we're in now – that was Brann's land and is still ruled by one o' his descendants, Dughall MacBrann.'

'I meant t'other. The one that made everyone shiver.'

'Gearradh? Oh. She is the one who cuts the thread, the third of the weird sisters, that we call the Three Spinners.' Seeing Rhiannon's puzzled face, Lewen tried to explain again. 'She . . . I suppose she is like the goddess o' death. She decides when it is time for us all to die.'

'No wonder everyone shivered.'

'It was as much at the idea of Brann the Raven living again,' Lewen said. 'He was a scary man.'

Nina laughed at their sombre faces and bade Iven play something to cheer them up while she served the stew. 'Ye willna fancy ye hear ghosts crying on the wind with a bowl o' hot stew in ye,' she said.

Iven strummed his guitar and sang lustily:

'O Eà let me die,
wi' a wee dram at my lip,
and a bonny lass on my lap,

190

and a merry song and a jest,
biting my thumb at the sober an' just,
as I live I wish to die!
So drink up, laddies, drink,
and see ye do no' spill,
for if ye do we'll all drink two,
for that be the drunkard's rule!'

Despite the merry tune and the hot stew, the shadow of the tale lay on them all still. That night, as she lay rolled in her blankets by the fire, Rhiannon could still hear the wind sobbing in the trees and feel the dark gaze of the mountains upon them. It took her a long time to find sleep, and she heard the sighs of the other apprentices as they too sought sleep that would not come.

The next day they were all tired and heavy-eyed, and quick to snap at each other, but no-one demurred when Iven began harnessing the carthorses to the caravans before any of them had even finished scraping their porridge bowls clean. All were eager to leave the Broken Ring of Dubhslain behind them.

They rode hard that day, for clouds were pouring in over the great peaks like a grey flood, dimming the thin spring sunshine and swallowing the steep banks of pines and hemlock. When the road rolled out before them Rhiannon challenged them all to race and, to her great delight, beat every one of them. Her pocket began to jingle with coins and she often slipped her hand inside to caress them, liking the cool round perfection of them.

Most of the day they all rode quietly, though, pacing the horses and nursing along their saddle sores. Rhiannon kept close and quiet, listening to the conversation and later asking Lewen to explain anything she did not understand. Hardened by her upbringing, she did not suffer as much as the other girls from the long hours in the saddle and so she was glad to look about her with hungry eyes, and listen to everything that was said, sucking out its pith of knowledge. Rhiannon was determined to never again be mocked for her ignorance. If learning was the currency of power in this land, then Rhiannon would learn all she could.

They came to a town late on the third day, as the gloom of the cloud-hung day darkened to dusk.

'Thank Eà!' Fèlice cried. 'A proper bed tonight! Proper food!'

'Ye do no' like my cooking?' Iven said, pretending to be hurt.

'Well, ye ken ye canna do much with a pot hung over a fire,' Fèlice said disarmingly. 'Stew, stew, or stew.'

'Och, but such delicious stew!'

'Aye, the very best. It will be nice to have something different, though, don't ye agree?'

'Mmm, a wee dram o' whisky would be nice,' Iven agreed. 'Ye girls take up so much room with all your fimble-fambles I havena any room for anything but a keg o' ale and that just doesna quench a man's thirst the way a dram does. Let's hope there's an inn.'

The town seemed quite large and prosperous, sprawling round a square of green grass with a big old tree at one end and a small white rotunda at the other. Behind the houses were little walled fields devoted to vegetables and orchards and a few grain crops, running up to steep hills that disappeared into forest. The mountains behind were hidden in mist.

Many of the houses had large gardens, some hidden behind walls overgrown with ivy, others with nothing but a low wooden pole fence to separate them from their neighbours. Coming down a low hill, the travellers were able to see how the town sprawled along a small river, following its curve. At the far end of the main street they saw a water-mill, and a hunchbacked stone bridge across the river, and then, away from the houses, in a big garden all bright with spring blossom, a small round turret built of stone.

'Aaah, they have a tower witch,' Nina said, pleased. 'She'll give us a bed for the night if there's no' room for us all at the inn.'

Rhiannon stared about her with interest. Six boys, two girls and a mob of goats surrounded their cavalcade now, all the children chattering happily in high, piping voices, the goats bleating and leaping about madly. A woman came to the door of one of the little grey cottages, wiping red, damp hands on her apron, a cluster of children peeping out round her skirts. She exclaimed aloud and called to her neighbour. Soon there were faces at every doorway or window, pointing at the long-billed, iridescent bird perched on Nina's shoulder and the arak leaping about on the roof of the red caravan, and exclaiming with awe at the magnificent winged horse. Blackthorn curved her neck in pleasure, lifting her feathered feet daintily. Rhiannon smiled and waved at the crowd, but did not answer any of the shouted questions, not knowing what to say.

They came down the main road by the village green, past a row of shopfronts with big glass windows filled with all sorts of amazing things. One, with the sign of a bee hanging above it, had windows filled with candles of all shapes and sizes and colours, many lit so the window glowed golden, and jars of honey with fabric tied over the top, some pale as sunlit water, some yellow as pollen, others dark as a forest pool. There was a honeycomb dripping with fresh honey, and large jars filled with round dark things Lewen said were toffees.

Another shop was filled with tools of all descriptions, hoes and scythes and enormous two-handled saws, and sacks of flour and meal, and bright saucepans and kettles and ladles, and mops and brooms and feather dusters, and brown bags of seeds tied with string. Another had stiff brown dried fish hanging from hooks alongside smoked hams, and huge round cheeses, and jars of preserved fruit and pickled vegetables and jam.

There was a tired-looking baker, giving away handfuls of sugar-dusted pastry twists to the children before locking up his shop for the night, and an apothecary's shop, the window filled with jars of pills, and bottles of potions, and bowls of dried herbs and flowers and muslin spell-bags, and hooks hanging with bunches of bright feathers to sweep away bad dreams, and myriad charms and talismans dangling from leather thongs.

Next to it was a shop filled with bolts of lovely coloured material, spread out to show their silky weave. In one corner of the window was a headless wooden mannequin wearing a gorgeous dress made of blue shimmering fabric tied up with silver ribbons. Rhiannon gazed at it longingly. Though she pretended not to care, it bothered her that she had to wear hand-me-down boy's clothes when Edithe and Fèlice were always so beautifully dressed in fabrics as soft as thistledown. It was a constant irritation to her, like a burr under a saddlecloth, and her only consolation was the embroidered shawl that Lilanthe had given her, which she wrapped around her shoulders every night as they sat round the campfire talking and singing.

'It'd look bonny on ye,' Lewen whispered shyly with a nod of his head towards the dress. Rhiannon scowled at him. She hated the way he always seemed to know what she was thinking, no matter how carefully she kept her feelings hidden. She gritted her teeth, waiting for one of the others to mock her, but they had not heard above the noise of the crowd and so she was able to pretend Lewen had not spoken and ride on, head held high.

They came to the inn in the very centre of town, facing the village green with its big old oak tree and its pretty white rotunda where, Lewen explained, the musicians would sit to play for weddings and festivals.

The inn was small and quaint, with an enormous blue-painted door, big windows with blue wooden boxes filled with herbs and flowers, and a very steep roof with two gabled windows in it like beetling eyebrows. Outside the inn were long benches where old men were sitting, hunched up in their heavy coats against the evening chill, smoking long pipes. Over their heads hung a brightly painted sign depicting a cat playing a fiddle.

The innkeeper stood in the doorway, beaming. He was a solid, red-faced man with a big apron tied over his breeches. Behind his square shoulder stood a thin woman, her hands clapped together in glee. It was clear they saw a good profit ahead of them that night.

Everyone was very chilled and stiff, and glad to dismount.

'Jongleurs!' the woman cried. 'We havena had jongleurs in Ardarchy for years. And such a large company! Will ye be putting on a show for the town? Ye may have the use o' our taproom, for sure. Everyone will come. And a flying horse! Gracious me! Does it perform too? Och, I dinna ken if we have room for it in here!'

'My wife and I are minstrels and will be glad to give ye a show, but I'm afraid our companions are only travelling with us and willna be performing,' Iven replied. 'They are apprentices journeying to the Theurgia at the Tower o' Two Moons.'

'Witchlings? What are they doing in Ardarchy? There's naught here but goats and geese,' the innkeeper asked. His voice rose incredulously. 'Ye do no' mean to cross the Stormness River, surely?'

'Aye, we do,' Iven answered. 'Why shouldna we?'

'The bridge is barricaded shut,' the innkeeper answered. 'No-one goes that way anymore. The land across the river is haunted, did ye no' ken?'

Nina and Iven exchanged a glance. 'Surely the barricade can be taken down for us?' Nina said gently.

'Och, ye willna want to be doing that,' the innkeeper said. 'Ye'd be best off riding back to Barbreck-by-the Bridge and crossing there.'

'But no' tonight,' his wife said firmly. 'Ye're cold and weary, and will be wanting a sup o' something hot, and happen a dram or two to warm your blood. And no point wasting a good audience. The whole o' Ardarchy will turn out to see ye perform – it's rare we see a minstrel or jongleur here. A shame ye're no' all performers, but no doubt the witchlings will still want a meal and some ale too, and will watch the show with the rest o' us. We'll want a cut o' the takings, mind. And ye'll want stabling for the horses, no doubt, and that's a few extra pennies too. I'll call my laddie to come take the horses for ye.'

'We'll see to the horses ourselves, thanks, but if ye could rustle up some hay and happen some bran mash for them, we'd be grateful indeed,' Iven said. Fèlice moaned audibly. He grinned at her. 'Come, lassie, surely ye were no' expecting to eat and drink until ye've cared for your horse yourself? She's had a long hard ride today and she's chilled through. What if this lad kens naught about horses? Ye wouldna like to think o' her shivering in a cold draughty stall without her blanket and nothing but a bit o' auld musty straw to chew on, would ye? No', o' course, that I'm wishing to cast aspersions on our good host here,' he added with a charming smile to the innkeeper. 'I'm sure your stable is warm and snug enough for a prince. It's just the principle I'm wishing to teach.'

'Och, and fair enough,' the innkeeper replied jovially.

He turned to the crowd of followers then and motioned away with his hands. 'Go on, get along home, there'll be no show now. Come back after supper.'

Iven had vaulted down from the caravan to speak to the innkeeper but now he turned and faced the crowd, his voice ringing out clearly. 'Good people o' Ardarchy, I am Iven the Magnificent, and I have great pleasure in introducing the incomparable Nina, called the Nightingale by the Rìgh himself for the indescribable sweetness of her voice. You may wonder what we do here, so far from the royal court, but only a few days ago we heard we were called back to Lucescere by royal decree, for Nina to sing at the wedding o' the royal heir Donncan MacCuinn to his bonny cousin Bronwen.'

There was a murmur of delight and astonishment.

'Aye, I am glad to be the one to tell ye the happy news . . .'

As Iven continued on, captivating the crowd with his patter, the innkeeper helped Nina down from the caravan, saying: 'I'll go and stoke up the fire for ye, and pull ye all some ale, and add a few extra potatoes to the roasting pan, and we'll have all ready for ye when your horses are seen to.'

'We do no' eat meat,' Nina said. 'Would ye have some vegetable broth or stew that we may eat instead?'

'I have bean stew,' the innkeeper's wife said, her voice falling in disappointment, as bean stew was worth quite a few pennies less than roast mutton and potatoes. At the word 'stew' an audible sigh was heard from the apprentices.

Nina flashed them an admonitory glance and allowed the innkeeper to show her into the warmth of the taproom.

Lewen helped Maisie down from her fat pony and, leading his horse and hers, followed the innkeeper's plump son round the back to the stableyard, the others trailing tiredly behind.

'I wish my groom was here to look after Regina for me,' Fèlice grumbled. 'I am so cold and so tired. Cameron, will ye no' do it for me?'

Before Cameron could reply, Maisie said in her gentle way, 'Och, we're all cold and tired, aren't we, Cameron? And poor Regina must be even tireder, for she was the one that did all the walking.'

Lewen looked at her with approval and she blushed and did her best to take off her pony's tack by herself. Lewen helped her, and then unsaddled Argent, who was looking very bad-tempered, not liking being ridden for such a long time on such stony roads. Fèlice sighed and started to undo the buckles and Cameron left his own horse standing with steaming hide and hanging head to help her.

By the time the horses were unsaddled and groomed and tucked into their blankets, with fresh straw forked into their stalls and buckets of warm bran mash and fresh water to lip at, and all the tack cleaned and hanging on hooks, and the caravans secured, it was fully dark and everyone was weary indeed. The work had kindled some sort of camaraderie between them, however, and they all talked and joked comfortably as they made their way back to the welcoming warmth of the inn.

'A proper bed tonight,' Fèlice sighed in ecstasy.

'I just hope they've aired the sheets,' Edithe said.

'I doubt there's room for all o' us here,' Lewen said, looking up and counting the number of windows streaming light. 'Some o' us will have to go and stay at the witch's, I think.'

'I will,' Edithe said. 'Less chance o' bedbugs, I bet.'

'She'll probably rather have Nina and Iven, so she can hear all the news from court,' Fèlice sighed regretfully.

'I doubt the innkeeper and his wife will let them go,' Edithe said. 'I'd say Iven the Magnificent is the most exciting thing to happen round here in a decade, and they'll want to be the ones to hear all the gossip first-hand.'

'Forget Iven, it's Rhiannon and her fabulous winged horse that's attracted most o' the attention,' Rafferty shot back, with a quick sideways grin at Rhiannon. 'I bet Iven is wondering how he can incorporate ye into his show. He'll have ye doing levades and caprioles by the next village we pass through.'

Rhiannon had no idea what he meant but she smiled back anyway, deciding she rather liked Rafferty. At least he did not leer at her, or sneer at her, or compare her breasts to mountain peaks.

'Well, I'm happy to stay at the inn,' Cameron said. 'Ale, ale and more ale for me, please!'

'I'd like to see the witch's tower,' Maisie said wistfully. 'I've never seen one afore, ye ken.'

They came into the taproom and hurried to warm themselves by the fire, the boys gratefully accepting the mugs of foaming ale the innkeeper tapped for them, the girls sipping hot spiced wine. Rhiannon had never tasted mulled wine before and drank deeply, feeling a pleasant euphoria fill her veins. By the time they had been served a substantial meal of bean stew and roast vegetables, fol-lowed by a surprisingly delicious treacle pie, she was feeling quite light-headed and was surprised to find herself giggling at one of Edithe's sarcastic asides. Edithe was equally surprised but rather gratified, while Lewen surreptitiously moved the jug of wine away from Rhiannon's elbow.

The boys began a game of chance with some dice which Cameron pulled from his pocket, and Rhiannon went eagerly to join them. Soon their corner was noisy with laughter and the calling of bets, Rhiannon's face alight with eagerness as she challenged Cameron to another toss. Lewen was content to sit back and watch her, sipping his ale and enjoying the warmth of the fire on the soles of his boots.

'I just canna understand why it is we have to travel round Eileanan in this ridiculous fashion,' Edithe said as she watched Roden and Lulu practising their juggling and Iven walking round the room on his hands. 'It really is naught better than a circus. My father would've happily paid for me to travel to the capital in comfort and it would no' have taken me months to get there! Do ye no' agree, Lady Fèlice?'

'Well, it's true my *dai-dein* was no' very happy about it,' Fèlice said. 'He wondered how safe it was, particularly, ye ken, with the boys . . .' She nodded towards Cameron and Rafferty, who were eagerly gesturing for the landlord to refill their ale tankards. 'But the Coven insists on it, ye ken. Diantha, the court sorceress at Ravenscraig, says it knocks any nonsense out o' us afore we get to the Tower and gets us used to doing things for ourselves and rubbing elbows with all kinds o' people.'

'Well, that at least is true,' Edithe replied and for once her voice was free of scorn, sounding only resigned.

'Diantha told me that the council o' sorcerers believe it was because the Coven had grown arrogant and isolated from the common people that the Day o' Betrayal was able to happen at all. So now all apprentices must travel slowly through the countryside afore they ever reach the Tower, learning what it means to be cold and hungry and afraid. We are lucky we are allowed to ride. Diantha said the council debated whether it would be wiser to make us walk the whole way on our own two feet.'

'Eà forbid,' Edithe said faintly.

'Probably if each country had its own Tower, we would have had to, but as the only Tower in all o' western Eileanan is the Tower o' Horse-lairds and their wisdom is no' what most wish to learn, we all have to travel a long way and so they allow us horses. Indeed, she said we were lucky indeed to get to travel with Nina and Iven, for they at least are great fun to be with, and will teach us much along the way. Besides, she said we should be honoured to be travelling in their company, and somehow I do no' think she was joking.'

'Honoured?' Maisie and Edithe echoed.

Fèlice shrugged. 'So she said. Iven is some sort o' war hero, ye ken. He fought with Lachlan the Winged in the rebellion against the Ensorcellor, and was there when they rescued Daillas the Lame and many other adventures they now sing about. And Nina . . . well, Diantha would no' say too much about Nina but there was this note in her voice that made me wonder . . .'

'What kind o' note?' Edithe said sceptically.

Fèlice shrugged. 'I dinna ken. Awe. Respect.' She turned to Lewen, favouring him with her most dazzling smile. 'Lewen, your family kens the royal clan. What can ye tell us?'

'About what?' Lewen said warily.

'About Nina. She's no' just an ordinary jongleur, is she?'

Lewen choked back a laugh. 'Well, ye only need to hear her sing to ken that,' he said.

'I mean more than that,' Fèlice coaxed. 'Ye should've seen the way the MacBrann himself bowed to her. The new MacBrann, I mean, no' the auld mad one who's dead now. There's some mystery about her, I just ken it.'

Everyone was staring at Lewen now. He wondered how to respond. If Nina wanted her family history told, would she not tell it? But perhaps it was hard for her to tell, just as it was hard for Lewen's own father to talk about his part in the war. And if they knew, these arrogant aristocratic brats, would they not treat her with more respect? He glanced at Nina, warming her voice at the far end of the room with the most exquisite rills of music, her sunbird trilling away with her in sublime accompaniment. She glanced at him with her bright dark eyes, and Lewen realised she knew exactly what they spoke about, huddled here in their own fire-lit end of the inn. She smiled at him ruefully, shrugged her slim shoulders, and turned away.

'So?' Edithe demanded. 'What's the big mystery?'

'Ask her to sing the song o' the three blackbirds tonight,' Lewen said at last, his chest muscles constricting tight.

'Why?'

'Because no-one sings it more beautifully, my mother says. And because her brother wrote it.'

'But . . .' Edithe sounded puzzled.

Fèlice, court-bred, knew at once. 'Ye mean the Earl o' Caerlaverock?' Her voice came out in a squeak. 'The Rìgh's own minstrel?'

'Wasna he the one who found the Rìgh, when he was still a blackbird, and saved him, and helped transform him back into a man?' Landon asked, eyes shining.

'It was Enit Silverthroat who did that,' Lewen said. 'Dide and Nina's grandmother. Dide was still only a lad and Nina little more than a babe. Lachlan travelled with them for years in their caravan, learning to be a man

202

again. Dide was the first to swear allegiance to Lachlan and promise to help him win the throne.'

'Wasna Enit Silverthroat the auld Yedda who master-minded the rebellion against the Ensorcellor?' Edithe said. 'And then taught Jay Fiddler the song o' love, which he played at the Battle o' Bonnyblair, enchanting the Fairgean into peace?'

Lewen nodded. 'Though she was no' a Yedda,' he said. 'She was a jongleur.'

They all turned and looked up the room at Nina, her head bent over her shabby old guitar, her messy chestnut curls tumbling down onto a gaudy orange and gold brocade dress, stained around the hem and darned here and there with mismatching thread.

'Ye're telling me *Nina* is the sister o' the Earl o' Caerlaverock?' Edithe's voice was dazed with amazement.

Lewen nodded. 'And Roden is his heir, for he has no children o' his own, ye ken.'

'*Roden* is a Viscount?'

Lewen could not help smiling as everyone stared at the grubby little boy juggling balls back and forth with the arak, his chestnut curls uncombed and his grimy jerkin missing a couple of buttons.

'Well!' said Edithe at last. 'I would never have guessed it.'

Edithe's expression of dazed wonderment stayed on her face all through the jongleurs' performance, which was concluded with a storm of clapping from the townsfolk crowded into the long smoky room. Nina was begged for encore after encore, but at last she had to desist, hoarse-throated and heavy-eyed. Reluctantly the crowd filed out into the frosty night, talking and marvelling, and Nina sat down limply, drinking one last cup of honeyed tea, Roden nestled sleepily against her side.

A tall woman in a flowing white gown came to sit next to her, talking quietly. Her brown hair was tied back in a long plait that hung to her knees, and as she lifted her hand to gesture, light flashed off the rings on her right hand. Rhiannon came shyly closer and, at Nina's welcoming smile, sat next to the woman on the bench.

'Come, ye must be weary indeed,' the witch was saying. 'Will ye no' bring yon lassies and come spend the night with me? Arley Innkeeper has only two rooms here, no' nearly enough for all o' ye, and I have room to spare.'

'I thank ye,' Nina answered. 'Indeed we are all worn out. We've been riding since dawn and had a day like it yesterday and another one ahead o' us tomorrow.'

'I do no' understand why ye have come this way,' the witch said. 'Do ye no' ken the road past here is rough indeed, for none o' us travel that way? It is a dark and evil land across the bridge. Ghosts walk there, and evil spirits. Ye would be better off travelling back up the river to the bridge at Barbreck and crossing there, to travel down the western bank o' the river. There is another bridge at Tullimuir where ye can cross again, and then ye need no' travel under the shadow o' the Tower o' Ravens.'

'But we would lose weeks in the travelling,' Nina said wearily. 'We would have gone that way from Ravenscraig if we had not had to go up into the highlands to pick up young Lewen and Rhiannon here. But since we had to go that way, it made more sense to cut through the hills and save crossing the Findhorn again twice. This way we can travel close round the base of the hills to Rhyssmadill, and then up along the flank o' the Whitelock Mountains to Lucescere. It will be much faster than having to follow the Findhorn south again, and then cross the river at Tullimuir Bridge, right at the mouth o' the firth.'

'But have ye no' heard? Do ye no' ken? No-one goes that way anymore. It's a cursed land. They say the dead walk again there and what few people are left keep their shutters closed and their bolts shot, even in the heat o' summer, for fear o' what may come knocking on their door.'

Nina frowned and unconsciously nestled her sleeping son closer to her. 'We've heard the tower is haunted, o' course, but we do not intend to go there, just pass through the gap in the hills at its foot.'

The witch shuddered and made an odd gesture with her hands, circling the thumb and forefinger of her right hand and crossing it with the forefinger of her left hand. 'Truly, it is no' safe, my lady, no' even to pass under its shadow. The people o' Ardarchy do no' go that way at all – we go north to Barbreck-by-the-Bridge and south again on the far side of the river with our goods, aye, even to go to the ports we go that way, rather than cross the Stormness.'

Nina looked troubled. 'I thank ye for your warning, Ashelma, but we do no' have time to retrace all our steps. As I'm sure ye've heard, we've been summoned to the palace for Prionnsa Donncan's wedding on Midsummer Eve, and I would no' miss it for anything. And I do no' fear ghosts. Ye o' all people should ken that ghosts do no' have the power to hurt us, they are naught but memories.'

The witch Ashelma looked very grave. 'Memories have as much power to hurt as any sword, if they are cruel enough,' she said. 'And it is no' just ghosts that haunt the land beyond the Stormness River. We have heard tales o' corpses that will no' rest in their grave but seek to return to warmer beds, and children stolen and found murdered.'

Nina looked down at her sleeping son and smoothed his tangled curls away from his flushed cheek. 'Does the MacBrann no' ken o' these tales?'

'Aye, o' course, but his hands are full enough already, having only just inherited the throne from his father. Auld Malcolm was no' a good laird, ye ken, being more interested in his dogs and his experiments than in the problems o' the people. He grew more vague and eccentric with every year that passed, and by the end was raving mad, by all accounts.'

Nina sighed. 'It's hard to ken what to do. Your news troubles me greatly, but I ken the people o' Ravenshaw and how melancholy and superstitious they are. There have been wild stories about the Tower o' Ravens since the time o' Brann himself, and that's a thousand years o' unfounded supposition. And two days o' hard riding and we are past the tower and into the lowlands. And I am no' without magic, as ye ken. I think we must risk it, though I thank ye for the warning.'

Ashelma sighed and rose to her feet. 'Well, let me see what I can do to make ye comfortable tonight, at least.'

Nina rose too, lifting Roden in her arms and laying him across her shoulder. 'My thanks,' she said. 'Rhiannon, will ye call the other lasses? We shall spend the night with Ashelma and meet up again with Iven and the lads in the morn. Is there aught ye need for the night?'

'I canna leave Blackthorn,' Rhiannon said. 'She fret without me. I sleep in the stable.'

Ashelma looked at Rhiannon for the first time. Her eyes were dark and very serious, and seemed to see everything there was to see in a single searching glance. 'Are ye the rider o' the winged horse I've been hearing so much about?' she asked.

Rhiannon nodded.

'Ye may bring your horse too, if ye ken,' the witch said. 'All beasts are welcome in my tower, as ye will see.'

Rhiannon thought for a moment, reluctant to rouse

her drowsy horse and take her out of the warmth of the stable into the cold night. She felt a great desire to see the witch's tower, however, and so she nodded abruptly and went to rouse the other girls from their sleepy repose by the fire. They got up, yawning and stretching. Fèlice and Edithe wrapped themselves up in their fur-trimmed cloaks and pulled on their gloves but Maisie had nothing but an old shawl to wrap around her against the cold. She pulled it close about her round face, her eyes shining with excitement at the thought of staying with a real witch.

'Sweet dreams, my ladies,' Cameron said unsteadily, looking up from the depths of his empty mug. 'Dinna miss me too much.'

'Miss ye?' Edithe said haughtily. 'I doubt we'll notice ye're no' around.'

She saw Rhiannon's mouth curve and flashed a quick smile at her, so that Rhiannon was unable to help smiling back.

Lewen stood up and looked at Rhiannon a little anxiously. She frowned at his look, and he quirked his mouth, saying severely, 'Ye willna stab anyone, will ye?'

She laughed at that, and said, 'Nay, o' course no'. No' unless I have to, that is.'

'Nina will have a care for ye,' he said.

'Me need no-one to care for me,' she snapped back and then, when he grinned, realised he was teasing. She would not relent, however, scowling at him as she pulled on her blue tam-o'-shanter and huddled the thick, warm cloak about her.

'Good night,' he said. 'Sweet dreams.'

She looked back at him from the doorway and her expression softened.

'Good night to ye too.'

THE WITCH'S TOWER

It was bitterly cold outside, with a nasty snippety wind that found every gap in their clothing and sent the fog swirling up around their ankles. Rhiannon led Blackthorn, the big blanket still flung over her withers and concealing her wings. Ashelma had a small two-wheeled trap pulled by a sturdy, shaggy-maned pony. She tucked Nina and Maisie and the sleeping boy up under some soft goat-hair blankets, saying to the other girls, 'Ye're well wrapped enough to walk a few blocks, I think?' as she took the pony's bridle and began to lead the way.

As they went down the ill-lit street, past dark shop windows and sleeping houses, a lantern hanging from the pony-trap's seat flickered into life by itself, making every hair on Rhiannon's body stand erect in sudden superstitious terror. No-one else seemed to notice, though, except Blackthorn who shied sideways, almost knocking Rhiannon over.

'It's hard to believe it is spring,' Fèlice said with a shiver. 'It feels like winter. Look, I'm breathing smoke like a dragon.'

'It's always cold in the Ring o' Dubhslain,' Ashelma said. 'We have a saying here: "Do no' put your plaids away, until the last day o' May".'

'It's more than a month to May Day!' Fèlice said. 'I would've been crowned May Queen if I had stayed in Ravenscraig, ye ken. I was hoping, if we got to Lucescere in time . . .'

'Indeed?' Ashelma turned and gave Fèlice that grave, penetrating glance so that the girl flushed a little and lost her smile.

'Well, I was,' she said a little defiantly. 'Though I hear the Banprionnsa Bronwen is all the rage there now. Apparently she's quite a beauty, though no' in the usual style. Anyway, never mind. There would no' be much o' a May Day celebration in Ravenscraig this year, anyway. The auld laird had just died and the court's in mourning.'

'There'll be other May Days,' the witch said, quite kindly.

They came to the Stormness River, moving sinuously under the mist like a great black-scaled snake, and turned to walk down a smooth narrow road along its bank. Trees and well-clipped hedges loomed over them. The last few lights fell behind and all was dark and quiet and cold. Their lone lantern bobbed along, its light little more than an orange blur through the fog. Rhiannon shivered inside her cloak. The words the witch had spoken in the inn echoed in her mind. *Tales o' corpses that will no' rest in their grave but seek to return to warmer beds . . . children stolen and found murdered . . .*

She looked across the silent river but she could see nothing but wisps of mist floating up from the darkly glinting water like the ghosts the witch had spoken of. She wished they did not have to cross the bridge in the morning but she would have cut off her tongue before she ever admitted it.

They came to a high stone wall with an iron gate standing open. The witch led them inside and the gate shut itself behind them. On either side stood tall trees covered in frail white blossoms like new snow. The air seemed suddenly warmer and sweetly scented. Through the mist Rhiannon could see lights shining towards them, golden as sunlight. They came into a wide cleared area before the house, a long, low building built of grey stone with a peaked roof covered in silver-green lichen, beside a tall round tower that rose higher than the trees. The light came from the windows and door of the house. A young woman stood in the doorway, the light of the lantern she held throwing bright colour up onto her face and hair.

'Come in!' she said. 'Ye must be chilled to the bone. What a dreadful night. Morogh says bad weather is coming and indeed I think he's right. It's cold as winter.'

Her voice was soft and kind with a warm undercurrent as if she had just this moment stopped laughing. She came running down the stairs, wrapped in a woolly red shawl, and took the pony's bridle. 'I'll look after Drud,' she said. 'Ye go on in and get warm. I've got the kettle whistling on the hob if ye'd like some tea.'

'Lovely,' Ashelma said. She helped a drowsy Maisie down from the pony-trap and up the stairs. Edithe and Fèlice followed her eagerly, Nina bringing up the rear more slowly, carrying the heavy weight of her sleeping child.

'I will stable my horse myself,' Rhiannon said.

'O' course,' the girl answered. 'What a bonny beast she is! So tall and finely made, and with such magnificent long horns. I have never seen a horse like her.'

'No' many like her,' Rhiannon said.

'Nay,' the girl agreed. 'A rare beast indeed. Ye and her are akin, I can see that.'

They had walked round the side of the house and in through a stable door as they spoke, and so when Rhiannon looked up in sudden keen interest, she was able to see the other girl clearly in the light of the lanterns hanging on either wall.

Rhiannon's first emotion was one of surprise. She had thought the other girl young and beautiful but now she realised she was at least six years older than Rhiannon, and quite short and plump, a big-boned young woman with mousy-brown hair, a round face and fresh, rosy skin. She looked with great frankness and openness at Rhiannon, however, and as soon as she spoke again the illusion of beauty returned, for her voice was so warm and merry, and her smile so wide and friendly. 'My name is Annis. I am Ashelma's apprentice.'

'My name is Rhiannon,' she answered, hearing the ring of pride in her own voice.

'And ye have tamed a winged horse,' Annis said admiringly. 'Och, the town was full o' it. I am so glad ye came to stay the night here for I would have been sad indeed to miss my chance to see your bonny horse and meet with ye. I could no' come to hear Nina the Nightingale sing, for I couldna leave the children, so I was hoping ye would all come home with Ashelma.'

'Children?' Rhiannon asked.

Annis had been swiftly unharnessing the pony from the trap, rubbing it down with a cloth and filling its bucket with grain. All her movements were quick and neat, and she was surprisingly light on her feet for such a big-boned girl. Rhiannon noticed she wore the white luminous stone on the middle finger of her right hand

211

that they all seemed to wear, as well as one made of some dark green stone.

She nodded. 'Aye, we run an orphanage here, ye see. We have two bairns from Ardarchy, but the others are all from across the river. No' all are orphans. Some were brought here by their parents for safekeeping. Mainly boys. For some reason it is boys that are in the most danger over there, we do no' ken why.'

Annis pumped some fresh water into a bucket for Blackthorn, who had settled comfortably into a straw-filled stall, her head drooping drowsily, and then quickly checked the water buckets of the other animals. Apart from the shaggy pony Drud, there were a tall chestnut mare, three goats, a tabby cat, and a large number of fat hens with glossy feathers.

'It snows heavily here in winter,' Annis explained, 'and so it is easier to keep them all under the one roof and close to the house. The hens have had to learn not to lay their eggs under the horses' hooves, but otherwise they are all friends and get on well.'

She led the way through an internal doorway into a long fire-lit room. Overhead were carved wooden beams holding up an arched ceiling, and tall gothic windows looked out on to the garden all along one side. An immense scarred table ran down the centre of the room, decorated with fat, sweet-scented candles and vases of spring flowers. Around the fire at the far end were drawn some deep, shabby, cushioned chairs where Nina and the witch Ashelma were sitting, drinking tea and talking like old friends. Another cat lay sleeping on Ashelma's lap and by her feet was a large hairy mass which, on closer inspection, proved to be three dogs, one of them a huge deerhound and another a tiny white terrier, smaller than the cat. The other was some kind of mongrel, spotted and brindled and patched with black, and missing one leg. An owl sat hunched on one of the rafters, while a bandaged hare lay sleeping in a box by the wall.

Maisie, Edithe and Fèlice were sitting curled together on a couch, covered by a soft blanket. Only Edithe was still awake, and she had her head pillowed on her hand and her cup resting in her lap, looking as if she would slip off into sleep at any moment.

Annis led Rhiannon to the only remaining chair, made her sit and poured her a cup of some kind of pale, flower-scented hot tea. Rhiannon sipped at it suspiciously.

'Chamomile,' Annis said, smiling. 'It will help you sleep. Go on, drink it up. Ye all look worn out.' She sat down on the ground at Rhiannon's feet, fondling the spotted ear of the three-legged mongrel, and nodded at her encouragingly. Rhiannon drank obediently.

Ashelma turned to her and smiled. 'I was just telling the others about all the animals. They think I keep some kind o' menagerie but indeed it is no' my fault. Annis collects wounded animals but somehow, once they are healed, they do no' wish to leave. The only creature that is mine is Strixa the owl, and believe me, it is only because o' the deep love she bears me that she tolerates all the other animals. Particularly Serena the hare, our newest guest. We have to keep a close eye on Strixa in case she forgets herself and swoops on her for her supper.'

The owl hooted contemptuously and spat a hard pellet towards the sleeping hare, who at once sat up, her long ears twitching nervously.

'The orphanage is Annis's idea also,' Ashelma went on. 'I do no' ken quite how it happened, but we now have nine boys and one girl staying here with us. Most are from across the river. Nina, I do no' wish to alarm ye but ye must ken that it is dangerous for little boys over there.

All o' the murdered bairns were boys, most around five or six years auld. Quite a few o' our lads were brought here by their parents for safekeeping. I wish ye would reconsider crossing the Stormness. I ken ye wish to reach the capital in time for the royal wedding, but surely your wee laddie's safety is more important?'

Nina was white. 'That's no' fair, Ashelma,' she said angrily. 'Ye must ken Roden is the most important thing in the world to me. O' course I feel anxious with all these tales o' lads going missing and being found murdered. But we are only passing through. In two days we'll be gone. I think Iven and I can keep Roden safe till then. We shallna let him out o' our sight.'

'I'm sorry, I dinna mean to offend ye,' Ashelma said.

Nina took a deep breath. 'That's all right,' she said after a moment. 'The fact is, Ashelma, we did no' choose to come this way lightly. If our only concern was getting back to Lucescere in time for the wedding, we would've gone the usual way. We have plenty o' time, the wedding is no' until midsummer.'

Ashelma nodded, looking an enquiry.

'Nay, the truth is we were forced to change our plans. As we came through Barbreck-by-the-Bridge, we found the body o' a murdered Yeoman, one o' His Highness's most trusted and beloved men. He had been beaten and tortured cruelly afore he died. Both Iven and I kent him well. There will have to be an enquiry into his death. His Highness will be most anxious for us to make our report, and Connor's sister . . . she will want to ken all we can tell her.'

'How terrible!' Ashelma exclaimed. 'I'm sorry, I dinna realise.'

'How could ye?' Nina asked. 'Ye must see now that we shall save more than a week in the travelling coming this way. And I must admit it was in my mind to try to find

214

the Scrying Pool at the Tower o' Ravens and use it to speak to His Highness.'

'Och, nay, ye must no' do that,' Ashelma said. 'The tower is haunted, do ye no' ken? Few who go into the ruin come out again, and those that do are stark raving mad, they say. The ghosts there are malevolent and cruel, and hate the living.'

Nina frowned. 'I have heard that,' she admitted. 'I was hoping it was all an exaggeration, however.'

'Och, nay,' Ashelma said. 'It is all true. And only getting worse, it seems. The land that lies beneath the Tower o' Ravens has been an unhappy place since the Day o' Betrayal but recently it seems the whole valley is cursed. No-one is safe, no' man, woman or child. Particularly not young boys. Nina, in the twenty-five years since Lachlan the Winged won the throne thirty or more lads have gone missing.'

'Thirty or more boys? Vanished?'

'Murdered. Their bodies were found, but there's no sign o' what killed them and no witch or skeelie nearby to examine the bodies more closely. Do ye wonder that the mothers o' boys dare no' stay in Fetterness anymore? Those that canna leave bring their lads across the river to me, but I have no room for any more and besides, they shouldna be with me, they should be safe with their families. Indeed, I do no' ken what can be done.'

Nina shook her head, looking appalled.

'And that's not the worst o' it. Nina, the dead canna rest there. Graves both auld and new are found open and the corpses walk around in broad daylight, dragging their rotting flesh behind them, seeking to come home again.' She shuddered and wrapped her arms about her body in a vain attempt to warm herself. Rhiannon shuddered too.

'And we fear the evil shall find a way to cross the river and shadow all o' us here. Already we've found two graves robbed, or broken out o', though we have no' seen the dead they once contained walking about, thank Eà! And our town watchman has disappeared. We have his children here, Casey and Letty. He went out one night to investigate a noise and did no' come back. We never found his body. Since then the town reeve has put a gate across the bridge and locked it, and only those that come across in daylight and can satisfy him they have true business here are allowed through. Most are wanting work this side o' the river but we canna take any more, and so now they head south towards the ports. No-one has come knocking on the gate for close on two weeks now, and we've had no news since then.'

Nina looked shaken. 'I had no idea it was so bad!' she exclaimed. 'We heard rumours, o' course, but . . . surely the MacBrann should ken o' this?'

'We sent a message to Ravenscraig last market-day, but have heard naught from the laird. Who kens if he even heard it? When the carrier returned from Ravenscraig it was with the news o' Malcolm MacBrann's death and all the court was in mourning. Our messenger had no chance o' seeing the new laird. He passed the news on to a guard at the gate and came away. What more could he do? And I canna scry to the court sorceress, even though we are so close, for we are bounded by two rivers here and both are deep and fast. Just as it is too dangerous to try to cross in a boat, so it is too noisy for my thoughts to cross.' She sighed. 'So we do what we can to help the people o' Fetterness, those who have no' fled, and shelter their children and guard our own doors and hope the MacBrann will send his guards to investigate when he can. Happen ye will tell the Coven yourself, if . . . I mean, when . . .' Her voice trailed away unhappily.

'I will,' Nina said firmly. 'Now we must to bed, for my

lasses are asleep in their chairs and I myself am sick with weariness. I am sorry for your trouble. I will certainly tell the Keybearer and when she can, she will no doubt come herself to listen in the ruins and see what the ghosts have to say. For now, do no' fear for us. I ken the songs o' sorcery. We shall be safe.'

Ashelma nodded, looking tired and troubled. She stood up, gently tipping the cat in her lap to the floor, and helped Annis rouse Edithe, Maisie and Fèlice. Nina lifted Roden to her shoulder, his curly head nestling into her neck, and followed the witch and her apprentice up a broad flight of steps to a bedroom on the upper floor.

Rhiannon followed quietly behind, her head ringing with the witch's words. Satyricorns were afraid of nothing living, but had a profound horror of anything supernatural. They spilt a little blood every day in supplication of the dark fiends they believed dwelt in every shadow and cleft, and if they had failed in the hunt that day, they would open their own vein to make sure the sacrifice was made. Rhiannon had not spilt blood once since leaving her herd, having been determined to leave all of that part of her behind like a snake's cast-off skin. Her whole body was shuddering now, though, down to the very marrow of her bones. She swore she would slice open her vein this very night and make an offering to the dark walkers of the shadows.

There was only one bed in the room but it was enormous, standing on its own platform with a velvet canopy hanging overhead. Annis helped the other girls sleepily strip down to their shifts and climb up into the bed, which had been warmed by long-handled brass-lidded trays filled with hot coals. They were to sleep two at either end, with a trundle bed made up before the fire for Nina and Roden. Rhiannon allowed herself to be tucked up under the white counterpane, pretending to be almost asleep so Nina or Annis would not try to speak with her. The sheets were stiff and smelt of herbs, and the pillow was very soft. She was so very tired it took a strong effort of will not to succumb to the insistent weight of sleep on her limbs. She lay quietly, watching from under her eye-lashes as Nina tucked up her son, washed her face and hands, and shed her own clothes.

The jongleur did not climb into bed at once, though. She picked up the small bag she always wore tied to her belt and rummaged inside it, taking out a small stick and a few little cloth bags tied up with string. She opened one and threw what looked like dead leaves on the fire. Little green-hearted flames sprang up and curled away, scenting the smoke sweetly as they died.

She then drew her dagger from its sheath, a gesture that made Rhiannon's eyes open wider and her muscles tense. Nina hesitated and turned to look towards the bed, as if she had heard the subtle change in the rhythm of Rhiannon's breath. Rhiannon breathed slowly, pretending to sleep.

After a moment Nina knelt before the fire and gathered together a little handful of ashes from the hearth, spread-ing these around her in a circle. She shook salt from one of the bags and sprinkled it on top of the ashes, then sprin-kled water about her as well. Then, with her back straight, she swept the stick in her hand all round her, tracing the shape of the circle, then repeated the gesture with the dagger, muttering words under her breath. She knelt naked in the centre of the circle in silence for quite some time, unmindful of the cold, her unruly red-brown curls her only covering. At last she opened her eyes and rose up onto her knees, her wand in one hand, the knife in the other. Facing the fire, she chanted in a low, sweet voice:

'Goddess o' life, Goddess o' death,
Goddess o' all power that is the universe,
Shine your light o' white upon me and mine,
Shield all within this house from that which is evil,
Give to me peace and protection from harm,
By the power o' the fire, by the life in this blade,
By the power o' the earth, by the life in this wand,
By the powers o' air and water, cup and bowl,
By the powers o' stars and moons and cold distances,
Shield us, Eà o' the green blood, and keep us safe.'

She then reversed the movement of wand and dagger, and swept up the salted ashes with her hands, pouring them into a little muslin bag with some of the dead leaves. She tied the top of the bag with blue ribbon and then slipped the cord about the neck of her son, kissing him gently on the forehead. He murmured in his sleep and turned, tucking his hand under one round cheek. Shivering, Nina dragged her shift back on over her head and then crept into bed beside him, pulling the boy close against her body.

Rhiannon felt an odd prickling in her eyes, a hot ache in her throat. *It's the smoke*, she told herself irritably, and set herself to waiting till Nina was asleep. The jongleur seemed comforted by her little charade by the fire and soon slipped into sleep. Rhiannon waited patiently a while longer, listening to the sound of the wind in the branches outside, the sudden wash of rain. When she was sure all was quiet and still, she slipped out of the warm bed and went to kneel where Nina had knelt, in the half-obscured circle of ashes and salt. She gazed into the black and orange puzzle of glowing coals, unsheathed her dagger and slashed it quickly across her outstretched wrist. Blood welled up, thick and dark, and dripped from her wrist onto the flagstones.

Walk elsewhere, dark lords, Rhiannon said silently. *Drink this blood I freely offer you and seek not to take our souls. Walk elsewhere.*

Then she raised her wrist to her mouth and sucked at the cut, tasting the saltiness of her blood. She used her dagger to tear a strip of material from her shift, having nothing else to hand, and bound the wrist thoroughly. Almost immediately the white material was blotched with a growing stain. She shrugged, slipped the dagger back into the sheath strapped to her thigh, and crept back into the warmth of the bed, feeling faint and sick yet obscurely comforted, ready now to brave the falling shadows of sleep.

Next morning, the rain fell so heavily it was like a curtain of water drawn across the windows. Rhiannon had slept badly, her wrist throbbing and her dreams troubled. When she woke her eyes felt hot and scratchy as if filled with sand. It was so cold and grey outside, she could not find the will to throw off the counterpane and get up, and neither could the other girls. They all lay there drowsily, talking desultorily among themselves.

'Listen to that rain!' Fèlice murmured, and a while later moaned, 'Och, my legs! I swear I am chafed raw.'

'I wish I could lie abed all day,' Edithe muttered, 'but I guess there's no chance o' that. They'll make us ride all day in the rain, just to make sure we really ken what misery is.'

'Surely no'?' Maisie poked her head out from under her pillow, her plaits all tousled. 'I would like to bide here a wee. I was so sleepy last night I dinna see a thing.'

'Just a whole lot o' smelly animals and that disgusting owl that kept spitting things at me,' Edithe said crossly.

They all burrowed back under the counterpane and were quiet. Rhiannon cradled her wrist against her breast and, when no-one came to rouse them, allowed herself to hope they would not have to ride out that day. She closed her eyes, feeling herself slipping back into sleep.

The door crashed open.

'Rise and shine, slug-a-beds,' Nina called, holding the door open with her foot, a tray in her hands. 'It's long past dawn and time to be getting on our way.'

A chorus of groans met her.

'But it's *raining*,' Fèlice said.

'And I ache all over,' Edithe said.

'Surely we should wait for the rain to stop?' Maisie pleaded.

'Blackthorn does no' like the rain,' Rhiannon said firmly. 'And she is still tired. Niall said I must no' ride her too hard. He wouldna want me to ride her in the rain.'

'Is that so?' Nina said. 'So ye lassies think we should wait for the rain to stop?'

'Aye!' they all cried.

'What if it doesna stop for days?' Nina said. 'The Stormness is already swollen with the melting snows. If it rains like this for much longer it could break its banks and then we'd be marooned here for weeks and weeks.'

'Weeks?' Edithe cried in dismay.

'Aye,' Nina replied severely. 'Dinna ye notice how high it was last night? If ye wish to be witches, ye must learn to look about ye.'

'I was too tired to notice anything except how much my legs ached,' Fèlice said. 'No' to mention the chafing. I'm rubbed raw!'

Nina pushed the door shut behind her and put down the tray. They all sat up a little, their eyes brightening,

221

and one by one Nina passed them a steaming cup of tea. As they drank gratefully, Nina sat on the edge of their bed and regarded them with frowning black eyes, as dark as polished jet. Her face looked pale and haggard as if she too had been troubled by nightmares.

Refreshed by her tea, Fèlice said with her most winning smile, 'We really are tired. We're no' used to riding so far every day. Please, could we no' rest today, and wait for the rain to stop? I'm sure Ashelma willna mind.'

'Ye do look rather white, the lot o' ye. Especially ye, Rhiannon. Are ye no' feeling well? I would no' like any o' ye to take a chill.'

Edithe immediately coughed, and laid her hand on her chest. 'I am feeling rather unwell.'

Nina cast her a stern glance but turned back to Rhiannon, first laying her hand on Rhiannon's forehead and then lifting her wrist. Rhiannon flinched and Nina looked down, her eyes at once widening in horror. 'Rhiannon, what have ye done to yourself! Ye've cut yourself – ye're bleeding!'

The makeshift bandage was heavily stained and so was the sheet where Rhiannon had slept. Nina held Rhiannon's wrist in her cool fingers and stared into her eyes with a look as sharp and penetrating as a sword.

'What did ye cut yourself on?'

'My dagger.'

'How?'

'I cut.' She demonstrated with one swift movement.

'Ye cut yourself on purpose?'

Rhiannon nodded, not dropping her gaze. There was a long silence. Rhiannon was conscious of the other girls shrinking back.

'Why?' Nina's voice was neutral.

'To make peace with the dark walkers.'

'Ye cut yourself to make peace with ... the dark walkers? What – or who – are they?'

Rhiannon shrugged, unable to hold Nina's gaze any longer. Not knowing how to describe what she meant, she used the word she had heard so often in the last few days. 'Ghosts.'

Nina let go of her wrist. It was smarting cruelly, and Rhiannon cradled it in her other hand. Her cheeks felt hot and she knew she was perilously close to tears. She could not look at Nina or any of the other girls.

'Did ye bleed much?'

Rhiannon nodded.

Nina stood up. 'Stay in bed, Rhiannon. I will make ye a blood-strengthening tea. We shall no' ride anywhere today. It really is no' the weather for riding out. Ye other girls can get up or stay in bed as ye please. I should tell you though that I willna allow Annis to be bringing up trays to ye, so if ye wish to eat, get up, get dressed and come on down. I'll make an exception for ye, though, Rhiannon. Stay in bed and rest.'

Rhiannon refused to be singled out, however. She got up when the other girls did, though she felt a wave of dizziness wash over her, and washed and dressed herself and went downstairs with the others, holding on to the banister tightly. Nina made no comment at the sight of her, though her frown deepened.

The long room was raucous with the games and fights of ten small children, most of them no more than six years old. Roden was in the midst of it, shrieking with laughter, while Lulu was leaping about like a mad thing, having stolen the only girl's rag doll. The little girl was sobbing despairingly and trying to snatch it back, her younger brother enthusiastically helping. The three dogs were barking, and a white and black cat was hissing and spitting from the mantelpiece. Strixa the owl huddled on one of the rafters, occasionally spitting out a hard pellet at one of the children. Her aim was excellent.

Annis had a bowl of porridge in one hand and a dripping ladle in the other, and was trying to make herself heard above the racket, while Lulu and the little boy dodged round her. The arak was gibbering in rage, the rag doll cradled close to her breast. When the other boys joined in the chase, she suddenly jumped up onto the table, sending a jug of milk flying, and leapt up to catch hold of the iron-wrought chandelier, swinging from side to side till she was high enough to leap up into the rafters. There she crouched, rocking the doll and humming a tuneless lullaby.

'Oh, dear,' Nina said. 'I'm so sorry. Lulu! Naughty girl! Give back the dolly right now.'

The arak shook her head, mumbling something in her own guttural language.

'Lulu, I am ashamed o' ye. We are guests in this house. Come down now and give back the doll to the wee lassie.'

Lulu gave a sorrowful moan and very slowly and sadly swung down, hanging from her tail before dropping lithely onto all fours. She raised the doll and kissed its painted face and then offered it back to the little girl. The girl snatched it and cuddled it close, glaring at the hairy little creature, who was looking very shamefaced.

'Good girl,' Nina said. 'Never mind. I'll make ye a dolly o' your own if ye'd like one.'

Lulu immediately danced in joy, shrieking in approval.

'I am sorry,' Nina said. 'Lulu forgets her manners sometimes.'

'No' to worry,' Annis said, looking rather harassed as three of the boys raced past her, almost knocking her over. 'Would ye prefer to have your breakfast in the kitchen? Mealtimes are rather wild here, I'm afraid.'

'I think we would indeed,' Nina answered. 'That is, if ye young ladies do no' think it beneath ye?'

'No' at all,' Edithe said sweetly. 'Please, lead the way.'

'Thank ye, then, Annis, that would be grand,' Nina said. 'Roden! Settle down! Poor Annis should no' have to be worrying about ye as well as all the others. Sit down and eat your breakfast quietly, there's a good lad.'

Roden reluctantly gave up the chase and came to sit at the table, dragging Lulu with him, and Nina and the older girls thankfully made their escape.

The kitchen was a haven of peace and warmth. A skinny old man with doleful dark eyes and a very long straggly grey beard meandered back and forth, getting them bowls, stirring various pots on the squat little stove and occasionally shovelling in another spade of coal. A grey cat was sleeping on one of the kitchen chairs, and in a box by the fire were seven adorable yellow ducklings, all squawking and trying to climb out over each other's backs.

Breakfast was a simple affair – porridge ladled out into bowls, tubs of honey and jugs of goat's milk, and a big brown pot of tea. Rhiannon felt much better after she had eaten her second bowl of honey-drenched porridge, and Nina stopped regarding her with a crease between her brows. Rhiannon was just finishing her third cup of tea when the door opened and Annis came in, plumper and rosier than ever.

'Morning, everyone,' she sang out. 'I hope ye've all had a more peaceful breakfast than I did!'

'I'm sure we did. I hope ye do no' mind us abandoning ye,' Nina said.

'No, no, o' course no'. I kent Morogh would look after ye. It's bad enough that I have to suffer the bairns' commotion without inflicting it upon ye as well. I warn ye, though, it's only going to get worse. They're planning a re-enactment o' the Battle o' Bonnyblair, and are about to descend on the kitchen in search o' pots and pans to make armour. Ashelma is in the tower, if ye would like to go through and visit her there? She is no' teaching today so she's free, for the morning at least.'

'Thanks, we would like that,' Nina said, standing up.

They followed Annis down a corridor to a large, arched doorway that led through into the tower. Built of stone, the tower was three storeys high, with a staircase that wound up around the inner wall. On the ground floor was the witch's study and reception room, with another iron-bound door out into the garden and four tall arched windows that could be opened to let in fresh air and sunshine. There was a large desk littered with scrolls and calendars and writing implements, a few straight-backed chairs and, by the fire, two soft-cushioned, deep-seated chairs drawn close together, each with a little wooden table just large enough for a cup or goblet.

Bookshelves had been made to fit the curved walls of the room, and these were filled with spell-books and scrolls and maps, jars of dried herbs and powders and polished stones, bottles of precious oils and distillations, skulls and bones and sticks and lumps of crystals, and candles of all sizes and colours. The room smelt faintly of incense and dried herbs.

Ashelma was sitting at her desk, writing, but she rose with a smile as Nina and the four girls came in. She let them browse among the shelves for a while, exclaiming and asking questions. Edithe and Maisie were particularly fascinated, the first becoming absorbed in a leather-bound book of spells, the second busying herself looking through the jars of herbs and medicines.

After a while, Ashelma took them upstairs to show them the other two floors. The middle storey was a workroom and storeroom, with all the equipment necessary to grind powders, distill potions and prepare spells. The girls browsed around for a while, then followed Ashelma as she led them up the staircase to the upper level.

They all exclaimed in surprise. The walls and domed roof of the tower were made entirely of clear glass, supported by slender spans of steel, so that they could see for miles in every direction, including up into the black, roiling clouds of the storm. On the floor a mosaic of coloured tiles and thin strips of silver metal traced out the shape of a five-sided star set within a circle. The four directions were each marked upon the perimeter of the circle with arcane symbols in yellow, red, blue and green, and set at each of these symbols was a twisted wooden wand made of willow, a ceremonial dagger made of iron and moonstones, a silver chalice, and a beautifully made clay bowl inscribed with a six-sided star and filled with charred ashes.

'This is extraordinary!' Nina cried. 'It really is a miniature o' one o' the great towers. How on earth could Ardarchy afford such a well-set-up witch's tower?'

Ashelma smiled. 'I won a grant from the Coven,' she answered. 'I studied at the Tower o' Two Moons, ye ken, and heard about the grants while I was there. It's a new initiative o' the Keybearer, to encourage witches to go out into the countryside and help remote towns and villages and teach them the ways o' the Coven. Ardarchy has no' had its own witch since before the Day o' Betrayal so I've had a great deal to do since I came here. Certainly the townsfolk are proud o' their tower and they profited from the building o' it, because a condition o' the grant is that it must be used on local craftsmen and products. Only the glass had to be shipped in, o' course, which was enormously difficult and expensive, but worth it, I think.'

'Oh, do ye think I could apply for a grant like that?' Maisie said with shining eyes and clasped hands. 'My village is very poor and we have no-one to teach the children or do the rituals, or even help the women in their labour. My mother used to do what she could, but she got sick with the fever and my grandfather kens naught about healing, only about weather magic and blessing the crops, and so she died . . . oh, if I got a grant, I could go back and build a tower like this for us. It would mean so much to all the villages in the valley.'

'O' course ye could, that's what the grants are for,' Ashelma said. 'Most o' the common folk canna be travelling to the High Towers for help in times o' trouble, and so the Keybearer hopes that one day every town or region will have its own tower, and everyone will be taught to read and write, and have access to healers, and celebrate the Sabbats as they should be celebrated. It has made all the difference to Ardarchy. I've started a village school, and I sit on the town council, and I bless the crops, and organise the parades and festivals, and often I mediate between the villagers so that the reeve does not have to be called in.'

'And ye've started an orphanage and a hospital for injured animals,' Nina said with a smile.

Ashelma smiled back ruefully. 'A witch for all seasons, that's what I am!'

CROSSING THE STORMNESS

The storm raged so violently the next day that even Nina had to admit it would be dangerous to ride out. Hail rattled against the windows, and the trees swayed and bent like sword-fighters in a duel.

Iven and the boys braved the storm to come and join them, and arrived windblown, mud-splattered, and eager to get out of the pelting rain. Ashelma welcomed them warmly, helping them find dry clothes to put on, and advising them strongly against riding on.

'Once a storm like this sets in, it'll take a day or two for it to blow itself out,' she said. 'Stay and rest up, and set out again once it's blown over.'

Nina looked at the streaming windows and thanked her with a sigh.

They were all glad to have a respite from riding, even Lewen, who was used to spending hours of every day in the saddle. They sat in front of the fire, playing cards or dice games, cleaning their boots or, in Landon's case, writing in his dog-eared, ink-splattered notebook.

'Growing among trees o' blossom white, her tower shines out with blessed light . . .' he murmured to himself.

The girls all had a long soak in a hot bath, and helped wash and comb each other's hair. Their clothes were badly travel-stained, and so they took the opportunity to do their laundry, though Maisie had to show them how to use the boiler and wringer. Nina gave them all some more salve for their chafed thighs and bound up Rhiannon's wrist for her with fresh bandages.

The storm was fiercer than ever by nightfall, and so Ashelma made up pallets for the boys before the fire. They had a riotous meal with the orphans, who were bursting with energy after a day spent indoors, and went early to bed, hoping for a clear dawn.

Rhiannon had determined to undo her bandage and open her vein again that night, once all the others were asleep, but in the end this was not necessary, for Nina brought her a half-dead mouse one of the cats had caught. She gave the mouse to Rhiannon with a very grave face but said not a word, and Rhiannon was able to slit the mouse's throat and spill its blood without causing any commotion.

The next day was even wetter and wilder, and once again they delayed their riding out. Like the apprentices, Iven would have been quite content to lie around and read, or play with the orphans, or strum his guitar, eating and drinking to his heart's content, while the rain streamed down against the windows. Nina, however, was clearly anxious. She went out several times to check the height of the river, coming back drenched to the skin, shivering with cold and frowning.

The sorceress decided to put their enforced rest to good use, and so the apprentices had to spend the morning in the study and practice of witchcraft. Rhiannon found these lessons fascinating, though it made all the hair on her arms rise to watch the apprentices lift a wooden ball and set it spinning in midair without touching it.

Annis was set to listen to the students stumbling through the seven languages of birds and beasts, a skill Nina apparently thought they were all very weak in, then she and Lewen spent an hour brushing up their knowledge in mathematics and alchemy, subjects they obviously detested.

Discovering Rhiannon could not read or write, Ashelma undertook to teach her, and soon Rhiannon's eyes and head and wrist were aching, the witch being a hard taskmistress. If it had not been for Edithe's raised eyebrow, and Cameron's snigger, half-hidden behind his hand, she would have rebelled but, having set her will to prove them wrong, Rhiannon learnt surprisingly fast. By the end of the day she could recognise her own name and Lewen's, as well as a few key words like bread, horse, witch and school. This gave her immense satisfaction, only equalled by her triumph over Cameron in the wrestling ring after lunch.

A morning spent in study had made all the apprentices very cross and quarrelsome, and so Iven had decided they needed some exercise. He pushed the table in the dining room to one side and asked the apprentices to demonstrate *ahdayeh* to Rhiannon. Although primarily used by the Coven as a form of meditation through movement, *ahdayeh* was also a system of hand-to-hand combat, and Iven set the students to pitting their skills against each other. After watching a few rounds, Rhiannon was eager indeed to test her own fighting skills. It took her only a few seconds to throw Cameron flat on his back.

He was furious and sprang up at once, challenging her again. Three times she threw him down, until he was white-faced and dangerous with rage. Iven separated them then, and challenged her himself, and Rhiannon took great enjoyment in laying him flat on the carpet as well. After that the competition began in earnest. Rhiannon found the only one she could not throw down with ease was Lewen, something which gave her a degree of secret pleasure. They struggled together for close on half an hour, hot and panting, half-angry, half-laughing, before Iven at last stopped them and declared his intention to teach them all how to dance instead.

It took Rhiannon only a minute to decide dancing was not for her, primarily because she was taller than most of the other boys and had absolutely no sense of rhythm, having never heard music before she met the jongleurs. She had no desire to sit and watch Fèlice flirting and laughing with Lewen as he spun her round the room, and so as soon as the music stopped and everyone changed partners, she stepped forward and laid her hand on his sleeve, asking him in a low voice if he minded if she had a look at his longbow.

Rhiannon had been fascinated by Lewen's bow from the moment she had seen him strapping it to his pommel. It was the tallest bow she had ever seen, almost a foot longer than hers. The arrows he whittled for himself were also longer than usual, and she had longed for a chance to try her hand at them. Her determination was only piqued by Lewen's surprised laugh and shake of his head.

'Ye willna be able to draw my bow,' Lewen said. 'Few can, ye ken. Ye need to be very strong.'

'Me strong,' Rhiannon said indignantly.

'No' that strong,' he answered.

'Lewen's a famous longbowman, like his father,' Iven said, lifting his fingers from the strings of his guitar so he could join the conversation. 'It wouldna be a fair contest, Rhiannon.'

'Iven!' Edithe protested, as she and Cameron came to a halt nearby. 'Play on! We want to dance.'

Rhiannon lifted her chin. 'Me shoot ogres afore, bet Lewen hasna!'

'Well, no, I haven't,' Lewen admitted, 'but it still wouldna be a fair contest.'

'Oh, ungallant,' Rafferty jeered, taking his hand from Fèlice's waist so he could join the conversation. 'I'd put my money on Rhiannon any day.'

'Rafferty!' Fèlice cried. 'Do ye no' want to dance with me? Iven, please, will ye no' play on?'

Iven did not hear her, turning to Rafferty and demanding whether he had ever seen Lewen shoot. 'For I swear his arrows can fly round corners. Ye'd lose your money.'

'I'm a fair shot too,' Cameron said belligerently, eager to overcome his humiliation in the wrestling ring. 'I bet I can outshoot any lass, no matter how much o' a tomboy she is.'

'Let's set up a target,' Rafferty said eagerly. 'I wouldna mind trying my hand at Lewen's bow too. It's mighty tall.'

'Iven!' Fèlice wailed.

'I'll play for you, lassies,' Nina said, looking over from the couch by the fire, where she was busy writing in a leather-bound book. 'Ye'll never drag Iven away from a shooting contest.'

'But we need the boys to dance with,' Edithe said waspishly, glaring at Rhiannon.

'If ye can persuade them to keep on dancing with ye, I'll be happy to play for ye,' Nina said. 'But, indeed, Edithe, I doubt they'll pay ye any heed.'

Nina proved to have the truth of it. The boys hardly heard the girls' entreaties, being busy looking for something to make a target out of, and entreating Lewen to go and get his bow so they could all try their strength and skill. Lewen agreed with good humour, and he and Rhiannon went to get their bows and arrows out of the stables, where they were stored with the rest of their luggage. Iven, Cameron and Rafferty busied themselves rigging up a board at the far end of the room, drawing rough concentric circles on it with chalk. Edithe went to sit down next to Nina with a sour expression on her face, but Fèlice joined the others, asking questions with great animation and much laughter. Even shy Maisie grew interested, and found the courage to ask Lewen, when he returned with his bow and quiver slung over his shoulder, why his arrows were so much longer than usual and why he fletched them with green.

'My arrows are longer because my bow is longer,' he explained with a smile, 'and I fletch them with feathers plucked from my mother's rooster's tail. They are very even and strong, see?'

To Rhiannon's chagrin, she did indeed find it impossible to bend Lewen's bow. Her only consolation was that none of the other apprentices could either, not even Cameron, who almost burst a vein trying. Lewen grinned and obligingly gave them a demonstration of his bow's range and power. He was a superlative archer. No matter where he stood in the long hall, he was able to send arrow after arrow right into the heart of the target. He even, at Iven's laughing prompt, shot an arrow from outside the room, its flight path curving round the door-frame and flying straight to the target, splitting one of Rhiannon's arrows right down the middle.

'That's impossible,' Rafferty exclaimed in awe.

'It's witchcraft,' Cameron said, aggrieved. 'It shouldna be allowed.'

'I told ye he could shoot round corners,' Iven grinned.

'It's part o' my Talent,' Lewen said apologetically. 'Anything I make from wood with my own hands is sort o' . . . magicked. I did try to warn ye.'

'Shoot with my bow and arrows then,' Rhiannon cried. 'We'll see how good ye are with a bow and arrows ye havena magicked.'

'Magicked really is no' a word,' Fèlice pointed out apologetically, but they were all too excited to listen to her.

'It willna make any difference,' Iven said. 'I bet ye a whole gold crown Lewen still beats ye hands down.'

'I'm no' betting,' Cameron said sulkily. 'He's got an unfair advantage.'

'I'm no' betting either but only because I havena any gold crowns,' Rhiannon said, her cheeks flushed and her eyes bright. 'I'll back myself against ye, though, Cameron, any day. I bet ye three coppers that I can split your arrow down the centre just like Lewen did mine.'

'All right then,' Cameron cried, seizing her bow. 'You're on.'

'Deal?'

'Deal!'

Rhiannon spat on her hand and held it out and, his ears crimson, Cameron seized it and shook it angrily.

He took her bow, fitted an arrow to it and bent the bow, making a visible effort to calm his temper before firing a very neat shot into the centre of the target. Rhiannon applauded him along with the others, but then, with extraordinary swiftness, lifted and fired her bow in a single smooth movement. The arrow Cameron had shot fell apart, split neatly in two.

'Bravo!' Rafferty shouted. 'Beautiful shooting.'

'Go, lassie!' Fèlice cried. 'Ye show those cocky lads.'

Edithe said to Nina, who was watching the competition with as much interest as anyone else, 'Do ye no' find her forward behaviour very unbecoming? It is so very unladylike, don't ye agree?'

Nina cast her an irritated look. 'No, no' really. She is a very accomplished archer, why should she no' take as much pride in that as the lads do? Really, Edithe, witches do no' much care for archaic social proprieties. If ye wish to be a sorceress, ye must try to put aside such silly prejudices.'

Edithe flushed crimson and pursed her lips tightly.

Only Iven did not join in the general praise, standing back, his brows drawn over his eyes in a most uncharacteristic frown. He looked from the arrow, embedded deep in the centre of the target, back at Rhiannon with a sudden hard glare of suspicion.

'Where did ye learn to shoot, Rhiannon?' he asked. 'Longbows are no' usual among your people, are they?'

Rhiannon's bright colour faded. 'The bow was my father's,' she answered gruffly.

'And he taught ye to shoot so well?'

'My father dead. Me taught myself.' As usual in times of emotional stress, her newly acquired language skills deserted her.

'Ye taught yourself very well,' he said, still staring at her with those hard, angry eyes.

'Thank ye,' she said, her eyes flashing up to meet his, then dropping again. 'I did have help, to begin with. There was a man who showed me . . .' Her words faltered away.

'I guess the fact ye had to teach yourself shows that I was right, and bows and arrows are no' common among those o' your kind?'

'What kind is that?' Edithe asked Nina, her eyebrows raised. Nina motioned her to silence, looking distressed.

'No, no' common,' Rhiannon answered after a moment.

'Any other longbows in your herd apart from yours?'

'Herd?' Cameron asked derisively.

Rhiannon shrugged, turning away to gather up her quiver of arrows. 'A few, I suppose. I've never really noticed.'

Iven clearly did not believe her, but the restive curiosity on the other apprentices' faces seemed to check any other questions he wished to ask her. He picked up his guitar and went out of the room, and after a moment Nina rose and went after him.

Everyone left behind felt confused and dismayed, not understanding why Iven had been so curt and angry. Rhiannon finished packing away her arrows, and said to Cameron, 'Do no' forget ye owe me three coppers.'

He scowled and fished in his pocket, saying sharply, 'So where do ye come from, Rhiannon? What did Iven mean, calling your folk a "herd"?'

'I'm sure he was just speaking metaphorically,' Edithe said sweetly.

Rhiannon flashed her an angry look, hearing the barb beneath the honeyed tone even if she did not understand the figure of speech.

'Are ye o' faery kind, Rhiannon?' Fèlice asked with lively curiosity. 'A Khan'cohban or something, like the Banrìgh?'

'My mother was a horned one,' Rhiannon answered shortly, not looking at anyone.

There was a surprised murmur.

'A satyricorn, does she mean?' Cameron demanded.

Edithe said, 'Well, that explains a lot!'

'Shouldn't ye have horns?' Rafferty asked.

Cameron thrust his coins back into his pocket, saying

angrily, 'Ye should've told us earlier, it was an unfair contest! I'm no' paying ye anything.'

Lewen had been quietly packing up his own quiver of arrows, but now he looked up and said, 'What difference does it make if Rhiannon is half-satyricorn? Iven just told ye a longbow is an unusual weapon among the satyricorns. It takes naught away from Rhiannon's success to ken her background, in fact, it makes it even more remarkable. Ye owe her those three coppers, Cameron.'

'It wasna a fair contest,' he said sulkily.

'Yes, it was,' Fèlice said. 'Ye always kent Rhiannon was tall and strong, Cameron, ye only have to look at her to ken that.'

'That's true,' Landon said. 'It would be dishonourable to refuse to pay.' He spoke with such clear certainty that Cameron was abashed and thrust his hand into his pocket to retrieve the coins and throw them at her. Rhiannon caught them out of the air, again startling them with the speed of her response. Lewen looked at Landon and gave him his slow, warm smile, which the young poet returned shyly.

Maisie was looking at Rhiannon with frightened eyes, and Edithe looked as if she had just found something foul on the bottom of her shoe. Rhiannon's face had settled back into its sulky lines. She did not look at any of them but went out of the room, her back very straight.

'Ye will find folk o' all kinds at the Theurgia,' Lewen said in a voice made gruff with anger. 'Often those born o' mingled human and faery blood have the most extraordinary powers o' all. Like the Keybearer and the Banrìgh who, as Fèlice said, are half-Khan'cohban. Or the Banprionnsa Bronwen, whose mother was half-Fairgean. There is a Celestine in my class, and a corrigan, and a girl who is a tree-shifter, like my own mother. Ye will have to get used to seeing faery folk about at the Tower o' Two Moons.'

'Aye, but a *satyricorn*,' Edithe said. 'No wonder she is so uncouth.'

'Ye would be uncouth too if ye had been raised by satyricorns,' Lewen said angrily. 'We canna help our birth or our upbringing, but we can help the kind o' people we are now.'

Edithe raised her eyebrows, smiled coldly, and went to sit down by the fire. After a moment or two, Cameron went to join her, saying, 'Well, no wonder she's such a lanky longlegs. A satyricorn!'

'I wonder she was allowed to travel with us,' Edithe said. 'I hope she is no' dangerous.'

'She bloody well is,' Cameron said moodily. 'Did ye see the way she snatched those coins out o' the air?'

Maisie was asking Fèlice much the same thing, and the pretty brunette was saying doubtfully, 'No, I'm sure Nina and Iven would no' open us to any real risk. I'm sure she's a *tame* satyricorn.'

Lewen gritted his teeth together, and went in search of Rhiannon. As he expected, she had sought comfort with her flying mare. She looked up as he came in, and said sullenly, 'What ye want?'

'Naught,' he answered. 'I thought I'd come and visit Argent. I wish I could take him out for a gallop. It's always such a bore, being shut up inside four walls.'

Her expression softened. 'Aye, I wish too.'

'Happen it'll clear tomorrow and we can ride out again.'

'Happen so.'

He had got out his currying brushes and was grooming the grey stallion, which half-shut its great dark eyes in bliss. He said no more, and after a moment Rhiannon got out her grooming kit and began to pet and pamper her mare too, although Blackthorn's coat already shone like silk. They worked in companionable silence for some time, and Lewen was pleased to see Rhiannon's face lose its hard, angry lines. By the time they went back into the house for supper, she had regained her composure, though not the bright, open, merry face she had worn during the archery contest, an expression Lewen would very much like to see again.

As they went towards the hall, they saw Iven was waiting for them in the corridor. Rhiannon's step slowed. The jongleur stepped forward to meet them, saying, 'Rhiannon, I just . . . I need to ken. Was it ye who shot Connor down?'

She looked straight into his face and said angrily, 'Nay.'

'Who was it, Rhiannon? Can ye tell me? It was one o' your herd, wasna it?'

'I do no' ken who,' she answered. 'I was no' there.'

'But ye have his clothes, his daggers,' Iven said.

'I won them gambling,' she said.

His face relaxed. 'That'd be right! I should've guessed.'

She jerked her head and went to move past him. He detained her with one hand on her arm. 'I'm sorry, I did no' mean to imply I suspected ye o' murder. I just . . . I really did need to ken, Rhiannon.'

She nodded, removed his hand from her arm and went into the long hall, her head held high, her face set and expressionless.

Iven looked at Lewen and shrugged, his hands held wide. 'I had to ask her.'

Lewen nodded. 'I did too.'

'I'm glad it was no' her.'

'So am I.'

'Do ye think she's offended?'

'Wouldn't ye be?'

'I suppose so,' Iven said unhappily.

'Never mind,' Lewen said. 'It canna be helped. Ye had to ken. Ye could no' ride with her for weeks suspecting her o' murder. Better to get it out in the open.'

'I suppose so,' Iven said again. 'Nina thinks I'm hasty and indiscreet. Happen I am a blabbermouth after all.' He hesitated. 'How are the other bairns? Kenning she's a satyricorn, I mean.'

'It is naught to be ashamed o',' Lewen said stiffly. 'The satyricorns have shown themselves loyal and true to the Crown, just like any other faery.'

'Aye, but . . .' Iven halted himself mid-sentence, tugging at his forked beard with both hands. 'Auld prejudices die hard,' he said then, half to himself.

Lewen nodded.

Iven flung an arm about his shoulder. 'Let us go and eat,' he said. 'At least we're enjoying some variety to our diet staying here with Ashelma. That man o' hers is a very good cook.'

Together they went in to the long hall, where the dining table was back in its usual place and the babble of high, childish voices filled any awkward silences. Roden and Lulu had spent the afternoon with the orphans and seemed to have made lifelong friends with the two eldest boys. One of them had fashioned himself a slingshot and was amusing himself shooting Annis in the bottom with paper pellets, and pretending it was Strixa the owl, much to the other children's amusement.

Nina had drawn Rhiannon down to sit with her and was doing her best to banish the stiff wariness of her face. Rhiannon would not be coaxed, however, and ate her meal in unbroken silence, sat through the usual evening games and storytelling in unbroken silence, and went to bed in the same cold unfriendly silence. It was only when Nina brought her another half-dead mouse to sacrifice that her expression relaxed. She took the warm, limp body and said 'Thank ye.'

'I do no' like to see small creatures being killed,' Nina said. 'It is against everything the Coven believes in. But I ken it is the nature o' the cat and the owl to hunt and kill, and I ken ye do so, no' from some kind o' cruelty, but because ye truly believe ye are keeping yourself safe by doing so.'

'Not just me,' Rhiannon said. 'Us all.'

'Then I thank ye,' Nina said. 'I hope I can one day teach ye other ways to keep yourself safe from the dark forces o' this world.'

Rhiannon gazed at her for a long moment, then suddenly smiled, a swift, small, shy, surprising smile.

'Happen so,' she answered.

Overnight the steady thrum of the rain slowed to a mere pitter-patter, and by dawn it had stopped altogether. Nina roused them all early and bade them dress for riding, and come down for a quick hot meal, for she wanted them on the road by first light. By the time it was bright enough to see the road without the need for lanterns, the carthorses were harnessed to the caravans and they were making their goodbyes to Ashelma and Annis, who came out in the cold, sharp wind in their dressing-gowns.

'Have a care for yourselves,' Ashelma said. 'I hope ye have a swift, safe journey.'

'So do I,' Nina replied with her quick smile. 'Thank ye so much for putting us all up. I'm sorry it was for so long.'

'It was our pleasure, wasn't it, Annis? We rarely get to enjoy the company o' other witches. I hope ye will come and visit us again.'

'We'd love to. Until then, goodbye!'

'Goodbye! Thank ye!' the others all called and then, wincing as their boots sank deep into the mud, mounted up and rode away down the drive, the gates opening and shutting behind them of their own accord.

The lane from Ashelma's house was hock-deep in muddy brown water, and one of the caravans was bogged almost immediately. By the time they had heaved it free, they were all wet and filthy and out of temper, and they were not even out of sight of the witch's tower. They rode on, hunched in their cloaks, more than a little perturbed at the sight of the river, brown and foamy as gushing ale, and carrying along great broken branches at immense speed.

They came to the crossroads and paused for a moment, looking back along the road to Ardarchy. Warm golden light glowed in the windows, and wood-smoke rose from the chimneys, torn into fragrant rags by the wind. Some children were playing with hoops in the street, and a smell of fresh bread came from the bakery. A wagon was drawn up in front of the inn, with three men rolling big barrels down a ramp and manhandling them in through the huge door. Four old men sat on the bench in front, puffing on their pipes, while further down the street two women stood gossiping, laden baskets on their arms, as a little girl dressed in a red hooded coat jumped gleefully in the puddles, unnoticed.

They glanced the other way. Only a few feet away the stone humpbacked bridge crossed the Stormness River. A high, stout gate had been fastened across it, locked tight with heavy chains and an enormous padlock. The river flung itself against the bridge angrily, throwing up gouts of brown foam. Beyond was a desolate landscape, grim and drear and empty of all life. The mountains loomed over it, purple-hued and draped with thick cloud. The road wound down away from the river, narrow and rutted and stony, running with water like a stream-bed.

'Could we no' stay a few more days in Ardarchy?' Fèlice pleaded. 'Indeed, it looks like rain again.'

Nina nodded. 'Aye, I ken. But we've been delayed far too long already. Come on, my bairns. A little rain willna hurt ye. Two more days on the road and we'll be past the Tower o' Ravens and back in the lowlands, where the weather is fairer.'

'What about the ghosts?' Cameron said sullenly.

'Most ghosts are only memories,' Nina said gently. 'When a place has seen great sorrow or great joy, often the emotion soaks down into the very stones and leaves a shadow of itself behind – and those that have the gift o' clear-seeing or clear-hearing can pick up fragments o' those memories. Some people see ghosts everywhere, and must learn to close their mind's eye to them. The Tower o' Ravens is built on a place o' power, like all the witches' towers, and it has seen much horror and bloodshed. Because o' where it is built, the memories o' those killed are magnified and so even those with very little talent can sense or even see the ghosts that remain. It can be awful, I will admit that, particularly if ye are very sensitive to such things. Ye feel as if ye are there, watching the battle again, hearing the shrieks o' the dying. But it is only a memory.'

There was a short silence, everyone staring across the river at the barren windswept moors beyond.

'Ye said *most* ghosts are only memories,' Fèlice said waveringly. 'What about the others?'

Nina hesitated. 'It is true that sometimes a soul refuses to go on and be reborn, but clings to its life here, for whatever reason – hatred, grief, horror, even a thirst for life that canna be quenched. These ghosts are more than just memories o' a soul, they are the soul itself. They are trapped between worlds, unable to go on because they canna forget their lives here. That is tragic indeed, for then the circle o' life and death is broken and all is unbalanced. A trapped soul can be dangerous, I canna deny it. Even those that are no' malevolent but only racked with grief or horror can cause harm, for they press upon our nerves, they swamp our souls with their own negative energy, and can drive those already prone to melancholy to deep depression or madness.'

'What about the ones that *are* malevolent?' Edithe asked, her voice shrill.

Nina sighed. 'Few ghosts have the strength to actually harm ye, Edithe. They have no hands to hold a sword, they have no feet to kick or teeth to bite. Sometimes, if their will is strong enough, they can cause objects to move, just as a witch can, but just clinging to this world saps their strength and their will and so it is rare, I promise ye. Their only weapons are fear and horror. If ye do no' fear them, they canna drive ye to madness or infect ye with their misery. Stay close, stay strong, and naught can happen to harm ye.'

The only sound was the wind rattling the branches, the angry roar of the river and the occasional clink of metal as one of the horses shook its mane or stamped its foot. Then Edithe sighed and said facetiously, 'Very reassuring, thank ye, Nina.'

'My pleasure,' the witch answered, not smiling, and shook the reins so her patient horse leant into the weight of the caravan and began to draw it forwards once more.

The town reeve reluctantly unlocked the barricade for them, after shaking his head and telling them sternly it was his duty to warn them that the road that passed the ruined Tower of Ravens was not safe and he hereby abjured all responsibility for them. Nina thanked him with a strained smile, then one by one they crossed the bridge, the horses baulking at first, then shying nervously at the flying spray and the thud of storm-wrack sweeping against the pylons. The reeve locked the gate behind them.

It began to rain again half an hour later. It came down in long slanting lines, beating at their backs. There was nowhere to shelter and so they rode on, enduring in silence. The clouds were so dark and heavy it was like dusk, and all they could see ahead of them were the long, empty, winding road and the closing ranks of steep, bare mountains. They passed a ruined croft, its windows gaping like blinded eyes, its roof fallen in. A little further on they passed a broken fence, the fallen slats covered in brambles. The road was treacherous with mud and rocks, and the horses had to pick their way carefully, sometimes splashing into puddles so deep the water was up to their withers.

The riders had all unconsciously drawn together close behind the caravans, the hoods of their cloaks drawn over their heads. Rain spat in their eyes, and trickled down their necks.

'I do no' like this place,' Landon said nervously.

'It doesna inspire ye to poetry?' Cameron jeered, though it was clear he was edgy too from the way he turned his face from side to side, scanning the misty horizon, his hands fidgeting with the reins.

'I do no' like it either,' Fèlice said. 'I wish we had no' come this way.'

Blackthorn pranced uneasily, tossing her head and refusing to go forwards. Rhiannon leant forward to pat her neck. 'What is it?' she murmured.

All the horses had to be urged onwards, and Rafferty had to tug hard on the lead rein before Maisie's fat little pony would submit to following him. Ahead was another abandoned croft, its garden and orchard choked with weeds, its gate hanging off one hinge.

Blackthorn shied sideways, banging into Edithe's mare Donnagh, who reared and plunged sideways.

'Keep your horse under control!' Edithe snapped, bringing her mare round smartly with a vicious dig of her spurred boot, the reins drawn so tight the mare's chin was forced in to her breast.

Rhiannon's nostrils flared. 'Bad smell,' she said.

'I beg your pardon?' Edithe demanded coldly.

'Bad smell.' Rhiannon nodded towards the abandoned croft, her brows drawn in over her nose, breathing in deeply through her nose. She dug her heels into Blackthorn's side, so the mare leapt forward into a canter. 'Us get away from here.'

'What is it?' Lewen asked, as she cantered past him, leaping over the ditch beside the road to the rough soil of the untilled fields.

She looked back at him over her shoulder. 'Bad smell. Bad feeling. Something hungry. Us better get away.'

The other apprentices were alarmed and began to try to urge their horses forward, but they all plunged and reared, fighting the rein.

Suddenly, a pack of snarling, yammering dogs came hurtling out of the gate, skeleton-thin, with hunger-crazed yellow eyes.

Maisie screamed, and kicked her wooden clogs into her pony's sides. The pony bucked violently and Maisie fell off. The dogs leapt upon her, jaws gripping and tearing, and the shrill sound of her screams rang through the air.

A PALE HORSE

'And I looked and behold a pale horse: and his name that sat on him was Death.'

Revelations, chapter 6, verse 8

FOREST OF THE DEAD

Everyone shouted in horror and alarm. The caravans were all over the road, the big carthorses rearing in terror. The other horses were neighing loudly, and bucking wildly. Edithe and Cameron's horses both bolted, the apprentices clinging desperately to their pommels. Iven was almost run down as he leapt to the ground, his unsheathed sword in his hand. He had to press himself to the side of the caravan to avoid being trampled.

Landon and Rafferty's horses had shied sideways into each other, almost knocking Landon out of his saddle. The young poet grabbed his horse's mane and hauled himself upright again as his horse leapt the ditch and galloped away over the rough fields. He had almost lost his seat again, his stirrups bouncing against the gelding's sides, his reins flapping. Blackthorn flung open her magnificent wings and soared up into the air, as Rhiannon flew in pursuit.

Argent neighed a challenge and kicked out at the dogs, sending one rolling over and over, yelping. Lewen leapt from the stallion's back, catching one dog by the ruff of its neck and hurling it away, fending off another with his arm as he laid about him with his long dagger. One of the feral animals he killed at once. Others turned to attack him, bearing him down onto his back, and he struggled to keep them from ripping out his throat. Argent reared above them, lashing out with his hooves.

Then Iven was there, his sword flashing and darting. He ran through the dog at Lewen's throat and dragged the corpse away, so Lewen could roll over onto his feet, then turned to slash and stab at the dogs still tearing at Maisie's flesh. Maisie had instinctively rolled herself into a ball, her arms about her face, so the dogs had not been able to get at her throat or stomach. Her legs and buttocks and arms were badly bitten and bleeding heavily, however, and one ear had been half-torn from her head.

'Eà's sweet eyes,' Nina sobbed, flinging herself on her knees beside the moaning girl. 'Help me get her into the caravan!'

Fèlice had been struggling to bring her panicked mare back under control. One big dog had leapt up at her, seeking to drag her down from the saddle, but although her skirt was rent and muddied, she had not been hurt. She slid down from her horse now and, keeping a tight grip on the reins, ran to help Nina.

Rafferty's horse had slipped and fallen in the mud, but Rafferty had managed to fling himself free. Attacked by three dogs at once, he laid about him with his sword while trying to help his panicked mount to its feet. The rain made the ground so treacherous that he almost slipped and fell himself, but saved himself by hauling on the horse's reins. His gelding heaved itself to its feet, and Rafferty managed to kill one dog and wound the others enough that they ran off, tails between their legs.

'Someone, help us!' Nina wept, another dog worrying at Maisie's foot while she and Fèlice did their best to drag her away.

Rafferty let go of his horse's reins and limped forward, seizing Maisie under her armpits and dragging her towards the caravan. His gelding plunged sideways, and Fèlice caught hold of its reins and held both trembling horses still. She was white as skimmed milk.

Driven off their prey by sword and dagger, the dogs prowled nearby, snarling. As one darted towards them, Iven lunged forward and drove his sword through its breast. At once another one leapt and closed his jaws upon the jongleur's arm. Iven fell to one knee as Lewen fought to drag the dog away. For a moment all was confusion, Lewen stabbing the dog wherever he could, then at last its jaws relaxed and he was able to pull Iven's bloodied arm free.

'Iven, we need help!' Nina called frantically. She and Rafferty were trying to lift Maisie up the steps into the caravan, but the dogs were lunging and snapping at them, and the brown carthorse was rearing in her traces, sending the caravan rocking wildly. Roden had brought the other carthorse under control, and was staring round at them with a white, horrified face.

With his hand pressed over the ragged wound in his arm, Iven ran to her aid. Lewen, left to face the pack of dogs alone, crouched down and drew Iven's sword from the body of the dead dog, swapping his dagger to his left hand.

With his lips drawn back from his teeth and his powerful shoulders hunched forward, Lewen gave such a terrifying growl that the dogs paused, startled. They sniffed the air, then circled round him, snarling, the hairs on their skinny backs standing up in a ridge. Lewen growled again and suddenly lashed out at the largest and most ferocious of the dogs, drawing blood along its shoulder. It yelped and slunk back, tail between its legs. After a few more feints and a lot more vicious growling from Lewen, the pack of wild dogs suddenly turned and fled back into the ruined croft, a few limping and whining.

Nina and Iven together managed to lift Maisie into the caravan. 'She's been badly mauled,' Nina said, wiping tears from her cheeks. 'The poor lass! Lewen? We need to find the others, quickly.'

Lewen nodded, and whistled to Argent, who came up at an easy canter. Reaching up with one hand, he seized hold of the pommel and swung himself up into the saddle, no mean feat considering how very tall his big grey stallion was and how long his stride. Then they were off, galloping down the road.

Lewen caught up with Cameron fairly quickly, for his gelding Basta was generally a steady, well-mannered horse and had already slowed from his headlong pace. Lewen was easily able to catch his bridle and bring him back to a walk, acknowledging Cameron's curt thanks with a nod and a rapid question about Edithe. Cameron, who was sickly white and clinging tightly to his pommel, managed to raise one hand and point down the road.

'Go back to the others, get them moving fast. Those dogs are starving and will attack again. I'll try to catch up with Edithe afore that bloody skittish mare o' hers throws her.'

Without any discernible signal, Argent began to lope forward again, moving quickly into his thunderous gallop. Mud and stones flew up from his hooves. Lewen leant forward, anxiously scanning the mist-wreathed valley ahead. Finally he saw the silhouette of the running mare outlined against the sky as she bolted over the crest of a low hill. His heart jerked as he realised the mare was riderless. With a low murmur and a pat on Argent's shoulder he encouraged him to an even greater speed. Then he saw Edithe lying on the road before him. As he pulled Argent to a halt and jumped down beside her, she moaned and moved, lifting her hand to her head. He helped her sit up. Blood trickled from a nasty gash on her temple.

'Can ye stand? Any bones broken?'

She tried to stand, with his help, and grimaced with pain. 'Ow, my ankle!'

He helped her limp to the side of the road so she could sit on the low wall, then he knelt and took her foot in his hand. 'I'll have to take off your boot,' he warned.

Edithe nodded. He tried to do it gently but she cried out and began to weep as he managed to wrench it off. Her ankle was discoloured and swelling rapidly. 'I hope it's no' broken, only sprained,' Lewen said. 'I'm no healer, I'm afraid. Nina will ken better than me.' He glanced back up the road but the rest of his companions were still out of sight on the other side of the hill. 'Do ye have a dagger?'

Her pupils dilated blackly. 'I? Nay, I have no dagger. Why? What do ye want it for?'

He bent and drew the little black dagger from his boot and passed it to her, hilt forward. 'Just in case,' he answered. 'I must ride on and catch your mare afore she damages herself. I'll be back, never ye fear.'

She nodded, her breath a little unsteady. 'Ye expect trouble?'

Lewen gave her his lopsided grin. 'Better safe than sorry.'

He vaulted into the saddle again, gathered up the reins and gave Argent a sharp tap in the sides with his boots.

Argent neighed and took off, galloping down the road, ears pricked forward. The mare was still running, but was worn out with her terror and already beginning to founder. Argent was able to catch up with her before she plunged into a thick forest of dark trees that filled the bottom of the valley, where she might have hurt herself among the branches. Lewen caught her trailing reins and hauled her to a shuddering, blowing halt, her front legs stretched out before her stiffly. Her dark brown coat was scudded with sweat, and her breath was harsh.

Lewen dismounted slowly, not wanting to spook her into running again, and left Argent to recover his own breath as he sought to calm the mare. She was trembling violently and so he unpinned his cloak and laid it over her, damp and mud-spattered as it was, then began to coax her to walk slowly in circles. She stumbled wearily and he talked to her in a low, soothing voice.

As they circled closer to the forest he caught a whiff of something foul and wrinkled his nose. The mare smelt it too, for her nostrils flared in alarm, showing the red hollows within. She tried to shy away but Lewen held her firm. Argent whinnied and cantered round them in a big circle, as if striving to head them away from the forest.

Surprised, Lewen glanced towards the trees. He had thought the smell must come from some animal that had crept into the wood to die. Instead, with an instant shock of horror, he saw a half-rotting corpse shambling out from under the leafy shadows, one putrid decomposing hand held out as if in entreaty. It still wore the filthy tattered remains of a shroud. One shrivelled breast showed through the rags. Its eye sockets were empty, eaten out. Its hair hung down in long, dirt-caked waves. Slowly it stumbled towards Lewen, the stench coming over him in waves that made him retch.

The bay mare neighed and reared, tearing her head free of Lewen's loosened grasp, and bolting back in the direction she had come. Knocked off balance, he fell to his knees in the mud, the dead woman lurching closer to him with each ungainly step.

Rhiannon crouched on Blackthorn's back, forcing herself to watch as the ground fell away below her. Even after almost a week on the winged horse's back, she had not managed to control the instinctive cower of terror as she felt Blackthorn's muscles clench and release beneath her, felt substantial ground fall away and the precarious power of air lift and hold her. She had nightmares of falling, dreams so real that she would rouse with a jerk and have to open her eyes and reach out her hand and clench on to the roots of grass to reassure herself she was safe on the earth. The only fear more profound was the terror that the others might guess and mock her, saying she was no true thigearn.

Blackthorn beat her long powerful wings, rising higher in the air. The wind was cold and made tears start to Rhiannon's eyes. She pressed with her knees, directing the mare to veer left, as she rubbed away the tears, searching for some sign of Landon. Clouds were rolling down from the mountains, and there was a low insistent rumble of thunder. Rain washed over them, drenching them to the skin. The only sign of life was a raven flying high above the forest in the valley, occasionally calling out in his harsh, melancholy voice. Otherwise all was still.

Rhiannon crouched lower on the winged mare's back as Blackthorn shivered, her wingbeats faltering. 'No need to fear, my bonny,' she murmured, stroking the damp black hide. 'We just need to find Landon. Can ye see Nuinn anywhere?'

Blackthorn whickered and began to circle lower. Rhiannon leant forward and saw Landon below her, looking rumpled and muddy, leading his grey gelding back towards the road. Nuinn was limping badly. Landon heard the beat of wings and waved his hand in urgent greeting. Blackthorn landed lightly before him.

'Nuinn hurt his leg,' Landon said anxiously. 'It's bleeding. I dinna ken what to do, whether to make him walk on it or not.'

'Storm coming,' Rhiannon said. 'We walk him back slowly.'

Landon nodded. 'That's what I thought too. Oh, Rhiannon, I do no' like this valley. It makes me feel . . .' He gave a little shudder and tightened his grip on the bridle. 'I do no' ken how to describe it. My skin is all a-prickle.'

Rhiannon nodded. 'Me too.'

She dismounted and cast a quick eye over the gelding's foreleg. Blood oozed from a long red gash, and it was clear it hurt the gelding to put weight on that leg. Then she looked up at Landon. 'What about ye? Were ye thrown?'

Landon blushed and nodded. 'I'm no' a very good rider,' he said miserably. 'No' like ye.'

'Hurt?'

'Shaken up a wee,' the boy said, 'and bruised all over, for sure, but nay, no' hurt. I just wish Nuinn had no' been injured. If I'd been a better rider this wouldna have happened.'

Rhiannon shrugged, leading the way back towards the road. 'All riders thrown sometimes. Dogs' fault, no' yours. Horses no' like dogs.'

There was a quick flash of lightning, then a few moments later thunder growled again. The rain was coming in waves over the hills, flattening the grass and the brambles. A grey twilight hung over the landscape, and the encircling mountains were hidden in great, roiling clouds.

'Bad storm coming,' Rhiannon said sombrely. 'Bad feeling here.'

'I feel like someone's watching us,' Landon said with a shiver and pulled his damp, muddy cloak about him. They heard the raven cry again and looked up in sudden superstitious apprehension.

'Something is watching us,' Rhiannon said.

They felt very alone and exposed in the middle of that rough brown field, and unconsciously quickened their step, forgetting Nuinn's injury. The raven flew over their heads, and then the rain swept over them as if tied to the bird's black wings.

'There's the others,' Rhiannon said, seeing the two caravans pulled up haphazardly on the road. 'Let's hurry.'

They ran forward over the tussocks of grass, Nuinn limping badly. Iven came out onto the caravan steps and greeted them thankfully.

'We've driven the dogs away for the moment. Lucky for us Lewen can speak the language o' dogs!' he said. He glanced at the pack of feral animals crouching just inside the gate, their yellow eyes intent, the hair on their spines stiff. One crept forward a few steps, snarling. Iven frowned.

'It won't be long afore they attack again. Let's get moving. Roden, ye and Lulu get in our caravan and do no' come out for anything. Fèlice, ye go on in and see if ye can help Nina,' he said. 'Landon, ever driven a caravan? No? Och, there's nothing to it, just hold the reins and Sure will do the rest. Rafferty, can ye help Rhiannon lead the other horses? We must get away from here, those dogs are gathering courage to attack again, sure as apples.'

'Throw them some food,' Rhiannon said. 'That'll keep them busy while we get away.'

'Good idea,' Iven answered, as the growling rose in volume and ferocity. The horses all sidestepped nervously, ears laid back.

'Pity ye have no meat to feed them,' Rhiannon said with feeling. Iven cast her a rueful glance, knowing how much she had missed eating meat since joining company with the witches, and scrummaged in the store-barrels for something to throw the dogs.

As soon as Iven flung some hunks of cheese and bread and onion pie at the dogs, the starving animals leapt upon the food. At once the two carthorses began to jog away down the road, Rafferty and Rhiannon close behind, leading the other horses. They met Cameron at the crest of the hill, and after a hurried consultation he climbed up onto the driving seat of the red caravan, taking the reins from Landon, who was looking white and frightened. Behind them they heard vicious snarling and barking as the dogs fought over the remnants of the food. The carthorses quickened their pace, the caravans swaying precariously.

Halfway down the hill, they found Edithe, sitting white-faced and bleeding on the ground, a dagger clenched in her hand.

'My mare!' she cried. 'My horse! I just saw her, bolting away again. That way!'

'Where Lewen?' Rhiannon asked.

Edithe shrugged, pointing down the road, which dipped and then rose again over the crest of another low hill. Behind them they heard yelping, a lot more snarling, and then, ominously, the long, drawn-out howl of dogs on the hunt. For a moment they all froze, listening, then everyone leapt into movement. Iven half-carried Edithe up the stairs of the red caravan, shoving her through the door, then scrambled up into his driver's seat again. He brought the reins down on the gelding's rump with a thwack and the big, shaggy grey began to jog forward, whickering in distress.

'I get Donnagh,' Rhiannon said and thrust Basta's reins at Rafferty, before wheeling Blackthorn round and urging her into the air. The great black wings rose and fell rhythmically, horse and rider soaring high into the air. Rhiannon could see the terrified mare stumbling blindly across the rough fields, and followed her, calling out to her with her mind. *Stop! Ye will fall. Do no' fear. I come. Me and Blackthorn, we come. Stop . . .*

The mare's headlong pace faltered and she came to a halt, shuddering with exhaustion, her head down, her legs braced. Blackthorn folded her wings and went spiralling down, landing lightly next to her. Donnagh flinched but was too exhausted to shy away. Rhiannon reached out her hand, grasped the bridle and forced the mare to walk along beside her, her hide scummy with sweat, her legs trembling. As they walked, Rhiannon scolded the mare and she hung her head in shame. When the brown mare had caught her breath, Rhiannon coaxed her into a stiff-legged trot, conscious all the time of the howling of the pursuing dogs.

By the time they reached the road again the dogs were racing along just behind the caravans, which were swaying roughly over the ruts in the road, all of the horses galloping at full speed, necks stretched out. Rhiannon let go of Donnagh's bridle, warning her sternly to keep close and not bolt again, then unhitched her bow from her pommel. She drew an arrow from the quiver on her back and lifted the bow, aiming carefully. There was a twang and then a dreadful yelping. One of the dogs went

261

down under the wheel of the red caravan. Some of the pack turned on the injured animal, tearing it to pieces, but the others kept on running, snapping at the horses' heels, trying to hamstring them. Rhiannon shot another arrow, and another. Two more dogs fell.

Then Landon's horse stumbled, his injured foreleg giving way. He fell heavily into the road, almost dragging Rafferty down with him. As the dogs leapt upon the terrified horse, tearing out its throat, Rafferty heaved himself back into the saddle and forced his own horse's head around, whipping him forward. He had let go of all the lead reins but the horses were running together now, as a herd, and did not need to be led. Blackthorn galloped behind them, keeping them all together.

'Where Lewen?' Rhiannon called out, anxiously.

No-one could answer her.

Lewen scrambled to his feet just as the dead woman lurched forward, decaying arms held open as if to embrace him. As her bony fingers seized him and drew him closer, the foul stench almost overwhelmed him. For an instant he stared into the empty eye sockets so close to his, where he could see the wriggle of white maggots still feeding. Violently he pushed her away, staggering backwards. She fell, her mouth open as if to shriek, and as she hit the ground her skin burst open like an overripe plum, putrid flesh spilling out with a liquid splash that caused Lewen to bend and vomit violently. Again and again he retched, until his stomach had nothing left to give, and then he broke into a stumbling run.

Blinded by the heavy rain, he slipped in the mud and fell into a long shallow pit. The bottom of the pit was covered in water and he was drenched to the skin and smeared with clay. He hauled himself upright and dragged himself out of the ditch, clutching at the slippery muddy sides for purchase. Wiping the slimy muck from his face he saw he was right up under the shadow of the trees. There were other mounds of disturbed earth nearby, and a few long pits like freshly dug graves.

Lewen's skin was crawling, and he scraped away as much of the mud as he could, feeling sick. Something moved under the shadow of the low-hanging branches and every nerve in his body jumped. Lewen peered under the branches fearfully. Seeing a dark, man-like shape lurching towards him, he spun on his heel to run.

A corpse stood right before him. Lewen cannoned into it before he could help himself. He cried aloud in horror and recoiled, as the rotting cadaver reached out with pleading hands, grasping his arm. Lewen wrenched his sleeve away, feeling it tear. 'Stop it!' he cried. 'Leave me alone!'

For a moment he stared into the cavernous, half-rotted face, seeing beneath the grey skin and the staring hollow eye sockets something of the man it must have once been. The stench was so overpowering his breath snagged in his throat. He pressed his hands over his nose and mouth, trying not to vomit again, and backed slowly away. He felt something, or someone, right behind him, and froze. Very slowly, his limbs trembling violently, he turned.

Close behind him stood an old man. White hair still clung to his blackened scalp. Filthy scraps of shroud hung from his bony shoulders. Bones gleamed palely through the withered skin. He was crying, his mouth hanging wide open, his hands held up in entreaty. A horrible keening sound filled the air. Lewen thought he could hear words among the sobbing and wailing. 'Help us, save us, avenge us,' he heard. 'Heeelp us!'

Lewen backed away, turning on his heel. On all sides stood emaciated corpses, their hands held out pleadingly, their decomposing faces twisted in grief. More came shambling out of the forest. A few were mere skeletons, their jerking bones held together by some invisible force, their jaws clacking horribly. Many were no higher than Lewen's thigh.

He heard Argent's trumpeting neigh and ran that way, dashing tears from his eyes. The stallion was in a terrified sweat, the white rim of his eyes showing, his ears laid back. Somehow Lewen managed to haul himself into the saddle before his legs gave way. The stallion swerved and began to run. Lewen made no attempt to control the stallion's headlong pace, using all his strength just to stay in the saddle.

Then he saw the caravans hurtling towards him down the rough, stony road, swaying so violently it seemed they must topple over. He leant forward, pressing one knee into Argent's hot, damp side, pulling gently on one rein. Obediently the stallion veered round and came galloping alongside the blue caravan.

'Stop! Stop!' Lewen cried. He could not frame the words to describe what he had just seen, but knew only that they must not go any further.

Iven was driving the caravan. 'Lewen! What's wrong?'

'Must stop,' Lewen panted.

'Canna stop,' Iven shouted back. 'Dogs at our heels.'

Lewen glanced back over his shoulder. Behind the swaying caravans, behind the galloping wild-eyed horses, came the mob of dogs, howling with blood-lust.

'They took down Landon's horse, you'd think that would hold them off for a while,' Iven said. 'But they're mad with hunger, poor mutts.' One wheel of the caravan hit a pothole and he was almost jerked off his seat. He hauled himself upright and concentrated on the road, such as it was.

'No' safe ahead,' Lewen said. 'Iven, there's . . . walking dead ahead. Dead people, corpses, walking around in broad daylight.'

Iven's eyebrows shot up. He hauled back on the reins instinctively, but the grey carthorse had the weight of the caravan at his back and could not easily stop.

'Dead people?'

Lewen nodded. 'One took hold o' me.' He shuddered involuntarily, feeling nausea rise in his throat. 'I pushed her off me and she . . . sort o' fell apart. But there were others, Iven. I saw them moving in the trees and . . . arrgh, I smelt them.' His stomach won out and he leant over, retching. Argent neighed in protest and swerved sideways, almost unseating Lewen.

'Mad dogs behind, walking corpses ahead,' Iven said ruminatively. 'Delightful place, this.'

'What are we going to do?' Lewen cried. 'Look, those trees just ahead, that's where they are, the walking dead.'

Iven whipped his carthorse back into a ponderous gallop. 'Ride, Lewen!' he cried. 'Ride for your life!'

The road ran straight through the spinney of trees. Trees crowded close on either side, forcing them to fall into single file. Branches slammed into the sides of the caravans, scraping away paint and tearing free some of the decorative fretwork. They made no attempt to retrieve it, the horses behind driving it deep into the mud with their hooves. As the horses were forced to slow by the deep ruts and sucking mud, the dogs swiftly gained ground on them. Lewen and Rhiannon turned and fired arrow after arrow into the pack. Nearly every one found its mark and those that fell were meat for the other dogs to fight over. Soon there was only a handful of dogs still pursuing them, led by a big yellow brute with crazed eyes and blood-slavered jaws.

Rhiannon had only one arrow left. With her body twisted right round, rising and falling to the rhythm of Blackthorn's powerful gallop, she raised the bow and squinted along the arrow's length. Just as she was about to let the arrow fly, a low tree branch knocked her from her horse's back. With a scream she fell.

'Rhiannon!' Lewen shouted and brought Argent wheeling round on his haunches. Just as the big yellow dog leapt upon Rhiannon's fallen body, Lewen shot an arrow straight through its chest, knocking the dog head over heels. Then Lewen flung himself down on the road on his knees, pulling Rhiannon into his arms. With frantic hands he brushed away the tangled mess of her hair, looking down into her face. 'Rhiannon, Rhiannon,' he whispered. 'Are ye hurt?'

She opened her eyes and looked up into his face. 'No' me,' she said.

Lewen bent his head and kissed her.

The world went still and quiet, all the clamour of snarling dogs, stampeding horses and jolting caravans fading away. Rhiannon reached up her hand and cupped it round the back of Lewen's head, fingers threading through his curls. Lewen's breath caught and he pressed his mouth down harder upon hers, feeling her body curl into him.

Then a shrill neigh of anxiety penetrated his dazed senses. He jerked upright, in time to see another dog leaping upon them. Instinctively he felt for his *sgian dubh*, the dagger he wore in his boot, but as his fingers found the sheath empty he remembered giving his knife to Edithe. He had time only to seize the dog's throat in his hands and hold it off, even as the weight of the dog bore him down onto his back. Then suddenly the dog jerked and went limp, falling upon his chest, blood gushing all over his hands. He thrust the dog away and saw Rhiannon withdraw her dagger from its chest, and wipe its bloodstained blade on her breeches.

'Best go,' she said.

He nodded, bereft of words. Together they ran and vaulted up onto the backs of their horses, leaving the dead dogs behind for the remnants of the pack to fight over. Then they were galloping down the road again, eager to catch up with the caravans.

Lewen risked a glance at Rhiannon as they rode. Her black hair whipped out behind her like a living cloak and her hands and face and body were smeared with blood and mud. She turned and smiled at him, and he felt the hot clench of desire. He looked away, finding it hard to breathe. *So beautiful*, he thought. *So dangerous* . . .

Rhiannon laughed.

The next instant they were once again having to rein their horses in to a violent halt. The blue caravan had hit a deep rut and was bogged in the mud. Iven and the boys were desperately trying to drag it free, Rafferty pulling at the big gelding's head, Iven and Cameron trying to lift the caravan with their shoulders while Landon knelt in the mud, thrusting branches under the wheel.

Lewen dismounted. To his surprise his legs almost gave way beneath him. 'Here, let me help,' he said, coming across to put his shoulder to the wheel.

'Quick! Quick!' Iven cried.

'The dogs are all dead, or gorging themselves on their kin,' Lewen said wearily.

'It's no' the dogs I'm worried about now,' Iven said. Lewen looked up in surprise. Only then did he smell the rank odour of rotting flesh. Something moved in the grey dusk under the trees, something out of rhythm with the blow of leaf and rain.

'Oh, no,' he said blankly.

'Oh, yes,' Iven shot back. 'Now, heave!'

With a will Lewen heaved. The caravan came up out of the mud with a sucking sound and rolled forward. The boys scrambled back to their feet. Then all went still and quiet as stone.

All round them stood the company of the dead. Some were nothing but bones and staring skulls, others were freshly risen from their grave and bore only the faintest purple bloom of putrefaction on their chalky skins. Some even had eyes still, filmed over, their eyelashes clogged with grave-dirt. These were the ones who reached out their cold hands as if begging, who stretched their mouths into moans and shrieks, who groped their way forward, lifting their limbs in a grotesque parody of living movement. It was not the jerking skeletons that caused the most horror but those most newly dead, who had skin and hair and eyes still, and features recognisable still as old man or young woman or little boy.

Rafferty made a gagging noise and swayed where he stood. Iven strode quickly to stand by him, holding him up with one hand. 'Nina!' he called softly. 'Nina!'

The door of the red caravan opened and Nina stood upon the step, looking out into the twilight forest where, step by stumbling step, the host of the dead closed in upon them. She stood frozen for a moment, horror on her face, then she reached back into the caravan and pulled out her guitar. 'Close your eyes and your ears, my dears,' she said gently. 'And throw your cloaks about your horses' heads. I am going to sing the songs o' sorcery and I do no' want ye ensorcelled too.'

For a moment no-one moved, their muscles paralysed with dread. Then everyone sprang to obey. They wrapped their heavy, rain-wet cloaks about their horses' heads and then huddled their own faces under the muffling folds of cloth, pressing their hands over their ears. There they hunched for an excruciatingly long time, hearing nothing but the thunder of their own blood in their ears.

At last Lewen felt a gentle touch on his shoulder. He stifled a shriek and sprang away from the touch, fighting his way free of the folds of his cloak. Argent neighed and reared back, spooked by Lewen's fear. It was only Iven though, his fair hair and beard bedraggled with rain.

'All is well,' he said. 'Nina has sung the dead home.'

Lewen looked about him in amazement. Dusk had fallen. Lanterns had been lit at the front and back of both the caravans, casting a warm circle of light over the road. The dead lay in crumpled heaps where they had fallen. Nina sat on the steps of the caravan, her guitar drooping from one hand. She looked ill and haggard, with deep blue rings under her eyes. The sunbird stroked its long, curved beak against her cheek affectionately.

'How?' was all Lewen could say.

Iven shrugged. 'Ye think I ken, lad? I had my ears well plugged, I assure ye. I am naught but a jongleur. It is my wife who is the sorceress. All I ken is she has drained her strength. I have to get her to warmth and shelter, and quickly. I do no' want her getting sorcery sickness! Help me rouse the others and let us get away from this accursed wood.'

'Aye, away from here,' Nina said in a dull, flat voice. 'Away from the stench o' death. Oh, Iven! Find us a house, a barn, somewhere with walls and a roof. For there are more out there, I can sense them. I do no' want to camp in the open tonight, when we are all so weary.'

Iven swallowed and rubbed his hand over his face. 'Go and rest, my darling. I will find us somewhere safe, I promise.'

She nodded and stood up, swaying for a moment as giddiness overcame her. Moving like an old, sick woman, she hauled herself up the stairs, the guitar dangling from her hand.

FETTERNESS VALLEY

L ewen went to Rhiannon, gently drawing away her cloak. He was surprised to find her sickly white and trembling all over, her pupils so widely dilated her eyes looked black in the flickering lantern light. To his surprise and pleasure, she flung herself into his arms, choking on sobs.

'Why, what's wrong, *leannan*?' he asked, stroking her back.

She shuddered, unable to speak.

'Dinna be afraid,' he said. 'All is well. Look, Nina has sung the dead to sleep, or true death, what, I really do no' ken. But they are quiet now and willna bother us again. All is well.'

She pulled herself away from him, her hands clenched into fists. 'No' afraid,' she said.

Puzzled, he put his hand on her arm, trying to draw her round to face him. 'No, o' course no'. Naught to be afraid o' now. Come, ye're shivering. Ye're wet through with rain, and the wind is cold. No wonder ye canna stop shivering!'

271

He put his arm about her, but she jerked away. 'Call this cold?' she jeered. 'It's no' even snowing!' She huddled her arms about her body, trying to control the shudders that racked her.

Nina paused on the top step of the caravan. 'Let her come into the caravan with me. I canna heat us a hot drink, but I do have dry clothes and warm blankets. We're all exhausted.'

'No' exhausted,' Rhiannon said stubbornly. 'I fine.'

'Rhiannon, ye're trembling,' Lewen said. 'Go in with Nina and get dry and warm.'

'Nay. I stay with horse, I ride. Ye go in and get warm, if ye so cold.'

'But Rhiannon . . .'

'I said I ride!'

'But it's raining . . .'

'Ye think I melt in a wee drop o' rain?'

'Nay, o' course no'! I just –'

'Ye no' worry about rain, why must I? I just as strong and brave as ye.'

'O' course ye are, I dinna mean to –'

'Then shut up and ride. Horses get cold.'

'What's all this clishmaclaver?' Frowning, Iven came up to them, the other boys close behind him. 'What's wrong?'

'Naught,' they both said stiffly, moving away to grasp their horses and swing themselves back up into the saddle.

'Rhiannon?' Nina called from inside her caravan. 'Will ye no' come in and get warm?'

'I plenty warm,' Rhiannon said through her chattering teeth. 'I ride.'

'Are ye sure?' Iven said.

'Aye, I sure,' Rhiannon snapped, wheeling Blackthorn round abruptly. 'Why ye doubt me?'

'I do no' doubt ye,' Iven said, taken aback. 'I just –'

'Talk, talk, all any o' ye ever do is talk,' Rhiannon said and kicked her mare into a gallop. Mud sprayed up from Blackthorn's hooves and splattered against Iven's face, but by the time he had indignantly wiped his face clean and opened his mouth to retort, girl and horse had vanished down the road.

'She's got a shocking bad temper, that lass,' Iven said, shaking off gobs of mud from his hand. 'Well, we'd best get after her. It's a bad night to be galloping about in.' He cast a shrewd look at Lewen, who was so baffled and angry that he felt unable to speak or look at anyone, then sighed.

'I guess she doesna like admitting she's afraid,' Iven said to no-one in particular. 'Silly lass. Everyone feels fear sometimes. May as well admit it. It's like love. No point trying to hide what ye feel. It'll break through in the end, regardless.'

Lewen felt a slow burn of shame and embarrassment spread over his body. He stared through Argent's ears grimly, saying nothing.

'Come on, let's get on the road,' Iven said, clambering up into the driver's seat and clicking his tongue at the big, grey horse standing so patiently between the shafts. Landon was hoisted back onto the driving seat of the girls' caravan, and the other boys forced themselves to remount, groaning as their aching muscles complained. Only their fervent desire to get away from this place of death gave them the strength they needed. They rode on into the damp gloom of the wood, staring all around them, flinching at every creak of branch or rustle of wind. Lewen could not help peering anxiously down the shadowy road, looking for Rhiannon, but when she came cantering back up to them, jeering at them for being so slow, he neither spoke nor looked at her, instead concentrating on spying out the road ahead. She fell in behind the caravans on the other side, as far away from Lewen as she could get. Lewen's chest tightened with misery.

He did not understand what was wrong with her. One minute she had been fighting by his side, kissing him passionately, laughing as they galloped side by side through the rain-swept forest. Then, the very next instant, she was cold and angry, rejecting him fiercely.

Lewen did not know what he had done to offend her. He hoped it was not his kiss that had changed her so profoundly. He had not meant to kiss her. He knew how much she hated to be touched. He had longed to take her in his arms from the very moment he had seen her, but she was like a wild creature caught in a trap, ready to bite any who tried to free her. He knew she needed gentleness and patience before she could be tamed, not the urgency of desire that sometimes threatened to overwhelm him. And she was only a lass, and she had been placed under the protection of one of his mother's best friends.

It did not matter that Rhiannon was unlike any young lady he had ever met, half-wild, and innocent of society's etiquette. He knew that if Nina should find him kissing Rhiannon, she would be troubled and upset. He knew his mother would be horrified.

If he was to do what society expected of him, he would wait till Midsummer and then ask her to jump the fire with him. When they were properly handfasted, he could take her to his bed and keep her there, at least for a year, when he would ask her to jump the fire again. If she said yes, then they would be wed, and he could have her in his bed for ever after. He could not imagine anyone approving. Not his parents, nor his Rìgh, nor the Coven, who liked their apprentices to finish their training before they got distracted with affairs of the heart. Certainly not Dillon of the Joyous Sword, captain of the Blue Guards.

Yeomen of the Guards swore to serve the Rìgh as their first and only master, and those who wished to marry usually left the Rìgh's service, as Lewen's father Niall had done when he jumped the fire with Lilanthe. Often they were given a small estate to manage, or given some other role at court, but they forfeited the right to wear the blue cloak and the badge of the charging stag.

He did not need to marry her, of course. The people of Ravenshaw were not like the Tìrsoilleirean with their fear and hatred of the natural desires of the body. Indiscretions of the heart were usually smiled at, unless there was a babe, and even then neither party was reviled if they chose not to marry. Witches of the Coven were even more relaxed in their attitudes. If Lewen decided to stay with the Coven, he could do as he pleased, as long as his affairs did not cause too much disruption. The Yeomen did not have the same freedom. Dillon of the Joyous Sword kept very strict discipline and would frown on any amorous indiscretion. Particularly one with a wild half-satyricorn who was suspected of being implicated in the murder of a Yeoman of the Guard. Lewen could not imagine it helping his career prospects.

Lewen would never have kissed Rhiannon if he had not spent the last few hours at the very extremities, fighting for his life and facing death squarely in the face. She had not seemed to mind. She had kissed him as passionately, opening her mouth to his, pulling him closer with an urgent hand, curling her body into his. The memory of it was enough to make hot blood flood Lewen's groin. He stifled a groan and shifted in the saddle, glancing sideways at her cool patrician profile. She did not glance back.

On and on the horses plodded with hanging heads, following the swaying lantern at the back of the caravans. They came out of the false dusk of the wood into the true dusk of the sinking sun, the sky behind them flaming with brilliant reds and oranges that slowly faded to crimson, and then to pink and at last to violet, as they rode through untilled fields, past abandoned crofts and ruined cottages, all gaping open to the wind and rain.

On and on they rode in the darkness, till Landon was asleep on the bench, the reins flapping loose, and Rhiannon and the boys were jerking about on the backs of their horses, only kept awake by the cold rain trickling down their necks.

Then the jongleurs' caravans ground to a halt. Lewen, jolted awake by the cessation of movement, looked up, rubbing his eyes. They had come to a gate in a high wall, topped with upright shards of glass that glinted in the light of the lanterns. Inside the wall was a steep, peaked roof, and a low window from which candlelight shone, welcoming and warm, and the soft sound of voices.

Shivering in their damp cloaks, the boys watched hopefully as Iven climbed down from the caravan and went up to hammer on the gate. Lewen smelt wood-smoke on the breeze and something delicious that made saliva spring in his mouth. He had not realised he was hungry.

At the sound of Iven's fist, the faint murmur of voices faded away. Iven hammered louder. There was no response. At last he cried out angrily, 'For pity's sake, open the gate! We have an injured girl ·here and we are all exhausted. Please, let us in!'

There was an exclamation and then a swift exchange of low voices. Then they heard a soft, cautious step, and a man said, 'Who's there? What do you want?'

'Just shelter for the night,' Iven said, his voice hoarse with exhaustion. 'We were set upon by a pack o' ravening dogs and were hard pressed to fight them off. One o' us was badly mauled, a girl. She's no' yet sixteen. Please, let us in!'

There was no response.

'Please!' Iven called. 'It is raining and we are all cold and hurt. We can pay. We have money.'

'Who are ye?' The man's voice was surly with suspicion.

'I am a jongleur, called Iven Yellowbeard. I have my wife and son here, and a party o' lads and lasses, who have ridden far and fought hard today. Some o' us are hurt. Please, for Eà's sake, have mercy and let us in.'

'A jongleur? Here in Fetterness?' They heard the bolt scrape back and the gate opened barely a crack. A man's face peered out at them. He was dark-eyed and dark-haired, like most people in Ravenshaw, and carried a long double-bladed sword, nearly as tall as himself. He held it out threateningly, his eyes running over the garishly painted caravans, the weary, mud-spattered horses and the hunched shapes of Rhiannon and the boys, the youth of their faces evident in the glow of the lanterns. The doors of the caravans had opened, Nina looking out of one and Fèlice out of the other, her dishevelment not disguising her fresh young beauty.

'By my beard and the beard o' the Centaur!' he exclaimed. 'Well, ye look live enough. I suppose ye can come in.' He dragged the gate open, staring suspiciously out into the darkness, his sword held high. Gratefully they rode through and the man shut the gate quickly behind them, slamming home the bolts.

'The stable is over this way,' he said. 'Ye'll have to pay me for the hay. We have little enough left after the winter.

Your horses look fair foundered. Come, I'll help ye unharness them and rub them down. Look, those lads are riding in their sleep! What on earth are ye doing out after sundown? Do ye no' ken the dead walk these hills?'

'Aye, we ken . . . now,' Iven answered heavily.

'I guess ye meant to make Fetterness afore they shut the gates,' the man said. 'They willna open after the sun has gone, no' even for the laird o' Fettercairn himself. Here, lad, take this bucket. There's a well in the yard. We'll just get these horses settled and ye can come in and rest by the fire. It's late, we've eaten our supper already and were readying ourselves for bed, but I'm sure my wife can find something for ye to eat. There's always bean soup.'

Bean soup sounded heavenly.

They were all so tired, the settling of the horses seemed to take forever. For once Iven did not insist on every piece of leather and steel being polished to a high sheen, but let them wipe away the worst of the dirt and hang the tack on pegs to be cleaned in the morning. He then carried Maisie out of the caravan and into the house, trying hard not to jolt her as he hurried through the pelting rain. Maisie was white with shock and pain, and the bite wounds on her arm and legs and head were still bleeding sluggishly through their bandages. The others trailed behind, too worn-out and hungry to notice more than the warmth of the fire in the candlelit kitchen and the good smell of soup.

The farmer was named Tavish MacTavish, and his wife, all bones and cavernous hollows, was named Alice. For a while all was bustle and hustle, as Maisie's ugly bite wounds were cleaned and re-bandaged, Iven's arm and Edithe's head and sprained ankle attended to, home-made healing potions and a few mouthfuls of soup swallowed, and the two injured girls tucked up to sleep in the sitting room, where the fire still glowed on the hearth. The others were allowed to wash in the scullery and then fed black bread and soup in deep bowls. Nina was so exhausted that she sat in silence, Roden asleep on her lap, wrapped warmly within the shelter of her plaid. Iven managed to coax her to eat a few mouthfuls of the soup, and then Alice, noticing her pallor, got down a bottle of goldensloe wine and poured her a tiny glassful. Nina drank it obediently and a little colour came back into her cheeks and she stirred, reaching for her spoon. The plaid fell away from Roden's head of chestnut curls, nestled sweetly into Nina's breast, and Alice stopped in mid-movement, staring at him, her sudden pallor making her face seem gaunter than ever.

'A wee laddie,' she whispered. She put down the precious wine bottle with such nerveless fingers it almost toppled from the table. Tavish reached out and caught it.

'Now, now, Alice,' he said anxiously.

She sat down, staring at the sleeping boy with an expression of such pitiful yearning on her face that her husband came round to stand behind her, resting both hands on her skinny shoulders.

'We lost our boy,' he explained awkwardly. 'Just afore Hogmanay. She grieves still.'

'I'm very sorry,' Nina said, so tired and overwrought that quick tears of sympathy welled up in her eyes.

'What are ye doing riding the moors at night wi' a laddie?' Alice said accusingly. 'Do ye no' ken? How can ye no' ken?'

Nina made a helpless gesture. 'We heard stories but . . .'

'No lads are safe in this valley, do ye no' understand, ye fools?' Her voice rose hysterically. 'We thought we could keep our boy Dooly safe, with our high walls and our long sword and the strength o' our love, but nay! He was taken from his bed, even while I slept only a few feet away, and though we searched high and low, calling and calling, we did no' find him, no' for weeks, and when we did he was dead.' She began to weep, slow desperate tears that did nothing to relieve the hot knot of her grief. 'I should have kent! I should have kent! The moment he began to toddle about and call me "mam", I should've taken him and gone.'

'Alice had a brother that was stolen too,' Tavish said. 'When she was just a lass o' six or seven.'

'Twenty-six years ago, he disappeared,' Alice said, raising her gaunt face from her hands. 'By the Truth, ye'd think I would've kent better than to stay near that witch-cursed tower. It casts its foul shadow over us all.'

Iven frowned at her words. 'Why did ye stay?' he asked.

Tavish flashed his wife an unhappy glance. 'My father farmed this land afore me, and his father afore him, and his father afore him. There has been a Tavish MacTavish living in this house for six generations. I could no' just abandon it.'

'There'll be no Tavish to inherit when ye're dead and gone,' his wife said brutally. 'Our wee Tavish would be alive still if ye'd only agreed to go. I should've taken him and the lasses and gone. But like a fool I stayed with ye and now we have no son, no wee Dooly!' She began to weep again.

Everyone was silent, not wanting to even move or cough, embarrassed to be witnessing this scene.

Alice turned to Nina, her face ugly with grief and spite. 'Have ye no care for your wee laddie that ye risk being out after dark? Do ye no' ken the dead will no' sleep here, but walk the hills, looking for live bodies to take wi' them? We buried our Dooly, when we found him, but he would no' rest in his grave, did ye ken that? He dug his way out and came sobbing back home, wanting us to let him in, though the flesh rotted on his bones. We shut the gate on him but he knocked and cried all night, every night, for a month, until at last my man could bear it no more and cut his head from his body with his sword. Can ye imagine doing that to your son?' Her eyes turned feverishly from Nina's horrified face to Iven's. 'We buried him again, head and rotting body together, but his spirit will no' rest. I hear him sobbing outside every night, crying for his mam. Do ye wonder that every croft in the Fetterness Valley lies abandoned, when our dead will no' rest, no matter how often we kill them?'

There was a long, strained silence. The wind howled in the chimney and rain rattled the shutters. Rhiannon, her nails cutting into her palms, thought she could hear a little boy's voice, crying pitifully outside the wall.

'I'm so sorry, I'm so very sorry,' Nina said at last, helplessly.

'Why should ye be sorry, when your son still lives?' Alice said. She stared longingly at the profile of the sleeping boy, his soft curved cheek flushed and rosy. 'Ye canna love him like I loved my Dooly, when ye bring him into our valley without a care.'

'We are just passing through,' Nina said pleadingly. 'We heard the stories but . . . I thought I could keep him safe.'

Tavish gestured towards the window. 'Keep him safe against *them*? No-one is safe!'

Nina frowned. 'Do ye mean the dead who walk? But they are no' the ones who took your laddie. It is no' the souls o' the living they seek, but peace. They have been ensorcelled from their natural rest, those poor dead people.'

'What would ye ken?' Alice said scornfully.

'We met with some in the wood,' Nina said gently. 'They came to us begging us for help. They did no' seek to hurt us. I went down among them and I saw they walked against their will, compelled by some unnatural spell. So I sang the spell o' reversal, to unbind them from the enchantment, and then I sang the songs o' death and o' farewell, so their bodies could rest and their spirits go free.'

Tavish and Alice stared at her, taken aback and horrified. Then a dark mottled flush spread up Alice's thin, bony face. 'Ye sang spells? I thought ye were jongleurs!'

'We are,' Iven said. 'Though that is no' all we are. My wife is also a journeywitch, who travels the land working on behalf o' the Coven. These bairns that travel with us, they are apprentices travelling to the Theurgia to study.'

'A witch!' Alice spat. She got to her feet, backing away from the table. 'Get out,' she cried. 'Get out o' my house and take your witch-brats wi' ye.'

Nobody moved, all stunned with surprise.

'Ye heard me! Get out!'

'But . . . it's late, it's raining,' Iven said. 'Ye canna mean to turn us out into the storm.'

Alice's face was distorted with hate. 'I can indeed. Witches! I should've kent. No-one else would be riding out on the moors after dark, wi' the ghosts and evil spirits and walking dead. Get out, get out, afore ye curse this house.'

'But where could we go?' Nina asked, nonplussed. 'Maisie is hurt sorely, and needs to rest, we all need to rest, we are exhausted. We have done ye no harm.'

'No harm! Harm is all ye witches ever do.'

'Ye canna believe that! Why, since the Coven threw down the Ensorcellor it has done nothing but good, surely ye must ken that? Why do ye hate witches so?'

'Nothing but good!' She snorted with scorn. 'All the evil that has ever happened in this valley is because o' the meddling o' those blasted witches. Go on! Get out o' my house.'

Nina rose hesitantly. 'Please, may we no' sleep in your stables? It is so late, and listen to that rain! We have ridden so far already today.'

'No, no! I want ye gone!'

'Ye canna throw us out into that storm,' Iven said angrily. 'It would no' be right.'

'Ye're witches, surely ye can drive away the storm?' Tavish said sarcastically. He took a few belligerent steps forward, a big burly man with clenched fists.

Nina shook her head. 'I am no weather witch to command the storm.' Her voice was very tired and sad. 'Even if I could, I doubt I'd have the strength now. I've already worked strong magic today. Please do no' drive us out. I am sorry if we have distressed ye . . .'

Tavish shook his head. 'Alice wishes ye gone. Gather up your things and get out.'

'I will go if ye wish, but my wee laddie? Ye would no' turn him out into the storm? And Maisie . . . and Edithe . . . they are sore hurt . . . will ye no' shelter them for the night at least? They are naught but lassies, and sleeping. And the other bairns? They are all so weary. There is no' room for them all in the caravans. Please, will ye no' let them stay?'

Alice shook her head, eyes red-rimmed, arms folded.

Nina's black eyes sparked with sudden anger. 'Ye ken I could force ye to shelter us, I could sing ye to sleep, or compel ye against your will, or I could even tell the boys to draw their knives and force ye into some cold store-room to spend the night thinking about the meaning o' kindness and compassion. But I shallna do any o' those things for that is no' the way o' the Coven. I will wake those poor injured girls, and I will take these poor weary bairns, and we will all go out into the rain and the storm and the darkness. But I hope ye never rest easy in your bed again, for ye are a cruel, hard woman.'

Alice's face twisted and she tried to speak, but her grief and rage and hate were like a boulder in her chest and she could not draw breath around it.

Nina looked round at the pale, miserable faces of the apprentices.

'Come on, my dears. I ken it is hard, but I for one do no' wish to spend another minute under this roof!'

As everyone slowly and unhappily got up, and gathered together their wet cloaks, Nina took out her purse with fingers that trembled. 'Here, for the hay, and the soup, and for your trouble.'

She held out a heavy gold coin.

Alice reached out and snatched it.

It was close on midnight and a foul wind was blowing. The horses refused to go out into the storm, and they had to whip their flanks and drag at their heads, all the while the rain beating on them through the open stable door. It was not until Lewen and Rhiannon seized their bridles and whispered cajolingly in their ears that the horses at last consented to leave the warmth of the stable.

Cocooned in blankets, Maisie and Edithe had been carried through the sleet by Lewen and Cameron and deposited on their narrow bunks in the cold, draughty caravan, frightened and questioning. Fèlice ran behind them, cloak over her head, tears running down her face. At Rhiannon's insistence, Landon took the fourth bunk and he was so exhausted he did not argue, just thanked her and lay down, huddling the blanket about him.

'Ye'll have to hold on tightly,' Cameron told them grimly. 'It's as black as Brann's waistcoat out there, and the roads are rough. I'll do my best, but I canna promise ye won't be jolted.'

He then put up the hood of his cloak and climbed up into the driver's seat, gathering up the reins dourly. Rafferty climbed up next to him, too weary to ride any further. Iven was driving the other caravan as usual, having first made sure Nina and Roden were safely tucked up in their bunks inside. Nina had protested, feeling she should drive the caravan since it was her fault they had all been turned out, but Iven simply told her not to be a goosecap, and to get in and comfort Roden, who was wailing in the thin, high tone used by very tired young children.

So that left Lewen and Rhiannon, the horse-whisperers, to lead the horses and keep them calm in that thunder-rumbling, lightning-stalked night. It was a difficult job. The horses shied at every crack and flash, sometimes rearing up on their hind legs in terror, sometimes trying to bolt and almost dragging their arms out of their sockets. It was so dark they had trouble seeing the road, and so the horses stumbled into every pothole and water-filled rut. Only the swaying orange blur of the lanterns in front of them kept them from wandering off the road altogether.

They stumbled along for half an hour, shivering in the icy wind. The road was covered with water now, swirling around the horses' hocks and sometimes splashing up to their withers. Once Edithe's nervy bay mare Donnagh reared as a great white sheet of lightning illuminated the sky. Lewen realised with a shock that they were making their way round the shore of an immense, wind-tossed lake. He only had time for one quick glance before he had to leap out of the saddle to drag Donnagh to her feet, the mare having slipped in the mud and fallen on her side. That one glance had been enough, though. Lewen knew where he was. That lake filled the mouth of the valley, spilling down through the gap in the Broken Ring of Dubhslain to fall in an immense roaring waterfall called the Findhorn Falls.

Somewhere on the far side of the lake, hidden behind the spray thrown up by the roiling waters, was Ravenscraig, built on its high crag of rock. That meant they must be coming close to the Tower of Ravens, for Brann had built his witches' tower on the crag facing the castle across the waterfall. Once, the castle and the tower had been joined by a great arched bridge of silver-bound stone, like a cold grey rainbow, so that Brann could cross as he willed. So high was the bridge, and so terrible the fall, that few had ever dared cross with him, the old stories told, even though it was the only way to cross from one side of the lake to the other. The waters were simply too wild and the currents too strong for any boat to risk crossing so close to the waterfall, which was more than one thousand feet wide from crag to crag and fell almost three hundred feet to the lowlands below. The bridge across the waterfall had been a marvel of engineering, but was destroyed on the Day of Betrayal by the Ensorcellor's Red Guards, toppling down into the maelstrom below and taking with it a hundred fleeing witches.

Knowing where to look now, Lewen waited for the next flash of sheet lightning then raised his head, peering through the driving rain. Involuntarily he cried out, for ahead he could see the walled town of Fetterness, built against a high ridge which rose and rose and rose into a great, forbidding pinnacle of stone. Perched high on this bare, stern crag was the ruin of a huge building, its stone blasted black with fire. Only for an instant could he see it, then the lightning was gone, leaving coloured midges dancing in Lewen's eyes, and he could see no more.

'What is it? What wrong?' Rhiannon cried.

'Naught,' he answered, his lips stiff with cold. 'Look, ahead, there's the town. Fetterness, they call it. Happen we'll be able to rouse someone to open the gate and let us in. There must be an inn where we can stay, even so late as this.'

But the town of Fetterness would not be roused. Though Iven pounded and pounded on the gate, and shouted until he was hoarse, no sleepy gatekeeper or surly guard came to open it up and let them in. At last they had to admit defeat.

'We'll find a croft somewhere,' Iven said, his hair dripping into his eyes, his shabby clothes wet through to the skin. 'Do no' worry, Nina, there must be somewhere we can shelter, even if it's only an auld ruin. Why, if the worst comes to the worst, we'll brave the tower! It canna all be burnt and broken down.'

Nina, standing in the caravan doorway with a gorgeous green-and-gold shawl wrapped round her head, shuddered and shook her head. 'No, thank ye! I've had enough o' ghosts for one night. Iven, that farmer said something about the laird, do ye remember? The laird o' Fettercairn, he said. If there's a laird, there must be a castle.'

'Aye, Fettercairn Castle,' Iven said slowly. 'I remember hearing about it, ages ago. It guards the pass down into the lowlands. It canna be far away. Do ye really wish to look for it, at this hour o' the night?'

Nina nodded. 'Surely the laird willna have forgotten all the laws o' hospitality, no matter how surly his people? And I need to sleep, Iven, we all need to sleep. It's impossible to rest with the caravan jolting and swaying the way

287

it does, and we canna all cram in, the vans are simply too small. I hate to think how poor Maisie is doing, all torn and bitten as she is. Let us find this castle and if they willna open to us, I swear I'll sing the gate open, if I have to! Never have I been in such an unhappy place!'

So on they trudged, following the road past the town and zigzagging up the side of the ridge. The wind plucked at them with icy fingers, dragging at the caravans as if seeking to throw them off the side. The road was steep and narrow and cobbled with stone, all slick and wet from the rain, and in the darkness it was hard to see their way. Iven got down and led the grey gelding, afraid they would miss a turn and drive right over the edge of the cliff. Nina got out and walked with him, to relieve the strain on the horse, and called to those who were not injured to do the same.

The higher they climbed, the more vicious the storm became. The wind sent their cloaks fluttering and snatched Iven's hat from his head, taking it whirling up into the sky. Thunder grumbled all around them, and flash after flash of lightning tore the sky from end to end. The horses were terrified, rearing and neighing and fighting to be free of the firm hands that held them steady. They came to the last turn of the road and, in a great stabbing stroke of lightning that made them all jump and swear, saw before them a long driveway, running through tall gateposts topped by stone ravens.

'No' that way!' Iven called back to Cameron. 'That must be the way to the haunted tower. Turn this way. Down the road. Down!'

The road wound down the side of the ridge, protected by tall battlemented walls all the way along. Lewen could only see over the wall by standing up in his stirrups, and he sat down abruptly again for the drop down into the valley below was many hundreds of feet.

The road was so steep they had to lean on the brake to stop the caravans from sliding down on top of the weary carthorses, who could barely lift one great hoof after another. Down another turn of the road they went, and then the road ended at a tall gatehouse with an enormous iron door. They looked around them, suddenly feeling trapped in that narrow ditch of a road, and realised that they had been passing under the outer wall of the castle, which reared grim battlements and towers far above them on the left side.

'Well, we found Fettercairn Castle,' Iven said. He cleared his throat, smoothed down his wind-ruffled hair, twirled his fair beard into its usual fork, both twists dripping water down his front, and tried to brush away some of the mud.

'Big castle,' he said.

'Plenty o' room for all o' us,' Nina answered.

Iven squared his shoulders and strode up to the enormous door. A bell hung beside it and he rang it loudly, catching his breath as echoes sounded from the abyss below. Again and again he rang the bell, and was just turning to Nina with a dismal shrug when a little doorway cut into the gate opened. An old, stooped man dressed in a nightgown and nightcap peered out, holding high a lantern. 'Aye?'

'Please, we're travellers, in desperate need o' shelter,' Nina cried out. 'Please, let us in!'

'O' course, o' course,' the old man said. 'Bad night to be lost in. What are ye doing here, o' all places? Och, ye canna go wandering round here at night, it's a bad dangerous place, it is. Come in, come in, out o' the rain. What have ye got there? Caravans? I'd best open the big gate.'

With a loud groaning noise, the gate swung open, revealing a narrow passage beyond, guarded by a portcullis. Looking up nervously at the sharp iron prongs above his head, Iven led the carthorse along the passage into a large stone room, the others following close behind.

Rhiannon slipped off Blackthorn's back to lead her through last of all, feeling a shiver run through the mare's delicate frame that she felt in her own bones. This was a grim, dark place indeed, the gatehouse of Fettercairn Castle. Its walls seemed to ooze fear and misery as much as they did dampness. Rhiannon imagined she could hear cries and groans and the clash of arms, and looking round at the white, anxious faces of her companions, she thought they heard them too. There were no windows, only small apertures in the ceiling and walls through which arrows could be shot, or boiling oil poured. Weapons were hung all over the walls, broadswords and axes and spiked clubs and flails. On the far side of the room, the cramped passageway continued along to another great iron door, which presumably opened out onto the road down into the lowlands.

To the left, the room opened out into the ground floor of the barbican. An enormous hearth on the eastern wall lay cold and empty. The old man opened another fortified door beside it to show a narrow grassed area between the inner and outer walls.

'The stables are along that way,' he said. 'I willna take ye, I have no desire to get soaked to the skin. Rouse up the grooms to help ye. Do no' fear, ye canna get lost. There's no way in to the inner ward from here. Ye'll have to spend the night here in the gatehouse with me, o' course, I dinna wish to be waking my laird at this hour and I canna take ye through to the castle myself, I'm just the gatekeeper. It's rather rough and ready, but there's plenty o' room. We dinna keep men-at-arms here anymore, no' being at war, ye ken, so there's just me and a messenger lad, who's still sleeping, despite all the racket ye lot made.'

'Oh, I canna thank ye enough,' Nina said. 'We've had a long day o' it, and a few o' us are injured, and we have no' been able to find shelter anywhere.'

'Aye, so I can imagine,' the old man said. 'Bad times in the Fetterness Valley, these past few years. Anyone who wishes to leave must come past me, and I've seen many o' them, all o' them weeping and wringing their hands. Och, well, it's keen I am to get back to my bed, for it's awful cold and my bones feel it these days, indeed they do. Come, I'll show ye where ye can sleep. There's firewood if ye wish to light a fire, and some blankets in a chest. Let the horses bide a wee, while I show ye. In the morning I'll send the lad up to the castle to tell the laird ye're here, for he'll want to ken.'

Nina nodded dumbly, and they followed the old man's flickering lantern up a spiral staircase to the second floor, where he showed them into a bare dormitory with rows of narrow beds.

'Ye'll be comfortable enough here, I imagine,' the old man said. 'Better than camping out in the rain.'

'Aye, indeed,' Nina said gratefully. 'Thank ye!'

'Och, it's my job,' he answered with a shrug of his skinny shoulders. 'No' that I've been roused at night for a long time, mind ye.'

He kindled a candle on the mantelpiece, nodded good-night, then went out, leaving them staring at the cold, bare room, while outside the wind howled like a flight of banshees. Rhiannon shuddered and wrapped her arms about her body, feeling a dark foreboding pressing on her spirits.

Nina sighed and looked at Iven.

'We've slept in worse places, my love,' he said.

'Och, I ken. I just hope those mattresses aren't full o' lice.'

'Doubt it, looks like they havena been slept in for years.'

'They'll be damp, for sure.'

'Well, so are we all. Come, *leannan,* this is no' like ye, ye're worn to a shadow. Let's get a fire going and get ourselves dry and warm, and tomorrow we can drive on, and shake the mud o' Fetterness off our feet. It's only one night.'

The wind shrieked in the chimney, as if in derision.

FETTERCAIRN CASTLE

Rain lashed at the mullioned windows, an occasional sheet of lightning irradiating the sky, before the heavy gloom descended again.

'I have never kent such foul weather,' Fèlice said discontentedly. 'Is it always like this?'

Nina was trying to blow the sullen coals into flames with the help of wheezy old bellows. She looked up and tried to smile. 'No' always. If I did no' ken better, I'd think the Broken Ring o' Dubhslain sought to keep us here. At least it is no' hailing.'

'In April!' Fèlice cried.

Hail suddenly clattered against the glass.

'I spoke too soon,' Nina said, and sat back on her heels, wiping one hand across her brow and leaving a dirty smudge.

It was midmorning already. Everyone had slept late, for little light penetrated the thick walls of the gatehouse and they had all been exhausted. It was the sound of Maisie's moans that had woken them in the end. She was sick with fever, and when Nina carefully dampened and peeled away the bloody, grimy bandages, it was to find the wounds beneath festering and green. Landon was unwell also, racked by a hacking cough, and aches and pains in all his joints. When Nina felt his forehead, the little crease between her brows deepened and she bade him stay in bed. Cameron was also coughing, and complained he had not been able to get warm all night, so he was abed also, and Edithe too, while Iven had gone to ask the gatekeeper for water and a kettle, and any herbs or medicines he might have.

'I'll go and check the horses, Nina,' Lewen said, pulling on his boots. 'We were so tired last night it was all we could do to get their tack off them. I want to make sure the grooms have fed and watered them properly.'

'I'll come too,' Rafferty said.

'Me too,' Rhiannon said. She had been standing by the window with her forehead pressed against the glass, staring at the hail, but now she turned and looked at the others.

'Ye'll get wet,' Lewen said to no-one in particular.

'Think I care?' she answered.

'We willna melt,' Rafferty said with forced cheerfulness.

Nina nodded and gave a ghost of her usual merry smile. 'Thanks. Would ye mind bringing me some stuff from my caravan? I'm worried indeed about poor Maisie. I wish I were a better healer. I wish Isabeau were here, or your mam, Lewen.'

'Me too,' he said. After Nina had told him what she needed, he led the way down the dimly lit stairs and out the door into the outer ward.

'Poor Maisie!' he said. 'Even if Nina can clean out the infection, she'll be left with nasty scars. It's such a shame, she's a sweet lass.'

Rhiannon frowned, but said nothing. Rafferty made a murmur of agreement, then said anxiously, 'Do ye think Maisie will be fit to ride out soon? Because glad as I am to be safe behind high walls, I canna wait to get away from here. It's creepy. I wish we'd never come this way.'

'I'm sure everyone does,' Lewen answered. 'But how were we to ken? I mean, they may have tried to tell us, back in Ardarchy, but who was to ken how bad it really was? I am just glad we've come through safely.'

'We're no' through yet,' Rhiannon said harshly.

'No,' Lewen answered, looking at her thoughtfully. Rhiannon did not return his gaze. They came to the door to the outer ward and pulled up their hoods against the rain.

Rhiannon could not have explained why, but she was angry with Lewen, and with all the others too. When she thought over the tumultuous events of the previous day, she felt such a confusion in her emotions that anger and fear, her two most familiar emotions, were the only ones she recognised. Since Rhiannon hated to feel afraid, or to have others know that she felt fear, her only refuge was anger. She stayed angry all through the trip to the stables, a vast stone building constructed within the double ring of walls that encircled the castle, and protected by its own gatehouse and bailey. In times of war, the horses could be fed and exercised within the outer ward, and if the first wall was breached, either taken inside to the castle grounds, or used to escape through the back gate. The stable itself had room enough for a hundred horses, though most of the stalls were now empty.

An old, wizened groom called Shannley, with a face set in lines of sour suspicion, grunted at the sight of them. He and his stablehands had not been pleased to be roused in the early hours of the morning, and by the expression on his face, he was not pleased to see them now. Even Lewen, who could win over most people with his deep warm voice and pleasant ways, could not soften the head-groom's manner. Shannley showed them where the bins of grain were with a jerk of one spatulate thumb, then shuffled back to his rooms, grumbling under his breath. The stablehands, meanwhile, got on sullenly with their work, casting many a curious look at Lewen, Rhiannon and Rafferty.

The horses were tired and bad-tempered after their hard usage, and so Rhiannon tried to work away her own ill-temper with a stable rubber, curry-comb and tack-brush. She groomed horses and carried buckets of mash and polished tack till her arms ached and her head throbbed, but it did not help. She was in a fouler temper than before, with most of her rancour directed at Lewen. If it was not for him, she would never have made this ill-starred journey into a land haunted by evil spirits and the walking dead. All night she had thought she could hear the sound of a young boy crying, and sobs of grief, and wails of fear, and the moans of the dying. It had done no good telling herself it was only the wind, or Maisie crying out in her fevered sleep, or her own overwrought imagi-nation. Even driving her fingers into her ears or pulling the musty-smelling pillow over her head had not helped. She had not been able to silence the echoes in her brain.

Rhiannon was shaken to the core by these supernatural terrors. Dark walkers stalked her imagination, and not even the slicing open of her wrist and the spilling of her own blood on the hearth had relieved her dread.

As they went about their business in the stables, she often felt Lewen's eyes on her face, puzzled and questioning, but in his usual fashion he did not say anything, which only infuriated her more. By the time they were making their way back to the gatehouse, loaded down with supplies from the caravans, even unobservant Rafferty was shooting her anxious glances, and beginning to be wary of addressing remarks to her.

They came into the dormitory to find Fèlice doing her best to keep Roden and Lulu occupied and out of Nina's way as the witch tended to the sick and injured. The sunbird was asleep on the back of a chair, its head tucked under one iridescent green wing as it was so dark and cold in the long room the bird thought it was still nighttime. The fire flickered dully on the hearth, for all the wood was wet, and sent out unpleasant puffs of smoke every time the wind shifted.

'Iven's gone up to the castle, to speak with the laird,' Nina said, looking tired and pale. 'I dinna ken what we are to do, for Maisie is only getting worse, and I havena all the medicines she needs, and I'm worried about Landon too, he's no' as sturdy as ye other lads, and he was chilled through last night. I do no' ken if we should go on, and seek help from the apothecary in the nearest town, or wait here until the bairns are feeling better. I must admit I'd rather no' stay. This place makes me uneasy. It's like a fortress! The laird sent down soldiers to insist Iven attend upon him, and the gatekeeper seems to dread his displeasure. If only it would stop raining! I canna feel easy about going on in such weather but I just want to get away from this place!'

Seeing how anxious they all looked, Nina laughed ruefully, saying 'I'm sorry, I'm all out o' sorts from such a late night and the anxiety over poor Maisie. I'm sure there is no need for us to worry.'

Poor Maisie, Rhiannon mimicked and then realised that Lewen had been watching her, as usual, and had seen her expression. He frowned and she glared at him, wondering what right he had to disapprove of her behaviour. His frown deepened, and she turned away and went to stand by the fire, pretending to warm her hands before its sullen glow. Tears prickled her eyes.

'The laird sent down soldiers? That seems odd,' Lewen said.

'I suppose it's no' so peculiar when ye think o' all those missing and murdered,' Nina responded. 'They must be suspicious o' strangers. I must admit I dinna like to see Iven go, however, flanked on all sides by guards armed to the teeth. If they decided to keep him, I'd never get him back!' She sighed, unconsciously pressing her hands together in a gesture of rare anxiety.

'I canna help but wonder how it was the Red Guards were able to take the Tower o' Ravens by surprise on the Day o' Betrayal,' Lewen said. 'If the only way in and out is through the castle's own gatehouse, ye would've thought the witches' tower impregnable to surprise attack.'

'They could've come over the Stormness River like we did,' Rafferty pointed out.

'Aye, I suppose so. Only . . . well, the tower looks over the Fetterness Valley, any force o' arms coming that way would have been seen. And they would've had to have passed the town.'

'There was some kind o' trickery, or betrayal,' Nina said. 'I do no' remember the tale. It all happened afore I was born.'

'Heavens, that long ago?' Fèlice said teasingly.

Nina cast her an amused look. 'Aye, hard to believe, is it no'?'

They heard Iven's quick steps running up the stairs and turned to him expectantly as he came in, looking a far different figure than the drenched and dishevelled man of the

298

night before. He had changed into his very best coat, a long-tailed blue velvet and silver-buttoned creation, over a fresh white shirt with a fashionably soft and flowing collar. His boots were rather worn but had been freshly polished, and he wore baggy black satin trousers tied under the knee with ribbons. The ends of his moustache curled upwards and his beard had been forked and plaited into two, with his long hair tied back with a ribbon.

'So what was the laird like?'

'What did he say?'

'Was the castle very grand?'

'Iven, what did he say? Those guards were so grim-faced, I've been afraid ...' The last question came anxiously from Nina, who had gone to him and grasped his arm tightly.

'What, did ye think he meant to throw me in his dungeon? Nina! Ye must be tired to fall prey to such imaginings.'

Nina quirked her mouth. 'I ken, I'm sorry. I am tired, I must admit, and this place is grim enough to make anyone imagine horrors.'

'Well, that's true enough,' Iven said affectionately, and looked around the circle of expectant faces, as always enjoying having an audience. 'The castle is just as grim, and very grand – or may have been, half a century ago. Now it is damp and cobwebby, and very much out o' style. The servants are either auld and grouchy or young and nervous, and there are far too few o' them for such a large place. The laird himself is a very affable gentleman and surprisingly well informed on court matters, consid-ering how far away from anywhere we are here. He was most distressed to hear o' our misadventures and has offered us his hospitality until we are all fit to travel again. Indeed, my love, even if Maisie was well enough to travel we couldna leave, for he says the storm has caused a big auld tree to fall across the road, which may take a few days to clear, as it's awkwardly placed. We are stuck here, willy-nilly, and so I thanked him most graciously. He is having rooms made up for us, and has promised to send over some sturdy footmen with a pallet for Maisie, and some auld nurse who he says is as good as any skeelie with her herbal remedies, that he swears will break the infection quick smart.'

'Well, that at least is a relief,' Nina said. 'I am no healer, as ye ken, and I'd begun to imagine us wandering the countryside looking for succour while gangrene ate away poor Maisie's leg. I suppose, if we must be marooned somewhere, it may as well be at a castle! Come, lads and lassies, let's pack up our things and make ready. I wish we could have a bath and scrub ourselves clean afore we need meet this laird. I feel damp and itchy and slovenly indeed, even with a quick wash and a change o' clothes.'

'Ye look most bonny,' Iven said.

She seized his nose and tugged it. 'Why, thank ye, sir! I could say the same about ye.'

Iven twirled his moustache. 'Aye, indeed ye could,' he answered complacently, so even Rhiannon had to smile.

Fettercairn Castle loomed high behind its battlemented walls, a great grey fortress with narrow slitted windows and two round towers, one looking into the Fetterness Valley, the other down into the lowlands of Ravenshaw, many hundreds of feet below. It had stopped raining, though the sky still looked ominously dark and the wind was strong enough to drag the girls' skirts sideways and blow their hair wildly.

300

The gatehouse led into the inner ward, a large square courtyard surrounded on all sides by lofty walls. To the south were the kitchens, staff quarters and workshops, all built no more than one storey high so that the sun could strike in over the peaked roof and fall upon the garden built in the centre of the yard.

A long, green rectangle of lawn with an apple tree at one end and a greengage tree at the other, the garden was surrounded by low hedges and bushes sculpted into balls and spirals. Narrow beds ran the length of the garden, filled with white roses underplanted with blue lavender and thyme. An old lady bent over the storm-ruined roses, tying them up with some twine. She turned her soft, crumpled face towards them as they made their awkward progression round the courtyard, all of them carrying bags and bundles, and craning their necks to look up at the crenellated towers looming over them.

'A garden planted for peace,' Maisie murmured, gazing at the sweetly scented flower beds with pleasure. She was lying on a makeshift stretcher carried by two footmen, and had been much more comfortable since drinking a pain-killing elixir given to Iven by the lord's old nurse. In fact, since swallowing the elixir, Maisie had had a strange, dreamy smile on her face and had even hummed a few bars of an old folksong as she was carried along. Only the fever-ish glitter of her eyes and her scarlet cheeks showed the insidious advance of the poison through her bloodstream.

'There's another garden behind the kitchen,' Iven told her, walking along beside her, holding her hand. 'When ye are better I'll take ye there and show ye. Ye'll like it. It's full o' herbs as well as vegetables, for the laird's nurse is as skilled a skeelie as any I've seen. She has hyssop and sage and pennyroyal planted there, and comfrey and feverfew, and many others I do no' ken.'

'Hyssop, sage, pennyroyal, feverfew,' Maisie repeated vaguely. 'A garden for healing. Will I ever walk there? Will I ever walk again?'

As she hummed a few more bars of music, Iven said uncomfortably, 'O' course ye will,' and exchanged a glance with Nina, who walked on the other side of the stretcher, Roden skipping along beside her.

'Can I go play in the garden, Mam? Please?' he asked, pulling against her hand. The old lady was regarding them with great interest, the twine falling from her hand, and he smiled at her brilliantly, for she looked like the sort of old lady that kept a box of sweetmeats in her pocket.

'No' now,' Nina said absently. 'Remember we are guests here, Roden.'

'Aye, Mam,' he answered in a long-suffering tone.

The procession rounded the garden and came into the paved area before the main part of the castle. Surrounded by a square of chains was a pyramid of rocks, a little higher than Rhiannon's knee. A raven perched on top of the cairn, head tilted, regarding them all with one bright black eye. The deep, plaintive cry of ravens echoed all round the courtyard and, glancing up, Rhiannon could see black-winged birds circling the towers far above.

'Have ye heard the tale o' the ravens o' Fettercairn?' a deep, melodious voice said at her elbow.

Rhiannon turned. An elderly man stood beside her, dressed in a black kilt under a black velvet jacket. Under the skirt he wore long black hose and black brogues with silver buckles. Only his stiff white collar and the criss-cross of fine white and grey lines in the kilt broke the severity of his dress. He was clean-shaven, an unusual trait in a country where men were proud of their beards, and his short dark hair glinted with silver.

'Nay, I have no',' she answered warily.

302

'It is said the first laird o' Fettercairn was a page in the service o' Brann o' Ravenshaw. One day, during the building o' the Tower o' Ravens, Brann and his retinue came to oversee its progress. As always, Brann had his familiar with him, a large raven he called Nigrum. He had brought the raven with him in the journey from the Other World, and so it was a very auld bird but still went everywhere with Brann, sitting on his shoulder and whispering cruel nothings in his ear. Or so they said, those who served him. They also said Brann loved this bird more than his own children and indeed, as ye ken, his eldest son did in time rebel against him, and so their saying may be true.'

Rhiannon did not know, but said nothing, regarding the old man gravely.

'The raven Nigrum flew from Brann's shoulder, whether because he was hungry and wished to find food, or because he was bored, who kens? Anyway, a screech o' gravenings nested nearby and saw the auld bird and came flying out to attack. My ancestor, who was then a lad o' sixteen, picked up a large rock and flung it at the gravenings, striking and killing the one which had seized the raven in its claws. Rock after rock he threw, until the gravenings fled and Brann's raven fluttered back to Brann, injured but alive.'

Everyone was listening now, and the old man moved his piercing black eyes, set deeply under strong black brows, from face to face, smiling a little as he noted their interest.

'The sorcerer was most impressed with his page's quick thinking and strong arm, and knighted him then and there, naming him Sir Ferris, which means "rock". He then promised the lad a nestling from the raven's next breeding which, given the bird's age, was to be his last.

"Ye shall stand guard over my witches' tower as ye stood guard over my raven," Brann said then, and ordered that a great castle be built to defend the approach to the tower, and that Sir Ferris be its laird and protector. The rocks Sir Ferris had thrown were gathered together and made into a cairn to mark the spot where the castle was to be built.' He indicated the little pile of mossy rocks with a graceful gesture and everyone turned to gaze at it.

'Brann always had a wry sense of humour, and so he decreed the castle be named Fettercairn, for Sir Ferris and his heirs would be bound here for always, guarding the pass. Then he made a prophecy, as Brann was wont to do. He said, "As long as ravens on Fettercairn dwell, tower and castle shall never be felled." So we let the ravens nest on our towers and feed them and protect them, so that Fettercairn Castle shall always stand. They are quite tame. Look.'

The old man held out his arm and whistled, and the raven on the cairn spread its wings and flew across to land on his outstretched wrist. It was an enormous, glossy black bird, with a cruel curved beak and knowing eyes. Fèlice gave a little shriek and jumped back, and everyone else exclaimed in surprise. The old man smiled and stroked the raven's back.

'But the tower did fall,' Rhiannon said abruptly. She was frowning, for while the old man spoke the air had seemed to thin about her so she could hardly breathe. She had heard faint cries and screams and the clash of arms, and the sound of a woman wailing in such terrible and profound grief that every hair on Rhiannon's body had sprung erect and she had shivered with sudden acute cold. She was shivering still.

The smile faded from the old man's face. After a moment he said, rather curtly, 'Aye, that is true, but then

Brann the Raven also prophesied that he would outwit she who cuts the thread and live again, and that is most manifestly untrue.'

He was quiet for a moment, preoccupied with thoughts that caused his thick dark brows to draw down and his mouth to twist, and then he looked at Rhiannon again and smiled. 'Besides, the tower did no' really fall. It was built too well. Despite all the efforts o' the Red Guards, and close on forty years o' neglect, most o' it still stands. Happen one day it will be rebuilt and witches will study their craft there once again. If ye listen to village gossip, which I urge that ye do no', they will tell ye the witches have never really left, that one still lives somewhere in the ruins. They say they have seen lights and smelt smoke, and even seen a mysterious hooded figure in the forest, gathering herbs and mushrooms.'

'Is that true?' Nina asked, raising one brow in quick interest.

The old man sighed. 'We o' the Dubhslain are said to be more superstitious than most, and those o' the Fetter-ness Valley more superstitious than any. Ye really canna believe aught that is said in the town or valley. The winters are long, and the auld folk tell tales to amuse and frighten the young, and seek to outdo the tale that was told afore. It is all fables and fabrications, nothing more.'

'The dead that walk are no' mere fabrications,' Nina said. 'We all saw them, and I myself went down and walked among them and tried to speak with them. And we have all heard the tales o' the lads that disappear from their beds at night. We met one who had lost her son that way and her grief was real enough.'

The old man's piercing black eyes went from her face to her son's. Roden was standing quietly for once, holding on to Nina's hand and listening with great interest.

'Aye,' the old man said slowly. 'That at least is true.'

The old lady had come out of the garden to join them and now she reached out a gentle hand to ruffle Roden's chestnut curls and stroke his cheek. 'What a bonny lad,' she said.

Roden submitted to the caress, though reluctantly.

The old man drew the old lady to him, tucking his arm through hers. 'But I have been most remiss,' he said. 'What are we doing, standing here and telling dusty auld tales? Please, come in and be welcome. I am Malvern MacFerris, laird o' Fettercairn, and this is my sister-in-law Lady Evaline NickKinney, who was married to my brother who was laird afore me, and is now chatelaine o' my castle.'

'Ye are most welcome,' Lady Evaline said sweetly, smiling round at them all. 'We do no' get visitors very often, I am afraid. I hope ye will be comfortable, and that the ghosts do no' disturb ye too much.'

Everyone had begun to murmur an answer, and move towards the door, but at Lady Evaline's last words every head swivelled to look at her.

'Ghosts?' a chorus of voices repeated.

Lord Malvern looked uncomfortable. 'I am sorry. My sister-in-law is getting elderly now. She was always rather a daydreamer, but in recent years I'm afraid ...' He paused, searching for a kind way to say what he meant.

Lady Evaline turned to him reproachfully. 'But Malvern, ye hear the ghosts too, I ken ye do!'

He shrugged a little and smiled. 'Come in out o' the wind, my dear, and let me call Harriet for ye. Please, everyone, come in, come in. Harriet!'

At his call a big-boned, red-faced woman came bustling along the hall and took the old lady by the arm. 'Time for your nap, Lady Evaline,' she said firmly.

'But our guests! I must see them to their rooms and make sure all is comfortable.'

'The maids can do that,' Harriet said.

'But that would hardly be very hospitable.' Lady Evaline looked distressed.

'Ye will see our guests again at dinner, my dear,' Lord Malvern said. 'Ye must rest, else ye will be too tired to preside over the table tonight.'

Lady Evaline resisted for a moment longer, her face looking more crumpled than ever, then submitted unhappily, allowing Harriet to lead her away towards the stairs.

The entrance hall was a vast, shadowy room, with large doors leading off on either side, and another set at the far end, under the stairs. The walls were hung with ancient shields and spears, stag heads, and a tarnished genealogical table adorned with swathes of black and grey tartan. A big man with greying hair and beard stood to attention a few steps away from the lord, wearing a metal breastplate and shin-guards, and a claymore strapped to his back. As Lord Malvern led the way down the hall, he fell into place a few steps behind him, his face impassive.

Footmen stood against the walls, staring straight ahead, and another man stood before the stairs, his head bowed, waiting for his orders. He was dressed in immaculate, dark livery, and his very large, very white hands were folded before him.

'Could our guests be shown to their rooms, Irving? I am sure they would like to wash and rest awhile.'

'Certainly, my laird,' Irving replied in a smooth, unctuous voice. He made a gesture with one hand, and at once a skinny young woman came scurrying forward to make an awkward curtsy.

'Wilma is the chambermaid assigned to care for your needs, sir, madam,' Irving said without actually looking at

Nina and Iven. 'If ye should require aught, please just ring the bell and she shall come to assist ye. Wilma.' He jerked his head.

At once Wilma bobbed another curtsy and said rather breathlessly, 'If ye could come this way. Please. Sir and madam. Ladies and gentlemen.'

'I hope ye will find your rooms comfortable,' Lord Malvern said and, with a nod and a smile, he walked through into the next room, the armed man following silently behind.

'A laird o' the auld school,' Iven said to Lewen in a low voice, as they followed the maid up the stairs. 'It is usually only the prionnsachan that still keep a gillie-coise at their heels.'

'What's that?' Rhiannon asked, not recognising the word.

'A bodyguard, I suppose. Once upon a time all the lairds had one, for times were dangerous, but we have been at peace now for years and most dinna see the need for them. I ken the MacSeinn has one still, and the NicBride, for their lands are troubled still, but the Mac-Thanach never does. I bet the laird has a cup-bearer too. Even the Rìgh does no' use one nowadays.'

The maid Wilma cast them a curious glance over her shoulder and Iven said no more, falling back and allowing the others to exclaim over the rich, ornate tapestries and artifacts that crowded the dimly lit gallery. They were led through a veritable maze of dark, damp halls and rooms, and up another flight of stairs till at last they reached a corridor with a number of rooms opening off either side.

The footmen carried Maisie into one of the rooms and shifted her to the bed, which had been freshly made, and Iven helped Edithe hop in and sit down gratefully in a big chair by the unlit fire, Lewen finding her a footstool on

which to rest her sore and swollen ankle. The maid
Wilma kindled the fire deftly, kneeling on the flagstones
and blowing the sparks with a pair of bellows until the
kindling caught and yellow petals of flame burst open all
along the sticks. She then stood and, curtsying, offered to
show the others their rooms.

Landon and Cameron, both heavy-eyed and hoarse-
throated, were glad to be tucked up in their beds in the
room next door, but the other apprentices followed Nina
and Iven into the large chamber they were to share, with
views across to the waterfall and the burnt-out hulk of
the tower. The room was cold, for the windows had been
flung open to allow fresh air in, and the floors had
been freshly scrubbed so were damp and chill underfoot.
Wilma frowned at the view and drew close the windows,
so that the shapes of crag and tower were obscured
behind small, thick, rippled panes of glass. The room was
immediately filled with a greenish gloom, for the glass
was so old it tinted the air like water. Wilma knelt by the
fireplace and pulled out her tinder and flint, chasing away
the watery shadows with warm golden flames.

The sight pleased her. She stood up, smiling, and
rubbed away the smudges of charcoal on her stiff white
apron.

'Ye need no' worry about the sheets, we aired them this
morning,' she said proudly. 'And Lady Evaline came
through to check all was nice for ye. She picked the
flowers for ye herself.'

Looking at the pretty tussie-mussies laid on the
pillows, white roses tied with lavender, newly opened lily-
of-the-valley and silver posie thyme, Nina exclaimed with
true pleasure. 'That was kind o' her,' she said.

'Lady Evaline loves her garden,' the maid said with
a sigh.

'It's a lovely wee garden, no' at all what one expects to find inside these grim grey walls,' Nina answered.

'Nay,' the girl agreed with a giggle, then added, 'Dedrie tends the garden for my lady.'

'Who is Dedrie?' Nina asked. 'Is that the laird's auld nurse?'

'The auld nurse, aye,' Wilma answered, 'though she was never the laird's nurse. Why, she'd have to be ancient! Nay, she was nurse to the former laird's son. Lady Evaline's son.'

'Lady Evaline had a son?' Nina asked, unconsciously drawing Roden to her and wrapping her arms about his shoulders. He was young enough still to press close and return the embrace.

'Aye. He died, och, a long time ago. Afore I was born.'

'And that was such a long time ago,' Iven teased, and the maid giggled again.

'Well, 'twas,' she insisted. 'I'm seventeen now. Lady Evaline's son died twenty-five years ago. He was just a bairn.'

'Och, that's sad,' Nina said. 'How did he die?'

The maid shrugged and grimaced. 'In the wars,' she said vaguely. 'Poor Lady Evaline, she's never got over it really.'

She seemed about to say more but a sound from the corridor startled her and she blushed, dropped her eyes, fiddled with her apron, and then said with a hasty curtsy, 'But if ye'll excuse me, madam, sir, I must be getting back. I'll bring ye up some jugs o' hot water so ye can wash. I hope ye'll all be comfortable.'

'I'm sure we shall,' Nina said and Wilma went out, bobbing another curtsy at the door.

'Indeed, I think the Rìgh should be paying ye, no' me,' Iven said. 'Ye are far better than me at loosening people's tongues, my love.'

310

Nina smiled a little ruefully. 'Happen it's just habit,' she said. 'Though, Iven, are ye implying . . . do ye think we are upon the Rìgh's work here?'

Iven hesitated, then shrugged. 'Happen we are,' he said slowly. 'Though I do no' ken why I feel so. My skin is all a-twitch, though. That crofter's wife last night and her talk o' cursed witches – and she called upon the Truth, remember? Maxims like that, they stay in the language, they can be hard to shake, we all ken that . . . but still, she said it fervently, as if the words meant something to her.'

Nina nodded but raised her finger to her mouth, casting a quick glance at the door. Iven nodded and turned to smile at Rhiannon, Fèlice, Lewen and Rafferty, all warming themselves by the fire and listening with interest. 'Go on, bairns, go find your own fires,' he said cheerfully. 'Have ye naught better to do than hog all the warmth?'

Fèlice dimpled at him and moved away from the fire, shaking out her skirts so the hot material would not burn her legs. 'We do no' ken where our own fires are,' she said.

'Go find one!' Iven said, flapping his hand at her. 'There seemed to be plenty o' room in this castle, there must be some way Nina and I can be rid o' ye. We need some adult time, away from all ye young things.'

Fèlice sketched a curtsy. 'O' course, we understand. Shall we take Roden for ye?' she said cheekily.

'Now there's an idea,' Iven said, his blue eyes kindling.

'No!' Nina said and then coloured as everyone, including her son, looked at her in surprise. 'I'm sorry. I just want to keep Roden near me. Until we are out o' the valley.'

'Och, Mam,' Roden said in disgust.

'I'm sorry, laddie. It's just . . .' she trailed away, not wanting to put it in words, her hands unconsciously tightening their grasp about her son's shoulders.

There was a knock on the door. Iven raised one eyebrow at his wife and sauntered over to open the door. After a low murmured conversation, he turned his head and called to Nina, '*Leannan*, it is Dedrie, the skeelie I told ye about. She has been to see Maisie.'

'Och, ask her to come in, please, and tell me how Maisie does,' Nina said eagerly. 'I've been worried indeed.'

Iven stood back and held open the door for a small woman dressed in a crisp white apron and cap, with a heavily laden basket on her arm. Her eyes were brown, her hair was brown, and her dress was brown, her cheeks as round and rosy as apples. She came in with a quick, supple step, looking round her with great interest. As her eyes fell on Roden, both her step and her smile faltered.

'Och, no' a laddie,' she whispered.

'Aye, a laddie,' Nina answered stiffly, her own welcoming smile fading. 'What o' it?'

'Has no-one told ye?' Dedrie said, her face creasing in anxiety. 'Och, my lady has no' seen him, has she?'

'Your lady? Do ye mean Lady Evaline? Aye, she saw us all arrive. She seemed quite taken with my boy.' Nina's voice was still stiff and offended.

Dedrie sighed. 'Aye, well, she would be, wouldna she?' She put down her basket blindly, groped in her sleeve for a handkerchief and wiped her eyes.

Nina regarded her curiously, while Roden looked red and uncomfortable. All the conversation in the room had stopped. Dedrie was oblivious of their curious glances. She blew her nose thoroughly, tucked the handkerchief away, and went to kneel by Nina's side, reaching out a rather tremulous hand to touch Roden's ruffled curls.

'Ye should no' bide here,' she said. 'This is no' a happy house. Ye should pack up your things and go.'

'Are ye saying we are no' welcome here?' Nina replied in a cold voice.

Dedrie shook her head impatiently. 'Nay, nay, I'm saying this is no' the place to bring a young boy. Particularly one with red hair and dark eyes. Our boy Rory, he had hair this colour. Happen a wee redder, though it's been so long, it's hard to remember.' She sighed and took out her handkerchief again, wiping her eyes.

'Rory was Lady Evaline's son?' Nina asked, her voice and manner softer now.

Dedrie nodded.

'Her son that died?'

The nurse nodded again.

'Ye are afraid the sight o' my lad will hurt your mistress? Stir up unhappy memories?'

'Aye, my lady,' Dedrie said, and hesitated for a long moment as if wanting to say more but unable to formulate the words.

'I'm sorry for that, truly I am, but what are we to do? Maisie is sorely hurt, ye've seen her, ye ken she should no' be travelling, and besides, Laird Malvern says the road is blocked. We canna go on until it is cleared.'

Dedrie looked up, alarm on her face. 'The road? Blocked?'

'Aye, that's what he said. Why? Do ye mean it isna blocked?'

'Nay, nay, I just ... if my laird says the road is blocked, o' course it is. I do no' go away from the castle much these days, I wouldna ken about the road.' She stopped and took a corner of her stiff, starched apron and began to pleat it between her fingers. After a moment she said awkwardly, 'I do no' wish to alarm ye but I am wondering if ye have heard the tales . . . did ye come past the town on your way here?'

'Nay, the town had closed its gates for the night and would no' open for us,' Iven replied, a trace of anger in his voice.

Dedrie seemed to consider. 'Happen ye have no' heard then. I wish I did no' need to say this, but my conscience would no' rest easy if I did no' tell ye. It is no' safe here for young boys. Lads – many lads – have gone missing from hereabouts . . . for years now. If I were ye, I'd be on my way just as fast as ye can.'

'But surely we are safe here, in the laird's own castle?' Iven said. 'This place is a fortress!'

'Nowhere is safe,' she answered harshly.

'Lady Evaline's son . . . is that how he died?' Nina asked gently. 'Did he go missing too?'

Dedrie hesitated, then said roughly, 'He was the first to die.'

Nina would have asked more, but the nursemaid got up, blowing her nose defiantly. 'I have done what I can for the lassie. They are nasty bites, deep and unclean, but I have washed them with water boiled with adder's tongue and St John's Wort, and bound on a poultice o' bruised wintergreen, a herb which grows freely in these parts and which is very effective for healing open wounds. I have given her a hot tea I made myself, with feverfew and powdered willow tree bark for the pain and the fever, and chamomile and valerian to help her sleep, and devil's bit to expel the poison. I gave my borage syrup to the lads, washed down with a dose of elderflower wine, with peppermint and vervain in a basin for them to steam their faces. The lass with the sprained ankle, I made a poultice o' elder leaves, trefoil and figwort. An afternoon's rest and she'll be walking by nightfall, I promise ye.'

'Thank ye,' Nina said, sounding dazed. 'So when . . .'

Dedrie snorted. 'There is naught wrong with the laddies that a little rest and warmth willna help, but the lass . . . rattling round in a caravan willna do her any good, she's in pain and shall be for some time. I did no' wish to give her too much o' the poppy and nightshade syrup, for it shall give her nightmares, and too much can be dangerous, but if ye find ye must be gone quickly, I will give ye a bottle o' it and it shall help her endure.'

Nina nodded. The blood had ebbed away from her face, leaving her eyes black and glittering. She looked down at Dedrie, saying in a constricted voice quite unlike her usual melodious tones, 'Will ye ask about the road for us, Dedrie?'

'Aye, that I will,' the nursemaid answered. 'I will come back at dusk, to change the lassie's poultice. I will speak with ye again then.'

'Thank ye,' Nina said.

As soon as Dedrie had curtsied and taken her basket of medicines away, Nina turned to the others. 'Go and rest, my dears,' she said. 'I think we will be setting out again in the morning, Eà willing, and so ye should enjoy a soft bed and warm fire while ye can.'

They all nodded and murmured, without a smile or a joke between them, and went quietly to their own rooms, where the dancing flames of a freshly kindled fire helped, to some degree, to drive away the sudden chill that had shadowed them.

THE NURSEMAID

Rhiannon woke slowly from a strange dream.
She had been in the castle garden, sitting under the
apple tree, watching a young boy dressed in stiff, formal
clothes rolling a hoop along the pavement with a stick.
He had run to her, laughing, and she had held out her
arms, gathering him in close for a kiss and a hug. At first
she had thought he was Roden, but when she held him
away, she saw it was some other boy. He had tugged at
her hand and, smiling, she had got up and followed him.
As they passed through the great door into the castle hall,
chill air had struck at her, the bee-humming sunshine
behind her swallowed. There was a confusion of noise,
shouting, steel crashing, screams of pain, and she was
running, the little boy's hand in hers. 'All will be well,'
someone whispered. 'I'll be back soon.'

Then she had been kneeling in a dark, icy space, stone
walls pressing close all around. Weeping, she had beaten
her fists on the stone, screaming to someone to release
her. 'So cold,' the little boy sobbed. 'Mama, I'm so cold.'

Small, cold hands touched her face. Somewhere ravens were crying. 'So cold,' a voice whimpered in her ear. 'Please, I'm so cold.'

Rhiannon woke, tears on her cheeks. It took a while for her shivering to ease. She rubbed her damp eyes, realising she was lying in a warm bed under a soft quilt, with firelight playing on tapestry-hung walls. She sat up. Rain drummed on the diamond-paned windows and the sky was dark. Ravens were calling weirdly. Fèlice was sitting in a hipbath by the fire, her hair twisted up into tight knots all over her head, washing her arms and softly humming. Rhiannon watched her for a while, unable to completely shake away the cobwebs of the dream. There had been a boy, she remembered, a crying boy. She shivered.

Fèlice looked across. 'Och, ye've woken at last. Ye've slept all afternoon.'

Rhiannon was surprised. 'Have I?'

'Aye.'

'I was exhausted.'

'Ye slept like the dead. No' even the servants bringing in the bath roused ye. I was debating whether to try to wake ye for dinner or let ye sleep on.'

'The dead do no' sleep in this valley,' Rhiannon said.

'Och! Must ye remind me? I was just beginning to feel a wee bit better. Come, have a bath and borrow some o' my perfume. That'll take your mind off such gruesome things.'

'I had a dream . . .' Rhiannon clutched the coverlet to her chin.

'What kind o' dream?'

Rhiannon shook her head. 'Gone now. Something about cold hands touching me . . .'

'Gruesomer and gruesomer. Mind ye, this castle's creepy enough to give anyone nightmares. I'm glad we're leaving tomorrow, even if it does mean poor Maisie shall be all rattled about.' Fèlice stood up, water streaming off her, rosy in the firelight. She shivered, clambered out of the bath, and hurriedly wrapped a bath-sheet about her. 'Come and have a bath, and I'll wash your hair for ye,' she said winningly. 'Do ye want me to put it into ringlets?'

'Is that why ye have all those knots in your hair?' Rhiannon climbed reluctantly out of bed.

Fèlice put one hand up to her head. 'O' course. Dinna tell me ye've never seen anyone with their hair papered afore?'

Rhiannon shook her head.

'Gracious me, where have ye sprung from, my sweet?'

Rhiannon's mouth shut firmly, but Fèlice had no real interest in an answer. She went on gaily, 'I'll do it for ye now, if ye like.'

'Doesna it hurt?'

'Well, yes,' Fèlice admitted. 'It does make my scalp ache a wee, and I canna lie down and sleep like ye did very comfortably. But it's all the fashion, ye ken. The Banrìgh and the Keybearer both have the curliest hair ye ever did see, apparently, and now it is all the craze to have curls too.'

'I canna,' Rhiannon said. 'I must go and see to Blackthorn. She shallna like being confined within these high stone walls.'

'Ye canna go now, it's close on dusk already,' Fèlice said in alarm. 'The laird keeps country hours here, we were told to be ready for dinner at sunset and it's nearly that now, look at the sky.'

Rhiannon looked out at the bruise-coloured sky, hesitating.

'Do no' fear, Lewen was going out to check on the horses when the servants came with my bath. He

318

would've come to rouse ye if he was concerned, ye ken he would.'

Rhiannon bit her lip but submitted, knowing Fèlice was right. She stripped off her chemise and stepped into the bath, which was cooling fast. Dressed in petticoats and pantaloons, Fèlice brought her soap, but stopped abruptly at the sight of Rhiannon's wrists, which were roughly and inexpertly bandaged, the cloth stained with seeping blood.

'Eà forbid! Rhiannon! Why do ye cut yourself so? It's horrible. Look at your poor wrists. Have ye done it every night? Why? I do no' understand.'

Rhiannon said nothing at first, but she liked Fèlice and found to her amazement that she wanted Fèlice to like her too. This was a new experience for Rhiannon, and it caused her to blurt out unhappily, 'It's the only way I ken how to . . .' She searched for a word. 'Quiet down . . . the dark walkers. They demand blood.'

'Ye said that afore, the dark walkers. What does it mean? Ghosts? Ye think ghosts want to drink your blood?' There was incredulity in Fèlice's voice.

Rhiannon tried again. 'Dark walkers the things that lurk . . . evil spirits . . . unhappy spirits . . . they hungry . . . they angry . . . they hunt at night, want blood. Spill blood, they drink, go away.'

Fèlice shook her head. 'Who told ye all this? It's rubbish. Ghosts do no' want to drink your blood. It's naught but an auld faery tale.'

'Happen dark walkers no' ghosts,' Rhiannon said. She searched for the best word. 'Happen they gods.'

Fèlice stared at her then came and knelt by the bath, taking Rhiannon's sore, abused wrists in her hands. 'None o' it is true, Rhiannon, I promise ye. Whoever told ye this was tricking ye. Wounding yourself like this does ye no good. Ye will make yourself ill and scar yourself, to no avail. Please do no' do it any longer.'

Rhiannon looked stubborn. 'Must. I see dark walkers at the edges, everywhere. They want blood.'

'Must it be yours?' Fèlice asked helplessly.

Rhiannon looked surprised. 'Nay. Any blood will do. Only I have no time to hunt. Ride, ride, ride all day, all night, and no eating meat, no hunting. So only my blood left.'

'I will find ye something else tonight,' Fèlice swore. 'If no', ye can cut me.'

Rhiannon looked at Fèlice's soft white wrists, with the blood pulsing gently through a delicate tracery of blue veins. 'Och, nay,' she said. 'I couldna do that.'

'That's good,' Fèlice said rather tremulously. 'Because I really do no' want ye to. We'll find something else, much as it hurts me to wantonly kill another living creature.'

'Why?' Rhiannon was perplexed.

Fèlice shook her head, all her tight ringlets dancing. 'Where did ye come from, Rhiannon? Do ye ken naught about the Coven?'

Rhiannon set her jaw. 'No' much,' she admitted angrily.

'Well, a conversation for another day. We're late and ye're still very grimy. Let me wash your hair and bandage your wrists and make ye bonny, and we'll worry about all this serious stuff tomorrow.'

Rhiannon submitted to Fèlice washing her hair and then tying it up into hard little knots that made her feel as if her hair was being pulled out by the roots. Fèlice then laid her hot little hands over Rhiannon's head, explaining as she did so that this was one sorceress trick she had learnt at court, to hasten the drying of the hair. 'Otherwise it can take hours to dry, when our hair is so long.'

Rhiannon was amazed at this magic trick, and so Fèlice amused her by causing the candles on the mantelpiece to flicker out, then spring back into life again, and then warmed the cooling water by swirling her finger round and round. 'Surely ye must've seen such tricks afore?' she asked. 'The challenge o' the flame and the void is an elementary exercise – any novice can do it. Can ye no' do it yourself?'

'I do no' think so,' Rhiannon answered.

'Have ye had no lessons in magic at all?'

Rhiannon shook her head.

'Nina must think ye have Talent though, else she'll no' be taking ye to the Theurgia,' Fèlice said thoughtfully. 'O'course, ye've tamed a flying horse and no lass has ever done that afore.'

Rhiannon smiled at the thought of Blackthorn. She hoped her horse was safe and comfortable in that great, draughty stable. She stared at the candles on the mantelpiece and imagined putting them out with the power of her mind alone. Nothing happened. She scowled.

'It takes time,' Fèlice said, dressing herself in a long dusty-pink evening gown and hanging a delicate, sparkling necklace about her slim neck. 'Ye need to learn how to draw upon the One Power, and that is no easy task.'

'What's the One Power?'

Fèlice hesitated. 'It is the life-force o' the universe, the energy that exists inside all matter, whether it be stone or tree, star or moon, wind or water. It is the wheel that drives the motion o' time and the seasons. It is in us too, our soul or our spirit, and when we die, our life-force dissolves again in the world's life-force, bringing with it all the gifts o' wisdom we have acquired in our life, to be born again in another shape, another time.'

She fell silent and Rhiannon was quiet also, thinking.

'What about ghosts?' she asked after a moment. 'Why do the spirits o' ghosts no' dissolve?'

'I'm no' sure,' Fèlice admitted. 'Happen they are no' ready to go.'

Rhiannon thought she could understand that. She too had a hunger for life that she could never imagine being satiated. If she was to die now, in her youth, before ever having had all the things she wanted, would she not cling to her empty shell of a body with fierce hands, refusing to let go?

Fèlice noticed her shiver. 'Hop out now, that water's getting cold and I do no' want to use all my energy keeping it warm for ye.'

Rhiannon climbed out obediently and huddled herself into the warmed bath-sheet Fèlice held ready.

'So these witch-tricks o' yours, they take energy, just like running or fighting?' she asked.

Fèlice nodded. 'O' course. Working magic is very exhausting, and no' just for the witch. The greater the magic, the more energy ye draw upon – and no' just from your own reserves but everything around ye, even other people if ye are no' careful. That is why witches must be taught to be canny in their use o' the One Power, for misuse can be very dangerous. That is why we go to the Theurgia.' She gave herself a little shake, setting her ringlets dancing. 'But all this talk is very boring. Let's let your hair out and see what it looks like.'

With Fèlice's help, Rhiannon put on her green silk dress, the other girl smoothing away the creases with her witch-warm hands. Then Fèlice took out the papers from her hair, Rhiannon biting the inside of her mouth to stop crying out in pain. By the time Fèlice had finished fussing, Rhiannon's hair hung in long, dusky ringlets to the small of her back, and her mouth and cheeks had been subtly rouged.

Looking at herself in the mirror, a device she had never before seen, Rhiannon smiled, and for the very first time saw the flash of her dimples in her cheeks. They surprised her and, after a few more tentative smiles at herself in the mirror, pleased her. The face that looked back at her looked nothing like the stern, unhappy face that she had sometimes glimpsed in the satyricorns' lake.

'Well, ye scrub up well,' Fèlice said, sounding very pleased with herself. 'Though the dress is a wee bit too tight for modesty. If ye were no' so tall, I'd lend ye something o' mine.'

Rhiannon stood up, conscious of how much bigger she was than the dainty dark-haired girl beside her. Fèlice smiled up at her. 'Here, let me fold down your sleeves to hide those bandages. We do no' want anyone to see ye've been wounding yourself again. Now, look, are ye no' bonny? Let us go show the lads!'

Together they left their room, going next door to Nina and Iven's room, where they could hear the sound of voices and low laughter. Rhiannon felt eagerness rise in her. She felt so much better after her sleep and a bath; it had made her realise how tired she must have been, and how very cranky and bad-tempered. She felt sorry now, and resolved to smile at Lewen as soon as she saw him.

But although Lewen looked up when she came into the room, he only coloured and looked away when she smiled at him. Rhiannon scowled at his averted profile and smiled at Rafferty instead, who went scarlet and jumped to his feet, saying incoherently, 'Ye look bonny indeed, Rhiannon, like a narcissus. All slim and green, I mean, not narcissistic. No' that ye're green, o' course, except in the dress. I just mean ... ye look bonny. Like a lily-of-the-valley.' He gulped and managed to stop himself, and Rhiannon laughed and let him pull out a chair for her next to Nina.

Both Cameron and Landon were there also, exclaiming over the efficacy of Dedrie's herbal remedies, and telling Nina she must get the recipe for the elderflower wine.

'It was the most delicious thing I've tasted, and cleared my head something marvellous,' Cameron said. 'I feel so much better now.'

'Aye, happen so, but drinking too much o' that willna help any,' Nina said pointedly, looking at the glass of whisky in Cameron's hand.

He flushed but drank a mouthful defiantly, saying, 'Och, my granddad said a dram o' whisky is the best thing for any ailment. That's why they call it the water o' life.'

'And your granddad was a healer, was he?'

'Well, nay, but he lived to be sixty-four years auld,' Cameron said defensively.

'Well, my lad, let's hope ye live to be a lot aulder,' Iven said, taking the glass out of Cameron's hand. 'Do no' forget we are guests in this castle and I doubt the laird wishes drunk and rowdy young men at his table.'

'I'm no' drunk,' Cameron said angrily.

'No' yet,' Iven answered, still smiling. 'But I'll wager ye two gold crowns that Dedrie's elderflower wine is as potent as it is effective, and ye look like ye've been drinking it all afternoon.'

'I had a few glasses,' Cameron replied, on his dignity. 'To clear my head.'

'To muddle your head,' Iven teased.

'I must give this wine a taste,' Rafferty said. 'Any left, Cameron?'

'O' course! I dinna drink the whole damn bottle.'

'Well, when we come back up after dinner I'll come and have a swig,' Rafferty said.

'Maybe I should have custody o' this famous bottle o'

wine?' Nina said. 'I'm sure Dedrie did no' mean for ye all to get sozzled on it.'

'Ye just want it for yourself,' Rafferty said teasingly.

'No' I,' Nina said. 'My father was both a fire-eater and a drunkard, a combination that does no' work well. I will drink Isabeau's goldensloe wine at Midsummer, but naught else, ever.'

Her words cast a pall of sobriety over the room. She looked up and smiled. 'Do no' fear, he did no' burn himself to death or anything awful like that. He just could no' work his trade, and he was a jongleur to the bone, it hurt him to have to leave the travelling life. Luckily my brother Dide had a house where he could stay and do his best to drink the cellars dry. He died comfortably in his bed when Roden was a babe.'

'Thank Eà for that!' Fèlice said. 'I was imagining the worst.'

Nina smiled. 'I think my da would probably have preferred to go out in a blaze o' glory. Dying in bed is no' the way a jongleur wishes to go.'

'What is it about this place that makes us keep talking about death?' Fèlice wondered. 'Canna we find aught else to talk about?'

'I was happy talking about the wine,' Cameron said. Fèlice laughed and moved to sit down next to him by the fire.

Nina smiled at Rhiannon. 'Ye look the very picture o' courtly fashion. I fear it is wasted on the laird o' Fettercairn. Did ye notice he wears his hair short and his chin clean-shaven? He wears the fashion o' thirty years ago. He willna like all the long curls and soft clothes o' today.'

She cast a rueful hand down her own gown, a low-cut, cap-sleeved orange velvet dress that brought out fiery tones in her long chestnut hair. Round her neck she had clasped an amber and gold necklace. Roden stood between her legs, squirming and protesting as she tried to comb out his unruly curls. He was neatly dressed in a clean white shirt with a flowing collar and full sleeves, under an embroidered brown velvet jerkin.

'If the laird willna like it, why do I have to wear it, Mam?' the boy complained, tugging at his collar. 'It's tight. It itches. I dinna like it. Ow! Mam!'

'Sorry!' Nina freed the comb from his hair and tried again.

'Please, Mam? I dinna want to.'

'We're guests here, Roden, and must mind our manners. I canna have ye coming down to the drawing room all in a tangle, and wearing a shabby auld shirt.'

'I dinna like this one. I want to take it off!' He pulled violently at his collar and a button pinged free.

'Roden!' Nina sighed in exasperation and pulled him onto her lap, as Lulu uncurled her long, dexterous tail, retrieved the button from under the chair, and gave it back to Nina, all without moving from the table, where she sat eating her way through a bowl of small green apples.

'Can I have my sewing kit too, please, Lulu?' Nina said, twisting Roden round so she could see where the button had come loose. Obligingly Lulu leapt across the room, rummaged through one of the bags, and brought back a little floral-topped basket. Roden had become engrossed in looking at Nina's necklace and so his long-suffering mother was able to deftly sew back the button without any more trouble.

As Rhiannon sat down next to them, he turned and showed her the pendant. Frozen inside the large amber stone was an orange-and-black butterfly.

'Mam says it's thousands o' years auld,' he whispered. 'It must've been sipping at the sap o' the tree and got stuck, and slowly the tree-sap flowed all over it and set hard, and the butterfly was trapped inside. We do no' have butterflies like this here in Eileanan, Mam says. This necklace came over with the First Coven. From the Other World, ye ken. So it's no' just thousands o' years auld, it's from millions and millions o' miles away! Is that no' amazing?'

As Rhiannon nodded in agreement, Nina turned to her and smiled, dropping a kiss on Roden's curly head. 'He loves this necklace,' she said. 'It belonged to my grandmother. I do no' ken where she got it from, but I remember her telling me the story when I was just a bairn. I always loved it too.'

'It's beautiful,' Rhiannon said, putting her hand up to her bare neck. For the first time in days she thought of her necklace of teeth and bones, hidden away inside her saddlebags, and felt a cold shudder of revulsion. Her face must have reflected her feelings, for Nina's brows contracted and she leant forward, her eyes asking a question. Rhiannon shook her head and tried to smile, pushing away the memory forcefully. She was not a satyricorn anymore, she told herself. She would throw the necklace away the first chance she got.

The door opened and Edithe limped in. She had put her hair into ringlets too, and was wearing a striking dress of gold lace, with a beautifully worked amulet hanging on a long gold chain round her neck.

Cameron whistled. 'Going all out, Edithe! Trying to impress the laird?'

'What, with this auld thing?' she replied coolly, though the colour rose in her cheeks. 'No' at all. I only brought a few clothes, we were no' allowed to bring more than a trunk each, as ye ken. The material o' this dress is so fine, it folds very small and doesna take up much space.' She twirled about, holding the skirt so the material glimmered in the dim glow of the candles.

'Well, ye look mighty grand,' Cameron said.

Edithe smiled and thanked him, genuine pleasure on her face.

'A daffodil, a rose and a lily,' Landon said. 'The spirits o' spring.' A thought struck him and he groped in his coat pocket for his notebook and the disgracefully chewed quill. Finding he had left them in his everyday coat, his face fell, but Iven tossed him a scroll of paper and a quill, and it lit up again. He went to the desk, found an inkbottle and began to scribble, his handwriting looking like an insect had fallen into the ink and managed to scrabble its way free.

There was a soft knock on the door. Lewen got up and opened it, to let in the nursemaid Dedrie. She came in briskly, looking with approval at Edithe and saying, 'Och, your foot is all better, I see. That's good. And ye lads? A lot more colour in your cheeks this evening, I'm glad to see.'

'I think that may be due to the elderflower wine,' Nina said apologetically, putting Roden down so she could rise to her feet. 'Cameron has taken rather a liking to it.'

Dedrie smiled. 'He wouldna be the first young man to sneak a few extra glasses o' it. It is delicious indeed, and will do him no harm. No' even a headache in the morn.'

'I must have the recipe!' Cameron cried. 'Dear, dear Dedrie, will ye no' write it down for me?'

'I canna write, sir. But if ye like, I can tell ye the recipe, which is simple enough, and ye can write it down yourself.'

As Cameron thanked her exuberantly, Nina said to her softly, 'Were ye never taught to write nor read, Dedrie? Do they no' have a school here?'

'No' since the fall o' the witches' tower,' the nursemaid answered stiffly. 'That was nigh on fifty years ago, when

328

I was but a bairn. There has been no school since then, nor any healers, which, Truth kens, we have need o' here. That is why I set myself to gathering what skill I could in herb-lore and healing, since there was no-one else to do it.'

'I will let the Coven ken,' Nina promised. 'Ye have no need o' a healer, for ye clearly ken your craft well, but the bairns need a school, and Eà kens ye need a good exorcist!'

She spoke lightly, but Dedrie did not smile. 'What do we need a school for?' she said bitterly. 'There are no bairns left to teach.'

Nina's smile faded. 'Happen there will be in the future,' she said gently. 'Eà willing.'

Dedrie looked up at her. 'My lady, I would no' be so quick to throw around your witch-words, if I were ye.'

'Ye are the second person to say so to me,' Nina said, drawing herself up to her full height, her face stern. 'Why so?'

Dedrie looked away, the rosy apples of her cheeks darkening. 'Witches have brought naught but trouble to Fettercairn,' she said roughly. 'I mean ye no disrespect, my lady, I ken you are a sorceress and I am sure ye mean well. But . . . we have long memories here, and Fettercairn has no' been well served by witches. There are those that will mislike ye for your powers, and it would be wisest no' to remind them.'

'But why are witches so disliked? What have they done?'

'Och, it was grand in the auld days, when the Tower was strong and people came from everywhere to study here,' Dedrie said. 'We were a rich valley then, and able to put up with the wildness o' the students and the arrogance o' the sorcerers for we had money in our pocket. But then the Red Guards came and burnt down the

Tower and put all the witches to the sword, and anyone who protested was killed too, without hesitation.

'They bided here in the castle, the soldiers, and no-one in the valley could mumble a witch-word in their sleep without them hearing it. We soon learnt to mind our tongues, we did. And the Seeker walked among us and told us all the wickedness the witches had done, under our noses all the time, and promised we would be rewarded for keeping faith with the blessed Banrìgh, as she was called. So we did what we were told, and it was true, we all prospered better than ever afore, for the Banrìgh came to live in Ravenshaw, at the blue castle by the sea, and needed guards and servants and food – and we are close to the blue castle here, only two days' ride away.

'But then the witch-rebels came and attacked Fetter-cairn Castle, and our laird was killed and his son too. Since then it has been a cold, unhappy place, filled with ghosts, and each year it only grows worse, so that no-one dares put their nose outside their doors after dusk. Ye've seen the walking dead, I ken, and heard the tales o' robbed graves and murdered children. All o' that has hap-pened since the witch-loving rebels stormed the castle and killed our laird. It is said the witches have long memories, and will no' forgive or forget our support o' Maya the Blessed.'

'The people o' Fetterness blame the witches? But that makes no sense! Why would the Coven rob graves and murder bairns? That is ridiculous.'

Dedrie shrugged. 'If it was no' for them, the auld laird would still be alive, and our dear Rory too.'

Nina was silent, though her black eyes glittered with anger under her knotted brows.

Dedrie looked at her appealingly. 'So ye see, they do no' like witches here, and though it is mostly foolishness and superstition, ye canna blame them. I do no' mean that ye should hide what ye are, it is too late for that, but just . . . mind your words. Words can jab as sharp as any thorn and, when the wound is already deep, cause fresh blood to flow.'

'That is true,' Nina said evenly. 'I must admit I mislike hearing ye call upon the Truth. That was one hypocrisy I thought never to hear again.'

Dedrie went scarlet.

'Enough!' Nina said, taking a quick step away. 'I heed your warning and thank ye for it. I will mind my tongue. Tell me, how does Maisie? I sat with her a while and she seemed to sleep easy enough. I did no' dare remove the poultices to see the wounds, no' wanting to undo your good work.'

'She does well. She is young and strong and will heal quickly. There will be scars, there's naught I can do about that, but the one on her face is only small and will no' mar her too much.'

'Will she be well enough to ride out tomorrow?'

Dedrie pleated the edge of her apron. 'I fear the road shall no' be cleared in time, my lady. It would be dangerous to try to leave afore the tree is taken away.'

Nina regarded her with frowning eyes. 'Happen Iven and I shall ride out tomorrow morn and inspect the road for ourselves,' she said silkily.

'As ye please, my lady.'

'Thank ye for enquiring.'

'No' at all, my lady.' Dedrie curtsied, then said, with colour again rising in her plump cheeks, 'My lady, if I may be so bold . . . happen your laddie would rather have his dinner up here, on a tray? I've already asked the kitchen to bring up some broth for the poor wee lass. It would be no trouble for them to bring up some more for the boy. 'Tis just . . . my laird is rather auld-fashioned in his ways, he has had no bairns o' his own, he is no' much used to their ways . . .'

Nina hesitated. 'Normally I'd agree like a shot,' she said. 'Roden is no' good at formal dinners. But . . .'

'Och, please, Mam?' Roden cried. 'I wouldna have to wear this bloody shirt then!'

'Roden!' Nina cried. She cast a vexed glance at Iven, who shrugged and held up his hands.

'If ye like, I could stay here with the lad?' Dedrie said. 'I'd like to stay close to the lass too, her fever still worries me.'

'I want to keep my laddie near me,' Nina said, almost inaudibly. 'I'm afraid . . .'

Dedrie nodded. 'Aye. I understand. I'll have a care for him, though, my lady, I promise.' There was a fierce note of passion in her voice.

There was a long pause. Just before it grew embarrassing, Lewen bent his head and coughed into his hand. 'Och, I fear I've caught Cameron's cold,' he said. 'Do ye think I could be excused from dinner too, Nina? I really am no' much good at formal dinners, either, and I do no' want to cough all over my laird.'

Nina looked relieved. 'Very well. O' course. Happen ye feel well enough to sit up with Roden for a wee while and tell him some stories afore he goes to bed?'

'Yippee!' Roden shouted. 'Lewen, will ye tell me some o' the tales from when your *dai-dein* was a rebel with the Rìgh? Please?'

Lewen grinned at Roden. 'Sure!'

Dedrie was frowning but when Nina turned back to her, one eyebrow raised, she nodded her head, smoothing down her crumpled apron with work-reddened hands. 'Sure, and that's a happy solution for everyone,' she said. 'Happen the young man can help me with the lassie too. I thank ye all. My lady . . . my lady forgets sometimes, ye ken. It is no' good for her to be reminded o' the past. She is happy enough, in her own way, if she does no' remember.'

Nina nodded, her dark eyes softening with sympathy. 'It is a terrible thing, to lose a child.'

'Aye,' the nurse said and, for one moment, crushed her apron between her large, red hands. Then she smiled ruefully, smoothed it down again, and moved towards the door, which Iven opened for her. Just before she crossed the threshold, she turned back and regarded them all with those troubled dark eyes, at such variance with her round, rosy cheeks and brisk step.

'Ye'll all stay close, won't ye? Fettercairn's a big place, and very auld. Ye willna go wandering about, will ye, or play any silly games like hide-and-seek?'

Rafferty and Cameron exchanged mischievous glances and Fèlice had to bite back a giggle, but they all agreed solemnly that they would stay close to their rooms.

'Och, good,' Dedrie said. 'I wouldna want aught to happen to ye. Wait here, I'll send Wilma to direct ye. She willna be but a moment.'

The door shut behind her.

'What a weird auld lady,' Fèlice said. 'I swear my blood ran cold when she said "stay close", with *such* a meaningful look. What do ye think she's afraid will happen to us?'

'Ye might get lost and spend the rest o' your life wandering the halls o' Fettercairn, looking for a way out,' Rafferty said solemnly.

'Happen they have dungeons. Or an oubliette,' Cameron said. 'Ye could fall in and no-one would ken where ye were. Someone would find ye in a hundred years, naught but a skeleton wearing a rose-coloured gown.'

'Happen the ghosts would get ye,' Roden said in his high, treble voice. 'Ooooh, oooooooooh.' He pulled his shirt up over his head and ran round the room, wailing and flapping his arms.

Fèlice shuddered. 'Enough!'

'Aye, that's enough, laddie,' Nina said. 'Ye can go and get out o' your good shirt now. I just wish I hadna asked for it to be ironed. Look at ye! Ye're grubby already. Ten minutes on your back, and it looks like ye've slept in it. I dinna ken how ye do it.'

Roden whooped with joy, dragged the hated shirt over his head and flung it on the ground. Lulu leapt on top of it, jumping up and down, howling with glee. Laughing, Roden joined her, the little bag of muslin he wore about his neck bouncing up and down on his thin chest.

'Roden!' Nina cried in exasperation. 'Ye've got your boots on! Look at it now. It'll have to be washed again. Why do ye do these things?'

'I don't have to go to dinner!' Roden sang. 'Yippee!'

'We'll go and check on the horses,' Lewen said, 'and give them a bit o' a walk in the grass, then have dinner just the two o' us.'

'And a story.'

'Sure, and a story.'

'Ten stories!'

'Three,' Lewen compromised. 'And only if ye do no' give me any cheek!'

'I wouldna do that,' Roden said in all sincerity, his eyes wide. 'Would I, Mam?'

'Never,' she said with a smile, and drew close to Lewen so she could thank him.

'I do no' wish to upset anyone, but I canna be easy about leaving Roden with a stranger,' she said softly. 'I ken I'm probably over-anxious but all these tales we've been hearing . . . and those poor ensorcelled corpses . . . I just canna be easy in my mind.'

'Och, that's grand,' Lewen said. 'I'm happy to have a quiet night by the fire. *I* have no desire to get myself all fancied up.'

He caught Rhiannon's eye and looked away, and she turned her back, feeling unaccountably snubbed. She smoothed down her green silk, shook back her ringlets, and smiled at Rafferty, who shielded his eyes, saying, 'All this beauty, I am blinded!'

Rhiannon did not glance at Lewen again as she allowed Rafferty to show her out of the room.

THE GREAT HALL

The maid Wilma was waiting anxiously outside to show them down to the dining room. They went down two-by-two, and were shown into a huge, gloomy room panelled from floor to ceiling in wood so dark it was almost black. Each lofty wall was crowded with the stuffed heads of dead animals – stags, hinds, boars, sabre-leopards, snow-lions, woolly bears, hoar-weasels – their glass eyes shining awfully in the dull flicker of the iron chandelier suspended from a chain in the centre of the ceiling.

Nina's step faltered as she took in the sight of all the disembodied heads and antlers, and Fèlice made a face. Rhiannon looked round in interest. She had never seen the taxidermist's art before but she understood the desire to display such trophies of one's hunting prowess.

In the centre of the room was a long table spread with a yellowing linen tablecloth and decorated with ornate silver candlesticks and an enormous silver epergne. Lord Malvern sat at one end, looking with displeasure at his watch, and Lady Evaline sat at the other, her face unhappy. There was an old man wearing round eyeglasses sitting on her right hand, and a thin, brown, drably dressed woman sitting on her left, fiddling with her fork. Another elderly man with thin gnarled fingers and anxious, grey eyes sat a little further along, a middle-aged man with the same grey eyes sitting beside him. All the other guests looked apprehensive, and Lord Malvern was frowning heavily, two white dents driven down from his hooked nose to the sides of his mouth.

'I'm sorry, are we late?' Nina said, crossing the room swiftly.

'Your maid's fault, no doubt,' Lord Malvern said, standing up and bowing stiffly.

'Nay, I'm afraid we were all rather tired and slow to get ready. I am sorry.'

'No matter,' Lord Malvern said.

The seneschal Irving was there in his sombre livery, carrying a white-tipped stick in one hand. He bowed to Nina and lightly touched the back of the chair on Lord Malvern's right hand. At once a footman sprang forward and pulled out the chair for Nina, who sat obediently. Irving touched another chair, and a footman pulled it out for Iven. One by one, the seneschal indicated where each person was to sit, showing himself uncannily aware of the order of precedence owed to each and every one of them.

Rhiannon found herself sitting right down the end of the table, next to the old man with the eyeglasses. He peered at her over their rim, mumbled, 'My, my!' and then introduced himself as Gerard the Sennachie. Not knowing what this meant, Rhiannon smiled and nodded her head, and discovered, in time, that this meant the old man looked after the family history and papers, and kept the clan registers and library in order. He rambled on for what seemed like a very long time, telling Rhiannon all about the long and distinguished genealogy of the Mac-Ferris clan. They were one of the few great families of Eileanan to have an unbroken line of inheritance, father to son, for a thousand years, he told her.

'Is that important?' Rhiannon asked, bored.

He was surprised. 'O' course! Though the line is broken now, unhappily. Hopefully my laird can repair the break and restore the line. I ken it is his dearest wish.' Just then the first course arrived, and he thankfully subsided into silence.

Lady Evaline was scanning all their faces with anxious eyes. 'Where is the lad?' she asked piteously. 'Did I no' see a lad with ruddy hair and dark eyes, just like my wee Rory? Is he no' here? Was he a ghost too?'

Nina hardly knew how to answer, and everyone else sat feeling troubled and uncomfortable. Then Lord Malvern said very lightly, from the far end of the table, 'There's always lads running about, my dear, ye ken that. It must have been some pot-boy ye saw.'

Lady Evaline shook her head. 'I never see lads anymore,' she said sadly. 'No' anywhere. No' living boys, anyway. Ghosts, only ghosts. Sometimes it is my Rory that haunts me, sometimes other boys that come and go like will o' wisps, never here for long but always crying, always cold and crying.'

Lord Malvern stood up, the white dents appearing beside his mouth. 'My dear, ye are unwell. I shall call Harriet.'

Lady Evaline shrank back. 'Nay, nay, I am well, indeed I am,' she said. 'No need to call Harriet. I am sorry, it's just . . . I'm sure I saw a lad, a living lad, but no' to worry, never mind, I must've been mistaken. I am sorry.'

Lord Malvern sat back down again, his face unreadable. He indicated with a jerk of his head that the footmen continue serving the soup and everyone was able to hurry into comments about how hungry they were, and how good the soup smelt, and how lovely was the table setting.

Lady Evaline's clouded gaze moved back to Nina's face plaintively. Nina smiled at her, and turned her gaze to the soup bowl being placed before her.

Rhiannon found her composure unbalanced by the mention of the cold, crying boys, which brought her own dream back to her vividly. She also found the table settings very intimidating, for there were at least four spoons and knives, some quite oddly shaped, and any number of glasses and bowls and platters and tureens. She wished fervently that Lewen was there to show her what to do. She watched what the other girls did and tried to mimic them, with mixed results, since this line of defence was complicated by the fact that Fèlice and Edithe, as apprentice-witches, were not permitted to eat meat. There was barely a dish on the table without the flesh of some animal in it, which made it hard for Nina and the apprentices to eat without discourtesy. The soup at least was made of some sweet orange vegetable, but otherwise there was a large roasted fish on a bed of spinach, a chicken and leek pie, baked pigeons with asparagus and fennel, a dish of lamb and minted peas, and a buttered freshwater lobster. Rhiannon had been hungry for meat since leaving the herd and so she made an excellent meal despite never being quite sure if she was using the right knife and spoon. She noticed that Cameron and Rafferty also tasted many of the dishes, even if rather surreptitiously, and that Nina noticed too and was displeased.

The drab woman on the opposite side of the table from Rhiannon watched her chomp her way willingly through everything on offer, and said faintly, 'Heavens, the appetite o' the young. How one forgets.'

Rhiannon regarded her thoughtfully, but said nothing. The old man with the anxious grey eyes, who was apparently the clan harper, smiled at her, and said, 'I always enjoy watching young people enjoy their food. I wish I could eat with such joyous abandon, but that is one more pleasure lost to me, I'm afraid.'

'Here, *Dai-dein*, try some o' the fish, that is no' too rich,' his son said.

Further up the table, Lord Malvern was enjoying a lively conversation with Edithe, who had been placed at his left hand, in accordance with her noble birth. The young apprentice was smiling demurely as he said, 'But what is your father thinking, to let ye go off to court all by yourself, with no-one to protect ye?'

'It is the way o' the Coven,' Edithe said with a sigh. 'Indeed, my father was concerned but I was determined to go to the Theurgia and so at last he gave in and let me have my way.'

'Indeed, I can see it would be hard to resist ye,' Lord Malvern said. 'But why must ye go to the Theurgia? Surely a lovely young lady like yourself must wish to be married?'

'To whom?' Edithe asked, raising her eyebrows. 'There is none with whom I would wish to jump the fire.'

'But surely ye must be inundated with suitors?' Lord Malvern said.

'None my father considers suitable,' Edithe said, wrinkling her nose.

'Too auld or too young?' Lord Malvern asked with a smile.

'Too poor,' Edithe answered.

Lord Malvern laughed. 'Och, well, that is a problem for any father. I pity him. Ye say ye have three sisters? No wonder he has permitted ye to go to the Theurgia. To spend eight years so close to court, it'll be a wonder if ye do no' meet some handsome young laird who will sweep ye off your feet.'

'One can only hope,' Edithe replied.

Lord Malvern laughed again, causing both Lady Evaline and her drab companion to look up the table at him. 'Och, if I was just forty years younger, I'd be wooing ye myself.'

Edithe replied sweetly, 'And if ye were forty years younger, I'm sure I'd be most flattered, my laird. Tell me, do ye no' have a son or nephew as charming as ye, that ye could introduce me to?'

'I have no son,' he answered harshly. 'And though I had a nephew once, he died afore ye were born, my lady.'

'I'm sorry,' Edithe said, looking down at her plate.

The smile returned to his face. 'Och, no matter. Ye will have to make do with me, as ancient and creaking as I am.'

'Ye're no' ancient!' Edithe responded with an arch smile.

'Compared to your young loveliness, I'm auld indeed, though I do no' feel it, basking in the warmth o' your smile. Indeed, it is a shame ye must ride on as soon as the road is cleared. If ye and your friends were to bide a wee, I swear I would shed years each day ye were here.'

'That would be lovely,' Edithe said with a giggle, 'but I am afraid we must go. We have a wedding to attend!'

'Och, aye, the wedding o' the young prionnsa,' Lord Malvern said. 'To his cousin, the deposed Banrìgh. That is a canny political liaison. I canna be the only one in Eileanan that remembers she was named heir to the throne when her father died.'

'She ruled for only six hours,' Iven interjected angrily. 'And she was only a newborn babe at the time.'

'But the only offspring o' the Rìgh,' Lord Malvern reminded him. 'I have never heard that youth was a reason for disinheriting the rightful heir to the throne.

Eleanore the Noble was only eight when her father died and she inherited the Crown and the Lodestar, if I remember correctly. Her mother ruled as Regent till she was twenty-four. And Jaspar himself was only fifteen when he inherited the throne. Why should his daughter be disinherited just because she was a babe-in-arms?'

'We needed a strong man to rule,' Iven said quickly. 'We were at war on every front, a land divided.'

'True,' Lord Malvern answered, 'but why could the Banrìgh's uncle no' act as Regent and rule in her name until she reached her majority? Which I believe she has done just recently. No wonder her uncle wishes to marry her off to his son.'

Iven half-rose. 'She is the Ensorcellor's daughter!' he roared.

'And Jaspar's,' Lord Malvern pointed out. 'If the fact that she is the Dowager Banrigh's daughter sticks in his craw so much that he will no' allow her to rule, why is Lachlan the Winged marrying his son to her?'

Iven said nothing, though his blue eyes blazed with anger. Nina laid her hand on his arm.

'Besides,' Lord Malvern continued, unperturbed, 'when has it ever mattered what evil acts one's parents have been accused o', as long as one's right to the throne is legal? Donncan the Black was no' disinherited simply because his father Feargus was accused o' terrible crimes.'

'Ye seem to ken your history well,' Iven said coldly.

'We were taught well when I was a lad,' Lord Malvern answered. 'It was thought that if we kent history, we could try to avoid the mistakes o' the past. That is obviously no' what is believed now.' There was a trace of bitterness in his voice.

'Come now,' Lady Evaline said in her sweet voice. 'I was taught it is rude to discuss politics at the dinner table. Tell me, my lady, how are your sick bairns? Has Dedrie been o' use to ye?'

'Aye, indeed,' Nina answered, her cheeks rather flushed. 'As ye can see, the boys are both well enough to join us here for dinner, and Edithe is only limping slightly. Dedrie seems to ken her craft well.'

Lady Evaline sighed. 'Aye. I do no' ken what we would have done without her all these years.'

'She's a skilled healer, ye are lucky. So many remote villages and towns are still without properly trained healers, even so long after the witch-burnings. Indeed, it was an evil thing, the killing o' so many harmless skeelies and cunning men. Most o' them had done no more wrong than do their best to help the poor and auld and sick.' Nina's eyes sparkled with anger. It was clear the lord's comments had cut her on the raw too.

Another uncomfortable silence fell. All of the castle folk stared at their plates, and Lord Malvern's thick, dark brows were drawn down angrily. He laid down his knife and leant forward, as if about to speak.

Lady Evaline spoke first, hurriedly. 'But ye have no' yet told me what ye do, travelling through Fetterness Valley? We are so pleased to have guests, it has been a dreadfully long time since anyone has come to visit us. Ye say ye are travelling to Lucescere, for the wedding? Why come this way? Most people seem to prefer travelling down the far side o' the Findhorn, where the roads are so much better and where there are no ghosts.'

Lord Malvern's frown deepened and once again he made to speak.

Iven cut across him. 'Indeed, we would normally have chosen to go the other way too, my lady, since it is difficult travelling with caravans on rough roads. However, we have news we were most anxious to take to His

Highness, and so we decided to come this way, since it is so much shorter. Or so at least we hoped. We have had nothing but bad luck and foul weather since we chose this road.'

'What news may that be?' Lord Malvern demanded.

Iven turned to him politely. 'One o' the Rìgh's Blue Guards was found murdered in the highlands, my laird. He was one o' His Highness's most trusted lieutenants and both Nina and I kent him well. His sister is the head of the healers' guild and is a dear friend o' ours. We wished to take the news to her, and to His Highness, as quickly as we could.'

'Oh, I see,' Lord Malvern replied, his frown relaxing.

'How very sad,' Lady Evaline said and the other castle inhabitants murmured also.

'How did he die?' the harper's son asked.

'He was shot,' Iven replied.

'And ye kent him well?' the drab lady asked.

Nina nodded. 'I've kent him since he was just a lad. He was one o' the League o' the Healing Hand. Have ye heard the tales about them? They were a band o' beggar children that joined the rebellion in Lucescere, och, many years ago, and did many brave deeds to help Lachlan the Winged win the throne.'

'The League o' the Healing Hand?' the harper asked with great interest. 'What a strange name.'

'One o' the lads, Tòmas, had the power to heal with the laying on o' hands. He was only a wee laddie, six or seven, perhaps. Connor, the Yeoman whose body we found in the highlands, was just his age and his best friend. They formed the League to help and protect Tòmas.'

'Where is this lad now? He must be a man grown?' Lord Malvern asked with sudden quick interest.

'He died at the Battle o' Bonnyblair,' Iven said. 'It was a great tragedy. He died saving the Rìgh's life.'

Lord Malvern turned his attention back to his lobster. 'Very sad,' he said.

'It was his second death,' Iven said, noticing the eager interest in the eyes of the harper and his son, who were naturally stirred by such a story. 'There is a beautiful song about him, written by the Rìgh's minstrel, who is now the Earl o' Caerlaverock. I will sing it for ye later, if ye like.'

'I would like that,' the harper's son said eagerly. 'We hear so few new songs here.'

'What do ye mean, it was his second death?' the harper asked, his grey eyes alight with curiosity.

'Tòmas died earlier, during an ambush by the Bright Soldiers. He had used all o' his powers to save the Rìgh, who was sorely wounded. Lewen should tell this story, it was his mother Lilanthe who saved him. She had been given a flower o' the Summer Tree by one o' the Celestines. The flowers have immense power in them, it is what gives the Celestines their magical ability to heal by the laying on o' hands, an ability that Tòmas had inherited. Lilanthe roused Tòmas enough so that he could eat the flower, and it brought him back to life and made his miraculous powers even greater. He saved the lives o' thousands o' soldiers during the Bright Wars, so many I think it is fair to say we could never have prevailed without him.'

Lord Malvern had looked up from his plate again, his gaze intent. 'So those *uile-bheistean* – the faeries ye call Celestines – they can bring people back to life?'

Nina and Iven both stiffened at his use of the word. Nina in particular looked outraged, her cheeks flushing red, her black eyes shooting out dangerous sparks.

'We do no' call those o' faery blood *uile-bheistean* anymore,' she said coldly.

Lord Malvern waved his hand dismissively. 'Whatever. Ye were saying they can bring people back to life?' His gaze was fixed with disconcerting intentness upon Nina's face.

'They can heal,' Nina said stiffly. 'Particularly those o' Stargazer blood. The Stargazers are those who have eaten o' the flower o' the Summer Tree. They are like the royal family o' the Celestines.'

'I see,' the lord said thoughtfully. 'But they can heal even those so sorely wounded they are close to death?'

Nina nodded. 'If they are powerful enough.'

'What a fascinating story,' he said, beginning to eat again. 'We must certainly hear the song after dinner. Some music would be a most pleasant diversion. And perhaps the young ladies would like to dance? My piper and my harper would be glad to play a few reels.'

Fèlice clapped her hands in delight. 'That would be wonderful!'

'I'm sure my ankle will be able to stand a few turns,' Edithe said.

'Then it's arranged. In the grand drawing room after dinner, Borden!'

'As ye wish, my laird,' the old harper said, bowing slightly.

Once the meal was cleared away, Lady Evaline and her companion rose and left the room, Nina and the three girls following her. They sat in one of the drawing rooms and drank tea, and made stilted conversation. As soon as the seneschal had indicated the footmen could remove the tray and had left the room himself, shutting the door behind him, Lady Evaline leant forward.

'My dear madam, please will ye no' tell me, ye did have a boy with ye, dinna ye? A laddie with red hair?'

'My lady,' the drab companion protested weakly.

Lady Evaline kept her eyes on Nina's face. The journey-witch pressed her lips together and reluctantly nodded. 'My son, Roden,' she answered.

Lady Evaline clapped her hands. 'I thought he was no' a ghost! Och, I am glad. I had begun to think I must really be going mad.'

'Evaline, my dear,' her companion said anxiously.

Lady Evaline waved a hand at her. 'I just wanted to be sure, Prunella. Tell me, did he no' come down to dinner because they warned ye to keep him away from me?'

Nina nodded, looking very uncomfortable.

'I knew it!' Lady Evaline cried. 'They do worry about me. But ye must no' worry, my dear. I would never hurt your son.'

'I hope no',' Nina said steadily, a spark igniting in her black eyes. 'For I am a sorceress, ye ken, and one should never enrage a sorceress.'

Lady Evaline nodded wisely, though her companion looked scandalised. Edithe and Fèlice exchanged glances, trying not to giggle.

'Believe me, I ken how to protect my son,' Nina went on, her colour high.

'More tea?' Miss Prunella asked, lifting the teapot. She had a soft downy moustache above her lip, which quivered.

'Nay, thank ye,' Nina answered, putting down her cup. 'I think I have had quite enough.'

'I thought I could protect my son too,' Lady Evaline said. 'I thought the strength o' these walls and the strength o' my husband's arm, and my own love, would be enough to keep him safe, but I was wrong.'

'Evaline,' Miss Prunella quavered. Nina and Lady Evaline both ignored her.

'I'm sorry for that,' Nina said gently. 'I ken how much ye must grieve for him.'

'They try to make it up to me, but there's naught they can do,' Lady Evaline said in her soft, plaintive voice. 'A mother kens her own son, dead or alive.'

Edithe rolled her eyes and made a little corkscrewing gesture beside her ear that almost made Fèlice giggle out loud. Nina shot them a fierce look. 'O' course,' she said.

The door opened and Lord Malvern came in, smiling.

'That was quick,' Lady Evaline said. 'Would ye like some tea?'

'None o' my guests were smoking men,' he answered equably, scanning them all with his fierce black eyes set under bristling grey brows. 'Do we feel like some dancing? Shall I send for my harper and piper?'

Edithe and Fèlice squealed and clapped their hands. Lord Malvern rang the bell and Irving came, bowing, to smoothly arrange the removal of various chairs and tables from the large drawing room.

'We have a ballroom, but that is too large for only a few couples,' Lord Malvern said. 'For a friendly little dance, this is more comfortable, I think.'

Then the harper and his son came, carrying various instruments, and an old man with a set of bagpipes, and for the next hour, the time passed merrily enough, with no more talk of ghosts or dead boys. Rhiannon was the only one of the girls not to enjoy herself thoroughly, for she could not dance. Also, she could not rid herself of the weird feeling that all this talk and laughter and music was a sham, and that under the smiling faces and lively chatter, other darker thoughts hid, like a snake in the grass. She felt like she was being watched all the time. Refusing every exhortation to join the dancing, she sat against the wall, listening and observing. The candlelight wavered in her tired eyes, and she thought for a moment she saw a little boy standing forlornly in the shadows. She started and blinked, and the mirage was gone, but she could not shake the nervous tension that kept her muscles all in a knot.

Landon did not much enjoy dancing, either. Dutifully he danced with Edithe, managing to tear the hem of her gauzy gold gown, and with Fèlice, who laughingly pretended to limp away afterwards, declaring her feet were black and blue with bruises, and then he thankfully sat down against the wall too. After a while, when he thought no-one was paying him any attention, he drew out his dog-eared notebook and his quill and, balancing the inkpot on the gilded, satin-covered chair beside him, began to scribble with great intentness.

Rhiannon watched him with interest. She had begun by thinking Landon a very peculiar young man, but she had grown to like him very much, something which surprised her. He was not strong, or fast, or brave, or handsome. He sat on a horse like a sack of potatoes, and showed no interest in wrestling or hunting. He did not like being wet or cold or tired or hungry. He was, in fact, the sort of person she would normally view with contempt. Yet, despite his physical frailty, despite his shyness and oddities, there was something about him that made her warm to him, and want to look out for him and keep him from hurting himself.

After a while she slid along the seats towards him, noticing with amusement that his inkpot was leaving a round dark stain on the lord's straw-coloured satin chair.

'What ye write?' she asked.

He glanced up at her, looking a little cross, but then when he saw it was Rhiannon interrupting him, he blushed and stammered and almost tipped his inkpot over. Rhiannon rescued it with a grin, and he said shyly, 'It's only rough still, but I could read it to ye if ye like?'

When she nodded, he cleared his throat and read aloud,

'How dark this place, how grim!
Where the black wings o' ravens shadow the sky
Where the wind sobs round the tower high
Like the desolate cries o' a murdered child.
My own life, once so keen and bright, grows dim.
My own song falters; my pulse is wild.
In my dreams I hear the toll o' death's bell,
Beneath my feet yawns a bottomless well.'

Rhiannon stared at him in true amazement. 'Ye feel it too?' she whispered.

He stared at her in surprise and pleasure. 'My poem means something to ye?'

She nodded. 'I hate this place. I wish we could get away.'

'Me too. But I dinna ken why. It's all dreams and shadows. I dinna like to say aught, I ken the others would just laugh at me, but . . .' He paused, and then said, 'It's no' a happy place, this castle.'

'No,' Rhiannon agreed. They sat in silence for a while, watching the dancers twirl about the room, then Landon said, very shyly, 'I'm so glad ye liked my poem.'

After Lady Evaline and her companion had retired for the night, and the musicians had packed up their instruments, Lord Malvern offered to show them around the castle and they agreed eagerly. He led them through various vast picture halls, a ballroom with a music gallery, a library filled with books and maps and a great desk piled with papers, the grand dining room which was far larger than the private room they had just dined in, and then, lastly, the great hall. This was an immense cold shadowy room that made Rhiannon shiver and edge closer to Nina. The witch seemed to find the atmosphere of the room unpleasant also, for she hugged her arms with her hands and looked about her with troubled eyes. 'Do ye use the hall much?' she asked politely.

'No' these days,' he answered. 'It has unhappy memories.'

As Lord Malvern spoke, Rhiannon felt a strange, disturbing thinning of the atmosphere. Her breath puffed out white. For a moment her companions faded away, and she saw a room filled with men, weary and bloodied with battle. One wore long red robes, others wore the livery of the MacFerris clan, but a few were dressed in shabby, stained motley, little better than rags. Two men faced each other across the points of their swords. One was young and dark, with a hunched shoulder, and a surly, unshaven face, wrapped in a filthy black cloak from head to foot. The other was older and dressed formally in a velvet doublet and black kilt, with embroidered stockings and neatly combed hair and beard. Rhiannon heard a snatch of voices, shouts, curses, a hysterical-sounding ranting from the man in red. Then the swords rose and clashed, there was a sharp cry of horror, and then the older man slowly fell to his knees, both hands clutching his stomach. He toppled sideways and blood spread across the paving-stones.

'Blood,' Rhiannon said, and clutched at Nina for support. 'Blood was spilt, just there.'

'Blood spilt, here?' Nina repeated, and looked at the floor as if expecting the stain to remain. Edithe gave a little shriek and leapt back.

'Aye,' Rhiannon said. 'A man was killed.'

351

'She is right,' Lord Malvern said unwillingly. 'It was my brother's blood that was spilt. He was murdered here on this very spot.'

Everyone exclaimed in shock and moved back uneasily.

'It was a very long time ago,' Lord Malvern said. 'I do no' like to come here myself, but I am surprised the lass should be able to sense aught. I daresay she has the witch-sight, though, heh?' His voice was heavy and sarcastic.

'I daresay,' Nina said, drawing Rhiannon close.

'Was no' murdered,' Rhiannon said in a clear, calm voice that sounded to her own ears as if it came from a very great distance away. 'Was fair fight.'

Lord Malvern turned on her in sudden rage, two white dents on either side of his mouth. 'A fair fight!' he cried. 'The laird o' the castle, cut down in his own hall by a mob o' filthy rebels? How is that fair or right?'

Rhiannon was coming back to herself in racking shudders. She leant heavily on Nina, her voice as tottery as her legs. 'I do no' . . . ken the laws o' your land. In my land, if one raises hand or weapon against another with same and . . . is killed, is no' called murder. Is called fair fight. Fancy man . . . your brother . . . he struck first blow . . . was no mob . . . fair fight with dirty man . . . dirty man won.'

'Indeed, the dirty man did win,' Lord Malvern said very softly, looking away into the gloom. There was a long silence. Rhiannon tried to still the trembling of her arms and legs. She saw nothing now, but the memory was vivid in her mind's eye. Half-fearful, half-curious, the others glanced about the ill-lit room, its hearth swept clean and bare as if it was never warmed with dancing flames.

'Did ye see aught?' Cameron whispered to Fèlice, who shook her head reluctantly.

'I *felt* something,' she whispered back. Landon nodded, eyes wide.

'Sure ye did,' Edithe said caustically. 'The damp and the cold.'

Fèlice cast her a cutting glance but dared say nothing else, for Lord Malvern had stirred and brought his stern gaze back to them.

'It is cold in here. Let us withdraw to the drawing room,' he said with great politeness. 'May I offer ye some mulled wine, my lady?'

'No' for me, thank ye, my laird,' Nina said just as politely. 'I find I am rather tired still and would like to retire to my bedchamber. I thank ye for a most delicious meal, though, and for your hospitality.'

'Tell me,' Iven said, 'what news o' the road? For we are anxious to be on our way, as we explained. We really must get to Lucescere as fast as we can, the Rìgh will be looking for us.'

Lord Malvern grimaced and shook his head. 'No good news, I fear, sir. The road was badly damaged and is hard to repair because o' the steepness o' the slope. I have all my spare men working on it though, and hope ye will be on your way again as soon as can be.'

Iven inclined his head. 'I ken something o' such things, my laird. Happen I may be able to help?'

'Thank ye for the offer but I'm sure my men have all under control,' he answered.

'Nonetheless, I would like to have a look, my laird, if only to give me something to do while we wait. I fear I am unused to much rest.'

'Ye should enjoy the chance to relax while ye can,' Lord Malvern smiled.

Iven sighed. 'True, but I fear a lifetime o' habit is hard to overcome in only a few days. And I am curious. It must indeed be a difficult job, to repair a road in such conditions. Happen your men can teach me something.'

'Very well.' Lord Malvern bowed stiffly. 'I shall instruct my men to show ye the road in the morning.'

They had come back through to the main wing of the castle and stood now at the base of the grand stone staircase that led up to their rooms. Lord Malvern bade them a rather grim goodnight and rang for a footman to show them the way back, even though Iven protested that there was no need, they knew the way.

'It is a very large castle, and much o' it is empty these days,' Lord Malvern responded. 'I would hate ye to become lost, particularly so late at night when most o' the servants are sleeping.'

'Then thank ye,' Iven said, allowing a footman carrying a great branch of candles to lead them towards their rooms. Rhiannon felt odd, as if her feet were weighted with lead and her head was as light as a bellfruit seed. It was very dark and quiet in the corridors, and bitterly cold, so all were glad to reach Nina's warm suite, lit generously with scented candles and a roaring fire. Roden was fast asleep in Nina and Iven's great canopied bed and Lewen was sitting drowsily before the fire, his boots off, his shirt undone at the collar and rolled up to show his powerful brown forearms. He had been whittling arrows, a great pile of them lying beside him, waiting to be fletched.

'How was dinner?' he asked, standing up and yawning.

'Creepy,' Fèlice answered, coming to stand close to the fire, and smiling up at him. 'No' as creepy as the great hall, though. Rhiannon had a fit, and saw blood everywhere, and ghosts, and the laird was furious. He doesna like talk o' ghosts, it seems.'

'Who does?' Lewen answered, looking past her to Rhiannon, who was now so exhausted she could barely stand upright on her own feet. 'How are ye yourself?' he asked.

'Grand I am, indeed,' she answered, and fainted.

THE DREAM

Rhiannon woke with a jerk. For a moment she was disorientated. Everything was dark. The fire had fallen into ashes. She lay still, temples throbbing. Her mouth was dry.

Someone stood by the bed.

Rhiannon's heart slammed hard, and she said with a sharp rise in her voice, 'Roden? What's wrong?'

The boy said nothing.

'Roden?'

'So cold,' he whispered. 'So cold.'

Rhiannon lay very still. 'Who are you?'

He stepped closer. In the darkness he was nothing more than a pale shape. She could feel him trembling. 'Please . . .' he whispered. Then an icy cold hand touched her face.

Rhiannon screamed.

Fèlice sat bolt upright beside her. 'What is it? What's wrong?'

'A boy . . . a ghost!'

355

'Ye're just dreaming,' Fèlice mumbled. The candles on the mantelpiece flickered into life, showing the bed-chamber was empty. 'There's naught here. Ye were just dreaming. Ye're sick. Go back to sleep.' The candles snuffed themselves out, and Fèlice rolled over and was instantly asleep again.

Rhiannon lay, every muscle rigid. Then she slowly brought one hand up to cover her cheek. It was chill to the touch. She shuddered.

After a moment she very slowly and carefully put back the bedclothes and got up. In the darkness she pulled on her woollen stockings and boots, and wrapped her cloak about her. It was so dark she had to feel her way to the door, but the hallway was lit dimly by a lantern left on a side table, turned very low. For a moment she stood, listening. Then she picked up the lantern, turning up the wick so it cast a circle of warm light into the frigid darkness. Immediately her heart began to slam against her ribs again.

At the far end of the corridor the boy waited. He was dressed in formal clothes, and his feet were shod in buckled brogues that seemed to rest solidly enough on the carpet. He had dark, sombre eyes and ruddy hair. He was shivering, and had his arms wrapped tightly about his skinny body. He looked back at her, then made his way slowly round the corner. Rhiannon followed him.

He led her away from the guest quarters towards the northern tower, which Rhiannon knew was set aside for Lady Evaline's use. He went swiftly and steadily, but not so fast that Rhiannon had trouble keeping up with him. She was just beginning to think that he was perhaps a real boy, a pot-boy who liked to play silly tricks on guests, when he passed straight through the great oak door that led into the tower. This discomposed her so much she stopped, fighting to regain her breath, her heart galloping like a runaway horse. Her nerve almost failed her, but her hunger to understand was greater and so she went on again, opening the door as silently as she could. There was no sign of the ghost, and she was angry with herself. She moved on through the narrow stone corridor anyway, its walls hung with faded tapestries. She came to a spiral staircase and began to climb it, her shadow preceding her up the round walls like some black, formless giant. Then she rounded the central pillar and saw the ghost standing there, only a few steps ahead, staring at a door half-concealed behind a tapestry. As she shrank back, instinctively shielding the light of her lantern, he looked back at her, beckoned urgently, then stepped forward and vanished through the solid wood.

It took Rhiannon a long time to find the courage to open the door. Her hand was trembling so much the lantern's flame flickered and shook, sending shadows swinging everywhere. She steadied it at last, and saw a sight which chilled her to the very marrow of her bones.

Inside was a boy's bedroom. There was a little bed with a patchwork counterpane, a rocking horse, a wooden castle with tiny soldiers lined up along the battlements, a puppet theatre, and a basket filled with balls and wooden animals and toy swords. There was a big barred window with a cushioned window seat and faded curtains covered with prancing red horses. Against one wall was a cupboard painted with stars and moons, and against the other was a toy chest, its lid propped open.

The room was filled with the ghosts of boys. One rode the rocking horse back and forth, back and forth, its rockers creaking. Another examined the puppet theatre, a few more were crouched over the castle. One was curled up in the big chair, looking at a book. One crouched on the window seat, sobbing into his arms. Another lay weeping on the bed. One boy was dripping wet, sitting in a puddle, shivering and crying. Another rocked back and forth in silent terror beside the door. Some were dressed in nightgowns, others in rough homespuns, a few in neat suits with collared shirts, a few others in heavy winter coats and red woolly hats. The more she looked, the more ghosts she saw, some as insubstantial as heat rising from a sun-baked stone, others looking like living boys, except that as they moved about the room, their bodies merged into each other and materialised again on the other side, like flickering shadows.

The ghost Rhiannon had seen first was standing in the centre of the room, his arms huddled about him. He turned his face towards her and said pitifully, 'All lost. Canna find their way home. Lost.' He shuddered violently and said in a thin whisper, 'So cold. Mama, I'm so cold.'

It was cold. Rhiannon's inner ears ached painfully. Her breath came out in frosty plumes, and she was shivering so violently the oil in the lantern slopped about and the flame sank away into darkness. All she could hear was the muffled whimper of crying and the creak, creak of the rocking horse.

Slowly Rhiannon backed out of the room, the lantern dropping from her nerveless fingers. The sound of it breaking went through her like a shock of lightning. She slammed the door closed, then ran down the stairs. She felt faint and sick, so faint she was afraid she might lose her wits again. Back through the dark hallways and galleries she ran, and ran, and ran, down unlit stairs and through cavernous chambers, banging into furniture, becoming entangled in hanging curtains, bruising her hips on unexpected hall tables, and, horribly, coming face to face with the gloomy eyes of ancient paintings, until the stitch in her side forced her at last to slow, fighting for breath. Only then did her panicked mind admit that she had no idea where she was, or how she was to get back to her room. She was lost.

For a while she huddled on a couch in an immense, high-ceilinged room, her cloak wrapped tight around her, overcome by such terror that unconsciousness passed over her in black, roaring waves. The muscles of her urinary tract had relaxed involuntarily, so that she felt a sopping patch on her nightgown grow, the initial warmth passing to bitter cold. All she could do was fight to get breath into her paralysed lungs and try not to lose control of her other bodily functions, which threatened to shame her further. No-one could endure such extremities of emotion for long, though, and eventually she was able to control the shudders that racked her, wipe the tears from her face and get up. She felt her way to the paler oblongs of the tall windows, looking for some clue as to where she was in the vast, silent castle. There was no moon to help her but the sky swarmed with stars. She wrenched the window open and leant out, breathing in great gulps of fresh, cold air, fixing her eyes on the familiar constellations above. When her eyes adjusted to the darkness, she was able to see the shape of battlemented walls and the pointed roofs of towers silhouetted against them. She gave a smile of pure relief, realising she was back in the main part of the castle, looking across the inner ward to the gatehouse.

She made her fumbling way through the room and out to the gallery above the main stairs. Here another lantern glowed softly in the darkness, lighting the landing. More light spread out in an arc from a door down on the next floor. Rhiannon hesitated for a moment with her hand upon the lantern. With its help she thought she could find her way back to the warmth and safety of her own bed. But she could not help wondering who in the castle was awake at this late hour, and what they were doing. Since seeing the ghosts of so many little boys, Rhiannon could feel nothing but the deepest horror and suspicion of everyone in the castle, but it only sharpened her desire to know, to understand. So she made her slow, tentative way down the stairs and put her eye to the crack of the door.

She saw high shelves of books, flickering in the dancing shadows of flames, and the high back of an old leather chair, and the gleam of a wooden desk. The air breathing out of the room was warm and smelt pleasantly of smoke. Everything was quiet.

After a while she gently pushed the door open. Still there was no sign or sound of life. She looked about her warily. Long wooden cabinets lined the walls. She pulled open a drawer. Inside were hundreds of old bones, all laid out neatly and tagged. Another drawer held a collection of desiccated claws and paws. She recognised the black massive hand of an ogre and the yellow claw of a goblin, a snow-lion's heavy white paw, and a scaly webbed hand that she guessed must belong to one of the sea-folk. In the drawer beneath it were rows and rows of human hands, all severed at the wrist. Some were badly preserved, some bare bones, but most looked as if they had just been cut away from a living body. Her stomach quivered uncomfortably. Rhiannon touched one. It was cold and hard and left an oily residue on her fingers. She swallowed and wiped her fingers on her nightgown. She felt, suddenly, very cold and frightened.

The warmth of the fire drew her irresistibly. It had only just been built up with fresh wood and roared away merrily on the hearth. She tiptoed towards it. A dead baby floated in a jar on a shelf. An ogre's head glared from another jar. Nailed to a board was a glittering scaly skin in the shape of a man. In another jar was a pile of strange white round things. Rhiannon could not bring herself to examine them closely. She stood before the fire and warmed herself, wondering what kind of man would surround himself with such things.

The hands of the clock on the mantelpiece were moving towards twelve o'clock, the only time Rhiannon could tell. She held her icy hands to the fire, watching the smaller hand tick round, wondering why the room was all lit up and the fire burning, when no-one was there. When the front of her body was so hot she had to hold the cotton of her nightgown away from her, she turned and basked her backside.

A huge woolly bear stood in the corner of the room, muzzle snarling, claws raised. Rhiannon bit back a shriek. Wildly she looked round for a weapon. Her daggers were back in her room. She cursed herself for leaving them there, even as she seized a heavy silver ornament from the mantelpiece. As she swung back round to face the bear, her impromptu weapon raised, she wondered in amazement what a woolly bear could be doing here, in the lord's own library. Lewen's parents had kept one as a pet, though, so she supposed it was not as uncommon as she would have imagined.

Breathing fast, she stared at the bear, who stared back at her with glassy eyes. For a long moment they eyed each other, then Rhiannon slowly lowered the ornament and took a tentative step forward. The bear did not move. She took another step forward. Still the bear did not move. She crossed the room warily, and reached up a hand to its stiff, cold snout. The stuffed bear stood frozen, yellow teeth exposed, huge claws curved. Rhiannon shook her head in wonderment.

Then she saw something that made her eyes widen and her breath catch. One section of the bookshelves had swung sideways, revealing a narrow doorway. She would never have seen it if she had not gone to examine the stuffed bear. Rhiannon tiptoed to the secret door and looked inside. All was black and chill. It smelt like a grave.

Rhiannon stared at the secret passage for a long time, her breath coming short. Every instinct in her body bade her flee back to the warmth and safety of her own bed. Her brain, however, told her that the gaping hole in the wall must hold some clue to all that was wrong and malevolent in this castle.

Rhiannon was not deceived by the affability of their host, or the sweet face of their hostess. From the moment she had ridden in under the portcullis, Rhiannon's skin had been prickling with an awful sense of dread and horror that had only grown with every moment spent inside the massive walls. Terrible things had happened here, she knew that as surely as if blood oozed from every stone. Everyone who lived within these walls felt the weight of disquietude and fear. She had seen it in the nervous mannerisms of the maid Wilma, in the belligerent stance of the castle guards, the surly sideways glances of the grooms, the nervous obsequiousness of the gatekeeper, the awkward deference of the dinner guests to their short-tempered lord. The sight of that dreadful playroom, haunted by the ghosts of dozens of murdered little boys, had only confirmed what she had already feared.

And whatever secret was hidden behind the lord of Fettercairn's smiling face threatened Rhiannon and her companions, she was sure of it. The satyricorn girl had lived all her life in the Broken Ring of Dubhslain. She knew this foul weather was unnatural. She knew gales of such ferocity did not last day after day after day, at a time when the skies were normally fair and the winds warm. She had watched the eyes of the lord and lady follow young Roden about, and she had seen the anxiety on the nursemaid's face as she begged them to take the boy and get away. She had come to recognise the white dents that appeared beside the lord's mouth when something was said to displease him, and knew that all about him dreaded that tightening of his jaw.

On the desk were a decanter of whisky and a glass. Rhiannon put down the silver ornament and swigged half a dram for courage. She knew she could not go back to her bed without finding out what secret Lord Malvern hid behind his smooth manner. If danger was threatening them, Rhiannon wanted to know from which direction it would come, and when. Though she coughed and spluttered, the whisky did give her both warmth in the pit of her belly and the nerve to go into the hidden passage. Remembering Lilanthe's words, she turned her cloak inside out, so that the grey camouflage was on the outside. Then she took one of the branches of candles and the tinderbox off the mantelpiece, for she was more frightened now of the dark than anything, and went through the narrow portal.

Freezing cold, musty air flowed over her. She walked quickly, trying to warm herself. The passage was only narrow, but high enough for her not to have to worry about hitting her head. The walls and floor and ceiling were all made of the same massive grey stone blocks as the castle. She thought she must be passing through the middle of the thick walls, and wondered where the passage was taking her. The floor began to angle downwards, and she noticed the walls were now rock, damp and slimy to the touch.

Then the passage opened out into a sizeable cavern. Passages and antechambers ran off on different sides, and Rhiannon could hear the roar of running water. She thought she must be coming close to the waterfall. She hesitated, not knowing which way to go, and unable to see very well because of the violent flickering of the candle-flames. A cold draught breathed on her neck, lifting her long tendrils of hair.

Suddenly the candles were snuffed out. She scrabbled to light one again. As the flame ignited, illuminating the cavern more fully than before, she saw, crudely etched on the far wall, the shape of a raven. Breathing quickly, she hurried that way and found another passage built by human hands, leading up at a slight angle. Rhiannon followed the passage and soon found herself climbing broad, even steps that rose steeply ahead of her. On and on she climbed, panting a little, the backs of her legs aching.

Fresh air blew coldly against her cheek. She came to another swivel door, standing sideways on its pivot. Shielding her candle with one hand, she crept out into the ruins of the Tower of Ravens. It could be nothing else, this edifice of crumbling stone with grass and brambles growing through cobblestones, and crooked walls rising like broken teeth high into the sky. It was very dark and her candle made only a small circle of light, but she held it high and examined the ancient marks of fire on the walls, the tree growing out of a crevice twenty feet above her head, the untidy ravens' nests high in the tower.

Rhiannon could hear the sound of chanting and she crept towards it, blowing out her candle and putting it down on the ground so the light would not reveal her. In the numb arc of frozen sky above her, the stars blazed whitely.

She came to a broken archway and looked through, her heart pounding.

Standing in a circle in the central courtyard of the ruined tower were nine people, all dressed in long red hooded robes. Holding hands, they were chanting in a low, monotonous tone. Rhiannon was not close enough to hear the words. A sullen fire burnt in a clay dish in the centre, reeking of strange incense. Nine enormous black candles in iron cages cast a flickering, uncertain light. As Rhiannon leant forward, trying to hear, the nine people stopped their chanting and stood in silence for a moment, all looking up at the sky, and then they broke apart. One man turned and knelt to the north, laying his forehead on the ground, his arms outstretched. Another figure came up behind him and bent to unfasten his robe, stripping it down so his back was laid bare. The red-robed figure then drew a whip with nine knotted lashes out of its sleeve. After a moment spent in ritual prayer, the figure began to whip the half-naked man, slowly, rhythmically. Nine times the nine-lashed whip rose and fell, and when at last it was laid down, the victim's back was running with blood.

He lay still for a moment, shoulders heaving, then struggled to his feet, drawing his robe up to cover his abused flesh. Then he turned to face the others. Eager to see who it was, Rhiannon leant right forward, but all she could see under the hood were glittering eyes, a mouth clamped shut with pain, and a clean-shaven chin. The man gestured imperiously and one of the other anonymous figures came forward, carrying a sack. The man who had been whipped took the sack, plunged his hand inside, and withdrew a rooster by its spurred feet. Its raucous protests were loud enough for Rhiannon to hear, and she watched as it struggled to break free, pecking at the hand that held it hanging. The other hand came up, there was a flash of silver, and then blood sprayed from the rooster's neck. Immediately everyone began to chant again, in high, hysterical voices. Desperate to hear more, Rhiannon lay down on her stomach and wriggled slowly across the cold, muddy ground until she reached a broken colonnade of arches closer to the circle of chanters.

'... By the power o' the dark moon, by the power o' spilled blood, by the power o' darkness and the unknown, by the mysteries o' the deep, I summon and evoke thee, spirit o' Falkner MacFerris, long dead brother and laird o' Fettercairn. Arise, arise from the grave, I charge and command thee ...'

Three times they repeated the charm. To Rhiannon's horror, by the end of the third repetition she saw a frail shape lift out of the ground in the centre of the circle, its head bowed, its arms folded about its chest. It lifted a haunted, cavernous face and said: 'Why will ye no' let me rest?'

'Falkner!' cried the leader, the man who had been whipped. 'Falkner, we come close to finding the secret. I beg o' ye, do no' despair yet. I ken it has been a long and weary time, but I swear to ye, we come close.'

'A long and weary time, aye, that it has. Why do ye hold me to this world? I want only to rest now. Let me be.'

'Do ye no' want vengeance?' the leader cried. Rhiannon was almost certain it was Lord Malvern, but she could not be sure, for this man's voice was high and shrill and desperate.

'Vengeance?' the ghost asked in mild curiosity. 'It is all dust and ashes to me now. What do I care?'

'But do ye no' wish to live again? Do ye no' wish to embrace your loving wife, do ye no' wish to hold your son in your arms? What would ye no' give to feel the sun hot on your skin and fill your lungs with sweet air, to drink cool water and eat your fill o' the fruits o' the earth? Falkner, once ye raved for these things, ye begged me . . .'

'They are all good things,' the ghost said slowly. 'Indeed, I had almost forgotten.'

'Falkner, Falkner, how could ye forget!' one of the others cried, stretching out trembling, age-spotted hands. The ghost turned his face towards her.

'Evaline,' he whispered.

'Falkner, my love!'

'It has been so long. I had begun to let go, to drift away, to forget.'

'It has only been five months, Falkner,' Malvern said impatiently. 'We last raised ye on All Hallows' Eve, as we have done every year since ye died. Tonight is the spring equinox, the night when the hours of darkness equal the hours o' light, and tonight the moon is dark. It seemed too good a chance to waste. We canna raise ye too often, ye ken that. It is too dangerous . . .'

As if his words were a key to unlock a door, the candle-flames suddenly wavered and were snuffed out as a bitter-cold wind swept round the courtyard. The fire whirled away in a blast of sparks and ashes, plunging the courtyard into darkness. There were a few terrified screams.

'Hold fast!' Lord Malvern shouted. 'Hold the circle o' protection!'

All Rhiannon could hear were the shrieks of panic and fear, and then every hair on her body stood erect and quivering. She could sense something new in the court-yard, something huge and cold and malevolent. She shrank down, hiding herself, as afraid as she had been when lost in the castle.

Suddenly nine tall pillars of pale greenish fire shot up from the candles. Mist was roiling everywhere, dank and foul-smelling. The ghost of a woman stood in the centre of the circle, regarding the cowering figures with amusement. In the one glance Rhiannon took before she pressed her face back down again, she saw only that the woman seemed richly dressed, and that her skin was white and her hair dark.

'Ye seek to raise the dead, ye fools?' the ghost said. 'With a slaughtered cock-a-doodle-doo and a handful o' powdered nightshade? Amateurs!'

Lord Malvern struggled to his feet. 'Begone, foul spirit!' he cried. 'Ye were no' invited here. By the power o' the sacred circle, I command ye to return to the world o' the dead.'

She laughed, and raised her hand. The bitter-cold, uncanny wind blew up again, strewing the salt and charcoal of the circle they had drawn across the stone.

'If ye open a portal to the spirit world, ye must expect some uninvited guests,' she said. 'Look out into the darkness. Can ye no' see the ghosts that swarm about your pitiful circle o' protection like a hive o' angry hornets? Ye stand here upon a Heart o' Stars and call upon the dead, and think ye can open and close the door at will?'

The nine hooded figures looked fearfully out into the darkness, cringing in their fear. Rhiannon looked also and had to bite her knuckle to stop from crying out, for a host of dead were indeed crowding close round the circle of candles with their strange, green flames. The ghosts seemed made of starlight and shadow and bone, only barely visible in the darkness, yet as they pressed forward eagerly, Rhiannon could see their faces, some grave and terrible, others cruel and greedy, others distorted with grief or rage. The longer she looked, the more she saw, hundreds of phantasms melting into each other like pallid marsh-flames.

'They are angry,' the woman said. 'I wonder why? So many spirits o' the dead, eager to kick open this door ye have opened and swarm upon ye like maddened bees. Do no' tell me. I can guess. Ye have been experimenting, haven't ye? Ye've been trying to discover the secret o' resurrecting the dead. Ye have dug up corpses and tried to reanimate them, ye have killed others in order to study the moment o' death, to understand how and when the spirit is severed, to find out how long it lingers, to study the psychic memory o' bones, to use them as objects o' power for your rituals, to seek to know death. Were ye never taught that it is no' for us to decide the time o' a man's death, but for she who cuts the thread?'

'Who are ye?' Malvern said in a high, desperate voice. 'What do ye want o' us?'

'For ye to bring me back to life, o' course,' she answered. 'That is what all these ghosts want, crowding round your door. I am the only one who kens the secret though. I am the only one who can help ye.'

'Who are ye?' he asked again.

'Never mind who. All ye need to ken is that I can help ye raise your beloved ones from the dead.'

'Ye can help us?' Lady Evaline asked in a quavery voice.

'Aye, I can. I have waited long for this chance, I have clung to life with tenacious hands, I have refused to go on to the final dissolution o' self, in the hope that somewhere, somehow, I would find someone with the will, the wit, to evoke the spell o' resurrection. I will tell ye where to find this spell, if ye promise that I will be the first spirit ye raise.'

The hooded figures were irresolute. Some looked out at the darkness with terrified eyes, others huddled together, muttering.

Lord Malvern was not hesitant. He stood up straight, looking the ghost in the eye. 'I have waited twenty-five years for this chance!' he cried, exultant. 'Twenty-five years I have sought to find the secret o' bringing the dead back to life, and always I have failed. We have done such terrible things – we have dug up corpses in all stages o' putrefaction and cast all manner o' spells upon them. We have tortured men to watch how many times they can be killed and revived afore the spirit flees forever. We have tried every way imaginable, and always we have failed. O' course we will help ye, my lady, whoever ye are. We will be glad to help ye!'

'Excellent,' the ghost said in her low, rich, purring voice. 'First let us drive away some o' these listeners, and then I shall tell ye where ye may find the spell.'

Rhiannon was suddenly convinced that the ghost knew there was a quick soul listening as well as a host of dead ones. She felt an overwhelming need to escape before she was discovered. She began to slowly creep away, keeping as low and quiet as she could, until at last she reached the shelter of the wall. She was trembling in every limb, but at last she managed to light her candle and find her way back through the secret passage and into the library.

She dared not warm herself before the fire, but hurried back up the stairs and through the maze of corridors and galleries till she at last reached her own room. By now Rhiannon was so cold and weary she could hardly put one foot before the other. Her legs threatened to buckle beneath her, every limb trembled, and black specks danced before her eyes. She came into the bedroom at last, and stripped off her cloak and boots so she could creep under the warmth of the eiderdown, shaking and prodding the sleeping Fèlice until at last the other girl yawned and half-woke.

'Fèlice! We must get away from here. Fèlice! Wake up! Fèlice!'

'What is it? What's wrong?' Fèlice said sleepily.

'We must get away from here. They mean us evil, I ken it. We must wake up Nina and Iven, and the others, and get out, somehow, I dinna ken how, we must get away as fast and quiet as we can . . .'

'Rhiannon, ye're gabbling! What's the matter with ye?'

As Rhiannon tried to explain, Fèlice sat up and laid a hand on her forehead and then on her cheek. 'Rhiannon, your hands and feet are like ice! And your head is boiling hot. Look at ye, ye're shivering.'

'Cold, so cold,' Rhiannon muttered, and shuddered as she realised she had echoed the refrain of the ghostly boy.

'Let me put some more wood on the fire, get ye warm.'

'Never mind about that,' Rhiannon said impatiently, though she gratefully huddled under the counterpane Fèlice pulled close around her. 'We have to get away. There are ghosts, Fèlice, hundreds o' them . . .'

'Ye and your ghosts,' Fèlice said, suppressing a yawn. She dragged her dressing-gown around her and got out of bed. 'This is the second time tonight ye've woken me gabbling about ghosts. I wish I'd slept with Edithe, ye're a most unrestful bed partner.' She threw some wood on the ashes of the fire, stirred it once or twice with the poker, and then caused the logs to burst into flame with a wave of her hand. She yawned again, so widely that Rhiannon could not help yawning also, and climbed back into bed.

'Nay, nay, we have to get up, we have to go,' Rhiannon said feverishly.

'It's the middle o' the bloody night, for Eà's sake! We canna go anywhere. Now go back to sleep and in the morning I'll get ye some o' that wine Cameron kept raving about. I think ye must've caught the boys' cold.'

'I do no' want wine,' Rhiannon said, sitting up in bed, clutching the bedclothes to her chin. 'Are ye no' listening? They're murderers, the lot o' them.'

'Who? Who are murderers?'

'Everyone! Everyone in the castle.'

'Oh, Rhiannon! Go back to sleep, please.'

'Sleep? How can I sleep? Did ye no' hear me? I saw ghosts, the ghosts o' murdered boys, and then I saw them, the laird and lady, working some kind o' evil to bring back the dead . . .'

'Ye were just dreaming, Rhiannon. Come, ye're not well, and this place is enough to give anyone nightmares. Lie down, and let me tuck ye up, ye're shivering. In the morning ye'll feel better, I promise.'

'I must tell Nina . . .'

'Ye can tell her in the morning. There's naught ye can do now. Ow, your feet are freezing! Let me warm the bedpan for ye. There, that's better. Go to sleep now.'

'No! I must tell Nina now. Do ye no' understand? They mean us evil!'

Fèlice hesitated. 'Happen I'd better wake Nina. I think ye're really ill.'

'Aye, aye, wake her,' Rhiannon said desperately.

Fèlice nodded and went quickly out the door. Rhiannon sighed and let her head sink down onto her pillow. Her bones felt as heavy as stone. In a few minutes, Nina came hurrying into the room with Fèlice close behind.

'Rhiannon! What's wrong?'

Rhiannon dragged herself away from the pillow. 'We must get away from here,' she said, clutching at Nina's hand. 'Oh, Nina, it was awful.' She did her best to describe what she had seen that night, but her tongue seemed more wooden than ever and she was so very weary she could hardly keep her head from drooping back down to the pillow. It was like talking through mud. Nina took her wrist in one hand, and felt her forehead with the other.

'Your pulse is tumultuous,' she said. 'Lie back, Rhiannon. Here, have a sip o' water.'

Rhiannon drank gratefully, for she was indeed parched, then she tried again to describe all she had seen to Nina, plucking at her sleeve with nervy fingers. Nina seemed not to understand the dreadful urgency of Rhiannon's news, patting her soothingly and telling her not to fret, to lie down and rest.

'Nay, nay,' Rhiannon cried, resisting all attempts to push her down on the pillow. 'We must flee, now!'

'How can we?' Nina said reasonably. 'It is dark, and raining still, and Maisie is very sick. The road is blocked by that fallen tree, remember, and even if it wasn't, how could we get away without rousing the whole castle? It would be unpardonably rude.'

Rhiannon laughed wildly. 'Rude! She worries about being rude!'

'Rest now, my dear, and we'll make ready to leave as soon as we possibly can. As long as ye're well enough.'

'Me fine!' Rhiannon felt hot tears of frustration scald her cheeks. A sudden paroxysm of coughing shook her. When at last it passed she could not speak for exhaustion.

'Lie back, my dear. I'll just be a moment.' Nina pushed her back onto the pillows gently and went out of the room, telling Fèlice to stay with a quick gesture. Rhiannon scrubbed her cheeks dry and laid her arm across her face, hiding her hot tender eyes. She felt Fèlice stroking back her tumbled hair and was obscurely comforted. For a long while there was silence, and Rhiannon felt herself sliding towards sleep. She tried to cling to consciousness, but the gentle stroking hand on her forehead and the irresistible softness of her pillows dragged at her. She let herself drift for a moment.

The sound of quick footsteps roused her. She felt peculiar, as if she had fallen into a dark well of time where minutes, perhaps even hours, had passed without her knowing. She struggled to sit up, opening her bleary eyes.

Dedrie was leaning over her. At once Rhiannon cried out and cowered away.

'I'm sorry, I startled ye,' the nursemaid said. 'Ye have a fever. Here, have a sip o' this.'

Rhiannon clamped her mouth shut and shook her head. The motion caused pain to shoot through her temples.

'It will make ye feel better.'

Rhiannon put one hand to her throbbing head, and shook it again, more gently this time. Her head felt strangely large, and her feet seemed a long way away. Her arms were so limp it took a great effort to move them.

'My lady? Would ye mind? Our wee patient willna take her medicine from me. Happen she will from ye.'

Nina came into Rhiannon's field of vision, leaning over the bed. She held the cup for Rhiannon to sip, but Rhiannon still refused. She would have liked to have pointed at Dedrie and accused her, but she dared not. Had Dedrie been one of those red-cloaked figures in the ruined tower? Rhiannon did not know, but she viewed any intimate of Lord Malvern's with great suspicion now. She did her best to communicate her distress with nothing but her eyes and facial muscles, but Nina only looked puzzled and alarmed, saying in her beautiful voice, 'Do no' fear, Rhiannon, it is only something to ease the cough and the fever. It'll make ye feel better.'

When Rhiannon persisted in her refusal, Nina stepped back, looking troubled. Dedrie stepped up to the bed briskly, saying, 'She's delirious, look at her! See how much her head aches, the way she turns her face on the pillow. We must bring down her fever.' Then, so suddenly Rhiannon had no time to react, the nursemaid clamped her hand over Rhiannon's nose, the heel of her palm pressing Rhiannon's head back into the pillow. Rhiannon tried to heave herself away but the nursemaid was surprisingly strong. Rhiannon opened her mouth to protest, and immediately Dedrie tipped in the medicine, then grabbed Rhiannon's chin, forcing her mouth shut so she could not turn her head and spit the mixture out. It tasted foul. Rhiannon choked and spluttered, but the hands on her forehead and chin were inexorable, and the weight of the nurse's upper arms pressed so heavily upon her body that she could hardly move.

Rhiannon heaved her body upright, sending the nurse-maid sprawling, and spewed the medicine into her face. She gasped for breath, the inside of her mouth and throat feeling as if they had been blistered raw.

Dedrie cried out and groped for the damp face cloth, urgently wiping her face clean.

'She's trying to poison me,' Rhiannon cried.

'Rhiannon!' Nina said in gentle reproof.

'Nay, nay, that's no poison, though I'll warrant it tastes foul enough,' Dedrie said. 'It's my borage syrup. It has thyme in it as well, and various other things, but no poison, I promise ye. Och, ye're burning up, my lass. No wonder ye're so wild.'

Rhiannon swatted away the nurse's hand, scowling ferociously. Her mouth tasted disgusting.

'Here, have some o' my elderflower wine, to wash the taste away,' Dedrie said soothingly. 'It'll ease that cough too.'

'No!'

'It's your choice but I promise ye it'll help.'

'Nina!'

'There, there, Rhiannon, ye're ill. Have a sip o' the wine then lie back and try to get some sleep.'

'Get that cursehag away from me. She's trying to kill me!'

Dedrie shook her head sorrowfully. 'Completely delirious. The fever can take ye like this sometimes. It makes them very hard to nurse. She really needs to swallow some o' the syrup, my lady. Such high fevers are dangerous. Will ye help me hold her down?'

'Is that really necessary?' Nina asked.

'Aye, it is. Fever o' the brain is very dangerous. Ye do no' want it to kill her, do ye?'

'Kill her? O' course no'!'

'Then help me get some o' the medicine into her. I canna break her fever without it.'

Nina looked at the small dark bottle in Dedrie's hand in perturbation. 'Is she really that ill?'

'Look at her, she's raving!'

'I no' raving!' Rhiannon said desperately. 'Nina, ye must believe me. Do no' listen to this cursehag! She's one o' them. She's trying to kill me. She kens what I saw . . .'

The nursemaid suddenly stepped forward and deftly tipped another measure of medicine into Rhiannon's mouth. Taken by surprise Rhiannon choked and spluttered, involuntarily swallowing a mouthful. It tasted like slime. Incoherent with anger, she swung at the nursemaid, punching her so hard Dedrie went flying back and crashed to the floor. The medicine bottle flew out of her hand and smashed in the hearth, the fire leaping up like hissing green adders.

Dedrie sat on the floor in a welter of skirts, one hand to her temple, the other bracing her on the floor. For a moment her face was white as paper, her eyes looking like hard brown pebbles, her lips drawn back and stiff with

376

rage. She took a deep gasping breath as Nina flew to her assistance. Dedrie's eyes bored into Rhiannon's with such unmistakable enmity that Rhiannon could not believe Nina was helping her up and stammering apologies. The very next instant the colour came back to her cheeks and the rigidity of her features relaxed.

'Obh obh!' she said reassuringly. 'Never ye mind, my lady. It's no' the first time a delirious patient has struck out at me. Never ye mind about me, I'll be fine. I'll rub in some arnica cream later and the bruise'll soon fade, never ye worry. But she's gone and broken the bottle and all the borage syrup is spilt. Luckily I have some more. It may take me some time to find it, though. Ye go and get yourself ready for breakfast, and leave the poor lass to me.'

'I am so very sorry,' Nina said again. 'I do hope ye are no' hurt.'

Dedrie rubbed at the purpling bruise. 'I must admit she took me by surprise. Never ye mind. What she needs now is sleep. I'll bring up some more medicine later, and one o' the maids to help me, and she'll be fit as a fiddle in no time.'

'Tell her to go away, Nina! I need to talk to ye,' Rhiannon said desperately.

'No talking,' Dedrie said firmly to Nina. 'Hear how hoarse her voice is? She needs peace and quiet. She'll feel much better after some rest.'

'Dinna need rest!' Rhiannon said forcefully and tried to sit up. The movement made the pounding in her head come back, but she ignored it, reaching out her hands to Nina. 'Nina, please, listen to me.' Her throat was so sore it was hard to speak.

Nina hesitated.

'Later,' Dedrie said firmly. 'She's delirious, canna ye see that? Let her sleep, and she can tell ye about her nightmares later.'

'Very well then,' Nina nodded, and allowed Dedrie to usher her and Fèlice from the room. Rhiannon moved her head restlessly on the pillow, tears choking her so she could not, for a moment, cry out or protest. By the time she had swallowed her tears, Dedrie had gathered up the dirty washing, taken the spent lantern, and gone quietly away, leaving the room dim and quiet.

Tears spilled over. Rhiannon scrubbed them away furiously, and cautiously heaved herself upright. She did feel very odd indeed. Her chest hurt, her head ached, and she felt utterly exhausted. When she swung her legs out of bed, a wave of dizziness washed over her and she clutched at the bedpost to steady herself. She sat for a moment, waiting for her vision to recover. Then she looked for her boots, but they were gone from the side of the bed. Her cloak was gone too. This frightened her. She was trembling all over with the cold, despite the fire glowing in the hearth. Slowly Rhiannon made her way to the cupboard where she had hidden her saddlebags, holding on to the furniture to steady herself. She found her shawl and wrapped it tightly round her grubby, mud-streaked nightgown. Then she made her way to the door, opening it a crack and listening. There was a low murmur of voices from Iven and Nina's room.

When she felt certain she could not hear Dedrie's voice, Rhiannon went down the hallway, one hand on the wall, and opened the door.

Nina and Fèlice were there, and all of the others too, even Maisie with her head swathed in bandages. The shutters were open, showing a clear sky just brightening with dawn. Outside the windows, ravens hovered in the wind, calling sadly. Roden sat up in bed, drinking a cup of milk. Nina, looking distressed, was telling everyone what had happened. Everyone was talking excitedly. As

Rhiannon came in, they turned in surprise. Nina got at once to her feet and came forward swiftly, remonstrating with her. Lewen stood up also, looking worried.

'Ye should be resting,' Nina scolded.

Rhiannon took a deep breath. 'Canna rest. Nina, can ye no' see what's going on? We canna stay here, we must get away just as fast as we can. They're evil, every one o' them. I heard them . . . what the word? Say true?'

'Confess?' Lewen said.

'Aye, confess. I heard them confess to murdering people, lots o' people. And I saw their ghosts.'

Cameron shook his head. 'That was some nightmare.'

'No nightmare! I saw truly. Boys, lots o' dead boys. And in the Tower, more ghosts, hundreds o' them, thousands o' them. Too many to count.'

'Rhiannon, my dear, indeed ye are no' well,' Nina said, putting her arm about her. 'Please, ye must get back to bed.'

Rhiannon broke free. 'No! We must get away. Canna ye feel how evil this place is? Why do ye no' believe me?'

'It's no' that I do no' believe ye, dear,' Nina replied, her voice as troubled as her face. 'It is just . . . well, we canna get away now. Ye are unwell, and Maisie too, and the road is blocked . . .'

'It is a trap,' Rhiannon said with conviction. 'They want to kill us too. He said . . . the laird said . . . they like to see how many times they can kill a man and bring him back to life.'

A shocked murmur rose.

'When?' Edithe said sceptically. 'When did the laird say this? To ye? He confessed all this to ye last night? Oh, please!'

'No' to me,' Rhiannon answered. 'He did no' ken I was there. I was listening, watching.'

'Spying?' Edithe said nastily.

'Och, aye, spying,' Rhiannon said impatiently. 'They were there in the Tower, nine o' them . . .'

'Nine?' Nina asked sharply.

'Aye, nine, all dressed in long red robes with hoods. I could no' see their faces.'

'But ye ken it was the laird and lady,' Edithe said.

'Aye, o' course. They raised a ghost, a man, the laird's dead brother. They said it was too good an opportunity to miss, it being a dark moon. But then another ghost came. A lady.'

'I thought ye said there were hundreds o' ghosts,' Cameron said, nudging Rafferty and smirking.

'Aye, there were.' A fit of coughing came over Rhiannon, so fierce she thought she would cough up her heart. Nina supported her, rubbing her back. When at last it subsided, Rhiannon was too exhausted to speak. She leant on Nina and listened to the others' scepticism.

'Loss o' blood will do that to ye,' Cameron was saying, grinning. 'She's been cutting herself every night, Fèlice says. Seeing ghosts everywhere. Barmy.' And he rotated one finger round and round near his ear.

Fèlice cast Rhiannon an apologetic glance. 'She's sick,' she said defensively.

'No wonder,' Cameron replied.

'It was just a nightmare,' Edithe said. 'Ye slept with her, Fèlice. She was there all night, wasn't she?'

Fèlice shrugged, looking uncomfortable. 'I think so. I mean, I was asleep. She woke me a few times, thrashing round and calling out. She thought she saw a ghost standing over us.'

'Delirious,' Edithe said.

'People have rotten dreams when they're sick,' Landon said defensively. 'And we've heard so many terrible stories since we came here. I dreamt o' ghostly boys too, last night.'

'Dreams can seem very real sometimes,' Iven said comfortingly. 'Especially when ye've got a fever.'

'No' a dream,' Rhiannon said angrily. She unwrapped her shawl. 'Look at my nightgown! Would it be this dirty if I had no' been crawling around in the mud in it?'

Cameron sniggered, and Rhiannon felt blood surge up her face.

'Walking in her sleep?' Edithe hazarded.

'No, walking awake! The laddie came and took me to his room, and showed me all the dead boys. He wants me to help them.'

'Och, sure, indeed,' Cameron said. 'He came to ye. Why no' Nina, or Iven, I wonder?'

'Because I can see him, I think,' Rhiannon said flatly, and sat down abruptly. She clenched her hands together to hide their trembling.

There was a well of silence, and Rhiannon spoke into it, trying to choose her words with care. 'I was frightened. I ran away. I saw light coming from the laird's library. I went down. There's some kind o' hidden doorway in the bookcase. It leads to a hall between the walls. I followed it. It goes to the auld Tower. They were there, the nine people in hoods. Chanting. They killed a rooster.'

'Indeed?' Nina said, exchanging glances with Iven.

Rhiannon was encouraged. She tried to remember more details to tell. 'One o' them whipped the laird all bloody. The whip has nine . . . what would you call them? Strings?'

'A cat o' nine tails,' Lewen exclaimed.

Rhiannon was puzzled. 'Nay, no cat. A whip.'

'A whip with nine thongs is called a cat o' nine tails. I dinna ken why. Happen because it makes the victim yowl like a cat.'

381

'The laird did no' yowl. He dinna make a noise. It must've hurt, though, for his back was all bloody.'

'Ye are sure it was the laird?' Edithe asked, scandalised.

'I did no' see his face, he had his back to me. But he had no beard, and when he spoke it sounded like the laird. And I'm sure he called the ghost "brother".'

'Which ghost?' Edithe said. 'Ye've seen so many it's hard to keep track.'

Rhiannon stared at her in cold, white anger. 'The first ghost to come, the one they seek to bring back from the dead. He called him "Falkner", and then "brother and laird o' Fettercairn". He is the same ghost I saw in the great hall last night, the one that was killed by the young, rough-looking man. They chanted these words, I dinna remember what, and then he just sort o' . . . floated out o' the shadows.'

'Laird Malvern wants to resurrect his brother? But he died so long ago,' Nina said.

'Twenty-five years they've been trying to bring him back to life. I heard them say so.'

'Twenty-five years?' Iven repeated thoughtfully. Cameron went to say something and the jongleur shushed him with an upraised hand. Rhiannon went on wearily.

'They are the ones that have been messing with all the dead people, digging them up and trying to learn how to make them come alive again. He said so, I heard him. And killing people, experimenting with them.'

'How awful,' Landon said, whey-faced. Maisie gave a little moan and raised one hand to her bandaged head.

'Then the other ghost came, the woman. She mocked them for standing on a heart o' stars and calling the dead. They were all frightened o' her. She said she would tell them the secret o' raising the dead if they promised to raise her first.'

'Indeed?' Nina said again, exchanging an incredulous glance with Lewen.

'Gracious, ye canna believe her?' Edithe burst out. 'Look at her, she's sick as a dog. She canna even stand. How can ye believe such things o' our host? He was a most charming and cultured man, and she's accusing him o' necromancy, and torture, and murder most foul. She must be mad!'

'She's been seeing ghosts everywhere,' Cameron said, and Rafferty gave an unhappy murmur of agreement.

'There are ghosts everywhere,' Rhiannon said thickly.

There was silence. She saw Edithe roll up her eyes and gritted her teeth together, her eyes burning with tears. She looked defiantly at Nina. 'Do ye believe me? Or do ye think it's just a dream too?'

Nina chose her words with care. 'I do no' ken, Rhiannon. It's true ye are sick and shaking with fever, and dreams are often more vivid when ye're feverish, but even so, dreams can be true sendings at times. And though I do no' see the ghosts ye've seen, that does no' mean they are no' there. I have felt troubled and uneasy since I came into this castle, and have fancied I've seen curtains lift when there is no breeze, or heard voices crying in the night. Happen ye have the gift o' clear-seeing, more strongly than any o' us. I do no' ken what to do, though. This needs investigation. Edithe is right. These are serious allegations. I would no' like to accuse a man o' necromancy and murder without strong evidence. And my heart misgives me greatly, for if your dream be true . . .'

'It was no' a dream,' Rhiannon said stubbornly.

Nina went on as if she had not spoken. '. . . then we may be in grave danger. I wish we had never come this way, but since we did, and we are here in Fettercairn Castle, I think we should do our best to leave as quickly as we can. This is a matter for the Rìgh's men to investigate. We must try to send him a message now, just as soon as we can, for if Rhiannon is right then we are in a trap and may have trouble getting out o' it. Iven, why do ye no' take the boys and go and inspect this damage to the road? See if we canna make our way past it, even if it means leaving the caravans.'

Iven nodded. 'Good idea.'

'Rhiannon, my dear, go back to bed, please. The sooner ye are well again, the sooner we can go. Lassies, I think we should go and see what we can find out. If Rhiannon is right, then the castle is the source o' all the evil and trouble in this valley and the Rìgh will need to ken o' it.'

Nina's voice was coming in waves, loud, soft, then strangely loud again. Rhiannon felt warm hands on her arms and looked up, her head feeling heavy and large on a thin, weak neck. Lewen bent over her. She looked up into his face and, to her surprise, tears sprang from her eyes.

'Come on, *leannan*,' he said softly. 'Ye should be in bed.'

'Do ye believe me?' she whispered urgently, fixing her eyes on his.

He nodded, and gently wiped away her tears with his thumb. 'O' course I do. Come, let me get ye to bed.'

He bent and gathered her up into his arms. Rhiannon was too tired to argue. She put her arms about his neck, rested her head on his shoulder, and let him carry her from the room.

COLD COMFORT

When Lewen came out of Rhiannon's room, it was to find the maid Wilma hovering in the corridor, her ear bent to the door into Nina and Iven's suite. She started at the sound of his step and moved hurriedly away.

'I'm sorry, sir,' she gasped, twisting her apron in her hands. 'I've been sent to wake ye all and bring ye down to breakfast. I dinna ken if Master Irving warned ye . . . I ken it is early . . . I dinna want to intrude . . .'

'It is early,' Lewen agreed. 'It's barely cockcrow.'

'My laird likes to rise early,' she said. 'I was worried . . . I ken it is no' what is done at court, dining so early, I mean, but my laird does hate anyone being late.'

'Does he?' Lewen said genially. 'I imagine no-one dares ever keep him waiting then.'

'Oh, no, sir,' she breathed.

'Well, witches rise early too,' Lewen said cheerfully, 'so we are all awake.'

'Och, so it's true then!' she blurted and then turned crimson. 'About ye all being witches, I mean. I dinna believe it. I mean, ye all seem so nice, and my laird has let ye all stay and . . .' Her words trailed away.

'No' all o' us are witches,' Lewen said. 'Most o' us are mere apprentices. Why, does my laird no' care for the Coven?'

'Oh, no, sir,' she said in surprise. 'Why, he used to hunt witches down and burn them, my da told me!'

'Is that so?' Lewen said, turning his head to stare at her.

Immediately Wilma was thrown into confusion. ''Twas a long time ago . . . times change, they say . . . I dinna ken if it be true . . .'

'Times do change, and we must change with them,' Lewen said, with no change to his affable manner. His veins were swelling with rage, though, and it took an effort to keep his voice steady.

Wilma looked at him doubtfully. 'Yes, sir.'

'Is that tea I see there on your tray?' Lewen gestured to the laden tray on the hall table. 'Ye'll be welcome at any hour if ye bring Nina tea. Come, bring it in, and tell us where we are to go for breakfast and when.'

'I'll show ye all down,' Wilma said. 'Master Irving said I was no' to let any o' ye go wandering off by yourselves. In case ye get lost, I mean.'

'O' course,' Lewen said, opening the door for her. She picked up the heavy tray with a visible effort and carried it in, staring at Nina with apprehensive eyes as if suddenly expecting her to have sprouted horns and a tail.

Nina was sitting wearily by the fire, Roden on her lap, while the other apprentices were still all heatedly discussing Rhiannon's news. Nina was not listening to them, but was staring into the flames as if their ephemeral, many-tongued shapes could speak to her. She was so entranced she did not notice Wilma at first, but as silence fell, she glanced round and smiled and thanked her.

Wilma poured the tea, Lewen and Landon helping pass the cups around, and then she said diffidently that she would be back in an hour to take them down to the breakfast hall.

'Is that a different hall to where we ate last night? Thank Eà! I do no' think I could manage to eat a mouthful if I had to do so under the gaze o' all those poor slaughtered animals,' Nina said.

Wilma gave a shy smile of sympathy. 'I do no' like them much either,' she admitted. 'Us maids hate having to clean the dining hall late at night. Their eyes gleam so, it looks like they're still alive.'

'Does the laird eat there every night? I wonder he does no' suffer indigestion!'

'My laird likes such things,' Wilma said. 'He has a whole stuffed bear in his library, and drawers and cabinets full o' strange things – a webbed hand and the head o' an ogre, and a braid o' witch's hair, and the jaw o' a dragon, and the skin o' one o' the sea-folk, and a pickled baby –'

'Urrk!' Fèlice cried.

'A pickled baby?' Rafferty and Landon both echoed.

'Surely no'!' Edithe said.

Wilma nodded. 'Aye. He collects such things. Folk hereabouts are always on the look-out for curiosities, for he pays well for them. He has drawers and drawers o' old bones and stones and skulls, and lots o' dead paws and hands. I seen them once. Normally us maids do no' clean his library, his gillie does that for him, but I was sent to fetch something for him and I saw the bear, it's near twice as tall as me and looks like it's alive! And some o' the drawers o' the cabinet were open, and so I couldna resist having a quick peek. I had nightmares after, though, I tell ye what! O' dead hands creeping after me –'

'Wilma, have ye naught better to do than stand here gossiping?' Dedrie spoke sharply from the doorway.

Wilma jumped as if she had been stuck with a pin, and made a hasty curtsy. 'Sorry, ma'am, o' course, ma'am, I'll go now, ma'am,' she squeaked, and hurriedly clattered everything onto the tray and made a hasty exit, almost tipping the whole lot to the floor in her discomfiture.

Dedrie shook her head indulgently. 'Lasses! They are all the same. Will stand around all morn repeating idle gossip instead o' getting their work done.'

'Is there something I can do for ye?' Nina asked in a cool voice. 'We were just about to get ready for breakfast.'

'Och, naught. I've just brought yon lassie some more borage syrup.' Dedrie lifted her basket of medicines, but did not come in. 'I would no' have disturbed ye, but I heard young Wilma chattering on, and did no' want her bothering ye. It is so hard to get reliable servants nowadays!'

'Rhiannon is sleeping peacefully,' Nina said, her brows drawing together. 'I do no' think she should be disturbed.'

'I'll only be a moment,' Dedrie said with a warm smile, and turned to go.

'Nay!' Nina cried, getting to her feet.

Dedrie looked round in surprise. As the light of the room fell upon her face, Lewen saw in surprise that, as well as the nasty bruise blooming on her temple, the nursemaid's skin was badly blistered and raw all down one side, as if she had been burnt.

'I do no' want her woken,' Nina said, with a fair attempt at a smile. 'Sleep is the best thing for her. Leave the medicine with me and I'll offer it to her when she wakes.'

Lewen smothered a grin. He knew that witches all took an oath of truth-telling when they joined the Coven, a restriction that often irked those who worked in secret on the Rìgh's behalf, like Nina and Iven, or Finn the Cat and Jay the Fiddler. He recognised an evasion of the truth when he heard it. Nina may offer Rhiannon the medicine, but both she and Lewen knew that Rhiannon would most certainly refuse it.

By the look on Dedrie's face, she knew it too.

'Och, my lady, no need to trouble yourself,' she said. 'Ye go on down to breakfast and I'll look after the lass. That's my job, after all.'

'No need,' Nina said pleasantly. 'Ye have done enough for us all. I'm sure a morning in bed will work wonders for Rhiannon, and we will hopefully all be out o' your hair by this afternoon.'

Dedrie's smile was unnaturally rigid. 'But my laird . . . I mean, what about the fallen tree? It has proved difficult to move with the weather so rough.'

'Today looks set to be fair,' Nina said, glancing out the window. The sky was crystal-sharp and azure-blue, and the windblown leaves of the trees glittered as if they had been polished. 'I am sure the laird's men will have no trouble moving the tree now that the storm has blown over.'

'The ground is still very wet and slippery,' Dedrie said sharply.

'Och, we will go and lend a hand or two,' Iven said cheerfully. 'I'm sure we'll manage. We have trespassed long enough on your laird's hospitality.'

'But the lass with the dog bites . . . ye canna mean to move her so soon. In those rough, jolting caravans!' Dedrie sounded scandalised.

'Maisie is much better,' Nina said firmly. 'Aren't ye, dearling?'

'Aye,' Maisie said uncertainly.

'She shall spend the morning resting too, and then when the tree is gone and the road clear again, we'll be on our way. We'll make sure Maisie is as comfortable as possible.'

'I canna agree to ye moving the lass with the fever,' Dedrie said. 'I dinna think ye realise just how sick she is. I've seen fevers like that afore. Expose her to a nasty wind like that, and all the jolting o' those caravans, and ye could kill her, I warn ye.'

'I think ye underestimate Rhiannon,' Nina said. 'She's very strong and her fever really does no' seem that bad. I think she's just caught a chill.'

'Well, on your own head be it,' Dedrie said angrily. She turned to go.

'Happen ye had best leave the medicine with me,' Nina said, holding out her hand.

Dedrie grasped her basket tightly to her. 'Och, no need,' she answered. 'If the lass is sleeping I'll leave her be. I'll look in on her later. Ye had best all be getting ready for breakfast, my laird does no' like to be kept waiting.'

'So we've gathered,' Nina said dryly. Dedrie gave a curt nod of her head, a quick fake smile, and left.

Nina went and shut the door behind her. 'Did ye see her face?' she said quietly to Iven. 'I told ye that Rhiannon spat her medicine out all over her. Do ye think . . .?'

'Surely no'! Imagine what such medicine would do to your insides if . . . Eà's green blood! I see what ye mean. Do ye really think so?'

Nina stood for a long moment, pondering, then turned to the apprentices, milling uncertainly near the fire.

'Maisie, my dear, I do no' think ye should go down to breakfast, ye're still rather unsteady on your poor auld pins. Do ye want to go back to bed for a while, and I'll arrange to have some food sent up to ye?' Maisie nodded and got up stiffly from her chair. One heavily bandaged arm was in a sling and she limped painfully. 'Rafferty, help Maisie back to her room, will ye?'

As Rafferty offered the injured girl his arm, Nina rubbed her forehead as if it pained her.

'I do no' feel happy about leaving Rhiannon all by herself, or Maisie either,' she said abruptly. 'Rhiannon did not seem delirious to me. Landon, would ye mind staying with them? Ye still have a bit o' a cough and shouldna be out in that cold wind. I'll leave Lulu with ye too. Send her to me if aught happens to worry ye.'

'Ye think Rhiannon's wild tale is true then?' Cameron asked in some surprise. 'Ye suspect we truly may be in danger?'

'I have a very bad feeling,' Nina said. 'I want to get us all away from here just as fast as I can.'

Iven put his arm about her. 'Your wish is my command, dearling,' he said cheerfully. 'Besides, I have a strong suspicion that whey-faced seneschal o' the laird's waters the wine. That stuff he inflicted on us last night was undrinkable!'

'Well, I never thought I'd say this but personally I'll be glad to ride on,' Fèlice said. 'This castle gives me the creeps.'

'I think ye are all absurd,' Edithe said with an angry titter. 'The MacFerris clan is one o' the oldest and most respected families in Ravenshaw, and Laird Malvern was perfectly charming. Rhiannon is obviously a hysteric who canna bear no' being the centre o' attention. Personally I find her behaviour absolutely appalling. From the moment she joined our party she has done naught but cause one scene after another. It is all an act, I'm surprised ye canna see that, Nina. She is nothing but a scheming, conniving little cat . . .'

'Thank ye for your opinion, Edithe,' Nina said wearily. 'I think we ken your position on the subject. Shall we all go and dress for breakfast now? I would no' like to be late.'

Iven grinned at her. 'I wonder what the penalty is for being late to both dinner and breakfast? The dungeons?'

'Do no' joke about it,' Nina said with an involuntary shiver. 'Happen it's because I'm a jongleur born and bred and have no liking for high stone walls, but I really do no' like this place. I feel most uneasy. Let's just get through breakfast as pleasantly as possible, and get on the road again! Bairns, can we no' talk about what Rhiannon thinks she saw last night? Let's all pretend everything is fine. If by horrible chance any o' it is true, I do no' want to rouse their suspicions.'

The apprentice-witches nodded their heads solemnly, all except Edithe, who sighed and rolled her eyes.

While the others went to wash and dress for the day, Nina beckoned Lewen to come and help her. 'I am worried about that stuff Dedrie gave Rhiannon,' she said to him quietly. 'Did ye see the blistering on Dedrie's face? She forced some o' that stuff down Rhiannon's throat. I fear it's some kind o' poison. I may no' be a healer but I ken something about the art, as all witches must. I'm going to mix up an emetic and give it to Rhiannon. It'll make her very sick but at least it'll get that stuff out o' her stomach. The thing is, I'll need your help to get it down her. She trusts ye more than anyone. Will ye help me?'

'O' course,' Lewen answered, feeling light-headed with the rush of instant anxiety. 'Will it have done her any harm already?'

'I dinna ken,' Nina answered. 'I do no' ken what was in the potion. I hope no'. I think it would no' work too quickly, they'd want her death to look natural.'

Lewen's skin crept with horror. He hurried to

Rhiannon's room as quickly as he could, while Nina made up her emetic. The satyricorn lay in her bed, her black hair spread out all over the pillow, damp with perspiration. Her face was damp too, and flushed crimson, and he saw in dismay that her lips were badly blistered. She moaned and turned her head restlessly on her pillow, her hands clutching at the counterpane. Suddenly she jerked upright and said something in a loud, guttural voice, in a language he did not recognise. Her eyes stared straight at him but did not recognise him.

Lewen soothed her, laying her back on her pillows, then wrung out a cloth in cold water and laid it on her forehead. She flung it from her irritably. He picked it up again and gently dabbed her face and neck with it. Within seconds it was warm to the touch.

'She's feverish,' he said shortly to Nina, as she came hurrying in with her hands full of bottles.

Nina felt her forehead and then her pulse. 'Aye. I hope I willna be doing her more harm than good by giving her the stonecrop. It's hard to ken what's best to do. Am I maligning that nursemaid, suspecting her o' trying to poison Rhiannon? Happen she saw the coming o' the fever better than me.'

Rhiannon moaned and twisted in the bed, uttering more unintelligible gibberish.

'Her mouth is blistered,' Lewen said.

Nina looked closely, then gently slid her fingers into Rhiannon's mouth so she could open it and inspect her tongue and gums. Rhiannon grimaced and tried instinctively to bite. Nina withdrew her fingers quickly.

'Aye, and so are her gums. Poor lass. Here, lift her up and hold her still, Lewen. I'm going to give her the stonecrop, and then I'll try to dab on something to ease those ulcers.'

Lewen did as he was told. Rhiannon shrieked and flung herself back when she felt his hands on her, but he spoke softly in her ear and she calmed, seeming to rouse a little.

'Here, Rhiannon, swallow this for me, sweetling,' Nina coaxed, holding a beaker of some thick, green liquid to her lips. Rhiannon moaned and moved her head away. Lewen shifted his grasp so he cupped the back of her head in his hand. The nape of her neck was damp and hot. He slid his other hand round to cup her chin and swiftly Nina tipped the beaker up.

Rhiannon went mad with fear, and Lewen had to hold her tightly to keep her still. He pushed her mouth shut and she swallowed instinctively, though her body twisted and flailed like a trout on the river bank. One hand caught him a glancing blow on his face, but grimly he held her firm until she had swallowed every drop. Then he relaxed his grip and tenderly laid her down. She opened her eyes, staring at him with such a look of terror that his heart lurched.

'I'm sorry, I'm sorry, it had to be done,' he said.

She gazed at him with a blank, wild-eyed look then suddenly began to vomit. Nina and Lewen flinched back, then hurried to support her, Lewen holding her upright while Nina thrust the bowl she had brought under the satyricorn's face.

For almost ten minutes Rhiannon retched, until there was nothing left in her to lose. As each paroxysm passed, she would stare up at Lewen with such a heart-wrenching look of hurt and betrayal that he felt quite miserable and choked in the throat. At last the vomiting eased, and Nina was able to give her something to help her sleep, and soothe some balm onto her blistered lips and gums. Rhiannon was so exhausted by then that she barely resisted. Lewen was able to lay her down, and wash her face and hands while Nina quickly tore off the soiled counterpane and covered her up with the cover from her own bed.

'I'll wash this out and hang it to dry afore the fire,' Nina said. 'We do no' want Dedrie to guess what we have done. Hurry and get dressed, Lewen, and make sure ye wash well. We both stink o' vomit.'

Lewen quickly did as he was told, but even so, by the time he had cleaned himself up and dressed, Wilma was already waiting anxiously at the end of the corridor. Nina came out of her room, looking ruffled, buttoning up one sleeve as she came.

'Are we late?' she asked. Wilma just bit her lip, cast them a scared look, and hurried them down the stairs. She had drawn her cap down low over her forehead but, walking close behind her, Lewen could not help but notice that one ear was red and swollen as if it had been soundly boxed.

The breakfast room was another long, gloomy room with dark panelling and a massive fireplace with an ornately carved mantelpiece. No stuffed animal heads stared down from the walls, but an enormous trout was mounted above the fire and ancient fishing lines and nets were hung all around the rails, above a number of dark paintings depicting limp pheasants with wrung necks, or dead fish with palely gleaming eyes. Lewen and Nina exchanged wry glances.

Lord Malvern sat stiff-backed at the head of the table. He was pale, with deep lines graven from his nose to his mouth, and heavy pouches under his eyes. He looked like a man who had not slept well.

Lady Evaline, her companion Miss Prunella, the librarian, the harper and his son were also sitting silently in their customary places round the table. They too looked strained and tired. As Irving the seneschal bowed and led

Nina and the apprentices to their places, the clock on the mantelpiece struck the hour. Without volition they all quickened their step, and Fèlice gave a nervous giggle as she collapsed into her seat. As soon as the last chime died away, the doors swung open and a procession of silent servants came in carrying covered plates and tureens. Once again meat dominated the menu. There was bacon and eggs, smoked haddock, a side of beef, a plate of kippers, a very pink ham, and eggs scrambled with salmon.

'Just some toast and honey for me, thank ye,' Nina said quietly. 'Or happen some porridge, if ye have any?'

Lord Malvern nodded at Irving who bowed and jerked his head at one of the servants.

'Oh, please, do no' make it just for me,' Nina said.

'I'm sure the cook will have made porridge for the servants,' Lord Malvern said coldly. 'It is no trouble.'

Fèlice giggled again, then bit her lip and looked down at her plate.

'I believe ye are anxious to deprive us o' our company,' the lord said to Iven, signalling to his gillie to fill his plate with beef. 'I am sorry for it. I was hoping to persuade ye to bide a wee longer.'

'We would love to stay, but indeed, we have been delayed far too long already,' Iven said. 'I was wondering what progress has been made on clearing the road?'

Lord Malvern made an expansive gesture. 'The weather has been most inclement,' he explained.

'Aye, indeed, it has,' Iven agreed. 'But today has dawned fair, thank heavens.'

'Aye. I have ordered some men to get to work clearing the tree but indeed, we have all suffered a lot o' damage from the storm, the people o' the valley as much as we here at the castle. I fear my men will be kept busy all day mending roofs and fixing fences.'

'Aye, o' course,' Iven said. 'And the weather is so chancy here in the highlands, I imagine ye must all be anxious to do what must be done afore another storm blows up.'

'I'm so glad ye understand,' Lord Malvern said.

'We must no' sit idle while all around us work, though, must we, lads?' Iven said, turning with a grin to Lewen, Cameron and Rafferty. 'Happen we can relieve my laird o' having to clear the road for us? Why do we no' walk down and have a look at this pesky tree after breakfast?'

Lord Malvern looked annoyed. 'There is no need, I assure ye.'

'Oh, no trouble,' Iven assured him airily. 'In fact, I'm sure we'd leap at the chance to stretch our legs, wouldn't we, lads!'

'Aye, indeed,' they chorused.

'But what kind o' host would I be, allowing my guests to undertake such hard manual labour?'

'Och, we are no' afraid o' work,' Iven said. 'These are big, doughty lads, my laird. The exercise will do them good.'

'But I fear it may be dangerous,' Lord Malvern said. 'It is a very big auld tree and it has fallen awkwardly across the road, bringing down a pile o' rocks and mud with it. Indeed I think ye had best leave it to my men, who are experienced in such things.'

'Och, no need to fear for us,' Iven said cheerfully. 'Yeomen o' the Guard are used to turning their hands to all sorts o' work, and Lewen here is the grandson o' a woodcutter and probably kens more about how to move the tree than any o' your men. We'll take a look at it, and I promise if I think it's dangerous, I'll no' lay a finger upon it.'

Lord Malvern inclined his head. 'Very well. I thank ye for your offer o' help. Durward, will ye accompany my guests down to examine the tree?'

The gillie-coise inclined his head. 'Aye, my laird.'

While Iven and Lord Malvern had been talking, a footman had brought in a big tureen of porridge and had ladled some into everyone but Edithe's bowl, the blonde girl obviously taking Lord Malvern's jibe about it being food fit only for servants to heart. She was daintily eating toast with honey, and sipping at a cup of lukewarm tea. Everything was somewhat cold, the kitchen being a long way away from the breakfast hall.

An awkward silence fell while everyone ate. Lord Malvern did not seem aware of it, frowning down at his plate with a preoccupied air, while Lady Evaline seemed even vaguer than before. Miss Prunella cleared her throat nervously and hurried into speech.

'Perhaps, while your husband rides out to look at this tree, ye and the lasses would like to have a turn about the garden? It is Lady Evaline's habit to sit there most fine days, and I am sure she would enjoy some company this morning. It is so pleasant to see the sun again, is it no'?'

'Thank ye, I am sure we would enjoy that,' Nina replied politely.

'I want to explore the castle,' Roden said. 'I want to find that room with all the toys.'

Nina's eyes flashed up from her bowl. 'Ye need some fresh air, my lad,' she said. 'Why do ye no' go with your father to look at this tree?'

'I could do with some help, laddie,' Iven said solemnly.

Roden looked pleased. 'Och, aye, that sounds like fun. Can I have a go at the saw?'

'Maybe,' Iven replied.

'I'll go and look for that boy's room later then,' Roden said, causing Nina to flush a little and bite her lip. Lord Malvern stared at him coldly, and Lady Evaline looked up from the scrambled eggs she was pushing round and round her plate.

'Do ye mean my boy Rory's room?' she said into the silence. 'Do ye want to play with his toys? I've been saving them, ye ken, for when he comes back. I do no' think he would mind ye playing with them.'

'Oh goody!' Roden said.

'I hope ye are no' scared o' ghosts,' she said. 'He's still there, ye see, he plays there still sometimes and all the other boys too.'

'Evaline,' Lord Malvern said forbiddingly.

'What, Malvern?'

'Ye must no' frighten the lad with your ghost stories,' he said. 'He's at an impressionable age and I'm sure his mother would no' thank ye for telling him scary tales.'

'I like ghost stories,' Roden said. 'And I'm no' scared o' anything.'

'No' even ghosts?' Lord Malvern said with such heavy meaning in his voice that Nina looked up the table at him, startled.

'Nay,' Roden said scornfully. 'Ghosts canna hurt ye, Mam says.'

'Are ye sure o' that?' Lord Malvern said, still staring at him from under beetling brows.

Roden looked troubled. 'I guess so.'

'Then ye canna have heard any true ghost stories,' Lord Malvern said, with such a strange note in his voice that Nina looked alarmed. 'Believe me, I could tell ye a few tales that would have ye whimpering in your bed at night and begging your mother no' to take the candle away. I could tell ye tales that would freeze your blood in your veins –'

'My laird!' Nina cried.

He turned his fixed, intent gaze towards her.

'Ye are right! He is but a lad and I would no' thank ye for scaring him.'

Lord Malvern laughed. 'No, that I warrant.'

Lady Evaline said kindly, 'Ye need no' be scared o' Rory, laddie. He would no' hurt ye. He was just a boy when he died, no' much aulder than ye.'

'How did he die?' Roden asked curiously.

'It was cold,' Lady Evaline said in a whisper. 'Och, it was so very cold and we could no' get out . . .' Tears filled her eyes.

'Fettercairn was attacked by some very bad men,' Lord Malvern said harshly. 'They used foul sorceries to trick and overwhelm us, and my brother Falkner paid for it with his life, and with the life o' his little boy. They will pay, though. Och aye, they will pay, and one day soon too!' He laughed and Lewen felt an uncomfortable tightening of his scalp. Everyone sitting round the table was staring at the lord in fascination, all except Lady Evaline, who was nodding her head in placid agreement.

'I do hope ye will come and see us afore ye leave,' the harper said suddenly to Iven. 'I did so enjoy hearing some o' the new songs and stories last night. I wish ye had time to teach us more.'

'Why do ye and the lassies no' take morning tea with us in the north tower?' Miss Prunella said just as hurriedly to Nina. 'I'm sure Lady Evaline would like to show ye her embroidery.'

As Nina and Iven both turned to answer politely, Lord Malvern laughed on. His face was white, the dents beside his mouth very deep. 'They say revenge is a dish best eaten cold,' he said to Lady Evaline. 'Well, we are used to cold comfort, aren't we, my dear?'

400

She nodded her cloudy white head in sad agreement. Lord Malvern laughed, so strangely that no-one could pretend all was well. 'Soon,' he said. 'Soon we shall have –'

The harper's son said sharply, 'My laird!'

Lord Malvern whipped round to stare at him, his face suddenly transformed with rage. 'Ye dare interrupt me!'

'My pardon, my laird,' he said with lowered head.

'Never interrupt me again,' Lord Malvern hissed, 'else I'll have your entrails fed to the ravens.'

There was a long silence. Iven stood up. 'Well, thank ye for breakfast but I hope ye'll excuse us. The day's running away with us and I'd like to get to work. Come on, lads!'

Lewen, Cameron and Rafferty all stood up immediately. Lord Malvern turned to stare blankly at them, almost as if he had forgotten who they were, then suddenly his brows snapped together and he cast a quick look around the room, as if realising he had revealed something he meant to keep hidden.

'I beg your pardon,' he said. 'An auld family joke.'

'No' at all,' Iven said just as politely.

After a long, frowning moment Lord Malvern stood. Lewen noticed he moved slowly and stiffly, and kept his shoulders very still. He wondered if the back under the black velvet coat was whipped raw and bloody.

'Durward will take ye to the fallen tree,' he said heavily, and jerked his head at his bodyguard. Immediately the big, quiet man moved to stand at Iven's shoulder. 'Take care, won't ye?' the lord then said to Iven. 'I would hate any accident to occur while ye were guests in my home.'

Nina threw an anxious look at her husband and stood up too, pushing her plate away from her. She had eaten very little. Iven smiled at her 'Och, thank ye for your concern,' he said to Lord Malvern. 'But there is no need to worry. We'll take very great care indeed.'

'What about the other lad?' Lord Malvern asked suddenly. 'Was there no' four o' ye? Where is he?'

He cast a piercing look at Irving, who bowed and said expressionlessly, 'The other young man is resting in his rooms, my laird. Apparently his cough worsened overnight. I ordered a tray to be taken up to him, and to the two young ladies who were both still sleeping.'

'Aye,' the lord said thoughtfully. 'The air o' Fettercairn does seem rather unhealthy to those o' your party, does it no'? It is very damp here, it is true, so close to the Findhorn Falls, and cold too, at nights.' He flashed a look at Nina. 'I understand one o' your young charges went sleepwalking about the castle last night and has caught a bad chill. I am sorry. I do hope she will feel better soon.'

'I'm sure she shall,' Nina replied.

'My nurse Dedrie will take excellent care o' her, I assure ye. She kens better than anyone what harm the damp night air can do.'

'Thank ye, my laird,' Nina said flatly.

He inclined his head. 'No' at all.'

Nina nodded to him, glanced round at the other inhabitants of the castle, who all sat as if frozen, and then went swiftly from the room. Iven and the apprentice-witches followed, the soft-footed bodyguard close behind.

'I will just go up and check on Rhiannon and Maisie,' Nina said. 'Have a care for yourself, won't ye, Iven? And for Roden. Do no' let him do anything reckless.'

'I'll do my best,' Iven said cheerfully. 'Though he's as much o' a madcap as I was at his age.'

Nina smiled wanly.

'Try to have a rest, my love,' Iven said tenderly. 'Ye're all worn out. We'll come back for lunch, and I hope to see some roses in your cheeks by then.'

'Aye, dearling,' Nina said submissively and turned towards the stairs. Before she had taken more than a few steps, Irving had moved smoothly ahead of her, bowing and showing the way with a fluid motion of one of those large, white hands.

As Nina and the girls went up the stairs, Iven turned to the gillie and said, 'Now, let's have a look at that tree, shall we?'

Durward bowed his head and led them down the hall.

THE HAUNTED ROOM

It was very quiet up on their floor of the castle. Maisie and Rhiannon were both asleep, the first peacefully, the other tossing and turning and muttering incoherently. Landon had been doing his best to soothe and comfort her, but was very glad to leave Rhiannon alone for a moment and come and join them in the main suite.

Nina moved restlessly about the room, standing at the window for a while, and then coming across to pet her sunbird, who sat on the top rung of the chair-back, head cocked.

'I just wish we could get out o' here,' the journeywitch said unhappily. 'I hate being confined within four walls all the time.'

'Personally I'm enjoying being back in civilisation,' Edithe said, smoothing the velvet of her skirt over her knees. 'I canna understand why ye wish to spend all day riding through the rain in preference to being here, in the lap o' luxury.'

'I canna help feeling we're caught in a trap,' Nina said.

'I canna even call a bird to my hand to take a message to the Rìgh! I've been trying since we arrived, but the ravens just chase any bird that comes away. I'd feel happier if someone kent where we are!'

The sunbird gave a long, melodious trill.

Landon looked up. 'She's a brave bird, volunteering to fly to the Rìgh for ye. It's a long way for such a wee bird.'

'Is that what she said?' Fèlice exclaimed. 'Ye're good, understanding her. I just canna get my head around the language o' birds. It sounds awfully pretty but working out what it means!' She shook her head ruefully.

'It's too dangerous,' Nina said. 'I couldna bear to lose her. She kens the way, o' course, she has been to Lucescere hundreds o' times, but never alone and never across the mountains.'

The sunbird trilled again, derisively.

'Could ye really give her a message to take?' Edithe was incredulous. 'She's naught but a silly little parrot. How would she ken where to go?'

Nina said angrily, 'She may be small but she's smart as anything, and she kens the Rìgh well. *He* speaks the language o' birds, and has always taken the time to converse with her.'

'Then should ye no' send her?' Landon asked. 'I mean, if that's our only chance o' getting a message to the Rìgh?'

Nina stroked the bird's iridescent cheek. 'She's no' strong enough to fly across the mountains.'

The sunbird squawked indignantly.

Nina smiled faintly. 'I ken ye are a mountain bird, my pretty, but ye canna tell me a sunbird is strong enough to cross the ranges here, they're very high.'

The sunbird shook out her brilliant tail-feathers and puffed up her wings, looking cross.

'Are ye sure?' Nina said. 'For indeed I am anxious to tell the Rìgh o' our suspicions. Though we will be able to tell him ourselves, o' course, once we get to Lucescere. But just in case . . .' Her voice died away.

There was a long silence. Fèlice looked rather scared. 'We're no' in any danger, are we, Nina?' she asked at last. 'Ye do no' suspect . . .'

Nina got up, shaking out her skirts determinedly. 'I'm sorry, my bairns,' she said with a return of her usual manner. 'I'm all on edge from being kept cooped up in here. A jongleur to the bone, I am, I'm afraid. We like the rolling road and the open air. Do no' mind me. I'll send the Rìgh a message, just to put my mind at peace, and then I'm going to go out and get some fresh air!'

She sat down at the desk and tore a thin scroll of parchment from the writing paper stacked there. She quickly wrote a brief message on it, and then rolled it up, inserting it into a message-tube that Lulu brought her from her bag.

'Is it safe, to just send a message like that?' Fèlice asked, wide-eyed.

'I wrote in code,' Nina said. 'Believe me, Lachlan and Dide and I have been sending each other messages by bird since we were bairns. He will understand.'

She held out her hand to the sunbird, who flew across to her with a flash of its brightly coloured wings. Nina crooned to it lovingly as she attached the little steel tube to the sunbird's leg. 'Fly swift and safe, my pretty,' she said, opening the casements wide and throwing the sunbird out. Higher and higher the little bird flew, up towards the sun, carolling joyfully to be out riding the winds again.

Suddenly there was a loud, harsh cry. A raven dropped down from the castle's northern tower, its wings so black and glossy in the sunshine they seemed to flash silver. Nina cried out in alarm. The sunbird ducked and dived, but the raven was too fast for it. It seized the little green bird in its claws and pecked it cruelly, once, twice, thrice. Then it let go, calmly circling back up to its tower. The sunbird fell in a welter of bright feathers.

Nina cried out, then she turned and ran from the room. They all hurried after her, distressed. It was a long way down to the courtyard below, and they brushed past countless surprised servants and a very displeased seneschal on the way, almost toppling him over. When they finally reached the courtyard, with its green oblong of garden set in the centre, it was to find Nina on her knees, cradling her dead bird, weeping. None of the apprentices had ever seen the sorceress break down before and, appalled, they crowded round her, trying to comfort her.

Nina got to her feet, wiping away her tears with an impatient hand. 'I should have kent better,' she said grimly. 'O' course the ravens would no' let her pass.'

She kissed the dead bird's limp head and then turned to Landon. 'Will ye help me bury her?'

He nodded, looking white and shocked.

'Edithe, I do no' want Rhiannon and Maisie left alone. Can ye go and sit with them, please?'

Edithe was displeased, but she nodded reluctantly and went back into the castle, while Fèlice slid one arm about Nina's waist. 'I'm so very sorry.'

'Me too,' Nina answered. She turned her face up to the sky, where ravens wheeled ceaselessly around the two looming towers, cawing loudly as if in mockery. 'I hate this place,' she whispered. 'Oh, when can we get away from here?'

The road down to the lowlands was enclosed on both sides by high stone walls so Lewen felt as if they walked along a tunnel. Although the sun shone and the wind blew briskly, it was cold as ice inside the walls and the stones wept water.

Gradually the wall on their right grew lower, until Lewen was able to see glimpses of the valley below if he stood on his toes. It looked impossibly benign in the sunshine, a rolling landscape of freshly tilled fields, green meadows and fluffy white sheep.

At last they came to the edge of the castle, and the high stone wall turned at a sharp right angle, continuing up a steep, rugged cliff. Only a few steps past the end of the wall, a massive tree lay right across the road. It had smashed the low wall on the right-hand side, its branches hanging out above the precipice. Its bulk completely filled the road.

'It'll take forever to saw through that,' Cameron groaned.

Durward glanced at him and the heavy muscles beside his mouth moved infinitesimally. Lewen wondered if that was what passed for a smile on the gillie's face, and wondered why the man should be pleased.

Iven raised an eyebrow at Lewen, who shrugged and stepped forward to lay his hand on the thick, mossy trunk. It was an oak tree and immensely old. In the innumerable rings of years the tree carried within its core, he could still sense the slow song of growing, of wind and rain and sunshine and birds singing, the deliberate groping down of root and groping out of branch and twig, the swelling of life in countless acorns then lost to the immutable laws of gravity. That solemn song, that could have been intoned for another century or more, had been broken in a shriek of metal, shuddering branches, and then the slow inevitable topple and crash of the living giant.

Lewen stepped away from the tree, glanced at Durward's impassive countenance, and then at Iven. Then he went to the smashed wall and swung himself up into the branches, making his way out past the wall and leaning perilously above the abyss. It was a fall of several hundred feet to the river below, the steep cliff broken only by the regular lines of the road switchbacking its way down the cliff-face.

'Be careful!' Iven called. Roden jumped up and down, saying, 'Can I climb out there too, *Dai*, please? I want to see!'

Even hanging as he was so dangerously above that dreadful drop, Lewen did not climb back at once, transfixed by the sight of the Findhorn Falls roaring down the cliff so close by. It was truly a magnificent sight. The waterfall looked as wide as an ocean, all foaming white and bursting in cataracts around outcrops of rock that broke the seamless curtains of water. The spray was so thick he could barely see the towering shape of Ravenscraig, built high on its crag of rock, on the far side of the river.

'Lewen!' Iven cried imperatively.

'Coming,' he called back, and began to carefully make his way back to the road, clinging tightly to the massive branches. The tree rocked a little with his weight, causing Cameron and Rafferty to cry out in alarm. Lewen shifted his weight, leapt down lightly onto the trunk of the tree and ran up its length towards its roots.

'Ye should get down, lad,' Durward suddenly called. 'That tree's no' safe.'

It was the first time they had heard the gillie-coise speak. He had an oddly light, shrill voice for such a large man. Lewen ignored him. He caught hold of the massive roots and pulled himself up so he could look down into the muddy pit where the tree had once clung to the cliff-side. Then he thoughtfully made his way back down the slippery trunk and jumped down to land with a heavy thump in the ditch of the road.

'Well?' Iven said.

'Cameron's right, it's a big job to cut through the trunk,' Lewen said. 'That oak will be as hard as iron. I reckon we can lever it over the edge, though.'

The muscles in Durward's forehead contracted slightly.

'Will it no' just crash down on the road below?' Iven asked.

'No' if we get enough momentum up. We'll use Sure and Steady to help us drag the tree forward, and weight the branches, and lever up the trunk. It should flip right over, with all that weight, and fall down into the river. We may need to help drag it out o' the river once we get down there, in case it causes an obstruction, but that willna be too hard a job.'

'Excellent,' Iven said. 'Let us go and get Sure and Steady, and some tools, and get to work. I'd like to be on our way by this afternoon, if we can.'

Durward's brows inched closer together.

As the men began the walk back up to the castle, Lewen fell back behind the others with Iven and Roden. The little boy was engaged in jumping in all the puddles, splashing mud and water high into the air, and it was not hard to let the others hurry on ahead with exclamations of annoyance as their boots and breeches were wet through.

'The tree was felled,' he said to Iven in a low voice. 'It dinna fall naturally.'

'Ye mean it was cut down? On purpose?'

'No' cut down, as such. The ground beneath the tree was loosened, with picks and shovels, it looks like, and some of the tap-roots severed. Then the tree was hauled down with a rope. The scars o' it are clear on the trunk.'

'Are ye sure?'

410

'Sure I'm sure. Working with wood is my Talent, remember. This tree did not fall down and block the road naturally, that I'm sure o'.'

'So happen the laird did mean to keep us at Fettercairn,' Iven said slowly. 'But why?'

'For his experiments in death, o' course,' Lewen said. 'Ye heard what Rhiannon said.'

'So ye really think Rhiannon is telling the truth?' Iven said curiously. 'It's a lot to swallow, dinna ye think?'

Lewen dropped his voice even lower as he noticed Durward turn to stare at them. 'She kens nothing about witches or the Coven. How could she ken necromancers use a circle o' nine? Or sacrifice a cock? She dinna ken what a cat o' nine tails was, remember?'

'I suppose that's true. Though it would be easy enough to pretend no' to ken details like that.'

'She kent the name o' the laird's dead brother,' Lewen pointed out. 'How could she possibly have kent that without overhearing it?'

'True.'

'And she said something about the tower being built on a Heart o' Stars. How on earth could she ken what that was? A satyricorn lass that has never left the mountains afore?'

Iven quirked his eyebrow. 'Lewen, we only have Rhiannon's word for it that she is a wild satyricorn girl from the mountains.'

Lewen stared at him in surprise. 'But . . .'

'Och, I agree that it would be an elaborate deception and I can see little reason for it, but ye must no' always be taking things at face value. One thing ye learn in the business I am in is that people very rarely tell the truth. That's one reason Connor will be so sorely missed. He had an uncanny ability to convince people to tell true.'

Lewen was silent.

Iven grinned at him. 'I'm no' saying I think Rhiannon has been lying to ye every step o' the way, my lad, I'm just saying no' to believe everything ye hear, from anyone. No' even me.'

Lewen took a deep breath. 'Fine, happen that's so, but still, what Rhiannon says she saw last night explains an awful lot, dinna ye think? About what's been happening in the Fetterness Valley?'

Iven nodded. 'Aye, it does. Enough to make me wary o' shadows. But Lewen, why would the laird o' Fettercairn try to keep us prisoner here? Do ye really think he plans to murder us? All o' us?'

Lewen was troubled and unsure. 'After twenty-five years, it must be hard finding people to kill and then try to raise again. The people o' Fetterness Valley are frightened now, and do no' go out alone anymore. He must've thought a caravan o' wandering jongleurs a gift from Gearradh.'

'Ye're right. No-one would've kent what happened to us. We would've just disappeared. So why then has he no' killed us?'

'Happen he did no' ken who ye were when he had the tree felled,' Lewen answered. 'It's one thing to waylay any auld traveller, but the sister o' the Earl o' Caerlaverock, the Rìgh's best friend? And a former Yeoman? Escorting a group o' witch-apprentices, some o' them nobly born? He would no' dare. We would be missed and eventually tracked here to the castle. Nay, I reckon once he found out who we really were, he decided it would be too dangerous to just murder us out o' hand.'

'But still he does no' want us to clear away the tree,' Iven said, pretending to smile as the gillie once more turned to stare at them.

'No. I wonder why?'

'Ye'd think he'd want to get rid o' us fast, once he decided it was too dangerous to kill us.'

'Happen he realises that we have begun to suspect him,' Lewen said. 'Certainly they must ken Rhiannon saw something last night. They canna ken how much, surely.'

'We will need to be very careful. If he realises how much we already ken . . .'

'*Dai! Dai!* Look!' Roden called, and jumped with both feet into such an enormous puddle that brown water flew up everywhere, splattering them from head to toe.

'Roden!' Iven said in exasperation. 'Look at ye, ye're soaked! Your mama will be furious. Come here!'

He bent and brushed off the worst of the mud, then took Roden's wet hand. Lewen took the boy's other hand and between them they swung Roden back and forth, moving up the last stretch of road to where Cameron, Rafferty and the gillie waited for them, the gillie's face hard with suspicion. Roden squealed with excitement.

'We must act as if we ken naught, suspect naught,' Iven said rapidly over Roden's head. 'And we must get a message to the Rìgh, just in case something happens . . .'

'But how?'

'The Scrying Pool at the Tower o' Ravens,' Iven said decisively. 'The MacBrann used it during the Bright Wars. If the pool worked then, happen it still works now. Lewen, ye must go and see. We must think o' some excuse. Take Roden, go tell Nina what we ken. Tell her to do whatever she must to soothe their suspicions. If the laird thinks we ken, we'll never get out o' here alive.'

'Again! Again!' Roden cried, and they swung him high into the air.

'Ye are nothing but trouble,' Iven said to him as they came up beside the others. 'Look at ye! Your boots are wet through. Your mother will have my head.'

Roden looked down at his boots in surprise.

'Lewen, will ye take this wicked laddie back to his mam? The last thing we need is Roden coming down with a chill.'

'Sure,' Lewen answered.

Roden was furious. 'No! I dinna want to go back. I want to see the tree crash down.'

'No, laddie. It's too dangerous, and I do no' want ye getting underfoot. Go on back to your mam.'

'No! I won't!'

'Och, aye, ye will, my lad,' Iven said sternly. 'Ye're soaked through and it's cold. Now do as I say.'

Roden began to cry. 'No! I dinna want to! Please, *Dai*, I want to stay, please, please?'

'Nay, laddie. Go on back with Lewen now.'

'Come on, Roden,' Lewen said winningly, but Roden dragged his hand away and sat down obstinately in the middle of the road.

'I'm no' going!'

Iven jerked his head at Lewen, who bent and picked Roden up. 'Never mind,' he said consolingly. 'Let's go and see what we can find for morning tea. I bet I can rustle up some hot chocolate for ye. That'll warm ye up again.'

Roden wept noisily, squirming like an eel. Lewen carried him swiftly through the gatehouse towards the castle. As he went he heard Iven say to the gillie, 'Bairns! Have ye any yourself?'

By the time they reached the inner ward, Roden had insisted on being put down so he could walk. 'I'm no' a babe,' he said furiously.

'Then stop acting like one,' Lewen said, and Roden thrust out his bottom lip and stalked ahead with a great air of injury.

Looking white and unhappy, Nina was sitting with Lady Evaline under the apple tree, while Fèlice and Landon wandered along the lawn. Miss Prunella sat a short distance away, working on some embroidery. Nina rose at the sight of Lewen and her mud-splattered and highly indignant son.

'Roden!' she cried. 'What's wrong?'

'*Dai* willna let me stay and watch the tree crash down,' Roden said with a quivering lip and flung himself in his mother's arms.

'Iven thinks it's too dangerous,' Lewen explained, 'and he was worried about Roden catching a chill. He was jumping in puddles.'

Nina looked rather puzzled. 'Och, Iven doesna normally even notice things like that.'

'He doesna want Roden to catch a fever,' Lewen answered. 'It does seem as if Laird Malvern is right when he says the air here is unhealthy.'

Nina glanced up at him, her brows twitching together. 'Well, let's go get ye dry and changed,' she said to her son, then cast a rueful glance down at her own gown. 'And me too, now. Look at my skirt! I've got mud all over it.'

Lady Evaline had been gazing at Roden with a look of longing and now she reached out a frail, blue-veined hand to ruffle his curls. 'Och, he's such a bonny lad.'

Roden gave her a look of disgust. 'I'm no' bonny, that's for girls!' he retorted. 'I'm doughty!'

'Indeed ye are,' Nina said with an apologetic smile at Lady Evaline. The old woman smiled back wistfully, her gaze returning to Roden's face.

'A big doughty lad like ye must be hungry,' she said. 'Would ye like to come and have tea with me when ye're changed? My cook makes some very nice honey cakes.'

'Lewen said I could have hot chocolate,' Roden said winningly.

'O' course, the very thing to drive out the chill. Miss Prunella, could ye ask the kitchen to heat up some chocolate milk for Rory?'

'My name's Roden,' he said crossly, the scowl returning.

'O' course. I'm sorry. I get muddled sometimes. For Roden.'

'O' course, my lady,' Miss Prunella said, folding up her embroidery and rising. She looked as if she had been sucking on a lemon, her face was so sour.

'I'll come up with ye,' Lewen said to Nina. 'As ye can see, I got rather wet too.' He cast a rueful hand down his mud-splattered clothes.

Fèlice and Landon had both drawn near and waylaid Lewen a few moments with questions about the fallen tree and what the others were doing. He escaped them as quickly as he could and hurried after Nina, who was climbing up the stairs hand-in-hand with her son, who was still very cross at being made to come back inside the castle. Thankfully there was no sign of the ubiquitous Irving, who was normally so careful to make sure they were escorted anywhere in the castle. He was able to tell Nina about the deliberately felled tree, and what conclusions he and Iven had drawn. She agreed that he must try to escape the castle and find the Scrying Pool at the Tower of Ravens.

'I tried to send my sunbird with a message but one o' the ravens killed her,' she told him unhappily. Lewen exclaimed, and she pressed her hands to her eyes.

'Aye, I ken. I loved my wee bird, I canna believe it happened. I should no' have tried to send her.' She let out her breath in a great sigh and blotted away another tear. 'Anyway, what canna be changed must be endured. We must focus now on getting all o' us out o' this blaygird castle alive. Lewen, I think Iven is right. We must get a

416

message to the Rìgh and the Scrying Pool is the only way. Though how we are to do so without arousing any more suspicion, I do no' ken,' she said. 'They must no' guess what ye are about.'

'I'll think o' something,' Lewen said. 'How is Rhiannon doing?'

'She's sleeping still. The fever does seem to have eased. Landon says Dedrie came to look in on her but went away again once she saw him sitting there. Edithe is there now. I thought poor Landon needed a break.'

But when Lewen opened the door into Rhiannon's dim, fire-lit room, it was not Edithe he found leaning over her bed, but Irving. The seneschal swung round abruptly at the sound of the door and Lewen saw with horror that he held a pillow in his hands.

'What are ye doing?' he cried sharply.

'Just adjusting the young lady's pillows,' Irving answered suavely, turning back to the bed.

'Get away from me!' Rhiannon cried, her voice rough and breathless. 'Lewen, Lewen, he try . . . he put pillow on me . . . I couldna breathe . . . Lewen!'

Lewen came swiftly to the bed. Rhiannon gazed up at him, her eyes so dilated with terror they seemed black. Her cheeks were red and had faint creases pressed into them. Her breath came harshly.

'Get away from her,' Lewen hissed.

Irving looked surprised and stepped away from the bed. 'I assure ye, the young lady is mistaken. She has been most feverish and I merely sought to make her more comfortable.'

'He try kill me,' Rhiannon gasped.

'Where's Lady Edithe?' Lewen demanded, sitting beside Rhiannon and pulling her into his arms, stroking the damp tangled hair away from her face.

'The young lady was rather bored when I came to bring her some morning tea and I suggested she go down to the library to find herself a book to read. My laird has a very extensive library.'

Lewen was so furious he could not speak for a moment. Irving moved away, fluffing up the pillow and placing it on a chair nearby, looking as suave as ever.

Just then, Nina came in. 'What on earth is the matter?'

'He try kill me,' Rhiannon said, her breath still coming short. 'He put pillow on me, held me down so I couldna breathe.'

'That's ridiculous,' Irving said, his colour altering just a little. 'The young lady is delirious.'

'Oh no, has her fever got worse?' Nina asked in concern, coming across the room quickly. 'She was quite incoherent this morning, but I had hoped ... och, ye poor man! Ye must no' mind her.'

'No, he try kill me!' Rhiannon protested.

'Oh, dear, she really is quite crazy with this fever! What are we to do? She hit poor Dedrie, did ye hear? And Lewen too.'

Rhiannon shrank away from Lewen. 'That's right,' she said in a horrified voice. 'I had forgotten ... I thought it but a dream. Ye poison me too.'

'No, no,' Lewen said in distress, trying to draw her back into his arms. 'We were trying to help.'

'Ye all try kill me!' Rhiannon stared from one face to another with huge, terrified eyes.

Nina shook her head sorrowfully. 'Dedrie said the fever can take one like this sometimes, but it's very distressing, isn't it? Look at her, the poor deluded lass!'

Rhiannon clutched the sheet to her. 'Why ye want kill me? Why?'

'Nay, nay, *leannan*. Ye're safe, I promise ye,' Lewen

soothed her, torn between his desire to comfort her and his dismay at having forgotten they were meant to be damping down the suspicions of any of the lord's minions.

Rhiannon did not believe him. She sat very still, her breath coming fast, her eyes darting from one face to another. Lewen could see a pulse leaping in her throat.

'I am so very sorry,' Nina was saying to Irving, drawing him away from the bed. 'I do feel dreadful. First Dedrie hit in the face, and accused so wildly, and now ye. I hate to think what the laird must think o' us. I do hope ye will forgive us. Rhiannon is . . . well, she's difficult, there's no gainsaying that. The best thing for her now is peace and quiet.'

Nina's voice faded as she escorted Irving from the room. Lewen tried to draw Rhiannon back into his arms. She resisted violently.

'*Leannan*, no, do no' be afraid,' he said in distress. 'Indeed, I ken what ye must think but it's no' like that. Ye must ken I would never hurt ye.'

'Ye made me sick,' she accused. 'Ye poison me!'

''Twas no' poison,' he protested. 'We . . . we were trying to make ye better.'

She made a disgusted noise. 'Go away,' she said, pushing him with her hot, damp palms.

'Rhiannon, indeed ye are sick. Please, lie back, let me sponge your face. I ken . . . he's a bad man, that Irving, I ken that. It's just we need to pretend for now . . . until we can get away from here . . .'

She listened to him, and after a while let him lay her back down, and smooth back her hair, and dab her face with the cool cloth. After a while her eyes closed and she fell asleep again. He sat watching her, feeling such a hot painful feeling round his heart it was as if the organ was actually bruised.

Nina came quietly back into the room. 'Is she sleeping? Poor lass! I could strangle Edithe. What was she thinking, leaving Rhiannon alone like that?'

'Nina, he had a pillow over her face, I'd swear it!'

'I do no' doubt it,' Nina said. 'We canna leave her alone. Maisie says she will come and sit with her a while now, she's feeling much better after a sleep, well enough to sit up for a while anyway. I'm going to go and find Edithe and rip shreds off her!'

'I'll sit with Rhiannon,' Lewen said.

'Ye canna,' Nina replied. 'Ye must find some way to slip out and get to the Tower o' Ravens. Noon and midnight is the best time to use the Scrying Pool, or dawn and sunset, and I do no' want ye there at night. I'm beginning to believe all those tales about malevolent ghosts that haunt the tower! So it'd be best if ye went now, and got there afore noon.'

Lewen nodded and got reluctantly to his feet, casting one last look at Rhiannon's flushed and sleeping face. She looked soft and vulnerable. He marvelled how this had the power to hurt him. He would have liked to have lain down with her, and curved his body to hers, pressing his mouth to the arch of her neck. He did not want to wake her, though. He did not want to watch her flinch away.

The door opened and Edithe came in, absorbed in a thin, vellum-bound book she held in her hand.

'Where have ye been?' Nina at once exclaimed furiously.

Edithe looked up in surprise and chagrin. 'I was only gone a minute!'

'A minute is more than enough,' Nina snapped. 'And it was much longer than that. We've been here for close on ten.'

'Well, I'm sorry, but I got chatting with Laird Malvern. He really is a very interesting man, so cultivated and so learned. His library is absolutely fascinating. I would have liked to have stayed and let him show me his collection, but I came hurrying back here because I kent ye wanted someone to sit with the satyricorn girl.' Her voice was filled with self-righteous indignation. 'Really, I canna think why, ye all seem to have got infected with her hysterical nonsense . . .'

'Edithe, until we arrive at the Tower o' Two Moons, I am your teacher and mentor. If I tell ye to stand on your head in a graveyard all night ye do as I tell ye, without question and without hesitation.' Though she spoke softly, Nina's voice had an edge to it like a whip. 'I have never kent an apprentice with less o' the qualities the Coven thinks necessary in a witch. Ye do no' listen, ye do no' watch, and ye do no' learn. Sit down in that chair and do no' move until I say ye may. And be glad your stupidity has no' had more dire consequences.'

Edithe's colour was high and her eyes glittered with angry tears, but she swept to the chair and sat down as ordered, disposing her skirts about her feet with exaggerated care. She then opened her book and began to read with an air of great interest.

'I'll just tell Maisie she can bide a wee longer in bed, I want her as strong and well as possible for the journey ahead,' Nina said as she led the way out of the room.

Lewen nodded, his mind already busy with plans for getting away from the castle without arousing suspicion. He took one last look at Rhiannon, sleeping restlessly in her bed, then followed Nina across the hall and into Maisie's room. She was out of bed and limping about, but it was obvious her deep festering wounds still troubled her. She was glad to get back into bed and have Nina give her another draught of pain-killing poppy syrup and tuck her up in her eiderdown. Lewen stoked up the fire for her, and moved the cup of water closer to her hand.

'Call out to Edithe if ye need anything,' Nina said gently, 'and try to get some sleep.'

Maisie nodded gratefully and shifted onto her side, trying to find a comfortable position to lie in.

'I wonder where Lulu is,' Nina said anxiously, as they went out into the hall again. 'I would've thought she would have been quite happy playing with the doll I made her and no' gone wandering off. She doesna like Edithe, though. Happen I left her too long and she went looking for Roden. We'd better go find her, Eà kens the trouble she could be causing!'

She put her head in the door of the big suite. 'Roden? Roden?'

There was no answer.

Nina went in, and hurriedly searched the room, her face growing whiter by the second. 'He's gone!' she cried. 'I left him only a moment, just while I looked in on Rhiannon. Och, the wicked boy! Where has he gone?'

Lewen came in too and searched in the cupboards and under the bed. There was no sign of Roden.

Nina was so white he thought she might faint. He supported her with one hand and went to pour her some water but she refused it impatiently. 'We must find him!' she cried. 'Och, this is no' the place for a wee laddie to be wandering round by himself. Oh, Lewen! Do ye think someone took him? That sly-faced Irving!'

'We'll find him,' Lewen reassured him. 'Nina, can ye sense where he is? Close your eyes, concentrate. Ye ken him better than anyone. Canna ye sense him?'

Nina tried to calm herself. She sank down on one of the cushioned chairs, sipped at the glass of water Lewen passed her, and closed her eyes, resting her face in her hands. The only sound was the cry of ravens outside. Lewen saw one had come down to perch on the window-sill. He went to the casement, threw open the window and violently shooed the bird away. It cawed mockingly and flew off with slow flaps of its enormous black wings.

'I think . . . he's over that way somewhere,' Nina said, waving her hand to the north. 'Oh, Lewen!'

'We'll go and find him now,' he said, leaning down to help her up. 'Do no' fear, Nina. He's bored and restless, and angry he wasna allowed to watch them move the tree. He's gone off exploring, that's all.'

'Happen he's gone to find that room with all the toys,' Nina said. 'I'll skin him alive!'

Together they went quickly along the hall and down the stairs, keeping a wary look-out for any servants. They heard voices from one room and passed it silently, then hid for a moment in an antechamber as some footmen went past, carrying some silver down to the kitchens to be cleaned. Otherwise all was quiet.

'I wonder where the laird is?' Lewen whispered.

'Still in his library, I'd say.'

'I hope Edithe kept her mouth shut!'

'Unlikely, but I do no' think it'll matter. She dislikes Rhiannon so intensely she would've done a better job than any o' us in discrediting her. I'm sure she told the laird that Rhiannon is half-satyricorn and quite wild and a constant trouble to us all. By the time she would have finished, the laird would be sure we suspected no ill o' him!'

'I hope so,' Lewen said grimly.

They came to a thick oak door that stood ajar. They could hear nothing beyond so eased it open a little further and slipped through. They tiptoed down a stone-floored corridor that led to a spiral staircase, winding upwards into gloom.

'He's here somewhere,' Nina whispered. 'Upstairs, I think. It's so hard to be sure. These thick stone walls confuse my witch-sense.'

Then they heard the low murmur of voices from a room to their right. Moving very carefully they pressed themselves close to the door to listen.

'Someone has been sneaking about and spying,' Lord Malvern said angrily. 'Irving found a smashed lantern on the steps near Rory's room, and I swear someone has been in my library! Ye ken I canna bear to have things out o' place, and things have definitely been moved. None o' the circle would've done it, they all ken better!'

Lady Evaline murmured something about sleep-walking.

'Sleepwalkers do no' take lanterns with them,' Lord Malvern cried. 'Nay, that girl knew what she was doing. The question is, how much did she see?'

Another low murmur from Lady Evaline.

'Dedrie says her boots and cloak were all muddy. She must have gone outside at some point, and I canna help thinking she may have found the secret way to the tower. If so, who kens what she may have seen and heard! We canna risk her telling a soul. Thank the Truth the witch suspects naught.'

Lady Evaline made some kind of protest.

'It's a little late to get cold feet now, Evaline. We're so close! Do ye no' want Falkner and Rory back? After all these years, all this trouble, ye canna get squeamish now!'

'There've been too many deaths,' Lady Evaline said unhappily.

'But the things we have learnt! And now we are so close, ye canna say it has no' been worth it. The secrets o' resurrecting the dead! That is a prize worth sacrificing for.'

Lord Malvern's voice came closer, as if he were striding around the room. Nina and Lewen flattened themselves on either side of the door, but were too eager to hear more to retreat. 'If we can just stop her from telling them all she saw! I'm sure they do no' suspect anything. Lady Edithe says she's some half-breed faery girl that is quite wild and hysterical, so happen they will no' believe her, no matter what she says. We canna take that risk though. We must stop her mouth somehow.'

Lewen gritted his teeth together in rage and Nina cast him a warning glance.

'What about the lad?' Lady Evaline said pitifully.

'Och, he's just too perfect,' Lord Malvern said with a strange note of longing in his voice. 'It canna be coincidence that a boy just the same age and height and colouring as Rory comes riding through our gate the very day we finally get the secret o' resurrecting the dead into our hands!'

'But they'll take him away! Once they ride out o' here we may never see him again.'

'Aye, o' course we will. We'll find him again when the time is right.'

'How can ye be sure?' she asked. 'Oh, Malvern, he's so like Rory, so bright and bonny! I wish I could take him into my lap and hold him, but that witch keeps him so close I have hardly been able to touch him. I wish we could keep him here a while longer.'

'Aye, aye, I ken, but we canna take the risk, Evaline. Surely ye see that?'

She said something low and he sighed in exasperation. 'Our first priority is getting hold o' the spell. I do no' ken how long that will take, Evaline.'

425

Again they heard the soft pleading murmur of her voice and then Lord Malvern's voice, as loud as if he was standing next to them, 'Och, very well, Evaline! Anything to keep ye happy! I must go now and find out what is happening. Do no' weep, now. We are closer than we have ever been.'

They heard his quick impatient stride, and both Nina and Lewen whisked themselves away from the door, making it into the shelter of the staircase scant seconds before the door opened and Lord Malvern came out. He went away down the hall, as tall and stiff and black as a pillar of obsidian, and Lewen heaved a sigh of relief.

Nina's face was pinched and angry. 'We have to find Roden and get away from here! What do they have planned for him? Oh, it canna be good, Lewen!'

Lewen nodded in agreement, and pressed her hand in comfort. 'Where is he? Can ye sense him?'

Nina pressed her hands to her temples. 'I'm so afraid I canna think straight.'

'Lord Malvern mentioned something about a broken lantern on the stairs. Let's go up and have a look around.'

Nina nodded and led the way up the spiral staircase. 'Why, oh, why did I ever come this way?' she murmured. 'Again and again we were warned, and I did no' listen!'

The staircase wound up to a narrow wooden door, half-hidden behind a faded tapestry curtain. They heard the sound of a boy's voice and quickened their step, though both felt a sudden superstitious chill that raised the hairs on their arms. 'Let it be Roden and no' that poor wee ghost,' Nina whispered, then pushed open the door.

Roden and Lulu were sitting together on the floor, playing happily with some toy soldiers. He looked up at the sound of the door opening and smiled. 'Hi, Mam,' he said.

'Ye naughty, naughty boy!' Nina cried and flew across the room, dragging him to his feet. 'What are ye doing here! Don't ye ken ye scared me half to death?' She gave him a good hard smack across his bottom, then pulled him into her arms, hugging him tightly.

Roden looked sulky, and Lulu jumped up and down, gibbering in distress. 'And as for ye!' Nina cried, turning on the arak. 'I told ye to stay! What are ye doing wandering all over the castle?'

The arak hid her face in her hands, peered round in abashment, then covered her eyes again.

'Lulu was bored,' Roden said defensively. 'She wanted to find that little boy's room too. She came and got me when she'd found it. O' course I had to come and have a look. See, Mam? There's a castle and everything.'

'I told ye to stay in your room!' Nina's wrath had not abated.

'Ye're just mean,' Roden burst out. 'Why canna I play with the toys? We've been stuck in this boring auld castle for days and days, and I wasna even allowed to watch the tree go crashing down. I just wanted to look at the toys.'

Nina took a deep breath. 'Thank Eà ye're safe,' she said. 'Please, please, do no' do that again, Roden. No' here, in this castle.'

'All right, Mam,' he said in long-suffering tones.

She drew him close to her and caressed his dark red curls. 'I ken ye're bored, dearling. Let's go and see how *dai-dein* is doing moving that tree, all right?'

He brightened at once, and Lulu skipped about joyfully.

'Leave the toys here,' Nina said sternly, and reluctantly the boy and the arak put the toy soldiers back into the castle.

'It's certainly just as Rhiannon described it,' Nina said, glancing round the room.

'Except for the ghosts,' Lewen replied with a slight grin.

'Och, the ghost is here,' Roden said unexpectedly. 'Canna ye see him?'

Nina and Lewen stared at him, their flesh creeping. Roden pointed at the rocking horse. 'He's there. He doesna want me to go. He's so sad and lonely.'

They stared at the rocking horse. There was nothing to see.

Roden lifted a hand. 'I got to go now, but happen I'll come back later. Bye!' Then he took Nina's hand and went out of the room with her, Lulu scampering on ahead. Lewen followed, the nape of his neck prickling as if someone had blown on it with icy breath. He could not help looking back over his shoulder. The wooden horse had begun to rock backwards and forwards, creaking gently. Lewen shivered and shut the door firmly behind him.

Rhiannon woke and lay for a while, staring about her room. Everything was quiet. On the hearth the fire had fallen into coals that gleamed dully. Somewhere ravens were crying. Edithe sat in the cushioned chair, one foot swinging, reading a book and sighing every now and again as if bored to distraction.

Rhiannon gently put back the bedclothes and slid her legs out. A wave of dizziness overcame her as she stood up. She leant her hands on the bed and let her head hang forward till it passed.

Edithe turned her head. 'Oh, ye're awake. I thought ye were going to sleep all day!'

Rhiannon said nothing, just stared at her with suspicious eyes.

'They brought ye food if ye want it.' Edithe jerked her head at a small pot of soup set in the hearth to keep warm.

'I eat naught they bring me,' Rhiannon said sullenly.

Edithe rolled her eyes. 'I suppose ye mean ye are afraid it's poisoned? Really, I think ye are quite mad. What do ye intend to do? Starve yourself to death? I'd expect anything from a girl who cuts herself for amusement.'

'Dinna do it for amusement,' Rhiannon growled.

'Well, it certainly doesna amuse any o' us! I'm quite embarrassed to be one o' your party. What the laird o' Fettercairn must think, I canna imagine.'

'He bad man,' Rhiannon said sullenly.

'He's a perfectly charming gentleman, and the laird o' one o' the auldest and most respected clans in Ravenshaw,' Edithe said sharply. 'And if ye think anyone will believe your wild accusations and slanders ahead o' his word, ye are very much mistaken.'

Rhiannon lost her temper and rushed at Edithe, knocking her down with a great shove. Edithe went down with a scream, knocking over the fire-irons and bashing her head hard against the wall.

'How dare ye!' Edithe cried, pressing her hand to her head. 'Ye're naught but a wild animal! Ye should be locked up in a cage like a snow-lion. Wait till I tell what ye've done. My father shall make sure ye pay!'

She scrambled to her feet and ran from the room, her face red with rage.

Rhiannon's eyes smarted with tears. Her legs were so wobbly she had to grip the back of the chair to stop them giving way. She waited a moment, breathing deeply, then made her way across the room, leaning on the furniture for support. She dressed, her fingers fumbling over the buttons and ties, and drew on her boots, which she found clean and freshly polished in her cupboard. Her cloak hung there too, and she slipped it about her shoulders, the camouflaging grey side outwards. Then she picked up her saddlebags and slipped them over her shoulder.

The morning had been one long, horrible blur to Rhiannon. She remembered most of it in weird disconnected flashes, mostly red-hued and throbbing. Her sleep had been tormented by strange visions and nightmares, and she found it hard to remember how much of it was true. Had Lewen really held her down while a grim-faced Nina forced poison down her throat? She knew it had made her sicker than she had ever been before in her life. She did not want to believe Lewen and Nina could do such a thing, but the vomiting had been no nightmare, the stink of it was still in her hair and she tasted it still upon her tongue. And she knew Lewen had seen Irving with the pillow in his hands, and yet he had done nothing to defend her. Rhiannon had to escape from this place.

It was easy enough to make her way through the castle without being seen. The sun was high and everyone was at lunch. Rhiannon did not go out into the inner ward, but found the back way to the stables. They too were empty, except for the horses that drowsily lipped at the straw or put their heads over their stalls to greet her.

Blackthorn whickered eagerly. Rhiannon felt a rush of tears to her eyes at the sight of her, but brushed them resolutely away, stroking her muzzle and murmuring love nonsense to her till the ache around her heart eased a little.

Then she opened the stall and let Blackthorn out. The winged horse came out prancing, restless after so much time confined. Rhiannon buckled on the soft pad and the saddlebags, then led Blackthorn over to the mounting-block. She was still feeling so very weak and dizzy she did not think she could mount without assistance.

Once she was astride the mare's back, she looked about her one more time and noticed that Sure and Steady were both missing, although the caravans were still drawn up to one side of the big barn. Then she realised Argent was gone too. She felt a jolt of disappointment and rage. 'He left me here,' she murmured. 'He doesna care one little bit.'

The thought spurred her on. She pressed her heels into Blackthorn's sides and the mare went daintily out into the courtyard. A groom was there, lazily forking manure into the muck heap. He straightened at the sight of her and said, 'Oy!'

Blackthorn danced sideways, then broke into a trot. The groom ran towards them, arms spread wide, shouting, 'What ye think ye're doing? Where ye going?'

Rhiannon urged the mare into a canter, then lifted her weight from Blackthorn's back. Obediently the mare spread her wings and soared up into the air.

Canna keep a thigearn trapped inside walls, Rhiannon thought with satisfaction.

The groom leapt out of the way hurriedly, landing face first in the muck heap. Rhiannon gave him a mocking salute as he sat up, furiously spitting and wiping clean his face. Then he was on his feet and running to raise the alarm.

Blackthorn wheeled in the air, tilting her wings, then rose higher, leaving the grim grey castle behind her. Rhiannon leant forward, enjoying the view. She could see the vast expanse of lake, whipped into shining waves by the breeze. The wind was very strong today, dragging her hair all over her face, sending her cloak whipping and

Blackthorn's mane swirling. The mare had to fight to keep her course steady against its rough buffeting.

As they came over the ridge, Rhiannon saw the distant grey bulk of Ravenscraig on its pinnacle of stone, and the broken arch of the old bridge across the lake, and the great clouds of spray flung up where the water bent its great weight over the lip of the cliff. She watched it in fascination, never having seen such a magnificent sight.

A distant cry caught her attention. She looked down. Below her was the gatehouse. On the far side of it, Rhiannon saw the massive old tree across the road, and men swarming over it with ropes and tools, and the carthorses dragging at the ropes patiently. Someone had seen her and was pointing up at her. She brought Blackthorn about, heading back towards the mountains, away from all those faces turning up to stare at her. The mare's black wings beat steadily.

Below her were the broken spires of the Tower of Ravens. Beyond she could see the small walled town of Fetterness built at the foot of the hill, and the green of the forest curving all round, and the brown of the untilled fields running down to the water.

The mare was tiring in her battle against the wind, and so Rhiannon looked for a place to land. She brought Blackthorn down near the road, and then saw, under the shadows of the trees, another horse and rider cantering along. At once she urged Blackthorn up into the air again.

Someone called 'Rhiannon!' behind her.

She glanced back and saw the rider was Lewen, standing up in his stirrups, calling to her. Rhiannon's heart was filled with anger and bitterness. She leant forward, urging Blackthorn to fly faster. But the wind was simply too wild and turbulent. Blackthorn whickered in distress, and Rhiannon brought her down the ridge to land lightly on the lower curve of the switchbacking road. She thought she had left Lewen far behind her but then she heard the thunder of Argent's hooves as he galloped round the bend. Rhiannon bit her lip and kicked Blackthorn into a gallop.

Down the steep winding road the two horses raced, the trees tossing wildly overhead. Every now and again Rhiannon glanced back over her shoulder and saw to her dismay that Lewen was gaining upon her. She urged the mare on, even though the mare skidded at one of the hairpin turns and almost fell, the road still being very wet and muddy. Here and there branches lay across the road, blown down in the wind, and Blackthorn leapt them nimbly. The wind was so cold it brought tears to Rhiannon's eyes. She had to hold back her hair with one hand. At last the road began to level out, leading past the walled town and along the lake shore.

A girl was herding geese along the road. Blackthorn plunged into the flock, sending indignant birds honking up into the air. They had just settled back to the road when Argent came thundering past, sending them all up into the air again.

Rhiannon leant lower over Blackthorn's mane, murmuring encouragements, then she glanced back one more time. Lewen was close enough for her to see his face. It was set and grim and angry, and her heart gave a strange little lurch. She urged the mare to run faster but slowly, inexorably, Lewen gained upon them.

Faster and faster the two horses galloped, moving fluidly, silver and black together, like one horse and its shadow. Really frightened now, Rhiannon tried to bring Blackthorn swerving away, to find room to rise into the air again, but with a curt command, Lewen brought Argent round, cutting the mare off and forcing her to slow. They came to a shuddering halt in the shade of a giant hemlock.

Lewen threw himself down from the stallion's back and seized Rhiannon round the waist, dragging her down from the mare's back.

'What in blazes do ye think ye're doing!'

Rhiannon leant her head against his chest, trembling in every limb.

He shook her, none too gently. 'Ye should be in bed! Ye're ill!'

'Me need escape,' she said. 'They try kill me.'

He had her up hard against his body, holding her so she could not escape. Now he twisted his hand in her hair and pulled her head up so he could see her eyes. 'O' course they tried to kill ye,' he yelled. 'Ye idiot, if ye die o' pneumonia they'll have succeeded! Ye should be in bed, no' out in this freezing wind.'

'Ye kent they tried to kill me? And ye still left me?' The hurt of his betrayal was bitter in her voice.

'Ye were safe. The others were watching over ye. I had to go . . .' His voice trailed away. 'Did ye think I was no' coming back? Rhiannon, I would no' leave ye. I promise.' He bent his head and kissed her.

Tears sprang to her eyes. She wound her arm about his neck and kissed him back.

When he spoke again, his voice was unsteady. 'Rhiannon . . .'

'Why ye go?' she demanded. 'Why ye leave me?'

'I have to find the Scrying Pool, at the Tower o' Ravens. I meant to find it by noon but we're too late now. I was going to tell the Rìgh what we have learnt . . . in case the laird tries something . . . in case we all disappeared.' His voice was grim.

'So ye did believe me?'

'O' course I believe ye!'

'And Nina? Iven? All the others?'

'Nina does, I'm sure. Iven . . . I do no' ken. It does no' matter. Once the Rìgh kens what we ken, he will send men to investigate and they will find the truth o' it all. For now, we just have to get away from here safely. Oh, Rhiannon, why did ye run away? The laird will be suspicious now, and happen we have lost our chance to talk our way out o' here. Ye should've trusted me.'

She moved away from him, her face set in its old wary, sulky lines. 'How was I to ken?'

He drew her close to him again, tipping up her face so he could kiss her again. 'I ken. I'm sorry.'

The wind whipped her hair across his face, and he smoothed it down, cradling her face in his hands. He felt as if he were falling down a deep hole, from which there was no way of climbing back to the life he had imagined for himself. She was stiff in his hands, her face sullen. He bent his head again, determined to kiss her into pliancy, but she leant away from him, her eyes suddenly widening. 'Look at that storm!'

Lewen turned and immediately gaped in surprise. To the north immense black clouds were building over the distant peak of Ben Eyrie. Lightning played eerily along its belly, then Lewen heard a low rumble of thunder.

'Mighty Eà!' Lewen cried. 'It was such a beautiful day! Where has that storm come from?'

'It's those necromancers,' Rhiannon said in a low, husky whisper. 'They've called the storm up. They want to keep us trapped here.'

'Och, surely no',' Lewen said, even though he half-believed her. 'They are no' witches there, what would they ken o' weather magic?'

'They can raise ghosts,' Rhiannon said flatly.

435

'We'd better start back,' Lewen said. 'We dinna want to be caught in that.'

Rhiannon nodded. She seized Blackthorn's mane and let Lewen lift her up onto the mare's back. 'It's cold,' she said. 'I'm shivering. That storm is no' natural, I swear to ye.'

'Nina said storms can blow up fast around here,' Lewen said, bringing Argent round so he could mount.

'Aye, that's true. I lived all my life in these mountains, remember. But this cold, that makes all the hairs on my body stand up, and makes my ears ache, that's no' natural. It happens whenever magic is worked. I ken. I have felt it every time.'

Lewen turned to stare at her. 'Ye can feel a chill in the air when magic is worked?' he said slowly. 'Ye must be very sensitive to it.'

'Lucky me,' Rhiannon answered, and wrapped her cloak tightly about her.

The horses broke into a restive trot, the wind blowing their manes and tails into banners. Thunder grumbled through the valley. The clouds chased them all the long ride home, along the shore of the loch and up the road towards Fetterness. The labourers were coming in from the field, looking anxiously up at the sky, and shop-keepers were pulling closed their shutters. By now the clouds had raced to cover the whole sky, and the trees were bending over in the wind, which crackled and roared with lightning.

'Should we stop here?' Lewen called. 'I do no' want ye to get caught in the rain, when ye've been so sick. There'll be an inn where we can take shelter.'

Rhiannon frowned. 'Nay, let's get back. We could be stuck here all night, if the storm is as wild as the last one.'

'Let's hurry then,' Lewen shouted back, the wind catching at his words, and kicked Argent into a canter.

It was tiring fighting against the wind, and the horses reared and whinnied as blown branches whipped against them. Rhiannon was soon so weary she could barely keep her balance. Lewen lifted her from Blackthorn's back, holding her before him. For once Rhiannon made no protest, huddling the cloak against the bitter cold that struck into the very marrow of her bones.

As they reached the top of the ridge, they saw the rain sweeping across the valley below like advancing ranks of grey-clad soldiers. Lightning flashed, making the horses rear in terror, and seconds later there was an enormous clap of thunder that seemed to make the ground shake.

'We'll never make it to the castle,' Lewen cried, as the first scud of rain spat into their faces. 'We're going to get soaked to the skin! Let us go to the tower. Ye can rest while I try to find the Scrying Pool. Sunset is a time o' power – I can try to reach His Highness then.'

'There'll be no sunset tonight,' Rhiannon said through chattering teeth. 'Only storm.'

THE TOWER OF RAVENS

A head of them loomed tall stone gateposts, with iron gates lying broken and open. The wind tore the hood from Rhiannon's head, and sleet lashed her face. She coughed, the paroxysm so severe she could not catch her breath.

Lewen kicked Argent forward into a gallop. 'Come on then.'

They rode helter-skelter through the gateposts, head bent against the vicious wind that seemed filled with thousands of little needles of ice. Within was a rising avenue of dark yew trees, growing so close overhead it gave them some protection from the storm, though they could barely see to avoid the ruts and potholes. The driveway led straight as an arrow up the hill and through a great arched gateway in a wall. As they passed through the archway, the rain hit them again like a hammer and Lewen spurred Argent on, Blackthorn cantering close behind, through courtyards and broken colonnades and blackened ruins, until at last they burst through a

438

doorway and found themselves in a dry, dark place.

Lewen dismounted, trying to catch his breath, and wiped his face with his sleeve. A sudden sphere of light suddenly winked into existence above his head, making Rhiannon gasp with alarm. 'It's all right, it's just me,' Lewen said. 'I wanted to see.'

He looked about him. They were in a long low building, very grimy and filled with old, cobwebbed contraptions that once would have been carts and carriages. A row of stalls stood empty, but Lewen saw with interest that one near the door was filled with fresh straw and had been cleared of the worst of the spiderwebs. The trough was clean and half-filled with water, and against the wall was a row of clean, shiny bins that must be filled with grain.

'So someone keeps a horse here,' Lewen said. 'Let us hope he doesna return soon. There's no muck heap, so I'd say it's only an occasional visitor.'

Rhiannon lifted a tired hand and pushed back her hood. Her cloak was dripping wet.

'Here, let me help ye,' Lewen said, lifting Rhiannon down. She was shivering with cold, and so he led her to sit down on one of the bins, and unfastened her cloak. Lewen shook it out and spread it to dry over one of the low walls between the stalls. He did the same with his own cloak, then turned his attention to the horses. Rhiannon's saddlebags and her precious bow and quiver hung from the pommel of her soft saddle-pad. He unbuckled these from Blackthorn's back, and hung them on the wall, then gave the mare a quick rubdown with a wisp of straw. He unsaddled Argent and rubbed him down too, then put the horses together in the stall. He gave them a bucket of oats to share, and then turned his attention back to Rhiannon. She looked pale and hollow-eyed, and coughed every now and again.

'Let's try to get ye warm,' he said. 'Wait here, I'll just have a little scout around.'

He looked out the doorway, where the rain was still teeming down, then went through the stables into the next building, which seemed to have been some kind of quarters for the stablehands. There was a kitchen with a big hearth, and a table and some old broken chairs, a few old pots, filthy with dust and spiderwebs, and a scullery with a sink and pump. After a few energetic jerks, there was a spurt of filthy water that then ran pure. Lewen rinsed out the sink, washing away myriad dead spiders, then tasted the water, which was sweet. He explored a little further, finding a couple of dark, smelly rooms above and what once would have been a kitchen garden beyond, but was now just weeds. The best find was a pile of fire-wood outside the kitchen door, protected from the rain by the eaves. It was filled with all sorts of creepy-crawlies, but Lewen banged it all together and built a fire in the old hearth, which he lit with a snap of his fingers. With fire-light dancing over the walls, the old kitchen began to look almost hospitable.

He went back to the stable and gathered together armfuls of straw, cheerfully telling Rhiannon what he had found. She followed him through to the kitchen and he made her a bed on the floor before the fire, then hung their cloaks out over the back of the chairs to dry.

'Are ye still damp?' he asked. 'Happen ye should take off your coat and stockings, and let me hang them afore the fire to dry.'

Rhiannon did as she was told then, dressed only in a loose white shirt and breeches, huddled closer to the fire, her hands held out. The wind moaned and sighed all round the ruins, and they could hear the occasional growl of thunder. An early dusk was falling.

'Happen we're stuck here for the night,' Lewen said. Rhiannon looked back over her shoulder at him and smiled.

He smiled back at her and stripped off his own coat and boots, arranging them over the back of old chairs so they could both stop the draughts and receive some of the warmth of the fire. His shirt was damp as well, but he was too shy to take it off in front of Rhiannon so he simply undid the collar and sleeves, and ruffled his damp hair, and looked about for the cleanest pot. 'I dinna think to bring any food,' he said. 'But I can make us some sort o' porridge from the oats, and I saw some herbs out in the garden, I'll go and pick some to make us some tea when the rain dies down a wee.'

Rhiannon lay back in the straw, looking dreamy. 'It does no' sound as if it's ever going to stop.'

Lewen looked down at her, and felt an absurd desire to say that he wished it never would. He bit the words back, and busied himself with practical matters. He scrubbed out a pot, then went into the stable to scoop a couple of handfuls of oats out of one of the bins. While it cooked, he quickly whittled them a rough spoon from a piece of firewood, porridge being too difficult to eat with the fingers. He and Rhiannon then put the pot of porridge between them and took turns to eat. It was rather taste-less, but it was warm and filling, and both felt much better after eating.

'I hope there are no ghosts here,' Rhiannon said. 'I never want to see a ghost again.'

'I doubt whether anyone died in this room,' Lewen said. 'The Red Guards did no' kill the servants o' the witches, only the witches themselves. Most o' the battle would have taken place in the actual Tower, no' here in the stables.' He reached out a lazy hand and threw another log on the fire. A small lump of wood fell down from the pile and rolled across the floor and he picked it up, and examined it in the fitful light.

'I think this is rowan,' he said in surprise, and scratched at it with his nail, then lifted it to his nose and sniffed. 'Ye do no' usually burn rowan,' he explained to Rhiannon, taking his knife and beginning to whittle. 'Rowan is one o' the sacred woods. It is thought to be particularly powerful protecting against evil spirits.'

'Why?' she asked.

He shrugged. 'I dinna ken. It just is. They plant it in graveyards, along with yew, to stop the spirits o' the dead from wandering, and countryfolk often hang it above their door to keep the house safe. In the Other World, they often used it to beat suspected witches, or make crosses out o' it to try to repel the devil. All nonsense, o' course, naught but auld-fashioned superstition, but still it is a powerful tree. I'll make ye something from it, a charm against evil.'

'All right,' she answered, pleased. 'What will ye make?'

'I dinna ken yet. Something to hang about your neck, I think. That is the best way to wear a charm.' He lifted the knot of wood, and turned it first one way, then another. 'A star,' he said softly. 'A star for my starry-eyed lass.'

She smiled at him.

In companionable silence, they sat together before the fire, listening to the constant wash of the rain, as curl after curl of white wood fell to the floor. It did not take him long to make. As large as Lewen's hands were, they were deft and nimble, and he wielded the knife with great confidence. A five-pointed star set within a small hoop soon emerged. His focus grew more intent, his movements more careful and studied. Soon the amulet was smooth and silvery-pale.

'I wish I had some beeswax to polish it with,' he said at last, passing the amulet to Rhiannon. 'I'll polish it for ye when we get to Lucescere.'

'It's bonny,' she said, turning it in her fingers. The hoop was about as large as the circle made by thumb and forefinger, the star within as delicate as thorns. 'Will it really protect me against ghosts?'

'Ghosts and sprites and things that go bump in the night,' he answered with a grin. 'Ye should wear it against your skin, just here, above your breast bone.' He touched her gently with one finger, and felt her take a startled breath. 'See, I've drilled a little hole here for ye to thread a ribbon through.' He reached behind his head and pulled loose the black cord that bound back his unruly hair. It fell loose about his face as he threaded the cord through the aperture and knotted it together. 'There you are,' he said, pleased. 'I'd like to see ye wear it. I've noticed ye have no necklace like the other girls.'

Her face suddenly darkened.

'What's wrong?' he asked.

'Naught,' she said, but he saw how she shivered and he at once built up the fire so sparks flew up the chimney. 'Ye're cold,' he said. 'Come warm yourself by the fire, and I'll make ye some tea.'

She obeyed, huddling her arms about her knees, the pentagram hanging about her neck.

Lewen pulled his cloak over his head and ran through the storm to grab a few handfuls of weeds. He saw peppermint, thyme, and chamomile, and a woody old lavender. There may have been more, but the rain was coming down so thickly he did not wait to see. He came back into the warm peace of the kitchen, and saw Rhiannon sitting staring down at the star charm in her hands. She gave him a radiant smile as he shook off the rain, and Lewen felt warm happiness well up through his body.

He sat next to her, poking at the fire and throwing the herbs into the water. 'I wish we had some honey,' he said.

'Canna have everything,' Rhiannon said. 'I think we doing well, all things considering.'

He nodded and smiled. 'Warm enough?'

'Lovely and warm now, thanks,' she said and rested her head on her hand. 'Will they be worried about us?'

Lewen nodded. 'If I find the Scrying Pool I'll try to scry to Nina,' he said. 'The storm may make it hard, and I am no' very skilled at scrying. I do no' ken if it'll work.'

'What is scrying?'

'Talking mind to mind,' Lewen said.

Rhiannon stared at him in amazement. 'Ye can talk to Nina, when she is there in the castle and we are here?'

'Maybe,' Lewen said. 'I ken Nina well, and she'll be listening for word from me. True witches can scry at a distance, but I canna, no' yet. I'm still learning.'

'I'm amazed,' Rhiannon said. 'Is there aught ye canna do?'

Lewen flushed. 'O' course.'

'I've yet to see it,' Rhiannon said. 'Ye can make a spoon out o' a lump o' wood, or a charm against ghosts, ye can light a fire with a snap o' your fingers, ye can talk to birds and dogs and horses and faeries, ye can make us a meal out o' weeds and horse food, and ye can outride and outfight any man.' Her voice was full of pride.

Lewen leant on his elbow. 'I've only managed to out-ride ye once.'

'Aye, that's true,' Rhiannon said complacently.

He smiled. 'Well, at least I beat ye at archery.'

'Aye, I ken,' she said and flashed her dimple. 'Ye strong.' She lifted one hand and felt his arm muscles approvingly.

Lewen shifted his weight, flushing. 'The water's boiling, let's have some tea,' he said. 'Oh, no! We have naught to drink out o'. Dinna say I have to whittle us a cup as well!'

'I have a cup in my bag,' Rhiannon said. 'We could use that.'

'I'll go and get it,' he said and sat up.

She frowned. 'I'll get it,' she said.

'I tell ye what, I'll get your saddlebags and ye can find the cup,' Lewen said, grinning at her. 'I ken how ye feel about people looking through your things.'

Her frown did not lift. 'No looking,' she warned him.

'No looking,' he promised. He got up and went out of the circle of light, into the chilly darkness beyond. When he came back, a few minutes later, he had Rhiannon's saddlebags in his hands. He tossed them to her, and warmed himself by the fire as she surreptitiously looked through her things. By the time he had swung the pot off the fire and thrown on a few more logs, she had drawn a silver goblet out of the bag. Simply made, it had a wide cup set on a smooth, slender stem. In the centre of the stem was a large crystal that caught the light of the fire and glittered with rainbow prisms.

'It's lovely,' Lewen said. 'Where on earth did ye get it?' She said nothing and he looked at her sharply. 'Was it Connor's?'

She nodded, looking anxious and guilty.

'I thought ye gave my mam all o' Connor's things, to give to his family.'

'She asked me for his *clothes*,' Rhiannon said.

He could not help laughing, though the admission troubled him. 'What else did ye keep?'

She drew out a pretty music-box that played an ethereal tune when she opened the lid, and the small golden medal with the device of a haloed hand. Lewen touched it with one finger. 'The League o' the Healing Hand,' he said, sounding sad. 'Ye canna tell a story about the Bright Wars without hearing tales o' the League. They are almost all dead now.' He lifted his gaze. 'Ye canna keep these things, Rhiannon. Truly ye canna. They belong to Johanna now. If Connor carried them in his travel-pack, it means they meant a lot to him, and they will to her too. Do ye understand?'

'I suppose so,' Rhiannon answered crossly.

He took the goblet. 'We may as well drink out o' it now, though, although it's far too precious for thyme tea!'

Very carefully he managed to pour some of the fragrant tea into the goblet. 'This will help warm ye, and will ease that cough,' he said. 'Drink up.'

She took the goblet between her hands and sipped at the hot liquid within. After a few mouthfuls she passed the goblet back to him. 'Ye now.'

He drank deeply, though the draught was quite bitter without honey, then passed it back to her, watching as she lifted the cup to her mouth and drank again. Her black hair was kindled with gold and bronze light where the fire struck through it, and her eyes were shadowed. He thought she was the most beautiful woman he had ever seen. As if sensing his thought, she looked up and smiled at him.

'Thank ye,' she said. 'I am warm all through now.'

Unable to help himself, Lewen bent over and kissed her. She caught her breath in surprise, then drew his head closer, one arm sliding up round his shoulder. Lewen lost himself in sensation. Her skin was just as satiny-smooth as he had imagined, and warm from the fire. Her mouth was soft and sweet, and she kissed with an intoxicating combination of ardour and inexperience. When Lewen entwined his tongue with hers, he felt her shudder and sigh and creep closer, and he felt such a desperate eagerness he surprised even himself. He tried to draw back, but she would not let him, raising herself to follow him.

He sighed and folded her under him, feeling their bodies shift and curve to each other's shape. One of her hands slipped down under his collar and caressed the skin of his throat. He closed his eyes and let his own hand slide under her shirt, finding the naked skin of her back, slipping round to caress her slender waist, and then finding at last her breast. She moved in sudden surprise and he heard her breath catch and sigh. He had to draw away then, to look down into her face, to watch as he undid her buttons with shaking fingers. Her eyes were closed, her face as soft and vulnerable as he could ever wish for, and a smile curved her lips. As he drew away her shirt, cupping her breasts with both hands, the smile deepened and her elusive dimple flashed in her cheek. He drew a deep, shaky breath and brought his mouth down to the creamy curve of her breast. She arched her back.

'Rhiannon, Rhiannon,' he whispered at last, managing to lift his mouth away. He felt drunk.

'Lewen,' she whispered back, and kissed his ear.

'Rhiannon, I canna . . .'

'What?'

'Rhiannon, if we go on, I willna be able to stop. I dinna think I can stop now.'

'Stop? Why?' she asked in surprise.

He kissed her again, drew back to look at her, swooped down to kiss her again. The feel of her half-naked body beneath him was drugging all his sense.

'Rhiannon . . . are ye sure? Is this what ye want?'

She turned her head blindly, seeking his mouth. He took her head in both his hands, his fingers tangled in the silkiness of her hair, and pressed her to him. They lost themselves in each other's mouths for what seemed a very long time. Then Lewen managed to disentangle them from their clothes, each discarding revealing a new source of joyous sensation. Rhiannon's body was just as beautiful as he had imagined, slim and lithe and milk-white, with a flowing curve from breast to hip that he marvelled over with mouth and hand. She was as eager to touch and explore his body as he was hers, and Lewen's urgency was so great he feared the mere touch of her hand would be enough to undo him. So he captured both her hands in his, stretching them out above her head and holding her still with the weight of his body.

'Please, dearling, *leannan*, please, lie still,' he begged.

She smiled up at him and obeyed. Cautiously he let go of her hands, but she did not try to move. Very slowly he put his hand down between their bodies and pried her legs apart. She was wet and warm and slick. He bit his lip, then drove into her. She cried out in shock, but Lewen was beyond hearing her. Again and again he thrust into her, crying aloud in pleasure, and she raised her hips, thrusting against him, so that he felt a great roar of blood race through him, deafening him. He raised himself high on his hands, his groin fused with hers, his head flung back, groaning. They were still a moment or two, Lewen slowly moving in and out of her again, then he bent his arms, laying his weight upon her again, utterly relaxed and replete.

'That was beautiful,' he said at last. 'Ye're beautiful, Rhiannon.'

She sighed. He said her name again and turned her face with both hands so they could kiss again.

'I love ye,' he said. 'I love ye so much.'

She looked up at him curiously, the firelight playing over the planes of her face. Her eyes looked very blue, and her lips were red and swollen.

'Ye're so beautiful,' he said again, kissing her very gently.

Still she was silent. He shifted his weight to the side, so he was not crushing her, and felt himself slide out of her. He sighed with disappointment and pressed himself as close to her as he could get. She cuddled against him, and that gave him the courage to ask, against all his better judgement, 'Rhiannon? Do ye love me too?'

She looked him in the eyes. 'I do no' ken what love is. Is this love I feel?'

'What do ye feel?' he asked, threading his fingers through hers and holding their entwined hands up against the golden glow of the fire. He was so afraid he dared not meet her eyes.

'Happy,' she said wonderingly.

'Me too,' he answered gladly and kissed her. She wrapped both her arms about his neck, her breasts spreading against his chest. At once he felt his body stir and smiled ruefully, lowering one hand to caress her inner thigh, then stroking his hand up towards her breast. To his surprise he left rust-coloured streaks on the warm creaminess of her skin. He looked down, and saw blood trickling down her thigh.

'Rhiannon!' he cried.

'Aye?'

He leant up on his elbow, winding her hair around one finger. 'Have ye never lain with a man afore?'

'Me? O' course no'. Who would I have lain with?'

He was taken aback. 'But I thought . . . ye said . . .'

'I No-Horn,' she said. 'The favours o' the men were kept only for the leaders o' the herd. I saw them mate often. It was no' like this, I think.'

Lewen sighed. He lay quietly, thinking. 'I'm sorry,' he said after a moment. 'I should've stopped.'

'Why?' she asked again.

He could not explain to her. She wriggled a little closer, and traced a circle on his hard belly with her finger. 'It worries ye, this blood?'

He sighed. 'Aye. Though I must admit, it pleases me too, that I was the one to deflower ye. I dinna ken why I tell ye so.'

'Deflower?' Rhiannon was puzzled. 'I girl, no' plant.'

Lewen laughed and traced round and round her nipple, watching it harden. 'Indeed, ye are, my dearling.' He closed his mouth over her nipple and the sound of her sigh went into him like a sword. He slipped his hand down between her legs and felt the hot stickiness of her, and then, his own desire quickening fast, slid down and tasted it. He had himself well in hand this time, determined to take his time over the loving of her, but her own desire was so swift, and her expression of it so honest and free, that once again it was a quick, hard, passionate coupling they had in the straw before the fire. Afterwards, he lay with his head on her stomach, feeling her hand twirling his hair, feeling exhausted, replete, and very happy.

'Ye mine now,' Rhiannon whispered. 'Do ye hear me? Mine.'

He rolled over, reaching out one lazy hand to trace down her brow, her nose, across the soft pads of her lips, down her chin and throat and the bare cleft of her breasts to her belly button. 'Aye, I hear ye,' he said softly, and kissed her. 'I'm yours.'

'Always,' she said.

'Always,' he repeated.

'So is this love, what I'm feeling?'

'Aye,' he said and kissed her again. 'This is love.' They kissed lingeringly. 'Say it,' he commanded. 'Say, "I love ye, Lewen".'

'I love ye, Lewen.'

'I love ye too, Rhiannon.'

They smiled, and then, for no reason, laughed. The fire was dying down, and outside the storm still howled. Rhiannon gave a little shiver.

'Ye're getting cold,' Lewen said remorsefully and sat up, looking for something to cover her with. 'Look, it's dark. We've missed sunset. Oh well, it's teeming down out there. I doubt I could have found the pool anyway. I'll have to try again at dawn.' He got up and felt the edge of her cloak but it was still damp, so he threw some more wood on the fire and then poured her some more tea, warming the goblet between his hands until steam wisped up. 'Drink this, my love, and I'll find something to wrap ye in.'

She took the goblet from him, smiling, and he was compelled to kiss her again, quickly, before getting to his feet. 'My shawl is in my bag,' she said, and drank the hot tea gratefully.

Lewen went over to the saddlebag and pulled out the embroidered shawl with a flourish. Something came rattling out of the bag with it, and he bent and picked it up from the floor. His entrails knotted. In his hand was a necklace made of bones and teeth. Even in the subtle, changeable light of the fire he could see most of the teeth were human. He stood still, frozen with shock, while his mind neatly put all the pieces of the puzzle together and made a whole. Even while he tried to deny and make excuses, his analytical brain turned the puzzle over and examined it from every angle. There was no mistake.

He turned and went back to the fire. Rhiannon sat in the straw, her arms about her knees, her hair streaming down her naked back, looking more bewitching than ever. He tossed her the shawl, and she caught it and smiled, wrapping it about her shoulders. When he did not

451

smile back, her expression turned grave. She looked up at him questioningly.

He held out the necklace. 'Is this yours?'

All the soft, warm, living flesh of her turned slowly to stone. She lifted eyes that had gone huge and dark. 'Aye,' she answered reluctantly.

'Are those Connor's teeth, his finger?'

'Aye.'

'So ye killed him? Ye lied to me?'

'Aye,' she answered again.

He suddenly became conscious of his nakedness. He dropped the necklace on the table with as much horror as if it had been a snake, then came back to the fire pulling on his shirt and his breeches, which were still unpleasantly damp. He then sat down on the floor to pull on his stockings and boots. 'Why?' he asked, not looking at her.

Her voice shook. 'He would've told them I'd helped him to escape. They would have torn me to pieces.'

'So ye killed him.'

'He had my mother, he was going to kill her!'

'But ye hated your mother.'

She nodded, tears welling up in her eyes. He thrust his hands into his pockets. She looked at him pleadingly but he would not look at her, and the tears overflowed. She buried her face in her arms.

'Why dinna ye tell me afore?' The words burst out of him.

She raised her miserable face. 'They said whoever had killed him would hang. I do no' want to hang!'

'Nay, I guess no',' he said bitterly and got to his feet. He did not know where to go, or what to do, so after a moment he prodded the fire, saying over his shoulder, 'Ye'd better get dressed, your clothes are dry now. Ye should try to get some sleep, it's late.'

She did not move. 'Lewen?'

He did not answer.

'Lewen?' she said desperately.

'What?' he said harshly.

'I sorry. I dinna want to hurt him. I had to, canna ye see that? Please, dinna be angry. I couldna help it, truly I couldna. I dinna ken!' The words came tumbling over each other and she held up both hands to him imploringly.

He did not reply.

She tried again. 'Lewen, dinna be angry. Please, please.'

'Ye should have told me,' he replied, prodding at the fire even harder.

'I couldna tell ye. Do ye no' understand? Lewen?'

He turned on her, his face twisted with pain. 'Ye are a murderess! A liar and a traitor! Ye killed my friend!'

She tried to speak, but could not. Weeping, she pulled on her clothes and huddled herself into the shawl. Lewen got to his feet. 'I'll sleep in the stable,' he said. 'Hopefully the storm will have blown over by morning.'

Catching up his cloak, he went away from the dim, warm room into bitter cold and darkness.

THE SCRYING POOL

He passed in and out of uneasy sleep all the long, unhappy night. The sound of the wind in the broken stone worried him like icy teeth, so that only the imprecise memory of nightmares showed he had slept at all. Yet when he finally woke, feeling a great weight of misery, it was to find a clear, cold dawn and the winged horse gone from the stall. Argent stood there alone, his head sunk, eyes shut, one hoof relaxed.

Lewen stared in stupefaction, then turned and ran into the kitchen. It was grey and empty, smelling of smoke. On the table were the silver goblet, the music-box, the golden medal, and the gruesome necklace of teeth and bones. There was no sign of Rhiannon.

Lewen could not believe she had gone. How had she managed to get Blackthorn out of the stall, when he had slept in the straw right next to the horses? He imagined her creeping out into the dark and the storm, and felt such a pit of loss open up inside him he came the closest to weeping since his roan pony Aurora had died when he was still a lad. Anger and grief together make a bitter brew, and Lewen was so angry he was blind and deaf with it. He did not know what to do. He sank to his knees and covered his face with his hands, trying to hold back the howl that seemed to be gathering inside him. At last the howl knotted itself into a hard lump in his chest, and he was able to get up. He filled the goblet with water and drank deeply, trying to wash the knot away, and then splashed his face again and again. A longing to speak to his mother came over him. He imagined her distress and felt his stomach quiver. Hurriedly he gathered up Connor's treasures and shoved them in his own saddlebags, then he led the big grey stallion out into the courtyard.

It was almost dawn and the sky was clear. Puddles gleamed everywhere, and the courtyard was littered with broken branches and torn leaves. High overhead ravens wheeled in the wind, hundreds of them, calling harshly. They looked like ashes blown from a bonfire. Lewen moved slowly through the ruin, the stallion following. Much of the main body of the building had been destroyed by fire, leaving nothing but blackened stones all overgrown with brambles and nettles. He found the gate that had once led out to the bridge across the waterfall, and looked out over the dizzying chasm, able to see nothing of the castle on the far side of the river for the great gusts of spray that dashed him in the face. He left Argent lipping at weeds in what once would have been a pleasure garden, and climbed an old stone staircase to explore the wreck of a vaulted gallery where once great sorcerers and prionnsachan would have walked together. He came down again carefully, feeling desolate and alone. Nowhere was there any sign of Rhiannon.

Then he and the stallion came to the central courtyard and found there a round pool of water, shimmering with reflections of the dawn sky. Despite the wrack of the storm that littered the cracked paving-stones, not a single leaf spoiled the sparkling perfection of the silver-lined pool. It was enclosed inside stone arches fretted with entwining lines and knots, and guarded by large stone ravens.

Lewen sighed and sat down heavily on the curved bench encircling the pool. He had half-hoped, half-dreaded finding the Scrying Pool.

He remembered hearing Dughall MacBrann tell the story of how he had crept here to the Tower of Ravens one bitter winter's night so he could scry to Lachlan and tell him news of the war against the Bright Soldiers. 'It's a wonder my hair and beard are no' as white as my father's,' he had said. 'For the tower was thick with ghosts and evil memories, and all I could remember was that old story about Brann the Raven and how he swore he would outwit Gearradh in the end and live again. I swear I felt him breathing down my neck the whole time!'

If the MacBrann had been able to use the Scrying Pool twenty-five years ago, the chances are the pool would be useable now. The fact that it was still brimming with crystal-clear water, untarnished after fifty years of neglect, indicated that the magic of the pool was unbroken. Lewen badly wanted to speak to someone. He felt as if his inner compass, that had led him true all his life, was now spinning out of control. He did not know what was right and true anymore. Rhiannon had lied to him, she had tricked and deceived him, she had made a fool of him. The thoughts spilled through his mind like acid. He looked back over the past few weeks and writhed in internal torment, seeing how easily he had been seduced by her air of wild and innocent beauty. Had it all been a lie? He could not tell anymore. He longed to be able to tell someone, and have them set him straight again. He longed for comfort and reassurance, for someone to say to him, 'But she is naught but a wild child, she did no' ken what she did, how could she? O' course she loves ye, o' course her heart is pure and true, o' course she is no' a cold-blooded murderess, how can ye think such things o' her?'

So he sat cross-legged before the pool, staring into its silvery depths, calling to Nina in his mind. It took only a few seconds for her image to appear to him in the pool. She looked white and anxious and he heard her voice in his mind.

'Lewen, where are you? What happened to ye?'

'We were caught in the storm. We took shelter in the auld tower.'

'Are ye all right?'

'Aye, we're grand. At least, I am . . .'

'What do ye mean? Where's Rhiannon? Is she with ye? She's disappeared!'

'Nay. I mean, I do no' ken. She's gone.'

'Gone? Do ye mean she *was* with ye? Where has she gone?'

'I dinna ken. She crept away last night, while I was sleeping . . . she's run away.'

'But why?'

'I found out . . . something.' He took a shaking breath, then the words burst out of him. 'Oh Nina, it was Rhiannon who murdered Connor. She confessed it all to me last night, and now she's gone. I dinna ken where, she disappeared during the night.'

Nina was silent for a long moment, then she said steadily, 'We all kent it may have been her, Lewen, we've suspected it from the beginning. Even Lilanthe feared so, and ye ken your mother always thinks the best o'

457

everyone. We will have to find her, we need to take her to Lucescere to be tried and judged.'

'But, Nina, they will hang her!'

'Maybe no'. If it was an accident . . .'

'It was no accident,' Lewen said harshly.

'That will be for the court to decide,' Nina answered. 'Lewen, come back to the castle. We will find her, dinna ye worry.'

'I am no' sure I want to find her,' Lewen said, his voice breaking.

Nina looked troubled. 'I canna just let her fly away, Lewen, no' if she is responsible for Connor's death. The Rìgh would want us to make every effort to find her.'

He said nothing, and she said again, with deep concern in her voice, 'Come back to the castle, Lewen. We've all been very worried about ye. Ye must be cold and hungry indeed. Come back, and we'll talk about it then.'

'But what about Rhiannon?' Lewen said. 'I do no' want to just leave her. She went out into the storm, and she's been so sick, and Blackthorn is so nervy . . .'

'The laird sent out search parties for the two o' ye, happen they will have had sight o' her. We'll talk about it when ye are here.'

Lewen sighed. 'All right.'

'Are ye using the Scrying Pool? For indeed your face and voice are clear as if ye were standing afore me.'

Lewen nodded, feeling sick at heart.

'Thank Eà! Have ye spoken to the Rìgh? What did he say?'

'I havena contacted him yet.' Lewen's voice was dull and a trifle defensive. 'I have only just found the Pool.'

'Then will ye scry to the Rìgh now? I think he should ken everything we do, just in case we fail to make it back to Lucescere. My heart troubles me . . . the laird is angry and suspicious indeed about ye and Rhiannon going missing.' She paused, then went on more strongly, 'Tell His Highness all ye can, Lewen, he needs to ken.'

'But it is so far . . . I do no' ken if I'll be able to reach him. I am no good at scrying.' Lewen knew he was making excuses. He did not want to have to face his Rìgh and tell him he had fallen in love with a murderess.

'The Scrying Pool will help ye, Lewen, that's what it's for. Remember your scrying exercises. Empty your mind, control your breath, and imagine his face. Reach out to him. Ye will reach him if ye focus strongly enough.'

Lewen nodded reluctantly and closed his eyes, emptying his thoughts. He waited a few minutes, then stared once more into the pool, imagining the dark, stern face of Lachlan MacCuinn, the Rìgh of Eileanan. 'My laird,' he called in his mind, 'can ye hear me? Can ye hear me, my laird?'

The shadows in the pool gradually shifted into the shape of a man, black-haired and black-bearded, with the curve of black wings rising from his shoulders. Lewen heard the startled mind-voice of the Rìgh.

'Lewen, my lad?'

'Aye, my laird, it is me.'

'What on earth is the matter? Why are ye calling me?'

'I have news, my laird, I thought ye should ken.'

'If it is the news o' Connor's death, we received word o' it, thanks to a very tired and bad-tempered golden eagle. It is unhappy news indeed, we are all most distressed.'

'Aye, my laird. I'm glad the eagle made it, we were no' sure he could cross the mountains, the weather has been foul indeed.'

'Has it? I'm sorry for that. Are ye delayed?'

'Aye, my laird, we are.' Lewen took a deep, shaking breath and forced himself to go on. He felt quite sick with the conflict of emotions inside him. 'There's more news than that, though, my laird. We have found out who killed him, Your Highness. It was a girl we found in the mountains, dressed in his clothes, a satyricorn girl.'

'A Horned One killed him?'

'She's no' horned, my laird, but a satyricorn nonetheless.' Lewen heard the bitterness in his own voice. 'She was travelling with us but when I discovered the truth . . . she fled, my laird.'

'Ye must find her, and bring her here,' the Rìgh commanded. 'The satyricorns have signed the Pact o' Peace, they are subject to the laws o' this land. The murder o' a Blue Guard is a heinous crime indeed, and Connor the Just was one o' my best and most faithful men.'

'I ken, my laird,' Lewen said unhappily.

'Ye must capture the murderess and bring her here to face trial, do ye hear me, Lewen? The whole city grieves his death. Where are ye? Are there men ye can call upon to help lay this murderess by the heels?'

'I think so, my laird. I am at the Tower o' Ravens.'

'Ye are using the Scrying Pool? Good lad! No wonder your face just popped up in my wash-bowl. I was wondering how ye managed to scry across the mountains so clearly, I thought ye must have found some way to fly across like the eagle. I could wish ye were closer, we are all keen indeed to charge the murderess and deal with her afore the wedding. We want no unpleasantness to mar the festivities.'

'No, my laird.'

'Well, fare ye well, then, my lad, and good work.'

'Your Highness, there is more. I think ye should ken it all, just in case something happens to us . . .'

'Happens to ye? What in Eà's green blood do ye mean? Are ye in some kind o' danger there? Is it that satyricorn girl?'

'Nay, my laird. It's just . . . my laird, in our effort to return to ye quickly, we came down the eastern bank o' the Findhorn River, through the Fetterness Valley.'

'Aye, o' course, ye must've, if ye're at the Tower o' Ravens. A bare, bleak place, if I remember rightly. We fought a battle there, at Fettercairn Castle, many years ago.'

'That is where we are now, my laird. We've been trapped here for some days –'

'Trapped? Held against your will, do ye mean?' The Rìgh spoke urgently.

'Nay, no' entirely. The road was blocked, though we suspect it was on purpose. Things are no' right here, though, my laird. There is much talk o' murders, and children missing, and corpses that will no' rest, and there seems to be necromancers using the auld tower . . .'

'Necromancers!'

'Aye. Trying to raise the dead. Rhiannon saw them invoke a circle, my laird, and sacrifice a cock, and speak with the spirits o' the dead.'

'Who is Rhiannon?'

Lewen's heart sank. 'The satyricorn, Your Highness.'

'The murderess?'

'Aye, my laird.'

'Did anyone else see this so-called necromancy?'

'Nay, my laird, but –'

'She could be seeking to deceive, to throw suspicion for her nefarious deeds onto others.'

'I do no' think so, my laird.' Lewen saw the Rìgh's frowning eyebrows shoot up and went on quickly, 'Please, I havena much time. Your Highness, there has been much evil done in this valley, evil much greater than Rhiannon is responsible for. She killed Connor high in the mountains, my laird, up under Ben Eyrie, no' here in Fetterness.

461

She has never been here afore. The murders and the necromancy, that is the work o' others, and I fear it means some danger to ye, my laird. The laird here talks o' seeking revenge for the death o' his brother – I think ye may have killed him, sir. Or one o' your men. A little boy died too.'

'I do no' remember a boy,' the Rìgh said.

'I think Connor heard something, knew something o' the laird o' Fettercairn's plans, though I do no' ken how or what. Connor was just across the loch, at Ravenscraig, when the auld MacBrann died. We were there too, for my mother to help ease him. The MacBrann was very ill, raving o' ghosts and auld prophecies and evil deeds. We all thought him mad. All except Connor. My laird, the very night the MacBrann died Connor took his horse and rode out for the Razor's Edge. That is a pass through to Rionnagan, your Highness . . .'

'I ken the Razor's Edge, I walked it myself once, long ago,' the Rìgh said gruffly. 'It is no' a road one would take lightly.'

'Nay, my laird. I think Connor must've heard something that made him fear for ye, or for your kingdom. Why else would he ride that way? He died afore he could tell ye his news . . .'

'Fettercairn Castle,' the Rìgh said broodingly. 'That is a name I have no' heard for many years, but I remember it well. A place o' blood and treachery.'

Lewen nodded.

'Ye have done well,' the Rìgh said abruptly. 'Ye must go. If there are sorcerers there strong enough to raise the dead, they will be strong enough to eavesdrop on your scrying. Get out o' there, Lewen, as fast as ye can, and come here to me. I will hear all your news and judge then what is best done.'

'Aye, my laird,' said Lewen and sat back on his heels. A wave of dizziness washed over him, and he felt tired enough to weep. He had not realised what a great effort of will and focus it took to scry so far, for so long. He ground the heels of his hands into his eyes and then got to his feet. Only then did he realise he was not alone.

The tall, quiet man who usually guarded Lord Malvern's back was leaning on his claymore only a few feet away, with a handful of men that Lewen recognised from the castle. There was Shannley, the old groom who had tended the horses, and his assistant, Jem, and a few of the footmen. They all looked surly and uncomfortable.

'Glad we are indeed to have found ye, young sir,' the laird's bodyguard said in his oddly feminine voice. 'We've been searching since dawn. My laird has been most anxious about ye.'

'I'm sorry,' Lewen stammered. 'We took refuge from the rain.'

'And ye so close to the castle,' he marvelled.

'Rhiannon has been sick,' Lewen said defensively. 'I did no' want her to get wet through. It was sleeting down.'

'And where is the young lady now?'

'I dinna ken,' Lewen said sullenly. 'We quarrelled and she ran off.'

There was a little rumble of laughter from the men, and a quick nudging of each other's ribs. Lewen went crimson.

'We need to find her,' he said. 'I was just about to head back to the castle to ask for some help.'

'Is that so?' Jem sneered. 'It looked like ye were mooning about, staring at yourself in the water.'

There were a few more sniggers. Lewen cast him an angry look, but said nothing. He could only hope that none of them there had any witch-skills, to eavesdrop on his silent conversation with the Rìgh. It seemed a futile hope. Some at least of these men must be part of the necromancers' circle of nine.

They all rode back to the castle, Lewen feeling like a prisoner in the midst of the other men. He was escorted silently through the gatehouse and the garden to the entrance hall, where Nina and Iven were both waiting with Lord Malvern. Nina flung her arms about his neck.

'Thank heavens ye are safe! We've been so worried about ye.'

'I'm sorry,' Lewen said defensively. 'Indeed I could no' help it.'

'O' course no', laddie,' she said. 'It was a wild storm! It seemed to blow up out o' nowhere. I'm just glad ye could find somewhere to shelter.'

'Where is the lass?' Lord Malvern demanded.

'I dinna ken,' Lewen said. 'We quarrelled, and she ran off while I was sleeping.' He turned to Nina anxiously. 'We need to find her,' he said.

'A lovers' quarrel, eh?' Lord Malvern said with a stiff, unnatural smile. 'I see, I see.'

Lewen ground his teeth. As his anger and hurt cooled, he was increasingly anxious about Rhiannon and sick with fear at the possible consequences of his telling Nina and the Rìgh about her confession. He wished he had not told anyone. He could not understand why he had. Now the Rìgh demanded Rhiannon be found, and brought to Lucescere to face trial. Lewen could not bear the thought that she might be found guilty and hanged, but then neither could he bear the thought that she had flown out of his life, never to be seen again.

Surely the court would understand? Surely they would not condemn such a young and beautiful woman to hang? Lewen moved restlessly. He wished he had never found the necklace. He wished he had slept all night with Rhiannon nestled into the curve of his body, and woken in the dawn to marvel at the peace of her sleeping face. He wished he had never met her.

But he had met her, and fallen in love with her, and promised himself to her, and then betrayed her. He could not ignore that. Though he still felt gutted with pain at her deceit, he could not bear to be instrumental in bringing her to the hangman's noose. Rhiannon may have killed Lewen's friend, and hacked out his teeth and chopped off his finger, and stolen his clothes and his treasures, and lied to Lewen, but he still loved her, Eà save his soul. He thought he always would.

Lewen turned to Nina desperately. 'Where is everyone?'

'Lewen . . .'

'Where's Iven?'

'He's gone to bring her back,' Nina said softly. 'Ye must've kent he would have to do so, Lewen.'

'She'll be long gone by now,' Lewen said.

Nina shook her head. 'She's no'. I scryed her out. She's up on the ridge behind the castle, watching. I do no' ken why she did no' fly further away. It would no' have made any difference in the end, though. Iven would still have ridden out after her, it just would've taken longer to find her.'

'Nina,' he said pleadingly. 'Canna we just let her go? She's only a lass. I should no' have told ye.'

She rose and came to him, taking both his hands in hers. 'I ken how ye must feel, Lewen, but Rhiannon killed a Yeoman. She must face the consequences o' her actions. Ye ken she must.'

He saw Lord Malvern's eyes narrow and wrenched his

hands away from Nina so he could press them against his eyes. 'She dinna ken!' he cried. 'She was just protecting herself.'

'Then she must tell the court so, and they will judge the right o' it,' Nina said with inexorable calm. 'Come, Lewen, ye are worn out. Do no' be fretting so. The men have found her and will soon be bringing her back. Ye can speak to her then.'

Lewen stared at her incredulously. Did she not realise the danger Rhiannon was in? He could say nothing with the lord of Fettercairn standing just there and listening, and the hall full of footmen, and Irving the seneschal, hovering nearby with his stiff, white, unpleasant face set as usual in an unctuous smile. Lewen felt as if he had strayed into a nightmare, the sort where you tried and tried to run but found your body would not move.

He turned and strode away down the hall, leaving Lord Malvern frowning after him.

Nina picked up her skirts and ran to follow him. 'Lewen, where do ye go? Lewen, ye're worn out, and starving hungry! Do no' be silly. Lewen!'

He was tired and kept having to stop to rub his filthy hand across his eyes, which smarted with angry tears. She caught up with him in the inner ward. 'Lewen, ye must leave it be,' she said softly. 'It is out o' our hands now.'

'It's all my fault. If I hadna told ye ... if I hadna ...' He broke off, unable to speak another word.

Nina stepped closer, holding his arm with both her hands. 'I'm so sorry,' she said inadequately. 'Indeed, I see how hard this must be. But she did kill Connor, Lewen. She shot him through the back, and hacked out all his teeth and mutilated his hand, and then tossed him into the river like a load o' garbage. She is no' the lass ye thought she was.'

Lewen took a deep breath. 'But she is,' he said gruffly. 'I always kent what sort o' a lass she was. She's wild and fierce, I ken that, but oh, Nina, she is brave and loyal and loving too, I swear to ye, and she's been treated cruelly all her life. She kent no other way to be.'

'Then we'll tell the judges so,' Nina said, and lifted her hand to wipe her eyes. 'Oh, Lewen, I wish . . . but it's too late. The men have ridden out to find her and bring her back, and they will, ye ken they will.'

'She'll no' come easily,' Lewen said sombrely. 'She'll fight for her freedom, and she fights dirty, Nina. Someone else may die.'

'I hope no',' Nina said.

'I do no' want it to be her,' Lewen said and tore his arm out of her grasp, striding away across the courtyard.

'Where are ye going?'

'To find her, o' course,' he said grimly over his shoulder. 'Ye think the laird's men will let us take her to Lucescere, to tell her story and throw suspicion upon them? O' course they willna! They mean to kill her!'

'But Lewen, Iven is there, he willna let –'

'What can Iven do? Besides, he is still a Yeoman himself at heart, ye ken that, and he loved Connor well. He willna save her.'

Nina protested again but Lewen did not wait to listen. He broke into a run, sprinting towards the stables. Argent had been unsaddled and put into a stall. Ignoring the curious groom who sought to waylay him, Lewen seized his bow and quiver of arrows and then grabbed Argent's bridle off its hook.

'Which way did they go?' he said through his teeth.

'Durward, ye mean?' the young groom said nervously.

Lewen dragged the bridle over Argent's head. 'Which way?'

'Out the back gate.'

'Open it for me.' Lewen vaulted onto Argent's bare back, kicking the stallion into motion.

'But . . .'

In a single swift motion Lewen had pulled an arrow from his quiver and had it aimed directly at the groom's heart, the bow's string quivering with the strain.

'Open it for me else I'll shoot ye!'

The groom ran to open the gate.

Argent galloped through before it was fully opened. It was easy enough to follow the other men. They had left a wide trail of hoof prints churning up the mud. The path was steep and slippery, and Argent almost fell once. Lewen dragged his head up and spurred him on. They reached the top of the ridge and came out on a wide, windswept moor. Rhiannon was struggling against four men. One was Cameron, the others were men from the castle. Her nose was bleeding. Blackthorn reared and plunged nearby, while Rafferty and a few other men sought to throw a rope around her neck. Iven was seeking to intervene, calling, 'Rhiannon, do no' resist! They'll only hurt ye. Rhiannon!'

Durward stood watching, a bow and arrow raised high. Rhiannon sent Cameron sprawling with a well-aimed kick between the legs, then wrenched herself free of the hands that sought to constrain her. For a moment she stood, struggling to regain her breath, then she whirled and ran a few steps towards Blackthorn. Durward released the arrow.

It raced through the air towards her, swift and merciless. The spin of the world on its axis seemed to slow about Lewen. He put back his hand, seized an arrow and cocked it to his bow. He bent the bow and raised it. He released the arrow. It sprang from his bow like a bird, soaring up, up, up into the sky. It reached the apex of its flight and began to descend, singing a little in the wind.

Then his arrow smashed into Durward's, snapping it in two. Both arrows fell harmlessly to the ground.

Amazed faces turned towards him, mouths hanging open. Lewen felt the world lurch back into motion again. He ran forward a few steps, his hand outstretched to Rhiannon. She had seen him knock the arrow out of the sky and her step had faltered as her eyes flew to his. The moment's hesitation cost her dearly. One of the castle men threw the noose of rope over her, and dragged her off her feet. In a minute they were all upon her, punching her with clenched fists and kicking her with their boots. One drew his dagger

'Stop! Stop!' Iven cried, and threw himself into the fray, dragging the laird's men away. 'We do no' want to kill her! Stop, ye fools.'

Reluctantly they all stood back. Rhiannon lay still on the ground. A few feet away, Blackthorn neighed and pawed the ground in agitation. As the men turned towards her again, she spread her wings and soared away, the sound of her unhappy whinnies ringing in the wind.

Lewen fell to his knees by Rhiannon's body. He turned her over, lifting her into his arms. Her face was smeared with blood and mud. He could see bruises springing up on her pale skin. With shaking fingers, Lewen opened her shirt. The charm he had whittled for her fell out, so that he almost cried out in his pain. He put his hand on her chest and felt beneath his fingers the rapid beating of her heart. For a moment he could not speak, his relief was so great, then he looked up at Iven. 'She lives,' he said.

Iven nodded, looking very grave. 'Well done,' he said. He stared round at the castle men with anger sparkling in his blue eyes. 'If ye had killed her, I would've had ye all arrested,' he said. 'This is a matter for the Crown!'

'My laird would never have let ye,' Shannley sneered.

469

'He has no' the power to stop me,' Iven replied. 'Come, let us take her back to the castle. We shall ride for Lucescere immediately!'

Lewen saw how all the castle men bit their lips and muttered among themselves, but they did not try to interfere as Iven lifted Rhiannon and trussed her to the broad back of the grey carthorse. Rafferty bent and picked up Rhiannon's saddlebags, and her bow and arrows. She had not even had time to try to defend herself.

Silently they made their way back to the castle, Durward striding ahead and looking very grim. All the men were muddy and dishevelled, and Cameron, who sported a nasty black eye, was limping painfully.

'Is she badly hurt?' Nina asked quietly, coming to Iven's stirrup and looking up into his set face as they rode back through the gate.

'I do no' ken,' he said. 'She would be dead if it was no' for Lewen. The laird's gillie tried to shoot her down.'

Nina's gaze flew to Lewen's face and then to the gillie's. 'I'm glad ye got there in time,' she said to Lewen.

Iven dismounted with a sigh and drew Nina to him and kissed her hair. 'She's unconscious. I'd say she'll be out for some time, *leannan*. Will ye help me put her to bed in the caravan? We'll have to shackle her to the bunk, I dinna want to risk her escaping.'

Nina nodded and beckoned to Cameron and Rafferty to help carry the unconscious girl to the caravans. Lewen watched as the two boys carried Rhiannon's limp form up the steps and into the red caravan, Nina following close behind. He felt powerless to move. It was as if all the will and desire in his body had been drained away, and he was left just a husk of man, unable to even lift a finger.

The stableyard was crowded with people. Landon, Maisie and Fèlice looked shocked and unhappy, while

Edithe looked very smug and self-righteous. Lord Malvern had been congratulating his men and hearing their account of the capture, which made Lewen grind his jaws together and clench his fists. Now the lord turned back to Iven, saying affably, 'Well, now your miscreant is caught and the road is clear, ye will no doubt wish to be on your way. I've arranged for the kitchens to pack up some supplies for ye, including for some bottles of Dedrie's elderflower wine, which I believe was very popular with your young folk. I do hope ye have enjoyed your stay with us.'

'Ye have been most hospitable, thank ye,' Iven answered. 'We are indeed eager to be on our way.'

'So I understand.'

'I thank ye again for your hospitality and your help,' Iven said rather shortly. 'If ye would be so kind as to arrange for all our luggage to be brought down?'

'O' course,' Lord Malvern answered, waving one hand at Irving, who was as always hovering in the background. Irving bowed and went silently away.

'I'm sure ye willna mind if I pack up my own belongings?' Nina said, coming down the caravan steps and shutting the door behind her. 'I do like to make sure I have everything in place. Lewen, happen ye could accompany me, while the other lads get the horses ready?'

'Shannley, Jem, ye will o' course assist?'

'O' course, my laird,' the old groom said with an obsequious bob of his head.

'Cameron, ye stay here and guard the prisoner,' Iven said. 'Maisie, my dear, happen ye had best go and lie down, ye are looking very pale.'

'I dinna want to go in there with *her*.' Maisie shrank back.

'She'll sleep a while yet,' Iven said wearily, 'and even when she wakes, she's tightly secured. She canna hurt ye.'

471

'Still,' Maisie said.

'Very well, ye may rest in our caravan, if ye like. I do no' want ye trying to ride yet.'

Maisie nodded and limped over to the blue caravan and hauled herself up the stairs with great difficulty. The door shut behind her.

Lord Malvern smiled and inclined his head, and Nina gathered up her skirts and followed him. Just as she passed through the doorway, she turned her head and said sternly, 'Roden, stay with your *dai-dein*, do ye hear? No more running off!'

'Aye, Mam,' Roden answered in long-suffering tones and, hand-in-hand with Lulu, he dawdled along behind his father.

Nina was obviously eager to cross-examine Lewen but she could not speak because Lord Malvern had turned to them and asked them a polite question about their plans. As Nina answered, just as politely, they came up the side of the central garden and Lewen saw Lady Evaline sitting under the apple tree. She looked at him and raised one lace-mittened hand to beckon him. Reluctantly Lewen approached her, the scent of sun-warmed lavender rising around him.

'Ye are all leaving now?' Lady Evaline asked wistfully.

'Aye, the road is clear and we must be on our way.'

'The laddie too?'

'Aye, o' course Roden is coming too,' Lewen said.

'Aye, best get him away quickly,' she said. 'Too many ghosts here already.'

'Aye,' Lewen agreed, not knowing what else to say.

'Such a bonny lad he is,' she said sadly. 'Such a shame.'

'What's such a shame?' Lewen asked, confused and unnerved by this peculiar old lady with her crumpled, vacant face.

'That he must die,' she answered. 'They all die, ye ken.'

'Do ye mean, everyone? Everyone must die?'

'Aye, everyone must die in the end,' she said with a sigh. 'I hope they let me rest when I die.'

'Evaline!' Lord Malvern called. 'Ye must no' keep the young man gossiping. Lady Nina wishes to be away.'

'Away,' Lady Evaline murmured. 'I wish I could be away also.'

'Why do ye no' go then?' Lewen asked, his sympathy stirred.

She raised her soft eyes to his. 'Where would I go?' she asked simply. 'At least here I have my ghosts.'

'Evaline!' Lord Malvern called impatiently.

She patted Lewen's cheek. 'Goodbye, lad. Have a care for yourself.'

'And ye yourself,' he answered and broke away so he could rejoin Nina and Lord Malvern by the steps. He felt shaken and unnerved by his conversation with the old lady. She was indeed quite mad, he thought.

'I must apologise for my sister-in-law,' Lord Malvern said, smiling. 'She is very auld now, and quite vague.'

Lewen nodded, smiling perfunctorily. He had a sudden overwhelming desire to be away from this cold, vast pile of stones and out in the fresh, clean air. It took a strong effort of will for him to force himself to follow Nina up the stairs and into its front hall, and he glanced over his shoulder as he went in, for a last glimpse of sunlit green. He thought he understood why Lady Evaline spent so much time sitting under the apple tree.

It did not take long to pack up all their belongings and help the footmen carry them out to the gatehouse. All the horses had been saddled and bridled, and were eager to be off. Irving had supervised the loading of sacks and barrels of fresh supplies, and Dedrie had come down to say farewell to her patients. She looked pale and tired, and did not have her usual brisk manner as she pressed a basket of herbal remedies upon Nina, as well as a fresh tussie-mussie of lavender and herbs.

'Lady Evaline picked them for ye,' she said. 'She wants . . . she wishes . . .'

'Aye?'

Dedrie cast a quick glance at Lord Malvern, who was chatting with Iven some distance away. 'She says to have a care for yourselves and for the lad,' she said then, in a fierce, low voice. 'Get him away from here, my lady! This place is no good for laddies.'

Nina opened her mouth to say something and then shut it. 'Never fear, we are out o' your hair now,' she said lightly. 'Thank ye for your help.'

'I'm glad I could do something to help. Have a good journey now,' Dedrie said.

Nina quirked her mouth in sudden ironic amusement. 'Let us hope it is a quick one,' she answered, then turned to give her hand to Lord Malvern as she thanked him again. Then the apprentices all mounted, Nina was handed up to the driving seat of the red caravan with Roden beside her, and Iven leapt up to the seat of the blue, clicking his tongue at Steady. The massive gates groaned open, and the cavalcade rode out from the shadowy gloom of Fettercairn Castle and into the quick bright windy day.

TO THROW A PRINCE

'They say princes learn no art truly
but the art of horsemanship. The
reason is, the brave beast is no
flatterer. He will throw a prince as
soon as his groom.'

Ben Jonson (1573–1637)

TALES OF THE PAST

The road went down at a steep angle, so they had to go carefully, Nina and Iven both leaning on their brakes. For quite a long way they were enclosed within high walls, then gradually the wall dropped away and they were able to see down into the lowlands, which spread before them, the river winding away like a broad silver ribbon.

'Look, was that the tree that fell? Isn't it enormous? No wonder it took so long for ye all to clear the road!' Fèlice called, pointing down the hillside. An immense oak tree lay tumbled to one side of the road, smashed and broken. They could see where it had fallen through the undergrowth, tearing up bushes and scarring the ground.

'Ye ken, I wronged the laird,' Rafferty called back. 'I really had begun to suspect him o' making up the fallen tree to try to keep us at Fettercairn.'

'Me too!' Fèlice said.

'What rubbish,' Edithe said. 'Ye people have such imaginations. Laird Malvern is far too noble and upright a man to stoop to such a subterfuge. Why on earth would he want to do such a thing?'

'Why indeed?' Landon said. He was sitting up next to Iven on the seat of the caravan, having no horse to ride.

'Next ye'll be telling me ye believed all those terrible lies that satyricorn girl made up!'

'I do believe her,' Landon said defiantly.

Cameron snorted. 'Ye would.'

'Well, I believe her too,' Fèlice said. 'Even if she did kill that Yeoman, doesna mean she wasna telling the truth about other things.'

'My dear Fèlice, what an innocent ye are,' Edithe said.

'That's enough, Edithe,' Nina said sharply. 'I think we should leave any discussion o' Rhiannon's guilt or innocence to the judges in Lucescere. Let us just concentrate on getting her there safely.'

Lewen said nothing. He felt very tired.

They came to a sharp corner, the road doubling back on itself, and now they rode back towards Fettercairn Castle, which loomed high overhead, ravens wheeling above its two grim towers. The vast expanse of white, falling water dominated the view. The shadow of the cliff fell over them, cold fingers of spray stroking their faces and hair. At last the road turned again, the cobblestones dangerously slippery with the damp, and they faced out into the sunlit valley again, feeling an immediate sense of relief. Six more times the road switchbacked, and then they came down a long, low decline that led them gradually out into rolling meadows where goats grazed by the river. They were able to quicken their pace until the great brooding cliff was lost to sight behind them, and on all sides there were only open pastures, small copses of trees and tilled fields, with the broad river winding through the middle. The air smelt sweetly of apple blossom.

Rhiannon woke during the afternoon. Lewen had been riding close to the red caravan, straining his ears for any sound from her, but for hours everything had remained quiet. Then he heard a cry of pain and alarm, then a sudden banging noise, and knew she had woken. Nina heard it too, and compressed her lips. Lewen made a move as if to go to her, and Nina shook her head at him sternly. For a while, they listened as Rhiannon fought to free herself, then Nina handed the reins to Landon and swung round to the steps, opening the door and going inside. Riding as close as he could, Lewen could hear nothing more than a rising and falling murmur of voices. Argent sensed his unhappiness and danced restively, but Lewen hardly noticed. After a few minutes Nina came out again, her face expressionless, and swung herself back to the driving seat. Everything was quiet.

The sun was getting low in the sky when Argent suddenly pricked his ears forward, whickering loudly. Lewen was roused from his miserable abstraction to look about him. He felt a sudden jolt of excitement as he saw a familiar black winged shape flying behind them, keeping close to the dark line of the woods. At once he glanced about but no-one else had noticed. After that he saw Blackthorn often, though the winged mare was taking care to keep herself hidden. It cheered him immensely, knowing Blackthorn had not abandoned her rider, and he wished he could let Rhiannon know.

They soon came to a village, and Nina and Iven decided to make camp for the night near the safety of its lights. Nina was eager to buy fresh supplies, being determined not to touch a single mouthful of the food given to them by Lord Fetterness. The apprentices were all glad to dismount, looking towards the village lights eagerly. None of them had been fully able to shake the unease they had felt while staying at Fettercairn Castle, and the idea of having a few drams in the village inn and talking with ordinary people cheered them all. All, that is, except for Lewen, who was racked with misery and guilt. He would have liked to stay with the caravans and try for a chance to speak with Rhiannon, but Nina would not let him.

'Let her be, lad,' she said, as she poured away every drop of the soup and wine and medicines that the castle servants had packed up for them.

'But I need to try to explain to her . . .'

'I'd rather ye left her alone, Lewen,' Nina said, a stern note hardening her voice. 'To be honest, I'm no' sure I can trust ye no' to help her escape. As sympathetic as I am to your distress, she is an accused murderess and the Rìgh has trusted us to bring her to the courts.'

'Please, Nina . . .'

She shook her head. 'Nay, Lewen. I want ye to stay away. Come with us to the village, and drown your sorrows with the other lads. There are times it can do ye good. Besides, this is the closest lowland village to the castle. They must've heard tales o' Fetterness. I want to hear them.'

So Lewen found himself accompanying Nina and the others to the village, while a rather cross Rafferty was left behind with Iven and Lulu to guard the camp and their prisoner.

It was a clear, cold evening, with the wind shaking the black branches about and the sky over the mountains very red as the setting sun stained the clouds. Everyone was full of talk and conjecture, for nobody had felt free to talk freely while under Fettercairn Castle's roof. Only Lewen did not speak, even when Edithe said she had always thought Rhiannon a sly hoar-weasel or when Maisie wondered if it hurt to be hanged.

Linlithgorn's inn was small and rough, but it was

crowded with farm labourers, milkmaids, eel-fishers and plump crofters' wives with red hands and cheerful faces. The talk was all of the weather and the spring sowing, and despite himself, Lewen found his mood eased as he drank his dram of whisky, ate a solid vegetable stew with dumplings, and listened. The strangers were all greeted with jovial good spirits, and Nina told them a much edited version of their adventures.

The news they had come from Fettercairn Castle was met with great interest. 'Och, they're an odd people, up there in the highlands,' the innkeeper's wife said as she ladled them a second serve of stew. 'Keep themselves to themselves, they do. Every now and again we get a family coming through, heading for the ports and hoping for work. Terrible stories they tell. We dinna believe most o' them, o' course, those highlanders are all a wee touched in the head, but still . . . enough to make ye check your doors are locked twice over. Ye can never be too careful.'

Under Nina's gentle questioning, she expanded like dough in the warmth. She had nothing much new to tell them, except that a few travellers had gone missing in recent years, along with one lazy farmer's boy, who was prone to leaving his goats to wander as they pleased while he went fishing or fell asleep in a hayrick.

'If it's stories o' Fettercairn ye want, ye should ask auld Martin. He came down from the castle nigh on twenty-five years ago, and married a local girl. He's full o' stories, like all those highland dreamers.'

'I'd like to hear his stories, if we have time,' Nina answered. 'Where can I find him?'

The innkeeper's wife jerked her head towards the fire. 'He'll be entertaining the drinkers,' she said dryly. 'I'd ask him now, afore the whisky muddles him more than usual.'

'Thank ye, I will,' Nina replied and rose and made her way towards the fire, Roden swinging off her hand, Lewen and Landon following close behind. The others stayed where they were, Cameron calling for more whisky, though Fèlice turned to watch them with curious eyes.

A group of men sat before the fire, some playing trictrac, others gambling on the roll of the dice. A tall, thin man sat folded up on a chair, staring into the flames. He had a crinkled brown face and melancholy grey eyes, and was dressed in a rough smock and leather gaiters. He was telling some tale, which he illustrated with dramatic gestures of his hands. As Nina approached there was a sudden roar of laughter, and one of the men cried, 'Och, pull the other one, Martin! Ye and your auld tales.'

'I've heard ye're a grand storyteller,' Nina said gently, pulling a stool towards her and sitting down at the thin man's gangly knee. 'Will ye tell us a tale?'

'Give me a dram o' whisky and I'll tell ye two, and happen throw in a song as well,' Martin said, lifting his dreamy eyes to Nina's face. 'Ye're a witch, ye are. I like witches.'

'That's good,' she answered. 'We've just come from a place where witches were hated, and I dinna like that at all.'

'Och, ye've been at Fetterness, have ye? Bad place. Very bad place.'

'Why? Why is it such a bad place?'

He stared down at his empty cup and ruminated. Nina glanced at Lewen, who went back and took the whisky decanter from Cameron, despite his howl of protest, and brought it to top up the old man's clay mug. Martin tasted it thoughtfully, swirled it round his mouth, swallowed, then sipped again. When his cup was empty, Lewen filled it up again.

'I was born in Fetterness, ye ken. More than fifty years

ago. They were the good auld days, indeed they were. The Tower o' Ravens still stood and the town was filled with laughing students who bet on which cockroach would scuttle away the fastest, or which raindrop would reach the bottom o' the pane first. Lairds and prionnsachan came to the valley to consult the witches' wisdom, and the MacBrann could often be seen crossing his silver bridge, his cloak flying in the wind, his guards and servants trying to keep up. He was no' mad then, nay, he was sane as ye or I. But then that was afore the Day o' Betrayal, when the whole world went mad.'

Martin stopped and drank some more, then looked round the little circle of rapt faces. He was indeed a master storyteller.

'Jaspar, who was the Rìgh then, he had married for love, like all young men, and like all young men, he found love can be a cruel joke.' His grey eyes came to rest on Lewen's face. 'His pretty wife Maya had her own plans, and one cold winter's day the whole world found out what they were. Jaspar had given her a legion o' soldiers for her own, and she dressed them in red, like she wore herself, and smiled at them and young men came flocking to serve her. That cold winter day her soldiers struck at every witches' tower in the land, and threw them down, and Maya declared the witches were traitors and should be killed, every one o' them.'

He looked back at Nina. 'Ye are too young to remember, but I, I remember it well. My family worked at the tower and so I was there, a lad o' only five. I remember the screaming, and the black smoke everywhere, and the way the soldiers went through every room and hall, killing every witch they found, and any who dared to defy them. Most were put to the sword, or were crushed under the falling masonry as the soldiers used their machines to drag down the walls. Some they dragged to the garth, and tied upon a great pile o' firewood and burnt them to death, feeding the flames with the books from the library. I hid down the well, and so they dinna find me. My parents both died, though neither were witches. So, ye see, it is no' a day I'd forget easily.'

Nina nodded, her mouth twisting.

'When at last I crept out, I dinna ken where to go or what to do. At last I went to the laird. Where else would I go? They gave me a job scrubbing pots in the kitchen. I was grateful. At least I was warm there, and had food. It was there that I heard what had happened. For the Tower o' Ravens was very strong, ye ken. No pretty red soldiers should've been able to throw it down, no' with those high walls and lookout towers and all those witches with their far-seeing and clear-seeing skills inside. And then there was Fettercairn Castle itself, built to guard the road. How had the soldiers got through? I myself did no' much care, being too young and full o' misery to wonder, but the servants at the castle wondered very much, and I listened as they talked, like young boys do.'

He rested his gaze now on Roden's mop of bright, curly hair, nestled in against his mother's side as he sat on the floor at her feet. Then he looked back at Lewen and suddenly his gaze seemed very clear and intent.

'The laird's younger brother was then staying in the castle, and I heard many mutters against him. He had been an apprentice once, just like ye, my lad. A witch's apprentice at the Tower o' Ravens, but he had been disgraced somehow. Cheating at exams, I think, though it was so long ago, I canna be sure. Happen it was trouble over a lass. There's always trouble over lasses. Anyways, he'd left the tower and gone to the capital, and by all accounts he was very sore at the witches who had been his teachers and fellow students and swore revenge on them. When he came back, he wore a long red robe and said he was in the Banrìgh's pay now.'

'A Seeker?' Nina breathed. 'Laird Malvern was once a Seeker?'

The old man flashed her a glance. 'We called them witch-sniffers, for they sniffed out magic, but I've heard them called Seekers too.'

Nina nodded, her dark eyes burning bright. 'So he was a Seeker! Och, that explains a lot.'

'The red soldiers were his friends,' the old man continued. 'He had brought them to visit Fettercairn, and they had gradually filled up every spare room, till the laird was very impatient and told his brother they must go. But they did no' go, they attacked the Tower o' Ravens instead, and though I dinna ken whether it be true or no', it was said Malvern, who's laird now, showed the redcloaks the secret way to the tower, so they could come in darkness and stealth, and attack from within.'

Nina and Lewen exchanged quick glances.

'Later, after the laird and his son died, Malvern put aside his red robes and became laird himself. For a while all went well, for he was a favourite o' the Banrìgh. But once the Banrìgh was thrown down, well, he retreated inside his castle and I hear he hardly ever comes out now. That was when things in Fetterness went from bad to evil, I heard, though I had left by then, hoping to leave evil things behind me.'

'How did the laird and his son die?' Nina asked persuasively, and Lewen topped up the old man's cup.

He drank deeply, then sighed and wiped his mouth on his sleeve.

'Another sad tale, that one. Would ye no' rather I told ye the tale o' Bessie and the runaway pig?'

Nina shook her head. 'Nay, please, we really do want to ken.'

He held out his cup again. 'To tell a sad tale like that I need to wet my whistle again,' he said. 'It's a tale to make ye weep.'

Lewen obligingly filled up his cup, and put the empty decanter down. Martin was quiet for a moment, staring into the flames. Nina was about to prompt him again when he stirred and began again to speak.

'Your wee laddie there has a look o' the laird's young son about him. It's the ruddy hair and black eyes, ye dinna see that very often. He was born about ten years after the fall o' the Tower o' Ravens. The laird had taken a young girl for his wife, a pretty wee thing, half his age. They loved that laddie, and spoilt him half to death. Now, at the time Maya the Blessed ruled the whole country with an iron hand concealed in a velvet glove. But no' everyone loved her, and rebels worked to bring the witches back. I must admit I loved to hear the tales o' those rebels, and often used to dream o' running away and joining them. The rebels were led by a man they called the Cripple, for he had a hunch to his shoulder and a twist to his spine, and could scarce walk a step. The things that Cripple did! He must've had magic o' his own, for they never managed to catch him, even when he rescued a cartload o' witches from right under the Banrìgh's nose.'

Nina and Lewen exchanged a smiling glance. They knew better than most the many stories about the days when Lachlan the Winged had hidden himself in the guise of a hunchback, working to overthrow Maya the Ensorcellor and bring back the Coven of Witches. It had been Nina's grandmother Enit who had masterminded many of those daring rescues and many a witch or a faery had, like Lachlan, been hidden in the jongleurs' caravan as they roamed around Eileanan. Lewen's mother Lilanthe had herself travelled that way, the jongleurs keeping her safe from Maya's Seekers, who would have burnt her to death if they had found her.

'Now the witch-sniffer Malvern hated witches and rebels, and he hunted them down far and wide. Every village skeelie and cunning man on this side o' the river was burnt alive, and anyone who had auld books, or who swore by Eà, or even protested that the witch-hunts were too brutal. And he seemed to have an uncanny way o' kenning what ye thought, so none o' us dared ever look him in the eye, or mutter under our breath. He had us under his fist, from Barbreck-by-the-Bridge down to Tullimuir and right round to Rhyssmadill itself. It was a sad day for us all when Laird Falkner let his brother come home to stay.

'One day he had his soldiers bring in a lass who was accused o' witch-talent. Her mother had been burnt as a witch and her grandfather too, but she had been taken in by neighbours and brought up as one o' their own. Her name was Oonagh and she hated the witch-sniffers for what they had done to her family. She saw one in the marketplace one day and had some kind o' fit, and thunder and lightning came out o' nowhere, and hail. She was sick as a dog after, and they arrested her and took her to the castle for questioning, which we all kent meant torture. They were dark days at Fettercairn.' He sighed and shook his head.

'Somehow the Cripple found out about this poor lass and that very afternoon they came to the castle, some hidden inside the dung-cart, some disguised as labourers or farmers bringing produce. There were only a dozen or so o' them but somehow they managed to lock up the castle garrison and rescue the girl. They could no' get out again, though, for Laird Malvern sniffed them out and attacked them with his own men. There was vicious fighting, all through the castle. Me and some o' the other pot-boys helped the rebels, for we hated the witch-sniffer and his cruel ways. We took the Red Guards by surprise, and locked them in one o' the halls, and then the Cripple caught the sniffer and held him hostage.

'It must've been about then that Laird Falkner took his lady and son, who was about five, I think, and hid them for safety. But then he was captured too and taken to the great hall, where the Cripple accused the witch-sniffer o' murder and torture and treason and all sorts o' other things, and held a trial. Truly it was amazing. The rebels had won the castle with only a handful o' men! We all kent we were in the presence o' greatness, even the fat auld cook felt it. Those rebels, though they were all filthy and stunk to high heaven, they were brave and bold and laughed as they fought, and they made no move to hurt us or molest any o' the maids, or even steal the laird's gold. The Cripple himself was only a few years aulder then me, and I must admit I admired him, for doing what I could only dream o' doing.'

Lewen was enraptured. He wondered if his father had been one of those men. Niall the Bear had turned rebel as a young man, and had worked with Lachlan the Winged to rescue witches and undermine Maya for many years before they at last succeeded in overthrowing her and regaining the throne. Swiftly he did the arithmetic in his head. If the Tower of Ravens had been thrown down by the Red Guards forty-odd years ago, and the rebels had attacked the castle fifteen years later, then it was highly likely his father would have been fighting with Lachlan, for he had not yet been twenty when he had joined the rebels.

Martin had paused only long enough to drain his cup. His eyes were unfocused now, and his words slurred, but his voice still had power to cast a spell. 'The laird was furious and called the rebels cowards and cheats and traitors, but the Cripple only mocked him, and told him that he was the coward and traitor, to kidnap and torture a young lass near to death. The laird had no' kent about the witch-lass, he tried his best to turn a blind eye to the things Malvern did, and he was horrified, ye could see it on his face. Laird Falkner shouted that it was no' true, it was all lies, and attacked him with his sword. The Cripple was clumsy on his feet, being a hunchback, and no' the best fighter, but the laird was mad and blind with rage. They fought and the Cripple killed him, though I dinna think he meant to.

'It was all confusion after that, and the battle broke out again, for the laird's bodyguard went mad and attacked the rebels with naught but his bare hands. Somehow, in all the fighting, the laird's brother slipped away, I do no' ken how though I was there, watching it all with my own eyes. We found his red robe in the library.

'It was only then that we discovered the lady and her son were missing. The boy's nurse set up a great screech and the castle was searched from top to bottom, but no sign o' them was found. We all thought they must've escaped with the witch-sniffer. Half o' us joined the rebels, and the others were allowed to leave, which they did right gladly, for everyone had expected the rebels would kill anyone who disagreed with them. But they dinna. There was a great feast instead, and singing and dancing, and the Cripple opened up the laird's treasury and gave it all to the poor folk. It was like a mad dream. A week or so later, the witch-sniffer returned with a big army to take the castle back, but the rebels saw them coming and went in the night, for after all, there was only a dozen or so o' them, and thousands o' the Red Guards.

'I went with them, so I wasna there when they discovered the lady and the young boy had no' fled with Malvern but had been hidden in a secret room by the laird. More than a week they were locked in that room, in the dead o' winter, with no food or water. By the time Malvern opened up the secret panel, it was too late. The boy was dead and his mother was quite mad. They say Malvern was stricken with grief and guilt, and indeed he quit the Banrìgh's service after that, and stopped his witch-hunts. I never went back to Fetterness, but I've heard the shadow o' those dark days still stretches across the whole valley and that the ghost o' the wee lad haunts the castle, crying aloud from the cold.'

There was a short silence, then Roden lifted his sleepy head and said, 'It's true, there is a ghost o' a little boy there, I saw him. He has the bonniest rocking horse. There are lots o' boys there, and all o' them cry 'cause they want to go home.'

'Is that so, laddie?' Martin said slowly. 'Obh obh, it's an evil place, Fettercairn. I'm glad I got away from there.'

'So are we,' Nina answered, cuddling Roden close. 'I canna tell ye how much.'

IN THE NIGHT

R hiannon lay in the darkness, slowly rubbing her
cloth-muffled chain back and forth against the
timber post of the bunk-bed. She had to control her desperate impatience, for if she jerked the chain too hard it
rattled, and she did not want to alert anyone to her wakefulness. She had only these quiet hours of the night to
wear away the wood till it was weak enough to snap,
setting her free. If anyone discovered what she was doing,
her chance would be lost.

A muted sound outside made her pause and turn her
head. Then she felt the caravan shift as someone put their
weight on the steps. Rhiannon found it hard to breathe.
With all her muscles tense, she listened as someone very
gingerly turned the door handle first one way, then
another. There was a pause, and then she heard the
furtive sound of someone fumbling with the lock. Rhiannon tested the chain between her hands. It was not long
enough to wrap around a throat and garrotte someone,
but perhaps, if she pinned them to the bed with it, she

could hold them down long enough to choke them. She raised herself onto one elbow, holding the chain rigid so it would not rattle, then managed to get up onto her knees, pressing herself back against the wall.

The tiny sounds from the doorway continued, then she heard a click as the lock sprang free. The door swung open, and someone slipped inside and closed the door behind them. Rhiannon listened as they took a step or two towards her, her heart hammering so loud she thought they must hear it. A dark, faceless shape loomed over her, and she tensed, ready to strike.

'Rhiannon?' a deep voice whispered.

She launched herself at him, burying her head into his shoulder, jerking her wrists painfully as she tried instinctively to throw her arms about his neck. 'Lewen!' she gasped, and then, as his arms closed about her, felt the painful swelling in her chest burst as tears gushed from her eyes.

'Hush, hush, my dearling, my sweet, they must no' hear,' he whispered, stroking her hair. She buried her head deeper into his shoulder, trying to control her shuddering sobs. Murmuring endearments, he pressed her back so he could lie beside her on the bed, his arm cradling her close. He felt something hard between them, and realised, with a little jerk of his pulse, that she wore the amulet he had carved for her hanging between her breasts. Eagerly he sought her mouth, cradling her head in both his hands, desperate to tell her how sorry he was for betraying her.

She tore her mouth away. 'Ye told them! Ye helped them hunt me down!'

'I'm so sorry, my dearling, I'm so sorry, I dinna mean for this to happen, I dinna want this.' He kissed her wet face and she recoiled away from him.

'Ye told.'

'It just happened, I dinna mean to.'

'What do ye mean, it just happened?'

Lewen buried his face in her hair. 'I'm so sorry, Rhiannon. Really, I dinna mean for them to hunt ye down or cage ye up like this. I just . . .' Words failed him. He could not explain. After a moment he said again lamely, 'It just happened.'

She was silent for a moment, then he felt her lay her head down on his chest again. 'Like me and the soldier,' she whispered. 'I never meant him harm. It just happened. I wish it never had.'

They lay in silence for a while.

'Will they hang me?' she whispered.

'I willna let them,' Lewen burst out, the desperation in his voice telling her more than he meant to. She shivered and clung to him.

'I have to escape,' she told him. She heard him sigh and shift his weight. 'I canna stand it in here,' she went on wildly. 'I feel like I canna breathe! The air presses down on me and chokes me. I canna stand it! I canna! Help me get out o' here!'

'But how?' he said at last. 'I only managed to get in here to see ye by putting a sleeping spell on Rafferty, but I am no' strong yet in such Skills, there's no way I could ensorcel Nina or Iven, I daren't even try. And even if ye managed to get away from the camp without anyone seeing ye, Nina has only to call out to the birds for help and she'd find ye in minutes.'

'I want my horse,' Rhiannon said passionately. 'If I had Blackthorn, I could escape!'

Lewen hesitated, then said, 'Blackthorn is near, she follows the caravans. But oh, Rhiannon!'

She pushed herself away from him, her chain rattling. 'Blackthorn follows?'

'Aye, she follows, but Rhiannon, I do no' think . . .'

'Lewen, unchain me! Please!'

'I canna,' he said unhappily.

'Why no'? Are ye afraid?' Her voice was thin with contempt.

'Aye, o' course I'm afraid,' he answered crossly. 'I risk being charged with treason just by being here with ye, do ye no' ken that! But I canna unchain ye just because I'm scared, Rhiannon. I havena got the key, and these chains are too thick for me to break, no matter how much I want to. And Iven is asleep just outside, and he'll wake at the slightest noise. So please, stop rattling those chains and hissing at me! I've been thinking and thinking what's the best thing for us to do, and I canna think that running away is it. Sssh! Please, just listen. Rhiannon, if I managed to free ye now, what would ye do?'

'Find my horse and fly away,' she answered promptly.

'Where?'

'Anywhere,' she answered impatiently.

'Back to the mountains?'

She hesitated. 'I dinna ken. Maybe. I'd find somewhere.'

'And what about me?' Lewen asked.

'Ye could come with me,' she said, seizing one of his hands.

'How? Blackthorn canna carry us both, I'm much too heavy.'

'Ye could come and meet me.'

'If I kent where ye were, and if I was no' arrested for setting ye free.'

She sighed. 'They wouldna arrest ye, though, would they? No' ye.'

Lewen shrugged. 'I dinna ken. If the Rìgh was angry enough . . . it doesna matter. I'd be ruined anyway.

There's no way I'd be allowed to join the Blue Guards or be the Rìgh's squire if I had helped an accused murderer escape, and happen they'd throw me out o' the Theurgia as well. That doesna matter. I'd do it if I thought it'd help. But I do no'. All it would mean is that ye'd be on the run for ever after. There'd be bounty hunters galore eager to catch ye if the reward was big enough, and I'm pretty sure the Rìgh would set Finn the Cat on your trail and she *always* finds what she hunts. It's her Talent.'

He took a deep breath and drew her close to him again. 'It's no life, *leannan*, always on the move, starting at shadows, waiting for someone to bring ye in. And there'd be no chance o' mercy if ye made the Rìgh hunt ye down. Nay, I think it would be best to go willingly to court and try to explain to the Rìgh what happened. I'd stand behind ye, and I'm sure Nina and Iven would vouch for ye too.'

'But they hunted me down!' Rhiannon cried.

'Sssh!' He put his hand gently across her mouth. 'No' so loud, *leannan*, ye'll wake Iven and then I'll really be in the soup. I ken they caught ye, my love, and chained ye up in here, but they were following orders. Iven was once a Blue Guard, remember, and he still works in the Rìgh's service. He could no' let ye go, but I swear he feels bad about it, and Nina too. I'm sure they'll speak up on your behalf, and they are good friends o' the Rìgh's and will have influence over him, I'm sure. And I ken His Highness would no' want to hang such a bonny young lass.' He bent and kissed her mouth. She sighed and kissed him back, tasting the salt of her tears on his skin.

At last they drew apart. 'So ye will no' help me escape?' she said in a very low voice.

He shook his head. 'Rhiannon, I love ye. I love ye so much. I want a life with ye. I do no' want to be a fugitive the rest o' our days, sick at heart 'cause I betrayed my

Rìgh's trust. I do no' want ye just to fly away into the blue yonder, never to be seen again, either. This is the only way I can think o' to make sure we can be together. If ye swore service to the Rìgh, as penance, perhaps? There must be something we can do.'

'What if there's no'? What if he says I must hang?'

'Then I will free ye then, and we'll run away somewhere together, I promise. I will no' let ye hang.'

Rhiannon nestled her head on his chest. She was so tired, it was a relief to murmur an agreement and let her muscles sag and her eyelids close. She felt like she had been running and fighting for so long, and all to no avail.

Lewen kissed her forehead. '*Leannan*, I must go. My sleeping spell willna last forever.'

'Do no' go,' she murmured, not opening her eyes. 'Please, do no' leave me.'

His chest rose and fell under her cheek as he took and released a deep breath. His arm came tightly round her, holding her close, and Rhiannon sighed and slipped into sleep.

She woke drowsily some hours later, as Lewen stiffened and tried to sit up. Rhiannon would have rolled over but the shackle on her wrist prevented her. The painful tug of the chain jerked her to wakefulness, and she opened her eyes and levered herself up on one elbow.

Iven stood in the doorway of the caravan, regarding them thoughtfully. Behind him stood a tousled and indignant Rafferty.

'I thought Nina told ye to leave Rhiannon be?' Iven said.

Lewen nodded jerkily. 'Aye, she did, but I needed to talk to Rhiannon, I needed to explain.'

'I see,' Iven replied. 'I suppose Nina and I have no real authority over ye, Lewen, but ye were placed in our care and so I would expect ye to listen to us and obey us.'

'I had to see Rhiannon,' Lewen repeated. 'Nobody could have stopped me.'

Iven stroked his beard.

'I dinna help her escape,' Lewen said defiantly. 'We are both still here.'

'Aye, I can see that.'

'Rhiannon's promised she willna try to escape,' Lewen said, with a quick glance at her. 'Ye do no' need to leave her locked up in this stinking caravan anymore. It's no' right. She hates being confined. Will ye no' let her come out and breathe the fresh air and sit in the sunshine? It's cruel to lock her up like this.'

Iven's brows drew together. He looked consideringly at Rhiannon. 'I hope ye will no' take this the wrong way, Rhiannon, but I canna feel sure that a promise from ye is to be trusted.'

Rhiannon did not reply.

'I will stand warranty for her,' Lewen said.

'I ken how ye must feel, Lewen,' the jongleur said after a long pause. 'But ye must remember Rhiannon's crime is a serious one, and she has lied to us and tried to flee afore. I canna allow ye to take such a responsibility. If she fled, ye would hang in her place, do ye understand that?'

Lewen swallowed convulsively.

'What if ye shackled her to me?' he said after a moment. 'She can ride with me, she can lie with me. I will keep her close, I promise.'

'I'm sure ye will,' Iven said, with a faint smile. He scratched his cheek, regarding them with thoughtful eyes. 'How am I to be sure that she will no' hurt ye to try to escape?' he asked, half under his breath. 'We have seen how ruthless she can be. It takes a cold head and heart to hack out a man's teeth and his finger.'

'I had to do that!' Rhiannon cried indignantly. 'If I had no' claimed blood-right, I would have lost everything, and I'd have been scorned by the herd. Worse, they would've been suspicious and watched me, and I could never have escaped. Ye think I enjoyed doing it? It made me sick to my stomach, and I shook all over. I could no' bear to wear the necklace afterwards. I had to do it, though. Have ye never done things ye wished ye did no' have to do?'

Iven nodded. 'I'm a soldier,' he said wryly. 'O' course I have.'

'Well then,' Rhiannon answered, her voice losing none of its passion. 'Why judge me so hard? Ye do no' ken what it was like in the herd. Any sign o' weakness, and they would have killed me. I was fighting for my life.'

'It is no' for me to judge ye at all,' Iven said coolly. 'That will be the court's job. Mine is to bring ye to them safely.'

Rhiannon lay back, covering her face with her arm. 'I canna bear it in here,' she whispered. 'I canna.'

Lewen drew her closer.

'Lewen, truly I do no' think this wise,' Iven said warningly.

'If ye willna let her out, I will stay in here with her,' Lewen said. 'We may no' have much time together, I willna be parted from her.'

'Lewen . . .'

'Please, Iven.'

Iven sighed. 'Rhiannon, ye must give me your solemn oath that ye will no' try and escape. And do no' think I willna be watching ye.'

'I will swear a blood-oath, if ye will give me a knife to cut myself with.'

'No need for that,' Iven replied, wincing a little. 'Ye have wounded yourself enough, I feel. Very well then, if ye promise.'

'I will no' try to escape while I am in your care,' Rhiannon said. 'After that, I will no' promise.'

'Fair enough,' Iven replied. He put his hand in his pocket and pulled out a key. 'I will shackle ye together, though,' he warned. 'I'm not taking any unnecessary risks.'

'All right,' Rhiannon said, so thrilled at the idea she might be allowed out of the caravan that she would have accepted far stricter preventative measures.

Lewen slid away from Rhiannon and stood up. As Iven stepped past him, Lewen touched his arm briefly. 'Thank ye,' he said.

Iven nodded and unshackled Rhiannon. As she rubbed her bruised and chafed wrists, he unwound the chain from the bedpost, pausing to examine the damage she had done to the wood, then quickly and deftly snapped one of the shackles around Rhiannon's wrist and the other around Lewen's. 'I hope I'm no' being played for a fool,' he said to no-one in particular and stood back to let Lewen lead Rhiannon out into the dawn.

The other apprentices lay in their sleeping rolls around the fire, which had sunk into grey ashes. Although it was light enough to see, the sun was not yet up and no birds called. The horses stood with sunken heads and relaxed forelegs in their hobbles. Even Lulu slept in a little round huddle.

'That was some sleeping spell ye cast, Lewen,' Iven said wryly. 'I felt like I'd been hammered over the head when I woke. Your teachers at the Theurgia must be pleased with your progress if ye can cast a spell as strong as that already.'

'Me?' Lewen asked in amazement. 'I canna cast sleeping spells that strong. Most o' my power lies in wood-working, ye ken that. My spell should have kept Rafferty sleepy for half an hour at most.'

Iven raised one eyebrow. 'Look at the horses,' he said. 'Look, even the bird in that tree is asleep. Happen ye're stronger than ye thought.'

'I ken my strengths and weaknesses well,' Lewen argued. He glanced at Rhiannon. 'Happen it was Rhiannon,' he said, frowning. 'She has Talent, we ken that, but she's never been tested. We have no idea what she can or canna do.'

'A sleeping spell is no' the easiest o' Skills,' Iven said. 'Ye have to be very subtle if it is to work, and no wild talent is ever that subtle, no matter how powerful they may be.'

Lewen shrugged. 'It seems very odd,' he began.

Just then the door of the blue caravan opened and Nina stood with her shawl wrapped tight about her nightgown, her dishevelled hair hanging almost to her knees. 'Roden!' she cried, in a voice made shrill with anxiety. 'Roden! Where are ye?'

Iven started forward. 'Nina! What's wrong?'

'Where's Roden?'

'Is he no' with ye?'

'No, no, he's no'. I canna believe I did no' feel him getting out o' bed.' She put her hand to her head, swaying a little. 'I feel so sick, so heavy-headed. I slept so very deeply. Maisie is still sleeping, I couldna wake her. Oh, that naughty lad! Where can he be?'

Nina called her son's name again and again, and began to search through the bushes, though her feet were bare and the grass icy with dew. Iven and the others began to search too, everyone feeling a creeping sense of dread. There was no sign of the little boy. Nina became increasingly distressed.

'He was sleeping right beside me, I had my arms about him, and Maisie slept on the other side. No-one could've stolen him, it's impossible.'

'Unless a very strong spell was cast indeed,' Iven said grimly. 'We all slept heavily, every one o' us. I could no' believe it when I woke and it was dawn. I was meant to wake and relieve Rafferty o' guard-duty in the dark hours. I have never no' woken afore.'

'I slept too,' Rafferty admitted shamefacedly. 'I could no' help it.'

'Me too,' Lewen said. 'I dinna think I'd sleep a wink, I had so much on my mind, but I slept like the dead.'

They all looked at each other, ashen-faced, then Nina began a strange, low keening. 'Nay, nay, no' my baby, no' my laddie, nay, nay, I canna believe it. They canna have got my baby.'

'If they have, they'll be sorry for it,' Iven said. 'They must have left a trail o' sorts. Do no' worry, my love, we'll find him.'

'The birds!' Nina said wildly. 'The birds may have seen something.'

Iven pointed to a nearby tree, where two small birds slept still, their heads tucked under their wings. 'A strong and subtle spell,' Nina said, unnaturally calmly, when the implications of the sight had sunk in. 'There's a sorcerer at work here.'

'Laird Malvern?'

'I fear so,' she answered. 'Remember, he was an apprentice at the Tower o' Ravens once, and they said his witch-sniffing powers were uncanny. Oh, Iven! Please, we must hurry! I fear for my Roden.'

Rhiannon had been standing still, the chain between her and Lewen drawn taut, looking intently at the ground. 'I see a footmark here,' she said then. They all crowded round her, but could see nothing but a faint smudge in the damp soil. Rhiannon ignored their questions and exclamations, walking slowly away towards the wood. Lewen followed her, tugged along by the chain between them. 'He went through here,' she said, examining a broken twig, then bending to look at the leaf litter.

'Are ye sure?' Nina asked helplessly, unable to see any marks on the ground.

Rhiannon glanced back at her. 'One thing a satyricorn kens is how to hunt,' she answered, her voice warm with compassion. Nina's eyes filled with tears.

'Rafferty, rouse the others,' Iven cried. 'Get the horses saddled up, get my sword.'

'And my bow and arrows too, please,' Lewen added.

'And mine,' Rhiannon said, giving Rafferty a very clear, direct look out of her blue-grey eyes. Rafferty hesitated and looked at Iven, who waved him on impatiently.

'Rhiannon, where now?' he cried.

She led them deep into the wood, through a maze of trees and thorny bushes. At last she came to a small clearing. 'Horses tethered here,' she said. A mound of fresh horse droppings galvanised them all into excitement. 'Three horses,' Rhiannon said. She suddenly bent and picked up something from the ground. It was a small wooden soldier.

Nina's face crumpled. 'He took it to bed with him last night. Oh, my laddie! Where are ye?'

'Fettercairn Castle,' Iven said in a murderous voice. 'I will raze the place to the ground if I have to, to get my son back.'

'Aye, with a handful o' lads and your sword,' Nina said in a voice blank with despair.

'We may be able to catch them afore they get back to the castle,' Lewen cried.

'We must be quick!' Iven said, gripping his hands into fists. 'Rhiannon, which way did they ride?'

Breaking into a run, Rhiannon led them through the trees to the other side of the wood. Beyond was a long meadow stretching back to the north. They could all see the deep indentations the horses' hooves had made in the damp soil. 'They were galloping hard,' she said, bending to touch one hoof print. 'At least half an hour ago.'

Nina was white and trembling.

'I bet they canna run as fast as Argent,' Lewen cried.

'Or Blackthorn,' said Rhiannon. She put her fingers in her mouth and whistled piercingly.

'Ye'll have to unshackle us,' Lewen said. 'Argent canna run if he is carrying both o' us.'

Iven did not hesitate. He put his hand in his pocket and pulled out the key. 'I'll be right behind ye. I'm sure the boys willna mind me taking one o' their horses. My auld Steady is too big and slow for this task.' He unlocked the shackles and the chain fell at their feet.

A shrill whinnying rent the air, and Blackthorn came galloping out of the wood, her tail held high, her mane rippling like a black satin banner. Rhiannon flung open her arms, her face radiant, and the mare came to a plunging halt before her, to blow grass-stained slobber all over her shirt. Her wings were unfurled, flashing blue as a kingfisher, and her horns cut through the air like rapiers as she tossed her head, pawing the ground. Rhiannon embraced her passionately.

Then Rafferty came up at a run, Cameron close behind him. They led their two geldings, and the girls' two mares. Argent cantered close behind, neighing in excitement, unsaddled, unbridled and untethered.

'He would no' let me saddle him,' Rafferty panted. 'I'm sorry.'

'That's all right, I'll ride bareback,' Lewen said. He vaulted up onto the stallion's back. Rafferty handed up Lewen's longbow and quiver of arrows, which he slung over his shoulder. Then the boy turned to Rhiannon and, without a word, passed over her bow and arrows, and her beloved silver and black daggers. Rhiannon took them with a quick shining smile and a nod of thanks, and quickly hid them about her person.

'Rafferty, I want ye and the girls to ride to Linlithgorn and raise the reeve. Tell him to get as many men as he can on short notice and ride for Fettercairn Castle. We canna allow the laird to escape the Rìgh's justice any longer. Take my courier's badge from my caravan, and show the reeve. It gives me His Highness's authority.'

Rafferty nodded, though it was clear he would rather be riding to the rescue with the others.

'May I borrow your horse?' Iven asked him. 'I'm too heavy for the mares, over such a distance.'

Rafferty nodded. Iven mounted with the easy grace of a one-time cavalier, taking his sword from Cameron with a nod of thanks. Then he and Lewen were off, galloping across the meadow. Rhiannon swung herself up onto the black mare's back with a wild whoop, then the mare bounded after them, her wings half-unfurled.

Nina seized the bridle of the brown mare, then she was up into the saddle too and galloping away, her unbound hair whipping behind her. Cameron grimaced at Rafferty, and then swung himself up onto Basta's back and kicked him into motion. As the gelding broke into a run, Lulu came scampering out of the forest, whimpering in distress. She leapt up Basta's tail and onto the back of Cameron's saddle, clasping his belt. Cameron cried out in shock and almost fell off.

'Get off!' he cried, but Lulu clung on, gibbering loudly.

He scowled but did not try to shake her off, bending low as he tried to catch up with the others.

The horses were fresh after their long stay in the laird's stables and the easy ride of the day before. Their heavy hooves seemed to eat up the miles. Rhiannon rode ahead, following the trail left by the kidnappers. There was no doubt the trail led towards Fettercairn Castle.

By midmorning the castle was in sight, frowning down from the great height of its cliff. They had been alternating between a trot and a canter for the last few hours, so as not to exhaust the horses too much. Argent and Blackthorn were some distance in front, the others trailing behind.

Suddenly Rhiannon shouted and waved her arm. She could see three horses riding up the long green slope towards the road. One of the riders carried something before him. Everyone kicked their horses on to a new spurt of speed. There was a flash of a face as someone looked back at them, then the three horses broke into a gallop again. The race was on.

Up the steep, cobbled road the horses thundered, striking sparks from their steel-shod feet. Stride by stride Argent and Blackthorn closed the gap between them. The kidnappers reached the first switchback corner and took it fast, one of the horses almost slipping on the damp stones. Rhiannon dragged up Blackthorn's head, urging her into the air. With a whinny, the mare spread out her wings, tucked up her legs and rose swiftly off the ground. She landed in the middle of the road above, turning to face the three riders galloping towards her. Rhiannon saw Lord Malvern, his face twisted into a grimace of fury and hate, the seneschal Irving, and the laird's bodyguard, who cradled a small, cloak-wrapped figure in his arms.

Rhiannon unslung her bow and pulled an arrow from her quiver, setting it to her string and raising the bow high. She did not know who to aim for. If she shot the bodyguard, Roden might be severely injured in the fall. Yet she wanted desperately to save the boy for Nina. She had only a few seconds. In a moment the horses would be upon her. Rhiannon took a deep breath, aimed for Lord Malvern, and let the arrow go.

It sang out into the air. Lord Malvern cringed back, his horse faltering in its headlong gallop. Scant seconds before the arrow found its mark in his shoulder, his seneschal Irving brought his horse plunging across the road, throwing himself before his lord. The arrow caught him in the throat, and he went down under the horses' thundering hooves.

Lord Malvern managed to heave himself back in the saddle, and spurred his horse on, tumbling the seneschal's body aside. Blackthorn reared, then, with a great thrust of her hindquarters, managed to leap into the air just as the bodyguard's huge charger galloped past underneath her. Rhiannon leant down and made a grab for Roden, but the bodyguard had the little boy in too tight a grip. All she managed to do was drag the cloak from his head so she could see his bright curls, and the pale curve of a cheek. His eyes were closed and he breathed stertorously. The wind from Blackthorn's steadily beating wings caused the bodyguard's cloak to toss and twist wildly. Only this saved Rhiannon, for the bodyguard had his sword in his other hand, and as she reached down for Roden he brought it up in a great whistling swipe that would have taken off Rhiannon's head if the sword had not got caught in his cloak. As it was the sword nicked her arm, causing her to cry out in pain. She dragged Blackthorn's head up, and the mare rose higher, her wings beating strongly. The body-guard galloped on, Lord Malvern close behind, and Blackthorn came down to land lightly on the road again.

Rhiannon grasped her arm, trying to stop the blood. Argent came galloping up and she shouted, 'Go! Go! They have Roden, I saw him.'

'Ye all right?' Lewen shouted as the grey stallion raced past.

'Aye, aye, just go!' Rhiannon looked down at her injured arm and saw she had taken a nasty swipe. Cursing under her breath, she took her shirt between her teeth and tore away a strip, which she clumsily wound round and round the gash. She had to bend her arm to tie the ends into a knot and this caused her such intense pain she almost swooned. For a moment she leant forward, resting her head on Blackthorn's mane, trying to fight off the dizziness. Blackthorn stood steady, though her chest heaved and her legs trembled. The dizziness passed, and Rhiannon tucked her injured arm against her body and urged Blackthorn on. At first the mare baulked, exhausted by the effort of her flight, but Rhiannon insisted and so the tired mare broke into a canter, following Lewen and Argent.

She heard hooves behind her, and then Iven was beside her, astride the brown gelding. 'Are ye badly hurt?' he said. She shook her head. 'I hate this slug! I wish I had my auld war-charger. Then Lord Malvern would ken what a real horse can do.'

'Saw Roden,' Rhiannon panted. 'Tried to shoot . . . the laird down . . . Irving took the arrow.'

'Aye, I saw. It was a brave try. Come on! We must get them afore they reach the gatehouse.'

Iven spurred his horse on, and Blackthorn leapt to match the gelding's stride. Rhiannon was too weak and dizzy to direct her. She just hung on grimly, trying to protect her wounded arm from the worst of the jolts.

Back and forth the road climbed up the cliff, like a great stony snake. Often the sound of the kidnappers' hooves was so tantalisingly close, it felt as if they could reach up their hand and topple their horses by seizing their hock. Iven drew ahead, and Nina rode up behind, barefoot and clad only in a nightgown, her hair wild. She shouted a question to Rhiannon, who was too winded to reply. Nina shot her a look of deep concern but did not stop, racing on to catch up with her husband. Rhiannon's impromptu bandage was now red with blood, and her hands were slick with it. Suddenly Blackthorn's withers rose up and hit Rhiannon in the face. Blackness overwhelmed her, and she fell. She hit the cobblestones hard, rolled over and over, and came to a rest against the wall.

Rhiannon lay still for a moment, trying to get her breath. Her arm throbbed unbearably. A dark whiskery face bent down to nudge her and blow a worried query. Rhiannon laughed shakily, wiped her eyes and, clinging to Blackthorn's mane, hauled herself upright again. This time she sat for a moment, waiting for the red waves of pain to recede. *Ye're no' thinking*, she told herself. *Ye have a winged horse. Use her!*

Behind her she could hear Cameron approaching fast. She clambered up the wall and remounted Blackthorn, being too weak to vault up onto her back the way she usually did. Then she set Blackthorn at the wall. The winged mare took a few strides, leapt over the obstacle and spread her wings. They soared into the air, right above Cameron's startled head. Lulu, clinging still to Cameron's belt, gibbered and cringed. The valley tilted away below them, sunlit and golden. Blackthorn veered, beat her wings rhythmically, and began to rise.

Up, up, they went, passing one level of the road after another. They passed Iven and Nina, who were both whipping their foundering horses on mercilessly. They passed Lewen, crouched on Argent's neck, the stallion galloping on tirelessly. Then, just round the next corner, they passed the foam-flecked, blowing mounts of Lord Malvern and his bodyguard. The lord drew his sword and slashed at them as they flew past, but Blackthorn swerved nimbly so he missed. Rhiannon could only hope the lord had not seen how very nearly she had been unseated by the sudden move.

They landed on the road just outside the gatehouse. The gates were wide open, yawning blackly, but there was no sign of the gatekeeper. Rhiannon slid off Blackthorn's back, and leant against her for a moment, taking strength from her warm, sweaty flank. Then she straightened herself, turning to look at the road. At the far end, Lord Malvern and his bodyguard were just turning the corner and coming towards her. Both their horses were badly winded, barely managing a canter. It was cruel to whip them on, and Rhiannon told the horses so, as they came wild-eyed and foam-flecked towards her. *Ye deserve better masters than this*, she said silently. *How dare they whip ye and spur ye and drive ye to gallop up such a cruel, steep hill as this. Ye are Horse. Ye are not their slave. Stand still. Refuse to run anymore.*

For a moment she thought she had failed, for the horses came on at the same headlong pace, their nostrils flaring red, their eyes rimmed with white. Then the bodyguard's horse suddenly came to a juddering halt, legs splayed, head hanging. Though the big, grey-bearded man whipped it with his reins and slapped it with the flat of his sword, it refused to budge. Suddenly its legs folded and it sank down in the middle of the road. The bodyguard jumped off, the unconscious child lolling in his arms, and dragged at the bridle, trying to force it on. Meanwhile, Lord Malvern's horse was rearing and plunging, refusing to go forwards. He slashed at it with his sword, and it reared so precipitately the lord was thrown from its back. Rhiannon whooped with joy, and so did Lewen, who had turned the corner and was galloping up the cobbled hill towards the foundered horses. Nina and Iven were close behind him.

The bodyguard glanced back at him, then dropped the reins and began to run up the road towards the gatehouse, Roden's arms and legs flopping wildly. Lord Malvern rolled, got to his feet and began to run too. Both men had naked swords in their hands, and murder in their eyes. Rhiannon set an arrow to her bow with shaking fingers. Again her aim wavered between them. She did not want to risk shooting Roden, but if she shot down Lord Malvern, the bodyguard would be upon her, with the open gate only a few strides past her. She tried to steady her breathing, and shot the bodyguard in the thigh. He cried out in agony, but although his stride faltered and broke, he did not stop, lurching forward with the feathered haft of the arrow sticking out of his leg. Rhiannon shot him again in the same spot, and then, in desperation, in the other leg. He fell, Roden rolling out of his arms. Lord Malvern bent, caught up the little boy, and ran on. He was too close now for Rhiannon to shoot him down. She drew her slim black dagger from her boot and flung it at him. To her horror he simply raised one hand and the dagger spun away harmlessly. Then he raised his sword and swiped at her. Blackthorn reared and he shrank back instinctively, allowing Rhiannon to roll away under his sword. Then the winged horse bent her head and charged him. One of her long, sharp horns slashed him across the face. He screamed and dropped his sword, putting his hand up to cover the gash. Rhiannon reached out a hand to try to trip him, but he stumbled past her and through the gates, Roden still clasped against his chest. The massive gates clanged shut behind him.

Storming the Castle

R hiannon sat up slowly, sick with disappointment.
Argent came to a blowing halt a few feet away, and
Lewen jumped down and came to help her up.

'He got past,' Rhiannon said, her voice thick.

'Ye almost had him,' Lewen said. 'It was so close.'

'Now what?' she asked, tears stinging her eyes.

'We go in and get him out,' Lewen said, looking up at
the immense wall towering over their heads. Rhiannon
heaved a sigh that came from the very pit of her chest
cavity.

'First, we question the bodyguard,' Lewen said, letting go
of Rhiannon's arm as she leant against the wall. He drew his
knife and walked back down the road towards the bodyguard. The man was clutching his shattered leg, his face
twisted in pain. He looked at Lewen's set, determined face,
then back down the road, to where Nina and Iven were
cantering up towards them, Cameron close behind. With a
great effort he staggered to his feet, and then, before Lewen
could stop him, dragged himself up onto the wall and

launched himself into the dizzying space on the far side. They heard a thin wail, and then a sickening bone-crunching thud. Soon after, there came another, more distant thud, and then another. Then there was only silence.

Grey with horror, Lewen ran and looked over the wall. Then he turned back and sank to his haunches, his dagger dropping from his hand. Iven and Nina flung themselves off their horses and ran to look too. Nina was weeping.

'I guess he dinna want to be questioned,' Rhiannon said through the roaring in her head, then she slid down the wall till she too was sitting. Nina ran to her side.

'Rhiannon, Rhiannon,' she sobbed. 'Och, ye were so close! I really thought ye'd saved him.'

'I tried,' Rhiannon said. 'I'm sorry.'

'Nay, nay, ye did so well, ye were so brave, so clever,' Nina wept. 'Och, my laddie, my babe. We were so close!'

Rhiannon dropped her head onto her arms.

'Ye're sorely hurt,' Nina said, dashing the tears from her face. 'Let me look at your arm. Och, I have naught here, naught to ease the pain or stop the bleeding. What a hare-brained, madcap rescue this is, me barefoot and in my nightgown, and only a sword and a few daggers between the lot o' us. How are we meant to storm the castle like this?' Her tears began to flow again, but she unwrapped Rhiannon's arm deftly, examined the ugly wound with compressed brows, and then bound it up again with clean cloth torn from her nightgown. Her bandage was far more effective than Rhiannon's.

'I shall have to fly over the wall,' Rhiannon said slowly, cradling her arm against her. 'It's the only way to get in.'

'But ye're injured,' Nina pointed out, taking her shawl off and fashioning Rhiannon a gorgeous, many-coloured sling. 'And Roden could be hidden anywhere inside that castle.'

'It's too dangerous,' Iven said reluctantly. 'Unless . . .'

'Blackthorn is mine,' Rhiannon said. 'She willna carry anyone else.'

'No' even me?' Lewen said.

'Ye're too heavy for her,' Rhiannon said.

Lewen acknowledged the truth of this. It was a rare horse that could carry his weight.

Nina sat back on her heels. 'It's the only way,' she said. 'But can I let ye do it? What if they shoot ye down? I'd never forgive myself.'

'Better I die here, flying on my horse's back, trying to save Roden, than at the end of the hangman's rope,' Rhiannon said wryly. She managed to stand up.

Cameron was hanging back, wide-eyed and pale-faced. Lulu, who had ridden the whole way clinging to Cameron's belt, darted forward and seized Rhiannon's blood-slick hand in her tiny, leathery paw. She jumped up and down, gibbering, waving up at the castle with her other paw.

'She wants to go with ye,' Nina said. 'She wants to help ye find Roden.'

Rhiannon looked at the little arak doubtfully.

'She has a very precise sense o' smell,' Nina said. 'And she can climb anything. Happen she can help ye find Roden? For ye may be able to fly over the walls, Rhiannon, but how are ye to find my lad once ye're inside?'

'I do no' think Blackthorn will like it,' Rhiannon said. 'Lulu's awfully smelly.'

'She willna mind,' Nina said eagerly. 'Oh, please, Rhiannon. Ye do no' ken Lulu. She's very clever, and quick, and nimble, and she adores Roden. She'll help ye, I ken she will.'

'All right,' Rhiannon said. She looked up at the stone bulwark again and could not help a little shiver.

'I dinna even have water for ye and Blackthorn to drink,' Nina said remorsefully. 'No' a crumb to eat. After such a hard ride too!'

'That's all right,' Rhiannon said absently. 'I am used to being hungry.'

She whickered to Blackthorn, who whickered back, and led the mare over to the wall so she could mount. Before she could clamber up onto the wall, Lewen was beside her, lifting her in his strong arms and throwing her up onto the mare's back. She smiled at him, and he held up his hand to her. When she took it he drew her down so he could kiss her.

'Be careful, my love,' he said. 'Come back safely.'

'O' course I will,' she replied with an attempt at her usual jaunty manner. He unslung his quiver of arrows and passed it up to her. It was full of arrows fletched with shining, iridescent-green feathers. 'I have a Talent with wood, ye ken. I made all these arrows with my own hand, and they will always fly true. Take them.'

'I will, but no' because I need enchanted arrows to shoot true,' she said with a flash of her dimple.

'I ken, it's just . . .'

She nodded and passed him her own quiver with its handful of clumsily whittled arrows. 'Yours are much bonnier, I'll be glad to take them,' she said cheekily. 'Thank ye.'

Iven stepped up to give her his hand. 'Thank ye, Rhiannon,' he said gravely. 'Bring Roden back to us.'

'I will,' she said gamely. 'What will ye do now? Where shall I meet ye?'

'We will go now and bang on that door until someone lets us in.' Iven said. 'It's all I can think o' doing. In the meantime, let us hope the reeve from Linlithgorn is on his way. If Malvern refuses us permission to search the castle, surely he canna refuse the reeve?'

'Laird Malvern rules this land as if he were a prionnsa and this were his kingdom,' Nina said unhappily. 'I'm sure he will have no hesitation in refusing the reeve, and I doubt the reeve will have the courage to insist. After all, he does no' ken who we are and he would ken and respect the laird all too well, I think. All the laird has to do is deny everything.'

'He'll have trouble explaining the gash across his face,' Rhiannon said grimly. 'I think Blackthorn put out his eye.'

'We can but hope,' Iven said and stepped back, so Nina could come and embrace Rhiannon.

'Ye have power, lassie,' the witch said to her intently. 'I have sensed it in ye, and ye used it here, to bring the laird's horses to their knees. Trust in yourself, and draw upon it in need. It shallna let ye down.'

Rhiannon nodded sceptically, then waved her hand to Cameron. 'Bye, laddie!' she said. 'See ye soon.'

'Good luck!' Cameron replied. 'I hope ye find Roden.' He hesitated a moment, then said in a rush, 'That was amazing what ye did afore, with the horses and all, I mean.' As Rhiannon shrugged and smiled, he continued, 'I'm sorry I punched ye. Ye ken, yesterday.'

Rhiannon touched the yellowing bruise on her temple. 'Well, I'm sorry I kneed ye in the balls,' she replied.

Cameron grinned, though his brown cheek coloured. 'So am I,' he said.

Nina passed up Lulu, who clung to Rhiannon's waist with her skinny, hairy arms, gibbering a little and bouncing up and down with excitement. Blackthorn shied and spread her wings, dancing sideways.

'Shhhh,' Rhiannon said sternly to the little arak. 'Thigearns do no' bounce.'

Lulu immediately stopped bouncing, though Rhiannon could feel her quivering, whether with fear or excitement it was impossible to tell. She took a deep breath. She was trembling herself, and very definitely from fear. She smiled at the circle of upturned faces, determined they would not know how very scared she was, and then wheeled Blackthorn round and set her into a canter. After a few quick strides, the mare unfurled her blue-tipped wings and leapt into the air. The circle of faces fell behind.

Blackthorn was weary and the wall was high, so Rhiannon took the ascent slowly. They flew along the wall, away from the gatehouse, gradually gaining height, until at last they breached it near the end. All was quiet. Too quiet. Rhiannon could not see a single soldier or servant. The castle could have been deserted.

Rhiannon directed Blackthorn towards the northern tower. Roden would have been taken to Lady Evaline, she guessed, who had her quarters in that wing. Rhiannon was not entirely sure she understood the madness behind Roden's kidnap, but she felt sure Lord Malvern had done it for his sister-in-law. He had called Lady Evaline old and mad, but Rhiannon felt that it was the lord who was truly the mad one, the one obsessed with bringing his brother and his son back to life, and expiating the guilt he felt at their deaths.

Blackthorn was beginning to tire, and Rhiannon brought her in close to the tower. The castle had been built for defence and so the only windows were high up under the roof, and heavily barred. The length of the tower was broken regularly with narrow arrow-slits, however. Blackthorn hovered as close to one of these as she could get, while Rhiannon lifted Lulu and thrust her towards the tiny aperture.

'Find Roden, Lulu,' she whispered. 'And be quick!'

Lulu nodded, whimpering a little with fear, and leapt across to the arrow-slit. She crept through the gap and disappeared from view. Blackthorn then flew up and landed gratefully on the roof of the tower. This was steeply peaked, but there was a little flat edge just before the battlements where Blackthorn was able to stand, and Rhiannon could stretch out in the warm sunshine and rest.

She shut her eyes, feeling very tired after the long, hard ride. She almost fell asleep there, resting in the sun, the pain in her arm dying down to a dull throbbing. But then Blackthorn nudged her with her nose, blowing on her and nibbling at her shoulder. Rhiannon sat up rather groggily.

'What is it?' she asked.

Blackthorn looked towards the battlements curiously. Rhiannon looked too, and saw to her horror a small brown wrinkled hand reaching over the stone. She thought of all the dead severed hands she had seen in the lord's library and a cold shudder went down her spine. It was all she could do not to scream. Surely the lord could not animate those embalmed hands and send them creeping down corridors and climbing tall towers, hunting down his enemies and strangling them to death?

Another hand reached up and grasped the stone, then Lulu's anxious face, so like an old, old woman's, suddenly appeared. Rhiannon's relief was so profound she almost fainted.

The arak crept over the battlement and leapt to Rhiannon's side, seizing her hand urgently. She gibbered, dancing up and down.

'Roden? Ye've found Roden?'

The arak dragged her to the side and pointed down. Rhiannon leant over the battlements, clinging tight to the stone with her uninjured hand. The tower fell away to the courtyard so far below, the vast drop making her feel dizzy. Lulu gibbered again, pointing, then swung herself down. Rhiannon watched in amazement as she clambered down the sheer drop, clinging to the stones with hands and feet and tail-tip. She came to a deep window embrasure and hung above it, looking up at Rhiannon.

Rhiannon nodded her head and climbed up onto the battlements so that she could more readily reach Blackthorn's back. Her arm throbbed painfully and her head swam, but she ignored it and managed to slide her leg across the mare's back. Blackthorn leapt out into the air, Rhiannon shutting her eyes against the sudden spin of space. She wondered how long it took most thigearns to get over the involuntary spurt of terror that came from flying on a winged horse's back.

Blackthorn flew down so that she was hovering just below the window where Lulu hung upside down. Rhiannon could hear the sound of low, murmuring voices. She felt sure one of them was Lord Malvern. Her pulse quickened and she signalled to Blackthorn to fly closer.

She could just make out the words.

'Do ye no' care what I've been through to bring him back to ye?' Lord Malvern was shouting. 'Irving is dead and Durward too, and I was slashed across the face by that great horned beast. Look, I bleed! Does the spilling o' my blood mean naught to ye?'

'There has been too much spilling o' blood,' Lady Evaline answered in a wavering voice.

'But ye said ye wanted him! I've risked much to get him for ye, no' to mention losing two o' my most faithful men. It would've been much better to have let them ride away, suspecting nothing, and then to have stolen him later, when I had the spell in my hands and was ready to resurrect Rory's soul. Now we have to hide him and keep him safe from prying eyes for weeks, months even, until

I find the spell. Why on earth did ye weep and wring your hands at the thought o' losing him if ye did no' want me to take him for ye?'

'Ye do such mad, strange things,' the old woman said in a broken voice. 'I canna understand ye sometimes, Malvern. Och, I ken ye felt for me in my grief when I lost both Falkner and Rory so cruelly, I ken ye felt ye were to blame. But so much time has passed, and I grow auld. Such fury o' emotion seems odd to me now.'

'But ye wept!' Lord Malvern was furious.

'Aye, I wept, aye, I was sorry the laddie had to go, aye, I wished he could stay here with me and brighten my days,' Lady Evaline said just as angrily. 'I did no' mean for ye to go and steal him! Why do ye do these things? So many boys! Ye've stolen so many boys for me and in the end killed them all, for ye could no' stand the way they wept for their mothers, or shrank away from ye, frightened. This lad is no' Rory, he can never be Rory, canna ye see that?'

'Oh yes, he will,' Lord Malvern said in a cold, malevolent voice. 'We will kill him and Rory will take over his body, and then ye will thank me.'

'But will it really be Rory?' Lady Evaline asked unhappily. 'His body rotted away long ago, and Falkner's too. We have their bones, it's true, but we ken we canna reanimate them, we have tried and tried.'

'The body is but a sack to keep the spirit in,' Lord Malvern said impatiently. 'It is the soul that matters, and we have tied their souls here to us. All we need do is find appropriate vessels to pour their souls back into. And ye canna tell me ye do no' think this lad a good vessel for Rory. I have seen the way ye look at him and long to caress him. Soon, soon, ye shall have him again, your own darling son, back in a living, breathing body, as ye have longed for so long.'

'I just wish we dinna have to hurt this lad,' Lady Evaline murmured.

'We shallna hurt him. We do no' want Rory to wake to pain or a marred body. We will kill him very gently, I promise ye.'

Lady Evaline sighed. 'Sometimes ye make my flesh creep on my bones, Malvern, even after all these years.'

'Do no' dare stand there and stare at me with those wide, innocent eyes, Evaline,' he hissed. 'Ye may no' have wielded the knife yourself but ye have been complicit in each and every death! Ye think me mad? Ye think me evil? Everyone I have killed was killed to make ye happy!'

There was a cry from Lady Evaline. 'Look, he wakes! Sssh! Do no' frighten him.'

Then Rhiannon heard a high, treble voice, wavering with tears. 'Where am I? Where's my mam? I want my mam!'

'I am to be your mama now,' Lady Evaline said. 'Do no' cry, my love.'

'Ye're no' my mam! Ye're auld! I want my own mam!'

'I am your mama, Rory.'

'My name's no' Rory! I'm Roden. Go away!'

'Rory, do no' speak to your mother like that,' Lord Malvern said in a chilling voice.

'She's no' my mam! My mam is young and bonny. She's a witch, and she'll turn ye into a slug for this. And my da's a soldier and he'll step on ye and squash ye flat. They'll be coming for me, just ye wait and see!' The little boy's voice wavered and broke.

'No-one will come for ye, Rory. No-one kens where ye are. Ye would be best to keep a quiet tongue in your head, and be loving and respectful to your new mama else I'll squash ye as flat as a slug. Do ye understand me?'

There was a short, fraught silence and then Roden began to wail, 'I want my mam, I want my mam. Mam! Mam!'

'Shhh, no, sweetling, do no' cry. Ye will forget her soon, and we'll be so happy together. Come, will ye no' sit here on my lap and I shall read ye a story? Come, come, my darling, do no' weep. Uncle Malvern will go now and leave ye here with me, and we'll have a lovely cuddle and I'll play with ye. Malvern, go and leave me with my son.'

Rhiannon heard the faint sound of a door shutting, and then there was no sound except for Roden's sobbing and the anxious attempts of Lady Evaline to soothe him. As she kept telling him that he would soon forget his real mama and she would forget him, all she managed to do was drive Roden deeper into despair.

Rhiannon shifted her weight, wondering what she could do to rescue Roden. There seemed to be no way in to the little tower room except through the window above her head, which was heavily barred. Blackthorn was tiring quickly, her wings not built for hovering. Whatever Rhiannon was to do had to be done quickly.

Lulu turned her small, wizened face to Rhiannon anxiously, gestured broadly, and then swung herself down and into the windowsill. For a moment the arak clung to the bars, then she put her hand through and tapped gently on the glass. A moment later, Roden's chubby face appeared at the window. He saw the winged horse and rider, and shouted with excitement, jumping up and down and waving. Then he unlatched the window and flung it open. Lulu squeezed through the bars and flung herself upon him, dancing up and down on his shoulder with joy.

Rhiannon stared at the bars in consternation. She flew closer and reached out one hand to test them. They were stout and strong. Roden reached through the deep aperture and grasped her fingers. Behind him there was sudden movement.

Rhiannon took a deep breath. She had nothing on her that could wrench the bars from the stone. No rope. No chain. All she had was her desperate desire to free Roden, and her will. Rhiannon had listened to the apprentices at their lessons often enough to know the keystones to witchcraft were will and desire. Both of hers were strong. She grasped the bars with both hands, focused her mind with all the fierce determination she was capable of, and jerked them hard. To her surprise and wild joy, the bars wrenched free. They flew out of the window-frame at great speed, almost whacking her over the head, and tumbled down to smash into the courtyard below. Rhiannon almost followed them, jerked off balance. Only Blackthorn's speedy manoeuvre kept her on the mare's back.

Roden did not hesitate. In a second he was scrambling up onto the windowsill, then he climbed through the window. Rhiannon grasped his wrists and swung him onto Blackthorn's back, behind her. The little boy whooped with joy and excitement. The next second Lulu was leaping after him, landing on the winged horse's mane. Blackthorn wheeled and soared away.

A despairing scream came from the window behind him. 'Rory, no!'

Rhiannon looked back. Lady Evaline leant out of the window, her arms outstretched. 'My son! Ye're stealing my son!' the old lady cried, tears streaming down her face. Suddenly she climbed up onto the sill and launched herself after them, calling Rory's name. Rhiannon and Roden could only watch in numb horror as she fell over and over, tumbling down the great length of the tower to the ground. She hit the paving-stones and bounced once, then sprawled still like a broken doll. Slowly a tide of red crept out from her skull.

Roden hid his face. Tears started to Rhiannon's eyes. She wiped them away, then bent to stroke Blackthorn's sweat-lathered neck.

'Take us away from here,' she whispered. 'Find Lewen for me.'

Blackthorn wheeled and flew to the south.

The Chain Between Them

Rhiannon lay in Lewen's arms, feeling warm and comfortable and at peace, despite the iron chain that weighed down her wrist and rattled whenever she moved.

Firelight flickered over the trees, which seemed to lean over the camp like protective guardians. Nina sat on the far side of the flames, Roden leaning against her, her arms about him as she whispered silly jokes in his ear to make him giggle. Lulu was curled against him, one paw nestled in his hand. Both looked as if they never wanted to let him go again. At the sound of Roden's laughter, Iven looked up from the guitar he was gently strumming and smiled.

The other apprentices were playing cards by the light of a lantern propped on a box. All except Edithe. She sat by herself, reading a spell-book and looking very sour. She felt the arrest of the lord of Fettercairn to be a slur on her perception, and was adamant that it was all a dreadful mistake and the lord would be cleared as soon as they reached the royal court.

More than a week had passed since Rhiannon had snatched Roden from Fettercairn Castle. She had managed to stay on Blackthorn's back long enough to see Nina clasp her son in her arms. Then she had fallen.

The next seven days were nothing but a hideous blur. Strange nightmarish visions stalked her imagination. She was first burning with fire, then tossed in an icy waterfall, then dried out with merciless heat like a lizard on a rock. Her limbs seemed to grow like tentacles, reaching for miles across the countryside, and then she was very tiny, a pale crustacean pried from her shell and held dangling above an open mouth. Dark walkers haunted her dreams and bent over her waking hours, pinned to the heels of those who tended her.

They had tried to put her to bed at the Linlithgorn inn but she had fought so viciously against being taken inside stone walls that Nina had had to care for her in the open, with no more shelter than the leaves of the trees and a canopy of oilskins strung up with rope. In her rare moments of lucidity, Rhiannon was able to stare up at the shifting green pattern of sunshine through the leaves, or the great vault of the night sky starred with familiar constellations. Gradually, her soaring temperature cooled, the crippling headache faded, and the dark walkers stepped back into the shadows, leaving Rhiannon weak and useless as a newborn kitten but aware of who she was and where she was.

Nina said she had suffered from sorcery sickness, a very dangerous illness that could overcome anyone who drew too deeply upon the One Power. It was a wonder, she said, that Rhiannon had survived it. Many wild Talents, who had not been taught how to use their powers properly, died after such a display of magical strength, or at the least were left broken in mind and body. Rhiannon must have great inner reserves of strength, Nina said, for she had wielded powerful magic by wresting the iron bars out of the stone. Rhiannon had already been weakened by the poison Dedrie the nursemaid had forced down her throat, and worn out by the desperate chase after Roden, and the loss of blood from her injured arm. 'Indeed I think Eà was watching out for ye, my dear,' Nina had said, 'and I am so glad. I could no' have forgiven myself if ye had died rescuing my laddie, after all ye've been through this past week.'

Nina had insisted that the whole company wait until Rhiannon was strong enough to ride again before they left Linlithgorn, and she had not allowed anyone to talk to her about what had happened at Fettercairn Castle. At first Rhiannon had been grateful for this, for her dreams were still disturbed with visions of creeping hands, pickled babies, bloody puddles, the unhappy ghosts of murdered children and the dreadful scream of an old lady as she fell to her death. She was content to spend a few days sitting in the leafy glade, enjoying the tender ministrations of Nina, who could not do enough for the rescuer of her son, and watching the sorceress as she called birds and small animals to her hands, and sang quiet songs of peace and healing over Rhiannon's head.

Once Rhiannon had been strong enough to walk about the clearing, or to ask after the others, her peaceful time was over, though. Iven had come with the chain and shackles in his hands, and a most apologetic look, to fetter her limbs again. Nina had protested angrily, and Iven had said, 'I'm sorry, my dearling, I'm sorry, Rhiannon, but naught has changed. I still must take ye to Lucescere to face the Rìgh's justice. Ye ken I wish I could just leave ye be, and pretend I do no' ken ye were the one who killed Connor, but I do ken and so does the Rìgh. I canna take the risk that ye will decide to fly off once more.'

'But Iven!' Nina cried, almost in tears. 'If it were no' for Rhiannon, we would no' have our own boy back again. We are in her debt!'

'I ken, dearling, and believe me I shall make sure the Rìgh kens it. He is a fair man, and fond o' ye and Roden. I am sure he willna let the courts hang Rhiannon when he understands –'

Nina was aghast. 'Iven! Surely there can be no question o' . . . Iven, ye canna allow . . .'

Iven's face was troubled and unhappy, but still he clasped the shackles around Rhiannon's wrists and fastened the chain to the tree. 'I'm sorry. Believe me when I say I will do all in my power to make sure the courts deal fairly with ye, my dear. Your help in rescuing Roden and your testimony against the laird o' Fettercairn – these will no' mean naught, I promise ye.'

Rhiannon had not fought him, or protested in any way, but she had felt a heavy mantle settle over her shoulders, a sort of weariness and fatalism she had not previously felt. Nina was worried about her, she could tell, and had tried to argue that they must stay a few more days until Rhiannon was stronger. Iven had shook his head, though. 'We must ride on, my love, ye ken that. We have been delayed far too long already.'

So Lewen and the other witch-apprentices had at last been allowed to join them, and the obvious affection in the faces of most of them had bolstered Rhiannon's spirits, and made it easier to bear the heavy chain that rattled every time she moved. Lewen had brought Blackthorn with the other horses, and the sight of the mare had given her fresh strength and courage.

The apprentices had spent the afternoon fussing over her, giving her little gifts of flowers and honeyed cakes, and telling her how brave and clever she was. This had been sweet. Sweeter still was the sight of Lewen's stead-fast brown eyes and the warmth and strength of his hands, which he found impossible to keep away from her. She was able to lean against his broad shoulder, and rest her head on his chest, and feel his fingers entwined in hers, and felt a warm glow of happiness she would have thought impossible earlier that day. Lewen had, without the need to speak, unshackled the chain from the tree and clasped it round his own wrist and Rhiannon had under-stood this gesture as it was meant – he would stand by her, and support her, and help her bear her fate.

The company planned to ride on again the next day and Nina had prepared a feast to celebrate. The village of Linlithgorn had provided them with fresh fruits and veg-etables and ripe cheeses and newly baked bread, which everyone had enjoyed very much, and now Rhiannon was replete and drowsy, and ready to hear at last what had happened while she had been lost in nightmares.

'So what did ye do then?' Rhiannon asked Lewen.

'Well, it was just as Iven predicted. The gatekeeper opened the gate and was surprised to see us. He told us there must be some mistake, no-one had been in or out o' the gatehouse all day, but he sent his lad to fetch the laird when Iven insisted. The laird made us wait for ages, which made Nina furious, and she marched into the castle. When the gatekeeper tried to stop her, she sang the spell o' sleep, which was rather funny, particularly since Cameron did no' heed her warning to cover his ears and so he fell fast asleep too. She ensorcelled half the castle garrison and quite a few servants too, and at last found the laird in his library, much to his dismay. Ye should've seen his face when he called and called for his servants, and then found them all snoozing!'

'What did he do?' Rhiannon asked, grinning.

'He was all honey and poison, looking Nina up and down as if she was a madwoman and speaking to her very soothingly. I must admit she looked rather wild, being barefoot and dressed in a torn and bloody night-gown, with her hair looking like she'd ridden through a whirlwind. Nina dinna care, though, she looked and acted like the countess she is. I do no' ken what would've happened, if the auld lady's servant had no' come burst-ing in, sobbing and raving about Lady Evaline. That must've been so horrible, seeing her fall like that.'

'It was,' Rhiannon admitted. 'I wish she had no' done it. I canna help feeling it was my fault. If only I'd been quicker, happen I could've caught her or something.'

'Ye probably all would've fallen then, Blackthorn's no' strong enough to carry such a load.'

'Aye, happen so . . . still, I wish she hadna done it.' Rhi-annon pressed Lewen's arms about her more firmly, the star amulet pressing into the tender flesh between her breasts.

Lewen kissed her temple and went on. 'Anyway, after that, the laird had to change his tune. He acted all shocked and distressed and pretended he kent naught about it. He put the whole thing onto Lady Evaline and her companion. Miss Prunella confessed to helping the seneschal kidnap thirty-four boys over the past twenty-five years, and to helping him dispose o' them when they failed to make Lady Evaline happy. That was why they did it, she says. To make the auld lady happy.'

'And the laird is trying to pretend he's innocent in all this?'

'Very persuasively,' Lewen replied grimly. 'He has the reeve o' Linlithgorn more than half-convinced.'

'But I saw him!' Rhiannon said indignantly.

'Aye, but ye're no' the most credible witness, my love,' Lewen said. 'The laird has argued most compellingly that ye are trying to deflect suspicion away from yourself. Nina and Iven have had to admit, most unwillingly, that they never actually saw the laird's face. Ye were the only one.'

'What about his eye?' Rhiannon cried. 'How does he explain Blackthorn putting out his eye?'

'He says the seneschal did it. He said he'd been worried and suspicious about Irving for some time, since he was often no' there when the laird wanted him, and so he had lain in wait for him that night, wanting to see where he went and what he got up to. Except Irving pulled a sword on him and slashed him, and the laird was so sorely wounded he was unable to pursue him. The laird says Irving had been his brother's servant and was faithful to Lady Evaline, no' to him.'

'It's unbelievable!' Rhiannon was so angry and upset she sat up, and Lewen had to draw her down into his arms again.

'Unfortunately, it's all believable. For every accusation we've made, the laird has been able to come up with a most plausible explanation. And the fact that he has placed himself so willingly in the reeve's hands has worked in his favour too. All he asks for, he says, is a chance to go to the Rìgh's court and plead his case. He has offered to pay restitution to the grieving families for their loss, on behalf o' his sister-in-law, who he says was quite mad. He has offered to give any assistance he can to the Rìgh's officers in their investigation. All he asks for is a chance to clear his name.'

'It's very odd,' Rhiannon said after a moment. 'What about the necromancy?'

'Again, ye are the only one who saw that,' Lewen said unwillingly. 'Basically, he's put his word against yours. The reeve did find a chest full o' red cloaks, and black candles and so on, but that was hidden under the

530

seneschal's bed, and so Laird Malvern has been able to deny any knowledge o' it. A few o' the footmen have fled, and the auld groom, and a few others, making it seem as if they were the ones involved.'

'But I saw him! Laird Malvern! He called the ghost his brother.'

Lewen said nothing.

'But I'm a half-satyricorn accused o' murder and treason,' Rhiannon said glumly. 'And he's a laird.'

'The worst thing is, Miss Prunella, the auld lady's companion, canna be questioned about her role in all this anymore.'

'Why no'?'

'She's dead,' Lewen said shortly. 'She took poison . . . or someone gave it to her, we do no' ken which. We never thought . . . if we had only guessed what she planned, happen we could have stopped her somehow.'

Rhiannon was appalled. 'Ye mean, she just died? And now she canna tell anyone the truth o' it all?'

Lewen nodded. 'That's right. I canna help wondering how she got the poison. I swear the nursemaid Dedrie kens more than she's saying, but she's shut up tight as a clam and willna say a word, and neither will any o' the other servants. They have all been arrested too and face trial with the laird in Lucescere, but they do naught but swear their innocence most convincingly.'

'I guess they all fear the hangman's noose too,' Rhiannon said in an unhappy voice.

Lewen kissed her. 'They willna hang ye now, Rhiannon, surely? No' after ye saved Roden. He's heir to the Earl of Caerlaverock, after all, the Rìgh's dearest friend. Nina will testify on your behalf, and His Highness has a real soft spot for her, he's known her since she was a babe. I'm sure he'll pardon ye.'

'I hope so.' Rhiannon shivered.

'We ride for Lucescere tomorrow. We'll be there in a few weeks, and then we'll ken. Do no' fear, Rhiannon. With Nina and Iven and me all vouching for ye, the Rìgh canna condemn ye.'

'Well, we'll find out all too soon,' Rhiannon said. She looked up at the star-strung sky and the sliver of new moon hanging over the mountain. By the time the two moons were full, she would be in the Shining City, facing her fate. Despite Lewen's confidence, Rhiannon could not feel the same optimism. Satyricorns believed in dark walkers and fearsome gods. Happy endings were not part of their mythology. She had the space of one moon, though, to grasp what happiness she could. She slipped her hand under Lewen's shirt and caressed his bare back, her chain rattling.

'Since we are so tightly shackled together, do ye think Iven would notice if we slipped away to the forest? I have had enough o' ghosts and death. I want some warmth and loving.'

Lewen's breath caught and he bent his head and kissed her. 'I think he may turn a blind eye . . . for a wee while.'

'Let's go then,' she said and stood up, tugging him up by the chain fastened to his wrist. 'Though I think we'll need more than just a wee while.'

'Ye're a forward lass,' he said approvingly, getting up with alacrity. Hand-in-hand they went away from the flames and into the darkness of the wood, the chain swinging between them.

GLOSSARY

acolytes: students of witchcraft who have not yet passed their Second Test of Powers; usually aged between eight and sixteen.

ahdayeh: a series of exercises used as meditation in motion. Derived from the Khan'cohban art of fighting.

Annis: apprentice to Ashelma, the witch of Ardarchy.

apprentice-witch: a student of witchcraft who has passed the Second Test of Powers, usually undertaken at the age of sixteen.

arak: a small, monkey-like creature.

Arran: south-east land of Eileanan, ruled by the MacFóghnan clan.

Ashelma: the witch of Ardarchy.

Aslinn: deeply forested land, ruled by the MacAislin clan.

banprionnsa: princess or duchess.

banrìgh: queen.

Beltane: May Day; the first day of summer.

Ben Eyrie: third highest mountain in Eileanan; part of the Broken Ring of Dubhslain.

blaygird: evil, awful.

Blèssem: rich farmland south of Rionnagan, ruled by the MacThanach clan.

Blue Guards: the Yeomen of the Guard, the Rìgh's own elite company of soldiers. They act as his personal body-guard, both on the battlefield and in peacetime.

Brann the Raven: one of the First Coven of Witches. Known for probing the darker mysteries of magic, and for fascination with machinery and technology.

Broken Ring of Dubhslain: mountains which curve in a crescent around the highlands of Ravenshaw.

Bronwen NicCuinn: daughter of former Rìgh Jaspar Mac-Cuinn and Maya the Ensorcellor; she was named Banrìgh of Eileanan by her father on his deathbed but ruled for just six hours as a newborn baby, before Lachlan the Winged wrested the throne from her.

Candlemas: the end of winter and beginning of spring.

Carraig: land of the sea-witches, the northernmost land of Eileanan, ruled by the MacSeinn clan.

Celestines: race of faery creatures, renowned for empathic abilities and knowledge of stars and prophecy.

Clachan: southernmost land of Eileanan, a province of Rionnagan ruled by the MacCuinn clan.

claymore: a heavy, two-edged sword, often as tall as a man.

cluricaun: small woodland faery.

Connor: a Yeoman of the Guard. Was once a beggar-boy in Lucescere and member of the League of the Healing Hand.

corrigan: mountain faery with the power of assuming the look of a boulder. The most powerful can cast other illusions.

Coven of Witches: the central ruling body for witches in

Eileanan, led by the Keybearer and a council of twelve other sorcerers and sorceresses called the Circle. The Coven administers all rites and rituals in the worship of the universal life-force witches call Eà, runs schools and hospitals, and advises the Crown.

Craft: applications of the One Power through spells, incantations and magical objects.

The Cripple: leader of the rebellion against the rule of Jaspar and Maya.

Cuinn Lionheart: leader of the First Coven of Witches; his descendants are called MacCuinn.

Cunning: applications of the One Power through will and desire.

cunning man: village wise man or warlock.

cursehags: wicked faery race, prone to curses and evil spells. Known for their filthy personal habits.

dai-dein: father.

Day of Betrayal: the day Jaspar the Ensorcelled turned on the witches, exiling or executing them, and burning the Witch Towers.

Dedrie: healer at Fettercairn Castle; was formerly nurse-maid to Rory, the young son of Lord Falkner MacFerris.

Dide the Juggler: a jongleur who was rewarded for his part in Lachlan the Winged's successful rebellion by being made Didier Laverock, Earl of Caerlaverock. Is often called the Rìgh's minstrel.

Dillon of the Joyous Sword: captain of the Yeomen of the Guard. Was once a beggar-boy and captain of the League of the Healing Hand.

Donncan Feargus MacCuinn: eldest son of Lachlan Mac-Cuinn and Iseult NicFaghan. Has wings like a bird and can fly. Was named for Lachlan's two brothers, who were transformed into blackbirds by Maya the Ensorcellor.

Dughall MacBrann: the Prionnsa of Ravenshaw and cousin to the Rìgh.
Durward: Lord Malvern's bodyguard.

Eà: the Great Life Spirit, mother and father of all.
Eileanan: largest island in the archipelago called the Far Islands.
Elemental Powers: the forces of air, earth, fire, water and spirit which together make up the One Power.
Enit Silverthroat: grandmother of Dide and Nina; died at the Battle of Bonnyblair.
equinox: a time when day and night are of equal length, occurring twice a year.
Evaline NicKinney: widow of Lord Falkner MacFerris, former lord of Fettercairn Castle.

Fairge; Fairgean: faery creatures who need both sea and land to live.
Falkner MacFerris: former lord of Fettercairn Castle.
Fettercairn Castle: a fortress guarding the pass into the highlands of Ravenshaw, and the Tower of Ravens. Owned by the MacFerris clan.
Finn the Cat: nickname of Fionnghal NicRuraich.
Fionnghal NicRuraich: eldest daughter of Anghus MacRuraich of Rurach; was once a beggar-girl in Lucescere and lieutenant of the League of the Healing Hand.
First Coven of Witches: thirteen witches who fled persecution in their own land, invoking an ancient spell that folded the fabric of the universe and brought them and all their followers to Eileanan in a journey called the Great Crossing. The eleven great clans of Eileanan are all descended from the First Coven, with the MacCuinn clan being the greatest of the eleven. The thirteen witches

were Cuinn Lionheart, his son Owein of the Longbow, Ahearn Horse-laird, Aislinna the Dreamer, Berhtilde the Bright Warrior-Maid, Fóghnan the Thistle, Rùraich the Searcher, Seinneadair the Singer, Sian the Storm-Rider, Tuathanach the Farmer, Brann the Raven, Faodhagan the Red and his twin sister Sorcha the Bright (now called the Murderess).

Gearradh: goddess of death; of the Three Spinners, Gearradh is she who cuts the thread.
gillie: personal servant.
gillie-coise: bodyguard.
Gladrielle the Blue: the smaller of the two moons, lavender-blue in colour.
gravenings: ravenous creatures that nest and swarm together, steal lambs and chickens from farmers, and have been known to steal babies and young children. Will eat anything they can carry away in their claws. Collective noun is 'screech'.
Greycloaks: the Rìgh's army, so called because of their camouflaging cloaks.

Harriet: servant to Lady Evaline.
Hogmanay: New Year's Eve; an important celebration in the culture of Eileanan.
Horned Ones: another name for the satyricorns, a race of fierce horned faeries.

Irving: seneschal at Fettercairn Castle.
Isabeau the Shapechanger: Keybearer of the Coven; twin sister of the Banrìgh Iseult NicFaghan.
Iseult of the Snows: twin sister of Isabeau NicFaghan; Banrìgh of Eileanan by marriage to Lachlan the Winged.
Iven Yellowbeard: a jongleur and courier in the service of

Lachlan the Winged; was formerly a Yeoman of the Guard; married to Nina the Nightingale and father to Roden.

Jaspar MacCuinn: former Rìgh of Eileanan, often called Jaspar the Ensorcelled. Was married to Maya the Ensorcellor.

Jay the Fiddler: a minstrel in the service of Lachlan the Winged. Was once a beggar-lad in Lucescere and member of the League of the Healing Hand.

Johanna: a healer. Was once a beggar-girl in Lucescere and member of the League of the Healing Hand.

jongleur: a travelling minstrel, juggler, conjurer.

journeywitch: a travelling witch who performs rites for villages that do not have a witch, and seeks out children with magical powers who can be taken on as acolytes.

Kalea: a nisse.

Keybearer: the leader of the Coven of Witches.

Khan'cohbans: a faery race of war-like, snow-skimming nomads who live on the high mountains of the Spine of the World.

Lachlan the Winged: Rìgh of Eileanan.

The League of the Healing Hand: a band of beggar children who were instrumental in helping Lachlan the Winged win his throne.

leannan: sweetheart.

Lewen: an apprentice-witch and squire to Lachlan; son of Lilanthe of the Forest and Niall the Bear.

Lilanthe of the Forest: a tree-shifter; married to Niall the Bear, and mother to Lewen and Meriel.

loch; lochan (pl): lake.

Lucescere: ancient city built on an island above the

540

Shining Waters; the traditional home of the MacCuinns and the Tower of Two Moons.

Mac: son of

MacAhern: one of the eleven great clans; descendants of Ahearn the Horse-laird.

MacBrann: one of the eleven great clans; descendants of Brann the Raven.

MacCuinn: one of the eleven great clans, descendants of Cuinn Lionheart.

Magnysson the Red: the larger of the two moons, crimson-red in colour, commonly thought of as a symbol of war and conflict. Old tales describe him as a thwarted lover, chasing his lost love, Gladrielle, across the sky.

Malvern MacFerris: lord of Fettercairn Castle; brother of former lord Falkner MacFerris.

Maya the Ensorcellor: former Banrìgh of Eileanan, wife of Jaspar and mother of Bronwen; now known as Maya the Mute.

moonbane: a hallucinogenic drug distilled from the moonflower plant.

necromancy: the forbidden art of resurrecting the dead.

Niall the Bear: formerly a Yeoman of the Guard; now married to Lilanthe of the Forest, and father to Lewen and Meriel.

Nic: daughter of.

Nila: King of the Fairgean; half-brother of Maya the Ensorcellor.

Nina the Nightingale: jongleur and sorceress of the Coven; sister to Didier Laverock, earl of Caerlaverock, and granddaughter of Enit Silverthroat.

nisse: small woodland faery.

Olwynne NicCuinn: daughter of Lachlan MacCuinn and Iseult NicFaghan; twin sister of Owein.

One Power: the life-energy that is contained in all things. Witches draw upon the One Power to perform their acts of magic. The One Power contains all the elemental forces of air, earth, water, fire and spirit, and witches are usually more powerful in one force than others.

Owein MacCuinn: second son of Lachlan MacCuinn and Iseult NicFaghan; twin brother of Olwynne. Has wings like a bird.

prionnsa; prionnsachan (pl): prince, duke.

Ravenscraig: estate of the MacBrann clan. Once their hunting castle, but they moved their home there after Rhyssmadill fell into ruin.

Ravenshaw: deeply forested land west of Rionnagan, ruled by the MacBrann clan, descendants of Brann, one of the First Coven of Witches.

Razor's Edge: dangerous path through the mountains of the Broken Ring of Dubhslain, only used in times of great need.

Red Guards: soldiers in service to Maya the Ensorcellor during her reign as Banrìgh.

Rhiannon: a half-satyricorn; daughter of One-Horn and a captured human.

Rhyssmadill: the Rìgh's castle by the sea, once owned by the MacBrann clan.

rìgh; rìghrean (pl): king.

Rionnagan: together with Clachan and Blèssem, the richest lands in Eileanan. Ruled by MacCuinns, descendants of Cuinn Lionheart, leader of the First Coven of Witches.

Roden: son of Nina the Nightingale and Iven Yellowbeard; Viscount Laverock of Caerlaverock.

Rory: deceased son of Lord Falkner MacFerris of Fetter-cairn and Lady Evaline NicKinney.

Rurach: wild mountainous land lying between Tìreich and Siantan, and ruled by the MacRuraich clan.

sabre-leopard: savage feline with curved fangs that lives in the remote mountain areas.

sacred woods: ash, hazel, oak, rowan, fir, hawthorn, and yew.

Samhain: first day of winter; festival for the souls of the dead. Best time of year to see the future.

satyricorn: a race of fierce horned faeries.

scrying: to perceive through crystal gazing or other focus. Most witches can scry if the object to be perceived is well known to them.

Seekers: a force created by former Rìgh Jaspar the Ensorcelled to find those with magical abilities so they could be tried and executed.

seelie: tall, shy race of faeries known for their physical beauty and magical skills.

seneschal: steward.

sennachie: genealogist and record-keeper of the clan chief's house.

sgian dubh: small knife worn in the boot.

Siantan: north-west land of Eileanan, famous for its weather witches. Ruled by the MacSian clan.

skeelie: a village witch or wise woman.

Skill: a common application of magic, such as lighting a candle or dowsing for water.

Spinners: goddesses of fate. Include the spinner Sniomhar, the goddess of birth; the weaver Breabadair, goddess of life; and she who cuts the thread, Gearradh, goddess of death.

Talent: the combination of a witch's strengths in the different forces often manifest as a particularly powerful Talent; for example, Lewen's Talent is in working with wood and Nina's is in singing.

Test of Elements: once a witch is fully accepted into the coven at the age of twenty-four, they learn Skills in the element in which they are strongest, i.e. air, earth, fire, water, or spirit. The First Test of any element wins them a ring which is worn on the right hand. If they pass the Third Test in any one element, the witch is called a sorcerer or sorceress, and wears a ring on their left hand. It is very rare for any witch to win a sorceress ring in more than one element.

Test of Powers: a witch is first tested on his or her eighth birthday, and if any magical powers are detected, he or she becomes an acolyte. On their sixteenth birthday, witches undertake the Second Test of Powers, in which they must make a moonstone ring and witch's dagger. If they pass, they are permitted to become an apprentice. On their twenty-fourth birthday, witches undertake the Third Test of Powers, in which they must remake their dagger and cut and polish a staff. If successfully completed, the apprentice is admitted into the Coven of Witches. Apprentices wear black robes; witches wear white robes.

Theurgia: a school for acolytes and apprentice-witches at the Tower of Two Moons in Lucescere.

thigearn: horse-lairds who ride flying horses.

Tireich: land of the horse-lairds. Most westerly country of Eileanan, ruled by the MacAhern clan.

Tìrlethan: land of the Twins; ruled by the MacFaghan clan.

Tìrsoilleir: the Bright Land or the Forbidden Land. North-east land of Eileanan, ruled by the MacHilde clan.

Tòmas the Healer: boy with healing powers, who saved

the lives of thousands of soldiers during the Bright Wars; died saving Lachlan's life at the Battle of Bonnyblair.

The Towers of the Witches: Thirteen towers built as centres of learning and witchcraft in the twelve lands of Eileanan. Most are now ruined, but the Tower of Two Moons in Lucescere has been restored as the home of the Coven of Witches and its school, the Theurgia. The Coven hope to rebuild the thirteen High Towers but also to encourage towns and regions to build their own towers.

tree-changer: woodland faery that can shift shape from tree to humanlike creature. A half-breed is called a *tree-shifter* and can sometimes look almost human.

trictrac: a form of backgammon.

uile-bheist; uile-bheistean (pl): monster

Yedda: sea-witches.

Yeomen of the Guard: Also known as the Blue Guards. The Rìgh's own personal bodyguard, responsible for his safety.

DARK WINGS

Olwynne sat bolt upright in her bed, choking back a
scream. For a moment her nightmare beat around
her head with dark, suffocating wings. Then the dream
dissolved away, leaving her with little more than an
impression of overwhelming grief and horror.

The air was cold on her damp skin, and she pulled her
eiderdown up around her, trying her best to remember the
dream. Her aunt Isabeau said she should pay attention to
her dreams, that they were often messages sent to warn or
teach or illuminate. All Olwynne could remember,
though, was her father falling away from her into some
dark pit, his black wings bent over his face, and then
ravens, thousands of ravens, descending from the sky to
peck out her eyes.

She shuddered and lay back down again, pulling her
eiderdown over her head. The wind was keening round
her windows, rattling the old leaded glass in its frame,
and sighing through the trees outside. It sounded like
banshees wailing. Olwynne told herself it was only the

wind, but all the hairs on her body stood erect and quivering, and her pulse rate accelerated. Such a feeling of morbid foreboding came over she almost cried out again, but she bit her lip and wrapped her arms about her knees, her face pressed into her pillow. Still the strange, high wailing went on. As it grew louder, slowly Olwynne realised that it was not the wind making that unearthly keening cry but something else. Something living.

Shivering uncontrollably, Olwynne crept out of bed and went to stand by her window, pulling the curtain back a crack so she could peer out. It was a clear, starry night, with both the moons at the full. The sky was full of flying things, a whirling hurricane of bat-winged creatures that seemed to beat themselves against the bright coins of the moons like moths against the glass of a lantern. As they hurled themselves through the night sky, they screamed and sobbed, tearing at their wild manes of hair, beating themselves on their heads and breasts.

Olwynne stood transfixed. She had seen the nyx fly before, on nights when the moons were full, but never had she seen so many hundreds before, and never had she heard them sing. It was a lament of such wild grief that Olwynne felt tears start to her own eyes, and her breath catch in her throat. Though she did not know why they sorrowed, Olwynne slowly slid down to the floor and wept with them.

By the time daybreak came, creeping through the trees like smoke, the nyx had all gone. Olwynne released her clutch on her curtains and stood up stiffly. She was very cold. She dressed herself in the long black gown of an apprentice-witch, then splashed her face vigorously with water. She combed back her sleep-tossed hair into its usual long, severe plait and wrapped her plaid tightly about her body. Still she felt cold and stiff and weary, but she had been taught to ignore the demands of her body. Moving very quietly she opened the door to her little cell of a room, and stepped out into the balcony that ran the length of the building. Everything was deathly quiet. It was too early for the bell to have sounded to wake up the students. Only the occasional bird called out.

Olwynne went swiftly along the balcony and through a doorway into the Theurgia. She negotiated a number of stairs and corridors, coming at last to the northernmost tower, the building assigned to the Circle of Sorcerers. A magnificent spiral staircase wound up the centre of the tower, its stonework carved with the crescent shape of two moons and a single star, set amid intricate knotwork. Olwynne climbed the staircase all the way to the top floor, her feet settling into deep hollows worn in the centre of each step. Her aunt Isabeau had her rooms up here, far away from the noise and bustle of the Theurgia.

Olwynne stood for a while outside her aunt's door, listening. Although she was sure Isabeau would be awake, she hesitated to interrupt her. It was very early. Just as she raised her hand hesitantly to knock, the door opened and Isabeau stood in the doorway, smiling at her.

'Morning, Olwynne,' she said. 'Come in. The kettle is just boiling. Would ye like some tea?'

Olwynne nodded and came in shyly. She looked about her with pleasure as Isabeau went and swung the steaming kettle off the fire. She loved the Keybearer's room. Shaped like a bluntly pointed crescent moon, it took up half the top floor of the tower. There was a fireplace at either point of the crescent, one to warm the bed with its soft white counterpane and pillows, the other to warm Isabeau's desk and chair where she worked. Comfortable chairs upholstered in blue were drawn up before either fire. A spinning wheel was set up near one, with a little loom pushed up against the wall. A tapestry was half-woven upon it. Olwynne could see the pointed towers of Rhyssmadill overlooking a stormy sea, and wondered what Isabeau was weaving. Olwynne knew she loved to spin and weave the old tales and songs, but had little time for it with all her other duties as Keybearer of the Coven.

At the other end of the room, where Isabeau was busy making the tea, her desk was piled with papers and books. An old globe, so stained with age the lands upon it could hardly be seen, stood upon a wooden stand nearby. A crystal ball glowed softly to one side, set upon clawed feet. More books filled the bookshelves which rose from floor to ceiling all round the curve of the room. Set at regular intervals between the bookshelves were tall windows which looked out across the gardens to the golden domes of the palace, gleaming softly through the morning mist.

The windows were open and long white curtains drifted and twirled in the dawn breeze. More curtains draped the four-poster bed, but they were so light they would not cut out the air like most bed-curtains but simply shield the sleeper from night-insects. The bed was still unmade, but the Keybearer was dressed in her long white gown trimmed with silver, and her hair was neatly combed and bound away from her face. Once her hair would have been the same fiery red as Olwynne's, but its colour had faded to a soft strawberry blonde, with grey at the temples. Her eyes were as vivid a blue as ever, however, and her figure was still slim and upright.

Isabeau poured the tea into two delicate bone-china cups and beckoned to Olwynne to come and sit by the fire. Olwynne obeyed with alacrity, for she was still cold and shaken. She held the cup between both her hands and sipped the hot liquid, feeling some of her tension drain away.

'Ye heard the nyx fly?' Isabeau said tranquilly.

Olwynne nodded.

'Aye, it was uncanny, was it no'? I have never heard such a lament. It made all my skin come up in goose-bumps.'

'Me too,' Olwynne said eagerly. 'Aunty Beau . . . what was wrong? Why did they fly and sing like that?'

'Ceit Anna is dead,' Isabeau said after a moment, her face shadowing.

Olwynne lowered her cup. Although she knew of the oldest of all the nyx, who lived in a cave deep under the sewers of the palace, she herself had never seen the ancient faery. Stories were always told of her, though. Ceit Anna had woven the cloak of illusions that had kept Lachlan MacCuinn, the Rìgh and Olwynne's father, hidden in the shape of a hunchback for so many years. She had woven it from her own hair, as she had woven a pair of gloves to conceal the magical hands of Tòmas the Healer, and as she had woven the choker that kept Maya the Ensorcellor mute and powerless. Ceit Anna appeared in many of the MacCuinn clan's stories, and Olwynne knew her death would be greatly regretted, for she had been the most powerful and influential of all the nyx.

'The nyx live very long lives,' Isabeau said. 'I certainly have never heard the death flight afore, and I ken none who have. I was just reading about it in the Book o' Shadows.' She indicated the old and enormously thick book which lay open on her desk nearby. 'The last time one was recorded during the time o' Feargus the Terrible, when Aldus the Dreamy was Keybearer. O' course, we ken many nyx died during the Burning, but if the death-flight was flown, there was certainly no-one around to record it.'

Olwynne was silent.

Isabeau looked at her intently then bent forward to lay one hand on her knee. 'What is troubling ye so much, my dear? Is it just the funeral song o' the nyx or is there more?'

Olwynne shrugged and looked away, embarrassed her aunt could read her so clearly.

'Are ye still having those nightmares?' Isabeau asked.

Olwynne nodded, fiddling with her cup. 'Last night I was attacked by a flock o' ravens, hundreds o' them, beating all round my head and trying to peck out my eyes. All I could see was their black wings, and all I could hear was their screeches in my ear.'

'Ravens,' Isabeau repeated, her brows drawing together.

Olwynne nodded. 'I thought at first, when I saw the nyx flying last night, that it was their wings I had dreamt, all those black wings against the moon. And it seemed I had dreamt that too, only . . . it is so hard to remember. For there are other wings in my dreams. My father's wings. And Donncan's too, turning all black like *dai-dein's*. A dark shadow falling on him . . . like the shadow o' wings . . . or happen a black cloak . . . or a shroud. Sometimes I'm being suffocated by feathers. Or maybe I'm buried alive, in a tomb. Or Donncan is, I canna always tell. It doesna make sense. And I wake with this horrible sense o' foreboding, like something awful is going to happen, and happen soon . . .' Her voice trailed away.

'Can ye remember anything else?'

'*Dai-dein* falling into a dark pit . . . just falling . . . though sometimes it is me falling . . . or Bronwen. I dream o' Bronwen too.' Olwynne's voice quickened. 'I dreamt o' her diving off a high cliff and falling too, falling hundreds o' feet. And she was crying, I'm sure o' it. A waterfall o' tears. And I dream o' her and Donncan drowning in a great pool o' blackness, like ink spreading in water . . .' Her voice trailed away.

Isabeau's frown deepened. 'I have dreamt o' ravens also,' she said at last. 'Though I ken o' disturbing news from Ravenshaw, which could well have fed into my dreams, while ye have no'. I think your dreams are truly prophetic, though I fear what they foretell.'

'What news from Ravenshaw?' Olwynne asked. Her voice rose. 'News o' Lewen? Is all well?'

Isabeau smoothed the snowy folds of her gown over her knee. 'Lewen is well. He is on his way back to Lucescere. I expect him any day now.'

'But he is connected to your dreams o' ravens somehow, is he no'?' Olwynne demanded. 'What is wrong?'

Isabeau smiled rather ruefully. 'Ye have guessed it. Lewen is very much involved in these happenings in Ravenshaw, and I must admit he has been much on my mind as a consequence. I may as well tell ye, the tattle-mongers will have the news soon enough anyway.'

'Tell me what?'

'Lewen was to travel back to Lucescere with Nina and her caravan, as ye ken. On their journey they somehow stumbled on a plot to raise the ghost o' the dead laird o' Fettercairn, which you may remember is the castle that guards the way to the Tower o' Ravens. Some necromancers were using the Heart o' Stars at the tower to open a gate between this world and the world o' spirits, and it seems they have raised a stronger spirit than they meant to. I have no' got many more details than that, so I am naturally eager to question Lewen and this girl who saw the necromancers . . .'

'Girl?'

Isabeau looked at Olwynne sharply. 'Aye, some lass from the Broken Ring o' Dubhslain. She is named Rhiannon, I believe, and she rides a black winged horse . . .'

'More black wings,' Olwynne said hollowly. 'Is it her coming that I foretell? For I swear I can see only evil ahead.'

'I do no' ken,' Isabeau said, sounding troubled. 'Olwynne, how long have these nightmares been haunting ye?'

She shrugged irritably. 'I dinna ken. It feels like forever.'

'Ye first spoke to me about a dark dream on the night o' the spring equinox. Was that the first such dream?'

Olwynne moved jerkily. 'I dinna ken. Happen so. I dinna remember.'

'Your floor mistress tells me ye have woken several times screaming in your sleep since then. How often do the dreams come, Olwynne?'

'Every night,' Olwynne answered wearily. 'I have tried no' to sleep, but I'm always too tired and fall asleep anyway. I've tried taking powdered valerian roots and drinking chamomile tea to help me sleep more deeply, but it doesna work. It just makes things worse, for I canna wake myself when the dream gets too bad, and when I finally do wake, I'm groggy and sick.'

'I can close your third eye for ye,' Isabeau said gently. 'At least for a night or two, to help ye rest. Ye look exhausted, Olwynne, and they tell me your school work is suffering.'

Olwynne gazed at her aunt in dumb wonder. She could not believe her aunt knew so much about her when Isabeau was so busy with the work of the Coven. Olwynne's own mother did not know about the nightmares. She thought about what the Keybearer had offered and, after a moment, reluctantly shook her head. 'Ye say such dreams are sent as warnings, or messages. Should I no' listen and try and understand?'

Isabeau nodded. 'Aye, I do think so, under normal circumstances. But ye are still only an apprentice-witch, Olwynne, and ye have had a month o' it now. I worry about your health and about your schooling. Ye have been doing so well, I do no' want ye to fall behind.'

'It comes soon,' Olwynne said. 'Whatever it is will happen soon.'

There was a long silence. Then Isabeau stood up, one hand going up to grip the Key which hung on a ribbon round her neck. 'Then happen we should try and find out more while we can,' she said forcefully. 'I will get Ghislaine Dreamwalker to meditate with ye and see if she can travel the dream-road with ye. I should have done so weeks ago. I am sorry, it is just we have been so very busy.'

Olwynne knew everyone had been preoccupied with her brother Donncan's upcoming wedding to their cousin Bronwen, daughter of the Ensorcellor. She had not thought she had minded, but at Isabeau's words she felt a little knot of tension behind her breastbone loosen. She muttered a thank you, hoping Isabeau's witch-senses would understand just how grateful she really was.

'Now I think ye should go back to bed for a while. I'll write a pass for ye, excusing ye from the morning's classes. Then a walk in the fresh air and a proper lunch will do ye the most good, I think. Come, I'll walk ye back to your room.'

'Och, there's no need, I'm fine, really,' Olwynne gabbled, ashamed that she was trespassing on her aunt's good nature.

'It's no trouble. I wish to walk through the library anyway, and it's on the way. I'll be glad o' your company.'

Olwynne smiled shyly and stood up, putting her cup down on the little table. Isabeau went to her desk and shut the Book of Shadows reverently, then called to her familiar, the elf-owl Buba, who slept on the back of the chair, with her head sunk down into her wings. *Come-hooh with me-hooh?* Isabeau said in owl language. Buba opened her eyes sleepily, stared at Isabeau a moment, then flew to perch on her shoulder. She was tiny, no bigger than a sparrow, and white as snow.

Owl-hooh come too-hooh, she answered and rotated her head round so she could stare unnervingly at Olwynne. *Why-hooh you-hooh fret-hooh?*

I fear-hooh, but what-hooh, I know not-hooh, Isabeau answered.

She did look troubled, Olwynne thought, as she followed Isabeau out of her room and down the stairs. The Keybearer's face was pale and strained, and the little frown between her brows had not smoothed away. She kept one hand cupped round the talisman she wore at her neck, almost as if drawing strength from it. As they approached the library, which took up all of the great building between the northern and eastern towers, her pace quickened noticeably.

It was still too early for any of the witches or apprentices to be up and about yet, though Olwynne could hear sounds from the kitchen wing as the servants began to prepare the morning repast. Isabeau opened the heavy door into the library and they went into the long, dark room together. The lanterns all sprang into life at once, and the kindling laid ready in the fireplaces at either end blazed up into dancing warmth. Olwynne glanced at her aunt enviously. Olwynne wished she had such a ready facility with flame. Her strengths were in the elements of water and earth, not fire, and she had to concentrate hard to light a candle, or bring witch-light. Isabeau had not even flickered an eyelid, let alone waved a finger, all her attention focused on the glass cabinets lined up against the walls, in little alcoves surrounded by towering bookshelves.

These cabinets were used to display old relics and artifacts that might interest the students, or help them in their lessons. There were ancient scrolls, fragile as skin, old maps of other lands and other worlds, suits of armour, famous weapons and jewels, a clàrsach that was said to have belonged to Seinneadair the Singer, even the cast-off skin of a harlequin-hydra, its scaly coils glittering in the light, its hundreds of heads pinned up against the wall.

Isabeau strode straight to a glass cabinet on the far side of the room. She stood there in silence for a long time. Olwynne stood beside her. As far as she could see, the cabinet contained nothing but an old stick. It had not been cleaned for a long time, for the floor of the cabinet was thick with dust.

'What is it? What's wrong?' Olwynne asked at last, conscious of the tension in her aunt's slim body.

'This cabinet had your father's cloak o' illusions hanging in it,' Isabeau said tersely. 'That is his crutch. When I first met him, he had naught but the cloak and an auld stick to lean on. No' a stitch o' clothing, nor a knife or bowl, nothing. I gave him my spare pair o' breeches to wear, and much too tight they were for him too.'

Olwynne was puzzled. 'So where's the cloak now?' she asked.

'Gone,' Isabeau said. She waved one hand before the cabinet's lock and a symbol of blue fire flared up for a moment. Olwynne recognised a ward of protection.

'No-one could have stolen it, for the lock has not been tampered with.'

'So where's it gone then?' Olwynne simply could not understand her aunt's tension. Although she knew it had some historical interest, as a relic from the days when her father had been a rebel fighting to overthrow the Ensorcellor, it was nothing but a hairy old cloak that probably smelt horrible. Her father had worn it day in, day out, for years, to conceal the wings and claws he had been left with after being transformed from a blackbird back into a man. He had not been able to discard it until he had at last won the throne back from the Ensorcellor, and by that time, Olwynne guessed, he had probably never wanted to see it again.

Isabeau pointed to the pile of black dust on the cabinet floor. 'I imagine that's the remains o' the cloak there.'

'All that dust? How come?'

'Ceit Anna wove that cloak for your father, Olwynne, from her own hair,' Isabeau said impatiently. 'It took her seven days and seven nights, and he wore it for seven long years. It was a weaving o' great power. And now it is dust. All this time it has hung here, so people could remember the time when one o' the MacCuinn clan had to hide himself beneath a cloak o' illusions to avoid being hunted down and killed. All this time, and now it is dust. Why? Why now?'

Olwynne shrugged. 'It's been a long time. It must be twenty-four years or more, for *Dai-dein* won the throne no' long before Donncan was born.'

Isabeau turned and pointed to a tiny pink silk dress and cap in another cabinet nearby. 'That dress belonged to Meghan o' the Beasts as a child. It is much more than four hundred years auld. Why has it no' dissolved too, then?'

Olwynne's cheeks heated. 'I dinna ken.'

'Olwynne, have ye forgotten? Ceit Anna died last night. The cloak was hanging there yesterday, yet now it is gone.'

'Ye think it dissolved because Ceit Anna died?' Olwynne asked.

Isabeau nodded. 'Aye, I do. I must admit, I came because I wondered if her magic would outlast her life.'

'What a shame,' Olwynne said. 'I suppose ye'll have to find something else for the cabinet now.'

Isabeau clicked her tongue in exasperation and Buba swivelled her head to stare at Olwynne out of her round, golden eyes. 'Ye have no' considered, lassie. Think! What else did Ceit Anna weave for us, that we may regret dissolving?'

Olwynne's eyes widened in a look of horror. 'The Ensorcellor's ribbon, that binds her throat!'

'Aye! If Maya's powers are returned to her, just now, when Bronwen and Donncan are no' yet married, and there is still so much controversy over who truly has the right to rule . . .'

Olwynne felt a cold clutch of fear. Although she saw Maya the Ensorcellor nearly every day – a thin, scarred, middle-aged woman who could communicate only by sign-language and the writing of messages on a little slate she wore at her waist – Olwynne did not underestimate the power of the one-time ruler of the land. She had been brought up on the horror stories of the days of the Burning, when the Coven had been thrown down, its towers destroyed, and witches hunted mercilessly to death all over the country. She knew Maya's powers were so strong and so subtle she had ensorcelled many a sorcerer into doing her bidding, and had been able to sway crowds of thousands to her will. Maya had only been controlled by the binding of her tongue to silence. Olwynne could not even begin to imagine what might happen if she found that ensorcellor's tongue again.

Olwynne's father, Lachlan MacCuinn, had won the throne from Maya after the death of his brother and her husband, Jaspar. At that time, Bronwen had been only a babe-in-arms and the land had been rent by civil war. Everyone had been relieved to have a strong leader occupying the throne, and those that had argued that Bronwen was by birth-right the true heir to the throne had been pacified by her betrothal a few years later to her cousin Donncan, Olwynne's elder brother. If Bronwen had been a meek and biddable girl, the matter may well have ended there.

However, the Ensorcellor's daughter had inherited her mother's imperious will and mysterious charm as well as her wild, fey beauty. In the six months since she had turned twenty-four, the age she would have assumed the throne, Bronwen had turned the court upside down with her antics. There had been much rumour and speculation that the betrothal between the two rival heirs to the throne might fail. Olwynne knew that her parents were angry and concerned, and her brother Donncan furious and miserable, but the implications were far more serious than mere unhappiness within the family.

There were those who envied the MacCuinn clan's power, or hated the witches, or passionately believed that Bronwen, as the only child of the former Rìgh, was the true heir. If the cousins failed to marry, there was a strong chance that civil unrest may again trouble the land. Olwynne could only shudder at the thought of the turmoil Maya, unbound and vindictive, could cause.

'We had best go and see Maya at once,' Isabeau said. 'Happen she is still sleeping. It is early still.'

Olwynne nodded. She hurried after Isabeau as the Key-bearer strode through the library and across the garth to the servants' wing. Though the other wings remained shuttered and quiet, the clanging of pots and pans, the gurgling of water, and the sound of voices and laughter did not bode well. The witches' servants were used to waking early, for many rites took place at dawn and the witches were always keen for their breakfast afterwards.

Maya had a little dark closet of a room on the second storey, tucked in behind the stairwell. Olwynne felt no pity for her. Her own room in the southern wing was not much bigger, and she was the Rìgh's daughter. Many doors along the corridor stood open, as serving-girls bustled in and out with jugs of hot water, or stood in the doorway, gossiping, as they combed back their hair. They all fell silent as Isabeau came past, dropping curtsies, and murmuring respectful greetings. Isabeau nodded and smiled at them, but hurried on, Olwynne trailing close behind. Behind them rose a hum of curiosity.

Maya's door was shut. Isabeau rapped on it smartly. There was a short silence, then the former Banrìgh opened the door a crack, and looked out.

She was dressed, as usual, in a plain black gown, very like the apprentice's robe Olwynne wore, only hers was covered with a long brown apron. Her graying hair was pinned back under a plain white cap. One side of her face was badly scarred, while the prominent knuckles of the webbed hand holding the door were red and swollen with hard work. She looked old and tired and sad.

'Maya, I'm glad ye're awake,' Isabeau said. 'I need to speak with ye. May I come in?'

Maya raised an eyebrow.

'I wish to examine your nyx-hair ribbon,' Isabeau said bluntly.

With an eloquent gesture, Maya lifted one hand towards the black ribbon bound about her throat.

'I do no' wish to do it standing in the corridor,' Isabeau said impatiently. 'Why will ye no' let me in?'

Maya shrugged and stood back, allowing Isabeau and Olwynne to step into her room.

'Perhaps because she wishes to retain some illusion o' privacy,' a lilting, musical voice said very sweetly.

Bronwen was sitting on the edge of the dressing-table, swinging one foot. She was dressed in a diaphanous gown that exactly matched the soft blue of her eyes. The gown was tied over one shoulder with nothing more than a silver ribbon, leaving her arms and shoulders bare. Her skin gleamed with subtle scales, and frills of fins ran from the inside of her elbows to her wrists. Though her gown was loose, the slim naked curves of her body glimmered through the transparent cloth, a few flowers of appliquéd beading the only thing retaining any measure of modesty. Her hair hung down her back like a silk curtain, tied here and there with more silver ribbons and pinned with a diamond-winged butterfly.

'Bronwen!' Isabeau cried. 'What are ye doing here?'

'Visiting my mother. Or is that no' allowed?'

'At the crack o' dawn?'

'My mother works from sun-up to midnight, and is rarely allowed any breaks. When else am I to see her?'

'Oh, Bronwen, dinna exaggerate! She is no' a slave! She has plenty o' free time, like anyone else who works in the service o' the Coven.'

'A few hours once a week. I happen to wish to see my mother more often than that, and preferably when she is no' worn out and exhausted by her work.'

'Bronwen, ye ken ye can see your mother whenever ye want,' Isabeau said in exasperation. 'I would've thought midday a far more civilized time to come calling. Maya has a lunch-break, just like anyone else does, and ye could have gone into the gardens and eaten together.'

'Och, aye, the gardens at lunchtime. Very private, with five hundred squalling students running around.'

'I'm sure ye o' all people would be able to find a quiet corner,' Olwynne said.

Isabeau glanced at her with a slight frown, and she subsided. Bronwen tossed her head, shot Olwynne a sharp-edged look, and then smiled, as if deciding to accept the comment as a compliment.

Meanwhile, her mother had been standing silently by the wall, her hands folded together, her face impassive.

'Maya, I need to look at your ribbon,' Isabeau said.

'Why?' Bronwen cried at once. 'What has my poor mother done to warrant this . . . this intrusion . . .'

'Oh, Bronny, pipe down,' Isabeau said. 'I just need to make sure all is well. There's no need for these histrionics. It'll only take a moment.'

Maya inclined her head, allowing her hands to fall down beside her body. Isabeau led her to sit in the only chair, flame uncurling from the wick of every candle in the room. It was certainly a dark, gloomy little room, and even the candlelight failed to alleviate all the shadows. With an impatient gesture, Isabeau conjured a ball of light to hang above the mute woman's head, casting a strong steady light down upon her. Olwynne could clearly see the scaly texture of her skin, the network of scars marring one sunken cheek, and the flat slits of gills that fluttered slightly under her ears. Maya kept her face lowered as Isabeau carefully felt right round the black braid of ribbon bound about her throat. Isabeau was frowning, and Olwynne felt a sudden rise in tension. She glanced at Bronwen, who grimaced at her and stretched out one elegant hand to examine her nails.

Isabeau stood back. 'Maya, did aught untoward happen last night?'

Maya looked up at her and shrugged. She lifted the little slate hung from her belt and rapidly wrote, 'Heard nyx fly over,' with a piece of chalk she carried in her apron pocket.

'The sound woke ye?'

Maya put one hand behind her ear, then folded both hands and rested her head upon them, closing her eyes.

'But then ye went back to sleep?'

Maya nodded.

'Naught else?'

Maya shook her head.

'Very well. Thank ye. I'm sorry to have intruded upon your privacy.' Isabeau cast a mocking glance at Bronwen, who gave another expressive little grimace and jumped to her feet.

'Let me show ye out,' she said sweetly.

'Och, thanks, but I think we can find our way,' Isabeau answered. 'Come on, Olwynne, ye'll be late to breakfast if ye do no' hurry. See ye soon,' she said to both Maya and Bronwen with a nod and a little smile, and led the way out of the narrow, cheerless room, the witch-light winking out behind her.

The corridor was empty now, all the other servants gone to their work. Olwynne was able to ask, 'So the ribbon is still intact? Everything's all right?'

'The ribbon is very much intact, and I felt a tingle o' magic, as I should,' Isabeau said slowly.

'So, everything's all right? No need to fear?'

'I'm no' sure,' Isabeau answered. 'Things did no' feel right. It was a powerful spell Ceit Anna wrought for us, and nyx magic is strange and unknowable, I had always thought. Yet . . . the magic I felt seemed simple enough – spells o' binding and silence. And though there was magic enough that my fingertips still tingle, somehow . . .'

'What?'

The Keybearer shrugged. 'I dinna ken. It is a very long time since I last touched the ribbon. I do no' remember how it should feel.'

'As long as it's still intact, and the magic holds,' Olwynne said.

'Aye,' Isabeau agreed, her frown deepening. 'So long as the magic still holds.'

G.L. 12.12.05.

TIM COPE

ON THE TRAIL *of*

GENGHIS KHAN

AN EPIC JOURNEY THROUGH THE LAND OF THE NOMADS

BLOOMSBURY

LONDON · NEW DELHI · NEW YORK · SYDNEY

First published in Great Britain in 2013

Copyright © 2013 by Tim Cope
Cartography by Will Pringle

All photographs copyright © the Tim Cope collection unless otherwise credited

Bloomsbury Publishing Plc
50 Bedford Square
London
WC1B 3DP

www.bloomsbury.com

Bloomsbury Publishing, London, New Delhi, New York and Sydney

A CIP catalogue record for this book is available from the British Library

Hardback ISBN 978 1 4088 2505 1
Trade paperback ISBN 978 1 4088 4221 8

10 9 8 7 6 5 4 3 2 1

Printed and bound in Great Britain by CPI Group (UK) Ltd, Croydon CR0 4YY

MIX
Paper from
responsible sources
FSC   FSC® C020471
www.fsc.org

DEDICATION

IN JUNE 2004, at the age of twenty-five, I set out to ride on horseback from Mongolia to Hungary, approximately 10,000 km, across the Eurasian steppe. I called it the "Trail of Genghis Khan," referring to the inspiration I found in the nomadic Mongols, who under Genghis Khan set out to build the largest land empire in history. The aim of my journey was to honor and understand those who have lived on the steppes with their horses for thousands of years, carrying on a nomadic way of life.

When I reached the Danube more than three years later, in autumn 2007, one of the common questions people asked me was, "How did you cope for so long alone?" The truth is that I never thought of myself as being entirely alone. With me were my family of horses, two of whom, Taskonir and Ogonyok, carried me most of the way. Then there was Tigon, my Kazakh dog, who accompanied me on his own four feet. My animals were on the front line of this journey, bearing the brunt of the extremes of cold and heat, traversing deserts and mountains, and being subjected to the consequences of bungled bureaucracy and even horse thievery. It was through them I came to experience the tapestry of the Eurasian steppe, and in retrospect, I can think of no better explanation for my journey than the reward of riding with my steeds, Tigon running by their hooves, as we sailed over open steppe, where nothing—not thoughts, feelings, time, the earth, or animals—was fenced in.

It is also true that the journey would have been meaningless without the many individuals and families I met, several of whom joined me for parts of the way, and more than one hundred of whom took me and my animals in. Some of my hosts were desperately poor, others were rich, and many were afflicted by alcoholism or even involved in corruption and crime, but most cared for me like I was a friend and shared their food, fodder, and shelter generously—sometimes, as it turned out, for weeks and months. To be welcomed with a smile by a stranger after many

days of hard riding, even though I was usually in a state of disrepair, provided a sense of camaraderie and closeness that not only enriched my life
but in some cases saved me and the lives of my animals.

All of my hosts also shared the story of the circumstances of their lives,
their culture, and their history with great honesty and openness. I realized later on that in some of them I had met the modern guardians of the
steppe—those special people who are driving the culture into the future,
fueling the pride of the nomad, saving the traditions, and keeping the
memory of their ancestors alive.

This book is dedicated to all of these people I met on the Eurasian
steppe, and to my animals.

CONTENTS

UKRAINE

HUNGARY

LIST OF MAPS

Before us now stretched Mongolia with deserts trembling in the mirages, with endless steppes covered with emerald-green grass and multitudes of wild flowers, with nameless snow peaks, limitless forests, thundering rivers and swift mountain streams. The way that we had traveled with such toil had disappeared behind us among gorges and ravines. We could not have dreamed of a more captivating entrance to a new country, and when the sun sank upon that day, we felt as though born into a new life—a life which had the strength of the hills, the depth of the heavens and the beauty of the sunrise.

—HENNING HASLUND
MONGOLIAN ADVENTURE: 1920S DANGER AND ESCAPE
AMONG THE MOUNTED NOMADS OF CENTRAL ASIA

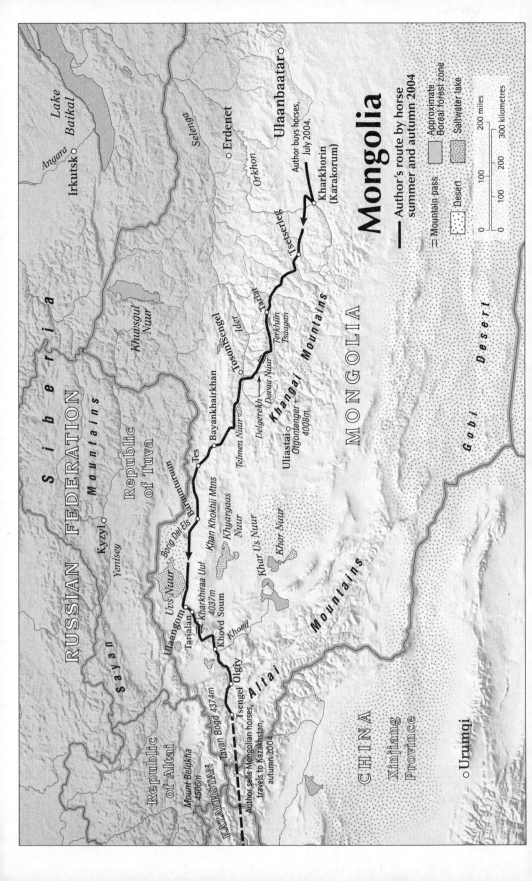

Mongolia

— Author's route by horse
summer and autumn 2004

═ Mountain pass:

▨ Approximate
Boreal forest zone

░ Desert.

▨ Saltwater lake.

0   100   200 300 kilometres
0   100   200 miles

Ulaanbaatar

Author buys horses,
July 2004.

Kharkhorin (Karakorum)

Tsetserleg

Erdenet

Selenga

Orkhon

Tariat

Tosontsengel

Ider

Terkhiin
Tsagaan

Delgerekh
Davaa Nuur

Bayankhairkhan

Khangai Mountains

Uliastai
Otgontenger +
4008m

Tes

Khuvsgul Nuur

Tes

Telmen Nuur

Baruunturuun

Bovig Dal Els

MONGOLIA

Khan Khokhii Mtns

Khyargaas
Nuur

Khar Us Nuur

Khar Nuur

Uvs Nuur

Ulaangom
Tarialan

Kharkhiraa Uul
4037m

Khovd Soum

Khovd

Tsengel Olgiy

Altai

Tavan Bogd 4374m

Author sells Mongolian horses,
travels to Kazakhstan,
autumn 2004.

Mountains

Gobi Desert

CHINA

Xinjiang
Province

Urumqi

RUSSIAN FEDERATION

Siberia

*Lake
Baikal*

Angara

Irkutsk

Sayan Mountains

Kyzyl

Yenisey

**Republic
of Tuva**

**Republic
of Altai**

Mount Belukha
4506m

KAZAKHSTAN

1

MONGOLIAN DREAMING

ONLY TEN MINUTES earlier we had been bent forward over our saddles, braced against the nearly horizontal rain and hail, but now the afternoon sun had returned and the wind had gone. As I peeled back the hood of my jacket, details that had been swept away by the storm began to filter back. Nearby there was the rattle of a bridle as my horse shook away a fly; around us, sharp songs floating through the cleansed air from unseen birds. The wet leather chaps around my sore legs began to warm up, and the taste of dried curd, known as *aaruul*, turned bitter in my mouth. Ahead, my girlfriend, Kathrin, sat remarkably calm on her wiry little chestnut gelding. Below, the rocking of my saddle as my horse's hooves pressed into soft ground was steady as a heartbeat.

In a land as open and wide as Mongolia I was already becoming aware that it took just the slightest adjustment to switch my attention from the near to the far. With a twist in the saddle my gaze shifted to the curved column of rain that had been drenching us minutes before, but which now sailed over the land to our left. Pushed out by the wind in an arc like a giant spinnaker, it crossed the valley plain we were skirting and continued to distant uplands, fleetingly staining the earth and blotting out nomad encampments in its path.

During childhood, I had often watched clouds such as this, feeling envious of the freedom they had to roam unchecked. Here, though, the same boundless space of the sky was mirrored on the land. Scattered amid the faultless green carpet of early summer grasses, countless herds of horses, flocks of sheep and goats, shifted about like cloud shadows. For the nomads who tended to them, nowhere, it seemed, was off-limits. Their white felt tents, known as *gers*, were perched atop knolls, by the quiet slither of a stream, and in the clefts of distant slopes. Riders could be seen driving herds forward, crossing open spaces, and milling by camps. Not a tree—or shrub, for that matter—fence, or road was in sight, and the highest peaks in the distance were all worn down and rounded, adding to the feeling of a world without boundaries.

Clutching the reins and refocusing my sights on the freshly cut mane of my riding horse, Bor, I wavered between this simple, uncluttered reality and the trials of a more complex world that were slipping behind.

For the past twelve months I had been preparing for this journey in a third-floor apartment with a static view over the suburbs of inner-city Melbourne, Australia. In theory, the idea of riding horses 10,000 km across the Eurasian steppe from Mongolia to Hungary was simple—independent of the mechanized world, and without a need for roads, I would be free to wander, needing only grass and water to fuel my way forward.[1] One friend had even told me: "Get on your horse, point it to the west, and when people start speaking French, it means you have gone too far."

In reality, there were complexities I needed to plan for. I knew, for example, that bureaucracy—getting visas and crossing borders with animals—would likely be a major obstacle, and taking the right equipment could mean the difference between lasting two hundred days on the road or just two. Perhaps more significant were the challenges ahead that remained unknown, and of a type unfamiliar to me. At that point, early in my planning, not only was the scale of the journey beyond my comprehension, but the sum total of my experience as a horseman amounted to ten minutes on a horse almost two decades earlier, when I was seven years old. On that occasion I had been bucked clear and shipped to the hospital with a broken arm. I was still deeply scared of these powerful creatures, and couldn't quite picture myself as a horseman—a feeling shared by my mother, Anne, who was a little bewildered when I first mentioned the idea.

Notwithstanding the uncertainties, I had pressed ahead with plans, and by the spring of 2004 I felt reasonably well prepared. With valuable direction from the founder of the Long Riders Guild, CuChullaine O'Reilly, I had studied the realities of traveling with horses and gathered together a trove of carefully selected equipment. I had also managed to make contact with people in embassies, visa agencies, and those who had promised to help me on the ground.

Not all preparations had proven fruitful. I hadn't managed to raise enough money to reach my target budget of $10 a day (for a journey I expected to take eighteen months), and assurances I would receive long-stay visas were vague at best. Since planning had begun, it was also true that I had not accumulated as much experience on horseback as I had hoped. In addition to that disastrous long-ago ride, I had managed to join a five-day packhorse trip through the Victorian Alps in southeastern Australia—courtesy of the Baird family, who were kind enough to take on the white-knuckled novice that I was—and a three-day crash course with horse trainers and an equine vet in Western Australia. Nevertheless, I was buoyed by the firm belief that because the difficulties of the journey ahead would prove to be of a scope beyond my imagination, not even another forty years of planning would have been enough. And besides, who could possibly be better teachers than the nomads of the steppe who I would soon be among?

From the time I booked my air tickets and canceled the lease on my apartment, there had been no turning back. Life as I knew it was disassembled, and I went through the process of farewells with my family. After saying goodbye to one of my brothers, Jon, I slumped up against the wall in my emptied apartment in tears. Setting off on such a long journey as the eldest of four close-knit children, I felt as if I was severing ties, and it frightened me to think how much we might grow apart. Finally, at Melbourne airport my existence was stripped down to an embrace with my mother. The longer I lingered in her arms, the more strongly I felt that, as a son, I was doing something that bordered on irresponsible.

After making my way to Beijing, and from there by train to Mongolia's capital, Ulaanbaatar, I had spent a few weeks persuading Mongolia's Foreign Ministry to grant me a visa extension (and very nearly failing), gathering together additional equipment, and, finally, searching for the horses that would be my transport, load carriers, and traveling companions.

A young English-speaking Mongolian man named Gansukh Baatarsuren had taken me to the home of a nomad family 300 km southwest of the city, where he promised to find me "hero's horses." The process had proven tricky. There was a general belief among nomads—in my case warranted—that "white men could not ride," and upon discovering the buyer was a foreigner, several previous offers to sell had been rescinded. No one wanted to be responsible for exposing a foreigner like me to danger, let alone risk maltreatment of their prized horses.

In the end I had been helped in my quest by a stroke of luck—there had been a general election, and voting was an opportunity for nomads to ride in from all corners of the steppe to socialize. Gansukh had gone to a polling place and put word out that he was looking for three good mounts. The following day, while I hid in a ger, he covertly negotiated with sellers on my behalf. In this way I had managed to buy two geldings and had purchased a third from the nomad family with whom we were staying.

Just six days ago I had assembled my little caravan and taken the first fragile steps, albeit most of them on foot, leading my little crew. Since then I had rendezvoused with Kathrin, who planned to ride with me for the first two months of the journey.

Lifting my eyes again to the steppe between my horse's ears, I felt the stiffness in my joints ebb away. Perhaps it was just the effect of *airag* seeping in—alcoholic fermented mare's milk that Kathrin and I had been served by the bowlful during lunch with nomads—but for the first time since I'd climbed into the saddle, a sense of ease washed over me. With reins in hand, compass set, and backpack hugging me from behind, all I could think was that ahead lay 10,000 km of this open land to the Danube, and across all of these empty horizons, not a soul knew I was coming.

WHEN THE SUN began to edge toward the skyline and the heat wilted, I watered the horses, then chose a campsite halfway up a hillside that overlooked the country we had ridden through. As would become my regular evening routine, I set about hobbling the horses and tethering them around the tent using 20 m lines and steel stakes. The camping stove was fired up, dinner was boiled, and Kathrin and I rested up against the pack boxes to watch herds of sheep and goats pouring over troughs and crests on their way back to camps scattered below. The sweet smell of burning dung and calls of distant horsemen carried through to us on the breeze, and when our dinner pots had been scraped clean, we lay down on mattresses of horse blankets listening to the crunch of horses chewing through grass. Thereafter the prospect of unbroken weeks and months of travel held me lingering in a dreamy state of semiconsciousness.

I must have eventually fallen into a deep sleep, for when I opened my eyes again, the bucolic scenes of evening had vanished. In their place the tent clapped and bucked in a roaring wind. Something had woken me, and although I wasn't sure just what, I crawled out of my sleeping bag and clutched blindly for my flashlight. When I failed to find it I lay still, held my breath and strained to listen for my horses.

Minutes passed. There were no telltale jingles of the horse bell that had been tied around the packhorse's neck, or indeed any other sound indicating the horses were grazing. I tried to convince myself I was experiencing a moment of paranoia and that the horses were sleeping, but then from somewhere beyond camp I heard muffled voices and the thunder of hooves. I forced my way out and ran barefoot to where I had tethered the animals, only to find my white riding mount, Bor, alone, pulling at his tether line and madly neighing into the black of night. Somewhere beyond the perimeter of camp the sound of galloping was fading fast.

Holding Bor's tether tight, I stumbled my way farther until I felt the other two tether lines between my toes. When I reached the end of one I fell to my knees clutching the only remaining evidence of the other two horses: the bell and a pair of hobbles.

Even as Kathrin woke and came running from the tent with a flashlight, warnings I'd brushed aside from seasoned nomads in recent days came flooding back: *What are you going to do when the wolves attack? When the thieves steal your horses? Are you carrying a gun?* In response I had naively pointed out my axe and horse bell. Sheila Greenwell, the equine vet in Australia who had so kindly helped me prepare, had suggested that if I put the bell on my horses at night I would wake up if thieves did approach, because the horses would become nervous and sound the bell. In reality, the sound of the bell as the horses grazed in the dark had led the thieves straight to my camp. They had quietly slipped off the bell, untied the horses, and made their escape.

As futile as it might have been, Kathrin and I continued to trawl the steppe in the hope we might have missed something. But by the time we returned to the tent, frozen, there was no denying that on just the sixth day of my journey some of my plans needed revision. In fact, I thought, perhaps the whole journey needed a rethink.

THE VISION OF riding a horse on the trail of nomads from Mongolia to Hungary had been incubating since I was nineteen. At the time I'd abandoned law school in Australia to study wilderness guiding in Finland. There I'd learned about the travels of Carl Gustaf Emil Mannerheim—the legendary Finnish general and explorer who began his career in the Russian Imperial Army and went on to lead Finland's move to independence, eventually becoming Finland's president during the final stages of World War II.

At the age of thirty-nine, in 1906, he set off on a two-year ethnographic expedition from St. Petersburg through Central Asia to Beijing, the last part largely on horseback. In truth, Mannerheim was not the ethnographer he was dressed up as, but a covert spy for the Russian tsar.

Nonetheless, he impressed me as someone interested in the continuity between the ethnic groups of Central Asia and the origins of the Finnish people. The Finns are part of the Finno-Ugric group of peoples, and are related to many different indigenous peoples that stretch right across the belt of forest and tundra regions of Russia and Siberia, as far as the Pacific. The story of Mannerheim's journey inspired in me the idea that connections between cultures, based on a common environment and way of life, transcend modern state boundaries.

After completing the wilderness course in 1999 I canceled my return ticket to Australia and set off with my friend Chris Hatherly to ride recumbent bicycles from Karelia, in European Russia, to Beijing. It was to be a fourteen-month journey during which we lived on a budget of $2 a day, surviving by camping in the forest, drinking from roadside ditches, and being rescued by kind villagers who took pity on us. The world expanded with every new challenge, from frostbitten toes to the dark clouds of mosquitoes that came with summer in Siberia. But most of all it was the people who left an impression on me. In the throes of the traumatic times of post-Soviet Russia and the more recent 1998 economic collapse, the people were resurgent with pride in their many varied origins, whether they were Buddhist Buryatians or the lesser-known Udmurtians of the pre-Urals. Above all, I found it astonishing that in the midst of an adventure I experienced more comradeship and connection with many of these people than with those where I had grown up in Australia.

It was more by necessity than by desire—it was the most logical and shortest route from Siberia to Beijing—that Chris and I found ourselves in Mongolia in the autumn of 2000.

While pushing our bikes through the sands of Mongolia's Gobi Desert we would pause, exhausted, and watch as horsemen materialized from the horizon at a gallop, their long cloaks flying, eyes trained forward, and sitting so composed it was as if they were not moving at all. After stopping to take a look at the two young Australians, bogged in the sand of the only track in sight, they would remount and gallop off in whatever direction they pleased.

I was struck by their world: unscarred by roads, towns, and cities, it was a place where even homes left impermanent marks on the land. Free of fences and private land ownership, the natural lay of the earth was unhindered, defined only by mountains, rivers, deserts, and the natural ebb and flow of the seasons. What's more, with little more than a thin piece of felt to protect them against annual variations in temperatures that spanned more than 82°C, the nomadic people had a connection to the land I had never dreamed existed in modern times.

Until that point of our travels, bicycles had been freedom machines for Chris and me, allowing us to break away from the pull of a conventional path in life. But it began to dawn on me that because we were confined to roads and wheel tracks, the realm of nomads was off-limits to us. I was merely a tourist passing through.

OUR JOURNEY TO Beijing was over rather quickly after reaching the Chinese border, and within a month of dropping down from the Gobi Desert to China's bustling megalopolis, my bike was gathering dust in my parents' garage. The memories of Mongolia still burned bright, though, and from that point on I not only craved to return to Mongolia but grew enchanted by the history of the Mongolians' ancestors, who had once ruled supreme under the leadership of Genghis Khan.

Drawing on the same hardy qualities that enable the nomads and their steppe horses to survive in the harsh environment of Mongolia today, horsemen of the thirteenth century had trotted out of the vast Mongolian steppe and thundered into Poland and Hungary, crushing some of Europe's most prestigious armies. I was captivated by stories of these warriors who were renowned for mounting up in the dead of winter, smearing fat on their faces against frostbite, and drinking blood from the necks of their horses when food supplies were low. The Mongolian armies were able to travel a remarkable 80 km a day, and among many military accomplishments they defeated Russia in winter—something neither Napoleon or Hitler could achieve. Later, when they conquered Baghdad in 1258, they also managed in one attempt what the Crusaders had been trying to do for more than a century, and which wouldn't be repeated until the 2003 American invasion.

Just as impressive as the military prowess of the Mongols was the ability of Genghis Khan and his successors to make the transition from conquering and pillaging to governing and administration. They established an empire that remained more or less intact for a century, and which left a sophisticated model of government and military that long outlived the Genghisid dynasty. Many contemporary historians point out how taxes levied by the Mongols during their reign were by and large used to serve the diverse people they ruled. They implemented legal codes, funded public works projects, patronized the arts and religion, and promoted international trade and commerce. Under their stewardship, trade routes and communication lines across Eurasia were perhaps safer and more efficient than they had ever been, enabling the first direct relations between China and Europe.

It is remarkable to think that at the zenith of Mongol power nomad herders of the little-known steppes of East Asia ruled an empire that included some of the most populous cities on earth and stretched from Korea in the east to Hungary in the west, the tropics of South East Asia in the south—the Mongols even campaigned in Java, Indonesia—and the sub-Arctic in the north. Western Europe could have become yet another corner of their lands if it weren't for a stroke of fate. In 1242 when Mongolian scouts reached Vienna, the great khan in Mongolia died—at that time it was Genghis Khan's son and heir, Ogodei—and the army packed up and went home to elect a new leader. Ambitions to rule western Europe were never revisited.

As I learned about the scale and significance of the Mongol Empire, I began to think the only thing more astonishing than the achievements of the Mongols was how little I'd known about them, not to mention my ignorance of the broader history of mounted nomads on the steppe.

When Chris and I were en route by bicycle to Mongolia, many ethnic Russians we met had hardly been enlightening. We'd been warned time and time again that Mongolia was an impoverished and backward country where the "primitive" and "uncivilized" people who still relied on horses would surely bring an end to our journey. There was a permeating sense of disbelief that these people who "didn't even know how to build a house" could ever have ruled Russia, let alone many of the great civilizations of China, Europe, Central Asia, and the Middle East. And yet at a time in history when most medieval Europeans were still limited to the distance they could walk in a day—the original meaning of the word *journey* in English—these Mongolian horsemen had been galloping across the globe, expanding their knowledge as rapidly as their empire assimilated the religions, technologies, and cultures of those they conquered.

Significantly, the Mongols were not some kind of isolated nomad phenomenon. To the contrary, they reflected a historic trend of nomadic empires that had begun thousands of years earlier with one of human history's most significant yet unheralded turning points: the domestication of the wild horse.

Recent discoveries suggest that this revolution began around 3500 BCE in what is now the northern steppe of Kazakhstan. There on the primeval plain where the steppe mingles with the southern edge of Siberian forests, hunter-gatherers first began to tame, breed, milk, and ride this four-legged creature with which they had shared the land since time immemorial.

On the sweeping, largely waterless tracts of land on the Eurasian steppe the marriage of human intelligence and equine speed enabled flat-footed hunter-gatherers to gallop beyond the known horizon and prosper in ways previously unimagined. Free to search out better pasture, water, and game, they rapidly expanded their concept of the world and revolutionized the way they communicated, farmed, traded, and waged warfare. As Bjarke Rink puts it in his book *The Centaur Legacy*, the union between man and horse represented "a qualitative leap in human psychology and physiology that permitted man to act beyond his biological means." In other words, the horse liberated humankind from its own physical limitations.

Over time the domesticated horse gave rise to nomadic societies from Mongolia to the Danube River in modern Hungary. The Greek historian Herodotus dedicated his "fourth book" to one of the first such known horseback people, the Scythians, who rose to prominence in the eighth century BCE and ruled the steppe from the Danube to the Altai Mountains.

The realm of the Scythians was at the very heart of what would become the platform for the countless nomadic empires that followed them—the ocean-like plain in the heart of Eurasia, where the horse had evolved over millions of years. On the northern shores of this land lay the boreal forests and tundra of Russia and Siberia, while to the south it was rimmed by the baking deserts of Central Asia and Persia, the great walls of the Tien Shan and Pamir ranges, and, farther to the west, the Caucasus and the shores of the Black Sea. Some areas of the steppe were rich grasslands and others semi-arid zones, deserts, high plateaus, and even forests, but far away from the moderating effect of any ocean, it was all characterized by a harsh continental climate.

For settled people who lived beyond the boundaries of this realm—clinging to the safety and protection of more-fertile soils, river systems, and plentiful forests—the steppe was a mysterious, inhospitable, and almost impenetrable world. For nomads such as the Scythians, however, who relied on grazing their herds of sheep, goats, cattle, camels, and horses, the steppe formed a corridor of pasturelands that linked Asia with Europe, and Russia and Siberia with Asia Minor and the Middle East. Apart from the Altai Mountains in the east and the Carpathians in the west, it was largely free of natural obstructions, and the east-west axis meant that despite vast distances the conditions varied comparatively little. Nomads could therefore apply very similar principles of pastoral farming in Mongolia as they could in Hungary.

It was inevitable that, once domesticated, the horse would carry nomads beyond the shores of the steppe and into conflict with sedentary society. Nomads, after all, could not survive exclusively on the milk, meat, and skins of their animals, but to a degree were dependent on trade with, and plunder of, the earth-tilling societies in the lands that bordered theirs. The horse gave the nomads a crucial military advantage, and a pattern of conflict began that would endure as late as the seventeenth century: nomads would make raids on settled lands and retreat to the steppe with their spoils.[2]

Among the many nomad powers to follow in the wake of the Scythians were the Sarmatians, Huns (who under Attila rocked the foundations of the Roman Empire), Bulgars, Avars, and eventually the Magyars, who founded the modern nation of Hungary in 896. Two hundred and fifty years later the greatest nomad force of all time, the Mongols (also known in the west as Tatars), were at the height of their powers.

Even after the breakup of the Mongol Empire in the fourteenth century, Turkic-Mongol peoples with nomad heritage took over much of the fallen Genghisid dynasty. The much-renowned Tamerlane modeled himself on the Mongols and went on to carve out his own empire of historical renown.

It wasn't until the advent of the musket in the seventeenth century that nomads began to go into permanent decline. The last great migration of nomads across the steppe took place in 1771, when the ethnically Mongolian Kalmyks migrated from the Caspian region in Russia to China and Mongolia. The final descendant of Genghis Khan to hold power was Alim Khan, emir of Bukhara, who was deposed in 1920.

OVER THE MONTHS and years following my bicycle journey I continued to read about the Mongols, and nomads more generally, and became struck by two disparate and rather extreme images of the steppe people.

On one hand, there was the entrenched stereotype of Mongols as primitive barbarians who, in their time of power, had senselessly pillaged, raped, and murdered before returning on their horses to the east. It is a reputation that, it should be acknowledged, is not without some justification. The Mongol tactic of conquest was brutal, designed both to decrease the population to prevent rebellion and to instill fear so that future enemies would surrender without a fight. There are, consequently, cities across Central Asia, Persia, the Middle East, Russia, and China that suffered irreparable devastation. When the city of Merv surrendered, historical sources suggest, nearly the entire population was put to death. Urgench was famously submerged by the waters of the Amu Darya after the Mongols broke dam walls. In Iran, the Mongols are still bemoaned for the destruction they wreaked on life-sustaining irrigation networks that took centuries to re-build; the famines caused by the devastation probably caused more people to die than did the initial conquest. There is even evidence to suggest that the early destruction by the Mongols under Genghis Khan left a problematic legacy for his successors. In China, Khubilai Khan—Genghis's grandson, who went on to become both grand khan and emperor of China—spent decades struggling to reconstruct towns, cities, and agricultural lands that had borne the brunt of the initial Mongol invasion.

Passing moral judgment on the Mongols based on their violent conquests is nevertheless not a fair way of interpreting the nature of the Mongol Empire or the Mongols as a nomadic people and culture. As historian Charles J. Halperin writes, "Empire building is an invariably destructive process, unwelcome to the conquered," and in this regard the Mongols were "no more cruel, and no less," than empire builders before or after them. It is important to consider that the history of the Mongol Empire was predominantly recorded by the vanquished, and filtered by religious ideology. Nomads were often judged on the premise of being pagan infidels and presented as harboring some kind of innate depravity. In 1240, the year before the Mongols crossed the Carpathians into Hungary, the renowned English monk of St. Albans, Matthew Paris, described the Mongols as "the detestable people of Satan" who were "inhuman and Beastly, rather Monsters than men, thirsting for and drinking blood, tearing and devouring the flesh of Dogges and Men."[3]

Such typecasting was not limited to the Mongols. The Roman soldier Ammianus Marcellinus described the Mongols' predecessors, the Huns, as "so prodigiously ugly and bent that they might be two legged animals, or the figures crudely carved from stumps which are seen on the parapets of bridges." Of the nomadic way of life, he wrote: "They have no home or law, or settled manner of life, but wander like refugees in the wagons in which they live. In these their wives weave their filthy clothing, mate with their husbands, give birth to their children and rear them to the age of puberty."[4] As late as the seventeenth century some Europeans still believed the myth—as recounted by the French traveler Beauplan—that Tatar babies were born with their eyes closed, like dogs.

On the other hand, the achievements of the Mongols, military and otherwise, have been widely lauded as evidence of a highly sophisticated and worldly people. The Mongols created not only the largest contiguous land empire in history but an empire that, despite the terror it raised, initiated broad social programs, showed remarkable religious and cultural tolerance, and ushered in a relatively stable era of economic prosperity. During Khubilai's reign over China he attempted to introduce public schooling, encouraged the widespread use of paper money (which was later used as a model by his Mongol counterparts in the Ilkhanate of Persia and the Golden Horde in Russia), provided grain to widows and orphans, and instigated the development of granaries across the country to ensure against famine and natural disasters. He set up governmental institutions to protect and promote the interests of traders, artisans, farmers, and religious faiths, and he used some of the tributes collected from conquered lands for state projects, such as the extension of the Grand Canal—a venture that never fully succeeded but employed an estimated three million laborers.

Mongols also administered urban centers of culture and commerce that are inconsistent with assumptions that Mongols—as uncultured "barbarian" nomads—conquered and ruled exclusively from the saddle. The purpose-built capital of the Golden Horde, Sarai, which lay on the Volga River, was a flourishing city exhibiting paved streets, mosques, palaces, caravansaries, and running water supplied by aqueducts. Khubilai's capital in China, Khanbalikh (also known as Ta-tu or Dadu), was symbolic of the way Mongol rulers amalgamated the diverse cultures, beliefs, and skills of their domains. In it were built a shrine for Confucians, an altar with Mongolian soil and grass from the steppes, and buildings of significant Chinese architectural influence. As historian Morris Rossabi points out, Khubilai "sought the assistance of Persian astronomers and physicians, Tibetan Buddhist monks" and "Central Asian [Muslim] soldiers." One can only imagine it must have been a city of grand cosmopolitan dimensions.

To me, these two somewhat conflicting portraits—the cruel barbarians bent on wanton destruction versus the empire builders with governing and administrative genius—were surely two sides of the same coin. But time and again I reflected that neither image bore relation to the hospitable herdsmen and herdswomen I had met in the Gobi.

Whenever a map of the world was in front of me, I couldn't help but be beguiled by the vast swath of fenceless land at the heart of Eurasia that stretched from Mongolia to the Danube River in the heart of eastern Europe. The history of empires aside, who were the people who had once roamed across this land? What must their lives have been like? What would it have been like for a young Mongol man to climb into the saddle and ride halfway across the world into Europe?

It was in 2001, about six months after arriving back home from my cycling expedition, that it first occurred to me to ride a horse across the steppe. Over time, the idea took shape and form, and I was excited by what appeared to be a very simple concept: using packhorses to carry my equipment, and camels where necessary, I would start from the former capital of the Mongol Empire, Kharkhorin (also called Karakorum), and make my way west through the heart of the Eurasian steppe until I reached the Danube. While this was a similar route to that taken a thousand years earlier by the Mongols under Genghis Khan and his successors, it wasn't my intention to follow any one trail, and I was not interested in visiting old battlegrounds, following a warpath, or even venturing to cities in the sedentary nations that once had been vassals of the Mongols. By climbing into the saddle, I wanted to discover the human face of the nomadic cultures, which seemed to have been lost in so many of the superlative-filled histories. The end goal of my journey, the Danube, represented the western boundary of the Mongol Empire, but more important, it was the very western fringe of the steppe, and therefore the end of the traditional nomad world.

From the beginning of my planning I was very conscious that I wasn't the first traveler to attempt a ride by horse across the Eurasian steppe. Apart from the untold thousands or perhaps millions of nomads who had crisscrossed the steppe through time, there were several standout examples

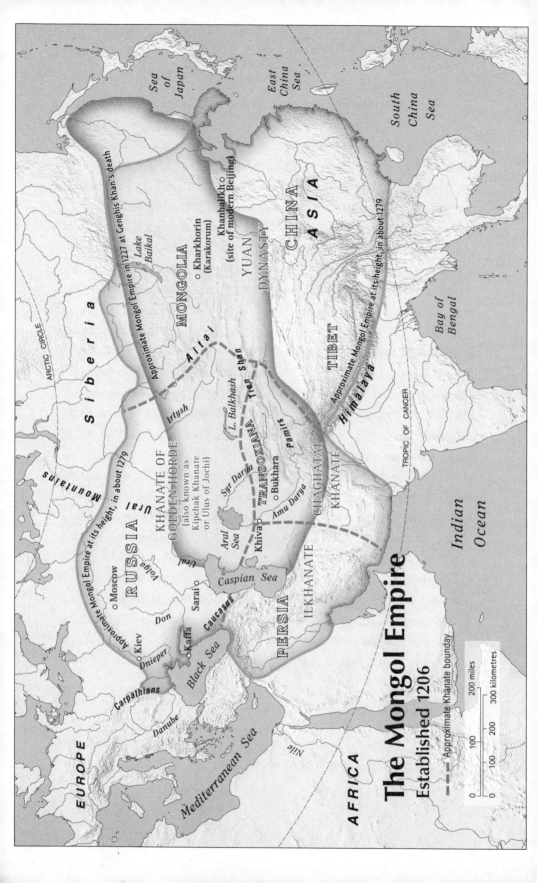

The Mongol Empire
Established 1206

EUROPE

Carpathians

Danube

Mediterranean Sea

Nile

Nile

AFRICA

Indian Ocean

0   100   200 miles
0 100 200 300 kilometres

- - - Approximate Khanate boundary

Black Sea

o Kiev
Dnieper
o Kaffa
Caucasus
Don
Sarai o
o Moscow
Volga
RUSHA
Caspian Sea
Ural
Ural

Mountains

Approximate Mongol Empire at its height, in about 1279

KHANATE OF
GOLDEN HORDE
(also known as
Kipchak Khanate
or Ulus of Jochi)

Aral
Sea
Khiva o
Syr Darya
Bukhara o
Amu Darya
TRANSOXIANA
Pamirs

L. Balkhash

Irtysh

Approximate Mongol Empire in 1227 at Genghis Khan's death

Lake Baikal

Altai

Tien Shan

MONGOLIA

o Kharkhorin
(Karakorum)

Khanbalikh o
(site of modern Beijing)

YUAN DYNASTY

CHINA

ASIA

Sea of Japan

East China Sea

South China Sea

Approximate Mongol Empire at its height, in about 1279

TIBET

Himalaya

Bay of Bengal

TROPIC OF CANCER

CHAGHATAI
KHANATE

IEKHANATE

PERSIA

Indian Ocean

ARCTIC CIRCLE

S i b e r i a

of intrepid Europeans who had made the journey at the peak of Mongol power.[5]

Among the more intriguing of these was a mysterious Englishman employed by the Mongols as a chief diplomat and intelligence adviser. A renowned linguist, he had accompanied the Mongol army during the conquest of Hungary in 1241 and was eventually caught by the Austrians during the Mongolian siege of Wiener Neustadt—where, remarkably, he was recognized by Austrian royals from the arena of the Holy Crusades more than twenty years earlier.[6] Had the Englishman been given an opportunity to write about his experiences, he would have been uniquely qualified to present history from the point of view of a nomadic regime at the height of its power. Unfortunately, he was hanged in Vienna, and the only glimpse we have of his life is from the writings of a heretic French priest who survived the siege of Wiener Neustadt.

Shortly after the death of the Englishman came the first two European travelers to make it to Mongolia and back to Europe and write accounts of their experiences—Italian friar Giovanni di Plano Carpini and, later, Franciscan friar William of Rubruck.

Carpini, who set out in 1245 from France with the Pope's blessing, traveled first to Kiev, where he was told to leave his European-bred horses because "Tartars have neither straw nor hay nor fodder, and they would all die." With various Mongolian entourages he carried on east through the steppes of what is Russia and Ukraine today, then onward to Mongolia through the Kazakh steppes, traveling an astonishing 3,000 km in just 106 days. No doubt still wrapped in the bandages that had apparently helped keep his body intact for such an exhausting ride, he arrived in the "Golden Tent" of the Khan in July 1246 and wrote:

> So great was the size of the tent which was made of white fabric
> that we reckon it could hold more than 2,000 men . . . they called
> us inside and give us ale because we did not like mares milk in the
> least: and so did us a great honor. But still they compelled us to
> drink so much that we could not stay at all sober, so we com-
> plained that this bothered us, but still they continued to force us.

Only five years after Carpini's miraculous return to Europe, William of Rubruck—on a mission to convert the Mongols to Christianity—set out on a route similar to Carpini's and became the first European to reach the capital of the Mongol Empire, Kharkhorin. His description of an animated debate that he participated in between representatives of the Buddhist, Muslim, and Christian faiths—and which was hosted by the khan—has gone down in legend.

Upon returning to Europe, both William and Carpini brought a wealth of information about the mysterious Mongolians, and their accounts are still a valuable resource offering historians and anthropologists a firsthand look at the inner workings of Mongolian society of the thirteenth century. It is also true, however, that as Dominican friars traveling from west to east, they inevitably interpreted the nomads and their way of life through the prism of their Catholic faith and their upbringing in sedentary Europe.

What I wanted to do on my journey was, in effect, the reverse. Leaving my Western baggage behind as much as possible, I wanted to start in Mongolia as an impressionable novice horseman, immerse myself in the lands and ways of the nomadic people, and travel steadily west to arrive at the far end of the steppe in Hungary, where I would try to view Europe firmly through a nomad's eyes.

In the twenty-first century a westward trajectory was all the more important for another crucial reason: the Eurasian steppe, and the western half in particular, was no longer the realm of nomads it once had been. In recent centuries the Russian Empire had reversed the trend of their subjugation to nomads and had come to dominate the vast bulk of steppe societies. The land between Kharkhorin and the Danube, albeit fenceless and much of it wild and remote, was now carved into modern states. In the west they included Hungary, Ukraine, and southern Russia, and in the east Kazakhstan, Mongolia, and those regions less relevant for my journey, western China and the Central Asian nations of Kyrgyzstan, Uzbekistan, and Turkmenistan. With the exception of China these were countries emerging from the shadows of Soviet rule, during which the people had been largely uprooted from their traditional way of life.[7] Only Mongolia, as a satellite Communist state, had been spared the full brutal effects of Stalin's collectivization policy. Partly by virtue of this, and the inherently isolated nature of Mongolian geography, the Mongols had managed to retain a vibrant nomadic culture, whereas their cousins in countries to the West had lost theirs.

Given this reality, the purpose of my journey wasn't just to understand how nomad life had once been on the steppe. I wanted to know whether there were still living, breathing connections between the nomadic and formerly nomadic peoples now scattered across Eurasia. Were Hungarians, for example, conscious of their nomad roots at all?

Even more important, what had happened to the nomadic societies during the violent upheaval of Stalin's industrialization campaign, and what did the future hold for them in the wake of the collapse of the Soviet Union? In the long run, would the nomadic way of life survive?

To have any hope of recognizing living traces of nomad heritage, I first had to come to understand it. And in reality, that was what had led me to Mongolia in the first place.

IT WAS HARD to know how many hours had passed since the horses had been stolen, but eventually my faith in the journey, like the dullest of pre-dawn light, began creeping back into the world. Still, I needed to do something. So I did what any modern adventurer might when in a bad situation: I picked up the satellite phone. The person I called for advice was my longtime friend Tseren in Ulaanbaatar.

"Well, Tim," she told me, "here in Mongolia we say that if you don't solve your problems before sunrise, then you will never solve them. You better get on that last remaining horse of yours and start looking!"

At 5:30 A.M. I pointed Bor into the pale hues of the eastern sky. Smoke had begun curling its way out from the outline of the nearest ger, and people were already emerging to milk the goats. Sitting high and straight in the saddle, I put on the most intimidating look I could muster and willed the horse into what I imagined was a gallop but was probably no more than a trot. As we approached the first ger, a large dog shot out, Bor reared, and I struggled to hold on as we followed it back the way it had come. Visits to other camps proved more elegant, but all brought little more than shrugs.

Then, around 8 km from camp, a woman waving from her ger caught my attention.

"Hello!" she called in English.

No sooner had I dismounted there came a herd of horses thundering over a rise, throwing clouds of dust into the path of the sun. Squinting hard, I could just make out the shape of two horses trailing behind, and beyond them a horseman. As he maneuvered the herd down toward us, I looked closer. My horses!

The herder, who was in fact the husband of this woman, approached, and I explained that two of those horses were mine.

"I know," he said. "They came to me themselves this morning. You must have tied them *really* badly."

In my poor Mongolian I asked him to explain how it was that my horses no longer had any halters or lead ropes. He shrugged. It was irrelevant now.

I was invited in to share a drink of fermented mare's milk while new halters were made from rawhide. The herder sat on the dirt floor looking me over, then said something in Mongolian: "Tanilgui hun algiin chinee. Taniltai hun taliin chinee."

With the help of a pocket dictionary I was able to translate: *A man without friends is as small as a palm. A man with friends is as big as the steppe.*

It was an old Mongolian adage, and in hindsight I would be left to wonder whether indeed the whole drama had been an intentional lesson. Gansukh even suggested that it could have been the original owners of my horses who had tracked me down and stolen them just to prove the truth of their warnings. Whatever the case, it didn't really matter now.

With the horseman from the family riding by my side, I cut a trail through the lingering dew of morning in high spirits. Somewhere during the search for my horses I had left my worries of the past twelve months behind. What mattered now was that my family was intact—I had been given a second chance—and I was returning to Kathrin and camp with two bits of newfound wisdom: if I camped alone I was fair game, and if I was to have any hope of making it another 100 km, let alone 10,000 km, my horses were not to be taken for granted.

2

THE LAST
NOMAD NATION

"To the mounted nomads who rode and resided along the Equestrian Equator [Eurasian steppe], possessions were for using, not hoarding. Life to them was a bridge; one should cross over it, not build a house on it."

—CuChullaine O'Reilly, F.R.G.S.,
  Founder of the Long Riders' Guild

AS I CAME riding back into camp with the reclaimed mounts, Kathrin emerged from the tent, her blond hair all wispy and her blue eyes aglow in the morning light. It was those eyes that had caught me off guard some nine months earlier. Two years older than I, she was a schoolteacher from Germany who had been living in Australia for a year to work and travel. We shared a passion for travel, and I'd been drawn at once to her down-to-earth humor and warmth. Our relationship got off to a quick start after she responded to an advertisement to rent one of the two bedrooms in the Melbourne apartment where I was living. For me, then twenty-four, it was the beginning of the most serious and important relationship of my life until that point, and in the time since we had met she had become the person who knew me better than anyone else probably ever had.

At the same time, it remained the case that our paths had crossed after I had set my sights on riding from Mongolia to Hungary. I had also long dreamed of traveling alone. Solo, I reasoned, I would be able to render myself more vulnerable, and therefore pledge a much greater trust in the humanity of strangers. With no familiar companion or culture to lean on, I would be forced to appeal to the better side of human beings no matter who they were. Doing so would offer me the kind of immersion—in the landscape and in the lives of people—that I craved.

Kathrin was aware of my plan and initially did not intend to join me, but she probably didn't expect the degree of my preoccupation in the intense six months of planning leading to departure. Kathrin felt neglected, and questioned at times what she was doing living with me, commenting that she might have been better off traveling around Australia, as had been her original plan.

Eventually we had decided to travel together for the first two months, until the end of August, when she was due to return to Germany to start a teaching job. It would be an opportunity to share this first part of the adventure and spend some precious time together after my prolonged "absence" at home.

Beyond these first two months together lay what I expected to be another sixteen months to Hungary, during which time we had rough plans for her to join me during her summer holidays. In the end, that's not what prevailed. The following summer Kathrin would be diagnosed with a life-threatening illness, Cushing's syndrome, triggered by a brain tumor that required surgery, and it would take me three and a half years to reach the Danube. By the time I was riding the last kilometres in the saddle, she would already be married. For the time being, though, that was all in the future.

Five days prior to the horse theft, Kathrin had emerged from a dusty van and dropped her bags onto the dirt in the town of Kharkhorin—the once proud capital of the Mongol Empire that lies in the upper Orkhon River of Central Mongolia. The following morning her humor helped me through a rather shaky start when my horse, Bor, went into a spin as I tried to mount. In front of a crowd assembled to send us off, I fell forward with my butt up and my face planted in Bor's mane. When the horse calmed down I leaped to terra firma and followed Kathrin's lead in towing my horse on foot out of town. Since then I had come to appreciate her presence and optimism, which made the trip's initial problems somewhat easier to bear.

⊞

THE MISADVENTURES OF our beginnings were hardly becoming of a journey in the spirit of the great horse people of the steppe. We could take heart, however, that we were setting out from a region of esteemed no-mad heritage.

Even before the time of Genghis Khan, the upper Orkhon River valley—in which Kharkhorin was built—had been the fabled seat of imperial power for successive steppe empires. Such was the veneration felt for the Orkhon that the Turkic Gokturks, who reigned over much of Mongolia and Cen-tral Asia between the sixth and eighth centuries, believed that he who controlled the Orkhon region had a divine right to be grand leader of the Turkic tribes. Later the Uighurs—who at one stage claimed to rule from the Caspian Sea to Manchuria—usurped the Gokturks and built their own capital, Khar-Balgas, on the same site, the remains of which still lie just 30 km from Kharkhorin.

Part of the significance of the Orkhon lay in a belief that a special power resided in the sacred mountains through which the Orkhon meandered. A glimpse of a map provides a more obvious strategic importance. Draining the gentle foothills of the Khangai Mountains, the upper reaches of the Orkhon lie near the geographic heart of Mongolia, where the main east-west and north-south routes pass and the three dominant land types of the Eurasian steppe very nearly intermingle—the deserts of the south, the forests of the north, and the grasslands of the center. With a plentiful sup-ply of water and its own relatively mild microclimate, the Orkhon River valley transforms in late spring and early summer into a carpet of olive-green grasslands where all five of the prized types of steppe livestock—horses, bovines (yak, cattle), sheep, goats, and camels, the five known collectively in Mongolian as *tavan tolgoi mal*—are grazed in abundance. In particular, the horse has always thrived here, roaming in the kind of free-running herds that one might imagine existed before its domestication. As such, the Orkhon has always been a cradle of the quintessential nomadic, pastoralist way of life once aspired to by peoples across the steppe.

Befitting a man who would create an empire that overshadowed all others on the steppe before it, Genghis not only designated the upper Orkhon the administrative capital but fought here one of the most important battles of his long path to consolidating power.[1]

In 1204, as the ruler of the tribes in the eastern half of Mongolia, Genghis had become aware of a plot against him by enemies in the west—the powerful Naiman tribe, which had formed an allegiance with, among others, his childhood friend turned archenemy, Jamukha. In anticipation of attack, Genghis rallied an army in the spring and set out west in a daring preemptive campaign. To reach the vicinity of modern-day Kharkhorin, they had ridden across vast distances, risking their horses becoming fatigued at a time of year when pasture was scarce and all livestock were at their weakest. His men were also greatly outnumbered by the enemy, who were under command of the leader of the Naimans, Tayang Khan.

Using tactics that would become associated with the Mongol Empire for centuries to come, Genghis ordered that every man light several campfires at night, therefore fooling the enemy as to the true size of his army. In the future, the Mongol army would also go to the additional effort of placing human-like dummies on reserve horses, thereby appearing to be at least two or three times their real number.

When scouts brought word of Genghis's advance to Tayang Khan, the Naiman leader considered retreating to the more familiar territory of the Altai Mountains in the west. Had the Naimans followed through, Genghis and his men would have had to pursue them for about 1,000 km, which could have proven disastrous given the weakened condition of their horses. However, Tayang Khan's son, Kuchlug, dismissed the idea as cowardly and convinced his father to commit to battle.

It was a fatal decision. The Naimans were cut down in vast numbers, Tayang Khan was mortally wounded, and Kuchlug, together with Jamukha, fled west into what is modern-day eastern Kazakhstan, where they were eventually hunted down.

Following defeat of the Naimans and the subsequent folding of the western tribes, Genghis Khan, now forty-three years old, was both reaching the end of a lifetime of struggle to unify the tribes of the Mongolian plateau and on the cusp of founding the Mongol Empire.[2] To come this far Genghis had overcome almost unthinkable odds. Twelfth-century Mongolia, into which he had been born, was a land engulfed in perpetual conflict as nomad tribes of mixed Mongol and Turkic origin engaged in an age-old series of tit-for-tat raids, as well as broader power struggles that were defined by ever-shifting alliances and an endless narrative of revenge and betrayal.

Genghis, originally known as Temujin, was a member of the Borjigin clan, which practiced a mix of hunting and pastoralism in the northern reaches of Mongolia where the southern rim of the vast Siberian taiga, the coniferous belt of subarctic forest, greets the open steppe.[3] Around the time of Genghis's birth, his father, Yesugei, was known to have killed a chief from an enemy tribe, the Tatars—in fact, it is believed Yesugei named his newborn Temujin after the slain Tatar.[4]

It was a killing that would have consequences.

When Temujin was but nine, Yesugei was poisoned by Tatars and died. Temujin's widowed mother, Hoelun, was abandoned by the other Borjigin families, beginning a tenuous existence in which Temujin fought with his elder kin to become head of the family, narrowly escaped violent raids, and experienced multiple spells in captivity.

Genghis Khan—whose new self-chosen title approximately translates to "grand leader of all"—had dealt with many enemies since that time. It was emblematic of how far he had come that just three years prior to the defeat of the Naimans, in 1201, he had exacted revenge on the Tatars, wiping them out as a future threat. According to various sources, male Tatars were put to the slaughter and the survivors distributed among other various tribes. And although the term *Tatar* has endured to the present as a general term for nomad people of the Eurasian steppe, European visitors to the Mongol Empire in the thirteenth century were told that the Tatars had once been a people, but that the Mongols had conquered them.

On a personal level for Genghis, the Upper Orkhon valley must have been a gratifying vantage point from which to survey this remarkable path to ascendancy. To the north and east among the mixed forest, mountains, and steppe lay his spiritual home, where he had spent his formative years and proven his ability as a charismatic leader. Southward from the upper Orkhon stretched the Gobi Desert, which spoke more of future aspirations. It was home to various nomadic and semi-nomadic peoples, including the Uighurs, from whom Genghis would eventually borrow a script for his previously illiterate tribe. Beyond all that sand and arid steppe also lay China—a land of immeasurable riches that would be the first in his sights once Mongolia had been consolidated. Genghis would eventually die in 1227, after falling from a horse during one of many campaigns to conquer his southerly neighbor.

For a shrewd leader such as Genghis Khan, though, who frequently implied that his rule was mandated by Tengri, the great god of the sky, it was the symbolic importance of conquering the upper Orkhon that would have been at the front of his mind. As long as he held sway over the Orkhon, he would have both an omnipresence among nomads that would help to keep the Mongolian tribes in unity and a strategic gateway to the corners of his growing empire.

Such was the significance of the conquest of the Naimans in the Orkhon River valley, in fact, that just two years later, in 1206, he had the confidence to declare himself the leader of the Mongols, or, more specifically, "The leader of all those who dwell in felt tents." Steppe history is complex, but of everything I'd read, it was this line about felt tents that gave my journey its primary sense of direction and purpose. Understood in the context of the modern day, this reference would only include Mongolians and a few scattered nomads in China, Russia, Kazakhstan, and other former states of Soviet Central Asia. In the thirteenth century, however, it would have applied to the plethora of nomadic tribes that inhabited the Eurasian steppe. While the vast majority of these nomads would never

have heard of Genghis Khan or the Mongol tribes at that time, the unifica-
tion of the Mongols was to lay the foundation for an empire that would
eventually encompass the steppe as far as the Danube and fulfill Genghis's
audacious claim to sovereignty.

Therein lay my journey: I wanted to ride from the symbolic cradle of
Mongolian nomadism, where Kharkhorin still stands, through countries
and cultures that shared a landmass and a common way of life. The end
goal of my journey, the Danube, not only represented one of the approximate boundaries of the Mongol Empire but, more important, the very edge
of the steppe, and therefore the farthest people who ever lived in felt tents.

IN 1204 GENGHIS KHAN might have been able to unite the warring
tribes of Mongolia, but eight centuries later on the same land, Kathrin and
I were content to successfully navigate our way out of the horse-theft valley intact. We spent the night camped hidden between the folds of some
hills, waking regularly to check on our trio. At dawn the shadows, like
our fears of thieves, began to retreat, but the sunrise only seemed to illuminate the scale of the task at hand.

In this first leg of the journey there lay approximately 1,400 km of
steppe, desert, and mountains to the Altai Mountains in the far west of
the country, and horse rustling was just one element of the greater challenge. To see out a single day safely we needed to learn to see other, less
obvious threats, such as an ill-fitting saddle that could fast injure a horse.
Without supplementary feed such as grain and hay, we knew one of our
main tasks would be learning to recognize and search out grasses that
were nutritious for the horses, not to mention learning steppe etiquette
and mastering riding. Viewed in this light, the coming three months of
summer were a narrow window to earn my nomad credentials. Beyond
Mongolia, if I made it, I would face the less forgiving conditions of winter
and the prospect of countries where nomadic life and wisdom had long
been in decline.

At the heart of the steep learning curve was coming to terms with the nature of the horse. Although all Mongolian breeds are stocky animals that survive the winters by digging through the snow to find feed, they apparently fell into two broad categories. The first included horses with a calm temperament; these were known as nomkhon. The second comprised wild, untamed horses that can nevertheless tolerate humans. Two of our horses—my old white gelding, Bor, and the chestnut gelding, Sartai Zeerd (the name meant "moon crescent chestnut"), were definitely of the latter variety. Just the touch of a brush or a blanket could send them into a wild display of bucking and rearing, and pig rooting—an Australian expression that describes the behavior of a horse when it kicks out with the hind legs while keeping the head down and forelegs planted. Grooming, blanketing, and saddling each morning were therefore nerveracking procedures. Packing the gear was another art unto itself. Even a small difference in weight between the pack boxes could risk saddle sores and injuries. The boxes subsequently had to be meticulously weighed using hand scales before being hoisted up onto our little bay gelding, Kheer, who by virtue of his calmer nature had become our designated packhorse.

A year would pass before I had learned enough to begin taking the rigors of riding and horse care in stride, and in these first few days it required all our energy and focus just to cope with getting from one camp to the next. The situation wasn't helped by a regime of night watch shifts that Kathrin and I had decided on. Nonetheless, the predatory feeling to the land did seem to fade with each passing day, and as the horses tired, they became slightly more agreeable.

After a week of straight riding, I found myself reawakening to the romance of the land and settling into a rhythm that was intimately involved with the moods of summer. Casting off from camp down onto a wide treeless plain on what was our twelfth day out from Kharkhorin, I felt the sun's early rays gently warming us from behind, while the pink hues of the western sky gradually flooded with incandescent blue. Ahead and around us the steppe spread out in vast sheets of luminescent green, appearing utterly empty until the sun revealed the white flecks of gers nestled at the base of tall mountains on the plain's perimeter. The agent for the changing of the guard from morning to midday was a breeze that came whispering over the young, supple summer grass, bringing a sortie of clouds, the shadows of which bent and twisted gracefully over the curvature of the earth. Also drifting across this sea-like grandeur were nomad riders sitting high in the saddle, their horses' legs a blur.

In a pattern that would become familiar, the climbing heat of midmorning coincided with a rising symphony of cicadas and the melting of the horizon into a haze. Herds of cattle, yaks, sheep, and goats disappeared in search of shade and water, and at the sun's zenith, when the temperature exceeded 30°C, the few horses we passed stood nodding their heads and swishing their tails. Nomad camps, meanwhile, appeared abandoned and lonely. Swept up in pungent clouds of dust and fine particles of dried animal dung, the only sign of movement came from foals lying flat, tied to tether lines, and big wooly guard dogs that lay low in whatever sliver of shadow they could find.

Come late afternoon, the sun had burned a path from our backs over our left shoulders and now dangled from the western sky before our eyes. Like the incoming tide, herds converged and piles of smoldering dung were placed around camps, keeping the swarms of mosquitoes at bay. Looking for a place to spend the night, we fixed our course on two nearly imperceptible gers that lay below a rounded peak in the distance.

By the time we reached the gers, the land was basking in golden evening light and the family in camp had been watching us through a spyglass for a couple of hours. Even before we could dismount, children came running with fresh bowls of yogurt, directing us to a place where we could set up our tent. While the horses were taken to a spring-fed trough, a team of young and old descended to help us unpack.

Ever since the horse-thieving incident we had been somewhat wary when it came to getting to know the people, but imbued with the magic of the day's ride, we happily surrendered. Our ensuing stay became typical of much of our time among nomads in the coming months, but particularly characteristic of central Mongolia, with its abundance of animals and summer dairy production.

With about eight pairs of helping hands, our tent was soon set up and the family piled in. An elderly man wearing a silky green *deel*—the universal long cloak of the nomads, fastened at the waist with a tightly bound sash—inspected the zips, fabric, and poles, then lay down on its floor as if he were a prospective buyer. Next he inventoried our horse tack and was particularly fascinated by my saddles and rope halters. Much to his disbelief, we had come riding in without a bit in the horses' mouths, instead using a rein tied to the rope halter. This was a technique the Watson family—who had given both of us our crash course in horsemanship— had encouraged us to do because it allowed the horses to eat and drink freely. The old man shook his head and waved his finger at this bitless riding technique, and was equally unhappy about the packsaddle with its heavy boxes. Horses were considered the aristocrats of the steppe, and by loading mine with deadweight, treating it as a beast of burden, I was breaking an ancient taboo. Today, just as in the time of Genghis Khan, horses were used only for riding, the task of haulage strictly delegated to camels, cattle, and yaks.

My riding saddle was an entirely different matter. The man fetched some spectacles held together with grotty old Band-Aids and ran his hands over the saddle's every feature, from the deep leather seat to the soft panels underneath. It was an Australian stock saddle with an adjustable gullet—a feature that enabled me to change the width of the front of the saddle according to the size of my horse's withers. Although I was still somewhat flummoxed by horse tack in general, the old man most definitely wasn't. He planted my saddle on his own horse and took turns trying it out with several of his sons. By the end of the session he came to me with what would be the first of hundreds of offers for my saddle right across the steppe. In some cases hanging on to it proved more difficult than keeping tabs on my horses, and often I was forced to sleep with the saddle inside the tent.

As the sun began to sink behind the mountains, the matriarch of this family group came out firing off orders, and within seconds everyone had scattered from our tent and returned to their duties. We now turned to the activities of the family with the same sense of fascination with which we had been inspected.

In this camp, which was nestled on a slight rise overlooking the plain, there were three gers that housed three generations. An elderly couple lived in one at the far end of camp together with their youngest, unmarried son, while the other two were home to two of their other sons and their wives and children. We found that keeping track of whose child was whose was especially difficult, since the number of children at any nomad camp swelled in the summertime, with relatives from the provincial centers and Ulaanbaatar sending their children to the countryside for the long school break. At the same time, babies seemed to be frequently handed from one mother to another depending on who was busy and who was not.

There was a distinct structure to nomadic family life, however, that had remained the unwritten law since the earliest records on the steppe. For one, daughters were required to move away to live with their husband's family, while males generally stayed closer to their parents. The youngest son was shouldered with the responsibility of looking after the parents in their elderly years, but was also given the title of otchigin— guardian of the family's home and livestock

Although Genghis Khan broke with many nomad traditions, he stuck ardently to the tradition of otchigin when dividing up the Mongol Empire between his sons. His eldest son, Jochi, was given the lands farthest from the center of Mongolia, "to as far west as our hooves have trodden," which at the time of Genghis's death included the area from the Irtysh River to the Ural River, in modern Kazakhstan. As the Mongol Empire expanded, Jochi's sons became the founders and leaders of what became known as the Golden Horde, which included modern-day Russia, Ukraine, and much of Kazakhstan.[5] Genghis's youngest son, Tolui, was entrusted with the heartland, Mongolia, and inherited the responsibilities of chief administrator after Genghis's death until one of the other sons, Ogodei, was elected grand khan.

Prior to our arrival, the boys of the family had driven immense communal herds of sheep, goats, and yaks back to camp, where the women were ready and waiting with their milking buckets and stools. The goats were the first in line to be milked, and as we watched, every member of the family took part in what was a nightly production line being repeated by tens of thousands of other nomad families across the country.

There were scenes of hysterics as the little children were tasked with rounding up the most mischievous goats. They sprinted after the animals, diving to catch whatever body part they could lay a hand on, whether it be the leg, ears, or even tail, but often ended up facedown in the dust. When one particularly large and courageous goat made a break for the open steppe beyond camp, one of the boys, probably no older than ten, swung up onto a horse bareback and, with his chest pushed out like a little man's, went galloping off with a shriek.

One by one the goats were tethered head to head with ropes made from yak- and horsehair. Young girls under the watch of their mothers moved from animal to animal, milking away until the pail was full, at which point it would be taken to a ready pot for boiling.

While nomads of the steppe rely largely on meat for survival, in the summer, dairy is a staple. From the boiled milk of goats, yaks, and cows—and, in desert areas, camels—they are able to make a diverse array of products, including creams, butters, cheeses, and yogurts. This is not to mention the renowned fermented mare's milk, airag—better known by the Turkic term kumys—that Marco Polo remarked was like "a white wine." It is known from archaeological digs in northern Kazakhstan, where the earliest horse culture has been discovered to date, that this drink, or unfermented mare's milk at the very least, has been an important part of the diet on the steppe since the earliest of times.

Perhaps the most universal food for horsemen of the steppe, however, was aaruul, which was what the grandmother of the family was preparing this evening. The fresh milk carted into her ger was boiled over a dung-fired stove, left to curdle, and then strained. The resulting curds were then compressed between pieces of wood weighted down by large rocks. These large pressed cakes would be made into various shapes and then put on the roof of the ger in trays to dry. Aaruul could be soft when fresh, but in the dry climate of the steppe it was often hard as rock, to the point where it was have to be sucked rather than chewed, and would last for a very long time. By carrying a bag of this bitter snack, it is said, warriors in Genghis's day were able to survive ten days without any other food. Kathrin and I had already been loaded up with aaruul by other nomad families, and although I found it overwhelmingly bitter, I eventually came to appreciate the way it staved off hunger during long hours in the saddle.

Midway into the milking process, Kathrin and I were beckoned into a ger and ushered to the grass at the rear, behind the hearth. One of the mothers, a bandy-legged woman with an angelic, youthful face but the creased, worn hands of someone in middle age, passed us cups of tea even before we were seated.

As I took a sip of the salty milk tea, the lingering sound of the wind in my ears died out. In this felt tent, just steps from the doorway, it seemed as though the vast land and sweeping sky that had so dominated our lives had vanished.

I looked across to Kathrin and said nothing. She sat with her cup cradled in her hands, her eyes wandering about the ger.

Feeling the teacup warm my fingers, I gazed up at the woman who stood next the stove. She was illuminated by a shaft of dying light that passed through the circular opening in the ceiling. She lifted a ladle of milk into the air and let the milk pour back down, then fluidly repeated the process. Steam wafted up, condensing fleetingly on her cheeks, which were as broad and splayed as wings, darkened by the sun but still soft. Her eyes were gracefully elongated, feather-like in shape, emanating femininity, yet her shoulders were wide, big-boned, and brimming with strength.

When the woman retired to an old steel spring bed to cradle her baby, my eyes shifted to the details of the ger. The frame was constructed with six collapsible lattice wall sections that could be swiftly dismantled and tied to the back of a camel or, as was the tradition in this region, strapped to a yak-drawn cart. From the top of the walls more than seventy intricately painted wooden roof poles—much like spokes—angled up to the circular opening at the apex of the ceiling.

Wrapped around the wooden frame like flesh on bone, thick sheets of felt were nearly impervious to sunlight, insulating against the cold and the heat. The felt so effectively damped the sounds from the world outside that one could easily converse in whispers while sitting at opposite sides of the structure, even in the midst of a storm—a quality I could only compare to what I had experienced in a snow cave.

When the milking was finished, everyone crowded into one ger for a dinner of meat and homemade noodles—known as *gurultai shul*—after which we passed around my photo album from Australia. The elder of the family, who had been so interested in my saddle, tried to ask a series of questions, but our poor Mongolian left us hanging. I was fluent in Russian, but like communism itself, it was a language that had never really held currency among a people who had remained more or less self-reliant through the centuries.

It was dark outside before we knew it. An oil lamp was lit, throwing a glow across to the woman who had been cooking earlier; now she sat with her husband, their little one fast asleep between them. Outside there came the almost inaudible sound of bleating and farting as the sheep, goats, and yaks settled in around the gers, adding to the sensation we were sitting in the nucleus of an extended family.

Although I didn't quite grasp it yet, much of my journey across the steppe to Hungary would be spent trying to imagine how life might have once been before the Russian Empire and the era of industrialization in Soviet times brought about an effective end to the nomadic way of life. It was also true that even now in Mongolia, the urban population, particularly in Ulaanbaatar, was growing exponentially, and there were whispers of multinational mining giants negotiating agreements to exploit Mongolia's untold deposits of gold, coal, copper, and uranium.

For most Mongolians in 2004, though, the looming mining boom and its potential impacts still seemed far off and unfathomable, and here, cradled by the ger, there was no thinking backward or forward, only a feeling of completeness, for this was nomadic life intact, virtually unchanged from the days of Genghis Khan eight hundred years before.

3

WOLF TOTEM

FROM THE NOMAD camp we continued northwest through the Khangai Mountains—a sprawling range that dominates central Mongolia and separates the dry deserts of the south from the Siberian forests. We were cutting through a narrow finger of the Khangai range to reach the gentler plains and river valleys on its northwestern perimeter. As we rode, I found myself absorbed by the unfolding terrain that grew in scale and wildness.

Meandering rivers led us among peaks as bony as the backs of malnourished old horses and past lakes where we watched the mist roll across the glassy water at dawn. The higher peaks were generally sleek, round-edged and emerald green, with dense clusters of forest concealing much of the upper slopes.

Perhaps it had something to do with a confidence newly found during our stay with the nomad family, but a feeling of cadence and routine emerged. Flecks of white on the horizon grew into gers as we rode, filling our day with characters, sound, and color, then melted over our shoulders just as the taste of fermented milk and dried curd faded from our palates. In a world without fences, where communities lifted and moved as unpredictably as the weather, our usual ways of keeping track of time and place were beginning to change. The only reference point for one particularly empty valley was a vulture pecking away at the flesh of a yak carcass under an oppressive sun. An entire day was defined by an incident when herders who borrowed Kathrin's horse to catch their own runaway mounts left us for hours wondering if, in fact, they had stolen it. A whole afternoon was marked out by one of many storms that came roaring through, breaking the heat and slamming us with a barrage of hail. For an hour we stood, like the horses, tail to the wind, shivering cold, yet within another half hour the black wall had given way to blue, and under the baking sun I was searching the sky for shade-giving clouds.

Ten days after our stay with the nomad family we made a decision to deviate from the main valleys and travel over a wild mountain pass known as Davaa Nuur (Mountain Pass Lake). Although we had begun to camp regularly with nomad families for the protection they offered, the grass around these camps was usually eaten down to dry stubble, and our horses were growing hungry and thin. Just as important, crossing Davaa Nuur would take us up away from the heat and provide a shortcut through the northern fringes of the Khangai Mountains to where the land promised to settle into broader slopes and plains.

Upon hearing about our plan, the family with whom we had camped at the base of the river valley loaded us up with dried curd and yak cheese. As we were on the point of departure, our host, a gruff toothless herder in a torn, threadbare deel that reeked of tobacco and mutton, emerged from the ger shaking his head and repeating, "It's dangerous up there!" The bowlegged elderly matriarch of the family waddled out carrying a bucket of milk. As we turned and rode away she flicked three ladles to the sky. "Ayan zamdaa sain yavaarai!" she called, wishing us good luck on our journey, as the milk rained down on our backs and the rumps of the horses. In a land where every journey away from home presented the risk of misfortune and even death, this was a ritual that had been preserved from ancient times long before the era of Genghis Khan. White represented luck and purity, and painting the road with this sacrifice of milk asked the gods to favor us with safe travels.

Several hours later, the family ger had contracted to an anonymous speck below, and what had been a wide river valley was a boxed-in ravine at the feet of giant mountain ridges that leaned toward one another. We had long lost any hint of a trail and followed a stream that cascaded down a trench through swamp and loose rock.

It was just coming on to evening as the tall seeding grasses gave way to dense, short alpine varieties cradling delicate colonies of dew and rain-drops. Not far above, 3,000 m peaks swam in frothing mist and cloud, revealing a different character each time I lifted my eyes. For one short period the sun bore through to the silvery scree slopes, highlighting orange and yellow lichens. Soon, however, the whole mountain was stained with dark cloud shadow, betraying no pigment at all. Then the clouds boiled over, and again all was lost in a soup of rain and mist. The sheer fragility of calm in this mountain environment brought a welcome clarity absent in hotter climes.

When we crested a final pinch of rock and grass, the source of the stream opened up. Davaa Nuur was a tawny lake nestled between the rocky peaks we had been aiming for all day. By now muscular black storm clouds had cut the sunlight short and banished any sense of romance.

In the morning we woke to waves of rain and hail that drove into the tent with such intense gusts that the tent threatened to tear apart. When it was particularly strong we sat hard up against the fabric feeling the blows from rain and hail pepper our spines. At last the wind abated somewhat and we lay cuddling in the sleeping bag. It was no secret that Kathrin had been looking forward to the sense of privacy to be found out here in the relative wilderness. It had become the norm to wake at the break of dawn greeted by children and adults sitting at the entrance of the tent watching our every move. When we packed up to leave, they would often inno-cently pull everything out of our boxes and sprawl things about. Men would also gallop in begging to see our saddles. Coping with this atten-tion, as well as managing the horses and everything else, left no room for romance. Our relationship had become a businesslike, working one, not helped by the fact that I could barely manage a weary "good night" before falling asleep each evening.

At around lunchtime, however, it seemed that even here in the wilderness time to ourselves was limited. Just as one of many thunderclouds surged over and the light went dim, two bedraggled men crawled in unannounced. It was a small, two-person tent—cozy at the best of times—but this didn't seem to concern the men, who unraveled tobacco bundled in old silk sashes, and began smoking.

"Where are you traveling?" they eventually asked.

I explained we were traveling to the Danube, but their eyes glazed over. "Tosontsengel," I then said, referring to a town on the far side of the pass. In turn, they explained they were searching for 150 missing yaks.

I offered them tea and aaruul. For the next hour or so they sat quietly smoking, flicking through our photos, and talking among themselves.

The rain eased, and the herders left the tent. I seized the opportunity to hike to the peak directly above camp. Perched on a rock that nearly breached the ceiling of cloud, I took in the land we had been riding through. First I cast my eyes over the lake. For a brief time the water was still, but then, brushed by the wind, it all went opaque and gray and an isolated rainstorm drifted across its breadth before smacking into rocky slopes on the far shore. To the north beyond the lake, where we planned to cross the pass tomorrow, mountains and clouds choked off the view, but to the south the horizon was indefinitely far. In places light spilled through patches of blue to the earth far below where flocks of sheep could be seen like fine grains of salt and pepper in a slow avalanche down the valley sides. Across on the opposing mountains patches of forest nestled into sheltered indentations, watched over by pyramids of green. I imagined the many hidden crevices and unhampered woods crawling with wild animals, which warily monitored the life of the humans below, just as I was doing.

The longer I concentrated, the more I became aware of the multitude of gers and the presence of horsemen, particularly on the bottom of the valley slopes. Together with their animals, nomads were carrying out a cycle of symbiotic life as old as the domestication of the sheep and the horse—the animals turned the grass into meat, milk, and dung, providing food, shelter, and heat. In return, the nomads offered their flocks protection from wolves and storms.

Some horsemen, however, like those who had been in our tent, could be seen picking their way up through the wild mountains to summits far from their homes and flocks. At the same time kites were diving down to clean away the tossed-aside remains of carcasses near gers and pick off rodents such as ground squirrels and mice from the grazing areas. Unlike where I had grown up in Australia, where the land was demarcated into national parks, logging zones, farmland, and residential areas, here there was an overwhelming sense that animals and humans coexisted on the margins of survival, each knowing its unique role.

By the time I made my way back down to camp, hail was beating down once more and the view had closed in. I was more than happy to return to a slumber in the tent, where the world was small and snug. The sun faded early behind the dense clouds, and we slept longer than we had since beginning our journey.

Two days later we were still confined to the tent by the weather and I was craving the long horizons of the steppe. With dwindling food supplies and only a sprinkling of diesel left for the stove, there was, in any case, no choice but to give the pass a try or retreat back down the way we had come.

We woke at 5:00 A.M. and by seven o'clock were skirting around the edge of the lake. A hint of sunlight that promised to break through the moody clouds stirred hopes of better weather, but there was no denying we had left summer behind in the valley. My toes turned to ice, and from the bare, wind-lashed slopes the only trees that dared grow were dwarf birch and willow, rising up all disfigured and little higher than ground creepers.

No sooner had I contemplated dismounting to warm up my toes than Bor fell knee deep through a frozen crust into a bog and I was very nearly thrown from the saddle. We dismounted and continued on foot, but time and time again were forced to backtrack from bogs with panicked horses, or became blockaded by fields of jagged rocks reminiscent of an old moraine. When Kathrin's horse suddenly flew at me with his back legs, hooves clearing my head by a hairsbreadth, we lay back in the bog to take stock. My hands trembled with adrenaline, and my vision blurred from hunger. Kathrin looked defeated. We had only just reached the northern end of the lake, and judging from my map, the pass was another 8 km away, the majority of which remained smothered by mist. Getting up there was beginning to feel beyond us.

As we sipped tea from the thermos, however, we noticed something that rekindled hope. Delicately marked out between two rocks was the unmistakable shape of a hoofprint. Sensing the significance, we leaped to our feet, and only a little farther on found a similar indentation. Then we laid eyes on something that told us all we needed to know: the butt of a cigarette.

Over the next three or four hours there were times when we lost all sign of the horse tracks, but just when we were convinced we had gone astray, they would materialize again. Meanwhile, a picture of this phantom rider grew. He was a gentle man, I decided, probably in his middle years, riding with a gun slung over his shoulder and a cigarette lolling in his mouth. At times he sang, but as he neared the pass he grew quiet and sober. In truth, though, nothing fazed him. While we pushed and fell and fought against every obstacle, he passed by with lightness and subtlety along a path that was clear as day to him and his horse. This grand adventure of ours was possibly an ordinary day's ride for a nomad returning home after a visit to friends.

Over the course of the journey, the companionship I felt from the sight of these hoofprints was something I would come to experience time and time again. In remote areas, the tracks of wild animals, horses, or humans provided solace, comfort, and clues to the puzzling lay of the land. It helped me ignore my fears, engaging me in a guessing game as to where the tracks might be headed and why. When finally we would depart from one set of tracks, it was like saying farewell to an old friend.

After six hours of heavy trudging, we were heartened when the mist dissipated slightly and the triangular silhouette of a cairn, known as an *ovoo*, came into view. It was a humble pile of rocks scattered with fragments of dried curd and a tattered blue silk scarf known as a *khadag*. A few craggy tree branches were planted in the middle of the pile. Ovoos like this had been a familiar sight on mountaintops and passes across Mongolia for centuries, if not thousands of years, possibly originating as marker cairns for navigation but also, and more important, functioning as sites of worship where travelers paused to venerate the mountains and offer acknowledgment and prayer to *tengri*, the eternal blue sky. The triangular structure, sometimes created with timber rather than stone, was, according to some, meant to symbolize the shape of the rising sun and pay tribute to its life-giving rays. This reflected the ancient animistic beliefs of Mongolians who, since time immemorial, considered the sky their father and the earth their mother. Ovoos were usually only found in the highest places, since it was there that sky, sun, and earth all married.

Following tradition, we walked around the ovoo in a clockwise direction three times, offering a new rock to the pile with each circle. In another context we might have felt like foreigners going through the motions of performing another culture's ritual, but here it provided a sense of comfort to know that something had borne witness to our presence there.

Just below the ovoo we dropped down a crumbly slope of clay and rock and emerged from a curtain of mist into daylight.

Boggy permafrost gave way to sturdy ground, and the sun's rays gently filtered down, bathing us with warmth that had been unimaginable in recent days. The only sign of storms here were wispy trickles of mist that boiled over the lip of the east-west-running ridge we had crossed, evaporating in the face of the sun. While the southern side had been treeless and windswept, the slopes here were thickly carpeted with larch forests that extended as far north as we could see. Following the tracks of the horseman, we descended at a good pace until the wind came to a standstill and we began to hear the bubbling of a stream, the cackle of birds, and the whine of cicadas. The cold and storms had become a memory, packed away like the rainproof coats and warm layers of clothing we had been living in for days.

We remounted the horses, and for the next few hours followed the twists and turns of the stream as it led us ever deeper into a forested valley. The horses pushed through the same waist-high grass where the phantom rider clearly had been, and I fell into rhythm with my horse, imagining that the mountain pass had delivered us into another time.

It was precisely this kind of high, forested backcountry that had so shaped the outlook and beliefs of Genghis Khan. Unlike nomads of the open steppe grasslands, he had grown up on the southern fringes of the Siberian forests, where reliance on grazing sheep and cattle wasn't possible. Hunting was a mainstay of his small tribe's survival, and whenever there was trouble in his life, he learned to retreat to the forest, where nature afforded him sustenance and protection. In one legendary episode, at the age of sixteen he managed to narrowly escape a deadly raid on his family by fleeing to the forested Khentii Mountains, not far from the place of his birth in present-day northeast Mongolia. There, surviving on marmots, rats, and whatever else he could find, he managed to evade capture. According to *The Secret History of the Mongols*, the future leader later voiced his gratitude to the highest mountain in the Khentii range, Burkhan Khaldun, by removing his belt and throwing it over his shoulder, then dropping to the ground nine times toward the south. "The mountain has saved my life. I shall not forget it," he said.[1]

Right up until the end of his days, Genghis would return to Burkhan Khaldun Mountain to worship and pray before going off to war or making any important decisions. Victory was always a sign that he had been given divine power and permission from Tengri, the eternal blue sky.

Just as the yellow disc of the sun began to touch the jagged skyline of the forest, our mood swung. We had lost the horseman's tracks, and the slopes of the valley side had become so steep we were forced to lead the horses along narrow ledges and crisscross from one riverbank to the other. The forest had been gutted by a wildfire, and where trees might have once bloomed with color and crawled with birds and squirrels, bare, sooty trunks fingered their way toward the sky. A sea of willow-herb had been the first to seed on the ground below us, and its millions of bobbing purple flower heads were the only living thing to catch the lingering light. No nomads had been here for a long time, and perhaps they had never grazed their animals in the upper reaches of this valley.

By the time dusk came on we were feeling marginally more positive. After negotiating the steepest section of the valley, we had reached a broad, open meadow on the riverbank, and set about making camp. Just as we were tying down the guy ropes, there came a howl from down the valley.

"There must a be a nomad family down there after all!" I said to Kathrin, fixing my eyes downstream, expecting to locate a nomad encampment. As I strained to focus in the fading light, the only white tinge to the landscape came from a ghostly rock that glowed from a slope of blackened, dead trees.

The howl came again, long and hound-like. From up the valley a similar cry echoed, then another from high in the forest on the far bank. Kathrin tripped over our canvas duffle bag, then sat where she had fallen with her panicked eyes skirting the forest. Nothing moved, and again things fell silent.

"You—you secure the horses! I'm going for firewood!" I stammered.

Nomads had long cautioned me about wolves and thought us mad to be traveling without a gun, but I had always dismissed their warnings as scaremongering. During my studies in Finland, I had learned that despite all the rumors and fear about wolves, there had only been a handful of recorded stories in history about attacks on humans, and even then the victims had been babies or young children.

It was only now that the real threat dawned on me. The wolves were interested not in us but in our horses. If the horses were frightened enough to break free of their tethers and escape, what would we do?

Night flooded in fast as I chopped away at standing trees, the axe first smashing its way through charcoal before hitting a core of dead dry wood that was hard as steel. After an hour's work I barely had enough wood to fill my outstretched arms, but nevertheless hurried back to camp.

Without a gun, there were only two courses of action available. I urinated near each of the three horses—a trick long suggested to me by veterinarian Sheila Greenwell. Second, I lit a fire and rationed out the meager wood supplies that would need to see us out until dawn. According to Mongolians, a fire would keep the wolves at bay.

Once the fire was going we relaxed somewhat and sat gazing into the flames, eating a mash of rice and rehydrated meat. As my tummy filled, I watched a deep blackness spill into the eastern sky and stars flicker on.

After an hour or two had passed with no sign of wolves, I collapsed in the tent while Kathrin took the first shift by the fire.

I woke after what felt like just minutes. Kathrin was shaking me.

"Relax, Tim! Apart from the fact that I'm freezing, everything is okay. No wolves so far. It's one in the morning, so it's your turn, you lazy Australian!" she said, her German accent, as always, more pronounced when she was tired.

I swapped my sleeping bag for the down jacket she had been wearing, and I settled in beside the gentle crackle and spitting of the fire. The flames licked the night air and cast a circle of flickering light that just reached the horses. All three of them had eaten themselves silly in the afternoon and now stood like statues, their heads hanging. The sky was giant above, yet as we nestled in this tall grass in the bosom of the hills, there was an intimacy that cradled us. I couldn't help wonder what it would be like after Kathrin went home and 9,000 km to Hungary yawned. The longest journey in the wilderness I'd ever done alone until now was a mere ten days.

By three o'clock an invisible heaviness tugged at my arms and legs. I rested my head on a rolled-up coat and drifted off.

When I felt the thudding of hooves vibrate through the soil beneath me, I thought sleepily that I was in the tent. I assumed Bor was attempting to move in the hobbles that bound his two front legs to his back left leg. While the others had mastered the art of walking at a reasonable speed with the hobbles on, Bor stumbled awkwardly.

Then, however, I heard furious pounding coming in toward me from all directions.

No sooner had I pried open my eyes than a howl shot through the darkness. This time it was from somewhere right behind us, perhaps no more than 100 m away, on the edge of the forest. I lay low, not daring to breathe. It was black all around—I had let the fire burn down to a few glowing coals.

When the fire was again ablaze I picked up the axe and checked on the ropes and tethering stakes. The horses' necks and withers were tense and their heads were raised high, ears twitching this way and that. Over thousands of years they had evolved as a supreme animal of flight, able to reach top speed within seconds and escape at the first hint of predators. By hobbling them, however, I had turned them into easy prey.

For the next few hours I sat, axe at hand, convinced our lives hung in the balance. When the fire sputtered and it seemed my pile of wood wasn't going to make it to dawn, I was sure I could make out the furry outline of wolves prowling the perimeter of camp. I even began to think there might be hundreds of them, half crazed by starvation in the cremated remains of the forest. Feeding my remaining branches into the fire piece by piece, I prayed for dawn and rued my formerly dismissive attitude. No matter what I might have previously thought about wolves, there was something deeply petrifying about these howls in the dark. Perhaps through thousands of years of coexisting and competing with the wolf, humans, like horses, had evolved an innate reaction to them—one that was surely not without reason.

I recalled what my friend Gansukh had once told me: "It's not for nothing you call a dog in your country 'man's best friend'—we Mongolians know they were the first animal to be domesticated! We believe the wolf is the wisest and most spiritual of animals. Look how cunning they are, how they survive in such tough conditions. To see a wolf, in our belief, is a good omen. It means you will inherit some of its wisdom. To kill a wolf is to be wiser than a wolf. We eat wolf meat for strength and use it for medicinal purposes."

The significance of the wolf for Mongolians went beyond Gansukh's words. There was a legend that the ancient Mongolian people had been born from a union between the blue-gray wolf and a deer. Wolves carried the spirit of the Mongolian ancestors, the link proven by what was called a "Mongolian spot"—a bluish patch found on the lower back of most Mongolians in their infancy. It was also understood that when a wolf howled, it was praying to the sky, making it the only other living being that paid homage to sacred tengri.

Perhaps most important for nomads was the belief in the symbiosis that existed between wolf and humans on the steppe. Wolves were an integral part of keeping the balance of nature, ensuring that plagues of rabbits and rodents didn't break out, which in turn protected the all-important pasture for the nomads' herds.

Although they caused havoc when they attacked sheep, when it came to horses wolves were known to mostly attack the injured and the weak, therefore aiding natural selection and ensuring that only the strongest horses lived on to breed. Reflective of the deep sense of gratitude and respect Mongolians reserved for wolves, there was a belief that only through wolves could the spirit of a deceased human be set free to go to heaven. When a person passed away, his or her body would be taken to a mountain and left for the wolves to eat. A good person would be eaten by wolves quickly, while a bad person would be left to rot for days. According to legend, wolves would fly up to the sky with the ingested human flesh and release the person's spirit.

As Kathrin and I would later discover, this "sky burial" was a practice still carried out among modern nomads. In Uvs province, only a day's ride from Ulaangom, we came across the skeleton of a young man on the steppe with only a few remaining pieces of sun-dried flesh and a torn khadag lying nearby.

In the safety and comfort of a nomad ger this philosophy might have made for engaging storytelling. But as the fire wavered it was difficult to feel gratitude toward the wolf. How could I reconcile the benevolent creature that Mongolians so worshipped with the ruthless animals that were surely about to attack my horses, and perhaps even Kathrin and me? And how was it that Gansukh could speak about worshipping the wolf and then in the same breath about killing and eating it?

I didn't know it yet, but these were questions that would linger for me well beyond the end of my journey. Over time I would come to believe that to dismiss the wolf as a bloodthirsty enemy would be akin to labeling nomads in the same ignorant way that Europeans had done for centuries.

The reality was that survival on the steppe was a fine balance, and wolves, like the humans, were no more cruel than was required to survive. Perhaps the relationship between wolves and nomads was best described in the fictional tale "Wolf Totem." In it an old Mongolian herder recounts to a Chinese student that the "wolf is a spiritual totem but a physical enemy." Of course, this understanding was still light-years from my mind where I sat now, barely a stone's throw from the beginning of my journey on the way to the distant Danube.

In the end, the test between night and my fire went down to the wire, and there were times when I was sure the fire would not hold out. When finally the night began to wilt away, however, there had been no howls for hours. I placed the last morsel of wood on the flames and lay until the sun's glow had eclipsed that of the coals. Soon the fire I had so clung to was nothing more than a gray bed of ashes.

By the time we were ready to go, the sun had painted out the shadows, and, just as the mountains around us appeared to shrink in the daylight, the threat of the wolves began to seem exaggerated. I started to think that had I been a more experienced horseman, I might have taken the night's experience in my stride. As if to leave us with a reminder of the danger, however, only a stone's throw from camp we passed the fresh tracks of a wolf on the muddy banks of the river.

In the future, particularly on the open steppe of western Mongolia and Kazakhstan, I would not have the advantage of firewood, nor the company of Kathrin. While carrying a gun seemed out of the question, it was clear I might have to come up with some kind of plan. For the time being, though, I was just grateful to be riding away.

4

A FINE LINE TO THE WEST

WHEN WE EMERGED from the forest into the grazed slopes of the lower valley, thoughts of the dangers posed by wolves faded and I was comforted by thoughts of a bigger picture of the journey. The mountain river we followed from the pass, known as the Delgerekh, was part of a greater watercourse I had crossed paths with during previous travels. Not more than three days' ride downstream it entered the Ider River, which in turn flowed east and north, joining the Selenga, and emptying into Lake Baikal in Siberia.

Four years earlier during the cycling journey across Russia, Chris Hatherly and I had crossed Baikal's pristine waters by ship and ridden our bikes along the Selenga. The following year I had returned to the shores of Baikal to join three others rowing a wooden boat more than 4,000 km northward through Siberia to the Arctic Ocean. Following first the Angara and then the Yenisey River and rowing twenty-four hours a day, we spent four and a half months meandering through steppe, then dense taiga, and finally frozen tundra. Having reached the Arctic coast at the river's mouth on the Kara Sea, we abandoned the boat with a reindeer-herding community and made our way home.

Now, three years later, riding alongside the humble waters of the Delgerekh that would someday make the same journey to the Arctic, I was on a very different trajectory. Heading west into the center of Eurasia, I could never hope for the abundance of firewood, water, and fish that had come to characterize those earlier experiences. For nomads, pasture held currency above all else, and so I was destined to remain on the steppe, picking a line between the boreal forests of the north and the deserts and mountains found at more southerly latitudes. Although the river tempted me with the possibility of greater plenty, I was looking forward to breaking away from its predetermined course and returning to open horizons. Just a few days' ride from here lay the prospect of exiting the Khangai Mountains, from where our route promised to take us into the broader and drier terrain of western Mongolia.

Before we could leave the valley and recover some rhythm, however, the Delgerekh had some important lessons in store for us.

We had only just made camp near one of the first gers we had seen in days when the distant rumble of a Russian four-wheel-drive from down the valley rapidly grew into a roar. I was attending a pot of boiling water when the headlights found us. As Kathrin ran to pull the horses in close to the tent, the car motored in over the tethering lines and jerked to a halt half a metre shy of my stove. The engine cut out and there was momentary silence, but then a door opened and from beyond the blinding glare of headlights the silhouette of a man stumbled into view, a waft of vodka preceding him.

"Do you have whiskey? Vodka? Airag?" he screamed in Russian, digging his index finger into my chest. Infuriated by my blank look, he lunged for the knife on my belt. When I resisted, keeping it out of his reach, he clenched his fist and drew it back, ready to punch.

"I take two of your horses now! They are mine!"

What had begun as a calm evening in what we assumed was the safety of peopled, wolf-free lands was about to become an all-night ordeal during which we managed to narrowly save the horses but had our crucial navigation maps stolen. When the attacker drove away, we took refuge with a nomad family, only to find ourselves in the throes of more drunken antics. Arguments, the odd prod and jab at Kathrin and me, and the coming and going of horsemen lasted until dawn, when, upon checking the horses, it was clear we were still not out of the woods. We found Bor sitting on his haunches trying to lick a swelling that had appeared on his spine. It was on an area of his back well behind my saddle, in a spot where I had earlier noticed multiple scars—signs, according to vet Sheila Greenwell, of a possible warble fly infestation. The larvae of this fly were known to burrow into the flesh, causing painful swellings and then sores when the mature flies resurfaced.

Staying to rest the horses was not an option, and so I loaded my backpack and set off on foot with Bor and the packhorse, Kheer, in tow. It was a relief when two young men rode up to us with the stolen maps, although they promptly threatened to tear them up unless we paid for their services. After negotiating a fee of $10, we carried on aware that while we had escaped serious misfortune this time, there was no guarantee we would always be so lucky.

Even before we threw ourselves on the mercy of a friendly nomad family that night, it was obvious that one of the main challenges of this journey would be treading the fine line between the dangers of the wilds and those of a human sort. More important, the coming days and weeks of travel would confirm that navigating between these perils was a defining reality of life and survival for the nomads themselves.

AFTER TWO DAYS' rest we parted ways with the Delgerekh, crossed the Ider, and headed northwest. As expected, the bottleneck of the Khangai Mountains gave way to open, barren plains and sleepy hills where the land faded from an early summer green to a brittle golden yellow. The temperamental weather of the mountains mellowed, and nomad camps, like our troubles, grew sparse and thin.

On the shores of a brackish lake known as Telmen Nuur, we were able to buy a new horse from a nomad family and thereby allow Bor to travel load-free. The new addition was a calm eighteen-year-old gelding, bigger than most Mongol horses, with a sharp odor and unusual coloring. His torso was white, speckled with rusty flecks of chestnut, while his hindquarters were splashed with large chestnut spots. Rusty, as we named him, led from the front with a fast pace, which, coupled with the wide-open land, enabled us to stride out and cover around 40 km a day—far more distance than we had previously.

It was just over a week after leaving behind the Khangai Mountains that our respite from trouble ended and the rigors of the land began to test us once more. The northwest of Mongolia, which we were entering, is part of a semi-arid basin known as the Great Lakes Depression. Dominated by desert, shallow saline lakes, and salt flats, it is a dry and sparsely populated corner of the country where the distance between watering points for the horses would turn out to be farther than we could cover in a single day.

The challenge began in earnest with a precarious route between a rocky range known as the Khan Khokhii and the southern fringe of the Borig Del Els, a desert renowned as the most northern in the world, which spreads out in a series of sand dunes beyond Mongolia's border into the republic of Tuva, in Siberia. According to nomads we had spoken to, there was no border fence, and, owing to the remoteness of the Borig Del Els and lack of patrols, the dunes were a favored route for horse thieves who specialized in smuggling into Russia.

Our departure from the river Tes coincided with a heat wave, and by 9:00 A.M. the temperature had already reached 30°C. Although our horses were hardy, while working in the heat they required a minimum of 20 litres of drinking water a day—more than we could ever hope to carry. For the next two days we saw no one and were only able to water the horses courtesy of a chance thunderstorm that left rainwater collected in a handful of puddles along the wheel tracks we followed.

Three days farther on, the heat was taking its toll. Kathrin's face was sunburned to nearly burgundy, her lips were swollen, and her hands were a mess of splits and cracks.[1] I had long lost my sunglasses and, after days staring into the raging sun, my pupils felt seared. We were both weary and dehydrated, and so were our horses.

Hungering for water and a day or two of rest, we stumbled into an isolated camp of two gers beyond the dusty village of Baruunturuun. A mother and her children took us to a well in a riverbed, then invited us to join in picking apart the boiled head, organs, and trotters of a freshly slaughtered goat. We were ravenous, and so the rubbery boiled scalp, lips, ears, and intestines—which only weeks ago I had found nauseating—slid down with ease.

For all the refuge this family offered us, they were in a particularly difficult predicament themselves. In the summer months they ordinarily retreated to the cool of the Khan Khokhii Mountains, but their remote pastures had been overrun with wolves, and so they had recently migrated to the slightly more populated corridor between the mountains and the Borig Del Els. As we would come to learn during our stay, however, life on these baking hot plains that lay wedged between the wolves and the dunes was by no means a perfect solution.

Early in the morning after our arrival I woke with my eyes glued shut by gunk and dust and a terrible throbbing at the back of my retinas. Trying to ignore the pain, I lay listening to what sounded like the soft patter of rain, but which I knew to be a thousand goats and sheep being herded out. The long grueling summer days were what nomads dreaded most—it was crucial to take the sheep and goats as far as possible to graze between dawn and dusk so that they would grow enough muscle and fat to see them through the winter. In some respects winter was an easier life—long dark nights meant lots of sleeping, and during blizzards the animals would not leave the pens.

After the sound of the sheep tailed off I put my head down for a bit more rest. When I woke again, I was struck by suffocating heat and the sound of an approaching motorbike. Kathrin came to as well, and together we ripped open the door to emerge dazed into the searing white light of midmorning.

As the motorbike hurtled closer, there was no mistaking the familiar sound of drunken singing. We fast retreated into the tent, from where we watched events unfold through a gap in the entrance zipper.

A short distance from camp, the driver expertly cut the engine and used the remaining momentum to steer his craft to the doorway of a ger. As it rolled to a halt, two men clinging on behind dismounted and staggered off—one lumbering away for a pee, the other falling unbalanced to the ground.

When all three had gathered themselves and dusted off their tattered deels, they charged inside, demanding vodka and food from the mother of five who had served us so generously the night before. Not having gotten what they wanted, two of the men went to the second ger, where her in-laws lived. There were several comings and goings before the young brother-in-law of our host ushered the driver out. An argument ensued, and after the driver carelessly knocked over the family's own motorbike, the gloves were off. A crack cut through the air as the young man's fist slammed into flesh and bone. The driver stumbled backward, clutching at his face, and fell, butt first, to the ground. Some uneasy moments passed while he recovered, but then he steamed forward, picked up his opponent, and drove him into the ground. No one emerged from the ger. The dogs lay low, unbothered.

Eventually the brother-in-law and the driver gave in to exhaustion, helped each other up, and then drove off together on the family's motorbike, leaving the other one there. All fell still and quiet. The white-hot sun crawled across the empty sky, and the dunes of the Borig Del Els wobbled on the horizon. Perhaps drunkenness and the trouble it brought, I speculated, was a welcome distraction in a land that was so desperately lacking in movement.

When the heat became unbearable we emerged from the tent and stumbled nervously into the mother's ger, where we found the two drunks fast asleep and the family drinking tea. One of the men was a special guest arrived from Ulaanbaatar, and the other two were family friends. The fight was never mentioned.

With time I learned that the drunken episode was not only an ordinary feature of steppe life but synonymous with summer. Coinciding with the peak production of milk, summer on the steppe is the nomad's age-old opportunity to partake in socializing—and drinking. The drunken men had been imbibing *nermel arkhi*, also known as "Mongolian vodka"—a clear, wine-strength drink distilled from fermented cow and yak milk. When Carpini arrived in Kharkhorin after his long journey from Europe, it is most likely this drink that he witnessed wreaking havoc. "Drunkenness is honorable among the Tartars, and when someone drinks a great deal he is sick right on the spot, and this does not prevent him from drinking more," he wrote. "In short, their evil habits are so numerous that they can hardly be set down."

Years earlier, Genghis Khan also had bemoaned the culture of drinking: "If there is no means to prevent drunkenness, a man may become drunk thrice a month; if he oversteps this limit he makes himself punishable of this offence . . . What could be better than that he should not drink at all? But where shall we find a man who never drinks? If however such a man is found, he deserves every respect." Despite Genghis's apparent will to curb alcohol consumption, his son and successor, Ogodei, was known as a lifetime drinker whose death in 1241—rumored to have occurred during a drinking bout—forced Mongolians to return to the homeland to elect a new leader, and in doing so abandon plans to invade Western Europe.

On the second morning of our stay I woke feeling overcome by nausea. The semi-broken-down trotters, lips, ears, and boiled intestines from the arrival feast seemed to be inching their way through my bowels like some slowly dying creature. Soon enough the sun surfaced with a vengeance. Stripped down to my underwear in the tent, I couldn't help but look on in horror at my bloated stomach. As my belly grew taut and round, it seemed to accentuate just how bony my arms and legs had become. After a mere seven weeks on the road, the muscle and fat appeared to have shriveled away, leaving my knees and elbows—knobby at the best of times— more skeletal than I had ever seen them.

By midmorning the temperature was 40°C. I staggered into the shade of the main ger and joined the family, who were lying on the dirt floor. To keep the ger as cool as possible, the felt was hitched up about 30 cm from the ground, allowing some limited airflow. Just beyond the collapsible wall in the sliver of shade cast by the ger, the mother of the family lay in dry dust and animal dung on her side, her young infant cradled in her arms.

For the remainder of the day I lay where I had fallen, taking in the world from ground level—every detail of which suggested that even in the paralyzing heat, surviving winter remained at the forefront of their minds. Directly above hung a curtain of meat strips being dried to produce what is known as borts. When dry, the strips would be cut into pieces, then ground into a fibrous powder, ensuring that the meat would be light, easy to carry, and would keep for months. Gansukh had told me that using borts in the old days Mongolian warriors could keep a "sheep in their pocket." Indeed I had discovered that a kilo of this—a portion of which each night we would add to rice—would last a couple of weeks between Kathrin and me. Next to me in the ger, under a bed, lay a cow stomach freshly filled with the cream known as urum, and beyond the door outside a pile of dried manure—the only fuel for cooking and heating in a land where the temperature could drop as low as −50°C.

There was no escaping the slim separation from the elements, and as compromised as this family might have been on the plains, where the pastures were thin, the heat was oppressive, and they were vulnerable to the intrusion of summer drunks, I was beginning to understand that there the herds weren't as threatened as they had been in the mountains. To lose animals, whether it be to wolves, frost, or drought, would be the undoing of any nomad family.

When finally I emerged feeling better in the cool of evening, both the remaining drunken guests had gone. The herds had arrived from another day of grazing, and children were busily tying up the goats for milking.

By dawn the next morning we were up and moving.

ALTHOUGH NOMADS DO not own land, there are some who are more fortunate with the land they inhabit than others—historically the cause of territorial conflict between tribes. One long day's ride west, we reached a nomad camp nestled into a relative oasis formed by a delicate brook flanked by slender shoulders of silky green grass. Where dust had reigned supreme the previous day, children splashed about in the water, and the women lay out their washing on a carpet of grass. Welcomed by five adult brothers and their extended families, who lived in five or six gers strung out along the stream, we felt a sense of life and prosperity sorely lacking in recent days—and, as would become clear, none of the drunken aggression we had come to expect. Such a camp was all the more welcome given that we were now just a day's ride from the driest and most challenging leg of the journey to the west.

By the time we had set up our tent and watched the family's herd of eighteen fat camels thunder down the steep, dusty banks for a drink, we knew it was a watershed moment for our little troupe. Although Bor, who had been running free without a saddle for two weeks, had improved, we were reluctant to put him back to work. More significantly, Kheer—our loyal packhorse and the mainstay of our caravan—was beginning to show fatigue and early signs of friction sores on his withers. It was nothing a few days of rest and a slight adjustment in the pack saddle wouldn't cure, but such was our affection for Kheer that we couldn't bear the thought of pushing him on longer than we needed to. Although it was true he was the kind of horse I would have liked to ride on with to the Danube, quarantine laws forbade the export of Mongolian horses on the basis that they are a "national treasure," meaning I would have to sell them before leaving the country.

The idea of trading Bor and Kheer for a new, fresh horse had only occurred to us in the past couple of days, but presented with such an idyllic setting, we were convinced we had found their new home.

There was great excitement among the families when they realized we were offering two horses in exchange for one, and by dusk children came galloping bareback into camp on an array of mounts. The first horse we checked was tame but had a fresh injury on its back hoof, and the second tore away and bolted to his herd before I had even looked him over. The third horse stole our hearts. A small bay gelding with a long matted mane and dark eyes, he was younger than Kheer at around six years, but equally calm. To prove he was a nomkhon—quiet-natured and tame—six children climbed onto his back, while another clambered underneath and gripped his penis. Through all of this the poor horse stood resigned to his fate, the only sign of any impatience the trembling of his rubbery lower lip.

The following day we stayed put and celebrated the exchange. Continuing a long-standing tradition, the herder took his horse out onto the steppe with his children, where they plucked hairs from its tail and mane. We too took our horses aside, pulling out a few strands, while stroking them, and whispering heartfelt thanks.

Mongolians believe the spirit of a horse can live on in its hair, even long after death, and in the past, nomad warriors collected the hair from their best stallions to weave into a *sulde* or "spirit banner," which served to bring good luck and as a way of harnessing the spirit of nature. Genghis Khan had famously used a white spirit banner in times of peace and a black banner for guidance during war, and it was thought that after death the soul of the warrior was preserved in these tufts of stallion hair.[2]

On this occasion, the herder selling us his horse simply strung up the hair in the ger so that a part of the horse's spirit would forever be with the family.

"You should keep the hair from your horses close to you as well, especially when in danger, for it will protect you from bad people. Also, do not give away your halters, or anything else together with a horse that you are selling, because it means you haven't entirely let go," he explained through the translated words of Gansukh via satellite phone. I pledged to keep hair from all the horses I used until the Danube.

After the horse exchange ceremony, we retired to the ger of the elderly parents, where we feasted on a meal of noodles and mutton, and sat watching a Korean soap opera on their shoe-box-size black-and-white TV. Like most well-to do Mongolian nomads, they had a satellite dish parked outside and a solar panel on the roof trickle-charging a 12-volt car battery, which in turn powered the TV. This cobbling together of the nomadic way of life with elements of the modern settled world had appeared a little incongruous to me at first, yet gradually I was coming to accept it as part and parcel of the evolving story of nomad life.

While the constant need to pick up and move had always ruled out any possession or technology that couldn't be carried on camels or yaks during migration, whenever something came along that was suitable and could improve their lives, it had historically been embraced with unique nomad ingenuity. In the twentieth century, for example, access to tight-weave cotton led to white canvas ger covers becoming the norm, whereas for thousands of years before, there had been no available material to protect the felt walls and ceilings from rain and wind. During the Soviet period, metal stoves and flues had also come to replace open hearths in gers, dramatically decreasing the prevalence of lung disease and lifting the average life expectancy of nomads. Although TV was perhaps more intrusive than these other innovations, the nomadic way of life out here was master and remained fundamentally unchanged.

Even if the advent of solar power, batteries, and TVs was an invasion of sorts, it certainly proved invaluable for me. By using a 12-volt adapter, I was able to recharge my video camera, satellite phone, and laptop computer. The system had its downside, though. As had happened on previous occasions, the family sighed and moaned when the TV went dead. My charging had flattened their battery.

With the TV out of action, dinner was washed down by nermel arkhi and the family's attention deftly switched from this modern, borrowed form of entertainment to one that was as ancient as nomadic life.

It was the matriarch of the family, a woman in her seventies, thin and creased as an old bedsheet, who pulled out a stringed instrument known as the morin khuur, or horsehead fiddle. Boasting a trapezoid-shaped box, carved horsehead at the top of a long stem, and two long, parallel strings—one made from 135 tail hairs of a stallion, the other from 105 of a mare's—it had been handcrafted in a tradition probably unbroken for at least a millennium. The morin khuur's predecessor, the chuurqin, was believed to date back to the sixth century, supporting a widely believed theory that bowed string instruments originated on the steppes somewhere in Central Asia. Once established by horseback nomads, the tradition is thought to have spread first through Persia and the rest of the Islamic world, reaching western Europe in the eleventh and twelfth centuries.

As this old woman moved the bow back and forth, the shaky, bony fingers of her left hand pressed on its two strings at the top of the stem, just below the green-colored carved horsehead. The sound coming from the wooden box between her legs was like a scratchy, drawn-out cry, but nevertheless her husband, a bandy-legged old man ignited by vodka and the special occasion, began swaying back and forth rhythmically, his hands and arms twisting this way and that. The music and vodka settled together in my own system and I found my eyes wandering from the fiddle to various points around the ger: the horsehair ropes that tied together the ger, the airag in the corner, and a piece of horse dung dangling from the ceiling for good luck. According to one Mongolian legend, the morin khuur had originated from a boy whose slain horse came to him in a dream to instruct him to make the fiddle using its body so that they would forever be together. In the present day, it was clear the morin khuur was a celebration of this crucial union between horse and man—a relationship that not only made life possible on the steppe but which, like string instruments, had been adopted in Europe and become a part of the making of history across the globe.

WHEN WE WERE saddled the next morning, the man from whom we had bought the horse came to our tent with his ten-year-old son. If the grief we felt in leaving our horses behind was difficult, then it was hard to imagine how it was for them. The horse we had bought, named Bokus, was the boy's favorite and had been raised from birth by the family. Over the years the boy had no doubt learned to experience and interpret the world around him from the back of Bokus. Now Bokus was abruptly about to leave for good, and as his father lifted the boy onto the horse for the last time he sat looking pale and bewildered.

Just before riding out, the boy's father pressed a gift into my hand—a wolf's ankle bone tied onto a necklace. "Keep it with you for luck," he whispered.

The boy cried at first, but by the time we had crossed the brook, I turned to see that everything was returning to normal. The camels had been released for a day of herding, and the boy was moving them out on a different horse. A woman was wandering down to collect water, and a sheep was being slaughtered in the morning cool. Bor and Kheer were mingling with the family's herd and didn't raise their heads from the grass as we moved away.

A DAY'S RIDE west from the family's oasis-like camp, the corridor between the Borig Del Els and the Khan Khokhii mountains widened to a thirsty plain extending west to where sand dunes in the north gave way to the shallows of the giant saline lake Uvs Nuur, and the Khan Khokhii in the south became the foothills of the greater Altai range. Not far from the southwest corner of the lake lay the provincial capital, Ulaangom.

Even before I'd left Australia, a quick scan of maps suggested that the greatest obstacle in traversing Mongolia would be crossing these wide, dry deserts and plains, which separate central Mongolia from the western provinces. I had trusted that a way through the driest zone would come to light en route, but nomads we had met of late had been adamant there were no gers or fresh water for at least 100 km. The only solution we could think of was to start in the evening, ride through the cool of night, and keep going for as long as necessary.

In theory, this first attempt at night riding—a routine that would become the norm a year later in Kazakhstan—was a prospect that excited me. In practice, it became a farce.

We started late in the dark and not far from camp became disoriented and rode into a swamp. Rusty sank up to his chest in mud, and it was a good half hour before he extricated himself. For a couple of hours thereafter we made swift progress, but then the absence of the moon and a suffocating cover of clouds conspired to render the world a soup of blacks and grays, inducing a feeling of motion sickness. The flashlight batteries went dead, and we spent a frustrating hour searching for my compass after I accidentally dropped it. Most unfair was the cold—expecting a sultry night in prelude to a searing hot day, we instead found ourselves hunched over in a damp breeze. The only way to stay warm, awake, and nausea-free was to walk.

When the world resurfaced, it came in a series of fragments between long periods when my eyes struggled to break open. At first an endless black, empty plain materialized, preyed upon by swirling gray clouds. A couple of hours later, the silhouette of mountains grew from the south, tapering off into the western horizon. To the north a slim flicker of silvery gray indicated the waters of Uvs Nuur, the hills beyond which lay in Russia. We had come far closer to the southern mountains than we intended but were still half a day's ride from their base. The lake was even farther.

Come midmorning, the sun suddenly seemed to be upon us, but with the air still cool, what might have otherwise been terrifying appeared exquisite. The mist lifted, revealing a band of fresh snow on the mountaintops, and a slither of blue in the direction of Uvs Nuur. The breeze died, and the pale, naked land we trod on turned mute, amplifying the sense that we were far from any shore. It was only after midday, when the crippling heat began to beat down and the horses slowed to a crawl, that our spirits withered.

In search of water, my eyes scanned the mountains to the south, where a web of cracks and crevices on the slopes promised to collect at the base in some kind of stream or river but was thwarted by what appeared to be the buildup of millions of years of rockfalls and landslides. Through these mounds a few rivulets thus reached the plains with barely enough momentum to limp out of the shadows into the baking sun.

By keeping my head down and focusing on the end goal of each day, I was ordinarily able to keep the bigger picture of traveling to Hungary at bay, but not today. The great plain that rolled out into a horizon of heat haze was inescapable. It was too big to fathom, yet amounted to nothing in the scheme of the overall scale of the steppe. It would have been easier to drift off into the anesthesia of half-sleep and let the horses carry me, but thoughts about the great distances the Mongols once traveled in their many traverses of Eurasia kept me bolt upright.

For a Mongol cavalry just to *reach* the enemy typically involved a journey of weeks, if not months. During these campaigns their armies were known to routinely travel 50 to 80 km a day. At the zenith of the Mongol Empire, horseback messengers could even gallop from Kharkhorin to Hungary in a matter of weeks, a legend seemingly confirmed by the great Venetian traveler Marco Polo, who wrote that Mongol couriers could cover 400 or even 500 km in a single day.

Reading historical tales about such exploits, one could be forgiven for imagining the steppe as a single flat grassland through which horsemen moved with a sense of freedom and ease. Here on horseback, though, it was clear the cavalry were negotiating deserts, mountains, rivers, swamps, heat, and frosts, and somehow keeping their horses fed and healthy, even before leaving Mongolia.

There were, of course, secrets to the Mongol ability to travel over such immense distances, which seemed all the more ingenious to me now. The much feted courier system, yam, which remains a great symbol of the efficiency and discipline with which the Mongol Empire was ruled, relied on staging posts known as ortoo every 30 to 50 km, where fresh mounts, food, and water were permanently stationed. As the rider approached, a special bell would warn the ortoo master of the impending arrival, and for urgent deliveries the rider would leap from one horse to the next and continue at a gallop. Unlike the Pony Express of the mid-nineteenth century in the United States, which was based on riders changing every 160 km or so, the Mongol messenger entrusted with the communiqué from the beginning was bound to deliver it to the very end. To protect his body from the rigors of such sustained rides and keep him upright, even when sleeping, he was bound in special strips of material and wore a thick leather belt around the waist. Today, the silk sash most Mongols wear performs a similar purpose, holding their lower abdomen tightly in place. The yam system reportedly remained in existence in Mongolia well into the twentieth century, until the Soviets began introducing roads and a mechanized postal service.

In terms of the great roaming campaigns of the Mongols, the sheer number of horses available to them was no doubt a key to their success. Historical accounts suggest that every Mongol soldier traveled with at least one spare horse, and up to three or four. This way, they could constantly rotate the horses and ride fresh mounts. Carpini even commented that "the

Tartar does not mount for three or four days afterward the horse he has ridden for one day; so they do not ride tired horses because of the great number that they have."

Carpini may have been describing the Mongol transport system rather than the mounted soldier, but in any case, by way of contrast with European armies at the time, the majority of European soldiers fought on foot, and their cavalry units used heavy warhorses reliant on hay and grain supplements. It is also true that the geography of Europe, with its forests, mountains, and fertile cultivated land, could not cope with the kind of large free-grazing herds that had always been an indigenous feature of the steppes. Not only was it the case that Europeans could never have hoped to achieve supremacy over the Mongols in the open terrain of the steppe, but they were also at a disadvantage when the Mongols attacked them on their own home ground.

We plodded on until late evening, at which point we had been moving without a break for more than thirty hours but covered little more than 50 km as the crow flies. Without the energy to carry on, we made camp and collapsed.

COME MORNING I was woken by a rather zealous Kathrin, who prodded and laughed until I peeled my eyes open. She had been up early to check on the horses and had scanned the distant lakeshore with our binoculars.

"Tim! I think I can see gers!"

I stumbled out of the tent, wiped away the dried toothpaste crusted around my lips, and brought the glasses to my eyes. Sure enough, there appeared to be nomad families on the shoreline.

Several hours later we stumbled into a camp and were led to a well. At first it was a relief to see the horses empty out several troughs of water, which were filled by hauling up buckets from a shallow well. As we rode on along the shore through more camps, however, we began to wonder why just 65 km earlier nomads had sworn there were no people or drinking water to be found on the shores of Uvs. We had been directed to follow the main way—a series of wheel tracks—to the capital of Uvs Aimag, Ulaangom, which cut through a largely waterless desert halfway between the mountains and the lake. Had the nomads intentionally misinformed us, or did they simply not possess enough knowledge of the region?

The experience remained a mystery until later on in the journey, when I realized that when modern nomads travel more than about 25 km from camp, they typically use mechanized transport.[3] This led me to consider the vastly different experience of riding a horse versus traveling via machine, and the effect this had on traditional knowledge of the land. On a horse, one was constantly monitoring the pasture and the general lay of the terrain, keeping an eye peeled for natural paths that might preserve the horse's energy. The slowness of the travel enabled the rider to absorb the details of each unfolding chapter of the landscape. It was inevitable, therefore, that nomads of the past would have possessed far more intimate knowledge of far greater tracts of land.

One might argue, of course, that the convenience of a motorbike or car outweighs the importance of traditional knowledge garnered from horseback. For those nomads remaining out here, where the elements have never really changed, I couldn't help feeling that the loss of knowledge was not to be taken lightly. In a drought or severe winter, nomads are routinely required to move beyond their usual pasturelands, and details such as being able to identify plants and their uses, or knowing where to take the animals to cover in the midst of a blizzard, can mean the difference between a herd being wiped out or clinging on.

HAVING EMERGED FROM the desert plain earlier than expected, we had reached the last chapter of this leg of the journey, which would take us along Uvs Nuur, then on to Ulaangom.

Uvs Nuur and the vast but dry basin it drains is one of Central Asia's most northerly depressions and thought to have once been the bottom of an ancient inland sea. While nowadays a relative puddle, the 70 km stretch of water is still the largest lake in Mongolia by area, and it transformed our perspective of the landscape. Panning out to the north, its flawless surface mirrored the pale blue above, creating the giddy feeling that if I stumbled, I might fall from the saddle into the depths of the sky. It was an illusion shattered only by herds of horses that forged into the shallows from time to time, and flocks of gulls that bobbed idly about. To the south, meanwhile, the plain that had so dominated our thirsty ride was reduced to a thin yellow line, overshadowed by the range beyond, which was still dusted with snow.

At the southwest corner of the lake we left the shore and reached the edge of a sprawling delta of salt marshes and dry, seasonal riverbeds. During an overnight stay with a prosperous nomad family, we discovered a drunken horseman attempting to steal our horses, providing another night of sleepless drama but also the consolation of affirming we had left the dry belt of land in our wake and returned to problems of a human-made kind.

Tired, but quietly proud that we had more or less taken the horse-stealing attempt in our stride, we rode on through lowlands of luscious tall grass that grew upon the salt marshes. There were Soviet-era bores where the horses were able to drink, and pastoral scenes of nomads grazing the prestigious tavan tolgoi mal (herds of five species). After the uncertainty of the desert, and with just 90 km to Ulaangom, we hoped to keep a low profile and settle in for a few excitement-free days. One encounter in particular, however, would prove to have far-reaching significance, although the importance wouldn't become clear to me until more than a year and 4,000 km later.

From a distance, there seemed to be nothing unusual when a horseman came galloping our way, his deel and whip flying, but up close I was intrigued by his unusual features. His eyes had the typical Mongol shape, long and slender, but they were a clear, translucent blue instead of brown. Assessing us, he sat groping a long gray goatee, baring some rather twisted, yellow Russian-like teeth. He wasn't the first Mongolian I'd seen with distinctly Turkic and Caucasian features, but combined with his obvious dialect, there was something so exotic I couldn't tear my eyes away. It wasn't long before we were sitting in the man's ger, where, over tea, he explained his origins.

"We are Oirats, and our ancestors traveled to the Caspian Sea and back here. Our brothers, the ones who didn't come back, still live there, so please bring greetings from us when you get there."

While Mongol is essentially an umbrella term that describes the many different tribes of the Mongolian plateau that were united under Genghis Khan, the history and identity of the Oirats, like the geography of western Mongolia, has always been somewhat distinct. A confederation of the Choros, Durvud (or Dorbet), Torghut, and Khoshut tribes, believed to have originated from the forests of southern Siberia, the Oirats fought fiercely against Genghis until the crushing of their allies the Naimans in 1204.

Over the course of the thirteenth century, the Oirats proved to be a loyal force for the Mongols, known for their role in the battle of Homs and as Genghis's personal bodyguards, but despite their loyalty they were never fully accepted within the circles of Mongol society.[4] The Oirats were certainly not considered to be of Genghis's lineage, and according to the unwritten laws of the empire, no Oirat could take the reins of power as khan.[5]

In the wake of the collapse of the Mongol Empire, the Oirats nevertheless rose to ascendancy on the steppe, establishing a vast empire known as Zhungaria. While the story of their empire is a history unto itself, it is really after the beginning of the demise of this empire in the seventeenth century that a fascinating tale of triumph and tragedy—and an important chapter in the history of the steppe—unfolds. I will recount the details later, but here suffice it to say that the Oirats eventually fled west to the steppes north of the Caspian Sea, where they formed a new khanate known as Kalmykia. Less than two centuries later, under repression from the Russian tsar in 1771, they embarked on a mass exodus back to their roots in Asia, during which more than half perished on the steppes of Kazakhstan. Those who survived the journey regrouped as the four Oirat tribes in western Mongolia and what is today Xinjiang province in China. Those who stayed behind in Russia remained known as Kalmyks.

The man who was now sitting before me was a Durvud, of the Oirat tribe that nowadays forms the majority in Uvs province, and whose name derives from the verb meaning "to escape." While it is true that it is nearly impossible to distinguish Durvud Mongolians from other ethnicities by physical characteristics alone, and the features of our host might well have been due to Russian heritage from the Soviet era, I liked to think those blue eyes might have been a remnant this man had carried from his ancestors in the distant Caspian steppe.

Taking his words seriously, I imagined for a moment relaying his greetings to his fellow countrymen on the steppes of Russia. It was, after all, a journey I was far more likely to make than this man or any of his family in their lifetimes.

Filing away his image for another time, we climbed back onto our horses, waved goodbye, and turned again to Ulaangom.

5

KHARKHIRAA: THE ROARING RIVER MOUNTAIN

A DAY'S RIDE from the camp of the Durvud man—whose name I never knew—we crested a rise at sunset to lay eyes on a glittering ensemble of mud huts, fence-enclosed gers, and a handful of Soviet-era apartment blocks. It was the end of August, and having traveled more than 1,000 km from Kharkhorin, we had reached the remote capital of Uvs province, Ulaangom.

For three days we stayed with a family on the outskirts, relishing the chance to sleep in and taking turns traveling to the town center. Symbolic of Ulaangom's isolation from Mongolia's more populated central regions—and a measure of how far we had come—it was a town that relied exclusively on electricity from the power grid in the republic of Altai, in Russia, which was closer. Due to unpaid state debts to Russia there had been a summer-long blackout, and owing to this the streets were particularly quiet. There were, nevertheless, some private generators in operation, and we were able to delight in such luxuries as ice cream, sweet biscuits, and carbonated water.

Our celebratory mood was tempered only by the fact that within a week Kathrin was scheduled to begin work as a schoolteacher in Germany. The dirt runway in Ulaangom was her ticket home, and so this far-flung town had come to represent not only a milestone on my journey to Hungary but the end of our trip together.

As we approached this crossroads, a feeling of unease had been growing in me, and I reflected with a sense of regret that in the last two months we had been so tested and stretched simply by coping with day-to-day events that we had spent precious little time concentrating on each other. More to the point, we had barely discussed the uncertainty looming over us as a couple: Kathrin was about to disappear to the other side of the world, while I would carry on for at least another sixteen months, and that was only if everything went according to plan.

"So what should we do?" Kathrin uttered nervously after darkness and silence had fallen on Ulaangom one night.

Although we had been together for almost a year, Kathrin well knew I was committed to my dream of riding across the steppes, and that the dream had only grown stronger along the way. There was no turning back, and so the only way to spend time together would be if Kathrin came to join me during her vacations. At the same time, while Kathrin was ready for a more serious stage in our relationship, to me the concept of real love involved a commitment I knew I wasn't ready for or capable of at this stage.

Perhaps I was wrong, but I had a feeling that Kathrin, like me, sensed that breaking up was the most realistic way forward. Yet I couldn't fathom casting off alone on this without Kathrin's support. From Kathrin's point of view, she was about to plunge into a new job and life in Germany, and the uncertainty she felt must have been far more immediate.

After buying a plane ticket for her to Ulaanbaatar, we spent our last day riding south across a vast plain that angled toward the base of a dark wall of mountains known as the Kharkhiraa-Turgen massif. We had been watching these mountains grow for over a week, the 4,000 m apexes of the glacier-encrusted peaks at times coming into view and inviting thoughts of alpine pastures and river valleys. The name *Kharkhiraa* itself was a word that describes the roar of a river's rapids.

As we had come to expect in the openness of western Mongolia, what appeared to be a short ride became eight hours. We spoke little but managed to articulate a desire to remain in a relationship and see how things worked out when I arrived in Hungary, or whenever she could join me again.

The following morning we hurried on horseback into the village of Tarialan, where we had arranged a lift back to the Ulaangom airport. Then it was all over in a heartbeat. The driver cranked the engine into life, Kathrin leaped in, and I waved goodbye. Within minutes the only visible sign that Kathrin had ever been with me was the sweat marks from her saddle on the back of her beloved Saartai Zeerd, who by now was the only remaining horse that had been with me from the beginning.

Even as the dust trail of the car carrying her began to fade, I turned my thoughts to immediate plans. Digesting the significance of what had just happened would have to wait for another time.

LIKE MY OWN state of mind, the village of Tarialan was a place on the edge of two very different worlds. Built on the banks of the glacier-fed Kharkhiraa River at the point where its waters spew from a gorge into the sun-baked plains, it was both the end of the road for motorized vehicles and the gates to the mountains.

From here I hoped to begin the first chapter of my journey without Kathrin by traveling west over the Kharkhiraa-Turgen range to the sandy basin on the far side. On one hand, crossing the mountains was a practical decision—the alternative was to make a lengthy detour around the massif to the north—but there was something more important that had led me to Tarialan. This humble little village was the central, and only, settlement of a minority known as the Khotons, who still live a traditional nomad life among the inaccessible slopes and valleys of Kharkhiraa-Turgen. Numbering no more than two or three thousand, the Khotons are thought to be descendants of a Turkic tribe that originated in Central Asia. Over time they had adopted the Oirat Mongolian tongue but remained distinct from other Mongolian groups, practicing customs and beliefs that are a mesh of Islam, Buddhism, and the shamanic faith of Tengrism.

Tseren Enebish, my longtime friend in Ulaanbaatar, had told me about the Khotons and suggested I find a local friend of hers named Dashnyam. I was hoping he might guide me through the high passes that would be impossible for me to tackle alone.

After being pointed in multiple directions, I found Dashnyam's ger near the mouth of the gorge. As soon as I dismounted, his children ushered me inside to the ger's back wall and slid a bowl of dried curd and stale pieces of deep-fried dough (known as *boortsog*) under my nose. While children from neighboring gers massed about the entrance, Dashnyam's wife ladled boiling tea into a cup, then, with her left hand supporting her right elbow, passed it to me in traditional fashion.

Dashnyam knelt, cradling a chipped teacup with an open palm, balancing his elbow on his raised knee, and brought his face down to drink.

"Drink tea, eat boortsog," he said gently.

Even at a glance, Dashnyam was different from other Mongolians. In the absence of the pronounced cheekbones that keep the skin stretched taut into old age for most Mongolians, his cheeks fell away in a series of saggy folds and wrinkles. His eyes were wide and almond-shaped, sunken deep in their sockets, framed by bushy eyebrows. The most prominent telltale of his Turkic origins, though, was the craggy, hooked nose that reached out from his otherwise rather hollow face.

Quite apart from Dashnyam's Khoton ethnicity was his gentle, kind character. Even as he looked me over, his eyes were thoughtful, betraying a sense of curiosity without hint of opportunism.

When the tea had begun to revive me I pulled out the map and asked whether he would guide me. At first he scanned the map with narrowed eyes and a pained look of bewilderment, but when I made myself clearer, he cast it aside.

"When do you want to leave? Today? Tomorrow? I need to fetch a camel!"

He agreed to travel with me for eight days—time enough to make it over the highest passes. A camel, he explained, was essential, since my horses were tired and unshod, and the way ahead was rocky. It was imperative we leave at the first opportunity, since the passes could soon be blanketed with snow.

Dashnyam, who was in his late forties but had the stiff, stringy body of someone ten years older, launched himself into action and rode with me into the village. After shopping for supplies, he sent me home. "Take the bag of flour back to my wife and tell her to make boortsog. I am going to find a camel."

I SPENT THE day preparing in camp and getting to know Dashnyam's family, who, it became clear, were sorely destitute.

The father of five children all under the age of fourteen, Dashnyam owned one old horse and seventeen goats. In the evening, when other families herded sheep and goats by the hundreds, Dashnyam's eldest son, Tsagana, walked up a slope not far from camp and shooed his flock home. Milking was over within twenty minutes, and the little pail it filled held barely enough for a day's worth of milky tea. There were no strips of drying meat (borts) hanging in the ger nor pouches of yogurt being stirred, or even the ubiquitous trays of curd drying on the roof. With so few animals, Dashnyam neither had the means or reason to migrate with his family from pasture to pasture, and so shifted no more than about 3–4 km between winter and summer camps. As such, he was caught between sedentary and nomadic lives, without the security of a "five-animal" herd or the safety net of town.

Come dusk, when Dashnyam returned with a small female camel, I had decided I wanted to give him a horse. With Kathrin gone, I didn't need a third animal, and Saartai Zeerd, who wasn't happy on rocks at the best of times, was not suited to the mountains.

When I first placed the horse's lead rope in his hands, both Dashnyam and Saartai Zeerd looked at me blankly. But as my offer registered, a nervous smile spread across Dashnyam's face, revealing a not quite full set of yellow, crooked teeth. Rather than make him a gift outright, I proposed trading the horse for two days of guiding, which Dashnyam said would normally cost $27 (I would pay for the other days in cash). There was a degree of dignity about such a deal that made us both happy.

AT DAWN DASHNYAM entrusted Saartai Zeerd to his son and told him to take the animal away to pasture. Then we packed the camel, Dashnyam's wife threw a single spoonful of milk in the air, and we were off.

Not far upstream we entered the head of the Kharkhiraa River canyon. Mountains drew like curtains over the sky, and the steppe shrank to a puddle behind. The river, which lower down had been nothing more than an unremarkable braid of channels leaching into the thirsty steppe, tumbled through with the momentum of a thousand ice-melt tributaries, carving out a gap through an otherwise impassable wall of rock.

In the initial stages of the canyon we avoided the river, riding along the bank beneath the shade of tall, elegant poplars still fragrant with the life of summer. After the monotony of the treeless steppe I was struck by the poplars' leaves, still supple, but turning bright yellow. Cast against the deep blue of the river, the pale sun-bleached river stones, and the red rock of the cliffs, they were an addition to a world full of contrast.

Where the trees ended, the canyon's walls drew in tight. Dashnyam forged paths from one riverbank to the other sitting casually with camel in tow, gently tapping the rump of his horse with a whip. I lifted my stirrups to avoid the rapids, gripped Rusty's mane with one hand, and tugged at Bokus with the other.

Eventually the river became so deep and concentrated we were forced to ride along a precarious ledge. I was beginning to lose confidence in

Rusty, whose hooves slipped about on the loose rock, but then, as abruptly as the canyon had begun, the cliffs parted.

The plains had now completely slipped from view behind, and before us lay a glacier-carved valley where the river was dwarfed by a wide, rocky flood plain. Within another few minutes, the canyon had become an imperceptible shadow between the overlap of ridges, and ahead grew a sight confirming we had been squeezed through a portal into a different world.

Weaving through a maze of river boulders came a camel train. From a distance these elegant animals seemed to move in slow motion, their long curved necks extending and retracting with each gait cycle, and their baggage-laden humps bobbing to and fro. The rapid rate at which they grew in size, however, suggested they were moving with remarkable speed. By the time my eyes had focused on the three or four men and women who led the caravan, they had drifted right before us.

"Good journey!" cried Dashnyam, overcome with such a smile that his pointy chin reached out to greet them.

"Good journey to you!" they replied, dismounting to join Dashnyam cross-legged on the earth.

I was too excited to dismount, and rode to the woman who controlled the lead camel. For nomads migration is a special occasion when the wealth and pride of a family is paraded, and this woman embodied the tradition. Sitting in a silver-coin-encrusted saddle embellished with yak horn and decorated with red velvet, she wore a silky golden and green deel with matching earrings and a fluorescent green sash pulled tight in around her thin waist. Traditionally, sashes and belts were important symbols of status and wealth. Men wore them low around the waist, while women wore them high. An unmarried Mongolian would not wear one at all.

I reached out to shake the woman's hand, and she obliged me in this unusual gesture with a giggle. Her hands were strong, wrinkled, and worn, yet the twinkle in her eye and the full set of blinding white teeth spoke of a woman younger than me, in her early twenties. When she smiled her eyes and mouth spread as wide as her broad fleshy cheeks, radiating a naivety and wisdom that in my experience are common among young nomad mothers who juggle giant responsibility with the gaiety of youth.

But the overwhelming emotion that flowed from this woman now was her pride. She motioned to the five camels behind, where, apart from the family's herd, which had been driven down a day earlier, her entire earthly belongings were on display. Each camel—carrying as much as 300 kg—was packed with segments of two family gers. Lattice wall pieces, cupboards, and milking buckets and cans were all packed on the sides of the camels, while the wheel-like ceiling structures were cast over the humps. On the heels of the last camel came a huge guard dog of the bankhar breed—the large Mongolian mastiff that is a quintessential of no-mad herders—with the beginnings of a new winter coat, and last year's still hanging off in dung-encrusted dreadlocks.

The woman pointed to the camel immediately behind her, where the kind of wooden baskets used to collect dung were brimming with odds and ends. Only when she dismounted and pulled the camel to its knees did I realize these baskets contained more than possessions. From the far basket, a young girl, perhaps three years old, raised her head shyly above the humps. Her hair was long and untamed, her cheeks rendered a deep red through exposure.

The woman lifted a sheet covering the basket immediately in front of me, and there, wrapped in a cocoon of sheepskin, was a newborn. Lying as placidly as the camel, the baby gazed up to a world framed by the wooly outline of the skin.

I was humbled by the thought that for much of the morning I had feared my horse might make a misstep on one of the narrow ledges or be knocked over by the river's current. This woman trusted her animals with the precious lives of her most fragile loved ones—showing more trust in those camels than many people in my own society would bestow on an-other human being. For these people, animals were part of the broader family, and, as such, they carried great responsibilities.

After bidding farewell to the family, we carried on buoyantly. Dash-nyam seemed immensely pleased I had witnessed the camel train.

"Up there in the mountain they live in the summer camp." He pointed to the high mountains. "Very, very good grass!" He shook his head passionately, then leaned down from the saddle, picked some grass, and brought it to his mouth.

Down on the lower steppes where I had traveled with Kathrin, the driving force behind migratory patterns was cryptic, but here it was relatively clear. Nomads spent summer in the high mountains, where the pasture was rich and they could avoid the heat and insects of lower down. The family we had met was moving to the plains for autumn, where dew promised to reinvigorate the grass. Some families would remain on the lowlands for winter, but many would return to camps here in the mountains, where it was marginally warmer. Where nomads moved to depended entirely on the needs of their animals.

It was, of course, this drive to search out greater pasture that had seen nomads and their animals spread out across the breadth of the steppe all those thousands of years before. And while families in this region might only have been migrating a relatively small distance a year, I was reminded that my journey was not only on the trail of nomads who might have ridden the steppe in the space of a lifetime but, perhaps more important, in the spirit of the people who had shifted across Eurasia on their horses through the space of millennia.

In the evening as the sun began to fall more steeply, the tips of the ice-encrusted peaks of Kharkhiraa and Turgen breached the horizon. We rode far above the river on a grassy shelf, marveling at cliffs on the far side smattered with splotches of white—signs of ancient kite and eagle nests. On this evening, though, it was signs of continuous *human* habitation that would leave the deepest impression.

On a particularly straight stretch, the shifting columns of light illuminated a series of embedded stones in a variety of shapes and patterns— signs of nomad grave markers. Dashnyam led me up the slope to a spot from which we had a bird's-eye view. The pattern below was a perfect circle, perhaps as much as 50 m in diameter. At the core lay a circular pile of stones from which four straight lines of stones spread out to the perimeter like the spokes of a wheel. As a whole, it resembled a giant sundial, or perhaps the circular wooden ceiling of a ger.

This was most likely a grave type known broadly as khirigsuur, dating back around 2,700 years to the Bronze Age. Some archaeologists theorize that the nomadic culture of the period was influenced by the Scythian tradition of burying horses and tack together with the deceased. I had read that during excavations of some burial grounds up to forty-five horses had been discovered in a single grave—a sign of the nomad's enduring belief that the horse carried them into life, through life, and beyond into the afterlife.

Beyond this grave marker lay many more, of tens if not hundreds of different types. Of the circular kind alone there were numerous intriguing variations. Some were surrounded by a square perimeter, while others were squares surrounded by circles. Many were circles filled out with a cobblestone effect, and still others were circles containing no central pile of stones or spokes.

While it was impossible for me to judge, some of these were probably those of the Xiongnu, a nomadic people who ruled an empire in greater Mongolia during the Iron Age from the third to the first century BCE. It was their constant attacks on China, including a war with the Han dynasty, that is thought to have triggered the building of the Great Wall of China. Although the origin of the Xiongnu is subject to ongoing controversy and debate, many historians believe they were the original Hunnic people, whose descendants charged into Europe centuries later under the helm of Attila.[1]

In a kind of collective cemetery that evidently spanned thousands of years, we rode through silently and slowly, taking in monuments from untold eras and peoples. Among them were long columns of around fifty small vertically standing stones. At the northern end of each column, facing the east, were the figures of men carved from granite. Each man held a cup in one hand and the dagger on his belt with the other. Flowing mustaches hinted at the Turkic origins of the makers, as did sculpted noses more resembling Dashnyam's features than the average Mongolian's. These were balbal stones—a kind of engraved headstone found across Central Asia and thought to be memorials to individuals of the diverse Turkic peoples of the steppe.

Just as remarkable were the large red standing megaliths, known broadly as deer stones, that stood solitary on the periphery of the cemeteries, thousands of years since their makers had placed them there. Although the particular stones we saw had no sign of engraving, other similar standing stones in Mongolia are renowned for extravagant depictions of deer and for some of Mongolia's—and Central Asia's—earliest known images of human beings.

At the far end of the cemetery, we stopped to examine some deer stones. When Dashnyam climbed back onto his horse, I watched him closely. Observing a custom universal among horsemen the world over, he carefully approached his black gelding from the left-hand side and eased into the saddle. Horsemen in the Western world believe this tradition originates from a time when cavalrymen carried swords on their right leg. On the steppe, however, among the descendants of those who introduced horses and cavalry warfare to the West, there is a belief about this custom that is probably older than both the Iron Age and Bronze Age. In a culture where the sun has always been worshipped and gers still strictly face south toward the life-giving orb, the word for "left" in Mongolian, baruun, is the same as the term for "east." To approach a ger from the east or mount a horse from the left is to approach in the same direction as the sun passes through the sky. To approach from the right and therefore the west is the sign of an enemy and can only invite trouble.

When the cemetery was behind us, I asked Dashnyam what he thought about the graves. With a distant look in his eyes, all he could tell me was they were in memory of his ancestors, and that those who lay here had been heroes.

IN THE MORNING we reached the confluence of the Turgen and Kharkhiraa rivers, then continued up the main Kharkhiraa River valley as it turned sharply south. The mountains grew taller and the valley sank so deep and narrow that we waited for what seemed an eternity for the shadows of night to peel away down the far western valley side, then up to where we rode high above the rapids on the eastern side. When finally the sun reached us, the frost burned away and my tense, cold muscles eased. Rather than ride alongside Dashnyam, I fell in behind the camel, too tired to speak.

After leaving the grave markers the previous day we had spent a sleepless night camped with a herding family. From the moment we put our heads down to rest, the mountains had come to life with howling wolves and the crack and echo of gunshots. Men had been coming and going to check on their animals, and every time I seemed to be falling asleep the ger door would creak open and bang close again.

Now, with the sun melting any remaining resistance to sleep, I leaned back in the saddle, let the horse guide me forward, and surrendered. Where the stars had been, kites and eagles circled against an incandescent sky painted with streaks of cloud. Where wolves had prowled, the herders from the family we stayed with pushed their flocks high to the lesser-eaten pastures. As my hands loosely gripped the reins, eyelids heavy with gravity, it all passed by in lucid fragments.

Several hours on, hunger pulled me from my slumber. The river had mellowed to a knee-deep meander, and we descended to ride along the water's edge through spongy alpine grasses. For the rest of the day the only person we saw was an old man out watching his yaks. He dismounted ahead of us and sat waiting with his sleeves hanging past his hands. I joined him and Dashnyam on the grass and watched as the man's horse leaned in with its bottom lip quivering and pushed its nose over its master's forehead. The horse groaned and lifted its head, and turds dropped to the earth in a series of muffled thuds. A waft of fresh dung mixed with the sweet aroma of horse sweat drifted between us. Just as the man appeared oblivious to the cold wind, he didn't acknowledge the horse, the smell, or the trail of saliva on his scalp.

Come midafternoon the snow-dusted shoulder of Kharkhiraa peak was emerging at the far end of the valley. I was eager to make progress and disappointed when Dashnyam pulled up at a lonely ger, insisting at first we were stopping for a cup of tea, but later suggesting it was too late to carry on. But my feelings of frustration didn't prevail long.

The dim interior of the ger hummed with a dung-fired stove, and a cauldron of salty tea breathed moisture into the air. The walls and ceiling were hung with antique rifles, a fresh wolf skin, rows of drying goat meat, and ornate horse tack. Dashnyam pulled out his stone snuff bottle and offered it with both hands to the elderly man of the family, Davaa. In return, Davaa, who had a long, narrow sun-blackened face and a white goatee, produced his. The two men sniffed each other's in a sign of respect, then sat back to drink tea and smoke from long pipes. Back down on the plains beyond the gorge, Dashnyam was a poor man, but here he could partake as an equal in the broader traditions of nomad life. It moved me to see how he was treated with a sense of high dignity.

Dinner was freshly boiled goat head and a cup of bouillon to wash it down. When our bellies were taut as drums, a silver bowl of nermel arkhi was passed around. Then we lay down our bedding—me my sleeping bag, Dashnyam an old winter deel—and passed out to the muffled sounds of settling sheep, goats, and yaks.

I slept heavily, and in the morning rode away feeling as sharp and crisp as the frozen needles of alpine grass that crunched under my horse's hooves. The sky was clear and the horses, alert from a good night of grazing, twitched this way and that, drawing attention to marmots and foxes that darted away from our path, and a kite that dove to earth in pursuit of a ground squirrel. Unlike on other journeys, when my own body had been on the front line, on this trip it was the horses that were in that position, and it was through their needs, senses, and toils I experienced the landscape. They had become my conduit with the land, and perhaps it was more accurate to suggest I was riding to Hungary learning to view the world through their eyes rather than those of a nomad.

Within an hour we reached a great sweeping corner of the valley where the river swung around in a right-angle turn to the northwest and split in two. The drama of 4,037 m Kharkhiraa slid into view. Gentle spurs climbed skyward to a craggy, indomitable peak entombed in a sarcophagus of glaciers. From the summit a cloud of wind-driven snow plumed into the sky, and, as I watched, it cascaded down the northern face past giant chunks of glacial ice that clung to the cliff midway down. Where the plume settled at the bottom, the main glacier slalomed through black rocky spurs, disappearing into the bowels of the mountain, then reappearing as a slender, cascading stream forming the headwaters of the Kharkhiraa River.

A little farther on Turgen emerged. Capped with a helmet of ice, its sheer northern face of dark rock looked more like the cross section of a mountain.

After pausing for lunch, we began climbing high above the respective valleys to the 3,000 m pass between the twin peaks. I leaned forward, gripping Rusty's mane, following Dashnyam along a zigzag of narrow ledges. The camel cried every time its soft, wide feet became wedged between rocks. Only the pain from the nose peg Dashnyam pulled was enough to egg her on.

The climb eased off abruptly when we reached an ovoo and rode out onto the broad grassy pass. Directly ahead, a series of hazy blue mountains aglitter with ice rose from the horizon. They were peaks of the Sayan range, on the distant border with the republics of Altai and Tuva in Russian Siberia.

We had made good time, so when we crested the highest point, we resolved to spend the next day and night camped just below the pass. The clear, stable weather provided an opportunity to explore the higher mountains on foot. Leaving Dashnyam with the animals, I trekked to a razorback ridgeline at around 3,700 m, where I spent a couple of glorious hours gazing down upon snaking glaciers, and a series of turquoise lakes at their tail ends. Up so high, it was as if life in the thinner air had been distilled. The sweat and difficulties of the last few months fell away.

On the second morning in the pass we woke to cluttered skies. Clouds like floating battleships had gathered, and wind tugged and pulled at our tents. Curved columns of snow raked across the slopes. We rode through scattered snow showers, passing hills pockmarked with hundreds of lakes, and in the evening maneuvered down a gully to arrive in camp ravenous and cold. As would become a ritual for me as far as Hungary, we sat with our eyes glued on the stove, waiting impatiently for the water to boil.

In the morning snow came thick and hard. Dashnyam was worried.

"The camel's pads will slip on this snow, and we will have a very bad accident if we continue. Better wait till tomorrow, when the snow might have melted," he explained.

I was more than happy to spend the day in the tent, using the undisturbed time to catch up on my diary entries, although it soon became clear we were not as alone as we thought.

After breakfast there came the standard Mongolian door knock—the clearing of the throat and a loud spit—before three men carrying rifles and bearing frozen, chapped cheeks clambered into Dashnyam's tent.

"How is your journey going? Good?" they asked.

"How is yours?" asked Dashnyam, offering them tea.

I sat squeezed up against the tent wall watching the tea breathe life back into the men. Like the snowflakes in their hair and eyelashes, which soon liquefied, sending rivulets of water running down their faces, their rigid expressions melted and the tent became abuzz with chatter.

The men—one in middle age, the others in their twenties—were marmot hunters who had been living for a week in a rock shelter not far from our camp. Their aim was to collect as many marmot pelts as possible, which they would sell to traders on the plains. All was going well, so they planned to stay another week.

In the late afternoon when the weather cleared we joined the hunters as they checked their marmot traps. With little emotion they hauled out their victims and methodically snapped their necks. When this was done we returned to the cave, where the limp carcasses were skinned and tossed into a pot of boiling water, and vodka was passed around. Before drinking, each man flicked a drop to the sky and one to the earth, then rubbed a little on his forehead. Dashnyam shared his snuff bottle and tobacco, talking with the men in the measured cadence I had become used to.

As the vodka set in I leaned up against the rock wall and studied my hosts. Their deels were shredded and impregnated with oil, dung, and soil. They had nothing to sleep on, and no food bar the marmots they caught and a few morsels of stale boortsog. The older man's face was a landscape to behold. His nose rose in a broad plateau from the steppe of his cheeks, below which a mustache as frayed as his deel grew unchecked. His life had clearly been hard, yet there was no hint of complaint. When he laughed, the features of his face parted elastically, giving vent to a happy soul.

When the meat was done, a single knife was produced, and fatty chunks carved out and brought to mouth. The older hunter chewed ungraciously on a jawbone. He then picked pieces up and slurped on them before licking his fingers and hands clean of the rich marmot oil. It was a scene that had played out through the ages. The same oil had once widely been used by warriors who would rub it over their skin to prevent frostbite during marches in the winter. Today the oil is still valued as a treatment for burns, wounds, and rheumatism, although eating marmots, as these men were doing, is frowned upon. A ground rodent, the marmot had been one of the first known carriers of the Black Death, which went on to contribute to the fall of the Mongol Empire and threaten entire civilizations from China to Africa. Marmots are still carriers of the disease, outbreaks of which occur annually in Mongolia.

"What about the Black Death? Are you scared?" I asked them through Dashnyam.

Their laughter said it all. Ignoring the taboo about eating marmot meat, I bent forward and accepted a piece of the fatty meat. As it slipped down my throat, I had no doubt these were the hardest men I had ever met—not in the aggressive, macho sense, but in their gracious acceptance of the difficulties and privations of their lives. On the steppe when the grass was rich and thick, herds flourished, and the people rejoiced and gave thanks to tengri. When the land was in drought, or stung by a bitter winter, their herds shrunk and the people accepted it. Life and death were at the whim of the earth and the sky, and there was nothing inherently wrong with that.

Their world fostered an uncomplaining attitude I would have liked to think I could adopt and carry forth to Hungary—but which I knew was probably beyond me.

TWO DAYS FROM the hunters' cave, we paused by an ovoo from which the mountains dropped away to a vast crater-shaped valley. Through the middle of this, a single wrinkle of a stream flowed its way to the west, funneled out by the mountains onto a distant desert-like plain where it spilled into a wide shallow lake. We were about to drop down to a rugged landscape of sand and rock where alpine grasses gave way to little more than hardy desert bushes.

On the horizon, beyond this immediate landscape there were too many layers of mountains to count, each riddled with thousands of shadowy crevices, gullies, and peaks that would absorb a lifetime of exploring. For now, though, my mind was sated by the journey that had just passed.

I rode behind Dashnyam, admiring the way he held the camel's lead rope with one hand and smoked with the other, still managing to tap gently at his horse's rear when necessary. "Aha aha," he called every time the camel threatened to slow or panic. I didn't have the heart to tell him that for days he had been wearing my backpack upside down.

In the evening we reached the abandoned summer community of Khovd Brigad, where a few old shoes and round circles of yellow grass indicated that the community had recently packed up and gone. We were still a good day's ride from where I could expect to find people again, but it was here that our journey together would come to an end. Dashnyam needed to return before the winter snows blocked the pass, and with only one serving of porridge, a handful of pasta, and some dried strips of meat remaining of our food stocks, one more day together meant that we would run out completely.

In light of our humble prospects for dinner, my heart sank when two men on motorbikes came to us at dusk. They were hunters, had been riding all day, and had no food or shelter. Dashnyam offered them half our meal, and we went to bed ravenous. The hunters lay down on the earth and pulled their deels over their heads. In the morning they stood up, dusted off the frost, and climbed back on their bikes.

Over breakfast, I took the time to appreciate the idiosyncrasies of Dashnyam's character one last time. As always, he ate his share of semolina by dunking his head into the buckled old pot and licking until it was shiny clean, his hooked Khoton nose needing a wipe afterward. I still couldn't work out whether he had forgotten to bring a spoon and was too proud to borrow mine or simply thought it unnecessary. Afterward he rolled a cigarette along the edge of his worn soldier's boots, and then, while he smoked it, took supreme care to fold up his tattered but treasured tent. When he was ready to pack, he ambled bowlegged to his camel and brought her over to his gear, tugging gently on the lead rope to make her sit.

Without my cumbersome equipment, the packing that had taken us over an hour required but ten minutes. I looked on with envy as he swung his tent, pot, brick tea, and tobacco up between the camel's humps. The distance that had taken seven days for us to cover together, he said, he could manage on the return in two and a half—and judging by his light load, I could partly understand how. In the end, I was a westerner and would never master the art of traveling light the way he did.

When he was ready to go, I gave him a packet of Russian cigarettes and paid him for an extra couple of days. He presented me with a packet of matches, which I accepted with two hands and brought to my forehead, according to custom. The packet hit the headlamp that was still strapped on my head, and went tumbling to the ground, to my embarrassment, since in Mongolian culture dropping a gift was a grave sign of disrespect.

Lastly, I split our meager rations—a few pieces of curd and some old sand-encrusted jellybeans from the bottom of the boxes. He lifted the collar of his deel over his head so he could tightly wind the sash around his waist. Then he mounted up and swung his arm in an arc to the northwest, indicating the way I was to travel.

I watched him shrink into the distance until he disappeared beyond a ridge. The melancholy cry of his camel lingered for a few moments, but then I was alone.

FROM THE KHARKHIRAA-TURGEN range, there remained about 250 km until the point where the borders of Mongolia, China, Kazakhstan, and Russia converge in the heart of the Altai Mountains—a two-week journey. Just two days after saying goodbye to Dashnyam, however, I crossed the Khovd River, and it was there that my Mongolian journey effectively came to an end. I had reached Bayan-Olgiy Aimag, at Mongolia's western-most extent, where Kazakh nomads have been in the vast majority since migrating to the region in the mid-nineteenth century. Nominal Muslims who speak a Turkic tongue, many I met gravitated culturally more toward my next destination, Kazakhstan, than to Ulaanbaatar, and certainly they were geographically closer to the former.

With hindsight, I would come to understand that because the Kazakhs from Bayan-Olgiy had been isolated during the period of Soviet revolution and Stalin's ensuing rule, these people had retained a more traditional and authentic culture than their brothers and sisters in Kazakhstan itself. At the time, however, I felt that Bayan-Olgiy simply represented the end of my Mongolian experience, and a prelude to a land that would dominate the next twelve months of my life.

Short of the border itself, I decided to finish up my journey beyond the village of Tsengel. There I managed to sell my horses to a Tuvan school-teacher who promised to use Rusty and Bokus as work animals and not slaughter them for winter meat. Since neither the border with Russia nor China in Mongolia's West was open to foreigners, getting to Kazakhstan by horse through either country was impossible. I had therefore decided to fly over the mountains into Kazakhstan and buy horses as close as I could to Kazakhstan's eastern border.[2] It would prove to be the only stretch of terrain—about 250 km as the crow flies—that I would not be able to travel by horse to the Danube.

KAZAKHSTAN

6

STALIN'S SHAMBALA

IN MONGOLIA I had ridden for more than seventy days and 1,4000 km from east of the old empire capital, Kharkhorin, to the far western province of Bayan-Olgiy. It had been a time crowded with challenges—among them learning to ride, familiarizing myself with nomad ways, and getting through the daily test of finding water and grass. And yet in the scheme of my journey to the Danube, it had been little more than a prelude to the challenges that lay ahead. I had, after all, been riding through the forgiving conditions of summer in a land where nomads were often nearby to lend a hand.

It was with feelings of trepidation and excitement that I looked ahead to the next broad chapter of my journey: Kazakhstan. The trepidation was because I knew Kazakhstan would be the make-or-break leg of the journey—not simply because of the sheer distance involved, the topography I could expect, and the fact that winter would be on my heels, but because of the social legacy of the Russian Empire and the Soviet Union, which I would confront in its many forms.

And yet I would also be heading into the heart of my journey—the remote center of Eurasia, which had been pivotal in the history of steppe nomads. Somewhere out there in the immense and sparsely populated deserts, steppe, and mountains—during a crossing that promised to be more than twice as far as that of Mongolia—there beckoned the kind of freedom of travel and cultural immersion I had dreamed of.

One of the first times I had heard anything about Kazakhstan had been in 2000 during the bicycle journey. Chris and I had stayed for some days with an ethnic German family in Siberia who had recently moved from the Kazakh steppes, where they had lived in exile since Stalin deported the Volga Germans during World War II. They had told of a land so hot in summer that Kazakh nomads wore heavy sheepskin coats and hats to insulate from the sun. In winter, the wind and the cold were more severe than in Siberia—compounded by the absence of the shelter and firewood found there in the dense taiga forest. Since that time, I had been fixated on maps of Kazakhstan, and my fascination with the country had steadily grown.

Almost equal in size to Western Europe, and the largest of the former Soviet nations behind Russia, Kazakhstan occupied what for many in the Western world is a geographical blind spot, stretching from the north Caspian Sea in the west (that technically lies in Europe) to China and the Altai in the east. In the south its borders pass through the legendary Central Asian deserts of the Kyzylkum and Karakum, and the ridgelines of the Tien Shan, China's "Celestial Mountains." To the north, sweeping grasslands merge with the beginnings of the Siberian taiga.

Significantly for me, Kazakhstan lay at the geographical heart of the Eurasian steppe, encompassing the most extreme terrain and climate of the nomads, and it was home to the world's oldest continuous horseback culture. Historians believe it was in the country's north, where present-day Akmola province lies, that an ancient people known as the Botai (c. 3700–3100 BCE) became the first humans to domesticate the equine.

Since that early period of nomad history, the Kazakh lands had played a central role in the rise and fall of steppe empires, including that of the Mongols. While the grasslands, desert, and mountains stretching from

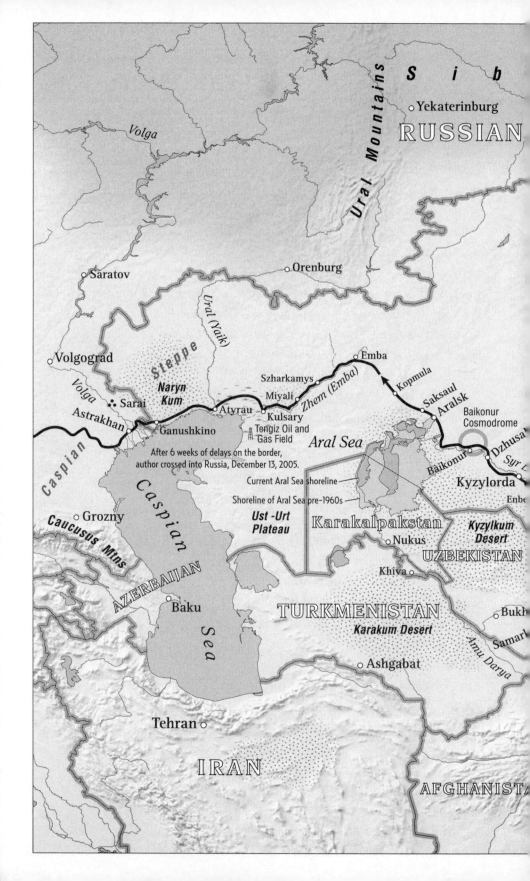

Yekaterinburg

S i b

RUSSIAN

Ural Mountains

Volga

Orenburg

Saratov

Ural (Yaik)

Emba

Volgograd

Steppe

Szharkamys

Zhem (Emba)

Kopmula

Naryn Kum

Miyali

Saksaul

Aralsk

Volga

Atyrau

Baikonur Cosmodrome

Astrakhan

Sarai

Kulsary

Ganushkino

Tengiz Oil and Gas Field

Aral Sea

Baikonur

Dzhusa

After 6 weeks of delays on the border, author crossed into Russia, December 13, 2005.

Syr L

Current Aral Sea shoreline

Kyzylorda

Shoreline of Aral Sea pre-1960s

Enbe

Caspian

Grozny

Ust -Urt Plateau

Karakalpakstan

Kyzylkum Desert

Caucusus Mtns

Nukus

UZBEKISTAN

Caspian

Khiva

AZERBAIJAN

Baku

TURKMENISTAN

Bukh

Sea

Karakum Desert

Samarl

Amu Darya

Tehran

Ashgabat

IRAN

AFGHANIST

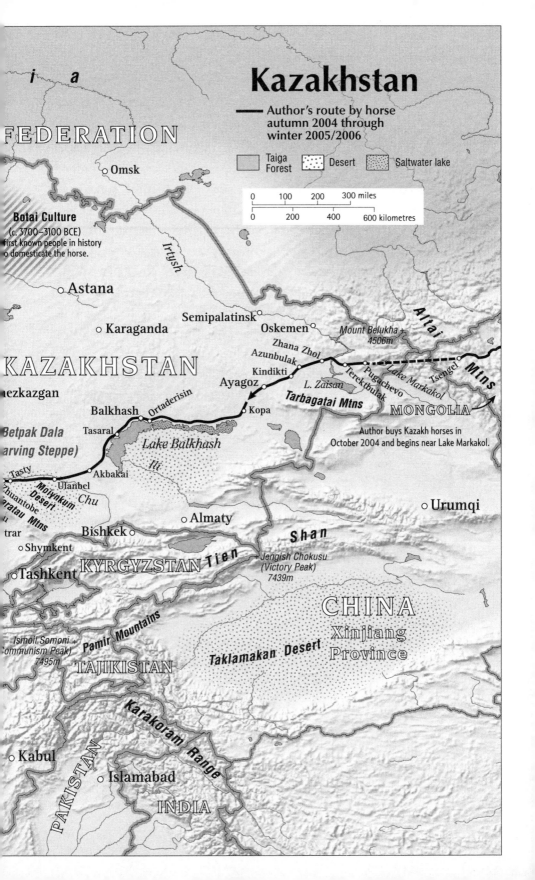

Kazakhstan

— Author's route by horse
autumn 2004 through
winter 2005/2006

Taiga Forest | Desert | Saltwater lake

| 0 | 100 | 200 | 300 miles |
| 0 | 200 | 400 | 600 kilometres |

i *a*

FEDERATION

○ Omsk

Botai Culture
(c. 3700–3100 BCE)
first known people in history
to domesticate the horse.

○ Astana

KAZAKHSTAN

○ Karaganda

Semipalatinsk ○

Oskemen ○

Mount Belukha +
4506m

Zhana Zhol
Azunbulak
Kindikti

Ayagoz ○

Terektbulak
Pugachevo
Lake Markakol
Tsengel

Altai Mtns

Irtysh

ezkazgan

Balkhash

Ortaderisin

○ Kopa

L. Zaisan

Tarbagatai Mtns

MONGOLIA

Betpak Dala
arving Steppe)

Tasaral

Lake Balkhash

Ili

Author buys Kazakh horses in
October 2004 and begins near Lake Markakol.

Tasty

Moiynkum
Desert

Ulanbel

Akbakai

Chu

huantobe
aratau Mtns

trar
○ Shymkent

○ Bishkek

○ Almaty

S h a n

○ Urumqi

Tien

Jengish Chokusu
(Victory Peak)
7439m

KYRGYZSTAN

○ Tashkent

CHINA
Xinjiang
Province

Ismoil Somoni +
ommunism Peak)
7495m

Pamir Mountains

TAJIKISTAN

Taklamakan Desert

Karakoram Range

○ Kabul

○ Islamabad

PAKISTAN

INDIA

the Caspian Sea to the Altai did not have the kind of treasures sought during the conquests of China, Europe, and the more fertile regions of Central Asia, it was a strategic steppe heartland that could be used as a horse highway bridging Asia with Europe, and a vast sanctuary where millions of horses could be grazed. In Genghis Khan's own lifetime, some of his most important conquests were launched from here, including the crushing of the Khwarezm Empire in Central Asia. These were also the lands that Genghis's oldest son, Jochi, had been given control of after his father's death, and which became entrenched as part of the Golden Horde.[1]

Just as important as the strategic nature of the Kazakh territory for the Mongols were the people who inhabited it. Tribes of mixed Turkic descent, they shared a common nomadic way of life with the Mongols, in some regions moving as much as 1,000 km a year in pursuit of pasture. The inherent rigors of this life made them formidable soldiers, and although the Mongols initially faced fierce resistance during their probing campaigns—most notably from the Kipchaks—historians estimate that the Mongolian army that invaded Europe consisted of only around 10 percent Mongolian soldiers; the bulk of the remainder were of Turkic extraction. In fact, as the Mongol Empire fractured into autonomous khanates in the late thirteenth and early fourteenth centuries, Turkic came to replace Mongolian as the language of the ruling class in much of the southern, central, and western regions, including the Golden Horde.

It is unclear when the identity "Kazakh"—a term that means "free rider"—emerged, but in the eighteenth century, three Turkic hordes, known as the Ula Juz (Elder Horde), Orta Juz (Middle Horde), and Kishi Juz (Junior Horde), united to form what would become the modern nation of Kazakhstan. Riding through their country would be to ride through the nucleus of the nomad's world—the original steppe melting pot.

IN A FORESHADOWING of the complex bureaucracy I would have to deal with as I traveled west, just getting to Kazakhstan proved difficult. As previously noted, the borders of China and Russia were closed to foreigners in western Mongolia. I'd tried nonetheless to wangle some way to transit the small stretch of Russia that lay between Mongolia and Kazakhstan by horse, presenting my visa invitation to an official at the Russian embassy in Ulaanbaatar. But he held up my invitation in anger and growled, "You understand Russian? The border is closed! And you know what? This invitation is toilet paper. That is what it is!"

With little choice, I bought a ticket on a charter for the short flight from Olgiy to the city of Oskemen (also known by the Russian name Ust-Kamenogorsk) in eastern Kazakhstan. My plan from there was to drive east, deep into the Altai—home of the mythical *shambala*, a paradise on earth that, according to Buddhist beliefs, will reveal itself upon the destruction of humanity—and as close as possible to the Mongolian border, to look for tough mountain breeds. From there, I hoped to quickly descend from the mountains before the winter hit and begin the long ride west toward the Caspian Sea. The complete crossing of Kazakhstan from east to west amounted to more than 3,000 km in a straight line—much more by horseback—and I estimated it could take anywhere between six months and a year.

I landed in Oskemen, a small industrial city that had once been a Russian fort town, during the first week of October, when the mountains were dusted in fresh snow. A couple of weeks later, a taxi driver known as Meirim was awash with excitement as we loaded his car in front of a central Oskemen hotel. With the trunk full and the backseat loaded to the ceiling, I handed over half of the agreed-upon sum of money—about $100—for him to drive me out of the city and begin searching for horses.

Meirim's eyes were alight like those of a young boy plotting an adventure. "I have told my wife that I will be away for just two days," he said. "When we are out there, I will call and explain we have been delayed."

It was not without reservations that I had agreed to hire Meirim. I had come to know the middle-aged father of two after accepting a ride in his taxi from the Oskemen airport. On the way into the city a speeding car had run down a pedestrian right before our eyes, and instead of stopping to help, Meirim had mouthed off at the traffic holdup, tooted his horn in fury, and then driven up over the curb and around the scene. There was a tough survival instinct just behind his disarming friendliness, and I wasn't sure I could trust him.

On the other hand, I had learned that Meirim was a Kazakh from Bayan-Olgiy province in western Mongolia. During Soviet times he had served as a tank operator in the Gobi Desert and gone on to become a professional translator for the Soviet army, specializing in Mongolian, Russian, and Kazakh. With the fall of the Soviet Union, he had spent several years trading marmot furs between Siberia and Mongolia before taking the opportunity to emigrate from Mongolia to the "motherland" in search of a better life.

Because I spoke Russian I could communicate freely with Meirim, and I was hoping his knowledge could help me reestablish a sense of continuity between Mongolia and Kazakhstan that had been broken not just by my plane flight and modern political boundaries but also by more than two centuries of dramatic social and political change. Although Mongolia and Kazakhstan might once have resembled each other as pastoral, nomadic societies, the Russian Empire had been encroaching on the Kazakh steppe as early as the latter half of the eighteenth century. By the 1880s most Kazakh lands were firmly under Russian control, and Russia's designs were such that the Russian commander in chief of the Kazakh headquarters in Almaty had the audacity to declare: "There is a requirement to admit with sincerity that our business here is a Russian one, first and foremost, and that land populated by Kazakhs is not their own, but belongs to the state. The Russian elements must force them off the land or lead them into oblivion."[2]

In the twentieth century Stalin initiated an intense industrialization of Kazakhstan that included the forced settling of nomads in collectives, the plowing up of steppe for grain production, and a process of cultural russification. Kazakhstan's remoteness also made it his favorite dumping ground for enemies. Some of the better-known prisoners of Kazakhstan's many gulags included Trotsky and Alexander Solzhenitsyn.[3] By 1989, the Kazakhs had long become an ethnic minority in their own lands, eclipsed by Russians, and it was estimated that 40 percent—mostly those living in urban areas—had lost proficiency in their native tongue.

Since then, of course, the Soviet Union had unraveled, and I was entering a country going through incalculable upheaval as it made the difficult transition to both independence and a free market economy. In these times of change it seemed likely that Kazakhstan's emerging identity would have less to do with its renown as the birthplace of horsemanship than as a resource powerhouse. The discovery of massive oil reserves on the Caspian Sea had attracted billions of dollars of foreign investment since the breakup of the Soviet Union, and some analysts were predicting that Kazakhstan would be among the world's top five oil producers by 2015.

If there was any chance of getting beneath the multiple layers of change that had coursed through Kazakhstan and reconnecting with the spirit of the horseback nomad, then Meirim, I reasoned, was surely a good start.

On the edge of the city a dacha village gave way to the open steppe—an undulating sea of pebbly earth sprinkled with hardy tufts of sun-bleached grass. The sky was gray and stagnant, casting dreary light onto the earth, which seemed to be resigned to the coming winter. I wound down the window, letting the cold air whisk away the mental cobwebs that had gathered around my senses in the city.

Meirim began to tell stories about the land around us. There was a mountain pass called Ayultai, which means "dangerous" in Mongolian. "When you ask the locals if they know what these names mean, they just say, 'Oh, there was a man called Ayultai.' They don't realize that so many of the places here have Mongolian names." As if to prove the point, we dropped into a valley thick with a pall of wood-fire smoke and came into a village hugging the bend of a shallow river. It was named Targyn— according to Meirim, a corruption of the Mongolian word targan, which means "fat" and is often used in describing horses.

"There are many Mongolian Kazakhs living here," said Meirim. "I lived here to start with for the first year as well, with relatives." He explained that many families occupied overcrowded homes while they searched for work and a new beginning.

The wooden homes were dark and gray, and the streets largely deserted. Among the locals, there were few if any Russians to be seen. Barely a soul acknowledged our car as we roared through.

The mass exodus of Kazakhs from Mongolia—and from other regions including China and Iran—to Kazakhstan began in the wake of the Soviet Union's collapse. In 1992, in a move to increase the native population, the president, Nursultan Nazarbayev, convened a kurultai, or council, and adopted a resolution appealing to all Kazakhs to unite under a single flag on the soil of Kazakhstan.[4] While sixty thousand Kazakhs had left Mongolia for Kazakhstan over the next few years, many had since returned to Mongolia, disenchanted. Many more likely wound up in impoverished villages such as Targyn.

AN ENGLISH LONG rider (equestrian traveler), Claire Burges Watson, who knew the area, had given me the name and address of a man who I hoped would be able to help me in Kazakhstan.[5] Ruslan was a herder and fisherman in his mid-twenties who at one time had traveled with her on horseback into Kyrgyzstan. Late in the evening, we arrived at his home in the village of Slavyanka.

Still smelling of fish, Ruslan and his brother met us with open arms. Ruslan was an athletic-looking man with coarse hands, thick eyebrows, and a strong jaw. Unlike Meirim, who had a classic, open face, Ruslan's was more chiseled, and he had a large, almost Russian nose. His charisma and strength must have made him popular among village girls, and when he spoke in his gentlemanly manner, I imagined he charmed the hearts of little old ladies. Meirim, by contrast, was a short, wiry little man with delicate hands who seemed to speak loud and gesticulate with his arms in order to enlarge his presence.

After a night in Ruslan's family home, we spent a day searching for horses in the nearby village of Terektbulak, to no avail. The horses we inspected were either old and scarred or untrained and dangerous. Without exception, they were also expensive, averaging $500.[6] Because I had been banking on a budget of $10 a day, the prices made my blood run cold. Ruslan did everything but soothe my concerns.

"Tim, if you want a really good horse, you will need $1,000. The price you are being offered is purely meat value." He explained how trucks from slaughterhouses in the city often came around to the villages. Whoever was in need of money sold their horses.

I wasn't ready to accept the high prices, so we set out early the next day east along the Kurchum River to a remote mountain valley near an alpine lake called Markakol. Meirim's spirits rose as we snaked through the rocky slopes. The territory had lain beyond the reach of Stalin's plans for Kazakhstan's north and looked more like the untamed environment of Mongolia. Ruslan, on the other hand, was becoming more anxious, perhaps because we had now gone well beyond his network of loyal friends and family.

The gentle slopes became sheer ridges that blocked out much of the low sunlight and the road gradually deteriorated. It was in the village of Maraldy that Meirim decided his city car could not go on. There we negotiated with a local who owned a Russian Niva with four-wheel drive to take us to Pugachevo—the end of the road and the last place in the valley where I might find horses.

The Niva lurched through puddles of snow and mud, often on the edge of a sheer drop down to the river. Eventually we pulled over a rise onto a wide, open stretch of the valley, revealing a vista of peaks rising seamlessly into brooding gray clouds. Pugachevo, a village of about 160 homes, lay nestled below, among the gentle slopes on the river's edge.

Our party was now four—me, Meirim, Ruslan, and our driver—and in Pugachevo, this became eight. The idea was to find someone who knew someone. We stopped at every second house, asked questions, then rolled on. Those who approached the car were obliged to shake each passenger's hand, which was becoming difficult, since we all had to lean through the driver's window. The standard greeting used by the nominally Muslim Kazakhs, "As-salam aleikum," was followed by the standard response, "Wa aleikum as-salam," and sometimes by "Zdrast-vuy-tye"—"hello" in Russian—when they realized there was a white man in the car.

Nurkhan, a short, robust man with a clean crew cut, wearing camouflage and Russian army boots, considered us his personal guests. He made sure word circulated that a horse buyer was in town. There was something tough yet fair about him. His long, slender Mongolian eyes set into a broad, open face conveyed the maturity of a patriarch. He bonded quickly with Ruslan, the two of them talking avidly in Kazakh; I could still understand much of their conversation, though, because they often swore fluently in Russian midsentence.

With Nurkhan yelling out demands to anyone who crossed our path, it wasn't long before the horses began to line up. There was an old nag, "the best in the village," that had a back sunken like an old couch. A mare that had open back wounds and a foal by its side was touted as "the perfect horse for the job." When I said that I couldn't possibly ride such an injured horse, they told me, "Tim, you can sell this horse for twice the price when you get down to the steppe and buy yourself another!"

Nurkhan promised better horses and after lunch took me to a man renowned for his workhorses, which regularly lugged 70 kg loads of fish from Lake Markakol for trading. The man seemed reluctant to sell, but Nurkhan and others urged him to consider. I was led to a white gelding in a yard, followed by half of the village men. The horse's withers and spine were thick with muscle, his legs tough and sinewy. Like Mongolian horses, he was a stocky, heavily built horse. With feigned confidence, I took a close look in his mouth—I had been given a crash course in reading horse teeth, but in reality had little experience—and took him for a ride. He seemed to have stiff legs. Perhaps the gelding was recovering from work, but more likely was very old. I was sure he was at least fifteen.

"He is ten," said the owner.

"But how could that be? I can see he is much older!" I replied.

A man from the crowd vouched for the owner.

"I remember when this horse was born. The horse is no more than ten."

I took another look at the teeth, then at Ruslan and Meirim. They were silent. After much mediation by Nurkhan and others, I accepted that I was probably mistaken and was offered a price of 65,000 tenge (about $550). But I wasn't buying yet.

As darkness fell, a man arrived on a young chestnut horse that he had brought down from a herd in the mountains. Named Ogonyok—which meant "small flame" in Russian, but was also the namesake of a local wildflower—it had short, stocky front legs and a powerful chest. Although the animal was flighty, I liked him, and the owner invited us home for dinner.

Messages were run to relatives near and far before they decided it was in fact for sale, and in the process vodka began to flow. It began as a three-shot toast, but whenever the bottle of vodka was near empty, another replaced it, and I lost count. Somewhere in the midst of broken flashes of detail, I agreed to buy the chestnut horse and return the following day with payment.

Before leaving Pugachevo, Nurkhan secretively ushered us into his home, where he pulled up a trap door under a rug and produced a glass bottle filled with a dark red liquid. "This, my friends, is a secret, worth a fortune. It is blood from deer antlers. You know, good for . . ." He pantomimed that it was an aphrodisiac. The three of us raised a toast and swilled down a shot of the stuff, followed by more vodka, then bundled into the Niva. It wasn't until we were sitting in the car that I wondered what good an aphrodisiac might do at that particular moment.

The Niva bucked and swayed in the night, and my head began to swim. I couldn't work out whether it was motion sickness or vodka, but I was overcome with nausea by the time we reached Maraldy and stepped out of the car into the freezing air. Meirim slumped into position behind the wheel of his own car, and Ruslan spread out on the backseat and fell asleep.

After negotiating just two bends, during which we very nearly veered off the edge of the road, I took over the wheel and guided the car down the winding valley road into the foothills. Meirim passed out, his head on the dashboard, where it rattled and rolled.

I must have been driving for a couple of hours when the shuddering of the car in the gravel suddenly became so violent it woke Meirim from his stupor.

"Stop!" he yelled. We stumbled out.

"Fucking Australian! If you were riding a horse and it had a broken leg, would you notice? This wheel is square! Don't you know they are meant to be round?"

The front right wheel had but a few shreds of tire remaining.

"Yeah, well, you didn't notice either, did you?" I retorted. "Because you are so drunk you can hardly stand up!"

Meirim took the tire off, threw it off the roadside in a rage, and fitted the spare.

"I will never let you drive again!" he shouted, handing the keys to Ruslan.

IT WAS WELL after midnight by the time we neared Slavyanka, but the night for us was only beginning. Eleven kilometres short of home Ruslan veered away to a ferry crossing point on the Irtysh River, where his wife-to-be worked twenty-four-hour shifts at a café. Inside, Ruslan greeted the patrons—mostly sleep-deprived truck drivers and local drunks—with a handshake, then announced to Meirim and me that we were his guests. I told him angrily that we needed to get home and back to Pugachevo by midday, but this only strengthened his resolve. On our table landed a bottle of vodka, which he and Meirim quickly finished . . . then another.

When Meirim began casting a steely stare at an aggressive-looking drunk in a soldier's uniform, I knew things were hurtling out of control. The soldier came and sat next to me, his breath heavy with alcohol. Ruslan stalled the face-off with a fresh round of vodka. I dragged Meirim outside.

"You know, Tim, I feel like I am young again! Those fuckin' Russians, these Russian Kazakhs, they know nothing! I just want to fight! You know that feeling, when you just want to break someone's nose?" I could only hold him out there for so long before he went back inside. It was the first of many close shaves when Meirim decided to pick a fight. Ruslan, meanwhile, ended up arguing with his girlfriend, then stealing her away in Meirim's car.

It wasn't until eight o'clock in the morning that we were back on the road, and upon pulling in at Ruslan's home I was so tired I could barely stand. I went straight to sleep, and when I woke, both Meirim and Ruslan had left.

A day passed before Meirim sheepishly showed up. I'd promised the villagers that I would be back within a day with the money for the horse, so by now they had probably given up on me. I had been paying Meirim a generous daily allowance, plus covering the fuel and food bills, and, sensing that I was ready to heap him with abuse, Meirim refused to look me in the eye, all the while protesting that he saw the situation differently.

"My wife needs me. I can't just drop everything for you! I have two children. They need to be fed. You need to pay me for the broken wheel, then I am going home." I gave him $50, and he drove off.

Ruslan, in the meantime, was nowhere to be seen, and although his father and brother tried to convince me that he would turn up sooner or later, panic crept up on me despite my resolve. I retreated to a pit toilet in the village, where among piles of frozen shit and cigarette butts I squatted, struggling to hold myself together. The first flakes of winter were beginning to fall from heavy gray skies, and I listened to the sounds of a drunken argument drifting over from somewhere nearby. Perhaps I was just coming to terms with my decision to travel alone, but the past few days had not been the kind of experience I had envisioned on my journey. I was overwhelmed by an unshakable feeling that journeying across Kazakhstan would be one long trial.

IT WAS TWO days before Ruslan showed up, and when he did, I was not taking chances. I helped him into the back of a 1960s Moskvich—a small sedan of the Soviet era—where he collapsed into a deep hangover-induced sleep. The smell of beer and cigarettes rising off him was worse than the cold, and so we set off with the windows wide open, rising and dipping along the same road where my journey had earlier disintegrated. Ruslan slept until well after dark and woke remarkably sober as we crashed our way through the last icy potholes and puddles to Pugachevo.

The locals complained that I had kept them waiting, with their horses standing around eating valuable hay, but I made them laugh with stories of Ruslan's antics, and any sense of guilt vanished when an old man approached me and whispered to me that the white horse was in fact fifteen years old—he had apparently wanted to tell the truth at the time, but it was a tradition to keep to the script of a fellow villager.

Though I'd agreed to buy Ogonyok, the chestnut horse, I announced that I was not leaving until I found two decent horses that could take me to Hungary. The wheeling and dealing began again, and every time a horse was offered I was told I "would not find a better one."

Eventually an elderly man trotted in on the back of a large bay horse. Nurkhan, who had again taken me under his wing, looked surprised.

"Take a look if you please. If you want it, buy it now. If you don't, I will release it back to the herd," said the man gruffly.

The horse's name was Taskonir,[7] which roughly meant "brown stone." His back was straight and sloped away at the hindquarters, while his mane was coarse and untamed. In his dark eyes was a look of fire I recognized as that of a wild horse, independent and strong-willed. Yet he was also comfortable and calm in the presence of so many people, suggesting he was a veteran work animal. Like most of the horses in Pugachevo, he was a breed known as *dzhabe*. Renowned for endurance and ability to hold their weight— and subsequently the choice of preference for horsemeat—Kazakhs say that their nation "rode the back of a dzhabe."

I took Taskonir for a ride with no bridle or bit, just an old goatskin thrown over his back, then fitted my Australian stock saddle. He moved instinctively, with only the slightest of commands, making me appear more of a horseman than I really was. I asked the owner, whose name was Altai, the price.

"Seventy thousand tenge!" he replied, quoting me a figure roughly equivalent to $520, before adding, "But for that price I keep the horseshoes!"

"How about sixty-five thousand with the horseshoes?" I asked.

"Fuck you!" he shouted. "What kind of person are you? Take your fucking saddle off my horse." He threw my saddle into the mud and stormed off with the horse. The crowd that had gathered fell silent.

Nurkhan came to my aid.

"He is an old, honored man. Maybe that is why he will not bargain."

The crowd followed me to Altai's home. Altai refused to come out. His son emerged, and I sent him back to make an offer of seventy thousand tenge—but only if it included the horseshoes. It was some time before the son appeared and waved us in.

I joined Altai at a small wooden table. In the light that drifted through the old warped glass, he sat still, glistening eyes shifting back and forth from the window to the cup of tea in his weathered hands. He had removed his fur hat and coat to reveal a bald scalp and a wiry figure that was sinking with age. In the wake of his temper, sadness filled his pale brown eyes. Later I understood that he was selling his horse to pay for medical treatments and his daughter's education at college. He was probably torn between a love of his horse and the need to support his family, and I was the unwelcome catalyst for deciding his loyalties. It wasn't just sentimentality, though. Horses here were essential for survival and work, and Taskonir had been a reliable work animal.

I wondered what Altai was thinking. Having lived his life true to the Soviet mantra that labor brought reward, he was selling his pride to a young foreigner who had not an inkling of the hardship he had seen. Like so many of his generation, he had entered retirement just as the Soviet Union collapsed, and now he found himself with nothing to rely on but his own hands, which were already worked to the bone.

I counted the money out onto the table, where it was counted again by his wife, then by his son.

"This horse," he boasted, "will take you all the way to Hungary."

"Will it?" I asked. "I will not forget your word."

I shook his hands, raised a shot of vodka, and reminded Altai: "In my culture it is a sign of disrespect to throw someone's saddle in the mud." He apologized, and then with a grin admitted the horse was probably twelve years old, not ten, as he had maintained.

We took photos together with Taskonir, and I promised to send a photo from the Danube. I could see now that I was taking away a part of his soul, and I pledged to myself never to forget the privilege of having Taskonir and the many years of training and wisdom that Altai had invested in him.

Negotiations for my second horse, Ogonyok, were more straightforward, but in the light of day, this big chestnut horse was more fiery than

I remembered. His eyes were untrusting, and he jumped nervously when I reached out to stroke his back. He was clearly the kind of horse that would bolt at the sound of his own fart and minutes after handing over the money I was told a story that confirmed my fears. It had been several months since anyone had ridden Ogonyok and the owner had been willing to sell only because Ogonyok had fallen on him and crushed his leg the previous winter.

Given the risk Ogonyok posed, I heeded Nurkhan's advice to have him shod with special studded winter shoes for gripping on the winter ice and snow. What I didn't know was that he had never been shod before. Only moments after being secured in a special wooden stall built for farrier work, he exploded in a frenzy of kicking. Nurkhan and the other men leaped for cover, and by the time they lifted themselves out of the mud Ogonyok had ripped apart the wooden frame and stood shaking his head.

The second time round they tied Ogonyok's tail to the top of the stall, then winched it up so high that his back legs barely touched the ground. Extra girths were fitted to his belly and every time he dared move a man beat his side with a steel pipe. This was still not enough to subdue Ogonyok, who managed to bust away the girths kicking back and forth until he was hanging upturned by his tail. It was only on the third attempt that they managed to tie his leg to a post and forcibly bang the shoes on.

During the fiasco I stood holding Ogonyok's bridle and peering into his eyes, which were wide with terror. Although monstrously strong, he was oblivious to his power. He was an honest horse, with none of the cunning of older, more experienced steeds. Even so, overriding any sympathy at this point in time was my own fear—how would I cope with Ogonyok on my own in the wilds?

RUSLAN, NURKHAN, ANOTHER villager known as Orolkhan (and nicknamed "the Chechen"), and I decided to get away from the village and find a fresh starting point for my journey in the loftier reaches of the surrounding peaks. I hoped to use this trip to purify my own spirits with something other than vodka, as well as to find some redeeming traits in Ruslan. I had hardly been able to look him in the eye since his misadventures with Meirim and was frustrated by the reluctance he had shown in helping me bargain during the negotiations over the horses. In the summer months Nurkhan lived and worked at a cooperative deer farm at a remote mountain station. The excursion into the mountains would double as a chance for him to return to his hut and gather the animals and goods he'd left behind.

We set out, and the village of Pugachevo shrank below in a mash of autumn browns and grays. After a heavy sleep in Nurkham's hut that night, Ruslan and I picked one of the peaks and set off to climb as high as we could.

Air gushed into my lungs as Taskonir attacked the slope. I sat snugly in my saddle, daypack hugging my shoulders, my eyes drifting from the few wisps of cloud that caressed the open blue to the freshly powdered crests that curved skyward. On the far horizon, the custodial pyramid of Mount Belukha—the highest peak of the Altai at 4,506 m—stood head and shoulders above everything else.

It was a relief to be looking at the world from horseback again. With every step, the self-doubt and snafus that had plagued me in recent times receded like a single tree in the landscape below.

When the slope became too steep we tied the horses to trees and set off on foot up a rocky spur and into the descending front of winter. After a couple of hours of scrambling through knee-deep snow we emerged from the cover of Siberian larch and pine and finished our climb on a rocky crag. From there I gazed over the land through a multitude of filters. Before us lay invisible trails of the original hunter-gatherers, their descendants who had spread out over the steppe with their horses, Mongol armies that had surged past these natural ramparts in their thousands, explorers who had arrived on a quest to find lost worlds, and imperialist Russians and Chinese who had only recently drawn up artificial borders. I imagined the enchantment for explorers who might have traveled here, beyond the Himalayas and Tibet, in search of shambala.

Some believe this Buddhist concept of a celestial kingdom, accessible only to those on the most evolved spiritual path, is a place of the spirit alone. Others write of a physical hidden world in the Altai, in Tibet, in India, or somewhere in between, where all inhabitants are enlightened. Whether or not the legend is true and there is a mysterious world that has camouflaged itself from modern-day cartographers, the Altai, encompassing a mix of taiga, tundra, glaciated peaks, and desert, would surely accommodate such a dream.

Yet to me, it was the view to the west over the steppe that most captured my imagination. I ran my eyes down the spurs to where they merged seamlessly with a sea of brown. There were no forests out there, or sheltered valleys of thick grass. Even rivers turned north on the edge of this exposed abyss. How many people had stood here like me and wondered just how far this land stretched, and what lay beyond the horizon? From here the open land continued unabated to the Carpathian Mountains on the fringes of central Europe. And regardless of the modern, post-Soviet reality of Kazakhstan and countries farther afield, I felt confident that the horses that would carry me were an ancient link whose primary needs, grass and water, had never changed.

"C'mon, Tim, I'm getting cold, and we have no food or water. Let's go!" I shifted my stare. Ruslan had finished his cigarette and, having thrown the butt in the snow, was trudging back down.

WE ARRIVED AT the hut after dark and found Nurkhan and Orolkhan cooking up the heads of freshly shot wild boar.

"Two wild pigs were guests in our home today. They left their heads behind but they themselves ran away," said Orolkhan as he plunked the two boiled skulls on the table.

We laughed, cutting away flesh from the jaws, eyes, and ears. The three men with me didn't have any problem enjoying the meat, even though pork is typically forbidden to Muslims.

"Mr. Cope," Nurkhan reminded me, "keep this to yourself. We are Kazakhs, but we can eat these pigs because they are clean, they are from nature!"

Our descent back to the valley in the morning was a fitting send-off. Nurkhan gathered some geese and a cat into a couple of potato sacks and loaded them onto an old cart that he harnessed to his horse. One tire was blown, so the cart moved precariously down the steep, icy trail. The geese honked, the cat meowed, and Nurkhan swore violently at them to shut up. I sidled up with my horse and pulled my camera out.

"Don't you dare! With geese and a cart people will think I am a bloody Russian!" he said.

By afternoon Pugachevo was behind us. We rode on after dark until we found refuge back in Maraldy with a family whose eldest son had served in the army with Ruslan. In the morning word reached the patriarch of the family that his brother had just died. Later we saw him, his wife, and their children huddled on the back of a truck rattling down the valley to the funeral procession.

Farther along the Kurchum River where it deepened into a gorge Ruslan led the way up into a maze of bald peaks riddled with rocky gullies. We spent the night at a remote herding station, where we were stirred awake in the early hours by an old man who strode outside and began howling. He had been wakened by a wolf, and this was how he scared them away. Before leaving the man offered us a gun for the remainder of Ruslan's time with me, but Ruslan refused the offer on the grounds that he didn't have a license. The man's question to us would be repeated many more times during the journey: "Why don't you carry a gun? What will you do about the wolves? Thieves?"

A long day of around 50 km brought us to the village of Terektbulak, where I bought my third horse, Zhamba. He was one of the old scarred workhorses I had seen during our first day of horse searching. For the remainder of the journey I regretted this decision. I bought Zhamba because he was much cheaper and in the short term would cause less trouble. This, however, meant forgoing a flighty young black gelding on offer that might have been expensive and dangerous but in the long term would have had what it would take for this kind of journey.

From here on, Ruslan felt he was on home territory, and with around 70 km to cover we moved at a trot, weaving our way up and over bare wrinkled hills and through frozen reed-choked gullies. Every now and then we caught sight of wild goats and deer moving like flecks being picked up on the path of a whirlwind across the slopes.

Ruslan was impressed with Ogonyok, whom he had nicknamed "The Tank."

"This is a great horse. I like him—he reminds me of my own. He is wild, that is true—all ginger horses and redheaded people are like that— but he will settle down after a few days on the road. If you teach him to trot and not be lazy, you will be able to cover a lot of distance every day," he said.

Taskonir was proving himself agile and determined as well. To the astonishment of Ruslan and others, I had ridden him without a bridle or bit, able to control him with a rope halter and the lead tied as the reins. With winter looming, I had extra incentive to dump the use of a bit, given how uncomfortable the freezing metal would be in a horse's mouth.

By contrast with Taskonir and Ogonyok, the third horse, Zhamba, was already struggling although he was carrying no load. We renamed him Maral, which means "roe deer," since he looked more like a mix between a deer and a donkey than a horse when he moved.

There was little time to settle into a walk and we seldom spoke, but during a short rest break Ruslan seemed anxious to talk. He had never acknowledged the days of riotous drunkenness with Meirim, and I thought perhaps he wanted to clear the air. With a look of sincerity he took a long drag on his cigarette and began.

"Tim, how much do girls cost in Australia?"

I tried not to look surprised.

"What do you mean?"

"Well, for example, Russians here, I have tried plenty of them. When I lived with my uncle for a while in Astana, I just watched TV during the day and could pay about a thousand tenge an hour when I needed it. I was even able to try a Korean—they are the most expensive at around three thousand. And the Germans come at a high price too."

He said it so solemnly that I wasn't sure how I could answer without either offending him or leading to the impression that I was homosexual.

"Well, I don't know, to be honest."

"But how do you fuck girls, then?" he interrupted.

I thought a while.

"Well . . . I guess you could say it is free."

Ruslan's eyes lit up, and he gave me a grin that showed his gold teeth.

"I thought so! You know Kazakh girls—they never put out unless you are married to them."

I didn't believe him, but I did know that many people I had met in the former Soviet Union during my previous trip had had conflicting views about Western women and very rarely had the chance to ask for themselves. The word in rural areas in particular was that either they "wore pants like men" and were highly nonsexual because of the feminist movement or they were all willing to offer themselves at will like in American movies. This was one of hundreds of such frank conversations that I would have with men, often herders in the saddle, right across the steppes. One colorful man later told me that Shymkent was his favorite city because "watermelons are twenty-five kopeks and Uzbek women two hundred."

I tried to explain to Ruslan that things were a bit more complex than what he had concluded, but another, more pressing problem had surfaced; Ruslan had clean run out of cigarettes, and he needed to think about going home.

THE MOMENTUM AND camaraderie of my time with Ruslan waned quickly in Slavyanka. Ruslan had his mind on other things. He was planning to get married, but more important, the next couple of weeks would be his last chance to fish before the Irtysh River weir froze over for winter. While I could only offer him $15 a day, which was a stretch for me, he claimed to be able to earn almost $100 with a good day's catch. Like many others in his village, he was able to pay off the fishing inspector and send his fish by car to Oskemen for lucrative sales at the market. (Later I was told that because of this kind of poaching, the Irtysh was headed toward being fished out within a matter of years.)

In truth, though, Ruslan's news that he could guide me for just two more days was a mutually convenient way of parting with our rapport intact. I was already tired of trying to understand the world as it was filtered through his eyes, and I was looking forward to a new chapter.

The remaining time with Ruslan was just long enough for us to cross the Irtysh onto the open steppe farther west, where my hopes of finding someone to travel further with me rested on locating a stranger I had met briefly during a taxi ride in Oskemen, and whose address I had scribbled on the back of an old cigarette box. Aset, as he was known, lived in the small village of Zhana Zhol, which happened to fall along my route.

7

ZUD

"Those who suffered as we did wept bitterly for their losses and cursed those who had introduced such inhuman laws: for people whose lives revolved around their animals, it was worse than being invaded by Genghis Khan's hordes. Their suffering was shared by their relatives in the aul, and the tears continued for weeks in these communities."

—Mukhamet Shayakhmetov,
   *The Silent Steppe: The Memoir of
   a Kazakh Nomad Under Stalin*

ACROSS HIS KITCHEN table, without the pitchfork in hand and heavy coat he had been wearing outside, Aset resembled the soft-natured man I remembered from our brief meeting in Oskemen. His face was broad and full, framed by a crop of silver hair above and patchy bristles that skirted his chin below.

He spoke in a husky, gentle voice that seemed poised to break into laughter.

"Ah, Tim! Tim! Don't be shy—drink, eat! This is Kazakh potato. Best in the world!"

It wasn't until I had filled my belly that I broached the subject of finding a guide to ride with me for a couple of weeks. He was excited and proudly recounted working as a horse shepherd for a collective farm in his youth.

"I used to work twenty-four hours moving with the herd to keep wolves and thieves away. At night I slept in the open holding the tethering rope of the lead stallion."

He recalled his experience nostalgically and suggested that although he hadn't ridden much in recent years and now worked as a laborer on demolition sites in the city, he was more than qualified to ride with me.

What impressed me more than Aset's credentials as a horseman were his qualities as a father. Aset's only child, Guanz, was a ten-year-old boy afflicted with cerebral palsy. When Guanz hobbled into the kitchen, Aset lifted his atrophied, buckled-looking frame into the air in an almighty embrace. Guanz giggled, and Aset's almond eyes squeezed into slender crescents, mirroring Guanz's own expression of joy. Over dinner Guanz clung to Aset's arm, stealing glances at me whenever I wasn't looking and burying his face in Aset's shoulder when I smiled back. Later, as he became a little emboldened, he attracted my attention by picking up the family cat and rubbing it against his cheeks, closing his eyes and laughing. In the grim reality of post-Soviet Kazakhstan it was hard to imagine a bright future for the young boy, yet Aset's visible love and affection seemed to transcend all else.

The evening took on a festive atmosphere as Aset's home crowded with villagers, and I spent hours sharing my photo album from Australia and telling stories. When it became late we went outside to mingle on the street. Guanz and many other children giggled, and dogs from all over the village brushed past my legs in the dark. It was only after most visitors had left that I felt two warm paws on my chest. The moist breath of a dog reached my cheek, and for a protracted moment the animal was still. I glanced down in time to see two white paws vanish into the night.

"He likes you," murmured Aset.

When the children began to tire, we returned inside, and Aset, his wife, and I settled in around the kitchen table. A little earlier Aset had told me that I needed to ask permission from his wife to have him accompany me. Now, when I put the question to her, she put on a serious face and replied with conviction: "You can take him all the way to Hungary if you like!"

TWO DAYS IN Zhana Zhol were set aside for preparations but became filled with leisurely hours drinking tea with villagers and visits to speak to students at the local school. In the company of Aset, who was a teetotaler with none of the coarseness or immaturity of Ruslan, I used the opportunity to slow down and let my nerves recover from the edgy, alcohol-fueled chaos of the past few weeks. A couple of long sleeps were enough for me to wake with a more measured eye and view my surroundings less through the prism of my own challenges and more in light of the recent history through which Kazakh society had passed.

Zhana Zhol—the name means "new road"—was a huddle of fifty or so tired timber homes cast in a sea of dreary gray steppe. Its one muddy street was lined with poplar trees that stood like skeletons against the opaque, clouded-in skies. Autumn was turning, and while in Mongolia nomadic families were no doubt preparing to migrate to winter pastures, Kazakhs here were instead gathering coal, firewood, and hay to see out the long months of cold. Most families had a milking cow, chickens, and even a horse or two, but there were none that boasted the kind of herds I'd been accustomed to in Mongolia. It was a life that closely resembled that of hundreds of Russian villages I had seen on previous travels.

At the school we met with young, wide-eyed children who had never seen the inside of a yurt and had only ever known the tumult of life in post-Soviet Kazakhstan. There were, however, others in the village, including Aset's elderly mother-in-law, who were just old enough to recall a time when Kazakhs lived and breathed a horseback life, moving with the seasons. For her generation, the collapse of the Soviet Union was just one of the many cataclysmic events that had not just changed the course of their individual lives but shaped the future of the country.

By any standards, the twentieth century was one of immense upheaval and tragedy for Kazakhs. It began on the back of more than a century of Russian colonization. In 1916, 150,000 Kazakhs—mostly nomad herders— were killed during a widespread but doomed rebellion against their colonial rulers, triggered by tax hikes, expropriation of livestock, and an order for men between the ages of eighteen and forty-three to be conscripted into the imperial army.

Only a year later, the Bolshevik revolution—which led to the formation of the Soviet Union in 1922—fanned hope that communism might bring equality and independence, but successive Soviet leaders came to see the steppe as an uncivilized backwater to be exploited, and the nomads as itinerant wanderers.[1] The seventy years of Soviet rule would prove an assault on almost every aspect of nomadic culture, the landscape of the Kazakhs, and ultimately their way of life.

For many Kazakhs, nuclear tests carried out at the Semipalatinsk test site, some 400 km northwest of Zhana Zhol, were indicative of the open disregard with which Kazakhs were treated. In 1947 a piece of land chosen for testing by the Soviet Atomic Agency was officially deemed "empty" although the area was home to nomads. During the first detonation in 1949 local teachers were ordered to take children outside the schools to watch the explosions, so their bodies' reaction could be observed and studied. A total of 116 atmospheric explosions were conducted before ground tests were banned, and another 340 underground tests had been carried out by the time the site closed in 1991. The United Nations believes that between 1947 and 1989 one million people were exposed to radiation, leading to high suicide and cancer rates, infertility, and deformities. Aset had grown up in a village adjacent to the testing zone and had only recently moved to Zhana Zhol. He believed that his disabled son, Guanz, was just one of untold thousands of children in the towns and villages of the region still being born with genetic abnormalities.

There were many other tribulations wrought by politicians in faraway Moscow, such as the decision to dam and siphon off the main river arteries of Central Asia—the Syr Darya and the Amu Darya—for cotton production, which led to the calculated death of the Aral Sea. There was also the so-called Virgin Lands Scheme announced by Nikita Khrushchev in 1958, which involved plowing up the steppe of northern Kazakhstan for wheat fields in one of the Soviet Union's biggest agricultural experiments. The steppe is a fragile environment, and although many of the wheat fields were initially productive, many eventually became abandoned dust bowls.

All of these calamities led in one way or another to an erosion of the traditional way of life, but ultimately none was as far-reaching as the early policies of Stalin. Above all, it was the collectivization that took place between 1928 and 1931 that spelled an abrupt end to nomadic life, a national tragedy from which Kazakhs have still not recovered. Although I couldn't yet grasp the scope of the upheaval, over the many weeks and months ahead I would come to realize that without an understanding of events that transpired in those years, any insight into modern Kazakh society was hollow.

The era of collectivization, which affected societies across the Soviet Union, began with the expropriation of property from the wealthy in the mid-1920s and was driven by Joseph Stalin's push for industrialization. The Soviet Union needed grain, plus gold and other minerals in order to buy foreign machines and tools. In 1927, when the grain supply dropped, Stalin blamed the wealthy peasants, or *kulaks*, for hoarding, and ordered them to increase supply. There began a terrifying period when anyone found with the tiniest quantity of bread was sent to prison—a policy that led to an artificial famine in Ukraine in the early 1930s, known as the Holodomor, that claimed the lives of five million.

For Kazakhs confiscation of land and the imposition of grain quotas did not have the same initially productive result as it did in Russia and Ukraine, largely because nomads did not own land. To remedy this, Fillip Isaevich Goloshchekin, a Russian dentist turned politician, was named secretariat for the Kazakh republic. He attempted to solve the problem by declaring that livestock was the equivalent of land for nomads, and in 1928 ordered animals confiscated from the rich (known in Kazakh as *bai*). The truly wealthy nomads—the real bai—had been dispossessed or incarcerated several years earlier, prior to collectivization, and so instead the middling nomads, and even poor ones, were accused of hoarding and forced to hand over their animals.[2] Around this time local Kazakh Soviet authorities—mostly Kazakh political activists who had sided with the ideals of communism, and were known as *belsendi*—became notorious for their pillaging. They often took everything from families, right down to blankets, clothing, and cooking utensils. Nomad families were left with barely enough animals to warrant traditional migration in search of pasture. Officially, the confiscated goods and animals were to become the property of state-owned collectives, but the real intent was for Kazakhstan to supply meat to the cities of the Soviet Union. From every region a quota was demanded, in some cases right down to the last animal.[3]

The scenes of mayhem during these times are difficult to fathom. Train stations across Kazakhstan became mass holding and slaughter yards, where livestock was jammed into rail cars to be sent to Moscow, Leningrad, and other large centers. There was no veterinary control, and an epidemic of brucellosis and tuberculosis broke out. In some cases, the carcasses of animals slaughtered in winter were not transported until spring, by which time they had begun to rot. As an indicator of how poorly Goloshchekin and his government understood the conditions of the steppe, wool quotas were demanded on the eve of winter, which led to entire herds freezing to death. Many nomads destroyed their animals rather than turn them over to authorities, and even animals in collectives died en masse because of mismanagement.[4]

The result of Goloshchekin's policy meant that from 1928 to 1932, cattle and sheep numbers declined by around 90 percent.[5] People began to go hungry in 1930, and it is believed that by 1933 somewhere between 1.7 and 2.2 million nomads—around a third of the Kazakh population at the time—had starved to death and another estimated 653,000 had fled to China. Simultaneously, most nomads ceased their annual migrations, and by 1933, 95 percent of Kazakhs had settled in collective farms. The term *aul*, which once had referred to a community of nomads who moved together from pasture to pasture, now meant little more than a permanent Kazakh settlement.[6]

Zhana Zhol was one such aul—a community anchored permanently on the steppe where their forebears had once roamed. And yet, although

Nomad encampment Arkhangai Aimag in Central Mongolia.

Me and Ochirbat, the elder of the nomad family with whom I stayed while buying my first horses. Packhorse recruit Kheer also pictured.

Kathrin, my girlfriend, traveled the first two months with me through Mongolia. KATHRIN BENDER-NIENHAUS

Kathrin heading off into the steppe, packhorse in tow.

Scenes at a family camp on the shores of Telmen Nuur lake, Zavkhan Aimag. The ger is being deconstructed for migration.

Ukher Tereg—Yak (or cattle) carts, traditionally used by nomads of Central Mongolia for haulage, particularly for migration.

A family helps me to set up camp not far from Uvs Nuur lake—the same night that a drunk attempted to steal my horses.

The Oirat man of the Durvud tribe who explained that his ancestors had traveled to the Caspian Sea, where they became known as Kalmyks, before returning to Asia in the eighteenth century.

Looking north to the Borig Del Els—a sandy desert sometimes described as the most northern desert in the world.

The horses grazing in camp on an idyllic Mongolian summer evening.

Churning fermented mare's milk, known in Mongolian as *airag* (or *kumys* in Kazakh).

Inside a family ger near the village of Tes. The meat cut into strips and hanging to dry is known as *borts*.

Dashnyam (center), a Khoton Mongol who guided me across the Kharkhiraa-Turgen Mountains, sits with his wife, several of his children, and a friend (left).

Dashnyam astride his one and only horse.

Dashnyam's oldest daughter, carrying her sister.

Dashnyam leading our hired camel towards Kharkhiraa Uul.

Rusty and I survey Khokh Nuur (Blue Lake) near the 3,000 metre-high pass between Kharkhiraa and Turgen Uul. (This photo—like many others—was taken on a tripod with a timer.)

A marmot hunter.

Dashnyam leading us toward the high pass, with Turgen Uul in background.

A proud Durvud Mongol woman leads her caravan down from the Kharkhiraa-Turgen massif to the plains for autumn camp.

Khoton family descending the Kharkhiraa River valley.

A Durvud Mongol man carrying his loved one in the saddle. Note the charcoal dust mark on the infant's face—a traditional marking for warding off bad spirits.

Kazakhs of Bayan Olgiy Aimag in Western Mongolia were isolated from the privations endured by their compatriots in neighboring Kazakhstan during Stalin's era. In Mongolia, they live a traditional nomadic life, reminiscent of what life might once have been like for Kazakh communities from the Altai Mountains to the Caspian Sea.

the events of collectivization had created the underpinning realities of everyday life, it was an era largely unspoken of. For Aset's mother-in-law and others her age, memories of the famine and dispossession were too painful to be recounted. Aset and others of his generation also spoke little about the subject, perhaps partly out of respect for their elders, but also because the effects of the more recent Soviet collapse for them overshadowed the difficulties of the past.

The very nature of the famine nevertheless remained one of raw contention. Academics, ordinary citizens, and politicians across Kazakhstan and abroad continue to debate whether the famine was accidental, a consequence of Goloshchekin's gross ignorance, or an intentional genocide of the Kazakh people. One traditional school of thought among internationalists—those Kazakhs who supported Sovietization—is that the heavy loss of human life, culture, and language under Stalin, while regrettable, was an inevitable part of modernization. But I couldn't help thinking that for the people in Zhana Zhol, such gross human sacrifice must have been all the more abhorrent, given that it was for a system that would ultimately fail its own people within just a couple of generations.

THREE DAYS AFTER my arrival in Zhana Zhol, Aset and I led the horses out onto the muddy street for a public farewell. The plan was for Aset and me to ride 250 km southwest across rugged steppe and hills to the town of Ayagoz. From there I would go on alone.

Many of the villagers who had assembled considered the prospect of our ride a death sentence. "The frost! The cold! It will be here soon, and it will hit you! There will be snow up to your neck," said one man, running his hand across his throat.

"Yes, but the most dangerous of all are drunks," an old babushka wrapped up in a shawl cackled. "We have many of them—don't go near them!"

This was too much for Aset's wife, who broke down in tears. Despite her joke earlier about my taking him all the way to Hungary, she had been fretting over Aset for the past two days, and today she had spent all morning helping to dress and equip him. To me it now appeared that the poor man was more likely to die of constriction than cold. Up top he wore two thick woolen sweaters, a neck warmer, and a denim jacket stretched so tight it couldn't be buttoned. For emergencies his pockets had been stuffed with sunflower seeds, pig fat, and garlic, and on the belt holding up his pair of thick Russian winter overalls was a knife big enough to chop down a tree. With only fractional movement possible at the knees and elbows, he waddled with great difficulty over to Ogonyok and heaved himself up.

When finally we turned to leave, the old babushkas and children alike didn't know whether to laugh or cry, and so most did both. The last image I caught before turning my attention beyond the village was of Guanz, standing with one arm hanging in a fixed clench and laughing ecstatically. He wasn't worried about the dangers out there in the wider world; he was only filled with feelings of pride to see his father set off on such an exciting adventure. When we pulled away from the crowd, he lifted his better arm in an attempt to wave, and called out in stilted Russian: "Write to us!"

From Zhana Zhol we headed for the open steppe, and within half an hour the drab timber homes had sunken into the creases of the land behind. The horses charged ahead, full of energy, and as the world around us seemed to expand with its wide, empty horizons, my own world shrank to the company of my animals and Aset. It was the kind of movement I had been craving. Bristling with impatience, I moved into a fast trot uphill.

"We can go at a trot on the flat, but not up! The road is long. We need to save the energy of the horses!" Aset called out.

"We also have to make the most of the good weather before winter sets in!" I replied.

It was then I noticed the little black dog with white front paws like socks running behind us. I recognized him as the dog from my first night in Zhana Zhol and had since learned it was Guanz's puppy. All ribs on long matchstick legs, he had a skinny trunk and snout followed by a frenetic wagging tail. From the skeletal frame rose two large ears, rather like that of a hare.

"Aset! What is this dog?" I demanded.

"Traveling on horse without a dog is incomplete," he replied.

"No! How will you take him home after we part?"

He said nothing, merely spitting out a few sunflower seed shells.

The way the dog peered up at me with those innocent, loving eyes was infuriating. I didn't know who was the more presumptuous, he or Aset.

That evening the sky cleared, and as the last light retreated, the breeze slowed to a halt and cold fell like a heavy blanket. I found my calm once more in the quiet of camp, and reveled in the feeling that there was little separating us from the stars. As the temperature dropped, Aset, on the other hand, grew nervous and withdrawn.

After dinner he looked worryingly into the food pot. "And for the dog?"

I reluctantly pulled out a can of meat. "If he is going to eat, he has to earn his keep. He must be a guard dog and stay outside."

My argument was nonsense. The poor dog, barely six months old, was a short-haired variety of sight hound, known as a *tazi*. He looked as if he might struggle to stay upright in a stiff breeze, let alone cope with sleeping in frosty weather. Later I pretended to be asleep when Aset pulled the poor shivering dog inside the tent to sleep at our feet.

In the morning, my hopes of making significant headway before winter were dashed. It was just the third of November, but when sunlight speared across the horizon it was hollow of warmth and splintered through a forest of hoarfrost on the entrance to the tent. A heavy panting from outside had woken me, and zipping open the door, I locked eyes with Aset, who was bundled up and jogging around the tent.

"It's freezing in there! It's much warmer out here!" he cried.

The temperature overnight had plummeted to around -15°C, and unfortunately we had just one sleeping bag and mat between us. Aset had shivered through the night under my horse blankets, and later he admitted it had been his first night in a tent.

When the sun rose higher there was some reprieve from the cold, and we rode out into a honey-yellow sea of wild grasses and heath. To the northwest a sliver of earth blanketed in snow rose across the horizon like a rogue wave. We met only one man during the day, a sheepherder who drifted across and away from us as if on the ocean currents.

It was the kind of autumn riding I had dreamed of, when the horses didn't overheat, there was plentiful pasture, and the air had such clarity it seemed that only the curvature of the earth prevented me from seeing what lay far ahead. As soon as the sun began to dip again, however, there was no more denying that winter was setting in. My leather boots froze solid and my feet became numb. I pulled out my knee-high Canadian-made winter boots and attached my wide Mongolian winter stirrups, which provided another layer of protection against the cold and wind.

At around four o'clock all concessions from the weather vanished. The grass howled with random, menacing strokes of wind, and the ambiguous sky of shifting clouds and scattered light was eclipsed by a dense, sweeping curtain of black and gray.

Terrified by the prospect of another night in the cold, Aset was determined to find somewhere indoors to regroup. Reluctantly I folded up the map and we moved into a fast trot toward the nearest aul.

IN THE LAST dying minutes of dusk we slowed the horses to a walk on the edge of Azunbulak. Aset wasn't familiar with this remote community and warned we might not find a place to stay. As we reached the sprawling carcass of Azunbulak's former collective farm, however, a young man came out on foot and greeted us with particular charm.

"What the dick? Yes, we have dick weather here, but true, we also have grass up to the dick!" he exclaimed. We could only take this as a warm welcome.

Even before we were led into the animal yards of the old collective farm I felt like I knew our host-to-be, Baltabek, who was steely and short, with a gold-toothed grin that belied his age, which was only twenty-one. It didn't come as a surprise to learn he had only recently been released from prison.

"Silly me! Young and stupid! I stole a few horses from the village! But I learned a lot in jail. In fact, that is where I learned Russian language. Before that I could speak only Kazakh!" he told us.

With the benefit of experience, I came to think that Baltabek's real crime had probably been not so much the stealing of horses as being young and, more important, getting caught. He was passionate about horses, and if he was to be believed, he had stolen them not to sell but because he didn't have enough money to buy the good ones he loved. That somehow seemed fair in a land where, until nomads were dispossessed of their animals during Stalin's era, Kazakhs had viewed their world almost exclusively from the saddle.

Nowadays Baltabek was getting on with his life. He worked for his father, who had established a small farm amid the wreckage of the defunct collective farm, and owned a black stallion that he couldn't wait to show us. Furthermore, his rather empty bachelor pad—the former administration office of the collective farm—was about to be transformed into a family home.

"My wife has just given birth, and if only you wait two days, you could join the celebration when she and the baby return from hospital!" he said feverishly. According to him, my arrival was good luck, and it was "crazy" for me to continue through the winter. There was a better option: I could live and work on the farm with him and his family.

We stayed up talking with Baltabek late into the night, and come morning his proposition to stay for the winter no longer seemed far-fetched. About 20 cm of snow had fallen, transforming the landscape, and the storm showed no signs of abating. Snowflakes choked the sky, blowing in horizontally, caking everything in their path.

There was no choice but to stay put, and as the day wore on, my disappointment at being delayed turned to one of morbid fascination. While in Zhana Zhol I had reflected on the effects of collectivization, here in Azunbulak I was offered a glimpse of the tragic fallout following the collapse of the Soviet system.

The small farming operation run by Baltabek's father, which involved modest numbers of horses, sheep, and cattle, was dwarfed by the graveyard of the original collective. Gutted buildings stood falling in on themselves, and scattered all around were dismembered combines, tractors, and trucks, lying twisted and rusting. So violent and swift had been the death of the Soviet era, it seemed, that its remains had not been given the dignity of burial.

"Yes, fuck your mother!" Baltabek told us, surveying the farm. "It has all gone to fuck."

His father, an old man whose body was used to working uncomplainingly, was a little more enlightening. In its prime during the 1970s and 1980s, the collective had employed 250 people and supported three hundred families in Azunbulak. Now just thirty families were involved in the new cooperative, and the village had shrunk to seventy homes. Baltabek's father couldn't really explain where all the animals and machinery had gone, but he did recall a time in the 1990s when the only way to acquire 1 litre of diesel was to trade 10 kg of meat. It had been in this disastrous era that the collectives were transformed from state-owned enterprises into collective entities, and later into largely failed privately run cooperatives. To pay off debts, farmers had flooded the market with mutton, causing the price of meat to plummet. Between 1991 and 1998 grain production also fell by over 50 percent and the transport system ground to a halt, meaning there was no longer enough fodder getting to livestock in state farms. Many animals either were slaughtered or simply starved. To make matters worse, many collective directors, as in Azunbulak, had taken the opportunity to steal or sell most of the collective's assets and abandon the community.

By the end of the 1990s the majority of Kazakhs in collectives had been left to scavenge among the remains for anything they could sell or use as spare parts. People such as Baltabek's father had turned to subsistence farming, surviving on the meager food rations they could produce themselves with animals they privately owned.

"In my father's time," Baltabek's father told me bitterly, "the Soviets dispossessed us of our animals and way of life. It was a terrible time, but over the years we grew accustomed to state-run farms. Now though, we have been abandoned by the Soviets and left without any of the skills of our ancestors. We feel betrayed."

Whichever way one looks at it—whether from the point of view of city dwellers or that of country folk—the chaos of the 1990s, during which

Kazakhstan emerged as an independent nation, was a staggering time of hardship and lawlessness. To the masses, perestroika meant the severe shrinkage of industry, the breakup of agricultural collectives, the dissolution of social services including pensions, and the departure of educated experts, largely to Russia, Germany, and Korea. Power shortages were rife and not helped by a burgeoning trade in scrap metal as organized crime groups stripped and sold huge lengths of power lines. Between 1991 and 2000, the population of Kazakhstan dropped by almost two million.

It was no wonder that most Kazakhs, like Baltabek's family, rued Gorbachev and recalled Soviet times with nostalgia, even though they knew full well the horrors that the Soviet era had inflicted on their people. Then again, as Baltabek's father later told me, a quizzical expression on his face, "To be honest, life, as far as I can remember, has always been hard, no matter who had the reins, Moscow or Astana."

In the evening we rode into the aul of Azunbulak proper for an extravagant dinner with Baltabek's family, and the appalling reality around us vanished. We swapped photo albums, sifting through each other's lives, and celebrated long into the night. Baltabek's father saw my arrival as a great omen and wished me luck.

THE STORM HAD lulled by the time we rode out the next day. Stony clouds swooped over the steppe, blocking the sun that seemed to begin its downward trajectory before the day had begun. The poor dog, experiencing the first winter of his short life, was suffering from frozen paws. Whenever we stopped for a break he whined and peered up with a look of bewilderment. Once, in a desperate attempt to escape the cold, he leaped up onto my back with his front paws clinging to my shoulders. I had dismounted and was taking a pee at the time, and he caused me to lose aim.

For an unbroken few hours Aset rode in front of me, singing sorrowful-sounding songs in Kazakh and spluttering between verses: "Ah, Tim, when you have vodka, you have a voice. No vodka, no voice!" I wondered if the soft rocking motion of his horse, the trackless land before him, and the presence of a loyal dog by his side was bringing his nomad roots out of dormancy.

In the late afternoon we cut across a plain and climbed through a tangle of snow-laden spurs toward a plateau. My legs were beginning to ache and I could think only of retiring in camp with dinner on the boil. But just as we were nearing the top of a gully the light dimmed and there came a gust of wind carrying a sortie of airborne shards of ice and snow. Then the cloud was upon us, like an avalanche from somewhere above, wiping out all before it. Aset stopped singing in the middle of a verse, and within seconds the world had hemorrhaged away all shape and form. There was no sky or earth anymore, just a swirling, soupy sea of white. The sun was still up, casting weak, diffuse gray-blue light onto the snow, but illuminated little. Leaning forward and clinging onto Taskonir's mane I flicked my head back to see Aset's silhouette melting in and out of focus. When he caught up, Taskonir nudged forward, uneasily probing for solid earth. I urged him on, but for every step forward our circle of vision closed tighter.

For the next hour there was no telling where we were or when this rushing cloud might dissipate. Several times I lost Aset, only to scream out for him, and he would reappear. Every ten minutes I checked my GPS and compass bearing. The horses plodded on up slopes, down into gullies, and up again.

Eventually we crested yet another hill, the terrain surrendered to a plateau, and there came an acute change in the temperament of the air, as if the world were drawing a breath. I stopped, and as the wind eased and the mist about me scattered, I looked to the west. Dark, jagged clouds on the wings of the wind began to lift, and a purple-blue light flooded over the wavy troughs and crests of the frozen earth. It glowed ever brighter until a shaving of cobalt-blue sky blinked into focus. The tail end of the sun had just slithered over the horizon leaving a trail of fading watercolors—blue on the clouds, purple on the ground, a hint of orange here and there.

The truce was short-lived. Darkness fell, the wind recoiled, and cold took its grip.

"The closer to people the better!" Aset ranted. While the raw feeling of this place had evoked in me a sense of awe, Aset was beside himself with fear.

For the hundredth time I stopped and spread the map out over the reins from the saddle, studying it with the light from my headlamp. We were aiming for the aul of Kindikti, two days' ride to the southeast, and were somewhere in the stretch of deserted hilly steppe in between. Since the map had a scale of 1:1,000,000, I could only hazard a guess at where we were.

"We have food, we have a tent!" I told Aset. "We can stop now, make ourselves warm, cook dinner, sleep, and see how things are in the morning light,"

"To hell with your tent!" he replied. "What if a snowstorm really comes in? What about wolves? We have to get to a kstau!" he replied, using the nomad term for a herder's winter station. Finding one would be a long shot, even with the GPS I carried and the approximate directions Baltabek had given us, but Aset was willing to bet his life on it.

One of my rules of travel was to stop before dark and, more important, before the horses were too tired and cold. On previous journeys I had learned that I was never lost as long as I still had food, my wits, and shelter. But I gave in, and we trudged on.

My hands turned stone cold and stiff. The horses became so exhausted they were immune to the kick of my heels. The sky cleared, but the wind was so ferocious it brought a stinging swarm of ice particles that hit like glass shards.

At half past ten we arrived at the coordinates where we thought the kstau might be, but there was nothing. I had given up trying to figure out the landscape.

"It's got to be somewhere here! We have to make it," shouted Aset, his words garbled by his nearly frozen face. At that moment he struck me as mad. His hankering for civilization was such that any sign of human life, even a piece of old horse crap that we stumbled on, sufficed to calm him.

As a last resort, he ordered that we release the reins and let the horses guide us. This is a custom found across the steppe—when lost or in search of water, always let the horses guide you. To my surprise, the horses seemed to know where they were going, and half an hour later we stumbled into the dark shape of something man-made. There was no one to greet us, but this was good enough to console Aset, who dismounted achingly. Hypothermic, he crawled into the cocoon of my sleeping bag and passed out.

In the morning I woke with the residual hum of wind in my ears. Stillness ushered in the new day, and as shadows turned to real shapes and lines, it became clear we had camped in an abandoned concrete pumping shed littered with frozen manure and graffiti.

Outside, nothing had escaped the fury of the storm. The stands of heath looked like a bleached, exposed coral reef, the intricate form of each twig entombed in finger-thick ice. Every blade of grass was also encased, rising from the earth in a million stalagmites. The horses stood stiffly in half sleep. As Taskonir turned his head to me, ice cracked and fell away from his mane. Ogonyok woke, automatically lowered his head, and crunched through a carrot of ice with his teeth.

When Aset woke, slit-eyed and puffy, he was worried. The storm had passed for now, but this kind of weather apparently foreshadowed the beginning of a zhut—a harsh winter, more universally known by the Mongolian term zud, that sweeps through the steppe every few years, traditionally ensuring that only the hardiest animals, and humans, survive.

"At first the ice weighs down the grass, snapping it off. If this is followed by a warm period, the ice and snow will melt before freezing again to form a cap of ice. On top of this may come deep snow, which means even if the animals dig to the ground they will only find ice and won't be able to break through. If any horses survive, they will be naked by spring because as a last resort they eat each other's hair," he told me.[7]

There were different kinds of zuds—some caused by an impenetrable layer of ice, others by the sheer depth of the snow, and others still when there was no snow at all. Common to all of them was that if they were preceded or followed by drought in summer, it typically meant the nail in the coffin for large numbers of livestock. By way of example, the year that

I had ridden across Mongolia by bicycle, Mongolia had been in the midst of a series of three consecutive zuds and droughts. Come the end of the winter in 2002, 11 million animals had been wiped out. There was one Kazakh in western Mongolia I was told about who had just one of three hundred horses remaining by spring.[8] Kazakh herders would later describe to me how, when the grass was particularly lean, they kept their animals alive by feeding them a combination of horse dung mixed with sheep tail fat and a grain by-product that was like wheat bran.

Given the carnage that zuds could wreak, it wasn't difficult to understand why for thousands of years zuds had been the common enemy of nomads on the steppe. In the case of the Kazakhs, a new foe, the Soviet regime, joined the zuds as threats to the people's survival. This new enemy proved unbeatable, and the famine that resulted from forced collectivization and the destruction of aul life remains known among Kazakhs as the "Great Zhut."[9]

After feeding the horses the remaining bag of crushed corn that we had picked up in Azunbulak, we loaded up and wrenched ourselves away from the shelter. The horses moved hesitantly, like barefoot children on sharp gravel. Spikes of crystalline ice shattered, popping and exploding under their hooves. The poor dog remained curled up in the pump shelter until it dawned on him that we were not coming back. He came whimpering, tail between his legs and whiskers all frosted up.

An hour of riding took us over the sweeping face of a hill where another scabby piece of civilization broke the emptiness. This time smoke tendrils rose timidly from it, and a herd of flea-like sheep and goats inched across the otherwise inanimate landscape. It was the kstau we had been searching for, and as we drew closer, a herdsman on horseback pulled away from his animals and approached.

"As-salam aleikum," he said, extending his hand. The man had swollen, chapped cheeks and was struggling to control a violent shiver. He looked how I felt. The wind cut like razors, and no matter how I slouched into my jacket and pulled the hood tight over my face, it was inescapable.

I was happy for Aset to take over the introductions, and as we rode I learned that the herdsman was originally from western Mongolia. He and his wife had decided to carry on a semi-nomadic existence, traveling to higher pastures with a yurt in the summer months—a camp known in Kazakh as the *jalau*—and retreating to the kstau in winter.

When we reached the cattle shelter of the kstau, I watched as our host skillfully climbed onto the roof of the shelter despite the wind and with a fork peeled off hay for my hungry horses. This man embodied the *chaban*— the iconic herdsman of the Kazakh steppe, who was fast passing into legend in the modern era. Using knowledge inherited from untold generations of experience, he was unequivocally hunkering down to survive the winter, zud or not. As I sat there immobile in the saddle, my elbows frozen at right angles and my feet freezing in the stirrups, I experienced a crisis of confidence. I could barely consider myself a horseman, I didn't know how to look after horses in such conditions, and I doubted I could manage alone with three of them.

We stopped in briefly with the herder's family, enjoying fresh deep-fried dough—known in Kazakh as *baursak*—and hot milky tea. I secretly hoped we might turn in for the day, but all too soon we were back into the cold and riding under a sky that was wilting into dark gray. The storm was gathering again, and as the frozen earth meshed with the sky, we pushed the horses into a trot. This time I had no objections to Aset's urgency—we would ride for as long as it took to find shelter.

THE LIGHT WAS fading fast and the snow was falling nearly horizontally when we came across the trail to Kindikti. First there came the muffled bellow of cattle and the cry of herders, then two figures materialized from the bleakness, hunched in their saddles, whips in hand, sweeping from one side to the other of a large herd of horses and cattle. Up close I could see they were wearing *valenki*, traditional Russian knee-high felt boots, and rode atop saddles with thick cushions—the kind that Aset had recently been encouraging me to get for my own saddle to prevent hemorrhoids.

From tightly drawn hoods, the men squinted against the snow and wind. Then, despite the conditions, they took off the mitts they wore and reached out to shake our hands. As luck would have it, we had caught the men herding the animals home to shelter for the night.

When the glow of homes emerged from the pall of snow, cattle peeled off to their respective owners and we followed a herder to a mud-brick house. Askhat, as he was called, dashed inside and came out with his father, a tall man named Bakhetbek. There were handshakes all around before we rushed to unload. Askhat was sent to the roof to gather hay, a young boy was given the job of preparing a barn, and Bakhetbek must have told his wife to prepare things in the house.

Accustomed to making sure the horses were cared for before I could think about relaxing, I was hesitant to go inside until everything was done. Ruslan had taught me that when we were finished riding for the day, it was unthinkable to remove the saddle and offer the horses water and feed until they had rested for two or three hours, or until their backs were warm and dry under the blankets. As I later understood, this was a kind of universal law on the steppe and possibly one that had been around since before the time of Genghis Khan.[10]

I began to explain to Bakhetbek how important this system was for my horses, but he interrupted me.

"Tim! Tim!" he said, almost angrily. "Don't even say it—it is offensive. Everything will be done, you don't have to worry about your horses. You are our guest!"

Aset pulled me aside. "Trust him and watch carefully—a sign of a Kazakh host who respects his guests is that he will feed the guest's dog before his own."

True to Aset's words, Bakhetbek fed our ribs-on-legs dog a pot of lamb innards and stale bread, sinking his boots into his own dogs when they tried to join in.

As tired as I was, somehow I got through dinner, and a few shots of vodka too, before tumbling into sleep. At some point in the night I woke in panic from a dream: we were on a creaking ship, but where was the exit? Then I remembered where we were and surrendered to sleep, confident that the horses, like us, were under the watch and care of the family.

BY THE TIME I woke it was late. Where Aset had been lay a pile of blankets, and from the kitchen drifted the homelike sounds of shuffling feet, muffled conversation, and tinny clanging of pots. Peeling my eyes open, I sat upright slowly. What I had assumed to be bright sunshine through the small window of our room was the glare of a snowdrift creeping up the windowpane. Outside, the storm, muted by the house's thick walls, raged on. Heavy clouds of snowflakes were being tossed about in violent gusts, and I could just make out the outline of an animal shelter, its timber frame encrusted by wind-driven snow and ambushed on one side by a drift banking up to the roof. On the shelter's lee side, a herd of sheep stood huddled in a pen, their wooly coats under a gathering blanket of snow.

The blizzard had all the hallmarks of a *buran*, the fierce winter windstorms of the steppe, accompanied by a whiteout, that could last for days, and which, I had been told, could bury livestock and people alive if caught in the open. It was for this reason Aset considered it reckless to camp alone on the steppe.

I found Aset and Askhat sitting idly by the softly crackling coal stove, looking over my Australian saddle. When he noticed me Askhat motioned to the window and joked, "You think this is winter? You should see winter here! There is usually *two metres* of snow!"

The family and I settled down with tea from the pot that was perpetually on the boil. I sat leaning up against the white-washed walls that were hung with nothing more than a couple of rugs and a horse whip. In the afternoon the blizzard briefly abated, and movement out a window caught my eye—a young boy riding bareback with a hypothermic sheep slung across the neck of his horse.

Bakhetbek was a tall and stately man in his fifties with leathery dark skin, green eyes, and a strong jaw line. When he moved, he did so measuredly, with grace and power. He was the father of four, and both he and his wife worked as schoolteachers. His passion was geography.

"Tim, if I am correct, you are not the first foreigner to travel here. An Englishman once came prospecting for gold and other minerals. That was about eighty years ago. I am fairly sure, though, that you are the first Australian," he said, eyes twinkling. His hands, broad and strong, shifted gently in their embrace around his cup of tea.

Bakhetbek's wife, wearing a scarf that accentuated her moon face, smiled. "Yes, that is true. But my Bakhetbek is a traveler, a foreigner even, of sorts, too."

Bakhetbek had been born near Urumqi in China's Xinjiang province, and fled to Kazakhstan after his brothers were murdered in the 1960s. Later his nephews, who remained behind, were also murdered. At his wife's gentle prod, Bakhetbek began telling his story himself, hesitantly, but was swiftly overcome with emotion.

"They killed us simply because we are Kazakhs," he said. "Back then, and even now, Chinese authorities don't protect Kazakhs. Actually, it was probably the police who did the murdering."

There was a bitter irony in Bakhetbek's return to Kazakhstan that he was well aware of. His own grandparents had originally fled to China among two hundred thousand others when the Russian imperial army violently quashed the 1916 Kazakh uprising. At the same time, though, Bakhetbek acknowledged that the tragedy of his family had been the experience of his ancestors through the ages—whenever the Kazakhs found themselves under oppression or attack, they would historically flee to Chinese Turkestan, Siberia, and other parts of Central Asia, only to find themselves under another oppressive regime.[11]

After telling his story, Bakhetbek looked spent, but there was a sparkle in his wife's eye. "Actually . . ." She looked over at her husband. "We still have one relative alive in China. She is Bakhetbek's niece, and she is studying in Urumqi. She wrote to us one year ago, but we have never met. She gave us a phone number, but we have never been able to call."

It was dark by the time everyone assembled outside in winter coats and fur hats. I pointed the satellite phone aerial to the sky and experimented with a few prefixes until the call went through. A woman answered. After a brief initial silence, all of Bakhetbek's family members took turns talking, struggling to hold back tears but smiling.

The occasion called for a feast, and after the phone calls it was all hands on deck. Bakhetbek's brother, who due to his balding head was nicknamed "the Kazakh Gorbachev," raced to get a sheep. In an outbuilding the men gathered with cupped hands to say a prayer before its throat was cut. Had I been of the Muslim faith, I would have been asked to bless the sheep, since traditionally guests were required to ask permission from the animal's spirit to partake of its flesh.

Late into the night we sat around gorging on meat and being plied with vodka. A *dombra*, the traditional two-stringed mandolin of the Kazakhs, was passed around.[12] When Bakhetbek played there was a fire in his eyes, and he sat with his back even straighter and prouder than usual. Strong fingers moved instinctively up and down the instrument's neck. In Kazakh they say a good player can make the dombra sing. I was sure I could hear the beating hooves of horses. It was as if a stoic, unfaltering rhythm prevailed through the harsh realities of life and the land. I looked across to Aset, who was welling up with pride. The last beat ended, and Bakhetbek looked at me. His eyes arched into crescents; from them tears spread into the many channels of his weathered face and disappeared.

Kazakhs believe that when a guest walks through the front door, luck flies in through the window. It is a good omen: the sheep will give birth to twin lambs in the spring. Looking back on this occasion, the magic of this belief was embodied by my meeting with Bakhetbek.

AS WE PREPARED to leave Kindikti, Aset was whistling and calling angrily, with an undercurrent of panic—the dog was nowhere to be seen. I felt guilty for rushing but still held resentment toward Aset for bringing the dog in the first place. We couldn't afford to wait any longer. If we didn't get out of Kindikti today and start heading south, there was the risk I would be stranded here until spring.

"If he doesn't come, let it be that his destiny is here," said Aset at last, playing down his distress. Just then there came a whoosh as a stringy heap of bones and elastic tendons leaped over the fence of a pen and came screaming toward us, eyes wild in panic. I had learned that the dog had been notorious in Zhana Zhol for stealing eggs from under chickens in the early morning, before they could be collected. As we rode out of the village, I thought with a shake of my head that if he kept this up in places such as Kindikti, he didn't have much hope of a long life.

For the first few hours we followed the compass southwest through a mire of deserted hills and gullies. Jagged rock fisted through unbounded white like compound fractures. Peaks of around 1,500 m gnashed at the horizon. To the south we could see the foothills of the Tarbagatai range, which slope from east to west out of the Tien Shan.[13]

The sky had been blown clear of clouds, but despite the white glow of the sun, cold tightened its grip. Even the slight breeze landed heavily, forging ice crystals in my eyelashes and nose hairs. On the horses it gathered as ice beards around their nostrils and chin. The air was powder dry, and beneath the horses the snow exploded in puffs, then fluttered back to earth in glittering clouds. Bakhetbek's tune strummed in my head.

When the sunlight withered we were stranded in the open. The earth froze to a standstill and the temperature dropped to around −20°C. Aset and the dog hung around my camping stove looking unconvinced we would survive the night.

"In these conditions you should not only consider leaving the saddles on the horses for three hours after you finish, but leave the saddle blankets on all night. We Kazakhs would even leave the saddle on for the whole night in this situation . . . And of course without vodka you won't survive. When your hands get cold, rub the vodka into your skin and drink it before you go to bed," Aset said. After dinner I unfolded my cotton blankets so that they covered the horses from withers to rump, and tied them on with spare belts and ropes.

Food and hot tea in our bellies, we climbed into the tent. Poor Aset bundled himself up in my down jacket under the remaining horse blankets and put on the insulated liners of my boots. The dog curled up at his feet.

In the morning it seemed that Aset had conquered his fear of camping in the open, or at least he could joke about it now. "Aaaaaawww! Tashkent! Tashkent down there!" he said, shivering and pointing to his feet, where the dog was still fast asleep. "But up here it is bloody Yakutsk!"

The inside of the tent was covered in hoarfrost, and any slight move sent a shower of ice down on us. Outside, the wind had picked up again, and the sky was streaked with shreds of blood-red cloud. Overnight one end of my tent fly had suffered a rip nearly half a metre long, and the small transparent windows at the entrances had turned brittle and shattered. When Aset went for a piss he came back with more worrying news—not more than 50 m away there were fresh wolf tracks.

Saddling up proved harder than usual as I struggled to find dexterity in mitts, yet when I took them off, even briefly, my fingers went numb. It was always a gamble putting Ogonyok's crupper on, and this morning as I lifted his tail and slid the leather down onto the sensitive skin above his butt he shied away and threatened to kick.

Inspecting the horses' hooves, we realized that Taskonir had one loose shoe, and all the horses had snow balled up under their feet, so they could hardly walk. We improvised with an axe head to solve both problems, but it took more than three hours, all told, to pack up, eat, and load the animals. By the time we settled into the saddle my feet were numb. I didn't want to think about the state of Aset's feet, since he was wearing only my hiking shoes.

For once the GPS and map proved correct as we passed through the tiny aul of Chubartas, a collection of twenty ramshackle homes and barns inundated by snow. Dogs came running, snarls of teeth and fur, and I watched our little guy scuttle away under the legs of Zhamba, tail between his legs and his back arching up like a skinny feline's. Aset lashed out at the attacking dogs with his lead rope. Not a soul came out onto the street.

Clouds crowded in, the temperature rose enough so that the frost on our faces melted, and the wind blunted. Following telegraph lines and tracks, we no longer needed the compass. Two days' ride to the southwest from here lay Ayagoz, where I would part ways with Aset.

In the aul of Saariarka Aset promised we would be able to stay with a relative overnight. As the sun set we were greeted by a thin, pale woman who looked terrified at the sight of us. She talked briefly with Aset over a cup of tea, and soon after we left in the dark. His relative—the husband of this woman—had recently died, and it was inconceivable to stay in the house with a woman when there were no men at home. Traditionally a strict custom was adhered to by which a whip was always hung adjacent to the yurt or kstau entrance. I was told that a whip hanging downward meant a man was home. If it was pointing upward, he was away and one should not enter.

Aset insisted we camp by an old Kazakh grave not far from town. It was a tall mud-brick dome, worn away at the top, the overall shape reminiscent of a giant, upright, cracked eggshell. Perhaps as much as several hundred years earlier the deceased had been laid to rest inside; as the structure eroded, his or her spirit would be given passage to the sky. This particular type of grave, often found in clusters known as "silent auls," had emerged in the fifteenth century when wandering Sufi dervishes succeeded in persuading nomads in the Kazakh steppe to adopt Islam. But the tradition of holding ancestors in great reverence was a far more ancient one among nomads, part of the shamanic religion of Tengrism once shared with the Mongols. For millennia they had believed that spirits inhabited the sky and land and could provide favor or disfavor depending on a person's action.

The next morning Aset turned to me hesitantly.

"We had a visitor last night. The old man from the grave. Nothing out of the ordinary; he was just here to check on us, to see what we were doing." Then he added, "My recommendation to you is that if you are alone, always try to find these graves. The old men of the steppe will protect you. If possible, the best thing is to even sleep inside the graves." He also pointed out that, as prescribed by Muslim custom, he had washed himself in the snow before going to bed.

For the rest of the day Aset seemed quiet but content. His eyes scanned the landscape longingly. His whip hung limply from his right hand. Every now and then he raised it and gently slapped Zhamba's hindquarters. He spoke little except once, when he pointed to the horizon across a wide plain.

"Many hundreds, thousands of my men lie here. Here there were big battles." He said it with pride and emotion, as though these events had happened recently, but he was talking about the invasion by the Zhungars—Oirat Mongols who ruled an empire known as Zhungaria after the collapse of the Mongol Empire—in the eighteenth century.

It had been dawning on me gradually, but now I realized that Aset felt a sense of approval from his ancestors at his being out here. On a horse, on the steppe, under the sky, he was living, even if fleetingly, by customs that he inherently knew but which meant so little in settled village life. Like most Kazakhs I would meet over the coming months, he had preserved a consciousness of Islam, but he clung even more closely to a belief in his nomadic heritage and the spirit of his ancestors—a blend that was symbolized in his behavior toward the grave we had camped by, and which defined the culture of the Kazakh nomad in recent centuries.

IN THE AUL of Karagash the specter of death followed us. We met a man called Kazibek who was out collecting firewood on his horse. He broke the news that Aset's relative in that aul, too, had just died. Kazibek, however, was more than happy to have us for the night, and his wife was kind enough to sew up my ripped tent.

Just shy of Ayagoz, Aset called home to Zhana Zhol and received more bad news: another relative of his had been run down by a tram in Oskemen and killed. The funeral would be the next day.

The caretaker of a dacha village not far from Ayagoz took us in. Aset pulled out the city clothes he had been carrying all along and suddenly our adventure together was over. It was sad to see him without his winter breeches, knife-laden belt, and woolen sweaters, and sadder still to see him on foot, horseless. He looked like a man dispossessed. At the local market I bought him some Chinese carry bags, a new watch—he had lost his during our trip—and a bus ticket to Zhana Zhol.

I expected Aset to be upset about his cousin in Oskemen, but he seemed to be resigned to the news and more worried about parting ways with me. There was something he had been waiting to tell me.

"Tim, you need a friend on the long road, someone to keep you warm at night and protect you from wolves. His name is Tigon. Tigon means 'fast wind' or 'hawk.' He is a hunting dog. His father was a tazi, a breed of hound that is not afraid of wolves and can run quicker than the wind.

"And in our country dogs choose their owners. Tigon is yours."

I was not in the mood. Only half an hour earlier at the market he had told me I should buy a packet of condoms because one never knew what might be around the corner. His ancestors surely hadn't relayed that advice to him! He had also convinced me to buy firecrackers to ward off wolves. He seemed to know everything that was best for me in a way I occasionally found patronizing.

"But what will I do with him? What will happen to him when I get to the border? I won't be able to take him further. Can't you take him on the bus?" I was frightened of the commitment of having a dog, and anyway, I had long since decided that if I was going to get a dog, it would be one of the big wooly mastiff breeds used by nomads as guard dogs.

Aset glanced down sadly at his feet and shrugged. "I don't know. You can give him to someone if you like." Then he looked me straight in the eye. "But there is one thing. In Kazakh culture there are some things that you cannot receive as gifts, that you must buy or steal: dogs, knives, axes, and wives. This dog is not mine. It is Guanz's. You need to give me something for him; it doesn't have to be money."

I paid Aset $120 for accompanying me; gave him a toy koala, some photos from Australia, and $10 for Guanz; and promised to print and send all the photos we had taken together. I needed a second packsaddle, and so he offered to sell me his own saddle, the one he had been riding in. I bought that for $50.

We locked Tigon inside the caretaker's hut for the time being, and waved down a car on the road into town. Then Aset was gone.

Aset had traveled only eleven days with me, but he knew so much better than I the challenges that lay ahead. For that I am indebted.

8

TOKYM KAGU BASTAN

I BROKE OUT of the tent into a landscape that resembled the open, rolling tundra of the Arctic. The scant moisture in the air had snapped frozen overnight into floating particles of ice that twinkled like quartz. Delicate crystals, light as cobwebs, clung to fine tussocks of grass that skewered up into the light. Underfoot the snow squeaked, but when I had finished my morning pee and stood still, there was utter silence.

I felt as if on a precipice.

The previous day I had said goodbye to Aset and nervously maneuvered the three horses around the southern edge of Ayagoz. In doing so I crossed the tracks of the "Turk-Sib"—a railway completed in 1931 to connect the cotton industry of Uzbekistan (set to rapidly expand under Soviet rule) with Siberia and Moscow. To me, these lonely black lines dissecting the steppe from north to south were a kind of frontier, beyond which the rest of Kazakhstan yawned—still more than 2,500 km of steppe as far as the Caspian Sea. The absence of fences, borders, and even mountain ranges, seemed to suggest endless possibilities as if I could ride in whichever direction I pleased. In truth I knew if I remained at this latitude, I would be ambushed by deep snow. Too far south, and I might find myself in a freezing desert without snow—which would be the main source of water for both myself and my animals during winter. Additionally, of the few rivers that lay between here and the Caspian, most flowed on a north-south line, or drained sluggishly into desert, or the Aral Sea, meaning that there would be no consistent access to water as I rode west.

Late the previous afternoon, after Aset's departure, I had called home to Australia on the satellite phone. I received bad news: our family dog of sixteen years, a blue heeler we called Pepper, had died. After the sun disappeared I had lain awake in the sleeping bag recalling the doe-eyed, tail-wagging presence that had filled our home throughout much of my childhood. At the same time I was aware of the curled-up ball of fur and bones pressing up against my thighs and snoring. It was hard to believe that earlier that day I had nearly decided to leave him behind.

With Aset gone but Tigon yawning by my side, I now stood with the morning sun on my back and gazed west. Yesterday I had dwelled on the challenge of finding water, pasture, and shelter through all that emptiness. This morning the overwhelming feeling was that I would have to do it alone.

IT HELPED ME somewhat to indulge in a fantasy, thinking of my journey as that of a Kazakh boy born into the rigors of life on the steppe. Under the guidance of parents and the circle of kinship, there were rituals that guided nomads from birth, equipping them with the knowledge required to rise to the challenges of their lives.

Central to the rite of passage for young boys was mastering how to ride a horse, graze and protect sheep, and in earlier times how to make and use a bow, hunt, and ultimately defend the family. One of the first important rituals was mounting *ashami*, when the boy was encouraged to emulate his father by taking a stick in place of a whip and riding out to see how the animals were grazed. An ashami was a special children's saddle without stirrups to which the boy's legs were bound so that he could not fall. Although this custom generally took place when the boy was seven years old, he would have been taught to ride much earlier; many children had their first experiences in the saddle before they could walk.[1]

By my reckoning, I had probably reached the metaphorical age of ten, and a custom known as tokym kagu bastan. At this age the boy was sent off alone on horse for his first long journey. The successful home return was anticipated with great fanfare—tokym kagu literally means "waiting for the boy to return"—and celebrated with a feast including the most sacred of drinks, kumys, fermented mare's milk. Aset had known that these first few days and weeks alone would be a great test, my own tokym kagu bastan.

In the absence of nomads to consult about my route, a hunting inspector in Ayagoz had offered valuable advice. On his suggestion, I had settled on the idea of traveling southwest toward the salty waters of eastern Lake Balkhash to beat the deep snow, before riding west along its northern shoreline into central Kazakhstan. There I would reach the Betpak Dala—a name that roughly translates to "starving steppe." My immediate goal was 150 km as the crow flies, to an aul called Kopa, where the hunting inspector had given me the details of a man known as Serik who might take me in.

After a pot of semolina, I set about the task of grooming, saddling, and packing, determined to overcome my nerves and set out in a positive frame of mind. Four hours later, however, I was still struggling to get the loads tied down on the two packhorses. Even when I finally got moving, the stiff leather of my seat had barely warmed before the load on Taskonir loosened and fell to one side. My original plan had been to use one packhorse and rotate load-carrying duties so that each day one horse was rested without a load. Recently, however, Ruslan and Aset had convinced me that it was better to spread the weight across two packhorses and carry 50 kg of grain whenever I could get it. Unfortunately, I had left in Mongolia the extra packsaddle that would have been ideal for this purpose. Aset's riding saddle, which I had bought to make do, was terribly ill-suited for carrying any load, let alone the wheat sacks I had rigged up as saddlebags. It was, according to my diary entry that night, "an absolute pig" of a saddle to pack.

It took another half hour to reload, but by then it was clear that the horses, tied for only the second time in a single caravan, had their own issues to iron out. I was riding Zhamba, with Ogonyok directly behind me and Taskonir bringing up the rear. But Taskonir, who had asserted his authority as the leader of my little herd, used every opportunity to take a bite of Ogonyok's butt. Ogonyok would suddenly bolt forward, the rattling green boxes brushing along Zhamba's flank and bashing into my right leg. Zhamba, who was the oldest but had retiringly taken middle ground in the hierarchy, was not pleased. His ears rested flat on his head while he bit and then kicked until Ogonyok was back in his place. I tried tying Ogonyok to Taskonir, making him last in our little caravan, but Taskonir continued the bullying by trying to kick Ogonyok in the head. Ogonyok pulled back until Taskonir came to a standstill and the lead rope was torn from my grasp.

Come darkness we had traveled only 12 km—and not particularly gracefully—but it was good enough that we had made it to camp intact. It wasn't until the horses had been staked out, hobbled, and fed, the stove turned off, and my stomach filled that everything felt remotely possible again. I sank back onto my big canvas duffle bag next to the tent and watched the crescent moon slope its way off the edge of the world.

For the next two days, any gathering momentum was interrupted by the same circus of hiccups, but even so I recognized the outlines of a routine that would become habitual in the coming weeks and months. In the morning Tigon bravely led the way. Then, when he tired, he followed behind like a tiny black shadow. As we rode through undulating hills, the cold white sun panned across our path and I took notice how in the morning the right side of the horses gathered a forest of sweat-frost, but by afternoon it was thicker on their left flanks. During the lunch break I knelt in the snow and watched the horses dig with their hooves and nibble on whatever they could find. Tigon sat in front of me, tail between his legs, bony spine in an arch, licking his chops and shifting his front paws. I tossed him rations of kolbasa, a Russian sausage, that disappeared in lightning snaps.

In the afternoon of the third day the air thawed and the snow grew thin and patchy—encouraging signs that I was making progress south and had begun to drop off the plateau toward the basin of Lake Balkhash. By dusk the vacuum of frozen silence had been filled with the sound of wind rustling through grass, and I trotted out along a rounded, dun-colored ridge.

Free of snow, the steppe turned black in the sinking light, and I made camp atop stony hills near the ruins of mud-brick graves. Only after setting up did it occur to me that without snow there was no water. It wasn't a prospect of great concern, though—I could make do with half a thermos of tea that night, and I was sure the horses wouldn't have to go thirsty for long. Winter was on our heels, and the scent of a storm brewing on the wind suggested that by morning it would have caught up.

That night I woke several times with sharp pains in my chest and the terrifying suspicion that the horses were gone. Each time it happened I unzipped the entrance and shot out, turning on my headlamp as I went. There was nothing unusual about this routine, which had characterized most nights since the horses were stolen in Mongolia. I had long since resolved to maintain a discipline of sleeping in my trousers with belt, knife, and headlamp fitted.

At some point after 3:00 A.M., however, the usual paranoia mingled with a powerful and lucid dream, the likes of which I had not previously experienced, but which would prove to recur almost nightly for the next six or seven months.

The dream began with me instinctually flicking my headlamp on and preparing to rip open the door. No sooner had I sat up, however, than Taskonir's head appeared in front of me. His eyes were as dark and shiny as maple syrup. There was a sheen to the long, dark winter hair around his face and under his chin. His floppy underlip quivered, and I had the urge to reach out and touch it. But then I realized Taskonir was looking not at me but over me, away into the night. In fact, now that I looked closer, all the horses were in front of me, their furry fetlocks at eye level, and I had all three of their lead ropes in my hands. They were pulling hard!

I held on for what felt an eternity, but just when I thought my arms and hands couldn't hold out any longer, I noticed the stranger. He stood in the darkness just around to my right—I could see him from the corner of my eye. He seemed old, I thought—balding, with gray hair and strong workman's hands. Unfazed, he walked toward me.

The rope began to slip from my grip, up and away. The heads of the horses lifted out of the beam from my headlamp and into the shadows. Before I could catch another glimpse of this man, my legs and arms gave way with heaviness. I closed my eyes and felt released into deep sleep. I had a strong conviction the horses were safe.

In the morning it was hard to get up. Outside, wind lashed the tent with thick wet snow. Inside, the dream hung around like a heavy fog. In time I would find the dream familiar and comforting—each time I would hold on to the ropes until an old man appeared and I would fall asleep. When I told Kazakhs about it, they were sure it was the spirits of the old men of the steppe, protecting me. This morning, though, the dream was still raw and frightening. I could still feel the tension in my arms.

In recent days, the steppe had spread out in a milky white and brown sea in which it was difficult to tell the difference between distant crags and clouds, the curves of both rolling sensuously out into emptiness. Now, as I moved on, the scale of the land contracted to depthless, throbbing squalls of snow. I caught only glimpses of the lay of the land—a warren of hills, a swamp, more hills, then a plain.

I had the feeling we had come in the wrong direction, but in the end my compass proved to be much better oriented than I, and at midday we stumbled on a track leading towards Tansyk—a village only 30 km from Kopa.

For the next two hours the tracks wound into fog and snow, and I shivered into a state of despondency. Stopping made me more aware of the wet sleet dribbling down my skin from neck to ankles, so I carried on without breaks.

I shouldn't have, but I caved in to tempting thoughts about spring and good times with Kathrin. Visions, smells, and distant feelings taunted— hot sand underfoot on the beach, the light-as-air sensation of shorts and T-shirt, Kathrin's soft, warm skin. They collided brutally with the reality around me. As I shifted my gaze to the snow in front, I thought I was dreaming. A snake was slithering feebly, incrementally, across our path. The odds against it seemed overwhelming.

Another hour of introspection passed, and when I lifted my head the tracks had turned to mud, it was raining, and there was no snow in sight. I paused to focus on a flock of sheep, tended to by a horseman—the first sign of life I had witnessed since leaving Ayagoz.

I could have taken hints from the herder and found someone to take me in, but this was my first stretch of the journey traveling fully alone in Kazakhstan, and I wanted to prove to myself that I could cope. That night I camped in sight of two large dome graves and shivered through till dawn in a wet sleeping bag. By morning the sky had cleared, and now, on my fifth straight day I took great satisfaction in pouring out the last of the bag of grain for the horses. The sun brought relief, and as steam poured off my thawing clothes I packed up for the first time in three weeks without mitts.

"Another half a day south to Kopa. It must be still summer down there!" I said to Tigon. The dog looked back at me, ears upright. He just wanted breakfast.

IN THE SAME way that Kopa would prove a fleeting but intense concentration of life and movement in the larger scheme of my winter journey, the aul of forty or so homes came into view as no more than an island dwarfed by a wild sea of brown and gray steppe.

Far out, a herd of sheep and goats was being driven home for the night, appearing from a distance like bobbing seagulls drifting in on the currents. I descended from the hills just as people emerged from their homes to welcome the animals and herders back. Had the animals grazed well today? No wolf sightings? Were all the animals accounted for? Then again things settled, the working horses in their corrals, the sheep in their pens.

I'd met two men on their way on foot to Kopa earlier in the day, and they led the way to a courtyard where others came out and helped unload the horses. There could be no mistaking my host, Serik, who motored into the aul and stepped out of a battered Soviet, crank-start jeep. He was a gentle but powerful man with a strong Russian nose, meaty hands that clutched on to me, and pale Kazakh eyes that looked at me intensely.

"Where have you been? We have been expecting you for two days!"

Serik was the akim of the aul and the local district, which meant he was at once an elected mayor and a man of recognized natural authority. It was a title reminiscent of leaders in nomad times, known as biys, who, along with batyrs—warriors—had been part of the old nomad aristocracy known as the "white bone" (ak suyet), which officially ruled outside the tribal system of nomads. In such vast territories, where loyalty always lay to circles of kin and not central administration, they were crucial for resolving disputes, especially over rights to grazing land.

Although there were historical parallels to be drawn, Serik oversaw a very different aul than that presided over by biys. In Soviet times Kopa had been a dedicated haymaking collective—a type of farming created under Soviet rule that saw collectives developed into monoculture farming productions and former nomads equipped with specialized skills such as haymaking, tractor driving, herding, and slaughtering. In post-Soviet times, this had left rural Kazakhs conditioned to be employees of the state but without the skills to practice the kind of wholesale farming introduced by the Soviets, yet also bereft of the knowledge that would allow them to contemplate a return to the nomadic pastoralism of their ancestors. Many Kazakhs had subsequently departed to regional towns and cities to look for work. Kopa, a victim of this trend, was now a largely deserted village, where the dwindling population survived on subsistence farming and the barter and sale of the hay that was still produced.

Despite the somewhat depressing conditions, the tradition of hospitality remained firmly unbroken. Without hesitating, Serik ordered the aul's fodder vault to be opened, whereupon two of his workers hauled out giant bundles of hay and laid them at the feet of my horses. Tigon was promptly thrown some bones, and after I had been treated to a sauna-like banya, a dish of meat, and a couple of shots of vodka, Serik compelled me to stay for three days. This was a traditional period of time during which a

Kazakh host was required to ply the guest with hospitality and had no right to ask who the guest was or what his business might be. Perhaps more to the point, there was due to be a wedding in nearby Tansyk, the aul I had bypassed the day before on the way to Kopa, and it was essential—compulsory, in fact—that I be there.

Two nights later the old *dom kultura*—the Soviet-era "house of culture"—in Tansyk was pulsating with a crowd of several hundred. Against the backdrop of a Soviet-era mural and some hastily strung up lights that flashed robotically, men with drab but impeccable suits and women in camel-hair vests mingled with a throng of teenagers clad in skin-hugging jeans. In a rising fervor of anticipation, many danced, including elderly men whose faces pursed in concentration, as if they were trying to remember a long-forgotten style. It didn't matter if the music was Madonna or traditional Kazakh—their dance moves did not change.

To announce the beginning of the ceremony, a musician made a dramatic entrance in a flashy suit with a dombra cradled in his arms. He roamed about the hall demanding attention with his furious strumming, and as he began to sing, people left the floor. In the past a musician such as he might have been known as an *akyn*—a talented performer chosen to represent a certain kinship group or family. For centuries, in the absence of the written word, the continuity of nomadic life and a sense of national consciousness rested heavily on such artists.[2] In the twenty-first century the akyn evidently had to have a broader repertoire than his predecessor. A tangle of amplifiers, microphones, and speakers was part of the modern arsenal, and in addition to traditional music, many of the songs he performed were slow love melodies to clunky backing music from a synthesizer.

When finally the bride and groom walked in, the musician serenaded the bride as part of a custom known as *betashar*, "revealing the face" of the bride. The formalities that followed were as eclectic as the musician's gamut. A mullah stood alongside a bureaucrat from the registrar's office, and as the bride and groom, dressed in a generic gown and suit, respectively, signed some papers, the dombra went quiet and Mendelssohn's "Wedding March" blared from the speakers.

Throughout the ceremony, Serik and several old men chaperoned me, making sure I was propped right up close to the action. As a foreigner wearing dirty hiking boots and faded travel garb, I found the experience a little awkward at first. When the official matters were over, though, I was carried into the dining room by the heaving spirits of the crowd. There I paused momentarily in disbelief.

Three rows of long trestle tables were laden with dazzling platters of fresh fruit, horse sausage, dried curd, pastries, confectionery, salads, and nuts. By every third plate shiny bottles of vodka and sparkling water provided additional polish. I had long since become accustomed to preserved meat, rice, and semolina as the mainstays of my diet, not to mention the frugal existence of the people I had met, so I found this at once overwhelming and perplexing. Noticing my sense of awe, Serik explained that it was a small wedding—only three hundred guests. Kazakhs, I discovered, put their life savings into wedding ceremonies.

I fell into it all. As a hundred different toasts were raised to the newlyweds, I relished the kaleidoscope of faces that seemed to reflect all corners of the steppe. There were men with large ears, sunken cheeks, and blue eyes, and others with broad faces and olive skin stretched taut over formidable fist-like cheekbones. A woman two seats up from me had large dark eyebrows, a slight red tinge to her face, and a pointy nose. A woman opposite had glowing porcelain skin that blanketed the rounded contours of her wide, open face like snow. Her eyes were almond-shaped, so, depending on her expression, she could swing from an Eastern look to a Western one in an instant.

After Serik had proclaimed his toast and the akyn made everyone aware over the PA system of the special guest from Australia, we moved back to the other section of the hall. The floors and walls there vibrated with a throng of old and young dancing to contemporary Kazakh music. There were middle-aged women twirling in shrieks of laughter, and grooving old men whose shirts had popped out from their belts and shook like flags in the wind. Judging by the number of empty vodka bottles lying around, there were a lot more festivities to come. Sensing this, and wisely choosing to censor my experience, Serik signaled that it was time to go.

MUSIC FROM THE wedding echoed in my head as I saddled up and rode out from Kopa. The horses were similarly buoyant—they had gorged so much under Serik's watch that I was forced to lengthen their girth straps. They were wound up, and happy to move into a trot with the gentlest of commands, but just as inclined to use their excess energy to misbehave. Something a Kazakh herder later told me was partially true: "It is dangerous to rest a horse too long, or a man, for they will soon relax and become weak, lazy, and disobedient."

Only a short distance beyond Kopa, a sobering headwind stole away any residual warmth from my stay. The horses also tired a little, and when they fell into line my sense of euphoria and companionship all but disintegrated. Reunited with my solo journey, I refocused my sights.

Just 50 km from Kopa lay the shores of Lake Balkhash, a long, narrow body of water stretching around 600 km from east to west. A geographical curiosity of the lake, the world's third-largest inland sea without an outlet, is that the eastern half is saline, while the western half, which curves in a crescent shape to the south, is freshwater.

My plan was to ride west, parallel to the shoreline, where the moderating effect of the lake would buy me some time before the onset of extreme cold. The challenge of this route lay in the arid and uninhabited terrain. There were no permanent streams or rivers feeding the lake from the north, and the eastern half was too saline for livestock to drink. My only hope in the event there was no snowfall was to rely on getting water from a remote industry-serving railway that ran just north of the shore. At regular intervals there were control points and sidings with camps of rail workers known in Russian as *raz'ezds*.

As I headed south from Kopa, then west, tracks and roads petered out, giving way to wide, cracked clay pans, between which grew tough, gray woody plants without foliage. Far to the north the escarpment of the up-lands was just visible, but ahead the horizon was one finger thick—so flat and deserted that nothing but Tigon with his tall pointy ears bridged it with the sky.

The routines of travel that had carried me to Kopa brought reassurance in such a wild setting, but on the evening of the second day I hadn't found any water or pasture and made for the railway line and a raz'ezd known as Zhaksybulak. During my time there it became clear that while I had left more populated territories behind, I had also departed from communities whose livelihood, like mine, was closely connected with the pursuit of pasture.

The single-track railway the raz'ezds served carried a cargo of oil and gas from the Caspian Sea in western Kazakhstan, much of which was bound for Druzhba on the border with China. Zhaksybulak itself—the largest siding I came across in the area, and the only one with any live-stock and permanent residency—was a disorderly handful of huts cling-ing to the rail line, laden with litter, broken glass, and a couple of rusting truck chassis. Most of the houses were either half-built or semi-demolished shells, and the rail workers eked out a living in rooms they had been able to improvise and close off to the elements with tarpaulins. Water supplies—even for the token sheep and cow—were brought weekly by train. Through an unbroken maelstrom of wind-whipped sand, dirt, and salt came the rumbling, and screeching of giant steel trains with tanks stained black with oil and grease. Long after they had been eclipsed by the horizon, acrid diesel fumes carried on the wind. With my animals freshly watered, I left as soon as I could.

The next five days—four riding and one resting—melted into one an-other. Two subtly different tones of gray offered the only contrast in a landscape of fading monochrome: the sky, which remained overcast and dim, and the featureless, color-drained steppe. There were no livestock, and only morsels of grass and wormwood plant to be found. The lake shoreline remained out of sight.

I rode a safe distance from the railway line but once a day made a trip to look for water at the raz'ezds that were spaced along the line at 20 km and sometimes 40 km intervals. Some raz'ezds had run out of water and the men had little or nothing to drink for themselves. Most were manned by only one or two workers.

At night I camped to the north, where there were tiny oases of grass, and retired to the tent, where the world was smaller and easier to comprehend. In Zhaksybulak stories of wolf sightings and attacks had abounded, so I began throwing firecrackers out the tent door before going to sleep as a precaution. One evening I tried to film myself with the firecrackers but forgot to open the tent door before I lit them. The result was a hole burned in the fly—an addition to a growing list of needed repairs.

Although I resented my dependence on the railway, I had nowhere else to turn when the horses tired and I clean ran out of grain. A day's ride short of a copper-mining hub called Sayak, I hesitantly approached a raz'ezd, two small buildings trackside.

In a room flooded with the stench of vodka and tobacco I found three men playing cards, heads down. At first they thought I might be a Russian illegally fishing the lake, but upon seeing my horses, they let loose with all manner of jubilant profanities and agreed to help.[3] I paid one of them to hitch a ride on a train to Sayak and bring back a sack of grain and some food supplies for me by evening.

Waiting a day amid the diesel stench, blackened earth, and scattered rubbish was not pleasant, but the only other possibility for resting the horses and getting supplies was to ride into Sayak myself—something I had been told to avoid at all costs. By all reports, this declining mining town was "full of bandits," unemployed "Oralmans"—Kazakhs who had recently emigrated from Mongolia, China, or elsewhere abroad—and competing Mafia groups.[4] More worrying for me were reports of the corrupt Sayak police. Apparently they were known to abduct people or arrest them on false grounds, drive them out onto a remote part of the steppe, steal their valuables, and leave them for dead. The police were said to be awaiting my arrival, and even though I suspected the rumor to be nothing more than scaremongering, I had managed to fly under the radar of the authorities until now and feared what they might make of my visa papers.[5]

After dark a sack of grain, some rice, and some canned meat were delivered. I settled into camp near the tracks, relieved that my time at the raz'ezd had passed without event. Just after tethering the horses, however, a special workers' train pulled in, and a group of around twenty men piled out. The workers, who had arrived from Sayak for a week of track maintenance, swaggered over to an empty dormitory hut, sniggering and swearing, smoking cigarettes. I was dragged into their smoke-filled den, where vodka was flowing and men sat on their bunks freely spitting onto the floor between drags.

One man with straw-like hair, pockmarked skin, and an unblinking stare poured me a glass. "Give me one of your horses! Or at least sell it to me cheaply! After all, what do you need three for?" When I refused, he backed off and replied in a gentler tone, "I have heard there are thieves in Sayak coming to steal your horses tonight, so be careful."

When I managed to extricate myself from the hut I found Tigon curled up by the door guarding my boots. He leaped up at me, paws on my chest, whining. I ran my hands along his snout, caressed his head behind the ears, and let him bury his moist nose in my coat.

It should have been obvious that I needed to stick close to my animals this night, but instead I took up an invitation for dinner inside the signal-control room with the engineers. This lapse of caution would very nearly prove the end of my journey.

I was partway through a slop of canned meat and fried potato when I stepped outside and heard a great thwack and muffled thump from the direction of my camp. Crouching, I could make out the silhouetted figure of someone scurrying away from Taskonir. As I ran toward him I tripped and fell over an object that proved to be my backpack. Even as I rushed to raise the alarm, the turn of events was becoming clear. The mystery figure had taken my backpack—which included my video camera, passport, and money—and leaped bareback on Taskonir for a brazen getaway. What he hadn't realized was that Taskonir was tethered on the lower front leg with a 20 m line. Taskonir had only made it to the end of the rope before he and his passenger somersaulted to earth.

It wasn't long before the would-be thief was dragged into the hut and revealed as the very same man who had warned me about thieves. Since our earlier meeting I had learned that he had been born in Mongolia and immigrated as a child to Kazakhstan, and was colloquially known as "the Mongol."

I had barely begun to make sense of these happenings when an engineer from the signal station took command. "You know what we do when there is a problem like this?" he announced. "There is just one solution." The men around him looked on, captivated. "To drink!"

They went back inside and raised toasts to anything they could think of. When their vodka ran out they demanded I hand over any alcohol I might have stowed away.

"Don't worry, Tim! Timokha! Tamerlane! Timurbek! This is the way we do it—this is the way we solve our problems. Don't be offended!" the men chanted.

Even the would-be thief, who was unapologetic, joined in for a drink.

I retired to the tent and packed so I could leave at the first hint of light, but the course of events still had a ways to run. At two in the morning Taskonir vanished, leading to a sortie of drunken men running clumsily through the dark on a desperate search. Someone tripped on an old wire and fell, and another face-planted on the train tracks. There were rumors that someone had *really* stolen the horse this time, and that it couldn't possibly have been the Mongol because he was asleep. But then, just as I was recovering my breath, the men wandered back, leading Taskonir. I tied the horses on short ropes for the rest of the night and lay in my sleeping bag on the ground among them.

At 6:00 A.M. I was up and saddling, and by sunrise I was ready to go. There was just one last issue to solve: Taskonir's hobbles were missing. I roused some men and told them to wake the Mongol. When he appeared looking sullen and disinterested, I was already sitting high up on the horse, so I was looking down on him.

"I don't care who stole my horse, but I need my hobbles!" I said sternly.

With a sigh he walked around to the rear of the hut and came back with them.

Other men came out, rubbing their eyes, to say goodbye as I set off into a fast trot. Tigon was already far ahead.

"Have a good journey! We hope you are not offended!"

I KEPT MY eyes straight ahead for hours and didn't stop until the railway had been so long extinguished from view that I felt beyond its orbit. I felt as though we were setting ourselves adrift back into the embrace of the steppe. I didn't care if it meant drinking salt water for a whole month; I was no longer going to be seduced by the illusion of security the railway suggested. It was true what I had been told: "The most dangerous wolf of all is that which walks on two legs."

By evening my pace slowed to a walk, and the adrenaline ran dry. Safely beyond the gaze of human beings, I felt more able to contemplate what had passed. Given the repercussions that might have ensued if the horse thief had been successful, I couldn't shake a feeling of dread and anger. Simultaneously, however, the farther I made it from the raz'ezd, the more the personal offense faded, and I began to find something curiously endearing about the thief.

In a kind of honorable way, the Mongol had warned me of the theft—an unspoken acknowledgment that he liked my horses, and a backhanded compliment. Most interesting was his choice of horse. Had he wanted to steal the most valuable mount for resale, Ogonyok would have been his pick. Instead, he chose Taskonir—a horse invaluable for herding, but long in the tooth and comparatively bony. If the theft was partly born of an appreciation of Taskonir's qualities, I believed there was some degree of honor in that.

More broadly, in the context of nomad culture and history, it was clear that my tendency to associate horse theft with the communities of the railway was misplaced. Horse rustling was an art as old as horsemanship itself, glamorized in oral epics of the steppe, and very much a part of everyday nomad life. Kazakhs had explained to me time and time again that he who has the skill to steal horses and cattle and get away with it deserves those animals more than the owner. One had to respect the daring and heroics of such men.

What was more, in getting my horse back from the Mongol, I had engaged in a centuries-old custom called *barimta*, which means "that which is due to me." It dictated that he who has been stolen from has the right to steal back, and if he is good enough, he can confiscate the offender's entire herd or even his wife until the dispute is resolved. Over time I came to think that the evolving history of this custom said a lot about the nature of the Mongol and the theft.

Prior to the colonization of Kazakh land, barimta was adhered to as a way of resolving conflicts ranging from unpaid bride-prices to contested grazing rights. It was condoned by the tribal justice system known as *adat* and governed by strict guidelines, such as that the confiscation had to take place in daylight so that the avengers' skill had to be exceptional and therefore honorable.

Like nomadic life in general, barimta began to erode with the arrival of the Russians, who gradually supplanted it with their own model of law. In 1822 they criminalized barimta as horse and cattle theft, and in 1868 they decreed that all land previously used for livestock grazing would be taken over by the state. In a move born partly of rebellion, but mostly spurred by the need to keep order among themselves, Kazakhs continued to recognize barimta. The term, however became more synonymous with the brazen horse thefts that Kazakhs carried out against tsarist emissaries.[6] These skilled Kazakh horse rustlers passed into legend and were rarely handed over to Russian justice.

In light of the background of barimta, I felt that the Mongol had stolen Taskonir in rough keeping with the spirit of his ancestors—a thought that offered cold comfort, but was at least a way of coming to terms with the theft. In the future, I would have to accept that if I wasn't good enough to look after my horses, then the thief probably deserved them more than I did. Ultimately, I would also have to understand that as a foreigner, without the protections of a traditional nomad society or colonial law, I was very much on my own.

9

BALKHASH

A GOOD 40 km from the raz'ezd where I'd nearly lost Taskonir, I crested a rise and brought the horses to a standstill. It was near sunset, and a low ceiling of dark clouds pressed down on the earth, rendering the steppe a uniform black. This had been the norm in recent days, but now to the south, east, and west, where the land ordinarily petered out into a smudgy embrace with the horizon, it merged with the broad, silvery waters of Lake Balkhash.

From a height and distance such as this, as vast as the lake appeared, it was not hard to imagine it was but a mere puddle on the canvas of the Eurasian steppe, draining the snowmelt of Central Asia's Tien Shan farther south. It was a reminder that although it was November 30, nearly five months since I had climbed into the saddle, I had come little more than a fifth of the distance to the Danube. West of Lake Balkhash still lay the most challenging landscapes of my journey—the Betpak Dala ("starving steppe"), then the deserts surrounding the Aral Sea. Even then, I would only just be reaching the halfway point to Hungary.

As I let my eyes be drawn in to the sense of space and grandeur before me, the bigger picture melted away and I became absorbed in the details of the land immediately in front of us. A series of peninsulas, coves, and bays formed an intriguing corrugated look to the northern shoreline of Lake Balkhash, the scale and drama of which could be more accurately described as an ocean coastline. For the next week or so I hoped to forget about the attempted horse theft and lose myself in the shore's furrows. We had traveled about half the length of Balkash's saline eastern half along the railway, and from here my aim was to avoid human contact for as long as I could manage and somehow find enough fresh water to be self-sufficient. I hoped that would prepare me—physically and mentally—to carry on farther west as the real winter set in.

ON THIS FIRST evening I camped on the highest hill I could find. Overnight it snowed heavily enough that by morning there was no need to find water. The next afternoon I felt my way down through gullies to the shore of the lake.

Close up, Lake Balkhash was even more spellbinding than from afar. When the sun came out, the water was a rich azure. Small swells arose and crashed onto veneers of ice that had formed around the lake edges. Soon, I surmised, both these vast bodies—the sea-like steppe and the lake itself—would fuse as one.

The period of on-and-off freezing—characterized by cold nights but warmish days—would prove a stroke of luck. There were polished pieces of relatively salt-free ice being washed up on the pebbly beach. There began a routine that would last for a couple of weeks—collecting ice during the day in plastic bags, and melting it in the evening for drinking water and dinner. The horses crunched on this ice as well, although they also began to drink water from the lake. It was a sign the lake was becoming less brackish the farther west we traveled.

As I rode, the evolving contours of the shoreline made for an engaging story. Flats grew into muscled hills, which in turn became stony ridges overlooking the lake. In places the earth below came to life with a smattering of red, green, yellow, and purple pebbles, but then these gave way to soft clay and patches of sand, where getting to the lakeshore meant fighting through marshes and tall reeds. The horses moved briskly, their pack boxes rattling rhythmically, hooves clipping the frost off plants. We trotted ten to twenty minutes each hour and set a fast walk in between.

At night when the dangers and fears seemed to crowd in, the growing sense of family with my animals provided comfort. The responsibility of being their leader and protector gave me more courage than I would have had alone. There was nothing better than falling asleep on a luxurious mattress of saddle blankets as the horses grazed around my tent. The sweet smell of horse sweat, hair, and leather permeated every waking moment.

Although my aim was to remain unseen, it wasn't possible to avoid people entirely. In places the railway hugged the shore, and I could see raz'ezds in the distance. There was also the odd mud hut camouflaged into the side of the hills, but the fishermen who inhabited them were just as reclusive and unwilling to be seen as I. I met only one of these men—a shriveled old Russian who came out to ask if I had vodka and if I was "migrating." Later I was told more about these poachers, and how the state authorities would sometimes send helicopters out to spot the illegal fishing shanties.

Especially in light of the scattered human presence, I relished the test of finding campsites hidden from prying eyes. The longer I evaded humans, the less likely it was that anyone would know to expect me, let alone look for or find me. It was rewarding to feel that only the land and my animals knew of my existence.

It was during a rest day, while I sheltered in the tent from flurries of snow and sleet, that I realized the wear and tear on my equipment had been creeping up on me. Much of my gear, which up until now I had considered new, was falling apart. My list of problems to solve, as I wrote it in my diary, went thus: *Trousers falling apart—winter hat needs sewing up—tent has another few holes (seems to be falling apart)—buckles broken on saddle—gloves need sewing up—hobbles need to be fixed—stirrup leathers almost knackered—zip on my jacket is going—tripod leg broken—stakes need straightening.* Oddly enough, perhaps, given the length of the journey that still stretched in front of me, I found it satisfying I had reached a stage of the journey when nothing was new and shiny and I had to persevere without the aid of the freshness with which I had begun. Some romantic part of me hoped all my foreign equipment would eventually fade away and I would be forced to borrow exclusively from the indigenous ways. Only then I could become part of the landscape like the nomads whom I so wanted to understand.

Eventually the steppe began to offer some more generous pasture. There were more signs of life, too. One frosty morning we came face-to-face with a herd of shaggy Bactrian camels. All three horses—which were from eastern Kazakhstan and therefore had never seen camels—reared, muscles tensing and nostrils flaring. I was riding Zhamba at the time and could feel his heart pounding through my lower legs. In a fraction of a second, I found myself a substantial distance from where we had been standing, holding on for life as the horses bolted away. Tigon, for his part, didn't help things when he began herding the whole group of camels toward us.

For the first time since leaving Kopa, I came across nomads' dome tombs. One in particular was at least 5 m high and made of well-preserved mud brick. Its entry was facing south, just like a yurt, and Tigon and I ate our lunch inside, huddled out of the wind. When I was moving again I scanned the surrounding area, imagining where camps might have been and herds might have grazed.

One week after we left the last raz'ezd, our bubble was finally broken. I was wakened at dawn by a whinnying from Ogonyok, and broke out of the tent. Two paces from the sleeping bag I stopped in my tracks: Ogonyok and Taskonir stood facing me with their ears back and hind legs flexed. Behind them in the half-light was the ghostly figure of a dark, wooly stallion. He snorted, demanding a confrontation. Beyond him, hidden among the shrubbery, were a hundred beady eyes and ears straight as nails. They were barrel-chested little horses with thick necks, coarse split manes, and brands on their hindquarters. Very Mongolian, I thought.

We all froze until Tigon came to his senses and sprinted over with the most aggressive bark he could muster. Foals, mares, and geldings broke into a gallop, and the steppe came to life with a thousand muffled thuds and the splintering of twigs. In their wake shrubs quivered, but even they soon returned to stillness.

It had been so long since I had seen another horse—more than two weeks—that I had forgotten the magic of it. In fact, the last two weeks had been the first time on the journey when the distant silhouette of a horseman hadn't been as common as the rising sun. I missed the cry of a herder, the rustle of a flock of sheep, and the movement of horses, all of which brought a sense of vitality to the steppe.

It was time to take a gamble with humans. Besides, the weather of late had been getting cold—around -10°C—and I was out of grain. And the next day was my twenty-sixth birthday.

FROM CAMP IT didn't take long to discover a kstau by following the converging trails of sheep and goats through tall tussocks of ak-shi, or white grass. Ever since coming across this grass the previous evening I'd known it was a good sign: a herdsman in western Mongolia had once told me that wherever ak-shi grew, Kazakh nomads have always lived. Sometimes towering taller than a rider in the saddle, it provided shelter for sheep and goats, survival food for horses, and an indispensable resource for nomads. Its woody husks became so thick and strong that the tallest blades were gathered, assembled in a mat, and placed upright between the collapsible lattice walls of the yurt and the insulating felt, acting as a natural screen to keep out flies and rodents when the felt was lifted up to let the cool air in. They were also used as drying trays and bird-proof covers for dried curd.

I sighted the kstau from the safety of the ak-shi, and it took some time before I mustered the courage to come out of hiding. Holding Tigon back and keeping his snout closed with my hand, I spied on the man who had his head down and was fixing an old motorcycle. Only after waiting for some herders in the distance to move out of view with their flocks of sheep and goats did I ride out into the open.

I was nearly on the man before he spun around and looked up at our caravan. I took the initiative.

"Who are you?" I asked. "Are you the owner? Do you have water? Do you have grain? Is there a trail from here to Balkhash? How far is the closest aul?"

Even as I spoke I could see Tigon out of the corner of my eye, sniffing around in reconnaissance. To my dismay when he pissed on things he did it crouching, like the puppy he still was, betraying his age and belying our fanciful cover as tough, hardened beings of the steppe.

The man, named Kuat, was the owner of this grazing station, and as he answered my questions ran his eyes meticulously over my horses. He began with the front hooves, then went up the legs to the mouth and across their backs to the rump before following the curves down from the hindquarters, finishing off with a peek underneath to confirm they were geldings and not stallions or mares. I was beginning to understand that you could read more about a person from his animals than his words.

There was a short silence thereafter, suggesting he was putting together the funny foreign equipment and my accent.

"So my dogs were not mistaken!" he said at last. "When they started barking last night we thought there were wolves. Your horses are hungry. I have some feed for them. Let's go drink tea."

Only inside the warm confines of his hut did I begin to relax. This was part of my plan to drop my guard cautiously, layer by layer. It became a protocol that I would adhere to religiously.

The first step was trusting the stranger enough to get out of my saddle. I kept in mind a saying that a Kazakh once told me: "When walking past the behind of a foreign horse, unless you have spoken first to its owner, keep walking."

If I felt comfortable after getting out of the saddle, I would risk unloading the animals and enter the home. Only over a cup of tea would I explain who I was and where I was headed. I also learned to monitor Tigon's reaction—if his tail shot down and he shied away from the host with a growl, it was better to move on. The ultimate shedding of defenses was unsaddling the horses, having some vodka with my host, and stripping down to thermal underwear for bed. To sleep without the hard handle of the knife on my belt digging into my hips—I never took my trousers off at camp on the steppe—was a luxury, but concurrently made me aware of being at the mercy of my hosts. I would then have no choice but to cave in to trust and exhaustion.

A couple of herders who worked for Kuat joined us for tea and bread. Although Kazakhs almost exclusively eat meat and dairy, bread and salt are considered sacred, able to draw guests from afar. Not eating or trying the bread shows disrespect.

As I cradled the tea and dipped the bread into some fresh *kaimak* (cream), we talked exclusively at first about pasture and the weather. This environment, with its soft sandy soil and vegetation, was a relative paradise and I recounted the harrowing land that I had been traveling through. They were impressed, but mostly intrigued to hear I had encountered their herd of horses. Had I seen the foals? Had I seen the stallion? What did I think about them?

With the second round of tea came the familiar questions: "Do you have parents? Where are your horses from? How did you find us?" And finally: "Where are you from?"

They tried to veil their excitement, but it was too much when I explained it was my birthday the next day. "Then it is decided. You must stay here to celebrate!"

I spent the rest of the day tinkering away with repairs and letting the adrenaline of the past two weeks turn to fatigue. Kuat, who had moved gracefully into his middle age with silver hair and was educated as an agriculturalist, had an authority born of life on the steppe, and I felt myself leaning toward trusting him. I knew it was risky, but I needed a rest, and so I accepted his invitation. It might have been an achievement to survive alone for some time, but not trusting in people wasn't sustainable.

At dawn the next morning I sat bolt upright, my recurring dream leaving a residue in my mind, and reached for the tent door. By the time I recalled where I was, I was fully awake, so I stepped outside to water the horses. Tigon, who was sleeping on a horse blanket next to my saddle, opened one eye briefly before tucking his nose further under his tail and pretending he hadn't seen me. I would have gone back to bed had I not noticed a shadowy figure coming out to the barn.

In the half-light Bazibek, a sixty-year-old herder, was limping bow-legged over to a camel. He had a gun slung over his shoulder and was wearing felt boots and a traditional fox-fur hat. His body looked as rigid and gaunt as an old skinny sheep, and wind had eroded his face, stranding his cheeks like broad boulders in a furrowed mess of landslips. For forty years straight he had worked as a chaban, and he set about saddling the camel, his motions sure as the rising sun, silent and unrushed. Age had worn away his agility, but everything he did, from fitting the felt blanket to tightening the girth and hanging the rifle from the front hump, was done with precision. I had the feeling he was trying not to wake the land. Even when he spoke to me he did so in a husky whisper. How was it that, despite its size and harshness, the land felt so tender at this time of day?

When the flock of sheep had been let out of a pen, Bazibek hauled himself into the saddle, and the camel rose. It was a dramatic transformation, he and the camel becoming one. Bazibek was now the eyes, the camel the legs, and in that moment the frailty of Bazibek's age vanished. As I was told by many, on the steppe men learned to ride before they could walk, and could still ride a stallion after they could no longer stand. Directing his sheep with a long pole and whip, Bazibek set off into the distance, calling rhythmically. Since the days were now so short, he would only step out of the saddle at dusk, when he returned.

Long after he had gone the look in his eyes stuck with me. There was a humble, faraway expression there that told something of the simplicity of the steppe. I had begun to feel it myself, out there all day—the steppe consumed and gently coaxed you into a motion and rhythm until you intuitively knew your place on this earth.

It was with this enchantment I returned to the hut for breakfast and Kuat said something that stirred me further: "Do you know that Genghis Khan and his men stayed here?"

I looked up at him, with his hair all awry and his mustache glistening wet above the steam pouring from his teacup. He looked a little nervous—perhaps it had taken courage for him to say it, as if it were a secret, or he was risking ridicule.

"Really? How do you know?" I asked.

"The old men know."

There was probably no written evidence to suggest the legend was true, but among a people for whom oral history had been the bedrock of knowledge, it was foolish to discard such legends. Within these stories was always an element of truth.

As I mulled over this conversation with Kuat in the coming days, I found several reasons to think it was possible that the area had borne the hoofprints of Mongols' horses. The ak-shi was a sign that the area was a relative oasis, suitable for a winter or summer camp, and I knew the region had long been home to nomads. And then there was the geographical location. It was here, at the very narrowest point of Lake Balkhash, that the fresh waters of the west flowed through the bottleneck into the saline eastern part. Because of the abundance of fresh water, this part of the lake would freeze over even early in the winter, and it would have been possible for an army to ride across the short stretch of ice to the southern shore.

Most important, the southern shore of the lake marked the northern border of the strategic Jeti-su or "Seven Rivers" region. The Jeti-su stretched from Lake Balkhash to the Tien Shan in the south; its extensive river systems traditionally supported a symbiotic mix of nomadic and more agrarian sedentary societies. From the Bronze Age to the present, aspiring empires—including those of the Usuns (a Turkic people in the third century BCE), the Huns, the Mongols, and Tamerlane—knew that whoever ruled the Jeti-su controlled a vast swath of Central Asia. This fact was not lost on the Russians, who in the middle of the nineteenth century established Almaty in the heart of the Jeti-su—it became Kazakhstan's largest city, and was the capital until Nazarbayev moved it to Astana in 1997.

The more I dwelled on it, the more I reasoned that this land just north of Lake Balkhash seemed like a logical retreat for armies between campaigns. It would have been a remote hinterland home to hardened nomads who had much in common with the Mongols, and ideal for grazing horses. In summer—the season for planning and grazing, not war—the lake would have offered natural protection from the south. In light of this, I wondered whether Kuat's herd of horses might have been the descendants of Mongol mounts. Still, it all seemed very farfetched, a romantic hope that I had stumbled on a piece of the nomad puzzle.

Weeks later I happened to be talking to Gansukh in Mongolia on the satellite phone and recounted the story, mentioning that the aul near Kuat's farm was known as Ortaderesin. In turn, he told me that *orta* in Mongolian means "tall," and *deres* is the Mongol term for ak-shi—something probably unbeknownst to most local Kazakhs, since *orta* is also a Kazakh word meaning "middle." Still, that piece of information made it seem all the more likely that this Mongolian hoofprint had withstood the test of time.

THE MEN AT Kuat's farm were ecstatic about the prospect of a birthday party and set about cleaning the hut in preparation. Kuat, meanwhile, agreed to drive me 50 km west to a market in the small copper-smelting city of Balkhash, and that night we returned in high spirits with delicacies such as fruit, salted fish, cake, salami, salad, the filled Russian dumplings called *pelmeni*, orange juice, and, of course, a few bottles of vodka.

As we pulled up at the farm, however, my spirits faded, for parked outside the hut was a military police vehicle. Word had clearly spread via the *uzun kulak* or "long-ear news" of the steppe. Kuat went silent.

Inside two inspectors stood in winter army garb. They ordered me over. "How can we understand your journey? What is your business here? Are you really Australian?"

I reached for my letter of introduction—which had been written in Russian on United Nations Development Programme/World Wildlife Foundation letterhead by Evegeniy Yurchenkov, who had given me invaluable assistance upon my arrival in Kazakhstan—hoping they wouldn't request my passport. I had never shown my "business" visa to officials, had not registered it, and wasn't sure it authorized my journey. Perhaps these men had a connection to the railway and the police in Sayak?

"We don't need papers. Just tell us, are you *really* from Australia?"

"Yes, I am from Australia, where kangaroos are from."

That was all they needed, and their expressions softened. "It's true! We have come to wish you a happy birthday!"

Like so many people I met during my travels, they had heard on the winds about my journey and wanted nothing more than to see me with their own eyes. My Australian saddle, in particular, was legendary, and I was more than happy to bring it in so they could look over it and try sitting in its deep leather seat. What's more, one of the men went out to the jeep and brought in a bag of barley.

"This is for you, a gift for turning twenty-six. My grandfather taught me that a palmful of this uncrushed grain is enough to keep a horse going when it is tired."[1]

After the police had gone, it was endearing to see the way the herders put on a proper feast with all the frills. They donned their finest for the occasion, including old creased dress pants, and combed their disheveled, unwashed hair. One of the young herders took on the role of tea pourer—something that was usually strictly for women.

In such a male-dominated environment there was a danger of falling into a pit of neglect and alcoholism, so it was admirable that they seemed to be consciously compensating for the absence of family. The men working here operated on shifts, returning periodically to homes in the aul. The exclusion of women was partly because of the paternal culture of the Kazakhs, in which men dominated physical herding work, and also because of Islamic influence, but mostly it was a legacy of Soviet collectivization. Nomadic life traditionally depended on family and kinship groups, and women were known to gallop alongside the men. Unlike in many parts of Muslim Central Asia, Kazakh women did not wear the veil, and the Koran was used selectively to support the role women play, as evidenced by a common saying taught to children: "To mother, to mother, to mother, and then to father." But collectivization meant not only that a sense of ownership was erased as herders became employees of the state, but also that farming was run divorced from the family unit.

The evening slid into night with the slosh of vodka and tea. The conversation meandered through quiet troughs of spiritual and political issues, boisterous highs of vulgar jokes, and chatter about horses. I marveled at the setting of our celebration—it was the first time since an evening with a chaban in the Altai that I was not dining at a conventional table with chairs. Just as Kazakhs had always done in the yurt, we sat on cushions on the floor around a low table called a *dastarkhan*. What I couldn't have known was that during my travels along Lake Balkhash I had crossed an invisible line, beyond which the influence of Russian ways had always been weaker. Although the dastarkhan had been an exception until now, I would barely see another set of table and chairs for the remainder of my journey in Kazakhstan.

FROM KUAT'S FARM the horses carried me swiftly across a landscape of frost-encrusted sand and ak-shi. We skirted the city of Balkhash to the north, then began following the arc of the lake as it turned to the southwest. My plan was to carry on along the shoreline for two weeks until I reached the lake's westernmost point, at which stage I would head west into the Betpak Dala.

Owing to the fresh waters of this end of Lake Balkhash and the scattered auls on its shores, I had speculated that the way ahead would pose no problems in terms of water supply. As we began to head southward, however, the conditions conspired to create new challenges.

A cold freeze fell on the land without any of the earlier ambiguity, and the sheets of ice that had been timidly creeping out from the shore now rapidly grew into vast expanses. At times when the sky was clear and the wind stopped it was an exquisite sight—a polished turquoise slab of ice meeting a distant glinting silver sea. Mostly, though, I was aware that as this sealing over progressed, the moderating effect of the open water waned, and the daytime temperature plummeted.

As always, Tigon's behavior was somewhat of a bellwether for these changing conditions, especially when it came to getting up in the morning. He would rise from my sleeping bag when I had finished cooking breakfast, and after wolfing down his porridge he would return to the tent and pretend to lie dead. To get him out, I would first roll him off the horse blankets, and he would lie on his back on the floor of the tent like a sack of bones, his neck bent at a right angle and his long legs crisscrossed in a tangle. After everything else had been packed up and it came to pulling down the tent, he would spring to life in fierce resistance. He refused to move of his own accord, so I would have to throw him out one end of the tent, only to have him sprint around to the other and leap back inside. Often the only solution was lifting the tent up and shaking him out, at which point he would go off and curl up in a ball until we were ready to go.

A day south of the city of Balkhash, I was confronted with more serious problems. While the water near the shore was frozen all the way to the bottom, there was still no snow on the ground. The only way to collect water for the horses was by tethering them to stakes onshore, walking out onto the ice, breaking a hole with my hand axe, and returning with pails. This process used much valuable daylight and was fraught with dangers. One day my thirsty horses broke free and went scuttling onto the ice. By now the metal studs on their shoes had worn down to nothing, and all tied up to one another, they skated uncontrollably out onto thinner ice, threatening to topple over.

Water issues came to a head one afternoon after the horses had gone thirsty for twenty-four hours. I detoured to an aul called Gulshat, where I found a well just as it was becoming dark. Zhamba was the first to drink, and by the time the third horse had finished he was shaking uncontrollably. You could see by his widening, despondent eyes that he was going into hypothermic shock, and soon Taskonir and Ogonyok started to rattle on their feet in the same way.

By nomad custom, it was sacrilege to water a horse in the cold immediately after a long ride—Kazakhs everywhere had taught me to restrain them for at least two hours before letting them eat or drink—but I felt there had been no option. I leaped back on Zhamba and took them off at a trot, continuing beyond darkness until they had recovered. If I had stopped and made camp any earlier, the horses could have been dead within hours.

As I rode onward, it was sad in a way to realize that the charm of Lake Balkhash was withering. This companion of mine that had offered a reprieve from winter would be sorely missed. At the same time, my window of opportunity to develop as a horseman in more forgiving conditions was fast passing. The snows of winter—the thinnest layer of which would make it possible for me to take the horses away from the lake, with no worries about water supply—could now not come quick enough.

10

WIFE STEALING AND OTHER LEGENDS OF TASARAL

IT WAS DECEMBER 17, and after more than 600 km and a month of riding along Lake Balkhash, I was three days' ride from its westernmost tip. The waters were now frozen as far as the eye could see, but the land was dark and empty—still no snow had fallen. If it did not come soon, then branching westward into the "starving steppe"—where there were no people or operating wells—was unthinkable.

Prolonged cold and dry conditions were known in Mongolian as *harin zud*, or "black zud," and were feared by nomads even more than deep snow cover and ice. Without snow or access to substantial underground water—which was rare on the arid steppe zones of Eurasia—livestock faced dehydration, then starvation in the early spring, when lack of snowmelt meant lean pastures.

My circumstances, of course, weren't that dire. I had just three horses and a dog, and in recent days had adjusted to the conditions by peeling off the scabs of ice that formed on my tent to melt for my own water supply. Public wells in the few auls scattered along the shoreline had sufficed for the horses. If it didn't snow, the worst scenario meant finding somewhere with a well to hole up for a while. By contrast, nomad graziers tradition-ally had thousands of animals to care for, and most did not have the lux-ury of a freshwater lake. The difficulties they faced—as did the Mongol armies and their tens of thousands of horses as they crossed these steppes— were beyond imagination.

Not long after breakfast I approached an aul called Tasaral, a gaggle of cigar-brown, blue, and white mud-brick homes barnacled onto the stony shoreline. Where the steely blue waters might have afforded a playground in summer, pressure ridges of ice were forming like frozen waves. Nearby, rusty old fishing boats rested at angles on their keels, their navigators retired to the indoors, where fires would now be chugging 24/7 until spring.

From the outside, where I sat hunched in the cold, this settled way of life beckoned with the immediate respite it offered from the rigors of no-mad life. If nomadic pastoral existence was an ongoing process of adapt-ing to the moods of the natural ecology, then a part of the legacy of the Soviet era was that people could now live with a greater sense of security against the fickle and uncontrollable trends of the weather.

From the interior of Tasaral, where I would stay for the next two nights, however, I was to discover a community that was, like me, precariously navigating through the midst of an awkward transition. Just as autumn had passed but winter hadn't arrived with life-giving snow, the old no-mad ways and the Soviet system were history, and ordinary people had not yet settled on a cultural identity or an economic model to follow.

My host in Tasaral was an unmarried thirty-year-old man named Shashibek. He had approached me on the lakeside and offered to sell me grain, and when I arrived at his home he insisted I stay for the night. Since leaving Kopa, I had found good grazing to be scarce, and the horses had lost weight. I seized the opportunity.

"I can only stay if you can promise my horses lots of hay, for they are hungry," I said. And, leaving nothing to chance, I refused to unload the horses until Shashibek let me inspect his family's barn. I was in luck. Shashibek was the son of the local akim, and their treasure trove of fodder included bundles of reeds—the primary winter fodder of the region, which was cut from the lakeshore in summer—and bales of hay that had been trucked in. Additionally, Shashibek promised that my horses would receive three meals a day of the grain of my choice. Before leaving the barn I was plotting to stay more than one night.

It took only a cup of tea with Shashibek and his parents to learn of the unique geography and historic pattern of life in Tasaral. Tás meant "rock," and aral meant "island"—a reference to a long, broad island rising in dramatic cliffs far offshore. For centuries, first nomads and then the settled Kazakhs of the aul had been herding livestock over to the island in the spring when the ice was still thick enough. The livestock would be left to graze there until there was adequate ice in autumn for them to be returned for winter.

The community in Tasaral continued this tradition, but a quick stroll around the aul was enough to know that animal husbandry was no longer at the center of life. A slew of cheap tangled Chinese nets strung up at the back of homes bespoke of the thriving contraband fishing industry, which most people relied on. In the wake of the collapse of the Soviet Union, fishing Lake Balkhash's waters had helped fill the vacuum of regional unemployment, and it was common knowledge that inspectors routinely took bribes to supplement their poor wages—a practice that had led to profits for all, but also to rampant overfishing. Shashibek's father acknowledged that the current levels of fishing were unsustainable, but he explained that people had few other options, and in any case, Lake Balkhash was under other, more serious threats. The metallurgical plant in the city of Balkhash was known for its emissions of lead, zinc, and copper, which contaminated the lake, and the main tributary flowing into the lake, the Ili River, had long been dammed, with 89 percent of its flow diverted for agricultural irrigation and industry across the border in Xinjiang province, China. The lake's water levels had been in decline for decades, risking the desertification of its immediate surroundings—as had happened to the Aral Sea. This, Shashibek and his family recognized, would bring an end to life in Tasaral.

For the middle-aged and elderly, the realities of the bare-knuckle era of capitalism represented a stark break with the past. For Shashibek, like all of the younger generation, however, it was a reality that had dominated his formative years. My experience in Tasaral was, above all, a fleeting opportunity to join him in his own personal journey through these times.

The evening of my arrival in the aul coincided with the grand opening of the new village tavern. Shashibek and two of his childhood friends took me to a room in the back of a mud-brick grocery decorated with strings of colored lights and a makeshift bar. From a portable stereo a CD of contemporary Kazakh tunes played on repeat.

Vodka was on the pour even as we stepped in, and it wasn't long before my entourage moved on to Russian brandy. As the alcohol sank in, Shashibek's fleshy cheeks turned red, his groomed mustache began to twitch, and the seniority he had exuded earlier receded. He and his friends broke out of their huddle and approached the only other group in the place— three or four girls on the dance floor—with rather imbecilic dance moves. One by one the girls, all of whom knew the men, rolled their eyes and slinked away. Sometimes Shashibek, giggling childishly, propelled me forward into the group of girls, but mostly I hung back, feeling a little embarrassed and out of place. I could see no signs of the evening finishing early, and so I kept throwing back the brandy handed to me. The party came to an end with my vomiting during the stumble home.

In the mist of a collective hangover the next morning, the male bonding session continued with a duck hunting expedition. All four of us squeezed into a Moskvich, a small Soviet-era car, and set off onto the steppe with a rifle pointed out the window, stereo blaring. The three Kazakhs— one of whom was a hunting inspector—took turns taking pot shots as we covered our ears. After scaring away the ducks and moving on to gunning down flocks of sparrow-sized birds—which were to be fed to the dogs—the highlight was when the Moskvich fell through the frozen crust of a salt marsh. We spent an hour digging it out, eventually pushing it free to wild yahoos of delight.

On the way back to the aul I sank back into the seat of the clattering car, cradling bleeding bird carcasses in my lap and watching the tangle of fishnets and boats grow on the horizon. Only a couple of generations ago, a hunt at this time of year—as still happens among Kazakhs in western Mongolia—would have been an event of significant prestige and celebration. In the late autumn, around the first winter snows, men of the community would have gathered on their horses, decked out in fox-fur hats, sheepskin coats, and ornate belts and whips, with a trained eagle at hand or perhaps a tazi dog by their side. It wouldn't have been uncommon for a grandfather, father, and son to take part in the hunt together—it was an opportunity for skills to be shared across generations.

Later Shashibek's neighbor was proud to unveil evidence of this past—his great-grandfather's saddle, which was more than a century old and had been hidden from the Bolsheviks at the height of the purges in the late 1920s. Covered with hundreds of intricate motifs engraved into a silver veneer, it was complete with stirrups carved from the antlers of an Argali sheep and silver-plated girth straps.

Just like this uncouth style of hunting, however, the saddle hinted at how strangely alien the old ways had become. It had been plunked unceremoniously on the floor of the house, wiped of dust, then awkwardly held up by Shashibek's neighbor with unaccustomed hands. It may have been testament to the deep sense of connection to the horse that its original owner had possessed, but this connection—unlike the saddle itself—had not survived to the present.

Even as Shashibek tore up the dirt doing burnout turns on the outskirts of the aul, a part of me could not help but feel dismay at the behavior on show, particularly by the son of a family to whom the community looked for leadership. On the other hand, the tide of history Shashibek faced as he forged his path and identity as a young Kazakh man could not be understated.

The forces eroding Kazakh culture had been multiple and complex. The seventy-year Soviet regime had not only dispossessed the Kazakhs materially and brought about the end to the traditional way of life but also cultivated an environment in which, in order to survive, let alone prosper, many Kazakhs had had little choice but to turn their backs on traditions and beliefs associated with nomadism and integrate into Soviet society.

In the wake of collectivization, dramatic transformation of the ethnic landscape coupled with unprecedented urbanization had had an incalculable impact on Kazakh society. The migration of foreigners to Kazakhstan—such as the 1 million people from European Russia resettled during the Virgin Lands Scheme—meant that by 1959 Kazakhs constituted just 30 percent of the population.[1] In the fast-developing towns and cities, where there were more opportunities to be found than in auls, Kazakhs found themselves not only in the minority but with nomadic traditions largely incompatible with urban life.

The corrosive effects that these changing demographics would have on Kazakh culture were not necessarily intentional, but Soviet authorities concurrently painted traditional culture as "backward" and "nationalistic"—and therefore counterrevolutionary—and sought to supplant it with Russian culture and values under the rubric of "internationalism."

The decline of the Kazakh language and the uptake of Russian is an example of how this doctrine played out with long-term effect. As early as 1949 Russian became the official tongue for all party meetings, and in the 1950s it was the mandatory language for university entrance examinations. According to research undertaken by Dave Bhavna for his book *Kazakhstan: Ethnicity, Language and Power*, even speaking Kazakh in public became socially frowned upon, as "it could invite allegations of nationalism and tribalism."

Within a generation of the Bolshevik revolution, the Kazakhs found that the language that had carried the heritage of their ancestors for centuries had become largely useless and even disadvantageous—without Russian-language skills, one could simply not climb the social or political ladder.[2]

In the present era of independence and "nationalism" into which Shashibek had been born, the climate had somewhat turned around. In the 1990s the Kazakh language was given official status alongside Russian, and as non-indigenous citizens emigrated, the population of Kazakhstan dropped by more than two million, leaving Kazakhs in the majority. Even as a sense of cultural identity and empowerment was emerging, however, a deep-set stigma of backwardness and disadvantage remained associated with traditional culture. Moreover, the fractious divide between rural and urban Kazakhs cultivated in Soviet times had calcified. The urban, russified life represented privilege, opportunity, wealth, and prestige, while to those in the towns and cities, the auls, where Kazakh was the predominant language, represented poor living standards and a relic of the past from which they had moved on. As I would later discover, there were Kazakhs in remote areas, particularly in the south and west, who could not speak Russian at all, and many Kazakhs in the cities who did not have any handle on their native tongue.

In Tasaral, nomadism was no longer a viable way of life, and many traditions associated with it had been lost, never to be reclaimed. In a society grappling with what appeared to be insurmountable hurdles to cultural revival, however, auls such as Tasaral were still a relative stronghold of indigenous language, knowledge, and culture where the old ways hadn't been completely displaced by the new. In this sense, it wasn't the degradation of Kazakh culture that came to define Shashibek and Tasaral for me, but the resilience of the people in maintaining pride in their heritage and, despite the odds, keeping the flicker of tradition alive.

⊞

ALL DAY WHILE hunting, Shashibek's friends had been discussing wife stealing. "It's time for Shashibek to get hitched! His mother needs someone to talk to in the evenings! Who is going to cook for his poor parents when they are old?" they had teased.

As the youngest son, Shashibek was bound by tradition to inherit the family home and take care of his parents. The wife of the youngest son was also traditionally responsible for all the housework. Having an unmarried thirty-year-old son, especially one who was the son of the akim, generated some sympathy for his mother and father.

I had of course dismissed the talk as empty ranting, but by dusk the plotting to steal a wife had turned serious. A Tasaral girl whom Shashibek was courting would be invited to meet me—the "Australian bait"—and someone would be sent to pick her up by car. Shashibek's home was a trap, where Shashibek's relatives and friends were gathering to watch him ask for her hand in marriage. The process was part of a tradition in which men could kidnap their desired future wife, with or without her agreement or prior knowledge. Shashibek and his friends joked about one woman whom they said had been stolen from America and was the sister of the boxer Mike Tyson—a tribute to her feistiness. Another woman had been stolen from Mongolia: "Here we have a real Mongolian girl! Look at her, she is so wild!" they said, pointing.

In a nomadic aul, abduction involved luring the girl from another community, or simply kidnapping her by horse. Once she was at the kidnapper's family home, a messenger would be sent to the parents, who would then send their oldest son and his wife, or oldest daughter and her husband. Across the steppe's nomad societies it had always been essential to marry someone who was not related along the paternal line for at least seven generations back.[3] Once it had been established that this was indeed the case and the girl had freely agreed to marry, then began the fierce negotiations for a kalym—a bride-price. This ordinarily involved livestock paid by the groom's family to the bride's, and it could be the cause of much contention, since an unpaid kalym was seen as grounds to wage reprisals including the use of barimta. Only once partial payment of the bride-price had been made did the groom have the right to begin discreet visits to the bride. From the bride's family a dowry was also expected, but this was negotiated later and usually paid in the form of a yurt.

These rituals had been a mainstay of nomadic society, but in the late 1920s and 1930s, as Kazakhs were collectivized, the paying of a bride-price had been specifically outlawed and used as a pretext to accuse families of being kulaks or *bai*—wealthy peasants who hoarded wealth rather than hand it over to the authorities. Regardless of whether a bride-price had been negotiated or not, in some cases merely having a married daughter had been enough evidence in itself to brand a family as an "enemy of the state," with the men sent to prison, their children denied schooling, and animals confiscated. As a result, ceremonies for betrothal and marriage in the aul went underground or were canceled altogether.

This was, needless to say, not the case today in Tasaral.

At eleven that evening the plan swung into action. Along with twenty or thirty of Shashibek's relatives and friends, I hid in another room as the girl entered the home. We gave her time to talk with Shashibek before breaking out and forming a huddle around them. It wasn't long before it was intimated that she had accepted Shashibek's proposal, and a woman stepped forward to place a white scarf on her head—a symbol that she had been embraced as part of the family. Then came a stampede as fistfuls of confectionery were showered on the couple and everyone fought for a turn to shake their hands. The old women were the most frenetic, fighting their way to the front amidst both tears and laughter. Children, meanwhile, raced to pocket chocolates and other sweets that had fallen to the floor.

I was nearly run down by the rush of people, and by the time I had collected myself, they had moved into another room, where the bride-to-be, a pretty girl who looked no older than eighteen or nineteen, was sitting with Shashibek on a *shumudrak*, a special settee-cum-bed adorned with curtains. As the realization of what was transpiring hit her, she alternated between tucking her hair behind her ears and drawing her hand over her mouth. Had she been expecting this? Did she love Shashibek? It was hard to tell, and I didn't get to ask her. Later in my journey, in southern Kazakh-stan, I had the opportunity to speak with two young newly wedded women who had become betrothed through the process of kidnapping. Both of them had hardly known their husbands, and one of them had been taken 300 km by car to the groom's herding station before her parents were informed. They explained that they had had the right to say no but had willingly agreed, and they maintained they lived happy married lives. If they later decided to leave, they had a right to separate, known as *kizdi alip kashu*.

Back in Tasaral, the intensity of celebration ascended with each step of the ritual, and when the signal was given, the bride-to-be stood up and led the crowd to the entrance of the house, where a special collection of twigs called a *baiyalish* was set alight. Cheering went up as she poured oil onto the leaping flames in a custom meant to bring warmth and luck into the home. Back inside, vodka bottles were decapitated with a symphony of cracking seals.

Things toned down again when the girl's older sister and her husband arrived to negotiate with Shashibek's relatives. While most people were asked to leave the room, including Shashibek and his new fiancée, I was allowed to stay.

In modern Kazakhstan, kidnapping was said to be more theater and symbolic ceremony than anything else, of course—technically, bride kidnapping was illegal—and when I later told the stories about what had transpired in Tasaral and other places to city Kazakhs in Almaty, they looked at me angrily. "You are wrong! We live in a civilized Kazakhstan now! That does not exist!"

Yet, based on the dark, angry look of the bride's brother-in-law and the uncontrolled sobbing of her sister, the wife steal was clearly anything but a staged event. Each person present said his or her piece gravely, followed by a toast. The emotions on display by the bride's family were apparently to be interpreted not as a disagreement, but as the grief of a family preparing to let go. Although I wasn't privy to the details since they spoke in Kazakh, a kalym was agreed upon, and planning for the wedding got under way—a celebration that, if it resembled even remotely what I had witnessed in Tansyk, promised to be of epic scale, lasting a full three days.

During the planning I was invited to give a toast of my own, and it dawned on me that I was being treated like an honored guest that they had long planned to be part of the events. Perhaps the theater of the kidnap was no less real than the role-playing of my journey—at some point it became much more than symbolic homage to ancient convention or nostalgic cravings for the past.

Indeed, that night as the vodka hit like a tremor from the gut, the actual and the acted, history and the present, seem to marry into one. The nomad life might have gone, but an opportunity to forge identity anew had been born. Customs carried through from history might have been juxtaposed in the chaos of modern times but were still every bit authentic.

11

THE STARVING STEPPE

UNBEKNOWN TO SHASHIBEK, his wife-to-be, and the other revelers who had partied into the early hours, a stealthy freeze had moved in under the cover of darkness. As I rode out at dawn, the ground underfoot felt as hard and cold as steel, and a sprinkling of snow, light as dust, brought a dull glow to the steppe. It was a promising development, given that in just 100 km I planned to turn west into the Betpak Dala, the "starving steppe," where I would need to rely on snow for hydration.

For the first day out of Tasaral the temperature hovered around −25°C. A headwind whipped up a pall of serrating snow. To meet the shift in conditions required yet another adjustment of my gear and riding routines. I pulled on all but my thickest down jacket and donned a balaclava and a pair of crude ski goggles I had picked up in a market. Even with thick mittens, my fingers quickly grew numb when gripping the rein, and so I held the reins one handed, alternating hands every few minutes. Fortunately, I had grown accustomed to the lead rope from the packhorses being threaded through a carabiner on my saddle, over my right leg, and under my butt, enabling me to ride with one hand free. Tigon delighted in chasing foxes and hares, but when he stopped his paws swiftly became painfully cold.

For three days we traveled south from Tasaral, settling into our new winterized routine. Just as I rode through an ever-changing terrain of hills and salt pans, so did my emotions go through highs and lows. When in the saddle and moving forward, I felt like I was floating, gunning toward the empty horizon as if in a dream, but when one or another of the saddles loosened and needed time-consuming refitting, frustration set in. Aset's saddle was still a constant hassle, and its narrow gullet had begun to irritate Taskonir's wither.

At night the tent offered more psychological warmth than real heat, and in the mornings the journey felt like a game of survival. To utilize daylight meant working by flashlight for two or three hours before the sun brought relief. The inner tent would be laden with hoarfrost, and ordinarily simple tasks such as pulling stakes and tent pegs out of the frozen earth became epic.

It was one of these mornings, as I lay in the cocoon of my sleeping bag, that I made a phone call to Kathrin in Germany. She was working eighteen-hour days in her teaching job and was boarding in the basement of a home near the city of Karlsruhe. I caught her, she told me, as she was stepping out of the shower. I imagined her standing there in a towel with her wet hair, and it reminded me of the cozy ritual of drying off and slipping into fresh clothing. She felt very far away.

It was about this time that a vision of the end of my journey crept into my mind, where it lingered for many months. When it was all over in Hungary, I imagined, I would pack Kathrin's little Opel station wagon with my green boxes and saddles. I could see myself closing the trunk, climbing into the passenger seat, and taking a deep breath. Then we would drive out, first into Austria and then Germany, and only with the steppe far behind would stories about my journey begin to trickle out.

The irony of contact with Kathrin, as with others in the outside world, was that while having the satellite phone was a luxury, even a godsend, it sometimes made the feeling of being alone and remote more acute. At the same time the phone could all too easily become a crutch—allowing me to vent and share feelings in moments of challenge that I would have otherwise had to overcome alone.

ON THE THIRD day from Tasaral I was faced with a dilemma. I had reached the westernmost point of Lake Balkhash, from where I planned to head west into the steppe, but a 40 cm rip had appeared in my tent. The fabric was so threadbare that if a storm came, the winds would probably tear it apart. It was foolish to go on until I had fixed it, but sewing the fragile material would be possible only if I could first patch it with gaffer tape—but that kind of tape wouldn't adhere in the extreme cold.

Erring on the side of caution, I headed into the raz'ezd of Kashkanteniz. It was the first time I had approached people on the railway since the attempted horse theft, and although this was a different line—the Almaty-to-Astana railway—my earlier dark impressions of its culture were reaffirmed. I moved from house to house looking for a place to stay but was met with glaring looks of aggression. Most of the workers kept stores of reeds and some hay but refused to sell even when offered a high price.

"No one knows how long winter will be. If I give you one bale, where will I get another?" a woman yelled.

By the time darkness fell, it was too late to ride out into the steppe, and I was hypothermic. A young railway worker let me inside his shack, which lay a stone's throw from the rail tracks. He convinced a family to take my horses in—for which I paid $30—and I stayed up late fixing the tent. But then all night I lay awake with asthma triggered by cigarette smoke, listening to trains bearing down on us, shaking the mud-brick walls as they passed. Tigon was an unwelcome guest and had to fend for himself—I hoped he had found a warm hayloft somewhere.

In the darkness of the next morning, while I was preparing the horses, Taskonir took a bite out of my hand. When I pulled back my gloves, the skin between the first and second knuckles came off like a sheath, leaving a raw, bloody ring. I stared back at Taskonir in bewilderment, struggling not to cry.

It was −28°C as I caught my last glimpses of Lake Balkhash and left the raz'ezd. The lake's blue waters were long gone. The ice had turned black, strangled in a web of frost. A week ago it might have been sad to say good-bye to this friend of mine, whose moods I had ridden out for more than a month, but now I felt no remorse.

From here to the west stretched the Betpak Dala. It was an immense swath of steppe stretching from Lake Balkhash toward the sands near the Aral Sea and as far south as the Chu River. Renowned as a desert of ex-tremes, with little water, it was empty even by Kazakh standards—a re-minder of the origin of its name, the "starving steppe." My aim was to trek 220 km as the crow flew across its southeast corner to a village on the Chu called Ulanbel. This probably equated to 300 km or more by horse.

Even as I set the compass west and climbed up a snow-encrusted slope, I could feel the cold and remoteness ratchet up the stakes. As if the earth had run out of breath, the wind died, and in the intense stillness, spar-kling ice crystals fluttered to ground like dead butterflies snapped frozen in flight. Ice rings formed around the horse's nostrils and clouds of frozen breath blew back onto their necks and flanks, spraying them white. The few pieces of hair that dangled out from my balaclava turned into icicles, and with every inhaled breath my nose hairs became needles. Even my eyelashes gathered frost, fusing together until I pried them apart and put on the goggles.

Soon there were no sounds, no trails, no people. Over the sea of pearly white, awash with frozen troughs and crests, I watched the sun creep into the empty sky, a pale, sickly yolk. In fact, I felt, it wasn't the sun at all, but earth, Australia perhaps. I was riding on an icy planet, drifting far away, flung out of orbit.

Later, as the sun dipped away, there came a phenomenon I had never seen. The sun squeezed vertically into an elliptical shape from which rose a golden column far into the sky. I could only assume that it was related to the particles of ice in the air.

There was much to think and digest, but little time for my mind to drift. One slip could mean trouble. My greatest fear had long been that one of the horses would lose its balance, sending me falling off, and that I would break a leg and be abandoned by the horses. Since there were no longer any functioning studs on my horses' shoes, this now seemed like a distinct possibility. As a precaution, I carried hot tea, my satellite phone, and a down jacket in my backpack, but when Ogonyok fell to his knees on an icy salt pan, I decided it was safer to get off and walk.

I carried on until sunlight had nearly vanished, then raced to make camp. The cold fell hard, and after unloading, my first priority was Tigon, who was whimpering inconsolably. I wrapped him in a spare horse blanket and zipped him inside my canvas duffle bag. Later, when the tent was up, I opened the bag a little way and dangled a piece of salted pig fat over it. Tigon's jaws swiftly snapped up the offering, after which he didn't stir until dinner was on the boil, at which point the bag began hopping toward the stove.

While I set up camp, a process that included driving in stakes, tying tethers, and barricading the side of my tent with the plastic boxes, it was vital to have the horses secured. To prevent them from eating snow initially—it was crucial to let the horses cool down before rehydrating—and stop them from running away, I had devised a system where I would make a rein from their lead ropes, then tie this to their saddles so that they couldn't dip their heads. The horses would then be tied alongside each other lengthways, facing in opposite directions, so that for them to wander off would involve near impossible coordination. Over the last couple of weeks I had noticed that after two hours of standing like this, their grumpy and impatient mood transformed into one of calm and composure. They had learned that this was an opportunity to rest and that patience was rewarded with a serving of grain.

When dinner was nearly ready I untied them and took off their saddles. Their bodies were as still as statues encrusted in ice, but under the blankets their backs were warm and dry. It had become routine when my hands were numb to place them under the saddle until they came back to life. As Aset had advised, I left the bottom blanket on this night, and folded it out so it covered the horses from wither to rump. This wasn't to warm them but to reduce the shock as their backs, heated and sweaty, were exposed to the cold.

The tasks at camp were unending, and with everything that needed to be done—packing tomorrow's lunch, eating half of the stodgy pot of canned meat and pasta (the other half was Tigon's) before it froze to the bottom, checking the maps, and marking my camp with GPS—there was little time to sit and absorb. One luxurious exception was feeding the horses. The mere rustle of a grain bag brought whickering from all three as they raced to the end of their tethers. This was the only moment of the day that lent itself to some affection, and although I spent twenty-four hours with my animals, it was also my only opportunity to truly acknowledge them. In the darkness I could tell them individually by smell and feel. I rubbed their necks and felt through their manes, under their hairy chins, and along their wooly bellies. Part of the routine involved lifting the blanket and feeling around for any problems. Apart from the sensitive spot on Taskonir's withers, their backs were clean.

By the time I finished feeding the horses, my feet were numb. I leaped inside the tent, where Tigon had been warming my sleeping bag, and took off my boots. To prevent moisture being absorbed and freezing in them, I wore large plastic bags over my outer socks, and a smaller bag between them and my thermal socks. As I took the bags off and shook them out, the pooled sweat instantly turned to ice. It took an hour for my feet to warm up in the sleeping bag. Tigon was covered in frost even though we were inside the tent. I tried running my hand down his bony spine, but he growled. Although I had grown to lean on him emotionally, I had hardly had a chance to show him much warmth. I felt guilty—how could I have alienated the one little creature who had stuck loyally with me through the tumults of the last eight weeks?

Before I pulled the drawstring of my sleeping bag tight I doused his paws in vodka—a technique to help prevent frostbite—and let him snuggle inside my down jacket. As he drifted off to sleep I had little doubt that he was thinking, *Well, thank God Tim is protecting me from the wolves.* I too was convinced I was safe in his hands, so we were at least able to get some sleep.

It seemed nonetheless as though I had barely slept when I woke at six o'clock, three hours before sunrise and at the peak of the cold. My body remained tense, and as I felt around my sleeping bag I realized my sweat had formed frozen clumps in the down. This was bad news, since down loses its insulating quality when wet. Once up, I shivered into my jacket and stepped out to check on the horses. Almost at once my feet turned to stone, and I spent the next twenty minutes jogging around the tent.

The horses, by comparison, didn't seem to be suffering—and for good reason. Descendants of horses that had survived natural selection over thousands of years, they were equipped with a physiology uniquely adapted to the extremes of the steppe. For example, their bodies had the ability to cut off the blood supply to their hooves in extreme cold to conserve heat. Their hairs, lifted slightly away from the body by special muscles under the skin, also gave them the ability to regulate heat loss. Later, in the Ukraine and Russia, where people had a more Western approach to horses, I was told that leaving horses in the open without winter blankets, as nomads did, was unimaginably cruel. I came to think that this view was based on one of several misconceptions that many Westerners hold in relation to the natural horse and therefore the culture of horsemanship on the steppe. Horses in Europe, after all, are blanketed largely to prevent the horse from growing a long winter coat, which is considered unsightly. And if a horse has been blanketed from a young age, the muscles under the skin that control the movement of the hair and thus regulate heat are not able to develop. The horses are therefore unable to keep themselves warm, the need for blankets being a human-induced one. Indigenous to the steppes, my horses had never known blankets, let alone stables, so there was nothing more natural than for them to be standing in the open.

Ahead of me like every morning lay the laborious task of brushing the horses, folding the blankets, saddling, cooking, and packing, a sequence rarely completed in less than three hours. Sliding my hands into textured rubber mitts and brushing the horses was not my favorite chore, but not to brush was sacrilege, since removing sweat, dust, and other matter was crucial for preventing saddle sores.

Getting everything done was a race against sunrise and required all my concentration. That morning, when I tied the last knot in Ogonyok's load, my feet were still numb and my balaclava an ice mask. Although my ther-mometer had broken, I later learned that a couple of days' journey to the north, the temperature had been below −40°C.

Before climbing into the saddle I unfolded the map and pulled my GPS out to double-check the bearing toward Ulanbel. The GPS refused to turn on. Then, when finally the screen flickered to life, none of the saved coor-dinates were there. The screen flickered a little more, then went blank. Until now the GPS hadn't been of great use, but in such a featureless envi-ronment, with the prospect of blizzards and a map with a scale of 1:500,000 that had been made for airline pilots, the prospect of relying exclusively on a compass was worrying.[1]

I tried to stay calm, but the predicament was undeniable. It was the twenty-third of December, just a couple of days beyond the solstice, which usually marked the beginning of the coldest period of winter. Ahead of me lay the loneliest section of my journey to date, and I had to get through it with a fragile tent, a frozen sleeping bag, a dodgy pack saddle, numb feet, and a damaged GPS.

No matter how positive I tried to be, the odds seemed to have closed in. The situation also made me think of a different milestone, which I had dismissed until now as unimportant. From the age of eighteen I had spent most Christmases abroad and never paid much attention to the holiday's significance—and, in truth, had come to think of Christmas as a hollow, commercialized convention best avoided. Now, however, I realized that in my juvenility I had missed the point: Christmas was about relishing the company of loved ones. The thought of being alone and freezing on the "starving steppe" on a day when my family was celebrating together was too much.

I opened up all my maps to see if there was anything remotely closer than Ulanbel. On my large tour map of Kazakhstan there was one dot on the "starving steppe," marked "Akbakai." Although it wasn't on my more detailed chart, there were some roads that converged on the same approximate area, which was about 75 km to the west. These road markings often represented nothing more than faded wheel tracks, and the absence of any marked aul made me think that perhaps Akbakai was an abandoned military base. Then again, it was my only hope. If I was good enough, I could cover the distance in two days and arrive on Christmas Eve.

It was a relief to get moving. Hooves squeaked and snow exploded in plumes. The sky was clear and the air eerily calm, with the snow cover little more than fetlock deep. We moved up the salt pan valley as it narrowed and rose through uplands. My aim was to follow it to a plateau, then beyond to a cluster of hills and small mountains where I hoped to find Akbakai.

Higher up, the valley split into a maze of shallow ravines choked with ak-shi, and in places dotted with thickets of a stumpy steppe tree known as *saksaul*. The danger of wolves began to prey on my mind. Midwinter was their breeding season—the time when they were apparently at their hungriest and the males hunted in packs. I had been promised by Kazakh herders that wolves would follow me unseen, possibly for days, before choosing their moment to attack. It was commonly said that a pack could take down a full-grown horse or camel. Stories about attacks on humans were also abundant—there was "a lady in the next aul who last year was killed," or "the boy who went to herd his sheep and never came home." One of the most common wolf stories was of an attack on a woman and her daughter who had been waiting at a bus stop on a lonely road in winter. The woman had saved her daughter by lifting her onto the roof of the bus stop. All that was found of the mother were her *valenki*, still filled with the lower part of her legs. The story bears a striking resemblance to one recounted by German explorer Albert von Le Coq, who, in the early twentieth century, was told a story about a girl who had run away from her older husband into the steppe of western China, and "all that was found later were blood-stained fragments of her clothing and her long top-boots with her legs still inside."[2]

I later met a Kazakh journalist who had spent months researching stories of wolf attacks on humans. After following hundreds of leads, he had been unable to find firm evidence that any had actually happened. It was always "another aul," "another time," and there was no official record of anyone having been eaten by wolves. Whatever the truth, all I had right now were the stories, and in the face of this cold and empty land my earlier skepticism seemed foolhardy.

Just after lunch, when the pale sun was limping toward the horizon, I found myself in the shadowy crevice of a gorge. Ogonyok's load had come loose, and I leaped off to reload, paranoid about an ambush by wolves. I felt like I was testing my luck to be riding out here alone, and I knew deep down that I shouldn't have been on the "starving steppe" in winter—the nomads who traditionally might have lived here in spring or summer would have long retreated to warmer, low-lying areas.

We continued on, and by early afternoon the horses had gathered more sweat-frost than I had ever seen. I was thankful I'd trained them to ride with a halter and rope rein instead of with a bridle and bit. Bitless riding, part of a modern trend of "natural horsemanship" in the Western world, had once been practiced widely on the steppe. Genghis Khan forbade the use of bits while armies were on the move. Not only was it beneficial because of the damage a cold bit could do to a horse's mouth, but the horses could eat and drink freely whenever there was an opportunity. This approach is voiced by the Kazakh saying "Only in an emergency should a young *dzhigit* [warrior] enter the water in his boots, or should a horse be allowed to drink in its bridle."

It was essential to cover at least half the distance to Akbakai if I was to make it by Christmas Eve, but in my rush I took several wrong turns up narrow, winding ravines and had to backtrack to the main valley. Feeling rushed, I pushed beyond nightfall under moonlight, willing the horses into a trot.

Tigon was soon exhausted. At one stage when I halted to check the map, he must have curled up under a grass tussock in the snow, thinking we had stopped for camp. I continued on without realizing he had been left behind—that is, until I heard a desperate whimper ring out through the frozen night air. He was sprinting to catch up.

By the time I made camp the temperature had fallen further and the snow glowed an ethereal blue. I struggled to hammer the tent pegs in, and when I inserted the tent poles they broke through the fabric sleeves.

My camping stove refused to ignite, and I spent half an hour pulling it apart and cleaning it—a task involving bare fingers.

There was a voice inside my head reminding me that as long as I took care and didn't rush or pin my hopes on Akbakai, then everything would be okay. Stupid decisions such as this—making camp long after dark and trotting blindly over snowy terrain—could prove disastrous. Yet I couldn't break my growing obsession with finding company for Christmas Day. Akbakai, I fantasized, would be an aul where the akim would welcome me in and I would take refuge in the embrace of a family. I imagined sitting around a table telling stories about my travels, in the security of a warm home bathed with the golden light of a fireplace.

I slept lightly, afraid that at any moment a storm would roll in from the mountains and knock down my damaged tent, or, worse, that I would wake to find the horses under attack by wolves.

At dawn we set off at a trot and rose to a plateau where the fragile calm was broken by raking winds. A great, hazy, white emptiness flowed down from all sides. There were no features, shadows, or depth to give any scale at all—the world had been distilled to pale blue, white, and the rumble of wind. Destinations and landmarks didn't seem to exist, the geography more a landscape of changing moods. Usually this emptiness instilled a sense of freedom, but now it brought dread. I tried to be conservative and plan for the event that Akbakai either didn't exist or was abandoned. Even if it was somewhere out there, my compass bearing had to be only marginally off target and I could pass it without knowing.

It was just as the sun was gliding into my line of vision that I caught sight of something through my monocular that gave me hope—a tower. The horses were tired, struggling to lift their hooves through the snow. I egged them on with the promise of hay and shelter.

For the next two hours there were times when I was sure Akbakai was just a derelict ghost town, then others when I thought I could see a tendril of smoke. I could make out strange buildings unlike any I had seen in farming auls, which made me think it might be, as I had suspected, an abandoned Soviet military base.

When Ogonyok's load came loose after dark, I lost my cool and let out a string of curses. The voice of common sense was still there and told me to stop rushing, but the intoxicating vision of hot tea and company possessed me.

I BEGAN TO stir from my stupor as we limped through some twisted scrap metal on the deserted outskirts. I was stiff as wood. The horses hung their heads in fatigue. As wind filled my ears, Tigon's whimpering rose in pitch. We had made it to Akbakai, but I'd forgotten that no one was waiting for us.

12

THE PLACE THAT GOD FORGOT

THE ONLY SIGN of life I could find on the edge of Akbakai in the failing light of Christmas Eve was the shadowy figure of a man hunched over a pile of firewood. Maksim, as he was known, suspected that I was a lost Russian geologist at best, and at worst an escaped prisoner on the run. After much pleading, he reluctantly led me to a half-built mud-brick shack. I tied the horses in the windowless end of the structure, then, together with Tigon, climbed into a small adjoining room. Inside, the flickering of a coal stove offered a fragmented picture of two old spring beds, mattresses, and cardboard-matted floor. Vitka and Grisha, the Russian laborers living here, were too inebriated to speak, but details didn't matter. I was out of the wind, I was warm, and I was not alone.

Christmas morning brought a more sobering reality. Wakened by a couple of puppies licking my face, I pried my eyes open to a panorama of dog shit, piles of empty vodka bottles, and a frying pan filled with ossified potato sediment and congealed fat. Lying under a pile of rags on the other bed, Vitka and Grisha were dead to the world but alive with the stench of body odor, tobacco, and alcohol. They were truck drivers from southern Kazakhstan who had been stranded in Akbakai since being caught drunk at the wheel and losing their licenses two years earlier.

Eventually they were stirred by their own snoring, and when they learned who I was, they cried: "Australian! We understand that today is your Christmas. By all means we will have a celebration tonight. A treat!"

When it was light enough I left the hut to search for hay and grain. Akbakai was not the herding community I had hoped for. The streets were littered with frozen clumps of rubbish, and lined with rubble and mangled machinery wreckage. Homes were a medley of mud-brick houses barricaded with tall fences. Some appeared to be semi-underground. There were few signs of animal shelters, and I only had to look to the edge of town to know why.

To the west and south heavy trucks labored through dirty, blackened snow. Beyond them the trapezoid shape of mine shaft headframes cast eerie silhouettes against the sky. Akbakai was a gold-mining town, and the livability of the environment had been an afterthought. Built on a range of rocky hills, the town had no natural water supplies, nor was water provided by the government. The handful of people who kept a milking cow were fiercely protective of fodder and water—both were precious resources shipped in from far away.

After hours of fruitless searching, I pried some concessions out of the local hunting inspector. He let me climb up his ice-encrusted water tank to fill pails for my horses, and agreed to sell me hay to last twenty-four hours—but no more than that.

I returned to the mud hut in the evening hungry and stiff as wood. Grisha and Vitka were rolling drunk. They had caught a couple of street pigeons earlier that day and had boiled them up for dinner.

"Everything will be fine! Sit down, lie back, have a vodka, a cup of tea, we will find you a wife . . . and you can use your horses as a bride-price!" they chanted.

I capitulated—on account of the vodka, that is—then watched as Grisha and Vitka argued, stumbled, and fought into the early hours. Both had dirt-ingrained skin, rotten yellow teeth, and untamed mustaches that grew animated by the candlelight of the hut. When they tired, they fell together onto a single bed and told of their tragic personal histories. Grisha's wife was as "honest as they come"—a quality proven by the fact that when she "butchered a man with a carving knife," she stayed with her victim and called the police. She was due for release from prison in five years. Vitka, on the other hand, had been deeply affected by the death of his only son, who had been hit by a car at age twelve. His daughter had run away to Russia and cut all ties.

To survive in Akbakai—a town they described to me as "the place that God forgot"—Vitka and Grisha worked odd laboring jobs, including felling saksaul trees on the steppe to sell as firewood.[1] The money they earned was spent on vodka.

When Vitka and Grisha passed out I lay awake listening to the wind, unable to sleep. On the far side of the wall behind me the horses had finished their hay and were standing hungry. When finally the vodka swept me under, I clung to fleeting visions of home and being close to my siblings, mother, and father.

I HAD URGED the horses on to Akbakai determined to find refuge with a family and a barn full of hay, but come the early hours of December 26—Boxing Day—that vision was in tatters. But things were about to get a lot more difficult.

My plan had been to stay two or three days in Akbakai, but when I woke to pack, Taskonir was holding his back left leg in the air. It was an abscess in his hoof—most likely the result of a stone bruise suffered during our rushed ride to Akbakai. He could barely walk, and the Australian vet, Sheila, warned via satellite phone that it would be many days before I could expect it to heal. The nearest village west from Akbakai, Ulanbel, was another five days across uninhabited steppe. Carrying on was not an option, yet with no feed for the horses and a precarious refuge with Vitka and Grisha, it was hard to see how I could cope here for any length of time.

I knew that the next few days were going to be tricky. What I could never have imagined, however, was that the abscess was to be the first of many hold-ups and failed attempts at leaving Akbakai. It would, in fact, be three and a half months before I was able to ride out of there, and while my personal struggle was uppermost in my mind at the beginning of my stay—and became a low point of my journey to Hungary—what emerged over time was that my troubles were merely reflective of circumstances in town immeasurably more difficult than my own. Through the many people I met—both those who helped me and those who hindered me—I came to see a dismal picture of social dislocation, survival, and corruption in this remote gold-mining society in the middle of the "starving steppe."

For two days I scrounged for fodder and water, to little avail. Neither the town's administrator or anyone else I met would so much as invite me past the front door for a cup of tea. When I approached Maksim—who was the owner of the mud hut where Vitka and Grisha lodged—for help, he retorted angrily, "What makes you think anyone should help you! You are better off selling your horses for meat before they are too skinny!" Traditions of nomad hospitality found in auls didn't widely function in Akbakai—most people simply didn't have the means.

Like many others, Maksim had come here lured by the promise of work but found himself unemployed and stranded far from his hometown. He lived in a derelict apartment block where he had rigged up a woodstove in a room on the third floor. To support his wife and two children, he had turned the basement of the building into a makeshift workshop where he made furniture to order out of scrap wood. Without a network of relatives or friends, it was hard to imagine what fallback he had if this venture failed.

This kind of scenario was unusual in the herding-based auls of modern Kazakhstan and would have been unthinkable for nomads in pre-Soviet times. A tradition called ata-balasy, which means "the joining of grandfather's sons into one tribe or family," was the bedrock of nomadic existence, and in many communities it is still only by banding together in wide circles of kin that it is possible to overcome the chaos of post-Soviet Kazakhstan and support those fallen on hard times.

Maksim's predicament was symptomatic of the widespread Soviet policy to develop entire towns and cities around a single industry or, in Akbakai's case, mineral resource. These monogorods, or "monocities," emerged largely in isolated environs that were unsuitable for agriculture, and drew on migrant workers from across the country. For Kazakhs, monogorods subsequently created even greater displacement from traditional lands and breakdown of traditional kinship structures than did farming collectives.

During the Soviet era, state-funded social welfare became the backbone of monogorods, substituting for the traditional safety net of family—but this also made them particularly vulnerable to the economic collapse of the 1990s. The failure of the state-run companies that held monopolies in these one-industry towns caused mass unemployment, and residents had neither an alternative economy to turn to nor a network of kin for support.

Three days after Christmas, Taskonir's leg was worse, the wind had picked up to gale force, and clouds were marching in from the north and east. Come what may, though, I had decided that anything was better than staying in Akbakai. After saddling up, I went inside the mud hut to say goodbye to Vitka and Grisha. They were sad to see me go and worried what would become of me. It was in the throes of this farewell that my fortunes changed.

Stumbling into our hovel came a short, squat man wearing thick, crooked glasses that magnified his eyes and pinched his red nose. I took the opportunity to slump back silently in the darkness and study him. From the weathered texture of his face I would have guessed he was in his sixties, but I knew in this harsh environment it probably meant he was a good ten years younger. His voice was deep and husky, and as he spoke, his defrosting mustache wiggled.

Curiosity eventually got the better of him. "Who is he?" he asked, pointing at me.

"We have a guest from Australia," Grisha related. "He came here to us by horse . . . from Mongolia."

The man stepped back, straightened his glasses, then leaned forward into the narrow shaft of light in front of the window. "Come to my home!" he exclaimed. "Why freeze here? I'll give you a sack of wheat to help you on your way!"

As I left the hut to take the horses to the man's home, Grisha and Vitka were excited for me. According to them, Baitak was a "millionaire" and a "king." I would surely be safe in his hands. Viewed later on with the benefit of a full stomach and grain for the horses, however, their description seemed like a bit of an exaggeration. His house was an underground one-room hut surrounded by a fence made of flattened drums that had once held sodium cyanide. He didn't own a car, had no washing facilities, and the toilet was a long drop full to the brim with frozen shit and just a tarpaulin to protect one from the elements. His water supplies were trucked in, like everyone else's, and the much talked-about cafe and bar he owned was a coal-heated hut that was within shouting distance of his house and backed onto a mountain of rubble.

At the time, though, to me everything about Baitak's empire shone. My first meal with him was a memorable example—I was presented with a series of fried eggs, and each time I chased the yellow from the plate, it would be replaced with another. Tigon ate buckets of stale bread and milk, until his little belly bulged out to twice its normal size and he sprawled out royally on the floor.

The true meaning of Baitak's wealth became clear over the weeks and months to come as my well-being and that of my animals came to gravitate around him. As one of the most established people in town—he had been in Akbakai since 1976, when mining operations were in their infancy—he had unique authority and knowledge. Above all, though, I think Baitak's status as a "king" was a measure of his generous heart, for certainly that is what would ultimately save my life, and those of Tigon and my horses.

After our meal, Baitak inspected Taskonir and shook his head. He knew I was in trouble, but he also knew what to do. He co-owned a fledgling kstau 6 km out of town—the only of its kind anywhere near Akbakai—where cattle were kept. "You can ride there and stay until your horse heals and the weather improves. Tell the herder there, Madagol, that he can feed your horses with my hay."

There were times in my journey when I felt like I was a captain, firmly in command, and steering my caravan on a course of my choosing. There were other times, however, when I simply had to let go of the reins and accept that the journey—or, in this case, Baitak—would guide me.

To REACH THE kstau, which was hidden in a valley between two knobby ridges, took two hours, by which time Taskonir was reluctant to move at all. In the midst of a windstorm I was greeted by Madagol—a gruff, wiry old fellow with tightly coiled graying hair and heavy, callused hands. He invited me in with a fusillade of curses regarding the weather.

"Wind is the worst thing in Akbakai! When it blows on the third day, you know it will blow for seven, and when it blows on the eighth day, it will blow for fourteen . . . after that it will blow for a month. It's not like that where we come from!"

Madagol was from Moiynkum—a regional center 250 km south of Akbakai—and had come with his wife to work as a chaban. Their new home was a shabbily constructed hut with such thin brick walls that despite a coal stove that burned 24/7 it was still below freezing indoors. When I entered I removed my coat and hat, but hurriedly I put them back on. Curled up on a bed under a mountain of blankets, Madagol's wife sat looking frail and utterly miserable.

Later I came to appreciate how terribly isolating it must have been for Madagol's wife. Although the town was not far away, few braved the weather to visit in winter. The main contact she enjoyed with the outside world was when Madagol rode a horse into town to sell milk and buy bread every second or third day. When the blizzards set in, there were some periods when they were completely cut off.

For me, the shortcomings of the hut were nevertheless a mere detail, and in fact the isolation was a godsend. The vet, Sheila, had suggested the abscess would pass within a week. All I had to do was sit tight.

It was, of course, wishful thinking to believe my journey was back on track.

After my first night in Madagol's hut, a man known as Abdrakhman—a friend of Baitak who owned shares in the kstau—came barreling down in his old Russian four-wheel-drive vehicle and hauled me back to Akbakai, exclaiming, "My daughter's birthday is tomorrow night. You will be an honored guest! We are chaining you to our home until the new year!"

Abdrakhman was a relative newcomer to Akbakai, and my presence was a drawing card for strengthening his network of friends. As the guest of honor, I was expected to raise a toast to the stream of guests visiting his home. In the coming days I fell into a whirlwind of feasts and drinking, culminating with a New Year's Eve dance in the snow to Kazakh, Russian, and Uzbek music, while Chinese firecrackers flew around like rockets, rebounding dangerously off the walls of the house. For me, as for the other revelers—including explosives experts, traders in contraband gold, and miners—it was a fleeting opportunity to forget about the realities of Akbakai.

The celebration was brought to an end by the onset of severe frost, and come New Year's morning there was a price to pay. I woke in a cold sweat and by afternoon was lapsing in and out of fever. Abdrakhman was exhausted and bedridden. He decided it was high time for me to leave.

In this way I once again found myself derailed and taking refuge with Baitak. He took me in without question and for three days insisted I sleep on the only bed in his home while he, his wife, and their son slept on the floor.

I intended to stay for one night, but as the flu took hold, this drew out to two weeks. In the beginning I was conscious of losing precious time, and concerned about how Madagol was coping with my horses and Tigon. At Baitak's insistence, though, I surrendered to the inevitable, and spent days lying disoriented while his wife, Rosa, fussed over me. As I lay there hour after hour, the underground hut felt like a ship berth. Far above there was the faint raking of wind. Only on rare excursions into the elements to relieve myself did I become aware the weather was closing in. A blizzard was gathering, and as the town battened down, visitors to Baitak's home dried up. Such was the isolating effect of the cold and snow that although Abdrakhman's house was only five minutes' walk away, as were Vitka and Grisha's hut and the lone apartment block, I never saw the alcoholics or Maksim ever again, and only met with Abdrakhman long after I had recovered. I could only begin to imagine what it was like for Madagol and his wife in the drafty hut at the kstau.

About a week into my sickness, Baitak too fell ill, and from that point on we lay side by side in our sickbeds, waited on by Rosa. We spent hours discussing politics, the contrasting realities of the Western world and Kazakhstan, all things nomad- and horse-related, and of course life in Akbakai. It was challenging to relate to Baitak and Rosa how I lived in Australia. Given that I had three horses and didn't appear to have a job, they assumed I was so comfortably rich that money was not an issue.

The reason for my journey was a topic on which Baitak and I could understand each other better. Baitak had grown up in the foothills of the Tien Shan Mountains near Almaty. He reminisced about how he and his friends used to catch the collective farm's horses from the herd and gallop bareback until they fell off. Although he no longer rode, he owned a herd of thirty horses that roamed the steppe around Akbakai. This was a source of great pride, and once every two weeks he set off by motorcycle to look for them. Later, when we had recovered from the flu, he pulled out two old saddles from a rusty trunk. "Not to have a saddle would mean becoming an orphan in my own land. Not to own horses would death," he said.

His respect for the nomad past and his understanding of my predicament delineated a significant difference between him and the majority in Akbakai who were severed from the land and more focused on trying to make money. Over time I decided that some of Baitak's wisdom must have been inherited from his father, who had been born in 1893, married a girl thirty-one years his junior, and survived the era of collectivization as a simple shepherd.

When Baitak and I finally were on the road to recovery, we regularly dined in his cafe. As breakfast, lunch, and dinner drifted into one another, it gave me a valuable opportunity to gather a broader picture of life in Akbakai.

Judging from the clientele, there were two types of locals. The first were pale, beaten-looking men who would arrive to eat and drink vodka after their grueling work in the mines. These were professional miners, some of whom were bused in from afar for fifteen-day shifts. Their work, by Western standards, was poorly paid and dangerous. Twelve people had apparently died in the mine shafts this year—a "very good" result, according to Baitak. Then there were those people, largely the permanent residents, who either had been established long before the Soviet era came crashing down or, like modern-day prospectors, had come seeking riches.

When I related my thoughts to Baitak, he described Akbakai residents somewhat differently. "There are two kinds of thieves in Akbakai: those aboveground, and those below."

It hadn't been obvious to me initially, but I came to see that there was an altogether "other" economy in Akbakai. Many of the "aboveground" thieves were workers in the processing plant who stole ore from the production line and sold it to locals to supplement their poor wages. It was standard practice for them to pay off their bosses and the security guards to get the material out of the plant. People who didn't work at the plant could also get ore and tailing debris by paying off security guards at night, and for this reason there was a raft of unemployed people from faraway regions who had come to try their luck.

Baitak pointed out that the real profits were being made not aboveground but by men who risked their lives below. Within the ranks of residents in Akbakai were a breed of men willing to rappel as far down as 400 m into disused shafts. According to Baitak, there were whole teams of skilled workers who put down the ropes and ladders and set up living quarters in the shafts. They had beds, kitchens, and even entire slaughtered cows down there, he said. Later on in the winter evidence of this came to light when twenty-eight illegal miners were discovered by police in a single shaft. One, it was said, fell to his death upon seeing the police near the exit.

Over the course of my stay I came to realize that almost everybody I met—except Madagol, Vitka, and Grisha—was involved in stealing ore and tailings in one way or another and processing it in crude backyard labs. I once walked in on Abdrakhman refining gold amalgam in a frying pan—a poisonous method involving the use of mercury, but one commonly used in most households in town. Abdrakhman was hoping to make a fortune before retiring to his hometown, Moiynkum. Several times in Madagol's cattle shelter I also encountered young men pulverizing ore in a metal tube and mixing it with sodium cyanide. It was part of what they called "secret business." At the end of the supply chain were traders who bought contraband gold for 1,000 tenge (about $8) per gram and then took it to Kyrgyzstan to sell on the black market.

Baitak estimated that 50 percent of the residents—most likely including himself—were actively involved in the contraband economy. Despite this, there was good reason to keep the activities hidden. Being caught by the police meant paying large bribes to avoid jail. The twenty-eight miners arrested that winter reportedly paid a collective $20,000 so that they could return to work. This made the post of police chief in Akbakai a very profitable one, and it was rumored that getting the job involved paying $10,000 to regional superiors for a two-to-three-year term.

As the scale of the operation and the complicity at every level dawned on me, I realized it was not possible to make an honest living in Akbakai and prosper. Perhaps, as might have been the case in other monogorods, the contraband economy was merely substituting for the breakdown of Soviet-era social security. At the very least, it was clear that unemployed and disadvantaged locals had little choice but to engage in this business and often had to take out loans at exorbitant rates to pay for bribes. Many of them were on the edge of survival, including one Russian family I came to know who could not feed themselves on their small share of the gold market and were forced to eat dogs to get by. They bred puppies exclusively for this purpose, eating them when they were still young, and leaving just one or two to mature from each litter.

The microcosm of corruption in Akbakai painted a bleak picture for Kazakhstan as a whole. Simple, everyday things such as getting a driver's license, a university degree, or even a seat on a train routinely involved paying a bribe. For those wanting a loan, the bank would approve the financing only if a cash-in-hand commission, known in Russian as an otkat—usually a percentage of the loan—was agreed upon. Everything, from securing a job to having enemies killed, was possible given the right price. A police officer in southern Kazakhstan later explained that in his

204 ON THE TRAIL OF GENGHIS KHAN

region, as long as you didn't kill someone within your own family, you could pay off the police to have them overlook it, or pay an extra fee and have the police do the murdering themselves.

All of these examples of corruption were trivial in the bigger picture of Kazakhstan, which was ranked by the International Monetary Fund in 2005, the year I was there, as one of the world's corruption hot spots, alongside Angola, Libya, Bolivia, Kenya, and Pakistan. Among Kazakhs it was widely known that the president, Nursultan Nazarbayev, and his extended family controlled all of the key sectors of government and the economy, including national security, taxation, the media, and the oil, sugar, alcohol, and entertainment industries. Less well known—since it was hushed up in the Kazakh media—was that Nazarbayev had made headlines around the world when he was implicated in a foreign bribery case involving American merchant banker James H. Giffen. Giffen, who worked on behalf of oil companies vying for access to the vast reserves on the Caspian Sea, was charged with channeling $78 million to Nazarbayev.[2] This was heralded as the largest bribery case in history against an American citizen.

Kazakhs were typically cynical when I brought this up. "Seventy-eight million?" one man told me. "That is just kopeks for Nazarbayev!"

Most Kazakhs I met nevertheless had a high opinion of the president and believed it was "those around him" who were "corrupt and conniving." Even then, Kazakhs who were disillusioned with Nazarbayev often commented: "At least Nazarbayev and his family have done all their stealing and are now giving back to the public. If we vote in a new president, then his family will spend the next ten years stealing for themselves before they start to help us!"

Politics and graft in Kazakhstan were beyond my comprehension and the scope of my journey. Baitak urged me not to even attempt to understand the system. He wanted me to focus on recovering from the flu and protecting my horses. "At this time of year the hunger begins, and one horse can provide food for a family for months. Every year, two or three horses will be stolen from my herd. This is normal. However I am afraid that your horses may be stolen and eaten as well."

During my illness, Madagol had run out of hay for my horses and had released them into the steppe. There was no other way for them to graze and have a chance at surviving the winter.

MOST OF MY stay in Akbakai was removed from any real experience of traditional steppe life. There were, however, some customs I was lucky to observe under the wing of Baitak.

After we both recovered from the flu, Baitak informed me there was a special occasion I needed to witness before leaving. It was *sogym*, the winter slaughter of animals—and not just any sogym, but the most sacred of all, the slaughter of a horse.[3]

On a relatively mild mid-January morning, Abdrakhman, Rosa, and others gathered at Madagol's hut armed with knives and axes. The horse in question was an eleven-year-old gelding that had been fattened on a diet of wheat, barley, and hay. "The fatter the horse, the better the *kazy*," explained Baitak. On many occasions I'd enjoyed kazy, the prized national Kazakh dish of horsemeat sausage made from the meat and yellowy fat that runs down from the spine along the ribs to the stomach. This meat and fat are cut into strips and stuffed into intestines with a mixture of garlic and salt before being boiled.

Specialists can tell at a glance whether a horse is "one finger," "two fingers" or "three fingers" fat for the purposes of kazy. I had become accustomed to Kazakhs routinely approaching me and prodding the ribs of my horses, specifically quantifying their fat. Ogonyok was always judged two or three fingers—a reminder that traveling with a fat horse through Kazakhstan was fraught with danger.

After the horse was led out of a corral, things swiftly got under way. At first the gelding's legs were bound together. When the horse lost balance and fell onto its side, the men hurried to roll it upside down.

Sensing my apprehension, Baitak talked me through it. "We have different horses for riding, racing, milk, and meat. But whatever the case, you won't find any horse dying of old age in Kazakhstan. It is sacrilege to let such precious meat go to waste—a single horse can keep a family alive for winter. More than that, to let a horse rot provides no dignity for the horse—it is like abandoning your animal, disowning it. And another thing, a horseman here will never slaughter his own favorite mount—it will be symbolically given or sold to someone else for the task. I could never imagine putting the knife to my own horse."

I stood back and watched the men heave the horse's head over a chopping block. Madagol cupped his hands in prayer. I focused on the horse.

At first the horse's eyes were wide. He labored to look back at the men who held him down. His nostrils flared, sending frozen breath shooting into the air. But then he stopped struggling and his eyes panned skyward.

Madagol cut back and forward with a long knife. I wanted to look away but felt cowardly. A gasping sound was followed by gurgling as a fountain of blood surged, filling a specially placed basin. Then it was all over. The unmoving head was flipped backward, hanging on by threads of skin and bone. Blood rushed back to my head and my heartbeat slowed. The men relaxed too, stepping in with knives and axes. The horse had gone.

Before long Madagol's wife brought a vodka bottle down to the men. Madagol drank first, followed by Baitak, then the others. Within a couple of hours the various cuts of meat were being sorted into hessian sacks. We sat around a table dining on kurdak, a traditional dish made of fried innards, including heart, liver, and kidneys.

Most of the horsemeat would be shared with people less fortunate than Baitak, including Madagol and Baitak's relations in the city. This was a nomad tradition known as sybaga, when the prosperous wing of a family shares the meat and milk from its herds with less successful kin. Sybaga also requires that the most respected and honored guests be given the best from the table.

At a visceral level, there was no denying I had disagreed with the horse slaughter. I'd grown to love my horses and could not imagine putting them to the knife. And yet as I sat chewing on freshly fried liver and watching the swelling happiness in the eyes of Baitak, Madagol, and others, I was overcome by the miracle of life on the steppe—that the morsels of grass the land offers can be turned into life-giving fat and muscle. Partaking of the flesh of the horse was a crucial part of the horse worship that had sustained nomads from the beginning of time. In full knowledge that their animals were traditionally the only link to survival, these people could appreciate the value of meat more than most of us could conceive of doing.

The celebration continued for two days, after which I prepared to leave. By this stage I had become so much a part of the family that the prospect of departure saddened me. Even Madagol, who seemed to have his reservations about me, had warmed somewhat. This was partly because I had let on that Australia had about half a million wild horses roaming in the outback. He had been dreaming of mustering a herd and bringing them home to sell for meat.

"That Indian Ocean, is it a shallow or deep lake?" he asked one night.

WHEN THE DAY came for my departure, Baitak was furiously opposed to my decision. Madagol, for his part, was angry that I would not cave in to his requests: "What do you need a dog for? Leave him here!" he demanded. Likewise he asked for my horses, ropes, clips and saddles.

Baitak's gripe with me was because Ulanbel, my next stop five days away, was a village renowned for its criminals. Moreover, this was precisely the time of year when wolves hunted in packs. He was afraid for my safety and concerned that I was rushing and being reckless.

It was nevertheless a relief to be alone again when I rode out from Madagol's kstau. I made good progress following little gullies and valleys, picking out features on the horizon and setting new bearings from there. By the time I made camp the mountains surrounding Akbakai were a blip on the horizon. But then came another blow. The seal on my fuel bottle split, and before I could begin cooking, the gas had all leaked out onto the snow. Furthermore, upon unsaddling I discovered that the sore spot on Taskonir's withers had once again swollen to the size it had been three weeks earlier. By morning a blizzard had come in, and the abscess in Taskonir's foot was back with a vengeance.

I packed up and turned back east, knowing it was the end of winter riding.

Upon my return to Akbakai I resolved to travel back to Oskemen, in eastern Kazakhstan, where I intended to pick up my second Canadian packsaddle—which had been mailed from Mongolia—and tackle visa registration issues before returning better prepared. Madagol was over the moon to receive advance pay to look after my horses, and Baitak was relieved to hear of my new plan. Within a couple of days I was on my way in a taxi, loaded up with 50 kg of raw horsemeat that I was to deliver to Baitak's relatives in Almaty before heading on to Oskemen.

I planned to be away from Akbakai for two weeks, but things became complicated. In Oskemen, where I was staying with Evegeniy Yurchenkov and his family (who had given me invaluable support on my arrival in Kazakhstan), I was summoned by the local immigration service for not registering my visa. They were aghast that I had traveled through so much territory—much of it close to sensitive border and military zones. I was either to be fined or deported, they decided (though this was eventually avoided with the help of a national TV correspondent who ran a story about me).

When I finally returned to Akbakai, toward the end of February, I found that winter had taken a heavy toll. The temperature there had stayed around −30°C for a month. It had, in fact, been one of the coldest winters in living memory, with a low of −52°C recorded near Oskemen, far to the northeast. In southern Kazakhstan there had been unusually high snowfall, and as Aset had predicted for times of zud, there were reports of horses that were practically naked after surviving the winter by eating their own hair.

Although I had arranged for wheat to be taxied out to Akbakai from the town of Chu, my horses had largely gone without fodder or shelter, fending for themselves on the steppe. Baitak and Madagol had lost track of the horses at one stage, and only after a week of searching discovered them in a gully sheltering from the wind. It wasn't long after this episode that Madagol had fallen off the roof of his animal shelter and snapped his leg in several places. His son had since taken over responsibility of the kstau. Madagol lay in traction in a hospital in Moiynkum.

Something I had already sensed from Oskemen was that the winter had not been kind to Tigon. One night I had been haunted by a dream in which Tigon was looking at me with big sad eyes. He was covered in grease and muck, trapped in a dark place, looking frightened. Upon my arrival Baitak and Rosa relayed the bad news. While on a visit with Madagol into town, Tigon had vanished for some time, and was feared eaten. One of the mines had gone bankrupt, and some of the hungry, unemployed workers were known to be hunting dogs. While Baitak searched for Tigon, his own pet dog had disappeared without trace. Eventually Baitak had heard a rumor that Tigon was being held by a Russian dog-eater named Petrovich.

"If that Australian's dog doesn't come back, I'll know it was you. Don't you dare eat him!" Baitak had told him. Seven days later Tigon had been found locked away in an old mining shed. He had been badly beaten and was covered in grease and muck.

"No one thought he would survive, so I arranged immediately for him to spend several hours in a sauna, then fed him raw eggs and vodka," Baitak told me. When I was reunited with Tigon he was all skin and bone and barely moving.

It took another three weeks before Tigon could walk, and during this time I was invited by CuChullaine O'Reilly of the Long Riders Guild to join what he described as an unprecedented international gathering of equestrian explorers in London. There I was to be made a fellow of the Royal Geographic Society.[4] Although I was initially opposed to the idea of going, I couldn't go back out on the steppe while Tigon was still sick, and my great-uncle and -aunt, John and Alison Kearney, offered financial support to buy tickets. I decided it was an opportunity I shouldn't refuse, particularly because I would have the chance to see Kathrin for a couple of days.

So I was more removed from my journey than ever by the time I arrived back in Akbakai at the end of March. What had begun as a two-day stopover for Christmas had become more than three months, and with the misery of midwinter fresh in my mind, I doubted I could pull through to Hungary. Even if I could, I wondered whether I would ever find a trace of the nomad spirit again.

Baitak, however—to whom, in hindsight, I owe my life, or at the very least the lives of Tigon and my horses—says he never once doubted that I would make it to Hungary.

13

OTAMAL

BY THE END of March, as the days began to draw long, there were signs winter had capitulated. Across northeast Kazakhstan the frost was broken by slush and rain, and in the south the snow was retreating to the high slopes of the Tien Shan. Some brave girls in Almaty were baring their legs, which, a Russian once told me, explained the high incidence of car crashes by male drivers near bus stops in spring.

The repressive hold that winter had on political life had also been broken. Neighboring Kyrgyzstan had just erupted in what would become known as the Tulip Revolution, making world headlines. The deposed president, Askar Akayev, accused of corruption and electoral fraud, had fled to exile in Moscow. To many Russians, and Russian-leaning Kazakhs in particular, this seemed to be part of a grand conspiracy of "color" revolutions that they assumed had been funded by America following the Orange Revolution that had swept Ukraine in the autumn and winter months and the Rose Revolution in Georgia a year earlier. It was all the talk on the street, at the markets, and on buses in the city, especially among pensioners who reveled in any whiff of news that could lift them from the drudgery of winter. The spring air seemed to be brimming with possibilities.

What would happen next? Was this the beginning of a greater rebellion across Central Asia? It was an election year in Kazakhstan, and Nazarbayev was reportedly paranoid about the sentiment of discontent spilling across the border. Word was that as soon as the Tulip Revolution had begun in Bishkek, Nazarbayev had ordered security forces to move south and be ready to quash any unrest. Spring was a dangerous time, as people no longer had to concentrate on surviving winter and their fervor was yet to be snuffed out by the heat of summer.

When I arrived back in Akbakai, people were emerging from their homes, pale, gaunt, and broken-looking, counting the costs of winter. In the wake of the snowmelt, the surrounding steppe had become a morass of impenetrable swampland, although I was told it would soon rise in a sea of red and yellow tulips.

I spent several days tweaking my equipment, gathering my animals from Madagol, and preparing them for travel, and during this time the steppe dried out enough to be navigable. With a new packsaddle, a healthy-looking Tigon, and a little extra weight on my own frame, I figured my window of opportunity had arrived.

It was with a sense of disbelief, then, on April 4—the day earmarked for my fourth attempt to depart Akbakai—that I stumbled out of Baitak's hut into a predawn blizzard. The thermometer read −15°C and by the time I had watered the horses I was chilled to the bone. So confident that I had seen the last of the cold, I had left my winter clothing behind in the city.

I didn't bother saddling the horses, and instead decided to return to bed. Baitak saw me come back in. "So Akbakai is still holding you here? It is you we blame for this weather. Only that man in the sky knows what is best for you, and he is keeping you in Akbakai for a reason. You have done the right thing."

Baitak had warned me about this seasonal phenomena, known by no-mads as otamal. It was a period of sudden cold that usually occurred in mid-March, just as it appeared the weather had turned the corner. Animals that had grown thin through winter could be polished off, and many people were known to perish, too, if caught unawares.[1] Spring,

Baitak told me, was the season of greatest weakness and vulnerability for all living things.

For me there was a larger message in all of this, summed up in a saying often repeated to me by Baitak and others: "If you ever have to rush in life, rush slowly." On the steppe, time was measured by the seasons, the weather, the availability of grass, and, most important, the condition of one's animals. To think I could hurry the seasons was as foolish as rushing with horses.

TWO DAYS AFTER the failed departure attempt, the sky had been blown clean and the sun glinted off the frozen streets of Akbakai. After a meal of horsehead, Baitak, Rosa, and Abdrakhman escorted me out of town for a departure ceremony. Baitak's farewell toast was simple: "I suggest you stay away from young people, and stick close to the elders."

Bundled up in an old woolen vest and buttonless coat that Baitak had given me to see me through the remaining cold, I hauled myself up into the saddle, whistled for Tigon, and hunched forward into the wind. When some time later that I took a peek over my shoulder the steppe was empty.[2]

Ahead of me now stretched nearly 150 km of the Betpak Dala to the aul of Ulanbel. In the wake of winter this formerly frozen wilderness had become a waterless desert, and to get through I hoped to find puddles of remaining snowmelt.

For the first three days we hugged the edge of brown silty salt flats, passing in and out of cloud shadows that wobbled and rippled over the land's undulations. Hills no more than bumps were akin to mountains in this exposed, flat land. They emerged from the earth in front of us, passed by our flanks, and then with time shriveled away behind.

Despite the cold and the ragged, ice-charred appearance of the earth— its many plants crushed and flattened by the snow—there were early signs of spring: yellow wrens jumping toward the tent door and V-formations of geese cutting the sky. What captured me most were the shoots of grass emerging beneath tough desert plants. Resilient enough to defy the odds of winter, here was the miracle sustaining life itself. The horses were electrified by the sight and spent much of their free time trying to reach the new growth, often succeeding only in scratching their noses on the tough, brittle plants above.

Tigon, for his part, was beside himself with excitement. The snow was nearly gone, so his paws didn't freeze, yet it wasn't too warm, which meant he could run forever and barely had to let his tongue out to cool down. He galloped about, digging, chasing, and sniffing, often running parallel with us on distant ridges. Periodically he returned to my caravan to check in and give the horses a lick on the face. Zhamba and Ogonyok didn't seem to mind this, but Taskonir, being the hardened old grump he was, usually snapped back and warned Tigon with a hoof pounded into the dirt. Tigon couldn't understand this unfriendliness and would peer up at me all concerned, his amber eyes aglow and his tail between his legs.

On the fourth day the temperature had risen and the remaining snow from the otamal had melted. Dust devils hurled across the flats, sometimes hitting us with a cloud of dust and sand. I became stuck in a series of salt bogs and was forced to retreat. The horses were thirsty, and the absence of sturdy ground made the going slow.

Late in the evening I put my compass away and followed a large bird of prey instead. It took me up into red rocky ridges, from where I could look down on never-ending salt flats to the south and at rising steppe to the north, where jagged little mountains cut the horizon. I reveled in the feeling that as the horizons were expanding, my own world was shrinking to the intimate family circle of animals I had known previously.

When I reached the top of the ridge the bird took off a little farther. Not only did it lead me straight to a set of old wheel tracks heading west, but it was now perched on one of two large round piles of rocks and earth. They were the unmistakable sign of ancient nomad graves.

Before moving on I dismounted and stood for some time. I couldn't help but wonder what it would have been like to make this same journey a hundred years ago. I had little doubt that in early times I could have made my way right across the steppe from aul to aul, directed by people who, from the saddle, knew every corner of their land. To some degree I had experienced this in Mongolia, where even in the most hostile of country it was rare that a yurt or a rider couldn't be seen somewhere on the horizon and approached for advice. I felt as though I was treading through the graveyard not only of the individuals who lay before me but an entire people and their way of life.[3]

After leaving the graves I found some snowmelt pooled in a rocky gully and the following afternoon reached the perimeter of the Betpak Dala. To the south, the plateau I had been on dropped away to a sprawling plain. A myriad of lakes and marshes and the Chu River glinted in the sun, and beyond them lay the burning red sand of the Moiynkum Desert.

We camped on the edge of this plateau, with the water tower and homes of Ulanbel on the horizon. At dinnertime the horses crowded around to pinch food from my pot, and Tigon barked indignantly at them to steer clear of what he thought was rightly his. I felt proud and relieved. If I could make it to Ulanbel, then maybe Hungary was possible.

EVERYONE I HAD spoken to in Akbakai warned that in Ulanbel not only would my horses be stolen, but I would be "stripped naked and left with nothing."

Abdrakhman had shaken his head ominously on the day of my departure. "Timurbek! Be careful! You won't find any Baitaks in Ulanbel!"

For such a small, isolated aul, it didn't seem credible that it could be full of bandits, yet there was a reason for its reputation. As recently as the year 2000, the Betpak Dala had been home to a unique migratory species of antelope known as saiga. Believed to be related to fauna from the era of the mammoth, and a living genetic link between antelope and sheep, the saiga was renowned for its speed, said to be around 95 kph. In Akbakai many had described to me how until the late 1990s Ulanbel had been swamped by hundreds of thousands of the animals as they swept through during annual migrations. There were apparently so many you could almost catch them by hand in the streets, people said.

For years now, though, in the middle of a region once called the "Serengeti of Central Asia," barely a single saiga had been sighted. The sad reality was that the collapse of the economy and of the rule of law in the 1990s had triggered an explosion in poaching, particularly of the male saiga, the horns of which are used to make cold and flu remedies in China. The estimated 800,000 saiga living on the steppes of Kazakhstan and southern Russia in 1990 were said to have dwindled to less than 40,000—almost none of which lived on the Betpak Dala.

The genocide of the Betpak Dala's saiga population had been partly coordinated from Ulanbel. Conveniently isolated from central authorities, it had had become renowned as a hotbed for traders, poachers, and contraband dealers. Nowadays—or so Baitak had heard—things had settled down because the poachers had run out of saiga to shoot. Baitak therefore reasoned that my horses would be in even greater danger of being stolen by "bored," "out-of-work" criminals.

With knowledge of this state of affairs weighing on my mind, I nervously crossed the Chu River to the southern banks where the aul lay. The bridge did not bode well—halfway across I had to dismount and lead the horses around holes big enough for a car to fall through. Safely on the far side, and still on foot, however, I was overwhelmed by an entirely different world. There were stone huts and fences, and mud-brick homes rising from wide, sandy streets. Cows wandered lazily about, a motorbike could be heard starting up somewhere, and there was even an old man with a few token teeth leading his donkey and cart to the river. I could hardly remember a place so positively blooming with life.

There was admittedly little time to indulge in a sense of reverie. No sooner had I reached the main street than a man came rushing from his home dressed in a green silky gown and fur hat. He stood at a distance, hands on hips:

"As-salam aleikum! Sell me your black horse! I like your black horse!"

"No! I need my horse! I will not sell!" I said, clambering back up into the saddle.

As the man drew near, Tigon sniffed at his crotch, and he raised his hands in fright. I came to my senses. The man's greeting to me had been a compliment, I realized, and in any case, the man's plump belly, rosy cheeks, and distinctive Kazakh mustache hardly presented a picture of intimidation. Five minutes later, I was in his family home drinking tea.

Temir, as he introduced himself, was adamant that I stay the night and proceeded to tell me that the name *Ulanbel* meant "red hillside" in Mongolian, which referenced the long sandy ridge seen to the south in the Moiynkum Desert. The aul had previously been home to a sheep farm collective that peaked at about 60,000 head but which had since been dissolved. About 10,000 sheep remained among private individuals. The herders who once had worked for the collective had turned their skills to poaching saiga, fishing, and digging up rock to be sold for the making of fences, homes, and animal pens.

The rumors I had heard in Akbakai about saiga seemed to be true. Temir asked me with a hopeful look whether I had seen any during my ride. I replied that I had not, and he shook his head sadly. Even now, with the saiga on the very brink, there were apparently instances of the odd kill, and locals were still trading in the horns they could find scattered out on the steppe.

Given what I had already learned about the pillaging of Kazakhstan's resources in Tasaral and Akbakai, this was really more of the same, but when Temir began to tell me about nomads and how they lived in the desert nearby, my ears perked up.

"You are in luck, Tim. Word is they are on the move, and will be coming through Ulanbel tomorrow on their way to the Betpak Dala."

JUST AFTER LUNCH the following day the idleness of the aul was broken by a wildfire of barking. A great cloud of sand and dust billowed in from the southern horizon like a main sail. Tigon, who had already joined a rabble army of local dogs, charged off in hysteria, his tail pointed sky high.

By the time I made it to the bridge I had been hit by the wafting aroma of livestock. What had been a desolate road angling into the aul from the desert was now throbbing with a tangle of five hundred sheep and goats, fifty horses, twenty shaggy camels, and a few donkeys. Ahead of them, breaking through a bow wave of dust, grunted a Russian truck full to bursting with belongings, and behind it a motorcycle with a sidecar brimming with wide-eyed toddlers. Bringing the group up from the rear were several men, one of them an old gray-bearded man who wore a purple fox-fur hat and sat astride a gray horse.

Upon reaching the bridge, the leaders in the truck lay down planks and boards to cover the holes. After a brief pause to let the animals drink, the whole caravan then rumbled over to the northern bank. Within half an hour the caravan had come and gone, and the dust had settled as if they had never been.

Eager to know more, I paid Temir's son to follow the caravan by motorbike to where they were planning to stop for camp. Tigon came with us, sprinting behind, leaving his own plumes of dust and sand.

What had been a silent steppe the previous day now bustled with movement. Toddlers played with baby goats in the back of the truck while large pieces of brown felt were unfurled and a team effort got under way to build a yurt. There were fifteen or so members of the extended family group to be accommodated between the yurt and a rusty old wagon that had been towed in by the truck.

First the collapsible lattice walls were put up, then the many roof poles to support the circular ring at the apex of the ceiling. After the felt had been pulled on, a young boy was sent scrambling up to the top to make adjustments. The silver-bearded elder directed with stern but soft commands.

When the yurt was erect the women set about decorating the insides with felt carpets and wall hangings. Outside, fencing for pens was set up, and a trench dug around the yurt. As proof that the pens were necessary, I was shown two horses with shredded rumps—the victims of a wolf attack.

By dark, the yurt was furnished, sheep were settling into their pens in a chorus of snorts, farts, and snuffles, and freshly slaughtered lamb sizzled on an open fire. In the midst of this camp scene, which had once been universal across the steppe, men came to earth with sighs of relief. I rested among them, savoring every detail.

One of the eldest men turned to me and grinned.

"You realize that the 'starving steppe' isn't really that hungry? There is good grass out here, and our animals always come back fat. It's just that you have to know when and how." His eyes were lit up, as if he were describing a feast.

I asked him to go on. He requested a pen and paper, so I handed him my diary, and in the light cast by the glow of the coals he drew a basic map.

"Every winter we live in the Moiynkum Desert. The soil is sandy and soft, there is little snow, and it is much warmer than other places." He sketched an east-west-running stretch of land that lay between the westerly flowing Chu River in the north and the Karatau Mountains in the south.

"Then just before the ticks come to life in the spring we pack up and leave. If we stay too late, the animals suffer from the ticks, and the grass won't have time to recover for the next winter. Our next camp is here, on the northern banks of the Chu River. As you can see, there are reeds to be eaten on the riverbanks, and grass is beginning to grow. We will stay here until the lambs and kids have strengthened. But eventually this river runs dry in the summer and the pasture gets burned by the sun. In just a few weeks, the grass will be long enough in the Betpak Dala, so we can go there."

At the peak of summer, the family would continue north nearly as far as the city of Zhezkazgan. There, in uplands that provided cooler weather and winds that kept the mosquitoes away, they would mingle with other nomad families who had migrated from other regions. Timing the return south was crucial—too late and there was the risk of getting trapped by blizzards, too early and the winter pastures would not sustain the herds until spring. By the time they reached the Moiynkum Desert for winter they would have completed a round trip of around 600 km.

The man finished his sketch. "This is my land, and that of my ancestors, the Naiman tribe, and we have camped in the same places for generations," he said. The completed map was an oval shape running from north to south bordered by the traditional lands of other tribes who had their own migratory routes. At the northern and southern ends the winter and summer stopping places overlapped with those of their neighbors. It was here families had the opportunity to socialize with other tribes and clans. Summer in particular was a time of festivity when horse races were arranged, feasts held, and courtship took place.

A piece of saksaul wood was rolled over, and a swarm of sparks spat into the sky like bees disturbed from a hive.

There had been times on my journey when it was tempting to imagine Kazakhstan as one great big swath of steppe and the nomads as living somewhat free-wandering, isolated lives. Now, however, I began to picture a sophisticated map of traditional grazing lands, stretching from the Caspian Sea to the Altai, the Kyzylkum Desert to Siberia. Each had clearly been home to generations of nomads, who, like this family's ancestors, had developed a unique migratory pattern according to the local ecology and who were connected to other groups by adjoining camps.

There was no official map, of course, and in the near absence of nomads in present times I must have unwittingly crossed many boundaries during my journey to date. But Kazakhs had never relied on fences or maps. Instead they had known their territory, history, and likewise their identity through detailed knowledge of ancestry, known as shezire.

I was already familiar with one important element of shezire—that before choosing a marriage partner it was a requirement to know the details of seven generations of the paternal line, for it was taboo to marry anyone within those lines. This information had been passed on through the centuries via epic poems that wove together a riddle of names, stories of land, and important historical events.[4] In the present day, as I witnessed in many Kazakh homes, it had survived in the form of family tree diagrams.

Also at the core of shezire was knowledge of clan, tribe, and juz (union of tribes)—three circles of allegiance that I had always found somewhat difficult to understand but which in the context of this family's ancestral grazing land was easier to grasp.

This family was part of the Orta Juz—the horde that traditionally lives in the north and east of Kazakhstan.[5] Within the Orta Juz they were Naimans—a tribe descended from the Naimans of Mongolia, whose defeat near Kharkhorin by Genghis Khan heralded the founding of the Mongol Empire. First and foremost, though, this man was of the Baganali clan.

"This here is Baganali land. We are the most honest clan. But see that woman over there?" the man said, pointing to a woman turning the frying lamb. "Don't trust her, because she is Tama!" There was much laughter.

"And when you get into an aul, Timurbek, be sure to find out which clan lives there. Then when you arrive and they ask who you are, you should tell them that you are one of them. They will take you in like a brother . . . but when you get down to the Karatau Mountains, don't tell them you are a Buzhban, because they are wild people!" There was more laughter.

For me, a foreigner, shezire would prove to be an icebreaker, just as the man advised, but had I been a Kazakh wandering the steppe, it would have been a much more integral part of greeting strangers. By asking, "What clan do you come from?" even today two Kazakhs can quickly gauge one another's geographical homeland, common ancestors, enemies, and living relations. It was becoming clear to me that shezire was much like a passport and a map combined, allowing people to understand who they were, the land to which they belonged, and even whom they could marry.

Tigon crept closer to the fire and sat straight-backed, licking his chops, his paws shifting restlessly. He sensed, as did I, that the lamb was almost ready to eat.

I had all but become absorbed by the man's story, but as hunger lifted my eyes beyond the glow of the fire, the distant lights of Ulanbel were a reminder that in a nation where nomadic life had been the norm for thousands of years, this family found themselves on the periphery of society.[6]

One of the men, who had been listening to the discussion, leaned in and said, "Life here was much better before this capitalism came! Back in those times we were all out herding. I used to be in charge of more than ten thousand animals! We had reliable wells, and everyone was employed, not like today. There were whole auls of yurts on the Betpak Dala until that idiot Gorbachev came along."

Until now I had overlooked the fact that arid land such as this—unsuitable for conventional farming or cultivation—had been grazed by animals from Soviet stock-breeding collectives, following the same migratory routes as their predecessors. Wells and concrete feeding troughs had been maintained every 20 km, even through the "starving steppe." In this way, Soviet doctrine had married successfully in part with traditional knowledge.

Come the collapse of the Soviet era, this surviving nomadic existence had abruptly halted, and I could see more clearly how things had unraveled. Most fundamental to the crisis was that with so few livestock remaining, the pasture in the immediate surrounds of auls and towns was adequate for them to graze on all year round. There was now no reason to migrate to the traditional seasonal pastures—a trend confirmed the following day in Ulanbel by people who spoke with bitterness and envy about the nomadic family I had met.

In fact, in Ulanbel one could find any number of hardened men playing dombras and singing melancholy songs. Crippled by nostalgia, they seemed to believe that the modern era was a temporary stage and that ultimately they would return to the life of the ancestors in the future. I began to see many of these sedentary Kazakhs as dormant nomads waiting for the day they had enough animals to justify a return to the steppe.

It must have been nearing midnight by the time Temir's son pointed nervously to his watch. The man with whom I had been speaking tried to persuade me to stay: "Timurbek! Maybe you could even travel with us into the 'starving steppe.' We could find you a Kazakh wife!"

If only I could. But then again, my animals were waiting, and the mild spring conditions beckoned with promise for travel in the coming weeks. I climbed onto the back of the motorbike and clung on for life as we crashed through the darkness.

A DAY'S RIDE west from Ulanbel I made camp by a lake flooded with overflow from the Chu River. Ducks whispered high across an orange sky, smaller birds darted acrobatically among reeds, and a pair of white swans milled at a safe distance from shore. As my mash of rice and canned meat boiled I watched the horses rubbing their sweaty backs in the sand. Taskonir went first, digging with his front hooves before falling to his knees and attempting to roll over. It took him more than a couple of tries before he managed to get up onto the ridge of his back where he thrashed about, his unkempt mane mopping up the sand. Once he had gone down, the other two followed. When they had all gotten up and shaken off, they, like me, stood gazing to the west.

For the next 200 km I planned to follow the Chu River as far as possible on its westerly course between the Moiynkum Desert and the Betpak Dala. Like many watercourses in Central Asia, it started off with great promise from the Tien Shan Mountains of Kyrgyzstan but withered as it flowed inland, finally disappearing ungraciously in a series of salt lakes and thirsty flats. Every year in spring, however, fresh snowmelt flushed through its system, bringing a fleeting abundance of life. For the first time on my journey this thin green line suggested the kind of reprieve I had only dreamed of previously: ready access to water for days on end and the prospect of plentiful grazing.

That first night out of Ulanbel I slept in the tent without a warm hat—the first time in six months—and rose in the morning feeling light and clearheaded. By sunrise I was in the saddle, and knew at once I was in for a good day. With a slight press into Zhamba's side we were moving forward across the sandy earth. I held the reins lightly in one hand and let the other go lax, twisting my torso at times to take in the full panorama. Following a series of horse tracks, we crossed empty flats, then threaded our way between tall desert bushes. There was always water to our right and grazing to our left. By lunch we had covered 20 km, by dinner more than 40 km.

The following day I was unwilling to lose the gathering sense of momentum and took a wide berth around an aul called Shyganak before hugging the shoreline of salt lakes. In the evening I descended to floodplains and brought the horses to a slow walk among a carpet of orange and red tulips that were backlit by the low sun. Between them crawled an engrossing sight—hundreds upon hundreds of tortoises. There were so many it was nearly impossible not to tread on them, and indeed, in coming days we encountered many corpses of those unfortunate ones crushed by horses and motorbikes. Tigon was fascinated at first by the plodding tortoises but soon decided they didn't play fair when they receded into their shells. Later, at our camp, he growled when they crossed by the tent through his territory, but invariably let them shuffle on.

That evening, as I sat glowing with the visions and feelings of our ride, I sensed that tortoises and wildflowers were not the only life unharnessed by spring. Tigon's ears rose suddenly to attention, and the horses went stiff and tall.

As I stood and turned, I locked eyes with a chestnut stallion standing resplendent in his shiny spring coat, tail raised like a war banner and ears speared forward. At first I watched, captivated, as he snorted, pawed at the earth, and marked his territory with droppings. But then he pranced forward, and my mind began to race. Spring was renowned as a time of chaos and conflict for horse herds, as maturing mares were expelled from the family and stallions fought for mating partners. I'd heard stories of competing stallions fighting to the death.

The stallion began circling, his focus bearing down on my horses, which stood defenseless in their hobbles. Tigon leaped to defend them, but the stallion charged anyway. All I could think to do was run between the stallion and the horses, taking aim with rocks and sticks. When finally a rock landed between the stallion's eyes, he retreated for a minute or two, but then came charging in again.

This routine went on until midnight, at which point I managed to chase him beyond camp. At dawn, he was back again, and just as I became absorbed in cooking porridge he took his opportunity.

When I looked up, a blur of mane, tail, and teeth was bearing down on Ogonyok. Ogonyok turned to run, but the stallion mounted him from behind, dug his teeth in, and dragged them along his spine from head to tail. Ogonyok reached the end of the tether that was tied to his front leg and somersaulted to earth. Almost at the same time, the stallion came crashing over the top, and the metal stake torpedoed overhead. It wasn't over yet, though. As Tigon took up the fight, the stallion caught him in the bushes and bit down on his back before flinging him through the air. Only after Tigon limped into my tent did the stallion recede to the bushes in the dunes. When the dust had settled I brushed Ogonyok down and uncovered two bloodied fang tracks from neck to rump. I cleaned the wounds and resolved to carry rocks in my pocket—a tactic that proved crucial for the remainder of my journey.

The stallion was not the only spring danger that seemed to have blossomed overnight. Even as I packed to leave, I noticed dozens of small bugs jumping aboard my boots and crawling up my chaps. They were ticks, and on inspection the horses had swollen specimens the size of grapes hanging off their chests, the sheaths of their penises, and under the tail around their anuses. It was dangerous work to pluck them off, especially from Ogonyok, who was sensitive at the best of times. In the process many ticks exploded, and by the time I had finished, dark oozing blood, thick as sap, had congealed with molting horsehair and stuck like glue to my hands.

It was a relief to eventually climb into the saddle and pick up the momentum of the previous day. Yet while the coming days would not turn out to be quite as eventful as the past twelve hours, it was clear that my encounters with the stallion and with the ticks were part of the many rhythms of spring I would have to learn to take in stride.

A WEEK'S RIDE west from Ulanbel we approached an aul called Tasty—a cluster of adobe houses on a peninsula of land that jutted out into a bend of the river. It was evening, and as I drew close, herders were returning for the night with sheep and cattle from all directions.

I decided to wait it out hidden among twisted desert shrubs before unpacking in darkness and making camp, but a herder spotted me with his binoculars and invited me to his home. The following day, while the herder's children took my horses out to graze, I joined him at a gathering of the aul's elders.

In the cool confines of a mud-brick house with whitewashed walls hung with rugs I squeezed in on the floor along a dastarkhan. Opposite sat men with faces as old and gnarly as camel-gnawn desert bushes. Most had patchy gray whiskers and wore traditional Kazakh hats. Women wore silky vests and were wrapped up in white head scarves. Most understood Russian, but few could speak it fluently.

On the table between us sat a freshly boiled camel's head surrounded by mountains of baursak (the deep-fried dough Mongolians call boort-sog) and plates of the national dish, beshbarmak.

"C'mon, Tim, eat!" the old men demanded.

Using the communal knife to cut meat from the cheek of the camel was one thing, but I was yet to master the eating of beshbarmak. The name means "five fingers," and it is a dish of meat and boiled squares of pastry often cooked with wild onion.[7] The technique of eating it involves scooping up the meat and angling it into the mouth so that the fat doesn't spill. When I tried, the hot fat and meat burned my fingers, and I sucked on my fingers to cool them. As I shoveled the food down, pieces inevitably dropped to the floor, and the elders laughed.

After the meal I lay anchored to the floor by my full belly watching the chiseled old faces and listening to the guttural sounds of Kazakh. Russian influence hadn't penetrated here as deeply as it had further to the north and east, and I sensed that these people were closer to the nomad past—a trend confirmed that night in my host's home.

Serik, as he was called, led me to his one-month-old baby boy, who lay in an old crib sucking on a piece of sheep tail fat.[8] As I bent over and smiled Serik gripped my arm and gently pulled me back. In silence we left the room. Once out in the kitchen he told me, "We Kazakhs believe that for the first forty days a baby has not been fully born and released by God to us, and must be protected from bad spirits, especially the evil eye of Zyn, which is like the devil. We would not usually show our baby to strangers during this time, only close relatives. We think you will bring good luck to our baby, but you should not look into his eyes."

I had often wondered why babies I had seen in Kazakhstan had black dots, usually from charcoal, on their forehead, and thanks to my host I now understood. "We make those dots to draw the attention of onlookers away from the baby's eyes. You would not even know yourself if you had the evil eye—don't be offended."

Traditionally, Kazakhs used all manner of techniques to keep bad spirits from harming the young. One involved giving the baby an unpleasant name that would make people laugh and therefore distract evil spirits.[9] An amulet called a *tumar* was also worn, traditionally filled with a sample of the baby's own feces, although nowadays with a prayer from the Koran. There was even a tradition known as *satyp alu* (buying a child), in which parents gave the baby away to an old woman dressed like a witch, and then went to her home dressed in rags to beg for a baby. The baby would be delivered through the door headfirst, as in birth, to ensure a long life and that he or she would eventually die while standing—traditionally considered honorable. In return, the parents would gift the old woman with several sheep, firewood, and a kettle.

FROM TASTY THERE remained just 40 km of riding along the Chu River to the town of Zhuantobe. During the two days it took me to get there, I never quite found my rhythm again.

Leaving Tasty was awkward after I discovered that my headlamp and watch were missing—it turned out they had been stolen by Serik's children. Then, just half a day from the aul, Tigon was hit by one of the first cars he had seen in his short life. At the time we had been forced onto the shoulder of a road to avoid floodwaters and had been transfixed by a solitary Lada hurtling in from the west. After the impact Tigon lay bleeding and unconscious. I was sure he would not survive, but the very next vehicle to arrive was a motorbike carrying the veterinarian from Zhuantobe. Tigon regained consciousness, and on inspection had a broken rib and concussion. The vet arranged for Tigon to be taken to Zhuantobe, where he would be looked after until my arrival.

When I reached the town I was greeted by a throng of barefoot children eager to lead the way to Tigon. I found him lying like a prince in the shade of an outhouse. He had been dining on bowls of fresh milk, meat scraps, and his favorite, eggs.

After two days Tigon was on his feet again, but it was clear that both spring and the respite of the Chu were over. The heat had arrived, and not far west of Zhuantobe the river came to a finish, spilling into a series of salt lakes and swamps. My immediate route lay to the southwest across 120 km of the Moiynkum Desert to the Karatau Mountains.

In what would prove a taste of the conditions and landscapes of central and western Kazakhstan in coming months, we covered this next leg in two long, hot days. At first I was guided by a local man and his friend on a motorcycle, but halfway across their fuel ran low, and we discovered that the artesian bores once used by nomads had been closed off—rumor had it that the water table had recently been poisoned by operations at a Canadian-financed uranium mine.

The last 60 km were the thirstiest to date for my little family of animals. I pushed them on across the shadeless steppe and desert until finally the olive-green ridge of the Karatau Mountains emerged from the dusty horizon. Beyond them lay the Syr Darya River, which I hoped would be my next lifeline, carrying me deep into central Kazakhstan.

Just at dusk we came to a gorge between the Moiynkum and the mountain ridge, at the bottom of which lay a cluster of adobe homes—an aul called Karatau. I hurried down and caught the last herder on his way home for the night. I didn't have to say a word before he led the way to a trough and invited me in.

14

SHIPS OF THE DESERT

IN THE LATE autumn of 1219 Genghis Khan rode along the freezing banks of the Syr Darya leading somewhere between 90,000 and 200,000 men and probably at least twice as many horses. He was drawing close to battle after the long journey from Mongolia, and one can only imagine that the cold air would have lifted the energy and alertness of his mount.

In Genghis's sights was the city of Otrar, which lay on the northern banks of the river, and beyond it Samarkand and Bukhara, at the heart of the powerful empire of Khwarezm.[1] A year earlier, Inalchuk, the governor of Otrar, had enraged the Mongol leader by executing a 450-man merchant caravan from Mongolia. The sultan of Khwarezm, Muhammad II, had added insult to injury when he beheaded an ambassador sent by Genghis to offer a peace agreement.

This was more than enough to invite the wrath of Genghis, and what lay in store was not just a hot-blooded act of retaliation but a carefully planned campaign to conquer all of Central Asia. It is well known that Genghis used a vast network of spies and diplomats to gather information prior to attack, and a mobile corps of Chinese engineers who built sophisticated catapults, battering rams, and siege engines. What is sometimes understated is that as a nomad, Genghis was also well aware that success of any campaign depended as much on timing, taking into account the seasons and the health of his animals, as it did on technology and intelligence. His early life growing up on the edge of survival had taught him to fear and respect Tengri, the eternal blue sky, over any living enemy.

Knowing that the journey from Mongolia to Otrar and beyond was going to be particularly hard on his horses, he had ordered that no one was to go hunting of his own accord, and use of horses was strictly minimized. Traveling in autumn with the object of conquering through winter was a crucial part of his strategy. That way he could avoid the heat of summer, with its increased risk of saddle sores, and because of dew on the ground there would be more pasture and less need for water. As rivers froze over in late autumn and winter, his army could also cross rivers at will.

Come the scorching heat of summer in 1220, Genghis Khan's timing had proven nothing short of genius, and it is little wonder he believed his aspirations to conquer the world were vindicated by Tengri. Otrar had been destroyed and its governor, Inalchuk, executed by molten silver poured in his eyes and ears. Following an unprecedented trek across the Kyzylkum Desert, a section of his army had also surprised the holy city of Bukhara, and after subduing the garrison, Genghis had entered the city and proclaimed to the ruling class that he had been sent by God to punish them for their sins. Samarkand was the next to fall before Genghis and his army retreated to the hills to rest and graze their animals for the summer. Sultan Muhammad II, meanwhile, was fleeing for his life, with a detachment of the Mongol army hunting him down. After an epic game of cat-and-mouse, Muhammad was eventually cornered on a remote islet on the coast of the Caspian Sea, where he died of exhaustion and pneumonia in the winter of 1220–21.

At the age of fifty-seven, having already conquered much of China and Turkestan, Genghis was now the ruler of an empire that stretched from Persia to Peking. Although his success in China to date had already proven his prowess, it was this crushing victory over the once powerful

Khwarezm Empire that set a precedent for the brilliance and terror that would characterize Mongol conquests in the future.

By contrast with Genghis Khan's first major foray into Central Asia, my approach to the Syr Darya was not going well. Two days' ride west from the aul of Karatau, I woke at midday slumped against a twisted tree root and listened to blood throbbing through my ears. The sun burned a rosette through my eyelids and pressed down on my cheeks like an iron. During my snooze the sliver of shade under the poplar tree had moved and the horses likewise had shifted, their bums facing the west, heads propped forward in the shade. Tigon had dug himself into a fresh hole for the third or fourth time and lay panting with his tongue out on the dirt and his eyes reduced to slits.

I felt lethargic and dizzy, so it took me some time to pull myself away from the tree trunk and reach for the battered plastic soft drink bottle that held my drinking water. Earlier I'd been lucky to find a well next to an abandoned winter hut and managed to lower my collapsible bucket 20 m to the water using tether ropes. As I pulled the bucket up it had broken away from the ropes, but I had managed to retrieve water by lowering this drink bottle, and had watered the horses from my cooking pots.

As this hot, algae-filled water now flushed out the dry bed of my throat, the stench of dry manure rose through my nostrils. It was a smell that would have been a comforting symbol of family and togetherness in the winter and early spring when there might have been hundreds of cattle, sheep, and horses milling about this tree, the only one I'd seen in two days. Now, though, the lingering fragrance of livestock was a sharp reminder that the people had moved away to the safety of summer pastures and I was alone under the tree.

The sickly feeling that I was traveling against the grain of the seasons had, in truth, been building ever since I'd met the nomads of the Betpak Dala some weeks ago. I'd tried to ignore it, but in recent days it had become unavoidable. Since I'd left the aul of Karatau, the land had been dotted with empty huts with boarded-up windows and abandoned yards. Horizons had crawled with nothing but heat mirage and billowing clouds of fine manure particles. The only people I had seen were a family who had just migrated from the Moiynkum Desert and were headed for the high pastures of the Karatau Mountains. They'd invited me to watch the final spring ritual for the year, camel shearing, and looked at me gravely when they understood my route. "Soon the flies will be here," they told me. "Down on the Syr Darya, where you are going, they will be even worse. If you leave your horse tied up for half an hour there, it will be dead."

The flies hadn't yet come, but although it was still only late April the temperature was reaching 30°C by nine o'clock in the morning and what pasture I could find was sun-fried and hollow. To avoid the heat—and decrease the risk of saddle sores that it posed—I had begun breaking the riding into two sessions, leaving before sunrise, then riding until mid-morning before unsaddling and finding shade, then doing more distance close to dusk. The conditions might have felt endurable had relief been in sight within days or even weeks, but everything I was now experiencing—the heat, isolation, and lack of water and grass—were merely precursors of what I could expect in coming months.

The ultimate goal of this leg of my journey was to navigate about 2,000 km through Kazakhstan's arid center and west to the Caspian Sea—a vast, sparsely populated region of open deserts and salt flats that lies midway between Mongolia and Hungary at the heart of the Eurasian steppe. It was here that Friar Carpini recorded the most harrowing leg of his journey from Europe to Mongolia, writing that it was so dry "many men die from thirst," and that he "found many skulls and bones about in heaps over the ground."

My original plan had been to make this traverse in the winter and spring, when the slightly warmer winter temperatures (at least slightly warmer than those found in the north) and a thin layer of snow would have been an advantage over a more northerly route. The holdups in Akbakai, however, had left me on course for one of the driest parts of the country at the hottest time of year—a prospect that any nomad, and certainly Genghis Khan, surely would have done all he could to avoid.

The big consolation in all of this—and one that would become my motivation in the months ahead—was that beyond the fiery core of the Eurasian steppe lay the relatively mild climate of the Caspian region and geographical Europe, where water and pasture promised to become pro-gressively more abundant. In the short term, I simply had to accept that things were only going to get harder.

⊟⊟

LATE IN THE afternoon, when the sun's heat waned, I lifted from slum-ber under the tree and rode on, determined to remain positive.

To tackle the trek ahead, I had broken my planned route into three stages, each of which I estimated would take a month. The first—and I reasoned the easiest—would be to drop south to the Syr Darya River and follow it about 500 km to the point where it spills into the Aral Sea. From there I would break away and track northwest around the northeast tip of the Aral Sea's old shoreline and continue as far as the Zhem River (known in Russia as the Emba). The final phase would be southwest along this minor—and partly seasonal—watercourse, which I hoped would see me through the western deserts to within range of the Caspian Sea. It was a very indirect route, at the mercy of where water lay, but if all went ac-cording to plan, I would cross the Ural River—into geographical Europe— and be entering Russia come autumn.

It took several more days of riding through abandoned pasturage be-fore I crossed through the Karatau ridge and began my descent to the Syr Darya. Viewed from a distance, the river appeared just as it did on my map: an improbable belt of water and leathery green vegetation that flows some 2,212 km from the Tien Shan down through Uzbekistan and Ka-zakhstan, snaking its way northwest through mustard-yellow desert to-ward the Aral Sea. In an otherwise inhospitable landscape, it was a fabled artery dotted with ancient towns and cities that have played theater to the aspirations of conquerors ranging from Alexander the Great to Genghis Khan and later Tamerlane.[2] In more recent times the Soviets had har-nessed the Syr Darya—in tandem with its sister river, the Amu Darya—to fuel a massive expansion of the cotton industry in Uzbekistan. The conse-quence of these developments was that while irrigated crops in the desert of the upper reaches had bloomed, further downstream both the Syr

Darya and the Amu Darya had slowed to a relative dribble. As predicted in 1959 when the water was diverted, the Aral Sea, which relies on the two rivers as its primary feeders, had now shrunk to around 10–20 percent of its original size—and was still receding.

It was not far west of the town of Shieli—about 100 km west of the ruins of Otrar—that I reached the riverbank and began the long journey west.

Initially the river environment offered reprieve. For the first two days I waded through a cluster of crop-farming communities where irrigation canals—predominantly for rice, corn, and cabbage—brought plentiful water and greenery. When navigating through the labyrinth of canals slowed my progress, I crossed to the less populated southern banks via a makeshift pontoon bridge—the last 15 m of which could be crossed only by laying down horse blankets and felt pads on a narrow ramp made from a grid of reinforcement wire welded to pipes.

Once on the far side I moved with a hint of rhythm along desert tracks. A typical day involved rising at 4:00 A.M., at which hour there were the whispers of a cool breeze. In the early morning the horses moved with purpose, their hooves shuffling quietly through sand. As the sky grew from purple to shades of crimson, I could see the glassy surface of canals and auls nestled among sand dunes with yurts set up outside permanent mud-brick homes. The Syr Darya forms both the eastern and northern boundary of the Kyzylkum Desert, and now and then I caught glimpses of this undulating landscape of tired-looking shrubbery and sand that angles away endlessly southward into the heart of Central Asia.

During the day it was suffocatingly hot, and I did my best to retreat to the shade of bushes and wait it out. The evenings, by contrast, were pleasant, particularly in the dusty, sun-baked auls. At dusk young children—already with dark summer tans—played about on the sandy streets, and old women sat on benches, chatting in their long, colorful gowns and scarves. Outdoor, dung-fired stoves and traditional samovars came to life, the bittersweet aroma of the smoke mingling with the smell of camels, which, naked and gray-skinned after recently being clipped, wandered freely through the streets. On my way through I was often offered fermented drinking yogurt, *airan*, which left a tangy flavor that lingered well into the next day.

In the scheme of things, this relatively smooth passage was nonetheless a fleeting one. After little more than a week, canals became less frequent and vegetation along the banks gave way to shadeless plains of clay and sand. Simultaneously, auls became rare, the days longer and hotter, and then, as I had been warned, the flies came.

My first encounter was one stifling morning as I attempted to descend the muddy banks of the river. The sludge was so thick there was a risk of the horses becoming bogged and so I had improvised a new bucket for carrying water to and fro. No sooner had I dismounted, tied the horses, and returned with the first pail, than a swarm descended. These weren't light, pesky mosquitoes, but meaty, gray, large-winged critters, and within minutes, each horse had trickles of blood running from their spines, down their rumps, ribs, and necks. I went about swatting as many as I could, but as numbers steadily built, I abandoned the river and rode out as quickly as possible. The river that brought life into the desert was, from now on, also to be a curse for me.

For the next three weeks—the time it took me to reach the old Russian fort of Kazalinsk (which Kazakh-speakers called Kazaly), near the river mouth—the trend of harshening conditions continued. Returning to the northern bank, I watched the silty brown water grow sluggish and the land fade to pale yellow. I adjusted my routine, starting earlier—usually by 3:00 A.M.—and spent more of the day attempting to escape the sun.

Every day during this period was different yet also somehow the same—a characteristic I found to be true everywhere in the desert during summer, when there were no crisp edges to the horizon, to days, or even to thoughts. It was also true, however, that there were two or three standout exceptions that punctuated the course of my journey along the Syr Darya.

Already by the time we had reached the Syr Darya, Zhamba, the fifteen-year-old horse that I had acquired in the foothills of the Altai, was looking underweight and weary. He had worked most of his years as a carthorse and his spirit was broken. Externally he exhibited large scars from all the haulage, and through his sad, submissive eyes emanated a melancholy soul. I'd known that sooner or later I would have to retire him.

While camped on the outskirts of the city of Kyzylorda I arranged to sell Zhamba to a man who agreed to keep him as a riding horse for his grandchildren. At dawn the next morning I went to the local livestock market to find a replacement. Among the hundred or so mounts brought in by herders from afar, I chose a rather gangling but strong-looking bay stallion. He was not an ideal choice given that it was still spring (and stallions were still in a very aggressive mood), but that was the only option in a region where castrations were apparently seldom practiced.

Three days' ride from Kyzylorda I left Zhamba with the buyer's relatives in an aul called Akkum and rode on racked with guilt. I felt like I had betrayed Zhamba by abandoning him in a place where the intensity of heat would have been foreign to him, a horse from the mountains and steppe of eastern Kazakhstan. Yet to take him further into summer would have been a death sentence for him.

In the scheme of my trip, it was not the first or last time I would be haunted by the decision to leave a horse behind, and although Taskonir and Ogonyok proved reliable, the new stallion was just one of several trades before I happened upon a good long-term third mount.

Apart from Kyzylorda, there was one other large center I passed along the Syr Darya: the city of Baikonur. A fenced-off cluster of apartment blocks on the northern banks, it lay in the same anonymous desert country that I was becoming accustomed to, although it had long risen from obscurity to international renown. In the 1950s, the featureless desert just north of the Syr Darya, about 200 km east of the Aral Sea, had been chosen as the launch site for the Soviet Union's space program. From here in 1961, the young Russian cosmonaut Yuri Gagarin was sent into orbit, becoming the first man in space. Today, the cosmodrome remained the nucleus of Russia's space program, catering to an array of scientific, military, and, increasingly, commercial missions. With the impending retirement of the U.S. space shuttle fleet, it also had a crucial role in servicing the International Space Station.

The city of Baikonur itself—built exclusively to service the cosmodrome—

lay on territory leased to the Russian government. A permit was required to enter the city, and inside, it was said, Russian roubles were the official currency.

Unable to ride through Baikonur, I took a northern route between the cosmodrome and the city. I began early but got caught out in the heat navigating through vast stretches of junk metal, some of which consisted of hundreds of thousands of empty steel cans. I passed satellite dish installations and crossed the northbound rails that are still used to transport the rockets to the launch pad. Above, a large, unusually shaped plane circled. There was something surreal about it all.

It was a matter of national pride that Kazakhstan continued to play an important role in the history of space exploration. In fact, the large map of Kazakhstan I consulted daily was emblazoned with a picture of the rocket launch pad. I had come to think of it as a symbol of a world ever more interconnected via satellite and Internet—an unlikely icon in a country of almost inconceivable open wilderness.

I took shelter that night with a herding family on the periphery of Baikonur. The young man who hosted me in his simple mud hut explained that in Soviet times no one had been informed about the rocket launches. His parents had apparently watched in terror from their yurts as the first rockets were shot skyward. Nowadays rockets had become a routine sight but remained part of an unfathomable, incongruous world of little relevance to most herders.

⧈

JUST SHY OF Kazalinsk I broke away from the Syr Darya and began the trek northwest around the northern tip of the remnants of the Aral Sea.

It was the end of May, and even as prospects of fresh water promised to be fewer and farther between, the temperatures were on the climb. To beat the heat and avoid dehydration I began saddling the horses at sunset with the aim of riding through the night and finding shelter by sunup. This routine, which would see me through the next two months of my journey, was fraught with its own difficulties and risks.

During my final camp along the banks of the Syr Darya, it became clear that one of the main issues of night riding was that getting rest during the day was virtually impossible. Although I had learned to insulate the tent with horse blankets and pads, laying them over the top, the interior still became so baking hot that it left me in a state of semi-delirium, feeling as if my blood were cooking in my veins. Keeping an eye on the horses was crucial, and at this particular camp a stallion that had pursued us earlier in the morning remained on the attack. Every time I felt a hint of sleep pulling me under, I found myself having to reach for the nearest stick and go charging off again.[3]

When the sun went down, my spirits lifted and I set out with conviction, but the lack of sleep soon took its toll and my body surrendered to weariness. In the hours that followed it was only the constant task of keeping a lookout for Tigon that kept me awake. He spent his time roaming far and wide, only homing back in every half hour or so. His black coat was nearly invisible in the night and kept me guessing.

When gray-blue light did bleed back into the landscape I was nevertheless half asleep and only vaguely aware of my surroundings. It was a dangerous state of mind to be in, especially this morning, as I found myself crossing empty canals via crude bridges made with parallel ramps of narrow, wheel-width steel.

Faced with such obstacles, I would have ordinarily led each horse individually on foot, but in my somewhat detached state I tried to cross without dismounting. Halfway across the bridge, I felt Taskonir's lead rope pull out of my hand. As I turned from my perch on the new stallion, Ogonyok—who was tied to Taskonir from behind—reared up, then planted his front hooves wide apart in an effort to reverse away from the bridge. Taskonir was pulled off balance, and I heard the scuffle of hooves on steel, then a visceral crunch as he fell between the two bridge ramps. Fortunately, the plastic pack boxes were wide enough to prevent him falling all the way through, but now he was wedged between the ramps, one leg caught up on the bridge, the other three dangling over the drop to the empty canal below. Ogonyok, still tied to Taskonir's pack saddle, was pulled forward by the short lead rope and now teetered on the edge of the bank, theatening to fall in on top of Taskonir at any moment.

I rushed back to untie Ogonyok, then cut Taskonir's girth strap and ropes. As 450 kg of horse went tumbling down, I shut my eyes. No sooner had I reopened them, however, than Taskonir darted out of the canal— saved by the soft canal bed. I couldn't believe how foolish I'd been, or lucky I was to escape with little more than some scratches and bruising on Taskonir's back left leg.

When I left the bridge my little caravan was shaken up and facing the kind of predicament I had endeavored to avoid. Although I had managed 38 km as the crow flies that night—a very good distance—the delay meant I was marooned in the open in temperatures pushing 40°C. It took another two or three hours to reach water and shade in the next aul, by which time the horses were caked in salt stains from all the sweat and looking shriveled and strung out. Come nightfall, when the whole cycle of night riding began again, I had once again barely rested. At this rate, it was difficult to see how I might make it as far as the Caspian Sea without coming to grief. And yet finding a more sustainable routine was a conun- drum—it was dangerous to ride sleep-deprived at night, but suicide to move through the heat of day.

Three more hard but less eventful night rides brought me to Aralkum, a small community that lay just east of the Aral Sea's original shoreline and one day south of the former fishing port of Aralsk. Invited in by Dauletbas, a retired train station manager who now made a living rearing camels, I accepted—it was an opportunity to take stock for a couple of days, while also coming to learn more about the Aral Sea.

Due to the diversion of the Amu Darya and Syr Darya for irrigation, the Aral Sea was a "sea" in name only. What had once been the fourth- largest inland sea of its kind, providing one-sixth of the Soviet Union's fish supplies, was now a series of deserts and unconnected lakes—one in the north fed by the Syr Darya, and a puddle in the south fed by the Amu Darya that was said to have split into three different lakes, the largest of which was already fast evaporating into a saline swamp.

During an excursion to Aralsk, Dauletbas accompanied me to the old waterfront where as children he and his friends used to jump into the cooling waters from the pier. Nowadays the harbor was nothing more than a graveyard of rusting ships sinking in the sand. The shoreline had receded by as much as 100 km, leaving most of the fishing fleet stranded in the desert and many of the forty thousand people who had once worked in the fishing industry unemployed.[4]

West of Aralkum we drove over the old seabed, which was little more than a shell-encrusted plain, and visited an aul where mud huts and corrals were under siege by wind-driven banks of sand. In a region where pasture was already very thin on the ground and life particularly marginal, the retreat of the sea had led to creeping desertification and more extreme summers and winters. Compounding these problems, the ever-dropping sea level had caused a dramatic increase in salinity in the remaining waters, which had killed off much of the lake's vegetation and aquatic life. Frequent windstorms, which once had brought a moderating sea breeze in summer, now whipped up clouds of salt, sand, and toxic chemicals—largely pesticide and fertilizer runoff from the cotton fields of Uzbekistan that had collected on the seabed. These toxic clouds, according to many I spoke to, had caused an epidemic of respiratory, liver, and kidney disease.[5]

It had been a calculated decision by Soviet authorities to doom the Aral Sea, and the upshot was that while the Kazakhs of the Aral Sea region had watched their health decline and their livelihoods disintegrate in the space of a generation, Uzbekistan had become one of the world's largest exporters of cotton. And if the Soviet authorities could not have cared less that up to 75 percent of the diverted water was lost to evaporation and seepage in open and largely unlined canals, there was perhaps even less political will from the now independent Uzbekistan to invest in solving the problem.[6]

It took two days of travel from Aralkum before the northern tip of the old Aral Sea passed behind. Ahead lay around 400 km of steppe and desert to the river Zhem. It was a stretch of particularly arid terrain renowned for claiming the lives of Russian and Cossack soldiers in what had gone down in history as one of imperial Russia's most humiliating military failures in Central Asia.

The campaign in question—still spoken about by Kazakhs of the region—was an 1839 expedition of five thousand men, untold numbers of horses, and some ten thousand camels that had set out from Orenburg in southern Russia with a mission to free Russian slaves from Khiva, deep in Turkestan.[7] The army general charged with leading the campaign, Alexander Perovsky, had planned a route through the Kazakh steppes to the Aral Sea, from where he would carry on through the Kyzylkum Desert. Before departure he was said to have proclaimed that "in two months with God's help we shall be in Khiva!"

Perovsky led his troops out in early winter, wisely choosing to avoid summer because of the heat and scarcity of water—there were limited wells right across the region, some possibly more than a day's march apart. Not long into the expedition, however, it became clear he had underestimated the Kazakh steppe (then known as the Kirghiz steppe). The expedition was hit by repeated snowstorms, and come February 1840 the column was forced to retreat, having barely made it halfway to Khiva. During the return, wolves attacked the column—attracted by the rotting flesh of camels that had succumbed to the harsh conditions—and soldiers fell victim to exposure, scurvy, and even snow blindness. By the time the expedition hobbled back into Orenburg, seven months after departure, fewer than fifteen hundred camels remained alive and more than a thousand men had perished, all without the army having reached enemy territory.

To me the tragedy said less about the nature of the landscape or even the incompetence of the Russian soldiers than it did about the skills and hardiness of the nomads who had carved out a livelihood in the region, not to mention the Mongols, who six centuries earlier than Perovsky had used the same region as part of a thoroughfare to Europe. The fact that Carpini, a portly friar from Europe, and later William of Rubruck had traveled through these regions so quickly and made it out alive points to the efficiency and skill of their Mongolian entourage.

In the present day the Moscow–Tashkent train line blazes a trail northwest from Aralsk to Orenburg over some of the very terrain where

Perovsky had failed. In the absence of nomads and the desert wells they once maintained, I had the luxury of relying on remote railway auls and sidings along its path for water. Even so, it proved a particularly challenging stretch of terrain.

During a month of travel that took me through to July, I would pass through a landscape of sand dunes, clay flats, and barren uplands with negligible shade. Unlike the Syr Darya, with its army of flies, such were the heat and the dryness that the pale, bleached clay and white sandy earth appeared sterilized of life. I rode exclusively at night, and learned that it was crucial to find water and shade by 8:30 A.M., at which time the great molten orb had well and truly returned over the horizon. When I did get caught out, my long-sleeved shirt, and my saddle became hot to the touch, and the horses' sweat dried off as quickly as it beaded. Tigon began a routine that would endure for the rest of the summer—sprinting ahead and furiously digging holes in which he would lie for a few minutes until I caught up. When this didn't help he whined endlessly, his paws burning on the sand and his tongue out, forever wanting water.

Since the only water to be found was in auls, I stayed with families and did not camp, although, somewhat ironically, I did not come to know the people very well. Typically I would stumble into a community feeling spaced-out and groggy and ask for somewhere to rest. My arrival was usually greeted with fanfare, but I could rarely last more than a cup of tea before passing out. The horses would be set free to find whatever grass was available in the vicinity of the aul. Sometimes I would be woken up by the family to be told that the horses had come to the front door of the house looking for their owner. The heat was so oppressive that the horses could do nothing but search out the slightest sliver of shade.

Then, just as everyone was preparing to roll out their mattresses on the floor of the mud huts—or, as was the case in many places, simply out under the stars—I would reemerge, saddle up, and ride on. It was a feeling of acute isolation that I knew would never leave me—moving while the rest of the world slept.

There was, on the other hand, a kind of dreamlike quality to this period of my journey that a part of me truly enjoyed. Although I was following the same path as the railway, I rode far away from it for most of the time, navigating by matching my compass bearing with star formations and following them until the sky faded to blue. At times I rode through auls under the rising moon, discreetly pushing the horses through the sand, disturbing little more than a few camels and dogs. It wasn't possible to remain awake right through the night; I regularly napped in the saddle, and woke to discover that the horses had taken me astray. At other times I dismounted and slept on the earth. Even rocks could appear as a comfortable mattress when weariness had gotten the better of me. Sunrise was a sublime time of the day, when it felt as if I were riding the waves across the steppe. Once the sun was up, however, the long hours of the doldrums would begin.

Despite being very much immersed in the landscape and occupied by the challenges of summer, I was by no means impervious to goings-on beyond the scheme of my journey. At some point during the past few weeks Kathrin had discovered that she was suffering from Cushing's syndrome, a deadly disease caused by a brain tumor that produces an elevated release of cortisol into the body. For months Kathrin had been suffering from horrendous symptoms, including rapid weight gain, back pain, and unusual mood swings. It had taken some time before a doctor had discovered the tumor, but he had told her that if it was left untreated, it would be fatal. Just as I was heading through this hottest part of the Kazakh desert, Kathrin was preparing to undergo brain surgery in Germany. I knew that in this region to leave the horses and dog would almost guarantee I would never see them again, and so I did not consider it an option to abandon the journey and travel to Germany. Kathrin did not try to persuade me to leave my journey behind, either, and was very understanding, although I imagine it must have been hurtful that I did not offer to come.

At the same time that Kathrin was preparing for surgery, on the other side of the world, in Cairns, Australia, my longtime friend Cordell Scaife and his partner, Cara Poulton, were readying to fly to Kazakhstan to join me for the month-long trek along the Zhem River. I had often spoken with Cordell—whom I had met at age of nineteen during my six-month stint at Australian National University—about the idea of his coming for one stage of the journey or another, and I was thrilled he could join me. Ironically, though, it meant that while I could look forward to the closeness of a friend during a stint of galling isolation, Kathrin was alone to deal with a far greater struggle.

Fortunately, Kathrin's surgery, which she underwent not long after Cordell and Cara's arrival, would prove successful, and she would be on the road to recovery by the time I was nearing the Caspian Sea.

CORDELL AND CARA joined me at the railway siding of Kopmula, little more than a week's journey short of the Zhem River. There we went about purchasing two extra horses and a pack camel that I hoped would reduce the burden on my mounts.

Two weeks later we were camped above the meandering Zhem. It was a shallow band of ale-brown water carving out a sunken gorge through wind-whipped hills dotted with dust-coated bushes and wormwood. Farther on, the river split into multiple channels among the curves and ripples of sand dunes.

From where we were, a day's ride from the junction of the river and the Moscow–Tashkent railway, the Zhem flowed some 600 km southwest through desert country to the Caspian Sea. At various points downstream it apparently dried up and went underground—particularly during the summer. I had also been warned that it was so brackish that only livestock could drink its waters. It had been a wet spring with heavy snowmelt farther north, though, and some had also suggested the river would keep flowing till August. My aim was to follow the river for a month as far as the oil town of Kulsary, 100 km from the Caspian.

Although we set out along the Zhem with the same night-riding routine I had followed since departing the Syr Darya, with water close at hand, we were not reliant on auls and could make camp along the riverbank to see out the heat of day. During the hottest hours, when the temperature breached 40°C, we rolled out of the tents and lay in the river's shallows. While the sun beat from above, I kept my head down, entranced by multicolored pebbles that shifted beneath the current and minnows that nibbled at my toes. Running as it did through the desert, the Zhem was a miraculous watercourse that the camel and horses also relished. They spent hours in the middle of the river, taking swipes at fresh green reeds and overhanging bushes. Even Tigon joined in, curling up in the water with only his nose and two tall ears poking skyward above the waterline.

When darkness fell, we became accustomed to feeling our way up the bank and onto the open plains, where the horses were adept at tapping into animal tracks that took us on efficient, direct routes, sometimes far away from the wide, arcing bends of the river but ultimately leading back to water. Harvette, as we had named our camel, brought a welcome new cadence and character to these long hours of riding. A seven-year-old female sporting the distinctive double humps of the Bactrian breed, she had a stoic rhythm and a sense of labored care to her every movement that made her very unlike the moody, short-tempered horses.[8] In camp, she was always in the mix, forever foraging around my kit bags. It was not uncommon to see her sucking on my sauce bottle or getting into other food—on one occasion she devoured an entire watermelon. When we slept, she often wandered a fair distance from camp, and it was quite some task to locate her and bring her back.

There was another shift in the nature of the journey that was evident in the early days along the Zhem. For two months I had been absorbed with the task of surviving summer. There had been precious little opportunity to get a real feel for the people, particularly while following the railway. Now, however, far from the economy of any main thoroughfare, and more accustomed to the rigors of summer travel (and greatly helped by Cara and Cordell), I could turn my attention to the nomad heritage of the region.

For some weeks I had been in the lands of the Kishi Juz, or the Junior Horde, a group of Kazakh tribes renowned as a hardened warrior people of the desert. Their territory stretches from the Aral Sea to the Caspian

Sea, and from Russia's southern border as far south as Turkmenistan. In the past, tribes of the Kishi Juz had wintered over in the deep south between the Caspian and the Aral, then migrated north to cooler climes for the summer.

For the first week and a half we passed typical examples of Soviet-era collectives that had brought together former nomads into settled communities. There were also permanent summer stations where families ran large herds of camel and sheep. At such a station beyond an aul called Szharkamys I inadvertently stumbled on an intriguing clue as to the fate of nomadic culture in the region.

While I lay in the family's mud hut nibbling on boiled lamb scalp, my eyes caught sight of a familiar curved piece of timber among a row of slats laid into the ceiling. It was a roof pole from the frame of a yurt—and an old one at that. I mentioned this to the herder of the house, and he looked at me sadly.

In this region of Aktubinsk Oblast, he explained, after the collapse of the Soviet Union, many herders, believing that independence and capitalism would usher in a new era of modernity, had hacked up their yurts—mostly family heirlooms from before collectivization—and used the frames for everything from firewood to building corrals. By the time they realized they would not be liberated from a life on the land, they were without yurts or the skills to make them. Now many herders who moved between seasonal camps made do in summer with rusty old wagons that were like tinderboxes in the heat.

It was hard to know how credible the herder's story was, but just two days downstream from the family's station—nearing the border between Aktubinsk Oblast and Western Kazakhstan Oblast—we entered remote country where the rhythms of nomadic life had certainly not faded.

At sunrise we rode out onto an elevated plain of powder-dry steppe looking for water. Long before we saw the river, there came a billowing plume of dust and the distinctive rumble of sheep and goats. After some time, the unmistakable figure of a man on the back of a camel came into view. Sitting wedged between the two humps, he wore a long scarf under his hat, and with a whip in hand, he rocked back and forth, pushing a sea of goats and sheep out to pasture. The gap between us rapidly shrank until the man was leaning down from his giant animal with a handshake, imploring us to return with him to his home.

The summer camp from which the herder had appeared was a sight to behold. We were led through a huddle of around two hundred camels in various states of leisure. Some sat on their haunches asleep, while babies frolicked on shaky stick-like legs and two or three bulls sauntered about, their front thighs thick as tree trunks, and humps the size of small refrigerators swaying to and fro. There was something dinosaur-like about their power and grace.

In the center of the huddle lay the camp itself—animal pens, a rusty old wagon, and an underground hut dug into the top of the riverbank. The camp overlooked the shallow waters of the Zhem and, beyond it, sweeping sand dunes and crusty plains. As I would witness during the remainder of the journey to Kulsary, many Kazakhs of the region spent summer squirreled away underground during the day, and the cooler nights sleeping in a yurt or simply on mattresses under the stars. All the work, which primarily involved milking camels, was done at dawn and dusk.

After unsaddling, we were led to a young woman who stood barely as high as the camel's back legs, her own right leg bent up to support a milk bucket on her thigh. While she milked, her infant daughter, who had barely learned to walk, stumbled about among the camels, unfazed as a couple of particularly gigantic specimens edged closer and gently sniffed at her hair.

When the milking was done, the full pails were whisked away for the production of cream, yogurt, dried curd, and fermented camel milk, known as shubat. Two teenage boys who had been lying in wait for the last camel to be freed mounted their horses and roused the herd with shouts and whistles.

As the boys and their horses worked like a tugboat, pushing and pulling at the vast herd, the camels rose reluctantly to their feet, then moved to the edge of the riverbank—a precipice where the steppe dropped away in a rather dramatic bank of eroding clay and sand. Only when the animals were bunched up did the first camels take the plunge. It began as a trickle—a few camels clambering down to the water—but soon became a torrent. Legs flew, saggy lips wobbled, the earth trembled, the sky filled with dust, and one by one they leaped into the river.

The boys continued after them, whistling and charging, urging on the lazier ones at the rear. From back up on the bank I watched as the herd crossed the river to the far side, where they rapidly shrank to nothing more than faint specks in a land of empty horizons.

Back at camp, the temperature was cranking toward 40°C, and what had been a hive of activity was now a picture of desolation. Hot wind gusted from the west, picking up dried dung from the empty pens and tossing it viciously through the air. A couple of dogs lay under the rusty wagon. Nothing moved. Tigon stuck close to my horses, which were standing still in the river below.

We were invited down some clay steps into the underground hut, where the glare and exposure gave way to darkness and intimacy. For some time we sat propped up on cushions, gulping down fresh bowls of fatty camel milk in the dark. But then our host, a man named Murat Guanshbai, lit a candle and the world reexpanded a little, revealing a room padded with felt mats and wall hangings and featuring shelves cut into the clay for the display of ornaments.

Murat was as exotic as his surrounds. He had a square, open face with a short flat nose, and his almond eyes were protected by bushy, overhanging eyebrows. Unlike most Kazakhs' hair, his was thick and curly as steel wool, and his jaw was masked with stubble. Murat and his family were Kozha, one of the tribes that composed the Kishi Juz. The Kozha were known as the descendants of Bedouin missionaries to Kazakhstan some thousand years ago.

More important for Murat than his tribal background, however, were his nomadic roots. Although he had an education in veterinary science, he had chosen to carry on the tradition of his family as camel herders. In fact, his family were herders of some local renown, owning somewhere in the order of five hundred camels—no small number, given that a large camel could fetch in excess of $1,500 at market. With a herd this size, it was crucial to migrate with the seasons, and Murat's family had five different camps. Soon he would move with his family to the August camp, which lay far away from the riverbank to the west.

I got along well with Murat, and he seemed to genuinely care about his animals. In light of this I decided to offer him the stallion that I had bought in Kyzylorda. My stallion was a tall, slender horse that many had offered to buy from me along the way because his build was seen as good for racing. Unfortunately, these same characteristics made him unsuitable for long-distance travel. In recent weeks he had been unwell, suffering diarrhea, and although I had wormed him and fed him more grain than the others, he had lost considerable weight. Murat promised me one of his horses in exchange—a quiet, fat little horse of Mongolian proportions—and made an additional offer that seemed like a godsend at the time, but which I would later regret.

I'd long planned to say farewell to Cordell and Cara in Kulsary before carrying on alone toward Russia. The horses, however, were in desperate need of a rest, and it had come to my attention that I would need to apply for a Russian visa in Almaty well in advance of reaching the border. I had decided to look for a place near Kulsary to leave the horses for the month of August. Upon hearing this, Murat warned that it was even hotter in Kulsary, and there would be no fodder for my horses in the area. He proposed instead that upon our arrival in Kulsary—where an uncle of his would host us—he would send a truck to bring my horses back here for grazing until September. All I would have to do is pay the costs. What I could never have foreseen was that Murat's plan would fall through, and so I would become trapped not only in a region without fodder, but the middle of an urban oil town with nowhere to go.

That was in the future, though, and for now I was intoxicated by the majesty of Murat's camp, where for two days more I drank in every detail, from the sound of the camels moving back under moonlight to the sensation of lying down under the stars at night and waking with not a drop of dew under an eternally blue and cloudless sky. There was a completeness, an intertwining of nature, animal, and man, that could not be replicated in an environment compartmentalized by walls and fences, and it rein-vigorated Cordell, Cara, and me for the remainder of the journey together.

FROM MURAT'S CAMP, there lay just 150 km to Kulsary. One day south of Murat's we met with his father, Guanshbai, and decided to sell him our little camel, Harvette. From there, the land became flatter, the pasture—as Murat had forewarned—grew thin and the ground metamorphosed into white clay pans with nothing but salt bush. The temperature climbed over 50°C, and the water became brackish—but still fresh enough to drink. There were times when we were so exhausted by the struggle to keep cool during the day that we'd saddle up the horses at night but then fall asleep until after midnight; when we finally woke, we gave up and unsaddled. It didn't really matter, though, for the end of my journey with my Australian friends was drawing near, and we had experienced the es-sence of steppe life that we had come for.

On July 27 we packed up for our last day of riding along the Zhem. I was thinking happily that my horses were about to be trucked back to paradise for a month of grazing. For the next month I could also look for-ward to some time away from the punishing routine of night riding, and come the cool of September, when I planned to return, my horses would be fat and rested. Never again, I thought, would I have to deal with the heat of the Kazakh summer.

15

THE OIL ROAD

SINCE DEPARTING AKBAKAI in April, my journey had taken me four months across the unbroken steppe of central and eastern Kazakhstan. During that time, the challenges of each and every day had been defined by the rhythms of summer, when daylight was cheap and the cool hours of night precious. On the outskirts of the oil town of Kulsary, 100 km short of the Caspian Sea, however, the steppe abruptly began to break up. The open desert and saltpans on the flanks of the River Zhem that had so infused in me a feeling of inner peace gave way to mangled earth that had been bulldozed into a maze of mounds and ridges. Then came twisted, rusty pieces of steel, shattered glass, and burned-out cars. On the asphalt road leading into the center, heavy trucks and SUVs hurtled past at unchecked speed, spraying gravel and leaving us in a wake of dust and fumes. The brave, indomitable Taskonir trembled.

I'd long known about the oil economy of western Kazakhstan, and in the past few weeks we'd glimpsed something of the industry—permanent gas flares on the horizon, the odd truck—but nothing on this scale.

Tanbai, the relative of Murat who had agreed to host us until the truck came to pick the horses up, met us on a street corner. As we came to a halt, he flicked his cigarette to the ground and looked us over.

"Where are your cars?" he asked, concerned. It turned out that Tanbai had mistakenly understood from Murat by phone that we were wealthy tourists traveling by jeep.

Tanbai begrudgingly led us to his house in the center of town, where we tied up the horses and took shelter from the heat. No sooner had we sat down for tea and bread than Tanbai's twenty-year-old son, also named Murat, shuffled in next to me and leaned over with a new Nokia phone. With his parents across the table, he covertly displayed a porn clip, and then a gruesome video of an American soldier having his head severed by Taliban. Oblivious to this, Tanbai said to us with pride: "My son can speak English, you know. He is studying to be an engineer, and is already work- ing for an American oil company."

In the light of morning it was clear that in the world in which the younger Murat had grown up, horses, the turn of the seasons, and grass held little currency. Tanbai earned a modest living as a bus driver and me- chanic, and their simple mud-brick home was hedged in by new two- story townhouses. Pointing to the house opposite, which had a brand-new black Toyota Land Cruiser parked behind the gates, Tanbai said of his neighbor, "He supplies concrete for the oil companies." Indicating another house, and then a third, he added, "And that one over there is a local politician . . . Him, his son is working for an oilfield."

A drive through the town of just over forty thousand people revealed mansions at all stages of hasty construction, most of which backed onto potholed dirt streets where camels wandered haplessly in the heat and piles of rubbish sat uncollected. There was little infrastructure for water or sewage—even the more luxurious homes had pit toilets in their yards. On the edge of town water tankers were lined up, ready 24/7 to deliver water at a rate of $200 for 3,000 litres.

In the past, the vast, sterile desert on the northeast shoulder of the Cas- pian Sea—at the center of which lay Kulsary—had been renowned for its warrior tribes, who kept their land impenetrable to invading armies. Nowadays, the mishmash urban landscape was the hallmark of a region in the throes of an oil boom, which had attracted a relative invasion of multinational oil companies. The scale and pace of economic transformation were difficult to fathom. Little more than an hour's drive south lay the Tengiz oilfield, which was built over the sixth-largest oil bubble on the planet and tapped by a joint venture between the Kazakh government and American-based Chevron. Tengiz was the single biggest contributor to the government's coffers, and combined with the Kashagan field in the nearby Caspian Sea—the second-largest known oil reserve in the world, and at the time of its discovery in the year 2000 the biggest find in thirty years—it placed Kazakhstan in a position to become one of the world's biggest oil exporters.[1]

The oil reserves of western Kazakhstan set the country's economy apart from many of its resource-poor Central Asian neighbors and had helped steer the country into a relatively prosperous and stable post-Soviet independence. Yet for all the potential and promise that oil brought, there were signs that the industry was a source of social division and corruption. In the early days of the boom, the president, Nursultan Nazarbayev, had been implicated in a scandal when it was revealed that billions of dollar in proceeds from a 1996 agreement between Mobil and the government were hidden away in Swiss bank accounts—and that $500 million of it had inexplicably vanished.[2] At the other end of the spectrum, the many herders and unemployed rural folk I had met in recent weeks were locked out of the oil economy and could only look on as their traditional livestock economy was pushed further to the fringes.

It is true that the oil industry offered lucrative opportunities for many regional Kazakhs, as evidenced by the pace of development in Kulsary. The corruption and lack of trickle-down wealth, however, contributed to a common perception that most of the oil money was being funneled to the east, where it ended up either in the pockets of officials or at the president's political disposal. Even among those workers employed at the coal face, there were recurring tensions over unsafe conditions and discrepancies of pay compared to that of foreign workers. There were instances when this had boiled over into violent rioting at the Tengiz field.[3]

Aside from this, there was also the view that foreign companies such as Chevron were taking more than their fair share of the nation's riches. "Back when the deals were made, Kazakhstan was desperate for money and the Americans paid too little," said Tanbai as we pulled up to the central market. "We were cheated. We didn't know the real value. Kazakhstan is a country surrounded by wolves on all sides—the Russians, Chinese, Turks, and of course the Americans!"

By the time we made it back to Tanbai's home it was 40°C, and the horses stood tied and sweating in the shade-less yard. I had paid for a water truck to fill Tanbai's tank, and hay was on its way, but Tanbai was unhappy about the growing pile of manure. In a town where I had long imagined that I could spend some time recuperating, it was becoming clear that while the most challenging terrain of Kazakhstan might have been behind me, my journey—like Kulsary—was at an awkward intersection between a life dominated by the natural elements and one in which survival would increasingly require navigation through the thickets of trouble brought on by industry, bureaucracy, and the every-man-for-himself attitude of the oil economy. Somewhat symbolic of this, my route from Kulsary to the Russian border—500 km of desert, punctuated by the central oil city of Atyrau—lay alongside the $2.2 billion oil pipeline that now pumped crude to the west as far as the Black Sea throughout the very untamed land once trodden by Mongol warriors and Silk Road traders.

BEFORE I COULD ride out of Kulsary I needed to travel 3,000 km to Almaty to apply for a Russian visa. To do this would first involve arranging for the horses and dog to be transported to Murat's farm for a month of grazing and finding buyers for Cordell's horse and the short, fat horse I had acquired from Murat. As a replacement for my third mount, I had settled on a gray horse named Kok, which Cara had been riding.[4]

In the end the agreement with Murat did not work out, and so instead I left the animals under the watch of a herding family in a nearby aul, Karagai. It was a community set in a mustard-yellow dustbowl with no grass to be spoken of. A herder there named Albek offered to buy Cordell's horse and assured me that, for a price, he could take the other horses out to graze at a summer pasture. Albek's elderly father promised to guard Tigon.

Five weeks later, I returned from Almaty pessimistic about my chances of finding the horses alive. I had been away longer than anticipated, and the only correspondence I'd received from Karagai was that the horses remained in the aul—they had not been taken out to summer pastures for grazing as agreed. Problems I had encountered in Almaty contributed to my gloomy outlook. The Russian embassy had refused my visa application. After much waiting I had mailed my passport to a travel agency in Finland instead—a risky move, since by law I had to carry my passport at all times.[5]

When I jumped out of a buckled old Russian jeep and landed my backpack in the dust and sand of Karagai, it appeared my worst fears had been realized. I found Taskonir tied up at the back of a corral with his head hanging and ribs resembling the corrugations I had just driven over to get to Karagai. The other two horses were missing, and the only person to be found at Albek's home was an emaciated shadow of a man who reached out to me from the doorstep for balance, then crashed drunkenly into the dirt.

After a tip-off from a neighbor, I was directed on foot east of the aul, where I found men cutting up two freshly slaughtered horses. They weren't mine, but the men knew who I was and waved me on further. I found Albek and a friend of his in the midst of a gallop—they were riding none other than Kok and Ogonyok, and explained that my horses had been entered in a baiga—a horse race—that was to be held the next day!

Back in the aul, the removal of saddles and blankets revealed fresh sores. Albek shrugged sheepishly and admitted that the 300 kg of grain I had left with his family had vanished within a couple of weeks—this, he explained, was why the horses were skinnier than when I had left them.

Albek's elderly mother tried to lighten my spirits: "Those sores are in memory of us! You will never forget us!"

Although I was angry, I was genuinely grateful that the horses were alive. I paid Albek the promised $300 and thanked him. Any mistakes were forgiven when I found Tigon. I spotted him from a distance dug into the sand under a wooden platform-cum-deck near Albek's house. On top of the platform, sitting cross-legged and guarding Tigon, was Albek's father. As I approached, Tigon's dusty ears sprang to life and his tail flopped about uncertainly. When I was nearer he sprinted to the end of his lead and leaped up with his paws on my chest. The old man straightened out his chicken bone legs, a smile opened up between his hollow, sun-blackened cheeks, and he rose to embrace me. "See! Everyone thought I was mad. They were sure you would never come back, but I didn't forget you!"

Departure from Karagai was one of the more vivid farewells of my Kazakh journey. Albek's father had gotten hold of a pink plastic gem-encrusted hair band and wore it over his bald scalp from ear to ear. As I saddled up to leave, he rose from a blanket on his platform, resplendent in this headwear, holding out a glass of vodka. As I went to accept, he pulled the glass back and fell back on the dirt in laughter.

"Whatever you do, don't rush!" he said, his eyes rolling as he slipped into another world.

The aul passed by in a series of wafts of dry dung until it had been eclipsed by the horizon and I was breathing in fresh, clear air. Then came silence and the empty steppe.

It occurred to me that the openness was like a big blank canvas, and being here after the turbulence of the past month allowed me to rebuild my picture of the world from the tiniest details. I closed my eyes, felt the swaying of the saddle and waited for the first sensations to bleed back in. It came as the sound of the horses brushing gently against the wormwood plants. Then came the feeling of the breeze lightly cooling the sweat on my back, and when I opened my eyes, I saw the saksaul trees coming and going like driftwood floating aimlessly by on the ocean.

After a short ride I made an early camp on the Zhem River. Tigon ran circles in the sand, pausing momentarily at times to come in close, roll onto his back, and demand a pat on the belly. The horses rested their necks on one another. Ogonyok let out long, breezy farts that tailed off lazily. Taskonir's condition was bad—he was all skin and bone—but at least he now looked at ease. I let my clothes drop to the ground and lay in the ankle-deep water watching the pink moon rise like a lamp into the sky.

In the morning I had ridden only a short distance when I slumped from the saddle with a banging in my skull and my stomach writhing— probably a consequence of the vast quantities of horsemeat I had consumed the previous day in Karagai. I managed little more than 13 km before heading for a herder's hut, where I feigned interest in finding water for the animals and swiftly collapsed on the floor inside. For the next three days I lay in a fever. I ate almost nothing but even so made frequent sojourns to relieve my stomach and bowels. At first I made an effort to do it discreetly, but eventually I let go of all pride.

I stayed a week in all, but only as I began to regain strength was I able to get to know my hosts and through them the curious farming arrangement they were part of. Aigul was a twenty-year-old woman with an open, round face, long brown hair, and a mischievous smile. The rigors of life on the steppe hadn't yet taken away the beauty of her youth, although her hands were wrinkled and callused, and the skin on her cheeks was freckled and dark from a lifetime of sun. During the day she brought me water and tea and in between chores scrutinized my photo album. She knew very little Russian. When her husband, Bulat, returned from herding each evening she would shrink away into the background and avoid eye contact. Bulat was a strong, handsome man in his late twenties with a thick mop of hair and light green eyes.

From a distance, the herding station that Aigul and Bulat managed, with its large herds of camels, horses, sheep, and goats, appeared like a traditional nomad camp. All was not as it seemed, though. The hut was neither a summer domain or a winter one but a permanent base, and Bulat and Aigul were not indigenous to the area but hired farmhands from neighboring Uzbekistan.[6] The owners of the farm and livestock were Kazakh businessmen from Kulsary who had taken out a forty-nine-year lease on the land.

"Kazakhs won't do this work—it's too little money. But for us, well, there is no work back home," explained Bulat, who spoke fairly coherently in Russian. I had heard about this type of farming from many Kazakhs, who complained the government was offering long-term land leases affordable only to city businessmen who didn't have skills or interest in animal husbandry.

This explained some of the glaring oddities of life at the hut. Every meal was a bland serving of rice or pasta mixed with a bouillon cube and onion. "Our employer won't let us slaughter sheep—we have to buy our own food. Meat is too expensive for us," they told me, as excuse for the fact that they had no meat to offer.

Their horse tack was as appalling as their food. Bulat's saddle was a crude construction of plastic and steel that left a permanent sore on his horse's back. Without investment from his employer in decent equipment, and no sense of personal ownership of work, there was little incentive for Bulat to take pride in herding. It was a pattern I had witnessed time and again in Kazakhstan, suggesting that the capitalist master had no more interest in the well-being of people and their animals than did the Communist predecessor.

The true nature of this style of steppe farming became clear the day before I departed. A Toyota Prado hurtling across the steppe signaled the arrival of the owners. They were two burly men dressed in city clothes and seemed to have come out for a bit of fun. For an hour or so they roared back and forth in pursuit of a terrified herd of horses, tooting the horn and flashing their lights. When the horses began to tire, a lasso was dangled out a passenger window and the vehicle closed in on a fat specimen. After being caught—and nearly strangled—the horse was bound by the legs, pushed upside down, and hauled up an old door used as a ramp into the back of a waiting van. For good measure it was kicked a few times before the doors were closed.

In a land where nomads had been perfecting horsemanship for at least 5,500 years, it was a saddening image that stuck with me.

OVER THE NEXT 500 km to the Russian border I took a direct route across the desert to the Volga River. It was a hard and gritty ride, characterized on one hand by the haunting beauty of the desert and on the other by the disruption brought by the oil industry.

In what proved a full month of travel, I spent the first two weeks picking my way through a morass of salt lakes, flats, and bogs known in Russian as *solonchak*. Following a web of narrow ridges I watched from the saddle as glassy shallow pools of water, glittering white crusts, and chalky plains unfolded, interspersed by carpets of yellow, pink and green plants. From this washed-out palette thousands of birds would lift in the distance like giant swarms of mosquitoes.

In the evenings we all rejoiced in the simplicity of our campsites—the horses rolling on their backs on the brittle, sun-bleached grass, and Tigon curling up asleep next to the tent. It was mid-September, and although the sky was pale and clear, the oppressiveness of summer had gone, meaning that for the first time since May, I was able to ride long hours through the day, and enjoy unbroken sleeps at night.

The downside of the barren landscape was that there was no fresh water to be found, and so I was forced to stray daily to local railway sidings and auls built around small-scale oil-extraction sites. These visits were invariably depressing, and when I rode out to reenter the open land I tried to leave the memories of them behind. Nonetheless, I couldn't stop my mind from filling with a tangle of thoughts. The nomadic life that had defined the people for eternity had clearly been pushed so far to the margins by oil, by the Soviets, and by the new era of capitalism that it was no longer on the radar. The more I stewed over what I had witnessed, the more the image of Kazakhstan as a land of hundreds of interlocking grazing territories, within which each nomad clan had its unique pattern of seasonal migration, began to crumble. In place of this a very different picture emerged. If the farm that Aigul and Bulat managed was the model of the future, then it was not difficult to imagine the rise of corporate-run farms that could one day carve up the land with fences. If this happened, then herders and nomads could be evicted from their ancestral lands and either be replaced by cheap imported labor or be forced into employment and lose the very independence that was the heart of nomadic existence.

The halfway mark to the Russian border from Kulsary was the city of Atyrau, the oil capital of western Kazakhstan, built on the banks of the

Ural River (a river historically better known by its Kazakh name, Yaik). Atyrau also represented the gateway out of geographical Asia into Europe.

After some preliminary work on veterinary documents for the border, I rode west, following the oil pipeline across flats and marshes on the northern fringe of the Caspian Sea. Next to me flowed untold riches on the way to powering the engine of economies in faraway countries. To me, what mattered was there were very few edible plants or grass for the horses. The only advantage of the oil pipeline for me was that every 20 km there were huts made of reeds and mud manned by security guards who were paid a pittance to patrol their stretch of pipe. Here I was usually able to find water and some advice about the terrain ahead.

Only a couple of days out of Atyrau my cooking stove broke and I went for the next eleven days without hot meals. The only comforting thoughts I could find lay in the nature of the harsh land around me. With such thin pickings of grass and limited fresh water, this kind of land would never be suitable for fixed farming. There were surely only two choices for land users of the future—abandon such steppe or return to some form of nomadic herding to utilize what little pasture there was.

My journey from Atyrau to the Russian border was broken by one unexpected discovery. Just beyond the aul of Isatai the land spread out into a sea of wavy sand dunes speckled with tussocks of grass and other desert plants. I had reached the southern edge of a desert known as the Naryn Kum. At a railway siding a gray-bearded herder took me in and spoke with passion about the land he had grown up in.

"I was raised as a nomad way out there in the dunes," he said, pointing to the north. "When I was young all nomads wintered over in the dunes and then migrated to the Caspian coast for summer. I didn't see a Russian until I was eighteen years old! In my day the best musicians in the area would turn up and volunteer for a wedding, not only looking for pay, like nowadays." There were few people who still lived in the Naryn Kum. According to rumor, this was partly because oil and gas exploration had destroyed many natural springs.

In the evening I retired to his home, and he brought out a remarkable-looking saddle blanket loosely woven with horsehair. "This is called a *kyl*

Ruslan descends from a peak in the Altai Mountains of Eastern Kazakhstan—the starting point for my year-long crossing of the country to the Volga delta on the Caspian Sea.

Nurkhan (far left) on newly purchased Taskonir, Ruslan (second from left) on Ogonyok, and friends, not far from Pugachevo, Eastern Kazakhstan.

Aset with his disabled son, Guanz, who is trying out my Australian saddle on Taskonir. Zhana Zhol, Eastern Kazakhstan.

Aset's mother-in-law—witness to the collectivization of Kazakh nomads and survivor of the resulting famine, believed to have wiped out 1.7–2.2 million Kazakhs between 1930 and 1933.

Aset leads off into a brewing *buran* (winter storm) a day before we took shelter in Kindikti, with a young Tigon in tow.

Tigon's first winter—he was desperate to get his paws off the snow.

Bakhetbek, our host in Kindikti, is an Oralman— an expatriate Kazakh born in the Xinjiang Province in China—whose family has since returned to Kazakhstan.

Aul of Kindikti, Eastern Kazakhstan.

The barren land along the north of Lake Balkhash. No snow, but freezing conditions.

Portrait of a Kazakh *chaban* (herder) near Ayagoz.

The *chaban* Bazibek and his camel near Ortaderesin, Lake Balkhash.

Lonely Kazakh grave on the north shore of Lake Balkhash—the kind that Aset advised me to sleep in so that the "old men" of the steppe would protect me.

Riding out onto the Betpak Dala (the Starving Steppe). I'm riding Zhamba, with Ogonyok and Taskonir in tow.

Self-portrait on the Betpak Dala, two days before Christmas. Temperature was dropping below –30°C.

Getting porridge cooking in camp on the Betpak Dala. Tigon is out of sight, curled up in my sleeping bag.

The grim gold-mining town of Akbakai on the Betpak Dala, where I was forced to hole up for the better part of three months.

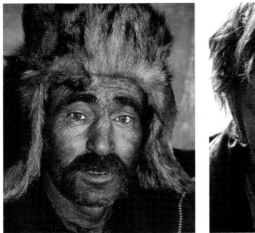 

Grisha and Vitka, the Russian alcoholics who took me in on Christmas Eve 2004 in Akbakai.

Baitak—the man to whom I owe the lives of my horses and Tigon, and the journey itself.

Spring has arrived. Children hold some freshly picked tulips next to their woolly camel near Tasty on the Chu River, Kazakhstan.

Taskonir shares my oatmeal porridge in one of my first camps on the Syr Darya River. Note the green spring grass.

A Kazakh woman from the family in Zhuantobe that nursed Tigon back to health after his run-in with a car.

Chilikti, a typical aul of adobe huts, a few days ride north of the Aral Sea.

After a long night ride I take refuge from the heat on the floor of a family's mud-hut, somewhere north of the Aral Sea.

Tigon and I often took naps during my night-riding routine. Here on the banks of the Zhem River, there is fortunately some shade to be found.

I film Murat Guanshbai's vast herd of camels being herded across the Zhem River.

A nomad greeting not far shy of Kulsary, Western Kazakhstan. In this region, people traditionally take cover in underground homes in the daytime heat and sleep in their yurts at night.

Nomad child amid the camel herd.

Bulat—the Karakalpak herder-for-hire—at the ranch near Kulsary where I fell ill with food poisoning.

terlek," he told me. "My father's father taught me how to make it, and he was taught by his father. We make them by cutting off the tails and manes of three horses in early winter when the horses no longer need to swish away the flies. In all my life using a kyl terlek, I have never had a sore on my horse . . . even in the heat of summer!"

I fondled it carefully, the significance beginning to dawn on me. In this blanket was a genius I could now appreciate.

"In the past, all Kazakhs used a kyl terlek. It drains away the sweat, allows air in, and is the most natural fiber available. When crossing a river, or in the rain, unlike wool felt, this blanket doesn't stay wet for long, and is never heavy!" he said.

Throughout my journey, I'd been asked whether I had ever seen or heard of a mysterious saddle blanket made from horsehair. No one had seemed to know how to make it, although everyone, from Kazakhs on the Betpak Dala to Mongolians in the central Khangai Mountains, knew that a horsehair blanket was the best option for long distance travel.

I had always wondered how campaigning Mongolian armies were able to swim across rivers with their horses, then get back on and keep riding. Although there were known methods the Mongols used, such as bundling clothes and saddles into a buoyant sack of leather that was tied to the horse's tail and towed across the water (such as is described by Carpini), it was inevitable that their saddle blankets would have often become wet in this process. And, as any nomad of the steppe knows today, a soaked felt saddle blanket remains wet for days and can rub a horse's back raw within hours. A kyl terlek, on the other hand, would drain almost instantly, allowing horsemen to continue without detriment to the horses. Could this kyl terlek—a term that coincidentally approximately means "summer deel for horse" in Mongolian—have been one of the Mongolian nomads' secrets to their long campaigns?[7]

It was a long bow to draw, but later when I informed CuChullaine O'Reilly of the Long Riders Guild about it, he was overcome with excitement. Only months earlier he had received a report from Swedish long rider and adventurer Michael Strandberg, who had made the same observations about horsehair blankets made by indigenous Siberians for

Yakutian ponies. Had the horsehair blanket once been used throughout Central Asia and the steppes of Eurasia? If so, why had the knowledge disappeared?

FROM THE NARYN Kum I dropped down onto flats near the town of Ganushkino. There, on the verge of the Volga River's vast delta, the Kazakh steppe I had known for so long came to an end.

A year earlier, and more than 4,000 km to the east from here, I had set out from the Altai with Ruslan and my new troupe of horses. With winter bearing down and the colossal steppe of Kazakhstan yawning, I'd been overwhelmed by the bare nature of the landscape, which seemed to have been scoured clean through sheer exposure. Since then I'd become accustomed to the arid, sharply continental climate of the Kazakh steppe, where the air was dry enough to parch the throat and clouds evaporated before they had a chance to germinate. Now I was descending into a warm breeze that brought thick, humid air. The smell of wetlands was all around, and the sky carried clouds in full bloom.

As gulls, ducks, and swans tracked above, the horses dipped their heads, stealing mouthfuls of luminous green grass. Tigon porpoised through reeds near the edge of a stream, and as if to mark the milestone finally cocked his back leg to urinate on a grass tussock instead of squatting on all fours.

In the scheme of things we had not yet technically reached the end of the arid steppe zone—that still lay ahead, about 300 km to the west of the Volga—but the natural riches of the delta signaled that the bulk of the harsh center of the Eurasian steppe was nevertheless behind us. From here onward to Hungary the conditions promised to grow milder and more fertile.

The next day, only a short distance from the border with Russia, I left the horses in the care of a man named Muftagali and took a taxi back to Atyrau to finalize my veterinary documents. Initially I thought things were looking up—my passport had arrived with the Russian visa, and I met with the director of the local Ministry of Agriculture, Kosibek Erzgalev, who promised to help. After a week, however, the permits were not yet ready, and being in the city forced me to confront issues that I had been conveniently avoiding while in the saddle.

In a city where the oil boom was giving rise to flashy new hotels and apartment blocks, my daily budget of $10 was looking particularly feeble. The cheapest accommodation I could find—an old Soviet-era studio apartment plagued by mosquitoes—was $250 a week. Recent repairs to my video camera had cost $487, my Russian visa had been $229, and I was accumulating a daily debt for the keeping of my horses. At this rate, even if I could pull my horses through as far as the Danube, my budget would not stretch that far.

Beyond my financial worries, though, there was a greater anxiety that had been welling up in me for months, and which was now impossible to ignore. In an Internet cafe I read an email from Kathrin with a sense of dread: *Why is it that I feel sick in the pit of my stomach and hollow after our phone calls?* she wrote.

After saying goodbye to Kathrin in Mongolia, I had long clung to a dream of reuniting with her in Hungary and spending some weeks getting to know her again. The journey would be behind me, and I could be present in a way that I hadn't been, even since before I left Australia.

In recent months, though, it was a dream that had faded, and the truth was that underneath I had always harbored some sense of unease about remaining with Kathrin. It would always be challenging to maintain a serious long-distance relationship such as ours by relying on satellite phone connections, but it also felt incongruous with the very nature of my journey. There was a tinge of irony that the very shared attribute that had brought us together—passion for travel—was also the thing drawing me away from her.

As time had gone on and the journey had become more uncertain and drawn out, the feeling of unease in me had grown, and in the process it had become abundantly clear that keeping our relationship alive was not among my priorities—that much had become obvious when Kathrin had been admitted for brain surgery and I remained riding through the desert instead of abandoning my journey to be with her.[8]

There was another feeling that had grown, too, though, albeit a selfish one—I had come to feel that I did not want or need any fixed horizons. I was happy to be dedicated to my journey and immersed in the experience. Not only could I not envisage life after Hungary—at this stage I couldn't even imagine getting there—I simply didn't want to.

After one of many sleepless nights I called Kathrin and told her that I wanted to break up. It was a difficult and painful conversation, and I was riddled with a feeling of guilt that I had entered into a relationship promising more than I could have given.

I spent most of my remaining time in Atyrau shuffling between the Ministry of Agriculture and an Internet cafe where I traded emails with Kathrin. Being unable to see each other in person must have been so much harder for Kathrin, especially in the midst of her recovery from surgery, and also because she had already waited so long. To add to the feelings of being apart, Kathrin planned to spend her upcoming school vacation in a remote village in northern Italy where there was no Internet or phone. We would each have to deal with everything in isolation, and in the circumstances I desperately wanted to get back out on the horses, where I hoped the sense of movement, the feeling of progress, and the company of my animals would make the pain easier to deal with.

AFTER TWO WEEKS in the city, I was able to pick up my veterinary permits, and I returned to the border. Although the Ministry of Agriculture was adamant that I had the right documents, riding horses into Russia was an untested thing, and I was nervous.

Nevertheless, things at first appeared to go smoothly. Not far beyond Muftagali's aul, Kuegen, I passed through a police post just before the border, where my only issue was that Ogonyok ate the roses from the post's one and only flowerpot. At the border, the presence of a familiar veterinary official from Atyrau put me at ease. "What took you so long?" he said. He arranged for the processing of my documents, took me to lunch, and then escorted me through immigration.

The customs officer showed no concerns. "Now, what model horse do you have? What year is its release?" he joked, waving me through.

Come afternoon I had left Kazakhstan, been ferried across a branch of the Volga River on a barge, and was approaching Russia. Tigon led from the front, bristling with optimism.

At first the Russian border personnel were friendly. I was led through to the customs inspection bay, where an officer called out in jest, "You know we will have to take the wheels off to check for narcotics!" The inspections were all over in a few minutes, and then all that lay before us was a simple boom gate leading into Russia.

It was just as the guards began to wave me through that my luck changed. From an office in a shipping container marked "Vet Control and Transport on the Border," a woman who appeared to have none of the joviality of her colleagues came my way. I broke the ice with a handshake and a smile, but as the horses edged closer her eyes widened, and the shaking of her head, which had begun hesitantly, became vigorous and full of conviction.

"I don't know what to do! I am in shock! My God, what problem has fallen on me tonight?" she cried.

I followed her to the shipping container, where she sat under a framed portrait of Vladimir Putin and made a phone call.

"I have a Hungarian traveling from Mongolia on Mongolian horses without documents!" she yelled. There was no opportunity for me to intervene and correct her misapprehensions. I could hear the reply that came down over the line from her superiors in Astrakhan: "What a nightmare!"

The woman hung up and regained some composure. "I must impound your horses! I cannot grant you permission to pass!"

I reassured her that I had all the right papers and that she had misunderstood my story, but she wasn't listening, and several hours later I knew I was in serious trouble. The only official means to export live horses from Kazakhstan to Russia was to process them for sporting events or as meat. Even if I could overcome this issue, there was a crucial document I didn't have: a transit permit from Moscow that would allow me to follow a strict route through Russia to Ukraine.

I called my contacts in Russia—Anna Lushchekina of the Russian Academy of Sciences in Moscow, and her friend and colleague Liudmilla Kiseleva in Astrakhan—but to no avail. According to the vet official I had two choices: "You can leave your horses and dog impounded with us, and go alone into Russia . . . or you can go back to Kazakhstan, where you came from." It was nearing midnight by the time I gave up and rode back into the no-man's-land between the two borders. The Kazakh border would not reopen until eight o'clock the following morning, and so I found a grassy hollow and made camp.

Come morning I was confronted with a fresh shift of Kazakh immigration, veterinary, and customs officials who accused me of horse rustling and illegal export of the horses. An eight-hour stand-off ensued, resolved only by negotiations between customs and the head of the Ministry of Agriculture in Atyrau. After this I dove back into the core of the problems from the day before.

MY HORSES WERE again left in Muftagali's care, and within twenty-four hours I had returned to my purgatory in Atyrau, where I was warned that to get transit permits from Moscow could entail a two-month wait. Given that my visa was only valid for six more weeks and I no longer had the funds to pay for rent, my situation was all the more tenuous. Additionally, unlike any other time on my journey, there would be no sympathetic ear from Kathrin—even if she was prepared to listen, she was in Italy and unreachable.

I got through the first week or so consumed by my frustration at the bureaucracy, which at least fueled my determination to beat the system. I spent hours each day at the Ministry of Agriculture learning about the laws and protocols, sending faxes to Moscow and Astana. Soon I was fluent in the kind of bureaucratic jargon used by the staff. During the daytime I was spurred on by the feeling that I was actively doing something about my situation. Each evening when the ministry closed its doors, however, I felt helpless and lonely.

As the days wore on, it seemed that my internal battle between clinging to optimism and being tempted to fall into dejection was mirrored in
the city around me. Everywhere I looked burgeoning wealth from oil that
spoke of a bright future collided with sectors of the economy that had
been left behind. The Ministry of Agriculture was clearly not part of the
economic boom—it was situated in a gloomy building cast among other
Soviet-era structures, all in a state of decay. Staff wages were pitiful, and
many had to come up with other ways of earning money to support their
families. By contrast, the city center showcased upmarket apartment com-
plexes and new office buildings. The city square had recently been rebuilt,
and opposing it was a newly constructed mosque of palatial proportions. All
around, billboards boasted advertisements by mining companies, banks,
and investment groups. Among these the face of President Nazarbayev was
unavoidable. A presidential election had been announced for December,
and his lavish campaign was in full swing. "Forward with Nazarbayev!" his
slogan read, as if claiming credit for all the visible affluence.

Two weeks passed, the miniature budget I had allowed myself for rent
had run out, and there was still no whisper about permits. I had nowhere
to go.

Then, as I was sitting in a cheap cafe having lunch, a young man
dressed in stylish designer clothes approached and introduced himself in
English. "I was just curious to know why a Westerner would be eating in
this kind of cheap place and wearing such bad, worn clothes. I thought
you were reaching out for communication with people, so I thought
I would come to talk," he said.

Azamat, as he was known, was my age and worked for a local oil firm.
We exchanged stories for a couple of hours and I learned that he was a
devout Muslim, and yet almost exclusively spoke in Russian.

"I feel ashamed that there are Kazakhs who do not understand Russian
language. I love Russia. I can't understand that there would be people interested in Kazakh culture," he said.

It was a curious perspective that I had observed in other cities like Almaty, but which I had never heard being articulated. For Azamat, Russian
culture represented modernity and sophistication, while nomadic life was

as alien as it would have been to a city dweller anywhere in the world. "I think you are the only man still wanting to be a nomad in my country! Why would you want to leave your home and come here?" he said, a little aghast.

While he could not quite identify with my journey, he was fascinated and could see I was in trouble. His aunt owned the cafe, and so he made a generous offer: "You are welcome to eat for free here as often as you like for as long as you need!" The only condition was that I would meet with him so he could practice his English. Later that evening he turned up at my rented apartment with a solution for my accommodation. Azamat's friend Dauren was a soft-spoken man who worked in security at Tengiz-Chevroil's head office.[9] He had just bought a new apartment near the city center. "It's unfurnished, and you will be alone, but you are welcome to stay," he said.

In the coming weeks my friendship with Dauren and Azamat not only gave me immeasurable comfort and support but provided an absorbing insight into the multiple realities of Atyrau. On occasion Dauren invited me to visit him at work in Tengiz-Chevroil's headquarters. A modern of-fice block fronted by immaculate green lawns ticking twenty-four hours a day with sprinklers, it was an environment far removed from the brutal-ity of Kulsary. Opposite the headquarters lay a secure living compound for Western workers that boasted row upon row of two-story cottages com-plete with double garages. The only life on its dust-free streets appeared to be security guards and company vehicles shuffling workers safely to and from the compound. Through Dauren's contacts I was invited inside to spend an evening with a Canadian engineer and his family. Over dinner the sense of insulation from the outside world was complete. We sat at a table using knife and fork and dined on broccoli shipped frozen from Canada. Afterward we drank beer on the couch in front of a wide-screen TV. At one stage the engineer's son came tiptoeing down the stairs in his pajamas to ask about a problem with his homework.

Back at Dauren's office, the reality of the oil business was less masked. During my first visit, he was irritated and stressed. "They've just found a murder victim at one of the Tengiz accommodation villages . . . and there has been another terror threat against the compound here in the city," he complained.

Violence among Kazakh workers at Tengiz was an ongoing problem, and there were some elements within Kazakh society, particularly of the Muslim faith, who were ideologically opposed to Western companies working on Kazakh soil. Kazakh security guards working outside the gates of the Atyrau compound were frequently threatened for working for the Americans and sometimes warned of potential bomb attacks.

Although Dauren worked in the oil industry, he was nevertheless sympathetic to many of the concerns of his fellow countrymen. "The oil industry is destroying our natural environment," he told me. "Bribes are paid to government agencies to cover up bad practices. The air is so bad at Tengiz that westerners are not given permission to work there for more than a year before they are sent home . . . but Kazakh workers stay there for years on end."

His views about President Nazarbayev and the looming election were equally cynical. "Nazarbayev considers himself the father of Kazakhstan. His political party is the Kazakhstan brand. The only true opposition is in exile in London, and Nazarbayev has a monopoly on the media. Yes, we will have a democratic election . . . but do you think that the government doesn't take note of which party people vote for? Anyone working for the state who chooses to vote for the opposition will lose their job."

When the election was over, Nazarbayev would prove to have won around 99 percent of the vote. Given this iron grip on power and his popularity, I wondered why he had bothered spending so many millions campaigning.

AFTER MORE THAN five weeks in Atyrau, I had a greater understanding of this urban society, but I had little to celebrate in terms of a breakthrough for crossing into Russia. With two weeks left on my Kazakh visa, a permit had been faxed through from Moscow but was quickly followed by a qualifying phone call from the border: "If Australian Tim Cope arrives on horseback we will turn him back. The permit only allows him to transport his horses and dog by truck or train through Russia."

My only success in Atyrau had been to convince the head of customs for western Kazakhstan to guarantee smooth passage out of the country. Technically, to send Kazakh horses abroad required a wild-animal export license, but to overcome this he had ordered his assistant to classify my horses as "house pets."

Now, with just five days remaining on my Kazakh visa, I lay on the floor of Dauren's apartment with the small of my back knotted up. It was Wednesday, December 7, my twenty-seventh birthday, and I felt more like sixty.

If, by the end of the working week, Moscow hadn't issued a new permit specifically allowing me to *ride* horses across the border and through Russia, then all hope was lost. I would have to give away my animals, but I didn't have the money to buy new horses in Russia. It was surely the end of my journey.

Friday, December 9, permit or no, would be my last day at the agricultural ministry. Like every day, I was there starting at eight in the morning, on the fax and the phone. By lunchtime there was no permit and my frustration was boiling over. I refused to let Kosibek's secretary leave on her lunch break. "Please, let's just call Moscow one last time," I begged. "If we don't get it now, then we will never get it."

She looked at me with a small smile, trying to keep the tears out of her eyes. Like everyone else in the office—which was labeled, in English, "Exsperts Room"—she had battled my problem every day for six weeks. Everyone from Kosibek down had given it their all.

"Tim, I'm sorry, we have done everything we can."

I reluctantly exited the office, and she locked the door on her way out to lunch.

I had a miserable last meal at Azamat's aunt's café. Azamat had remained upbeat and believed I would get the permit somehow, and now I had to disappoint him. The many meals his aunt had provided me had all been in vain. I called Muftagali in Kuegen and explained we would need to find new owners for the horses. Then I spoke with Dauren and promised to be moved out within a day.

Finally I made my way back to the ministry. I needed to say goodbye to Kosibek and the other staff who had put their hearts into helping me.

As I reentered the building I noticed something odd. Lunch hour was not yet finished, but the door to the "Exsperts Room" was ajar. I pushed it open, and there, looking pale and sunken, was Kosibek's secretary. She looked up at me, and though there were tears in my eyes, I approached to console her. She whispered something.

"What?" I asked.

"I got it." She held up a fresh fax in her trembling fingers: *This is to certify that in addition to the permit of the 29th of November Australian traveler Tim Cope can transport his three horses by riding them. His one dog can be carried by its four legs.*

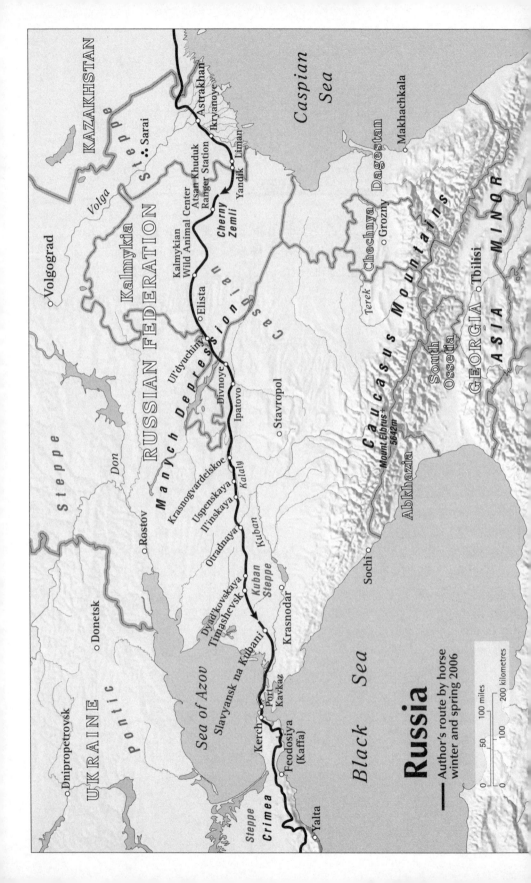

KAZAKHSTAN

Steppe

Volga

KALMYKIA

RUSSIAN FEDERATION

Volgograd

Steppe

Pontic

Don

Rostov

Donetsk

Dnipropetrovsk

UKRAINE

Sarai

Astrakhan

Ikryanoye

Liman

Yandik

Cherny Zemli

Atsan Khuduk Ranger Station

Kalmykian Wild Animal Center

Elista

Ul'dyuchiny

Divnoye

Ipatovo

Stavropol

Manych Depression

Krasnogvardeiskoe

Uspenskaya

Il'inskaya

Kalaly

Otradnaya

Kuban

Kuban Steppe

Krasnodar

Dyad'kovskaya

Timashevsk

Slavyansk na Kubani

Port Kavkaz

Kerch

Feodosiya (Kaffa)

Sea of Azov

Yalta

Steppe

Crimea

Black Sea

Caspian Sea

Makhachkala

Dagestan

Grozny

Chechnya

Terek

Caucasus Mountains

South Ossetia

Abkhazia

Sochi

GEORGIA

Tbilisi

ASIA MINOR

Mount Elbrus 5642m

Russia

— Author's route by horse winter and spring 2006

0   50   100 miles

0   100   200 kilometres

16

LOST HORDES
IN EUROPE

When in the steppe I stand alone
With far horizons clear to view,
Ambrosia on the breezes blown
And skies above me crystal blue,
I sense my own true human height
And in eternity delight.

The obstacles to all my dreams
Now shrink, appear absurd, inept,
And nothing either is or seems
Except myself, these birds, this steppe . . .
What joy it is to feel all round
Wide open space that knows no bound!

—Unknown Kalmyk poet

ON A BLUSTERY morning, when sleet and snow clogged the air and wind careened across the freezing waters of the Volga delta, I found myself once again at the Kazakh border post. The same workers who had given me such a hard time on the way back from my failed crossing were on duty.

"You cannot export the horses—you do not have the necessary permit. These are commercial export!" the official in charge told me.

I'd anticipated this and had a plan. I used the public phone booth to call the head of customs in Atyrau, who was waiting and ready. No sooner had I replaced the handset than the official in charge at the border post took a call and turned pale. Shortly he came cowering apologetically: "Don't worry, everything will be done."

Later that evening, with just a matter of hours remaining on my Kazakh visa, I rode through and made camp in no-man's-land. Come morning the visa had expired and there was no way back.

This time around the Russian officials proved friendlier than their Kazakh counterparts, and within a couple of hours I sailed under the boom gate into freedom. Tigon led the way, chest puffed out, tugging hard on his lead, tail pointed high "like a pistol," as the guards joked.

Once through, I refrained from looking over my shoulder and covered as much distance as possible before dark. Only from the safety of camp did I dare pull out my satellite phone to break the news to my family. It was the thirteenth of December, my father's fifty-fifth birthday, and I could claim to be inside Russia.

For the next couple of days I was paranoid about still being within the web of influence of the border officials, and so I kept up a brisk pace. I seldom stopped during the day and hid my camp at night. It was only after I had crossed a few channels of the Volga that I began to relax. Liberated from the impasse, it was a luxury not only to be with my family of animals but to once again lift my sights to new horizons.

In the scheme of my overall journey, the Kazakh-Russian border was just the second of four international borders to be navigated on the way to the Danube, but it was a milestone greater than all the others. With time I would come to see that the Kazakh-Russian border demarcated two broadly different cultural spheres of the Eurasian steppe—and therefore split the experience of my journey into two distinct halves.

In the east were Mongolia and Kazakhstan—both countries deeply affected by the Soviet era and, before that, the Russian Empire (Kazakhstan to a much larger degree), but nonetheless self-ruling, sovereign nations where nomadic culture remained predominant. Even Kazakhs and Mongols who lived in cities were only a couple of generations at most removed from the saddle.

In the western portion of the steppe, from the Russian border to the Danube, the nomadic way of life had long since faded out. Hungarians had abandoned their nomadic way of life even before the Mongols' appearance in the thirteenth century, and the so-called Pontic and Caspian steppes—encompassing the grasslands stretching from the Volga to north of the Black Sea—which had been a historical stronghold of nomad culture and a key to Mongol rule in Europe, had been subjugated long ago by the Russian Empire and was now incorporated into modern Russia and Ukraine. The many steppe peoples that lay ahead of me, including Kalmyks, Cossacks, Crimean Tatars, and even the Hutsuls of the Carpathians, formed ethnic minorities with only limited autonomy. Most of them had been singled out under Stalin, and some had shared the experience of mass deportation to Siberia and Central Asia. In post-Soviet times they were experiencing cultural revival—in the Crimean Tatars' case, return from exile—and their lands were in varying states of stability.

The first of these formerly nomadic nations was one I had anticipated with particular intrigue. The Caspian steppe, which has at its heart the rich pasturelands of the lower Volga, had once been ruled by the Kalmyks, an ethnically Mongol people of the Oirat confederation of tribes, whose arrival in the region in the early seventeenth century heralded the last migration of a nomadic people from Asia to Europe. In 1771 there had been a catastrophic attempt by Kalmyks to flee en masse back to Mongolia to escape oppression under the Russian Empire. Almost two-thirds of those who set out had perished on the very Kazakh steppes through which I had ridden in the last twelve months.

The first I had known about the Kalmyks came from Oirat Mongols in western Mongolia who had claimed to be descended from Kalmyks who survived the exodus. "Thousands of kilometres from here in Russia near the Caspian Sea, you will meet our relatives who never came back. They are our Mongol brothers and sisters, and they are still stuck in Europe," they had told me.

What remained of the once powerful Kalmyk khanate was a small, semi-autonomous republic known as Kalmykia, situated to the west of the Volga River and nowadays renowned as the only Buddhist republic in geographical Europe. Legend had it that Kalmyks there were descendants of those unable to cross the partially frozen Volga in the mild winter of 1770–71.[1] Whether coincidence or not, the name *Kalmyk* originates from a Turkic root word that roughly means "to remain." I'd been waiting to lay eyes on the fabled steppe of Kalmykia for what seemed an eternity, but even now, when it lay less than two weeks of travel in front of me, it was premature to set my sights on it. Before reaching the Kalmyk steppe, I first needed to cross through the labyrinth of bridges and towns that are dotted along the braided channels of the Volga River delta.

Crossing the main channel in particular proved difficult. The only bridge lay smack in the middle of Astrakhan, a Russian outpost city founded in the sixteenth century by Ivan the Terrible. The historic fortress walls that are still a feature of the old city center served as a reminder that for centuries it had come under attack by nomadic horsemen. In the modern era, though, Astrakhan was a bustling metropolis of more than half a million, and on horseback it was my turn to be terrorized. A marathon day saw us weaving a dangerous path through a sea of trucks, trams, and cars. At times when we were forced onto narrow sidewalks, there were hordes of pedestrians and lethal, ill-fitting manhole covers to deal with.

Upon reaching the far side of the city after dark, my horses were so spooked that no sooner had I dismounted to make camp than they bolted, still packed and saddled. I was left with nothing but my thermos, video camera, and satellite phone.

Local police and emergency services came to my aid, but after a fruitless all-night search we retired empty-handed to the police station. It was only due to the intuition of a policeman of Kazakh descent that my journey was rescued. At 6:00 A.M. I was awakened by shouting and opened my eyes to see him leaning over me, his machine gun slung over his shoulder. "Wake up! You have to get in the car! I have had a dream that I went fishing and caught three fish—a brown, a gray, and a red one, the same color as your horses. I just know we are going to find your horses this time!"

An hour later we came across a long trail of equipment leading to my horses. It was a remarkable sight as the policeman, machine gun and all, strode over to Ogonyok and planted a kiss on his nose.

AFTER PULLING MY caravan back together I spent a week riding from Astrakhan south along the banks of the Volga through a tangle of fishing villages. When the Volga's waters began to freeze I crossed the last bridge and turned west, leaving the web of roads, towns, bridges, and traffic behind.

I was now on the western fringes of the Volga delta, and as I rode through a landscape of marshes, lakes, and broad flanks of open pastureland, my thoughts returned to the Kalmyks. It was precisely this combination of reed beds, open land, and low-lying pastures irrigated by spring overflow that had drawn the Kalmyks' forefathers to the Caspian steppe. Those early pioneers had been war-hardened Oirat Mongols, who, like waves of nomads before them, had been prompted by conflict in their Inner Asian homeland to pick up and ride out across the steppe in search of new beginnings.

More specifically, the powerful empire ruled by the Oirats, known as Zhungaria, had begun to decline by the turn of the seventeenth century, and one Oirat tribe, the Torghuts, had sent scouts west to locate a refuge for their people.[2] As early as 1608, encampments on the vanguard of this mass migration were spotted along the Zhem River. By the 1640s Kalmyks had driven out the nomadic Nogais from the Caspian steppe and established their own khanate, the center of which was located around the Lower Volga.[3] In Zhungaria their Oirat brethren would mount a resurgence and hold power until the mid-eighteenth century, but the Oirats who had migrated to the Caspian steppe generally became known as the Kalmyks.

For the better part of the next century the Kalmyks utilized the unique river ecology and pasturelands of the Caspian steppe and more or less lived by the traditional nomadic patterns that had long defined life in the region. They lived in yurts, roamed seasonally with their livestock, and indulged in the age-old nomad pastime of raiding their neighbors. Horse rustling and slave trading were important parts of the Kalmyk economy, and Russian captives in particular could be sold at lucrative prices in the markets of Khiva, or returned to Russia for ransom. Unable to pacify or control the Kalmyks, the Russian tsar took advantage of their fearsome cavalry skills, hiring them to defend Russia against the Ottoman Empire.[4]

By the mid-eighteenth century the Kalmyks' fortunes had well and truly turned. For thousands of years, nomads had enjoyed military dominance as horseback archers of unmatched prowess, but the Kalmyks had arrived on the Caspian steppe at a time when the advent of cannons and muskets was eroding this supremacy. More generally, the seventeenth and eighteenth centuries were an era that marked the demise of nomads and the emergence of powerful sedentary societies on the fringes of the Eurasian steppe—namely, those of China and Russia.

As Russia's might grew, the tsar's demands on the Kalmyk cavalry's services increased, and southward colonization pushed into the lush pastures of the lower Volga. Traditional Kalmyk grazing lands were turned into hayfields and put to the plow, driving the Kalmyks to less fertile steppe. By 1740 the number of livestock kept by the Kalmyks had declined dramatically, and around ten thousand Kalmyk "tents" (families) were without enough animals for subsistence. To survive, Kalmyks resorted to more frequent raids, sold their children as slaves, and even took up fishing.

It was these oppressive conditions that, in 1771, gave rise to the exodus of Kalmyks back to their roots in Asia—after which the Kalmyk khanate was all but absorbed by the Russian Empire.

More than two centuries on, in January 2006, it was hard to imagine that very much remained of this once fiercely reputed people—particularly because the descendants of those who stayed behind at the time of the exodus had since been deported en masse to Siberia by Stalin during World War II. And yet, as I approached the modern border of Kalmykia, there were signs suggesting that the pattern of tension and conflict between Kalmyks and their neighbors was an ongoing one.

It was late on New Year's Day when I reached Liman, a sleepy village on the very edge of the Volga delta where marked roads came to an end and a series of marshes and lakes gave way to wild, waterless steppe. This kind of unique intersection of environments had no doubt been a pillar of the local nomadic economy, but it also had long attracted settling farmers, and nowadays lay outside Kalmyk territory.

Through my friend Anna Lushchekina, a local Russian man, Anatoliy Khludnev, had agreed to guide me through the Stepnoi nature reserve to Kalmykia itself. Anatoliy, a retired lieutenant colonel who nowadays worked as the director of the reserve, was quick to point out the issues of his region: "The land here has long been disputed between Kalmykia and Astrakhan Oblast, and there is still no agreement as to where the official border lies."

Still, the border dispute was trivial in the scheme of things. A wider problem, or at least the issue of the day, was the friction between Kalmyks and the growing Chechen population. "Chechens who are fleeing their own country on resettlement programs are taking over. They are the new settlers of the Kalmyk steppe," Anatoliy complained.

Racked by conflict and unemployment, Chechnya lay little more than 100 km from Kalmykia's southern border. In the past decade thousands had migrated here seeking work and a safer life. According to Anatoliy, their presence had scared many Russians into moving out of the area. "It's not too bad for us, I guess, though," he reflected. "We have all of Russia to go to if we want. The Kalmyks, on the other hand, have little elsewhere if they want to be among their own. I don't blame them for getting into conflict with the Chechens."

Anatoliy may well have been projecting some of the prevailing prejudices against Chechens, but violence between Chechen migrants and Kalmyks in the area had recently made headlines. In August, in the village of Yandik, not far from Liman, a Kalmyk girl had been shot dead by Chechens. In retaliation a crowd of five hundred mourning Kalmyks returning from the funeral had rioted through the village, torching homes and forcing the Chechens to flee. The situation had threatened to spread into a wider ethnic conflict until the Russian army was brought in to ease tensions. The peacekeeping force had rolled out a week before my arrival.

Things had apparently settled down for the time being, and the plan was for Anatoliy to escort me from Liman through Yandik, then across 70 km of wild steppe known as Cherny Zemli, or "Black Lands," that straddle the disputed border region.[5] Anatoliy explained that he would lead the way in the patrol vehicle and stand guard at night. He would take his gun in case we ran into wolves or poachers.

On a freezing morning when curtains of light snow raked the land I packed a week's supply of food and set off out of town. Half an hour later there was a distinct air of unease as I followed Anatoliy through Yandik. Many houses lay in burned ruins, the streets were largely deserted, and those people I did see peeked out shyly from half-opened doorways. At the far end of the village I rode past the cemetery, pausing briefly by the fresh grave of the murdered Kalmyk girl.

For three days from Yandik I followed Anatoliy through a landscape of wild, frostbitten grasslands. Our route followed a centuries-old trail once used by merchants to ferry fish from the Volga across the steppes to more temperate Stavropol. By day Anatoliy told tales about the grueling journeys of these merchants, who had come under constant attack from Kalmyk brigands. By night, as the temperature plummeted to around −20°C, Anatoliy was less cheerful. He tried to sleep in his vehicle but was forced to repeatedly restart the engine to keep warm.

The only people we met along the way were a couple of old shepherds who worked for a Chechen sheep farmer.[6] One of them was a Volga Tatar who had spent the best part of his days in prison. In colorful language he warned me about the dangers of Kalmyks, and told a running joke: "What could possibly be worse than a drunk Kalmyk? Only a drunk Kalmyk woman, of course!"

On our third morning we entered the nature reserve. The sun was creeping into a solid blue sky, sending an orange light angling across a still sea of pale, bleached grass. It was the seventh of January, and although there was no snow cover, evidence of winter could be seen in the form of frozen shallow ponds that sparkled like silvery discs embedded in the land.

As frost gathered around my sheepskin hat and the horses moved briskly across the frozen sandy soil, I couldn't help but think it might have been a morning like this on January 5, 1771, when the Kalmyks had embarked on their exodus back to their origins in Zhungaria. On that day Ubashi Khan, the Kalmyks' young leader, had set out east from the Volga to lead an estimated thirty thousand nomad families, somewhere between 150,000 and 200,000 individuals, with their untold camel caravans and probably more than a million head of livestock.[7]

For those who departed, it was the beginning of an epic journey that would prove to be a tragedy of extraordinary scale. Traveling a route similar to the reverse of the one I had followed across the Kazakh steppe, they had to deal with the inherent environmental challenges, compounded by attacks waged by Kazakhs who took the opportunity to settle old scores. When finally the Kalmyks arrived on the Ili River in what is today Xinjiang province in China, around a hundred thousand men, women, and children—as many as 75 percent of those who had started off—had perished.

For those Kalmyks who survived, dreams of refuge in Zhungaria were swiftly quashed. Little more than a decade earlier, the Qing dynasty had embarked on a campaign to exterminate the Oirats, with some historians suggesting that as little as 7 percent of the population had survived. Ubashi and his people were dispersed throughout Xinjiang, and in the words of historian Michael Khodarkovsky, "the Kalmyks had escaped Russian tentacles only to be ensnared in Chinese ones."

AT AN ABANDONED hut we had a late lunch and decided to part ways. We had, by now, crossed an invisible line into Kalmykia, and besides, Anatoliy was short on fuel.

"See this trail here?" Anatoliy said, pointing to a vague line of ruts and hollows that was more sketch than road. "If you follow it and keep your compass between 270 and 290 degrees, then you should come to a hut called Atsan Khuduk—it's manned, and the caretaker there should be expecting you ."

After watching his four-wheel-drive vehicle shrink back the way we had come, I sat still in the saddle long enough for the sound of the engine to peter out and a sense of aloneness to bite. When I turned and pulled away, silence was replaced by the swishing of sixteen legs—Tigon included—brushing through frozen grass.

For the next three hours I rode with urgency, wanting to reach the hut as soon as possible. The sun sank into a smudge of black cloud, the shape and texture of the land faded into pastel grays, and the cold drew in like a noose. I called Tigon in close and kept an eye on my compass. When the moon rose, and my caravan cast dim shadows across the frosted grass, my transition to an older world felt complete. I slowed to a walk, snuggled deep into my winter coat, and opened the bell on Taskonir's neck—something I always did at night in case the horses broke free (so I would be able to hear where they had gone) and in this case, also because it as was an old steppe tradition along courier and trading routes to have a horsebell to warn rest stations of the approach of a horseman. After traveling nearly 40 km into the cold of evening, I was beginning to worry I had missed the hut, but around 11:00 P.M. three dark shapes emerged from the moonlit steppe. From one came the faint flicker of an oil lamp.

I was greeted by an old man reeking of vodka who introduced himself in Russian as the caretaker. Word hadn't reached Atsan Khuduk—a station for rangers and scientific researchers—about the special permission I had received to ride through the reserve, but it didn't worry him. I was led inside to a mattress, where my body withered, my vision blurred, and I collapsed into sleep.

Some time later I woke to another world. I heard banter and heavy footsteps and opened my eyes to a group of four or five men clambering into the hut, dusting off the frost from their army fatigue coats. The dull flicker from the lamp caught the profile of broad, chapped red cheeks with skin drawn taut over the bone. The men's eyes were long and slender, and when they spoke I was astonished to hear the familiar sounds of Mongolian.

I joined the group around a wooden table, where Mongolian salty milk tea was on the pour, and with the last remaining battery power in my laptop showed video footage of Oirat Mongols whom I had met in the far west of Mongolia fourteen months earlier. The men leaned in and listened intently:

"They speak a purer Oirat dialect than we do, and clearer than Oirats we have met from China! You know what we say about those who went back to Asia: 'Tasarsan makh'n, usersen tsus'n'—it translates to 'Split flesh and spilled blood' and means 'We are one people with you.' But how was Kazakhstan? What was it like to ride where our ancestors perished?"

As I sat there sharing stories about the steppe, with the salty tea warming my insides, it was as if Kazakhstan had merely been a bridge between these two disparate nomadic Mongolian societies. One could almost be convinced that these men were nomads who had just returned from a wolf hunt. Symbolic of modern-day Kalmykia, however, the men were Kalmyk scientists and rangers who had come back from a fox count as part of a biology study. One of them was the deputy director of the Cherny Zemli reserve, Boris Ubushaeva—a professor whom I would later see dressed in a suit and tie at a university in Kalmykia's capital, Elista. Impressed by my journey, he promised to take me out to see the very reason the reserve had been founded.

In the morning we left the hut when the sky was still dark and a residual glint of stars remained. It was an hour later, as we crested a subtle swell of sand, that the professor told me to crouch down. In the still conditions the faint twitching of a grass tussock had been enough to betray the presence of an animal, and as I focused closer a shaggy creature the same pale color of the grass darted away.

By the time the professor had handed me the binoculars a whole swath of grassland before us shimmered to life and a flock of these creatures lifted like startled sparrows. The animals possessed goat-sized bodies draped in a thick winter coat and were scuttling along on twig-like legs. They were saiga.

Since first learning about the saiga on the Betpak Dala in Kazakhstan, I had heard untold numbers of stories about these enigmatic antelopes of the Eurasian steppe, which could migrate hundreds of kilometres in a single day and which as recently as 1990 had numbered around 800,000. But the herds of the Cherny Zemli were the first I had seen on my travels. "We have around eighteen thousand saiga left on the Black Lands," the professor explained. "Our efforts to catch poachers are working, but saiga are nomadic, and when they leave the boundaries of our reserve we have no jurisdiction, and often they never return . . . In 1998, during a cold winter, around a hundred thousand saiga migrated south into the Republic of Dagestan, and only a few came back. They say that the snow in Dagestan was painted red by the slaughter."

A short way past my first sighting, we startled another herd, this time much closer to us. Not more than 100 m ahead stood a male saiga. His horns, set above bulbous eyes, struck me first. Backlit by the sun, they rose with a slight inward curve and a ribbed texture, looking like a set of glowing amber pincers. Below this spectacle hung a long curved nose that functioned to filter out dust and heat the winter air during inhalation. The head and trunk were so large and heavy-looking it seemed his matchstick legs might give way. So peculiar were the features that it was not hard to believe this was a surviving ice age species that had once coexisted alongside the likes of the mammoth and the saber-toothed tiger.

When the male and his herd sprinted away, I was left mesmerized, yet also aware of how the empty steppe that I had ridden through in the past twelve months had been lacking in saiga. I understood that the saiga's presence, like the magic of a horseman set against the sky, had been a quintessential part of steppe life.

Back in the hut, where we warmed up with more tea, the professor turned to me thoughtfully. "In the past we Kalmyks used to hunt saiga in our everyday lives. In fact, hunting saiga was how we honed our skills for battle. The key tactic for getting a saiga was to feign retreat, then lure the animals into an ambush—the very technique used so well by Genghis Khan. Ever since the exodus of our brothers back to Asia, however, it has been Kalmykia itself under ambush."

Like the saiga's once vast habitat, Kalmyk land had contracted to a small island of steppe where nomadic life was nearly impossible. Not only this, but Kalmyks had faced cultural extinction during World War II, when they were accused of sympathizing with the Nazis and deported to Siberia. More than a third had died in the cattle wagons en route, and, unprepared for the terrible conditions of the Siberian winter, thousands more had perished on arrival. In their absence the Republic of Kalmykia had been dissolved and Kalmyk livestock wiped out so comprehensively that the Kalmyk horse became virtually extinct and the fat-tailed sheep would never again graze the Kalmyk steppe.[8] It was only in 1957 that Kalmyks had been allowed to return from exile and had begun to rebuild a sense of their homeland.

A product of this turbulent history, the professor's life story mirrored that of untold thousands of his compatriots. He had been born in Siberia and studied at a university in the city, never having experienced or witnessed the traditional way of life of his ancestors. "We can no longer live as nomads, and for the saiga it's a similar story—they have been decimated and no longer run free across the steppes. Nevertheless, we have not lost everything and we know that the Kalmyk steppe without saiga would be like tea without milk—very poor indeed. To protect the saiga we need to preserve our culture, and draw on modern science as well as our heritage."

Over the coming days and weeks, the sentiments expressed by the professor were repeated by many Kalmyks I met. The plight of the saiga had become a metaphor for the fate of the nation. The efforts to bring the four-legged nomad back from the brink reflected a broader struggle to revive all facets of Kalmyk heritage and culture.

JUST THREE DAYS' ride beyond the wardens' hut, I had traversed half the territory of Kalmykia, yet in that time encountered just one Kalmyk family living out on the steppe—a former schoolteacher and his wife who had decided to try cattle and sheep farming for a living.

In a land so reduced in width, it was perhaps inevitable that like the modern-day culture of the Kalmyks, my journey through Kalmykia was destined to be more spiritual and academic than a physical one. Fifty kilometres shy of the capital, Elista, I was welcomed at the Kalmykian Wild Animal Center by a Kalmyk professor of biology, Yuri, who had been charged with the task of breeding saiga in captivity. Dr. Anna Lushchekina, who had flown from Moscow, was also there to meet me. She headed a UNESCO project, "Human and Biosphere," in the pre-Caspian region and was responsible for much of the effort to preserve the saiga. For the next week, Anna and Yuri became my chaperones, introducing me to the many faces of modern Kalmykia. With the horses resting at Yuri's farm, most of that time was spent in Elista, where I would come to understand that the revival of Kalmyk culture was being promoted not on the steppe by horseback nomads but from the urban environment of the capital.

From a distance Elista appeared like any other Soviet city—a drab series of dilapidated apartment blocks and ramshackle homes barnacled to the bare, snow-dusted slopes of a valley. Up close, however, the unique eastern identity was hard to miss.

The city's main park was dominated by a giant wooden archway decorated with impressions of saiga, wolves, and mounted horsemen gazing over the city. On the central square a statue of Lenin had been moved aside to make way for a Buddhist prayer wheel housed beneath a towering pagoda. On the street the Russian language seemed to be predominant, but there were places where only Kalmyk could be heard. A cheap Kalmyk eatery was one of these, where Kalmyks of all ages congregated to dine on nomad food including boortsog, Mongolian milk tea, and an assortment of mutton dishes.

These may have been rather anecdotal examples of ways in which Kalmyk culture was being reasserted, but as Anna guided me around it became clear they were signs of a wider groundswell of cultural reclamation driven by a dedicated and diverse group of individuals.

At the Kalmyk Institute of Humanitarian Studies I was introduced to a young Kalmyk woman, Kermen Batireva, who was writing her doctoral dissertation on traditional Kalmyk costume. She gave me a tour of a museum that displayed original Kalmyk yurts, horse tack, and Buddhist art. In the same institution where she studied I came to know the eighty-one-year-old librarian, Praskovi Erdnievni. Standing not much higher than her desk, this pint-sized woman had single-handedly been gathering written resources about the Kalmyks for more than fifty years. Her stories of lugging suitcases of books from as far afield as Moscow at a time when there were no paved roads to Elista and many of those who were returning from exile lived in tents were legendary. When she was unable to take books back to Elista, she had copied them by hand or on a typewriter.

There were many other individuals who, with characteristic pride and vigor, were pursuing one aspect or another of Kalmyk culture. Two in particular, however, came to take on particular significance for me.

Stepping out of his office in the newly opened monastery, known as the Golden Temple, Erdne Ombadykow did not look anything like what I had imagined. The fresh-faced thirty-three-year-old who wore a chic suit and tie and spoke English with an American accent was the supreme lama of the Kalmyks, recognized by the Dalai Lama as the reincarnation of the Buddhist saint Telo Rinpoche.

"My father was born here in Kalmykia, and my mother was born in a refugee camp in Yugoslavia, but I grew up in Philadelphia. I didn't see my homeland until I was nineteen years old," he said softly.

At the age of seven, Erdne had decided he wanted to become a monk. His parents supported his wishes and sent him to India, where he was to live and study in a monastery for thirteen years. It was in 1991, as part of a delegation with the Dalai Lama, that Erdne had first been to Kalmykia. The following year he returned to live in Elista, elected as the first supreme lama of the Kalmyks since the Bolshevik revolution.

"The task to revive Buddhism here was so challenging that in the first two years it drove me to despair. When the Communists destroyed the monasteries in Kalmykia, they didn't leave one brick at the site—everything was rooted out. When my people returned from exile in Siberia, we started from zero, both materially and culturally."

As I stood with Erdne on the top floor gazing down at a golden Buddha 9 m high, I could see that those early days were a far cry from the present.

The monastery, at 63 m tall, dominated the skyline just west of the city center and was now considered to be the largest in all of Europe. On December 1, 2004, little more than a year before I visited, the Dalai Lama had consecrated the building site—an old Soviet metal factory—and only a month before my arrival the temple had opened to the public.

I couldn't help thinking that the significance of this temple, and the thirty-three others across Kalmykia that Erdne had overseen the building of in recent years, went beyond a mere revival. Ever since the Kalmyks' arrival on the Caspian steppe, maintaining a connection with Tibet had symbolized self-determination in the shadow of the Russian Empire. In the early years a lama from Tibet had been sent to Kalmykia to be the spiritual leader, and until the mid-eighteenth century pilgrimages from Kalmykia to Tibet were common. These pilgrimages ended due to the increasing dangers of crossing through hostile Kazakh territory and control by Russian authorities who saw links to Tibet as a threat to their own supremacy. In the present day, Moscow was no doubt keeping a close eye on developments in Kalmykia. In a move that perhaps reflected suspicion about growing independence in Kalmykia and other republics of the Russian federation, Russian president Vladimir Putin had recently revoked the right for citizens to elect their provincial governor or president, bringing control of all republics directly under Moscow.

With Erdne I toured the monastery from top to bottom, marveling at the impressive construction. But by the time we had returned to Erdne's office it struck me that there was an absence of reference to the nomadic way of life. I pressed him on his thoughts.

"Just because the world is modernizing, it doesn't mean we should forget our past," he replied, "but it's also true that it's unrealistic to think we can return to being nomads." Because he had grown up without a connection to horses, the steppe, or a lifestyle of herding livestock, it was, perhaps, understandably difficult for him to identify with the nomad culture of his ancestors.

In a relatively luxurious house on the other side of the city, I met another Kalmyk who was perhaps equally as influential in reviving Kalmyk culture, but whose philosophy was strongly at odds with Erdne's. Okna

Tsahan Zam (who also used the Russian name Vladimir Karuev) greeted me in a deel and colorful Mongolian winter boots. His hair was trimmed to a crew cut halfway back along his skull, and at the back plaited into a ponytail that dangled as far as his bottom

"As Kalmykians, the earth is our mother, Gazar Eej; the sky is our father, Tengri Etseg; and traditionally, where it was good for horses, we lived, and where our animals went we followed. Buddhism is not our faith—it was introduced after we arrived on the Caspian—so we must look to our more ancient nomad heritage and belief in Tengri for strength and inspiration," he told.

Okna was a renowned musician and singer whose traditional songs about life on the steppe, combining throat singing with contemporary music, had topped the pop charts in Mongolia and captivated live audiences in Europe. But he hadn't always lived this way.

"I graduated in Moscow as a nuclear engineer and worked for years at a nuclear plant. In my twenties, I suffered a personal crisis. To heal myself I turned to my culture, and my heritage, and began reciting the prose of our national epic, *Zhungar*," he said. He opened a bottle of vodka, poured a shot, then dipped his ring finger in the liquid three times, rubbing a little on his forehead, sprinkling a bit over me, and throwing the rest in the air. "If people know their history, their traditions, they understand the value of experience that our people have collected over thousands of years. When we know who we are, our place in the world, and why we exist, we are happy and have a purpose in life!"

After the customary three shots, Okna offered to sing for me, and for the next half hour I sat engrossed by his deep, gravelly voice and the haunting otherworldly harmonics of throat singing.

As we made our goodbyes, he said to me, a little somberly, "I used to believe in politics, but I had a falling-out with the president. I am not happy here in Russia. Even now we Kalmyks are feeling the pressure, the suffocation of Moscow. It's time for another mass exodus, which I will lead . . . What do you think—maybe Australia next time?" he chuckled. "Anyway, may the sun always shine on your horses."

When my week in Elista was over I returned to the Kalmykian Wild

Animal Center, where the city gave way to empty, snow-blanketed steppe, but my mind continued to churn with the color and intensity of all I had witnessed. I'd swum in euphoria at the thought that Kalmyks were meshing the realities of modern life with wisdom from the past. The passion of the people I had met made me reflect that Kalmyks seemed to be more conscious of the value of their heritage than Mongolian nomads, who still lived the very traditional lives that Kalmyks pined for. But I wondered: was the romantic, nostalgic view of nomadic life held by many Kalmyks possible only for a people who were an educated, urbanized generation removed from the horse and the yurt? How far could the revival go in this modern world?

In a vast fenced enclosure at the saiga farm I spent a day battling snow and wind to film the saiga that roamed within. They came to feed at special troughs and kept a wary eye on me at all times. At one stage saiga were caught and hustled into a barn for blood sampling. Under Yuri's supervision, the blood was put into test tubes, spun on centrifuges, and whisked away.

It occurred to me that, like the saiga at the Wild Animal Center, Kalmyk culture was fenced in and under the microscope of intellectuals. This guaranteed preservation, but how would it be for future generations of Kalmyks who would be born, like these saiga, into relative captivity?

THE SEASON'S FIRST blizzards had only just begun to set in, but the saiga farm was destined to mark the end of my winter ride. Unfortunately, the six-week delay on the border meant I had just days remaining on my Russian visa—not nearly enough to cross southern Russia to its borders on the Azov and Black Sea. I had no option but to leave the horses behind and travel to Ukraine to apply for a new visa.

Yuri, who had a hardened team of workers at the saiga farm, was eternally helpful. On the condition I pay for hay and grain, he offered to put the horses under the watch of his workers for the time I was away. So on January 17 I boarded a Crimea-bound bus, waved goodbye to Anna and Yuri, and promised to return within a month.

17

COSSACK
BORDERLANDS

ON A FREEZING evening in early March 2006 I was back on the horses and riding into a headwind with a Kalmyk man named Anir. Reawakening to life in the saddle after the winter break, I was acutely aware of the fine mist particles turning my cheeks numb and the sound of long, brittle grass fracturing beneath the horses' hooves. We had departed the Kalmykian Wild Animal Center three days earlier and, just as it had been during the first few days of spring in Kazakhstan a year earlier, my body felt a little stiff, the horses were wound up, and I was seeing the land afresh.

Framed between Taskonir's ears, the ridge we'd been following for most of the day angled southwest, turreted every so often with the silhouetted domes of ancient kurgans, mounds of earth and stones raised over graves that probably dated back to Scythian nomads.[1] Further on, the ridge gave way to empty plains where the sun was nestling into a golden haze. Empty and uncluttered, it was the kind of vista that could easily be mistaken for the steppe of central Mongolia, where I had begun two years ago. In fact, it was the kind of landscape that had defined most days of the journey since. It was difficult to imagine, then, that within the next twenty-four hours, it would pass behind.

Not long before descending from the ridge, Anir took me to a lone tree. Covered in prayer flags and ribbons, it had been planted on the grave of a lama. Following Anir, I led the horses around it in a clockwise fashion three times. Anir threw vodka into the air. "You might think the hardest part of the journey is behind you, but it is only beginning. Ahead are towns, fields, and roads—down there not even a wolf would find cover, and I don't know where you will camp. This is for good luck."

Forty kilometres ahead lay the Manych Depression, a system of rivers and lakes that in ancient times connected the Sea of Azov with the Caspian Sea. A historical crossroads of Asia Minor and Europe, it nowadays forms the southern border of Kalmykia and the northern reaches of Stavropol Krai that lie in the forelands of the Caucasus.

Significantly for me, the Manych represented the end of the arid and somewhat wild belt of steppe that stretches from Mongolia to Kalmykia. Beyond the Manych I could expect arable and more populated steppe.

The immediate leg of my journey lay along a corridor between the restive Caucasus and the uplands of southern Russia. Stretching west beyond the Manych as far as the Azov Sea, it once was a highly sought-after nomad hinterland that the Russian Empire had since fought hard for and plowed up under Stalin.

From the holy tree we pushed beyond darkness. Our aim was to reach Stavropol Krai, from where Anir would return home. To get there involved crossing the Manych via an artificial embankment controlled by a police checkpoint. In theory, this should have been a rudimentary procedure. In practice, things had become complicated in recent times.

On my return to Russia in late February, I had learned that Kok, my hardy gray packhorse from central Kazakhstan, had stepped on a 12 cm rusty nail that lodged deep into his hoof. It had gone unnoticed for many days before being removed. When I arrived he was sitting on his haunches, unable to stand on the injured limb. Sheila in Australia advised me that if the infection had reached the bone, he would probably never recover; if he did, it might take six months. I treated him for two weeks to no avail before deciding to leave him behind.

Losing Kok not only meant I needed to find a new packhorse but also complicated the fine line I had to tread with the Russian veterinary and quarantine authorities. Technically I had to remain in transit with the Kazakh horses and have them inspected in every province en route. Recently I had also learned that officially stationing my horses at the Wild Animal Center over winter required the center to apply for a permit—something neither the director of the center, Yuri, nor myself had been aware of. Even so, the fate of Kok might have been easily explained to authorities but for one further complication—the head of the provincial veterinary authorities in Elista apparently held a grudge against Yuri and had heard on the winds that Yuri was harboring my horses. In my absence, inspectors had visited the center but Yuri had managed in the nick of time to have the horses ridden away and hidden; he told the inspectors I had passed through in the winter, had long exited Kalmykia, and never stopped at the center. If the truth was discovered, the ramifications for Yuri could be significant, and so to help me get out of Kalmykia unnoticed he had agreed to supply a replacement horse—a fine-featured chestnut gelding I had named Utebai. Utebai would travel on the existing papers of the fallen Kok.

At around 11:00 P.M. we rendezvoused with Yuri by the edge of the still-frozen waters of the Manych. He had transported Utebai in the back of a truck, and now he opened the back gate. Already terrified by the ride, poor Utebai nearly fell out before we slapped a packsaddle on him and got under way.

Yuri had earlier made an audacious plan to guide me below the embankment out of sight of police, but the tangle of crushed-up ice pushed up against the edge made this impossible. There was nothing we could do but try riding straight through.

As I approached the boom gate under the glare of floodlights an armed policeman strode into the middle of the road. I came to a halt at the point where I was looking directly down at him, then offered a handshake. There was a moment of silence as the cold, unblinking man looked on. At this crossing in particular, Yuri had warned, they routinely checked the transit papers of live animals, particularly because of the prevalence of rustling.

Gradually, however, the policeman's face melted into a smile.

"Hello, Genghis Khan! Welcome!"

WHEN DAWN BROKE Anir and Yuri had gone, and like my new horse, I watched nervously as the sun illuminated a new world.

Somewhere during our crossing in the night, the unbridled steppe had given way to fields, canals, and endless lines of poplar trees. I rode through lingering mist on the outskirts of the town of Divnoye, passing residents emerging to till their backyard plots. Out in the larger fields a horse and cart rattled its way along a lane, and an old Soviet tractor pushed through plowed earth. They were scenes reminiscent of an ancient cradle of agrarian society, yet the history of the area belied this picture of settled life.

For most of the last few thousand years the land that stretched ahead to the Azov Sea had been rich, open grasslands, home to nomadic societies. Wave after wave of horseback peoples who inhabited the region had benefited from trade and from close cultural and political ties with their northerly Slavic neighbors. History, however—Russian history in particular—has overwhelmingly remembered them for using the strategic nature of their territory to exploit the southern underbelly of Slavic lands. Violent raids, which often involved taking Slavic peasants into slavery, had in part led to Russia's obsession in recent centuries with subduing the region.

The pattern of nomads penetrating Slavic lands from the south was no better demonstrated than by the Mongols when they made their first appearance on European soil in 1223. What has since become known as one of the most remarkable military campaigns in history—and which ended with the humiliation of Russia's armies—began as nothing more than a manhunt. Following the Mongol defeat of the Khwarezm Empire in Central Asia, Genghis Khan had sent twenty thousand soldiers under the guidance of generals Jebe and Subodei to hunt down the deposed Khwarezm leader, Muhammad II. I have recounted this episode earlier, but after pursuing him west to the Caspian Sea, where he died, the generals were granted permission from Genghis to return to Central Asia via the Caucasus along the north Caspian coast. There began their foray into Europe.

After conquering armies twice their size en route and plundering vast regions of Iraq-Ajemi, Azerbaijan, and Georgia, this roving band of hardened nomad warriors crossed the high passes of the Caucasus and rode down onto the steppe between the Caspian Sea and the Azov Sea. At the time the region was under the rule of nomads known as Kipchaks—a powerful Turkic people who at times held sway from Siberia and Central Asia to the Balkans, and who would feature prominently in the expansion of the Mongol Empire. After persuading the Kipchaks to honor the brotherhood between Mongols and Turks, Jebe and Subodei turned on them and pursued their fleeing armies northwest into Slavic lands.

Although the Kipchaks were not allies of the Russians, one of the Kipchak khans, Kotian, was the father-in-law of Prince Mstislav of Galich—the ruler of one of the most important princedoms of Russia. Afraid that if the Mongols conquered the Kipchak Empire they would invade his own land, Mstislav enlisted the support of several princedoms, including powerful Kiev (whose prince was also named Mstislav), to fight the Mongols.

In an attempt to halt the Mongol advance, a Russian army of around thirty thousand was assembled on the banks of the Dnieper River. The Mongols melted away into retreat in what must have appeared as a sign of capitulation but which was a classic nomad tactic—the likes of which Herodotus had described more than a thousand years earlier. Lured into a sustained pursuit for nine days, the Russians were weakened by the rigors of travel and taken far beyond their borders. When Mstislav of Galich became overconfident and crossed the Little Kalka River ahead of the main Russian army, the Mongols seized their chance.

Prince Mstislav of Kiev could only look on as the Mongols turned on Mstislav of Galich's soldiers, who were no match for the Mongols in the open, marshy terrain. Realizing that retreat for his own army would be fatal, Mstislav of Kiev fortified himself on a hill and offered surrender on the grounds that his army be allowed to return home. When their weapons were put down, however, the army was slaughtered, and the bodies of Mstislav of Kiev and his fellow princes were crushed beneath planks of wood upon which the Mongols feasted and celebrated victory.

Little more than a decade later the Mongols, under Subodei, would return to subjugate Russia in its entirety and use the Pontic and Caspian steppes (also simply known as the Pontic-Caspian steppe) as a base from which the Golden Horde would rule over Russia for 240 years.[2] After this initial invasion, however—a sort of reconnaissance sojourn—the Mongols retreated as abruptly as they had appeared. Riding east via the Caspian and Aral Seas through what is modern-day Kazakhstan, they rejoined the main Mongol army in 1224. In a paltry two or three years the small, disciplined detachment had traveled at least 10,000 km, conquered armies at will, and created a reputation of invincibility that would endure for centuries.[3]

It was humbling to reflect that in roughly the same time it had taken Jebe and Subodei to achieve this military expedition from Asia to Europe and back, I had barely managed to reach Russia in one piece. In fact, before my first day of riding beyond the Manych Depression was out, I was feeling more depleted than at almost any other time on my journey.

Little more than 30 km from the checkpoint, I fell ill with a high fever. For the next three days I lay in the care of a Dagestani farmer, drifting in and out of sleep, haunted by a dream in which Kok appeared with his two front legs chopped off. He stood on the bloody stumps with terror in his eyes, searching for his family. I had imagined arriving in these settled lands infused with the courage of the big wide steppe, but without Kok I felt exposed and vulnerable. Utebai was a small, weak horse unsuitable for travel and sooner or later I would have to find a replacement.

Uncertainty was creeping up on me from another quarter, too. As a foreigner, I was required to receive official registration to account for every day of my stay in Russia. The hotel in Elista registered me for the days I had been there, but beyond that I had no fixed address or host. This hadn't been an issue in the Kalmyk countryside, but I was now in provinces closer to the unstable republics of Ingushetia, Chechnya, Dagestan, and Ossetia. The ongoing insurgency in Chechnya, raw memories of the

Beslan school hostage tragedy, and recently foiled terrorist plots had created a heightened atmosphere of suspicion. I had experienced an indicator of this during my bus trip from the Crimea to Elista, during which I'd been ordered out for document checks eleven times. Almost every intersection in Stavropol and Krasnodar Krais— krai is a term that is the equivalent of oblast but historically used for territory on Russia's frontier—were manned by heavily equipped police, some even with light tanks. Because I was a foreigner riding three horses (one of which was not the same one listed on the papers I was carrying), carrying a satellite phone and GPS (technology that also required a permit), and traveling on an unregistered visa, things felt a little precarious.

After recovering from the fever, I set off gingerly. Fixing a westerly course and trying to avoid unwanted attention, I began by resisting any attempt to conform to the reality of fields, roads, and villages and took direct routes via compass. But it wasn't long before the hidden dangers of this environment were revealed. In the deep, soft soil of plowed fields, the horses tired fast, and I became hemmed in by a web of irrigation canals. While trying to jump across one such canal Taskonir fell up to his chest in muddy water and spooked the other horses. As I tried to calm them down Tigon ran off chasing a hare and did not return. An hour of searching led me to a railway track where he was tangled dangerously by the collar.

The next evening I thought my luck had changed when I crested a hill to find myself looking down at a green sea of virgin spring pasture. It was sweet, thick, grass—the kind I could only have dreamed of in the arid steppes of Kazakhstan and Kalmykia. I found a hidden hollow for my camp and the horses ate until morning and their stomachs were as tight as drums.

In the morning, I had only just emerged from the tent when a Russian jeep came barreling down on us. The driver was on his feet before the engine cut out. "So, you think you've found some good pasture?"

I nodded. The man angrily explained I had destroyed his autumn-sown barley—there were apparently hefty fines for such "vandalism." I couldn't bring myself to apologize and instead explained it was one the first fields

I had seen since leaving Mongolia. But the man didn't leave until I had tied the horses to a row of trees on the edge of the field. As he drove off he shot me a venomous look and left me with these words: "I hope you *do* keep grazing fields. Soon the mouse and rat poison will kill your animals anyway."

Over the coming days remnants of open pasturage became increasingly rare, and just as Anir had warned, the only grazing to be found was among the single-file rows of trees so narrow I could barely fit a tent on them. I could no longer afford to let the horses graze free, and tethering ropes had to be especially short. Afraid that Tigon, who loved catching mice and rats, might be poisoned, he too was permanently tied. I put him on a long leash and let him guide from the front of the caravan.

As I rode I cast my eyes sadly over Taskonir. With his coarse, tangled mane, stormy eyes, and untamed spirit, he was a living descendant of wild horses that had only ever known the freedom of open steppe. I felt guilty for bringing him to a land where he did not belong.

A WEEK BEYOND the Manych I passed the town of Krasnogvardeiskoe and crossed out of Stavropol Krai into Krasnodar. I was now about 400 km from the Azov Sea and had arrived on the Kuban—the most fertile and heavily cultivated steppe in southern Russia.

Given the intensity of farming onward from here, I expected conditions to grow more difficult. Instead, I found respite by following a series of rivers that flowed on an east-west line—some draining eastward into the Manych Depression, and others westward to the Azov Sea. I was able to locate pasture along the banks and enjoyed the cover of reeds. Most of all, I took heart that I had reached the home of the Kuban Cossacks—the legendary horseback warriors of Russia's frontier who had evolved on the very kind of crossroads of sedentary and nomadic society that I now rode through.

The most accepted version of Cossack origins holds that they were lawless Tatar bandits who began to fill the power vacuum left behind on the steppe after the disintegration of the Mongol Empire. Living in unclaimed borderlands between the Turkish, Russian, and Polish empires, the borderlands that were once so important for the Golden Horde, they were joined by Russians and Poles and emerged in the fourteenth century as a loose federation of military societies. Although Cossacks came to adopt the Russian language and Orthodox Christianity, their oft-worn Asiatic-style forelock on a shaved head, known as a *khokhol*, was a symbol of their unique place on the crossroads between the perceived "wild" East and "civilized" Europe.

Most Cossacks fought for whoever paid them, and so their alliances changed like the seasons. The free Cossacks—those not registered as soldiers in service to the tsar—commonly made raids on both Ottoman and Russian territory, and the ruler of one often asked the other to curb the attacks. Ivan the Terrible's reply in 1549 to the Turkish sultan was typical of such exchanges: "The Cossacks of the Don are not my subjects, and they go to war or live in peace without my knowledge."

At the end of the eighteenth century Russia moved to expand its empire and defeated the Cossack armies, after which Cossacks served the tsar and went on to become the imperial army's most feared cavalrymen, playing crucial roles in Russo-Turkish wars and the colonizing of Central Asia and Siberia.[4]

The Cossacks' dogged, independent spirit nevertheless endured, leading to a series of uprisings. In the twentieth century they had fought for the Whites and the Reds, the Nazis and the Soviets, and consequently Stalin considered them unreliable, if not traitorous. Cossack Nazi collaborators repatriated after World War II were infamously executed en masse in what Nikolai Tolstoy (a distant descendant of Leo Tolstoy) labeled the "secret betrayal." They also were singled out for repressive measures during collectivization.

In the post-Soviet era these harms had been publicly acknowledged, and Cossacks were reportedly reestablishing their culture. This was something I had long hoped to witness, not least now, because I was desperate to believe that some spirited fight for freedom still existed in a land that had submitted to the plow.

TEN KILOMETRES SHY of the town of Uspenskaya I happened on a rich meadow along the banks of the Kalaly River. Hidden from roads and almost entirely encircled by reeds, it seemed an ideal place for a rest day.

I had only just unloaded the horses, however, when the sound of Soviet-era motorbikes—a model found universally in former Soviet states called a Ural—thrust rudely from behind the reeds, passengers in sidecars bouncing about wildly. It was too late to pack up and move, and my spirits sank as I contemplated a long, sleepless night.

One of the drivers nearly drove into me before he stopped. As his mop of curly ginger hair settled, he barked at me, "What the fuck are you up to?" Hugged by a much-darned woolen sweater, he hauled his heavy gut up against gravity and stood with hands on hips. With his sights trained on me, I told my story rather pleadingly.

"Fuck off. Did you fuckin' hear that, boys? Mongolia to Hungary. Fuck me!" he replied.

Two other men who had tumbled out of the motorcycle sidecar stood a breath away. They had hulking, fat shoulders, and their faces were sunburned landscapes of freckles and unruly stubble.

It turned out that I was apparently guilty of making camp in their private fishing hideout. A deflated rubber raft was bundled out of a sidecar and pumped up by hand. Meanwhile, a picnic of salami, cucumber, vodka, and beer was laid out, and two more motorbikes came roaring to the scene.

One of the newcomers was a mountain of a man with a face as broad as a wheat field and green eyes the size of eggs. His gargantuan head swam in an even bigger wobbling chin, and like the others he had chipped teeth and mismatched clothes. Bellowing expletives, he settled next to me, rested his head against my saddle, then tore the cap off a beer bottle with his teeth, saying, "This is the most important part. You know the saying: beer without vodka is like throwing money to the winds!"

The food and alcohol consumed, my new friends unpacked a pile of fishing nets and set about the main business of the evening. They had only just managed to paddle out from the reeds, though, when the large man received a call on his cell.

"Boys! Police! Quick! Let's get the fuck out of here!"

The raft was deflated in seconds, and everything was stuffed into side-cars before the bikes were push-started in a scramble of legs. As they tore away they yelled at me in no uncertain terms: "Don't say a word or else! As soon as those fuckin' police have gone, we'll be back with more vodka!"

Fifteen minutes later the headlights of a Russian police jeep jittered across the uneven land in the falling darkness until the reeds around my camp were lit up like an amphitheater. Three policemen stepped out stiffly. "You haven't seen any poachers around here, have you? On motorbikes?"

A skinny, pale officer with a wiry mustache butted in. "You know these damn Cossacks—you have to be careful. Remember, you are on the Kuban now."

The jeep had only just taken off when the roar of motorbikes came to life and I was assaulted with backslaps and wild shrieks of thanks. They had managed to collect wood in the meantime and went about establishing a roaring campfire.

When the nets were set, we bundled up in my horse blankets and lay on the earth roasting salami and preserved pig fat on sticks. Vodka and pure spirits flowed, and by the flickering light the cracked-tooth smiles and tough but boyish faces took on an air of celebration. They talked rude, freewheeling talk about women, fishing, and fights, creatively describing everything using variations of just a few obscene words.

Listening to the ebb and flow of the stories, I sank into my coat, relishing the feeling of pig fat warming my belly. Tigon sat among us all, one of the gang. For the first time since crossing the Manych two weeks ago I was not alone; it was nice to feel a sense of camaraderie.

For a time the conversation petered out, then the large man poked the coals and looked at me. "You know, we are Cossacks after all. We have to live free! Stalin turned our land into fields, took away our horses. Brave men became wheat farmers and tractor drivers! Now we're not even allowed to fish without permission!" In the pained expression that spread across his face, you could tell he was trying to appreciate the identity of his people, something he would never have the luxury of knowing as anything but legend.

Cossacks had been targeted by Stalin not just because of their split loyalties, but because they lived on the most fertile land of the Soviet Union. Stalin relied on grain production in the Kuban and other Cossack territories in Ukraine to fund his push for industrialization. During collectivization, hundreds of thousands of Cossacks were accused of sabotaging the grain procurement campaign and were either executed, exiled to Siberia, or sent to forced labor camps.[5] Another policy that aided Stalin in his long-term assault on the Cossacks was that private ownership of horses was declared illegal. When the Nazis advanced into Russia, horses and cattle were herded away from the Kuban and never replaced. With the Cossacks horseless, their land depopulated, and their militaries outlawed, any hope of a return to the former life was snuffed out when the Kuban was set upon by a large-scale project of irrigation and cultivation.

Nowadays Cossacks, like these poachers, were free to revive their culture but the overwhelming reality was that the grinding process of industrialization had long rendered the horseback way of life redundant. And this is now what these young men faced.

One of them who had been quiet until now spoke up. "Have you seen the wild dogs yet? You should be carrying a gun—they are even more dangerous than wolves."

At the very thought of these wild predators, the man's eyes were full of hope and expectation. It seemed to me he wasn't so much frightened by the idea of wild dogs as he was proud of them. The idea excited me, too, to think that somewhere in this land there was a wild spirit that carried on even if the wolf was long gone.

At some point during the night one of the fishermen traveled into the village, then at about 3:00 A.M. returned in a car with more friends. As the beat-up old Lada lurched drunkenly to a halt, eight or nine bodies were disgorged in a wave of cigarette smoke, techno music, and the stench of vodka and beer. The fisherman at the wheel grinned. "We have a gift for you, Timofei!" Reaching into his pocket, he pulled out three small purple packages, which he held up to the headlights. They read: "Contained: 1 condom. Fish flavored." A robust-looking girl stepped out of the car with a giggle. I was told to take her to my tent.

At the time my temper was frayed—the car had spooked the horses, and Ogonyok and Taskonir had managed to rip out their tethering stakes; I had narrowly managed to hold on to them—and I declined. They seemed quite offended, and later on I couldn't help but feel bad for rejecting their offer so emphatically.

Traditionally the free life of a Cossack—who was obliged to serve in the army until the age of forty—was incompatible with marriage. Until the eighteenth century, most Cossack men were single, and even when the domestic family unit was adopted with the influx of Russian settlers, it was custom for married men to walk some distance in front of their wives and children in public places. This was to symbolize the uncertainty that Cossack men lived under, since they could be sent away to war for many years at any time. Women had to be prepared to carry on raising the family without a husband, and to some degree it was acceptable for them to be unfaithful while their husbands were away. Many young Cossacks I later met spoke proudly of their grandfathers, who had been known to have many mistresses. Like the romanticized version of their forebears, it naturally followed in their eyes that my life as a single wandering horseman should entail a love interest—or at least a visit to a prostitute—at every watering hole from Mongolia to Hungary.

THE FISHERMEN HAD deflated their raft and taken away the nets by dawn, leaving me with the condoms for "another time." I continued along the Kalaly River for a day until it began to curve north, then cut across to another watercourse that flowed west toward the sea. Confident the Cossacks wouldn't turn me in to the police, I relished the prospect of riding through the long, trailing Cossack villages that clung to the banks of the rivers.

Known as *khutors*—a Ukrainian term used by Cossacks to describe new settlements—they were built by the original Black Sea settlers who arrived from the Ukraine in the late eighteenth century. Khutors consisted of single rows of timber and mud-brick houses and were traditionally not large enough to warrant a church. It comforted me that in the modern era most didn't have police or administration representatives, either.

Bypassed by major roads, these khutors seemed to belong to a bygone era. Each house had a healthy plot of land and a run of chickens, pigs, and the odd goat. As firewood was scarce, most families also had mountains of dried corncobs out front—the staple source of fuel on the Kuban. Babushkas bent permanently at the hip worked the earth, and old men rowed leaky flat-bottomed fishing boats into sleepy waters. The clop and rattle of a horse and cart sometimes rose and faded along the single, unsealed streets.

Initially I had hoped I could slip in and out of these settlements inconspicuously, but even the dead would have been woken by the wave of barking dogs and honking geese that preceded me when traveling the length of a khutor. The longest was 15 km but had a population of less than 1,000. The kerfuffle gave people time to ready themselves to greet me with jars of homemade vodka and preserved cucumbers, peppers, tomatoes, jams, honey, juice, pears, and *salo* (pork fat). The key to getting past was having at least one shot of vodka, although under duress this often became three. On one occasion I was told that if I wanted to become a genuine Cossack, I would have to drink a giant bottle of home-brewed vodka, known as *samohon*[6] and then "jump over a fence." It was a drinking culture that reminded me of a description I'd read in Leo Tolstoy's short novel *The Cossacks*:

"All Cossacks make their own wine, and drunkenness isn't so much a tendency common to all as it is a ritual, the non-fulfillment of which would be considered apostasy."

Within two days I had accumulated so much heavy produce that the offerings had become a serious danger to the packhorses. When I explained this, the gift bearers always glared back indignantly. More than once I was told, "If I have given it to you, you must take it! You know the saying: 'When they give, take. When they kill, run.'"

The fanfare in khutors sometimes delayed me long enough for Cossack men to dress up and greet me on the street in traditional regalia. Near Il'inskaya, a stanitsa (a town larger than a khutor, big enough to have a church), one such man stepped proudly into my path in a black Astrakhan hat, a golden embroidered cloak fitted with bullets in the chest pockets, and a whip and antique dagger on the belt. His near-royal refinement was strongly at odds with the uncouthness of the poachers I'd met a few days before.

"Welcome, Cossack! I am the ataman of the Il'inskaya Cossacks. Where are you migrating to?" he said, shaking my hand. "As ataman, I am the leader of the Cossacks here and responsible for getting young people enlisted in the Kuban Cossack army. But my job is also to instil the spirit of freedom, fairness, and independence that was crushed in the Soviet era."

I asked the ataman what relation he felt to the nomadic people of the steppe.

"Like nomads, we could always pack up and leave wherever we needed. In old times, like for nomads, the steppe gave us all we needed—horses, wild game, and fish." He cast his eyes over my gear and the horses with a look of envy. "I consider that Genghis Khan was a Cossack by definition. Although we did not live in yurts, we adopted the best of nomad custom: most important, their horses and horsemanship. We have a saying: 'Only a bullet can catch a Cossack rider.'"

As I rode on there was no doubt in my mind that Cossacks genuinely identified with my journey and were conscious of their history as great horsemen. I took great heart from this and was beginning to lose my fear of authorities. Nothing, however, could hide the fact that the essential ingredient of their past—horses—had disappeared. I felt the absence of the equine at every move. Most village atamans I met stepped out of cars or traveled on foot, and no one thought to offer me fodder—a meaningful gift for a nomad. The few horses I did encounter had never been saddled. Famous don breeds that had once been ridden into war were now used for pulling carts. When I passed them on the road they shied at the sight of my caravan and sometimes bolted off the edge of the road, the driver hanging on for dear life.

In another telling sign of the absence of horses, in all my time on the Kuban steppe only one family ever invited me to stay. Very few had horses or the facilities to keep them overnight, and those who did didn't believe they had room or feed for three extras. Whenever I asked if there was somewhere I could lodge, I would be directed to a collective farm beyond the village. These ranches were depressing Soviet relics, many of which had been converted into piggeries and almost exclusively manned by poor men who lived in the village and worked out at the farm on irregular shifts. As it had elsewhere in the Soviet Union, collectivization had clearly driven a wedge between farming and family life. Horses had subsequently become associated with state farms and were no longer treasured family members.

Beyond Il'inskaya, the freshness instilled by the winter break wore off. My body began to ache, and the accumulated lack of sleep took its toll. At the first sign of hunger my mood would crumble. The horses felt heavy themselves, and during breaks they kept their heads down. Even Tigon was exhausted. He had learned that the most important thing while on the lead was keeping well out of reach of Taskonir, for whenever Taskonir caught up he would take a nip at Tigon's hind legs to remind him who was boss. Several times Tigon's lead became dangerously tangled in the horse's legs. The worst torment was when the front horse happened to step on the lead at a trot. It nearly strangled poor Tigon, who, pinned down and trampled by the caravan, was spat out the end in somersaults. How he came out of these scrapes without serious injury was beyond me.

Then came the rains. The lanes and tracks turned to sticky black mud—a telling sign that I was riding through chernozem, or "black soil"— the fertile soils that stretch from the Kuban across the southern steppe of the Ukraine, forming the breadbasket of Russia and the former Soviet Union. It was so sought after for its richness that, legend has it, when the Nazis advanced through southern Ukraine and Russia they took soil back to Germany by the shipload.

As mud, however, this precious soil balled up under the horse's hooves until they slipped and fell. I resolved to walk, but within minutes the buildup on my boots turned them into heavy clogs. The slightest tug from the horses on the lead rope toppled me into the mud. I walked the better part of three days, descending into a quagmire of filth. The horses were still losing their winter hair, and the shed hair combined with the mud to stick fast to my clothes, my skin, and my sleeping bag. But the dirtier and more desperate for hospitality I became, the less likely it was that anyone would let me in.

And then one night, while I was setting up camp in the pouring rain beyond a ramshackle khutor, a local drunk stumbled upon my muddy patch of earth and twisted the knife. "How dare you camp here on the Kuban, you foreigner! If I tell my friends about it, they will come in the night, take your horses to the meat factory, and drown you in the river for the crayfish to eat!" I swore at him darkly, and he stumbled away. But the look I caught in his eye meant that I slept the night in my filthy riding clothes and with my axe by my side.

Out of grain and low on food the following night, I was forced to camp on a narrow strip of grass next to freshly plowed earth. Despite tying the horses on short tethers, they managed to get out and roll in it. By morning they were all plastered in black grime.

As I sat there with my porridge, a thought dawned on me. I'd become the picture of a down-and-out, homeless wanderer that many westerners and Russians mistakenly associate with the word nomad. My condition reminded me of when I had been in Siberia at age twenty-one, riding a bicycle to Beijing. I had been living on a budget of $2 a day, had a single change of clothes, and hadn't shaved in more than four months. A village woman, who looked at me in horror, explained the word bomzh, which usually referred to a homeless bum, to me this way: "Well, Tim, bomzh . . . it's basically you, only without your bicycle."

How ironic, I thought, that this same mud that caked us all, the pride of the Kuban, had spawned the end of the nomad era and the downfall of the free Cossack way of life. Stalin had never trusted Cossacks and had needed grain to pay for his dreams of industrialization, and plowing up the chernozem had been a valid pretext to solve both problems. I understood it now: to dispossess a nomad, you take away his horse and plow up his land. Horseless and coaxed into a life between four walls, the once brave warrior becomes toothless and redundant in the space of a generation.

On a lighter note, as I noticed the tattered fabric hanging around my legs, I sadly concluded that the trousers I had been wearing since day one in Mongolia were close to the end of their own road.

18

THE TIMASHEVSK MAFIA

BEYOND THE STANITSA of Dyad'kovskaya, the rain came down in sheets. I slipped behind a row of trees and headed down a narrow track into some deserted wheat fields. Protected by the hood of my jacket, I kept my head bowed and considered my circumstances.

I was now only 250 km from the Kerch Strait, which lay between Russia and the Crimean peninsula in Ukraine, but before leaving Russia I needed to find a replacement for Utebai and start the process of getting my horses approved for passage through customs. To do either of these would require a miracle. Horses were a scarcity on the Kuban, and no one would ever agree to trade for a wimp like Utebai. In my filthy, disheveled state of late, it was also true that I would struggle to convince a shopkeeper to sell me a loaf of bread, let alone a border guard to give me entry into another country.

But when I lifted my eyes, columns of light peeled away the gloom, and it seemed my prayers had been answered.

The unruly beard of the man before me caught my eye at first, then his tall, burnished velvet hat and long black robes. He lifted a small broom from a bucket of water, flicking drops from high above his head into the field. Then he turned to me.

"We've come here to bless the wheat fields with holy water! Where are you going?"

He was the priest of Dyad'kovskaya, and he explained that since ancient times it had been the role of the Orthodox Church to bless every wheat field of the parish in the spring. As I went on my way, he showered my caravan with holy water.

It was only a few minutes later that proof of his friends in higher places materialized. Accustomed to noisy Russian jeeps and Ladas, I'd failed to notice the purr of a new four-wheel-drive Range Rover until it was right up alongside me. Tigon took a sniff, then retreated. As a tinted window slid down silently, a man who was polished but not as elegant as his car grinned out at me from the leather interior.

"So, fellow traveler, partisan, Kazakh, Cossack—how can I help you?"

I wiped mud and rain from my eyes and peered down as he stepped out and swaggered up to me. Standing only little taller than he was wide, he was adorned with flawlessly buffed shoes, a black jacket, sunglasses, and a silky tie in red, green, and white, the colors of the Krasnodar provincial flag. This was crowned with silver-streaked curly hair and a handlebar mustache. He might have been the second apparition in as many minutes, but there was no doubting it: this man was no priest.

"My friend! You do not know me, but soon, I think, we will be friends. I am Nikolai Vladimorivich Luti: ataman of this region, owner of ten thousand hectares of crops, and employer of eight hundred workers."

I stammered out my story. Luti, as he liked to be called, looked at me thoughtfully. Finally he said, "Thirty kilometres away at my friend's farm you will have all the services you need. Go there tonight, and tomorrow we will consider your problem. If we can find a new horse for you, we will."

Rain streamed down as I hightailed it through fields and villages.

Flocks of geese parted, avenues of dogs erupted, and goats tied on short chains nearly strangled themselves in panic as my caravan thundered by. It grew dark and cold, and my body ached, but sometimes I had to let the reins go—I had, after all, been promised hot food and a wash.

It was well into the night when I pulled up alongside a throng of Soviet harvesting equipment, peeled myself out of the saddle, and hobbled inside a cavernous machinery shed. There, under floodlights on a plastic table, lay a tub of freshly roasted meats, fruit, and salads, surrounded by a forest of vodka bottles. Around this table sat Luti and three other men, all clearly ravenous.

As I sank thankfully into a chair, Luti introduced himself as the "big farmer," and Sascha Chaika—the owner of the farm where we had arrived—as the "little farmer." Luti then rose with a glass of vodka and puffed out his chest. "I want you to know that you have fallen in with simple people. It's Easter, and although we are observing fasting, Cossacks were always allowed to eat meat and drink alcohol when on the road . . . and, well, we are on the road!"

The vodka had barely hit our guts before we swooped down on the food. Sauce exploded from the corners of our mouths, oil ran down our arms, and soon all that remained were empty disposable plates and a "tablecloth" of oily newspaper. Our attention then turned to drink, and soon the shed was filled with a cacophony of laughter, man-to-man talk, and heated arguments that were resolved by more drinking. It wasn't until the vodka ran out that the calm of night reclaimed the wheat field and the shed grew cold, then dark and silent.

In the morning came a message through Chaika that Luti would agree to see me again only *after* I had had a wash. Luti had booked me a hotel in Timashevsk for a night, and sure enough I soon found myself with rivers of black and brown mud flowing off me in a luxurious bathtub. Luti had suggested that a little love was in order as part of this "recovery package," and although I had turned the offer down, I had half expected to find a woman waiting in my room when I arrived.

Clean and sober the next morning, I knew it was time to face the challenge of finding a new horse and eking a way into the tangle of bureaucracy so I could leave the country with my animals. Luti was not fazed by this challenge. Timashevsk, he said, was the perfect base from which to organize everything.

Over the next six weeks, my problems would indeed be solved, but in this farming center on the main road between Krasnodar and Moscow, my time among the circle of Luti's friends and acquaintances would offer me an intriguing portrait of a society in which the void created by the collapse of the Soviet Union had been filled by endemic corruption. Partly in an effort to cope with the eternal uncertainty this created, but also as a celebration of the unregulated times they were living in, people had adopted a carefree approach to life and had a remarkable propensity to enjoy the moment—albeit with alcohol (and, in the case of Luti's men, the liberal use of prostitutes) at its core.

Much of my journey from Mongolia to Hungary was an external one, dealing with the elements and the horses. But here in Timashevsk, challenged by this culture, I would experience a chapter that would prove to reveal as much about me—and perhaps my naiveté—as it did about those around me.

THE FIRST PRIORITY was finding a place for my horses, and it wasn't long before Luti had made a few calls and come up with a solution: "I have the perfect place! My friend owns a scrap metal plant in town." When he noticed my blank stare, he added, "You will thank me for this, I promise!"

Later that day my blank look turned to one of extreme apprehension as I led my horses toward a run-down industrial building from which came violent booms and the screeching of metal. It looked and sounded more like a glue factory than a stable. I felt Taskonir tremble as we entered and navigated through a mess of twisted car wrecks and mangled steel. A man wearing grease-covered overalls waved urgently at me to stop as a crane swung a full-size truck through an arc just 5 m ahead of me. The truck was dumped in a huge steel bin with a deafening clang, then set upon by a gang of men wielding crowbars and sledge hammers.

Metal recycling had thrived in southern Russia since the 1990s, and plants like this had become processing facilities for the dismantling of seventy years of Soviet machinery. The metal business was also known to have a close affiliation with the Mafia. I was beginning to wonder just who my benefactor was when a blond woman in a figure-hugging dress and high heels emerged from an office and picked her way toward me through the dust and debris. She led me toward some stables in a corner of the recycling yard that I'd overlooked.

There, I met the owner of the plant and Luti's friend, Igor Maluti—a man who was half Tatar, half Cossack, almost 2 m tall, and bearing shoulders as wide as a draft horse's. Stooped forward, veins flaring at his temples, he wrenched rather than shook my hand while declaring that his life was devoted to the love of three things: horses, pigeons, and women. As I would soon learn, he was determined to introduce me to all three as soon as possible.

His horses were expensive breeds ranging from English thoroughbreds to ponies. He never rode them, but he made sure they were given the finest food, and he had the Gypsy stable master wash them weekly with special horse shampoo. "They are food for my soul," he explained in his coarse, dry voice.

Next he drove me to see his wife and mistresses, one after another, to whom he brought gifts and money. On the way home we came to a screeching halt on a bridge. Luti leaped out and managed to catch a pigeon from the ledge with his bare hands.

"Don't you see? Pigeons are freedom, intelligence, and peace," he said, canoodling with the bird, which he held against his powerful chest.

While I sensed that he could be brutal and cruel in different circumstances, there was a directness and honesty in Igor that I warmed to. Flexing his powerful hands over the steering wheel, pigeon tucked under his arm, he turned to me with a sigh and said, "Of course, Tim, to live your free life is my dream." He turned back to the road, and I saw the folds in his trunk-thick neck smooth out. There was a sad look in his eyes. "But alas, your life is not my destiny."

The hidden genius in leaving the horses with Igor was revealed later. The Gypsy stable master was an expert at bringing horses back to health. He professed to know when to feed and water them, and how much was needed to make a horse gain strength and weight. By the time I left, the horses were being prepared for the first shampooing of their lives.

On the other side of town Tigon and I moved into an industrial site of our own. Owned by Luti, it was a huge yard fenced in by concrete and barbed wire that contained a tile-making factory and a transit facility for gas and diesel.

My new home was located in a ramshackle security guard's hut, where I was given a room filled with old tires, car parts, and tools, and decorated with flaking stickers of naked women. In moving in, I had dispossessed Luti's head mechanic of his love shack.

To assist in finding a new horse and getting veterinary papers in order, Luti granted me two drivers. One was his loyal assistant, Aleksei, and the other was Edik. The two couldn't have been a more curious contrast. Aleksei was a tall handsome womanizer from Dagestan, who wore white leather dress shoes and a suit. His hobbies were women, vodka, smoking, cards, and more women, generally in that order. Edik, on the other hand, was a family man who worked as a tractor driver and wore nothing more glamorous than a pair of cheap Chinese-made sandals and threadbare track pants. Aleksei, or "Lokha," as he was known for short, took charge of finding me a new horse, while it was decided that Edik would look after my veterinary affairs.

Field trips with Lokha began well. We narrowed the horse search down to a farm 20 km out of town, owned by a proud Cossack named Nikolai Bandirinka. The stables of this onetime secretary of the local Communist Party was home to more than one hundred stud horses—the jewels of which were twenty prize stallions from lines famous for dressage, show jumping, and racing.

Although Nikolai generally did not keep workhorses, he did by chance presently have one: a four-year-old palomino stallion named Sokol, whose name meant "magpie." Sokol was about fifteen hands, broad and strong, with a flowing blond mane and an inquisitive nature. Although he had lived his whole life in a stable and had never been ridden, I liked him at once. There was only one problem: it was spring and Kok was a fully-fledged stallion. Luti offered to pay half of the $1,000 to buy the horse, and Nikolai agreed to organize a castration. The deal was agreed to, vaccinations administered, and blood samples taken.

Solving the issue of my veterinary and customs papers with Edik proved more complex. To get exit permits from Russia I needed cooperation from all levels of bureaucracy, including the regional Timashevsk veterinary and transport authorities, the provincial laboratory, the veterinary department in Krasnodar, federal authorities in Moscow, and the equivalents of all of these in Ukraine. Naturally, this had never been done before by a horseback traveler here, and so I faced the same labyrinth of red tape and confusion I had experienced on the Kazakh border. Edik explained that locals would never go through with such a torturous process—it was far easier to pay bribes. Because I was a foreigner, though, this was tricky territory, since no official wanted to be held accountable for making an error in relation to my case.

I persisted, and after establishing reliable contacts a semblance of routine developed to my life in Timashevsk. Two or three days per week I was ferried by Edik between the local veterinary department, the horses, and the laboratory in Krasnodar—there were twelve different diseases to be tested for, and for those tests that could not be done in Krasnodar, blood samples were couriered to labs in Moscow. Most days I also visited Luti in his office to fill him in on my progress. He sat in an executive chair, smoking imperiously, as he listened to my latest account. While there were fits of angry phone calls and times when Lokha was being ordered to do this and that, they were interspersed with long periods of silence during which he sat contemplatively, the one small window casting light onto his speckles of silver hair. "Tim," he would say at last, pulling a rolled-up $100 bill from his top pocket, "take some pocket money and go and buy yourself some cigarettes or something!"

On days in between the expeditions to Krasnodar, Lokha took me to Nikolai's farm to train Sokol, whom I had already renamed Kok. The new Kok, as it turned out, was not only unridden but had never even been tied to a fence nor been fitted with a halter, saddle, crupper, or girth strap. Unaware of this initially, the first time I tied him to a fence he panicked, reared, and ended up hanging by his throat with the rope wrapped around his neck. I had four weeks to get him ready to take his place in the caravan.

Using "approach and retreat" methods that the Watsons had taught me in Australia, I gradually accustomed Kok to my touch until I could rub him all over and he would stand still. The next step was to familiarize him with a girth strap. After initially taking it well, he let fly one afternoon with a fit of bucking and pig rooting, rearing up and punching his front hooves into the air. I had little experience with stallions, and he had a power and will that frightened me.

During the second week of training, Kok underwent castration. With his legs bound and Nikolai standing on his neck, his testicles were clamped and then twisted around until they sheared off. As Kok struggled in agony, Nikolai laid a fist into his nose to distract him from the pain. I went home feeling sick.

Despite also witnessing the castration, Lokha was unconcerned and had other things on his mind. The trips to Bandirinka's farm doubled as reconnaissance missions to find venues for the infamous weekends of debauchery he shared with his boss. Earlier that day he had discovered a suitable sauna retreat nearby and couldn't wait to get back to Timashevsk to share the news with Luti. "Oh, Tim. What more could you ask to relax? A good sauna, sex, drink, and sleep!" he said, one hand moving restlessly over the steering wheel, the other deftly pinching a cigarette. He and Luti were regularly sampling prostitutes, and conversations with Lokha generally orbited around this subject.

He had already invited me along for the weekend and, unhappy that I had declined, turned to me. "What are you resisting for? You can have your pick of the women, eighteen-year-olds, twenties, younger, whatever you please!" His pointy leather shoe drove downward on the accelerator, and we swerved out around a truck and zoomed ahead.

I was having difficulty coming to terms with the fact that Lokha, who indulged so openly with prostitutes, was also a family man with a wife and children. My discomfort with the subject surely reflected my upbringing in Australia, but in truth, I'd also never felt completely at home in a culture of masculinity in its more extreme forms. As a result, there was a part of me that felt out of place with the company I was keeping.

Whatever the reason for my feelings, the awkwardness with which I reacted to Lokha's offers frustrated him. This boiled over one day when I was explaining my deep reservations about a suggestion from Lokha that I should try to export Sokol to Ukraine on Kok's passport. "This is Russia!" Lokha expostulated. "This is the way things are done here! Listen to me and you will get your horses through without trouble! You should quit worrying and have some fun with some girls while the offer stands! Sometimes you think too much!"

A month went by, Sokol's wound healed, the air in Timashevsk grew thick and warm, and all around the wheat and barley crops began to bulge. Lokha raved about the coming summer, which would be filled with a good harvest, barbecues, drinking, and romance. Quite apart from getting the horses ready for the border, I found every minute of my day occupied. The industrial base that had become my home was a thoroughfare for workers, mostly drunken, who all had stories to tell.

Take, for instance, the security guard who worked night shifts from the shack where I slept. He was a balding man in his fifties, whom they all called Lisi, "Baldy." Security watch for Lisi meant a night away from his wife, drinking a bottle of vodka and having sex with a string of women in the hut's kitchen. All night he could be heard laughing hysterically as the level of vodka in the bottle went steadily down, then groaning and creaking as he made love on the tea table. One night I caught a glimpse of his lover storming out after a fight, pulling her dress on as she ran barefoot into the murky hues of the pre-dawn hours. Having let her go, he broke into my room, pulled me up by the arms, and, drawing his face close to mine, showered me with spittle as he said, "C'mon, Tim! What are you waiting for? Let's go to the highway!" When I protested sleepily and asked why, he shook me in a rage. "To get prostitutes, of course!"

I wasn't the only one who had to endure these tirades, although I was probably the only one who found them the least bit curious. Sharing the hut with me was Yura, an illegal immigrant from Georgia who worked at the tile factory. His passport and visa had long expired; afraid of what might happen at the border, he hadn't been home to see his family for four years. His situation had recently become more tenuous because of the deteriorating relations between Russia and Georgia. The nightly TV news was filled with stories condemning Georgia's president, Mikheil Saakashvili, who was drumming up support for Georgia to join NATO. Moscow had just banned all imports of Georgian wine, cut off diplomatic relations, and halted cross-border postal services. During the dead of winter a mysterious explosion on the gas pipeline had left the population of Georgia's capital, Tbilsi, freezing, and Georgia had accused Russia of sabotage. Georgians such as Yura who lived and worked illegally in Russia found themselves the focus of unwanted attention from authorities.

Yura's story would have resonated among hundreds of thousands of illegal immigrants in Russia who had come from former Soviet republics to work but were stuck with expired documents and cut off from family with no support or legal protections. Like everything in Russia, citizenship could be bought at a price, but few could afford the going rate, which apparently was around $5,000.

To make matters more complicated, Yura's girlfriend—a girl from a nearby village—had become pregnant, and he was doing his best to set up his shoebox of a single room as a family home. Yura was philosophical. "Life is different for everyone. For some it's easy, for others hard; some are rich, some are poor. At least when you are poor you have nothing to fear. If you are rich, the law means nothing—but for that, people will try to kill you," he said.

He often spoke of his dream to set up a car detailing business, raise a family, build a home in Timashevsk and live with a sense of normalcy. Every night when I came home he would greet me with his round, boyish face, some Georgian wine, and stories about his home on the Black Sea coast. On weekends he would lie on his humble little sofa bed with his girlfriend and watch TV programs ranging from *Who Wants to Be a Million-aire?* to the Russian version of *Big Brother*—shows that portrayed a life in Moscow that might have well been on another planet.

As days stretched into weeks in Timashevsk, it seemed that no matter whom I talked to, if they weren't being strangled by bureaucracy or in the thrall of prostitution, then they were certainly tangled in corruption, voluntarily or otherwise.

Chaika—the farmer who had hosted my arrival feast—said to me one day with a jaded look, "A couple of months ago the state prosecutor turned up to my farm and told me that I had broken some environmental laws. He offered me a choice, saying, 'If you want to take me to court, then you are more than welcome. But I can guarantee that you will lose, because I am the court! The fine will be three hundred thousand roubles'—about $10,000. 'But if you want, you can pay me thirty thousand roubles now and I will forget about it.'"

Chaika's muscular old body moved restlessly in the chair. One could sense the honest toil that had made up a good part of his life. Unlike Luti, whose transition from a collective farm director to big farmer was murky, he had built his farm up from scratch with hard work. He took a sip of his tea and continued. "So what am I supposed to do? If I don't pay, then he is sure to bankrupt me and sell off the machinery cheaply to his friends." Chaika, like so many other Russians, accepted as a given that the law was largely a tool for those in power to extract bribes and provide a pretext for convicting anyone the authorities pleased.

My only time out from the intense swirl of events and people in Timashevsk was when I was alone with Sokol. After three weeks of circle work inside the compound at Bandarinka's, I had finally been game enough to ride him. On the first attempt he bucked me clear and bolted back to the stables, but gradually he learned to trust me. During rides along a river out back of the farm I could feel his body bristling with wound-up energy as he moved nervously along, pausing and sniffing at flowers, grass, puddles, and trees. Unlike any other horse I had ridden, he had no problem negotiating fences, gates, tractors, even wire and steel, yet he was petrified of birds, the river, and the reeds that rustled in the wind. He was most at ease in his stable and around the roar of farm trucks. This couldn't have been more contrary to horses of the steppe, which were petrified of anything remotely unnatural. His behavior, like that of the people in Timashevsk, were simply a reaction to the world into which they had been born.

After nearly six weeks in Timashevsk, the feeling of tranquility and effervescence that I had had right after my arrival had faded. The constant battle with bureaucracy, on one hand, and the flagrant disregard for law, on the other, mingled with the culture of masculinity among my companions, had worn me down. One evening over a drink with Luti and Lokha my spirits bottomed out. They had been discussing Luti's only son, who was set to be married in just a couple of weeks' time. With a look of resignation Luti took a deep drag of his cigarette and eyeballed first Lokha, then me. "Yes, no matter how you look at it, it's true. Wives over time inevitably become just friends, partners. You are yet to learn this, Tim, but it is a true fact."

I returned that night alone to the grimy mechanic's shack where everything was imbued with the stench of alcohol and diesel. I felt as far away from the steppe as I had ever been on my trip. It was time to get back in the saddle and move on—a luxury that people living here did not have.

The next morning I had a meeting with the priest of Dyad'kovskaya, whom I had originally met in the fields all those weeks before. The derelict state of his church seemed symbolic of the spiritual condition of the people I'd been meeting. In fact, the church where he held services was an abandoned Soviet-era school hall where cardboard posters of saints, Mary, and Jesus Christ were stuck to the wall with Scotch tape. Although in his grandfather's day there had been three churches and a thriving attendance, his regulars at the Sunday service amounted to three old pensioners.

"The original churches were torn down by the Bolsheviks, and my church has become a three-day church," he said philosophically. "The only time people come to church is for baptism, marriage, and death. Money is the problem—if only people like Luti could give more generously, then I might be able to resurrect a sense of spirit in the local community.

"You see, Tim," he continued, "we are still suffering the destruction of the Soviet era. Modern-day Cossacks grew up as nonbelievers, and everything connected to ethics, morals, and spirituality takes a long time to resurrect. This is how I think of it: A wound on the body heals fast. A wound in the spirit might take ten years to heal. But if a wound is in the spirit of an entire people, it can take a hundred years. And what we experienced during the Soviet revolution wasn't just a wound—it was a killing blow, a death of the soul and spirit. I would like to think that Russia could again be great in more than just the size of its territory, but at the moment it doesn't seem to be the case."

I came away from my talk with the priest with my faith in the ability of people to transcend their social and political realities anything but restored. The truth was that the deeply penetrating corruption and the coping mechanisms of alcohol and prostitutes had personally affected me. It wasn't that any of this was unique to Timashevsk, of course; in fact, they were realities that I had witnessed throughout my horseback travels. At this stage of the journey, though, two years after setting out, I felt less able to step back into the role of an observer and more a part of society. Particularly because I was traveling by horse, I depended on the generosity and goodwill of people of all walks of life, and so I was both a victim and beneficiary of corruption. This left me feeling conflicted.

On the upside, the priest had got me thinking. Within the context of the upheaval of the twentieth century, there was a sense of cohesion among Luti's men—a genuine care for one another—that had endured through these times and was perhaps incorruptible. Some, like Luti, could to some degree create their own rules. But even then, whether it was Luti, Edik, or Yura, they were all people eking out their precarious lives the only way they knew and casting aside worries about the morrow they could not control. It was an attitude I could no doubt benefit volumes from.

WHEN FINALLY MY documents were in order, I gave Utebai to Igor Maluti at the metal recycling factory, who in turn donated him to a local riding school for children. Bandirinka gave me a royal send-off, dressed up in Cossack gear on one of his stallions, and Luti paid a visit to congratulate me on getting everything done.

Two weeks after departing, I found myself riding through the crisp air of morning watching the sun splinter through fractured clouds, turning the reeds by the roadside a luminous green. On the horizon I could see ships floating idly on the silky gray sheen of the Azov Sea.

I was a few kilometres shy of the ferry port of Kavkaz, where, if all went well, I was hoping to catch a ferry with my horses out of Russia and across the narrow Kerch Strait to Crimea. But I was under no illusions about my chances of getting through customs and immigration. Among other things, my unregistered visa remained an unresolved issue, and to reach the border I would have to pass through a police checkpoint.

As the boom gate, police cars, and a watchtower crept into view, I had the terrible feeling that my whole journey was about to unravel. When I reached the border crossing, the guards failed to appear, and I thought for a moment they might let me pass. But then a door opened and a large man sauntered out, machine gun dangling loosely against his belly. "Tie them up and come inside!" he ordered.

My passport was taken away by the superior officer, who went to run a check on their computer. He returned shaking his head. "What are we going to do with this lawbreaker?" he said, looking at his colleague. He was referring to the lack of the required registrations that would cover each day of my stay.

I started to explain the circumstances that had prevented me from getting the proper documentation, but after a while the boss pulled me aside. "Look, I'll tell you what to do. You see that registration date from the hotel in Elista that expired more than two months ago? Take this pen and put in today's date." He paused awkwardly. "Usually, for permission to write that, it would cost you eight hundred roubles . . ."

I pretended not to understand the hint, scribbled down the date, and carried on into immigration, where the veterinary officers were waiting. They were impressed with the thoroughness of my paperwork and told me, laughing, that it was the first time, to their knowledge, that anyone had completed all the required tests.

The last obstacle before boarding the ferry for Crimea was customs. Just as I pulled into the inspection bay, Ogonyok disgorged a gigantic turd. The junior officers laughed but their superior did not see the humor. "You are not leaving Russia until you clean that crap up!" he yelled.

"Okay, okay. But I'm not going to shift it with my bare hands. You will have to find me a shovel," I replied, disembarking from the saddle.

While he sent some officers off in search of a shovel, most of the customs people on duty came out to look at the spectacle. Meanwhile, I went inside to be processed and breezed through the screening post to have my passport stamped. Back outside, nobody had found a shovel, and the boat was due to leave. Within minutes I was casting off into the Kerch Strait leaving behind the cluster of officials still gathered around Ogonyok's parting present.

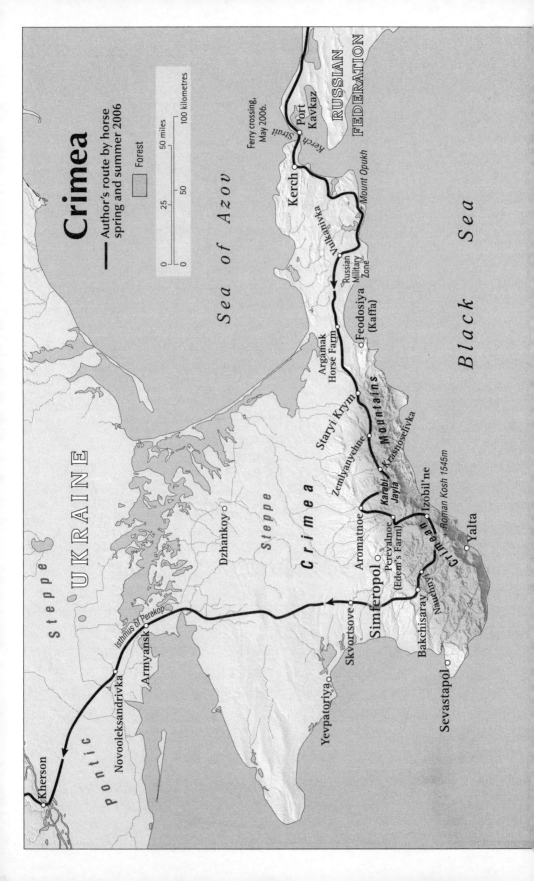

Crimea

— Author's route by horse
spring and summer 2006

☐ Forest

0   25   50
0   50   100 kilometres
50 miles

RUSSIAN FEDERATION

Port Kavkaz

Ferry crossing,
May 2006.

Kerch Strait

Kerch

Vulkanivka

+ Mount Opukh

Russian Military Zone

Sea of Azov

Feodosiya (Kaffa)

Arganak Horse Farm

Staryi Krym

Zemlyanyebne

Krasnoselivka

Mountains

Karabi Jayla

Izobil'ne

+ Roman Kosh 1545m

Yalta

Black Sea

UKRAINE

Steppe

Dzhankoy

Crimea

Steppe

Isthmus of Perekop

Armyansk

Novooleksandrivka

Pontic

Kherson

Skvortsove

Aromatnoe

Simferopol

Perevalnoe (Edem's Farm)

Crimean

Bakchisaray

Nauchnyi

Sevastapol

Yevpatoriya

19

WHERE TWO WORLDS MEET

A SHADOW SWOOPED from the solitary cloud in the sky, and the whole sleepy mountain in front of us dimmed to olive green. As the salty breeze gusted, my sweat cooled and Ogonyok's wild ginger mane flew in all directions.

From the saddle I watched Tigon's tail and ears cut through the tall swaying grass like dorsal fins. He'd been on long-ranging missions all day, drifting back at times to check in, looking up at me with his tongue lolling about and his amber eyes alight. It wasn't long before he reached the crest of the hill and stopped, ears bent forward, the sleek shaft of his snout fishing for scents on the breeze.

As the cloud shadow peeled back toward us I, too, was soon surveying the view. From a foreground of waist-high grass, red poppies, and white chamomile, the steppe dropped away in a sea of green, gleaming with the same vitality as my horses' spring coats. Directly below, a narrow sandy isthmus cut a straight line to the west between the sea and a series of pinkish salt lakes. Immediately to our north, smooth, rounded peaks reached down to the lakes and surrendered to a plain beyond them.

By the time we'd descended to the beach, the wind had eased and the sun was losing heat and gaining color. I stepped stiffly down and walked along the ridge atop the isthmus. A pyramid-shaped hill was casting a flawless reflection in the lake, and as I shifted my gaze to the sea, a dark shadow shattered its glassy veneer. A school of dolphins surfaced, their shiny torsos rising and dipping effortlessly as they cruised along the shore.

By nightfall banks of dark cloud hung heavily over the sea. I pegged the horses out and watched as they buried their heads in the grass, feeding like a pack of hungry lions. Over dinner the western sky faded from peach to deep blue, then black. Tigon and I lay on my canvas duffle bag. I meant to write in my diary and study some Russian, but I woke at midnight with rain falling on my face. I'd managed to pen one line: *We're in horse heaven.*

TWO WEEKS EARLIER, I had sailed away from the cultivated lands of Krasnodar Krai in Russia and landed in the port city of Kerch. In making the half-hour crossing of the Kerch Strait, we had reached Crimea—a peninsula of historic renown that bulges southward via a bottleneck from the Ukrainian mainland into the Black Sea, forming a distinctive shape resembling a wide-bottomed vase. The dry steppe interior of Crimea, cut off from the coast in the southwest by a band of forested mountains, had long been a favored home for nomads.

Since my arrival I'd been looking forward to this moment when our little family could once again range free on unplowed grassland. Getting here had not been elegant. For three days from Kerch I had tracked along the southeast coast joined by a Ukrainian man, Giorgi. On the first day we'd been interrogated by the border patrol, Giorgi's stallion had bucked him off, and finally we had been pursued by a runaway foal; when the foal's owner tracked us down he accused Giorgi of stealing it.

On the second day we came to a dead end at a fenced-off military zone. We spent the evening camped at a Ukrainian outpost where an officer made us dinner and explained that it was from this base a rocket had accidentally been fired in October 2001 and infamously blown up an airliner en route from Tel Aviv to Russia. On the third day both Giorgi and Buran were limping and turned for home.

Now, finally alone, I sank into thoughts about the Crimean land around me—the same setting that in 1223 must have induced in the battle-weary Mongol army a feeling of jubilation. During Subodei and Jebe's remarkable campaign through Central Asia and the Caucasus that culminated with defeat of Russia, they and their men had spent time in Crimea, where they had no doubt taken the opportunity to rest and fatten their horses. Somewhere in these lush grasslands the night would have been filled with revelry and the sounds of thousands of weary horses being set free to graze. As nomads whose moods, like mine, fluctuated with those of their horses, the sheer abundance of grass must have left a deep impression, and one can only imagine the tales they brought home to the harsher climes of Central Asia.

There was something more significant than pasture that had attracted the Mongols to Crimea, though, and which made this peninsula so unique. As nomads had known for millennia, the true wealth of Crimea lay in the strategic port cities on its coast where the Eurasian steppe greets the Black Sea. For the largely landlocked societies of the steppe, the coast provided unique access to trade, communication, and plunder.

Long before the arrival of Subodei and Jebe, a historical trend had been established whereby nomads of Crimea's steppe interior both coexisted and clashed with the sedentary societies of the coast. Kerch had even been built on the ruins of the ancient city of Panticapaeum, the sixth-century BCE capital of a kingdom known as Bosphoria, which itself had been a fusion of Scythian nomads and Greek traders.[1]

The history of Crimea subsequently read like an almanac of both nomadic and European empires. The steppe interior had been ruled by Scythians, Sarmatians, Huns, Khazars, and Kipchaks, and the coast had passed through the hands of Romans, Bulgars, Goths, Byzantine Greeks, Venetians, and finally Genoese. The appearance of the Mongols in Crimea in 1223 was fleeting, but when the Mongols returned on their full-fledged conquest of

Russia, Crimea would become a pivotal outpost of the Mongol Empire for well over a century.

In the morning I woke to a sky flooded with stormy gray. Rain eased down, gently brushing the poppies and chamomile flowers on its way to earth. I packed unrushed, marveling at how the petals righted themselves with a shudder after every drop. When the sun broke through we rode—or, rather, waded—on.

Visions of Mongols and Scythian horsemen had sunk in overnight, and without signs of the modern world, I savored the feeling that I had become part of a continuum of nomad history. We had only traveled a very short way, however, before the hulking shape of Soviet barns broke the spell.

Since the fracturing of the Mongol Empire, Crimea had weathered many winds of change. A Tatar of Mongol descent, Hajji Girei, had founded the Crimean Khanate on the steppe in the fifteenth century, and the Ottoman Turks had replaced the Genoese as rulers of the coast.[2] In the eighteenth century, the Russian Empire expelled the Ottomans and forced the Tatars to submit to their rule. In the nineteenth century, Crimea was the stage for another struggle when the Russians fought a bitter war with the British and French. Next to arrive were the Nazis, subjecting the earth to the tread of angry tanks and laying siege to Sevastopol. When Crimea was reclaimed by the Soviets, the Tatars were accused as traitors and deported by Stalin en masse to Central Asia and Siberia. In 1954 Crimea was gifted to the Soviet state of Ukraine, finally emerging in 1990 as a semi-autonomous republic of an independent and democratic Ukraine.

Only fifteen years had passed since the collapse of the Soviet empire, but already the barns in front of us lay like lonely shipwrecks, overgrown with chest-high weeds and roofs folding in. The empty corrals that had once sheltered hundreds of sheep and cattle were filled with nothing but breeze. Like so many empires before them, the Soviets had come and gone.

No sooner had the barn been eclipsed by the horizon than the figure of a horseman came charging toward us across the grassy plain. His whip flew in a frenzy on the left rump, then over his shoulder to the right, in Central Asian style. It was moments before his short black stallion stood in front of me, foaming at the bit, sweat-drenched chest convulsing.

Sitting straight-backed in his tattered saddle, this rider had all the confidence and authority of a custodian of this land. "Where are you going?"

I looked into his sun-blackened face but could barely make out his eyes, hidden in the shadow of a shabby baseball cap. As I began to answer he softened, and we rode on together for some time.

Rinat was born in Tashkent and had moved here in 1990, but soon after his arrival he had been imprisoned. He had been released three years ago. It was sad to see his proud sense of authority wither away as he recounted his story.

"There are three Russian men in my village who attacked me because I am Tatar. Finally they beat me so badly I decided to knife one of them. I wanted to get him in the butt but got him in the stomach." He looked away and spat. "It doesn't bother me now. I don't drink, I don't smoke. I have my cows and my sheep—I'm happy. Regarding those Russians—well, God sees everything from above."

Rinat was the first Crimean Tatar I'd ever met, and, as it turned out, the only one I ever saw on horseback. The Crimean Tatars had only been allowed to return from exile in Central Asia beginning in 1989, just before the end of the Soviet era. What I would learn in time was that Rinat's story reflected a broader conflict between local Russians and returning Tatars that belied the calm of this peaceful landscape. It was a conflict that echoed the pattern of Crimea's complex history as a place of hostility and cooperation between nomads and sedentary society—a history that would ultimately dominate my stay in Crimea.

Before Rinat rode away he pointed to the distant radio towers of a Russian military exclusion zone. "That's where my mother was born. Her village was there. God willing, I will see my true homeland again, but I doubt that will happen. The Russians won't let me."

THAT EVENING, A flotilla of Soviet apartment blocks on the horizon signaled the historic port of Feodosiya—a city with intriguing links to the curbing of the Mongol expansion and the eventual decline of the Mongol Empire.

Formerly known as Kaffa, the city had been an important slave trading post, through which the Genoese exported Slavic and Kipchak prisoners to the slave army of the Egyptian sultan. The Mongols benefited from this trade by demanding tribute from the Genoese, but what the Mongols could not have foreseen was that these Kipchak slaves—who were nomads with a wealth of experience in the tactics of Mongol warfare—would rise to become a powerful military caste in Egypt known as the Mamluks. In time the Mamluks would inflict the first serious defeats on the Mongol army, permanently halting Mongol advances into the Middle East and tarnishing their image of invincibility.[3]

The rise of the Mamluks is not the only historical event for which Kaffa became an unlikely catalyst. Although Mongol authorities had allowed the lucrative slave trading to continue during their reign, on occasion they had also sacked Kaffa and other Genoese cities in an attempt to shut it down. In 1345 a Mongol army had been preparing for one such attack when the plague reached the Golden Horde capital, Sarai, on the lower Volga. The plague decimated the Mongol armies and forced them to withdraw. According to one report, Yanibeg, the khan of the Golden Horde, ordered the dead bodies of the soldiers to be catapulted over the high fortress walls surrounding Kaffa. This tactic is unlikely to have succeeded in transmitting the plague, but it is believed the disease nevertheless spread from the Mongol camp into the city, and then via ships from Kaffa to Constantinople and on to Africa and Europe. Not only did the plague wipe out at least a third of Europeans, more than half of China's population, and twelve million Africans, but some experts, including anthropologist Jack Weatherford, argue that it contributed to the disintegration of the Mongol Empire.

By the time the plague hit in the fourteenth century, however, it must be acknowledged that the Mongol Empire had already begun to break down. Genghis Khan had established a remarkably robust system of rule and conquer that would outlive him by generations, but his heirs were racked by division. During the latter half of the thirteenth century, the four khanates of the Mongol Empire—the Golden Horde, the Chaghatai khanate, the Ilkhanate, and the Yuan dynasty—were well on the path to being independent states. In the 1260s, in fact, the Ilkhanate fought a war with the Golden Horde, and in the east, Khubilai battled with his brother Arikboke for succession to the throne of the grand khan.[4]

Nonetheless, even if the plague wasn't responsible for the fall of the Mongol Empire, then it certainly accelerated its demise. Ever since Genghis Khan proclaimed himself "the ruler of all those who live in felt tents," the empire had relied on an efficient network of trade and communication routes. This not only provided military advantage but also helped prevent vassal states from revolting by keeping the people happy with stability and thriving economies. Just as this complex network could carry a messenger or Silk Road trader from Mongolia to Europe without affray, it equally aided the passage of the plague. Just like a global pandemic would do today, the plague paralyzed the flow of trade, isolating cities and countries, and eventually entire continents. Mongolian aristocracies found themselves with depleted militaries, unable to procure the same kind of taxes that had funded the empire, and more outnumbered by subjects than ever before.

By the end of the fourteenth century, Mongolians in Asia had returned to a nomadic lifestyle in their homeland or were absorbed or killed by the rebelling Chinese. In Persia, the last Mongol successors to the Ilkhanate had vanished. The Golden Horde would hold together for much longer than elsewhere, but ultimately Mongols here became part of fractious Turkic nations, such as the Crimean khanate, which eventually fell to Ottoman and Russian rule.

COMPARED TO LAYING siege to a city of slave traders, my designs on Feodosiya were more routine. The main obstacle of my journey through Crimea was a set of rugged, densely forested mountains, which I would have to traverse as far as the old Tatar capital, Bakchisaray. To do this I would need someone to guide me. I also required a farrier—my horses had gone barefoot for the last eighteen months, but with the rocky terrain of the mountains, they needed to be shod. I'd been given the name of a Russian lady named Ira who ran a horse farm called Argamak near Feodosiya. She had promised not only to help with the challenges of the mountains but also to show me around the city.

I found Ira's sprawl of stables and yards in the open steppe about 20 km shy of Feodosiya. Locating Ira proved another matter. A wafer-thin woman with stringy, meatless arms, and a look of grit in her eyes stepped from a stable, and when I told her whom I was looking for, she said, "You must be Tim! Wait here."

Half an hour passed before the woman appeared again and led me to a muddy yard strewn with horse tack, empty vodka bottles, and half-eaten cucumbers. It was then I noticed a leg dangling out of a car door. I followed it up to a mop of curly blond hair slumped forward on the steering wheel.

Just then a burly man with balding white hair and an unruly beard approached. "Ira! You have a guest!" he shouted. The man swayed on his feet, hands fumbling with the buttons of his shirt, which was open down to the last sunburned rib. His name was Max, he explained, and it was Ira's birthday.

The foot dangling from the car wiggled. Then the car door swung violently open and the woman who had been collapsed against the steering wheel staggered into life. "It's very . . . very nice to meet you," she slurred.

Ira may have been blind drunk, but after steadying herself against me she charged past and ran her hands up and down the legs of my horses.

"Yep, sure thing, we will shoe them," she said, sitting down in the dust.

My stay with Ira was meant to be brief, but as had happened so many times before on my journey, I became engrossed by the goings-on of the place, and a sequence of events—namely, a misfortunate mishap with Tigon—saw me delayed for much longer.

The first evening was a precursor of how I would spend most of my time with Ira and her friend Max. I'd had my first shot of vodka even before my backpack and chaps were off, and we fell into a conversation that orbited around all things horse.

Ira had a background in equestrian sport and had moved out onto the steppe in the 1990s to pursue her dream of running a stud farm. Max, on the other hand, was a grazier whose father was a descendant of Bashkirian nomads in Siberia; he had set up a farm on neighboring land. By virtue of their divergent approaches to life on the steppe, they were of very different schools of thought when it came to horsemanship—Ira kept her horses in stables, while Max believed in the virtues of a fence-free life. It was a point of endless baiting.

"Fancy cooping her horses up like this in this glorious steppe!" Max told.

"Well, with thieves like you around, what choice do I have?" Ira tossed back.

Despite their differences—and their passion for horses, which to me embodied the spirit of nomads—they were united on one front: neither of them was fond of my interest in traditional steppe cultures, particularly when it came to Crimean Tatars.

Ira said to me, "Tim, Crimean Tatars are not to be trusted. They are not like you and me. The only reason they are coming back to Crimea is to steal our land and make lots of money. I watched a Tatar on horseback once—he was so cruel to the horse, no style at all. Never again will I invite a Tatar onto my property!" Over the coming days—and, as it turned out, weeks—I learned to avoid the subject.

On the third morning of my stay Max came charging into the farm. "Have you heard the news? Those damn Americans are here! Their NATO ship arrived in Feodosiya port last night! We are rallying as many boys as possible. We are not letting them ashore!" This bluster served as a thin veil for the real reason Max had blazed in: his wife had kicked him out, and he was hoping to sleep in Ira's barn for a week. But as Ira and I soon discovered, the ship had certainly caused a stir in Feodosiya.

After catching a ride into the city we stepped into the mayhem. Several hundred protestors waving flags and banners were heaving forward to the gates of the port. An elderly man leading them chanted slogans through a megaphone: "We know you Americans! You are not taking our land, now get out!" It was a simplistic assertion of a deeply complex conflict.

Although the Crimea had been gifted to Ukraine in 1954, it had been a Russian stronghold ever since 1783, when Catherine II defeated the

Ottomans. Even after the breakup of the Soviet Union, when Ukraine gained independence, the vast majority of the Crimean population remained Russian, with few cultural links to Ukraine. Critical to the issue was that Russia had always had its Black Sea naval fleet based in the strategic port of Sevastopol. Russia had signed an agreement with Ukraine to allow the fleet to remain stationed there until 2017, with the assumption that the lease would be extended. Viktor Yushchenko, however, the pro-Western leader swept to power on the tide of the Orange Revolution, had promised to make it his mission to break with Russian imperialism and join NATO. Not only were Russians facing the prospect of the fleet being expelled, but Yushchenko had refused to make Russian the second official language for Ukraine. So while Yushchenko and his prime minister, Yulia Tymoshenko, enjoyed popular support in mainland Ukraine, particularly in the west of the country, in Crimea they were detested.

After we battled our way through the crowd, the sounds of the protest faded as Ira and I took a walk along the esplanade in the shade of regal trees. We then turned into the old quarter of town. Competing with tsarist and Soviet-era architecture was a fourteenth-century stone church, built no doubt with the riches of the slave labor trade. Further on we pushed uphill through tiers of old stone homes with terra-cotta-tiled roofs until we reached a labyrinth of paths that took us to an old rampart. I climbed to the top, from where the protest and the ship had shrunken to mere details. In the hills around the old quarter, remnants of stone walls ran along the edges like vertebrae wearing through the earth. Out at sea the water was calm and glassy.

It seemed that through the millennia some things here had not changed. Whether threats of invasion came from the Mongols or NATO, Crimea remained a flash point in the geopolitical landscape. To bear witness to this land by horse felt like a way of bridging the past and the present day. And my adventure in Crimea had only just begun.[5]

꠵

IT WAS UPON returning with Ira from Feodosiya I learned of news that crushed hopes of carrying on to the mountains any time soon. Tigon had run off after being violently kicked by a visitor to Ira's farm. I found the dog lying semiconscious under some bushes and spent the ensuing night holding him in my arms. In the morning a veterinarian concluded he had internal bleeding and swollen kidneys.

It was two days before Tigon began to eat again, and three weeks before we could contemplate riding on. By that time the rich green of the steppe had waned to yellow, the days were unbearably hot, and mosquitoes were descending like fog at night. It was a seasonal transition that once would have signaled to nomads of the Crimea that it was time to escape the heat and migrate to the cool alpine meadows of the mountains.

I had long put the word out that I was looking for a guide, but most shied away when they considered the route. There were no Tatars in the area with knowledge of the mountains anymore, and the tracks in the forested approaches to the high plains were overgrown. The only man willing to try was Seryoga, a Russian friend of Ira's.

"The only thing to keep in mind is that Seryoga likes to drink," Ira warned.

On the day before my departure, I watched with anticipation as my companion-to-be arrived driving a horse and cart. From a distance his heavyset frame, weathered face, and tawny, sun-bleached hair cut a handsome figure. As he pulled in with a series of whistles and commands, though, my eyes were drawn to his disfigured upper lip.

"This is my trophy from an accident a few years ago, when I was even younger and even more stupid!" he said, pointing apologetically to his toothless upper mouth. "I was drunk and fell off my horse at a full gallop on the pavement!"

We spent the afternoon shoeing. Seryoga was particularly impressed with Taskonir. The walls of the horse's hooves were so hard that when he tried hammering nails in, they bent and had to be pulled out. "That's what you call a no-problem horse," Seryoga exclaimed. "You could have boiled a cup of tea in his hooves and then ridden another ten thousand kilometres without shoes!"

We agreed that such naturally hardened hooves would have been a big advantage for the Mongols when they rode into Europe. Their European counterparts, riding on large, hay-fed horses, would have been hampered by the need to constantly maintain their horses' hooves and shoes.

The next day we began our journey to the mountains in a fashion I came to learn was true to Seryoga's character. Overnight Seryoga had shared four or five bottles of vodka with Ira and had not slept. Nevertheless, we rode eight hours straight in the heat, which at its maximum reached 38°C. Seryoga was bareback on his bony old mare, Zera, and wore nothing but a pair of cavalry jodhpurs and a rope tied around his waist. His lean, muscled torso was red with sunburn, and he smoked tobacco rolled in pieces of newspaper, stubbing them out one by one on the soles of his cheap Chinese-made running shoes.

Late in the day we reached the forested foothills of the Crimean mountains and rode on to Seryoga's parents' home in the town of Staryi Krym. "Give me two days here, Tim. I have some things to sort out, then I will be able to come with you," Seryoga promised. Two days soon became three, and then this grew to a whole week. Although I had initially counted on Seryoga only as a guide to see me through the mountains—where mostly I hoped to learn about Tatar heritage—he became a story in himself.

Seryoga saw the journey with me as an opportunity to quit his job as a forest ranger, and each morning he would walk an hour into town with the intention of handing in his letter of resignation. On the way, however, he would buy a couple of bottles of beer. With each bottle his mood would turn, and ultimately he never reached the forestry department offices.

On the eighth day, when I was on the verge of leaving alone, he picked himself up and promised I had to wait just one more day. That morning he walked 20 km to the coast to shoe a dozen horses at a trail-riding farm—they were poorly trained animals that no farrier would touch. He stumbled home after dark, nursing terribly inflamed cuts and gouges across his wrists and palms, but reassured me, "Don't worry, nothing could be harmful to my body! Tomorrow morning, we leave!"

We were joined for dinner by two local prostitutes who were a mother-and-daughter combination—they had heard on the grapevine that Seryoga had earned some money. Later on Seryoga vanished with them to a local bar, and finally the following morning he turned up ready to go.

"Let's go, Tim!" he yelled triumphantly.

The morning air was cool as we packed and finally rode out among a mob of mooing cattle on their way to pasture. A babushka wielding a stick hobbled after them. "I'll moo you if you don't move, you bunch of bitches!'" she called affectionately.

When we left the village behind and entered the forest, I rode behind Seryoga, enjoying the sense of protection the dense canopy of oak, ash, and beech provided. The sun drifted down in slender cascades, fragrant leaves tumbled, and red deer flashed through the undergrowth. Every now and then a gust of wind creaked through the trees, reaching us as a soft breath of air.

For centuries, the forests of the Crimean mountains had been home to one of the three distinct subgroups of Crimean Tatars, the Tatas. The Tatas were renowned for their European features, believed to be inherited from Goths who had inhabited the same area in Crimea for well over a thousand years. The Tatas differed from their Tatar brothers on the steppe, known as the Nogais, who were descendants of a long line of steppe nomads, the Kipchaks. The Nogais in turn differed from the Tatars on the coast, known as the Yaliboyu, who lived as traders and fishermen. The existence of these distinct identities went largely unacknowledged by Russians, including Seryoga and Ira, who believed that Tatars had only ever inhabited the steppe regions.

I kept my thoughts to myself while Seryoga smoked in silence, gently tapping Zera's rump. Whenever he spoke it was about his beloved mare. "Oh, Zera, my love!" he would say with a heavy lisp. "We don't need anyone else, do we? Just you and me . . . you should see her pulling carts of timber up and down the mountain. She is one courageous lady."

By evening we were lost, and for the next three days we pushed on along winding trails laden with fallen trees, with little clue as to where we were. The slopes grew steep, giving way to gullies that twisted and turned, choked with ferns and cascading streams. At one point we stumbled into a small sunlit meadow where a stone memorial to Soviet partisan fighters stood masked in moss and grass.

"It was in these forests that the Soviet partisan heroes lived during the

Great Patriotic War," Seryoga said reflectively. As I looked at him sitting on his sheepskin saddle blanket, wearing khaki jodhpurs, chaps, and a commando vest, it wasn't hard to picture the partisans he spoke about. For almost three years they had famously fought against the Nazi occupation of Crimea until the Red Army retook the peninsula in 1944.

From a word etched into the memorial stone, we were able to locate ourselves on the map. As I remounted to leave, Seryoga remained standing there. His expression had turned to one of bitterness. "But those traitor Crimean Tatars, Tim, they fought against us, the partisans. If you speak with the old-timers here, you will hear the truth of what they did. They slaughtered innocent women and children—anyone, in fact, who was supporting these brave partisans."

In my short time in Crimea, I had learned that this was a point of contention. Stalin had ordered the blanket deportation of Tatars to Central Asia and Siberia on the basis that they had collaborated with the Nazis. Word-of-mouth stories about violence meted out by Tatars abounded, yet modern-day evidence suggests that only a minority of Tatars ever sided with the Nazis. According to what I had read, a large percentage of partisans were in fact Tatar but changed their last names to Russian versions during the war to avoid suspicion. I wanted to point out to Seryoga that even those who did fight for the Nazis should perhaps be forgiven; after all, between the Bolshevik revolution and 1941 the Soviets had banned Islam and murdered, starved, or deported around 160,000 Tatars—about half the Tatar population at the time. Could anyone really blame some of the Tatars for choosing not to fight on behalf of the Soviets? I said nothing, however.

Sensing my sympathy for the Crimean Tatars despite my silence, Seryoga continued. "I know one good Tatar, but mostly, Tim, they are bad people . . . It's not for nothing they were deported by Stalin, you know."

IT TOOK A full week to reach the steep forested slopes just below the high alpine plateau. By this stage Seryoga had run out of cigarettes and we were down to the last scraps of food.

Just as we were preparing to retreat down the mountain—we were once again lost—the sun speared through the trees uphill from us and we walked, blinking, onto the Karabi Jayla. The largest alpine plateau of the Crimean Mountains, the Karabi was a place so renowned for its pasture that nomads once traveled here from as far as Moldavia to fatten their sheep and cattle. Echoing the important role this high pasture played in nomad life of the region, *jayla* is a Crimean Tatar word with Turkic roots, similar to the Kazakh term *jalau*, meaning "summer place" or "summer pasture."

We rode on to where the plateau fell away in dramatic cliffs to the Black Sea about 1,000 m below. In camp I gazed out over broad grassy slopes, imagining huddles of yurts and the fragrant smell of burning dung. In the seventeenth century, European travelers Guillaume le Vasseur de Beauplan and Pierre Chevalier had painted a picture of a nomadic culture here that was essentially unchanged since the time of Genghis Khan. The Crimean Tatars lived in felt tents, were feared horseback archers, and, according to the Europeans' observations, rode small unshod horses, described by both as "ugly"—although Chevalier qualified this by saying that "nature hath very well repaired their ugliness by their swiftness."[6]

Russian occupation of Crimea in the eighteenth century saw Tatars making migrations of a different kind—primarily across the sea for refuge in Turkey. Suspected as collaborators with the Turks, a hundred thousand fled during the annexation in 1783, and even more in the 1860s in the aftermath of the Crimean War. Many drowned during the risky sea crossings.

Come the twentieth century, in 1944 any Tatars who had remained and survived Soviet persecution were shipped away by train across the vast ocean of steppe to Central Asia. According to some, the very last camels—descendants of those used by Crimean Tatar nomads on migrations—were herded out of Crimea in 1941 during the Nazi invasion.

I was lifted from my thoughts by Seryoga. "If we have run out of cigarettes and vodka, and we have almost no food, there is nothing for me to do but sleep!" He crawled inside the tent, covered himself with a horse blanket, and collapsed.

When he woke I offered him dried curd, peanuts, and dried meat that had been floating about in the bottom of my pack boxes for over a year.

We picked some wild herbs for tea and went to bed immediately to mask our hunger.

By the time we got moving the following day, Seryoga had sobered up. The heaviness that surrounded him had evaporated and he seemed to have lost years from his face. "If I don't come all the way to Hungary," he said, "which I would like to do, please promise me one thing: if you aren't able to get the horses over the border, let me know and I'll be sure to travel there and ride them back. Don't think about giving that Taskonir to anyone else!"

I agreed, and for the next couple of days we rode on in high spirits. I felt that we had become good friends. For a short time I even began to believe that he might come with me as far as Hungary, but his positive state of mind lasted only until we descended to the village of Aromatnoe for food. There Zera pulled up lame and Seryoga was back on the booze.

The next morning he hugged me goodbye and began the long walk home.

20

THE RETURN OF THE CRIMEAN TATARS

Crimea, Crimea, Mother Crimea,
We did not forget our name,
We did not, Mother Crimea,
Exchange our isle for another's.

—Rustem Ali, *Crimea* (1992)[1]

AFTER LEAVING AROMATNOE I rode for nine hours over a pass before reaching the village of Perevalnoe. There, against Seryoga's advice, I had prearranged to meet with a Crimean Tatar farmer named Edem.

Given the animosity expressed to me about Tatars, I was all the more curious to meet Edem and learn firsthand about the Tatars' return to the Crimea.[2] Not so secretly, I was already partial to the cause of these once nomadic people, and I had spent much of the past few weeks pondering the underlying reasons for the hostile attitudes.

The vilification of Tatars seemed cruel to me given the tragic circumstances of their exile. On May 18, 1944, without warning, around 191,000 Tatars had been escorted by soldiers from their homes and deported in livestock train cars to Siberia and Central Asia. Many died during the harrowing journey, their bodies, according to witnesses' accounts, often hauled out on the order of guards and left in open graves by the tracks in the deserts of Central Asia. The survivors of those chilling events—for whom the trauma was still raw—had waited all their lives to return from exile.

Ostensibly, the antipathy harbored by Russians stemmed from the Tatars' alleged collaboration with Nazis.[3] I'd decided, however, that attitudes probably reflected a deeper, more enduring prejudice, hints of which had been explicit in Stalin's strategy. When Stalin deported the Crimean Tatars he had labeled them not only traitors but descendants of Mongol invaders. Soviet authorities had even falsely reasoned that Crimean Tatars were Mongol in origin and therefore belonged in Central Asia. After deportation the category "Crimean Tatar" was removed from the official encyclopedia of the Soviet Union's peoples, and evidence of their history in Crimea—including cemeteries, literature, and even place names—was erased. The homes, livestock, orchards, and grain stores they had left behind were seized, and unlike other deported peoples such as Kalmyks and Chechens who were allowed to return to their homes in 1957, Crimean Tatars were forbidden to return to Crimea until 1989.

In associating Crimean Tatars with Mongolians, Stalin not only justified indefinite exile but preyed on Russian hostility toward Crimean Tatars that dates to the founding of their khanate in the fifteenth century—a hostility that, in all fairness, is worthy of consideration. Like a series of nomadic powers before them, the Crimean Tatars had been renowned for riding up through Russia's southern borders to take captives for trading as slaves through the port of Kaffa (present-day Feodosiya). Slave trading was in fact at the core of the Crimean khanate's economy, and in 1571 during one raid alone Tatars managed to burn Moscow to the ground and take up to 150,000 Slavs into captivity.

Many historians point out that hostilities between nomads and Slavs have been overemphasized. Evidence suggests that nomads and Slavs often inter-married, engaged in mutually beneficial trade, and struck military alliances. Nonetheless, the historic propensity for Crimean Tatars to inflict terror on the Russian people is undeniable, and something I was perhaps guilty of not paying enough attention to in my broader evaluation of nomad society.

In the last two centuries, of course, Russians had come to dominate Crimea and decisively reversed the trend of predatory steppe empires. Even so, the exploits of the Tatars had, somewhat understandably, left a deep scar on the Russian psyche. The very term *Tatar* could still rouse heated emotion, and the return of the Tatars had incited fears of a modern invasion. As I would discover in coming weeks this had created a tinder-box of ethnic tension and triggered a dangerous cycle of revenge.

For the last hour of the ride to Perevalnoe I felt my way down the mountains in the dark, relieved when a chorus of snarling dogs signaled my arrival at Edem's farm. The outline of men conversing in a Turkic tongue grew out of the darkness. Then a floodlight flicked on and I was met with a steel-gripped handshake.

"I'm Edem. Now c'mon, what are you sitting there for? It's time to rest and feed your horses!" the man said in flawless Russian.

In a rusty old worker's cabin I sat sipping tea with Edem and six of his employees who had recently migrated from Uzbekistan. Under dim light cast by a bulb shrouded in a haze of mosquitoes, the men ranged from a sun-blackened teenager with Russian features to a bandy-legged elder with deep-set eyes and a large Turkic nose, whose dark, freckled face had been sculpted far more by the harsh Central Asian sun than it could ever be now by the coastal climate of Crimea.

Edem himself was thickly built and balding with blue eyes, a narrow pinched nose, and a fine, pale mustache—classic features of his Tata ori-gins. He sat wearing leather sandals and an immaculate white shirt un-buttoned to the belly, exhibiting both the air of an aristocrat and the machismo of a worker. He had been in Crimea for twenty-five years and, like many of his generation born in exile, had moved to Crimea to pave the way for his mother, who had been deported as a child.

We had barely finished the tea when there came the roar of a truck grinding up the driveway. I went out and watched it come to a halt next to a half-constructed building before a bevy of women climbed down from the back laden with mops and brushes. The workers unloaded a bed, dresser, mirror, and mattress, while the driver personally carried a pot of hot plov (pilaf) to Edem.

Only after Edem and I had finished eating did I understand the goings-on. "Tim, you can move your things in now. I have been building this hotel for two years . . . and I want you to be the first guest!" Edem said.

In the light of morning I was able to get a better picture of where I had landed. Edem's hotel and farmyards were built into the slope above the village of Perevalnoe. Below, on the valley floor, the main road to the resort city of Yalta snaked its way toward the coast. Somewhere down there Edem had apparently built himself a two-story family mansion. In the other direction mountain slopes angled up in ramps of rock and craggy trees to alpine pastures. The teenager from the night before was high above, whistling and calling as he pushed a herd of sheep into cooler, thinner air.

After breakfast, when the yards were empty and the rising sun had taken the crisp edge off the morning, Edem and I sat in the shade with a cup of tea. To become this established as a Tatar in Crimea was a remarkable achievement requiring strong conviction—a fact not lost on Edem.

"For Tatars who are returning now, life is hard, but it is a fairy tale compared to what it was like for us earlier," he said, casting his gaze up to the high slopes. Edem had first tried to migrate in 1981—when it was still illegal for Tatars to live and work in Crimea. This discriminatory law had been enforced by denying Tatars a propiska, a residence permit, without which registration was not possible and employment prohibited.

"At first when I arrived from Uzbekistan in Semfiropol," the modern capital of Crimea, "I slept at the train station while I looked for a job. I was a communications expert and was offered work in the coastal city of Sudak. When my employer discovered I was a Tatar the police pursued me and I was beaten up and arrested. Eventually I managed to escape to the Ukraine," Edem explained.

Brutalization was a common experience of Tatars in those times and combined with the prospect of exile and imprisonment to create an atmosphere of desperation. Some returning Tatars had resorted to extreme measures to assert their right to live in Crimea, including acts of self-immolation. The most notorious case had occurred three years before Edem's arrival in 1978, when a Tatar named Musa Mahmut had doused himself in gasoline and lit a match as officers arrived to arrest him. He later died in the hospital and had come to be seen as a martyr for Tatars making the bold decision to migrate to Crimea. In fact, in the 1980s and 1990s many Tatars modeled their strategy on Mahmut's, keeping gasoline and matches at hand as a means to prevent eviction from lands and homes they were reoccupying. This proved effective—but it also drew great contempt from Russians.

Edem had been more fortunate than many others. "After one year in Ukraine I had gathered enough money to buy a car and drove back to Crimea. I was lucky to avoid authorities—with my blue eyes and fair hair, few people suspected me. Eventually I made friends with a city councilor in Kerch. He was one of the few Russians I have ever met who believed discrimination against Tatars was wrong, and he agreed to help me get a propiska. I remember when the lady at the registration desk noticed that I was a Tatar. She said, 'We can't register him!' but my friend yelled at her, 'Just do it!'"

This kind gesture had not been without consequences. Soon after Edem received the propiska, he was arrested and the Russian councilor was imprisoned. Nevertheless, Edem managed to escape following these events, and from that point on managed to find refuge in the Crimean mountains. Living up on the high plains I had ridden through, he had avoided the authorities for the better part of a decade, coming down "once in 1985 to get married to a Tatar girl." Only in 1989 was he given legal status, and he immediately began arranging for his mother and other relatives to migrate.

Nowadays, of course, Tatars had the right to return and were technically entitled to housing and land as compensation. Edem lamented, however, that Russian attitudes had not changed. In fact, he felt they might be growing worse. "These people who live in the homes that our fathers built, who eat the food of the trees that our fathers planted, drink water from the wells that were dug by our forefathers, of course they are not all that happy to see us again because it reminds them of what was done to us."

Edem was accustomed to insults from Russians and internalized most of his frustration. What he found most injurious these days was that his elderly mother, who had been the only survivor among her siblings during deportation, had to date been denied access to the home she had grown up in. "All she wants is to drink from the well that her grandfather dug himself, but the Russian occupants won't let her past the front gate."

I spent a week under Edem's wing, during which time I learned that while the struggle for early arrivals such as Edem was largely over, for many of those who had come later the battle had only begun. On the grassy flats by the Yalta road I visited one of hundreds of land claim sites established across Crimea. For four months Tatars had been living in an army mess tent, preparing to take the land by force. Surrounding the tent were hundreds of stacks of yellow bricks spread out over a large area. Each stack represented an individual family claim. The people here were waiting for a signal from Tatar leaders, at which point, according to the plan, building would begin at all sites across Crimea, and the numbers would be too vast for the authorities to contain. Inside the tent I spoke with aggrieved Tatars who complained that although the Ukrainian government had promised to provide homes, the program of resettlement had collapsed back in 1996, and of the 270,000 returned Tatars, more than half still had no land or housing of their own.

I had also been told the Russian side of the story: that the Tatars who were making claims already owned homes elsewhere, and after taking this coveted land they would build a house and flip it for profit. Edem had admitted that some of these Tatars were in fact abusing the system.

Whatever the truth, though, despite efforts by the Soviet regime to erase the identity of Crimean Tatars, it was clear that the Tatars' passion for their homeland remained stubbornly alive. Tatars such as Edem had even been prepared to risk life and limb to return. Perhaps it was this dedication that troubled Russians most, because it challenged the premise they had been sold that these people were not deeply connected to the Crimea, that they belonged somewhere in the savage East. The status quo reminded me of a phrase in Tolstoy's short novel *Hadj Murat*: "He [Tsar Nicholas] had done much harm to the Poles and to explain this it was necessary to believe that all Poles were scoundrels. Nicholas considered that to be so and hated the Poles in proportion to the harm he had done them."

Before leaving Edem's, I spent one day in the Crimean capital, Semfiropol, where I met with the deputy minister of culture of Crimea, Ismet Zaatov. Ismet put me in contact with leaders of the *mejlis*, the independent Tatar government, which in turn offered me the support of the Tatar community wherever I might need it. The most important connection he arranged was with the director of Tatar TV, Islyam Kishveye.

In an office at the back of the Tatar TV studio in Semfiropol—which Islyam later claimed was bugged by Russian and Ukrainian secret services—Islyam played me a video he had recently recorded in the old Crimean capital, Bakchisaray. It was there, he said, that the front-line battle was now being fought by Tatars.

Islyam skipped forward to footage of a wall of burly Russian men steaming toward a group of Tatar protestors. As they collided, the crowd exploded in fistfights. Some men were knocked to the ground and kicked, while others were chased away and beaten. Islyam had been attacked, too, and as his camera jerked from side to side there were flashes of bloodied faces and sounds of hysterical, wailing women.

At one point he paused the video on the image of a man with a shaven scalp in a gray suit. He had just moved in to kick a Tatar man who lay on the asphalt. "This is Medvedev," Islyam said. "He is the director of the market where this whole battle is taking place. He has hired these thugs that you can see now."

I didn't yet understand the reasons for the conflict I had seen, but I couldn't wait to get back to my horses and on to Bakchisaray.

FROM EDEM'S FARM I rode for three days along mountain and forest trails. It was the peak of summer, my third on the steppe, and a part of me was mentally weary and comforted by the thought it would be my last in the saddle. The mosquitoes stressed the horses, and the heat increased the risk of saddle sores. Additionally, I was beginning to feel claustrophobic in Crimea. In wider spaces, people bearing historical grudges with each other were separated by the muting qualities of distance. Here, trapped on such a small, sought-after chunk of land, cultures, layers of competing histories, and even environments were compressed, and I found myself bandied from one to another. There was no let-up, and ahead of me, things were only about to get more intense.

In the evening of my third day out from Edem's farm a Russian horseman led me as far as the edge of the forest, where oaks gave way to an old Tatar walnut orchard. Pressing on, I took the opportunity to enjoy a passing moment of aloneness. I slowed the horses to a walk, soaking in the way their hooves shifted quietly along a track of powdery white clay. I leaned back in the saddle, watching the outstretched branches of the walnut trees and their broad leaves glide over us. Like Tatar elders who had survived deportation and returned, these elegant trees had outlived the Soviet years and were obstinately rooted in Crimean soil.

Beyond the orchard we emerged from the shade and descended into the head of a gorge-like valley. Ears pricked and tongue out, Tigon craned his neck to look at the high slopes that now blocked much of the sky. Rising above were limestone bluffs running like ramparts along both our sides. The rock high up to our left was honeycombed with caves—the remnants of a seventh-century Byzantine stronghold that was taken over by the Tatars in the fourteenth century. The farther on we rode, the deeper we sank into this curious landform, and as the gorge narrowed we began to pass homes, stables, and even an Orthodox monastery carved out of the rock at the base of the bluffs.

Where the gorge seemed to have run its course, the cliffs converged and the track shrank to a narrow cobbled alleyway between old stone houses. Then, unexpectedly, it hooked sharply to the left, and a valley opened up, filled from wall to wall with a riot of minarets and red ceramic-tiled roofs. Right in front of us they mingled majestically with the bustle of cars and pedestrians in the dusty summer evening.

Bakchisaray was formerly the capital of the Crimean khanate and once an important crossroad of the Silk Road, where traders met from across the Black Sea, the steppes of Central Asia, Russia, and eastern Europe. In its heyday during the fifteenth and sixteenth centuries the town had boasted eighteen mosques and several important madrasas. Nowadays, it is the cultural center for returning Tatars and, as I would learn, a bottleneck of tourism, religion, and conflict. I would spend more than a week in Bakchisaray, but within the first twenty-four hours I had been introduced to the main settings and protagonists that came to dominate my stay.

Nestled among the cobbled streets of the old part of town lay the khan's palace. Known in Tatar as the hanssaray, it had been the seat of power for generations of Crimean khans dating back to the sixteenth century. On the one hand, the palace represented the sophistication of the Crimean Tatar khanate, which had once wielded much power, but on the other, now that it was a museum and part of a heritage park with a Russian director, it symbolized the passing of the Tatars' way of life into the archives of history and its once proud empire into subservience to Russia.

Out of sight of tourists at the other end of town—but still little more than a kilometre from the palace—lay the market. Here an ugly stand-off between Tatars and Russians was under way in which the same clashes of history documented at the palace were still being played out.

Lying between these two places, and caught in the crossfire, were my host, Volodya—impoverished, fiery, half Tatar, half Russian—and a Ukrainian girl named Anya, with whom I fell in love.

Ismet had arranged for Volodya to look after me in Bakchisaray, and so

I carried on down the steep cobbled street into the old town, where he led me through the grand wooden gates of the khan's palace. Inside, I rode Taskonir through an archway into the courtyard, where the last fragments of the evening sun cast golden light from over the cliffs above. As Tigon took the opportunity to bathe in a fountain, I lifted my gaze to the high wall of the palace and let my eyes wander down. Towering minarets inscribed in Arabic cast lean shadows across a courtyard of rose gardens, fountains, lawns, and shady trees. Adjoining the outer wall was the two-story palace itself, adorned with arches, long verandahs, and walls decorated with Islamic murals. In these luxurious headquarters the Crimean khans—blood descendants of Genghis Khan—had ruled one of the most powerful empires of eastern Europe. There was without question a sense of authenticity about the palace that transcended time and invited thoughts about what might have once been. At a closer look, though, tourist information signs nailed onto walls and museum-style displays were a reminder of the modern reality.

In 1736 Bakchisaray had been burned to the ground by the Russians, and when Catherine II's army completed the conquest of the peninsula in 1783, the last khan, Sahin Giray, took refuge in Turkey, where he was eventually executed. The palace had long become a defunct relic paraded by its captors as accommodation for important guests, including Catherine II herself. Two centuries on it was a major tourist attraction to which thousands of Russian tourists flocked each summer to marvel at the lair of their historic foe.

It was while the guards test-rode my horses that I noticed Anya. She stood by a rose garden in the back corner of the courtyard, busy brushing strokes onto canvas, her easel set up between us. Just from a glimpse of her bare, slender arms and golden hair I recognized her as a girl who had approached me as I had ridden down into the town. In fact, the image of her was still firmly entrenched in my mind: carrying an easel and a bag of paintbrushes, her blue eyes lit up by the low-angling sun, she had walked up to me and asked about my horses.

As I approached now she looked my way and put her brush down.

"About time you noticed me! You just walked into my painting!" she said, as we both struggled in vain to hold back smiles.

Anya was a twenty-four-year-old Ukrainian art student from Kiev. She had been given special permission to stay in the palace after hours to paint. I offered her a ride on Taskonir and for the next half hour nervously led her around the courtyard. Before I left, Anya and I agreed to meet in the city in the coming days.

At Volodya's house that night a rabbit was slaughtered in my honor, and we celebrated with cheap Russian vodka. My spirits were high: I had fallen for Anya, and in light of the last few hard days of riding, the rabbit was a veritable banquet.

Come morning, my feelings for Anya hadn't changed, but the reality around me was a lot more sobering. Volodya had been born in exile and now lived in a hovel he had built out of mud, reeds, scrap wood, glass bottles, and a few token bricks. Inside, there was just the one room with an old Russian divan that doubled as a bed for him, his wife, and their two children.

Volodya's mother, a Tatar, had been born in a house in the center of Bakchisaray, but on return from exile Volodya had been forced to settle in what had became known as the "seventh micro-region"—a self-proclaimed Tatar enclave (known in Russian as a *samozakhvat*) on the barren steppe above the gorge. To support his family, Volodya worked shifts at a tile factory in town, and his wife, who was Russian, made cushions stuffed with juniper shavings for tourists, receiving thirty kopeks for each. Their cross-cultural relationship did not make life any easier. "It's hard to hear when Tatar children tell my kids things like, 'We will butcher you. All Russians should be loaded up in cattle wagons and sent out, just as they did to us,'" Volodya's wife said. Compounding the difficult situation, as I would learn, was Volodya's addiction to cigarettes and alcohol.

Later that morning I visited the market for the first time. It was situated in the new center of Bakchisaray—a place with none of the allure I had seen the previous evening. Where the gorge spilled out into a wide dry valley, a hot summer wind blew dust through scattered Soviet apartment blocks and crooked wooden houses. Nineties-era shops were tacked on like afterthoughts, perused by token shoppers on foot. Beat-up Ladas drifted listlessly by.

At a central intersection, stretching across the road between an apartment block and a drugstore, was a picket line of demonstrators. Beyond them lay the entrance to the market and a makeshift barricade hung with the Tatar flag and an unmistakable banner: "Close the Market That Is Built on Our Bones!" To one side of the drugstore, a carpet had been laid down, and a group of men wearing traditional embroidered velvet skullcaps—known across Central Asia as the *tyubeteika*—were kneeling in prayer. A hundred or so elderly Tatars manned the picket line, and others gathered around a cauldron that filled the air with the aroma of boiled mutton.

Meanwhile, lurking in the shade of trees, in cars, and in buses on both sides of the picket line were dozens of heavily equipped *berkuts*, or riot police, their shields and truncheons at the ready. Another branch of police, special forces known as *bars*, were roaming about in flak jackets.

Ismet had informed the mejlis about my journey, and on approaching the protestors I found Akhmet, a high-ranking mejlis representative who had been expecting me. He was busy in negotiation with a local police constable but took the time to explain the crux of the issue. "There are eleven mausoleums here that house the graves of several generations of our khans and spiritual leaders who brought Islam to Crimea," he said. "They date back at least five hundred years. The market that was built on this holy site by Russians in the early nineties hasn't been around for more than fifteen years, and we want it removed."

Akhmet introduced me to a Tatar historian who took me beyond the picket line to the base of one of the mausoleums, a domed, octagonal monument built from stone. Nearby lay the vacant market, a ramshackle collection of insipid stands. Inside its buckled iron boundary fence stood another mausoleum—this one with a Russian-built pit toilet alongside.

The mausoleums were thought to be connected to the ancient city of Eski Yurt, which had been founded on the grave of the seventh-century Islamic saint Malik Ashtar—the first to have spread Islam in Crimea. It had subsequently become the cemetery for Tatar khans, and until Soviet times it attracted thousands of pilgrims annually.

In a provocative move, the market had been built during the death throes of the Soviet Union, and ever since then, Tatars had been lobbying the market's Russian director, Medvedev, to relocate it. They had put forth a plan for the mausoleums to be protected as part of the Bakchisaray Historical and Cultural Preserve. Medvedev had thus far refused, and only a few months before my arrival he had hired some men to start moving the boundary fence of the market out even further—with the rumored backing of the pro-Russian party Russki Blok and local Mafia.

It was this situation that had led to the violent confrontation I had seen on Islyam's footage back in Semfiropol. Medvedev had employed a band of thugs to smash through the protestors and reopen the market by force. Temporarily at least, Medvedev had won the day.

BY THE TIME I left the market the heat of the day had sapped the energy of the demonstrators and the tension had waned. Even the riot police had their helmets off and sat eating ice cream, their shields leaning up against trees.

I was determined to return to the market, but in the meantime I used the lull to meet with Anya. We spent the rest of the day together exploring the monasteries and ruins in the cliffs above the khan's palace. I talked a little about the problems at the market. As a Ukrainian accustomed to the imperialistic ways of Russia, she had some degree of sympathy for the Tatars, but on the other hand, like many Ukrainians, she had a poor understanding of the situation and was mostly impartial. I dropped the subject and savored the shady old quarters of the city, where there was little hint of conflict. Sunburned tourists flowed in on excursions from their resorts on the coast, and I was lost in the light, happy feeling of summer and romance. We spent the next two nights together in my tent, and hours in front of a campfire together with some of her student colleagues. In her arms I felt as though I were in a parallel world—a place where we could both have some time out from the palpable ethnic tension in Bakchisaray, and I could rest from my journey.

On our second morning together I accompanied Anya to the station for the train to Kiev and kissed her goodbye. Our time together had been brief, but nonetheless, when the train pulled out of sight it left me feeling alone. We promised to remain in contact, and to meet up if possible. Anya had a dream of joining me somewhere, although realistically we weren't sure if that was possible: she was in the middle of working toward her master's degree.

In a somber mood I trundled away from the station. When I arrived at the market, however, I was promptly pulled out of my funk. The scene there was very different from how I had left it two days earlier. Now the picket line was choked with protestors, and the group of men camped outside the drugstore with their prayer mats had grown into such a crowd that there was only sitting room. The riot police, in turn, stretched across the road between the picket line and the market and were facing off against the swelling crowd, brandishing their shields.

I became acutely aware of glares from both the riot police and the Tatars. It was a delicate balance, being a foreigner seen to have an allegiance with one culture or the other—something that my time with Anya, a Slav, had only accentuated. Underneath I had felt a little traitorous abandoning the cause of the market to be with her, and Tatars, including Volodya, had been noticeably silent upon learning about our romance. On this day, however, I was relieved when a man from the crowd in front of the drugstore stood up and waved me over excitedly.

It was Islyam, the director of Tatar TV. He was looking sweaty and frazzled. Apparently the prime minister of Ukraine had flown to Crimea, and the mejlis was negotiating the final order for the market to be removed. Overnight, Tatars had rallied from across Crimea and were bracing for a showdown. "We are waiting for a decision," Islyam told me, "but, signature from the prime minister or no, we are going to smash the market down today, by ourselves if necessary!"

Just as he said it, there came a high-pitched whistling from the picket line, and around me the whole crowd of men, Islyam included, leaped to their feet and rushed forward. Apparently someone had attacked the picketers. I dashed after the rushing crowd but fell behind in the thrusting mass of people. Suddenly I was yanked backward and fell flat on my back—someone had nabbed me from behind and pulled me to the ground.

"Hey! Go back! Move out, Russian!" screamed the man who had grabbed me, drawing back his fist above my face. A section of the crowd stopped and circled, but just as they closed in there came a woman's voice. "No, no! Leave him! He is one of ours. He is the Australian traveler!" The men helped me up and invited me to join them, but I decided to hang back.

Watching from a distance, I saw that it wasn't a thug who had attacked the picket line but a Russian pensioner. She was wielding her fists and screaming, "Let me through! God! This is my home! Let me through to my home!" According to Tatars, confrontations like these were part of a campaign by Medvedev, who paid local Russians to act as provocateurs.

Over the next few hours I stuck close to Islyam as more provocations unfolded and tensions rose. Tatar numbers were expanding. Rumor had it Medvedev had hired a legion of thugs from Sevastopol, and that a group of Cossacks—bent on fulfilling their historic role as protectors of Russia— were coming from as far as Russia. Using wire, wood, and whatever they could find, Tatars began to fortify their picket line in preparation for a tense night.

I was invited to camp out with Islyam, but I had to decline, as I had been invited to the khan's palace. The director of the Bakchisaray Historical and Cultural Preserve had arranged a special concert and dinner.

IN THE COOL of evening on a lawn at the back of the khan's palace courtyard, four musicians began to play. As I approached, wandering sounds from a traditional flute, a long-necked lute, and a cimbalon mingled with the energetic notes of a conventional violin. The resulting harmony filtered up through the shady trees above. I came to rest on the grass and felt my sweat chill.

I gazed at the four men, each with their black olive-shaped eyes and wearing a golden embroidered tyubeteika. At the end of each song, they bowed their heads, bending elegantly at their waists, which were tightly wrapped in red cummerbunds.

The oldest of the men explained they had studied music in their youth at the conservatory in Tashkent and now played for the Crimean Philharmonic Orchestra. Since their return to Crimea, they had set about resurrecting traditional Tatar music and during a visit to archives in Istanbul discovered pieces dating back to the sixteenth century. It was these tunes they now brought to life.

The concert came to an end when Evegeniy Petrovich, the tall, charismatic Russian director of the Bakchisaray Historical and Cultural Preserve, arrived to take us to dinner. It was he who would be charged with the responsibility of looking after the site of the mausoleums—Eski Yurt—should the market be removed. In his presence, the musicians lost their happy glow.

"Evegeniy, why do the Russian tour guides purposely avoid us with their tourists? Today we earned almost nothing!" said the elder of the group.

Evegeniy smiled, rocking drunkenly on his feet, and ushered us out of the palace grounds. His distinguished silver hair and charming smile had no doubt reassured many disgruntled souls in his time.

In the nearby cheburekery (chebureks being the ubiquitous Uzbek meat pastry found right across the old Soviet Union), Evegeniy had assembled a large group of visiting historians, Tatar palace staffers, and other employees of the Bakchisaray Historical and Cultural Preserve. With everyone settled for dinner, he stood at the head of the table and shakily raised a glass of wine.

"It's my great, great honor to introduce you to a very unique person." The guests hushed. "A modern-day Marco Polo, speaker of fifteen languages, employee of the Royal Geographic Society, traveler on Mongolian horses, he carries half a sheep in his pocket. I welcome here tonight . . . Kimofi Pope!"

With that he threw open the toast, and I sat down trying to avoid the looks of adoration that now turned on me. Not knowing what to say, I took a large sip of wine.

The most senior historian at the table—who was already looking at the world through the prism of his wineglass—stood up to tell a tale of a different nature. "They found Hitler in the Amazon and brought him to court in Paris this year," he began. "The English decided that death by firing squad should be punishment. The French, the guillotine. The Americans, a hanging. Yet when they couldn't decide, they turned to the representative of Israel. He coolly told them: 'I don't know what the argument is about. The solution is simple—marry him off to a Crimean Tatar!'" With that he erupted in a deep, croaky laugh and downed a shot of vodka.

The far end of the table where the musicians sat was deathly silent.

A vodka glass slipped and fell, and alcohol was quickly poured anew for everyone.

When dinner was over we loaded into a bus and went to a disco to continue celebrating. Evegeniy drank endlessly, and in his euphoric stupor demanded the musicians bring out their instruments and play. As they played, their music drowned out by Russian pop, fluorescent disco lights lit up their surly looks in fragments of purple, green, and nauseating white.

It was some time before I realized the disco we were in was located at the intersection directly opposite the Tatars' picket line. Somewhere out there Islyam and his crew were battening down for another night in the open. Meanwhile, the man who would be responsible for the site of the mausoleums should the market be removed sat before me clapping his hands and rolling with laughter.

At midnight, when the musicians refused to play on, he wobbled over to me with a crazed look. "Tim, do you have your own separate room where you are staying? I mean, if you need a girl, twenty years old, it's no problem . . . Or how would you like having fifteen or twenty girls in one room? They just come to you to sniff you and touch you."

He had by this stage leaned right over close to my ear and was whispering, but then slumped back in a drunken silence.

NOT ONLY WERE the worlds that I passed between in Bakchisaray all surreally parallel, but they seemed to be simultaneously reaching climactic crescendos.

Back at the seventh micro-region that night, I passed a friend of Volodya's, Eldar, who was stumbling off with his bicycle and clutching his jaw. Inside his hut, Volodya lay as if in a coma on the divan, speckles of blood down his shirt, a cigarette butt floating in the vodka glass next to his head. His freckled ten-year-old son rushed to me in excitement. "Dad's head flew off! First Eldar went down, then Papa, but they didn't share with us the reason for the fight!"

When Volodya rose, battered and bruised, he was still desperately drunk. With his remaining weekly salary, which he had received the day before, he went to buy beer and credit for his prepaid mobile phone. He then began calling strangers and speaking nonsense until the credit dried up.

If the signs were ominous at Volodya's home, then it was nothing compared to the situation at the market.

I headed off hoping to meet Islyam, but a kilometre from the picket line, it was obvious I wouldn't be able to get through. The roads and shops had been shut down, and hundreds of police and soldiers were being bused in.

At an outer police line, muscle-bound Russians emerged cut and bloodied, boasting about the Tatars they had bashed. Beyond the police, Russian men of all ages paced about wielding sticks and planks of wood and a crowd of Russian women chanted abuse. The Russian version of Rambo, a bare-chested hulking brute of a man, flexed his sunburned pectorals and screamed, "I am ready! I am mad! And I am ready to face death to fight you Tatars in the Russian way!" There was even a band of Cossacks in army fatigues. The Tatars, meanwhile, vastly outnumbered, were surrounded by hundreds of riot police, upturned cars, and wire.

I rang Islyam, who explained that three hundred "fighters" had stormed the picket line. When pushed back by police, they had begun hurling concrete, steel, and rocks. One Tatar had been hit on the head and had nearly bled to death in the crowd before being retrieved. Many cars, including Islyam's, had been smashed, and their tires slit. For the time being there was a relative lull, but there were no signs of a resolution yet.

"It's too dangerous for you now. I can't get you in," Islyam told.

I decided that it was safer to walk home to the relative sanctuary of

Volodya's home. On the way, buses and cars full of Tatar men rocketed past into town. The word was out, and vehicles were roaming Tatar enclaves to recruit volunteer fighters.

By the time I arrived at Volodya's, smoke had begun to rise from the market, accompanied by occasional gunfire. Volodya's wife was in hysterics, tears streaming down her sunburned cheeks. The seventh micro-region was eerily quiet—children were locked indoors and houses deserted of men. Later, reports suggested that around fifteen hundred Tatars moved in to encircle the Russians.

I sat down and watched the Russian news. Crimea was in the headlines, as usual. The journalist commented, to pictures of a beautiful coastline, "These people are coming back here to Crimea because they like it here and because they lived here before 1944." Then they showed footage of a Tatar man hurling a rock at riot police.

As I withdrew to my bed it seemed inevitable that Bakchisaray was on the verge of war. The market had become an opportunity for Russians to settle old scores, and for the time being there was no end in sight.

IN THE MORNING I woke early and gathered my things. I craved being back on the steppe.

Before leaving, I rang Islyam. Overnight the army had moved in and cleared out both the Russians and the Tatars. Islyam was recovering at home. He was jubilant. "The prime minister signed! The market will be abolished!"

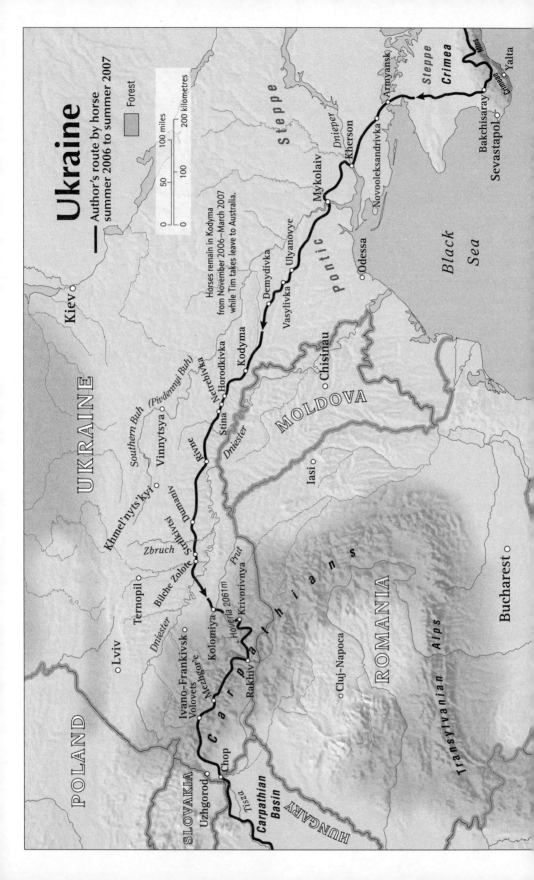

Ukraine

— Author's route by horse summer 2006 to summer 2007

▓ Forest

0   50   100 miles
0   100   200 kilometres

Horses remain in Kodyma from November 2006–March 2007 while Tim takes leave to Australia.

POLAND

SLOVAKIA

Uzhgorod
Chop

HUNGARY

Carpathian Basin

Tisza

ROMANIA

Cluj-Napoca

Bucharest

Transylvanian Alps

Lviv

Ternopil

Dniester

Ivano-Frankivsk
Volovets
Mezhgor'e

Rakhiv
Hoverla 2061m
Krivorivnya
Prut

Kolomiya

Carpathians

Bilche Zolote
Zbruch
Sudkhivtsi
Dunaivtsi

Khmel'nyts'kyi

Vinnytsya

Southern Buh (Pivdennyi Buh)

Rivne

Stina
Netrebivka
Horodkivka
Dniester

Kodyma

MOLDOVA

Iasi

Chisinau

Kiev

UKRAINE

Demydivka
Vasylivka
Ulyanovye

Odessa

Pontic

Steppe

Dnieper

Mykolaiv

Kherson

Novooleksandrivka

Armyansk

Steppe
Crimea

Nos

Yalta

Bakchisaray
Crimean
Sevastapol

Black Sea

21

CROSSROADS

FROM BAKCHISARAY I headed north through the arid steppe interior of Crimea and settled into a rhythm of riding by night, making camp by midday, and sleeping in the open under horse blankets. By following a canal that carried water from the Dnieper to the cities of Crimea, I was able to avoid towns and villages and make quick progress. As I rode, the tension and stress of the conflict began to dissipate.

Little more than a week took me to the far north of Crimea, where I woke late one night, half asleep, and gazed up at the dim profile of the horses. Taskonir stood over me, his ears bent forward, back leg cocked, and Kok's head resting on his wither. Tigon was curled up, breathing heavily, his bony spine hard up against my thigh. Time passed unmarked until a fart broke through camp. Ogonyok, who had evidently woken himself up with the noise, put his head down to munch on the sun-dried grass, followed by a quick shake of the mane and a stamp of the hoof. Tigon let out muffled barks in his sleep, and Taskonir's bottom lip quivered for some time until once again all was still.

It occurred to me that without the horses I would have lost my sanity on this journey long ago. Only from the solitude of the steppe, reconnected with them, did I feel ready to make sense of what had passed and make room for new horizons.

This night it was sinking in that after three intense months in Crimea, I would soon leave the peninsula for the mainland. Simultaneously, my third and final summer on the steppe was coming to a close. These milestones cemented the feeling that the vast bulk of the Eurasian steppe, which bulges out at its core in the oceanic spaces of Russia, Kazakhstan, and Mongolia, was now firmly behind, and all I had in front of me were the western fringes that taper off into a narrow prong in Hungary. With the softer climate of Ukraine nearly in my sights and the border of Hungary a mere 934 km away as the crow flies, it promised to be a piece of cake compared to what I'd been through. In fact, for the first time on my journey I was tempted by thoughts of the end. If all went smoothly, I could bank on crossing the Carpathians and reaching the Danube by early spring.

It was ironic, then, just how distant Hungary would prove to be in reality. What I could not have foreseen was that in Ukraine my journey would again be waylaid by events. In fact, another summer would come to pass before I could set my eyes on the finish, and this time the setback would be a personal loss far more profound than the journey itself.

For the time being, though, that was weeks away in the future, and as far as I knew, I was gathering momentum to make the final run. Gazing up at the stars, I felt a breath of cool air breeze through with its nightly relief, then rolled under the sweaty smell of the horse blankets and surrendered to sleep.

AT 3:30 A.M. the alarm clock sprang rudely to life, and as had become the routine, we were off within an hour, moving anonymously through the predawn darkness, the familiar dull ache throbbing up from my feet in the stirrups to my hips and butt.

When the black of the sky dissolved, it seemed the sun was rising just for us. Golden light spilled over the open steppe until I could check my bearing by the long shadows cast by our caravan. Tigon was off, a black speck bounding through the yellow grass, followed closely by dive-bombing birds. When I dismounted to pee, it triggered the three horses to do the same, and when Tigon homed back in he joined in, too.

The soft rays of friendly orange and yellow were deceptive. By 7:00 A.M. hot gusts thrashed at the grass and my eyes narrowed to slits. By lunchtime I had retired to the patchy shade of a lonely tree.

It took another day of riding through dry, hot conditions before we reached the narrow Isthmus of Perekop, which connects Crimea to the mainland. The modern territory of Ukraine that lay beyond was a land blessed with a relatively mild climate and an abundance of fertile soil, rivers, and forests—owing to which it was historically suited to an agrarian style of life.

Since the ninth century, the steppes of Ukraine had been a Slavic stronghold, and in the eleventh century they formed a key center of Kievan Rus, the most powerful state in Europe at the time. When the Mongols invaded in the thirteenth century, however, the state disintegrated, and for nearly three centuries Ukraine found itself under the rule of the Golden Horde. Ever since the dissolution of the Golden Horde, Ukraine had struggled to rekindle a sense of its greatness, forever in the shadow of Russia, Poland, and the Soviet Empire. Today it was a country ensconced in political chaos as the pro-national party that had been swept to power during the Orange Revolution of 2005 pitted its vision for integration with the European Union and NATO against those of the pro-Russian party that had recently gained control of parliament.

Kievan Rus and politics aside, what mattered to me at this point in time was that the perilous winters and scorching heat were safely behind us, and I was about to enter a world where I'd surely never have to worry about finding grass, grain, or water again. With Ukraine's many villages, I also hoped I could carry smaller loads of food and travel longer distances.

By contrast, I reflected, the prospects for Friar Carpini when he arrived in Ukraine in 1246 were altogether terrifying. Fresh from Europe and only just beginning his journey to Mongolia, it was in Ukraine that Carpini was warned about the treacherous lands ahead and forced to abandon his European horses because "Tartars have neither straw nor hay nor fodder, and they would all die." From Kiev, Carpini traveled southeast through the steppe of Ukraine and Russia on "the road to the barbarian nations." From there, he wrote, "we left with many tears, not knowing whether we traveled toward death or life." Ahead of Carpini stretched a land so vast and hostile that, on reading his account, one gets the impression that he went to painstaking lengths to convince readers he was telling the truth and not a fantasy.

The culture shock I anticipated, however, was essentially the reverse. Because I had traveled the long haul from Mongolia, Ukraine represented my first real glimpses of cultural Europe.

⊡

BEYOND THE INDUSTRIAL town of Armyansk I crossed onto the mainland and felt the first whisper of autumn. A cool breeze from the west rustled through the grass like some ghostly messenger and turned my sweat cold. The horses stopped to turn and gaze in its direction, and Tigon lifted his nose. The sun had done its summer's work and was moving on to new pastures. In its place thick, cottony clouds were filling the sky.

My own transition into autumn was not so subtle. On my first day on the mainland in Kherson Oblast a horse and cart spooked the horses into a wild bolt and I was forced to run 10 km to catch them. Ogonyok cut his leg badly on a broken glass bottle and was very nearly hit by traffic while crossing a bridge. Taskonir managed to run off with a full grain bag in his teeth and spread its entire contents on the ground.

Beyond the vast waters of the Dnieper River we were caught in an extraordinary deluge, and in the city of Mykolaiv my horses were confiscated by customs and veterinary officials, who said my permits were inadequate. After another round of vaccinations, being issued with Ukrainian animal passports, and a gift of a bottle of vodka to the head of veterinary control, the horses were released. It would be a month, however, before I got back in the saddle. Unexpectedly I had been selected as the *Australian Geographic* Adventurer of the Year, and as part of the award they were flying me to Sydney for the ceremony. The opportunity to see my family after two and a half years was too much to pass up despite the delays it would cause.

Leaving the horses at an equestrian center in Mykolaiv, I spent some days with Anya in Kiev, then, still dressed in my tattered riding boots and single change of shirt and trousers, found myself in front of a packed audience at the Maritime Museum in Sydney. A week passed in a whirlwind of media interviews, visits to sponsors, and two days at home, culminating with a luxurious dinner at the Australia Club in Sydney with Mum, Dad, and my great-uncle John Kearney. Although Dad in particular had felt uneasy about me throwing over my law studies at nineteen to pursue adventure, he had always supported me, and over oysters and champagne we celebrated the award as if it were ours together. He gave a short speech about what I had done, and in his swelling pride and approval I realized he had begun to see me as a man.

After staying together in a hotel on Sydney's Darling Harbor, I hugged Mum and Dad goodbye, then watched their taxi drive off until it was lost in the busy traffic of the city. It was the last time I would ever see my father.

BY THE TIME I had returned to Mykolaiv the air was crisp, the autumn leaves were alight with yellows and reds, and the horses had begun to grow their wooly winter coats. For the third year in a row I fitted my wide Mongolian stirrups, donned my winter boots, and prepared to set off with no one but winter expecting me beyond the horizon.

Anya had traveled down to Mykolaiv to see me off, and when the day came to leave, she walked alongside my caravan to a small forest on the outskirts, where we kissed goodbye. Both of us knew that we might never see each other again, and by the time we parted, both our faces were wet with salty tears.

From Mykolaiv I aimed to traverse southwest Ukraine before crossing the Carpathians and descending into Hungary. For the first few days

I charged across cultivated flats. The horses bristled with energy, and I sat high in the saddle watching Taskonir's wild mane thrash about and feeling his powerful chest absorb the shudders of pounding hooves.

We departed from all signs of main roads, and the flats grew into raised plains, dissected by deep, shadowy gullies and streams. Unlike on the Kuban in Russia, much of the land here that had been cultivated in Soviet times was overgrown and neglected, and those fields still in use had been deserted for winter. Sometimes I made my way cross-country using a compass, while other times I followed muddy lanes and tracks. Apart from the odd buckled Lada and horse and cart, only thin trails of smoke rising from villages in the valleys suggested signs of life.

The villages I did pass through presented a bleak picture of post-Soviet decline. Many of the houses had been hastily built in the 1930s and 1940s with tree branches, mud, and reeds and were now sinking unevenly into the ground. A great number of villages had only a handful of residents remaining, and some had been abandoned altogether. The majority of people who still lived in these hamlets were old babushkas and elderly men who looked as bent over and obsolete as the thatched-roof homes they stepped out of. Usually I would drift in during the morning or in the evening before camp in search of a well. As I rode through avenues of empty homes, it was clear the communities were receding as fast as the occupants were dying.

Beyond the village of Ulyanovye, where the only movement on the muddy street was a medieval-looking wooden cart, I rode through heavy mist and long grass until the land gave way to a valley. As the mist began to rise I looked down to a small huddle of homes chugging out smoke. The only person visible was a man walking behind a herd of cattle. He had not seen me.

From my vantage point in the saddle I was overcome by the vulnerability of the village. I felt I could have just pressed my heels into Taskonir's side and galloped down before anyone knew what or who was coming. The late autumn chill had lifted my energy significantly. The horses, too, had been raising their heads a little higher and were striding out with renewed alertness. Meanwhile, the settled world was withdrawing for a season of atrophy in the comfort of their homes. It occurred to me this natural trend had been exploited by nomads for thousands of years and perfected with cruel precision by the Mongols. It was, after all, in the winter of 1237, after the villagers had retreated from the fields and the Mongol horses were at their peak strength, that thousands of Mongol horseman emerged from the steppe to so infamously devastate the cities of Ryazan and later Vladimir. Entire towns were wiped off the map in those cold months when unsuspecting villagers retired for relative hibernation. In the city of Vladimir it is still remembered by Russians today that terrified townsfolk who had sheltered in the city's churches were burned alive.

For Ukrainians, the greatest moment of tragedy also fell in the wintry month of December. It was in 1240, as the frost settled, that the Mongols surrounded Kiev and within a matter of days laid waste to what had been the most powerful princedom of Russia and the capital of Kievan Rus. A measure of the devastation was recorded by Carpini some six years later, when he noted that the city was still littered with "countless human skulls and bones from the dead." "In fact," he wrote, "there are hardly two hundred houses there now."

It is true that this state of ruin was only part of the Mongol legacy. Conquest of Russia was backed up by 240 years of Genghisid rule, under which a sophisticated bureaucracy was introduced and commerce flourished. The Russian Orthodox Church, for instance, grew in material wealth during the Golden Horde period, and the fur trade was rerouted along north-south lines, allowing cities such as Moscow to enjoy unprecedented prosperity.[1] Nonetheless, the many benefits that Mongol rule would bring would have been cold comfort for those who endured the initial wrath.

After the crushing of Kiev, the Mongol army had continued across what is now Ukraine, setting up a summer camp just east of the Carpathian Mountains, lying in wait for the next winter of raiding and warfare to come.

The mist rolled back in, the village disappeared from view, and I rode on, unnoticed except by a couple of dogs that let out halfhearted barks.

Winter might once have been synonymous with the appearance of nomad hordes, but it seemed as though that chapter of history had long been forgotten here.

For another couple of days we continued on with energy and confidence, but unlike the Mongols and their army, I was alone and my feeling of empowerment waned. In the week since leaving Mykolaiv the horses hadn't had a rest and I had only been invited into a home once, and even then just for a cup of tea. When I asked the whereabouts of wells in villages, many would narrow their eyes and claim they didn't know. When I enquired whether anyone was willing to put me up for the night, the typical response was, "Sorry, I can't help you because I do not have space to shelter three horses."

One evening in a remote field I stopped by a broken-down truck. From under the hood, a hulking man emerged into the evening light. I noticed his powerful hands first, with their grease-stained, callused fingers—each as thick as a bratwurst. The way he fidgeted with a screwdriver as if it were as light and fragile as a toothpick suggested he had the potential for violence. Then came his face, bulging out of a long-necked woolen sweater, wide and round as a dinner plate. Set into the folds of his grimy skin were two small hazel eyes that now locked on to me.

He shook my hand absentmindedly as his cheeks, brows, and mouth began to bunch up in a way that didn't feel friendly. I started asking directions, but he cut me off.

"Give me at least one of your horses!"

"No," I replied. "These horses are going with me to Hungary!"

His eyes grew hard, and his face took on a righteous look. "Sure!" he grunted. "I know that you have stolen these horses, and so I will take them from you!"

There was a stand-off for a few moments, until he moved toward Ogonyok, behind me. Before he could reach the horse, I pulled on Ogonyok's lead rope, kicked my boots into Taskonir's side, and pulled away. I didn't turn around until the man and his broken-down truck had been swallowed up by the land.

That night I made camp in a hidden gully where I felt safe. In the coming days, however, I couldn't escape the feeling that while I might have shaken off this stranger, the land was imbued with the same sinister intentions as he was.

The following evening when I descended to the village of Vasylivka I was desperate. I had run out of grain and food, and the horses were exhausted. Some Uzbeks offered the horses a drink on the outskirts, but still no one was willing to put me up. Dark crowded in, sleet fell, my feet were numb in the stirrups, and I was told to go into the hills to the abandoned settlement of Mala Dvoryanka. "There is one man who still lives up there, and he can point you in the direction of water and grass," an old man told me.

The green beneath us turned to black, and after another hour's ride we were drawn to the lonely glow of a house. On our approach the sound of the door swinging open filled me with relief, but then two snarling dogs leaped out. Tigon launched into attack, a blinding flashlight flicked on, and above the raucous barking and snarling came swearing. I could just make out the silhouette of a man, then the pointy end of a rifle.

"Calm down, please! I came for advice on where to graze my horses and somewhere to camp!" I said angrily.

"Turn around, thief! Get out of here! I will shoot your dog just like that!" he screamed in a mix of Russian and Ukrainian.

I replied in Russian, "Okay! Okay! I'm leaving!"

I rode away and felt my way up a gully until safely hidden, and then I made camp.

My anger subsided only as the last of my pasta settled into my stomach. People here might have suspected me to be a thief or a Gypsy, but it gave me some sense of satisfaction that perhaps deep down in the Slavic psyche there was still recognition that horsemen from the east meant trouble.

IN THE MORNING the sun revealed thick, unruly pasture. Beneath the frozen yellow tops, the grass was still green near the roots. There was also a well in the old village of Mala Dvoryanka, and despite the risk of meeting the old man, I watered my horses there and decided to stay put for the day.

While the horses grazed I had just enough battery power to start my computer and connect the satellite phone to post an update to Australia. Before I could manage it, however, an email arrived in my inbox. It was from my father and addressed to me, my two brothers, Jonathan and Cameron, and my sister, Natalie. The subject line was "Sandy Point Van Sold," and it was written in a reflective tone I had rarely heard from him. In it he expressed his feelings about his early retirement. *As you know, he said, I took a step into the unknown last year . . . In retrospect the resignation probably wasn't a good idea financially . . . I struggle each day to try and determine what I should be attempting to reach forward for . . . and it is a major readjustment not having as a goal the care and maintenance of our children.*

For most of his career Dad had worked in outdoor education, first as a field leader, then as a lecturer, and eventually as founder of a degree program in sport and outdoor recreation at Monash University, Australia.[2] As children we were lucky to be taken out with university students on skiing, bushwalking, and sea-kayaking trips. But in the past ten or fifteen years the job had taken Dad into progressively more administrative roles, in which he had struggled with the internal politics of the workplace and a recent decision by management to relocate the program. These stresses were what had conspired to force him to consider early retirement.

The main subject of the email was the sale of his holiday cabin at Sandy Point—another point of sorrow for Dad. Sandy Point, a summer village on the Victorian coastline where his family was heavily involved in the local surf lifesaving club and owned a block of land, had been his stomping ground for most of his childhood and adult life. In 1999, however, his mother had pledged the block of land to one of Dad's brothers as a dying wish. This had caused a serious fracture between Dad's siblings and their father, who felt beholden to her promise. In the interceding years since then, Dad had, in part, resolved his feelings of dispossession by buying a simple cabin in Sandy Point caravan park—a permanently anchored caravan with built-on annex. But now he was writing to tell us he was forced to sell it for financial reasons.

Dad went on to press us to spend time with our grandfather while he was still clear of mind, and to learn from the schism between him, his siblings, and their parents. He wrote: *I can assure you that I do not want to be as isolated (distanced) from my children as mine have been as our family grew up . . . You are all in the prime of your life with many years of energetic activity to go, but once partnered and with children it would be fun to be near you.* The email finished, *I wish you well and look forward to sharing your ambitions, joys and sorrows and the sound of your voices in our house. Love, Andrew.*

The battery died and my screen went blank.

For most of the last two years, my home and childhood had seemed like another lifetime, a reality so detached it was in a parallel world that didn't belong. Now, however, I felt myself drawn into memories and feelings that cut to the present. My surroundings faded until I was back at Sandy Point, running along the beach and into the water with my brother Jon to catch a wave, Mum and Dad watching from the shore.

I recalled all the times that I had visited Dad at his university office and the long drives to get there and back home, when he would open up and vent all his frustrations, hopes, and ideas. It had been hard to weather his negative outbursts, but underneath there was a camaraderie during those trips that perhaps only a father and son can experience. He had resigned from his work toward the end of my stay in Kazakhstan, and I wondered with sadness and even guilt what it must have been like for him. We had all encouraged him to take the early retirement package he was being offered, yet now he was left at home alone, all four of his children pursuing their own lives.

What moved me most about the message, though, was the absence of anger. It disarmed all defenses and left me pining to tell him how grateful I was, how brave I thought he was for making the decision to resign, and how I sympathized.

My reflection was cut short by someone clearing his throat. Tigon woke with a growl, and I unzipped the tent door to meet the eyes of a startled cow herder.

"Do you have any cigarettes?" the man asked, trying to mask his curiosity.

⚎

I WAS THE first foreigner that Kolya had ever spoken to. He and his wife were from western Ukraine and had moved here to take up beekeeping. Later that evening when they had finished their village cow-herding duties, they returned to my camp to invite me to stay with them in Vasylivka.

My arrival at their home was a stark reminder of the settled world of Europe I had begun to enter. As I pulled in, Kolya invited my horses into a cramped barn, but even Taskonir pulled backward.

"Your poor horses!" Kolya exclaimed. "They have been out in the elements for so long they have forgotten what a stable is!"

I gave him a wry look. "The problem is that my horses have almost never been in a stable!"

Kolya shook his head and grinned, then took a longer look at my horses.

I'd become used to this misperception since arriving in mainland Ukraine. Some people had refused to take me overnight because they didn't have space in their barn and thought it cruel to make the horses stand out in the rain and cold.

Clearly Kolya had associated horses with stables all his life, and his innocent comment well illustrated that although Europeans had originally inherited horses from nomads of the steppe, they could not comprehend the extreme conditions that define the native environment of the horse, nor the horse's ability to survive in it. The horse, after all, evolved as a herd animal with a physiology honed for outrunning predators in the harsh climes of the Eurasian steppe. It was not naturally conditioned to either a stationary life isolated from other animals or a regimented diet of hay and grain.

It was difficult to explain to Kolya that to my horses his stables would have appeared more prison than refuge. Even more difficult to get across would have been that to me the stable symbolized the greatest difference between nomads and sedentary society: while nomads adapt their lives to the needs of their animals, migrating from pasture to pasture in symbiosis with nature, sedentary beings tend to control their animals and environment for their own convenience. In a similar vein, I felt it ironic that many times on my journey people had pitied me for living out in the elements. The truth was that after being so long on this journey, I found it hard to imagine living in a town or village, let alone a four-wall dwelling in a city.

That night I proudly tied the horses up outside and Kolya gave them generous piles of hay. In the morning, however, it was with a hint of hypocrisy that I found myself relishing the feel of my warm clean skin and the fresh sheets. The furnace was going and the smell of fried pork, buckwheat, and eggs wafted into my room. Outside, the first snow of the season had blanketed the earth. Life under the open sky wasn't as inviting as it had seemed the night before.

With some reluctance I saddled up and rode out over the frozen waves of mud in the streets of Vasylivka. Kolya walked with me to the outskirts, where my goodbye was marred when a man came hurrying up to us to ask if he could buy Taskonir. His dog attacked Tigon, and by the time we had separated them, blood was dripping from Tigon's mouth onto the snow.

Beyond Vasylivka I carried on through high open plains broken by the occasional gully. Bitten by frost, the land had lost its autumn gleam, and leaves on the odd trees that we passed were dull and brittle. By evening it was so cold I was forced to get off and walk to bring life back to my toes. It was only −2°C, but the moisture in the air and the ceaseless northwest wind were grinding me down.

The next day promised to be warmer, but by midmorning gray clouds swooped in and the headwind brought flurries of snow. My ropes turned stiff and frozen and the horses attempted to shy away.

Sometime in the afternoon we emerged from the plains like wild animals to cross the Odessa–Kiev freeway, then scurried our way back into the hills to the village of Demydivka. Ostensibly I entered the village look-ing for water, but the cozy homes under their wreaths of smoke broke the nomadic rebel in me.

At the first house a woman carrying the weight of middle age on her hips came out wrapped in a scarf and coat. She hurried back inside and emerged with a man bearing glazed, bloodshot eyes. He stopped a short distance away, corrected the angle of his fur hat, then broke out in stac-cato laughter.

"Tie up the horses! Fuck your mother and a donkey, too! This kind of traveler comes once in a hundred years!" His hands were up in the air as if praising the gods. "Nina!" he called to his wife. "We will feed the horses beets, hay, straw! Prepare porridge for the dog! Get the borscht ready! Tim, listen to me, I don't drink . . . Well, today I am because it is thirty years since my father died. Tomorrow I will also drink, and then I will stop. But come in, come in, you must be cold!"

Vasya, as he was known, had apparently only just raised a toast in mem-ory of his late father when my caravan came clopping into town. It was an event he wanted his children, grandchildren, and great-grandchildren to know about. Who was I to argue?

With the horses tied and beets, hay, and grain raining down, we rushed inside, where samohon (home-distilled vodka) was poured. There was apparently no need for me to worry about my horses. "I am a gun lover, you see!" he explained. "The special forces came to take away my guns, but everyone in the village suspects, rightly, that they didn't find them all! One *puck*," he said, pulling an imaginary trigger, "and the thieves will all be gone in a second!"

The vigor of his words made him quite a coherent and pleasant drunk—that is, until I stopped drinking and he carried on to finish the 2 litre soft drink bottle of home brew. By that time, I could not avoid con-fronting the circumstances in which he, his two young children, and their wife found themselves. The whitewashed walls and ceiling of their tiny two-room house were coated in years of grime, smoke, and cooking fat. It was better not to take shoes off, given all the muck on the floor. As I lay down to rest and the world faded away, I was vaguely aware that the boy had plucked out a gun from under Vasya's bed and was scampering about the house pretending to shoot.

After a shallow sleep I woke to suffocating wafts of stale samohon, body odor, and cigarettes. It was not the refuge, nor the sense of family, I'd been looking for.

For the next three days I rode into sleet and snow, became lost in a tangle of hills, and felt my spirits fall into a tailspin. In the town of Obzhyle I was greeted by drunken men driving a horse and cart. "Where the fuck! From where the fuck?" they hollered when they saw me. They were coarse and unhelpful, and I realized that while they marveled at my adventure, they did not identify with it—I had become a novelty.

I rode out fast, aiming to camp in the hills nearby, but as dark fell a Lada pulled up and a man in uniform stepped out demanding documents. I told him angrily that I did not have time, for it was getting late, but a second man emerged and took Taskonir by the reins. "Hand over your papers. Now!"

By the time they concluded I was legal, it was too dark to get safely out of town and find camp. Perhaps it was just the lack of sleep in the last few days, but I felt distraught and vulnerable. I told them that since they had held me up, they were responsible for finding me a place to stay. It was a mistake.

I was sent home with a drunk Gypsy bachelor, who after half a bottle of vodka outlined his plan to steal my horses. I broke out of his squalid hut in the middle of the night and slept on the frozen earth among the horses, which were tied up outside.

Another day took me to the town of Kodyma, where by chance Rodion, the brother of a Ukrainian friend of mine, had agreed to meet me. He had generously prearranged for my horses to be looked after at a collective farm with the help of the head of the local forestry department, Vladimir Sklyaruk.

For two days I enjoyed a respite, and when I left the weather had cleared somewhat. Still, when I rode out I felt directionless. The trees had finally been stripped of all life, and like my spirits, the autumn leaves skittered about in the breeze. I had a formidable distance to go to get to the Carpathians, and I wasn't sure how I could sustain my pace through the winter. I was also unsure how I fitted into this sedentary world. Irritated,

I tried calling Dad on his mobile via satellite, but time after time, the call went to voicemail. There was only one solution: it was time to grit it out and get this journey done.

⸝

TWO DAYS OUT from Kodyma I rode toward the sun as it was sinking from a clear peach sky. I passed a herd of cattle returning for the night, and noticed a horse and cart clopping along a track in the distance. A ways in front of us to the west the land planed off into a gully, and I reasoned that if I hurried, I could make it there for camp before dark.

Before speeding up, I reached into my backpack and pulled out the satellite phone. For some time now it had been beeping—a sign that I had accidentally left it on. As I went to switch it off, however, I noticed a new message.[3] It was from my brother Jon: *Tim! Call home please!*

I stopped, leaped from the saddle, and knelt in the grass. Clutching the handset, I dialed home and waited. When our family friend Peter Nicholson answered, it was obvious something was wrong. As the handset was carried to Mum, I could hear other familiar voices of friends.

Mum was in the bathroom when she picked up. "Tim?" Her voice crackled down the line, shaking. There was a long pause. I held my breath.

"It's Dad," she started, her voice strong, but in an instant it wavered and she began to cry. "He was in a car accident . . . I'm so sorry, Tim . . . he is dead . . . I can't bring him back."

⸝

IT'S NOT HARD to remember the first few moments after I hung up that evening, November 16, 2006, but they are hard to describe, and it's harder still to do them justice.

On the one hand, sitting there by the roadside at the feet of my horses, the journey that had consumed me for two and a half years evaporated as if it had never been. I couldn't breathe, and my back muscles heaved. I vomited two or three times, cried, and felt my body convulse. Inside, it was as if a bullet had ripped through me, cutting the tensioned cords that held me together, and they were recoiling, whipping at my interior.

But simultaneously there was a numbness and a surreal sense of calm and normality. I was still on a horse somewhere in the Ukraine, and I needed to camp, find grass, and unsaddle. I fragmented into two distinct parts from that moment—the practical, steadying me, and the passenger.

Among the myriad thoughts competing for space in those first few moments, the predominant one was that I had to be alone, to be away from anyone who had not known my father. Somehow I knew that if I was quick about making camp, out on the steppe under the stars I had a fleeting chance of communion with Dad before he was gone.

In a gully somewhere I worked fast. Poles broke through sleeves in the tent, Tigon whined for his food, and the horses tried to bolt. For a fleeting moment it felt as though the two disjointed parts of me merged to focus and get the job done. But then the horses were tethered, the food was cooked and eaten, and I crumpled onto my canvas bag. I gazed up at the sky, and suddenly it was so big and so lonely. Where could he be? Did he know how to find me?

I wanted to know when Dad had died, how many hours I had been pretending that life was normal. I computed what Mum had told me, weighed up the time differences: he had been alive when I woke up but dead by lunch. My lungs seized again at the thought.

How many times had I called? How many times had he not answered? I could imagine his phone lighting up, my name coming through. Maybe when I made that last call he had still been alive, trapped in the wreckage, watching the phone. And all I could do was get angry and leave a message to say how pissed off I was that he wouldn't pick up!

Sleep didn't beckon. To sleep would have been to abandon him, and he had to be aware of me, he had to know that I was here. And yet the steadying hand of the other me guided and caressed until I couldn't keep my eyes open any longer.

When I awoke again, I felt frozen—the sleeping bag was half on. There was ice on the tent, and outside a sea of mist was gushing in and devouring us. It must have been about four in the morning. I picked up the phone again. This time I got Jon. We just cried. Then I talked to my sister, Natalie. The first thing she asked was, "Did you reply to his email?"

"No, I didn't," I replied.

"I didn't, either."

THERE WAS ONLY one thing to do: go back. Back to the spot where I had eaten lunch after he died, back to where I'd camped the previous day, when he was still alive. Back home, where I could return to the life I'd had as his son.

I packed faster than I had ever managed. To stop and think would be to let time carry on.

We trotted through the village under the cover of heavy mist, and before the sun could illuminate a world without Dad we were lost in the folds of the land. The sun gradually melted through, a silvery disc suspended in space. Delicate, frost-encrusted birch limbs fingered their way into reality. I pushed the horses harder, into a canter. Mist began to swirl, then above me a circle of clear sky turned peach. I craned my neck and twisted around but urged the horses on.

Dad, I'm coming!

I was catching up with him. But then Ogonyok pulled at the lead rope, I slowed, and the mist began to rise.

I lost Dad for some time. Then, as we entered a tract of forest, he seemed to return. I slowed to a walk, breathing in the tang of rotting leaves that littered the ground. Dad walked to my left in his shorts and hiking boots, carrying one of his weathered old daypacks. We stopped momentarily as he leaned over and lifted a plant from under a tree. Cradling it in his palm, he brought it over to me and held it up. I was back in the Australian bush, one of the many times when he'd turned to me and said, "Tim, isn't life amazing?" Back then I hadn't understood what he meant, though I could see from the look of fascination in his eyes that he was right. Now he looked up at me in the saddle, his eyes alight with the same sense of enchantment. We rode on together.

So many times by phone and email we had talked about him joining me on this adventure. Since resigning from work he had taken interest in the histories and cultures of the countries I traveled through and read many books on the subject. Nevertheless, neither of us had committed to the idea of him coming over. The naked forest glared angrily—I had missed the season of opportunity—and as the edge of the forest drew near I began to sob.

WHEN I WAS halfway back to Kodyma, Vladimir Sklyaruk met me and took my gear back by car. I'd phoned his family in the middle of the night, and he had promised at once to find a way to look after Tigon and the horses in my absence. I galloped past the lunch spot and camp and rode another 15 km into town.

The following dawn I fell into Anya's arms at the Kiev train station and about thirty hours later walked out through Australian customs—the same gates I had recently passed with so much celebration.

Then they were there: Mum with her pale face and wet blue eyes, Jon behind her, nervously grinding his teeth. I was the eldest child, and Jon was my junior by two years, although from an early age he had been much stronger and more athletic than me. As he leaned over and hugged my skinny frame there was a seniority in him I hadn't recognized before.

Natalie and Cameron were there, too, but it wasn't until we made the two-hour drive home that it felt like we were all finally reunited. And Natalie had some good news: although neither she, Jon, nor I had answered Dad's email, Cameron had. He had also made sure, by looking at Dad's email account, that his response had been read.

In the coming days it was obvious that Dad's death meant something unique and different to each of us, but in some ways the four of us were together in our grief. There was no one who could share what Mum must have been going through, however. Mum and Dad had been married for thirty years and had lived in the same country house in rural

Victoria since the year I was born. On the previous Thursday, the day of
Dad's accident, Mum hadn't been expecting him home. He had spent the
week helping out at a surf lifesaving camp at Sandy Point and had promised to be back on Friday morning, as the two of them would be attending a wedding in Canberra on Saturday.

Sometime in the early evening of Thursday there had been a knock at
the front door. This was odd, since anyone who had been to our home
knew that the back door was in fact the proper entrance.

It was the police. At about 4:30 P.M. that day there had been a crash on
a stretch of the South Gippsland Highway—the road we traveled from
home to Sandy Point. A man carrying Dad's identification was deceased.

"It can't be him! There must be some mix-up!" she'd told them.

Our neighbors, who had come over after seeing the police car, had
helped Mum to an armchair and tried to calm her down.

In hindsight, Mum said, there were signs that something was going to
happen. Every day of their married life she had been picking up after
Dad—his clothes sprawled over the bedroom floor, the mess he'd left in
the kitchen, his Ventolin inhaler not where it should have been. Yet when
he'd left to go to Sandy Point, almost everything had been in its place. In
the final weeks before his death he had also met with an unusually large
number of old friends and acquaintances—mostly coincidental meetings,
such as in the supermarket or at various functions. Then there was the
email to us, and other subtle things—it was as if he had been unconsciously
preparing to sign off.

Out in the garden I joined Dad's brother Kim, who had been liaising
with the police, and learned something that Mum and the others had been
keeping from me. "First, Tim, I want you to know that there was little
chance for your Dad—it was a head-on collision," he told me. "People went
to his aid within a few minutes, but he was trapped in the driver's seat and
unconscious."

He took a deep breath.

"But not long after the crash, your dad's car started burning. They tried
to get him out, but it was impossible. I am still trying to get details from
the police. They think that someone checked for his pulse before the fire

and he didn't have one, but we don't know. Only the autopsy will give us the answer."

The accident had been a tragedy for those in the other car as well. One woman had died and her husband had been airlifted to the hospital. Their granddaughter, who had Down syndrome, had been in the front seat and had survived, but with possible spinal injuries. No one yet knew how the accident had happened.

I passed out for some time in the afternoon and woke feeling groggy and disoriented. The house was strangely empty, and I stumbled down the hallway into the living room. Surely if I sat there long enough, something would break the silence—perhaps Dad would talk to me, or walk through the door.

As I closed my eyes I could hear the screen door open outside. In my mind I heard his work bags land on the floor and his shoes come off, but when I opened my eyes and looked up it was Mum. She had come running to hold me.

ELEVEN DAYS OF life without Dad.

The house was filled with guests, and we spent much of our time organizing the funeral. Unlike out on the steppe, in our Western world dying was complicated. Dad's body couldn't be released until the autopsy was finished, and until the death certificate arrived Mum's bank accounts were partially frozen. We were not allowed to see Dad.

Finally, though, we had chosen a coffin, Dad had been returned, and on the eve of the funeral I lay awake hearing nothing but the odd creak of a bed and the rustle of possums on the roof. We had several large specimens living up there; they were nocturnal animals, and slept in the attic during the day, but at this time of night you could hear them venturing out for food.

I was still suffering jet lag, but more than that I craved the calm of night, which held me close to Dad. I knew that when daybreak came it would bring with it terror, sobbing, guests, and frantic preparations. I'd come to think of my nightly vigil as a duty.

The darkness moved slowly until a *cack cack cack* from a magpie sounded, then the warbling of a hatchling. An ever so pale light cracked through the fronds of the giant cypress trees, and a thrush hopped by the window—so innocent and unaware that the world had stopped.

I couldn't lie there any longer.

From the back corner of the wooded yard I gazed out over the paddocks toward the emerald hills of the Strzelecki range. A fox and her cubs appeared, moving stealthily across the dew-laden grass. They were hurrying back to their den before the magic of dawn was eclipsed by the sun.

To the east I fixed my eyes on large eucalypts that stood with their limbs outstretched, silhouetted against the blanket fog. These ancient trees were what Dad loved, so much so that they were somehow inseparable from him. How could they still be here, continuing to exist as if everything remained as it had always been?

Finally I sat on an old cypress stump and watched the sun grow near. For a while it seemed like an even race between it and the mist to reach the horizon, but in the end the mist won, rising like a cloak from the land, embroiled in pinks and reds that glowed brighter and brighter. From the gap between the mist and the horizon, subtle rays of golden light began to feel their way over the land, rendering the dew a million glinting marbles. The deciduous trees around the house behind me lit up with their translucent, wafer-thin spring leaves. Then came the sun, this lifting yellow orb of life, so full of spirit yet indifferent and coldly calculating. It was rising for another day, one of millions and millions of cycles.

Then the sun was gone, hidden behind the fog. The sound of a crow. A breeze. The leaves in the trees beginning to move—they were no longer translucent, but opaque and dull. Everything was returning to the mundane, to the passing of time.

THE FUNERAL PASSED, then the wake, then the memorial service at his university, and gradually the visitors and letters of sympathy slowed to a trickle.

Sometime after Christmas Jon and I decided to board up the holes around the house where the pesky possums were getting inside to sleep in the attic. We did it late at night when they were out looking for food. As dawn broke I was woken by the sound of possums frantically scratching to get back in before the sun exposed them. Their days had begun just like any other, yet they had returned to find that their whole life had changed, and try as they might, there was no way back.

Since receiving the news about Dad, there had only been room to confront his death and what it meant, but as time wore on the journey re-emerged. I received emails that Tigon was well but missing me. The horses, however, had been hastily left at the collective farm, where they were tied up in a barn with dairy cows. I wasn't sure if the men there had managed to remove their horseshoes, or how often they saw daylight. Fodder was scarce, and it was a big thing to ask strangers to feed three extra horses.

Come February I had to make a decision. If I left it much longer, I might not have horses to return to. But on the other hand, I was the eldest of four children and it didn't feel right to abandon everyone so soon. And in any case, my Ukrainian visa had expired, and I'd spent the last of my money on a plane ticket home. Underneath, though, I knew that Dad would have wanted me to continue, and I simply couldn't abandon my animals.

The answer came when I was offered work as the subject of a Discovery Channel promotion film. It was to be filmed over two days in March, and I was to be given a round-trip ticket to Dubai, valid for twelve months, as well as almost $2,000. From Dubai it was a relatively cheap and short plane trip to Kiev.

So on March 14, 2007, four months after arriving in Australia, I was back at Melbourne airport, feeling as if I had left my horses too long but was saying goodbye to Mum and the family too early.

***

ANDREW JOHN COPE, born on December 13, 1950, passed away on November 16, 2006. He was the oldest of five children. The autopsy report eventually determined that there was no sign of smoke inhalation in his throat or lungs; he had died on impact of a broken neck. At the coroner's hearing it was concluded that Andrew had veered into oncoming traffic. The coroner found that he had most likely fallen asleep at the wheel.

22

TAKING THE REINS

On a brisk spring morning in central Ukraine a small crowd of workers was assembling by the buckled iron gates of Kodyma's collective farm. I stood with them, a compass strung from my neck and dressed in the patched trousers and faded Russian army hat that I had lived in for the better part of two and a half years but which, at this moment, felt like objects from a former life.

Among those gathered were the many generous people who had looked after my animals during my absence in Australia. Incredibly, for the four and a half months that I had been away the director of the collective had not charged me a cent. I shook his hand and presented him with an Australian oilskin coat. In a gesture recalling the Mongolian tradition of throwing milk to the sky, he then raised three toasts of vodka for a fortuitous journey to Hungary.

It was at that point I hauled myself up onto Taskonir, shouldered my backpack, and, with Tigon choking himself to get moving on the lead in front, felt my journey pulled back into motion.

At first I rode slowly and carefully through the outskirts of town, my body settling back into the saddle, hands and feet feeling their way instinctually around the reins and into the stirrups.

It was early April, the time of morning when the frosted-over furrowed earth in the fields was acquiescing to mud and the pall of smoke from wood fires and coal stoves was beginning to lift. We passed graying timber homes and snow-trampled stretches of pastureland that were yet to spring back after the post-winter thaw. To me, everything about this mash of brown and grays signaled a land at its lowest ebb, and it mirrored the way I felt internally. It wasn't a pleasant analogy, but one I had grown comfortable with—after all, it wouldn't have felt right to return to the bloom of spring or the gaiety of summer.

If my state mirrored that of the land, then the condition of the horses was a good metaphor for where my journey was at as a whole. Two weeks earlier I had arrived in Kodyma to find Kok, Taskonir, and Ogonyok in a cavernous cow barn where they had been tied up for the better part of four and a half months. Their muscles had atrophied, their hooves had grown out, and their winter coats were matted with muck. When I saw them, it had sunk in that to reach Hungary would not be a simple a matter of picking up from where I had left off. Though I had already traveled around 8,000 km from Mongolia, the momentum had dissipated, and ahead still loomed over 1,000 km to the Danube River, including a crossing of the high Carpathian Mountains. These initial few weeks would be as much a journey of spiritual and physical recovery as a passage through the landscapes and people of central and western Ukraine.

There remained one last but important moment for pause and reflection before I could truly get moving. Not far beyond Kodyma I turned onto a muddy trail and pulled the horses into a familiar meadow. Winter had preserved the ghostly footprint of my tent from the previous year. I dismounted and lay on the earth. It was the last place that I had slept and woken while Dad was alive.

It was just an insignificant patch of grass and weeds near a railway, but it was also the place where my life had been broken in two—life with a father, and life without. For the past five months I had been dealing only with the latter, and time, like my journey, had effectively stood still.

Beyond this point lay horizons where I had never been while Dad was alive. Without him the road ahead seemed more fraught with dangers than before. My guts twisted at one thought in particular—that somewhere in a village ahead, at some point in time, I would be asked the inevitable question: "Do you have parents?" On the steppe it had been a standard greeting that I found odd and even amusing. I'd answered without thinking.

Before remounting I noticed a solitary dandelion that had blossomed. With it firmly pressed into my breast pocket I moved on.

THAT NIGHT A snowstorm swooped in, and I spent the following day in camp listening to the snow rap against the tent, the rise and fall of Tigon's chest pressing into my side. When morning came the snow had stopped, and anticipation hung as heavy as the frost. Tigon lay next to me, feigning sleep, with one ear cocked and an eye half open. When I rose, he rose with me, and together we jammed our heads through the tent entrance. The sun was nudging its way into a deep blue sky. Golden fragments of light splintered through the snow-covered grass. There was a stillness that beckoned with the promise of the kind of crisp, calm weather that a horseman could only dream of.

After packing up I rode quietly through empty meadows and woodlands. A couple of hours later I crested a hill overlooking the village of Horodkivka. Cupolas of an Orthodox church reached gracefully above a huddle of timber homes—rather like a priest towering over his flock. As I rode down the hill I met a procession coming up. I pulled over to yield the way.

Leading the march was an elderly man bent forward carrying a heavy wooden cross. His face was a haggard topography of shadowy ruts draining tears from glassy blue eyes. Beyond him women carried the lid of a coffin, followed by a priest, who, with his flowing black robe and beard, seemed to glide rather than walk. Next rumbled an old truck with an open coffin in the back. The deceased was an elderly woman, the skin of her pale, uncovered face lightly warmed by the sun. Two children sat in the back holding her in place as the truck wobbled and rocked its way up the road to the grave.

As I turned to move on, the land ahead seemed touched by the beauty and sorrow of this traditional passage. It felt as if we, too, were passing through the gates into another world.

From Horodkivka I tracked west. I rose to high plains, then dipped into deep, meandering river valleys that flowed southward to the Dniester. Hamlets drew me away from heavier thoughts. Most were nestled on the steep valley sides and on riverbanks, tucked away from the cold wind. They were places far from main roads where the only movement to be seen were dogs running to the end of chains and babushkas bent over scattering seeds in furrowed plots, looking as twisted and knotted as old birch trees. I seldom stopped, registering only the occasional greeting.

In Dakhtaliya an old man yelled, "Hey, sell me your horses."

In the next village, Netrebivka: "Hey, Gypsy, where are you going?"

On the cobbled, windy streets of Hnatkiv: "What's this caravan?"

In Stina, a lady pointed in horror at my packhorses: "Hey, stop! You have lost your passengers! They must have fallen off!"

There were so many villages that sometimes these greetings were the only means of making sense of where I'd been and when. Perhaps my lacking clarity of mind was also because I felt withdrawn, unable to engage as normal. I tried to let my mind go blank and allow thoughts and feelings to come without force, relying on the land, the animals, and people to lift me.

The first inkling of a smile surfaced one morning as I lay in the tent. It had been another cold night, and I cautiously opened the tent flap so as not to give myself away. Outside, the horses were making the most of their newfound freedom.

Ogonyok was irrepressible, erupting in fly kicks, shaking his neck, and teasing the others into play fights. Taskonir had his regal reputation to

A Kalmyk herder near Tavan Gashun, Kalmykia, Russia.

The Golden Temple in Elista, Kalmykia—the largest Buddhist temple in geographical Europe. Founded and completed in 2005. IGOR SHPILENOK

This Kalmyk man in the village of Ul'dyuchiny lived through the deportation of his people to Siberia during World War II, and their return to their homeland in 1957.

A male saiga (*Saiga tatarica*) on the Kalmyk steppe. Its horns, much sought after as a Chinese flu remedy, have made it the target of rampant poaching. Saiga are now critically endangered. IGOR SHPILENOK

Luti (left) and his driver, Lokha—my unlikely saviors in Timashevsk, Krasnodar Krai, Russia.

A Cossack Ataman of the Kuban with his son, both in traditional dress.

Ogonyok, Taskonir, and Utebai happily grazing in one of the first fields I had seen on my journey . . . only moments before I am told that they have ruined a winter crop of barley. Stavropol Krai.

Cossacks of the Kuban, a once proud horseback society, have become cultivators of the hallowed *chernozem* (black soils).

Taskonir, Tigon, and I stand on the edge of the Karabi Jayla, Crimea, overlooking the Black Sea. The high plains of the Crimean Mountain range were once a summer haven for nomadic Tatars.

Me bathing in the Black Sea waters with the palomino gelding, Kok.

Seryoga, a Russian from Staryi Krym, spent two weeks leading me through the forest and mountains of Crimea.

Three elderly Crimean Tatar women who survived the deportation of their people to Central Asia and Siberia in 1944 and have returned. Here, they sit in near the picket line in Bakchisaray, where Tatars are lobbying for the removal of a market, built in the 1990s, from Eski Yurt—the site of an ancient city dating to the seventh century, where generations of spiritual leaders and Tatar khans are buried.

Riot police try to keep the peace in Bakchisaray.

The old quarters of Bakchisaray.

One of the Tatar musicians, who played a concert in the Khan's Palace, Bakchisaray.

One of the last photos of our family taken together with my father. I am standing with my brothers Cameron (left) and Jonathan (right). My sister, Natalie, my father, Andrew, and my mother, Anne, are seated, with our family dog, Pepper, who died during my early weeks in Kazakhstan. Photo taken November 2003, eight months before I began my journey.

Tigon looking for a pat from Ferona, the ninety-three-year-old babushka in the village of Dumaniv, who learned to read at age eighty-three.

A Hutsul man in traditional dress at the church in Berezhnytsia on Saint Nikolai Day. The felt hats are known as *krysani*, and the heavy sheepskin vests are *kyptars*.

Ivan Ribaruk, the Hutsul priest of Krivorivnya who hosted me, finishes the ceremony in Berezhnytsia. With him is eighty-four-year-old hat maker, Vasil.

Yuri Wadislow carefully guides my horses over a snowdrift high on the Chorna Gora ridge of the Carpathians, Western Ukraine.

Tigon poses on a peak in the Carpathians. By this stage of the journey, he has grown into adulthood, run probably more than 15,000 km, and even become a father.

The tail end of the Svidovets ridge. I'm riding Taskonir and leading Ogonyok and Kok. Note the dog lead—sometimes necessary in Ukraine and Russia where there was a risk of him being shot by sheep herders or eating mouse poison in the fields.

Guardians of Hungarian nomadic heritage. Top left, Kassai Lajos, demonstrating his prowess as a horseback archer. Top right, Tamas Petrosko, who rode from Bashkiria in Russia to the Danube on horseback in honor of his ancestors. Below left, a Csikos horseman on the Hortobagy steppe. Below right, Istvan Vismeg, from Sarospatak.

Peter Kun's Kazakh yurt at his steppe ranch in the Hortobágy Puszta.

A Przewalskii stallion at a scientific reserve on the Hortobágy. The Przewalskii—a wild species of equine, known in Mongolian as *takhi*—is thought to be the closest living link to the original wild horse of the Eurasian steppe that was domesticated at least 5,500 years ago.

I dismount on the banks of the Danube—the end of the steppe, and the completion of my journey.

uphold, but Kok was more than happy to join in, rearing on his hind legs and softly biting at Ogonyok's neck.

As the sun rose, the brittle frost softened and the needling air turned friendly and ambient. Taskonir dropped to the ground with a sigh, then stretched out on his side and closed his eyes. Kok joined him, lying opposite, followed by Ogonyok. Together they lay breathing in the promise of spring. The snow and rain had washed away all traces of their ordeal in the barn, and their bodies rippled and shone with vitality.

It was rare when the horses were so benign, and sensing this, Tigon took the opportunity to get up close and sniff around them. Then, as if it were one of his first days out of prison, he wriggled around on his back, paws punching at the air, chewing lazily on grass. When he was done with that he sprinted circles around camp and cocked his leg on everything in sight. Eventually he lay upside down playing dead—legs in a tangle, tongue hanging slack out of his jaws, and back legs wide apart, proudly displaying his jewels to the sky.

It was to be a charmed day. Not long after setting off, a wiry, little man pulled up in his ancient Lada and surveyed me with astonishment. "What's this? It's my dream! I've always wanted to travel like a free Cossack!" he exclaimed, grabbing my hand with both of his and shaking like a madman. "You are coming to my village! To Rivne! Follow me!"

Yanked rather than coaxed from my withdrawn state, I found myself that evening at a long wooden table jammed with burly farmers. "Pork fat is life! Sport is your grave!" they chuckled, slapping their bellies and pouring vodka. "Eat and drink! This isn't Russia, where they drink a lot and eat little. We *eat* a lot and *drink* a lot!" It was the beginning of two days of utter embrace by the villagers of Rivne.

My time in the village was marked by a particularly special visit to the local school. At the school's entrance the principal—a fiery lady with red permed hair—had ordered the children out into the front yard. There, as she shook my hand and kissed me on the cheek, Tigon proceeded to stick his snout under her dress. Teachers and students alike erupted in hysterics, then descended on Tigon. While tens of pairs of hands reached out to stroke him, he sat like a prince, then surrendered to a lying position, spreading his back legs in an effort to direct scratches to his belly.

When things had settled down I was ushered into a classroom where children with wide, uncorrupted eyes divided their attention between this funny Australian and the dog. I fielded questions for over an hour: "How many kilometres a day do you travel?" "What do you eat?" "Do you have a girlfriend?" "When do you wash?" "Is Tigon a father?" Their questions were simple and the right ones to ask. Unlike adults, who were full of astonishment that I hadn't been knocked over the head and killed along the way, they saw my adventure in all its simplicity. It reminded me that in truth, before setting off from Mongolia, I had never worried about death, bureaucracy, conflict, drunkards, or robbers. I had wanted to come here out of curiosity, to appeal to the better side of people whoever they were, and live the kind of dream that most forget when they grow up.

I left the school feeling light and unburdened in a way that, after the past few months, I could not remember.

FROM RIVNE I carried on with such buoyancy that I was engrossed in thoughts other than about my father.

As I passed through back-to-back villages, it occurred to me the land was shrinking in scale, and with it the concept of the world held by local people. If in Kazakhstan the average distance between settlements had been 100 km, then here in Ukraine it was rarely more than a tenth of that. Yet it was often the case that people did not know the names of villages beyond the next one or two. A satellite image of the earth at night that I had with me well demonstrated the nature of the land I was entering. From Mongolia to Russia the Eurasian steppe was visible as one vast black empty space, ringed by a few dim lights on its fringes in Siberia and Central Asia. In Ukraine, the lights of towns, cities, and villages faded in, growing in intensity toward western Europe, which was ablaze. The higher the density of living, it seemed, the shorter were the boundaries of the known world for the people who lived there.

Another thing that began to strike me was that when I materialized in a village out of the forest, from across a field, or out of a gully, villagers were bewildered. Where had I come from? How? The penny dropped one day when I stopped to ask directions from a man on the edge of a village. I could see by the lay of the land, and from my map, that I could cut straight over a rise beyond the last houses, through a forest, and end up in the next little hamlet.

"No, you can't! I don't know about your map, but it's clearly wrong!" he said, a little angrily. "You need to go back the way you came and take the road over there."

I proceeded to follow my off-road route without issue. On the map I could see that the road he suggested would have taken me the long way round—almost twice as far.

Unlike a nomad, who from the back of a horse learned to read the lay of the land using its natural features, this villager had mapped out his world almost exclusively according to roads. This had blinded him to the natural paths in the environment. It would be easy to assume that this road culture was a modern product of the motorcar, yet that couldn't have been farther from the truth. After all, this man from whom I had asked directions had been at the helm of a horse and cart. When I asked him why he didn't ride, he replied, "Horses are for work! Not for fun!"

It was an apt illustration that Europeans from antiquity had been experts not at riding but in using carts, drays, sleds, and carriages. With a single animal, the settled farmer could transport hay, grain, and other produce, carry the whole family, and cultivate the land. For them this was a much more practical application of the horse than riding, although it did have one small drawback: they could travel only where their wheeled vehicle would go, and this limited their sensory experience of the landscape.

Riding on, I began to imagine the life of a villager as it might have been in medieval times. Most peasants would have been illiterate and would have rarely traveled beyond the boundaries of their parish—the root of the term parochial—and for those who did travel a considerable distance, they did so almost exclusively by road.

Meanwhile, for a nomad in the Mongol army in the thirteenth century, the world would have looked like a very different place. His concept of the world was an ever-expanding one as he traveled through diverse landscapes, experienced different cultures, heard a multitude of languages, and of course did so without being limited to roads. When the nomad horseman reached Europe, the knowledge and life experience he possessed would have been beyond comprehension of the insular European villagers. For them, just like for the man who rejected my map as being "incorrect," it would have seemed that the invading nomads were breaking the rules. In fact, the nomad ways, land, culture, and origin had been a mystery to Europeans for thousands of years before the arrival of Mongols and, despite the eternal waves of invasion, would remain so, it seemed, for centuries to come.

A WEEK OUT of Rivne I woke tired and hungry in a weed-infested gully. Tigon yawned, pricked his ears, realized there was no food on offer, and then tucked his nose back under his tail.

For five days straight we had been riding into bitterly cold wind and rain, and overnight fog had flooded the gully and snap-frozen my muddy boots and chaps. It might have been May, but winter was reluctant to let go.

After a breakfast of residual oatmeal scraped from the bottom of a pack box, I willed the horses down to a river valley in search of food and a rest. In the village of Dumaniv I had only just dismounted when a car pulled up at a cluster of adjacent homes. I approached nervously but had barely begun when the driver cut me off: "Don't even think about it! Sleep here! You will eat what we eat! Sleep where we sleep! We won't offer more, we won't offer less."

Valeri, as the man was known, led me home and doled out hay and grain. By nightfall I had scrubbed clean and sat reborn at the dinner table. Across from me sat Valeri, his father Volodomor, and his grandmother Ferona—three generations of a family, each of whom, I would learn over the course of the evening, was in some ways a unique product of their era.

Valeri, who was in his thirties, had recently come back from four years working as a laborer in Spain. Like thousands of others who had reached adulthood in the chaos of the 1990s, he had gone to the European Union in search of work but was now barred from returning because he had overstayed his visa. He was relying on the savings he had brought back to set himself up for the future.

In the formative years of Volodomor's life, such a scenario had been unimaginable. Born in 1950, he was schooled in the Soviet Union at the height of the Cold War and had served a long career in the army. In 1992 he had quit; in 1998 he "realized the big mistake" in his life and become Christian. Nowadays he was an evangelical preacher and had returned to the roots of his childhood in Dumaniv.

Both Valeri and Volodomor had fascinating stories to tell, but the person who interested me most was Volodomor's mother, Ferona. I'd been drawn to her ever since she greeted me at the doorway dressed in a black shawl that was as creased and wrinkled as the folds in her ancient face. She sat at the table practically jumping out of her skin. "I might be ninety-three, but I can still thread the eye of a needle, no sweat! And every day I go barefoot to the hills with my goats!"

Her body was miniature and shrunken, but in her eyes was the sparkle of youth. She opened a Bible. "I only learned to read at the age of eighty-three! My son taught me so that I could read the Bible before I die." With a giant magnifying glass trembling in her hand, she read aloud. I listened intently, astonished that before me sat a woman who had survived every violent convulsion of Ukraine's past century. By the time she turned thirty, she had witnessed the Bolshevik revolution, Ukraine's fleeting independence, Stalin's purges, and the horrors of World War II, navigating her way through these cataclysmic events in spite of, or perhaps partly because of, her illiteracy.

Like most survivors of her generation, she told me the event that had most affected her was the Holodomor, the famine of 1931 to 1933. Somehow most subjects of conversation with Ferona led back to her experience of this tragedy. Bearing parallels with the Great Zhut in Kazakhstan, the Holodomor had been triggered by the forced collectivization of Ukrainian farmers—a policy propagandized as a war on the kulaks, but which in reality was a means for the state to wrest control of agriculture, using the citizens as virtual slaves to produce grain that was then used to buy industrial equipment and patents from the West. Mass starvation began in the winter of 1931–32 after widespread crop failure. Stalin suspected sabotage and persecuted the farmers, who were now part of collectives.

"To keep us alive my father hid a bag of wheat in between the stones in the wall of our house. One day the Komsomols found it, and Papa was sent away to a labor camp in Russia. We never heard from him again. I survived on grass and the old leaves of sugar beets," Ferona told me.

As tragic as that winter had been, it paled in comparison to what followed. The summer harvest of 1932 was successful, but few collectives met the unrealistic grain quotas. Failure to meet targets was treated as treason and led to an all-out attack on the rural population. Grain was locked up in storehouses or sent to Russia while essential supplies to Ukrainian villagers were cut off. "Bread procurement officers" roamed villages searching for food. Mortars were ordered destroyed. By the middle of the winter of 1932–33, people in Dumaniv—like in thousands of villages and towns across the breadbasket of Russia and Ukraine—were dropping dead in the fields, on the roads, in their homes. Even then, Ferona explained, the authorities "came to ask for taxes on everything—the trees in our yard, our animals, all our possessions." When her family could pay no more they were evicted and locked in jail. The authorities stole everything remaining in their house, "even our sewing machine, bedding, and cooking items," she said.

Resembling the debate that goes on in Kazakhstan about the causes of the Great Zhut, there is broad disagreement—primarily between Russians and Ukrainians—about whether the Holodomor was a genocide or just a tragedy resulting from collectivization. For Ferona there was little doubt that the state did everything it could to thwart the survival of the rural Ukrainian population. At the height of the crisis, when the only way for many villagers to survive was to send their children to cities, a passport and registration system was introduced to keep collective farmers out of urban areas. The border with Russia was closed, and food imports were not allowed in.[1] Miron Dolot, in Execution by Hunger: The Hidden Holocaust, an eyewitness account from a survivor of the Holodomor, points out that when villagers resorted to eating cats and dogs, quotas for dog and cat skins were suddenly invented. Authorities went around shooting the animals, and the carcasses were guarded and left to rot. When people resorted to wild birds, rodents, and fish, Stalin proclaimed that all living things were owned by the state. In some cases, being alive was considered counterrevolutionary because it demonstrated that the collective farmers and their families were getting food from somewhere. By the summer of 1933, an estimated seven million Ukrainians had starved to death. Unbelievably, it was a tragedy unacknowledged by the Soviet Union until the late 1980s.[2]

In the morning Ferona took me down to the velvety grass by the riverbank with her four goats. She had promised to sing for me, and after tethering her little crew she put her hands together in prayer and wet her lips.

> I was born in Ukraine
> I lived here a long, long time
> Now they are sending me away
> What is happening to me?
> They will send me out of Ukraine
> They will send me away
> Oh, oi oi oi
> I am leaving small children behind
> And adults go away with me
> My small children are not ill
> Other people will feed them
> And I will be in Siberia
> Remembering my children.

From her crumpled, shrunken body came a deep, gravelly voice. It wavered a little at first but soon strengthened.

> And who's going to feed him
> When he'll be on his deathbed?
> And who's going to feed him?
> How is he going to live?

She brought her hands to her face, and, as though an unhealed wound were breaking open, her eyes cracked and tears came, running over her fragile eyelids and down the worn, eroded gullies of her cheeks. She edged close, clutched my hands, and searched my eyes for a fragment of consolation. But then her grip loosened and she surrendered to an empty gaze. Although millions had suffered with her, most had died long ago, lucky to survive just one of the tragic waves of madness that had swept Ukraine in the twentieth century.

THE SURROUNDINGS FELL away. Avoiding villages, I camped in hidden valleys and cut through fields and forests. At night I sat by the campfire feeling the cool air fall on my back and the glow of coals on my face. I listened to the horses grazing and watched the moon rise into clear, starry skies.

I tread a knife-edge of wonderment and gloom. While Ferona would probably pass away as peacefully as a fallen autumn leaf, Dad, who had lived in one of the safest countries on earth, had met a violent end. Was it destiny? Luck? Karma? Or was life's path random? How was it that Ferona embodied the optimism of the children from the school in Rivne even though she had seen the very worst of humankind?

It wasn't until one stormy afternoon several days west of Dumaniv that I was pulled out of my introspection again. I had reached the river Zbruch, a shallow flurry of water that had once been the border between the Russian and Polish empires. For many during the 1930s it had been a cruel demarcation line between life and death.

On the eastern bank, where I pulled up, Stalin's terror had reigned. On the far bank the churches had remained intact, the people had continued their farming traditions, and there had been little hint of a famine. Until World War II, in fact, the land west of the Zbruch had passed between the Austro-Hungarian and Polish empires but had never been part of Russia. It was only when the Red Army routed the Nazis that Ukrainian land as far as the plains of Hungary was absorbed by the Soviet Union. Nowadays the Zbruch is the border between Khmel'nyts'kyi Oblast and Ternopil Oblast and is one of the fault lines of the east-west cultural divide in modern Ukraine.

As I crossed the river and carried on through a village, rain bucketed down and dark brooding clouds swallowed the sun. Even in the dimness, through the frame of my tightly pulled hood, the atmosphere in the village at once felt different. There were tall two-story homes, a flaking old church that looked to be Catholic rather than Orthodox, and shopfronts built onto ornate buildings of an unfamiliar style. I rode through the main street, then up a muddy track between twisted wooden homes that took me out over a crop of winter-sown wheat. I hurried on another few hours toward the town of Bilche Zolote (the name means "white gold"). Ismet Zaatov from Crimea had contacted some friends along my route, and earlier I had received a message that the mayor of Bilche Zolote was awaiting my arrival.

The nature of my meeting with the mayor in Bilche Zolote proved characteristic of the man I came to know in coming days. Long after darkness had descended I was clopping along the main street wondering how I might find the mayor, when there came someone running into my path wearing a suit and tie. He had a chubby face, a stomach to match, and the stocky, square frame of a bulldog.

"Off you get! We're just about to start dinner!" he instructed in a raspy voice. Introductions had to wait as he seized me by the collar, asked someone to watch my horses, and ushered me inside a bar for a celebratory pint.

Come morning I was left with no doubt as to who was in charge. I had barely pried my eyes open when Yaroslav burst into the room in a frilly apron holding out a tray of steaming hot eggs, sausages, salad, bread, and tea. He dragged his nose over the feast in appreciation, then put it on my lap.

"Here you are, traveler! Courtesy of Bilche Zolote's first-class hotel!"

This was just the beginning of my time under the wing of the eccentric and at times overzealous mayor, who viewed my arrival as the chance to put his town on the map. Every moment was a photo opportunity, and in coming days he would treat me to aromatic baths, royal tours of the town's historical sights, feasts with local dignitaries, and even a school concert put on at his insistence. Although he possessed an overinflated sense of self-importance that tended to rub locals the wrong way, his enthusiasm and raw energy were infectious. I was more than happy for my journey to fall into his hands while I enjoyed the opportunity to recuperate physically and gather my first insights into western Ukraine.

My days in Bilche Zolote were centered on Yaroslav's office, where on my first visit he sat behind a large desk, directed me to a seat, and proclaimed that he was the "owner of this region" and that he didn't have to "answer to anyone." He was scheming to set up a national press conference based on my arrival and generally spent his time reaching for the phone and fax. His press release was titled "Great World-Famous Australian Traveler Arrives in Bilche Zolote." During the work session that first day, I trawled my eyes around his walls and shelves, which were plastered with flags, photos, books, and emblems, all in one way or another representative of the spectrum of Ukraine's divided politics and indicative of the crisis currently engulfing the country. Two small flags in a vase on his desk symbolized the main opposing forces at work: the flag of the pro-Western and NATO-aspiring Orange Revolution Party, and the flag of the Russian-leaning Party of the Regions.

Although the president of Ukraine at that time, Viktor Yushchenko, had been swept to power during the 2004–5 Orange Revolution, the Party of the Regions had since won a majority in parliamentary elections and installed Yushchenko's archenemy, Viktor Yanukovych, as prime minister. In the beginning of April 2007, only days before I flew back to Ukraine, Yushchenko had dismissed the government and called for fresh elections. Yanukovych was now contesting the decree in the constitutional court, and Kiev was once more flooded with thousands of demonstrators. In some Russian media there was talk of civil war and the potential for the country to split into separate states. The political deadlock reflected deep cultural divisions in Ukraine. In the west of the country, people were staunchly nationalist and identified themselves as European. In the Russian-colonized east and south, the population was predominantly Russian-speaking and -leaning.

As a western Ukrainian himself, Yaroslav's bipartisan display of flags was out of official decorum only—his true sentiment was embodied by a large black and red flag on the shelf. It was the historical banner of the Ukrainian Insurgent Army (UPA). Next to the UPA flag was a large portrait of the late Ukrainian nationalist Stepan Bandera. Lauded as a hero in the west but a villain in the east, Bandera was a divisive figure who had led a faction of the Ukrainian Nationalists Organization (OUN) whose ultimate aim in the 1930s and 1940s was to create an independent state in today's western Ukrainian provinces. The UPA was the military wing of the organization and had fought a guerrilla-style campaign first against the Poles and then against the Soviets until it disbanded in 1949. Bandera, who was eventually assassinated by KGB agents in Munich, had emerged in the wake of the collapse of the Soviet Union as a symbol of Ukrainian independence and anti-Russian sentiment.[3]

From here onward to Hungary I could expect more nationalist sentiment, and in the main I was sympathetic to western Ukrainians who were struggling to salvage their cultural identity. Most interesting for me, however, was that this cultural divide seemed broadly reminiscent of the fractious Slavic princedoms the Mongols had so famously exploited during their invasion all those centuries ago. Many Russians and Ukrainians had lamented to me that "if only" the Slavs could have unified, then the Mongols never would had advanced to Europe. Little, it seemed, had changed.

The first of many tours of Bilche Zolote got under way with typical gusto. In the "first-class" sanatorium I was ordered to strip off and enter a special pine-oil bath. Yaroslav stood over me cuddling one of the sanatorium's nurses, to whom Yaroslav had apparently lost his virginity in his youth. "That was thirty-seven years ago!" she yelped as Yaroslav moved to bury his face in her bosom. This was just one example of the mayor's rather lewd behavior, which went as far as climbing up a stone statue of an undressed woman and posing with his tongue caressing a giant nipple. On several occasions he told me that if I needed a girl, I only had to whisper the word.

Among the multiple other tours, one of the more memorable was riding through the countryside in a traditional horse wagon squeezed between two teenage girls dressed in traditional outfits. Yaroslav sat back, commanding the girls to sing. Between songs he told elaborate tales of his kingdom. The driver, who had been convinced to drag out his old horse and cart for the occasion, swore monotonously.

It was on the third evening that things began to spiral out of control. I was invited for dinner with the principal of the high school, and Yaroslav was adamant the horses remain grazing after dark on the soccer oval. "Don't worry! Nothing can happen in this town, it is mine! I will order the caretaker to guard the horses while we are gone!" But when we returned around midnight the caretaker was passed out, snoring. Ogonyok and Kok were gone.

In that moment Yaroslav's authority disintegrated. You could see a growing look of terror as it dawned on him that his grand PR plans were fast unraveling—half of the country's media were due to turn up for a press conference in the morning, and what they would get was a story about horse thievery!

As panic spread through us all, Yaroslav, the principal, and her husband took off in three different directions. The security guard was resigned. "What's the point? It's common knowledge that the horse will be at a meat factory by morning. You will never find them," he said.

I raced around blindly on Taskonir trying to pick up the scent, but after two hours all seemed lost . . . that was, until the sheriff phoned to report the sighting of a local leading two horses out of town. I later learned this person was an orphan with a history of crime who was currently on parole; being caught would have meant a long jail sentence. Word was that the sheriff managed to find him and convince him to return the horses, or at least that was what we came to believe, because at about 1:00 A.M. a mysterious figure came running through the street with my horses before letting them go and vanishing into the night.

Come the press conference I was itching to wrest control of my journey back from Yaroslav. After I finished giving interviews, there was one last event—the school concert. The poor principal, who had been told only the day before about the impending extravaganza, scrambled to get the kids in traditional dress. When the time came, Yaroslav changed into traditional clothes too and addressed the crowd with an exuberant speech. During the group photo, he leaped from the steps at the school entrance onto an unsuspecting Taskonir and paraded for the TV cameras with a fist punching into the sky.

In the afternoon I dug out my gear and attempted to ride off. It wasn't going to be that easy, though. On the way out I was serenaded by the local choir and offered vodka and food, and by the time I got going it was almost dark. I made it as far as a lake and thought I was in the clear—until 3:00 A.M., when there came shouting. I wearily zipped open the tent, and there in the pouring rain, with his leather jacket and "I Love Ukraine" T-shirt soaked through, was Yaroslav.

"It's such a beautiful place here, isn't it? I was so worried they would steal your horses! I came to protect you!" He had walked on foot for 10 km to reach me, and now looked in with crazed drunken eyes and dangled a pint-sized fish in my face. "Come and see the rest of my catch and I will make us fish soup! Only I'm wet—can I borrow a coat?"

I gave him my rain jacket and went back to sleep, but no sooner had I drifted off than I was woken by a bloodcurdling noise. Not far away under a little tarp shelter I discovered Yaroslav. He lay on the ground, covered in mud, curled up with his pet dog. The two of them had their noses pointed skyward and were howling a duet.

"Listen, Tim! This Bilche Zolote dog can sing! Where is your video camera?"

With what little strength I had left I rode out, and even when the howling faded I didn't look back.

A WEEK FROM Bilche Zolote I pulled into camp on the banks of the river Prut near the city of Kolomiya. The grass was long, the evening dry and dusty; the tender spring foliage on the trees fluttered in the breeze.

The last few days had felt like more of a recovery from Yaroslav than from Dad's passing, but either way the horses, Tigon, and I were rejuvenated. I felt ready to commit myself to the task at hand. As I gazed to the western horizon, there, embroiled in dark stormy clouds, was my first glimpse of the Carpathian Mountains.

23

AMONG THE HUTSULS

"Where there is a Hutsul, there you will find a horse."

Vincenz Stanislaw, 1936
On the High Uplands: Sagas, Songs,
Tales and Legends of the Carpathians

BEYOND THE VILLAGE of Sheshory the mountains closed in and the sky shrank to a strip. I followed a river in a deep, narrow valley where steep slopes barbed with spiny spruce rose around my little caravan. In the late afternoon dark gray clouds avalanched from unseen peaks, flooding the valley and blotting out the sun. Thunder cracked, a gust of cold air hurtled past us, and a heavy rain tore down.

In the evening the sun made a fleeting reappearance, backlighting a bedraggled babushka who hobbled along the roadside carrying a sack of hand-cut grass on her back. She looked up at me with great concern.

"Are you off to the *polonina?*" She put her hand on her heart. "You are brave! May God be with you!"

The following morning I was no wiser as to what the word *polonina* meant—that would come later—but I was beginning to appreciate the well wishes. At the head of the valley in the village of Shepit, the road gave way to ridges and peaks with no obvious way through. I could either take a three-day detour back the way I had come and ride on via a main road, or I could try my luck at finding a path over the top.

Opting for the latter, I dismounted and set off up a slope that soon became so steep I could almost lean on it. With each step my panicked lungs sucked for air. Behind, the horses heaved and moaned, sweat dribbling down from the back of their ears, hooves slipping as rocks were dislodged and went clattering down.

Higher up I found a chute used by timber workers for sending logs down from the forest. The rains had turned it into a muddy trench, and after many falls I reached a grassy ledge and collapsed at the hooves of my horses. At first I lay clutching the lead ropes, feeling my eyeballs throb in time with my chest, but as my heart rate subsided I lifted my sights, and the difficulties faded. To the east, back the way we had come, the mountainside dropped away to the foothills of the Carpathians. Lined up like ocean swells were row upon row of forested ridges. The sky was clear, and my eyes floated effortlessly over the same crests and troughs through which we had struggled in recent days. Eventually my focus settled on the horizon where the land tapered off into steppe.

Two and a half years earlier I had perched on a similar slope in the Altai of eastern Kazakhstan and gazed over the steppe from the opposite direction. From such a height the modern age of machines, highways, and state borders had melted into insignificance. The Eurasian steppe had beckoned as a fenceless space that carried on unbroken for a vast distance to the Carpathians. I had visualized it as one giant kingdom, guarded in the east by the Altai and in the west by the Carpathians, beyond each of which lay the respective outposts of Mongolia and Hungary.

Around 7,250 km later, Ogonyok and Taskonir, who had shared that moment with me, were still here, and none of my enchantment from those early days had worn off. Only now, looking to the horizon, what had been an unknown I could recount in vivid detail. When I closed my eyes I could visualize every camp, every lunch stop, the contours of the land, and the faces I had met from the Altai to here.

I reached up to Tigon and scratched his chest. As I did he swung his eyes from the steppe to the steep slope ahead of us. Speckles of his saliva dropped onto my face, and I rolled over on my stomach to share the view of a new unknown.

Above us a rising blanket of mist was snagged on dense alpine forest. Every now and then pointy treetops tore a hole through it, offering fleeting glimpses of craggy peaks that form the periphery of the second-longest mountain range in Europe—a range that stretches in a horseshoe embrace around the frontiers of Poland, Slovakia, Ukraine, and Romania like Europe's insulation against the East.

Through this terrain the Mongols had once forged a path on their way to conquering Hungary. Setting off in the deep snows of winter in early 1241, they had somehow been able to navigate the labyrinth of forests and ridges and surge through the guarded high passes almost as if the mountains presented no barrier.

When King Bela IV of Hungary finally became convinced of the impending invasion, he naively hoped that cutting trees across the paths of the Carpathians and sending extra troops to man the forts would be enough to stop the Mongols, or at least give him time to prepare an army. But, as a measure of the sheer speed of the Mongol advance, only four days after Bela learned that the Mongols had attacked the Carpathian passes, news that they had fallen reached Buda. Once over the mountains, the Mongols flew across Hungary, covering 65 km a day, their advance ending in battles that would see half of Hungary's population wiped out and the defeat of some of the most professional and prestigious armies of Europe.

Nowadays the Carpathians stood in a different era, crisscrossed by asphalt highways that connect Ukraine with central Europe. Some of the famous passes through which the Mongols had forged, are now little more than scenic overlooks where roadside souvenir and fast-food sellers take advantage of through traffic.

Riding along such roads, I could not hope to appreciate what the Mongols achieved, nor rekindle a sense of what it might have been like for these hardy nomads crossing into Europe. My plan was to avoid roads where possible and travel through the highest and most rugged section of the Ukrainian Carpathians, where, I had learned recently, there existed something that was more likely to capture the spirit of the nomads than was a ride along a highway.

Back in Crimea, the eyes of Ismet Zaatov, the Tatar deputy minister for culture, had lit up when I mentioned the Carpathians. "Our brothers live there—the Hutsuls," he told me. "They are an example to us all, keeping their culture alive under the fists of the Russians. Most important for you are their horses, which they say are descendants of those left behind from the Mongols when they retreated from Europe in 1242."

Where the Mongols had succeeded in crossing the Carpathians, the invasion of tractors, combines, bulldozers, and the penetrating policies of the Soviet machine had apparently failed. According to Ismet, the Hutsuls were a unique ethnic group who lived in the most inaccessible valleys and alpine plains, relying on the forest and the herding of sheep and cattle for subsistence. Their land, Hoverla, orbiting around the tallest peak of the Ukrainian Carpathians, was broadly known as Hutsulshchyna, and while there is no consensus as to the origins of the Hutsuls, the various hypotheses gave me reason to be excited.

Some believe the name *Hutsul* is derived from the old Slavic term *kochul*, which means "nomad," and that they are possibly a Turkic people who fled to the mountains during the Mongol invasion of Russia. The more contemporary belief is that the name comes from the Romanian word *hotul*, meaning "outlaw," and that they were descendants of a Slavic people who had lived in the Carpathians since the fourth century.

"When you get there, Tim, please give me a call," Ismet had said. "I know the governor of the region, and I will make sure I arrange a special greeting for you."

THERE CAME A shout from somewhere above in the forest, then the thud of an axe on wood. My horses stood to attention, their ears pointed forward like pistols. I pulled myself up in a hurry. From the mist above, four stocky men and their similarly built horses materialized towing freshly cut logs. They struggled to arrest the slide of the timber before coming to an unsteady halt.

"Good morning, men! Can you show me the way over to Berezhnytsia?" I called, referring to a hamlet marked on the map on the far side of the ridge.

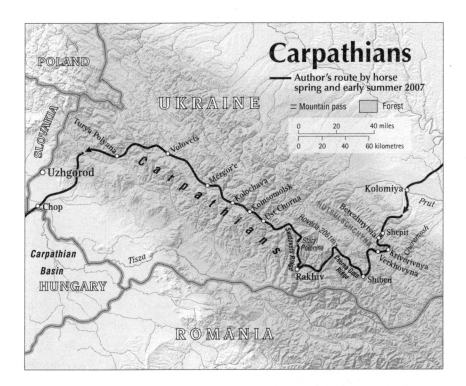

Like horsemen of the steppe, they took their time to respond, first running their eyes over my equipment and tilting their heads sideways to peer under the legs of my horses, checking their status. As always, attention narrowed down to Ogonyok, who they all agreed would make a fine timber-pulling horse.

It wasn't long before the youngest of the men unharnessed his horse, leaped on bareback, and led the way. We entered the forest via a track so narrow and crowded with crisscrossing branches that I was forced to dismount and follow the horses on foot. The fir trees and mist became ever denser, the sunlight withered, and Ogonyok struggled to squeeze between moss-laden trunks with his plastic pack boxes.

At the top of the ridge we came to a wind-raked saddle, then dropped beneath the cloud on the other side. When the mist had cleared, we brought the horses to a stop. From where we stood, the mountainside fell away into space. Across the valley on the opposite slopes, timber homes bordered by silver-gray fences and haystacks appeared painted onto a vertical canvas of green. The jingle of bells floated across to us from a flock of sheep making their way up toward an alpine meadow.

I had been accustomed to the drab, derelict collectives of Russia and Ukraine, and so Ismet's account of the Hutsuls had been hard to believe. But now, as I gazed down into this otherworldly valley, my doubts vanished.

Sometimes such rosy first impressions are fleeting. Not so here. Over the next month my developing picture of Hutsulshchyna would prove to remain true to this fairy-tale exterior—a place elevated from the realities of both my personal challenges and the issues of the societies I had passed through. I would find the land and its people so engrossing that I could temporarily forget about the past and live unconcerned about all that the future held.

My introduction to the Hutsul people began in earnest at a cottage practically at the tree line. The young horseman pulled up at the gate. "They will certainly take you in for the night—that's the Hutsul way!" he said, before using a twig for as a whip and galloping back up the slope.

True to the horseman's pledge, a portly woman followed by her sheepish husband and elderly father emerged and ushered me in. Even before they introduced themselves they had invited me to stay for a week. "First things first, though," the lady, named Maliya, said, hands on her generous hips. "You need a bath."

As it turned out, Berezhnytsia was not so much a village but a community of around eighty homes and corrals sparsely dotted about the high slopes at the head of this remote valley. To reach my host's cottage—like most others in Berezhnytsia—one needed to walk or ride along steep, ankle-breaking paths. The only evidence of the mechanical era was a deeply rutted track at the bottom of the valley, apparently bulldozed in the 1960s but rarely used.

To some it would have seemed a tough, isolated life, but not to Maliya. After I had washed, she fed me sour milk and blueberries and told me that they had "everything" in Hutsulshchyna. The cattle provided meat and milk, berries from the forest were plentiful, and every winter they harvested small fir trees, which they took to eastern Ukraine to sell as decorative New Year trees. Having traveled through regions where collectivization had wiped out untold thousands of hamlets and family farms, I found the independent life she described novel and difficult to comprehend.

I asked her how it could be, and Vasili, her father stepped in to explain. He told me that the Hutsuls had never surrendered their homes. After World War II the Soviet state had officially taken over the land, but when the Soviet Union fell, the property was returned to the original owners or their descendants. "We might be Ukrainian, but we are first and foremost Hutsuls," he said.

Judging by Maliya's two-story timber cottage built into a cutting on the slope, the Hutsuls had also dodged the attack on cultural identity and traditional craftsmanship that had devastated so many ethnic groups across Eurasia under Stalin. I let my eyes filter down from the steep angled roof of a structure that could only be described as a work of art. The ridging that ran along the hips of the roof was decorated with thousands of motifs cut from shiny zinc sheets. Most of these seemed to be in the form of eagles and men reaching to the sky. The zinc cladding on the gable was worked into an extravagant mural of circle, diamond, and star shapes and featured depictions of animals. There were lions—a tradition, according to Vasili, that dated to an era when these predators still roamed Europe—encircled by doves. Framing them were flowers, suns, and thousands of other patterns, the details of which were only obvious up close.

The interior of the house was something else. Doors featured multicolored glass panels, and the ceilings were awash with hand-painted peacocks, wrens, and a dizzying array of floral patterns. There were woven mats and rugs, hand-woven blankets, Orthodox Christian icons, wood carvings, and a range of hanging carpets. The centerpiece of the house was the furnace, painted a lurid purple with repeated themes of lions, birds, and deer.

With the two men shyly following in tow, Maliya took me to her room and pulled down a wooden picture frame with a black and white photo of a young couple in traditional dress. "These are my grandparents. Before deciding to build here, my grandfather watched carefully for the places where the cows liked to lie down. Once he found this place, he spent a night sleeping on the earth. According to Hutsul belief, if one dreams about cattle, then it is a sign the site is blessed."

Ivan, her husband, disappeared into the attic, then came back timidly holding an antique that wouldn't have been out of place in Mongolia. Carved with symmetrical lines, diamonds, and coils, it was a wooden saddle so small and delicate that Ivan could hold it up with two fingers. It was clearly designed for a short-backed horse. Vasili and Ivan were convinced of its origins: "Just like the horses and the saddles, there is Mongol influence among us Hutsuls! Some of us have high cheekbones and slanty eyes!" they chuckled.

There were untold centuries of history in this saddle, but Vasili sadly explained that the man who had crafted it had died thirty years before. "These days everyone in our valley rides bareback," he said. He now used the saddle for ferrying supplies to the house on a packhorse.

IN THE MORNING I stepped into the theater of high peaks and forest. I felt at ease. To see the horses grazing and Tigon off the leash brought a sense of calm and completeness I had not found in the villages and towns. I could sympathize with the words of Stanislaw Vincenz, an influential Polish writer who grew up among the Hutsuls at the turn of the twentieth century: "All they [the Hutsuls] know about towns is that they stink till you choke, that there is no water there, and nothing to be seen, and they are terribly short of room . . . A town is a calamity, a work of the devil." In the Hutsul uplands, according to him, "distances and journeys" were "not recounted in hours, nor—God forbid—in minutes, like trains, but in days and weeks." There was a sense of time here "not to be compared with foreign time."

For me there was nevertheless a pressing need to move on. For years I had been lobbying the Australian Broadcasting Corporation (ABC) to support a proposal for a documentary film about my journey. Just before my dad passed away, the ABC had promised a development grant sufficient to pay for veteran Australian adventure cinematographer Mike Dillon to join me and film the kind of shots impossible alone. He planned to spend two or three weeks with me on foot, and I had prearranged a rendezvous point not far from Berezhnytsia in a village called Krivorivnya. Although Mike wasn't due for a few days, word had it that the priest of Krivorivnya was awaiting my arrival.

It took a day to descend to the Cheremosh, a fast-moving river that carved a serpentine path through the bowels of the mountains. Compared to where I had just come from, the air was damp, the sky crowded in, and there was even an asphalt road. But as I rode into Krivorivnya, a string of homes built between the bottom of the slopes and the rapids of the Cheremosh, it was clear that the town was anything but the "work of the devil."

Striding up the street came a man so much larger than life that the mountains shrank around him. He stood 2 m tall and was built like an ox; his long, flowing dark hair and bushy beard were matched by a black robe dragging at his heels. He had eyebrows that spread over his face like the wings of an eagle, drawing attention to dark, deep-set eyes. In another life he had been a Hare Krishna devotee, but the large golden cross that bounced about his chest left no doubt as to his prevailing faith. In fact, if ever there was a reincarnation of Jesus Christ, then it was he who now had his eyes locked on me and was fast approaching.

"Ribaruk, Ivan, priest of Krivorivnya, welcome!" he bellowed. I surrendered my hand to his bear-like grip.

Ivan and I got along like old friends from the beginning. Nudging forty years of age, he was still bristling with a kind of rebellious youth, and out of his robes could well have been mistaken for a charismatic rock star. During his student days, mountaineering and travel had been his passion. In fact, it had been while climbing in the high Pamir Mountains of Tajikistan that he resolved to become a priest. "I reached a peak around six thousand metres high and realized that I didn't want to go down. Below it was full of problems that humans had created, and I just wanted to keep climbing up to the sky," he told me.

After completing theological studies, he had returned to the playground of his childhood in Krivorivnya, where at the young age of twenty-nine he was elected priest of the parish. He had since married a local poet, Oksana. These days Ivan did not have much time for mountaineering, but he still put his skills to good use. One of his chief responsibilities was to bless all the houses in the village and the outlying mountain communities—about six hundred—as well as the rivers, streams, and wells that were within the boundaries of his parish. To do this involved setting off on a two-week trekking expedition in winter every year.

I would spend a week in Krivorivnya, lodged at a guesthouse on the church grounds. During this time I came to appreciate that for Ivan, Ukrainian Orthodox Christianity—as opposed to the Russian denomination—was a profound symbol of Ukrainian independence. More specifically, his church in Krivorivnya had remained open since 1620, defying closures during Soviet times. With handwritten scriptures in the Hutsul dialect and traditions unique to the region, the church, as Ivan said, lay at the heart of Hutsul life and culture.

Only one day after arriving I returned with Ivan to Berezhnytsia, where a ceremony in honor of Saint Nikolai had been scheduled. To get there we joined a throng of babushkas, elderly men, and children hitching a ride on the back of a former army truck. On the last stretch of road before town the truck threatened to slide. Up on top we clung to swaying slabs of beer and soft drinks.

The wooden church where the celebration was to be held was situated at the base of the head of the valley. As we arrived, young and old were converging from the slopes. Elderly men steeled themselves down narrow paths on walking staffs, and babushkas straddled wooden fences. Some teenage boys rode horses down slopes so steep they nearly rested the back of their head on the horse's rump as they went.

It was the kind of clear day when the sky appears close, and in the unfiltered light, the traditional dress worn by the people glittered from afar. The men wore stiff bowler hats, known as krysani, and heavy, sheepskin vests, called kyptars, embellished with braided multicolored cords and all manner of shiny buttons, sequins, and metal studs. Some hats were more extravagant than others, covered by hundreds if not thousands of these bright spangles and topped off with feathers. The women wore long embroidered dresses and handcrafted jewelry ranging from gold and silver coin necklaces to glass beads fitted tightly around the throat. There was many a teary eye as this rush of color congregated. Ivan and Vasili—my hosts from earlier—were among them. "You see," Vasili said, "we Hutsuls don't just wear our clothes for show. They carry the soul of our ancestors and of our belief in God."

There was no clear-cut beginning or end to the proceedings. The hundreds of people who had come to celebrate could not fit inside the church, and so there was a slow shuffling queue moving in through the door at the front and out another. Inside, Ivan and two other priests went through an exhaustive series of prayers and songs, acknowledging those who reached the front with a swinging thurible casting thick incense smoke. The interior of the church was filled with the same overwhelming color as Maliya's house, but with the addition of a sophisticated network of fluorescent green, purple, and white disco lights flashing robotically around the icons of Saint Nikolai.

It must have been two or three hours by the time Ivan, sweating like a shaman in a trance, led the congregation outside and stood before a wooden barrel of holy water. There, adorned with a silky orange and golden mantle, he held up a cross to the sky and went into deep whispers of prayer. When this was done he lowered the cross into the water before again raising it and patting it dry. As his prayers came to an end the crowd descended to drink from the barrel.

After the ceremony Ivan changed into simpler vestments, champagne was popped, violins were brought out, and we retired to a nearby cottage, where dance and song hummed through the wooden floors and walls. Our celebrations were rounded off by a visit to an eighty-four-year-old hatmaker called Vasil, who had been making traditional clothing from the age of sixteen. In his remote mountain abode, he invited me to a dark, hidden room in the attic. When he turned on a flashlight I realized that the hard wooden shape pushing against my thigh was a coffin.

"This is older than you are, boy!" he said, grinning. "Made of light wood, too, so that when they carry me out of here, they don't drop me! Every real Hutsul must make his own coffin by the time he is forty." He lifted the lid. There, laid out, was a traditional costume including boots, trousers, and a hat. Vasil shuffled around and brought out a metal head-stone plate engraved with his name and birth date. A blank space was set aside for the day of his passing. "Hutsuls don't fear death. But we must prepare to meet God, and for that it is expected you will be dressed in your best outfit."

On the way back down Ivan described a Hutsul legend: "When God was giving out land the Hutsuls turned up late and all that was left were these harsh, infertile mountains. However to compensate, he gave them generous helpings of creativity."

ON THE EVENING of May 25 a rather jet-lagged Mike piled out of a car with his backpack and camera gear. The lanky sixty-one-year-old Australian cut a humble figure. Soft-spoken, with wide blue eyes and wavy silver hair, he was dressed in worn cargo trousers, creased old boots, and a checkered shirt. I'd warned him about weight limits for baggage on the horses, and he had kept to his word, bringing only two sets of clothes.

Ahead of us lay a crossing of the Chorna Gora, a wall of peaks that rise in the heart of Hutsulshchyna, including Ukraine's highest mountain, Hoverla, at 2,061 km. In my short time in Krivorivnya, I had learned it was a place enshrined in local legend through songs and folklore about tales of high adventure—such as that of the eighteenth-century outlaw Oleksa Dobosz, known as the Robin Hood of the Hutsuls.[1]

Hutsul shepherds and their families had been making annual migrations to the high slopes on and around Chorna Gora for centuries. There in the summer months they grazed their animals in alpine meadows known as polonina. Most of the older folk in Krivorivnya had worked as shepherds on the Chorna Gora in their youth, and while they admired my plan to cross the peaks, they had stern warnings. "Every year shepherds are killed by lightning! You could be caught in a snowstorm! Eaten by wolves! Or, God forbid, lost in the forest—there are such big, dense forests that you can easily get lost for days."

Our send-off from Krivorivnya was marked by a traditional ceremony—an event Ivan said was reminiscent of the annual farewell for shepherds and their families traveling to the high slopes. With Ivan leading on foot, a drumroll, violins, and a long horn known as a trembita heralded our approach to the front gates of the village school.[2] As I urged the nervous horses closer, a group of pretty girls in traditional dress stepped forward with wreaths of crepe-paper flowers to tie to the horse's halters. When the horses shied away, the girls found a more appreciative recipient in Tigon. As all three wreaths were tied around his collar, he sat with his chin raised high.

Ivan had insisted we take someone to help us find our way across the highest peaks, and at his request a veteran mountaineer, Yuri Wadislow, and a man called Grigori from the mountain rescue squad had agreed to come. For the final part of the ceremony, Yuri, Grigori, Mike, and I lined up to be blessed. Ivan came to us one by one, said a prayer, and doused us with holy water. He blessed the horses, too, and said a prayer for Tigon.

It took a long day's ride to reach the outpost village of Shiben, which lay at the feet of the Chorna Gora. Along the way a thunderstorm smacked into the mountains, followed by a torrential downpour, turning the Cheremosh into a dirty brown torrent. The river had broken its banks and torn apart several timber bridges. If the conditions were so turbulent down here, it was daunting to imagine what it was like up high.

In the morning Mike, Yuri, and Grigori shouldered backpacks and we heaved our way up a forest path. We were not the only people making for the polonina, however. Not far into the trek a squall of curses and neighing rang out through the forest. Near the base of a particularly steep track I came across two Hutsul horses harnessed to a heavily laden cart. The cart had jackknifed and sat at right angles in the mud. The drunken cart drivers were beating the horses with straps and chains. They wanted to borrow my horses to help pull the cart up, and when I refused, the abuse turned on me. A man with a balding head and fiery eyes flew at Kok and Ogonyok with his fist: "Come here or I will cut you down the Bandera way!" When I backed away, the men calmed down a little and explained they were heading to a polonina known as Vesnyak, where they planned to live for three to four months. Cattle and sheep from Shiben had been driven up ahead.

Mike, Yuri, and the others caught up, and we carried on. That afternoon we reached the alpine meadows, and after overnighting in a cluster of knotted pines we began the climb in earnest.

Not far above camp we moved into a shroud of cloud and onto the top of the main ridge. The mist was so thick it felt like we were burrowing our way through the mountains, but at times when it thinned out I caught glimpses of the abyss that fell away on both sides. We paused by memorials to two young boys who had died the previous summer during a lightning storm. Those markers were the first of many we would see in the coming weeks.

When evening came we had been moving for almost ten hours, the mist had not lifted, and we were all feeling a little frayed. Grigori and Yuri had begun to bicker between themselves.

After pitching camp, Mike and I climbed up to a peak just in time to see the mist fall away and reveal our first full view of the Chorna Gora ridge. Like the twisted torso of a serpent, it stretched ahead, joining a series of peaks. Along the edges scabby snowdrifts formed cornices. Above it all hovered the distant dome of Hoverla.

The Carpathians weren't the tallest peaks in the world, but from here they had a grandeur befitting the history they had played theater to. Not only had the Mongols surged across these mountains, but the plethora of nomads before them—Huns, Scythians, and the Magyars, to name a few. In more recent times, as evidenced by stone markers we had seen along the ridge, it had also been the shifting boundary between the Austro-Hungarian and Polish empires, not to mention the scene of fierce fighting between Nazis and the Red Army.

In the morning we were back on the ridge. Clouds were colliding with the east face, then hurtling up like waves, breaking over the lip of the cliffs, and crashing down to the west. Unperturbed, Tigon spent most of the time scouring the slopes, appearing from time to time poised over great precipices of ice and rock. More than once he disappeared for an extended time, and I was sure, as I had been so many times before on my journey, that he was gone forever.

Just after lunch we reached the first of several impasses. The ridge had narrowed to a razorback where one slip on steep rock or snow meant that the entire caravan would tumble down. After scouting the route, we took a line along the eastern side of the ridge. The first section was around 50 m of rock, leading to a snowdrift. I began with Taskonir, watching as he nervously inched his way forward. His hooves scraped and slipped across the broad faces of the rocks but, fortunately, caught on to cracks and gaps. The last 10 m were the most delicate, requiring navigation down a ledge to a small flat rock. Taskonir studied the way ahead, then came down in a controlled slide, coming safely to rest at my feet.

Ogonyok was less elegant. He stood on the point of a rock with his front legs together, his half-tonne frame and 50 kg load teetering over the edge. With a tug on the lead rope he scraped and slipped his way down, miraculously landing on all fours at the bottom. Kok followed in similar fashion.

The snowdrift proved impossible to negotiate, and so there began an operation to get the horses up over the ridge to the far side, where it was rocky but free of snow. The whole procedure took a couple of hours, by which stage Yuri, who was inexperienced with horses and accustomed to mountaineering in far more dangerous terrain, became impatient, shouting, "Those Mongols certainly didn't come over this way, did they?"

Yuri and Grigori's bickering escalated as we continued. In the end, Yuri strode out ahead, refusing to listen to Grigori, and made his way straight up to the summit of a peak. An hour later we were staring down a face of steep, jagged rocks. Grigori had had enough. "I am going home! I warned you, Yuri! My body can't take any wasted effort!"

By the time we retreated, the sky had turned dark and the heavens opened. Although Mike, Grigori, and I shrank into our raincoats, Yuri came to life. "Tim, you waste time like you are a rich man! In the mountains every second counts!" He had thinly veiled his feelings about this several times. For him, packing carefully and allowing time for the horses to graze and rest were unnecessary. The concept of a multiyear journey and the sustainable cadence and patience it required was beyond him. "We will not get through now! We will have to cut our way through these bushes! People have become lost and died here!" His words were lost in the thunder and rain as I tied the horses up, my mind elsewhere.

If Yuri, who had traveled widely himself, was unable to appreciate the scale of my journey, then how could anyone in Europe have comprehended the Mongols or the threat they posed on the eve of their invasion of Hungary and Poland? By the time the Mongols had reached the Carpathians in 1241, they had already created the largest land empire in history and developed what was arguably the most sophisticated army of the era. Their exploits had included a defeat of much of China, Central Asia, Persia, and more recently Russia.[3] Among the sixty thousand hardened horsemen who had crossed through these mountains, it is not hard to imagine there were men who had been on continuous campaigns for twenty years or more. For them, the Carpathians must have been more like the backwater hills commonly found at home in Mongolia.

In Europe at the time, the truth is that although there was clear evidence of the formidable Mongol threat, few took it seriously. The countries firmly in the Mongols' sights—namely, Hungary and Poland—were more concerned with domestic squabbles, and farther afield Pope

Gregory IX was at war with the Holy Roman Emperor, Frederick II. As a measure of the ignorance among European powers, Pope Gregory had suggested that the supposed Tatar advance was nothing more than a strategy on behalf of his enemies to "unite Christendom against the Lord Pope." When at the eleventh hour King Bela IV of Hungary finally realized the seriousness of the threat facing him, it was too late. Ironically, it seemed that the very Carpathians that ordinarily comforted Europeans with a sense of protection from the East had fatally insulated them from any real understanding of the foe that was approaching at a gallop.

The rain went on for two or three hours. I gave up waiting for it to stop and erected my tent. The horses stood stiffly. Mike retreated to his single-man, coffin-shaped tent, followed by Tigon. We went to bed too exhausted to cook a proper meal.

COME MORNING, THE tension between Yuri and Grigori had dissipated, and it became clear that the struggle of the journey across the Chorna Gora was also over. We found an easy path around the ridge and later passed below the mist-shrouded summit of Hoverla. Climbing the last short stretch to the top was out of the question with the horses.

At the first opportunity Grigori headed down a shortcut to the nearest village. Yuri, who had grown thin and tired, walked silently down the western flanks with us to a valley. The following day he hitched a ride into the town of Rakhiv with Mike and had gone by the time I arrived.

One last challenge lay ahead of me before the mountains promised to drop away to the more gentle mountains on the edge of the Hungarian plain: the crossing of a ridge known as Svidovets. I was confident of managing the Svidovets alone, and after the intensity of the experience with Yuri and Grigori I was relieved it would just be Mike and me for the next couple of weeks.

After restocking with supplies, Mike and I began the process of rising once more into the high mountains—I on horseback, he on foot. The summer heat was cranking up in Rakhiv, and it was a relief to return to the polonina, where the air was thinner and cooler and the sun's ferocity was vulnerable to as little as a single cloud.

On the second day we reached the exposed Svidovets ridge. The weather had stabilized, and we followed sheep tracks across soft green meadows. The terrain was less rocky than the Chorna Gora and better suited to grazing. The jingling of bells from sheep and cows was ever present, punctuated by the gruff commands of shepherds. Wiry men with the same jerky, bandy gait of their sheep sometimes stood in our way, resting on twisted old walking staffs. Their giant leathery hands looked too hardened to have any feeling.

On the evening of the second day we struck camp at a Hutsul summer station known as Staryi Polonina. We had planned to continue at first light, but by dinner Tigon was looking seriously ill. Curled up immobile on a horse blanket, he refused to stand or eat. His condition had been deteriorating for a couple of days. Mike joked that he was missing his girlfriend—a bitch from Krivorivnya with whom he had made friends— but it was more likely due to the raw pig lungs I had fed him in Rakhiv. For the next couple of days I rested Tigon and set the horses free to graze. The break proved an opportunity to learn about the life of the polonina we had heard so much about.

Staryi Polonina was separated into two quarters—one for a cow herding station, and another for sheep. We came to know the latter best. It was primarily run by two lanky seventeen-year-old boys, Bugdan and Vasil. Apart from guarding and grazing sheep, their job was to milk all four hundred animals three times a day—twice in daylight hours, and once at 4:00 A.M. After each session, they carried buckets of fresh milk to a cooking hut where milk was forever being boiled and churned, the curds and whey separated, and cheese hung up to drain. Once a week a horse and cart came to collect the cheese and take it down to the valley, where it was usually mixed with cow's milk and made into a feta-type cheese known as brinza.[4]

The boys had been coming to the polonina as long as they could remember, and the hardworking life in the mountain air had already sculpted them into distinct adult characters. Vasil, the most striking, had long narrow limbs and wore black jeans that fell straight as timber planks down his bony legs. His childlike body—so slight that when he crossed his arms it was as if his shoulders were touching each other—seemed incongruent with the aged look of his face. His front teeth were turning brown and his cheeks were so gaunt that when he smiled, his face collapsed into a series of deep, habitual wrinkles. He smoked regularly, and once I noticed him fiddling with a cigarette in the corner of his mouth while he was milking a sheep. He twitched it up and down until it fell out into the pail of milk. He then simply dipped his hand in, put the cigarette back in his mouth, winked at me, and continued.

After the evening milking session, Mike and I joined the boys for a meal of maize porridge and sour cream, known as *banosh*, washed down with homemade wine. Darkness was descending on the forests below, but the afterglow of sunset still lit up the polonina. A feature of the station was an old dead tree, the branches of which had been turned into a rack for hanging utensils. Pots, pans, sifters, stirrers, ladles, and many other items shone a ghostly silver against the sky. When the stars came out, Vasil pointed across the valley to a distant polonina where a fire lit up the night. "Over there they have bears. That's why they need to keep the fire burning," he said in a deep husky voice.

"And what about here?" I asked.

"Here? Wolves are a regular audience!" he chuckled. "But we aren't afraid of wolves and bears. And this work is a holiday compared to winter, when we work with horses hauling logs through the forest."

During daytime the polonina was a friendly place that would have beckoned with adventure and fun for any young boy. But as the blanket of cool air dropped and the slopes turned black, the sky loomed vast and the mountains became a place for grown men. Vasil and Bugdan fired up stoves in cubicle-like huts where they barely had enough room to lie down in. The sheep settled, and as all fell quiet the huts seemed to shrink until they were nothing more than specks, as lonely as the stars.

At 1:00 A.M. that night I listened from the comfort of my sleeping bag as dogs barked, my horses whinnied, and the sheep rose to flee. Come morning we learned that wolves had emerged from the forest edge. The boys had been up all night.

The responsibility carried by Bugdan and Vasil left a deep impression on Mike and me, and for days afterward neither of us could help reflecting that on their narrow shoulders also weighed the traditions of an entire people. In Ukraine, the people of the Carpathians were renowned as poor, and for every Hutsul boy like Bugdan and Vasil, there were probably ten who had left to try their luck in the cities.

WITH TIGON BACK to health we set off again, and a day and a half beyond Staryi Polonina we climbed beyond a snowfield to reach the highest point of the Svidovets. On the way a hailstorm converged and the mist closed in, stealing away the view in a single swoop. When the worst had passed I dismounted and led the horses along a narrow ridge, watching as the rain came in waves and mist ebbed and flowed.

Late in the afternoon the wind dropped and the mist began to sink. A freshened blue sky was unveiled and the grassy but sheer ridge glistened emerald, appearing to float above the clouds. Just as the sun angled down into our eyes there came an apparition—the shape of fifty horses rising through the mist, their silhouettes coming to a standstill right before us. After some time a horse stepped nervously forward with its head up and nostrils flaring. It seemed to be readying to strike, but then nibbled gently on Ogonyok's mane instead. Pressing on, the herd followed in a symphony of whinnies, snorts, and the rhythmic beat of hooves. Their coarse, split manes, large heads, and thick short necks were all outward signs of their Mongolian origins. Tigon strode out as if he were the proud leader, and when the herd lost interest and stole away at a gallop, he pretended he had gallantly chased them away, shooting an aggressive bark in their direction.

We walked on until the sky turned the same rosy pink as Mike's cheeks—we had both taken a shot of sugar beet vodka to warm up earlier in the day. Then in a small meadow atop of the ridge we called it a day. I sat admiring the horses as they rolled about the luscious green. Tigon came sprinting when he heard the ritual bang of my cooking pot, and we shared, as always, a slice of pig fat before putting on dinner to cook. All day I had been overwhelmed by the sense of freedom. Up here, away from roads and fences, it occurred to me that because my horses were free, they had nowhere to run. We had everything necessary—fresh air, water, open space, and an abundance of grass. In these circumstances it didn't make sense to tie a dog up or fence a horse in.

Mike set up the tripod to film the sun as it slid below the horizon. The mist had pooled deep below, and for the first time it was clear we had nearly reached the end of the ridge. Ahead of us it twisted and fell as a spur to the same kind of low, forested foothills through which I had entered the Carpathians from the east. Far beneath us was a river valley collecting tributes from the many converging slopes on its snaking path to the plains of Hungary.

"Tim, this might be your last real mountain campsite," Mike said, pulling himself away from the viewfinder.

I took out my diary and felt the cold fall. I thought about Dad; I thought about where I had come from in the last three years, and indeed what I had experienced in the last few weeks. Then I thought about going down from here. Mike was right—this tail end of the Svidovets was the end of the polonina, the end of Hutsulshchyna, and the last real mountain between us and the Danube. I was about to enter another world, and it was hard to think that I might not ever share this kind of wild landscape with my little family of horses again.

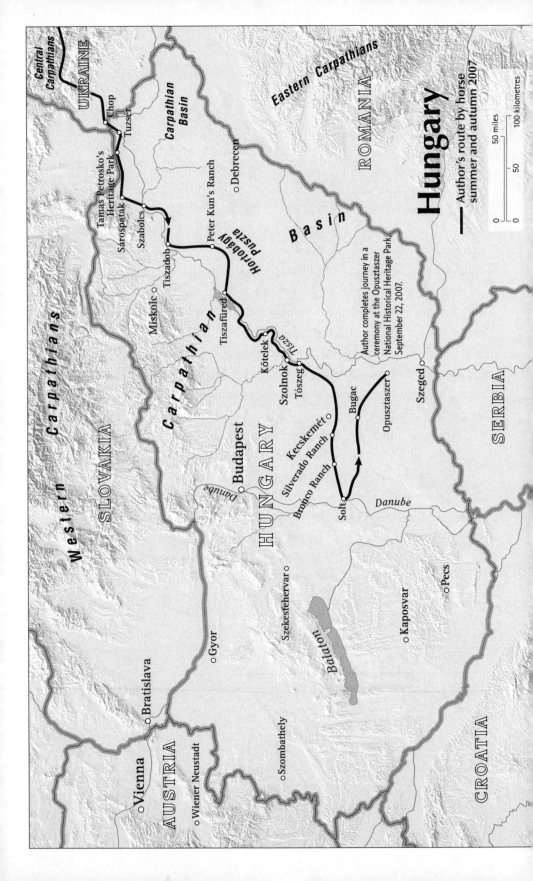

Hungary

— Author's route by horse
    summer and autumn 2007

UKRAINE

Central Carpathians

Chop
Tuzser

Tamas Petrosko's
Heritage Park
Sarospatak
Szabolcs
Tiszadob

Carpathian Basin

Carpathian Basin

Eastern Carpathians

ROMANIA

Peter Kun's Ranch

Debrecen

Hortobágy puszta

Basin

Miskolc

Tiszafüred

Kötelek

Tisza

Szolnok
Tószeg

Author completes journey in a
ceremony at the Opusztaszer
National Historical Heritage Park,
September 22, 2007.

Bugac

Opusztaszer

Szeged

SERBIA

Kecskemét
Silverado Ranch
Bronco Ranch

Budapest

Danube

HUNGARY

Solt

Danube

SLOVAKIA

Western Carpathians

Gyor

Szekesfehervar

Balaton

Kaposvar

Pecs

Bratislava

Vienna

Wiener Neustadt

AUSTRIA

Szombathely

CROATIA

50 miles
50
100 kilometres
0
0

24

THE END
OF THE WORLD

"The keeping of herds on free range is not more 'primitive' than the other method, nor is it more sophisticated. It is simply a quite different approach to the problem . . ."

—Miklos Jankovich, *They Rode into Europe:*
  The Fruitful Exchange in the Arts of
  Horsemanship Between East and West

IN THE SUMMER of 1240, the Mongol army was resting in the shadows of the Carpathians, poised to invade central Europe. Ever since the grand kurultai of 1235 in Mongolia, they had been steadily conquering territory to the west under the leadership of the veteran general Subodei and Genghis Khan's grandson Batu.[1] In 1238 they had defeated the powerful nomadic Kipchaks—known in Europe as the Cumans, and henceforth in this book by this name—and after fattening their horses on the rich steppe grasslands between the Sea of Azov and the Caspian Sea, they went on to subjugate Russia, culminating with the siege of Kiev.[2]

Despite overwhelming evidence of the Mongols' superior military and the threat they posed, the reality was that Europe was still a deeply fractured political landscape. The Mongolians—experts in gathering detailed intelligence—were fully aware of the infighting and ready to exploit it.

Hungary was first and foremost in the Mongols' sights. A country in the heart of the so-called Carpathian Basin, it offered the strategic gates to Central Europe and the most suitable country in Europe for grazing their army of horses. There was also a convenient pretext for invading: during the Mongols' conquest of the Cumans, forty thousand nomad families had fled to Hungary, where King Bela IV had offered them refuge in return for conversion to Catholicism. Aware of this, Batu had issued the king a grave warning: "I command you to send them [Cumans] away, for by taking them away from me you have become my enemy. It is easier for them to flee than it is for your people. They live in tents, while you live in houses and cities. So how do you escape my hands?"[3]

Although it is unlikely that Hungary's neighbors—Poland, Bohemia, and Germany—were capable of uniting to block the Mongol invasion of Hungary, Batu and Subodei were taking no chances. In early February 1241, soldiers under the command of the Mongol leaders Baidar and Orda were sent on a campaign into Poland. On March 18 they defeated the thirty-thousand-strong army of King Boleslaw IV, which had among its ranks some of Europe's most professional soldiers.[4] On Palm Sunday a few days later, the Mongols burned Krakow, then carried on into Silesia to face Duke Henry II, who was supported by German knights. Drawing the knights into an ambush near the town of Liegentz, the Mongols attacked with a technique of horseback archery not practiced in Europe, where close range fighting was the norm. The Mongols shot from afar, sometimes using smoke to disorient their enemy. Although the knights' heavy armor offered some protection, it proved cumbersome in the face of the speed, endurance, and agility of the Mongols, who were lightly protected and rode small but strong horses; the Mongolian conquest of Europe is thought to have heralded the end of heavy battle horses and knights and the beginning of light horse cavalry. By the end of the battle Duke Henry's head had been cut off and paraded on a pike. As evidence of the defeat, nine large sacks of ears were collected and sent to Batu and Subodei.

While the Poles were occupied with Baidar and Orda's forces, Batu and Subodei attacked Hungary. Batu's central column of soldiers descended from the Carpathians onto the plains and swiftly defeated a Hungarian army on March 11. Two smaller columns moved along Batu's flanks; the northern column was credited with traveling an astonishing 70 km a day through the snow.

As the Mongols advanced, Hungary fell into internal strife. The Cumans were already unpopular due to their nomadic ways, which clashed with the sedentary, agriculture-based way of life, and now King Bela's detractors spread a rumor that the nomadic Cumans were allied with the Mongols. Cuman royalty, including the leader, Kotian, were murdered, and an uprising against the unwelcome nomadic guests spread across the country. The Cumans, who were steppe nomads familiar with Mongol warfare and who under other circumstances might have bolstered the Hungarian defenses, fled south to Bulgaria, murdering Hungarians en route.

By March 15, Batu's forces had arrived near Buda on the Danube and were soon joined by the two other columns from the north and south. On the far bank of the Danube, Bela gathered his army, which some estimate was as large as eighty thousand. On April 9, the same day as the Battle of Liegentz in Silesia, Bela's army began moving north from Pest for an attack on the Mongols. In a tactic typical of steppe warfare, Batu and Subodei feigned retreat, leading the Hungarian army to the plain of Mohi—a place previously chosen by the Mongols—near the confluence of the Tisza and Sajo rivers. While the Mongol army melted away into the forests, Bela set up camp on the plain, fortifying the camp with a ring of wagons linked by chains. Bela reasoned the only access the Mongols had was via a single bridge across the river, which he arranged to be guarded by a thousand men.

Bela's actions played into the hands of the Mongols. The following day, when Batu began attacking via the bridge, Subodei took a troop of men upstream, where they crossed the river and set about surprising Bela from the rear. When Batu's army breached the bridge, the Hungarians inflicted

serious losses on the Mongol army, but when Subodei appeared from behind, Bela's army was trapped. With the Hungarians encircled, the Mongols withdrew and employed catapults, sending burning tar and naphtha
raining down inside the fortress of wagons. The Mongols then intentionally created a gap in their defenses to the west, encouraging Hungarian
soldiers to escape. As planned, what began as a few soldiers riding for
their lives became a mass retreat. The Mongols closed in on this spread-
out line of soldiers and cut them down. The killing is believed to have
gone on for two days, during which about sixty-five thousand Hungarian
soldiers were put to death. King Bela managed to escape to Zagreb, from
where he was pursued to an island off the Adriatic coast. The detachment
of the Mongols charged with the task of hunting him conquered their
way through Slovenia, Croatia, and Bosnia in the process.

The following winter, 1241–42, the Mongols were using Hungary as a
base for furthering their campaign into Europe. In what was an unusually
cold year, the army was able to cross the frozen Danube and carry on into
Austria, where they invaded the town of Wiener Neustadt, just south of Vienna. Eccentric accounts from a heretic priest who resided there provide
some insight into the terror and confusion Mongols wrought. Yvo de Nar-
bonne, as he was known, recorded the following about the fate of the locals:

> Without any difference or respect of condition, fortune, sexe, or
> age, were by manifold cruelties, all of them destroyed; with
> whose carcasses, the Tartarian chieftains, and their brutish and
> savage followers, glutting themselves as with delicious cakes, left
> nothing for vultures but the bare bones . . . the beautiful they
> devoured not, but smothered them, lamenting and scritching,
> with forced and unnatural ravishments. Like barbarous miscre-
> ants, they deflowered virgins until they died of exhaustion and
> cutting off their tender Paps to present for dainties unto their
> chiefs, they engorged themselves with their bodies.[5]

Regardless of the embellished and imagined details—some of which
were born of religious ideology, but also no doubt a result of Mongolian

propaganda designed to spread fear—such accounts provide some insight into what appeared to lie in store for the rest of Europe. It seemed nothing could stop the Mongols from carrying on deep into the heart of Catholicism and beyond. In the end, though, there will only ever be speculation, for in March 1242 news reached the Mongols that the grand khan, Ogodei, had died in Mongolia. Batu, Subodei, and their army began to withdraw east for the election of a new leader, reaching their homeland in 1243.[6] Although the Mongol Empire would hold together for another century, and the Golden Horde for 240 years more, the Mongols would never return to Hungary, nor realize their aspirations for domination of central and western Europe.

AS DEFTLY DESCRIBED by Jack Weatherford in his book *Genghis Khan and the Making of the Modern World*, the initial destruction caused by Mongols during their conquests usually "yielded to an unprecedented rise in cultural communication, expanded trade, and improved civilization." Although it is broadly true that the territories the Mongols conquered were incorporated into their empire and enjoyed the stability and relative prosperity that followed, Hungary could be considered an exception. Followed by the rapid withdrawal, the conquest must have appeared to be the kind of senseless murder and destruction for which Mongols (and nomads in general) have been largely remembered in Europe.

Given the devastation wreaked on Hungary, it might be expected that someone like me, arriving in the spirit of the Mongols, could not expect a particularly warm reception. Yet in the dying light of the warm summer evening on the Hungarian-Ukrainian border, the atmosphere was anything but unwelcoming.

Inside the veterinary control building that lay beyond immigration, János Lóska was excited. Within the tight coils of the Hungarian's short blond hair, there seemed to exist the same spring-loaded energy of his bulging forearms and legs. János was a horse breeder, a former member of the Hungarian national eventing team, and currently the president of the Hungarian Equestrian Tourism Association. For months I had been corresponding with him by email, and he had pledged to do all he could to help get my horses across the border into his country. In the few weeks since I had said farewell to Mike in the Carpathians and dropped down to the Hungarian plains, János's help had been instrumental in navigating the European Union's tough quarantine regulations.

Standing over the veterinarians as they inspected my animals and documents, János urged them on with a look of unwavering determination. When the last of the documents was stamped, he grabbed my sweaty arm with an iron grip and spoke to me in hushed English: "Nothing can stop us now! Nothing!"

We celebrated with beer that János's son brought to us, and I rode the horses to the nearby town of Tuzsér, where they were taken in by a family. Tigon and I climbed into János's BMW and were rocketed away to his home. I clung to Tigon in the backseat, drawn toward sleep yet determined not to miss a single waking moment. At one stage the journey was broken by a fuel stop, during which I stumbled into the gas station convenience store and picked up a hot dog. The bright lights, sanitized walls and floor, and plastic-sealed "food on the go" were a startling novelty and a measure of how far I had come.

In the morning the scale of János's support became clear. He had already promised a public finale for my journey, and now spread out a map of Hungary to plot the route he had prearranged. I was to travel southwest across the great plain of Hungary, known as Hortobágy, then roughly along the meandering banks of the Tisza River to the center of the country before turning west to the Danube. "I have ridden every corner of this country by horse, and I can ensure that you will never have to ride on a road if you follow my directions," he said proudly.

The vision that János had for this last chapter of my journey was one of my caravan being escorted and hosted by Hungarian horsemen and -women along a network of tracks and trails, and where possible cross-country. He had friends and acquaintances ready to take me in and guide me through, and planned to ride with me whenever he could. He estimated it would take between four and six weeks to make it to the Danube.

Although Hungary had been an eastern frontier for Catholicism since the eleventh century, and was indeed a sedentary society at the time of the Mongol invasion, it had for a much longer period of time been the western bulwark of steppe nomad culture. Forming the westernmost tip of the Eurasian steppe, its plains had, since antiquity, been roamed by nomads with their yurts, horses, sheep, and cattle in a fashion not dissimilar to those of the Mongolian plateau today. The Indo-Aryan Scythians were one of the first known nomads to reside in Hungary, and it is well known that in the fifth century the Huns, united under Attila, had used Hungary as their platform to invade the Roman Empire. Following them came the Avars, another steppe people who are believed to have introduced the stirrup (which had been developed in Asia) to Europe. Modern-day Hungarians are thought to be descended from the last known nomadic people from the east to migrate to the Hungarian plains, the Magyars.[7] There is an ongoing dispute about the origins of the Magyars, whose language is more closely related to the Finno-Ugric group than the Turkic languages that predominate on the steppe. It is safe to say, however, that they came riding out of their homeland somewhere in the vicinity of modern Bashkiria—also known as Bashkortostan—near the southern Urals of Russia. Under their leader, Arpád, the Magyars officially founded the nation of Hungary in 896 and spent the best part of the next century raiding deep into Europe, defeating armies of Italy, France, and Germany.

I had long read about the nomadic history of Hungary but hadn't held out high hopes of finding Hungarians with whom my journey resonated. By the time the Mongols invaded, Magyars had not been nomadic for almost three hundred years. This reflected a unique feature of Hungary—on the fine line between temperate Europe and the Eurasian steppe, it had always been a kind of bridge between two worlds, characterized by a fusion of both sedentary and nomadic customs. In the long run, a settled way of life had come to dominate, and in the twenty-first century Hungary was firmly part of the European Union, gravitating—politically at least—to the

West, and more renowned for its grand cultural capital, Budapest, than for its steppe heartland.

Yet there was little doubt that János's support for me came because I was honoring the heritage of his own ancestors by riding horses from Asia into Europe. With time I would learn that among many Hungarians, wounds from the Mongol invasion had long healed, and for them the Mongols, Huns, Scythians, and Magyars had all coalesced into a broad brotherhood of horseback, nomadic peoples.

Emblematic of the significance that my journey held for János was that he didn't hesitate to tell me where I should hold the ceremony for the end of my journey. "There is only one choice, if you really want to make it the Hungarian way. And that is Opusztaszer. There I will really be able to make you a hero!"

THE FIRST OF my hosts in Hungary was a man very familiar with Opusztaszer. I met Tamas Petrosko half a day's ride from Tuzsér. Wearing traditional regalia, he rode toward me in a saddle draped with a full sheepskin, tail and all. In his sixties, he had slightly sunken shoulders and a hard, toughened frame rounded out by a belly.

"You come the Magyar way! I also ride this route!" he said in a patchwork of English and Russian, leaning over from his horse and giving me a hug.

In 1996 Tamas had been part of a small group of Hungarians who carried out a 4,200 km journey in honor of the great migration of his people. With a backup truck carrying supplies, they had ridden horses from Bashkiria in the southern Urals through Russia and Ukraine before crossing through the Carpathians onto the Hungarian plain. The end of their journey had been celebrated with a ceremony in Opusztaszer, which, according to Tamas, was the "spiritual center" of the country. It was in this nondescript town on the sandy steppe, just 90 km east of the Danube, that the Magyars' leader, Arpád, had officially founded the modern nation.

Tamas's quest had by no means ended there. On return from his journey, he had been inspired to set up a tourist park in honor of his Hungarian ancestors. I would spend several days with him on a sweeping property that featured yurts, a Mongolian ovoo, and a shaman's hut marked at the entrance by the skulls of a horse and a cow. Out in the field flocks of long-haired Hungarian sheep and a herd of horned Hungarian cattle grazed. It was Tamas's dream to inspire young Hungarians to incorporate the spirit of their nomad ancestors into their identity—an aim that he fulfilled with summer camps where children came to ride and live as nomads might once have done.

In the context of greater Hungarian society, Tamas may well have been considered an eccentric, but as I rode onward over the coming days and weeks, I came to think it would not be an inflation of the truth to suggest that he was part of a groundswell of Hungarians—albeit a minority—who were not merely conscious of their nomadic heritage but hungering for a connection to the life of their horse-borne ancestors.

In Hungary, where there were no mountains or deserts and there was plentiful grass and water, my meetings with these people took over from the geographical challenges as the driving narrative of my journey. Joining me from Tamas's farm, for instance, was István Vismeg, a burly high school physical education teacher with unkempt, shoulder-length black hair and a hint of the East in his eyes. In a wild ride through backstreets, along forest trails, and across fields, he took me to a monument near the town of Sárospatak that had recently been built on an ancient Magyar gravesite. It was a pyramid onto which was embellished a mosaic of the path of Hungarians from horseback warriors who migrated from the East to settled Christians.

"Archaeologists discovered this important graveyard fifty years ago—they believe there was some kind of battle here when Arpád conquered the Carpathian Basin, but it was only two years ago that this site was rescued from farmers. Our governments have hidden and disrespected our history . . . they've protected the buildings of the Austro-Hungarian Empire, yet left the graves of our founding fathers to be plowed over," he told me.

The collapse of the Iron Curtain had provided freedom for Hungarians to reevaluate the Communist version of history, which had emphasized Hungary's rise as a sophisticated European society and treated nomads with some hostility. Now, as the country shifted its allegiance to the West, there was a determination to rediscover and preserve the unique nomadic identity of Hungarians before the tide of European cultural and economic norms swallowed the country.

From Sárospatak in Hungary's northeast, István guided me through rolling countryside to the historic town of Szabolcs and handed me over to my next host, a short, rotund man named Geyser. A self-proclaimed sha-man, Geyser greeted me with a ceremony complete with drums and chant-ing in the center of a thousand-year-old earthen fortress. I camped there and celebrated into the night with Geyser, István, and a saddle maker who specialized in Arpád-era saddles. After many glasses of the national drink, pálinka—a kind of schnapps—Geyser became even more animated. He ar-gued a point with the saddle maker that the true Hungarian origins were to be found in the Huns, rather than the Magyars, and began beating his drum and chanting. "The Hun way! You have come the Hun way. We are Huns! One sky, one big blue sky, the Huns, the stars, the sky. Earth, water, sky."

Among Hungarian horsemen and -women there was a raft of conflict-ing opinions about which era of history embodied the most authentic Hungarian culture—not unlike the competing philosophies I'd witnessed in Kalmykia among those striving to revive a sense of culture and identity. Another character I met who was convinced of his Hunnic origins was Kassai Lajos. Kassai had resurrected the art of horseback archery and turned it into an international martial arts discipline. Through years of research he had developed bows and archery techniques reflecting vari-ous nomad eras. He had become somewhat of a cult figure, with thou-sands of followers and his own institutionalized training center, called The Valley. Watching him galloping and shooting off six arrows in just ten seconds, hitting the target every time, one could only imagine the intimidating sight of a group of Mongols or Magyars charging into Eu-rope. Ironically, this horseback archery skill was one that Mongols had since lost. Among Kassai's many ambitions was to travel there and rein-troduce the art.

When I rode out from Szabolcs and waved goodbye to Geyser, I was still only four days' ride into my Hungarian journey. Ahead lay a further five weeks of encounters that are too numerous to recount here. Suffice it to say that the entourage—arranged by János—proved to include individuals ranging from wealthy businessmen to academics, stud farm owners, and simple farmers; though they often held opposing views, all had their own unique way of incorporating something of the steppe culture into their modern lives. Among these many people, one man in particular, Peter Kun, had a profound impact on me. My encounter with him was the kind of watershed moment I had not expected but nevertheless always hoped for.

At the time I met with Peter, I had ridden seven long days from the Ukrainian border, at first as far west as Tizsadob in Hungary's northeast, then rapidly south with János. On my second afternoon with János we rode out under the glare of the sun onto a vast golden plain. Squinting hard, I could make out the appearance of cattle and sheep inching across the horizon, cutting in and out of focus in the wobble of heat mirage.

We had reached the Hortobágy—a vast plain of eastern Hungary considered the last great remnant of arid grasslands in the Carpathian Basin and home to the only remaining mounted herdsmen of Hungary. The Csikós, as they are known, are to this day predominantly graziers of cattle and sheep, renowned as skilled horsemen who, among many tricks, can make their horses lie down on command—a tactic the Mongol army was famed to have done in order to remain unseen.

It was just as we idled up to a well and Tigon returned to his old trick of bathing in the drinking trough that Peter Kun came cantering in. Sitting straight-backed astride an Arab horse, his long hair neatly tied in a ponytail, the thirty-five-year-old cast his almond eyes at once to my horses, then to Tigon.

"Your dog is tazi! And your horses are dzhabe!"

I nodded in disbelief. Not a soul had recognized the very specific Kazakh breeds of my animals since I left their homeland more then eighteen months earlier.

It was not a lucky guess. Claiming to be descended from the nomadic Cumans, who had fought the Mongols before fleeing to Hungary for refuge, Peter had had a fascination for everything nomadic since he was a child. As a university student he had excelled in ancient Turkic history, learned to speak Mongolian and Kazakh, and at the age of seventeen spent a year living in Mongolia. He had gone on to complete a doctorate comparing Hungarian and Mongolian horsemanship and had produced a popular documentary about the Kazakhs of remote western Mongolia.

Peter had been offered a job in the Hungarian embassy in Ulaanbaatar but instead decided to follow what he called a "true Hungarian life." He had bought up cattle, sheep, and horses and moved to a traditional Hungarian homestead on the Hortobágy. Peter now split his time between lecturing at a university and tending his herds. "In Mongolia and Kazakhstan I can go to feel something of how my ancestors once lived. At the university in the city I can teach about our Hungarian heritage, and here on the *puszta*"—the Hungarian term for the steppe—"I can really live in line with my origin," he told. Leaning down out of the saddle, he plucked a piece of wormwood plant and brought it to his nose. "When I smell this wormwood, I feel like I am back out on the wild steppes of Kazakhstan and Mongolia . . . and that's because this is still the big Eurasian steppe, the same one where you began."

Riding onward, Peter and I passed shepherds tending to sheep and cattle, and lonely old barns and ranches with reed-thatched roofs. There were also traditional wells that operated using a weighted lever to extract water, nodding against the sky like majestic old oil well pump jacks. In such open and flat terrain the sky was dominating, and beneath us the earth a mere crust. From time to time, fine clouds of choking dust and pulverized dung wafted through.

With no paths, roads, or fences, we rode five abreast—János, his son Marti, Peter, myself, and Ogonyok, who had decided of his own volition to join us in the front. János, being his exuberant self, led us into a full gallop, and for a few fleeting moments it felt as if we were flying effortlessly over the land. Embodying the sentiment of all Hungarian horsemen I met, János veered over next to me and shouted: "The day there are fences in Hungary is the day that this is not my country. I will leave."

An hour or two brought us to Peter's ranch. It was a huddle of horse and sheep yards, with a barn and house cast like an island in a pale brown sea of steppe. A Kazakh yurt stood out front. At first I spotted what appeared to be a pile of old matted sheepskins lying in the shade of its northern wall, but these presently rose and transformed into the figures of two indignant-looking dogs the size of small bears. They were a breed known as komondor, which is a corruption of the Hungarian term for "Cuman's dog." Their long white dreadlocked coat, the likes of which I had never seen, was so thick, it was rumored even wolves were unable to penetrate to the flesh.

After János and his son had loaded their horses into a waiting trailer and departed, Peter brought me a piece of rope, slung it over my forearm, and began to tie a knot. I knew in advance what his special demonstration was going to be. On the very first night of my journey, now more than three years ago, a Mongolian herder, Damba, had spent an hour teaching a knot that he assured me I had to know. A kind of reverse bowline, it could be tied with lightning speed, always held fast, and no matter what force was applied, could be quickly and easily untied. It was an indispensable knot I had used for everything from tethering horses to tying improvised reins and fastening pack loads.

During my first winter on the steppe I had begun to realize the cultural significance of the special knot. In Kazakhstan, herders had looked on with astonishment and asked where I had learned it; it was, after all, a Kazakh knot. In Kalmykia, more than a year later, I encountered the same reaction from a Kalmyk craftsman, who termed it a Kalmyk knot. Now, just as I predicted, Peter tied the very same knot and claimed it for his own people: "You know, we say that if you don't know this knot, then you are not a horseman . . . In western Hungary, beyond the Danube and the great Eurasian steppe, no one knows this knot. We call it the Cumanian knot."

After a meal of mutton and a good serving of pálinka, I lay down to rest on a sheepskin in Peter's yurt. Outside, the wind gently pushed against the felt walls. A horse somewhere cleared its nose, and a bleating sheep stirred. Through a narrow gap in the felt of the ceiling, glimmers of moonlight filtered down, illuminating a wolf skin, horsewhip, and bow that hung from the wall. Next to me, his head resting on an old stirrup, Tigon was fast asleep and in a dream, paws twitching.

There were many connections that I had learned of between the modern-day cultures of the steppe, yet I had never dreamed that among them was something I had carried with me from day one. To me, this simple knot not only tied together immense stretches of steppe but symbolized the relationship between human and the horse that underpinned nomadic life.

AT SUNRISE I joined Peter as he saw off his herd of long-haired Hungarian sheep and gray cattle. A bandy-legged shepherd who wore a wide black hat slowly moved them out with the crack of a whip and a chorus of whistles and shouts. Then we opened the gates of the horse yard and watched as Peter's herd thundered off, leaving a cloud of dust suspended in the morning light.

By 9:00 A.M. everything had settled, and the sun brought such stifling heat it had quashed the spirits of the most exuberant young horses.

"It's too hot to step outside," said Peter mischievously. "In fact, it is so hot the only reason to step outside today is to see the takhi."

Unbeknown to me, Peter had arranged a visit to a rare reserve where herds of Przewalskii horses (known in Mongolian as takhi) live with minimal human interference. As the only surviving wild horse of Eurasia, the takhi may closely resemble the equines that were first domesticated by hunter-gatherers. Access to the takhi reserve was ordinarily restricted to scientists, but Peter had been able to get permission for me through his connections.

After we had followed hoofprints for half an hour or so, the crest of a slight rise fell away to a series of reedy waterholes and marshes. There, mingling by the water, were around sixty or seventy takhi, all of which displayed distinctive zebra-striped legs, short manes, and dun-colored coats.

Peter pointed to a commotion on the far side of the water hole. A stallion had set upon a younger competitor, which now galloped off. At first the younger horse darted right and left before plunging headlong into the water. The pursuing stallion crashed in behind, nipping at the fleeing competitor. On our side of the water hole the pursuit continued. The stallions shot past a mare that was leading her foals along the water's edge, and careened out into the steppe. My attention returned to the water hole, where there had been a collective decision to move on. The water's surface was shattered by a frenzy of hooves as the herd pulsated through the water, then out onto hard ground.

It was the first time I'd laid eyes on takhi, and it struck me that before us was a scene that could at once have been something taken from prehistory, but also still be seen in any given valley in Mongolia on a hot summer's day.

The takhi's barrel-like chests and trunk-thick necks were a feature of the constitution of my own horses, Taskonir and Ogonyok, reflective of the endurance and hardiness that had carried me safely to Hungary. The speed of the stallions was a reminder of the equine's unparalleled ability to take flight and reach as much as 70 kph in seconds—a trait that had developed as the horse evolved over millions of years and which eventually opened up a new era of communication, travel, trade, and warfare for humans.[8] Even the way the takhi opportunistically took bites at reeds on the move was reminiscent of the greedy Ogonyok. At heart, horses were nomadic, and their ability to travel long distances enabled them to roam far and wide for feed and water, eating on the move.

I could not help but reflect that the very qualities of the takhi I was bearing witness to had facilitated the creation of some of the world's greatest empires, from those of the distant past, such the Scythian, Roman, and Mongol, through to the making of the New World. Although nomadic life could not be sustained far beyond the Danube, the horse and a nomadic style of light horsemanship had been adopted by Europeans and taken to the Americas, Australia, and Africa, where men had conquered from the saddle with same advantage that earlier nomads had once used to great effect in Eurasia.[9] For better or worse, the horse, together with humans, had been on a journey through time that had not just contributed to the world but helped define society in every inhabited continent.

After the excursion to see the takhi I returned to Peter's place for several more days. When finally I saddled up to leave, he plucked hair from each of my horses, gifted me with a Mongolian sweat stick, and told me: "I am so happy to have met you, and I hope we have strong connections in future. In your mind, your head, you think and act like a nomad even though you are from Australia."

I rode on with my sails filled. With my mind lingering on thoughts of the takhi and the experience of sleeping out in the Hortobágy in Peter's yurt, the complexities I'd encountered in recent months and years seemed to melt away, and I found myself reunited with the basic ingredients of the land from which I had begun.

For seven days straight my caravan traveled south along the Tisza River, covering as much as 50 km from one host to the next. Tigon was a rod of muscle and could sustain long sprints at over 40 kph. A quick dip in any number of oases along the way—river, trough, drain, or puddle—and it was as if he had been recharged. At night the horses were spoiled with hay and grain, and in the mornings they routinely broke into frolic. Taskonir, who had once been so desperately thin that some people had said he would not make it to the Russian border alive, now pig rooted, thrashed his head about, and nipped at his juniors with mighty aggression. In the evenings, I took Taskonir out without so much as a saddle or even a halter. It had taken me a year on the road to feel confident enough to gallop, and another year before we reached the kind of fattening grass where I was tempted to try. Here, though, the issues of water, grass, and distance had fallen behind us. Holding on to Taskonir's mane, with my bare toes tucked into the fur on his belly, I took him for long, exhilarating gallops. As he leaned forward and the earth began to rush beneath, I was overcome by an uncanny sensation that time was slowing down. Details of the environment passed through my field of vision with lucidity. I sat straight and still, legs wrapped around Taskonir's chest, my rear not lifting a centimetre from his spine. These same animals that I had been terrified of in the beginning had transformed me. I could not imagine life without them.

The momentum of the ride from Peter's farm carried me to the village of Tószeg, from where I was escorted straight west for two days by a party of horsemen whom János had described as "cowboys." He was not exaggerating. Riding American quarter horses, they turned up with their lassos, long leather chaps, spurs, bulging belt buckles, and broad cowboy hats. Leading them was a man they called "Sheriff"—a wealthy software programmer who admitted to having watched too many John Wayne movies as a child. En route with them, I stayed in the unique Hungarian institution of a horse-friendly hotel. While the horses overnighted in stables, I slept with Tigon in the luxury of my own chandelier-hung room.

It was only as I rode on unescorted from Sheriff's ranch that my buoyancy began to wane. Immersed in the rush of movement and with my time filled daily with new characters, I had barely taken note of how rapidly I was crossing the country. It was hard to believe, but it was already September, and I was now just two days' ride from the Danube.

So often during the earlier part of the journey, when Hungary had seemed impossibly beyond reach, I had dreamed about a time like this, when I was nearing the end. Mostly I imagined the day my horses would no longer have the burden of carrying me. After all they had done, I wanted desperately to offer them a land where there would be certainty of pasture. There had been many times when it seemed that my ambition to give my horses a deserving retirement would remain just that—and some horses hadn't made it. I was still haunted by the gray horse, Kok, whom I had left behind with an infected hoof more than a year ago in Kalmykia. I hadn't had the nerve to call to find out what his fate had been. Somehow, though, I'd brought the rest of my team through. Ogonyok and Taskonir had been with me for almost three years—a prospect that had seemed improbable when the old man in Pugachevo from whom I had bought Taskonir asked me to send him a photo from the Danube. Yet now that I was in this place of relative richness, it felt all too soon, too quick.

After a gentle ride west from Sheriff's farm through undulating sand hills and forest, I craved setting up camp in the open steppe to take stock, but it was not to be. My last night before the Danube was to be spent at another Western-style stud farm, the Bronco Ranch. My arrival happened to coincide with a Saturday and a gathering of Western horseman. Instead of pulling into camp, I rode in among a throng of suburbanites and loudspeakers that alternately played country-western music and rang out with commentary. There was barrel racing, sliding, and a beer-swilling crowd adorned in the same outfits as Sheriff's cowboys.

After being met by a man called Tibor, who was one of Sheriff's train-ers and caretakers, I unloaded and took Taskonir and Tigon on a ride. I trotted out of the ranch and into the forest, where I found a small, sandy meadow and lay with Taskonir's rope lax in my hand. I tried to focus my concentration on the sunset and let the steppe soothe me as it had done so many hundreds of times before, but from one direction the constant hum of distant motorcycles and cars was unending, and from the other, music from the Bronco Ranch crept its way through the forest.

A legend I'd been told about the makings of Hungary gripped me. At the end of the Magyars' epic voyage from the East in search of a new homeland, it is said, they offered a white horse to the existing rulers of the land in return for a bundle of grass and a jug of Danubian water. It was a deeply meaningful exchange: water and grass were the essential ingredients of life, and the Carpathian Basin offered the kind of quantity that any nomad would yearn for. In the end, that eternal search for pas-ture and water, which tied people to the rhythms of the land, was what defined nomads for me—not their dual capacity for devastating feats of war and empire building, which can be found among the history of many nations and cultures.

Explicit in the Hungarian legend, though, was a conundrum that I was only now beginning to grasp: the quest for better pasture had ultimately lured nomads—just as it had me—to this land on the border of Europe and the steppe that was not suited to a pure nomadic existence. By buying into a world of abundance, the Magyars were trading away their white horse, a symbol of their nomad way of life and the animals that they had sought to nourish in the first place. Like nomads who had come before them, their saddles would be replaced over time with wagons, plows, and scythes, their vast herds with cultivated fields, and the yurt with perma-nent homes. In a land of such riches, there was, after all, no driving im-petus to keep moving.

I thought about it for some time—about what it meant for Hungary's unique past, then what it spelled for my future. Hungary was the high-water mark of the steppe—a place of historical stalemate between those of the saddle and those of the plow. Even the Mongols, who had struck deep into settled lands and administered their rule, had not been able to sustain nomadic life beyond the great grasslands and deserts whence they had come.

And therein lay my dilemma. The journey had changed me, and I'd fulfilled my dream of riding from Mongolia to Europe, learning to see the world through nomad's eyes. Yet if nomadism didn't belong in temperate Europe, or indeed my home in Australia, then could I really carry what I had learned beyond the Danube?

I wasn't at all sure, and it worried me that people back home might not be able to relate to who I had become. I found some cause for optimism in the example of Peter Kun, who seemed to have been able to embrace the advantages of the modern, settled world while also living according to his nomad heritage. But then again, I was Australian, with Anglo-European origins—wouldn't it feel contrived to live as he did? Then it occurred to me that perhaps part of the answer lay in the raucous music drifting through the trees from the Bronco Ranch. The truth was that a part of the nomad legacy had never stopped radiating beyond the steppe. In the deserts of Mexico and the mountains and prairies of the United States, a sophisticated horse culture had developed, resting on the accumulated wisdom of untold people over untold centuries. It was strange, in a way, that Tibor, Sheriff, and others were reimporting a style of horsemanship in which the shadow of their own ancestors was inextricably woven. And yet it seemed to me proof that the virtues of freedom and independence for which the cowboy of the American West had become glorified—and which were at the core of steppe life—were universal. It was a thought that would at least provide some comfort as I moved on from here.

FROM BRONCO TO the village of Solt on the Danube was a mere 25 km. It was to be my last day of westward travel, and my last alone.

As I traveled roughly parallel with the M52 freeway, the steppe came in dribs and drabs. When there appeared open spaces I went into a trot, but then a ditch, a road, or a cornfield would stop us. In the evening I passed through Solt, disturbing a few dogs, a cyclist, and a pedestrian. From there it was a hop, skip, and jump to the flood embankment, from which we soon dropped down to lush green flats and arrived at the river. In front of me lay a wide swath of silty brown water stretching to the far bank. Not much beyond that lay the beginning of fences, walls, roads, and cities. From the south, a tourist ferry was chugging up against the current. I resisted the pull of Taskonir's head at first, but then let the reins go and watched as all the horses drank. Even Tigon carefully walked his way in and lapped it up.

That night I camped for just the second time in Hungary. Deep into the early hours of morning I retraced in my mind every day of travel since I had set off three and a half years earlier. Give or take one or two campsites, I could remember every step of the way. It was not a journey as such, but had become my life. And yet there was no escaping the reality that it was already fading. The hoofmarks of my horses in Kazakhstan would have already long gone by now, the bushes I crushed rejuvenated, the grass my horses eaten regrown. Some of the people I had met had even passed away. Never again would the horses feel the packsaddle on their backs. Tigon would never again know the freedom of running day in and day out.

As I had felt when I was leaving my life in Australia behind and heading to Mongolia, I knew that a part of me was dying.

JUST AS IT was hard to say precisely when the summer came to an end and when autumn fully took hold, my journey did not come to a close in one time in one place. There were, rather, many endings, and later many new beginnings.

Originally I had flirted with the idea of coming to a close in Budapest, but decided that finishing in a metropolis where the Mongols were still remembered almost singularly for their destruction was not fitting. The rather anonymous stretch of Danube near Solt offered a personal finish and symbolized the edge of the steppe. It was, however, a very solitary and rather anticlimactic ending.

The other significant ending was to be in Opusztaszer—just as János had planned. As the site where Arpád had founded the nation of nomadic Magyars in 896, it was symbolic of Hungary's enduring role in the history of the Eurasian steppe. Perhaps just as important, it was a place where I could celebrate with others.

The day after reaching Solt and the Danube, I packed my things and made my way to Budapest's international airport. There, stumbling a little disoriented out through immigration, was my brother Jon. During my journey there were times when he had wanted to join me but didn't. In the wake of Dad's death, he had been determined to come for at least the finish.

For the four days it took to ride from the Danube southeast to Opusztaszer, he traveled with me. On the first day, he went by foot, running this way and that, snapping photos, and taking in all the details—it was only his second time outside Australia, and his first in Europe. At dusk he approached me with a smile. "Look, there are so many frogs! I have one!" He opened his hands to reveal a squirming, mud-coated little specimen. Standing there at my side, with his daypack on and face full of wonderment, he was the spitting image of Dad—or at least the vision I had had of my father walking by my side, the day after he had died.

For the second day of riding János came to lead us on a trail more than 5 km long. We carried on well after darkness, and just as we approached an equine-friendly hotel for the night, there came a familiar voice.

"Tigon! It's really you!"

Ahead of us, Tigon was the first of our troupe to greet my mother. Also waiting there was Graeme Cook, a longtime family friend and neighbor who had been the first person to put me on a horse four years earlier. My childhood mate Mark Wallace was there, too, with his partner, Nadia.

The next two days were something of a dream. To ride with family and friends by my side, with my caravan of horses still intact, gave me a feeling of togetherness that I knew would never be repeated in exactly the same way.

My last camp was a mere 10 km from the finish line. A night of what I had hoped to be reflection became one of minor drama: Tigon had rolled in something dead earlier in the day, and I spent hours trying to wash him with shampoo and water.

For the finale at the national heritage park in Opusztaszer, the Kazakh and Mongolian embassies had sent representations, along with the deputy ambassador from the Australian mission in Budapest. Gordon Naysmith, a roguish old Scot who in his youth had ridden from south to north through Africa and into Europe, arrived as the representative of the Long Riders Guild. Then there were tens and tens of others—some were friends from Europe, including old friends Sandy and Rita Cooper from Scotland, but mostly they were Hungarians who had hosted me along the way.

As the remaining distance of my journey dwindled, I felt carried forward on a wave of emotion. The last few steps were made through a guard of honor formed by Hungarian horsemen in traditional regalia.

When the formal side of the ceremony was over, the celebration moved to a yurt camp nearby, where that night the smell of goulash, the splash of pálinka, and the neighing of horses mingled till morning.

At one stage, Attila Cseppento, the owner of the yurt camp, pulled me aside with a gleam in his eye that was definitely part pálinka. "Tim Cook—first night of travel you sleep in yurt tent. Last night of travel you sleep in Hungary, yurt tent." He looked at me now, almost ready to cry, but shook his head slowly. "Beautiful, it's beautiful."

EPILOGUE

SEPTEMBER 22, 2007, the day I rode into the national heritage park at Opusztaszer in Hungary, was one of the most fulfilling of my life. More than three years after setting off from Mongolia, I had achieved my dream to ride by horse across the Eurasian steppe to the Danube. There to share the moment with me were my mother, my brother, friends old and new, representatives of cultures across the steppe, and of course my family of animals.

That same day, however, also marked the beginning of a process of what I could best describe as the surrender and shedding—not always voluntarily—of much of what had come to define my life on the steppe.

During my time in Hungary I had thought long and hard about what I would do with the horses after I had finished. I'd considered giving them to Peter Kun or Tamas Petrasko, but in the end I was persuaded by a suggestion from János Loska that I give them to an orphanage in the small village of Tiszadob. I had stayed at the orphanage en route, and the director, Aranka Illes, explained that they had been trying to set up a riding program for the orphans for many years. At the end ceremony I handed over the horses to Aranka and several children who had traveled to greet me. The next morning the horses were loaded into horse trailers and driven off, and I was left with a now useless array of horse tack.

It had never been within the realm of possibility to bring the horses back home to Australia, and so I had long expected this day. I had, however, harbored hopes of bringing Tigon home with me, so it was somewhat devastating to discover that getting him into Australia from Hungary would cost around $10,000—a nearly impossible sum of money at the best of times, but particularly at that point because I was broke. Additionally, Tigon would need to become a resident of the European Union before being eligible to apply for a permit to enter Australia's strict quarantine, and that would require him to stay in Hungary for a minimum of another six months. János took Tigon home, generously offering to keep him at his horse farm.

Six weeks later I put my bags down at my mother's country house in Gippsland, Australia, and entered a world where I savored being in familiar surrounds and close to my family. Still, a part of me felt in exile, and I found it difficult to understand the relevance of all I had learned and witnessed. I realized almost at once that readapting to life in Australia, particularly without my animals, would be much more difficult than the challenges of being a novice horseman on the steppe. The hardest stage was yet to come. Little more than a month after arrival, several of my journals—which I had cradled across the length of the steppe—were stolen from my car in St. Kilda, Melbourne, outside my sister's apartment. A campaign of appeals through media and with leaflets and reward posters proved to be of no avail. The grief I felt from this is difficult to describe, but suffice it to say that I felt as if someone had robbed me of a part of my life.

The months following the loss of these journals were a low I would never wish to return to, but they also became the turnaround point for me on the long path to reconciling a sense of the significance of the journey for myself, and, most important, beginning the catharsis of turning my experiences into something of relevance to other people.

With editor Michael Balson, my brother Cameron, and producer Richard Dennison, I began working through 140 hours of video that I had taken over the course of the journey, with the aim of making a film series for television broadcast. Simultaneously, I began putting my journey in writing—a process that was tinged with grief in the beginning because of the loss of some of my journals. As I began to write, however, I found myself so immersed in my experiences that I only had to feel the contours of my saddle—which is still infused with the smell of my horses and the steppe—get a whiff of wood smoke, feel the breeze wash over the hills near my mother's home, catch a glimpse of a horse in a paddock, or hear the sound of a distant dog barking to feel transported back to the steppe. Where diaries were lacking, I realized I was also fortunate to be able to draw on maps, photos, and other writings I had done at the time. Most important, I began reestablishing contact with many of the friends I had made across the steppe—both through correspondence and, in some cases, by visiting them. In the middle of 2008, I took up an impromptu request by World Expeditions to guide a trekking journey in Mongolia, at which time I met with many of the people who had seen me off in the saddle all those years before, including Gansukh Baatarsuren and Tseren Enebish and her family and relatives. It was to be the first of a series of trips to Mongolia I have undertaken annually since.

Toward the end of 2008, things began progressing quickly. In the fall I found myself in North America after accepting an invitation as a presenter to attend a travel and adventure festival in Montreal. On the way back to Australia, I stopped over in Washington, D.C., from where I traveled to New York with literary agent Gail Ross and met with several publishers in Manhattan, among which were editor Anton Mueller and publisher George Gibson of Bloomsbury. Within a couple of months I had a contract.

During 2008 I missed Tigon greatly and kept in close contact with János Loska about his well-being. There were many stories of mischief to be recounted, such as when Tigon followed a passing horseman for a day and took all the farm dogs with him. János lamented that he had had to send a taxi to pick them all up. True to form, Tigon became a father at János's farm, and one of the offspring was given to the Tiszadob orphanage, where he was named Tigi.

In November 2008, more than twelve months after I had last seen Tigon, I received a letter in the mail. It was from Australian Quarantine—a permit for Tigon to enter Australia had been granted! I was still without money, however, and the catch was that it would expire within a month. I happened to be in Perth at the time, staying with my friends Rob and Rachel Devling, and with the help of Mike Wood of Mountain Designs, I was able to arrange a special fund-raising presentation. The response was overwhelming, and with a sold-out theater of people who had come to listen to my story, $8,000 was raised in just one night.

In early December 2008, Tigon was taken from Budapest to the Vienna airport by Hungarian veterinarian Edit Budik. From there he was flown to the United Arab Emirates and loaded onto an Australia-bound flight to Melbourne. On December 12, 2008, Tigon showed no hesitation as he came bounding out of his quarantine enclosure to meet me (although he then ignored me for half an hour while he chewed on a marrow bone that I had brought as a welcome gift). In January 2009, when I sat down in earnest to begin the long journey of writing the book, Tigon was by my side, and I was well on the way to bridging the great divide between life in Australia and life on the steppe.

Since that time, much has happened, both for me and for the many people on the steppe with whom I still share a close connection.

In August 2009, I made the first of several trekking journeys back to the Kharkhiraa-Turgen mountain region of western Mongolia, in cooperation with Tseren Enebish and World Expeditions. There, we hired Dashnyam as our head camelier and guide to make the same trek I had done with him over the high pass. It was a wonderful experience to reunite with Dashnyam and his family and tell him news of my journey to the Danube. Dashnyam's circumstances had changed little since I had said farewell to him on a cold autumn morning in 2004. He was still living a marginal existence with very few animals to support his many children. I had hoped to see the horse I had gifted him, Saartai Zeerd, but he explained that the horse had become old and his family had eaten him the previous winter. More recently, his one and only other horse had been stolen, and so he was all but horseless. With the help of the trekkers on the initial 2009 journey, we raised enough tips additional to his salary for him to buy a new horse—and in later years a second horse and a camel. Since then, Dashnyam has become a grandfather—his daughter, whom I had photographed in 2004 (seen on page 5 of the first photo insert), gave birth to a boy in the spring of 2012.

Two other important things happened for me in the summer of 2009. After many trials and tribulations, I received news that ZDF, the national broadcaster of Germany, acting on behalf of the ARTE channel, had granted funding for a three-hour documentary series about my journey. ABC in Australia soon followed with their support of a version of the series, and I spent much of the next year working on the film, which was titled *On the Trail of Genghis Khan* (*Auf den Spuren der Nomaden* in German). The series has since been broadcast in several countries and languages.

The other important event was that I met a young Mongolian woman, Khorloo Batpurev, with whom I fell in love. I would spend the summers of 2010 and 2011 in Mongolia, guiding my annual trip and writing my book in Ulaanbaatar, where I shared an apartment with Khorloo. Since then, we have remained mostly in Australia—Khorloo concentrating on her studies, and me on my book.

During the writing, I have followed with great interest the unfolding circumstances of the lives of many whom I met on the steppe. None are more important to me than Aset from Zhana Zhol, who accompanied me in the winter of 2004–5, and Baitak and his friends in Akbakai.

It wasn't until a year after Aset traveled with me in Kazakhstan that he told me he had spent fourteen years of his life in jail. At the age of just twenty, while working as a taxi driver, he had been involved in a brawl and accidentally broken the jaw of a policeman. He hadn't mentioned it at the time because he feared it would scare me off. Since my journey with him, Aset has moved from the village of Zhana Zhol into the city of Oskemen, where he lives with his wife and disabled son, Guanz. Back in 2005 I was able to return the saddle that he sold to me, but it has to date gone unused in his new city life. Guanz is doing well, now studying at university. I have promised to send more updates about his former pup, Tigon, and hope to visit them again one day.

Baitak and his wife, Rosa, left Akbakai in 2006. After selling his horses and home, Baitak bought a herd of sheep and goats and at the time of this writing runs a cafe on the main highway between Almaty and Astana. When Baitak left Akbakai, he took the alcoholics Grisha and Vitka with him. Vitka continued his ways with vodka and returned to Akbakai, where he died in the autumn of 2006 of a combination of malnutrition and alcohol poisoning; Baitak arranged a funeral for him. Grisha worked as a welder for some time but then went missing, and Baitak has not heard from him since.

Madagol, the herder who looked after my horses that winter in Akbakai, never recovered from the broken leg he incurred in his fall, and he now lives in Moiynkum with his son and daughter-in-law. His wife died of cancer at age fifty-three in the winter of 2007–8.

In terms of gold mining in Akbakai, Baitak tells me that things have since been cleaned up. In 2004 about half of the city's three thousand residents apparently had been involved in gold theft. The mine is now in private hands and security guards are harder to buy out. He tells me that only 10 percent of people are now stealing, and that as a consequence, the black market price for gold has increased by more than 300 percent.

In the years between the finishing of the trip and the publishing of this book, it is worth noting some of the political and economic changes across some countries of the Eurasian steppe through which I traveled. In the political sphere, Vladimir Putin stepped down as president of Russia in 2008 to become prime minister but has since returned to his role as president. Of the many "color revolutions" among former Soviet states, all have been reversed. In Kyrgyzstan, the Tulip Revolution, which ousted President Akayev in 2005, brought some semblance of stability for just five years until the 2010 so-called Second Kyrgyz Revolution, which was followed by violent interethnic conflict in which as many as two thousand people, mostly ethnic Uzbeks, were killed. In Ukraine, Viktor Yanukovych, from the Russian-leaning Party of Regions, came to power in 2010 and has reversed many of the reforms of his Orange Revolution predecessor, Viktor Yushchenko. Yulia Tymashenko, who at the time of my travels in Ukraine was in a bitter power struggle with both Yushchenko and Yanukovych, is currently languishing in prison after being found guilty of abuse of office when brokering the 2009 gas deal with Russia—a case that is widely regarded as politically motivated. In Kazakhstan, on the other hand, Nursultan Nazarbayev remains in power and has essentially become president for life after the parliament passed a constitutional amendment allowing him to run for president as many times as he chooses.

These political changes I've outlined, as turbulent as some may have been, probably have not brought much influence to bear on the trajectory of life and culture of the steppe peoples as I encountered them during my journey (although in Ukraine it is true that the Ukrainian language and culture have undoubtedly been dealt a blow by Yanukovych's pro-Russian policies). In Mongolia, however, it may be a different story, for it is a country that has recently seen, and will no doubt undergo, a dramatic economic shift.

In 2001 copper and gold deposits worth an estimated $350 billion were discovered in the southern Gobi Desert. After many years of political wrangling and negotiation, an investment agreement on the development of the deposit—which is known as Oyu Tolgoi—was reached in 2009 between the government of Mongolia and the mining corporations Rio Tinto and Ivanhoe Mines (now Turquoise Hill). Commercial mining at Oyu Tolgoi, which is expected to be one of the five largest mines on the planet, is scheduled to begin operation in 2013, and at full production will provide an estimated 30 percent of GDP for Mongolia.

Oyu Tolgoi is not the only big mine under development in Mongolia. Tavan Tolgoi, also in the Gobi, is thought to be one of the largest unexploited reserves of coking coal in the world. This is not to mention the untold smaller mining projects currently under way across the country.

Given the scale of Mongolia's resources, and the investment that has been poured into the mining sector in recent times, it is not hard to imagine that a transformation must now course through Mongolian society. Nonetheless, the economic statistics are mind-boggling. In 2011 Mongolia was the fastest-growing economy in the world—the GDP had increased from $1 billion in 2001 to $11 billion just a decade later. Even compared to 2004 when I set off on my journey, the Ulaanbaatar of 2013 is unrecognizable. At rush hour, the city's roads are jammed with a chaotic sprawl of traffic, among which one cannot avoid the spectacle of fleets of luxury vehicles. The Soviet-era apartments that once loomed large over the city's suburbs are fast being outnumbered by new developments, which include gated communities and multistory office blocks in the city center—many of which have been built in anticipation of the mining production to come.

With a boom of this kind, it comes as no surprise that there are many allegations of corruption against Mongolia's politicians, complaints about the lack of transparency of deals with multinational mining companies, and rumors of foreign companies taking advantage of Mongolia's inexperience in dealing with such large-scale projects. Then there is the problem of high inflation and the growing wealth gap between rich and poor, and questions over the environmental impact of mining. For one, the scale of mining being developed requires vast quantities of water—a fragile resource in the Gobi and one that is key to the survival of nomads.

Much of what is happening in Mongolia resembles the early stages of Kazakhstan's oil boom, only in a country with a population of just 3.2 million—many of whom are still nomadic—the effect is bound to be more profound. And this inevitably raises the question of what this will bring to bear on the nomad's economy and culture. No matter how ethically mining is managed, there is, of course, a very real risk in the long term of the marginalization of nomadic life and, ultimately, its slow demise.

Whatever may await in the future, though, for many, such as Dash-nyam in western Mongolia, the fast pace of change in Ulaanbaatar is worlds away. And at the present time the constitution of Mongolia still prohibits the privatization of grazing lands—that is, with the exception of mining leases and areas suitable for crop farming. For the time being, the ancient rhythms of steppe life that revolve around the horse reign supreme in the Mongolian countryside.

Returning to notes of a more personal nature, in 2006, the year before I reached the Danube, Kathrin Nienhaus, with whom I had begun the journey, married Frank Bender. We remained in contact, and Kathrin has been a great support, ranging from her counseling at the time of my father's death to helping me trawl through details of our time together in Mongolia for the purposes of this book.

It is also of note that Gansukh Baatarsuren, the young Mongolian man who helped me buy my first horses, splits his time between Mongolia, and Australia with his Australian partner, Sonya. We remain good friends.

And a word about my animals in Hungary. In the years since I left the horses at the orphanage, Aranka has kept in touch, sending photos and updates of the horses, and the orphans who have learned to ride on them. Not long after I left Hungary, the soccer oval was permanently transformed into the horses' paddock. A measure of how long my book has been in the works, however, is that at the time of writing, Taskonir, who is now probably into his twenties, has been retired from work. Kok unfortunately suffered some kind of injury to one of his legs and is lame. Ogonyok continues to be ridden by the children. Tigi, Tigon's progeny, unfortunately went walkabout one day and never returned.

Lastly, plans for the future. I have many dreams of traveling in northwest China, Central Asia, and even Australia, mostly on foot, with animals. I'm also interested in the origins and migrations through time of the Roma people (Gypsies), and on a different note, I dream of writing a children's book about Tigon and visiting my horses. I have begun a program of taking Australian students to Mongolia and raising money for the school in the village of Khovd, and I hope to continue this.

In the meantime, however, I am going to take a breath and enjoy the experience of new and opening horizons with the completion of this book. After that, I will probably take a long walk with my four-legged companion to think about it.

—TIM COPE
APRIL 9, 2013

ACKNOWLEDGMENTS

WHAT BEGAN AS a plan to ride horses for eighteen months from Mongolia to Hungary has shaped and consumed my life for a decade.

Broadly speaking, there have been three stages—the preparation, the journey, and the digesting of the experience, including the making of a film series, but mostly the writing of this book. At every stage, help, support, and encouragement from others have allowed me to go forward.

Some of these people to whom I owe my gratitude I have lost contact with, partly because while I have been consumed with the journey, they have long moved on in their lives; others are still close friends; and some, I am sad to say, did not live to see the end of this project.

In the early stages I owe many thanks to my parents—Anne Cope, and the late Andrew Cope—and my then-girlfriend, Kathrin Nienhaus (now Kathrin Bender-Nienhaus). My great-uncle and great-aunt, John and Alison Kearney, have supported me throughout my travels over the years and offered crucial moral and financial assistance.

The horse world is a varied, and confounding one for the uninitiated, and there were individuals who helped guide me into it. CuChullaine O'Reilly, a founding member of the Long Riders Guild, responded at once to my request for advice, offering generous wisdom, a sympathetic ear, and encouragement that not only equipped me with the knowledge to travel by horse but inspired me to carry on with what I learned far beyond the Danube and write this book. His colleague, Long Rider and author Jeremy James, also offered some guidance.

In Australia, Cath and Steve Baird of Bogong Horseback Adventures generously gave me my first taste of horse riding—a packhorse trip in the Victorian Alps. In Western Australia, Brent, Sam, and Sascha Watson of Horses and Horsemen provided training, then advice throughout my journey. They introduced me to equine vet extraordinaire Sheila Greenwell, who donated a veterinary kit and throughout the journey offered life-saving vet services by correspondence.

Then there are those who helped me in the countries I traveled. Old friends Tseren Enebish of Mongolia and her husband, Rik Idema, Tseren's elderly mother, and her cousin Bayara Mishig hosted and guided me through the difficult early stages in Ulaanbaatar. Gansukh Baatarsuren, a young enthusiast of Mongolian history and horsemanship, helped me buy my horses and was an endless source of nomadic cultural insight.

In Kazakhstan I stayed with some seventy families, but in particular I'd like to thank Evegeniy and Misha Yurckenkov in Oskemen, Aset and his son Guanz (who generously offered me Tigon), Baitak in Akbakai, and Dauren Izmagulov and Azamat Sagenov in Atyrau. I'm also particularly grateful to Kosibek Erzgalev, the minister for agriculture in Western Kazakhstan, and his team, who helped me get my horses into Russia. In Almaty, thanks go to Rosa and Vadim Khaibullina of Tour Asia for visa- and logistics-related assistance, and to Gaukhar Konuspayeva for putting me in touch with many helpful contacts.

In Russia I was supported by Dr. Anna Lushchekina of the Russian Academy of Science, journalist Inna Manturova, and Dr. Liudmilla Kiseleva. Liudmilla, a professor of biology and an environmental activist, unfortunately was killed in a car accident in suspicious circumstances only a couple of weeks before the end of my journey. I'd also like to thank Yuri at the Kalmykian Wild Animal Center, the Kalmykian Institute for Humanitarian Sciences, and Nikolai Vladimorivich Luti and all his crew in Timashevsk. In the winter of 2005–6, I traveled to Crimea to renew my Russian visa. I was hosted for a month in Sevastopol by my surrogate Russian grandmother, Baba Galya, whom I had befriended in 2000 while cycling in northern Russia. Her daughter Shura, grandchildren Olya and Dima, and son-in-law Sasha Shishkin, kindly looked after me for a month. Sasha died suddenly of cancer in 2007. Baba Galya passed away on November 24, 2008, just shy of her eightieth birthday.

In Crimea, thanks go to Ismet Zaatov, deputy minister for culture of Crimea, and to Ira of Argamak Horse Center, near Feodosiya, and her helping hand Sascha, who has unfortunately since been killed in a horse accident.

In Ukraine itself, thanks to Anya Summets for her love and support, particularly during the period after my father's death, and to Vladimir Sklyaruk and his family in Kodyma, who arranged for Tigon and the horses to be looked after while I returned to Australia after my father's passing. In the Carpathians, Ivan Ribaruk remains a good friend. I was fortunate in Hungary to have broad support from many. I am indebted to János Loska, who single-handedly arranged my journey across the border into Hungary and then to the Danube, as well as the special ceremony for the finish in Opusztaszer. Peter Kun, István Vismeg, and Tamas Petrosko also deserve special mention.

The last stage of my journey, from the Danube until now, has been the longest, and in many ways the most trying. I owe great thanks to my mother, Anne, for sheltering me for the best part of two years after I returned home. Mum has supported me through the highs and lows I have experienced while coming to terms with the end of one journey and the beginning of new challenges. Likewise, thanks go to my brothers, Cameron and Jonathan, and my sister, Natalie. Family friends the Cooks, Wallaces, and Nicholsons have been great supporters of our family, particularly since the passing of my father.

It goes without saying that I owe much to my father for introducing me to the outdoors and doing everything he could to support me on my path to adventure and writing, even when it involved abandoning my law degree at university—something that did not sit comfortably with him at the time.

The book has been a major thread of my life for nearly four years. I have written it in many places. I began writing at the Drouin South home of our longtime family friends, the Wallaces, who kindly offered use of their study. Then I went off on solo writing "expeditions," such as when I was invited by Andrew Faulknor (aka Viktor) to his property in the Strzeleckis, where I wrote by day in a shed and slept in a tent at night with Tigon. Some of this book was written in Mongolia, and in November 2011 I was given a Fleck Fellowship to write in the artists' colony at the Banff Centre for Creativity, Canada. The last part was written mostly in Tawonga in the Victorian Alps, Australia, where I have had very understanding landlords in Helen and Glen McIlroy, forever patient and supportive friends in the Van der Ploeg family, and a trusty canine sitting on the couch by my side and demanding a run at the end of every writing day.

Through all of this time, I am thankful for the patience and belief of my literary agents, Benython Oldfield in Australia and Gail and Howard in Washington, D.C., and my publisher, George Gibson, in New York, who was willing to go out on a limb and commission this book from an unknown, rather disheveled Australian.

Anton Mueller, my editor, has lived through the journey, and although it has been via correspondence between New York and Australia, I feel like he has accompanied me for every hoofstep. Anton has both encouraged and challenged me during the writing process, and I feel indebted to him for the personal growth I have experienced as a result; the book simply would not be as it is without his input. During the writing of this book—and the cutting, which has involved reducing the original manuscript by almost half—I have also enjoyed the generous feedback of longtime friend and travel companion Dr. Chris Hatherly. Then there is the person closest to me, who has had to live through all the ups and downs. My girlfriend, Khorloo Batpurev, did not know me when I carried out the journey, but she has had to weather every challenge as I have relived them. It's also true that while I have long since returned from the steppes, I have not been 100 percent present at home, either. Thank you, Khorloo, for all your love and care, and for sticking this long journey out.

There are many other friends and supporters who have helped me greatly, including my former English and history teacher Rob Devling, longtime friends Cordell Scaife, Ben Kozel, and Todd Tai, and more recent friend Joss Stewart. Thanks to the many others not mentioned here.

Lastly, it would never have been possible to carry out this journey without the support of sponsors. I would like to thank the following:

MAIN SPONSORS
Iridium, satellite phone communications
Internetrix.net, particularly support from Daniel Rowan
Saxtons Speaking Bureau, especially Nannette and Winston Moulton
The Australian Geographic Society

MEDIUM-LEVEL SPONSORS

Bogong Horseback Adventures (Victoria, Australia)

Horses and Horsemen (Margaret River, Western Australia)

Odyssey Travel

Mountain Designs

Spelean Australia, distributors of such brands as MSR, Therma-Rest, and Platypus

Reflex Sports

Fujifilm, with special thanks to Graham Carter and Darren at CPL Digital Services, Melbourne. Fujifilm and CPL were responsible for supplying the transparency film for my photography (a range of Astia, Provia, and Velvia slide film) and the reproduction for this book.

Inspired Orthotic Solutions, with a thank-you to Jason Nichols

Equip Health Solutions

Dick Smith Foods, with special thanks to Dick Smith

Mobile Power

MINOR SPONSORS

Baffin Polar Proven, Nungar Knots, Ortlieb, Leatherman, Magellan, Mountain Horse, Bates Saddles, Energizer, Custom Pack Rigging, Lonely Planet.

NOTES

CHAPTER 1: MONGOLIAN DREAMING

1 This is only an approximate distance that I traveled, which is not to say that it is 10,000 km as the crow flies from Mongolia to the Danube River in Hungary.

2 In time sedentary society would also adopt the horse and use it to great advantage, but for those early earth-tillers who suffered the wrath of raiding nomad hordes, there is no doubt that the horse was an inseparable symbol of the devastation of war. It is surely no coincidence that in the New Testament it is horses that carry the four beasts of the apocalypse: conquest, war, famine, and death. The legend of the centaur—the mythical creature that is half man, half horse—is probably further indication of just how alien horses and nomads initially were to sedentary society. *Centaur* literally means "those who herd cattle," and while there are many theories as to its origin, one suggestion is that it originates from Scythian incursions into Thrace in ancient Greece.

3 Originally from the *Chronica Majora*, written by Matthew Paris in the thirteenth century. I read it in the Introductory Notice of *The Journey of William of Rubruck to the Eastern Parts of the World 1253–55, with Two Accounts of the Earlier Journey of John of Plan De Carpine*, trans. and ed. W.W. Rockhill (London, 1900; repr. Asian Educational Services, 1998), xiv, xv.

4 *Ammianus Marcellinus*, Book 31, trans. Walter Hamilton (Hammondsworth, UK: Penguin, 1986), quoted in Erik Hildinger, *Warriors of the Steppe: A Military History of Central Asia 500 BC to 1700 AD* (New York: Da Capo Press, 2001), 57, 58.

5 During the Mongol reign, travel from east to west was not limited to nomads and armies. A Nestorian Christian from China, Rabban Saums, who set out on a pilgrimage to Jerusalem, became the effective Mongol ambassador in Europe and had audiences with King Philip the Fair of France in Paris, King Edward I of England in Bordeaux, and the Pope.

6 This drew author Gabriel Ronay to speculate in his book *The Tartar Khan's Englishman* that the Englishman had probably been Master Robert Eracles—an

English knight and former adviser of King John who had been exiled and eventually picked up by Mongol talent scouts and taken to Mongolia.

7 It is worth clarifying that although Hungary was indeed emerging from Soviet rule, it had long been a settled nation. In fact the Magyars—who had arrived on horseback from the east in the ninth century—were already a sedentary Christian society at the time of the Mongolian invasion in the thirteenth century.

CHAPTER 2: THE LAST NOMAD NATION

1 Although the upper Orkhon was effectively Genghis Khan's administrative capital, particularly from 1220 onward, it was his son Ogodei who is considered the founder of Kharkhorin in the years following Genghis's death. Genghis's grandson Khubilai later built a capital for the Yuan dynasty (greater China and Mongolia), Khanbalikh (also known as Ta-tu or Dadu). Khanbalikh stood on the approximate site of modern Beijing.

2 There is some dispute about Genghis Khan's birth year. I am assuming his birth date is the same as that referenced by Mongolians today, 1162.

3 The Borjigins were part of the Mongol tribe, which also included the Taijut clan.

4 The Tatars were a tribe that had emerged in the eighth century as one of the most powerful on the eastern steppe, but their power had begun to wane by the twelfth century. They were one of the Borjigins' enemies.

5 The vast majority of my journey would be through the former territory of the Khanate of the Golden Horde.

CHAPTER 3: WOLF TOTEM

1 *The Secret History of the Mongols*—a mix of factual history and folklore documenting the rise of the Mongol Empire—was written for the Mongol royal family some time after Genghis Khan's death in 1227. It is the oldest surviving Mongolian literary work.

CHAPTER 4: A FINE LINE TO THE WEST

1 The severe nature of these fleshy wounds was later diagnosed as a symptom of Cushing's syndrome.

2 As recounted in Jack Weatherford's *Genghis Khan and the Making of the Modern World*, the wartime spirit banner, and therefore soul, of Genghis Khan was protected by his descendants until the Stalin purges of Mongolia in the 1930s, when it disappeared.

3 In retrospect, this concept of mine might have been a little unfair. In a tradition known as *tuvar*, nomad families in Mongolia are still known to leave their grazing lands and move out on extended horseback journeys with their herds in search of better pasture. This is particularly true of nomads from Uvs Aimag during times of drought. Tuvar dates back to the very earliest of nomads, whose eternal journeys in quest of better pastures took them across the breadth of the Eurasian steppe. Whether coincidence or not, the word *tuvar* is still used by Crimean Tatars; it means "cattle" or "livestock."

4 Hints of this can be found in the term *Oirat* itself, which some historians believe originates from an earlier name, Dorben Oord, meaning "the allied four." The Mongol tribes farther east, meanwhile, sometimes referred to themselves as the Dochin Mongols, meaning "forty Mongols."

5 In a possible throwback to this historical division, it is nowadays common to hear Mongolians from the central regions insult the Durvuds, who form the majority in Uvs Aimag, by calling them *Khun Bish*, meaning "inhuman."

CHAPTER 5: KHARKHIRAA: THE ROARING RIVER MOUNTAIN

1 *Hun*, pronounced "khun," is modern Mongolian for "person," and this has been used as evidence by some historians to prove the Mongolian origins of the Huns. In 2011, Mongolia officially celebrated the 2,200th anniversary of the Hunnic (Xiognu) empire.

2 This border between Uvs Aimag and Kosh Agach in Siberia was, ironically, opened for the first time to foreigners later the same year I was traveling. In 2011, the border with China in the southwest was opened for foreigners. China would have been my preferred route to Kazakhstan.

CHAPTER 6: STALIN'S SHAMBALA

1 The Golden Horde is also known as the Kipchak khanate or the Ulus of Jochi.

2. From Tom Stacey's introduction to Mukhamet Shayakhmetov, *The Silent Steppe: The Memoir of a Kazakh Nomad Under Stalin* (New York: Overlook/Rookery, 2007), ix.

3 This was not a policy unique to the Soviet era. Dostoyevsky was also sent to prison in Semipalatinsk in 1862, where he wrote *Memoirs from the House of the Dead*. The Ukrainian artist Shevchenko also served a term in Orsk in 1847.

4 A kurultai historically was a political and military council of ancient Mongol and Turkic chiefs and khans. The root of the word means "meeting" in Mongolian.

5 Claire Burgess Watson has since written a book about her journey from Mongolia to Turkmenistan, *Silk Route Adventure: On Horseback in the Heart of Asia*.

6 By contrast, at that time a horse in Mongolia started at $80, and a *good* horse there was no more than $150.

7 According to the formula I have used elsewhere in the book for transliterating Kazakh terms to English, Taskonir would more correctly be *Taskonyr* (*Tas* meaning rock, and *konyr* meaning brown). But in the interests of pronunciation, given how centrally this horse featured on my journey, I have stuck with Taskonir.

CHAPTER 7: ZUD

1 It is with an irony not lost on many Kazakhs, then, that it was Lenin's recognition of ethnicities—attachments that he thought would dissolve over time with the brotherhood of Soviets—that eventually heralded the independent state of Kazakhstan.

2 Many historians believe that if the initial policy had confiscated animals from just the bai, and not the middle class and poor, the famine would not have occurred.

3 The Kazakh professor Talas Omarbekov, who worked on the 1997 senate commission into the famine, came across a telegram sent in 1933 from the administration of Kostanai Oblast to the central government: "We cannot fulfill our quota of meat supply of pigs. In the entire oblast there is left just one pig."

4 Collectives run by ethnic Russians and Cossacks tended to have a much lower attrition rate, because their heritage as agrarian farmers allowed them to adapt to the conditions much better than Kazakhs, who knew only nomadic life.

5 Official figures from the time suggest that cattle numbers declined from 6.5 million to fewer than one million. Sheep declined from 18.5 million to just 1.5 million.

6 *Aul* was originally used for Kazakh settlements, as opposed to those founded by Russian settlers, which are known as *derevnye* (village), and separate from

collective farms. Up until the 1950s there was a substantial difference in living conditions between a village and an aul. Russians, with their history as cultivators, were much more easily able to adapt to running state-owned farms, while Kazakhs had neither the same equipment nor the experience and were given less-arable land, so their auls were much poorer. Therefore there was a stigma attached to the word *aul*, which still persists in some ways to the present.

From here on, for the purposes of the book, I will refer to any small Kazakh settlement based on agriculture as an *aul*, no matter whether it was initially a former state farm or collective, Russian-founded or not.

It is also worth noting that at the time of Soviet collectivization, anyone whose family was branded kulak or bai were forbidden to reside in collectives. *Aul* therefore also came to mean the forced settlements of Kazakh nomads outside the collectives.

7 Frederick Burnaby—a British soldier, writer, and undercover spy agent in the era of the Great Game—was told of a similar phenomena in 1875 during his horseback journey from Russia, south through the Kazakh steppes to Khiva. He wrote: "A tartar who is a rich man can find himself a beggar the next. This comes from the frequent snowstorms, when the thermometer sometimes descends to around −40 to −45°C; but more often from some slight thaw taking place for perhaps a few hours. This is sufficient to ruin whole districts. The ground becomes covered with an impenetrable coating of ice, and the horses simply die of starvation, not being able to kick away the frozen substance, as they do the snow from the grass beneath their hoofs." From Burnaby's *A Ride to Khiva: Travels and Adventures in Central Asia*, 148.

8 Since I finished my journey, Mongolia has been hit by another severe zud. In the winter of 2009–10, about 80 percent of the country's territory was covered with a snow blanket of 20–60 cm, and in Uvs Aimag a period of extreme cold, with nighttime temperatures as low as −48°C, endured for almost fifty days. Nine thousand families lost their entire herds, while an additional thirty-three thousand suffered a 50 percent loss. The Ministry of Food, Agriculture, and Light Industry reported 2,127,393 head of livestock lost as of February 9, 2010 (188,270 horses, cattle, and camels and 1,939,123 goats and sheep). The ministry predicted that livestock losses might reach 4 million before the end of winter. But by May 2010, the United Nations reported that 8 million, or about 17 percent of the country's entire livestock, had died.

9 Note that the famine in Kazakhstan under Stalin is known in Russian language as *Veliki Dzhut* (Great Zhut), but in Kazakh the famine is officially known as *asharshylyk*.

10 Later I heard that the Hazara of Afghanistan—descendants of Mongols who conquered the region in the thirteenth century—have the same horse care method, although the same can't be said for Pashtuns and other non-Mongol peoples in that country.

11 The most infamous flight for survival occurred in the spring of 1723 when the Zhungars—Oirat Mongols—nearly wiped out the entire Kazakh population of the Talas region in the middle of a seasonal migration. Those who survived fled to refuge in the overcrowded oases of Bukhara and Samarkand in present-day Uzbekistan. To this day the events are remembered as Aktaban Shubyryndy— "running" (fleeing) to "the bone" (of the foot)—a saying sometimes used in reference to the exodus of Kazakhs to China in the twentieth century during Stalin's collectivization policies and the subsequent famine.

12 There is a legend about the dombra that is linked to the Mongol Empire. The story goes that Jochi, the eldest son of Genghis Khan, promised to pour melted lead down the throat of whoever brought bad news about his son. His son was killed on a hunt by a stampeding wounded ass (known in Kazakh as a *kulan* and in Mongolian as *khulan*). Although everybody was afraid to tell the news to Jochi, there was one musician who agreed to advise of the accident by composing and playing a piece on a dombra. Jochi understood every detail and instead of pouring the lead down the musician's throat ordered it to be poured over the body of the dombra. The hot lead made the soundhole on the instrument that it has today.

13 In Mongolian, the name *Tarbagatai* translates to something like "marmot mountains."

CHAPTER 8: TOKYM KAGU BASTAN

1 Reflecting the blend of old beliefs with the more recently adopted Muslim customs, these days "mounting *ashami*" is often practiced in auls at the time of circumcision. The boys are paraded around the village on horseback to symbolize their coming of age.

2 Above the ranks of akyn were the *jyrau*, who represented an entire people and were advisers to the great khans. They performed *kui* or *terme* (musical recitatives) in everyday life, some of which were many thousands of lines long. Many of these *kuis* recall such events as Alexander the Great's arrival on the Syr Darya (classically known as the Jaxartes River), the Mongols, the Zhungars, and the arrival of Russians on their land.

3 Their observation was not without reason. They told me about a fisherman who had recently died of thirst after his motorcycle broke down during a poaching trip to the lake somewhere nearby. And in the afternoon that day two Russian men turned up briefly looking for water. They had been stuck out on the lake edge for more than a week after their motorcycle broke down. Emaciated and exhausted, they told stories of drinking the saline water, which had made them more and more thirsty, until they had miraculously gotten the bike going again.

4 For some time now I had been sensing that *Oralman* was a derogatory term, as if they considered these people an impure underclass who weren't genuine Kazakhs.

5 In a strange twist, three years later I met an Australian who cast some light on these rumors about police that I would hear time and time again during my travels in Kazakhstan. This Australian had set up a company in Azerbaijan and had once sent a Scottish employee to Kazakhstan on business. According the Scotsman, he had been arrested while near Aktau in western Kazakhstan, driven into the desert, and strangled before the police took off with his wallet. It was apparently only by feigning death that he had survived at all. He managed to wander back into an aul for help.

6 Most of the emissaries of the Tsar were Cossacks.

CHAPTER 9: BALKHASH

1 Over vodka I learned these policemen worked as security guards at a nearby abandoned military base. A year earlier the weapons storage facility at the base had exploded, very nearly killing the workers inside. I later spoke to a man who managed to rescue several military employees by car in the nick of time. For kilometres around there was still debris to be found, and many of the local people had discovered that shards of an orange substance could be used effectively as fire lighters. This was a reminder of hundreds of Soviet military relics

that remain in the steppes of Kazakhstan, where military zones occupy vast stretches of country.

CHAPTER 10: WIFE STEALING AND OTHER LEGENDS OF TASARAL

1 It is also true that existing Slavic settlers from colonial times already made up an estimated 40 percent of the population in 1917.

2 The loss of the Kazakh language was consequently rapid—by 1989, it was estimated that 40 percent of Kazakhs no longer had a proficient grasp of their own language, and three-quarters of Kazakh urban dwellers did not use their native tongue in daily life. Russian, as Dave Bhavna explains, was "more than just a survival tool; it also became a source of personal and collective empowerment and an emblem of becoming 'cultured' and 'civilized.' "

3 In Mongolia it is nine generations.

CHAPTER 11: THE STARVING STEPPE

1 The maps I primarily relied on were tactical pilotage charts that I had managed to buy from a map shop in Adelaide, Australia.

2 This is recounted by Peter Hopkirk in *Foreign Devils on the Silk Road: The Search for the Lost Treasures of Central Asia.*

CHAPTER 12: THE PLACE THAT GOD FORGOT

1 Saksaul was scarce and the wood so dense and twisted that the only way to split it was by smashing it on rocks in winter, when the frozen wood would shatter on impact.

2 According to Ron Stodghill's article for the *New York Times*, "Oil, Cash and Corruption," Nov. 5, 2006, the money was also allegedly channeled to the head of the oil ministry.

3 The autumn slaughter, known as *kuzdyk*, is also celebrated. In summer the slaughter is known as *szhazdyk*, although it is not usually celebrated with ceremony, as in summer dairy products become the staple.

4 CuChullaine O'Reilly regards this as the first international meeting of long riders in history, with riders traveling from all five continents. I was the first to be made a fellow while still on an expedition and "in the saddle."

CHAPTER 13: OTAMAL

1 There was a subtle warning about this in the saying "By spring, fat stock grows thin, and by spring thin stock's nothing" (from Mukhamet Shayakhmetov's book *The Silent Steppe*).

2 I later understood that long farewells, gazing after the departing guest, or the traveler looking back was considered bad luck. In western and central Kazakhstan in particular, I was regularly abandoned and left alone on the day of departure, and until I understood this lore, I felt that I had offended my hosts in some way.

3 Upon reading *The Silent Steppe* I was deeply moved by Mukhamet Shayakhmetov's description of riding alone through a deserted valley the year after nomads had been forced into collectivization: "Until the previous autumn, the valley had been crammed almost full of the nomadic aul who regularly spent each autumn and spring there, to the extent that there could be arguments over whose livestock had the right to graze where. But now it was completely deserted and eerily silent. The people who used to live here had all joined collective farms, and were mostly living together in centralised winter stopping places or in make-shift camps on the ploughed fields; and as there was now enough pasture near these farm centers for the depleted herds of livestock, it no longer made sense to drive them to deserted pastures such a distance away." Mukhamet Shayakhmetov, *The Silent Steppe: The Memoir of a Kazakh Nomad Under Stalin* (New York: Overlook/Rookery, 2007), 65.

4 In times past, anyone who could recount forty generations was held in particularly high status in society.

5 The Kazakh nation had emerged in the sixteenth century as a unity of three confederations of tribes or juzes: the Ula Juz (Elder Horde) in the Jeti-Su (Seven Rivers region) in southern Kazakhstan, the Kishi Juz (Junior Horde) of the arid deserts of the west, and the Orta Juz (Middle Horde) of the north, center, and east.

6 Statistics paint the scale of change in Kazakhstan through the twentieth century. In 1897—thirty years before Kazakhs were forced into collectives—only 7 percent of the Kazakh population had lived settled lives. Nowadays only 9.6 percent of Kazakhs worked on the land, roughly 5 percent of whom, like this family, were thought to carry on a nomadic or semi-nomadic way of life.

7 Beshbarmak is customarily followed by meat broth mixed with dried curd.

8 A fatty sheep tail is the equivalent of a modern-day pacifier and is still used that way among Mongolians as well. Kazakhs also believed that touching a baby's body with a fatty rump will bring wealth.

9 In Mongolia today, it is still in fact the custom never to compliment a baby but to call it "ugly" so as not to cast a spell of bad luck.

CHAPTER 14: SHIPS OF THE DESERT

1 The Khwarezm Empire, which bordered the Mongol Empire, stretched across what is historically known as Transoxiana, which roughly includes the modern states of Iran, Turkmenistan, Uzbekistan, and parts of Kazakhstan, Tajikistan, Afghanistan, and Pakistan.

2 Alexander the Great had in fact fought a famous battle on its banks in 329 BCE with Scythian nomads. Tamerlane (also known as Timur and "Timur the Lame"), of Turkic descent, attempted to evoke the legacy of Genghis Khan in the second half of the fourteenth century, restoring rule over much of the territory that the Mongols had earlier conquered, including the Chaghatai khanate in Central Asia, remnants of the Ilkhanate in Persia, and the Golden Horde on the Pontic-Caspian steppe as far as Russia. He also attempted to reestablish rule over China.

3 In the summer heat it was also the case that injuries to the horses were more prone to infection, and this kept me additionally occupied. At this point of the journey Ogonyok had an infected cut above his left eye, and a pressure sore on his back—probably the result of heat, combined with tying down the pack load too tightly. I gave him an anti-inflammatory and antibiotics, made some adjustments to the saddle, and could only hope his condition did not deteriorate.

4 Although by 2005 most of these ships had reportedly been salvaged for scrap metal, some still stood as sad memorials in what had once been Aralsk's busy port.

5 As some measure of the fallout caused by the shrinking of the Aral Sea, Anton Schneider, an ethnic German who grew up in Kazakhstan, has recently written to me, describing how, in the 1990s, desperate refugees from Aralsk—fleeing disease, and unemployment—turned up in his aul of lugovoy, about 1,200 km from the Aral Sea. From what Anton recalls, the Aral Sea refugees lived in tents

on the outskirts of their village. Anton's father and many others in the aul had great sympathy for these poor people. Eventually the local government gave them land to build new homes on.

6 To help address the situation from the Kazakh side of the border, in 2005 a scheme was under way to build a dam along the southern tip of the northern Aral Lake and hence capture all the outflow of the Syr Darya. This guaranteed some rebound in the northern lake and the potential for the limited reintroduction of the fishing industry.

7 The expedition was officially said to be a scientific expedition to the Aral Sea. The mission of rescuing slaves, however, was also a cover for the real intention, which was to conquer Khiva.

8 I will always remember one morning after a long night ride when we had been forced to divert from the river course. Upon discovering a shallow, spring-fed puddle barely a centimetre deep, Harvette had moved in slowly, dipped her long arched neck, and brought her lips ever so carefully to the surface, whereupon she began to suck in the water without stirring up any visible sediment. When the horses came galloping impatiently over, Taskonir stomped about, turning the puddle into a mud bath before the others were able to drink.

CHAPTER 15: THE OIL ROAD

1 Some commentators, such as Lutz Kleveman in his book *The New Great Game: Blood and Oil in Central Asia*, suggest that by 2020 Kazakhstan could rival Saudi Arabia, exporting as much as 10 million barrels of oil a day.

2 Lutz Kleveman in *The New Great Game: Blood and Oil in Central Asia* alleges that $120 million of this was discovered in accounts under the names of Nazarbayev's children and relatives. Soon after these revelations Nazarbayev had the parliament pass a law making him immune from prosecution for anything he may have done in office.

3 At the time of my journey there were several known incidents of rioting and violence. Weeks prior to my arrival in Kulsary there was a riot between Turkish and Kazakh employees at Tengiz. In December 2011, at least fourteen people were known to be killed when oil workers of the Ozenmunaigas company—based farther south in the town of Zhanaozen—went on strike due to unpaid hazard pay, rioted, and were fired upon by police.

4 In Kazakh, kok means "green," but it is also a word used to describe the color of a gray horse.

5 My visa eventually came through successfully, but not before I was taken in by police in the town of Ganushkino, who threatened to hold me until I could produce my passport. In the end I was rescued by a local former politician who agreed to be my guarantor.

6 They were Karakalpaks—a Turkic people closely related to Kazakhs who were nowadays a minority in their own semi-autonomous republic of Karakalpak-stan.

7 Kyl means "horse" and terlek means "summer deel" or, in old-fashioned language, can apparently also mean "underwear."

8 After her operation, Kathrin had also proposed visiting me in Almaty, but I had jettisoned the idea because I knew I would be occupied with the visa and other tasks.

9 Tengiz-Chevroil is the name of the company run by Chevron together with the Kazakh government to exploit the Tengiz oil deposits.

CHAPTER 16: LOST HORDES IN EUROPE

1 It is also acknowledged by historians that the majority of the Kalmyks who remained behind were of the Durvud tribe, and they had elected to stay there.

2 In the fifteenth century, the Oirats had usurped the Genghisid Mongols (also known as the Eastern Mongols) and gone on to found the empire of Zhungaria, which at its peak stretched from Lake Baikal in the northeast to Lake Balkhash in the west and the Great Wall of China in the south.

3 The Kalmyk khanate held sway from the Zhem, across the northern shores of the Caspian Sea, to the Terek River in what is present-day southern Russia.

4 In one campaign in 1711 the Kalmyks attacked the Nogais, who, since being pushed out of the Lower Volga, had moved west to the Kuban steppe and become vassals of the Ottomans. In four days of fighting it is believed the Kalmyks caused the deaths of almost 40,000 and wiped out the entire male population of the Kuban Nogais. They also took 22,000 people captive—the majority of whom were women and children—and stole 190,000 horses and 220,000 sheep.

5 It is so called because of the lack of snow cover on this steppe in the winter.

6 This particular Chechen farmer, whom I did not meet, was said to have lost two houses, a truck, and a semi trailer in the recent riots.

7 This works out to about 150,000–200,000 individuals.

8 I later met a Kalmyk man who told stories about his time as a teenager helping to herd Kalmyk livestock to the eastern banks of the Volga in an attempt to stop them from falling into the hands of the Nazis. "They were never returned to us after the war," he said sadly. "Probably those Kazakhs still have them."

CHAPTER 17: COSSACK BORDERLANDS

1 Kurgans are found across Central Asia, Siberia, and eastern Europe. They were common among many nomad societies on the steppe, including that of the Scythians. According to the *Oxford English Dictionary*, the word is derived from a Tatar term meaning "fortress."

2 The capital of the Golden Horde, Sarai, was established on the Volga River. The Pontic-Caspian steppe, where vast numbers of horses could be kept in close proximity to Russia, enabled the Mongols and their successors to preserve their military superiority over their vassals.

3 Nothing further is known of Jebe, and it is assumed he died soon after arrival back in Central Asia, but the young Subodei would go on for another twenty-five years, long after Genghis had died, expanding the Mongol Empire to its zenith and again wreaking devastation on the princedoms of Russia.

4 A decade after Russia defeated the largest Cossack army, the Zaporizhian Sich, the Cossack army was reinstated to help efforts in the Russo-Ottoman War of 1787–92. Russia later granted Cossacks the lands of the Kuban for their contribution. Twenty-five thousand Cossack soldiers moved to the Kuban, founding the Kuban Cossack society that still lives there today.

5 In one case the entire populations of three Kuban towns, totaling 45,600 people, were deported. Later, as more than 3 million tonnes of wheat were kept in government storehouses, up to 4.5 million peasants across the Ukraine and Kuban starved to death.

6 Home-distilled vodka in Russian is known as *samogon*, but Cossacks use the Ukrainian variation of the word, *samohon* (Kuban Cossacks generally speak a dialect closer to Ukrainian than Russian). The large bottles they serve with corncob corks are known additionally as *suliya*. Ordinary vodka in Cossack dialect is also known by the Ukrainian term, *horilka*.

CHAPTER 19: WHERE TWO WORLDS MEET

1 For me, the most intriguing symbol of the unique cultural dualism of Panticapaeum was an excavated tomb that lay in the hills overlooking Kerch. The so-called Tsar's Kurgan or Royal Kurgan, a 22 m earth-covered dome, appeared from the exterior like a typical Scythian burial mound—the kind I'd seen regularly elsewhere. Yet the excavated opening revealed an arrowhead-shaped tunnel and a chamber constructed with impressively hand-hewn sandstone blocks that bore the hallmarks of the ancient Greek. The tomb was not of a nomad but of a Bosphorian king.

2 The Crimean khanate was founded in 1430 by Batu Khan's brother's descendant, Hajji Giray.

3 After conquering Baghdad in 1258, Hulegu Khan (Genghis Khan's grandson), of the Ilkhanate declared war on Egypt. Mongol advances were halted by the Mamluks, however, who defeated them in the Battle of Ain Jalut. It was the first of several major battles with the Mamluks, including the First and Second Battles of Homs.

4 It is also true that Mongol aristocracies assimilated with the culture of their subjects—at the turn of the fourteenth century, for example, the Golden Horde officially converted to Islam, breaking the tradition of Mongol rulers adhering to shamanism.

5 After weeks of protests and blockades it was reported that the NATO ship sailed home without unloading. The day after my trip to the city, the front page of the newspaper had two headline stories: "Australian Reaches Crimea from Mongolia by Horse" and "Crimeans Say No to NATO."

6 Sourced from Erik Hildinger, *Warriors of the Steppe: A Military History of Central Asia 500 BC to 1700 AD* (New York: Da Capo Press, 2001), 205.

CHAPTER 20: THE RETURN OF THE CRIMEAN TATARS

1 Translated from an original Crimean verse by Rustem Ali. Sourced from Edward A. Allworth, *The Tatars of Crimea: Return to the Homeland* (Durham, NC: Duke University Press, 1998), 5.

2 From here on I will use *Tatars* and *Crimean Tatars* interchangeably, although Crimean Tatars are a distinct people from other Tatars, such as the Kazan or Volga Tatars.

3 There was wide agreement among historians that the real reason for Stalin's decision to exile the Tatars had been his fear of their historical alliance with the Turks.

CHAPTER 21: CROSSROADS

1 Contemporary historians, such as Charles J. Halperin, argue that even after throwing off the so-called Tatar yoke, Russia inherited Mongol military and economic models that helped enable the Muscovite state to unite the northeastern Slavs.

2 His most spoken-about experiences were during a year at Mankato University in Minnesota, where he studied for his master's degree.

3 Text messages could be sent to my phone via an email address.

CHAPTER 22: TAKING THE REINS

1 When reports of famine reached the West and relief supplies were sent to the border, they were turned back, and Moscow announced that there was no famine.

2 In November 2006, the same month that my father died, the Ukrainian president brought to power through the Orange Revolution, Viktor Yushchenko, had finally pushed through a decree that the famine had been genocide. At the time of this writing, however, Yushchenko's archenemy, pro-Russian politician Viktor Yanukovych, is in power and has reversed this decree, recognizing the Holodomor only as a human tragedy.

3 Such were the high emotions surrounding Bandera that one of Yushchenko's last acts as president in January 2010 was to posthumously award Bandera status as a "Hero of Ukraine." Months later Yanukovych had the award overturned. At the time of writing, the award has been officially annulled, although Stepan's grandson, who received it on his behalf, has not been asked to return it.

CHAPTER 23: AMONG THE HUTSULS

1 In times gone by, Hoverla had even been a site of religious sacrifice—the higher the Hutsul climbed to carry out the sacrifice, the more respect they would have from the community. There was one legend I heard about a man who had carried a white bull on his back all the way to the top to be slaughtered.

2 According to tradition, this unique horn was always made from a pine or spruce tree that had been struck by lightning, and it was bound by birch bark collected from trees growing beneath waterfalls. The trembita—which is quite unlike the better-known alpenhorn of the European Alps—was then used to send signals across the high slopes for everything from weddings to communication between herders.

3 Although Genghis Khan had died fourteen years earlier, his son Ogodei, together with Genghis's loyal general Subodei, had resolved to carry out Genghis's wish for world domination.

4 Later on I was approached frequently by villagers who asked how much I was selling brinza for—they assumed that I was a shepherd bringing it down from the polonina.

CHAPTER 24: THE END OF THE WORLD

1 Batu was the second son of Jochi, who was himself Genghis Khan's eldest son. Batu became khan of the Golden Horde.

2 The Kipchaks were known as *Cumans* in Latin and *Polovtsy* in Russian. For the remainder of this chapter, I will use the term *Cumans*, since this is historically how the Europeans referred to them. Those Cumans who survived the onslaught and accepted Mongolian suzerainty became central to Batu Khan's Golden Horde (also known as the Kipchak Khanate).

3 This is an excerpt from the letter delivered from Batu Khan to King Bela IV. The original is believed to have been in Mongolian, but this is part of one of many different versions—all subtly different—translated from Latin. Gabriel Ronay, in *The Tartar Khan's Englishman*, even suggests that it was possibly the Mongol's mysterious English diplomat who penned the letter. The translation version I have used here is sourced from Leo De Hartog, *Genghis Khan, Conqueror of the World*. Folio Edition. (Berkeley: University of California Press, 2005), 176. (Note however, Hartog did not include the last line that I have here: "So how do you escape my hands.")

4 Many of these elite soldiers had fought against the Seljuks during the Crusades and were part of military orders including the Knights Templar, the Knights of the Hospital of Saint John of Jerusalem, the Teutonic Knights, and the Brothers of the Sword.

5 Sourced from Gabriel Ronay, *The Tartar Khan's Englishman* (London: Cassell, 1978), 11.

6 It is also said that divisions between Batu and other family members influenced the decision to abandon plans for Europe. Additionally, the retreat may be partially explained by the fact that although the Hungarian plain was well suited for horses, it wasn't large enough to support the sheer number of Mongol mounts. This, some historians suggest, would have forced the army to eventually return to the more familiar steppe of the former Cumanian territories anyway.

7 In the centuries following the arrival of the Magyars in Hungary there was a belief that somewhere between the Volga and the Urals existed an ancient "greater Hungary. " In 1236, a Dominican friar, Julian, claimed to have reached it and met people who spoke fluent Hungarian. The following year he once more set out east but on arrival in Suzdal in Russia was told that the eastern Hungarian nation had been wiped out by the Mongols. The existence of this nation remains a mystery.

8 In his remarkable book *The Centaur Legacy*, Bjarke Rinke writes that the "neurophysiological merging of horse and man" resulted in a "super predator equipped with the ambition of man and the speed of the horse." Bjarke Rink, *The Centaur Legacy: How Equine Speed and Human Intelligence Shaped the Course of History* (Zurich: Long Riders Guild Press, 2004), 29.

9 In his book *Guns, Germs, and Steel: The Fates of Human Societies* (New York: W.W. Norton & Company, 1999), Jarred Diamond points out that "the most direct contribution of plant and animal domestication to wars of conquest was from Eurasia's horses, whose military role made them the jeeps and Sherman tanks of ancient warfare" (91).

In relation to the Spanish conquest of South America, he also writes of the "tremendous advantage that Spaniards gained from their horses." Reminiscent of the advantage that the nomads of the steppe had over the armies from sedentary Europe the "shock of a horse's charge, its maneuverability, the speed of attack that it permitted and the raised and protected platform that it provided left foot soldiers nearly helpless in the open" (76).

GLOSSARY

FOR THE BENEFIT of readers I have created a glossary of common and important foreign terms used in the text. I have categorized them according to the country of origin of the term. Separately I have provided a list of the Mongol khans and military leaders referred to in the book. There are also lists of other important historical figures, and steppe peoples and empires.

A note about transliteration: there are various formulas for transliterating Mongolian, Kazakh (which is a Turkic language), Russian, and Ukrainian to English. In some cases I have decided to stick with the most commonly found spelling in English, particularly for historical figures. Genghis Khan is a good example—that spelling is widely known in the English-speaking world, even though his name is more accurately transliterated from Mongolian as Chinggis Khaan or Jenghiz Khan.

For Kazakh terms, there is a convention of writing the Kazakh letter к as q, in English, but for ease of reading I have retained this as K. So for example, Qyzylorda becomes Kyzylorda.

In the majority of cases, whether they relate to people, places, or other terminology, I have tried to stick with the spelling that most closely resembles pronunciation in the indigenous tongue.

Note that the letter ы which is similarly pronounced in Kazakh, Russian, and Ukrainian as a hard, unrounded i (such as in the word silly) is transliterated in my book as y.

MONGOLIAN TERMS

Aaruul A traditional dairy product made from dried curd, commonly found among steppe cultures. Known in Kazakh as kurt.

Aimag Traditionally meaning "tribe" in Turkic and Mongolian; now describes administrative subdivisions of Mongolia.

Airag Fermented mare's milk. Also known across the steppe by the Turkic term kumys (sometimes spelled "koumiss").

Boortsog A deep fried dough common among steppe cultures. Known in Kazakh as *baursak*.

Borts Meat cut into strips and hung to dry from the ceiling of a ger or yurt, then crushed.

Deel Long-sleeved long robe traditionally worn by Mongolians and many other peoples of the steppe; held in place by a belt or sash.

Ger Portable tent of steppe nomads, constructed with collapsible lattice walls and roof poles that support an insulating layer of wool felt. More broadly known as a yurt (note that apart from my Mongolian chapters, I have used the term *yurt* in my book to refer to these tents).

Khan Title of a sovereign or military ruler among the Turkic-Mongol societies of the steppe and Central Asia. Also known in Mongolian as khaan or kahn, or by the Turkic term *kagan*.

Nermel arkhi Clear alcoholic beverage, usually distilled from yak or cow's milk; commonly known by outsiders as "Mongol vodka."

Nomkhon Calm, still; often used in relation to a good-natured, quiet horse.

Nuur Lake.

Ovoo Mongolian cairn of rocks and sometimes timber, often found on passes and mountaintops; sites of worship for travelers to pause and venerate the mountains, and offer acknowledgment and prayer to tengri.

Tavan tolgoi mal Five-animal herd (sheep, goat, camel, horse, and yak/cattle); symbol of wealth and prestige among nomads.

Tengri Supreme deity many ancient steppe cultures once worshipped, including Mongolians, many Turkic nomad peoples of Central Asia, and even Hungarians. "Tengrism," which has features of shamanism, animism, totemism, and ancestor worship, is recognized as once having been an organized religion. In what is now modern-day Kazakhstan, Tengrism survived an invasion of Christianity in the sixth century, then Judaism in the seventh. Between the twelfth and fifteenth centuries, Tengrism competed with Islam and was ultimately superseded. In Mongolia today, many Mongolians practice a blend of Buddhism and worship of tengri. Tengri—known as Tenger in modern Mongolian—is also the the term for "sky."

Uul Mountain.

Zud Particularly harsh winter of the steppe that usually leads to heavy losses of livestock. There are a variety of types of zud, ranging from very cold winters, winters with lots of snow or ice, or even *harin zud*— black Zud—when there is no snow at all. Zuds are known in Kazakh language as *zhut*, and in Russian as *dzhut*.

KAZAKH TERMS

Airan Fermented cow's milk.

Akim Mayor; head of local government.

Ak-shi A variety of grass (*Achnatherum splendens* or *Stipa splendens*) that grows on the steppe in tall, tight tussocks and which is used for many Kazakh handicrafts and practical applications in nomad life.

Akyn A talented musical performer traditionally chosen to represent a certain kinship group or family among Kazakhs.

Aul Historically, a community of nomads who camped together in vicinity of a single region, and sometime migrated together. Nowadays used to describe a Kazakh village.

Barimta Traditional form of justice in nomad society that ordinarily involved avenging a crime by stealing the offender's livestock and keeping it for ransom until the dispute was resolved.

Batyr Honorific title given to a Kazakh warrior hero. A baytr was part of the *aksuyet*, aristocracy of Kazakh nomadic society.

Baursak Deep-fried dough meal of Kazakh nomads. Same as boortsog in Mongolian.

Beshbarmak Meaning "five fingers" (because of the way the meal is eaten with one's hands), the Kazakh national dish of meal and boiled squares of pastry, often cooked with wild onion.

Biys Traditional title of elected leader or judge in Kazakh society; part of the *aksuyet*, aristocracy of Kazakh nomadic society.

Buran Fierce windstorms of the steppe, accompanied by a whiteout that can last for days. Known in Mongolian as *shuurgan zud*.

Chaban Kazakh nomad herder.

Dastarkhan Traditional low table of Kazakh nomads; also, table mat spread out on the ground or floor; or, more generally, Kazakh tradition of hospitality.

Dombra Traditional long-necked, two-stringed lute of the Kazakhs.

Dzhabe Kazakh breed of horse renowned for its endurance, strength, and ability to hold its weight even when fodder is scarce. My horses Taskonir and Ogonyok were both of the dzhabe breed. Kazakhs say that their nation was "built on the back of the dzhabe."

Jalau Summer pasture. Same as *jayla* in Crimean Tatar language.

Jeti-su Fertile region of southeast Kazakhstan between Lake Balkhash and the Tien Shan Mountains, known as *semirechye* in Russian. It owes its name to the "seven waters" (or rivers) that flow through the region from the Tien Shan to Lake Balkhash. The Jeti-su has historically been a strategically valued region for empires of Central Asia.

Juz A confederation of nomad tribes, of which there are three that make up the nation of Kazakhstan. The *Ula Juz* (Elder Horde), *Kishi Juz* (Junior Horde), and the *Orta Juz* (Middle Horde).

Kalym Bride-price.

Kstau Winter quarters of Kazakh nomads, usually a semipermanent mud-brick house with corrals for the animals.

Kumys Fermented mare's milk; also written in English as "koumiss." Same as *airag* in Mongolian.

Kurt A traditional dairy product made from dried curd, commonly found among steppe cultures. Same as *aaruul* in Mongolian.

Kurultai Political and military council of ancient Mongol and Turkic chiefs and khans. The root of the word *kural* or *khural* means "meeting" in the Mongolian language, as in "Great State Khural."

Kyl terlek Saddle blanket woven from horsetail hair. Although it is a Kazakh term, it roughly means "summer deel (or underwear) for horse" in Mongolian—evidence perhaps of a wide tradition of its use in the past.

Oralman Expatriate Kazakh whose ancestors fled Kazakhstan during times of war or to escape the privations of the Stalin era; expatriates who have returned to Kazakhstan since the collapse of the Soviet Union.

Otamal Sudden cold snap that usually occurs in mid-March, just when it appears the winter has passed.

Saksaul Small, bush-like tree (*Haloxylon* spp.) of the arid steppes and deserts of Eurasia; traditionally played an important role in nomad life as a source of firewood, shelter, and, in emergencies, even water.

Shubat Camel milk.

Tazi A sight hound of Central Asia renowned for its ability to run over long distances; traditionally used for hunting fox and hare. Due to its nature as a quiet, short-haired dog, it is the only breed Kazakhs—as nominal Muslims—allowed into their dwellings. Tigon's father was a purebred Tazi.

Zhut Particularly harsh winter of the steppe that usually leads to heavy livestock losses. Same as *zud* in Mongolian and *dzhut* in Russian.

RUSSIAN TERMS

Babushka Grandmother, old woman.

Banya A kind of traditional sauna used for bathing and washing.

Chernozem Rich "black soils" found in southern Russia, Ukraine, and some northern parts of Kazakhstan.

Dacha The summer villages of city people across the Soviet Union, used primarily for growing vegetables to supply families through winter.

Krai (Rus.) Administrative division of Russia, historically describes territories that were on the frontier of the Russian empire. Equivalent to a province or state, and holds the same status as an *oblast*.

Kulaks Originally used to describe independent and relatively prosperous peasant farmers of the early twentieth century in Russia, but after the Bolshevik revolution described any farmer not handing over his property to the state.

Lada Soviet (and now Russian) make of car.

Moskvich Small sedan car of the Soviet era.

Oblast Administrative division in Slavic countries (and Kazakhstan), equivalent to a province or state.

Solonchak Salt marshes, salt pans, salt flats.

Ural motorbike Sidecar motorcycle that was a workhorse in Soviet times and is still widely used across the former Soviet Union.

Valenki Traditional knee-high felt boots.

COSSACK TERMS

Ataman Leader; may range from administrator of a regional community to the commander of a Cossack army (as was the case during the Russian Empire).

Horilka Vodka; technically a Ukrainian term.

Khutor Traditionally meaning a single farming homestead but came to describe small Cossack settlements that were not big enough to warrant a church.

Samohon Home-brewed vodka; technically a Ukrainian term.

Stanitsa Traditionally, a unit of economic and political organization among Cossacks; has come to describe Cossack towns and regional centers large enough to support a church.

CRIMEAN TATAR TERMS

Jayla Summer pasture of nomads, generally used to describe the various alpine uplands of the Crimean Mountains. Same meaning as *jalau* in Kazakh.

Mejlis Central executive body of the kurultai of Crimean Tatars, founded in 1991; acts as a representative body for the Crimean Tatars to the Ukrainian central government, the Crimean government, and international bodies.

UKRAINIAN TERMS

Horilka Vodka.

Krysani traditional stiff bowler hats of the Hutsuls.

Kyptars traditional heavy sheepskin vests of the Hutsuls, usually embellished with colorful braided cords, buttons, sequins, and studs.

Polonina High alpine pastures of the Carpathians, used by the Hutsul people for summer grazing of their livestock.

Samohon Home-brewed vodka.

HUNGARIAN TERMS

Komondor Traditional Hungarian breed of dog renowned for its long, matted white coat.

Pálinka traditional Hungarian fruit brandy.

Puszta Steppe.

MONGOLIAN KHANS AND MILITARY LEADERS OF THE MONGOL EMPIRE MENTIONED IN THIS BOOK

Arikboke Grandson of Genghis Khan, the youngest son of Tolui. In 1260–64 Arikboke fought against his brother Khubilai for ascendancy to the throne of the grand khan of the Mongol Empire. He was defeated, and died in 1266.

Batu Khan Grandson of Genghis Khan, and son of Jochi. Ruler of the Golden Horde (including the territories of Russia) from 1227 until his death in 1255.

Genghis Khan United the Mongolian and Turkic tribes of the Mongolian plateau and in 1206 founded the Mongol Empire; considered to have conquered more territory in his lifetime than any other single conqueror in history. Born in 1162, died in 1227.

Hulegu Khan Grandson of Genghis Khan, son of Tolui, who founded the Ilkhanate of Persia. Hulegu died in 1265.

Jebe One of Genghis Khan's most important commanders, who, together with Subodei, led the first Mongol conquest of Russia in 1223. Jebe is thought to have died some time after this campaign en route back to Central Asia. In Mongolian, Jebe is *zev*, meaning "arrow."

Jochi Oldest son of Genghis Khan. After his father's death he was given the westernmost lands conquered in Genghis Khan's lifetime, from the Irtysh to the Ural River; his descendants went on to rule the Golden Horde (also known as the Ulus of Jochi, or the Kipchak Khanate.) Jochi died in 1227, the same year as his father.

Khubilai Khan Grandson of Genghis Khan, son of Tolui; became the leader of the Yuan Dynasty, the territories of which included China and Mongolia. Established the khanate's summer capital, Xanadu, and the Yuan Dynasty capital, Khanbalikh. Khubilai fought a brief war against his brother, Arikboke, in the 1260s for the ascendancy to the throne of the grand khan of the Mongol empire. Khubilai was victorious and is considered to have ruled the Yuan dynasty from the 1260s until his death in 1294.

Ogodei Khan Third son of Genghis Khan; ascended to the throne of the grand khan of the Mongol Empire in 1229, oversaw Mongol expansion into Europe. When news of Ogodei's death in 1241 reached the Mongol armies, the Mongols withdrew and retreated east to elect a new leader.

Subodei Genghis Khan's chief military strategist and commander. After the death of Genghis, Subodei oversaw Mongol expansion into Russia and eastern Europe and was later assigned to lead campaigns against the Song Dynasty in China. Regarded as one of the greatest military minds in history, he died in 1248 in Mongolia at the age of seventy-two. His name is transliterated more correctly from Mongolian as *Subatai*.

OTHER IMPORTANT FIGURES OF STEPPE HISTORY MENTIONED IN THIS BOOK

Alim Khan Emir of Bukhara from 1911 until 1920, when he was deposed by the Soviet army and forced to flee to exile in Afghanistan, where he died in 1944. Thought to be the last direct descendant of Genghis Khan to hold sway as a national ruler.

Arpád Nomad leader of the Magyars (Hungarians) from 895 to 907. Under his rule, the Magyars settled the Carpathian Basin and laid the foundations of the nation of Hungary.

Bela IV Ruler of Hungary at the time of the 1241 Mongol invasion of eastern Europe; escaped and returned to successfully govern Hungary after the retreat of the Mongols to Asia.

Hajji Giray Descendant of Batu Khan's brother; founded the Crimean khanate sometime around 1430. The Giray dynasty survived until annexation of Crimea to Russia in the late eighteenth century.

Inalchuk Governor of the town of Otrar on the Syr Darya River during the reign of Muhammad II and the Khwarezm Empire. He enraged Genghis Khan by executing a 450-man merchant caravan sent from Mongolia to Otrar in 1218. Otrar was the first city to be crushed by the Mongol campaign against Khwarezm in 1219–1220. Inalchuk was put to death by molten silver poured in the eyes and ears.

Kotian Khan of the nomadic Kipchaks (also known as Cumans) at the time of the Mongol invasion of Russia and Europe. During the initial Mongol raid in 1223, Kotian sought military alliances with several princedoms of Kievan Rus but was nevertheless heavily defeated during a battle on the Little Kalka River. In 1238 when the Mongols returned, the Kipchaks were again defeated, and Kotian, together with 40,000 nomad families sought refuge in Hungary. It was on the pretext of King Bela IV of Hungary harboring these Kipchaks that the Mongols invaded Hungary in 1241.

Muhammad II Sultan of the Khwarezm Empire, the territory of which stretched across Transoxiana, roughly including the modern states of Iran, Turkmenistan, Uzbekistan, and parts of Kazakhstan, Tadjikistan, Afghanistan, and Pakistan. Khwarezm was crushed by Genghis Khan's army in 1219–1220. Muhummad fled to an islet on the Caspian coast but died of pneumonia in the winter of 1220–1221.

Sahin Giray Last khan of the Crimean khanate.

Tamerlane Turkic ruler from Central Asia who attempted to evoke the legacy of Genghis Khan in the second half of the fourteenth century; restored rule over much of the territory Mongols had conquered earlier. Also known as Timur and "Timur the Lame," Tamerlane died in 1405.

Tayang Khan Leader of the Naimans, who were defeated by Genghis Khan's army in 1204. Also known as "Taibuqa," he was mortally wounded in this battle.

Ubashi Khan Eighteenth-century khan of the Kalmyks; led the disastrous exodus of Kalmyks from the Caspian Steppe back to China and Mongolia in 1771.

Yanibeg Khan Distant descendant of Jochi; ruled the Golden Horde from 1341 to 1357.

IMPORTANT STEPPE PEOPLES

Borjigin Clan that was part of the Mongol tribe that inhabited the steppe and forests of northern Mongolia between the Onon and Kherlen Rivers; the clan of Genghis Khan.

Botai An ancient steppe people of what is northern Kazakhstan today (Akmola Oblast); credited with being the first culture to domesticate the wild horse, c. 3700–3100 BCE.

Huns Renowned horseback warriors who appeared on the Russian steppe and the Hungarian plain in the fourth century CE and in the fifth century, under the rule of Attila the Hun, threatened the Roman Empire, Persia, and much of Europe with their invasions.

Kalmyks Descendants of Oirat Mongols who migrated to the Caspian steppe in the early part of the seventeenth century and formed the Kalmyk Khanate.

Khoton A small Mongolian minority, most of whom live a traditional nomad life in the Kharkhiraa-Turgen mountain region of Western Mongolia.

Kipchaks Powerful Turkic people of the steppe who at times held sway from Siberia and Central Asia to the Balkans. The Mongols defeated the Kipchaks during their westward expansion into Europe, and 40,000 Kipchak families fled to Hungary for refuge. The Golden Horde is also referred to as the Kipchak Khanate. Kipchaks are known as "Cumans" in Latin, and "Polovtsy" in Russian. Note I have used the term *Cumans* in the Hungarian chapter, for this is how they were known to Europeans.

Magyars Nomadic people believed to originate from somewhere in the vicinity of Bashkiria (also known as Bashkortostan) near the southern Urals of Russia; conquered the Carpathian Basin in the end of the ninth century and, under the leadership of Arpád, founded the nation of Hungary in 896.

Mamluks Powerful military caste of medieval Egypt who seized the sultanate of Egypt and Syria and dealt the Mongol some of its first major defeats. The Mamluks were primarily of Kipchak origin—nomads of the steppe with a wealth of experience in the tactics of Mongol warfare who had been traded to Egypt as slaves.

Naimans Turkic tribe of western Mongolia; one of the most powerful tribes on the Mongolian steppe at the end of the twelfth century at the time of Genghis Khan's rise. The Naimans and the Keraits alike were Nestorian Christians. After their 1204 defeat by Genghis Khan's army, the Naimans fled west into what are now the steppes of Kazakhstan, where, under their leader Kuchlug (the son of Tayang Khan), they struck alliance with the Kara-Khitans. The Naimans were again defeated by the Mongols during the conquest of Khwarezm. Today there are around 400,000 Naimans in Kazakhstan, mostly in the east. They are part of the Orta Juz (Middle Horde) confederation of tribes. I met with Naiman nomads migrating to the Betpak Dala from the river Chu.

Nogais Descendants of Mongol and Turkic tribes who rose to power on the Caspian Steppe in the wake of the collapse of the Golden Horde. Nogais were allied with the Crimean Khanate, and many migrated to Crimea, where they served as cavalry for the Crimean Khan (in fact Crimean Tatars who resided on the steppe of Crimea are known as Nogais). The Kalmyks displaced the Nogais from the Caspian steppe in the first half of the seventeenth century. Nogais today reside mostly in the northern Caucausus, Crimea, and Turkey. There is also a tribe of Nogais who are part of the Kishi Juz (Junior Horde) of Kazakhs.

Oirat Mongols A confederation of the Choros, Durvud, Torghut, and Khoshut tribes of western Mongolia, believed to have originated from the forests of southern Siberia; fought fiercely against Genghis Khan and later formed their own empire, Zhungaria. As the power of Zhungaria waned in the early part of the seventeenth century, some tribes migrated west to the Caspian Steppe, where they founded the Khanate of Kalmykia and became known as Kalmyks. In 1771, the Kalmyks made a tragic exodus back to Asia during which many died en route through the Kazakh steppes. The Zhungarian Empire was vanquished by the Qing Dynasty between 1755 and 1757. Today, Oirats primarily reside in western Mongolia and China, and in the republic of Kalmykia (Russia).

Scythians Diverse group of sophisticated nomadic and seminomadic cultures stretching from Hungary to the Altai Mountains from around the seventh to the fourth century BCE. Their war tactics of feigned retreat and skill as mounted archers—described by Herodotus—bear a striking similarity with the Mongols. The Scythians were renowned for their gold art and the elaborate burial mounds known as kurgans, still found widely on the steppe.

Xiongnu Nomadic people of Inner Asia who ruled an empire in greater Mongolia during the Iron Age from the third to the first century BCE. Although the origin of the Xiongnu is subject to ongoing controversy and debate, many historians believe they were the original Hunnic people, whose descendants charged into Europe centuries later under the helm of Attilla.

CRIMEAN TATAR TRIBES

Nogais Tatars who were primarily pastoral nomads on the steppe of Crimea.

Tatas Tatars who inhabited the forested mountains of Crimea, renowned for their European features.

Yaliboyu Crimean Tatars who lived as traders and fishermen on the coast of Crimea.

KAZAKH JUZES (HORDES)

Kishi Juz (Junior Horde) Confederation of tribes in the arid deserts of western Kazakhstan between the Aral Sea and Caspian Sea.

Orta Juz (Middle Horde) Confederation of tribes in the north, center, and east of Kazakhstan, and many of the Kazakhs of Xinjiang province in China.

Ula Juz (Elder Horde) Confederation of tribes in the Jeti-Su region in southeast Kazakhstan.

THE MONGOL KHANATES

Chaghatai Khanate Founded by Chaghatai, Genghis Khan's second son, and ruled by his descendants; extended from the Amu Darya to the Altai Mountains.

Golden Horde Khanate composed of territories of what is nowadays Kazakhstan, Russia, Ukraine, and the Caucasus, ruled initially by Jochi Khan but expanded to its zenith under his son, Batu Khan.

Ilkhanate Khanate primarily comprising territories of Persia, founded by Hulegu Khan (Genghis Khan's grandson) and ruled by his descendants until the mid-fourteenth century.

Yuan Dynasty Khanate that included approximate territories of modern China, Mongolia, and Korea; ruled by Khubilai Khan from 1260 to 1294.

SELECT
BIBLIOGRAPHY

NONFICTION

Allworth, Edward A. *The Tatars of Crimea: Return to the Homeland*. Durham, NC: Duke University Press Books, 1998.

Burnaby, Frederick. *A Ride to Khiva: Travels and Adventures in Central Asia*. Oxford: Oxford University Press, 2002.

Carpini, Giovanni di Plan. *The Story of the Mongols Whom We Call the Tartars*. Wellesley, MA: Branden Books, 1996.

Conquest, Robert. *The Harvest of Sorrow: Soviet Collectivization and the Terror-Famine*. New York: Oxford University Press, 1987.

Dave, Bhavna. *Kazakhstan: Ethnicity, Language and Power*. London: Routledge, 2007.

Dolot, Miron. *Execution by Hunger: The Hidden Holocaust*. New York: W. W. Norton, 1987.

Gray, John. *Kazakhstan: A Review of Farm Restructuring*. Herndon, VA: World Bank Publications, 2000.

Halperin, Charles J. *Russia and the Golden Horde: The Mongol Impact on Medieval Russian History*. Bloomington: Indiana University Press, 1985.

Hartog, Leo De. *Genghis Khan, Conqueror of the World*. Folio Edition. Berkeley: University of California Press, 2005.

Haslund, Henning. *Mongolian Adventure: 1920s Danger and Escape Among the Mounted Nomads of Central Asia*. Zurich: Long Riders Guild Press, 2001.

Hildinger, Erik. *Warriors of the Steppe: A Military History of Central Asia 500 BC to 1700 AD*. New York: Da Capo Press, 2001.

Hopkirk, Peter. *Foreign Devils on the Silk Road*. Amherst: University of Massachusetts Press, 1980.

———. *The Great Game: The Struggle for Empire in Central Asia*. New York: Kodansha International, 1992.

Jankovich, Miklos. *They Rode into Europe: The Fruitful Exchange in the Arts of Horsemanship Between East and West*. Zurich: Long Riders Guild Press, 2007.

Khodarkovsky, Michael. *Where Two Worlds Met: The Russian State and the Kalmyk Nomads 1600–1771*. Ithaca, NY: Cornell University Press, 2006.

Kleveman, Lutz. *The New Great Game: Blood and Oil in Central Asia*. London: Atlantic Books, 2004.

Maclean, Fitzroy. *Eastern Approaches*. London: Penguin Books, 1991.

Manz, Beatrice Forbes. *Tamerlane: His Rise and Rule*. Folio ed. Berkeley: University of California Press, 2005.

Martin, Virginia. *Law and Custom in the Steppe: The Kazakhs of the Middle Horde and Russian Colonialism in the Nineteenth Century*. Richmond, Surrey, UK: Routledge, 2001.

Rink, Bjarke. *The Centaur Legacy: How Equine Speed and Human Intelligence Shaped the Course of History*. Zurich: Long Riders Guild Press, 2004.

Rockhill, W. W. *The Journey of William of Rubruck to the Eastern Parts of the World, 1253–55*. Asian Educational Services, 1998.

Ronay, Gabriel. *The Tartar Khan's Englishman*. London: Cassell, 1978.

Rossabi, Morris. *Khubilai Khan: His Life and Times*. Folio ed. Berkeley: University of California Press, 2005.

Shayakhmetov, Mukhamet. *The Silent Steppe: The Memoir of a Kazakh Nomad Under Stalin*. New York: Overlook/Rookery, 2007.

Uehling, Greta Lynn. *Beyond Memory: The Crimean Tatars' Deportation and Return.* New York: Palgrave Macmillan, 2004.

Weatherford, Jack. *Genghis Khan and the Making of the Modern World.* New York: Three Rivers Press, 2004.

FICTION
Rong, Jiang. *Wolf Totem.* London: Penguin Books, 2009.

Stanislaw, Vincenz, *On the High Uplands: Sagas, Songs, Tales and Legends of the Carpathians.* Roy Publishers, 1955.

Tolstoy, Leo. *The Cossacks and Other Stories.* London: Penguin Classics, 2007.

EQUESTRIAN TRAVEL RESOURCES
For anyone interested in the practical side of equestrian travel, I recommend consulting the Long Riders Guild at www.thelongridersguild.com.

A comprehensive list of historical equestrian adventure and practical guides to horse packing can also be found at www.horsetravelbooks.com.

A full list of my personal equipment can be found on my website, www.timcopejourneys.com

INDEX

A NOTE ON THE AUTHOR

TIM COPE, F.R.G.S., is an adventurer, author, film-maker and motivational speaker with a special interest in Central Asia and the states of the former Soviet Union. He has studied as a wilderness guide in the Finnish and Russian subarctic, ridden a bicycle across Russia to China and rowed a boat along the Yenisey River through Siberia to the Arctic Ocean. He is the author of *Off the Rails: Moscow to Beijing on Recumbent Bikes* and is the creator of several documentary films, including the award-winning series 'The Trail of Genghis Khan', which covers the journey of this book. He lives in Victoria, Australia.

www.timcopejourneys.com